the PLAIN Janes

Cecil Castellucci and Jim Rugg

LITTLE, BROWN AND COMPANY

New York   Boston

Copyright © 2020 by Cecil Castellucci and Jim Rugg
Foreword copyright © 2020 by Mariko Tamaki
Lettering of parts 1 and 2 by Jared Fletcher; lettering of part 3 by Ching N. Chan

Cover art copyright © 2020 by Jim Rugg. Cover design by Ching N. Chan.
Cover copyright © 2020 by Hachette Book Group, Inc.

Little, Brown and Company
Hachette Book Group
1290 Avenue of the Americas, New York, NY 10104
Visit us at LBYR.com

First Edition: January 2020
The Plain Janes originally published in 2007 by DC Comics
Janes in Love originally published in 2008 by DC Comics

Little, Brown and Company is a division of Hachette Book Group, Inc.
The Little, Brown name and logo are trademarks of Hachette Book Group, Inc.

Library of Congress Cataloging-in-Publication Data
Names: Castellucci, Cecil, 1969– author. | Rugg, Jim, illustrator.
Title: The plain Janes / Cecil Castellucci and Jim Rugg.
Description: First edition. | New York ; Boston : Little, Brown and Company, 2020. | "The Plain Janes originally published in 2007 by DC Comics. Janes in Love originally published in 2008 by DC Comics." | Presents the full text of Plain Janes and Janes in Love, plus bonus content such as the evolution of the graphic novel and original cover sketches. | Summary: When Jane moves to the suburbs and thinks her life is over, she and three new friends form a club to make public art but are soon distracted by romance.
Identifiers: LCCN 2018050077| ISBN 9780316522724 (hardcover) | ISBN 9780316522816 (trade pbk.) | ISBN 9780316522748 (ebook) | ISBN 9780316522786 (library ebook edition)
Subjects: LCSH: Graphic novels. | CYAC: Graphic novels. | Friendship—Fiction. | Clubs—Fiction. | Street art—Fiction. | Dating (Social customs)—Fiction. | Schools—Fiction.
Classification: LCC PZ7.7.C375 Pp 2020 | DDC 741.5/973—dc23
LC record available at https://lccn.loc.gov/2018050077

ISBNs: 978-0-316-52272-4 (hardcover), 978-0-316-52281-6 (pbk.), 978-0-316-52274-8 (ebook), 978-0-316-52280-9 (ebook), 978-0-316-52279-3 (ebook)

PRINTED IN CHINA

IM

Hardcover: 10 9 8 7 6 5 4 3 2 1
Paperback: 10 9 8 7 6 5 4 3 2 1

ART SAVES

Foreword

It's possible that my love of The PLAIN Janes has something to do with the fact that I have no doubt that when I was a teenager, being an art nerd saved my life.

Before I was an art nerd, I was a weird kid. Before I was an art nerd, I was the kid who didn't like most people's music and was bad at parties. Before I was an art nerd, my culture was Entertainment Tonight every night at 7 P.M.

Then in tenth grade everything changed. I had a cool friend, Jen, who knew way more than I did about pretty much everything. She introduced me to improv theater, documentary films, music not produced by major labels, and, crucially, The Rocky Horror Picture Show. I discovered dressing up as a form of self-expression. Eyeliner as lipstick.

I discovered the joy of obsessing over the work of an artist who inspires you to make your own work, however rough that might be in the beginning.

I came to this book through Cecil Castellucci. The first time I ever saw Cecil, it was 1995 (ish), and she was rocking out on her guitar in a freezing, bare concrete warehouse in Montreal, in front of a crowd of college art geeks, with her band Nerdy Girl. I remember thinking that she was cool the way so much of Montreal seemed impossibly cool to me then. Cool like a pair of Doc Martens weathered to the perfect shade of worn. I immediately bought her CD and played it endlessly.

A decade later, I got to actually meet Cecil at a comic convention in Toronto. She was over the moon about her new graphic novel with artist Jim Rugg: *The PLAIN Janes*. Jim would bring the Janes to life with expressive style and impeccable detail (which you can also see in his other works, including *Street Angel*), capturing the glory and frustration of these characters. Jim rules.

The PLAIN Janes is the story of budding artist and suburban transfer Jane Beckles, who creates a community of friends and fellow artists (all also named Jane) to change the face of their part of the world.

I finished the book a giant fan of Cecil and Jim. It exemplifies and celebrates the power of collaboration, the coming together of minds, channeling inspirations and experiences into a story for young artists-to-be in the middle of that strange journey of being a teenager.

The PLAIN Janes is about finding your people, finding your voice, finding your future. It dives into art as expression, art as activism, art as resistance.

Art celebrates: the work of the nerds who came before us and the work of the nerds who are just now putting pen to paper.

Art saves. It saves you and me in little ways every day. We pass it forward to the people caught in torment and hope it shines a light.

Thank you, Cecil and Jim, for these incredible stories!

—Mariko Tamaki

Part 1
The PLAIN Janes

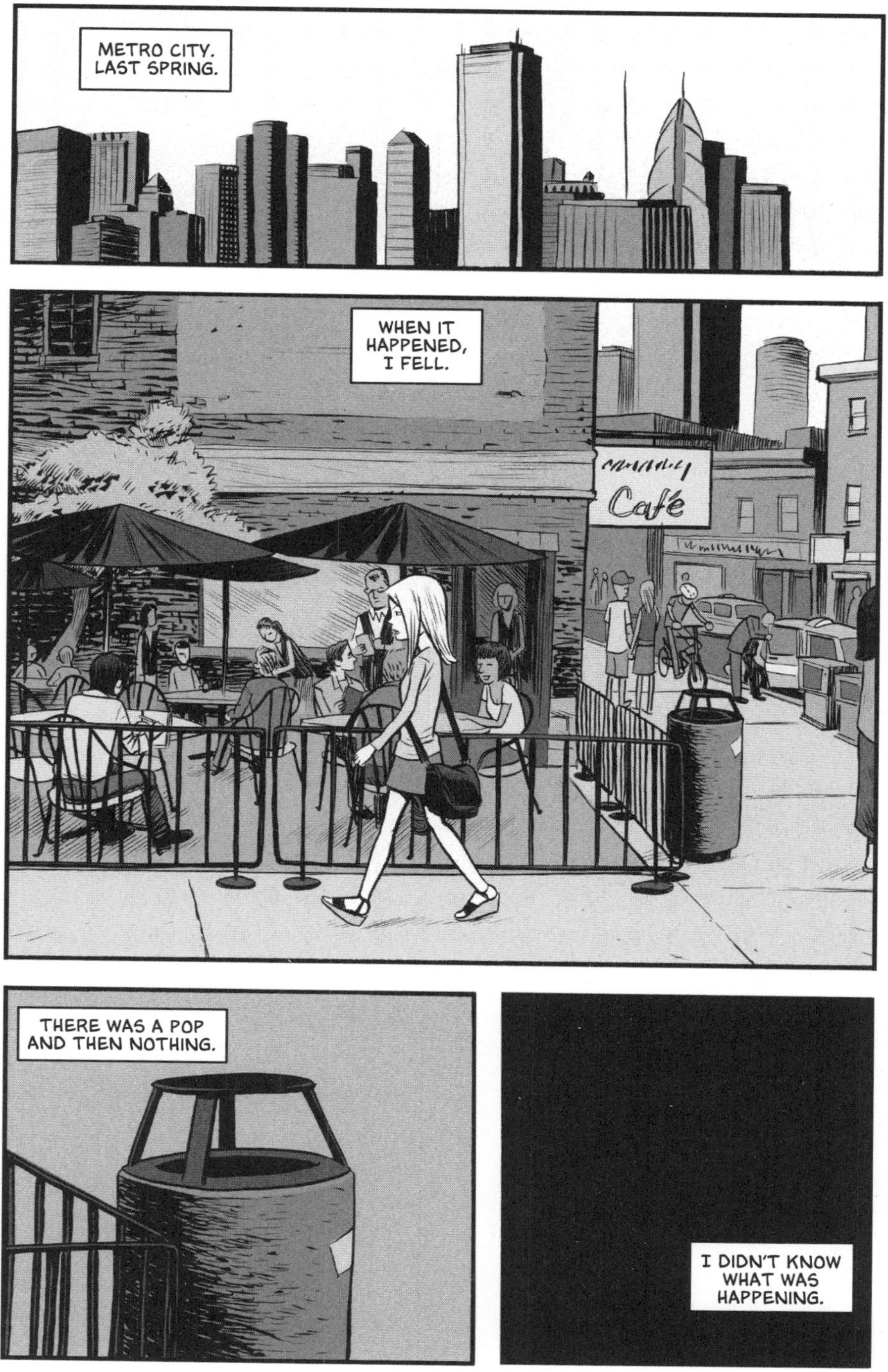
METRO CITY.
LAST SPRING.
WHEN IT
HAPPENED,
I FELL.
Café
THERE WAS A POP
AND THEN NOTHING.
I DIDN'T KNOW
WHAT WAS
HAPPENING.

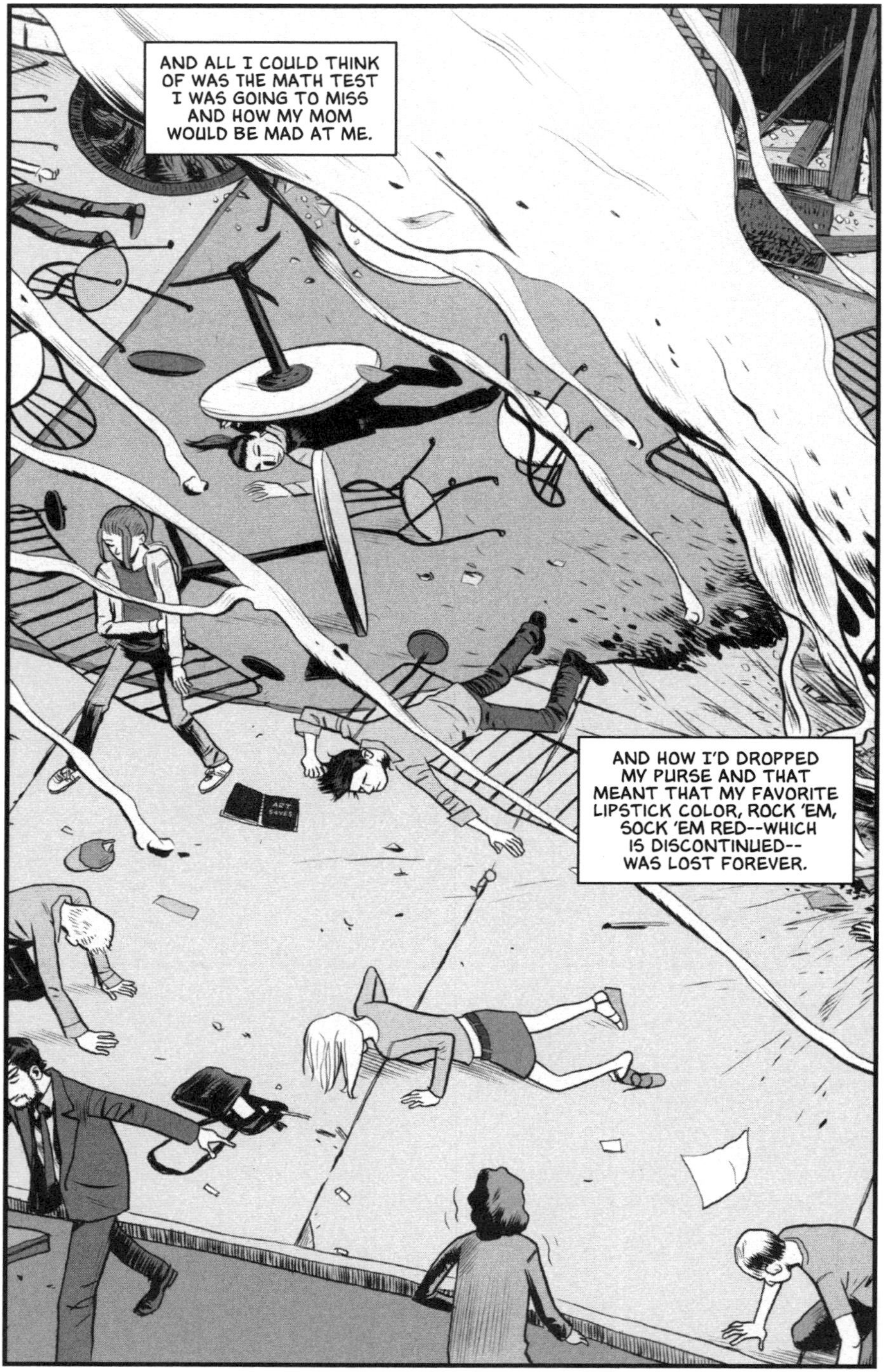
AND ALL I COULD THINK OF WAS THE MATH TEST I WAS GOING TO MISS AND HOW MY MOM WOULD BE MAD AT ME.
AND HOW I'D DROPPED MY PURSE AND THAT MEANT THAT MY FAVORITE LIPSTICK COLOR, ROCK 'EM, SOCK 'EM RED--WHICH IS DISCONTINUED--WAS LOST FOREVER.

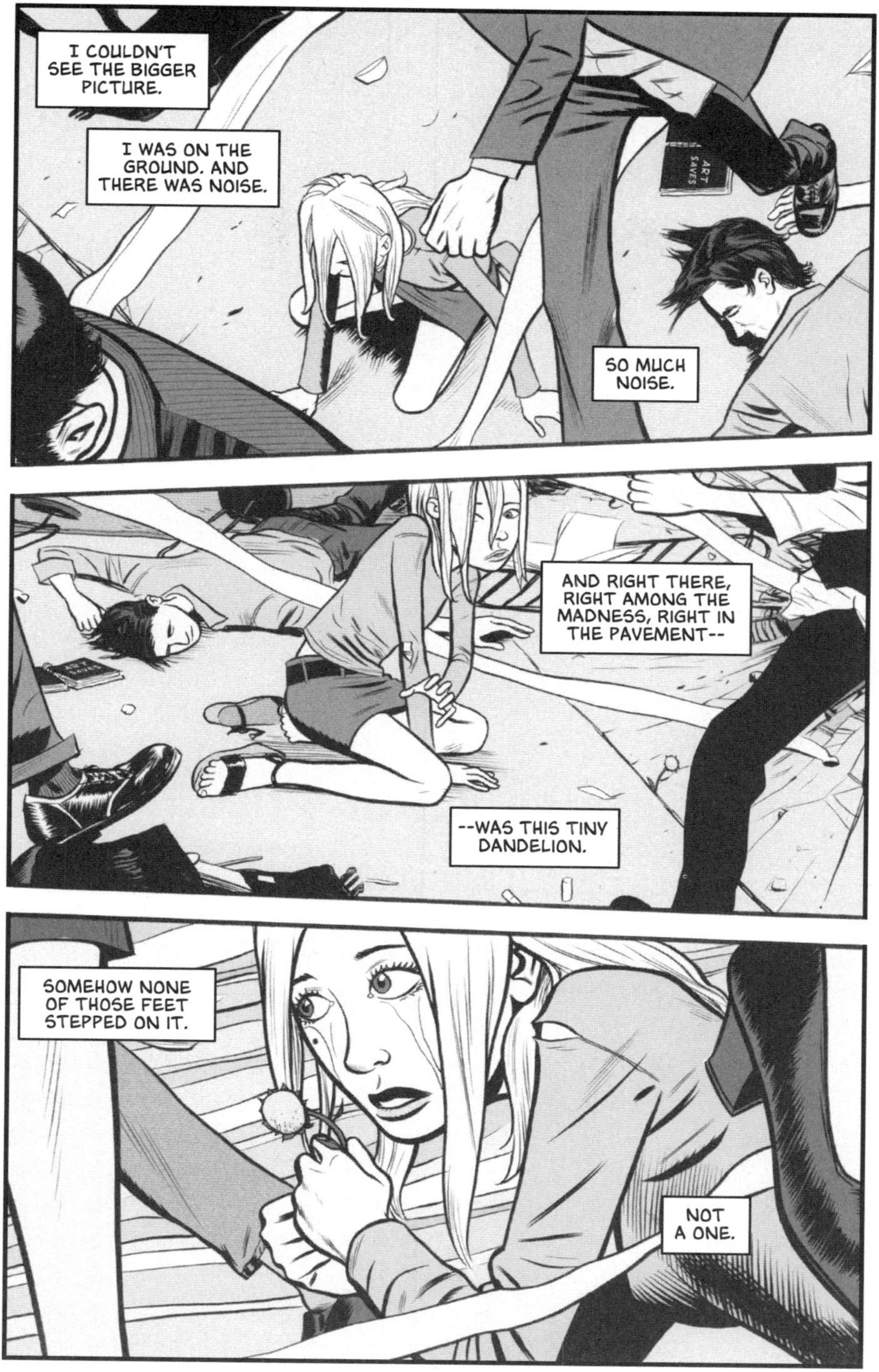
I COULDN'T SEE THE BIGGER PICTURE.
I WAS ON THE GROUND. AND THERE WAS NOISE.
ART SAVES
SO MUCH NOISE.
AND RIGHT THERE, RIGHT AMONG THE MADNESS, RIGHT IN THE PAVEMENT--
--WAS THIS TINY DANDELION.
SOMEHOW NONE OF THOSE FEET STEPPED ON IT.
NOT A ONE.

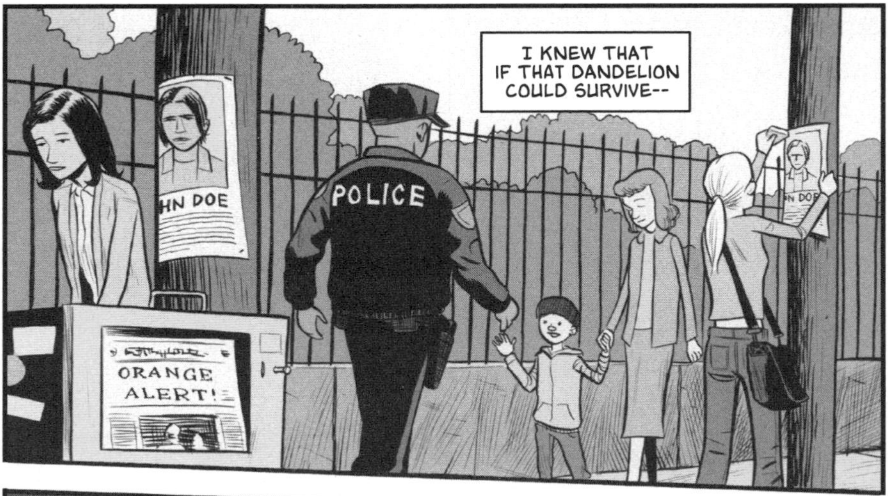
I KNEW THAT IF THAT DANDELION COULD SURVIVE--
HN DOE
POLICE
ORANGE ALERT!

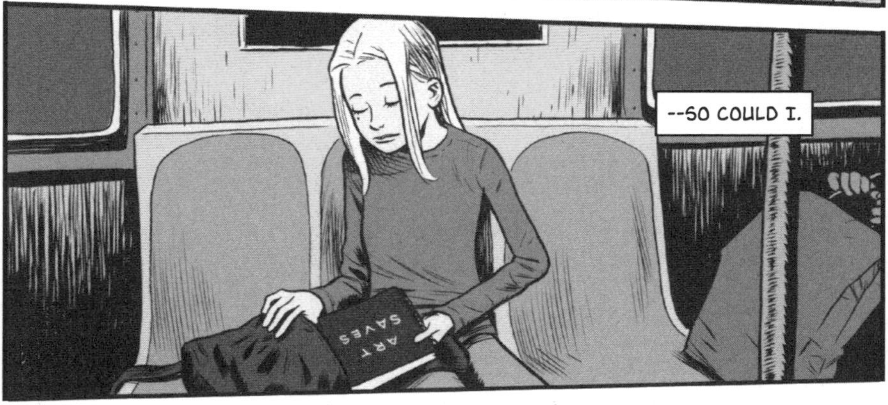
--SO COULD I.
ART SAVES

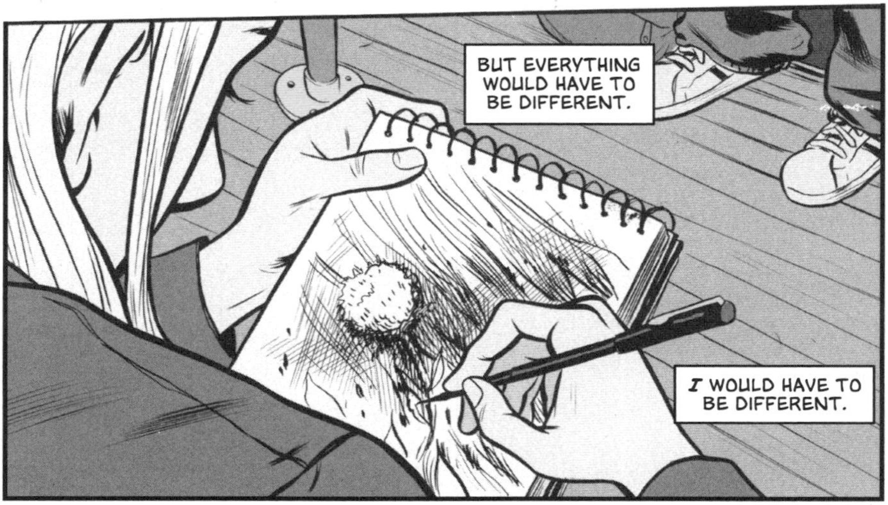
BUT EVERYTHING WOULD HAVE TO BE DIFFERENT.
I WOULD HAVE TO BE DIFFERENT.

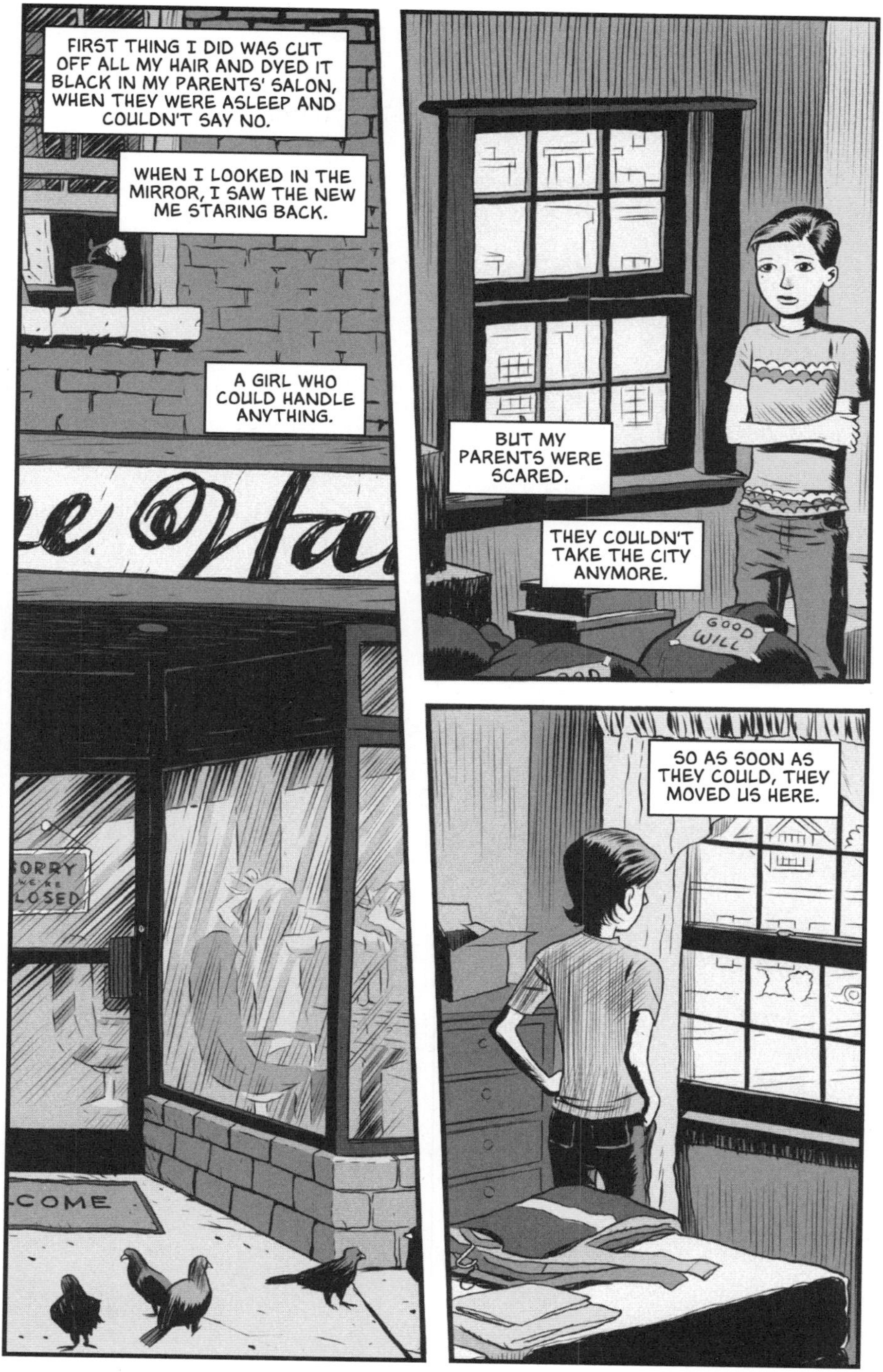
FIRST THING I DID WAS CUT OFF ALL MY HAIR AND DYED IT BLACK IN MY PARENTS' SALON, WHEN THEY WERE ASLEEP AND COULDN'T SAY NO.
WHEN I LOOKED IN THE MIRROR, I SAW THE NEW ME STARING BACK.
A GIRL WHO COULD HANDLE ANYTHING.
BUT MY PARENTS WERE SCARED.
THEY COULDN'T TAKE THE CITY ANYMORE.
GOOD WILL
SO AS SOON AS THEY COULD, THEY MOVED US HERE.

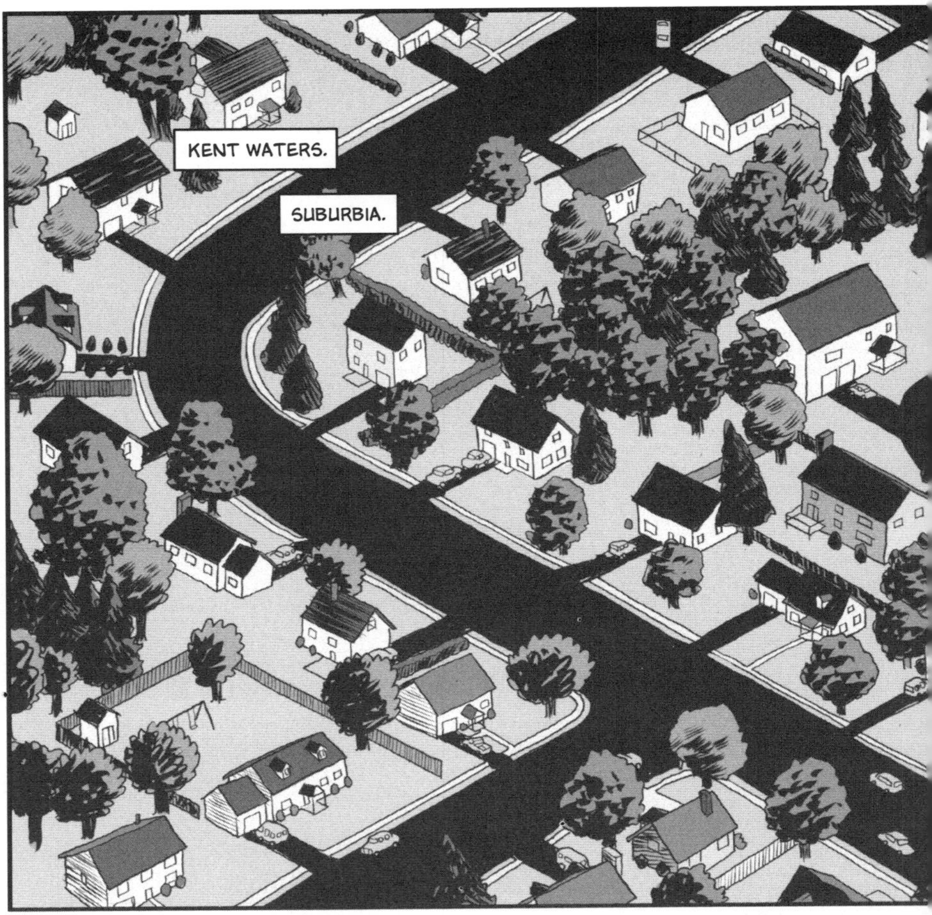
KENT WATERS.
SUBURBIA.

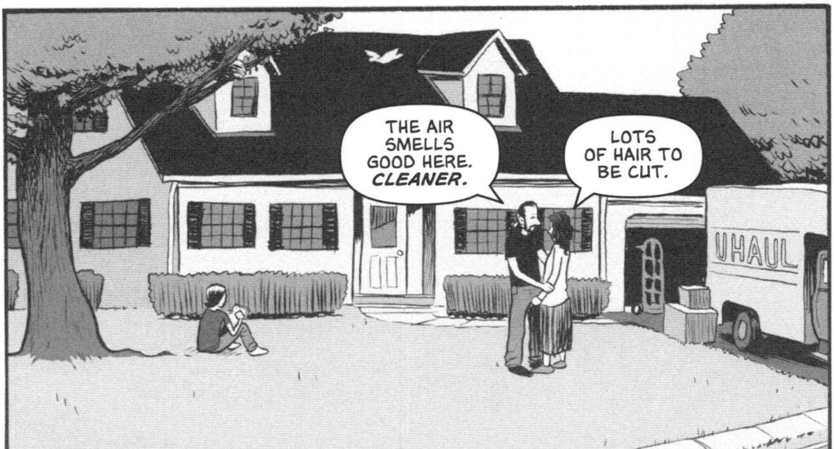
THE AIR SMELLS GOOD HERE. CLEANER.
LOTS OF HAIR TO BE CUT.
UHAUL

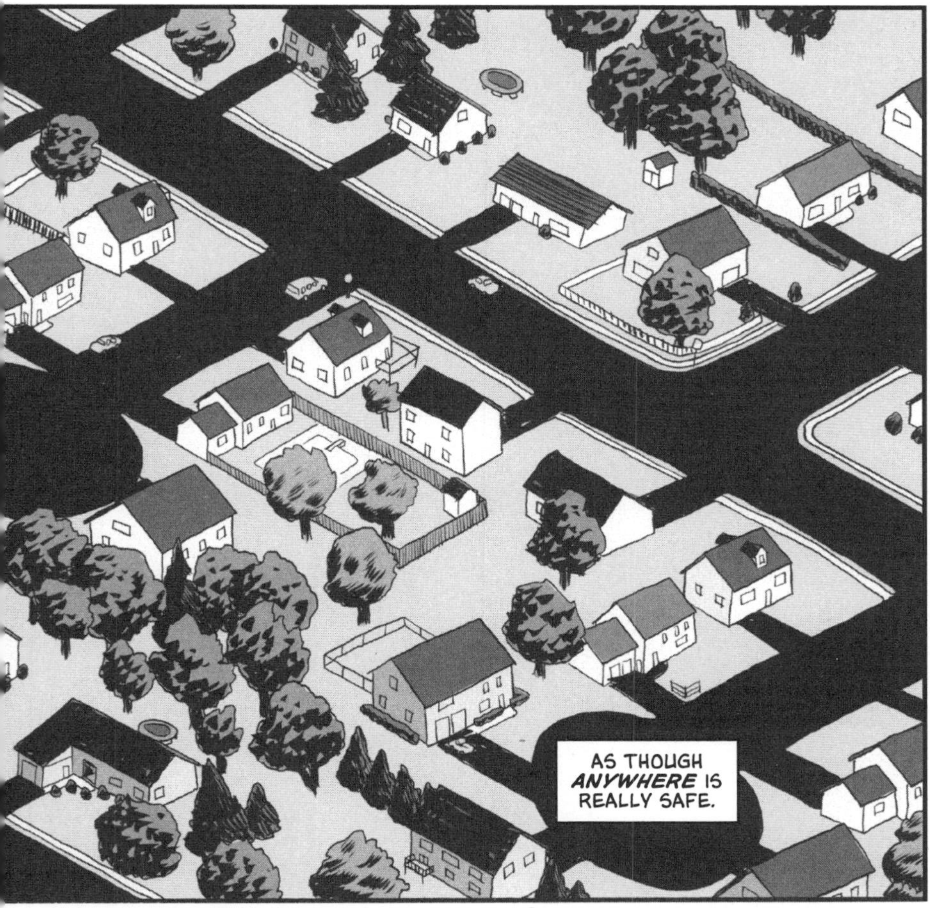
AS THOUGH *ANYWHERE* IS REALLY SAFE.

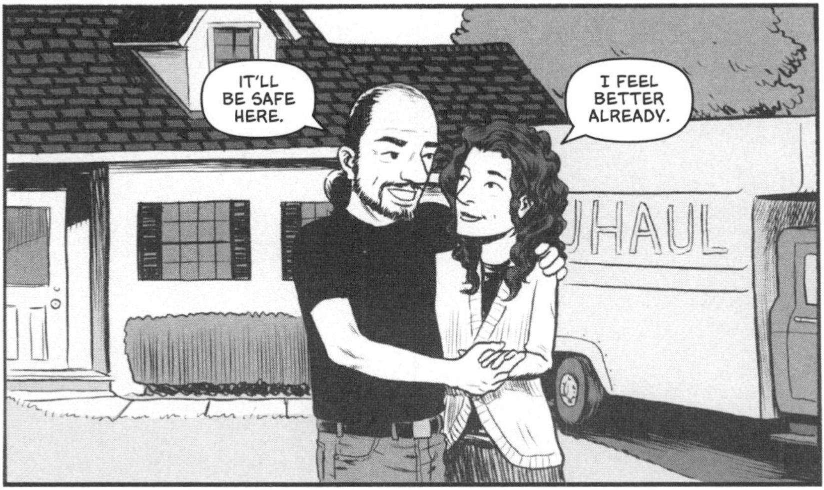
IT'LL BE SAFE HERE.
I FEEL BETTER ALREADY.
UHAUL

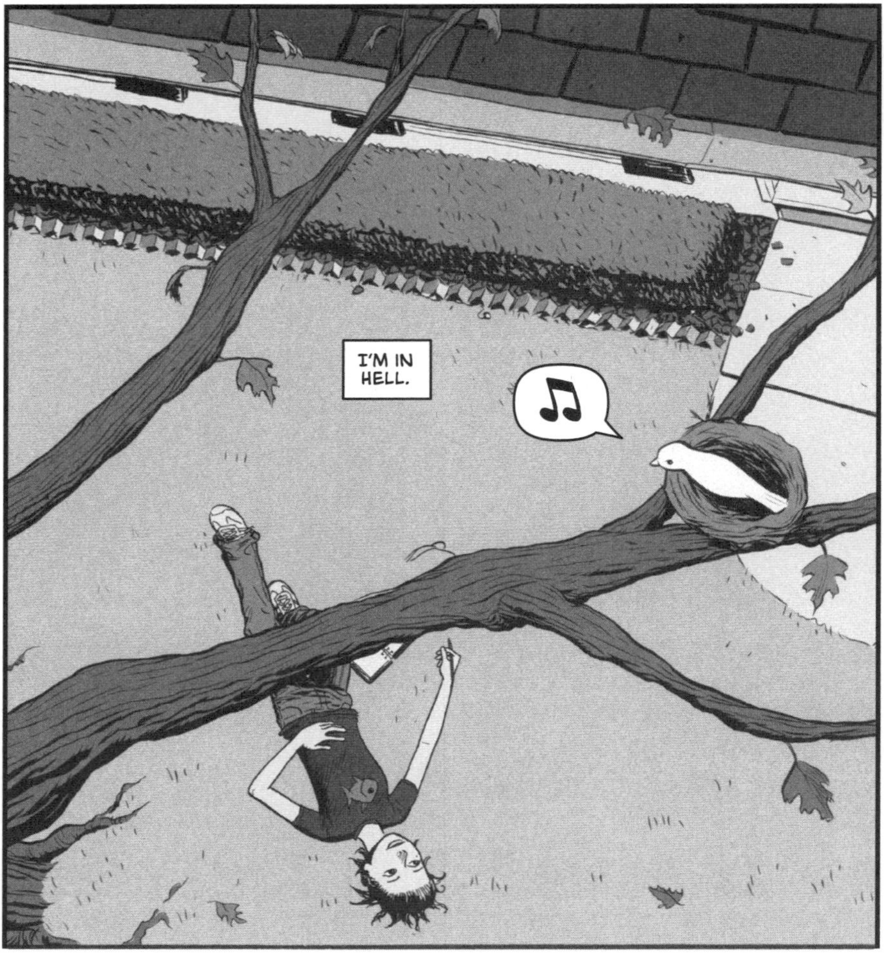
I'M IN HELL.
♫

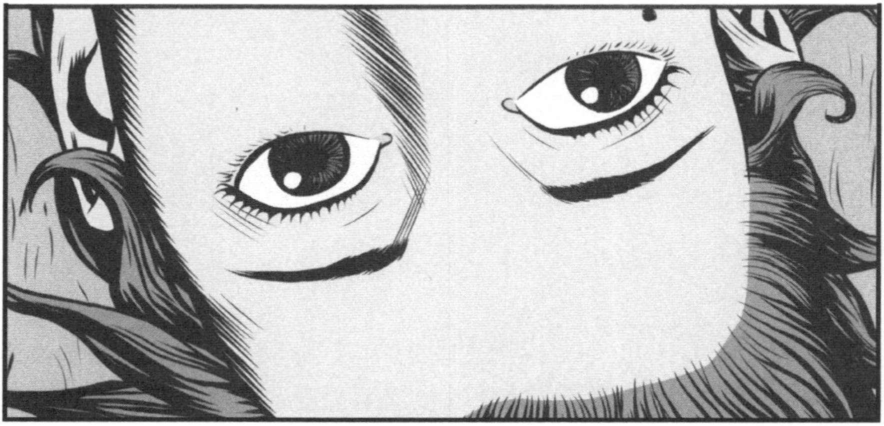

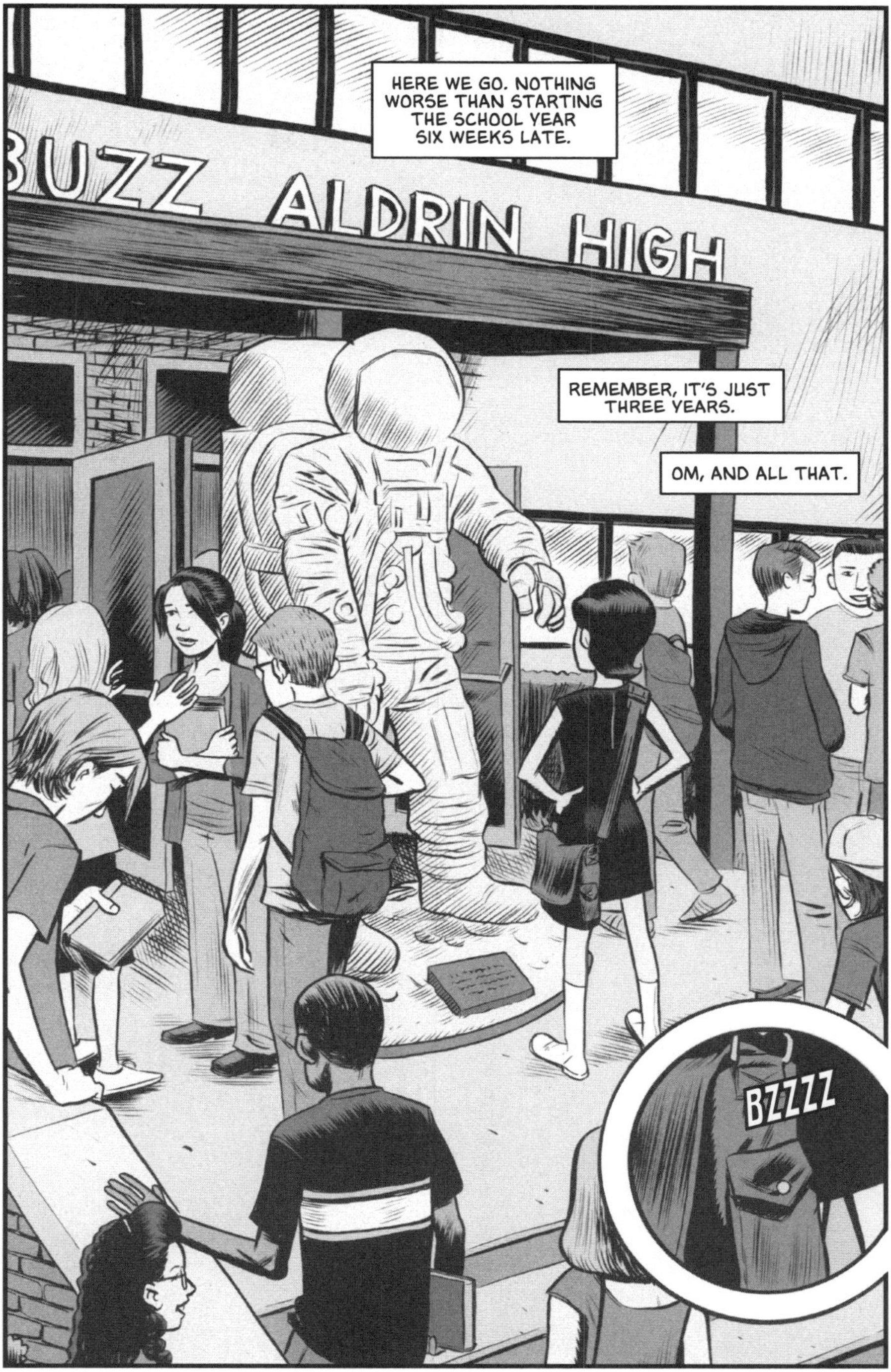
HERE WE GO. NOTHING WORSE THAN STARTING THE SCHOOL YEAR SIX WEEKS LATE.
BUZZ ALDRIN HIGH
REMEMBER, IT'S JUST THREE YEARS.
OM, AND ALL THAT.
BZZZZ

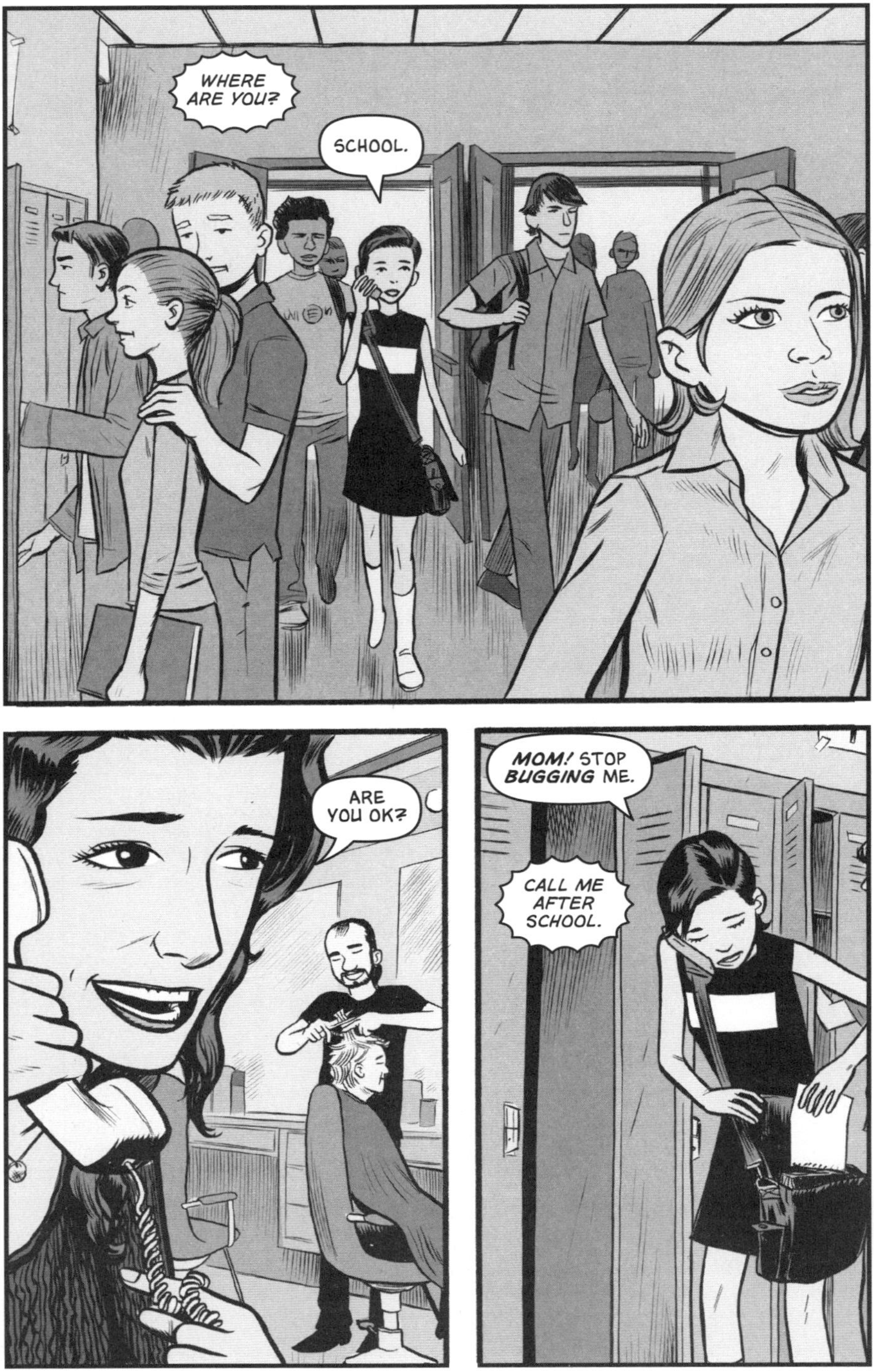
WHERE ARE YOU?
SCHOOL.
ARE YOU OK?
MOM! STOP BUGGING ME.
CALL ME AFTER SCHOOL.

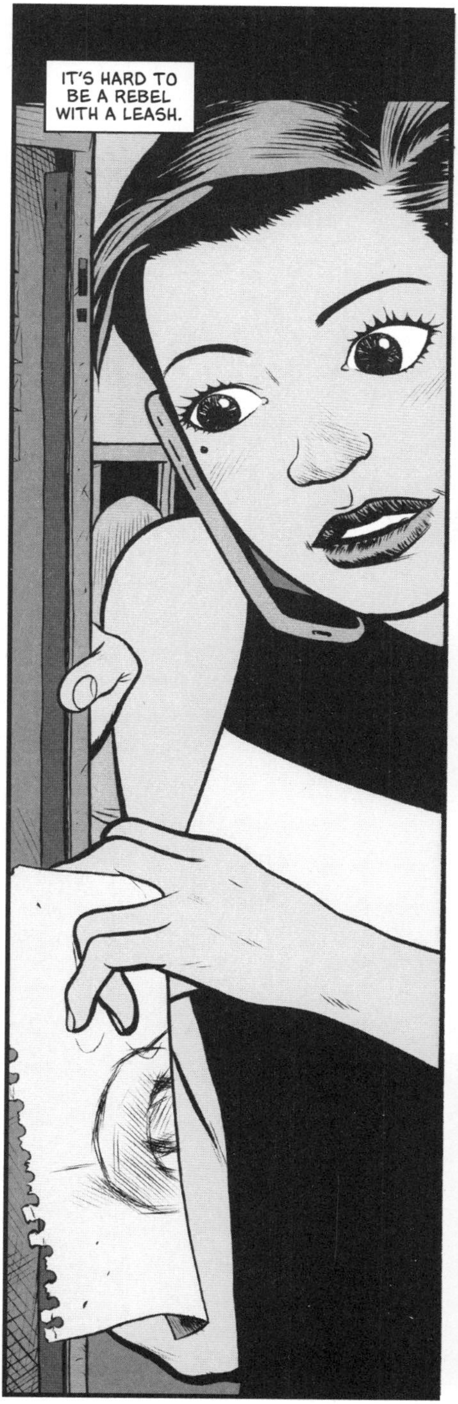
IT'S HARD TO
BE A REBEL
WITH A LEASH.

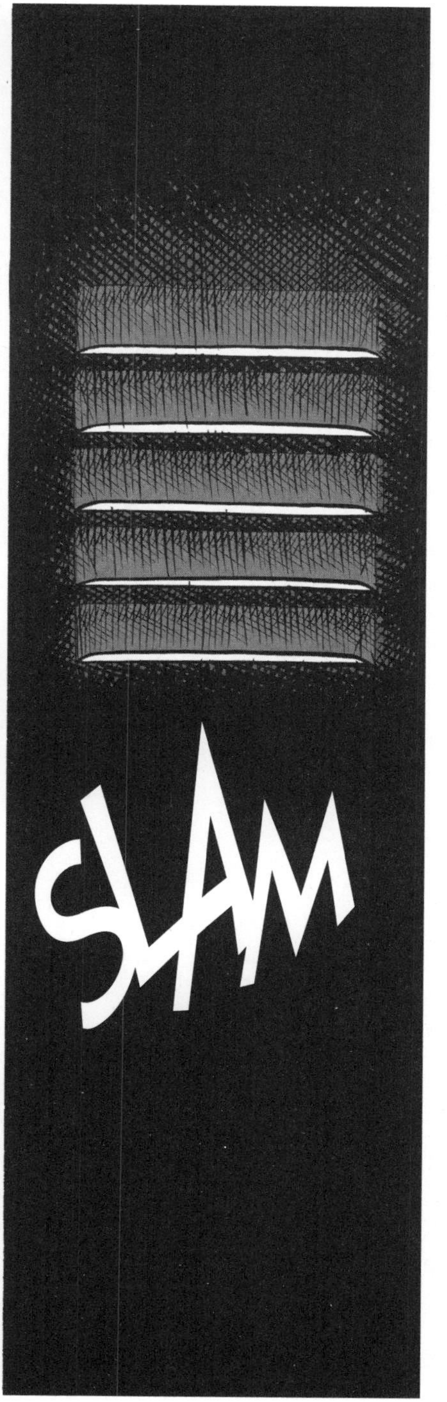
SLAM

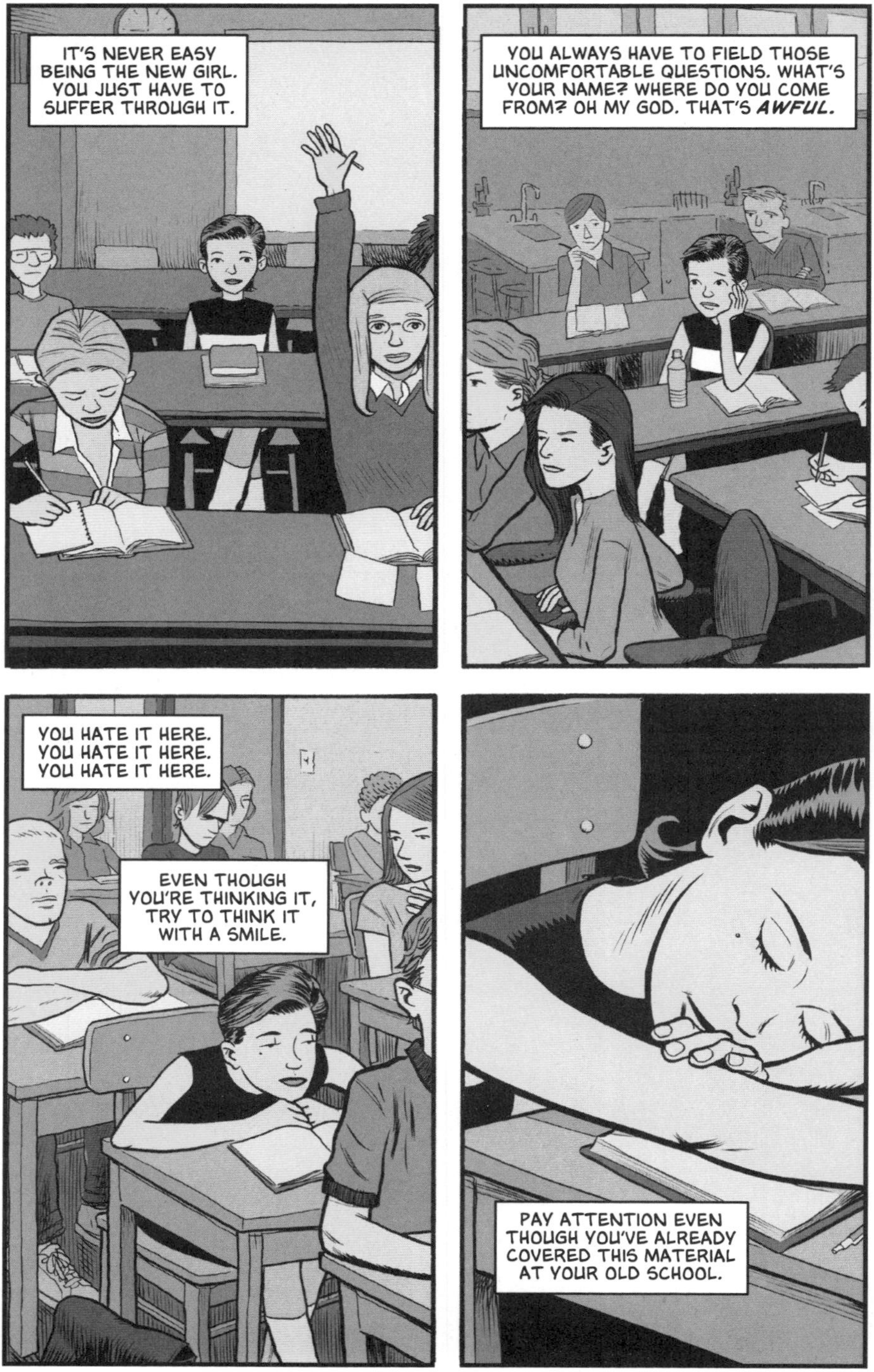
IT'S NEVER EASY BEING THE NEW GIRL. YOU JUST HAVE TO SUFFER THROUGH IT.
YOU ALWAYS HAVE TO FIELD THOSE UNCOMFORTABLE QUESTIONS. WHAT'S YOUR NAME? WHERE DO YOU COME FROM? OH MY GOD. THAT'S *AWFUL.*
YOU HATE IT HERE. YOU HATE IT HERE. YOU HATE IT HERE.
EVEN THOUGH YOU'RE THINKING IT, TRY TO THINK IT WITH A SMILE.
PAY ATTENTION EVEN THOUGH YOU'VE ALREADY COVERED THIS MATERIAL AT YOUR OLD SCHOOL.

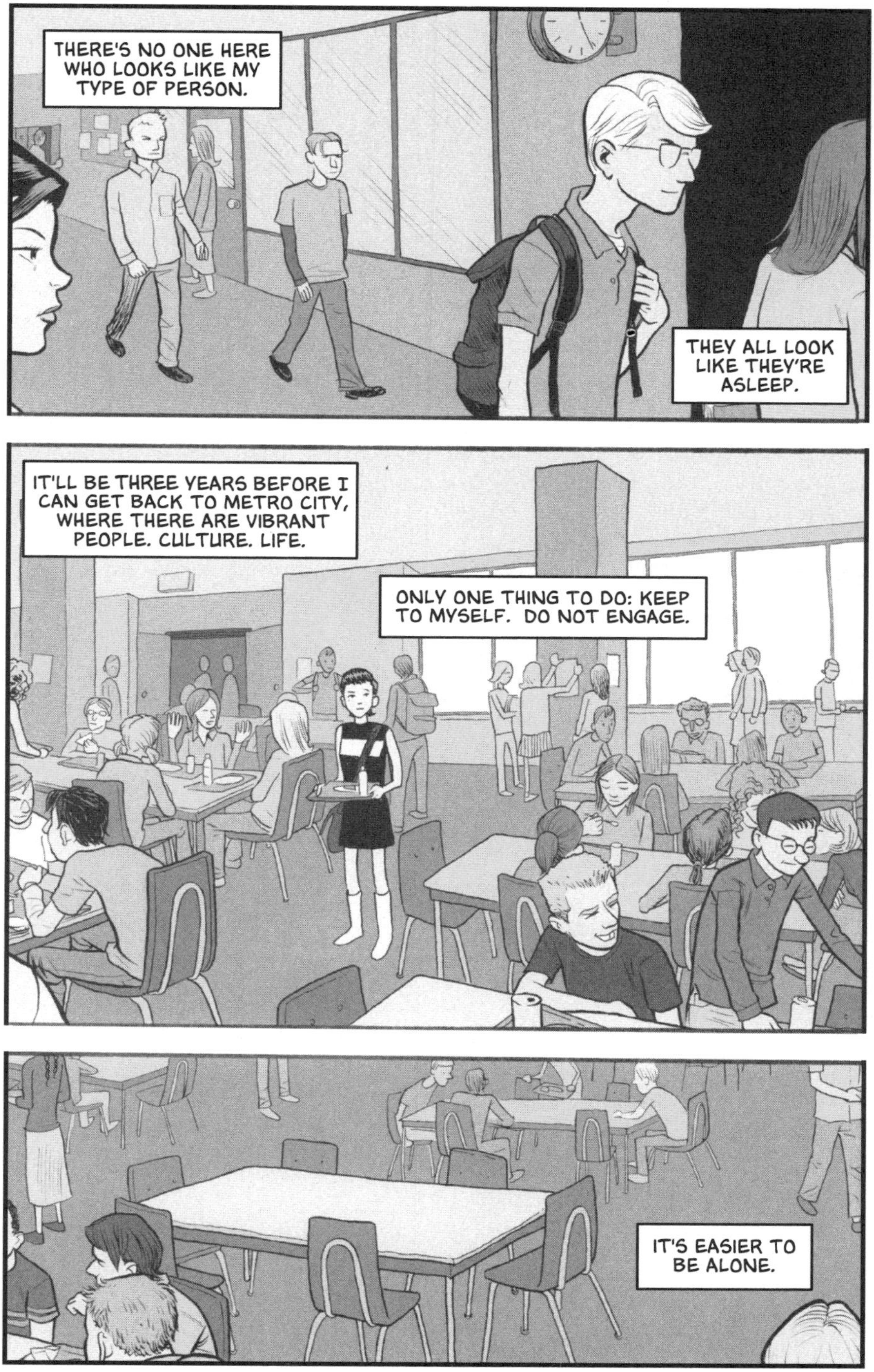
THERE'S NO ONE HERE WHO LOOKS LIKE MY TYPE OF PERSON.
THEY ALL LOOK LIKE THEY'RE ASLEEP.
IT'LL BE THREE YEARS BEFORE I CAN GET BACK TO METRO CITY, WHERE THERE ARE VIBRANT PEOPLE. CULTURE. LIFE.
ONLY ONE THING TO DO: KEEP TO MYSELF. DO NOT ENGAGE.
IT'S EASIER TO BE ALONE.

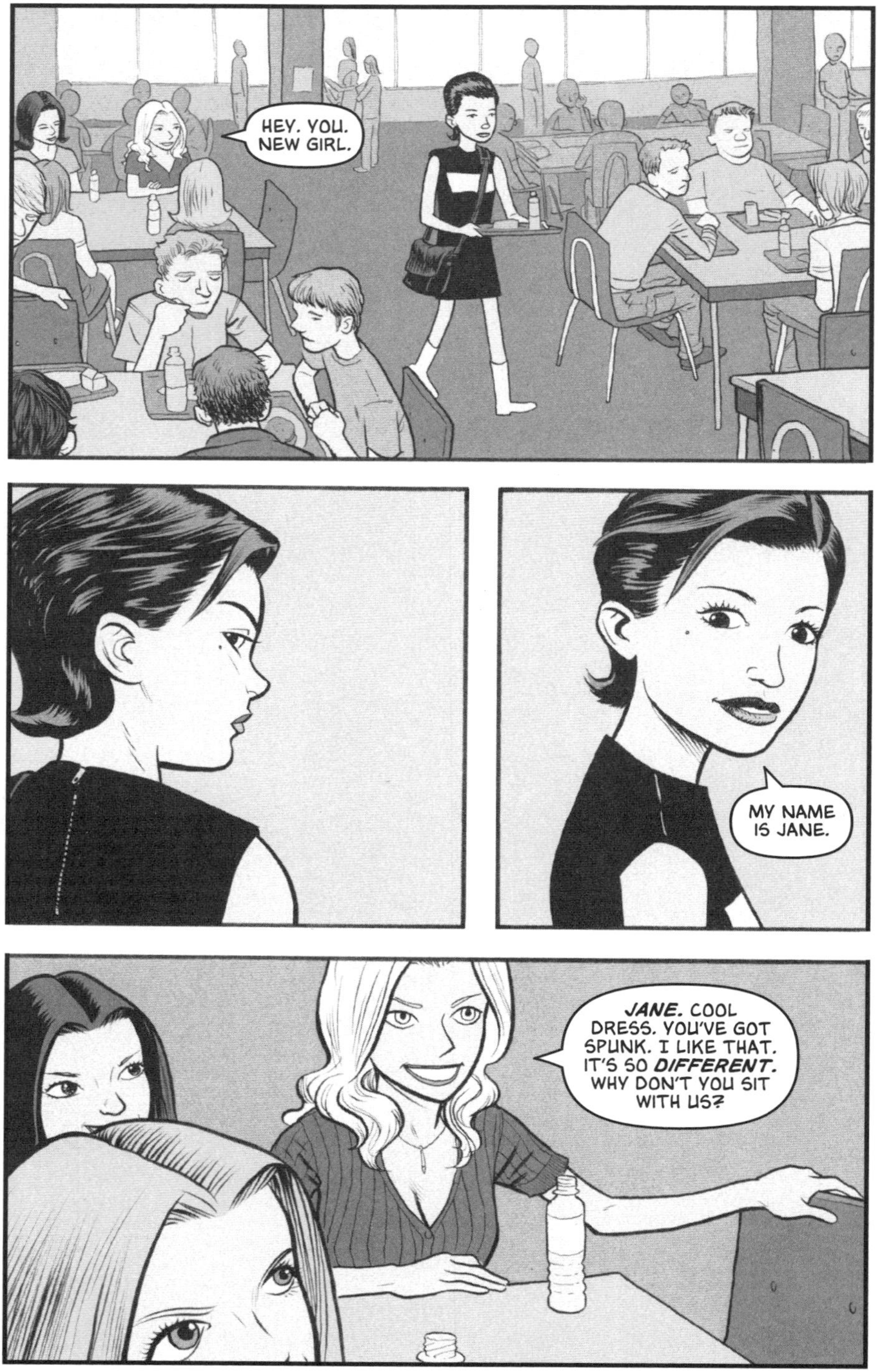
HEY. YOU. NEW GIRL.
MY NAME IS JANE.
JANE. COOL DRESS. YOU'VE GOT SPUNK. I LIKE THAT. IT'S SO *DIFFERENT.* WHY DON'T YOU SIT WITH US?

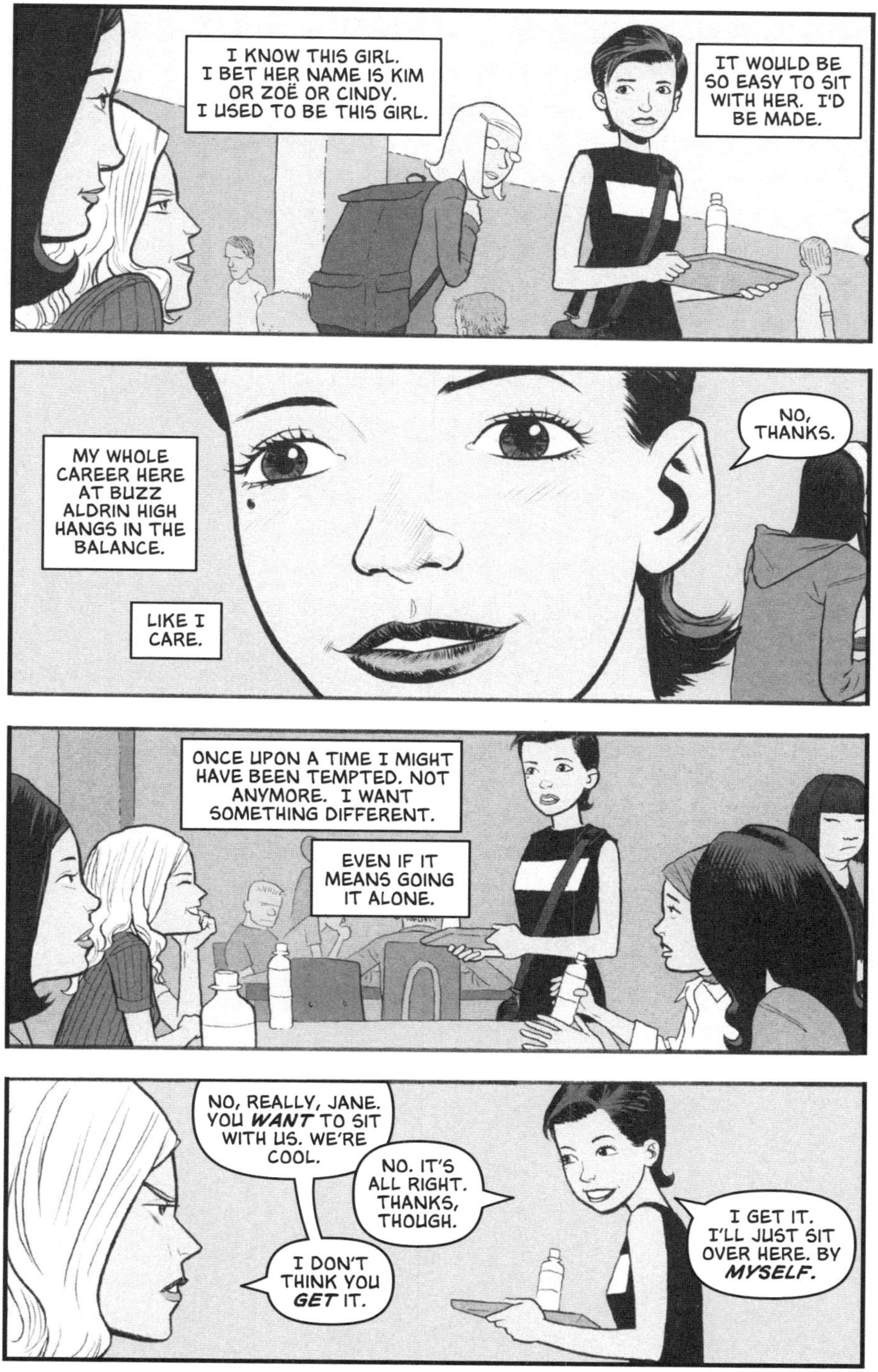

I KNOW THIS GIRL. I BET HER NAME IS KIM OR ZOË OR CINDY. I USED TO BE THIS GIRL.
IT WOULD BE SO EASY TO SIT WITH HER. I'D BE MADE.
MY WHOLE CAREER HERE AT BUZZ ALDRIN HIGH HANGS IN THE BALANCE.
LIKE I CARE.
NO, THANKS.
ONCE UPON A TIME I MIGHT HAVE BEEN TEMPTED. NOT ANYMORE. I WANT SOMETHING DIFFERENT.
EVEN IF IT MEANS GOING IT ALONE.
NO, REALLY, JANE. YOU ***WANT*** TO SIT WITH US. WE'RE COOL.
NO. IT'S ALL RIGHT. THANKS, THOUGH.
I DON'T THINK YOU ***GET*** IT.
I GET IT. I'LL JUST SIT OVER HERE. BY ***MYSELF.***

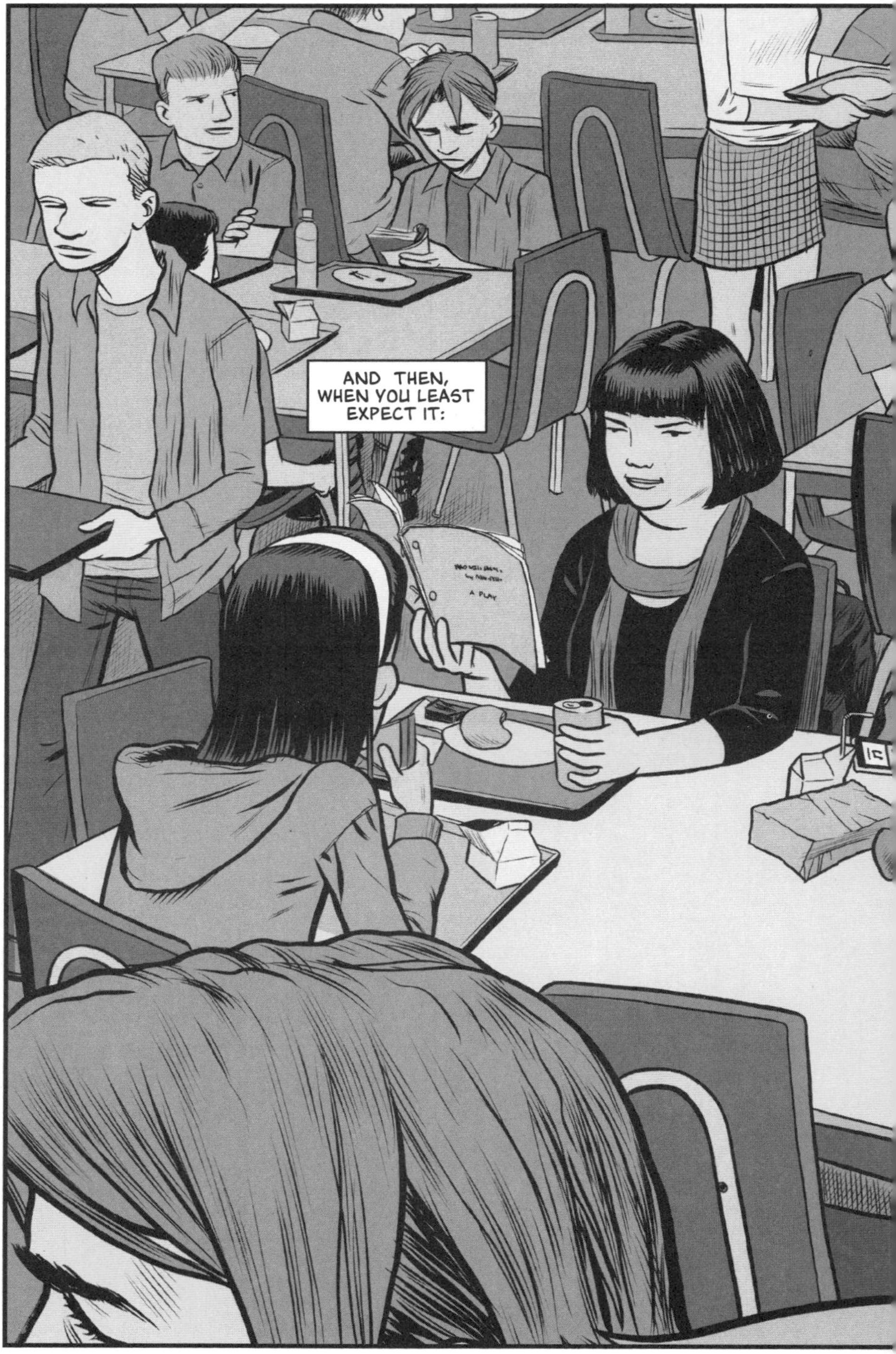
AND THEN,
WHEN YOU LEAST
EXPECT IT:

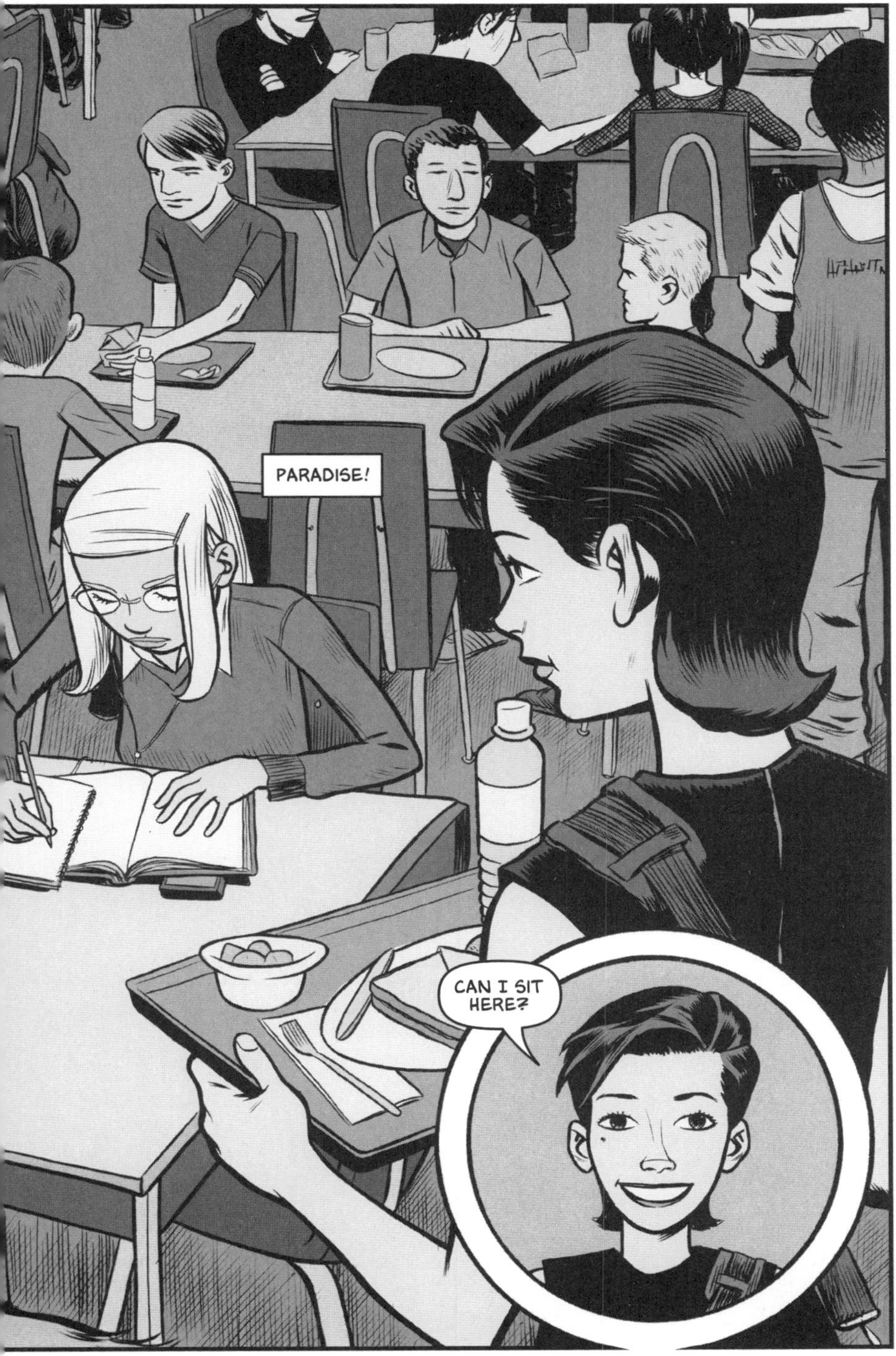
PARADISE!
CAN I SIT HERE?

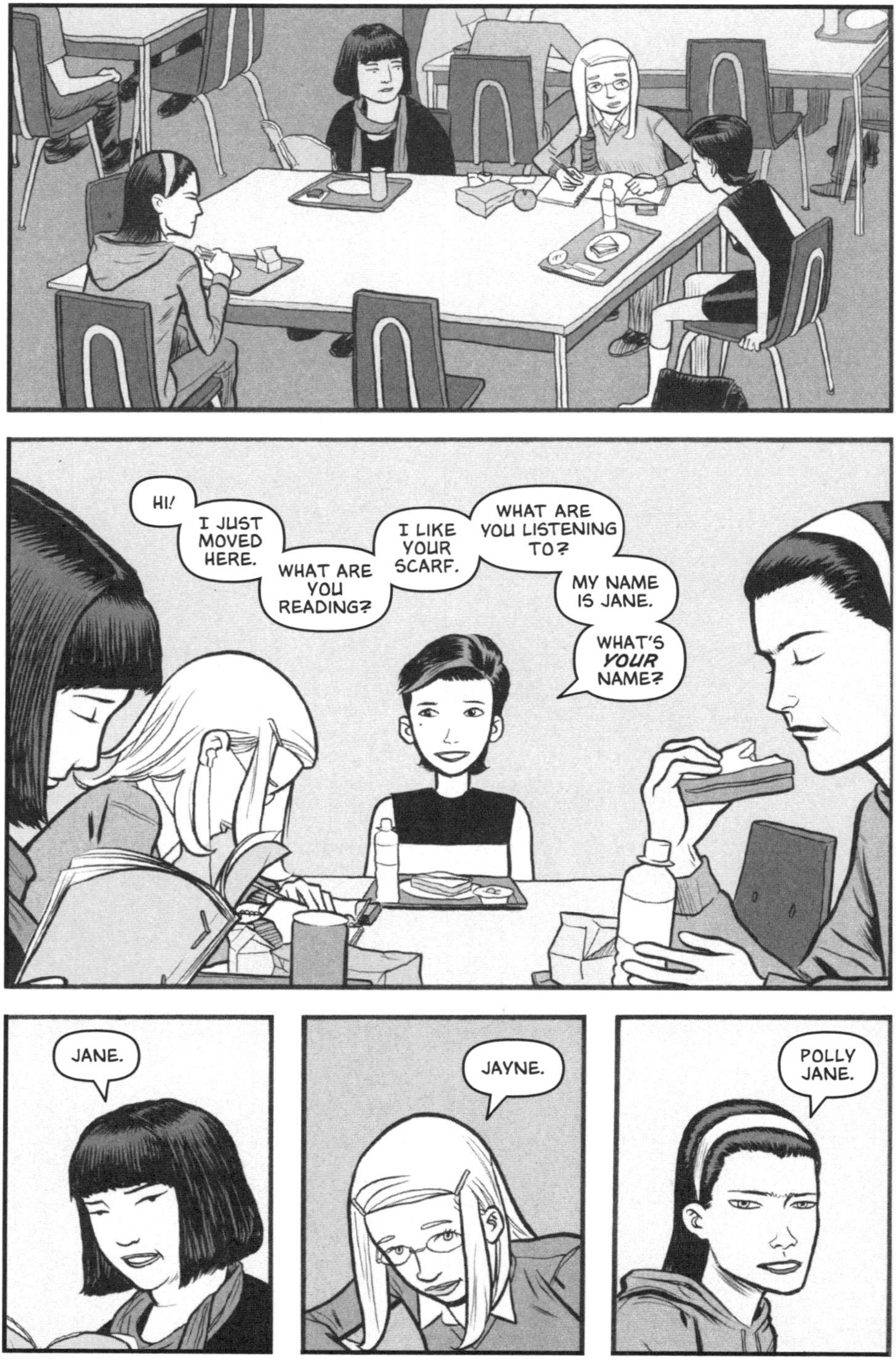
HI!
I JUST MOVED HERE.
WHAT ARE YOU READING?
I LIKE YOUR SCARF.
WHAT ARE YOU LISTENING TO?
MY NAME IS JANE.
WHAT'S *YOUR* NAME?
JANE.
JAYNE.
POLLY JANE.

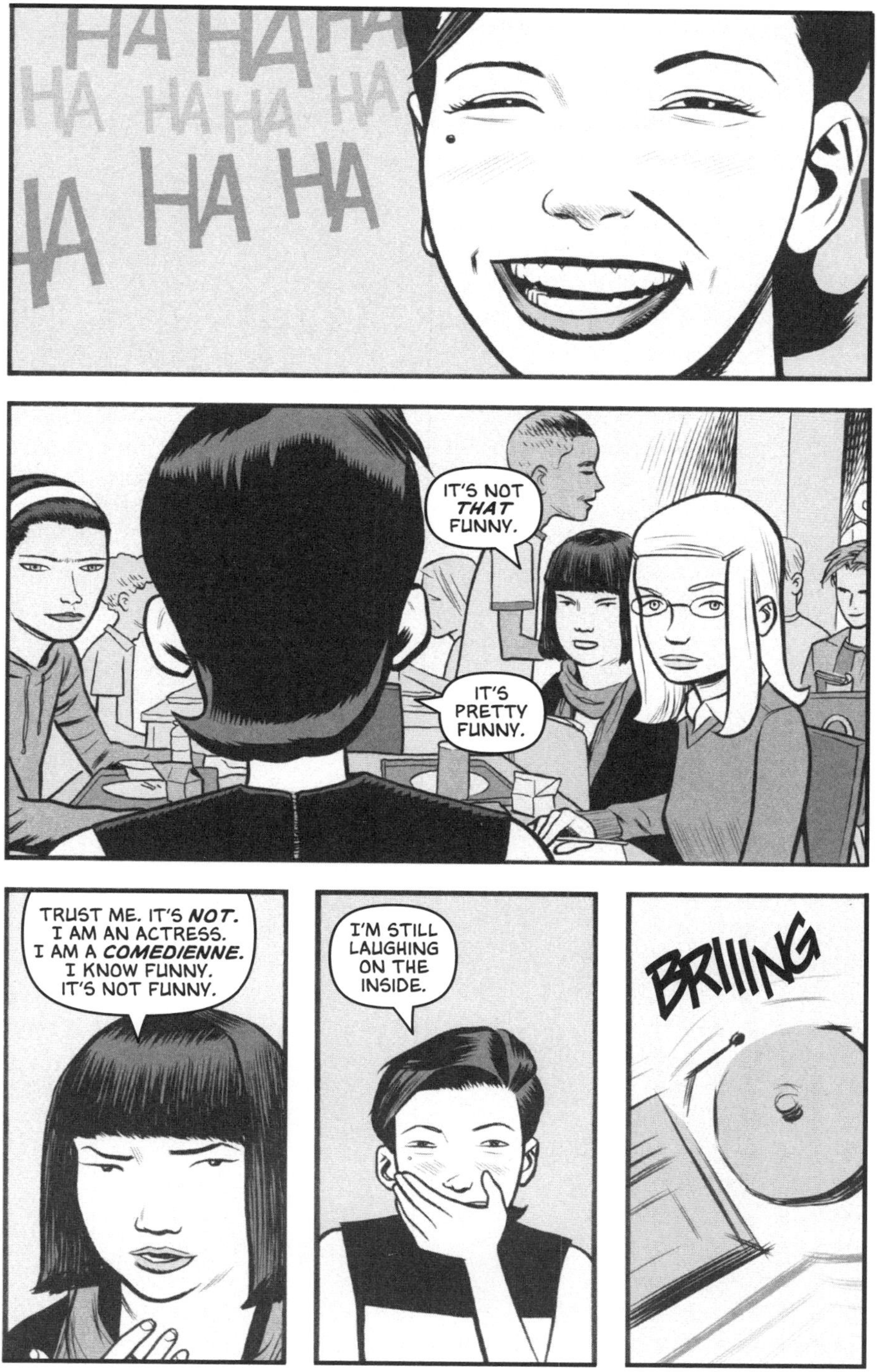
HA HA HA
HA HA HA HA
HA HA HA
IT'S NOT *THAT* FUNNY.
IT'S PRETTY FUNNY.
TRUST ME. IT'S *NOT.* I AM AN ACTRESS. I AM A *COMEDIENNE.* I KNOW FUNNY. IT'S NOT FUNNY.
I'M STILL LAUGHING ON THE INSIDE.
BRIIING

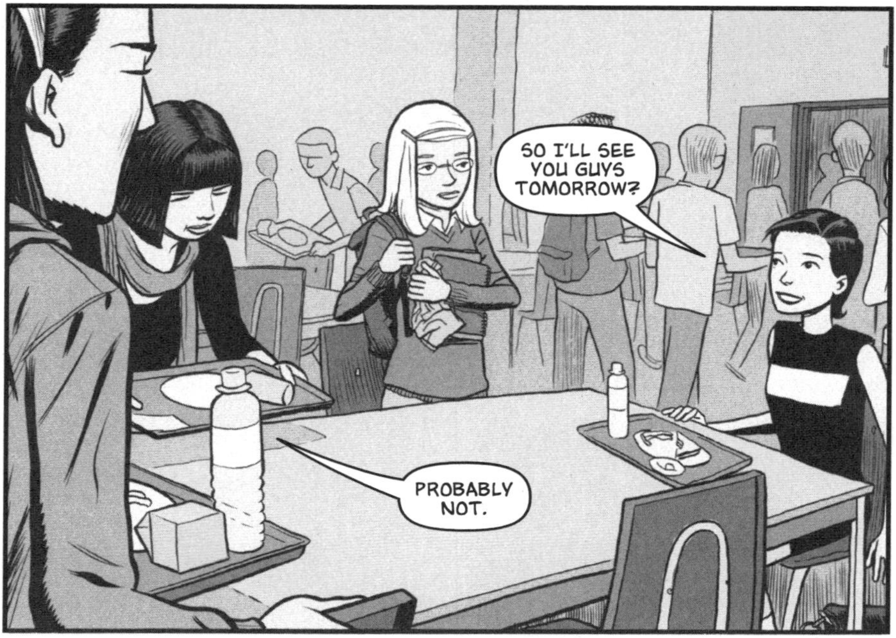
SO I'LL SEE YOU GUYS TOMORROW?
PROBABLY NOT.

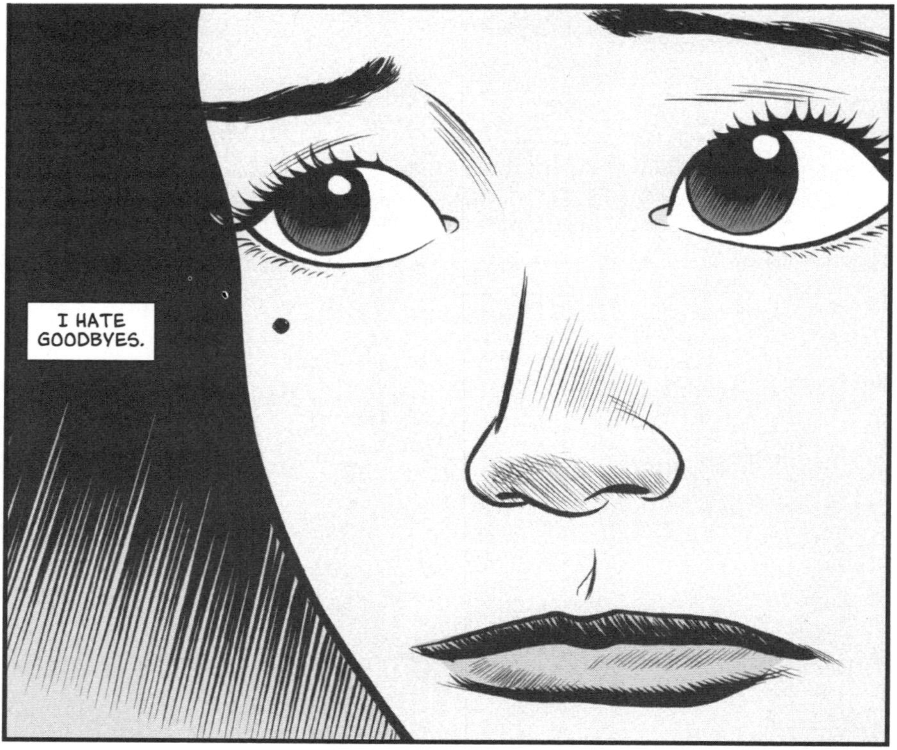
I HATE GOODBYES.

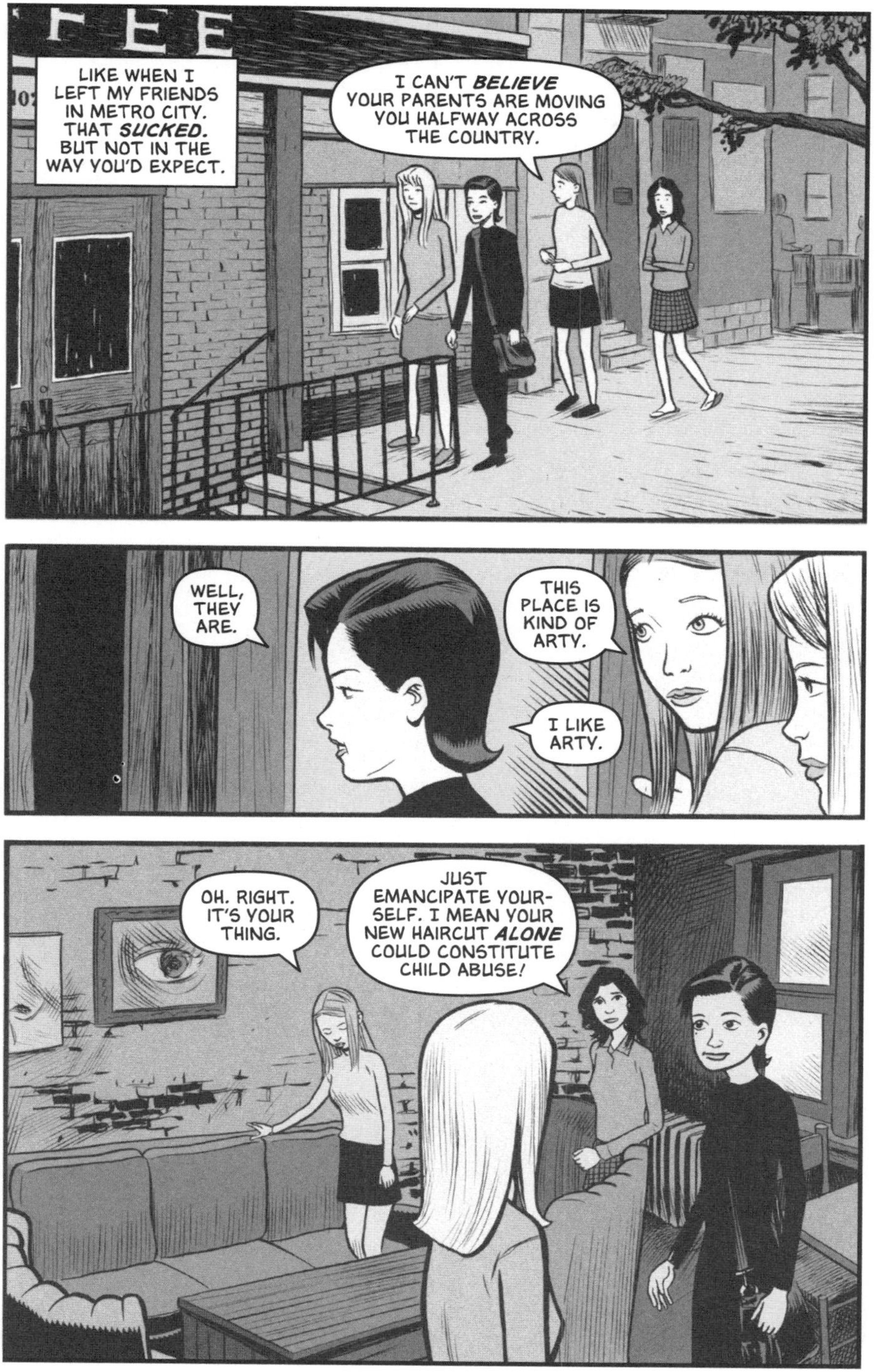

LIKE WHEN I LEFT MY FRIENDS IN METRO CITY. THAT *SUCKED.* BUT NOT IN THE WAY YOU'D EXPECT.
I CAN'T *BELIEVE* YOUR PARENTS ARE MOVING YOU HALFWAY ACROSS THE COUNTRY.
WELL, THEY ARE.
THIS PLACE IS KIND OF ARTY.
I LIKE ARTY.
OH. RIGHT. IT'S YOUR THING.
JUST EMANCIPATE YOUR-SELF. I MEAN YOUR NEW HAIRCUT *ALONE* COULD CONSTITUTE CHILD ABUSE!

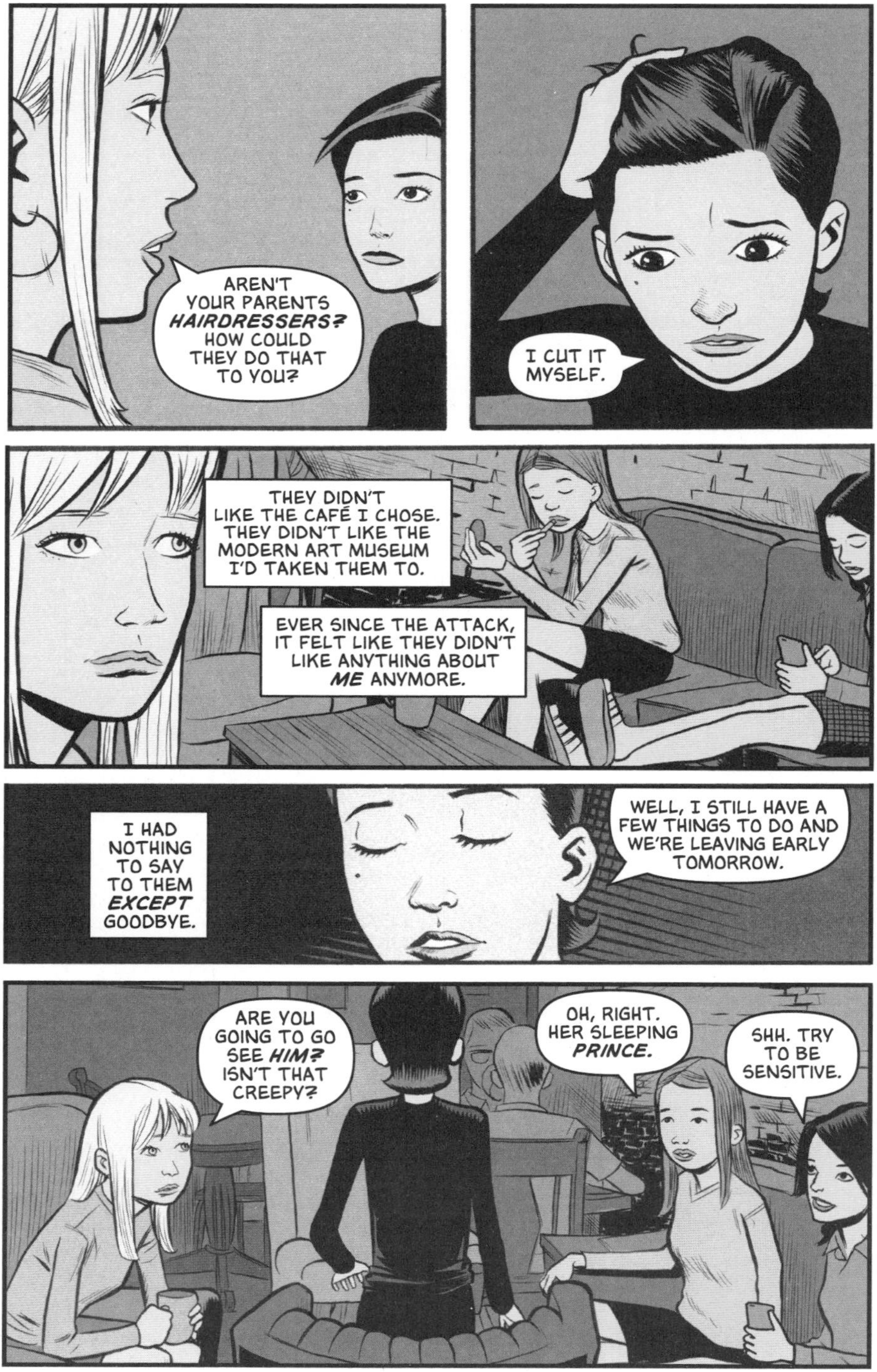
AREN'T YOUR PARENTS HAIRDRESSERS? HOW COULD THEY DO THAT TO YOU?
I CUT IT MYSELF.
THEY DIDN'T LIKE THE CAFÉ I CHOSE. THEY DIDN'T LIKE THE MODERN ART MUSEUM I'D TAKEN THEM TO.
EVER SINCE THE ATTACK, IT FELT LIKE THEY DIDN'T LIKE ANYTHING ABOUT ME ANYMORE.
I HAD NOTHING TO SAY TO THEM EXCEPT GOODBYE.
WELL, I STILL HAVE A FEW THINGS TO DO AND WE'RE LEAVING EARLY TOMORROW.
ARE YOU GOING TO GO SEE HIM? ISN'T THAT CREEPY?
OH, RIGHT. HER SLEEPING PRINCE.
SHH. TRY TO BE SENSITIVE.

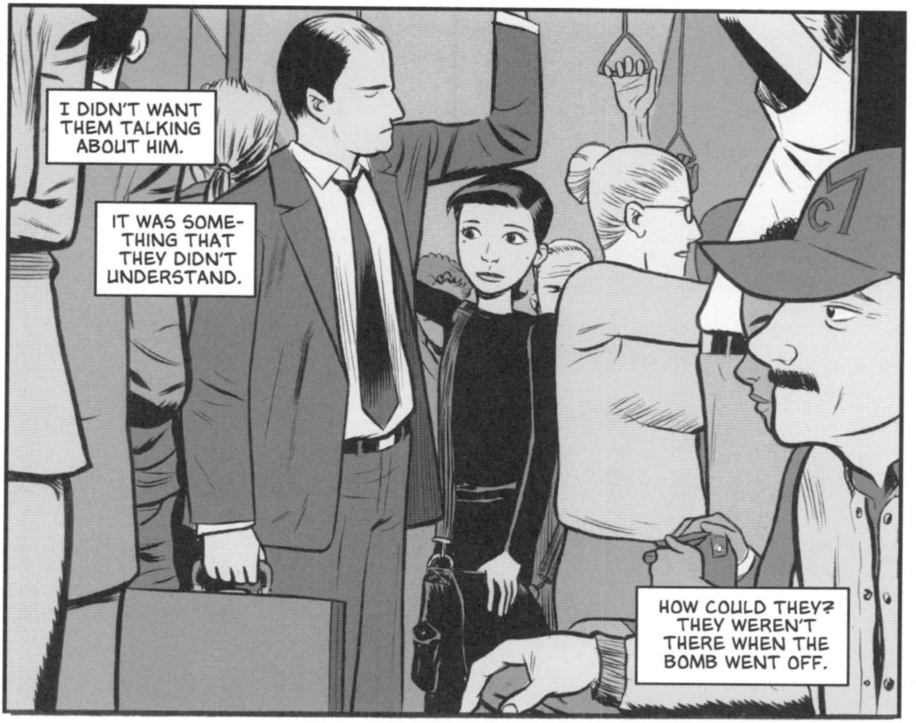
I DIDN'T WANT THEM TALKING ABOUT HIM.
IT WAS SOMETHING THAT THEY DIDN'T UNDERSTAND.
HOW COULD THEY? THEY WEREN'T THERE WHEN THE BOMB WENT OFF.

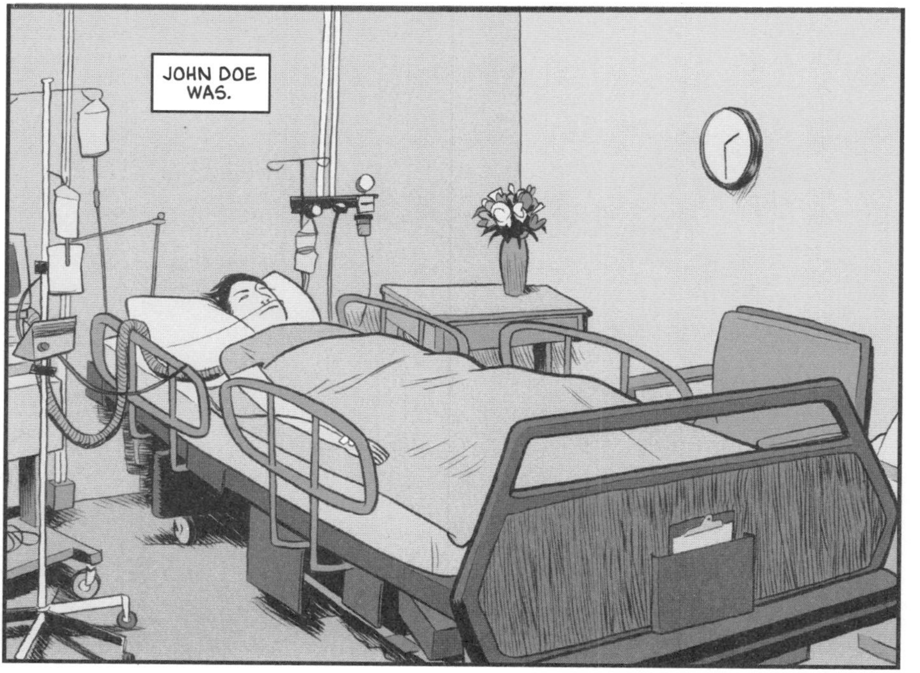
JOHN DOE WAS.

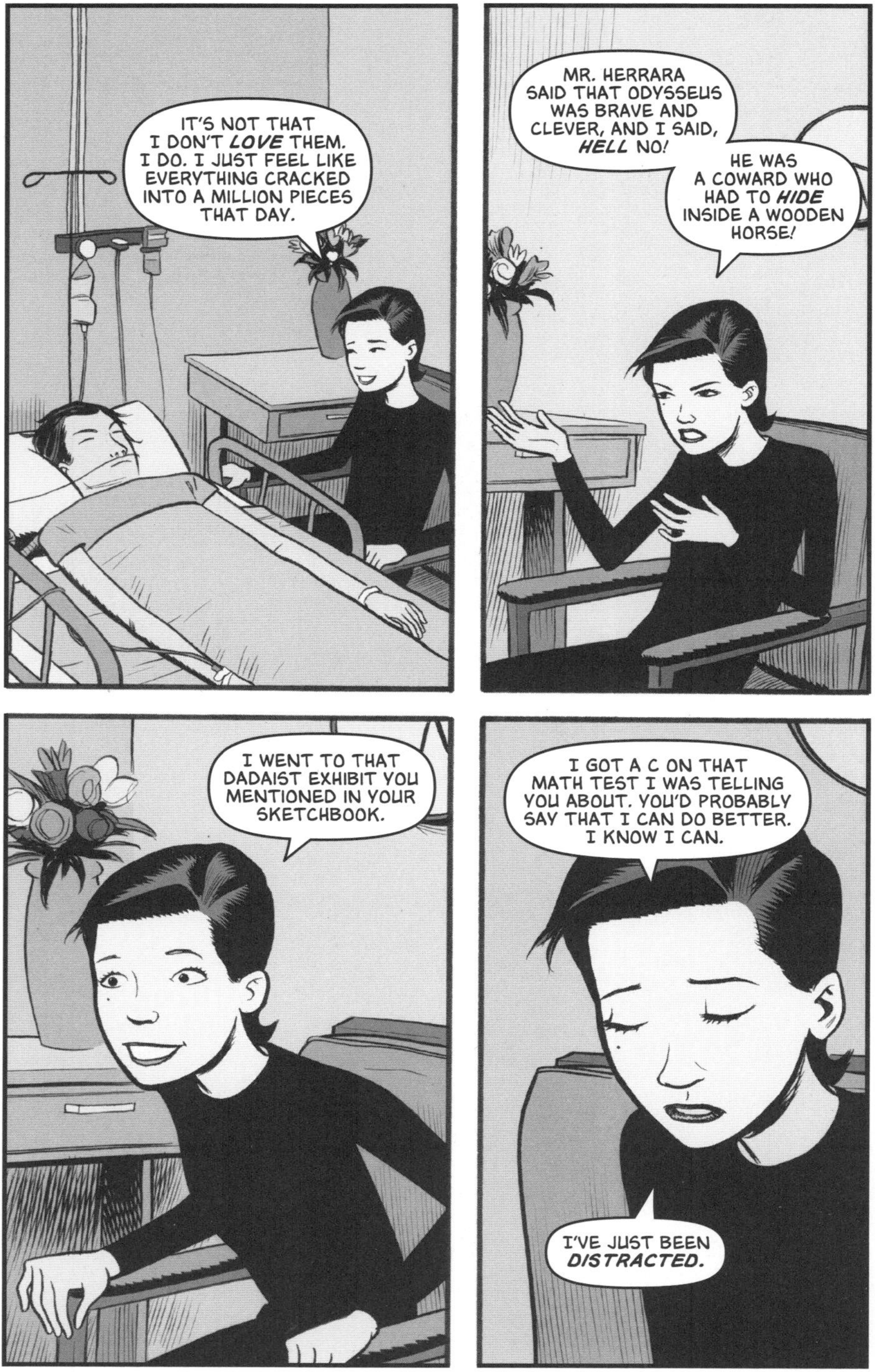
IT'S NOT THAT I DON'T LOVE THEM. I DO. I JUST FEEL LIKE EVERYTHING CRACKED INTO A MILLION PIECES THAT DAY.
MR. HERRARA SAID THAT ODYSSEUS WAS BRAVE AND CLEVER, AND I SAID, HELL NO!
HE WAS A COWARD WHO HAD TO HIDE INSIDE A WOODEN HORSE!
I WENT TO THAT DADAIST EXHIBIT YOU MENTIONED IN YOUR SKETCHBOOK.
I GOT A C ON THAT MATH TEST I WAS TELLING YOU ABOUT. YOU'D PROBABLY SAY THAT I CAN DO BETTER. I KNOW I CAN.
I'VE JUST BEEN DISTRACTED.

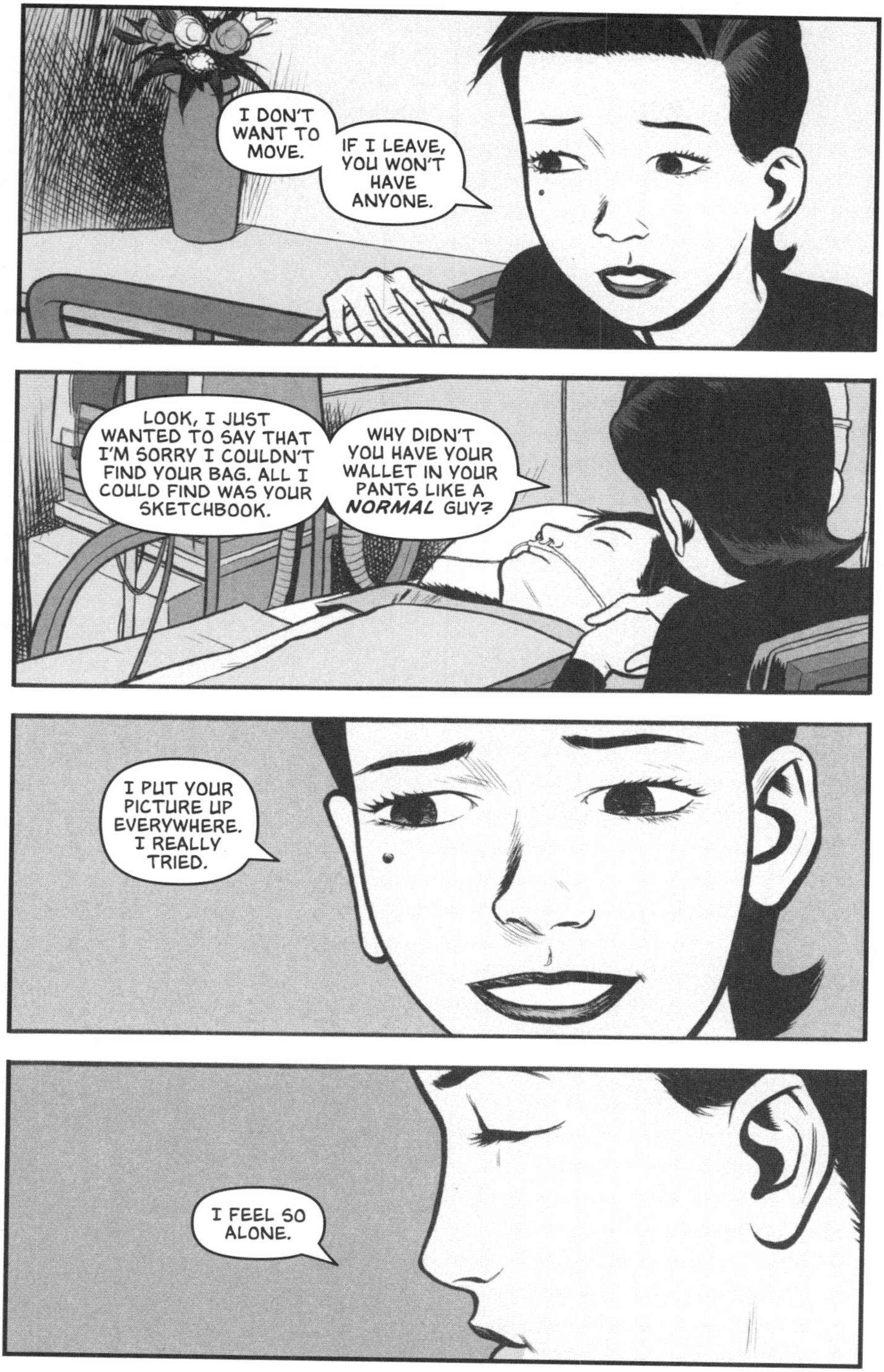

I DON'T WANT TO MOVE.
IF I LEAVE, YOU WON'T HAVE ANYONE.
LOOK, I JUST WANTED TO SAY THAT I'M SORRY I COULDN'T FIND YOUR BAG. ALL I COULD FIND WAS YOUR SKETCHBOOK.
WHY DIDN'T YOU HAVE YOUR WALLET IN YOUR PANTS LIKE A *NORMAL* GUY?
I PUT YOUR PICTURE UP EVERYWHERE. I REALLY TRIED.
I FEEL SO ALONE.

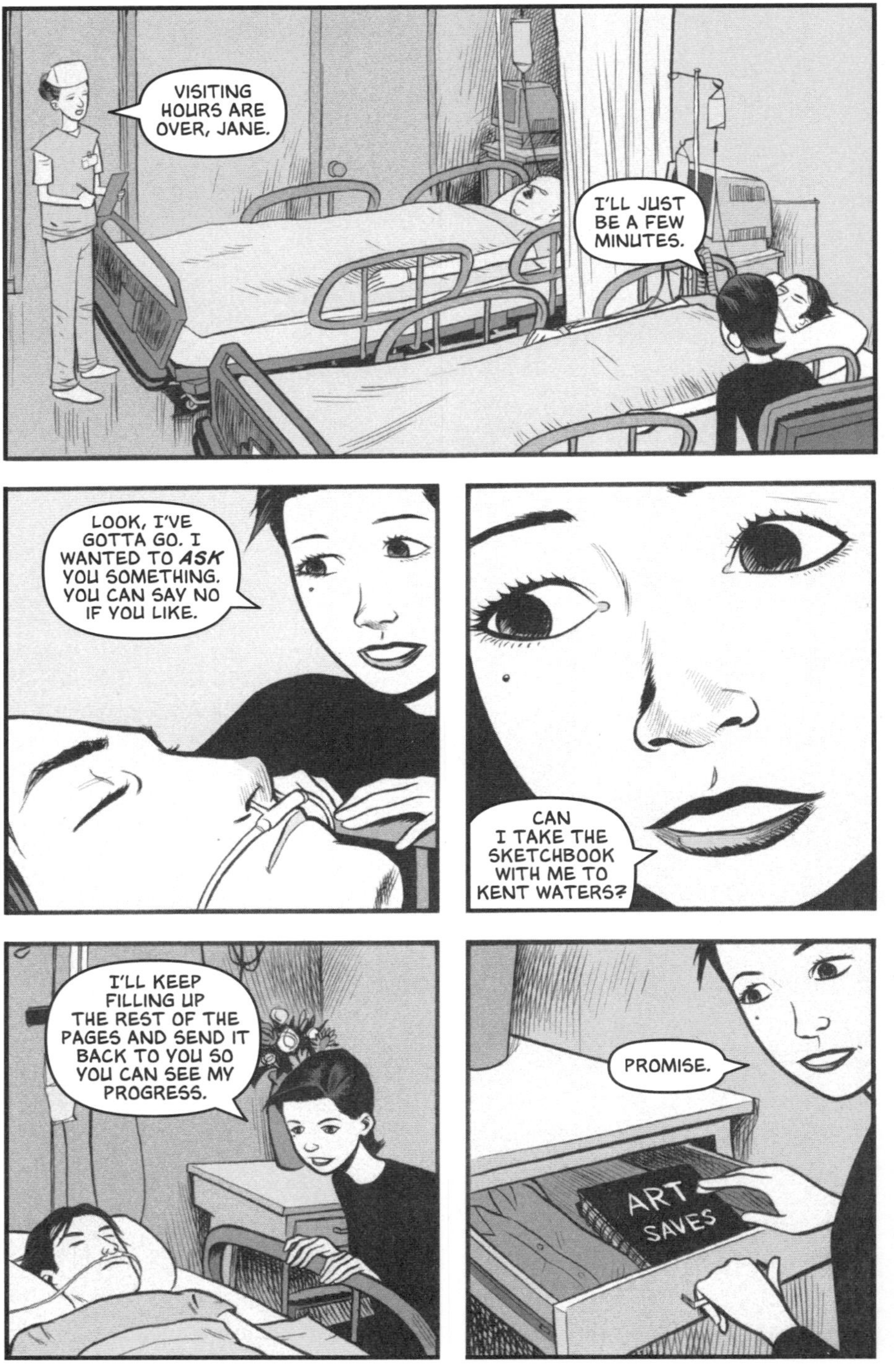
VISITING HOURS ARE OVER, JANE.
I'LL JUST BE A FEW MINUTES.
LOOK, I'VE GOTTA GO. I WANTED TO ASK YOU SOMETHING. YOU CAN SAY NO IF YOU LIKE.
CAN I TAKE THE SKETCHBOOK WITH ME TO KENT WATERS?
I'LL KEEP FILLING UP THE REST OF THE PAGES AND SEND IT BACK TO YOU SO YOU CAN SEE MY PROGRESS.
PROMISE.
ART SAVES

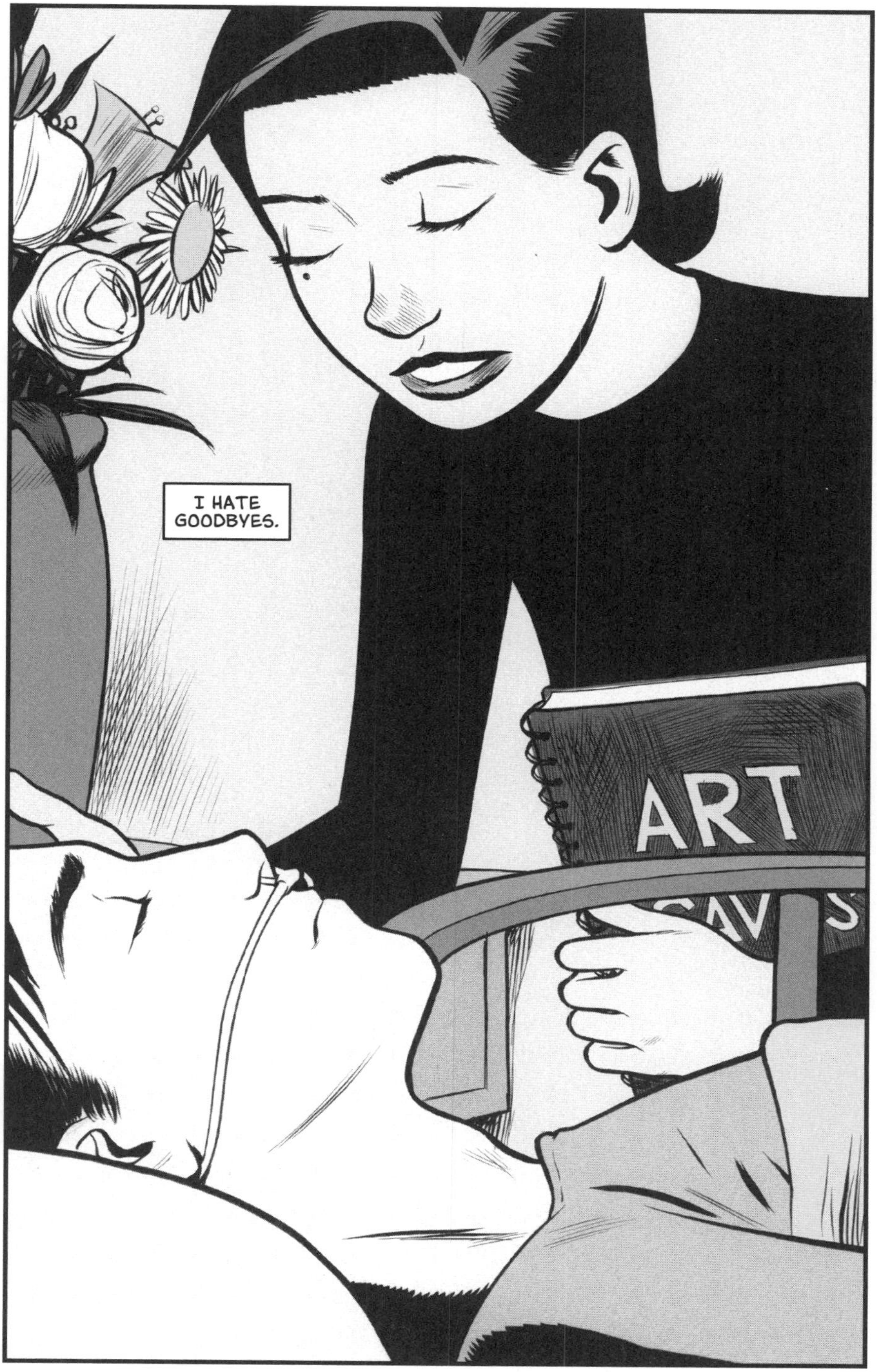
I HATE GOODBYES.
ART

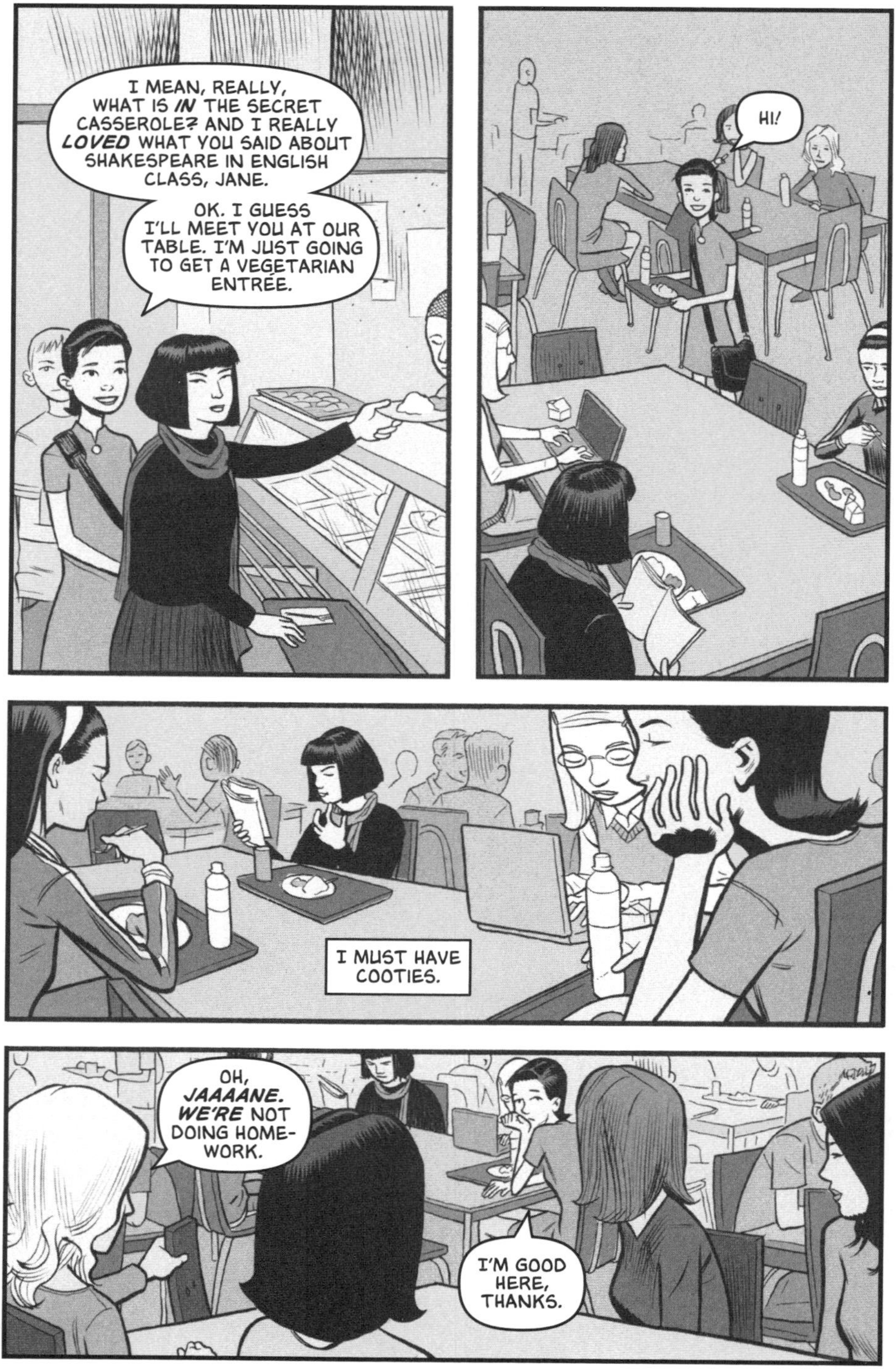
I MEAN, REALLY, WHAT IS *IN* THE SECRET CASSEROLE? AND I REALLY *LOVED* WHAT YOU SAID ABOUT SHAKESPEARE IN ENGLISH CLASS, JANE.
OK. I GUESS I'LL MEET YOU AT OUR TABLE. I'M JUST GOING TO GET A VEGETARIAN ENTRÉE.
HI!
I MUST HAVE COOTIES.
OH, *JAAAANE. WE'RE* NOT DOING HOME-WORK.
I'M GOOD HERE, THANKS.

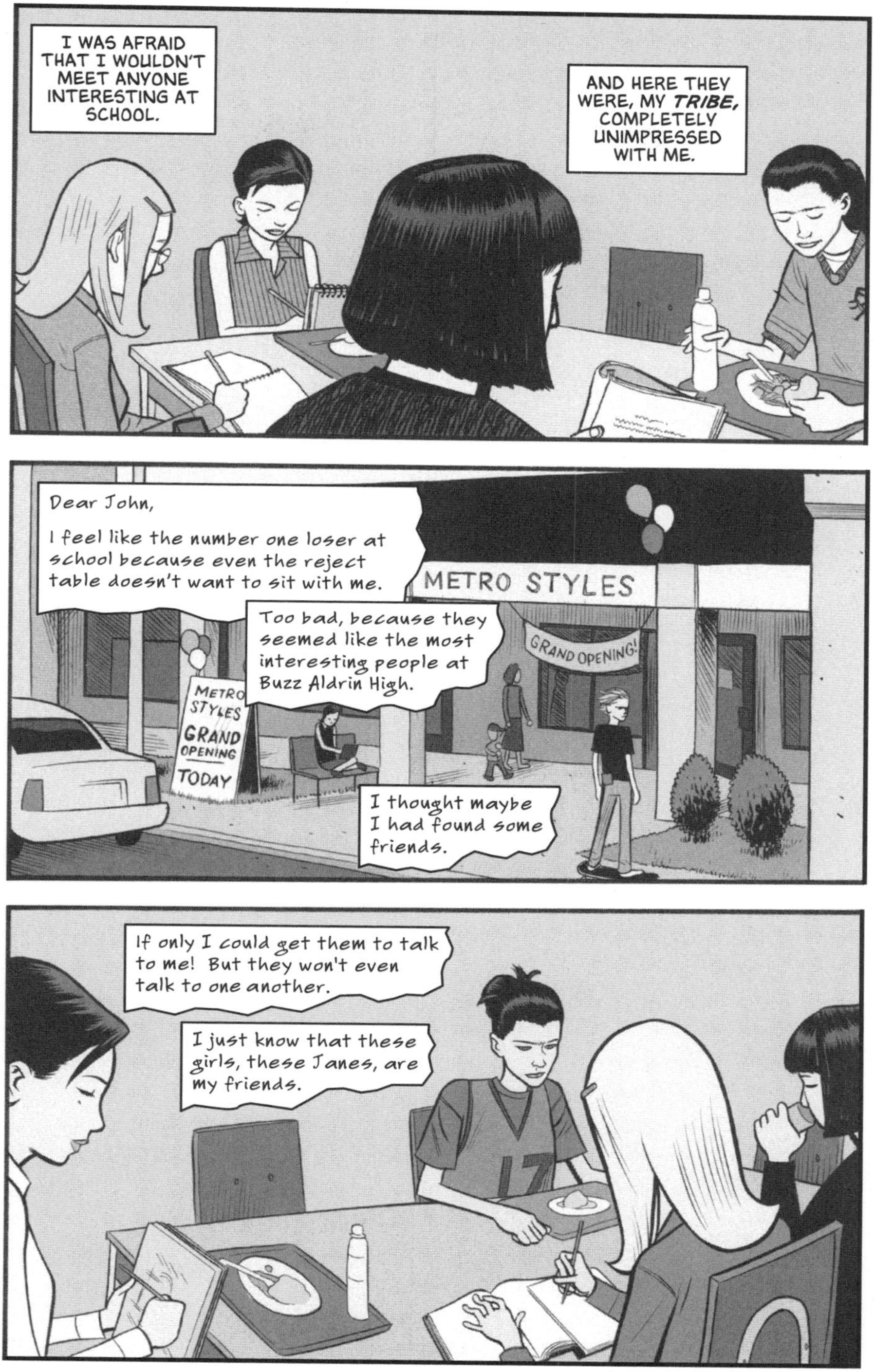
I WAS AFRAID THAT I WOULDN'T MEET ANYONE INTERESTING AT SCHOOL.
AND HERE THEY WERE, MY *TRIBE,* COMPLETELY UNIMPRESSED WITH ME.
Dear John,
I feel like the number one loser at school because even the reject table doesn't want to sit with me.
METRO STYLES
Too bad, because they seemed like the most interesting people at Buzz Aldrin High.
GRAND OPENING!
METRO STYLES GRAND OPENING TODAY
I thought maybe I had found some friends.
If only I could get them to talk to me! But they won't even talk to one another.
I just know that these girls, these Janes, are my friends.

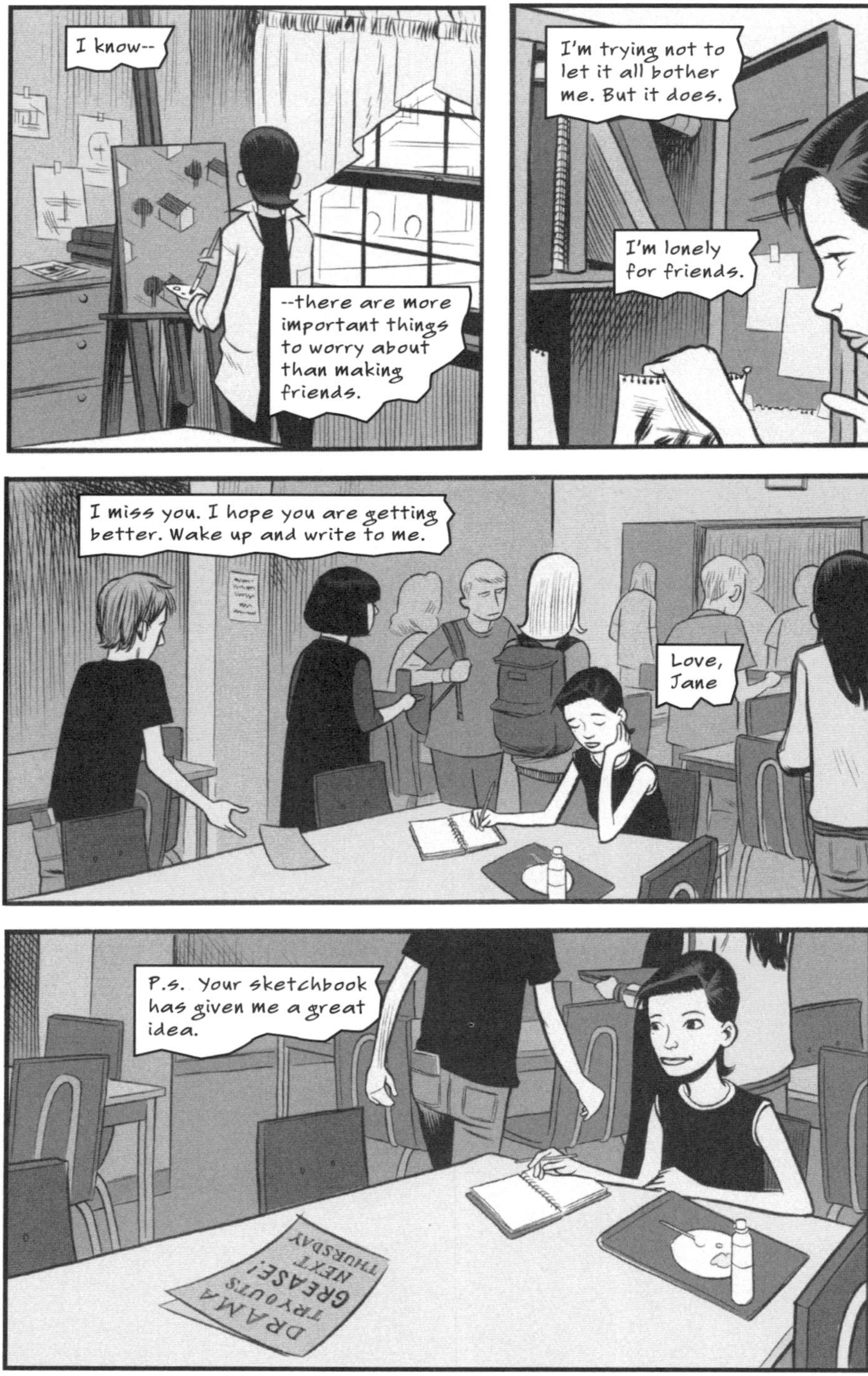
I know--
--there are more important things to worry about than making friends.
I'm trying not to let it all bother me. But it does.
I'm lonely for friends.
I miss you. I hope you are getting better. Wake up and write to me.
Love, Jane
P.s. Your sketchbook has given me a great idea.
DRAMA TRYOUTS GREASE! NEXT THURSDAY

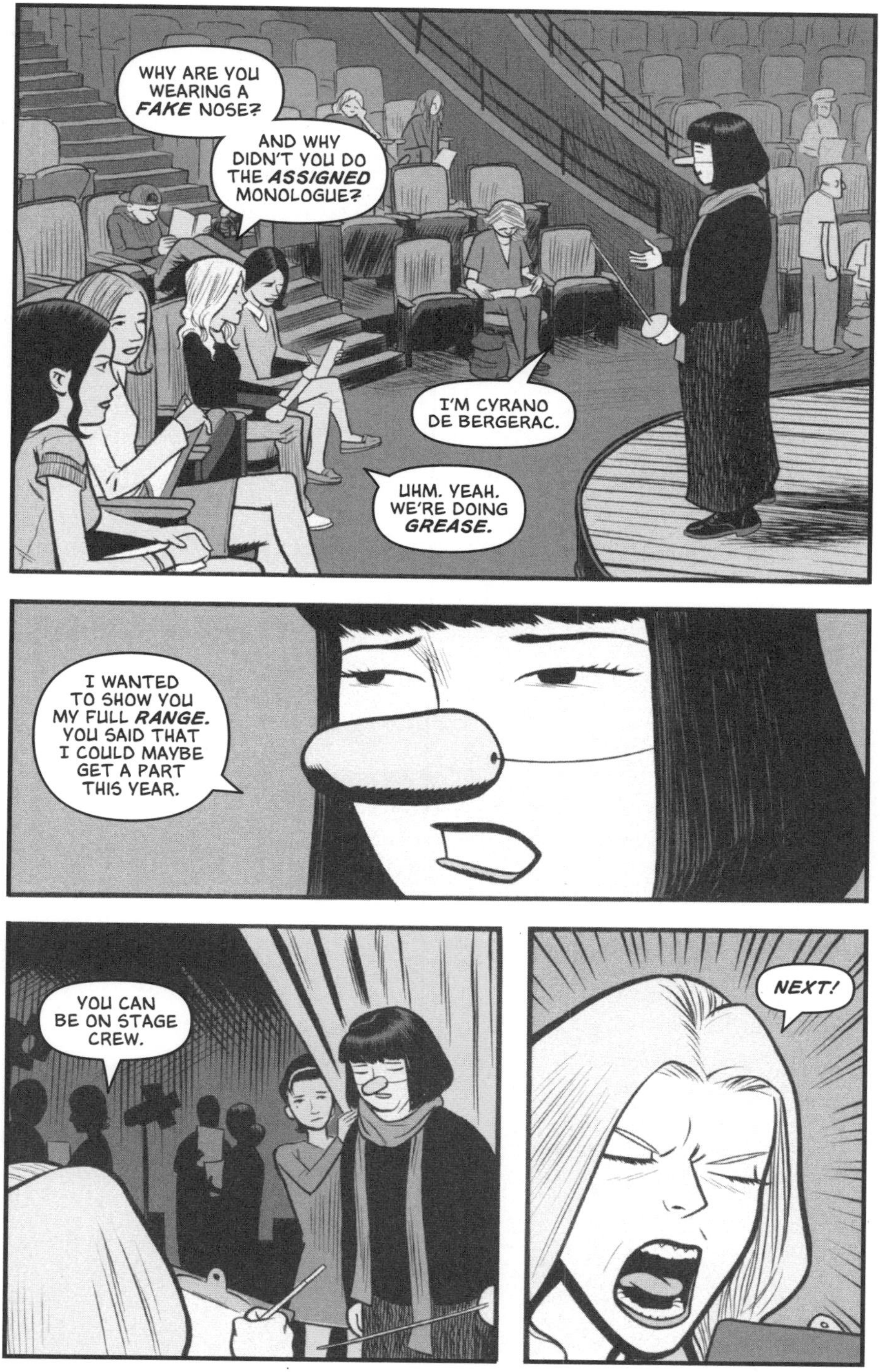
WHY ARE YOU WEARING A FAKE NOSE?
AND WHY DIDN'T YOU DO THE ASSIGNED MONOLOGUE?
I'M CYRANO DE BERGERAC.
UHM. YEAH. WE'RE DOING GREASE.
I WANTED TO SHOW YOU MY FULL RANGE. YOU SAID THAT I COULD MAYBE GET A PART THIS YEAR.
YOU CAN BE ON STAGE CREW.
NEXT!

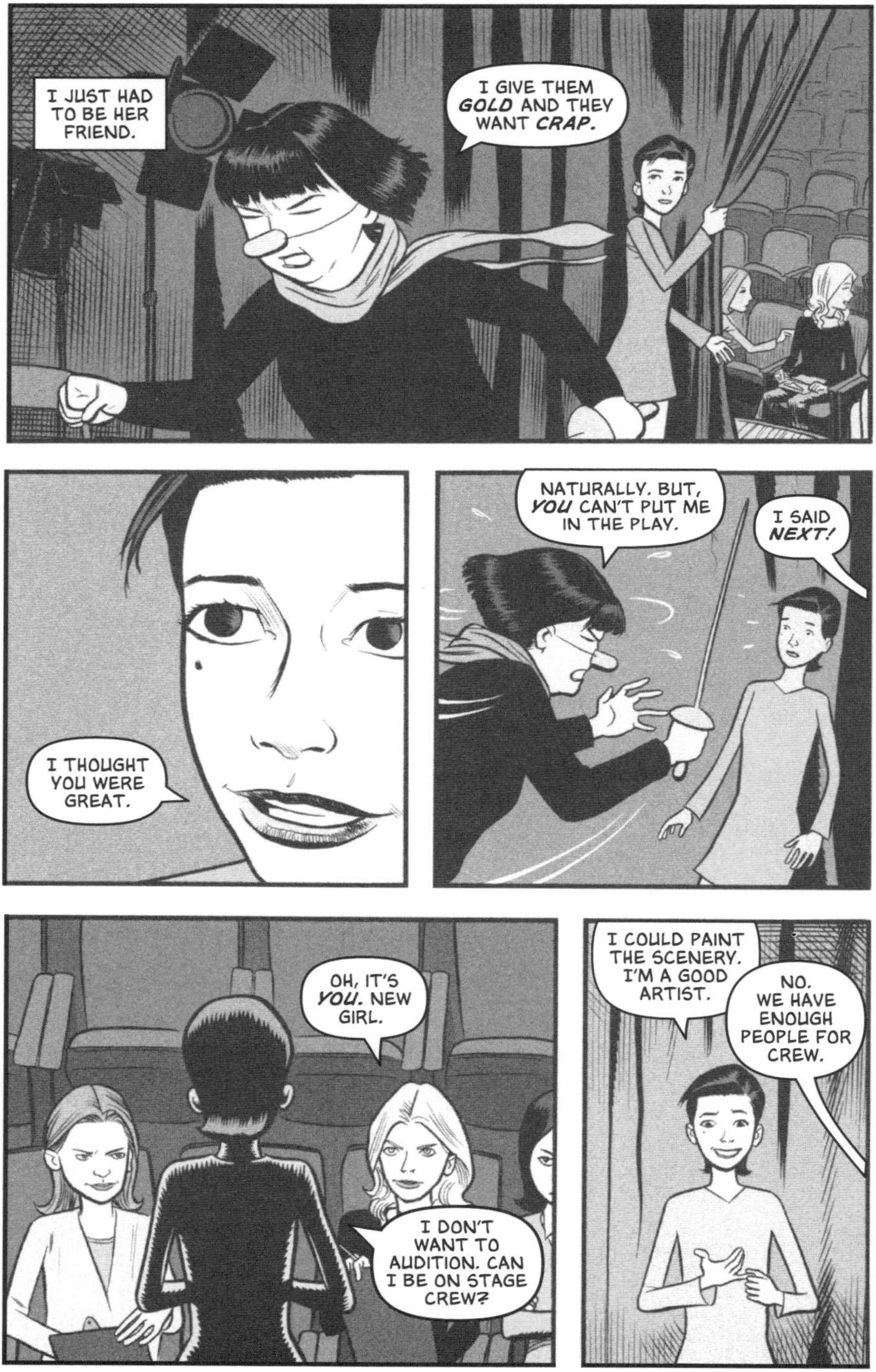
I JUST HAD TO BE HER FRIEND.
I GIVE THEM GOLD AND THEY WANT CRAP.
I THOUGHT YOU WERE GREAT.
NATURALLY. BUT, YOU CAN'T PUT ME IN THE PLAY.
I SAID NEXT!
OH, IT'S YOU. NEW GIRL.
I DON'T WANT TO AUDITION. CAN I BE ON STAGE CREW?
I COULD PAINT THE SCENERY. I'M A GOOD ARTIST.
NO. WE HAVE ENOUGH PEOPLE FOR CREW.

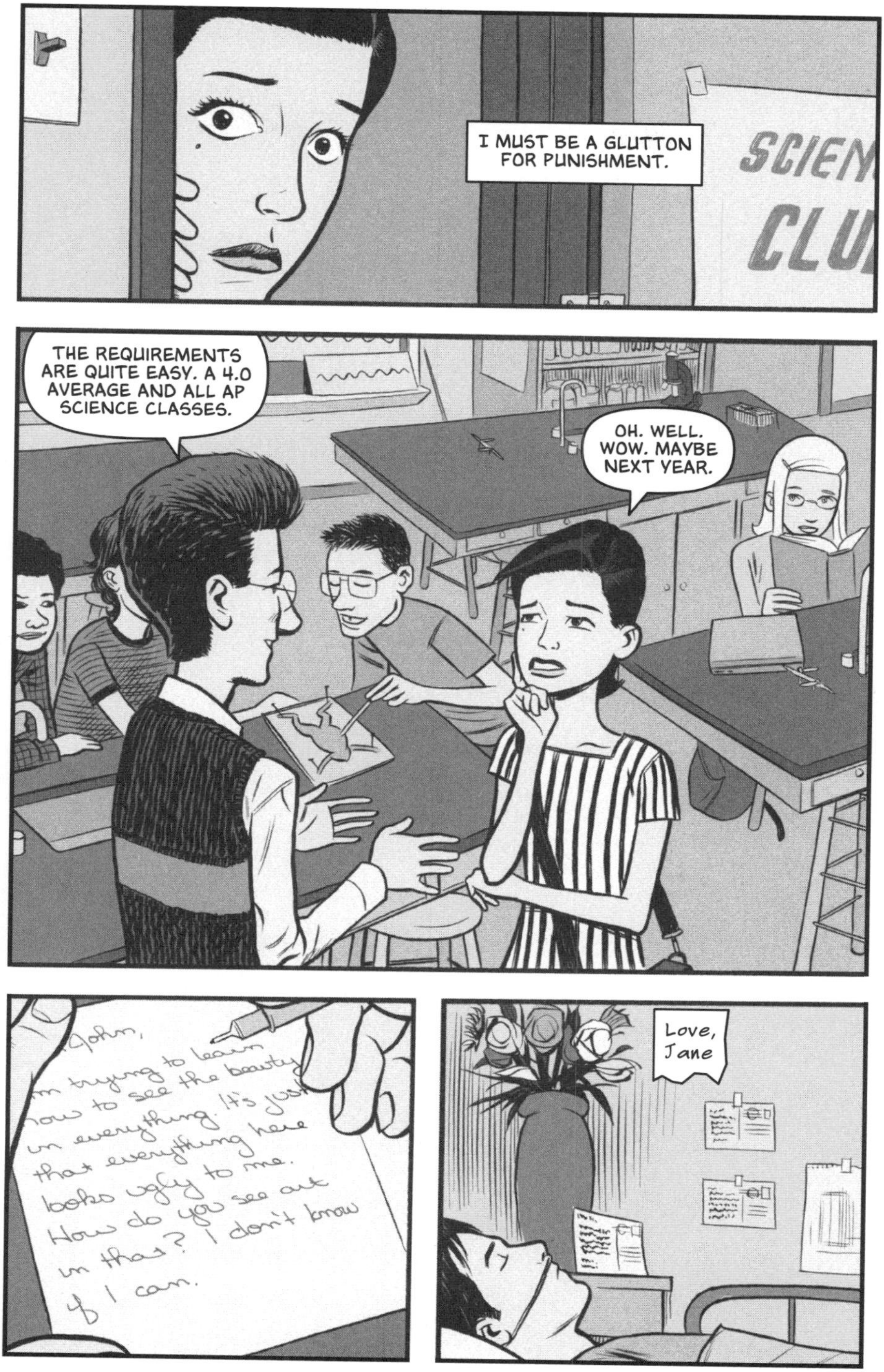
I MUST BE A GLUTTON FOR PUNISHMENT.
THE REQUIREMENTS ARE QUITE EASY. A 4.0 AVERAGE AND ALL AP SCIENCE CLASSES.
OH. WELL. WOW. MAYBE NEXT YEAR.
John,
I'm trying to learn
how to see the beauty
in everything. It's just
that everything here
looks ugly to me.
How do you see art
in that? I don't know
if I can.
Love, Jane

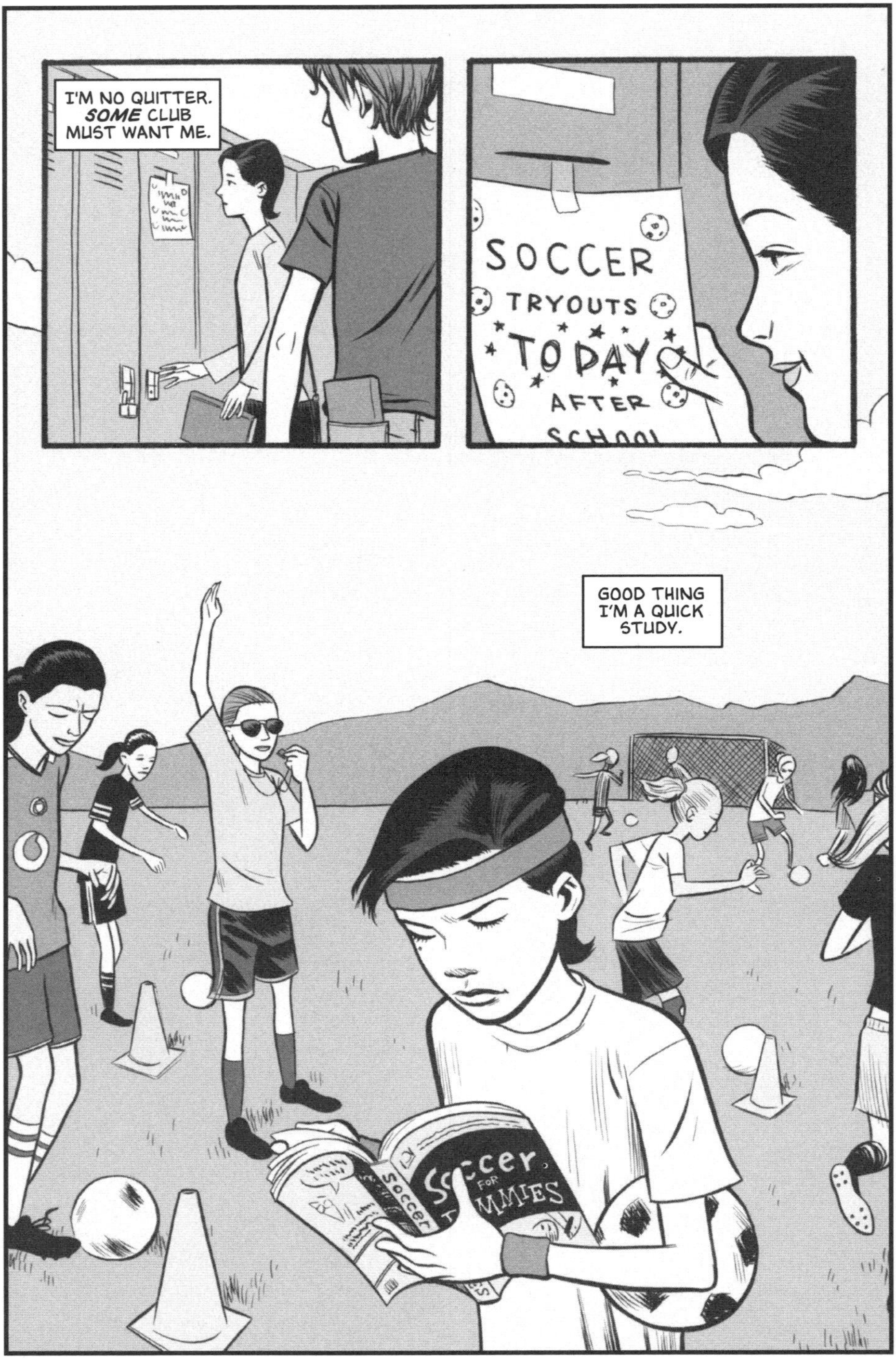
I'M NO QUITTER. SOME CLUB MUST WANT ME.
SOCCER TRYOUTS TODAY AFTER SCHOOL
GOOD THING I'M A QUICK STUDY.
Soccer FOR DUMMIES

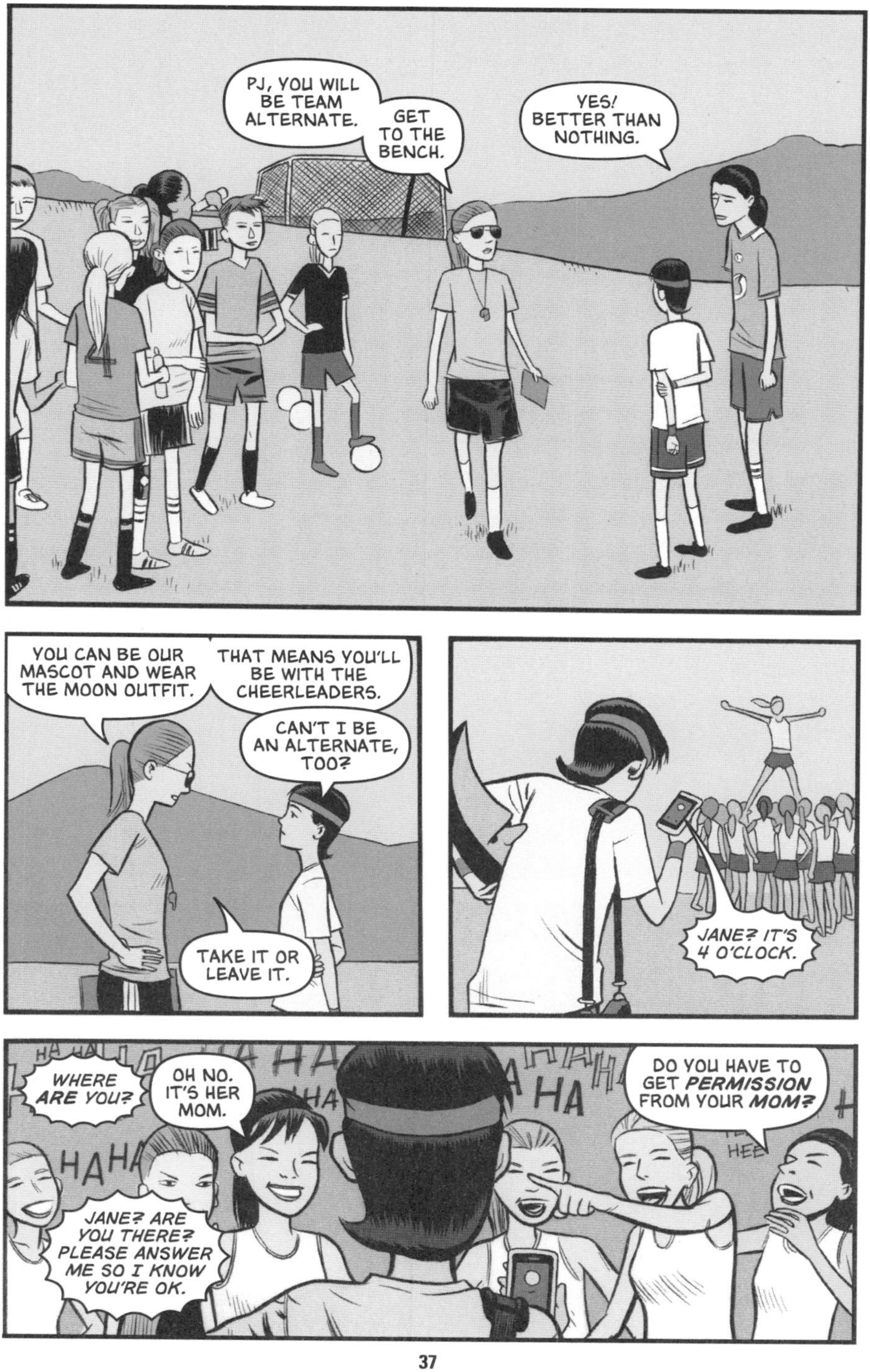
PJ, YOU WILL BE TEAM ALTERNATE.
GET TO THE BENCH.
YES! BETTER THAN NOTHING.
YOU CAN BE OUR MASCOT AND WEAR THE MOON OUTFIT.
THAT MEANS YOU'LL BE WITH THE CHEERLEADERS.
CAN'T I BE AN ALTERNATE, TOO?
TAKE IT OR LEAVE IT.
JANE? IT'S 4 O'CLOCK.
WHERE *ARE* YOU?
OH NO. IT'S HER MOM.
HA HA
DO YOU HAVE TO GET *PERMISSION* FROM YOUR *MOM?*
HAHA
HEE
JANE? ARE YOU THERE? PLEASE ANSWER ME SO I KNOW YOU'RE OK.

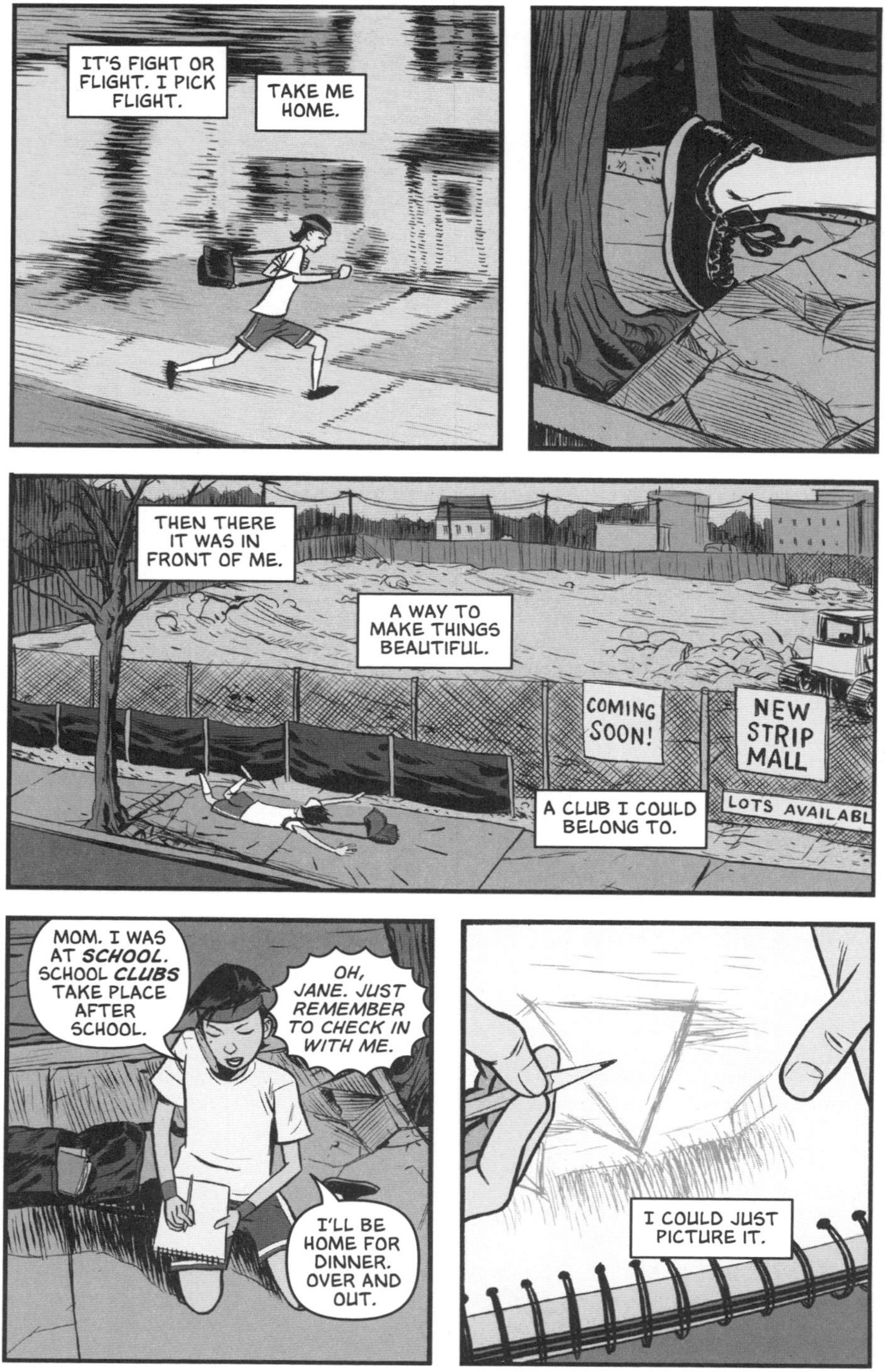
IT'S FIGHT OR FLIGHT. I PICK FLIGHT.
TAKE ME HOME.
THEN THERE IT WAS IN FRONT OF ME.
A WAY TO MAKE THINGS BEAUTIFUL.
COMING SOON!
NEW STRIP MALL
A CLUB I COULD BELONG TO.
LOTS AVAILABL
MOM. I WAS AT SCHOOL. SCHOOL CLUBS TAKE PLACE AFTER SCHOOL.
OH, JANE. JUST REMEMBER TO CHECK IN WITH ME.
I'LL BE HOME FOR DINNER. OVER AND OUT.
I COULD JUST PICTURE IT.

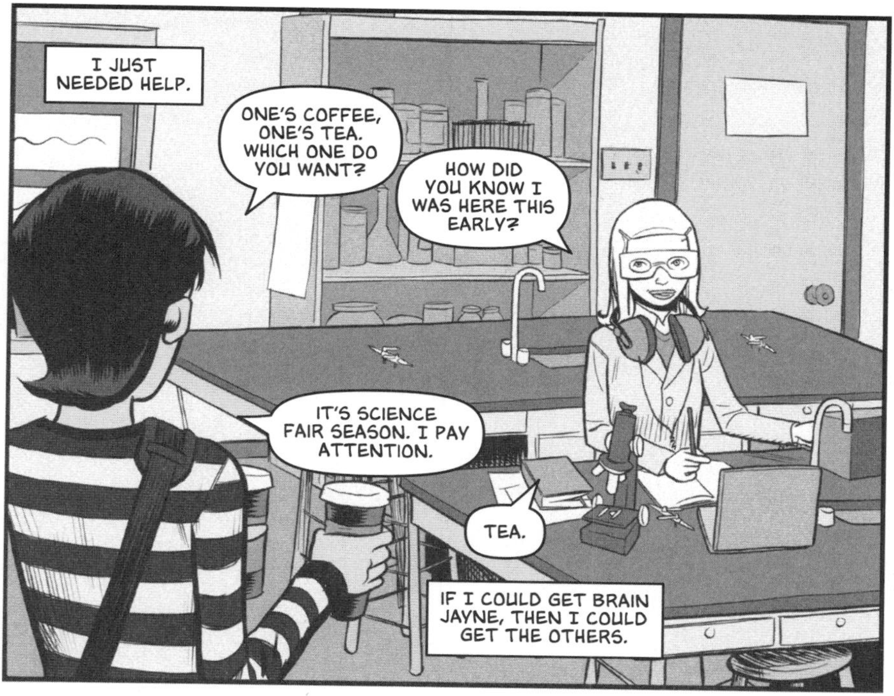
I JUST NEEDED HELP.
ONE'S COFFEE, ONE'S TEA. WHICH ONE DO YOU WANT?
HOW DID YOU KNOW I WAS HERE THIS EARLY?
IT'S SCIENCE FAIR SEASON. I PAY ATTENTION.
TEA.
IF I COULD GET BRAIN JAYNE, THEN I COULD GET THE OTHERS.

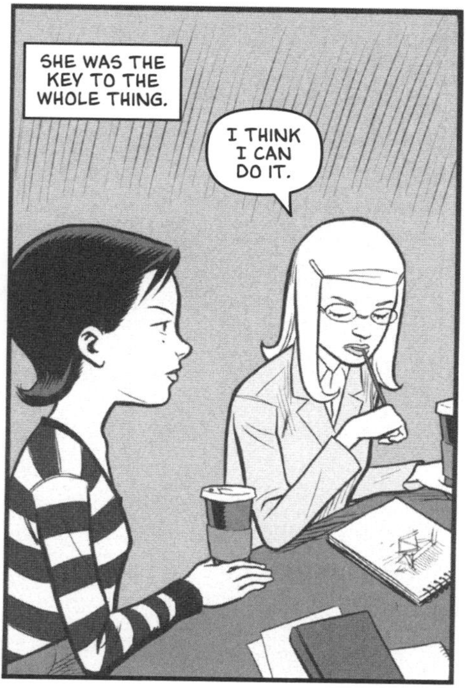
SHE WAS THE KEY TO THE WHOLE THING.
I THINK I CAN DO IT.

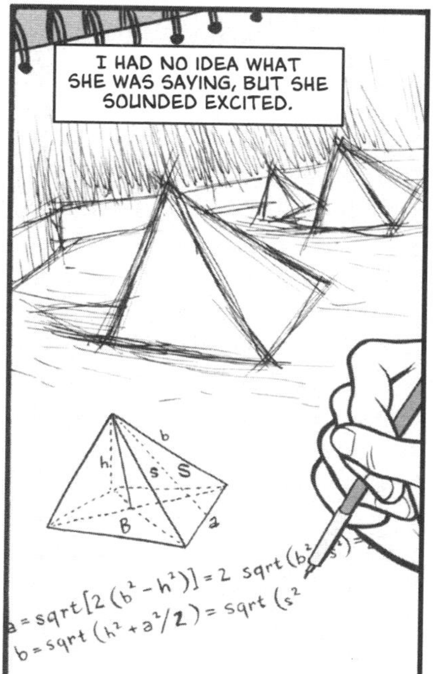
I HAD NO IDEA WHAT SHE WAS SAYING, BUT SHE SOUNDED EXCITED.
h
s
S
b
B
a
a = sqrt[2(b² - h²)] = 2 sqrt (b²
a = sqrt (h² + a²/2) = sqrt (s²
b = sqrt (h² + a²/2)

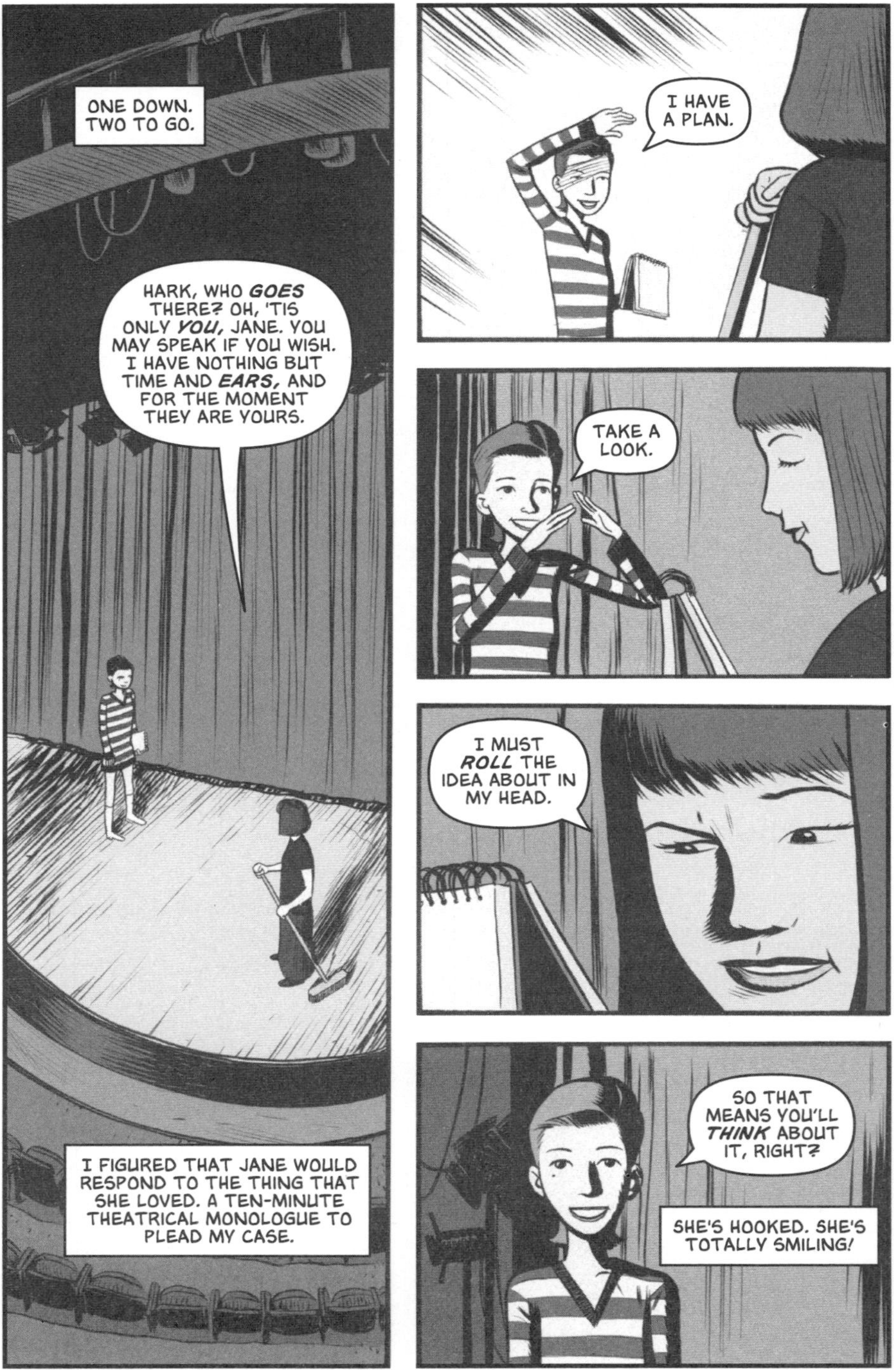
ONE DOWN. TWO TO GO.
HARK, WHO GOES THERE? OH, 'TIS ONLY YOU, JANE. YOU MAY SPEAK IF YOU WISH. I HAVE NOTHING BUT TIME AND EARS, AND FOR THE MOMENT THEY ARE YOURS.
I FIGURED THAT JANE WOULD RESPOND TO THE THING THAT SHE LOVED. A TEN-MINUTE THEATRICAL MONOLOGUE TO PLEAD MY CASE.
I HAVE A PLAN.
TAKE A LOOK.
I MUST ROLL THE IDEA ABOUT IN MY HEAD.
SO THAT MEANS YOU'LL THINK ABOUT IT, RIGHT?
SHE'S HOOKED. SHE'S TOTALLY SMILING!

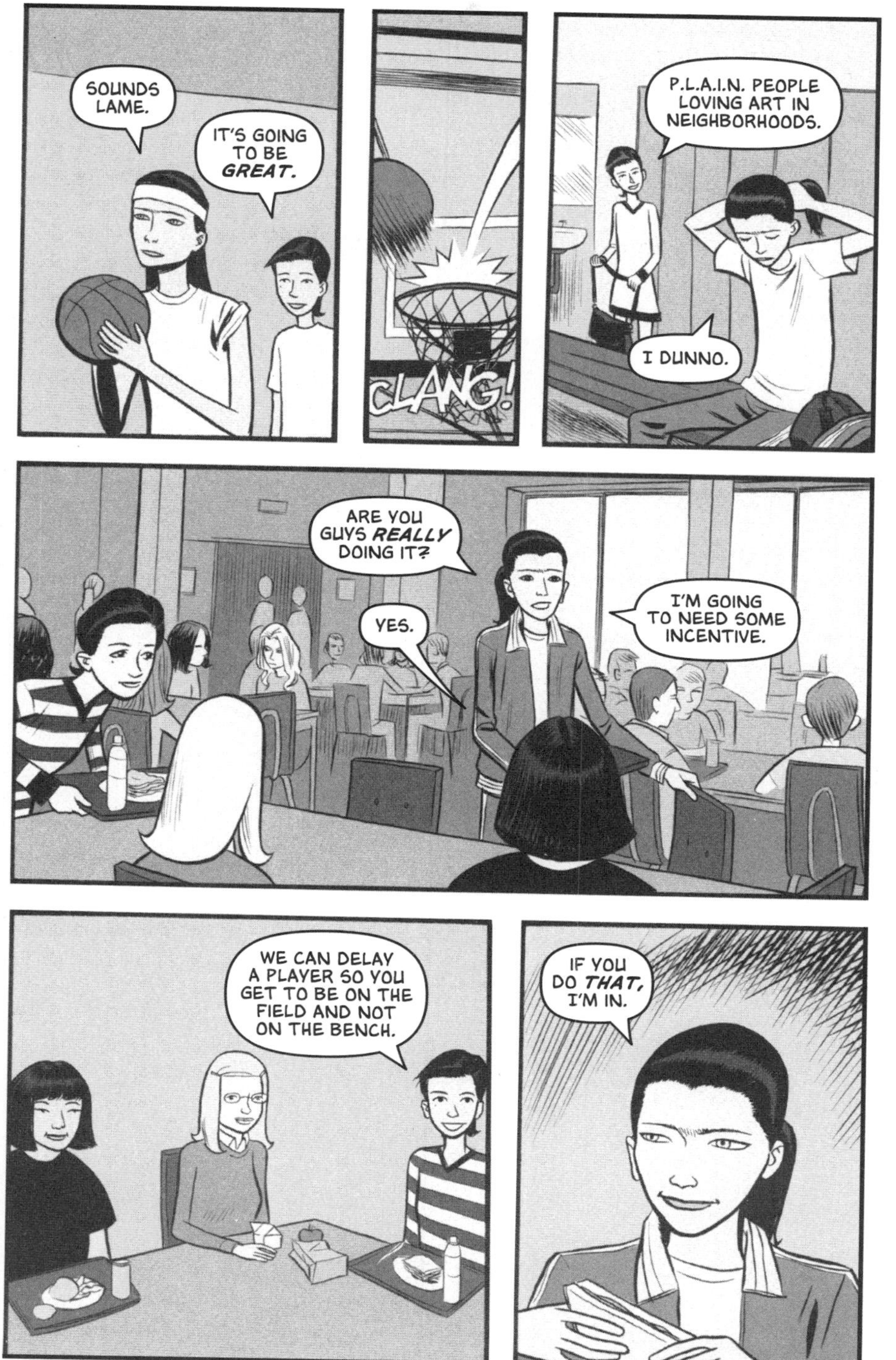
SOUNDS LAME.
IT'S GOING TO BE GREAT.
CLANG!
P.L.A.I.N. PEOPLE LOVING ART IN NEIGHBORHOODS.
I DUNNO.
ARE YOU GUYS REALLY DOING IT?
YES.
I'M GOING TO NEED SOME INCENTIVE.
WE CAN DELAY A PLAYER SO YOU GET TO BE ON THE FIELD AND NOT ON THE BENCH.
IF YOU DO THAT, I'M IN.

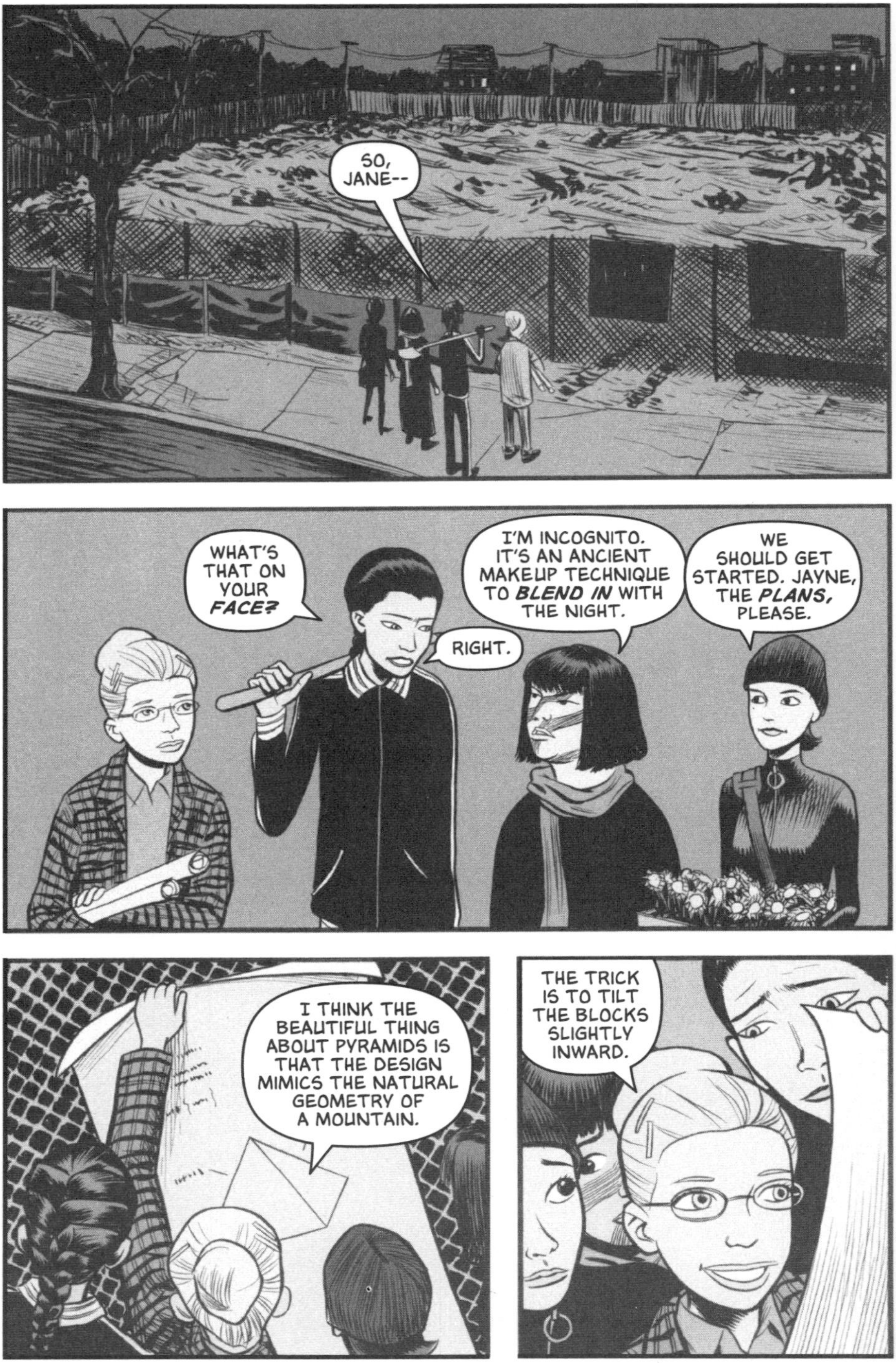
SO, JANE--
WHAT'S THAT ON YOUR *FACE?*
RIGHT.
I'M INCOGNITO. IT'S AN ANCIENT MAKEUP TECHNIQUE TO *BLEND IN* WITH THE NIGHT.
WE SHOULD GET STARTED. JAYNE, THE *PLANS,* PLEASE.
I THINK THE BEAUTIFUL THING ABOUT PYRAMIDS IS THAT THE DESIGN MIMICS THE NATURAL GEOMETRY OF A MOUNTAIN.
THE TRICK IS TO TILT THE BLOCKS SLIGHTLY INWARD.

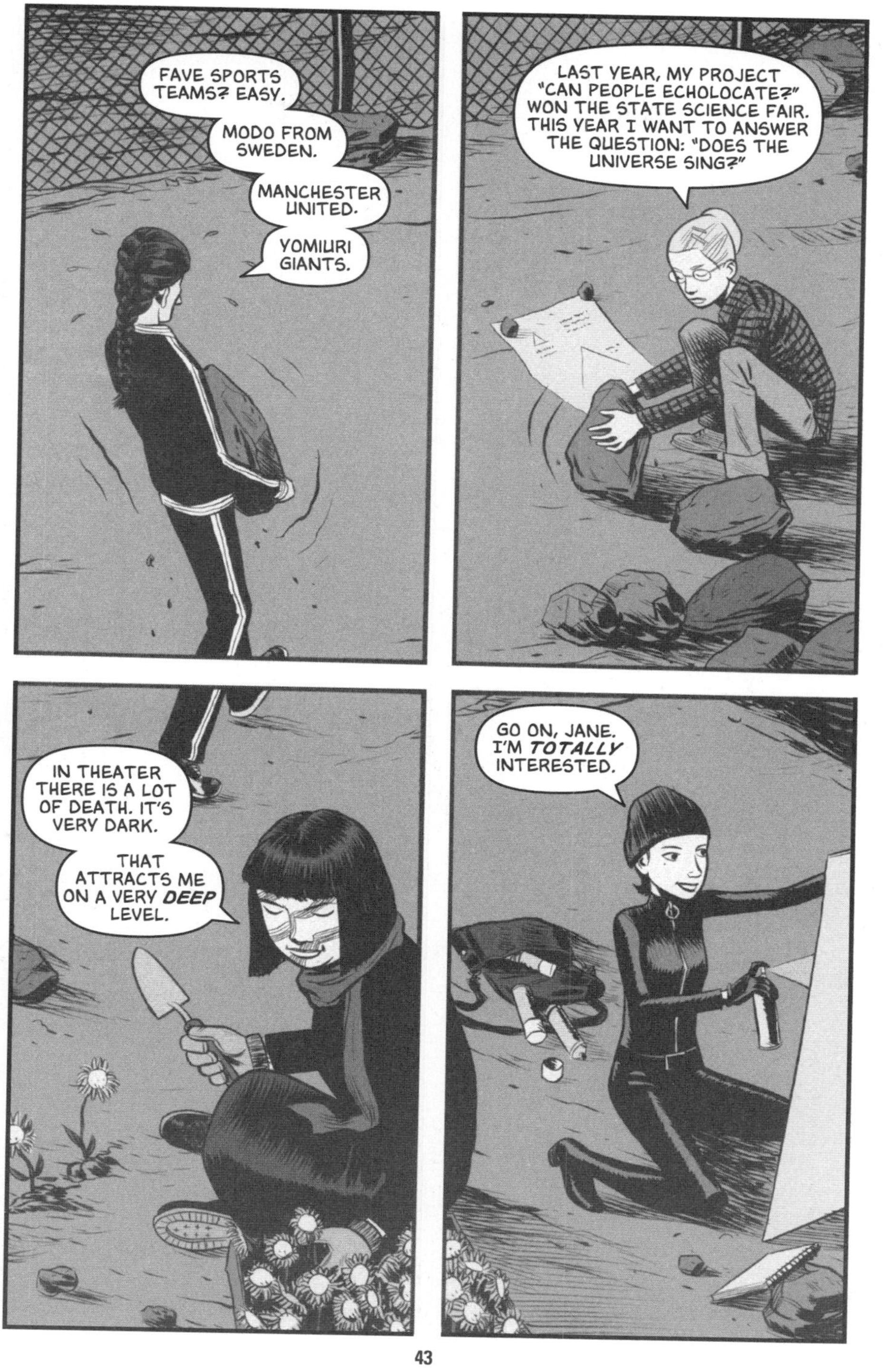
FAVE SPORTS TEAMS? EASY.
MODO FROM SWEDEN.
MANCHESTER UNITED.
YOMIURI GIANTS.
LAST YEAR, MY PROJECT "CAN PEOPLE ECHOLOCATE?" WON THE STATE SCIENCE FAIR. THIS YEAR I WANT TO ANSWER THE QUESTION: "DOES THE UNIVERSE SING?"
IN THEATER THERE IS A LOT OF DEATH. IT'S VERY DARK.
THAT ATTRACTS ME ON A VERY *DEEP* LEVEL.
GO ON, JANE. I'M *TOTALLY* INTERESTED.

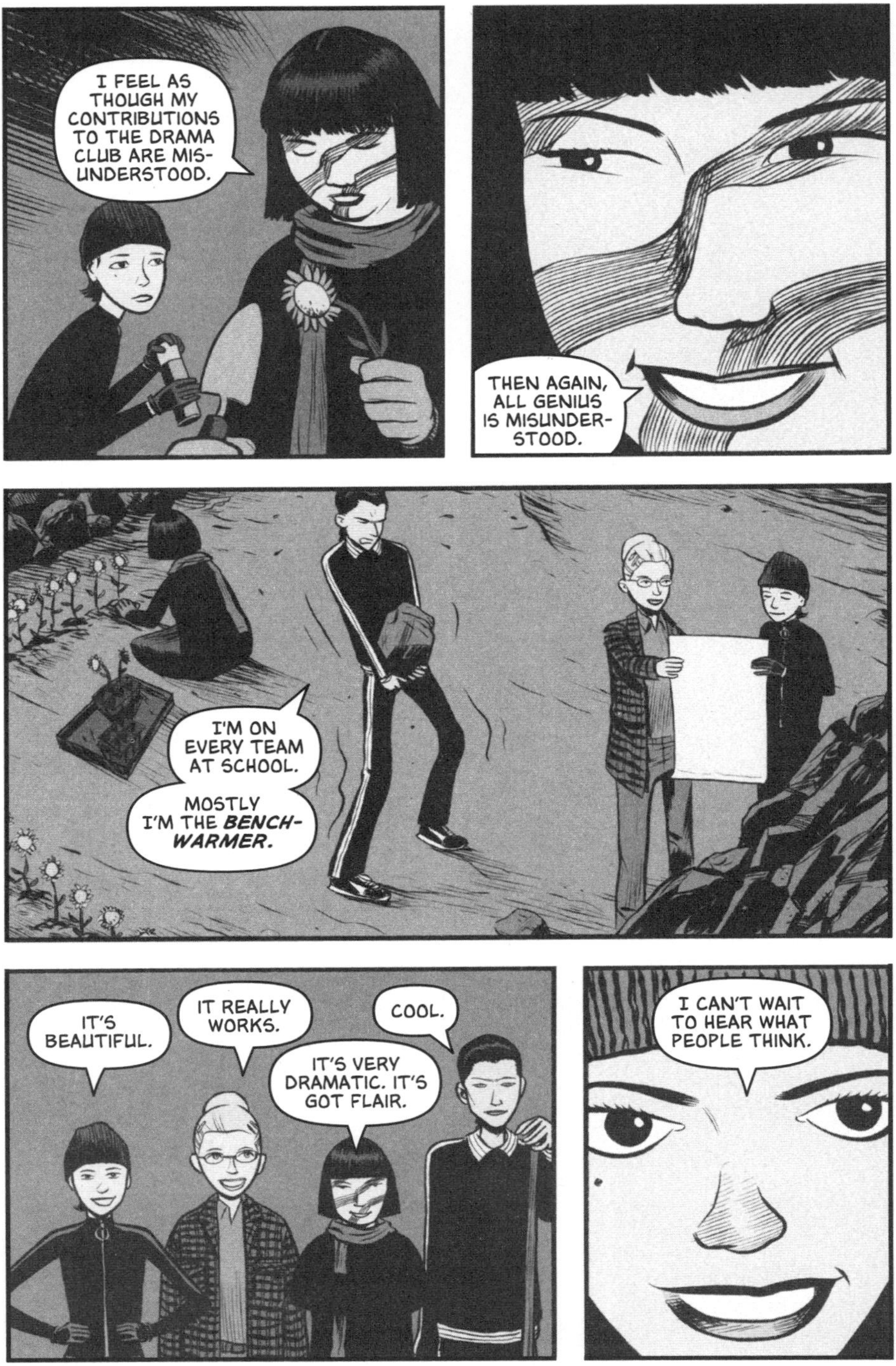
I FEEL AS THOUGH MY CONTRIBUTIONS TO THE DRAMA CLUB ARE MIS-UNDERSTOOD.
THEN AGAIN, ALL GENIUS IS MISUNDER-STOOD.
I'M ON EVERY TEAM AT SCHOOL.
MOSTLY I'M THE *BENCH-WARMER.*
IT'S BEAUTIFUL.
IT REALLY WORKS.
COOL.
IT'S VERY DRAMATIC. IT'S GOT FLAIR.
I CAN'T WAIT TO HEAR WHAT PEOPLE THINK.

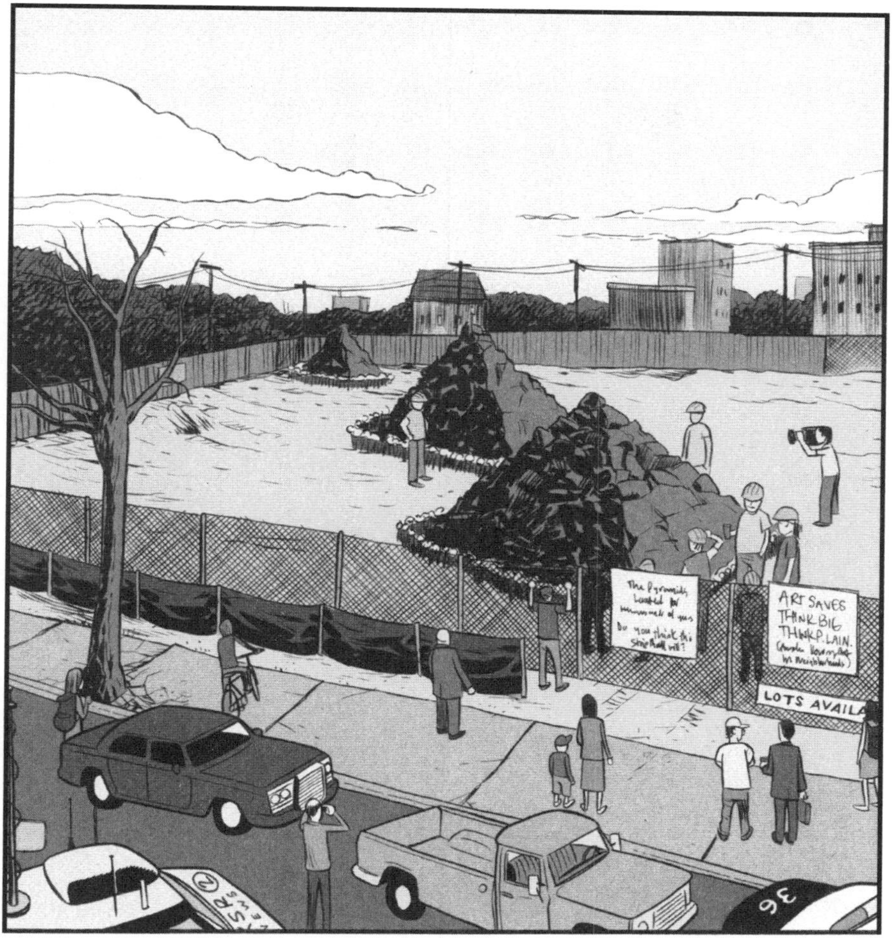
ART SAVES
THINK BIG
LOTS AVAILA

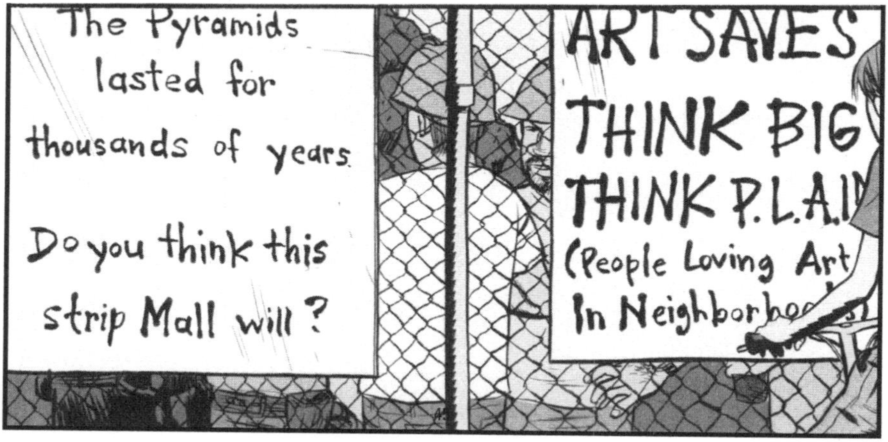
The Pyramids
lasted for
thousands of years.
Do you think this
strip Mall will?
ART SAVES
THINK BIG
THINK P.L.A.I
(People Loving Art
In Neighbor

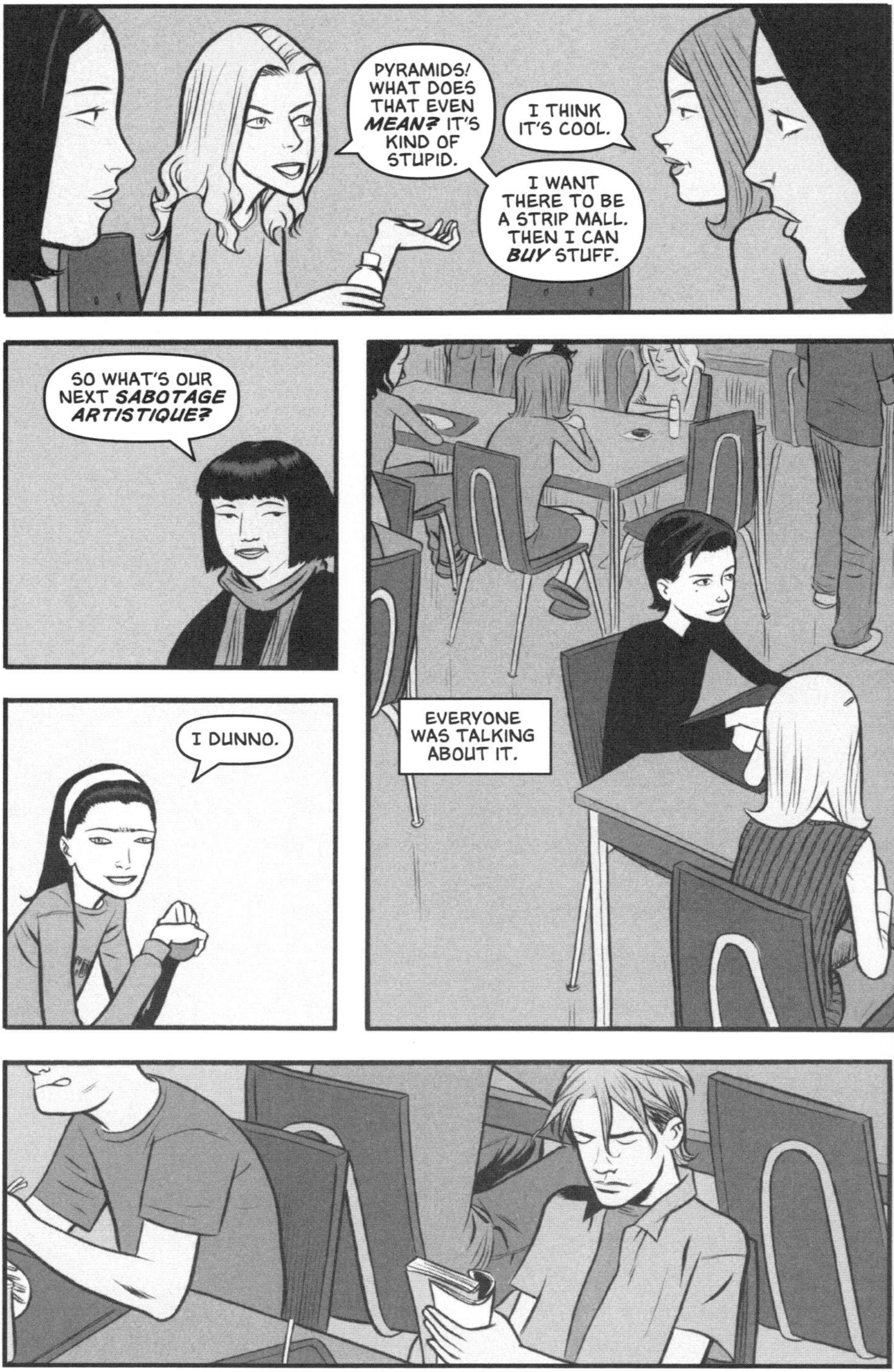
PYRAMIDS! WHAT DOES THAT EVEN MEAN? IT'S KIND OF STUPID.
I THINK IT'S COOL.
I WANT THERE TO BE A STRIP MALL. THEN I CAN BUY STUFF.
SO WHAT'S OUR NEXT SABOTAGE ARTISTIQUE?
I DUNNO.
EVERYONE WAS TALKING ABOUT IT.

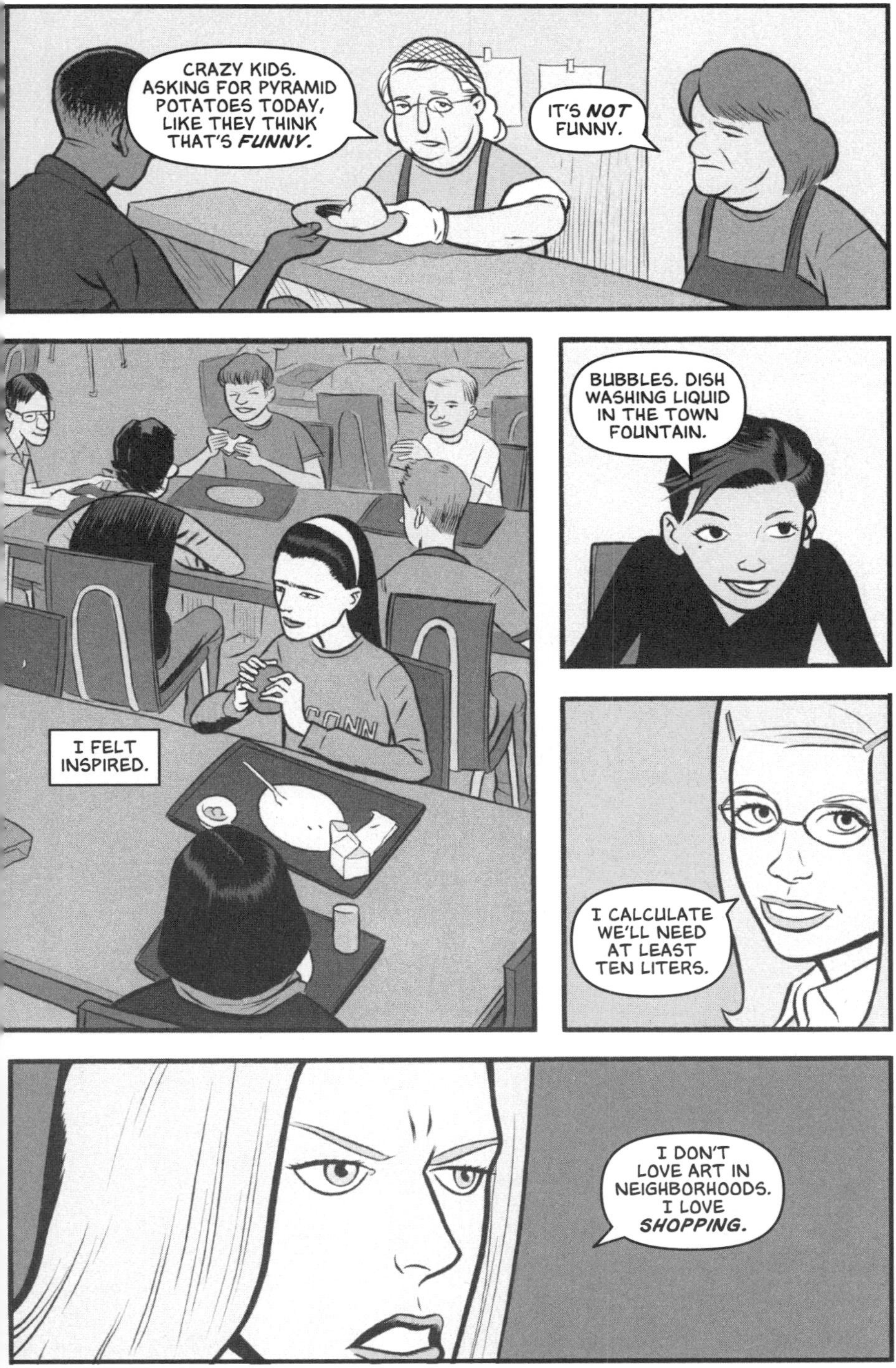
CRAZY KIDS. ASKING FOR PYRAMID POTATOES TODAY, LIKE THEY THINK THAT'S *FUNNY.*
IT'S *NOT* FUNNY.
I FELT INSPIRED.
CONN
BUBBLES. DISH WASHING LIQUID IN THE TOWN FOUNTAIN.
I CALCULATE WE'LL NEED AT LEAST TEN LITERS.
I DON'T LOVE ART IN NEIGHBORHOODS. I LOVE *SHOPPING.*

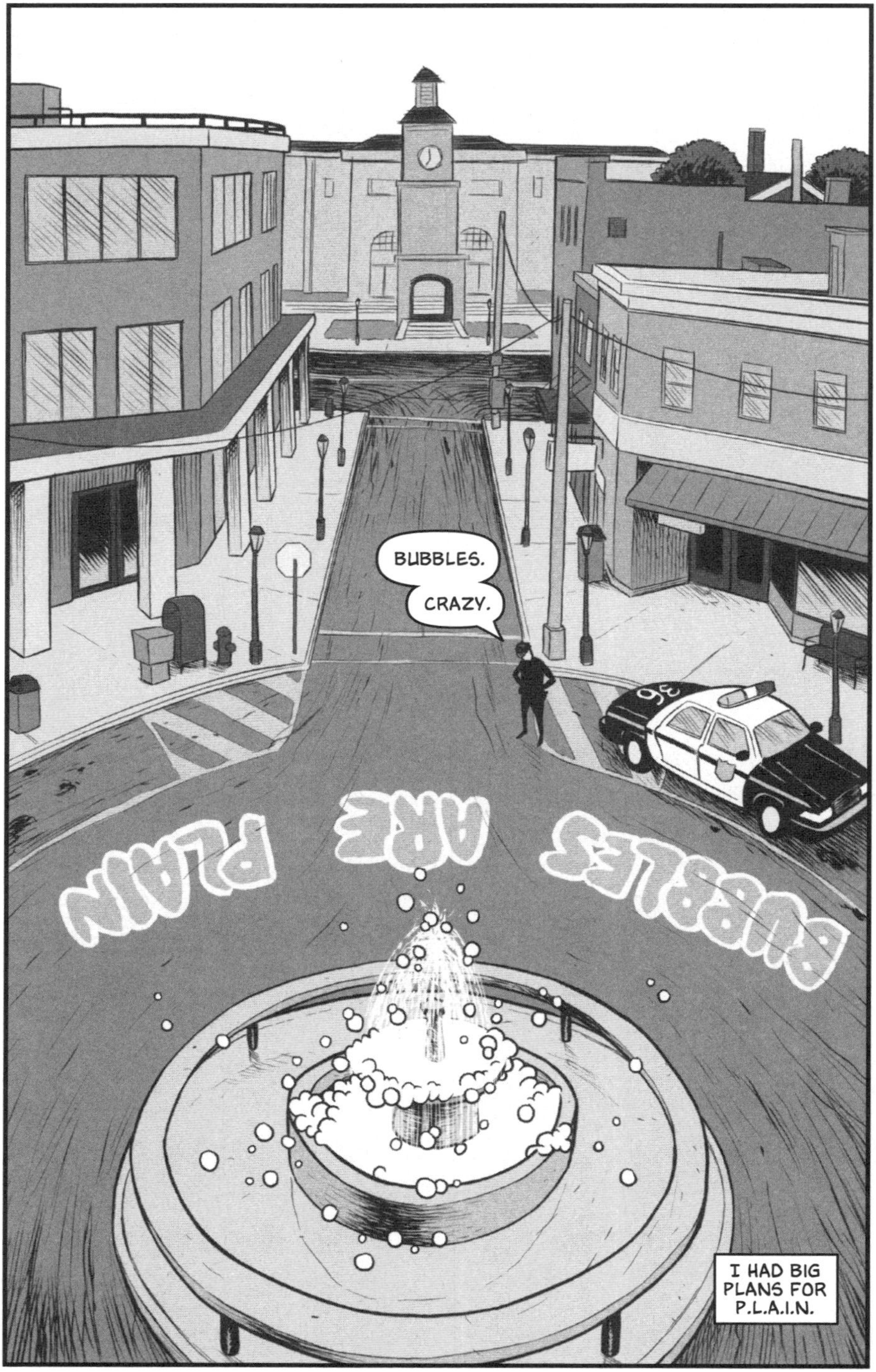
BUBBLES.
CRAZY.
BUBBLES ARE PLAIN
I HAD BIG PLANS FOR P.L.A.I.N.

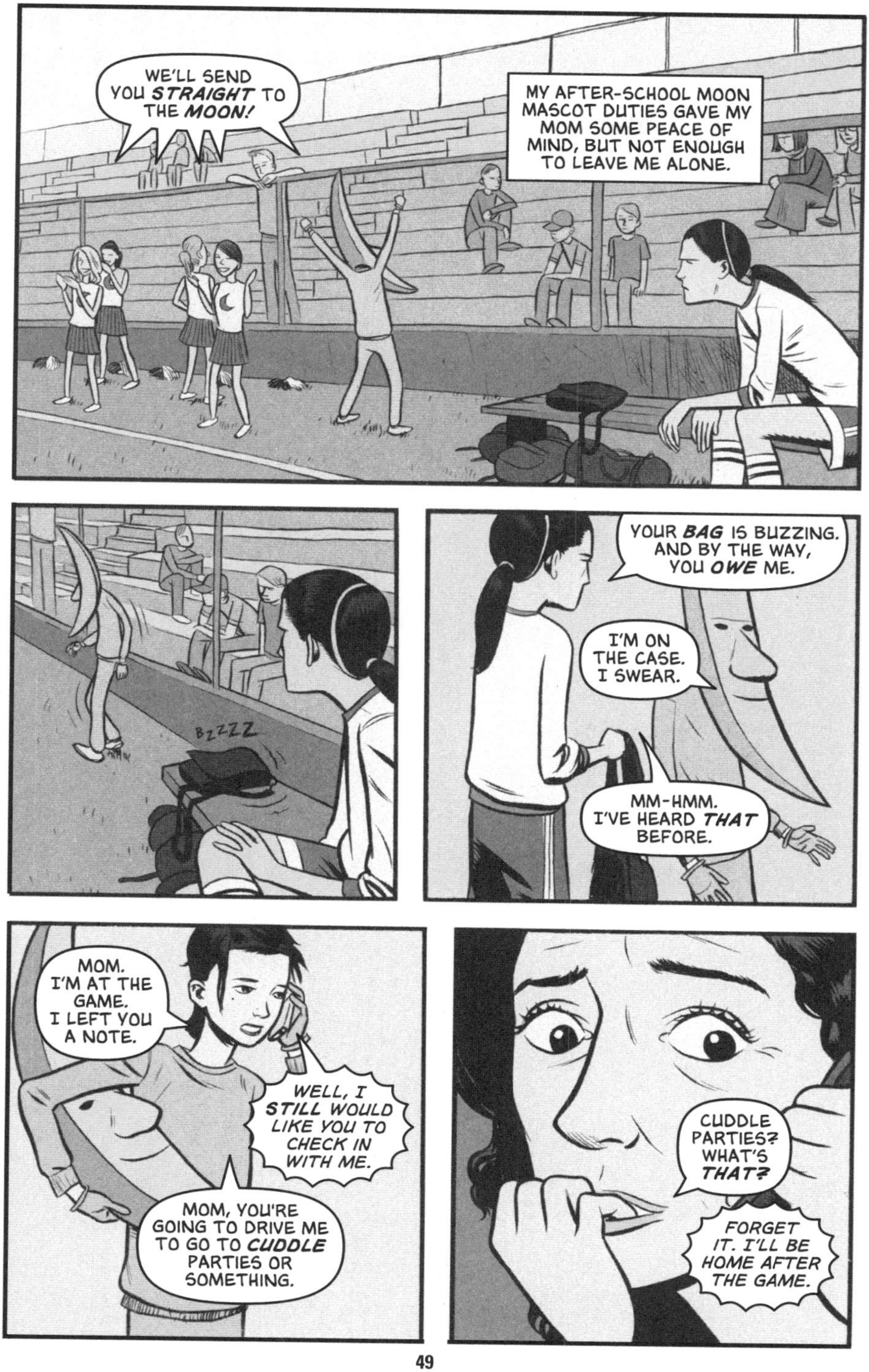
WE'LL SEND YOU STRAIGHT TO THE MOON!
MY AFTER-SCHOOL MOON MASCOT DUTIES GAVE MY MOM SOME PEACE OF MIND, BUT NOT ENOUGH TO LEAVE ME ALONE.
BZZZZ
YOUR BAG IS BUZZING. AND BY THE WAY, YOU OWE ME.
I'M ON THE CASE. I SWEAR.
MM-HMM. I'VE HEARD THAT BEFORE.
MOM. I'M AT THE GAME. I LEFT YOU A NOTE.
WELL, I STILL WOULD LIKE YOU TO CHECK IN WITH ME.
MOM, YOU'RE GOING TO DRIVE ME TO GO TO CUDDLE PARTIES OR SOMETHING.
CUDDLE PARTIES? WHAT'S THAT?
FORGET IT. I'LL BE HOME AFTER THE GAME.

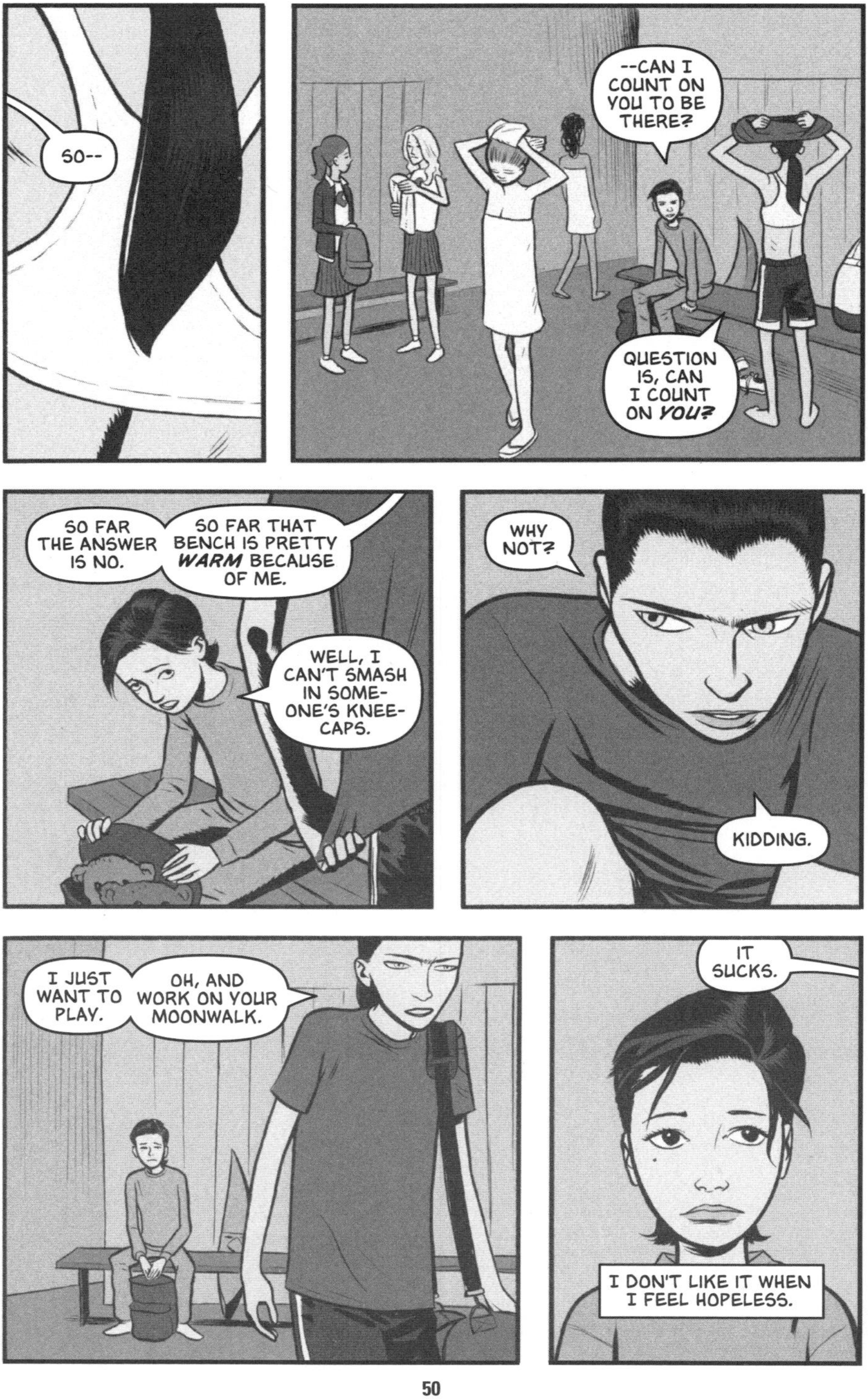
SO--
--CAN I COUNT ON YOU TO BE THERE?
QUESTION IS, CAN I COUNT ON *YOU?*
SO FAR THE ANSWER IS NO.
SO FAR THAT BENCH IS PRETTY *WARM* BECAUSE OF ME.
WELL, I CAN'T SMASH IN SOME-ONE'S KNEE-CAPS.
WHY NOT?
KIDDING.
I JUST WANT TO PLAY.
OH, AND WORK ON YOUR MOONWALK.
IT SUCKS.
I DON'T LIKE IT WHEN I FEEL HOPELESS.

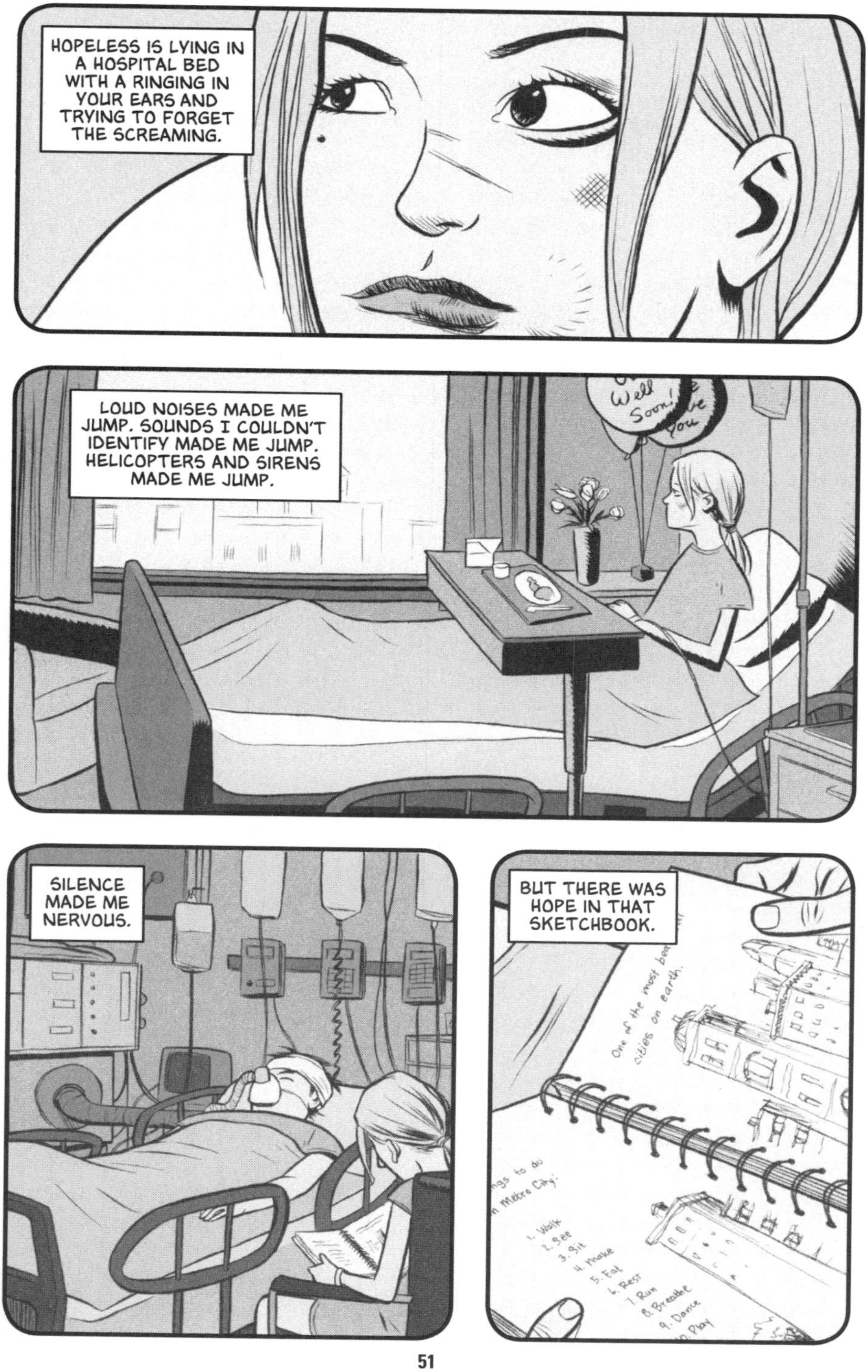
HOPELESS IS LYING IN A HOSPITAL BED WITH A RINGING IN YOUR EARS AND TRYING TO FORGET THE SCREAMING.
LOUD NOISES MADE ME JUMP. SOUNDS I COULDN'T IDENTIFY MADE ME JUMP. HELICOPTERS AND SIRENS MADE ME JUMP.
Well Soon!
SILENCE MADE ME NERVOUS.
BUT THERE WAS HOPE IN THAT SKETCHBOOK.
cities on earth.
1. Walk
2. See
3. Sit
4. Make
5. Eat
6. Rest
7. Run
8. Breathe
9. Dance

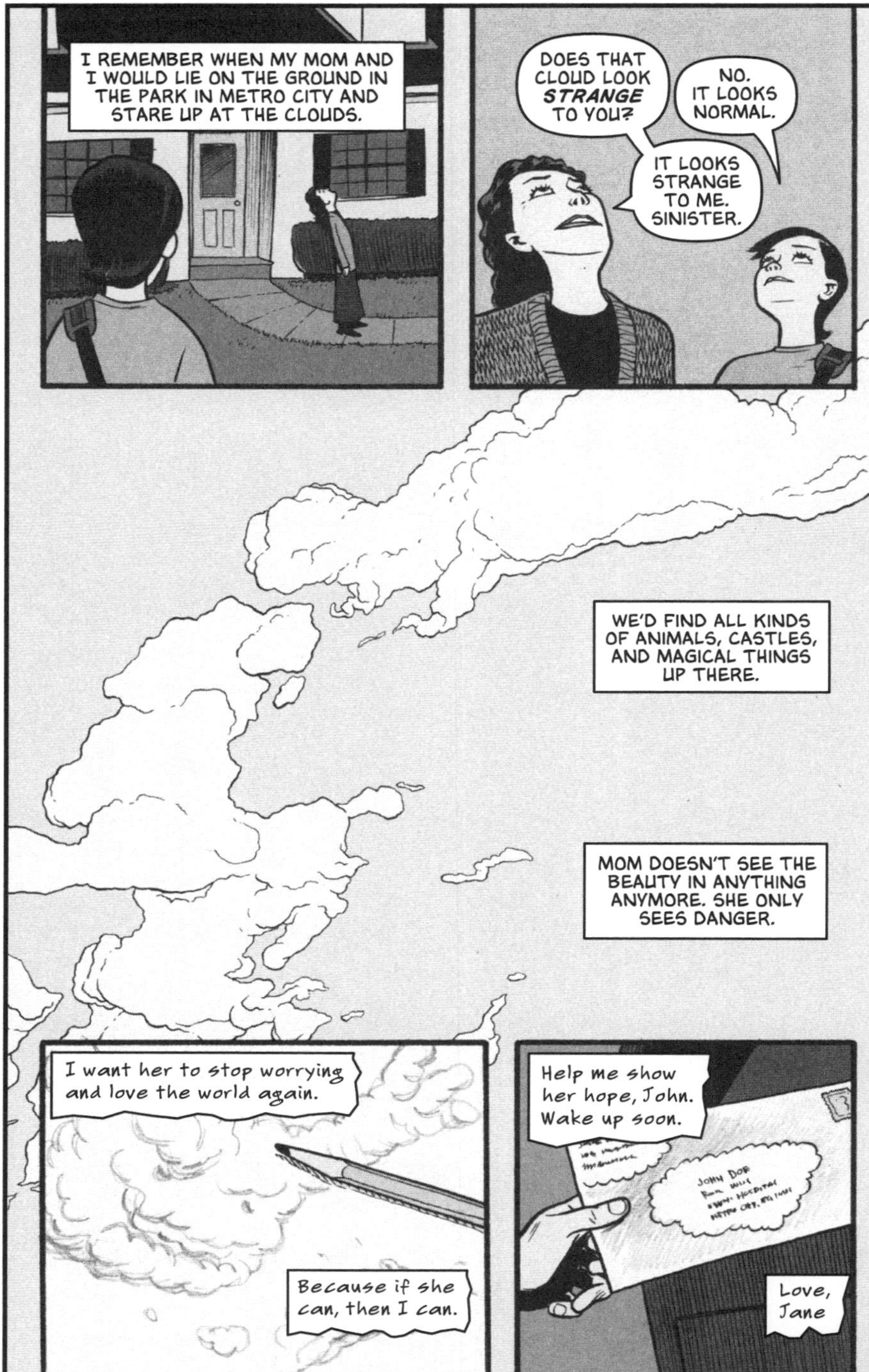
I REMEMBER WHEN MY MOM AND I WOULD LIE ON THE GROUND IN THE PARK IN METRO CITY AND STARE UP AT THE CLOUDS.
DOES THAT CLOUD LOOK *STRANGE* TO YOU?
NO. IT LOOKS NORMAL.
IT LOOKS STRANGE TO ME. SINISTER.
WE'D FIND ALL KINDS OF ANIMALS, CASTLES, AND MAGICAL THINGS UP THERE.
MOM DOESN'T SEE THE BEAUTY IN ANYTHING ANYMORE. SHE ONLY SEES DANGER.
I want her to stop worrying and love the world again.
Because if she can, then I can.
Help me show her hope, John. Wake up soon.
JOHN DOE
Love, Jane

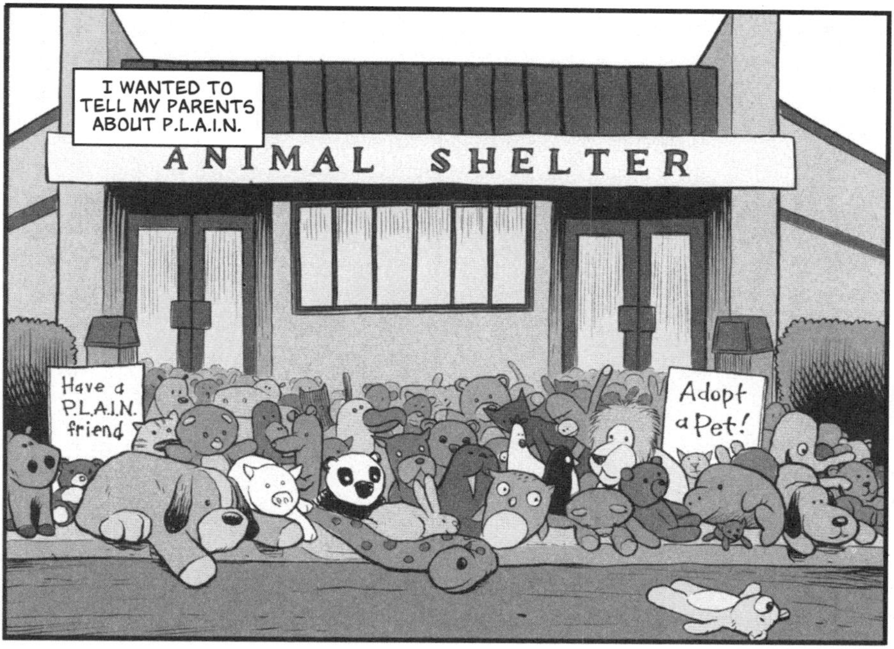
I WANTED TO TELL MY PARENTS ABOUT P.L.A.I.N.
ANIMAL SHELTER
Have a P.L.A.I.N. friend
Adopt a Pet!

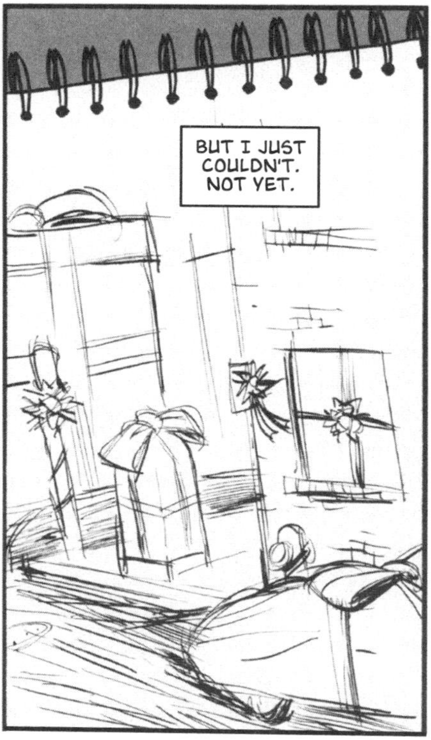
BUT I JUST COULDN'T. NOT YET.

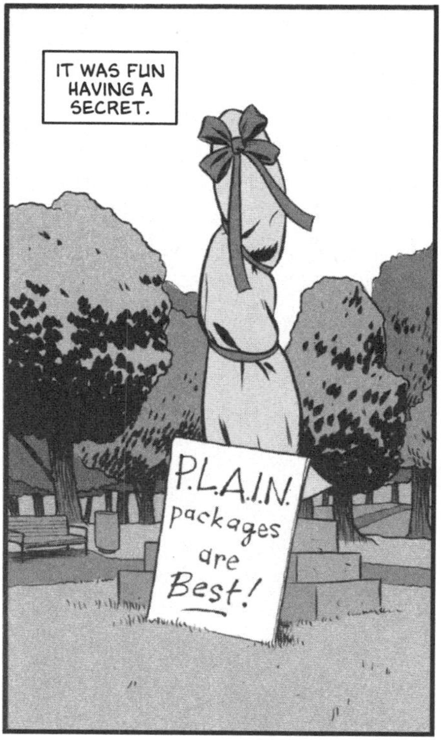
IT WAS FUN HAVING A SECRET.
P.L.A.I.N. packages are Best!

vol. 94   No. 192

Attacks in plain view!!!

Yet another art attack, this time hitting Main and Elm, where various objects were wrapped up like a present.

Who are these artists and what do they want?

"The scariest part of this whole incident, is that they could be anyone." Chilling words from the Chief of Police offers little hope that attacks can ~~happy~~ ending.

THE WHOLE TOWN WAS TALKING ABOUT P.L.A.I.N. EVERYONE HAD AN OPINION ABOUT WHAT WE WERE DOING.

EXTRA CREDIT

$\cos(\omega t + \phi) = A_1 \cos(\omega t + \phi_1) + A_2 \cos(\omega t + \phi_2)$

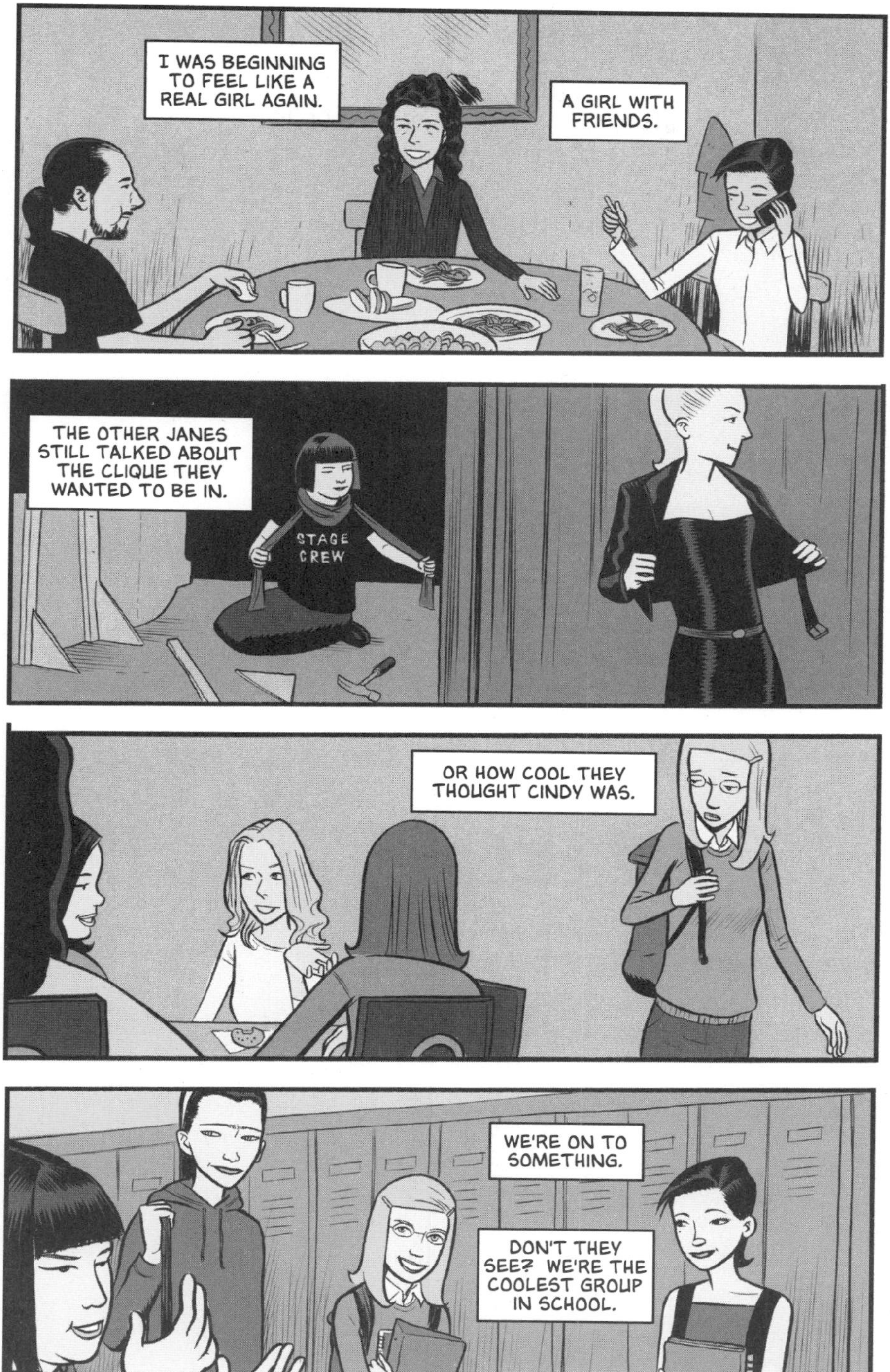
I WAS BEGINNING TO FEEL LIKE A REAL GIRL AGAIN.
A GIRL WITH FRIENDS.
THE OTHER JANES STILL TALKED ABOUT THE CLIQUE THEY WANTED TO BE IN.
STAGE CREW
OR HOW COOL THEY THOUGHT CINDY WAS.
WE'RE ON TO SOMETHING.
DON'T THEY SEE? WE'RE THE COOLEST GROUP IN SCHOOL.

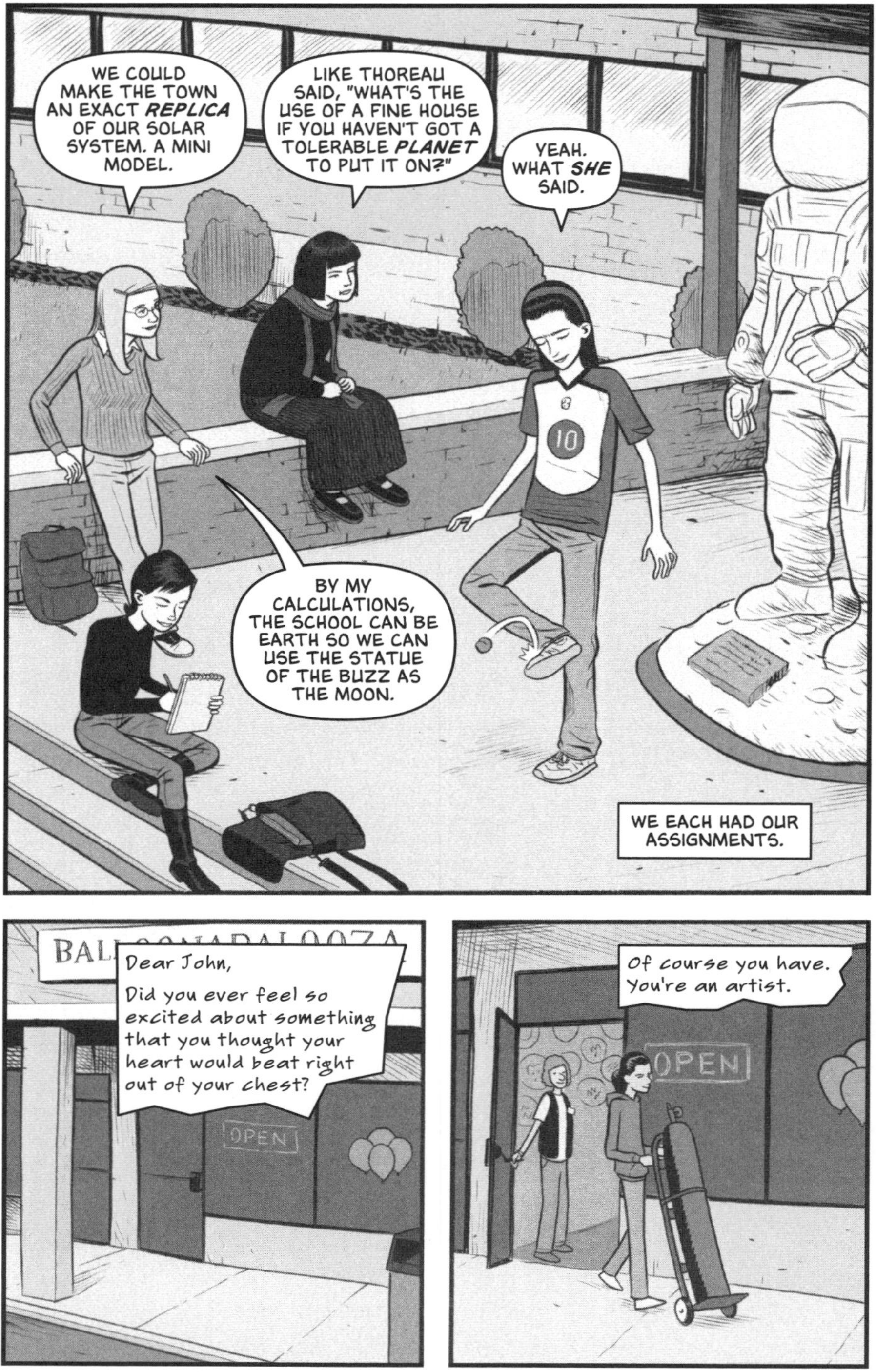
WE COULD MAKE THE TOWN AN EXACT *REPLICA* OF OUR SOLAR SYSTEM. A MINI MODEL.
LIKE THOREAU SAID, "WHAT'S THE USE OF A FINE HOUSE IF YOU HAVEN'T GOT A TOLERABLE *PLANET* TO PUT IT ON?"
YEAH. WHAT *SHE* SAID.
BY MY CALCULATIONS, THE SCHOOL CAN BE EARTH SO WE CAN USE THE STATUE OF THE BUZZ AS THE MOON.
WE EACH HAD OUR ASSIGNMENTS.
Dear John,
Did you ever feel so excited about something that you thought your heart would beat right out of your chest?
OPEN
Of course you have. You're an artist.
OPEN

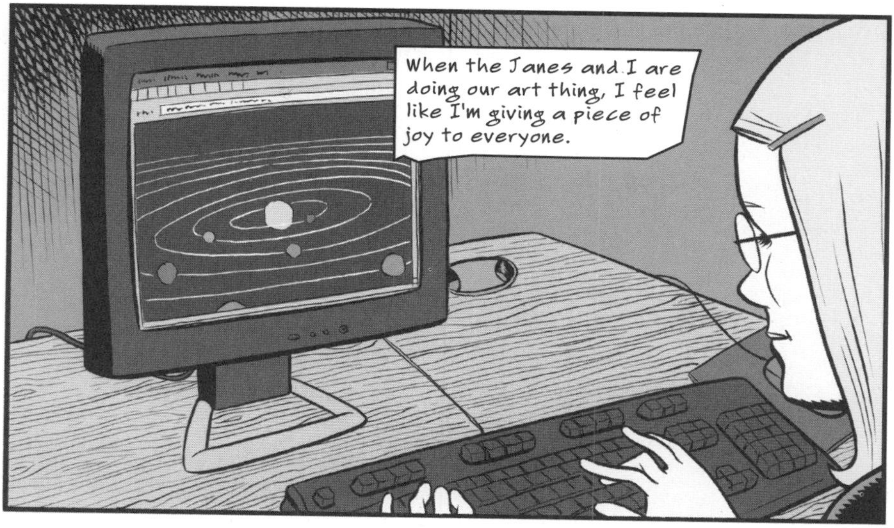
When the Janes and I are doing our art thing, I feel like I'm giving a piece of joy to everyone.

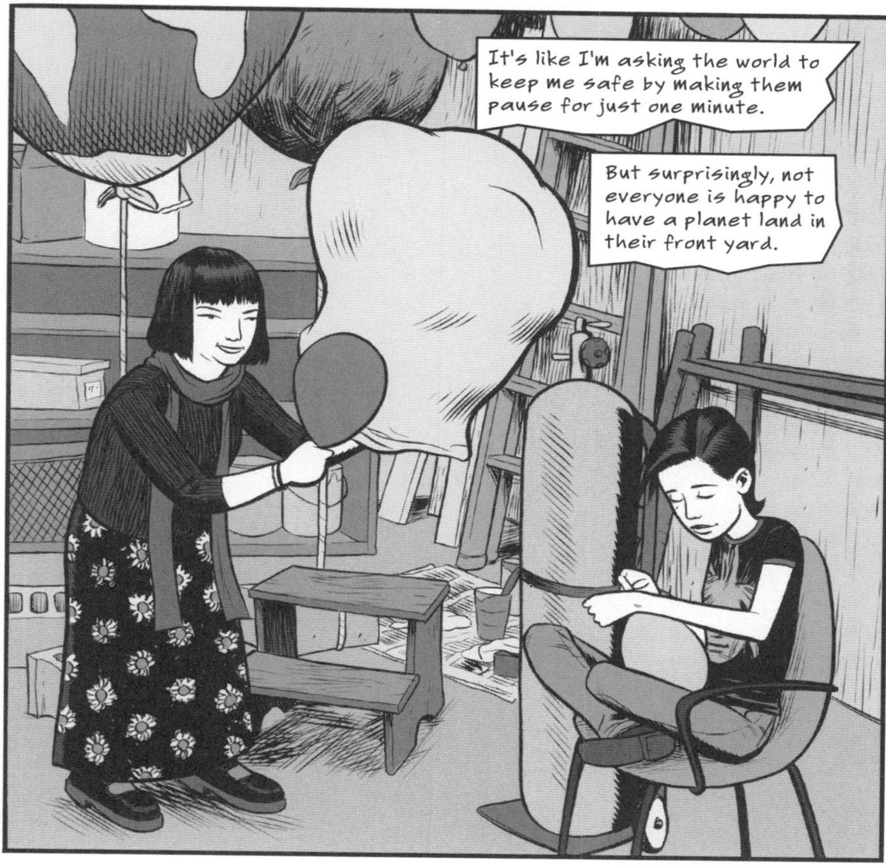
It's like I'm asking the world to keep me safe by making them pause for just one minute.
But surprisingly, not everyone is happy to have a planet land in their front yard.

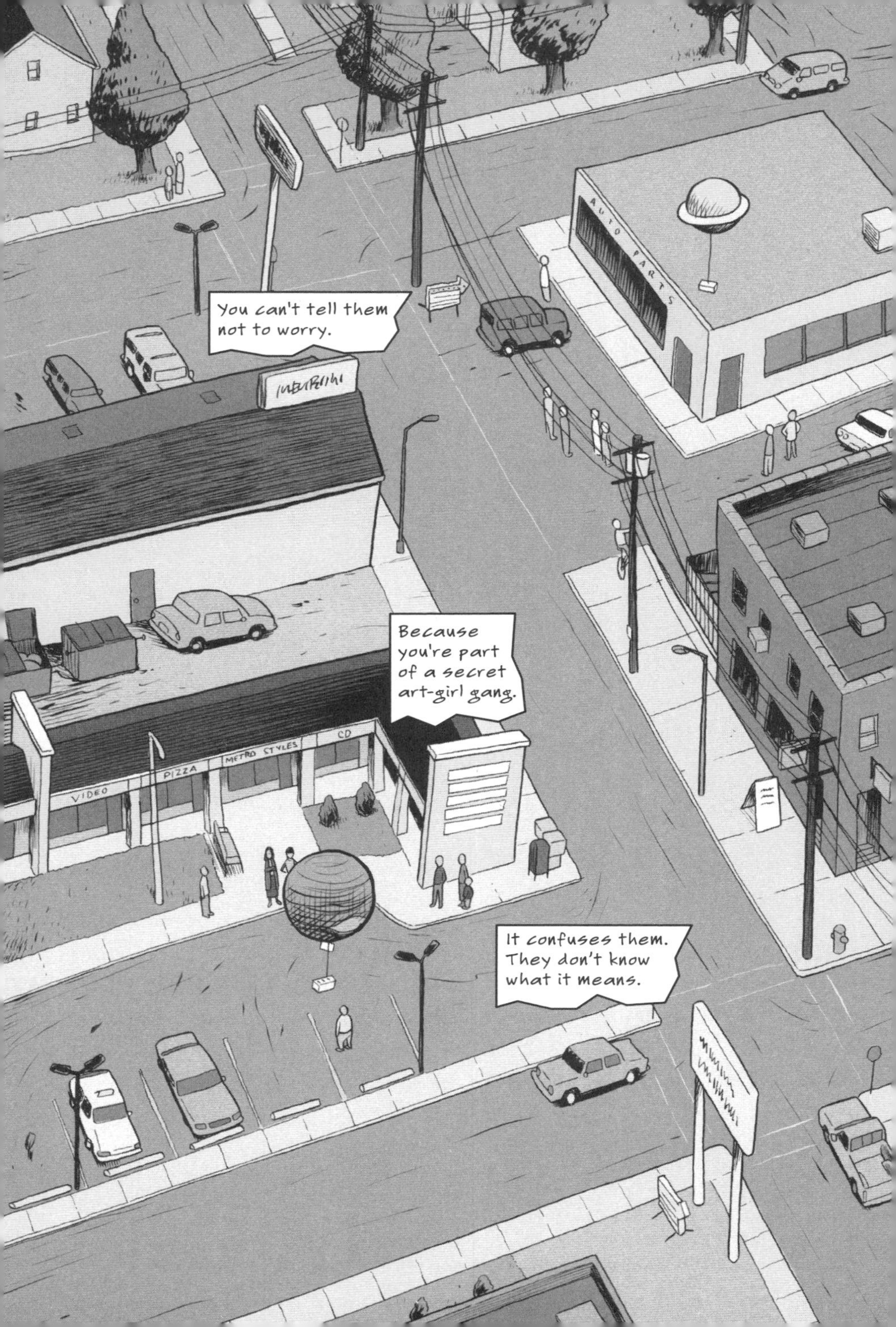

You can't tell them not to worry.
Because you're part of a secret art-girl gang.
It confuses them. They don't know what it means.
AUTO PARTS
VIDEO
PIZZA
METRO STYLES
CD

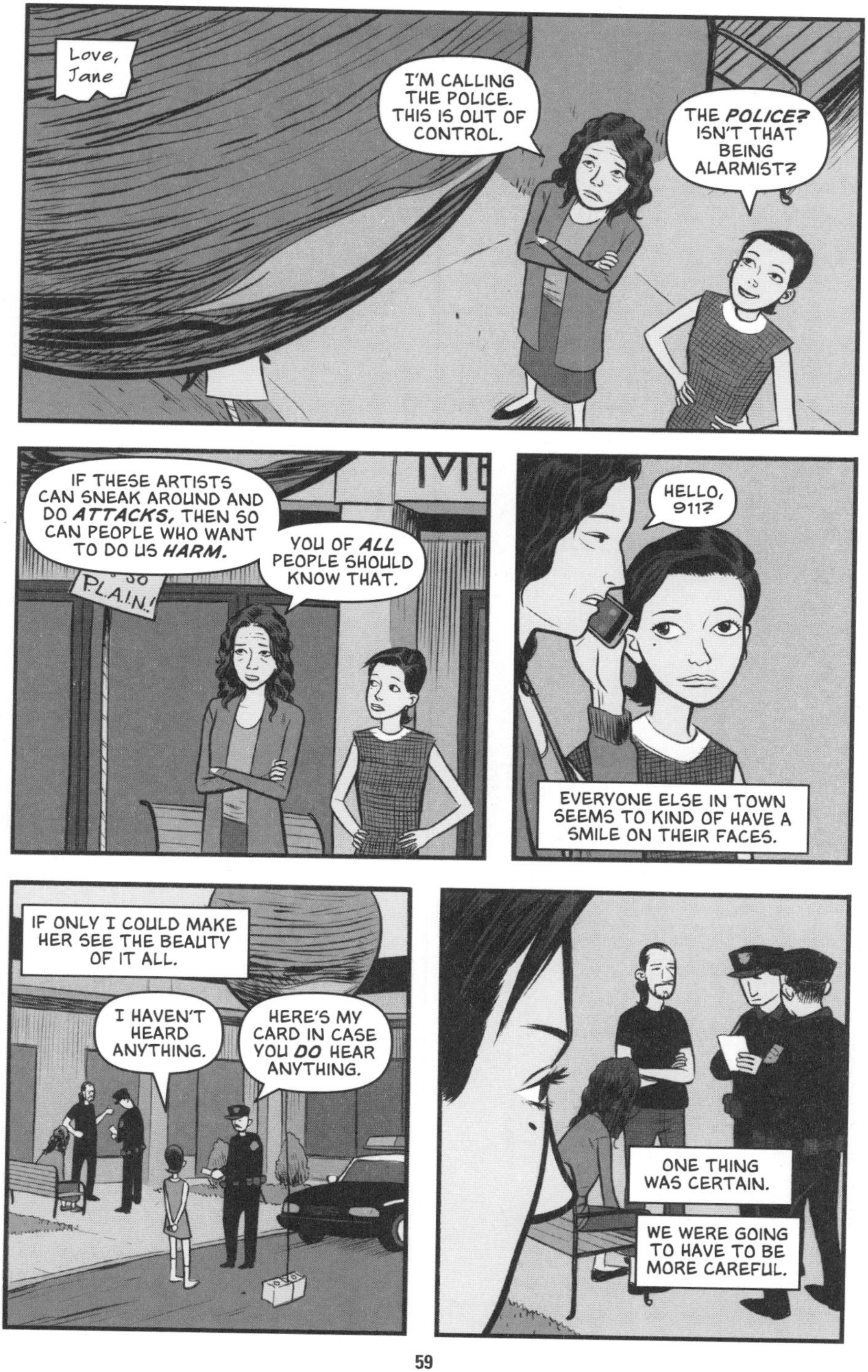
Love,
Jane
I'M CALLING THE POLICE. THIS IS OUT OF CONTROL.
THE POLICE? ISN'T THAT BEING ALARMIST?
IF THESE ARTISTS CAN SNEAK AROUND AND DO ATTACKS, THEN SO CAN PEOPLE WHO WANT TO DO US HARM.
YOU OF ALL PEOPLE SHOULD KNOW THAT.
P.L.A.I.N.!
HELLO, 911?
EVERYONE ELSE IN TOWN SEEMS TO KIND OF HAVE A SMILE ON THEIR FACES.
IF ONLY I COULD MAKE HER SEE THE BEAUTY OF IT ALL.
I HAVEN'T HEARD ANYTHING.
HERE'S MY CARD IN CASE YOU DO HEAR ANYTHING.
ONE THING WAS CERTAIN.
WE WERE GOING TO HAVE TO BE MORE CAREFUL.

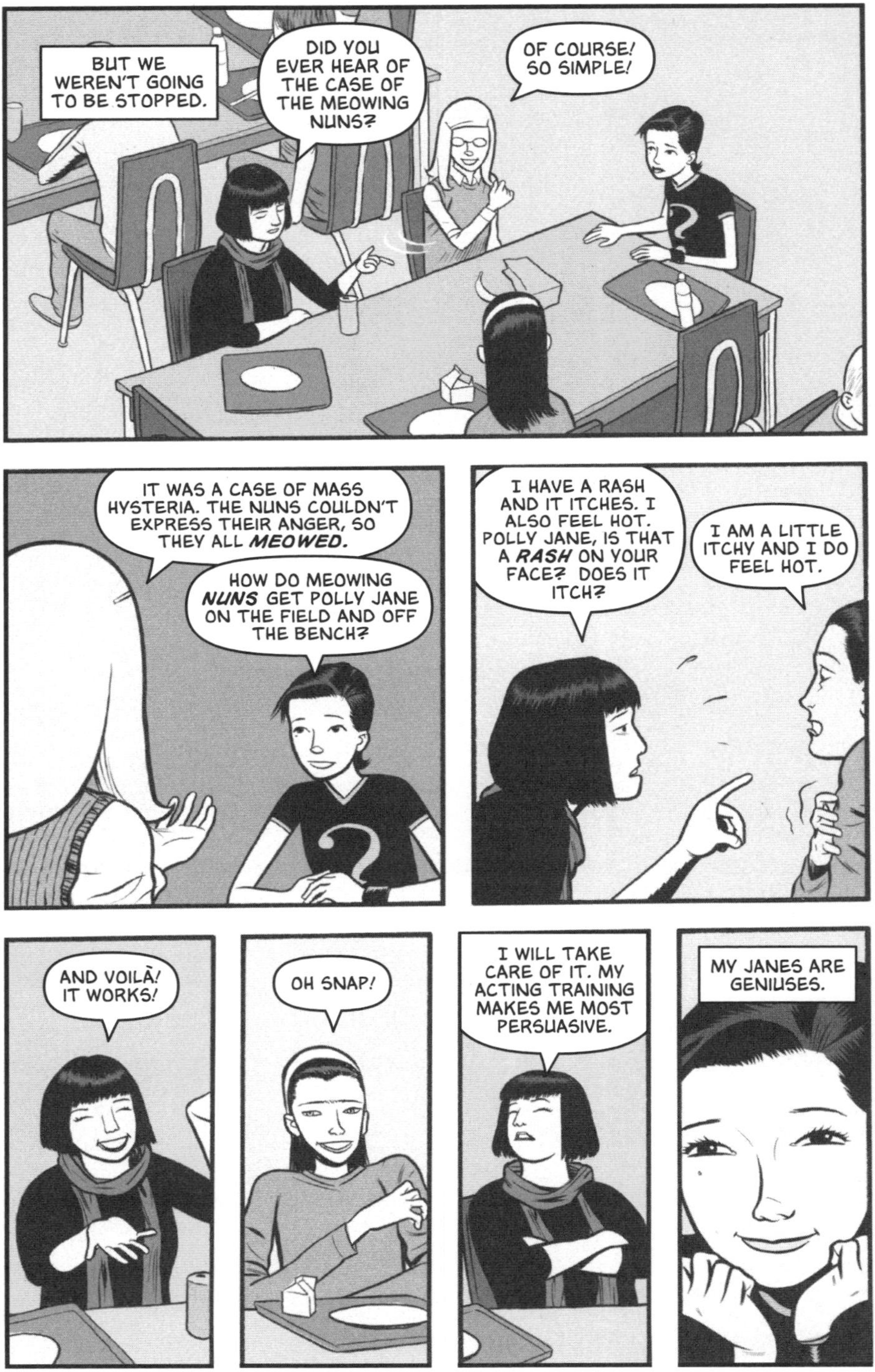
BUT WE WEREN'T GOING TO BE STOPPED.
DID YOU EVER HEAR OF THE CASE OF THE MEOWING NUNS?
OF COURSE! SO SIMPLE!
IT WAS A CASE OF MASS HYSTERIA. THE NUNS COULDN'T EXPRESS THEIR ANGER, SO THEY ALL *MEOWED.*
HOW DO MEOWING *NUNS* GET POLLY JANE ON THE FIELD AND OFF THE BENCH?
I HAVE A RASH AND IT ITCHES. I ALSO FEEL HOT. POLLY JANE, IS THAT A *RASH* ON YOUR FACE? DOES IT ITCH?
I AM A LITTLE ITCHY AND I DO FEEL HOT.
AND VOILÀ! IT WORKS!
OH SNAP!
I WILL TAKE CARE OF IT. MY ACTING TRAINING MAKES ME MOST PERSUASIVE.
MY JANES ARE GENIUSES.

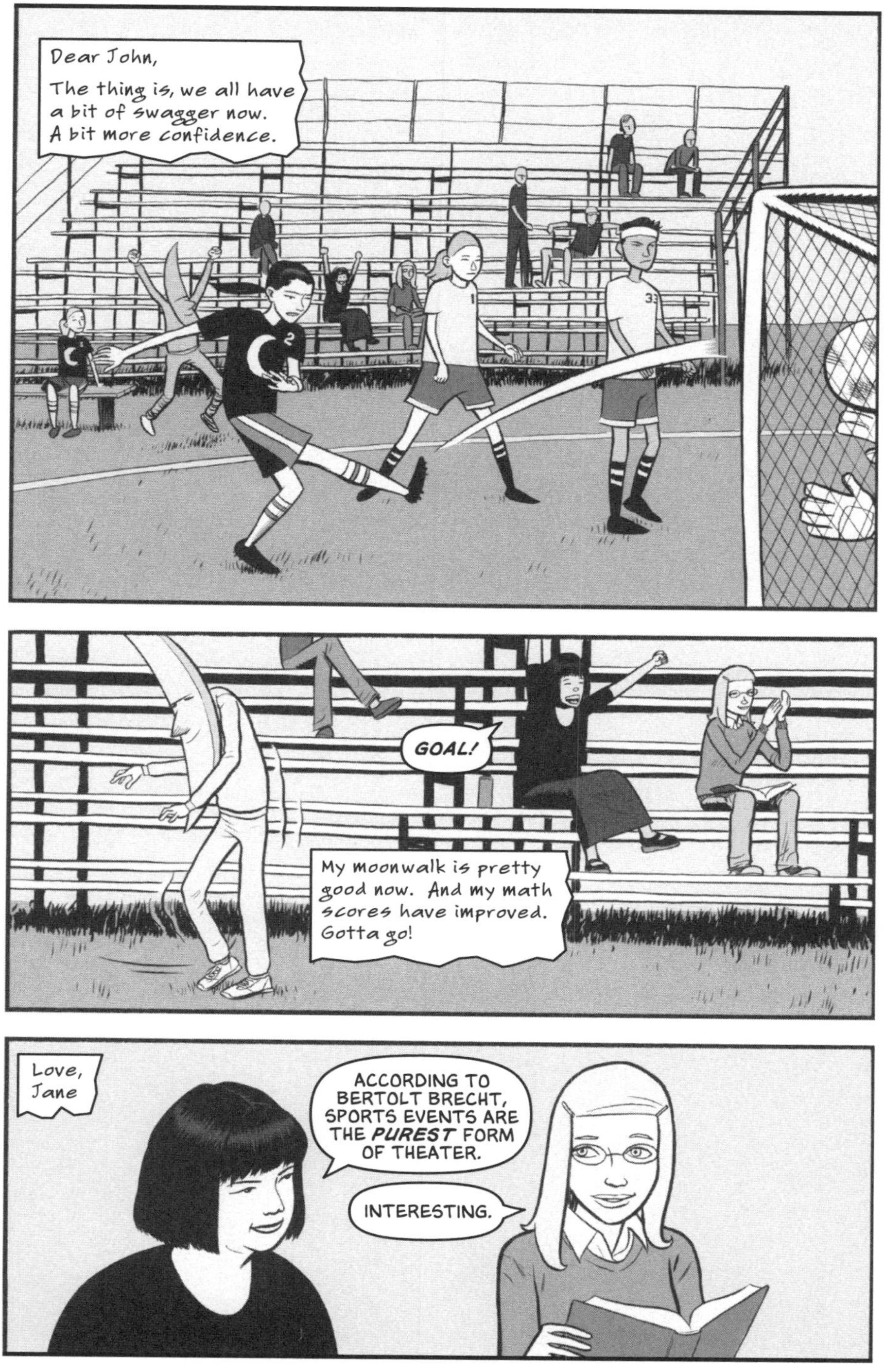
Dear John,
The thing is, we all have a bit of swagger now. A bit more confidence.
GOAL!
My moonwalk is pretty good now. And my math scores have improved. Gotta go!
Love, Jane
ACCORDING TO BERTOLT BRECHT, SPORTS EVENTS ARE THE *PUREST* FORM OF THEATER.
INTERESTING.

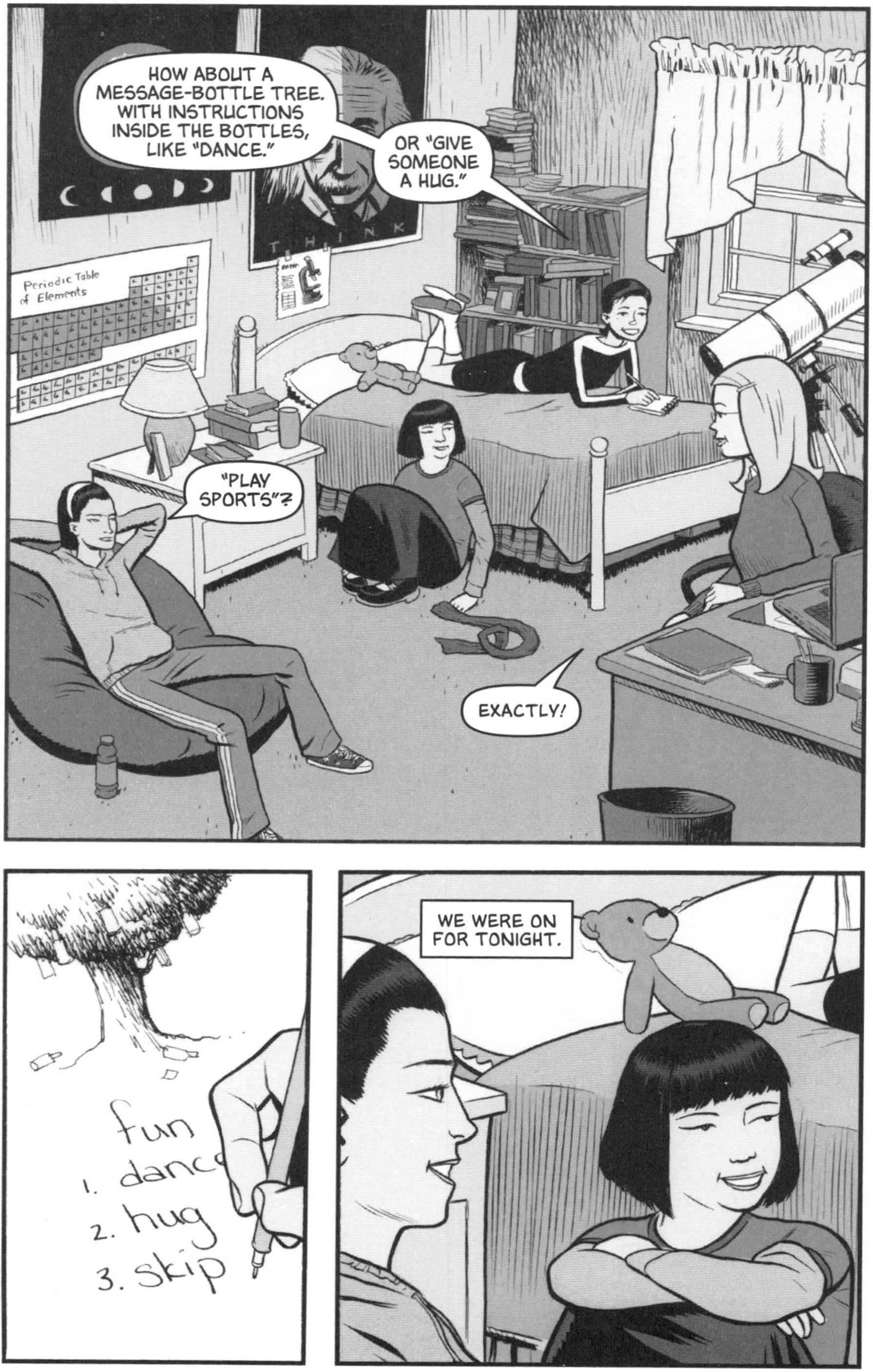
Periodic Table of Elements
THINK
HOW ABOUT A MESSAGE-BOTTLE TREE. WITH INSTRUCTIONS INSIDE THE BOTTLES, LIKE "DANCE."
OR "GIVE SOMEONE A HUG."
"PLAY SPORTS"?
EXACTLY!
fun
1. danc
2. hug
3. skip
WE WERE ON FOR TONIGHT.

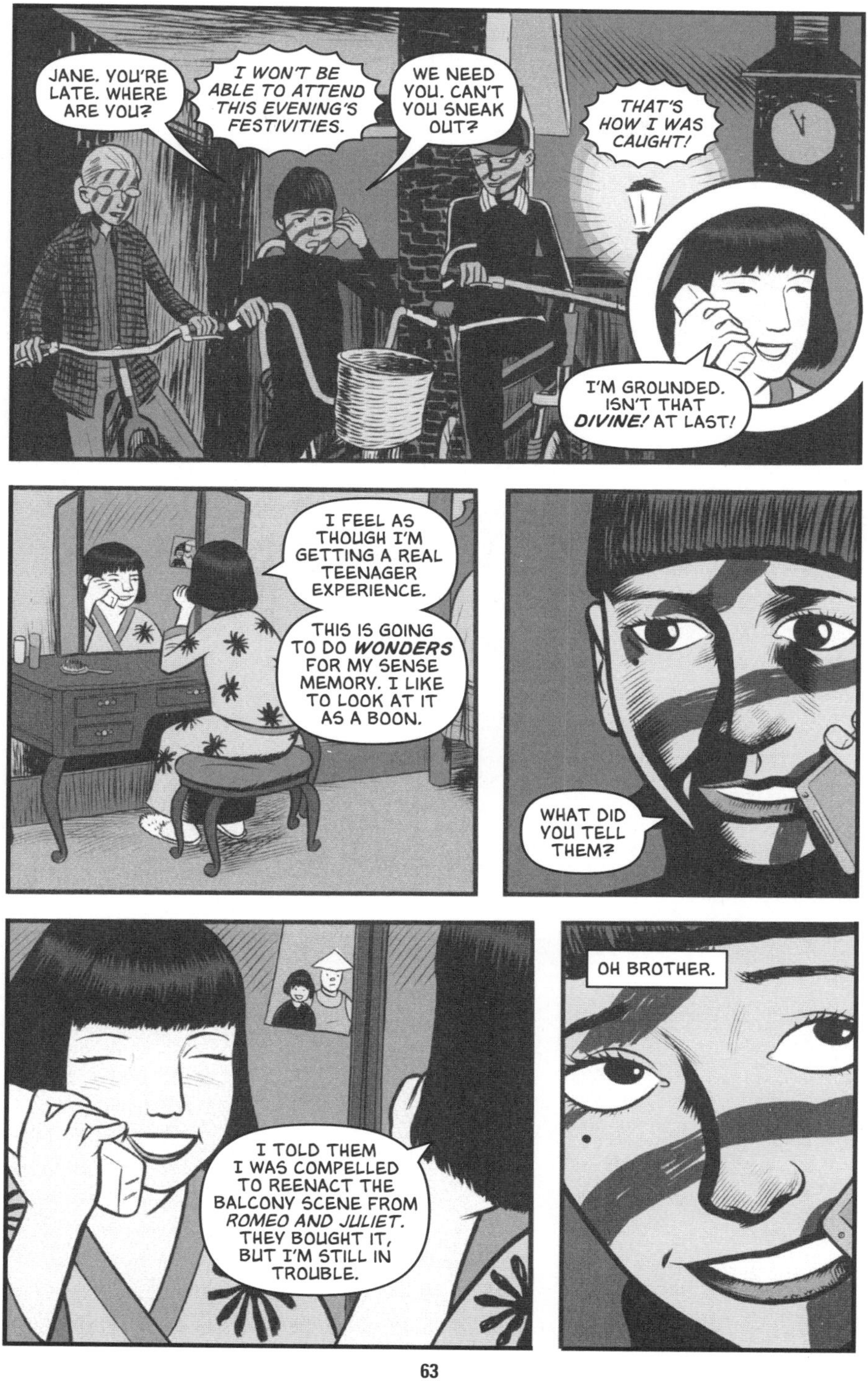
JANE. YOU'RE LATE. WHERE ARE YOU?
I WON'T BE ABLE TO ATTEND THIS EVENING'S FESTIVITIES.
WE NEED YOU. CAN'T YOU SNEAK OUT?
THAT'S HOW I WAS CAUGHT!
I'M GROUNDED. ISN'T THAT DIVINE! AT LAST!
I FEEL AS THOUGH I'M GETTING A REAL TEENAGER EXPERIENCE.
THIS IS GOING TO DO WONDERS FOR MY SENSE MEMORY. I LIKE TO LOOK AT IT AS A BOON.
WHAT DID YOU TELL THEM?
I TOLD THEM I WAS COMPELLED TO REENACT THE BALCONY SCENE FROM ROMEO AND JULIET. THEY BOUGHT IT, BUT I'M STILL IN TROUBLE.
OH BROTHER.

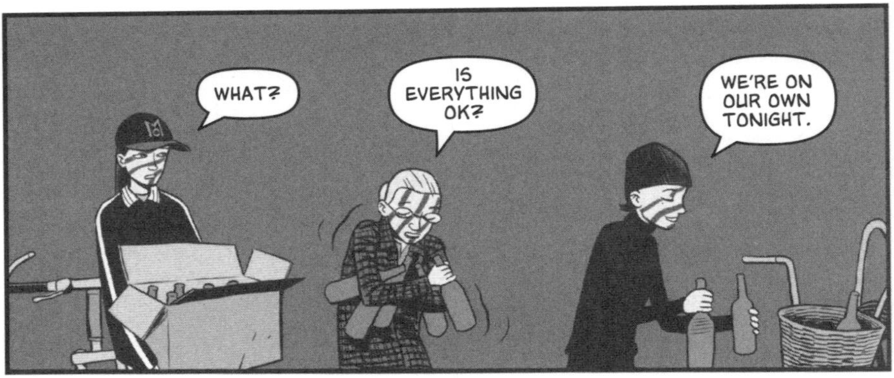
WHAT?
IS EVERYTHING OK?
WE'RE ON OUR OWN TONIGHT.

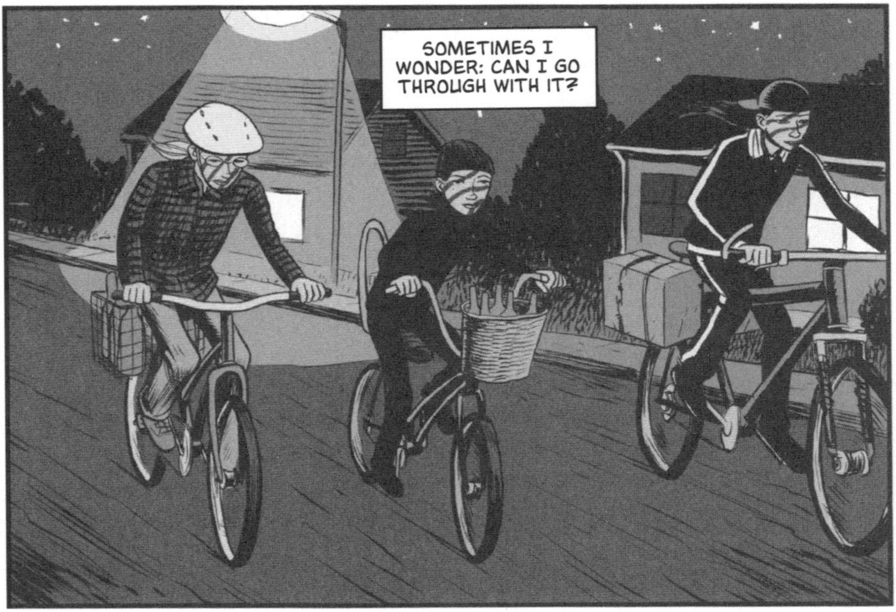
SOMETIMES I WONDER: CAN I GO THROUGH WITH IT?

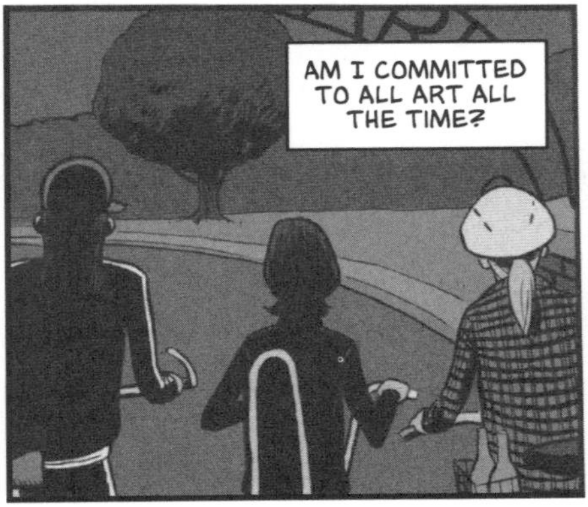
AM I COMMITTED TO ALL ART ALL THE TIME?

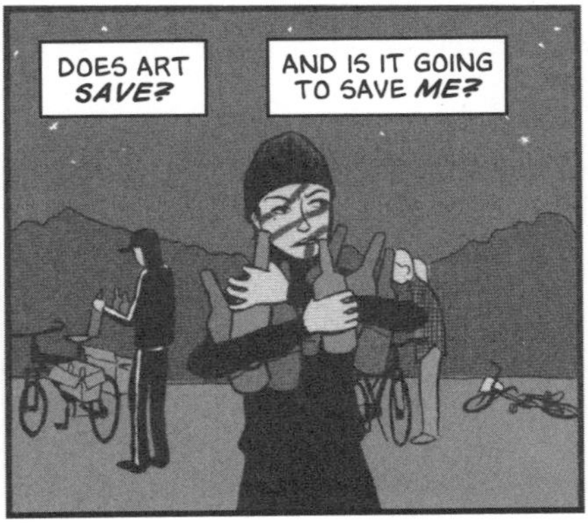
DOES ART *SAVE?*
AND IS IT GOING TO SAVE *ME?*

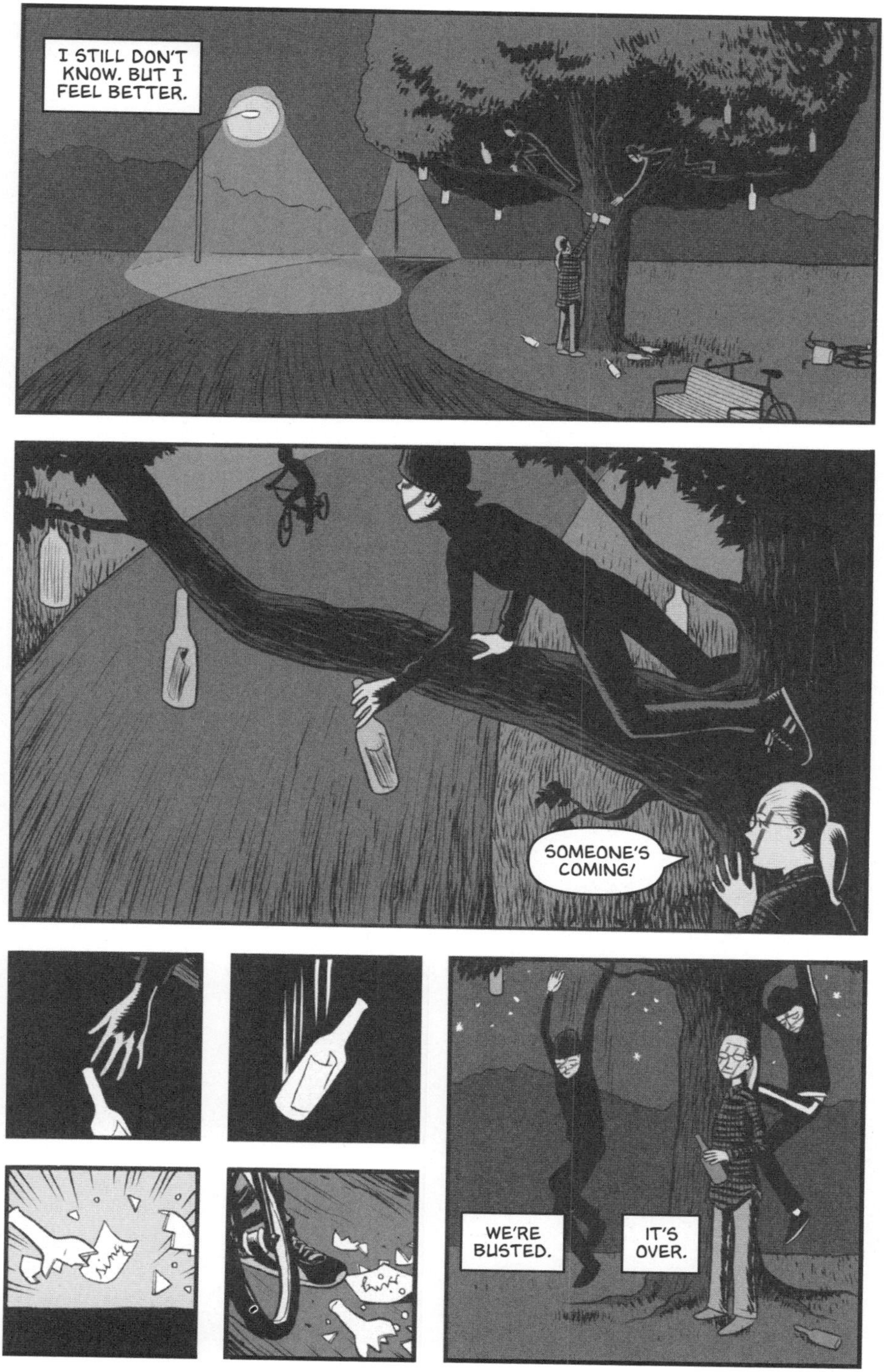
I STILL DON'T KNOW. BUT I FEEL BETTER.
SOMEONE'S COMING!
WE'RE BUSTED.
IT'S OVER.

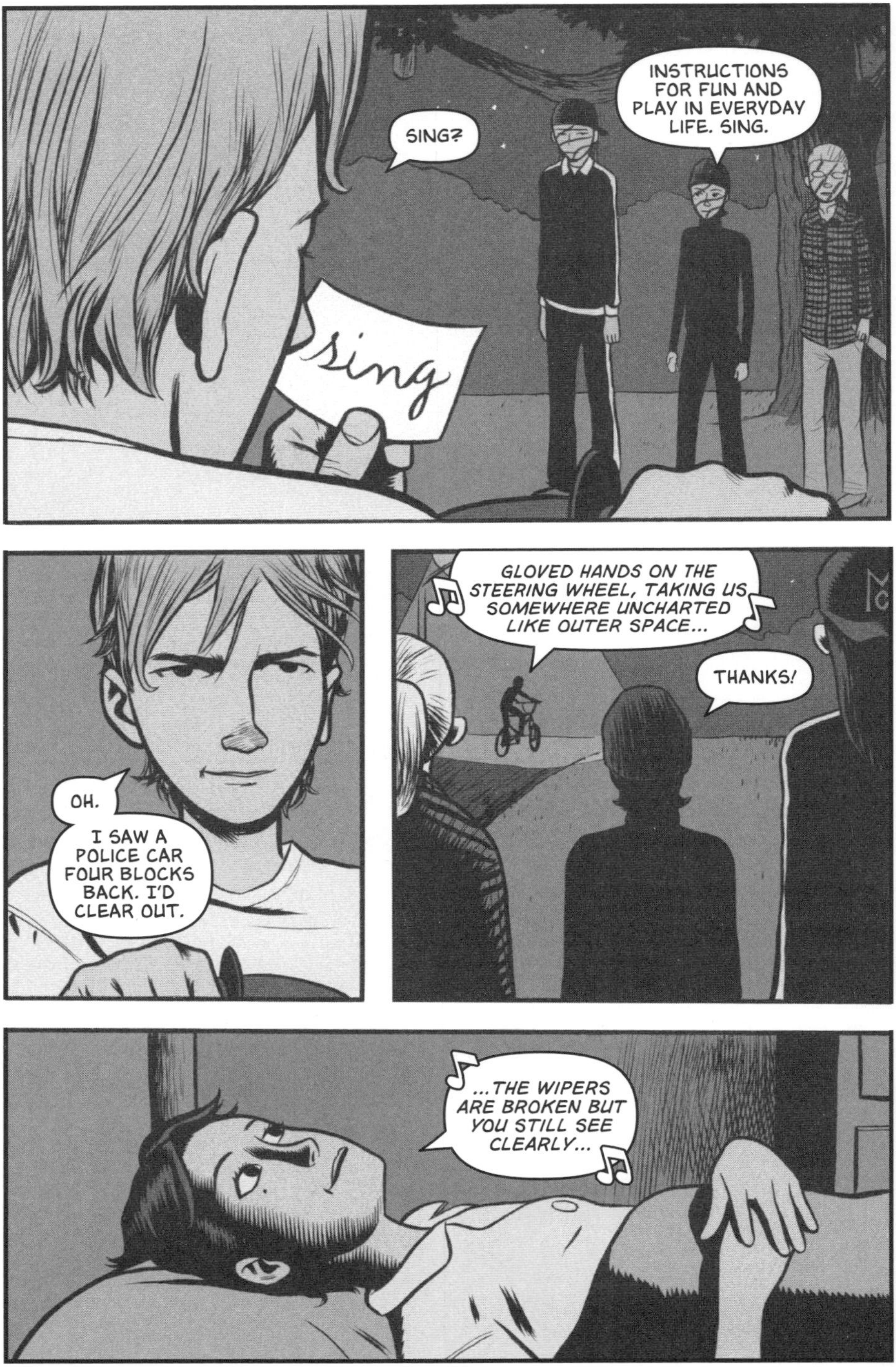
SING?
INSTRUCTIONS FOR FUN AND PLAY IN EVERYDAY LIFE. SING.
sing
OH.
I SAW A POLICE CAR FOUR BLOCKS BACK. I'D CLEAR OUT.
GLOVED HANDS ON THE STEERING WHEEL, TAKING US SOMEWHERE UNCHARTED LIKE OUTER SPACE...
THANKS!
...THE WIPERS ARE BROKEN BUT YOU STILL SEE CLEARLY...

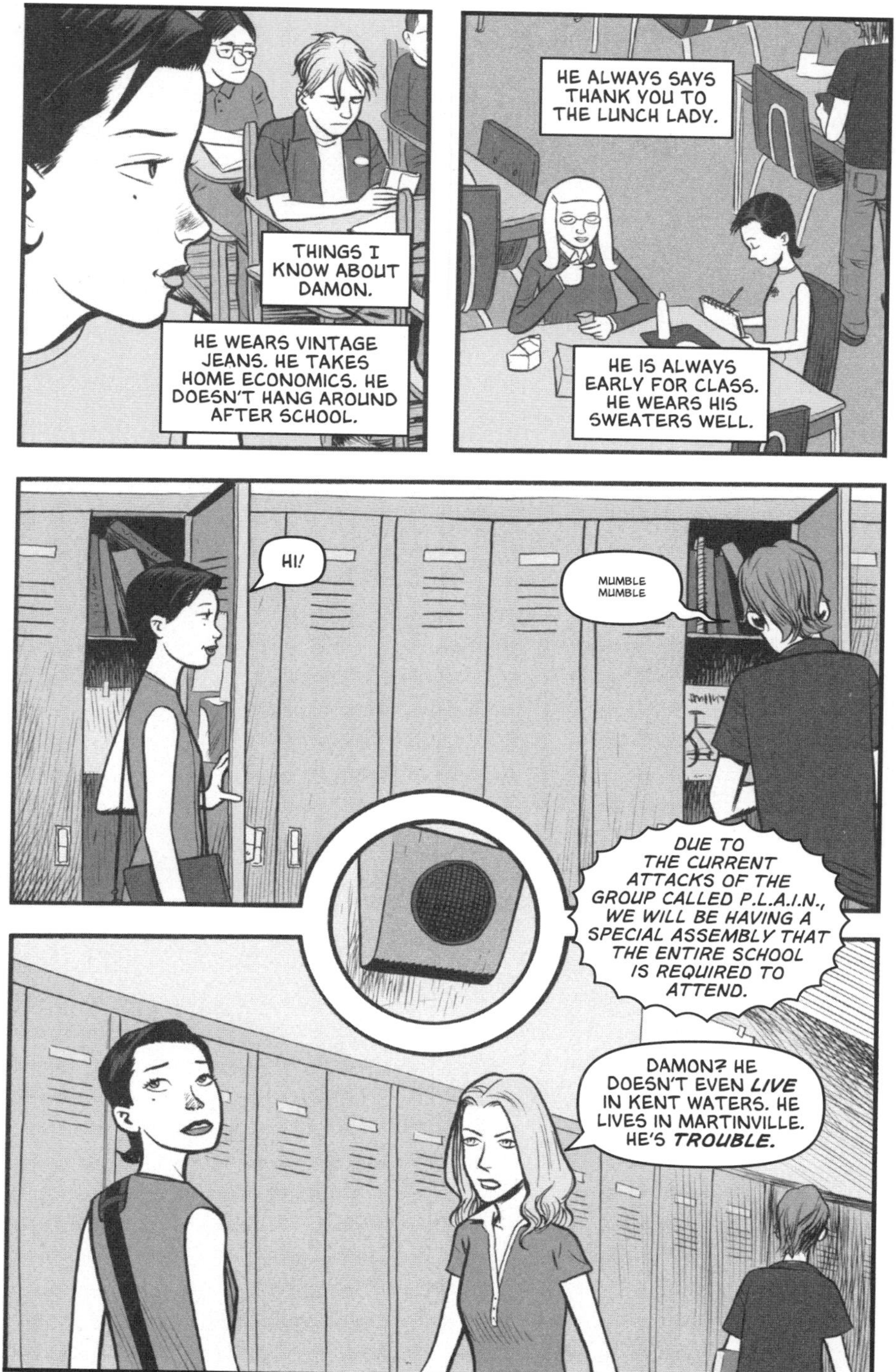
THINGS I KNOW ABOUT DAMON.
HE WEARS VINTAGE JEANS. HE TAKES HOME ECONOMICS. HE DOESN'T HANG AROUND AFTER SCHOOL.
HE ALWAYS SAYS THANK YOU TO THE LUNCH LADY.
HE IS ALWAYS EARLY FOR CLASS. HE WEARS HIS SWEATERS WELL.
HI!
MUMBLE MUMBLE
DUE TO THE CURRENT ATTACKS OF THE GROUP CALLED P.L.A.I.N., WE WILL BE HAVING A SPECIAL ASSEMBLY THAT THE ENTIRE SCHOOL IS REQUIRED TO ATTEND.
DAMON? HE DOESN'T EVEN *LIVE* IN KENT WATERS. HE LIVES IN MARTINVILLE. HE'S ***TROUBLE.***

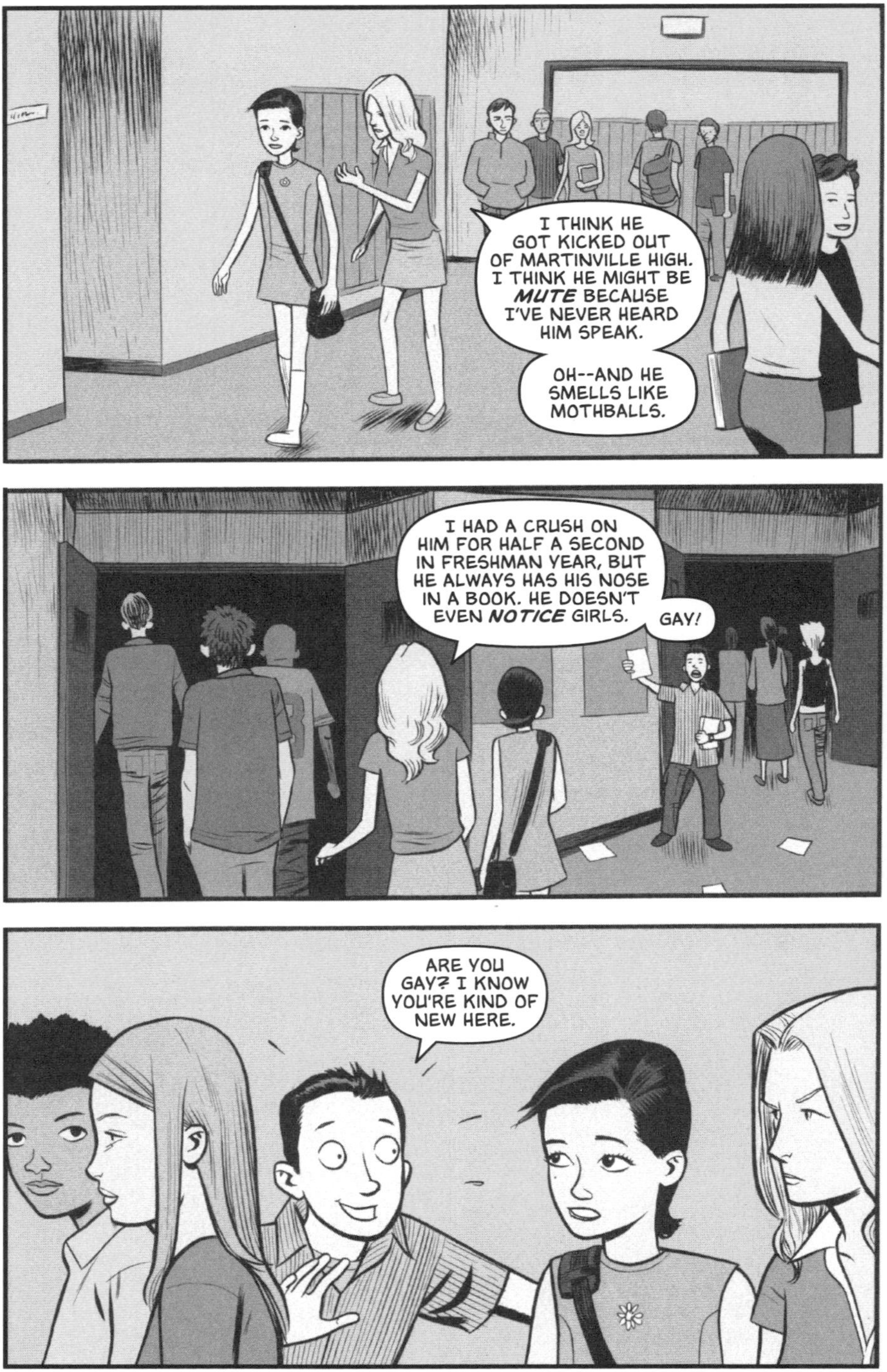
I THINK HE GOT KICKED OUT OF MARTINVILLE HIGH. I THINK HE MIGHT BE *MUTE* BECAUSE I'VE NEVER HEARD HIM SPEAK.
OH--AND HE SMELLS LIKE MOTHBALLS.
I HAD A CRUSH ON HIM FOR HALF A SECOND IN FRESHMAN YEAR, BUT HE ALWAYS HAS HIS NOSE IN A BOOK. HE DOESN'T EVEN *NOTICE* GIRLS.
GAY!
ARE YOU GAY? I KNOW YOU'RE KIND OF NEW HERE.

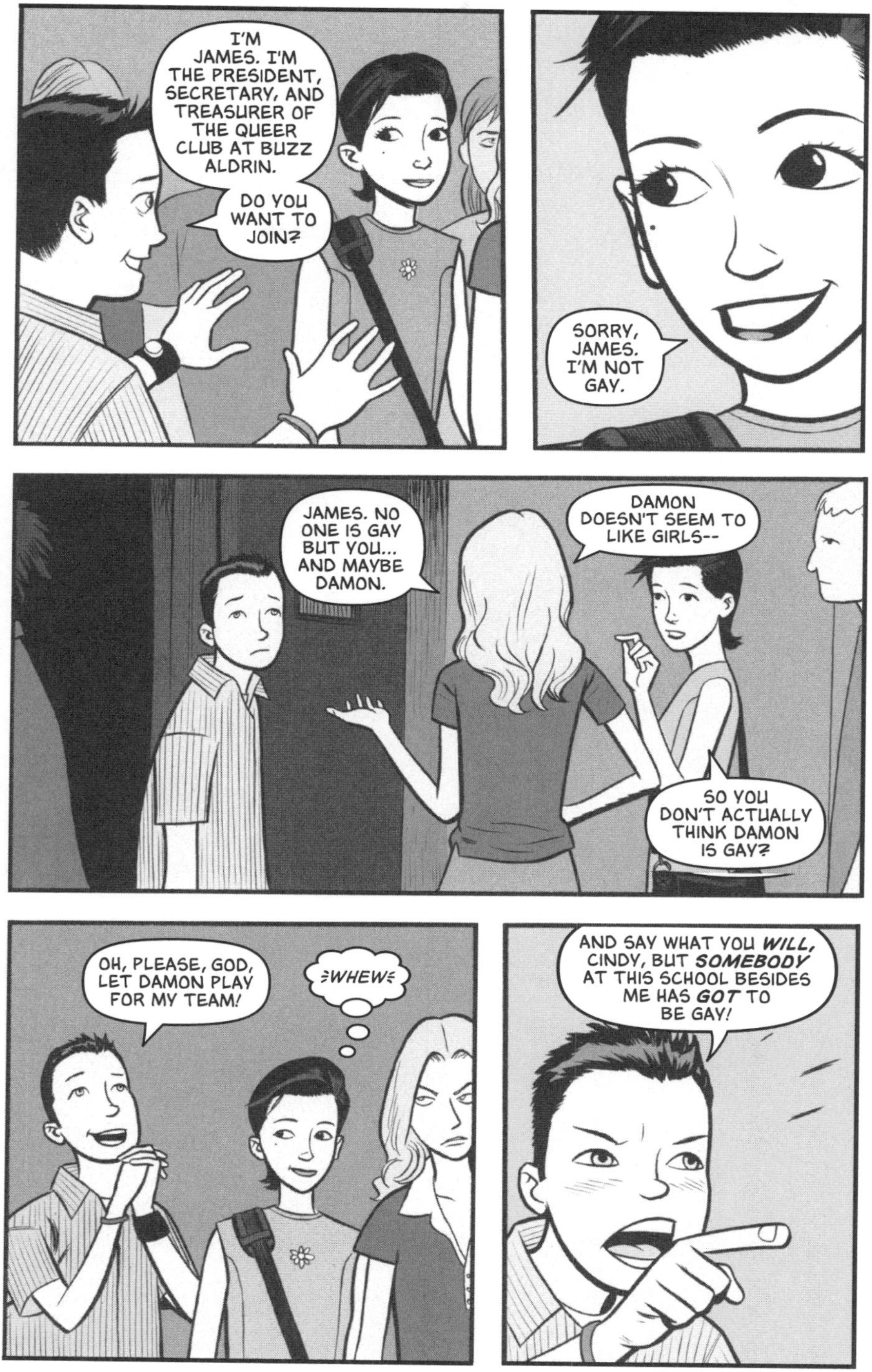
I'M JAMES. I'M THE PRESIDENT, SECRETARY, AND TREASURER OF THE QUEER CLUB AT BUZZ ALDRIN.
DO YOU WANT TO JOIN?
SORRY, JAMES. I'M NOT GAY.
JAMES. NO ONE IS GAY BUT YOU... AND MAYBE DAMON.
DAMON DOESN'T SEEM TO LIKE GIRLS--
SO YOU DON'T ACTUALLY THINK DAMON IS GAY?
OH, PLEASE, GOD, LET DAMON PLAY FOR MY TEAM!
WHEW
AND SAY WHAT YOU *WILL*, CINDY, BUT *SOMEBODY* AT THIS SCHOOL BESIDES ME HAS *GOT* TO BE GAY!

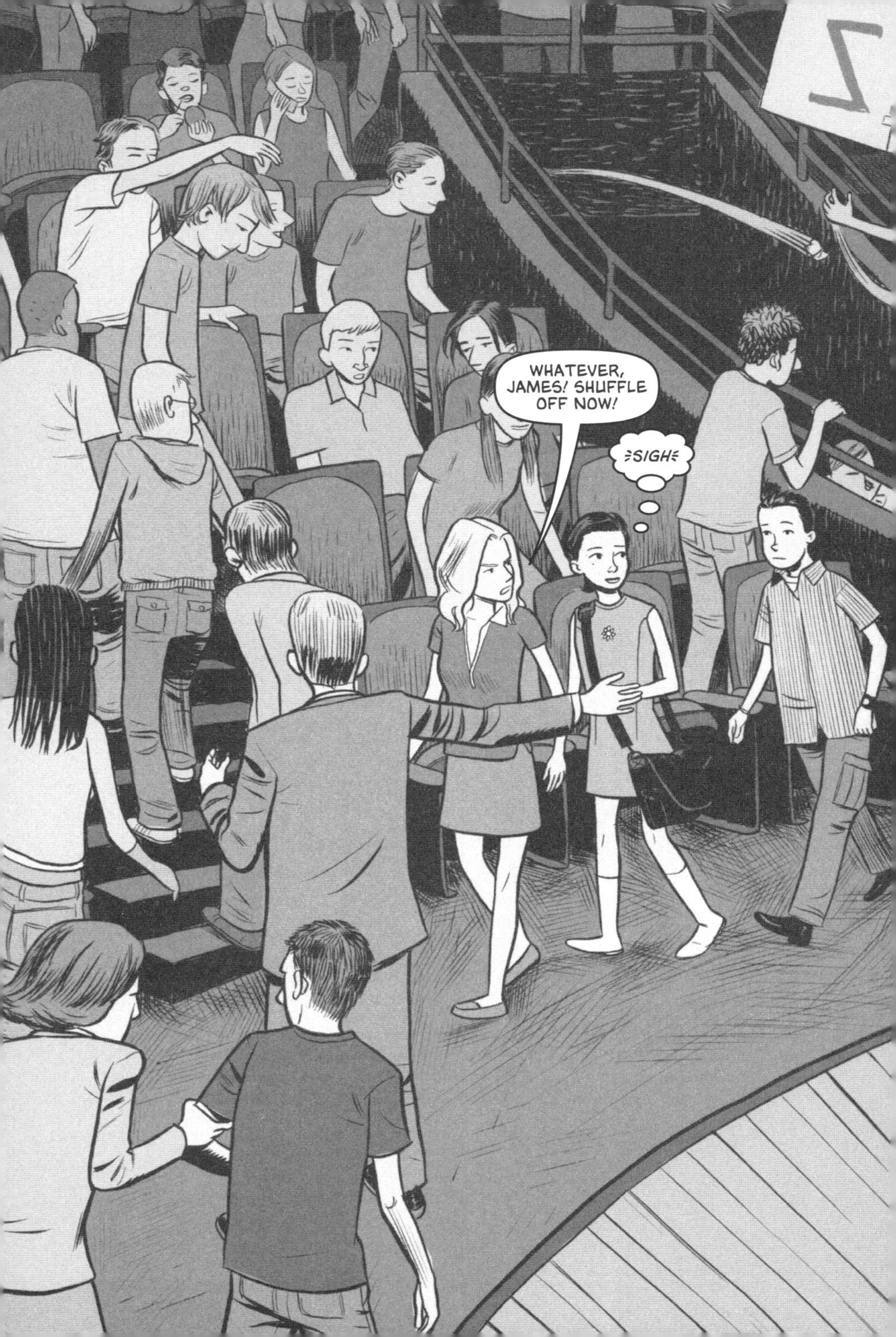
WHATEVER, JAMES! SHUFFLE OFF NOW!
SIGH

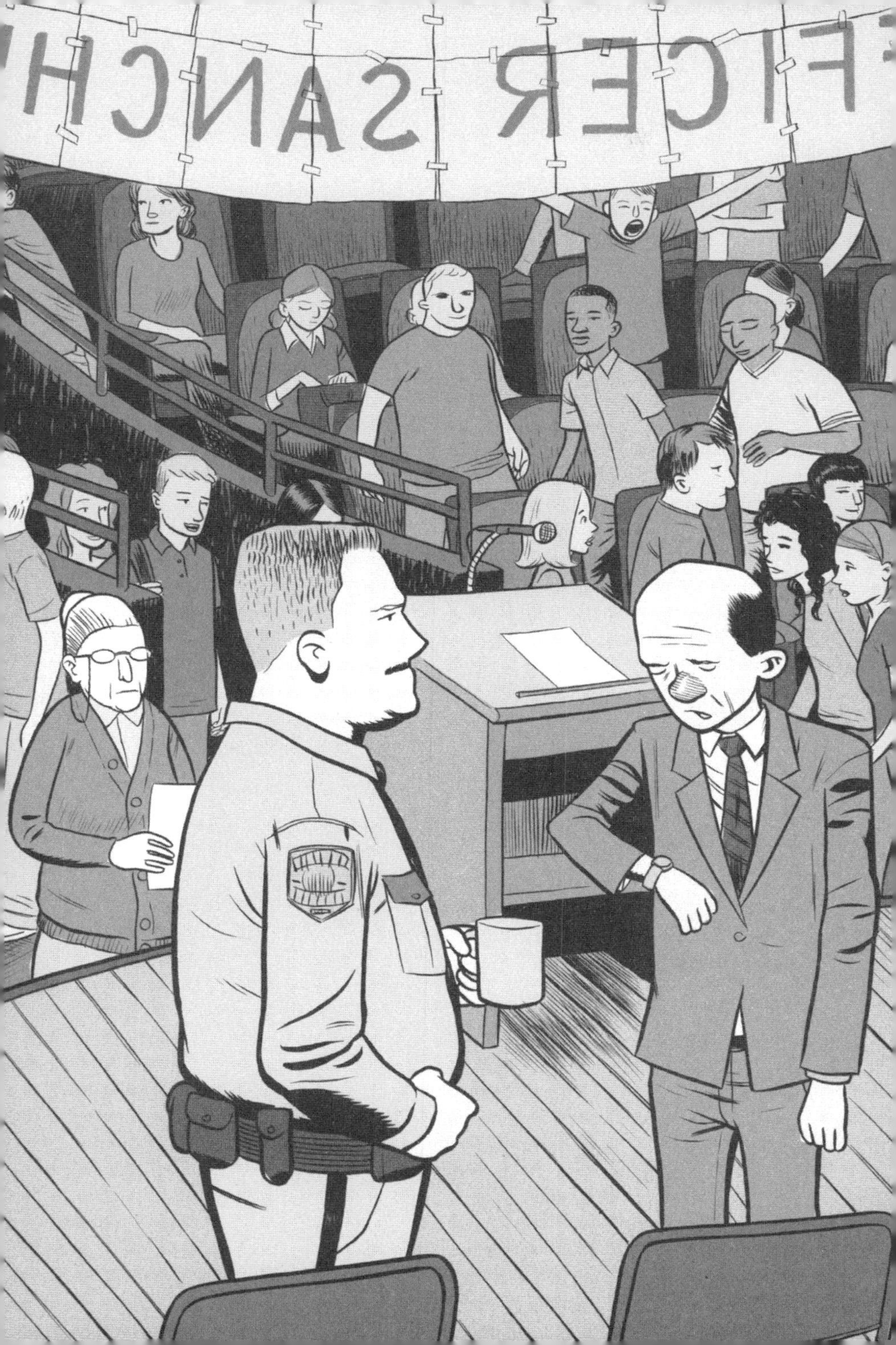

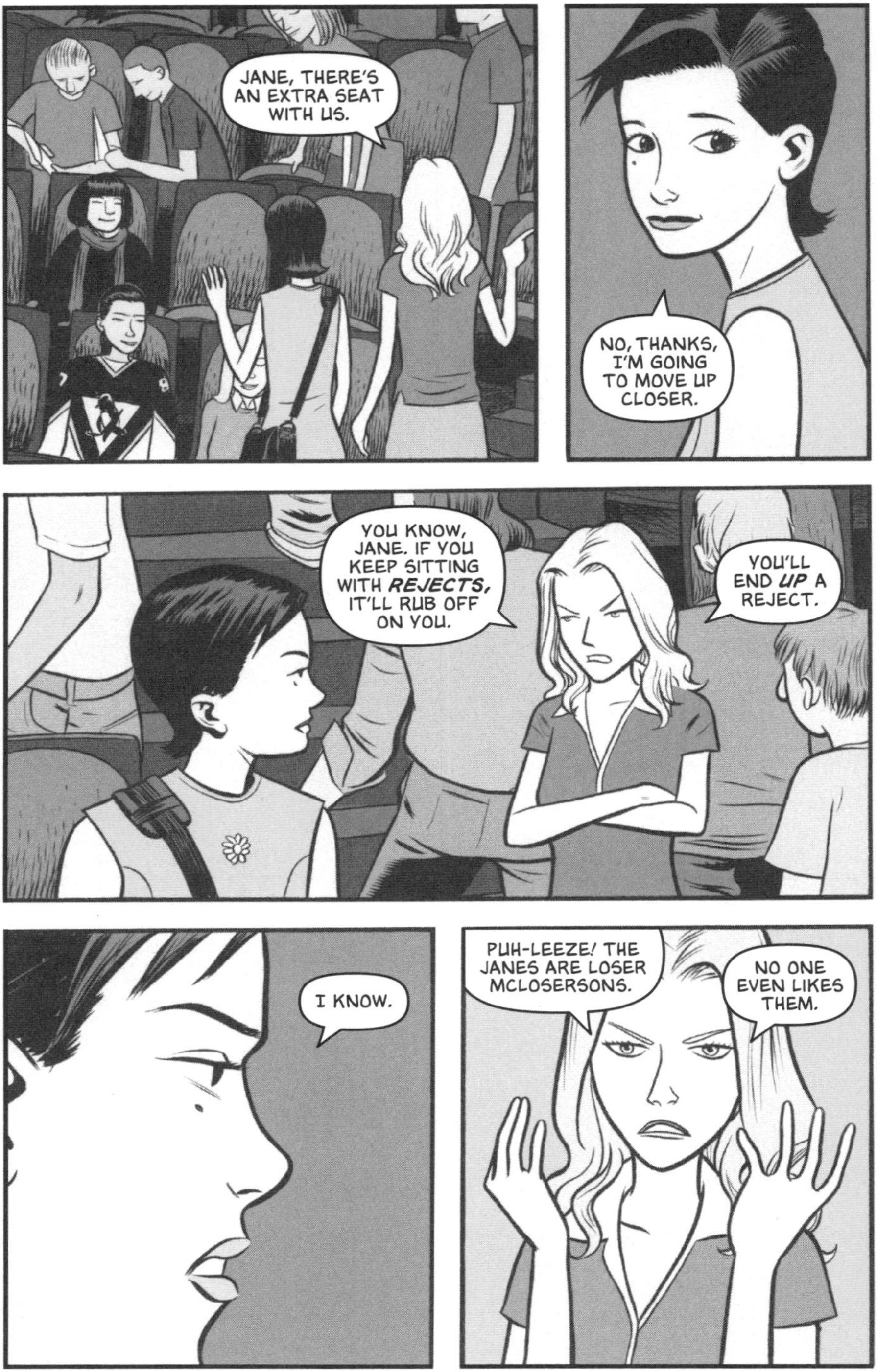
JANE, THERE'S AN EXTRA SEAT WITH US.
NO, THANKS, I'M GOING TO MOVE UP CLOSER.
YOU KNOW, JANE. IF YOU KEEP SITTING WITH *REJECTS,* IT'LL RUB OFF ON YOU.
YOU'LL END *UP* A REJECT.
I KNOW.
PUH-LEEZE! THE JANES ARE LOSER MCLOSERSONS.
NO ONE EVEN LIKES THEM.

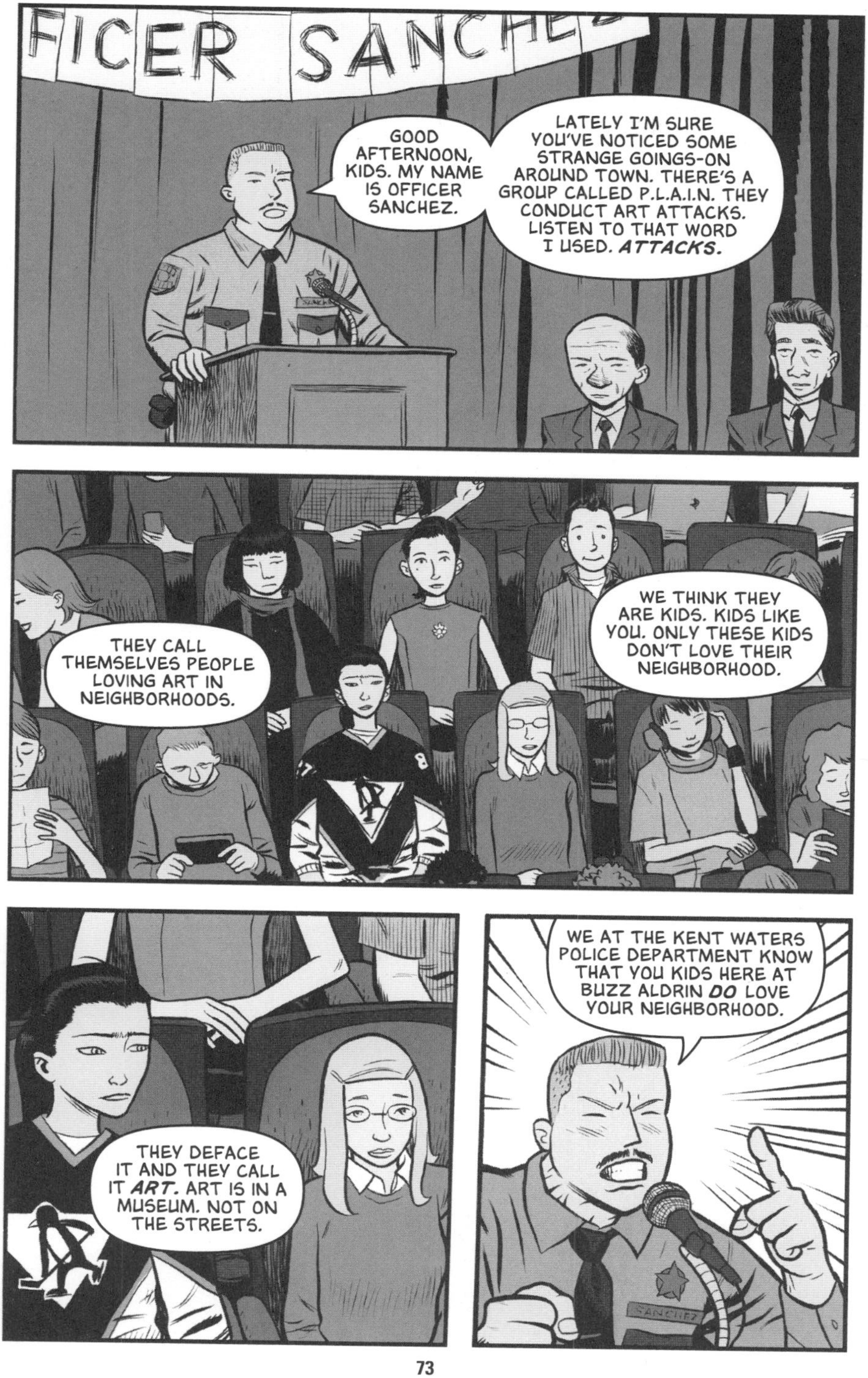
FICER SANCHEZ
GOOD AFTERNOON, KIDS. MY NAME IS OFFICER SANCHEZ.
LATELY I'M SURE YOU'VE NOTICED SOME STRANGE GOINGS-ON AROUND TOWN. THERE'S A GROUP CALLED P.L.A.I.N. THEY CONDUCT ART ATTACKS. LISTEN TO THAT WORD I USED. *ATTACKS.*
THEY CALL THEMSELVES PEOPLE LOVING ART IN NEIGHBORHOODS.
WE THINK THEY ARE KIDS. KIDS LIKE YOU. ONLY THESE KIDS DON'T LOVE THEIR NEIGHBORHOOD.
THEY DEFACE IT AND THEY CALL IT *ART.* ART IS IN A MUSEUM. NOT ON THE STREETS.
WE AT THE KENT WATERS POLICE DEPARTMENT KNOW THAT YOU KIDS HERE AT BUZZ ALDRIN *DO* LOVE YOUR NEIGHBORHOOD.
SANCHEZ

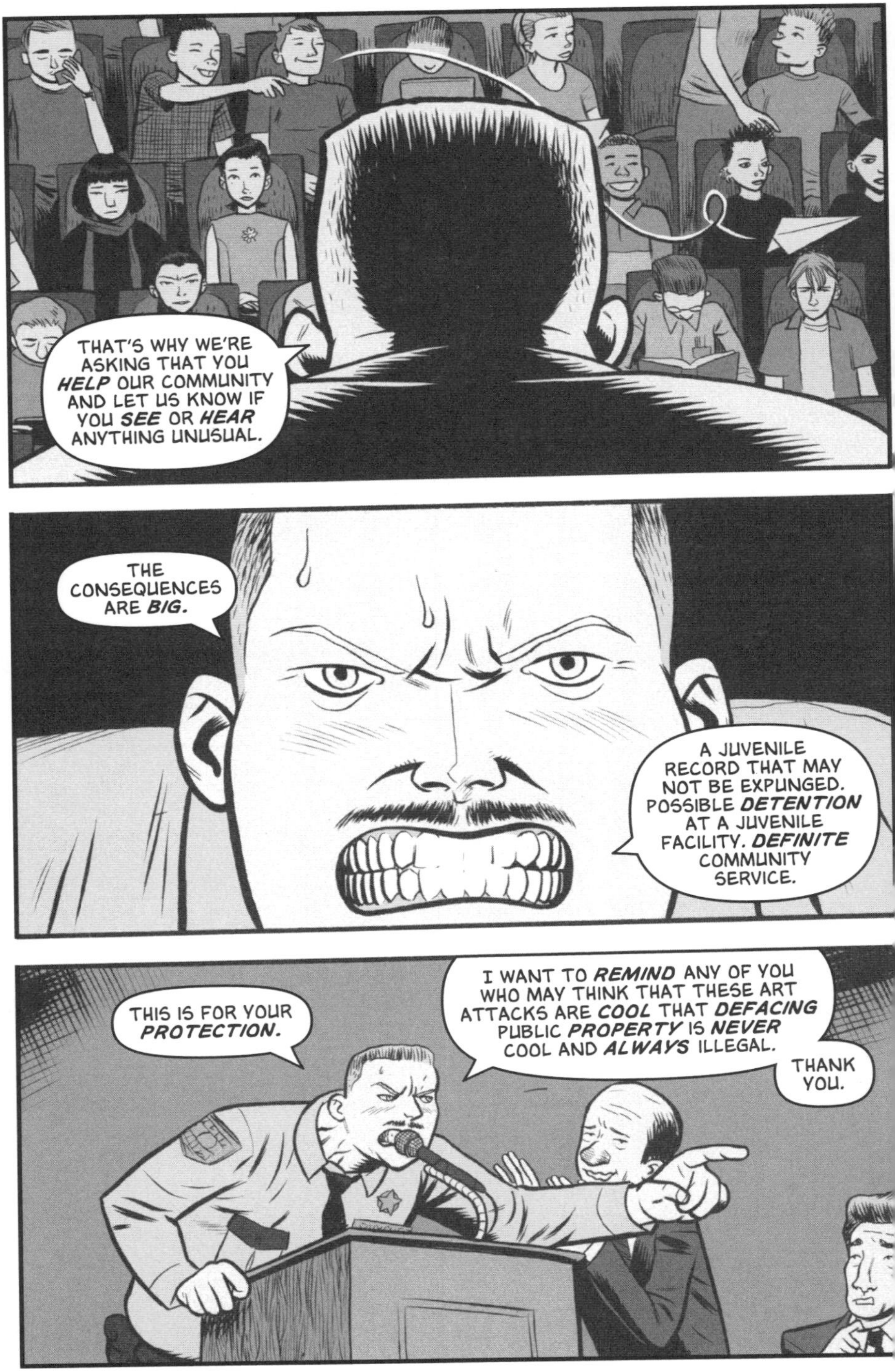
THAT'S WHY WE'RE ASKING THAT YOU HELP OUR COMMUNITY AND LET US KNOW IF YOU SEE OR HEAR ANYTHING UNUSUAL.
THE CONSEQUENCES ARE BIG.
A JUVENILE RECORD THAT MAY NOT BE EXPUNGED. POSSIBLE DETENTION AT A JUVENILE FACILITY. DEFINITE COMMUNITY SERVICE.
THIS IS FOR YOUR PROTECTION.
I WANT TO REMIND ANY OF YOU WHO MAY THINK THAT THESE ART ATTACKS ARE COOL THAT DEFACING PUBLIC PROPERTY IS NEVER COOL AND ALWAYS ILLEGAL.
THANK YOU.

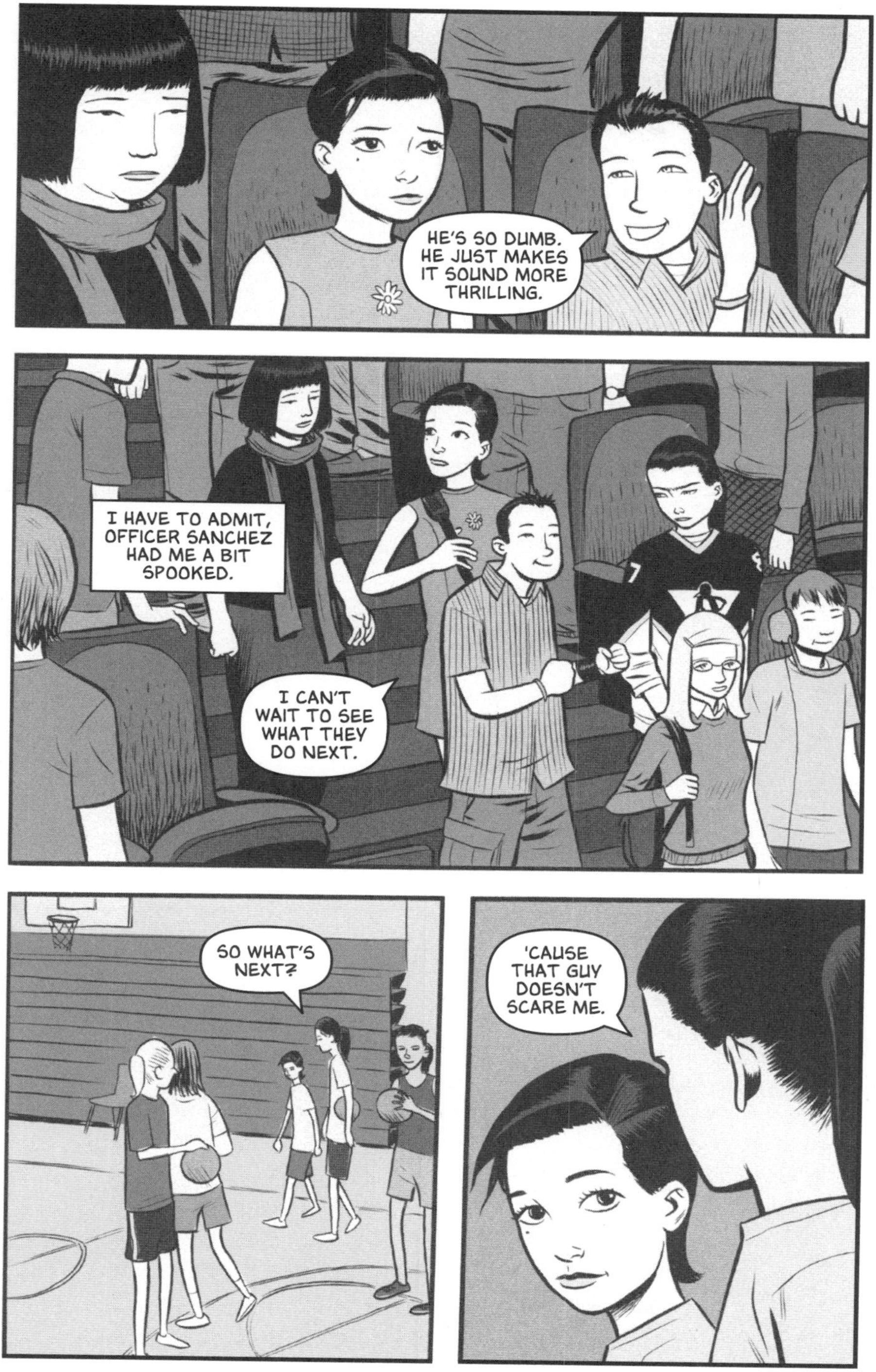
HE'S SO DUMB. HE JUST MAKES IT SOUND MORE THRILLING.
I HAVE TO ADMIT, OFFICER SANCHEZ HAD ME A BIT SPOOKED.
I CAN'T WAIT TO SEE WHAT THEY DO NEXT.
SO WHAT'S NEXT?
'CAUSE THAT GUY DOESN'T SCARE ME.

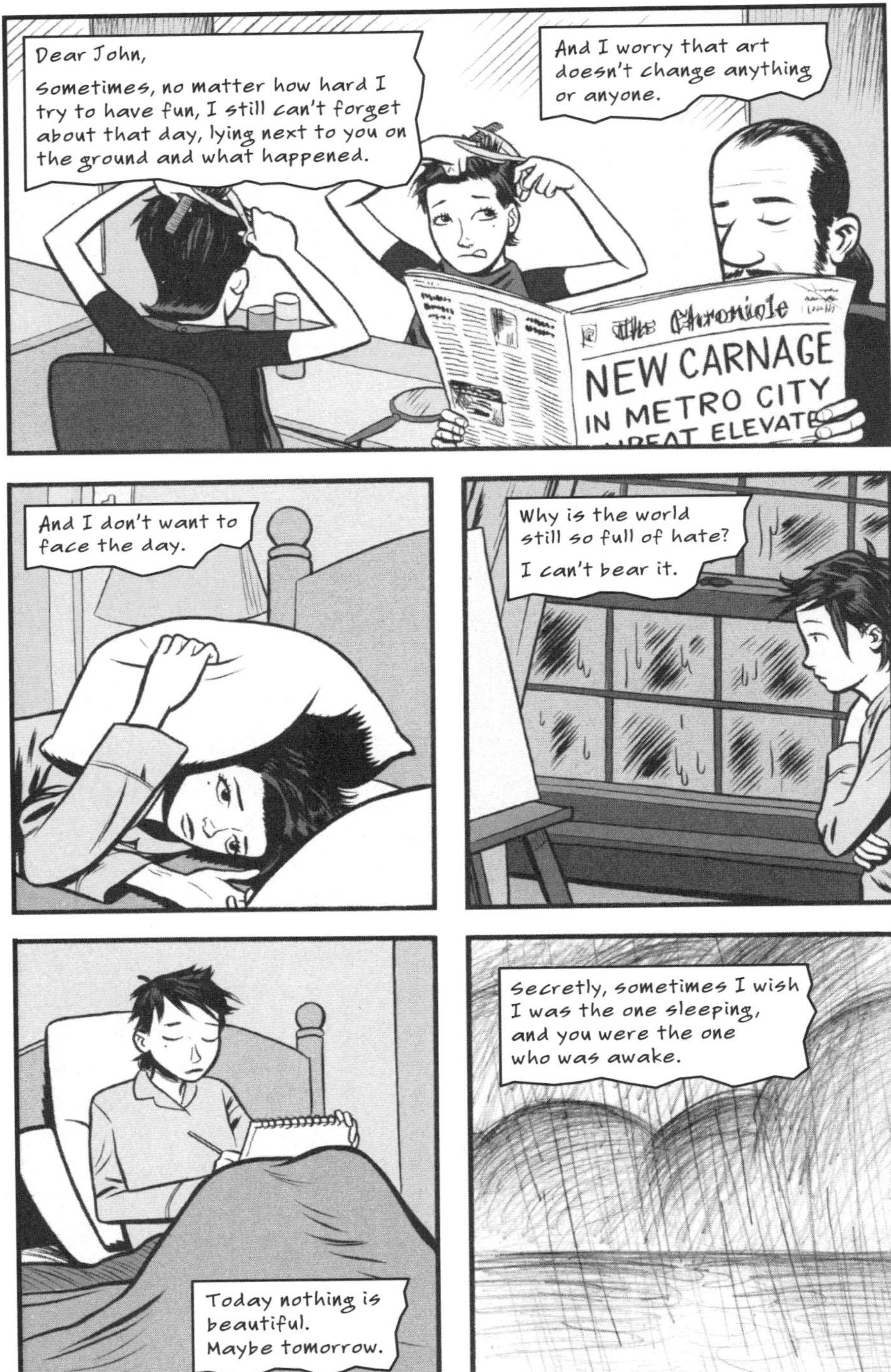
Dear John,
Sometimes, no matter how hard I try to have fun, I still can't forget about that day, lying next to you on the ground and what happened.
And I worry that art doesn't change anything or anyone.
The Chronicle
NEW CARNAGE IN METRO CITY
And I don't want to face the day.
Why is the world still so full of hate?
I can't bear it.
Today nothing is beautiful.
Maybe tomorrow.
Secretly, sometimes I wish I was the one sleeping, and you were the one who was awake.

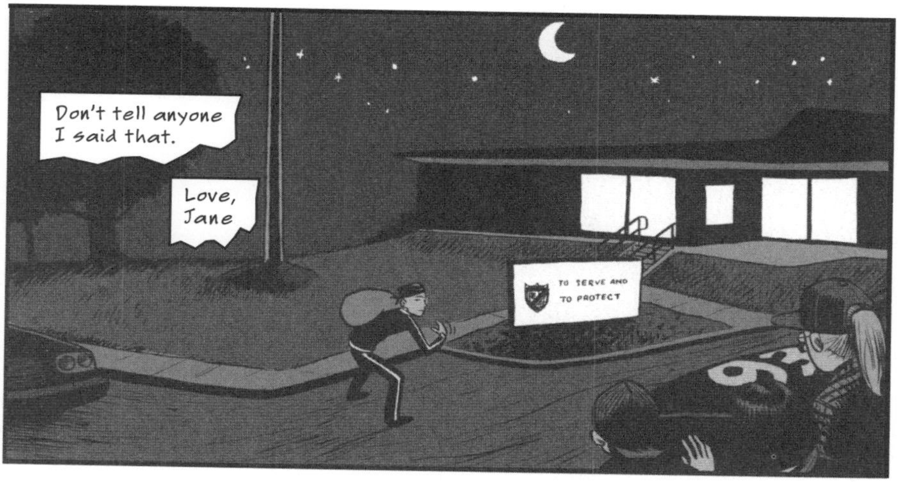
Don't tell anyone I said that.
Love, Jane
TO SERVE AND TO PROTECT

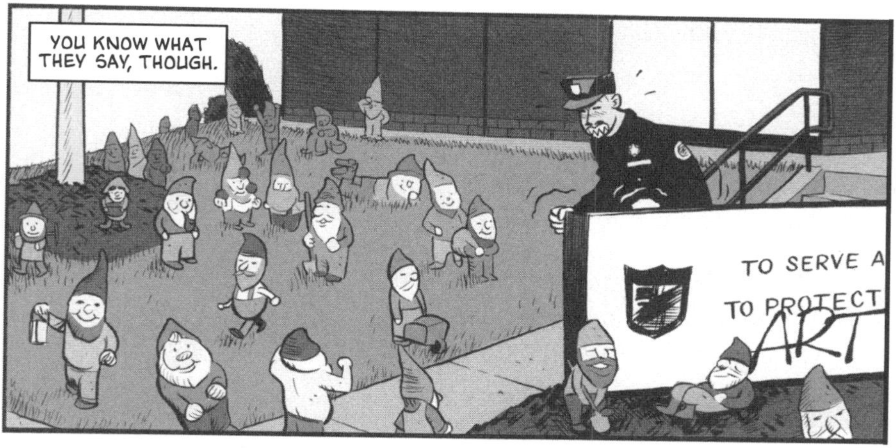
YOU KNOW WHAT THEY SAY, THOUGH.
TO SERVE A
TO PROTECT
ART

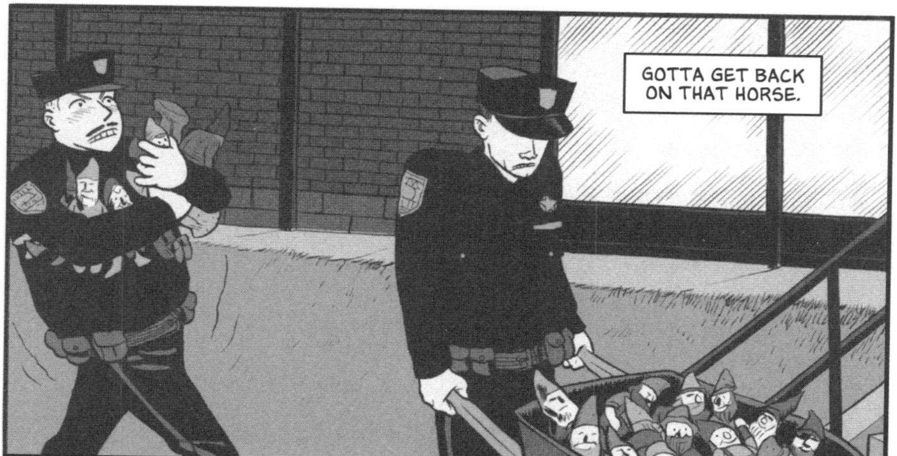
GOTTA GET BACK ON THAT HORSE.

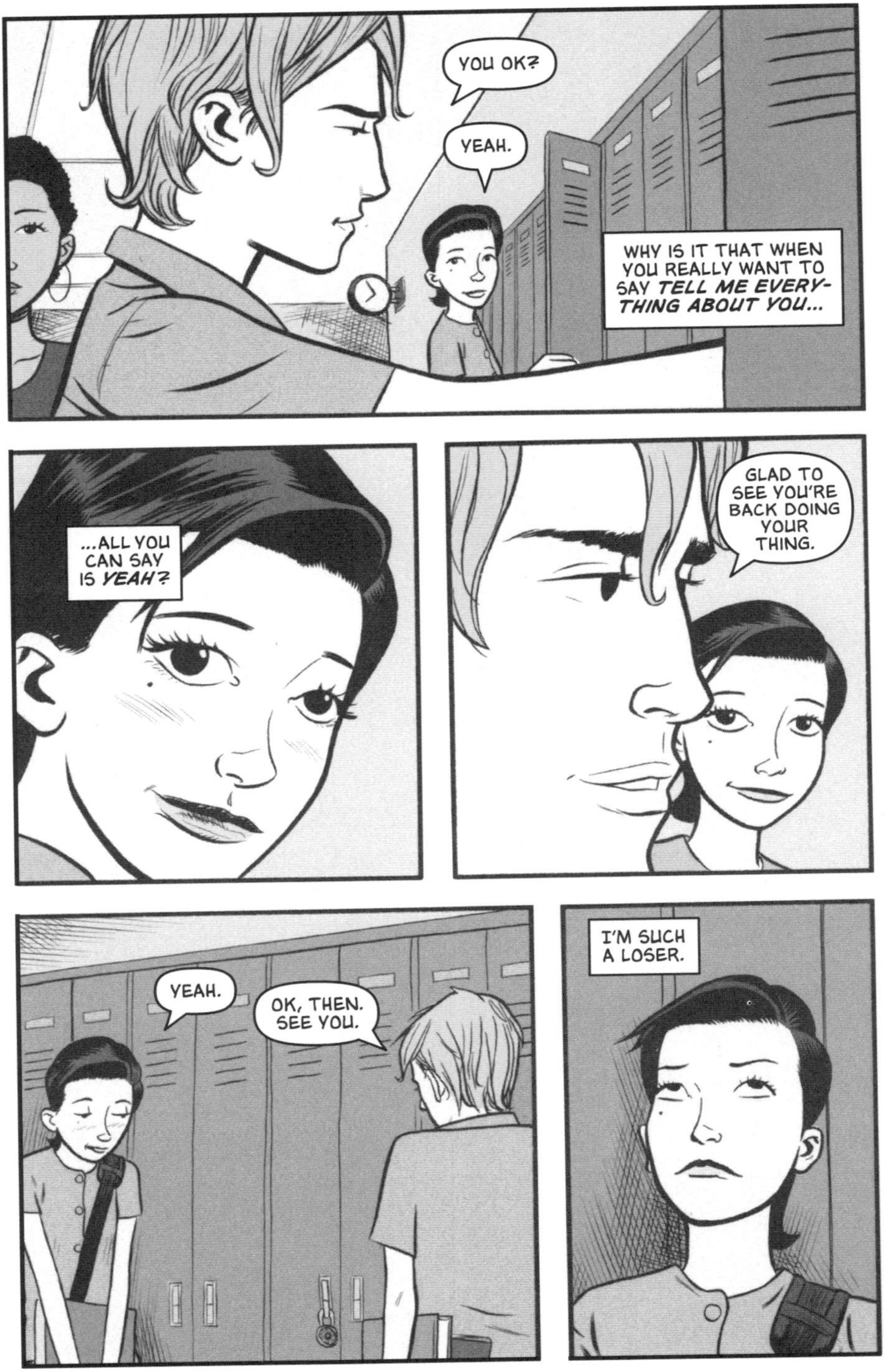
YOU OK?
YEAH.
WHY IS IT THAT WHEN YOU REALLY WANT TO SAY *TELL ME EVERY-THING ABOUT YOU...*
...ALL YOU CAN SAY IS *YEAH?*
GLAD TO SEE YOU'RE BACK DOING YOUR THING.
YEAH.
OK, THEN. SEE YOU.
I'M SUCH A LOSER.

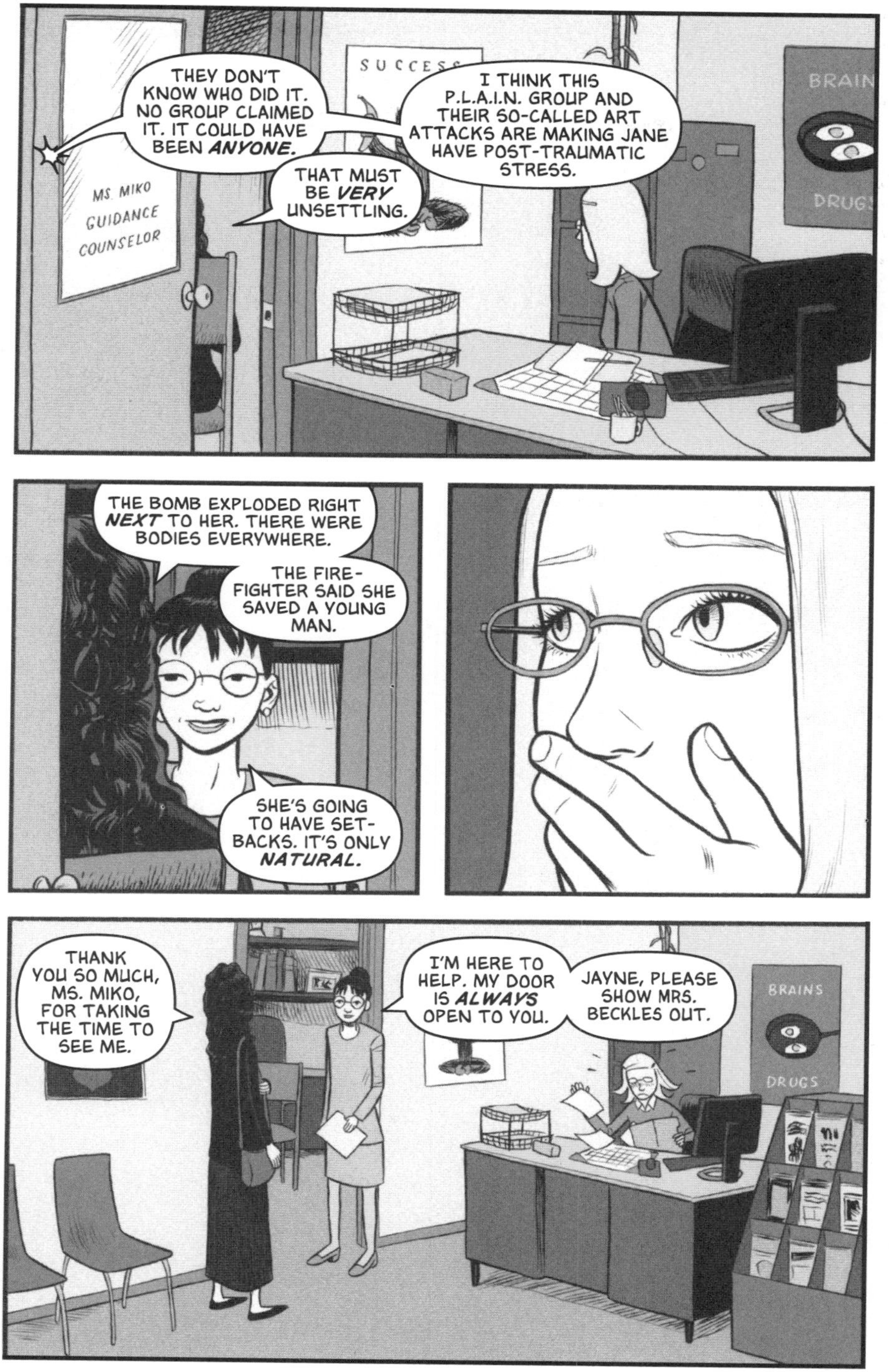
SUCCESS
BRAINS
DRUGS
MS. MIKO GUIDANCE COUNSELOR
THEY DON'T KNOW WHO DID IT. NO GROUP CLAIMED IT. IT COULD HAVE BEEN ANYONE.
I THINK THIS P.L.A.I.N. GROUP AND THEIR SO-CALLED ART ATTACKS ARE MAKING JANE HAVE POST-TRAUMATIC STRESS.
THAT MUST BE VERY UNSETTLING.
THE BOMB EXPLODED RIGHT NEXT TO HER. THERE WERE BODIES EVERYWHERE.
THE FIRE-FIGHTER SAID SHE SAVED A YOUNG MAN.
SHE'S GOING TO HAVE SET-BACKS. IT'S ONLY NATURAL.
THANK YOU SO MUCH, MS. MIKO, FOR TAKING THE TIME TO SEE ME.
I'M HERE TO HELP. MY DOOR IS ALWAYS OPEN TO YOU.
JAYNE, PLEASE SHOW MRS. BECKLES OUT.
BRAINS
DRUGS

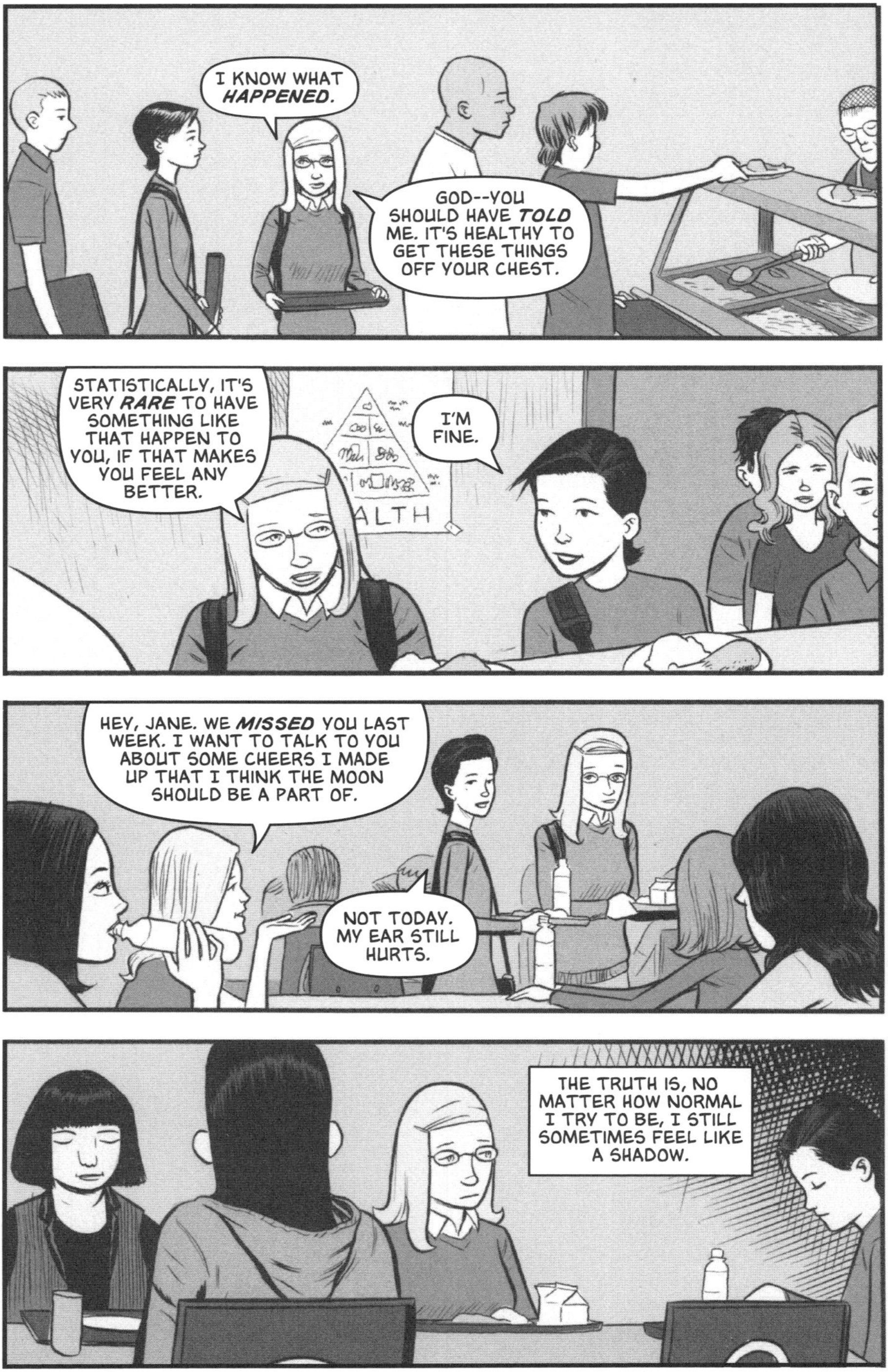
I KNOW WHAT *HAPPENED*.
GOD--YOU SHOULD HAVE *TOLD* ME. IT'S HEALTHY TO GET THESE THINGS OFF YOUR CHEST.
STATISTICALLY, IT'S VERY *RARE* TO HAVE SOMETHING LIKE THAT HAPPEN TO YOU, IF THAT MAKES YOU FEEL ANY BETTER.
I'M FINE.
HEY, JANE. WE *MISSED* YOU LAST WEEK. I WANT TO TALK TO YOU ABOUT SOME CHEERS I MADE UP THAT I THINK THE MOON SHOULD BE A PART OF.
NOT TODAY. MY EAR STILL HURTS.
THE TRUTH IS, NO MATTER HOW NORMAL I TRY TO BE, I STILL SOMETIMES FEEL LIKE A SHADOW.

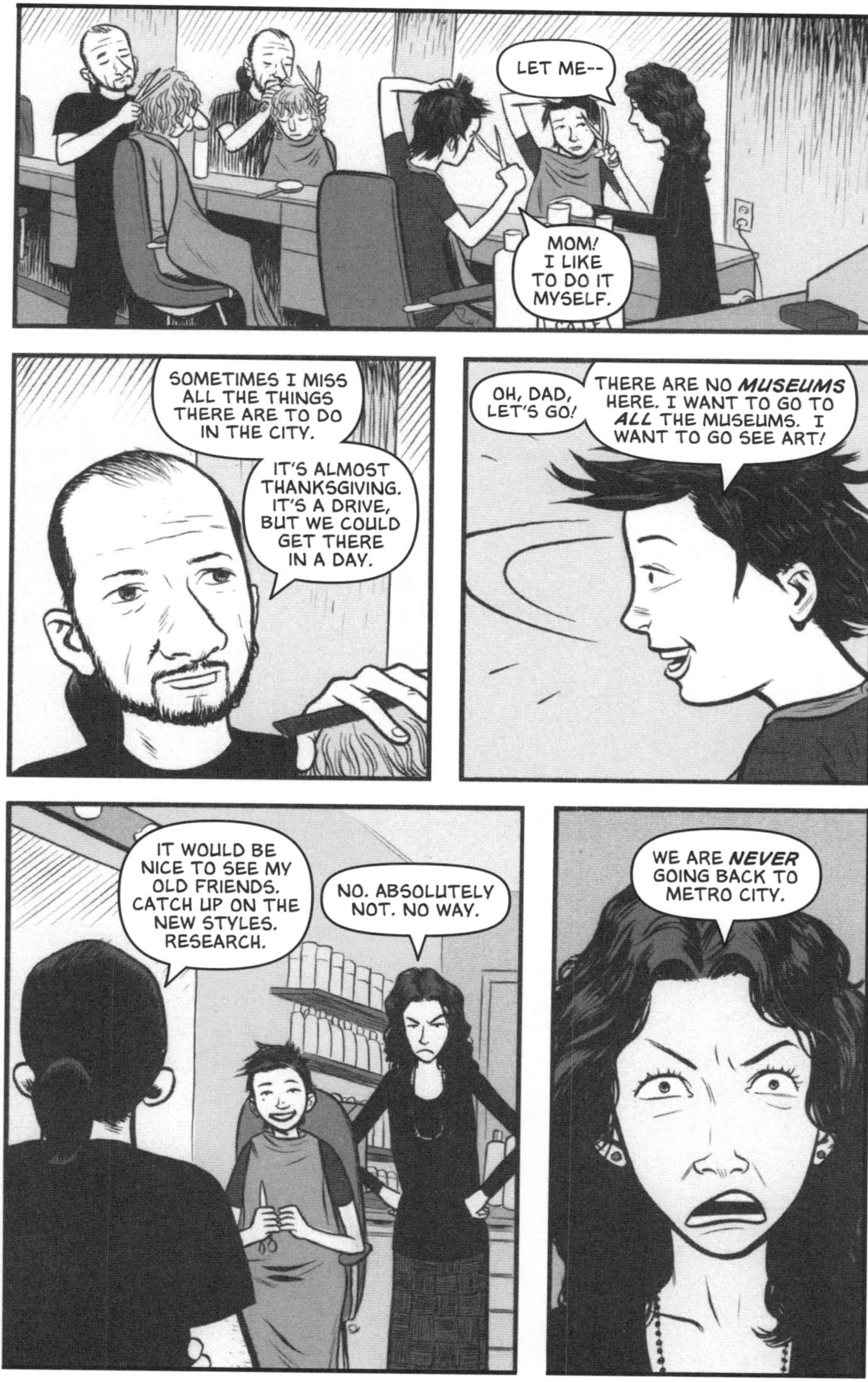
LET ME--
MOM! I LIKE TO DO IT MYSELF.
SOMETIMES I MISS ALL THE THINGS THERE ARE TO DO IN THE CITY.
IT'S ALMOST THANKSGIVING. IT'S A DRIVE, BUT WE COULD GET THERE IN A DAY.
OH, DAD, LET'S GO!
THERE ARE NO MUSEUMS HERE. I WANT TO GO TO ALL THE MUSEUMS. I WANT TO GO SEE ART!
IT WOULD BE NICE TO SEE MY OLD FRIENDS. CATCH UP ON THE NEW STYLES. RESEARCH.
NO. ABSOLUTELY NOT. NO WAY.
WE ARE NEVER GOING BACK TO METRO CITY.

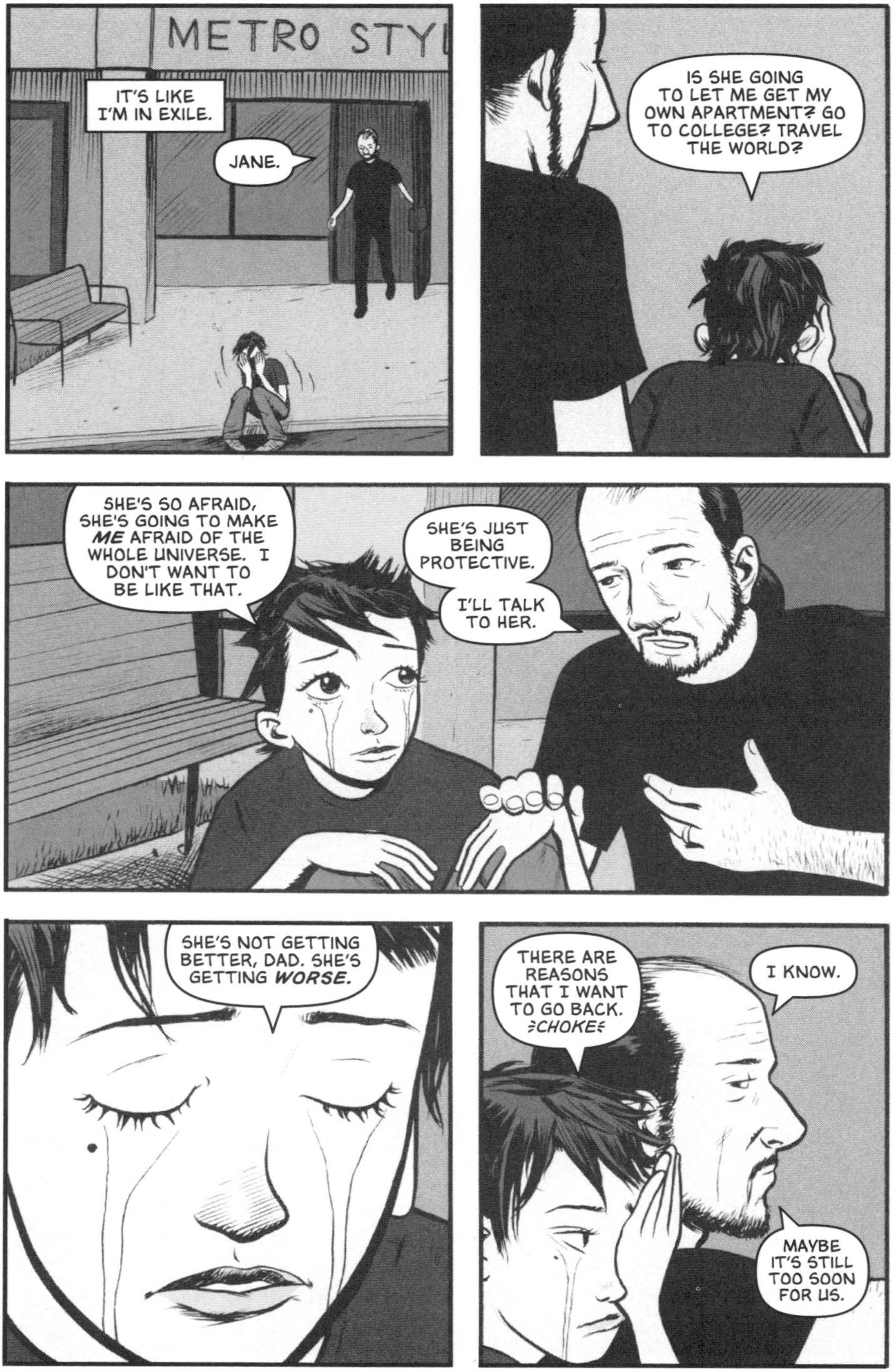
METRO STYL
IT'S LIKE I'M IN EXILE.
JANE.
IS SHE GOING TO LET ME GET MY OWN APARTMENT? GO TO COLLEGE? TRAVEL THE WORLD?
SHE'S SO AFRAID, SHE'S GOING TO MAKE *ME* AFRAID OF THE WHOLE UNIVERSE. I DON'T WANT TO BE LIKE THAT.
SHE'S JUST BEING PROTECTIVE.
I'LL TALK TO HER.
SHE'S NOT GETTING BETTER, DAD. SHE'S GETTING *WORSE.*
THERE ARE REASONS THAT I WANT TO GO BACK. *CHOKE*
I KNOW.
MAYBE IT'S STILL TOO SOON FOR US.

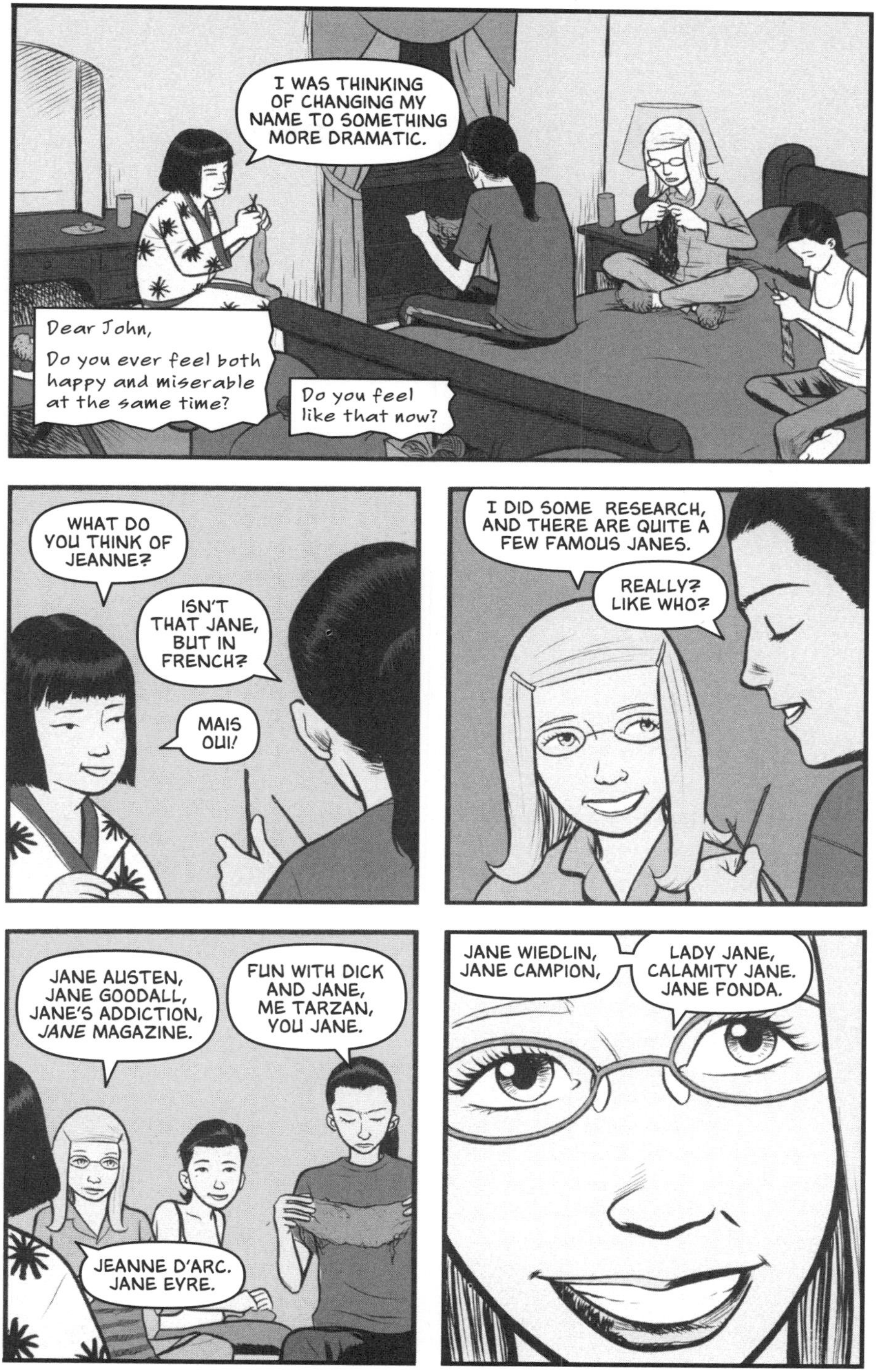

I WAS THINKING OF CHANGING MY NAME TO SOMETHING MORE DRAMATIC.
Dear John,
Do you ever feel both happy and miserable at the same time?
Do you feel like that now?
WHAT DO YOU THINK OF JEANNE?
ISN'T THAT JANE, BUT IN FRENCH?
MAIS OUI!
I DID SOME RESEARCH, AND THERE ARE QUITE A FEW FAMOUS JANES.
REALLY? LIKE WHO?
JANE AUSTEN, JANE GOODALL, JANE'S ADDICTION, *JANE* MAGAZINE.
FUN WITH DICK AND JANE, ME TARZAN, YOU JANE.
JEANNE D'ARC. JANE EYRE.
JANE WIEDLIN, JANE CAMPION,
LADY JANE, CALAMITY JANE. JANE FONDA.

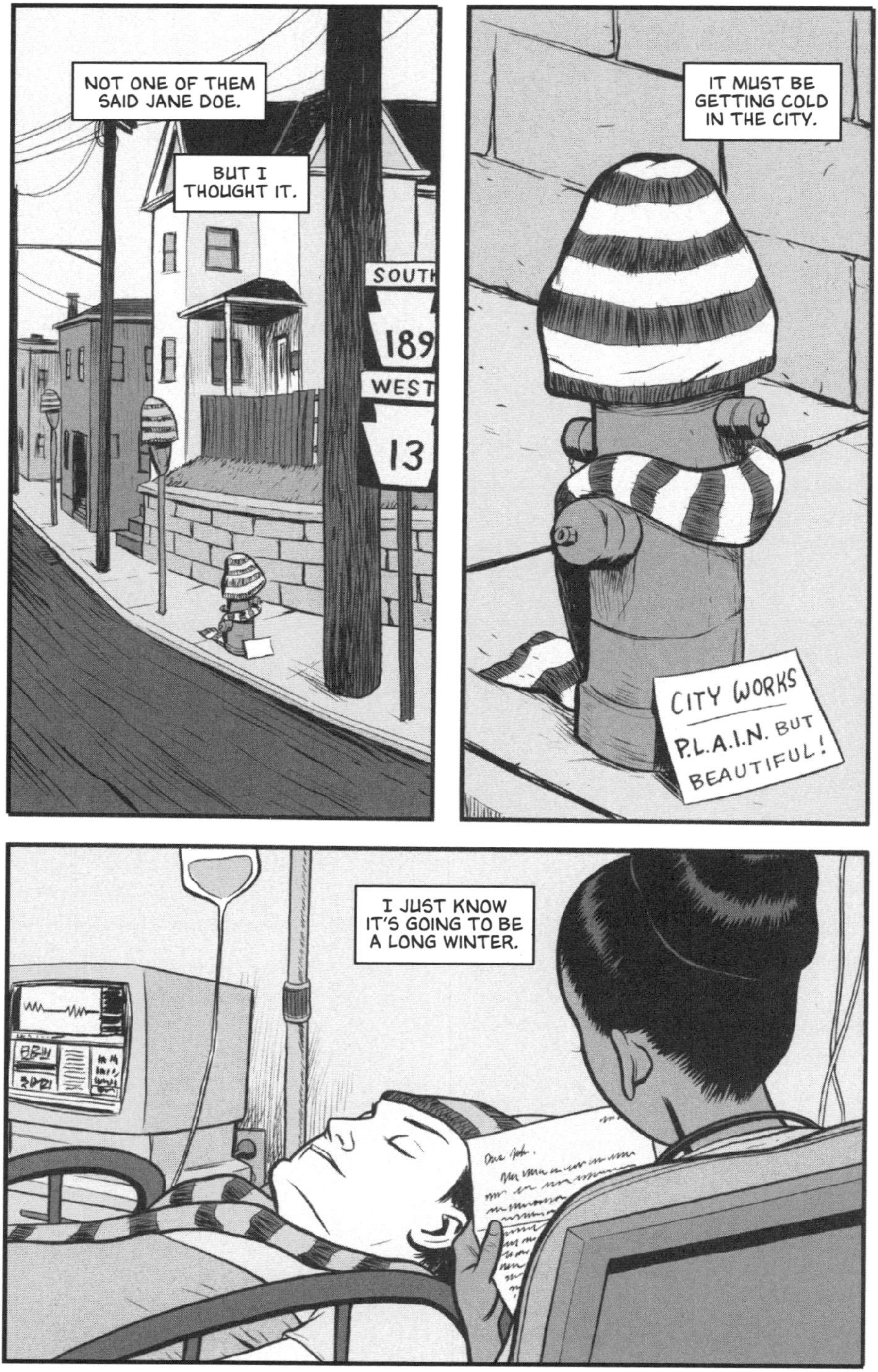
NOT ONE OF THEM SAID JANE DOE.
BUT I THOUGHT IT.
SOUTH
189
WEST
13
IT MUST BE GETTING COLD IN THE CITY.
CITY WORKS
P.L.A.I.N. BUT BEAUTIFUL!
I JUST KNOW IT'S GOING TO BE A LONG WINTER.

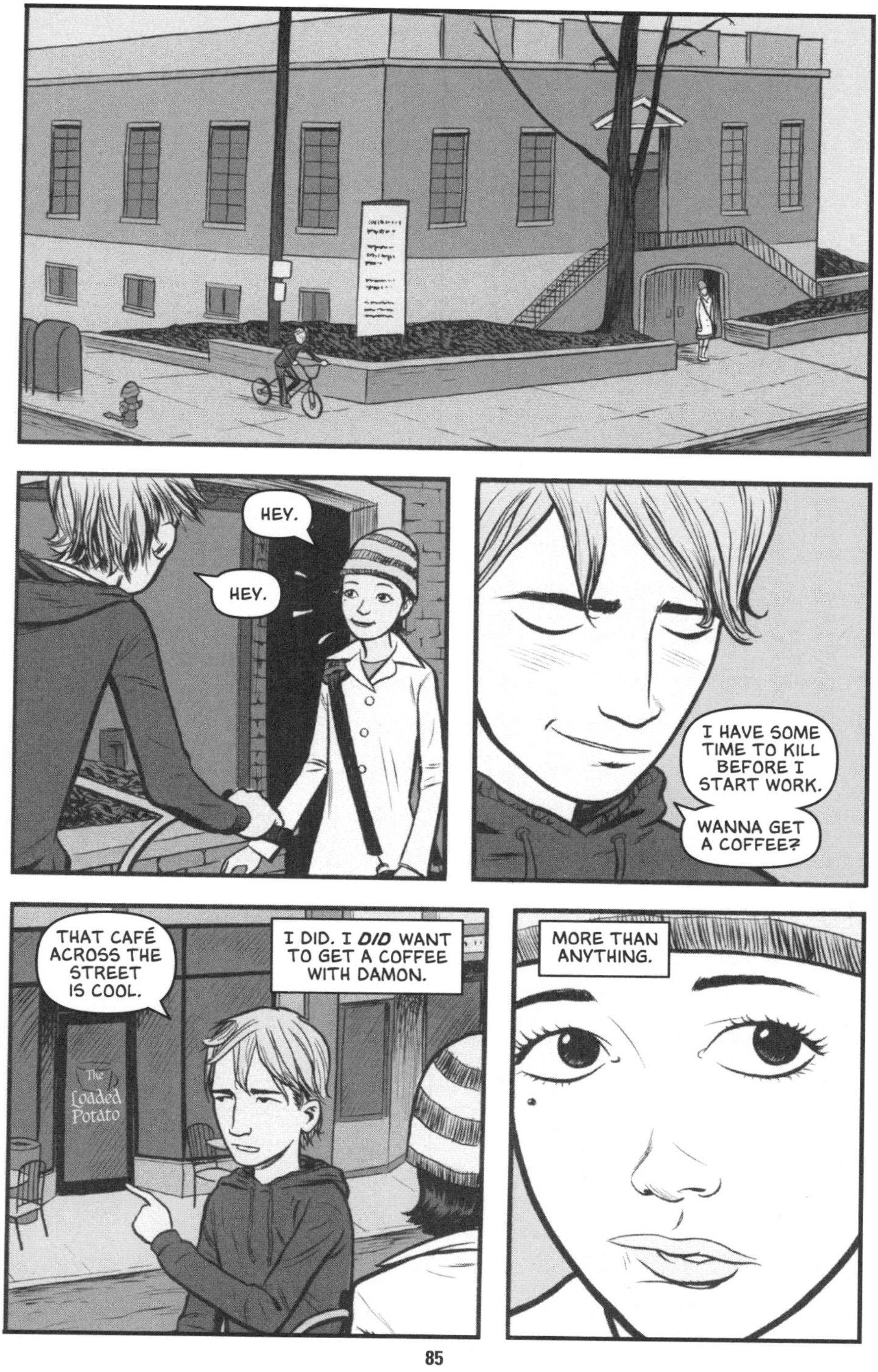
HEY.
HEY.
I HAVE SOME TIME TO KILL BEFORE I START WORK.
WANNA GET A COFFEE?
THAT CAFÉ ACROSS THE STREET IS COOL.
I DID. I *DID* WANT TO GET A COFFEE WITH DAMON.
The Loaded Potato
MORE THAN ANYTHING.

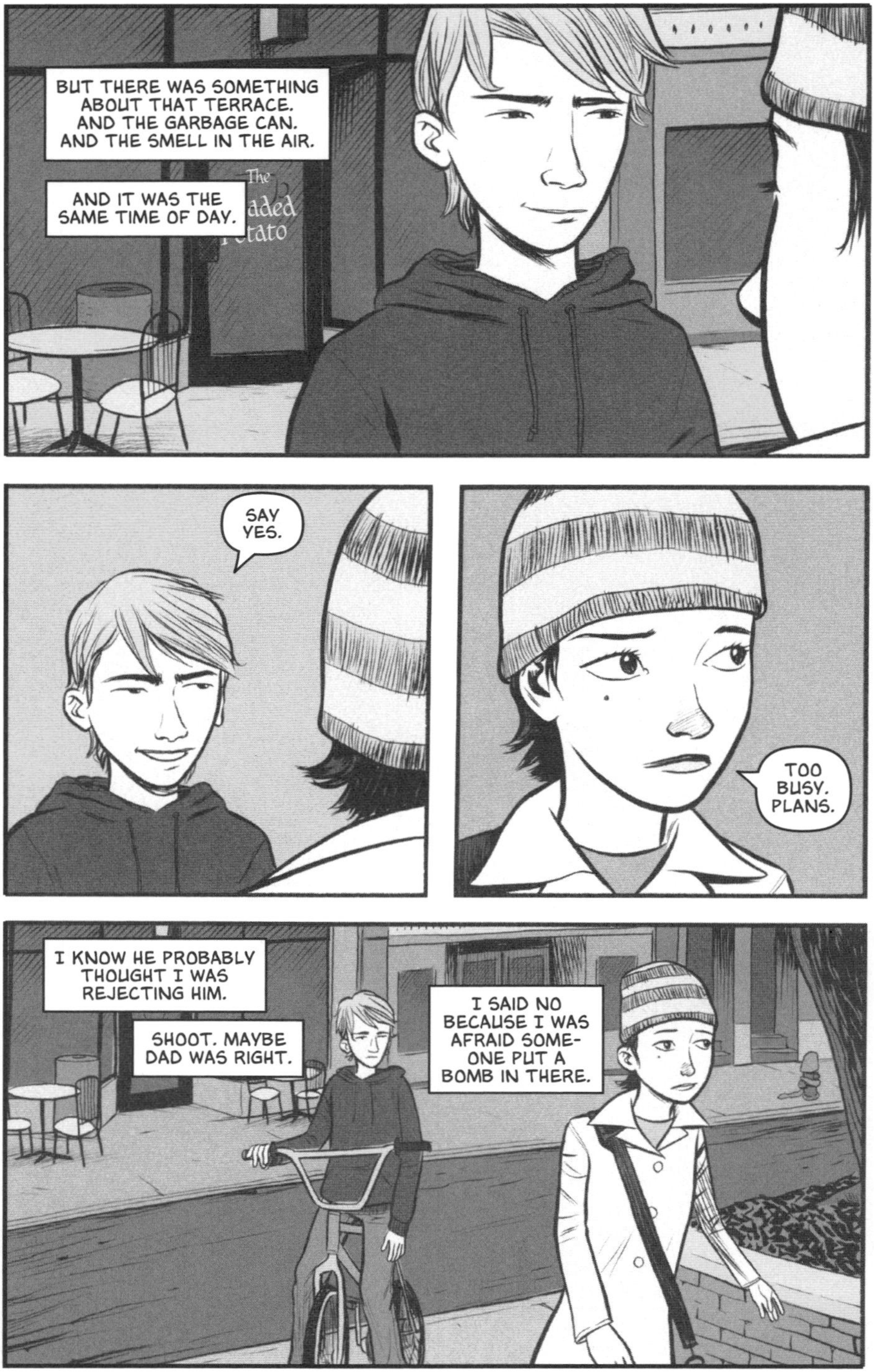
BUT THERE WAS SOMETHING ABOUT THAT TERRACE. AND THE GARBAGE CAN. AND THE SMELL IN THE AIR.
AND IT WAS THE SAME TIME OF DAY.
SAY YES.
TOO BUSY. PLANS.
I KNOW HE PROBABLY THOUGHT I WAS REJECTING HIM.
SHOOT. MAYBE DAD WAS RIGHT.
I SAID NO BECAUSE I WAS AFRAID SOME-ONE PUT A BOMB IN THERE.

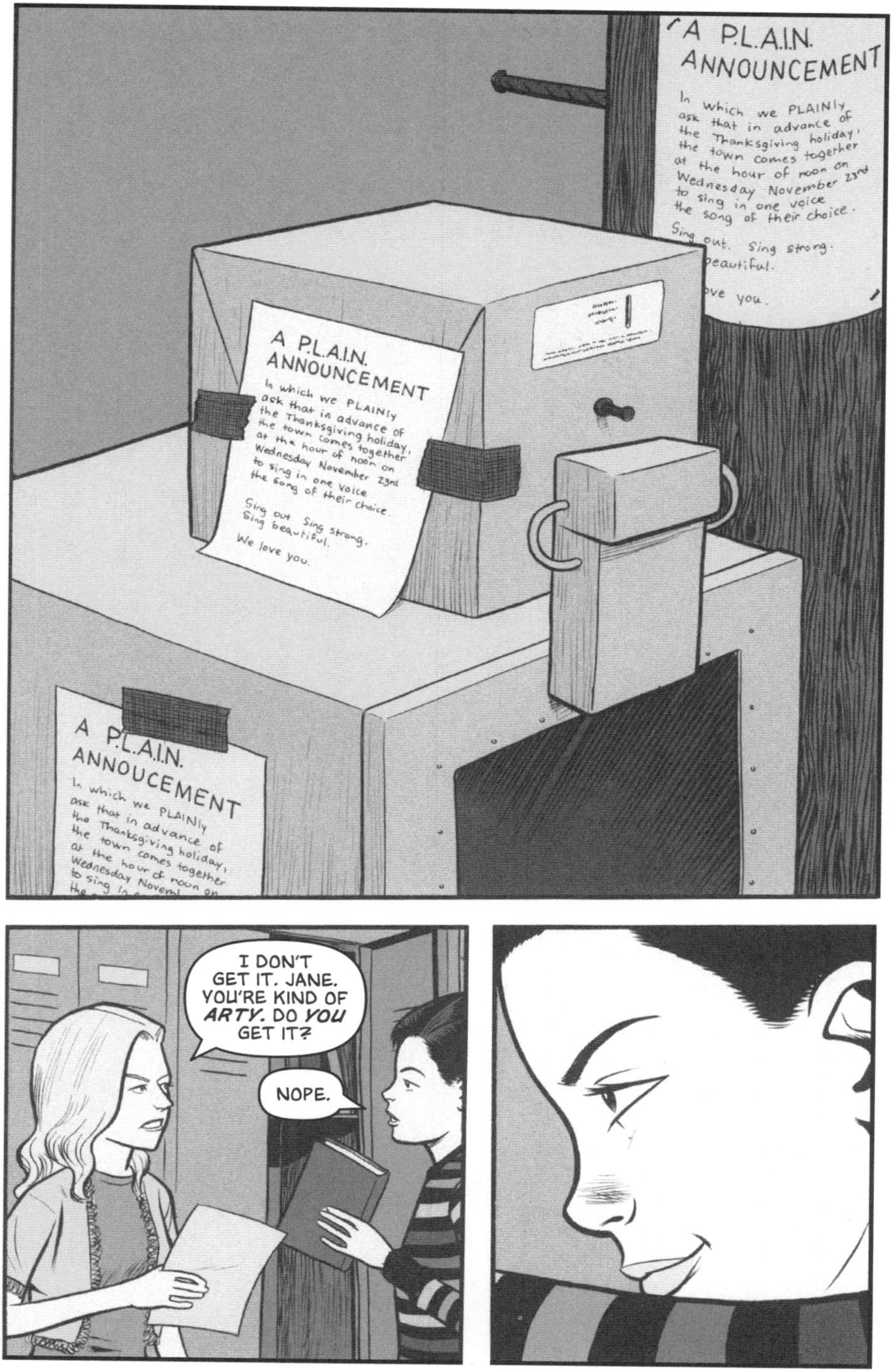
"A P.L.A.I.N. ANNOUNCEMENT
In which we PLAINly ask that in advance of the Thanksgiving holiday, the town comes together at the hour of noon on Wednesday November 23rd to sing in one voice the song of their choice.
Sing out. Sing strong.
A P.L.A.I.N. ANNOUNCEMENT
In which we PLAINly ask that in advance of the Thanksgiving holiday, the town comes together at the hour of noon on Wednesday November 23rd to sing in one voice the song of their choice.
Sing out. Sing strong. Sing beautiful.
We love you.
A P.L.A.I.N. ANNOUCEMENT
In which we PLAINly ask that in advance of the Thanksgiving holiday, the town comes together at the hour of noon on
I DON'T GET IT. JANE. YOU'RE KIND OF ARTY. DO YOU GET IT?
NOPE.

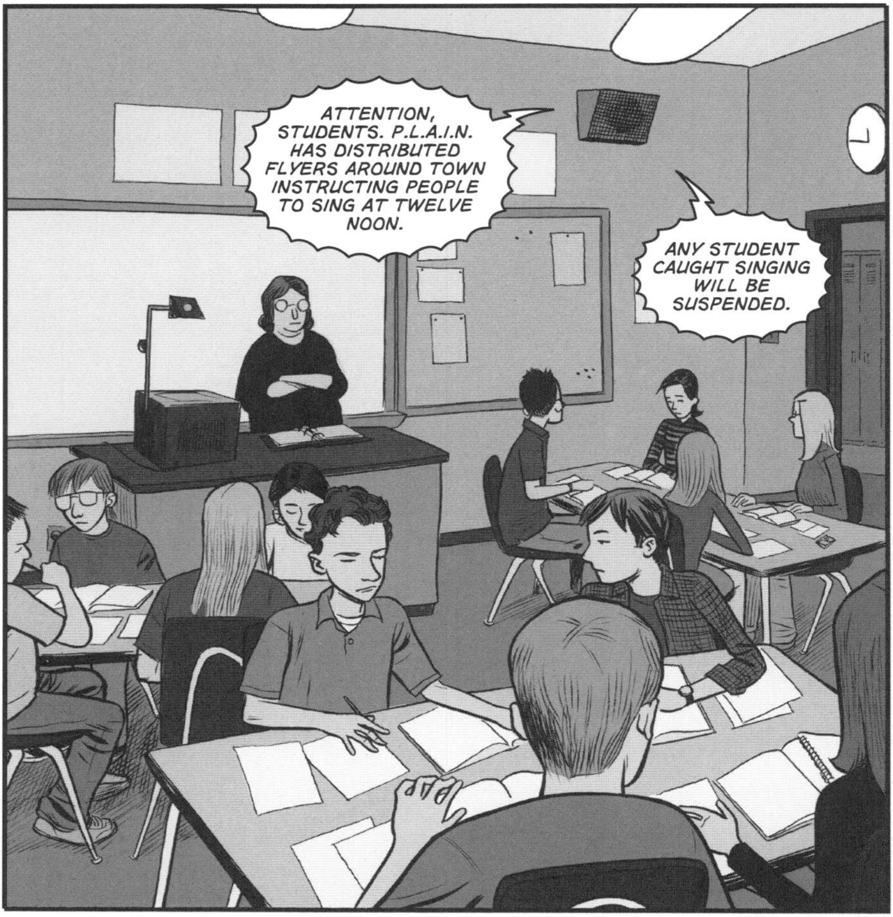
ATTENTION, STUDENTS. P.L.A.I.N. HAS DISTRIBUTED FLYERS AROUND TOWN INSTRUCTING PEOPLE TO SING AT TWELVE NOON.
ANY STUDENT CAUGHT SINGING WILL BE SUSPENDED.

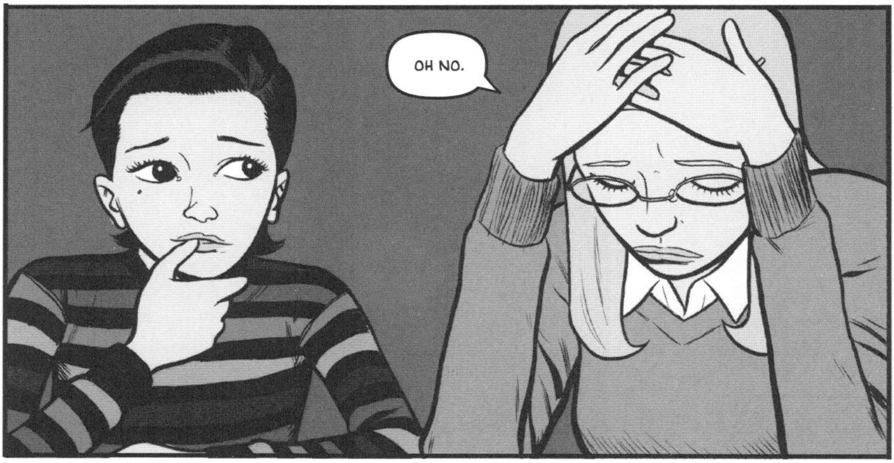
OH NO.

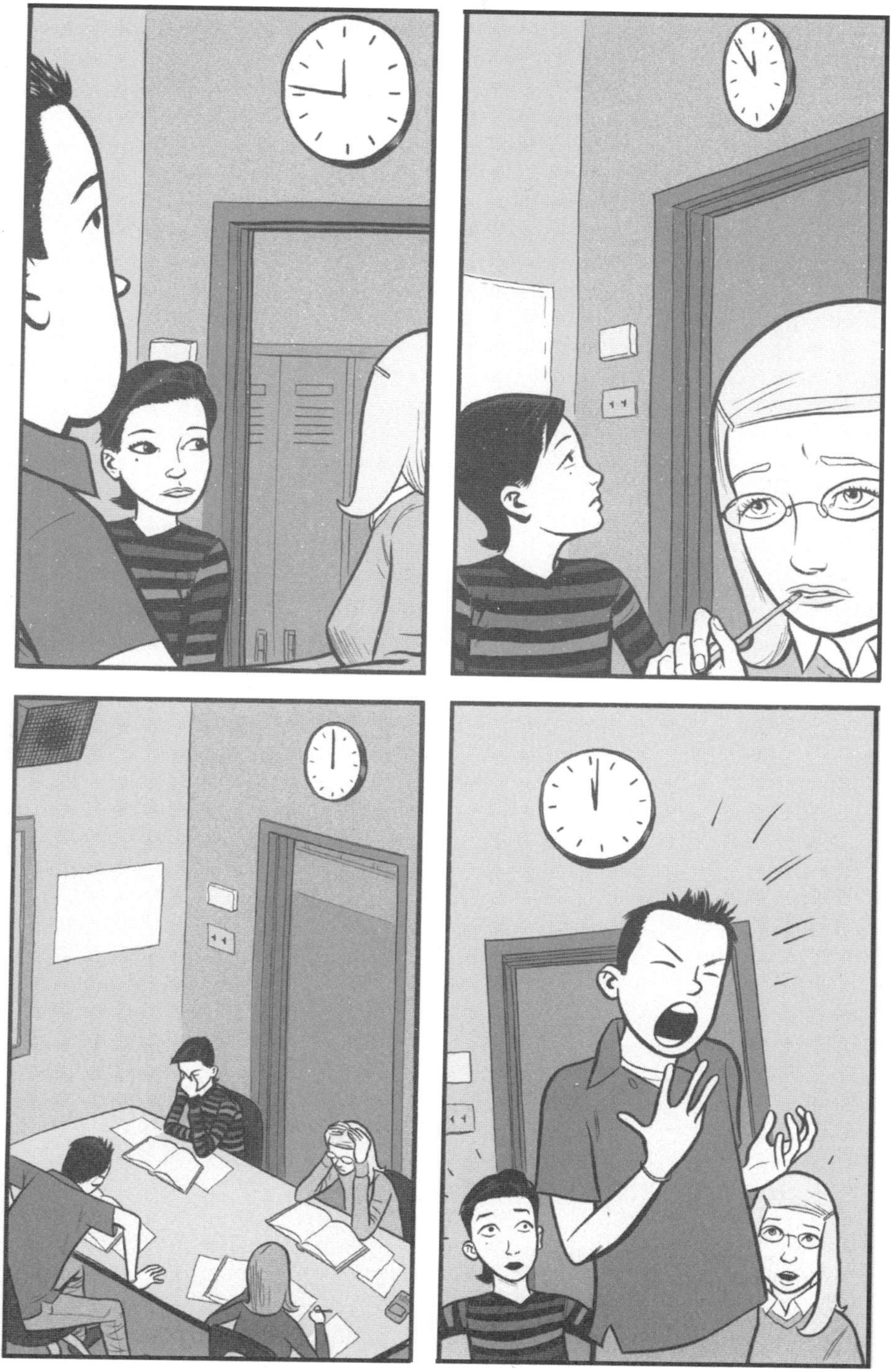

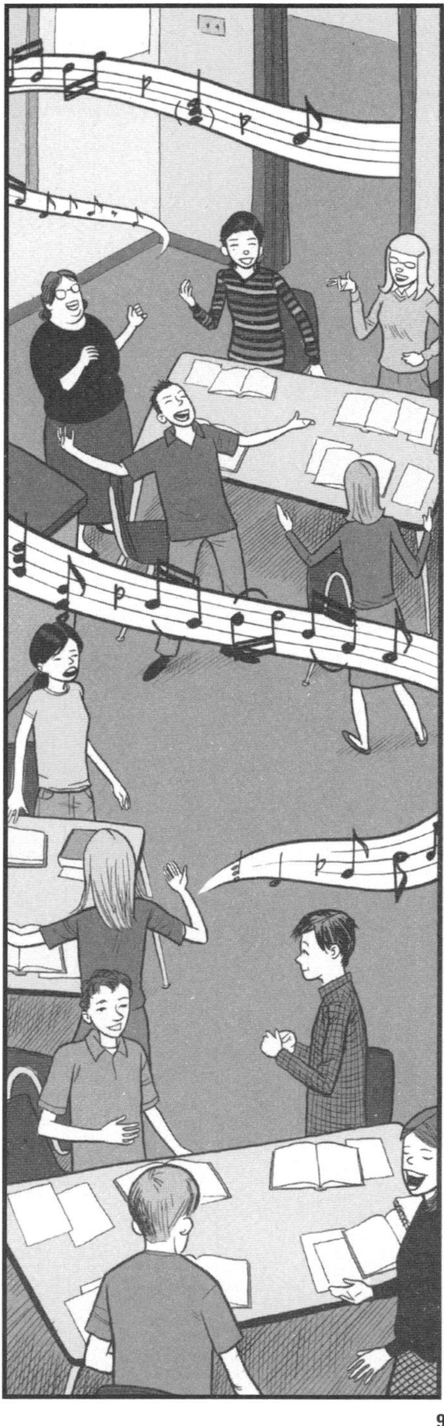

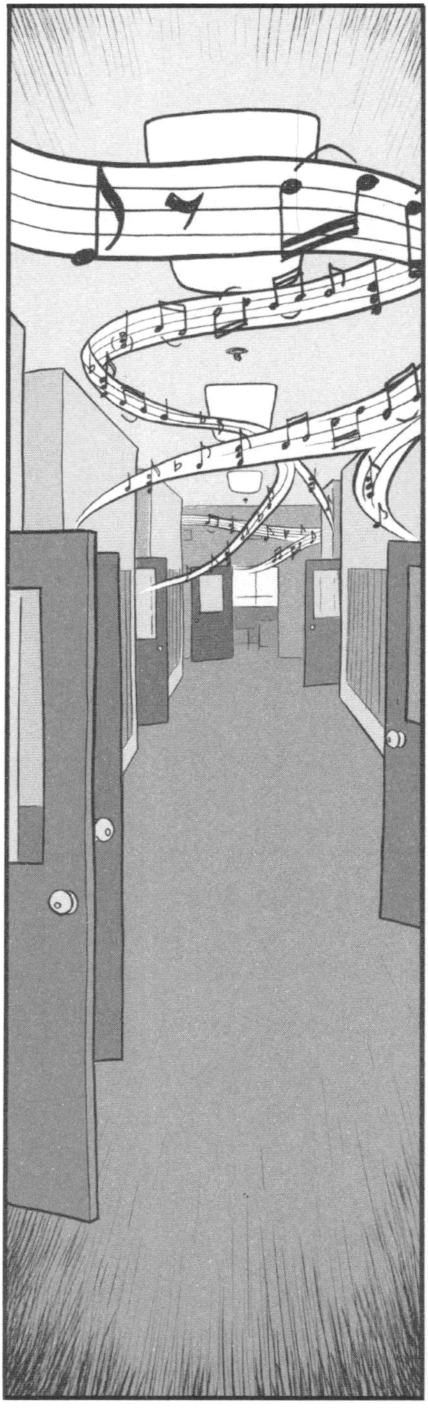

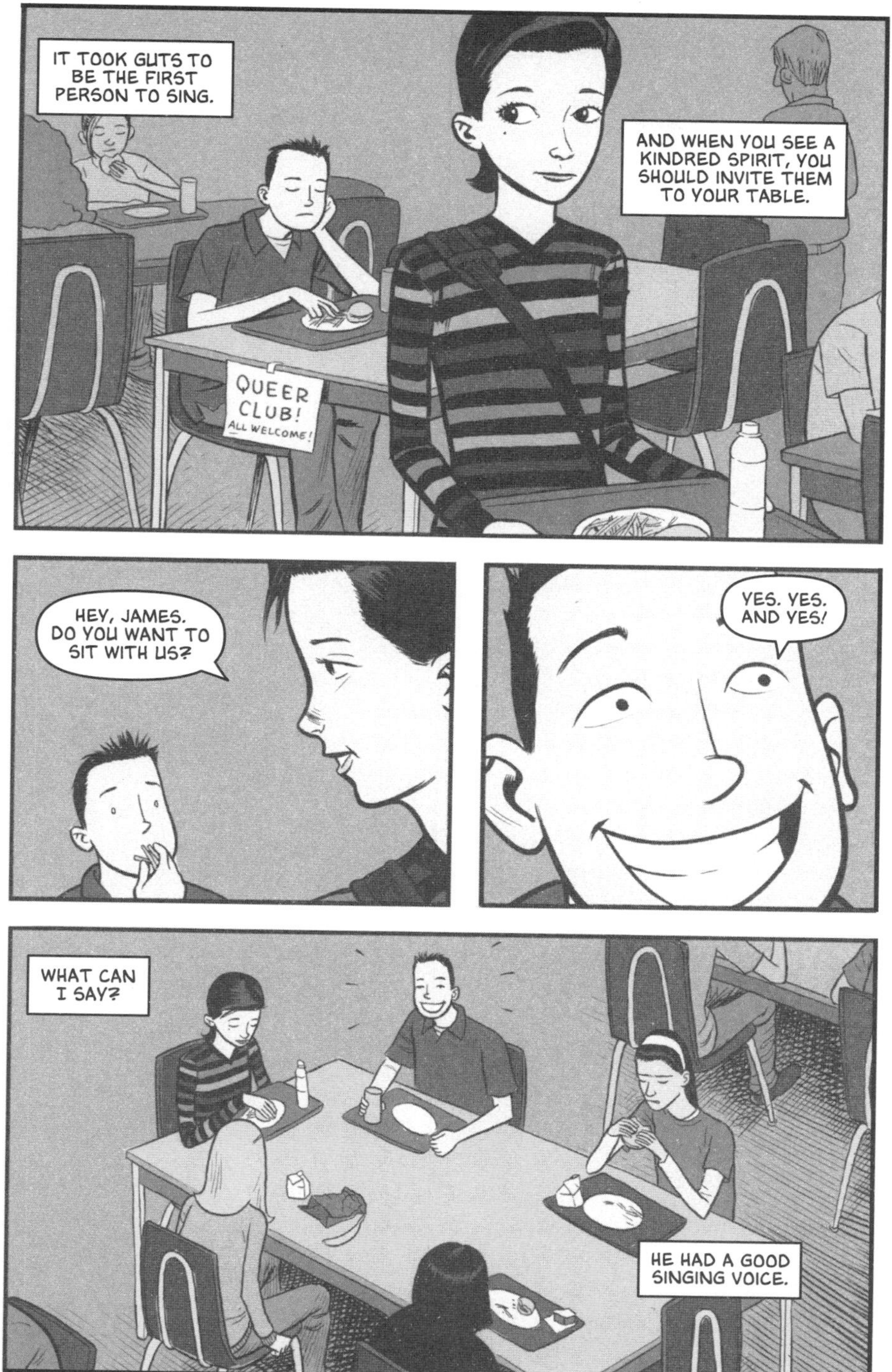
IT TOOK GUTS TO BE THE FIRST PERSON TO SING.
QUEER CLUB! ALL WELCOME!
AND WHEN YOU SEE A KINDRED SPIRIT, YOU SHOULD INVITE THEM TO YOUR TABLE.
HEY, JAMES. DO YOU WANT TO SIT WITH US?
YES. YES. AND YES!
WHAT CAN I SAY?
HE HAD A GOOD SINGING VOICE.

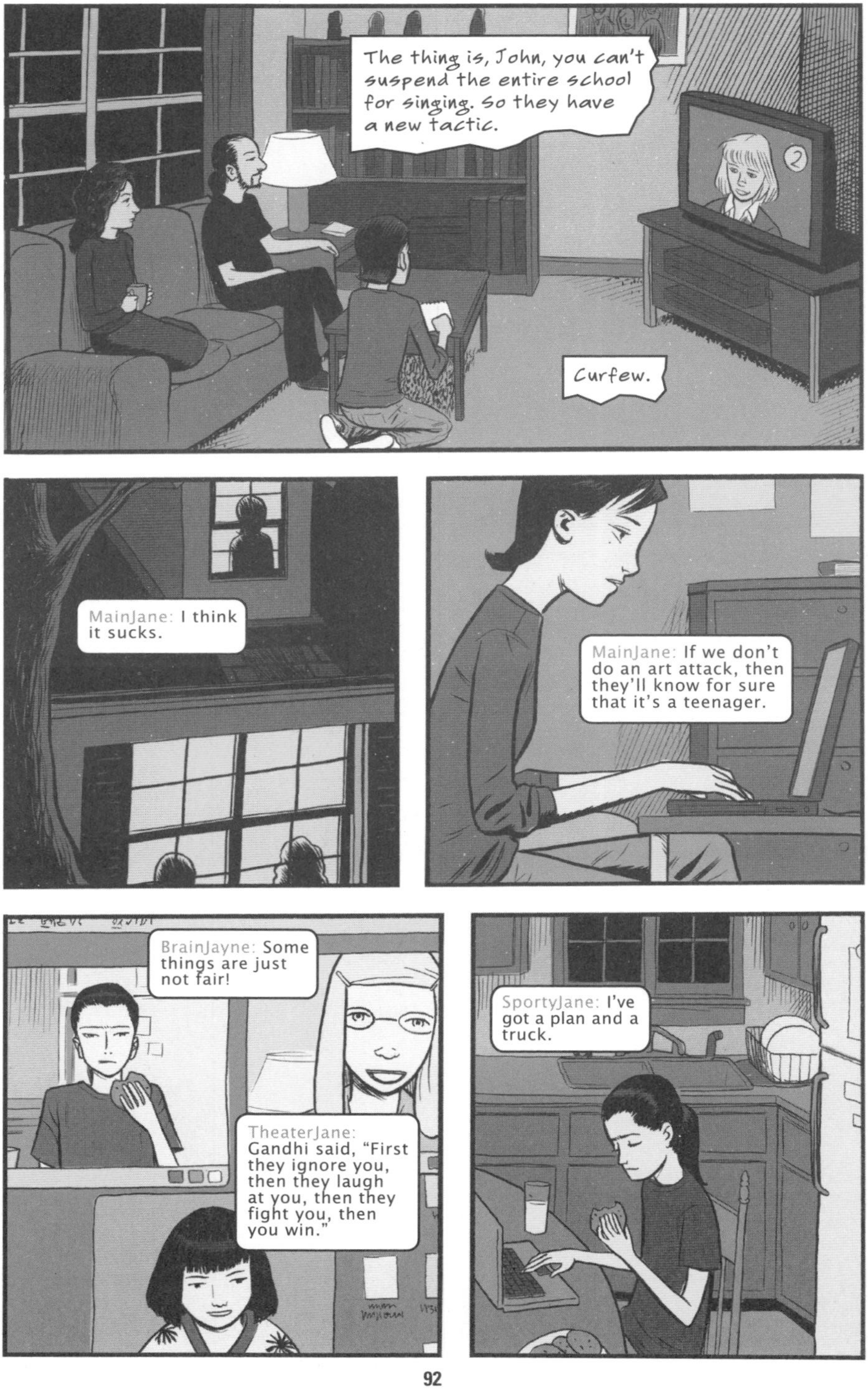
The thing is, John, you can't suspend the entire school for singing. So they have a new tactic.
2
Curfew.
MainJane: I think it sucks.
MainJane: If we don't do an art attack, then they'll know for sure that it's a teenager.
BrainJayne: Some things are just not fair!
TheaterJane: Gandhi said, "First they ignore you, then they laugh at you, then they fight you, then you win."
SportyJane: I've got a plan and a truck.

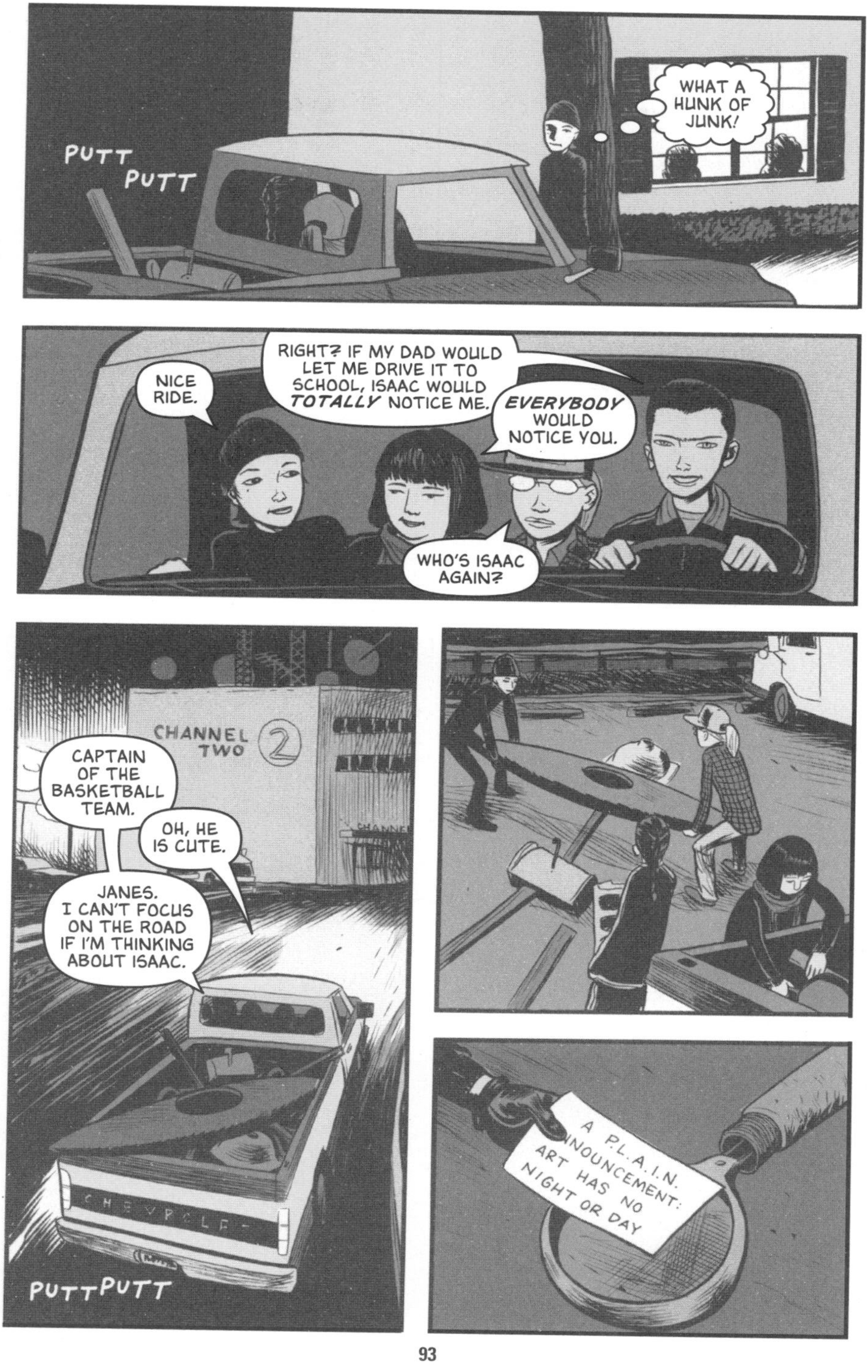

WHAT A HUNK OF JUNK!
PUTT PUTT
NICE RIDE.
RIGHT? IF MY DAD WOULD LET ME DRIVE IT TO SCHOOL, ISAAC WOULD *TOTALLY* NOTICE ME.
EVERYBODY WOULD NOTICE YOU.
WHO'S ISAAC AGAIN?
CHANNEL TWO 2
CAPTAIN OF THE BASKETBALL TEAM.
OH, HE IS CUTE.
JANES. I CAN'T FOCUS ON THE ROAD IF I'M THINKING ABOUT ISAAC.
PUTTPUTT
A P.L.A.I.N. ANNOUNCEMENT: ART HAS NO NIGHT OR DAY

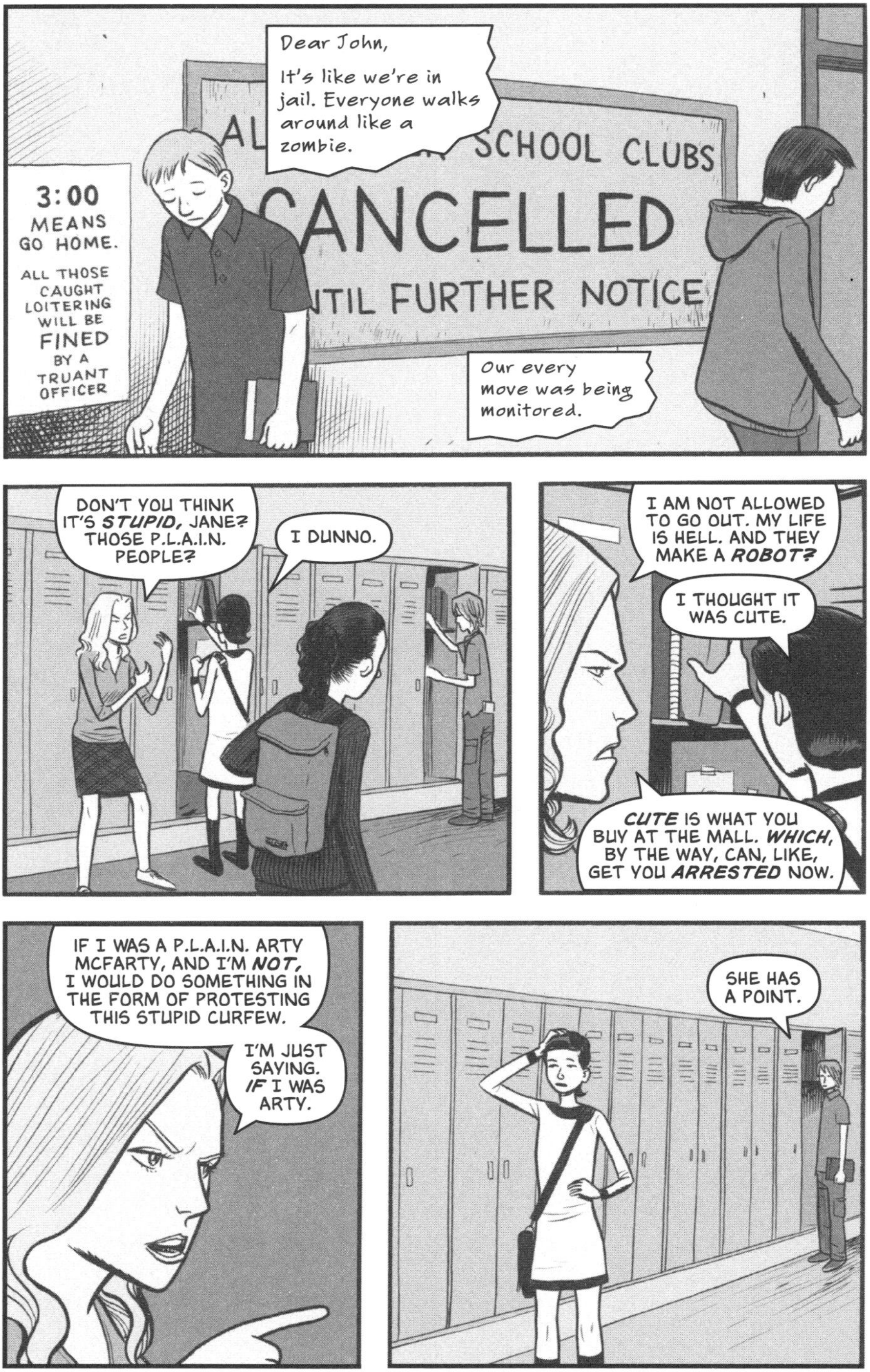
Dear John,
It's like we're in jail. Everyone walks around like a zombie.
SCHOOL CLUBS
CANCELLED
TIL FURTHER NOTICE
3:00 MEANS GO HOME. ALL THOSE CAUGHT LOITERING WILL BE FINED BY A TRUANT OFFICER
Our every move was being monitored.
DON'T YOU THINK IT'S STUPID, JANE? THOSE P.L.A.I.N. PEOPLE?
I DUNNO.
I AM NOT ALLOWED TO GO OUT. MY LIFE IS HELL. AND THEY MAKE A ROBOT?
I THOUGHT IT WAS CUTE.
CUTE IS WHAT YOU BUY AT THE MALL. WHICH, BY THE WAY, CAN, LIKE, GET YOU ARRESTED NOW.
IF I WAS A P.L.A.I.N. ARTY MCFARTY, AND I'M NOT, I WOULD DO SOMETHING IN THE FORM OF PROTESTING THIS STUPID CURFEW.
I'M JUST SAYING. IF I WAS ARTY.
SHE HAS A POINT.

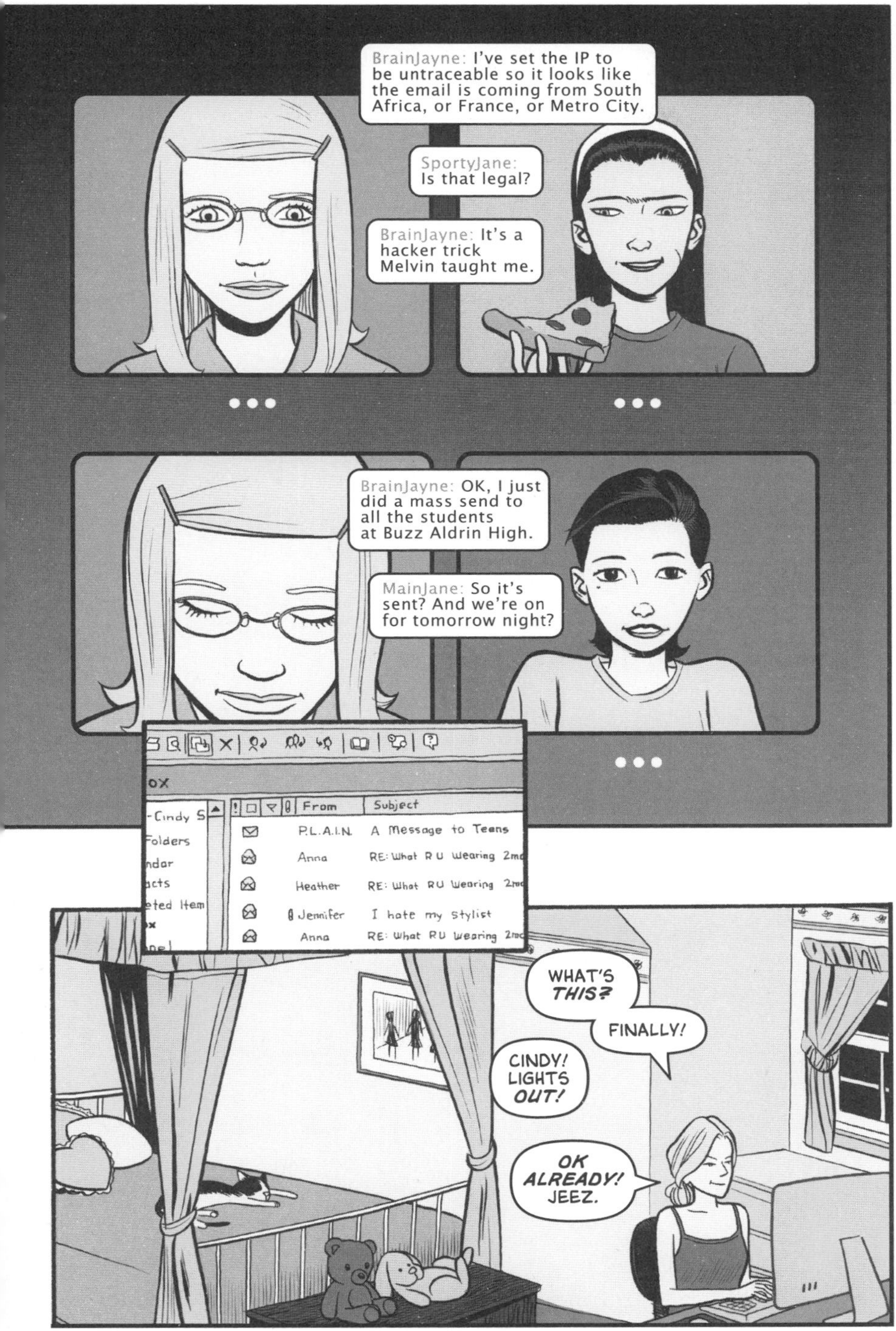
BrainJayne: I've set the IP to be untraceable so it looks like the email is coming from South Africa, or France, or Metro City.
SportyJane: Is that legal?
BrainJayne: It's a hacker trick Melvin taught me.
BrainJayne: OK, I just did a mass send to all the students at Buzz Aldrin High.
MainJane: So it's sent? And we're on for tomorrow night?
From
Subject
P.L.A.I.N. A Message to Teens
Anna RE: What R U Wearing
Heather RE: What R U Wearing
Jennifer I hate my stylist
Anna RE: What R U Wearing
WHAT'S *THIS?*
FINALLY!
CINDY! LIGHTS *OUT!*
OK ALREADY! JEEZ.

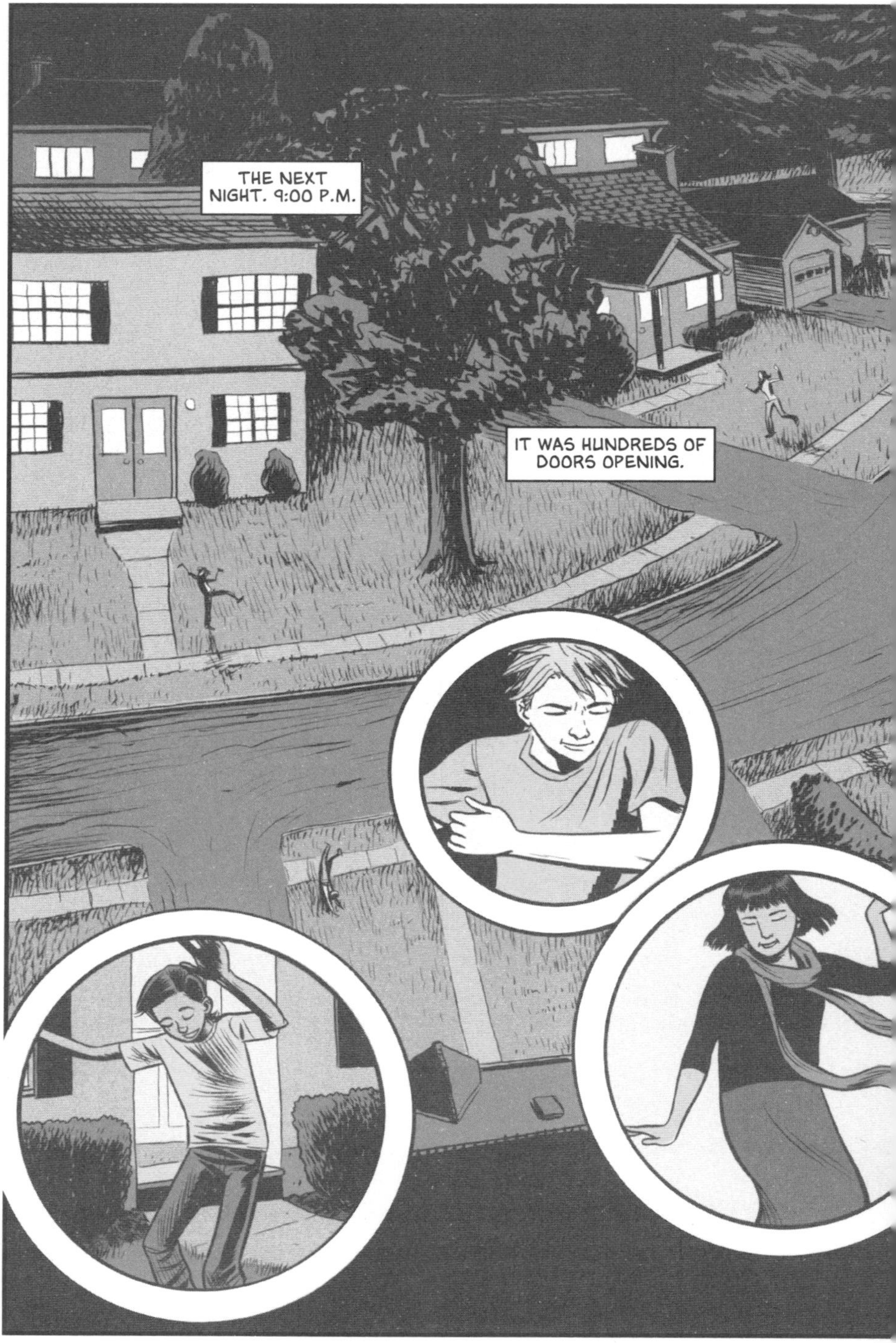
THE NEXT NIGHT. 9:00 P.M.
IT WAS HUNDREDS OF DOORS OPENING.

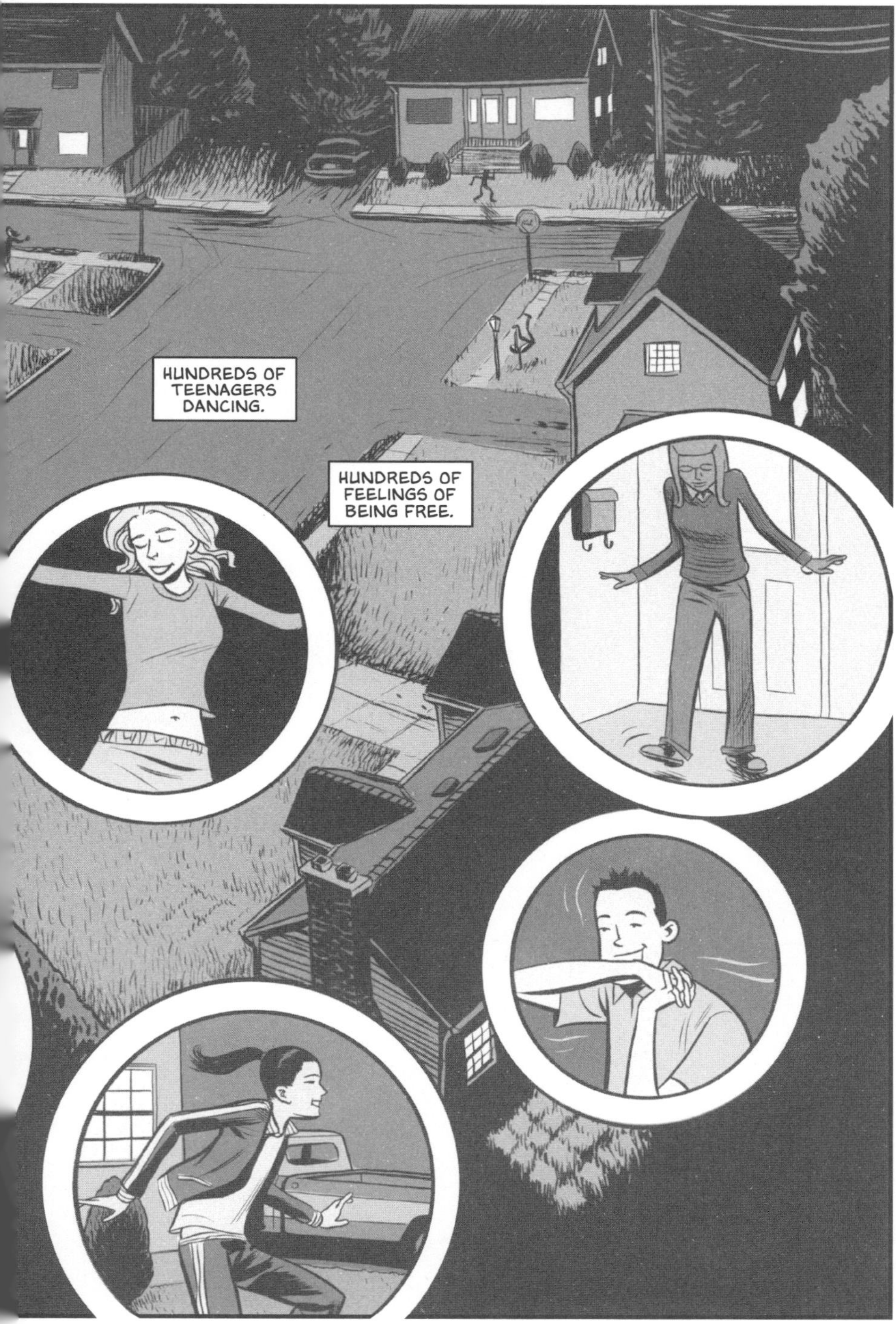
HUNDREDS OF TEENAGERS DANCING.
HUNDREDS OF FEELINGS OF BEING FREE.

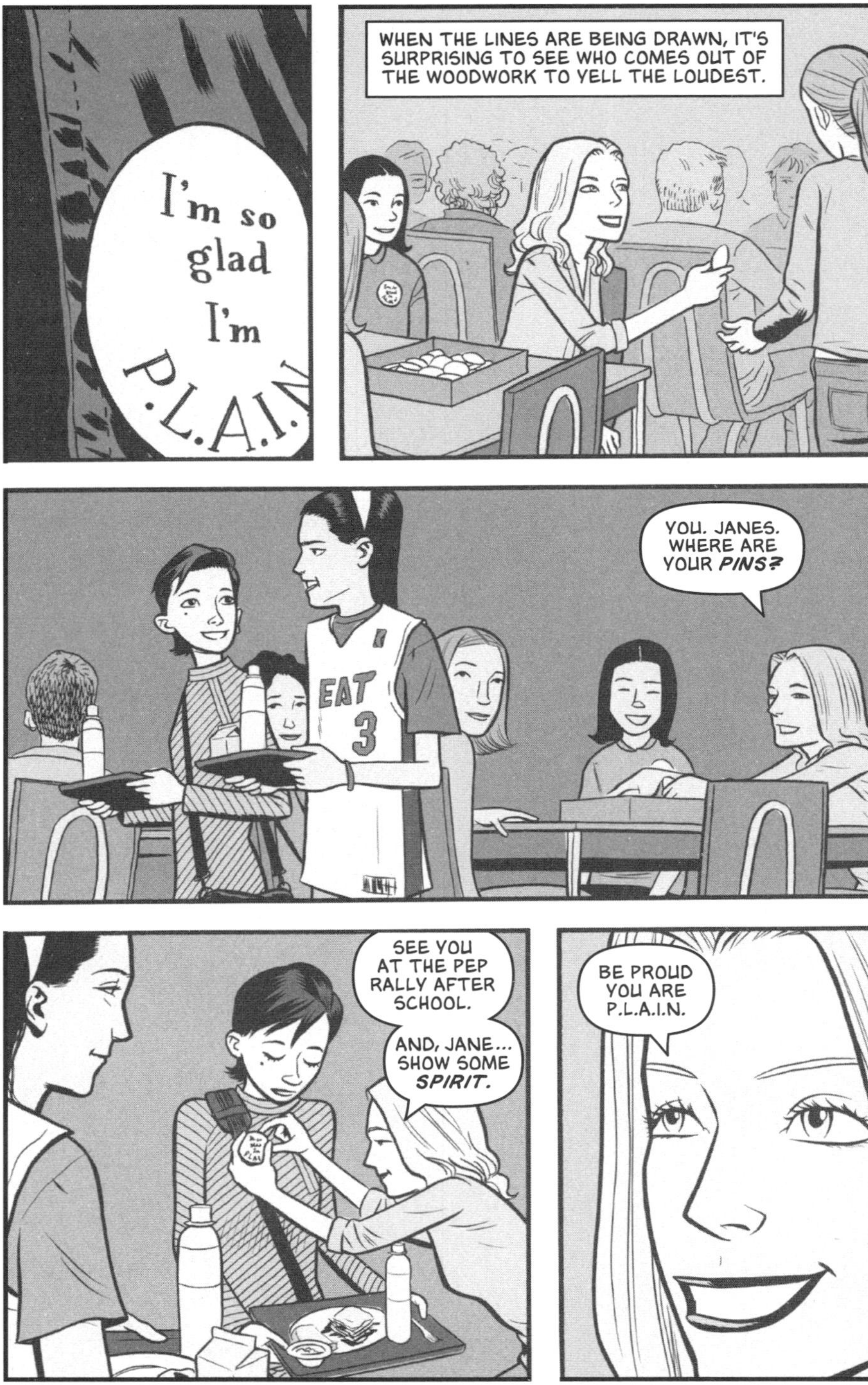
I'm so glad I'm P.L.A.I.N
WHEN THE LINES ARE BEING DRAWN, IT'S SURPRISING TO SEE WHO COMES OUT OF THE WOODWORK TO YELL THE LOUDEST.
YOU. JANES. WHERE ARE YOUR *PINS?*
EAT 3
SEE YOU AT THE PEP RALLY AFTER SCHOOL.
AND, JANE... SHOW SOME *SPIRIT*.
BE PROUD YOU ARE P.L.A.I.N.

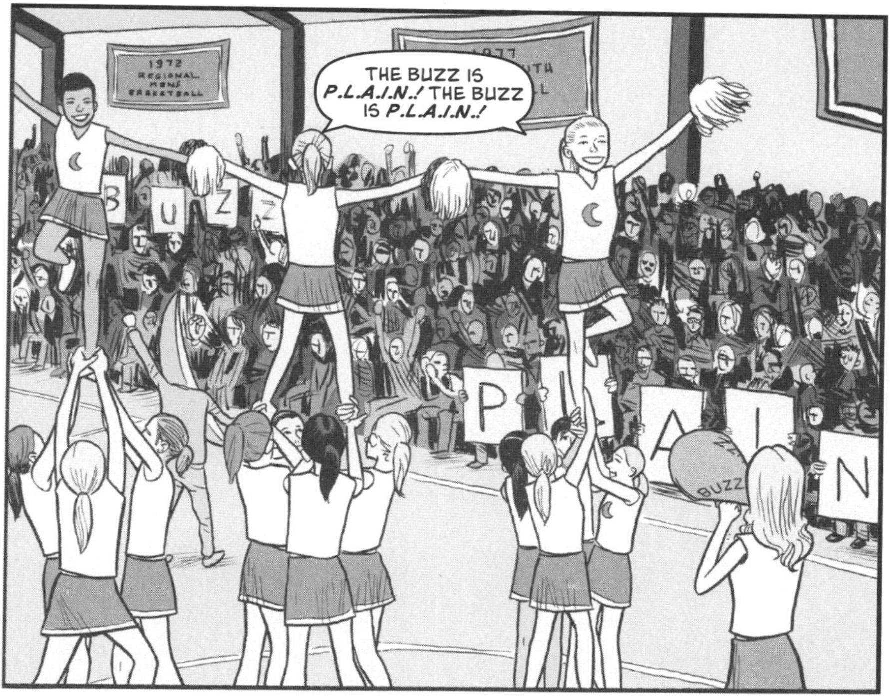
1972 REGIONAL MENS BASKETBALL
THE BUZZ IS *P.L.A.I.N.!* THE BUZZ IS *P.L.A.I.N.!*
BUZZ

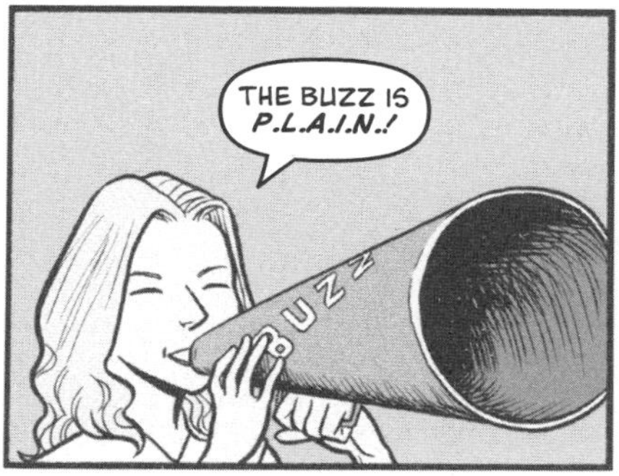
THE BUZZ IS *P.L.A.I.N.!*
BUZZ

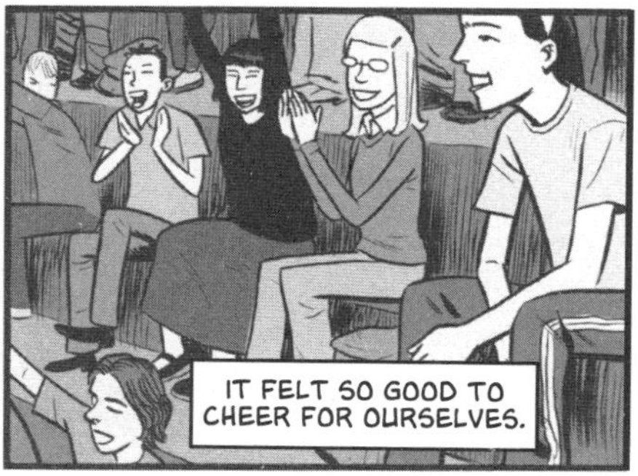
IT FELT SO GOOD TO CHEER FOR OURSELVES.

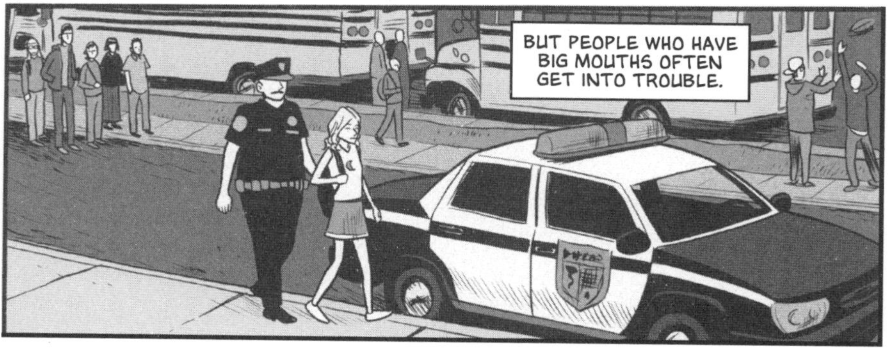
BUT PEOPLE WHO HAVE BIG MOUTHS OFTEN GET INTO TROUBLE.

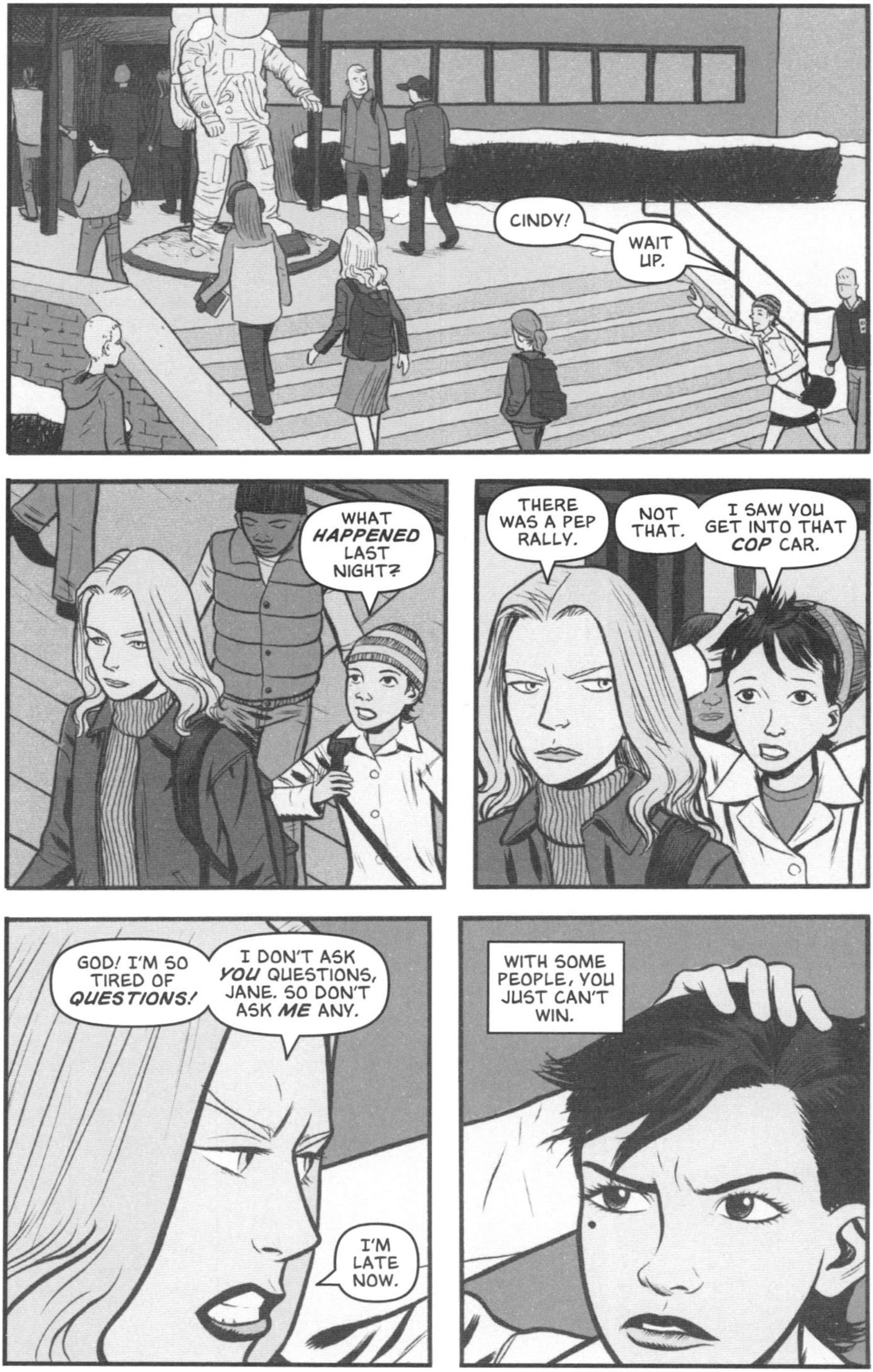
CINDY!
WAIT UP.
WHAT *HAPPENED* LAST NIGHT?
THERE WAS A PEP RALLY.
NOT THAT.
I SAW YOU GET INTO THAT *COP* CAR.
GOD! I'M SO TIRED OF *QUESTIONS!*
I DON'T ASK *YOU* QUESTIONS, JANE. SO DON'T ASK *ME* ANY.
I'M LATE NOW.
WITH SOME PEOPLE, YOU JUST CAN'T WIN.

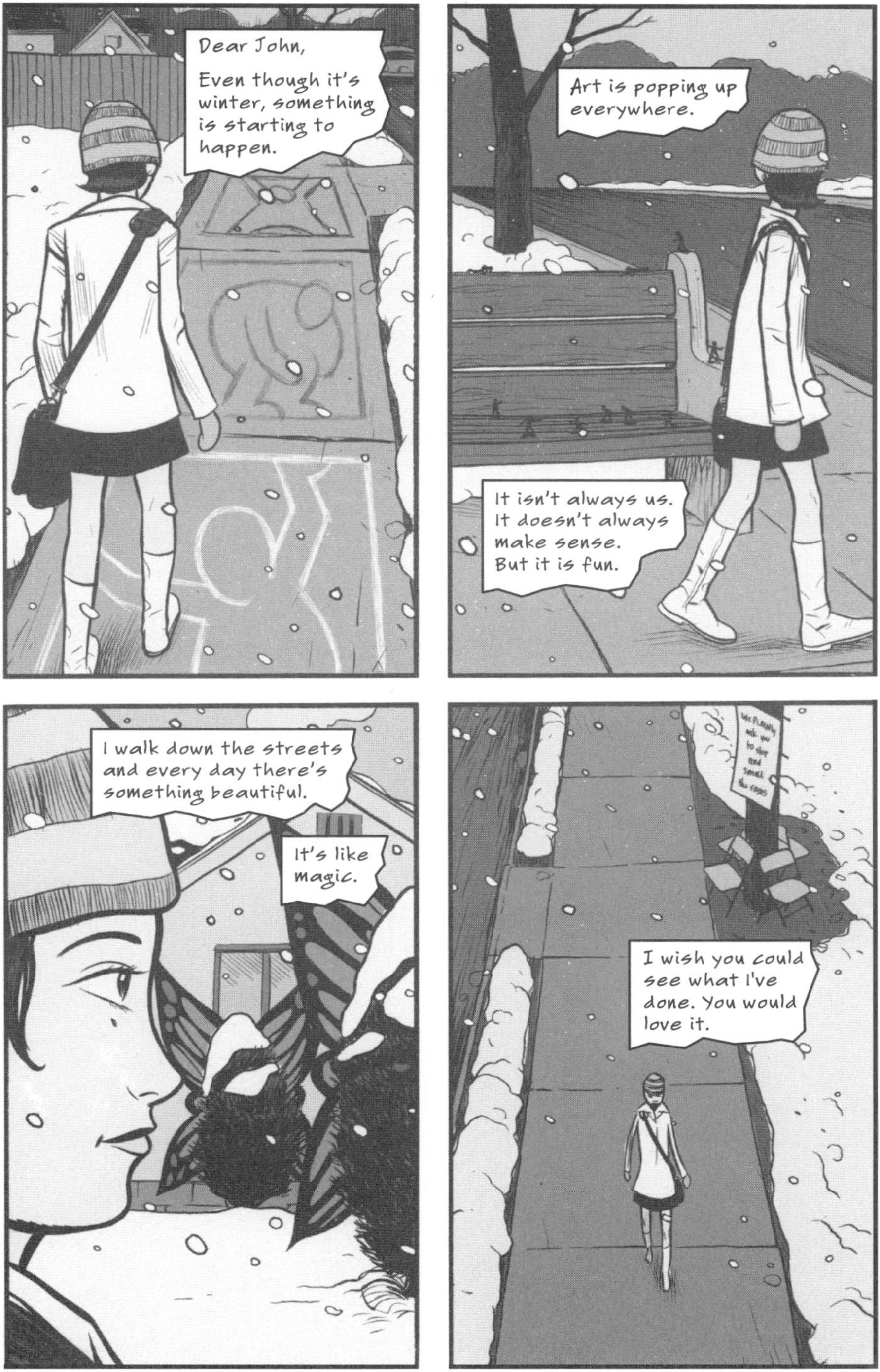
Dear John,
Even though it's winter, something is starting to happen.
Art is popping up everywhere.
It isn't always us. It doesn't always make sense. But it is fun.
I walk down the streets and every day there's something beautiful.
It's like magic.
I wish you could see what I've done. You would love it.

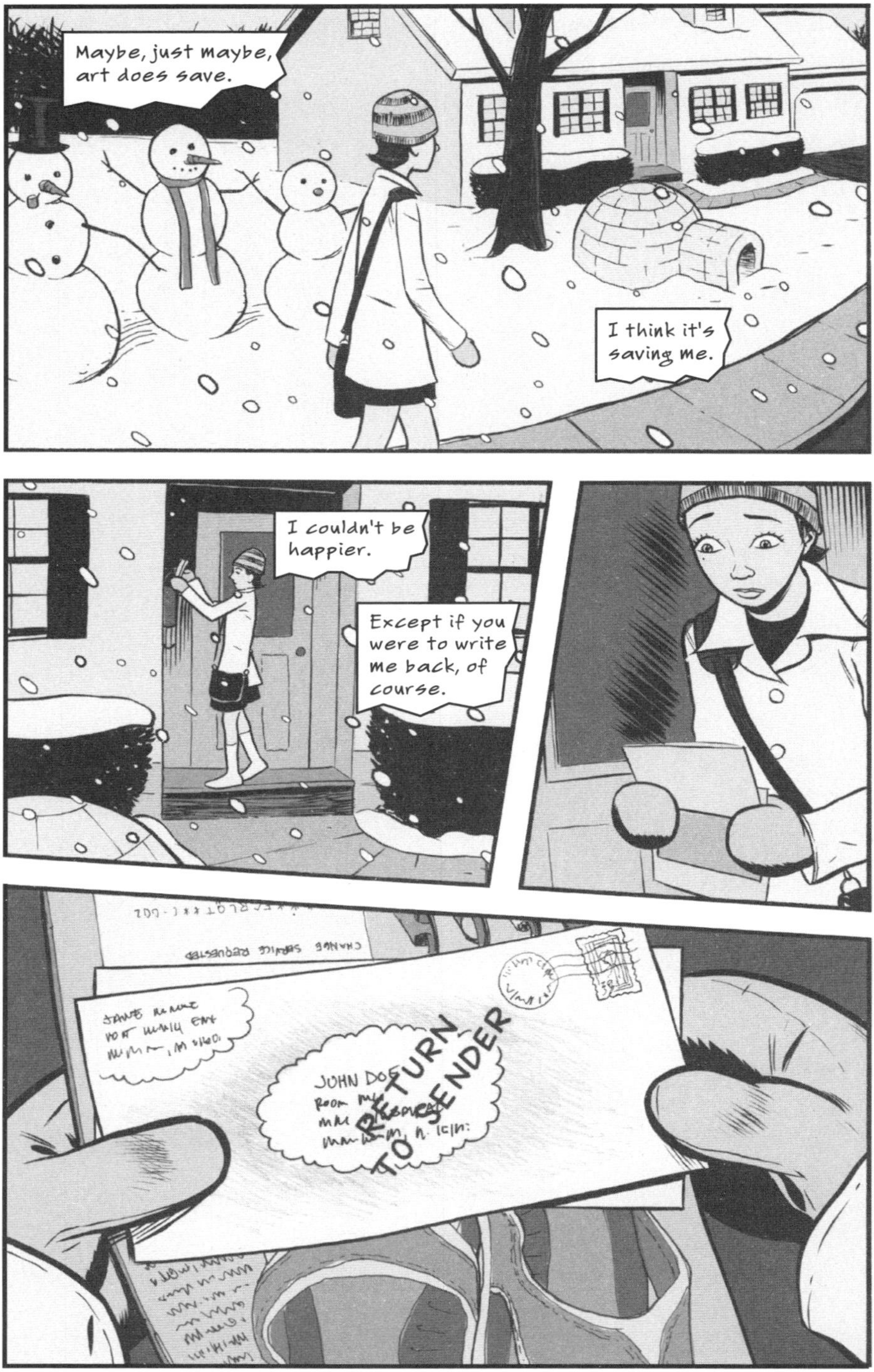
Maybe, just maybe, art does save.
I think it's saving me.
I couldn't be happier.
Except if you were to write me back, of course.
JOHN DOE
RETURN TO SENDER

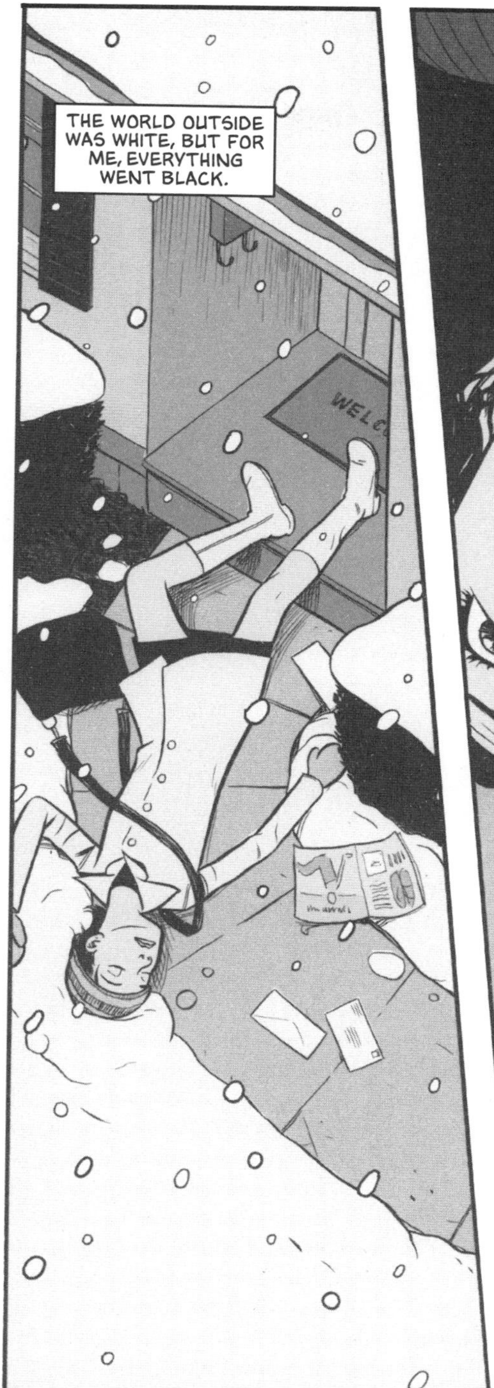
THE WORLD OUTSIDE WAS WHITE, BUT FOR ME, EVERYTHING WENT BLACK.

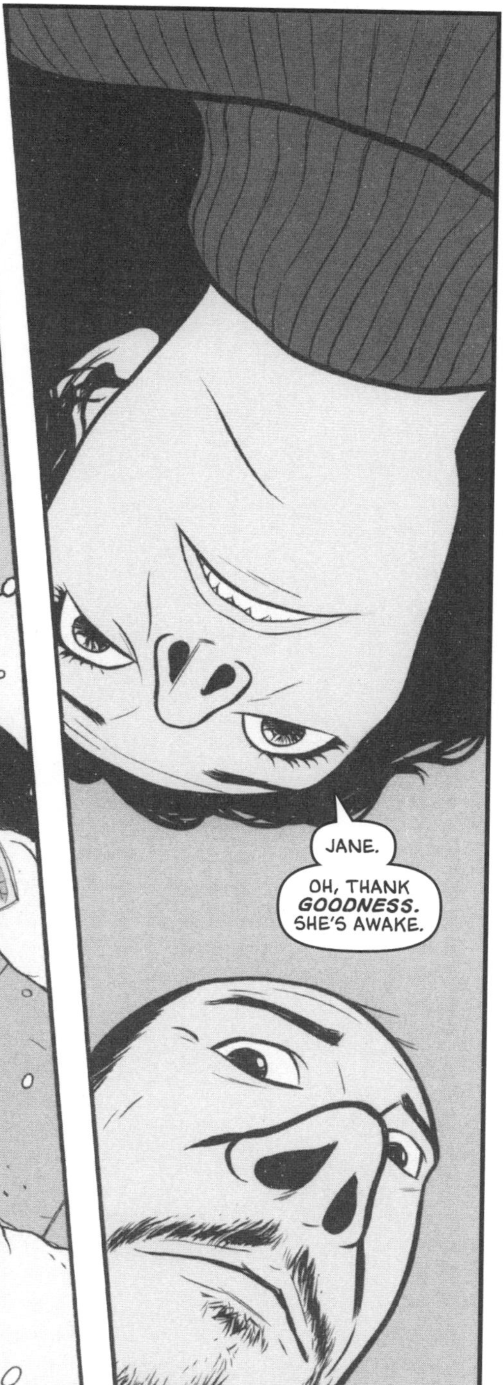
JANE.
OH, THANK **GOODNESS.** SHE'S AWAKE.

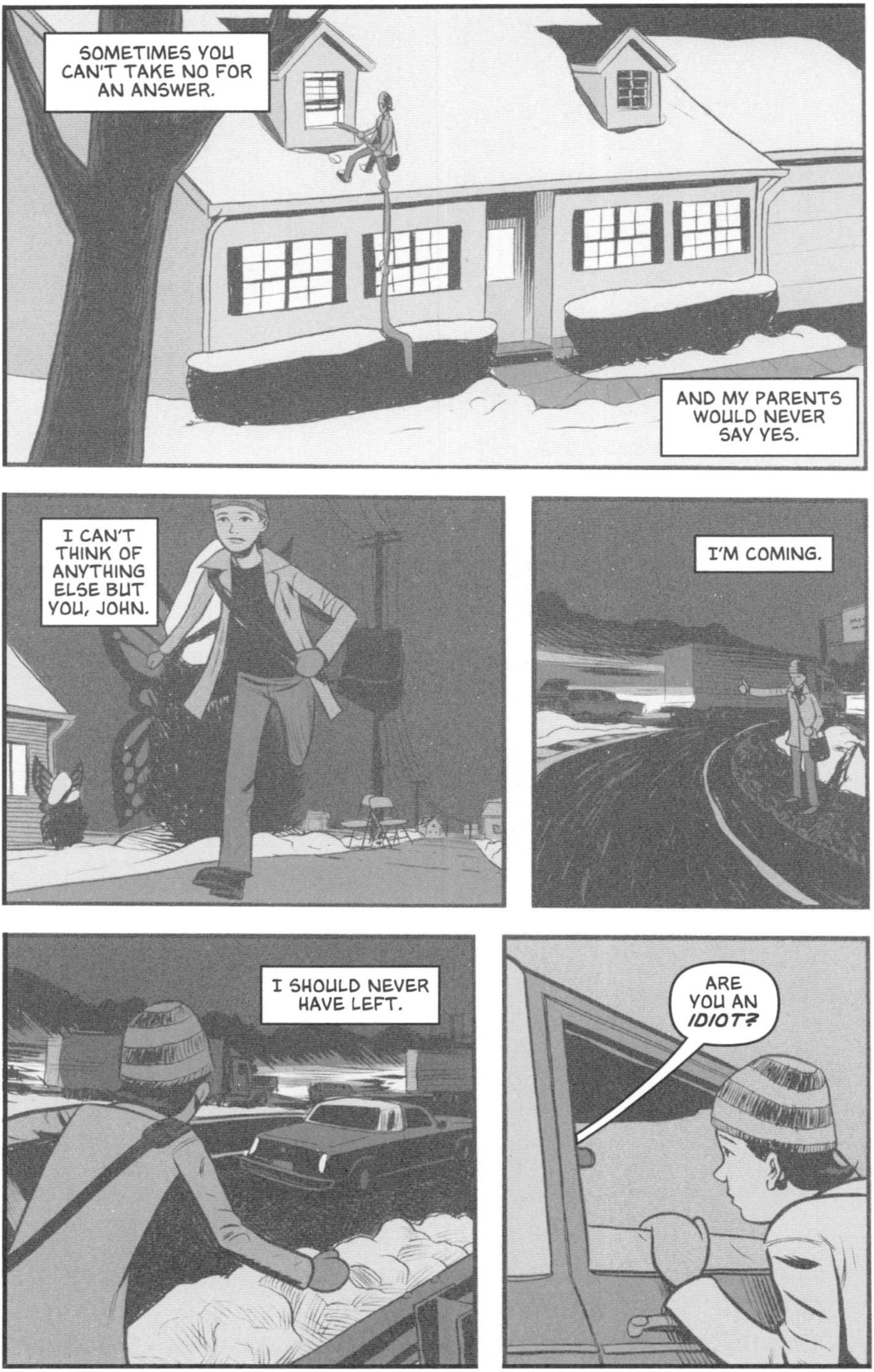
SOMETIMES YOU CAN'T TAKE NO FOR AN ANSWER.
AND MY PARENTS WOULD NEVER SAY YES.
I CAN'T THINK OF ANYTHING ELSE BUT YOU, JOHN.
I'M COMING.
I SHOULD NEVER HAVE LEFT.
ARE YOU AN *IDIOT?*

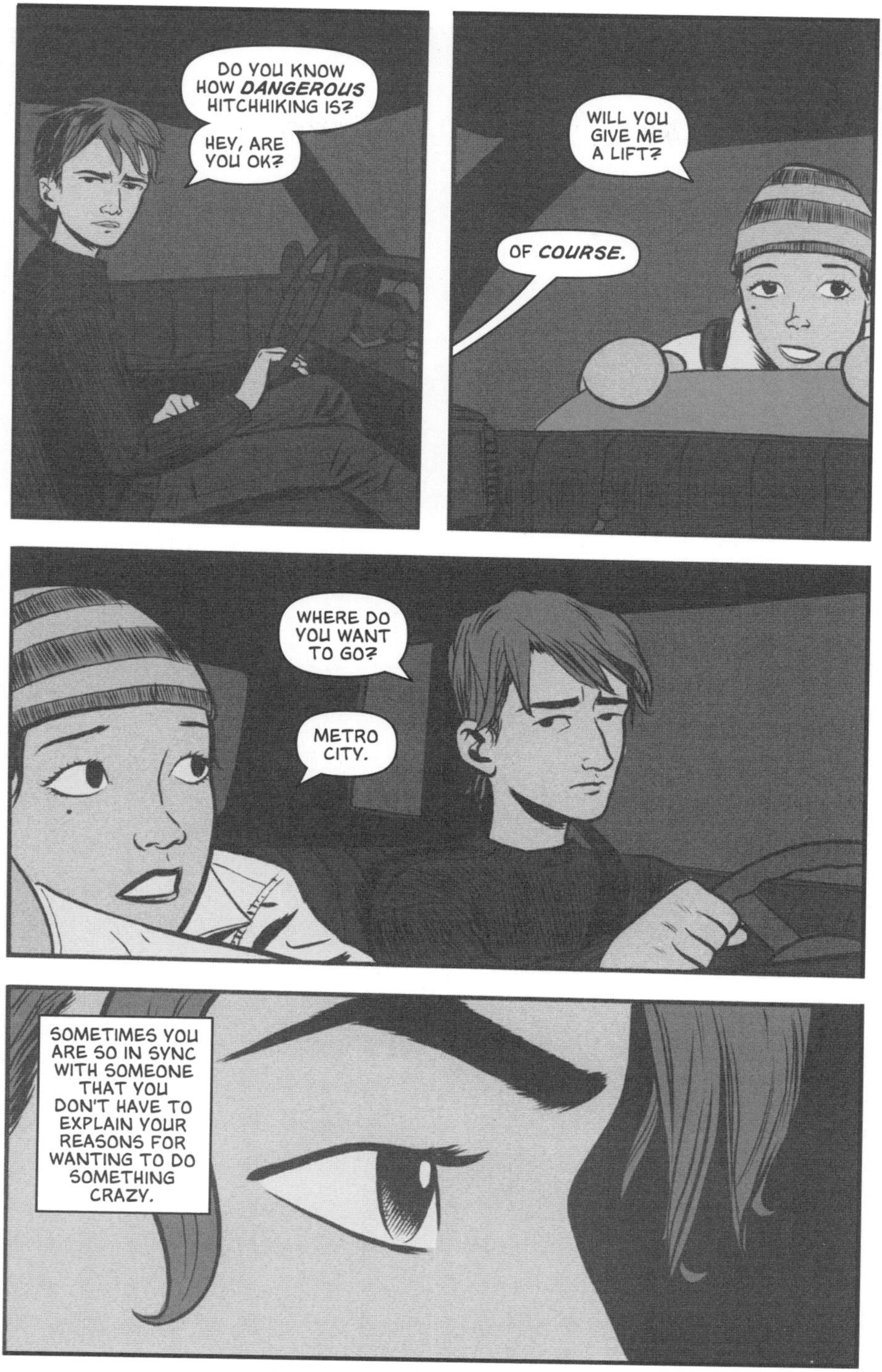
DO YOU KNOW HOW DANGEROUS HITCHHIKING IS?
HEY, ARE YOU OK?
WILL YOU GIVE ME A LIFT?
OF COURSE.
WHERE DO YOU WANT TO GO?
METRO CITY.
SOMETIMES YOU ARE SO IN SYNC WITH SOMEONE THAT YOU DON'T HAVE TO EXPLAIN YOUR REASONS FOR WANTING TO DO SOMETHING CRAZY.

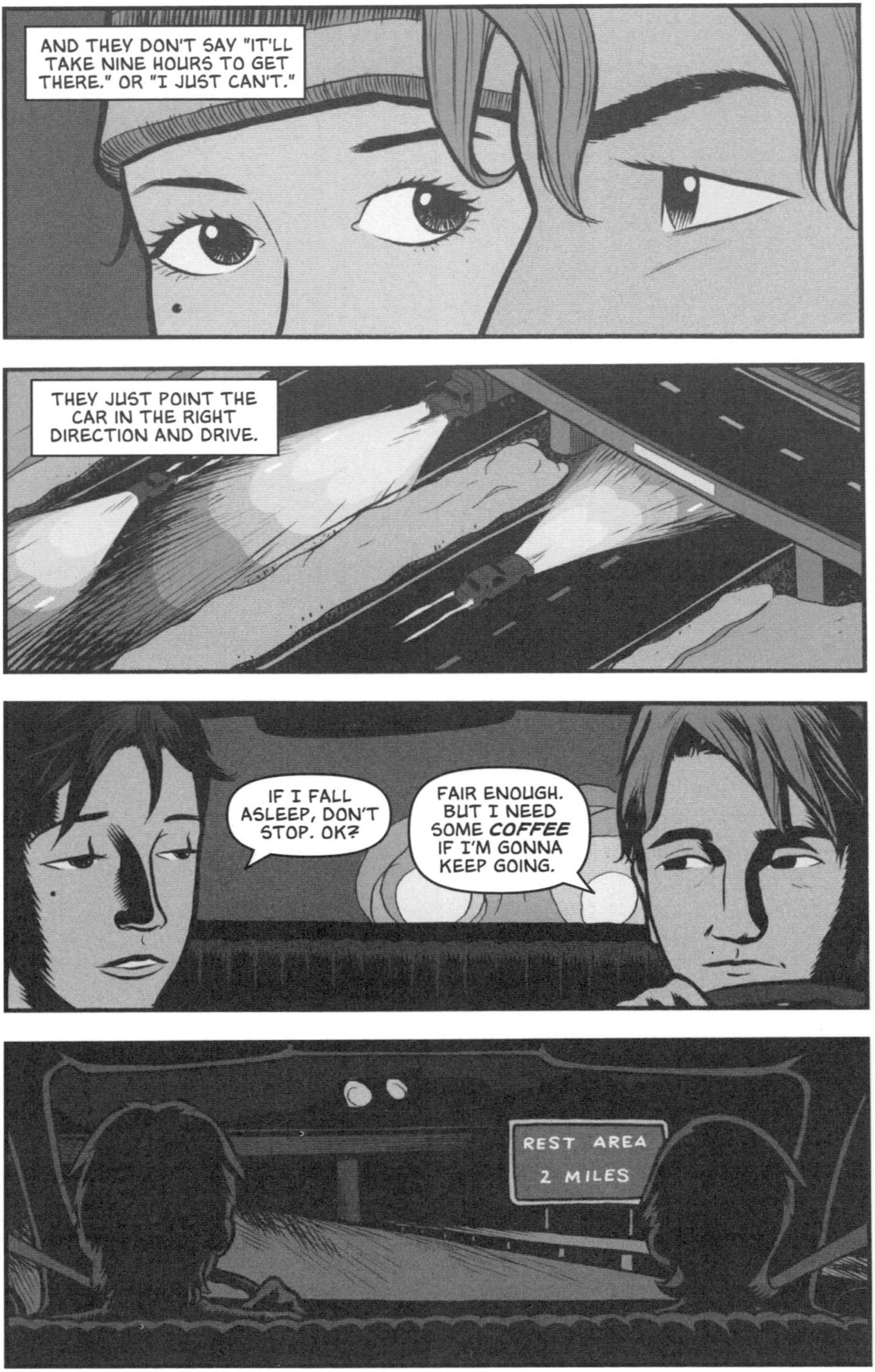
AND THEY DON'T SAY "IT'LL TAKE NINE HOURS TO GET THERE." OR "I JUST CAN'T."
THEY JUST POINT THE CAR IN THE RIGHT DIRECTION AND DRIVE.
IF I FALL ASLEEP, DON'T STOP. OK?
FAIR ENOUGH. BUT I NEED SOME *COFFEE* IF I'M GONNA KEEP GOING.
REST AREA 2 MILES

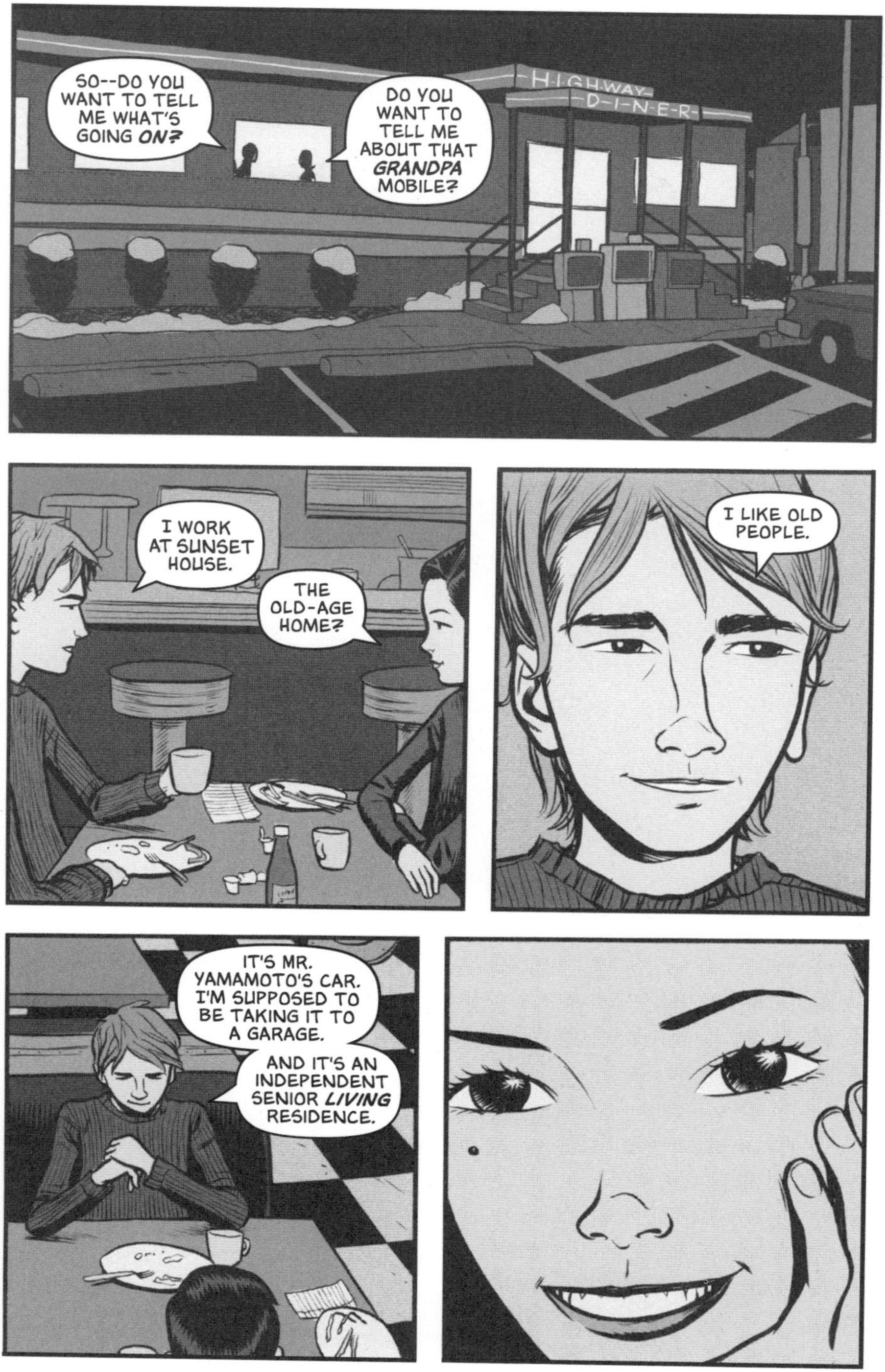

HIGHWAY DINER
SO--DO YOU WANT TO TELL ME WHAT'S GOING *ON?*
DO YOU WANT TO TELL ME ABOUT THAT *GRANDPA* MOBILE?
I WORK AT SUNSET HOUSE.
THE OLD-AGE HOME?
I LIKE OLD PEOPLE.
IT'S MR. YAMAMOTO'S CAR. I'M SUPPOSED TO BE TAKING IT TO A GARAGE.
AND IT'S AN INDEPENDENT SENIOR *LIVING* RESIDENCE.

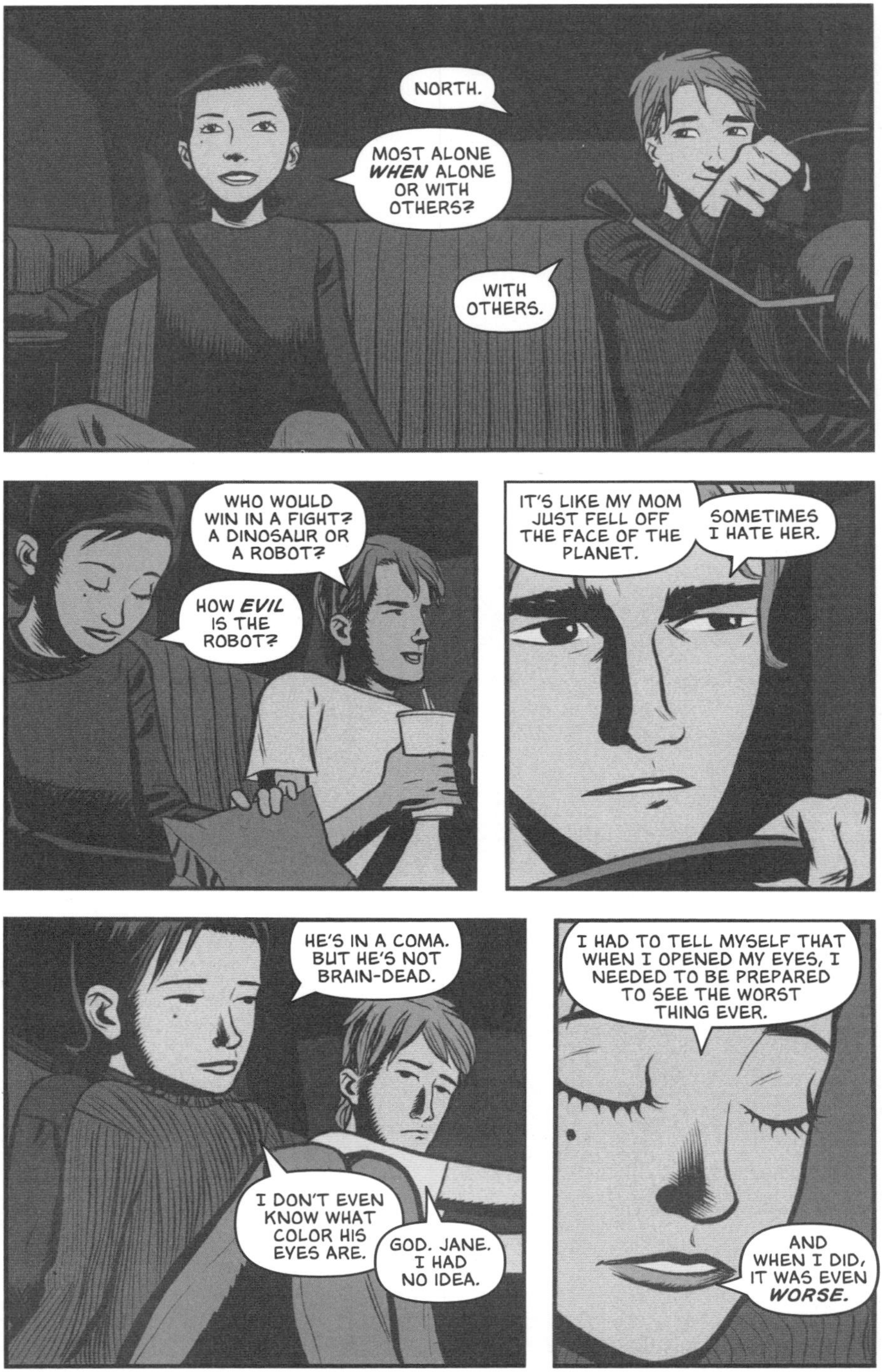
NORTH.
MOST ALONE *WHEN* ALONE OR WITH OTHERS?
WITH OTHERS.
WHO WOULD WIN IN A FIGHT? A DINOSAUR OR A ROBOT?
HOW *EVIL* IS THE ROBOT?
IT'S LIKE MY MOM JUST FELL OFF THE FACE OF THE PLANET.
SOMETIMES I HATE HER.
HE'S IN A COMA. BUT HE'S NOT BRAIN-DEAD.
I DON'T EVEN KNOW WHAT COLOR HIS EYES ARE.
GOD. JANE. I HAD NO IDEA.
I HAD TO TELL MYSELF THAT WHEN I OPENED MY EYES, I NEEDED TO BE PREPARED TO SEE THE WORST THING EVER.
AND WHEN I DID, IT WAS EVEN *WORSE*.

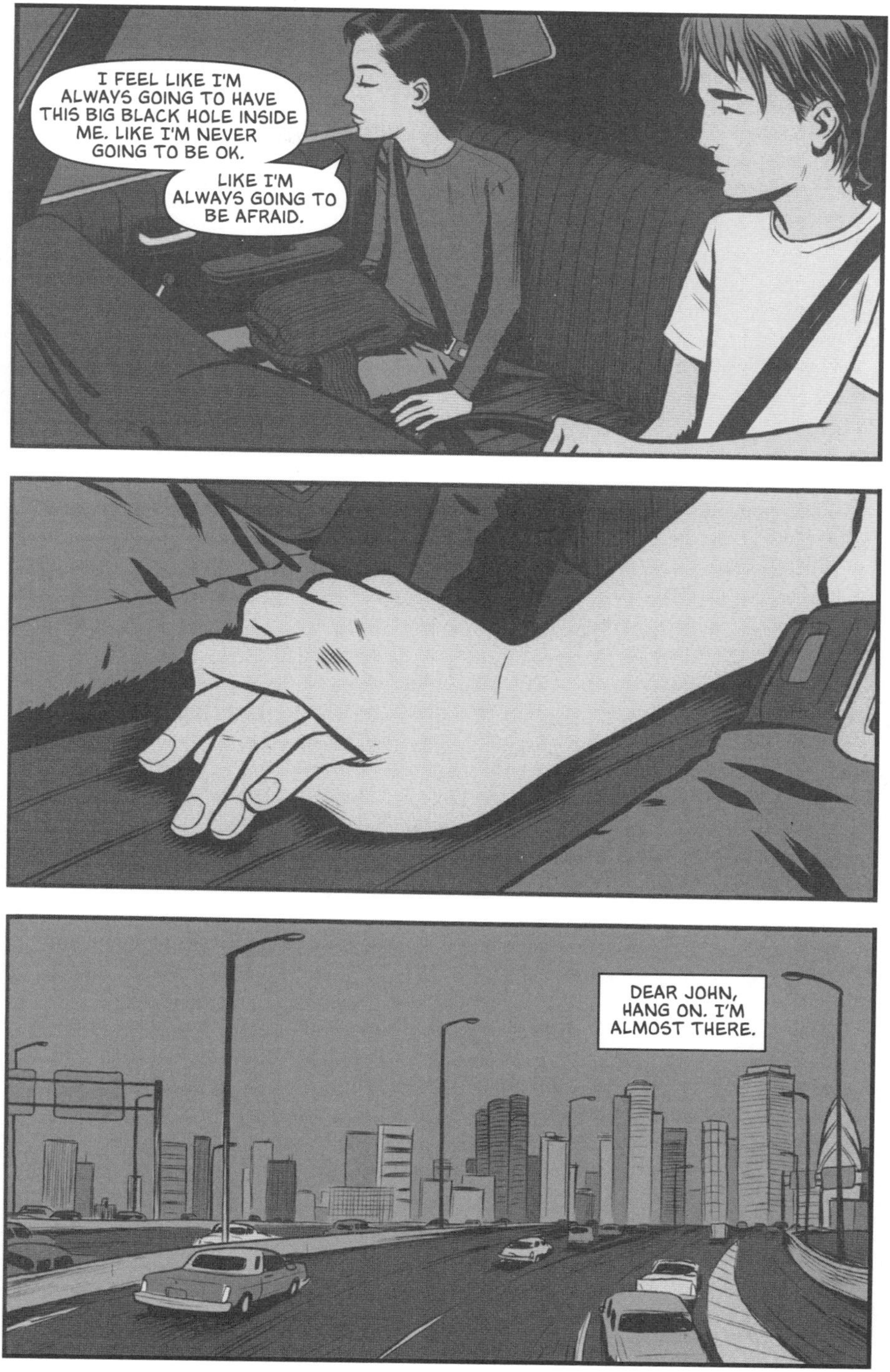
I FEEL LIKE I'M ALWAYS GOING TO HAVE THIS BIG BLACK HOLE INSIDE ME. LIKE I'M NEVER GOING TO BE OK.
LIKE I'M ALWAYS GOING TO BE AFRAID.
DEAR JOHN, HANG ON. I'M ALMOST THERE.

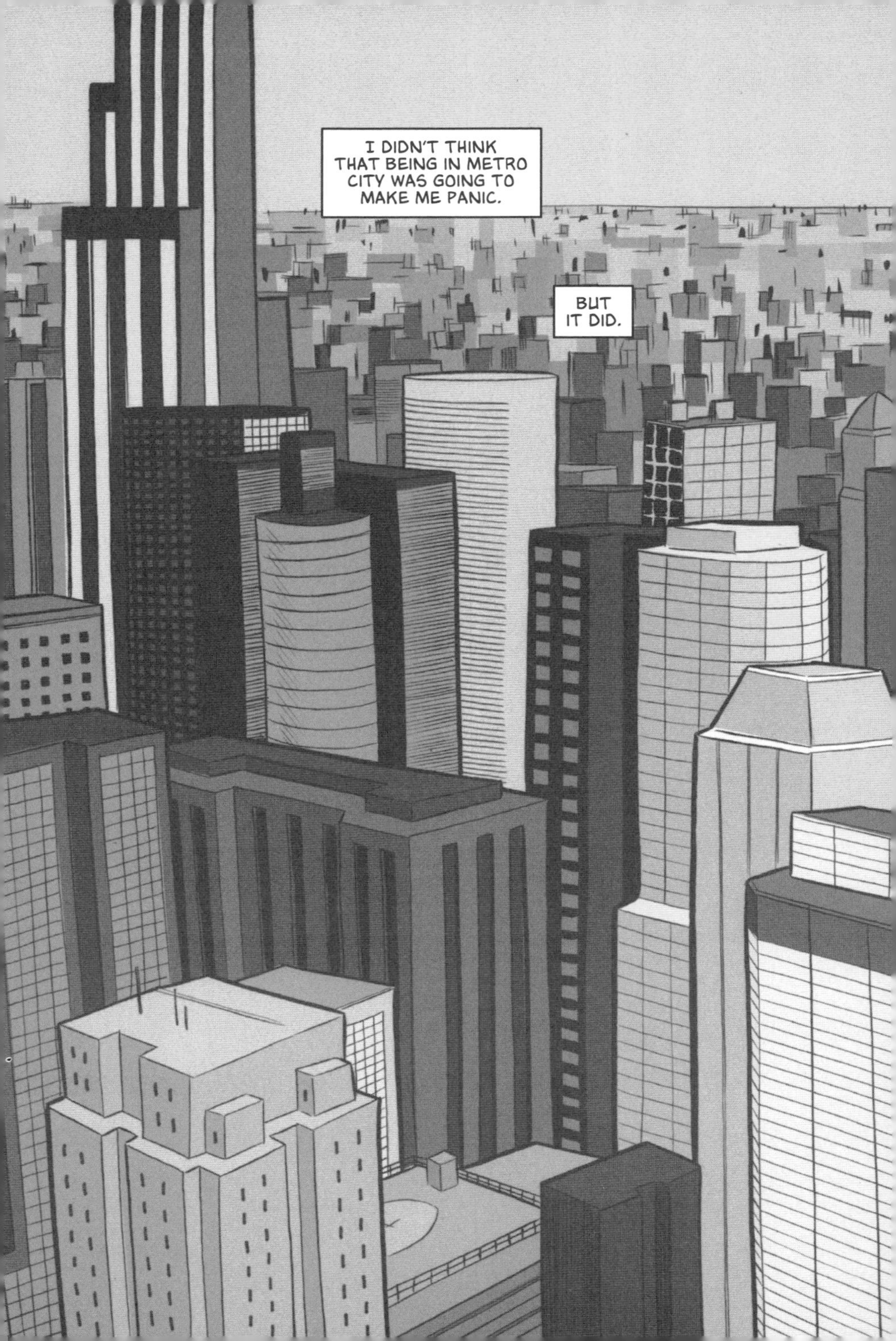
I DIDN'T THINK THAT BEING IN METRO CITY WAS GOING TO MAKE ME PANIC.
BUT IT DID.

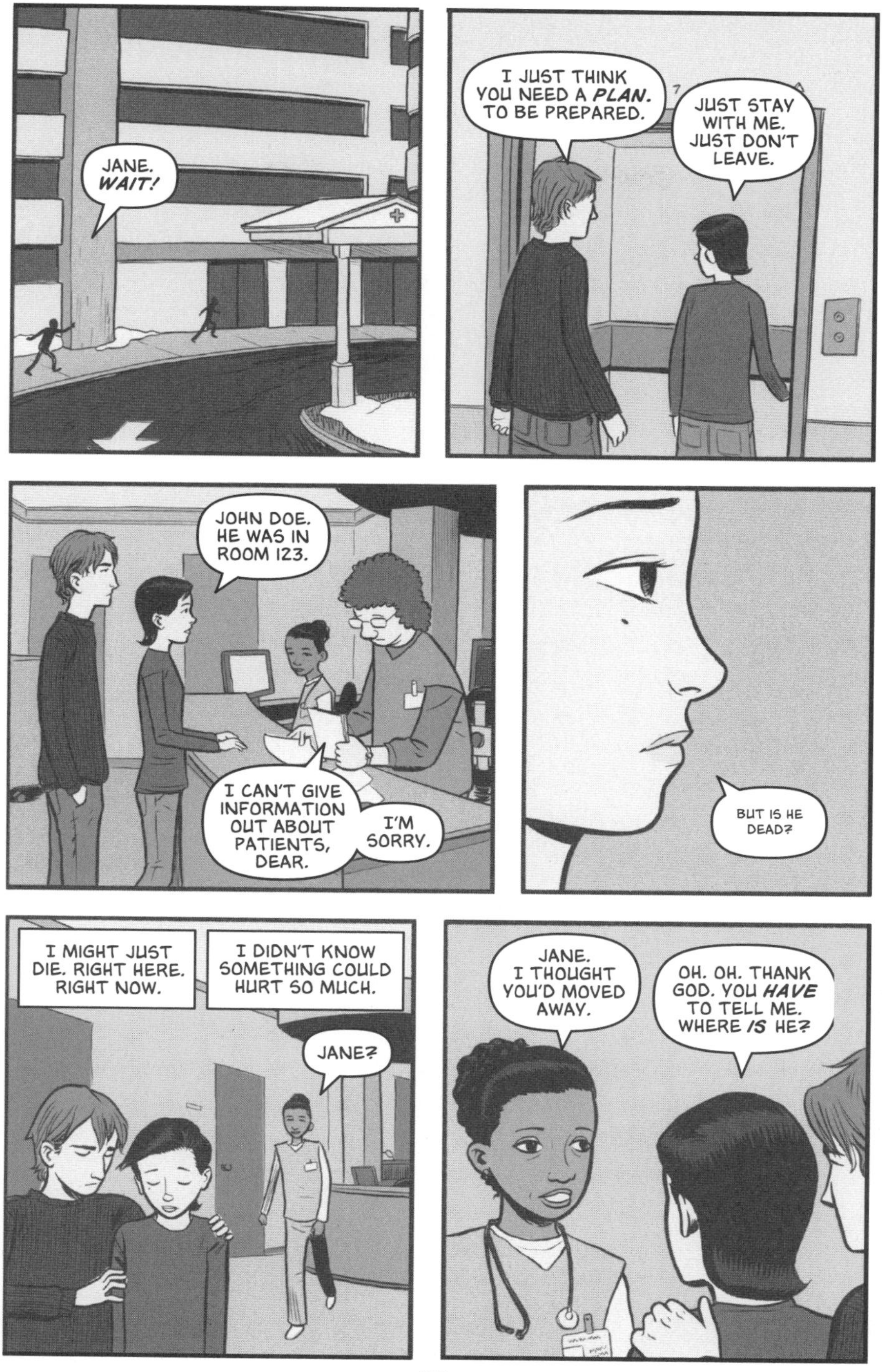
JANE. WAIT!
I JUST THINK YOU NEED A PLAN. TO BE PREPARED.
JUST STAY WITH ME. JUST DON'T LEAVE.
JOHN DOE. HE WAS IN ROOM 123.
I CAN'T GIVE INFORMATION OUT ABOUT PATIENTS, DEAR.
I'M SORRY.
BUT IS HE DEAD?
I MIGHT JUST DIE. RIGHT HERE. RIGHT NOW.
I DIDN'T KNOW SOMETHING COULD HURT SO MUCH.
JANE?
JANE. I THOUGHT YOU'D MOVED AWAY.
OH. OH. THANK GOD. YOU HAVE TO TELL ME. WHERE IS HE?

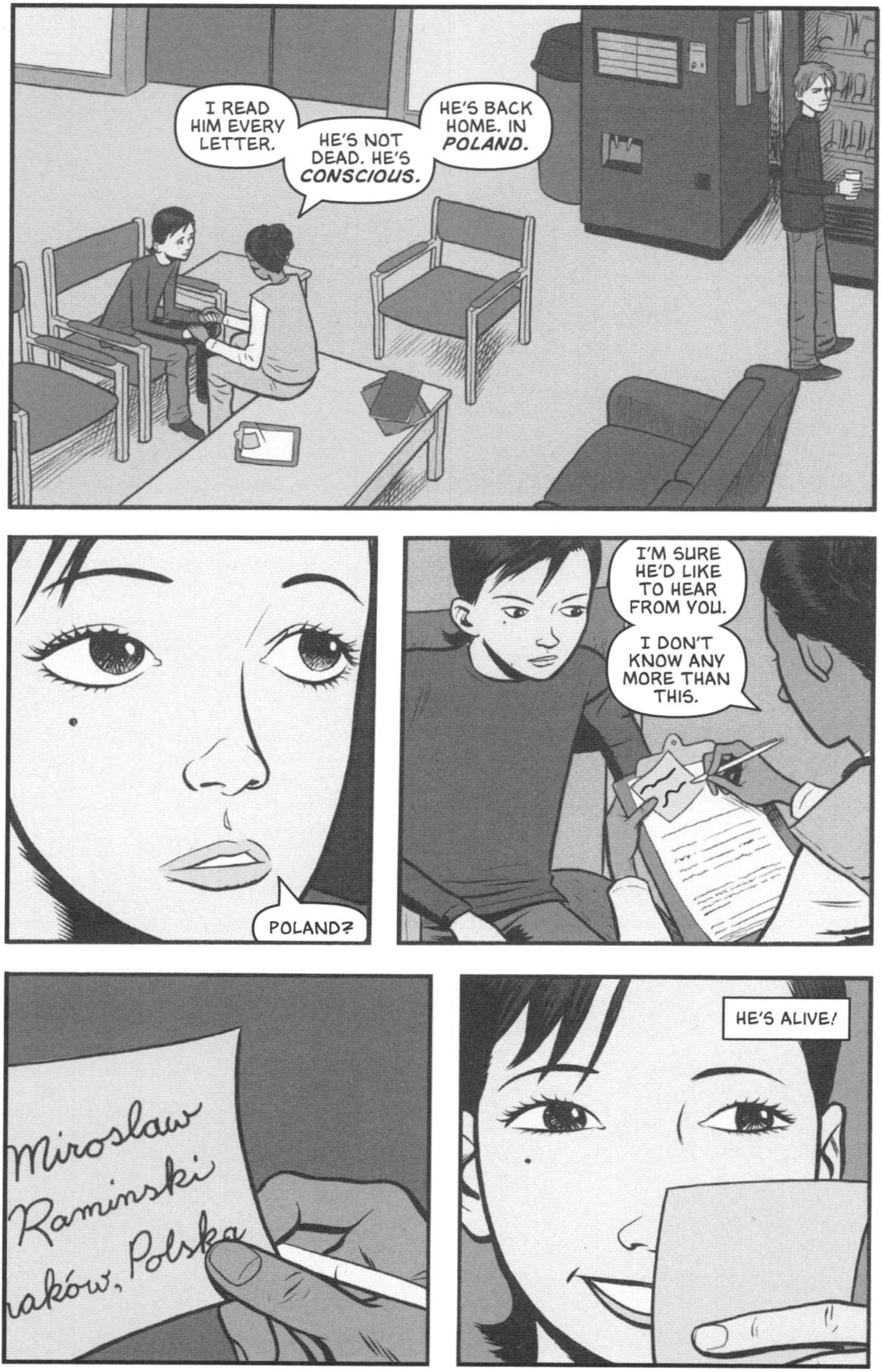
I READ HIM EVERY LETTER.
HE'S NOT DEAD. HE'S *CONSCIOUS.*
HE'S BACK HOME. IN *POLAND.*
POLAND?
I'M SURE HE'D LIKE TO HEAR FROM YOU.
I DON'T KNOW ANY MORE THAN THIS.
Miroslaw
Raminski
aków, Polska
HE'S ALIVE!

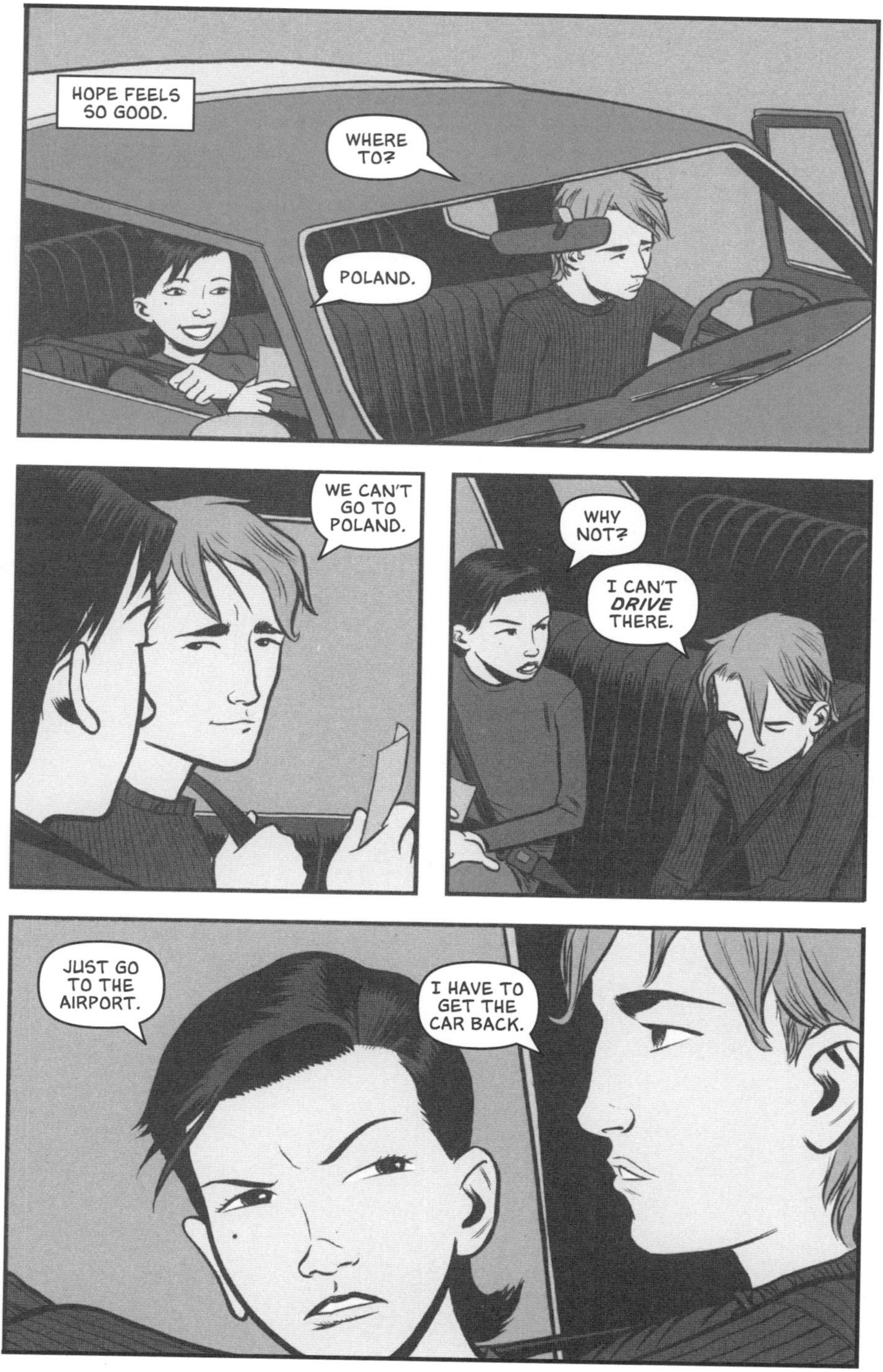
HOPE FEELS SO GOOD.
WHERE TO?
POLAND.
WE CAN'T GO TO POLAND.
WHY NOT?
I CAN'T *DRIVE* THERE.
JUST GO TO THE AIRPORT.
I HAVE TO GET THE CAR BACK.

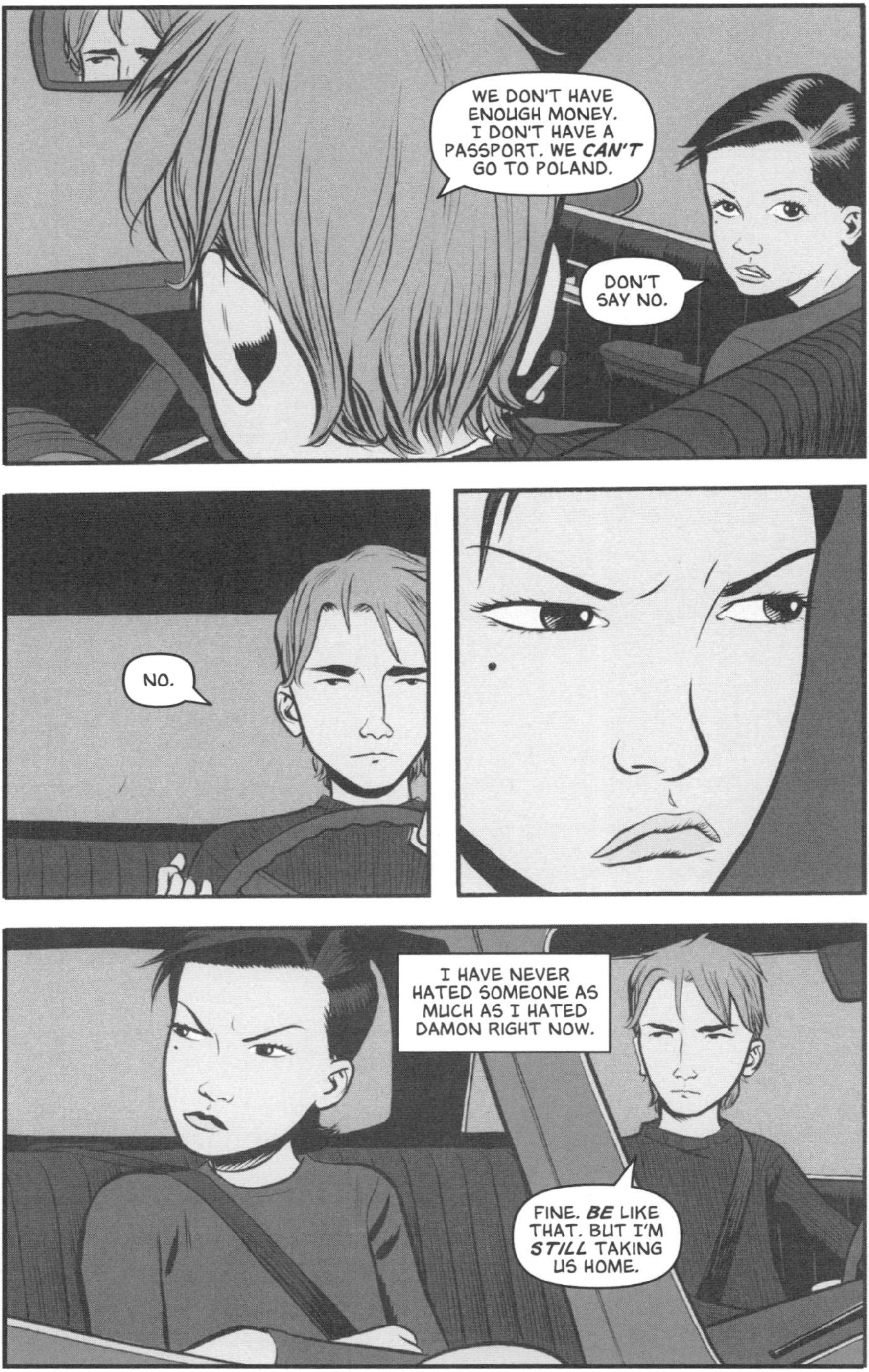
WE DON'T HAVE ENOUGH MONEY. I DON'T HAVE A PASSPORT. WE *CAN'T* GO TO POLAND.
DON'T SAY NO.
NO.
I HAVE NEVER HATED SOMEONE AS MUCH AS I HATED DAMON RIGHT NOW.
FINE. *BE* LIKE THAT. BUT I'M *STILL* TAKING US HOME.

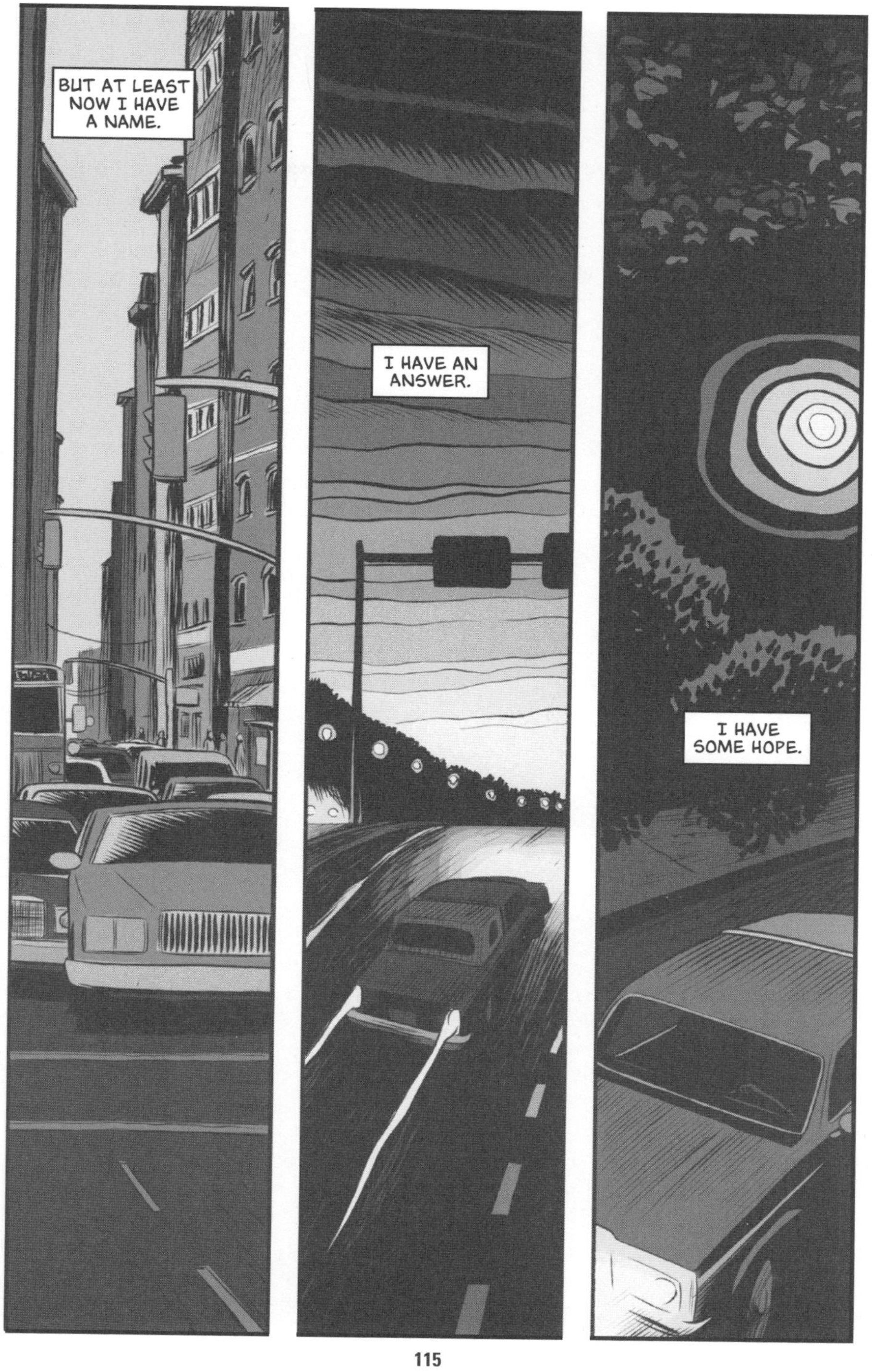
BUT AT LEAST NOW I HAVE A NAME.
I HAVE AN ANSWER.
I HAVE SOME HOPE.

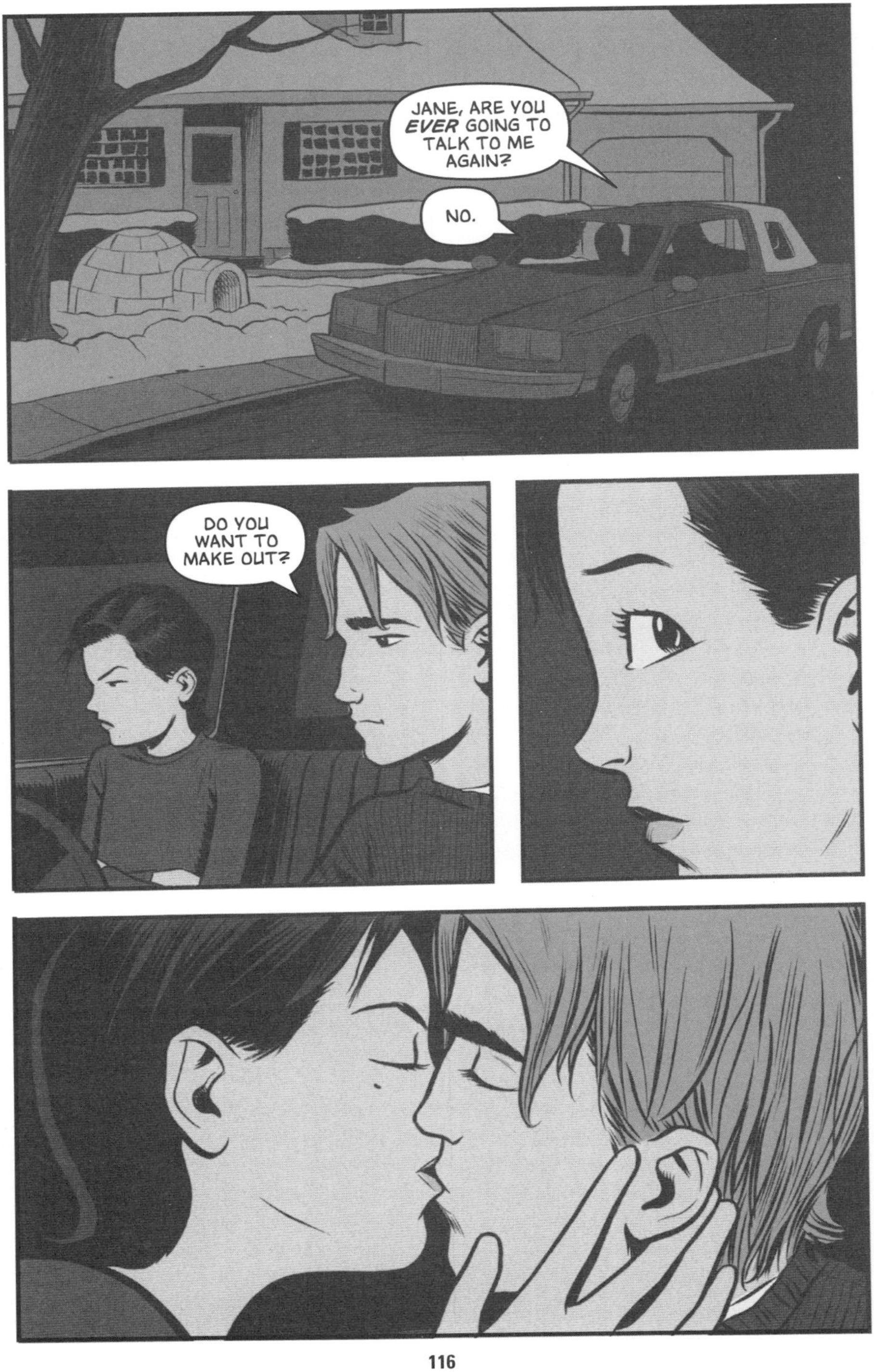
JANE, ARE YOU EVER GOING TO TALK TO ME AGAIN?
NO.
DO YOU WANT TO MAKE OUT?

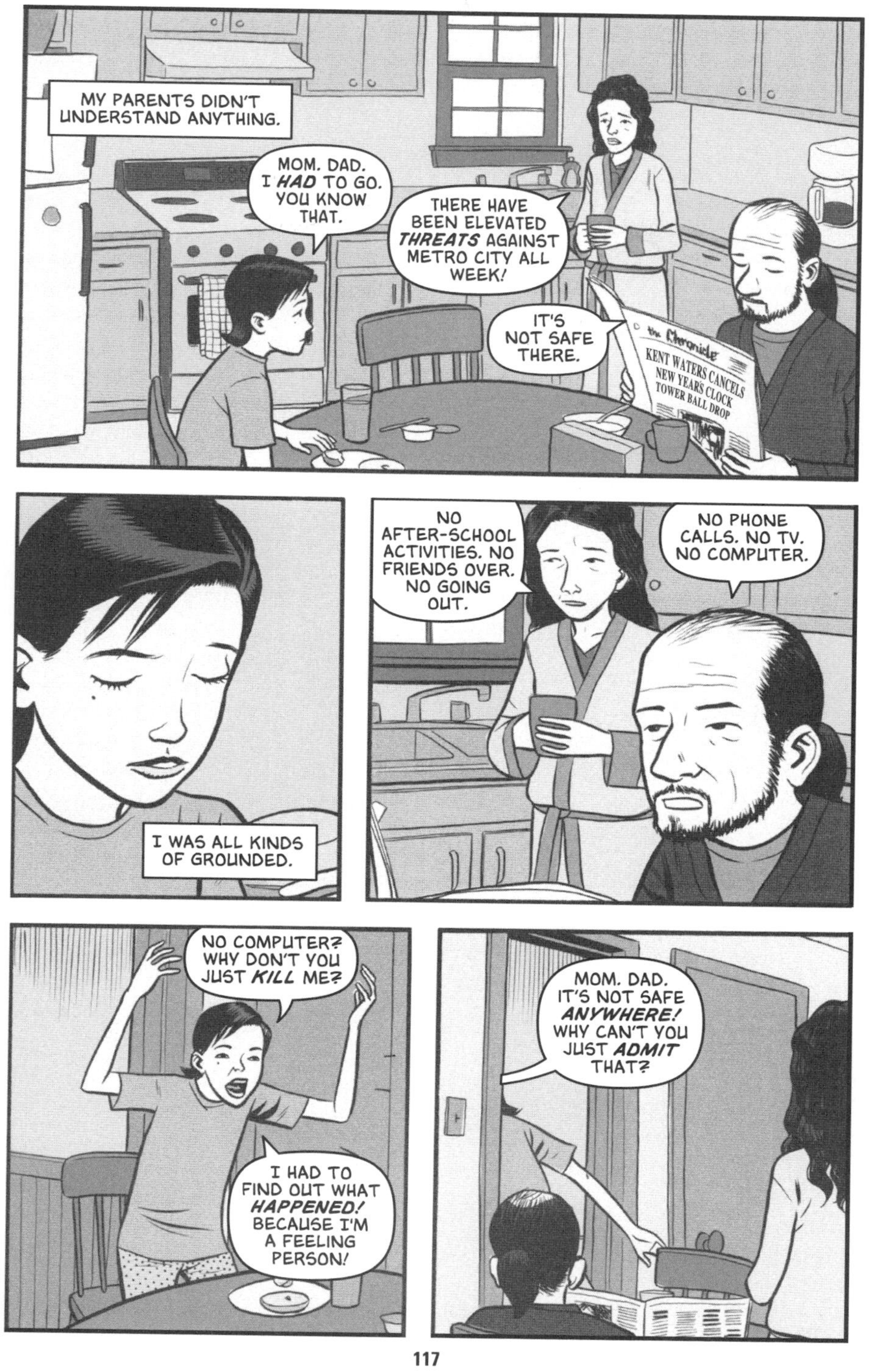

MY PARENTS DIDN'T UNDERSTAND ANYTHING.
MOM. DAD. I *HAD* TO GO. YOU KNOW THAT.
THERE HAVE BEEN ELEVATED *THREATS* AGAINST METRO CITY ALL WEEK!
IT'S NOT SAFE THERE.
the Chronicle
KENT WATERS CANCELS NEW YEAR'S CLOCK TOWER BALL DROP
I WAS ALL KINDS OF GROUNDED.
NO AFTER-SCHOOL ACTIVITIES. NO FRIENDS OVER. NO GOING OUT.
NO PHONE CALLS. NO TV. NO COMPUTER.
NO COMPUTER? WHY DON'T YOU JUST *KILL* ME?
I HAD TO FIND OUT WHAT *HAPPENED!* BECAUSE I'M A FEELING PERSON!
MOM. DAD. IT'S NOT SAFE *ANYWHERE!* WHY CAN'T YOU JUST *ADMIT* THAT?

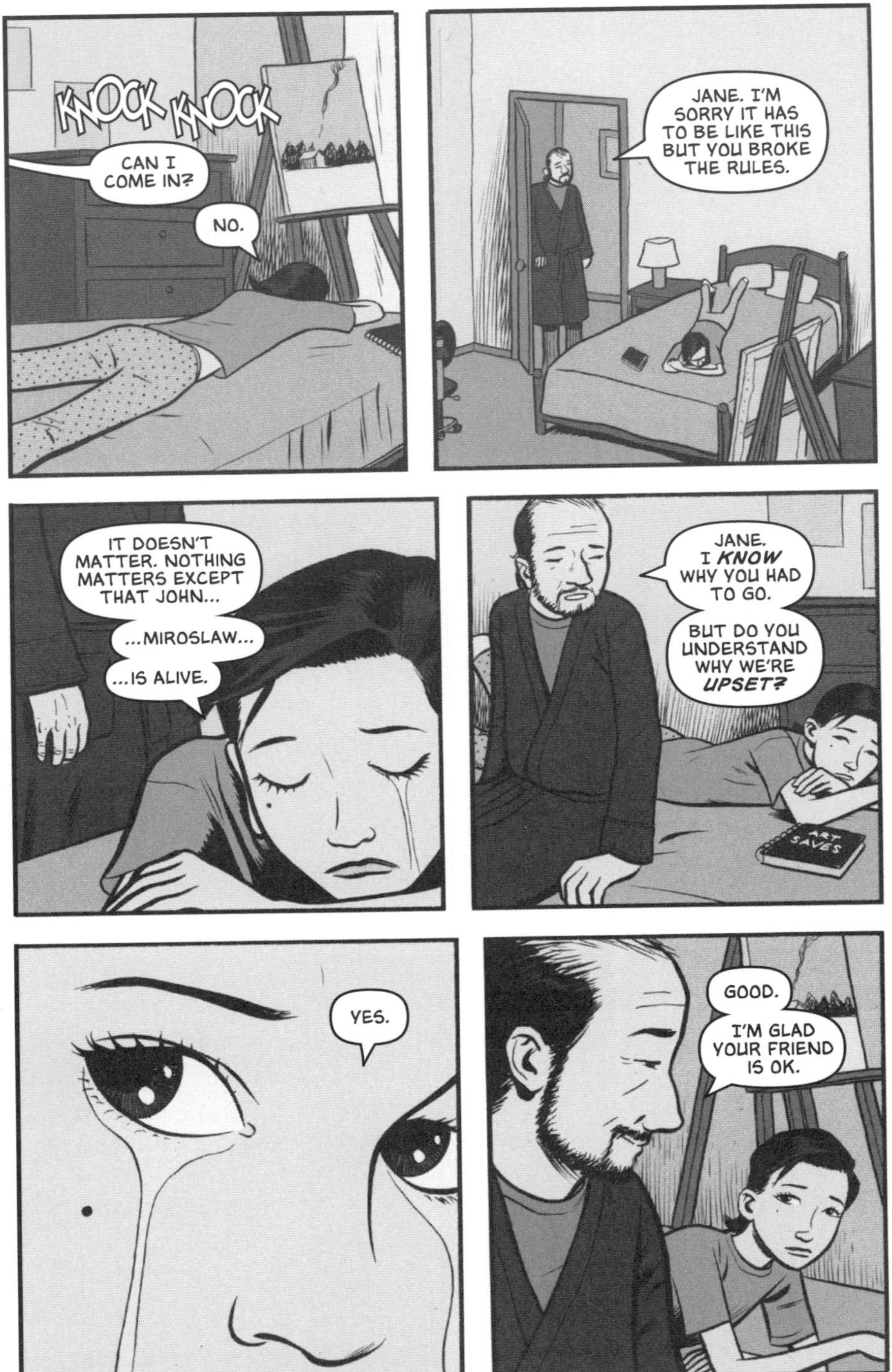
KNOCK KNOCK
CAN I COME IN?
NO.
JANE. I'M SORRY IT HAS TO BE LIKE THIS BUT YOU BROKE THE RULES.
IT DOESN'T MATTER. NOTHING MATTERS EXCEPT THAT JOHN...
...MIROSLAW...
...IS ALIVE.
JANE. I KNOW WHY YOU HAD TO GO.
BUT DO YOU UNDERSTAND WHY WE'RE UPSET?
ART SAVES
YES.
GOOD.
I'M GLAD YOUR FRIEND IS OK.

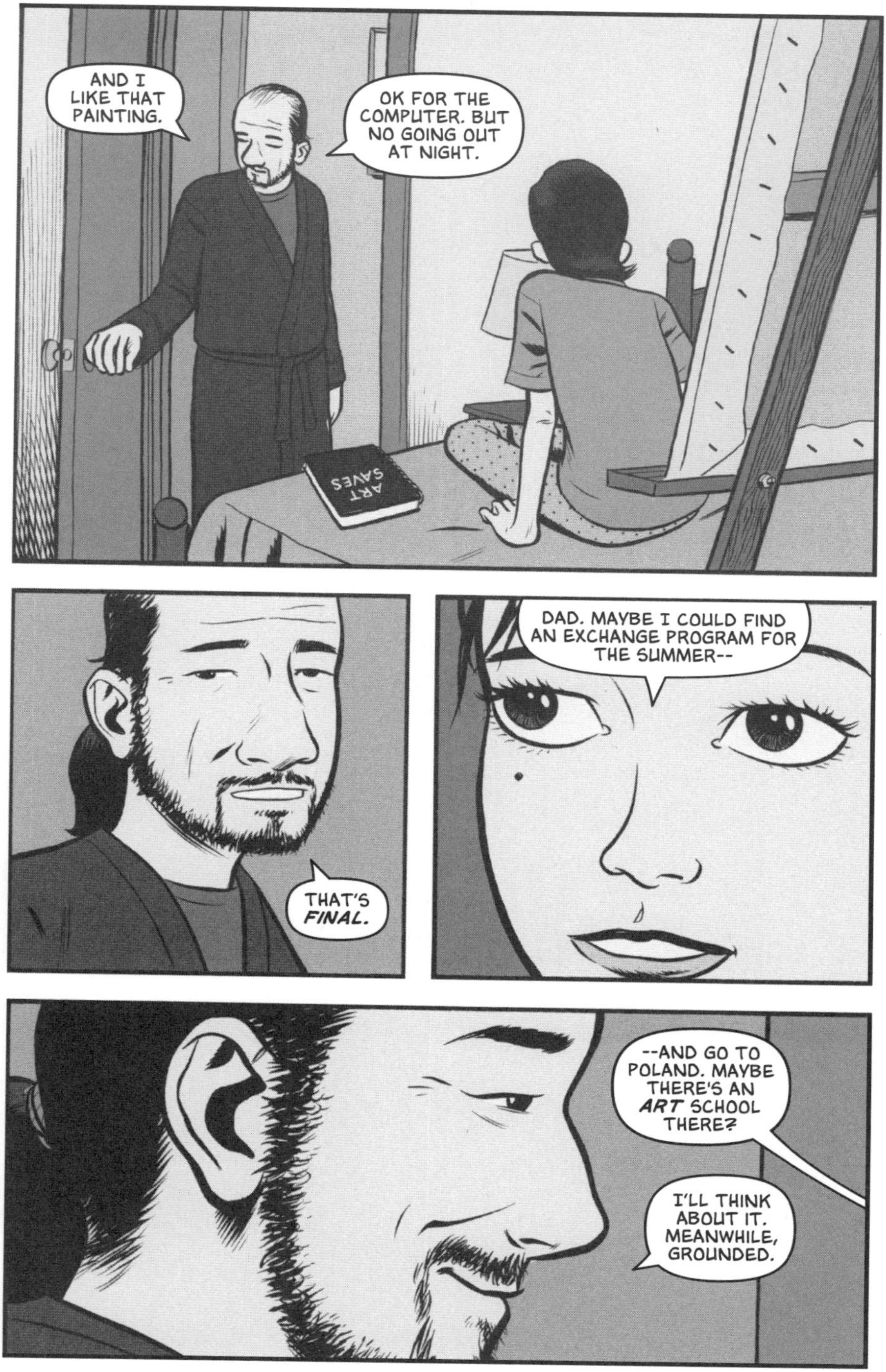
AND I LIKE THAT PAINTING.
OK FOR THE COMPUTER. BUT NO GOING OUT AT NIGHT.
ART SAVES
THAT'S *FINAL.*
DAD. MAYBE I COULD FIND AN EXCHANGE PROGRAM FOR THE SUMMER--
--AND GO TO POLAND. MAYBE THERE'S AN *ART* SCHOOL THERE?
I'LL THINK ABOUT IT. MEANWHILE, GROUNDED.

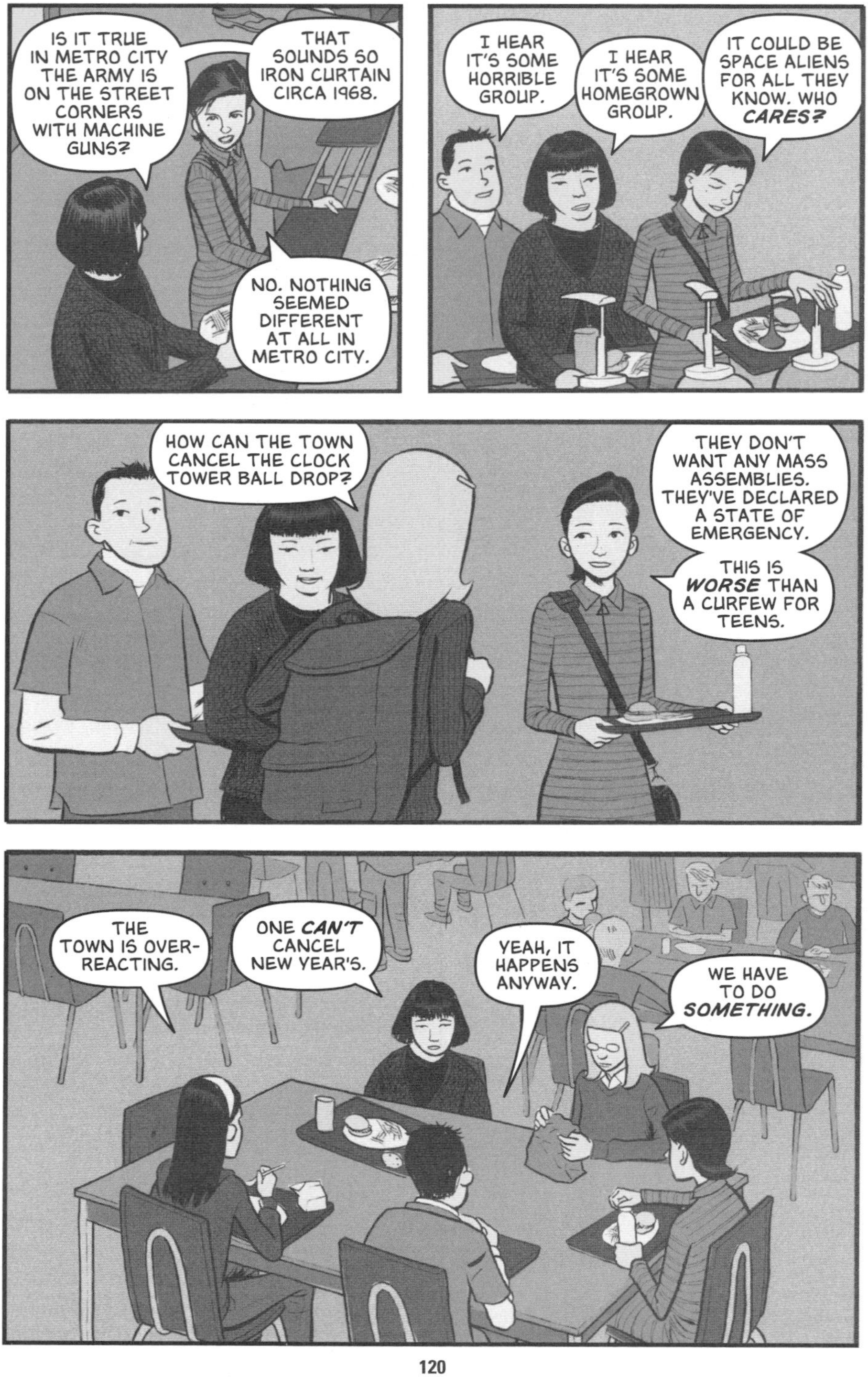
IS IT TRUE IN METRO CITY THE ARMY IS ON THE STREET CORNERS WITH MACHINE GUNS?
THAT SOUNDS SO IRON CURTAIN CIRCA 1968.
NO. NOTHING SEEMED DIFFERENT AT ALL IN METRO CITY.
I HEAR IT'S SOME HORRIBLE GROUP.
I HEAR IT'S SOME HOMEGROWN GROUP.
IT COULD BE SPACE ALIENS FOR ALL THEY KNOW. WHO *CARES?*
HOW CAN THE TOWN CANCEL THE CLOCK TOWER BALL DROP?
THEY DON'T WANT ANY MASS ASSEMBLIES. THEY'VE DECLARED A STATE OF EMERGENCY.
THIS IS *WORSE* THAN A CURFEW FOR TEENS.
THE TOWN IS OVER-REACTING.
ONE *CAN'T* CANCEL NEW YEAR'S.
YEAH, IT HAPPENS ANYWAY.
WE HAVE TO DO *SOMETHING.*

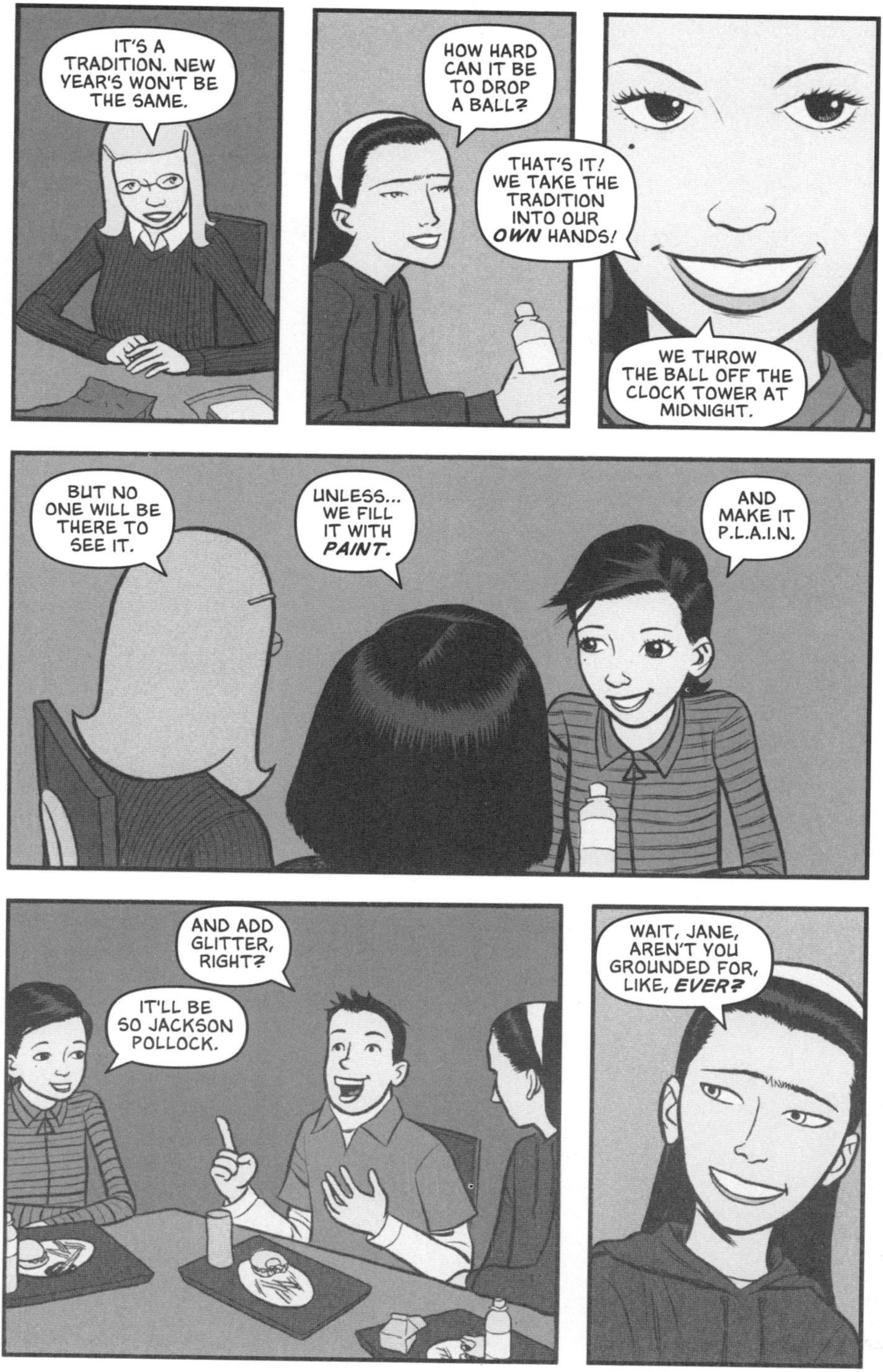
IT'S A TRADITION. NEW YEAR'S WON'T BE THE SAME.
HOW HARD CAN IT BE TO DROP A BALL?
THAT'S IT! WE TAKE THE TRADITION INTO OUR OWN HANDS!
WE THROW THE BALL OFF THE CLOCK TOWER AT MIDNIGHT.
BUT NO ONE WILL BE THERE TO SEE IT.
UNLESS... WE FILL IT WITH PAINT.
AND MAKE IT P.L.A.I.N.
AND ADD GLITTER, RIGHT?
IT'LL BE SO JACKSON POLLOCK.
WAIT, JANE, AREN'T YOU GROUNDED FOR, LIKE, EVER?

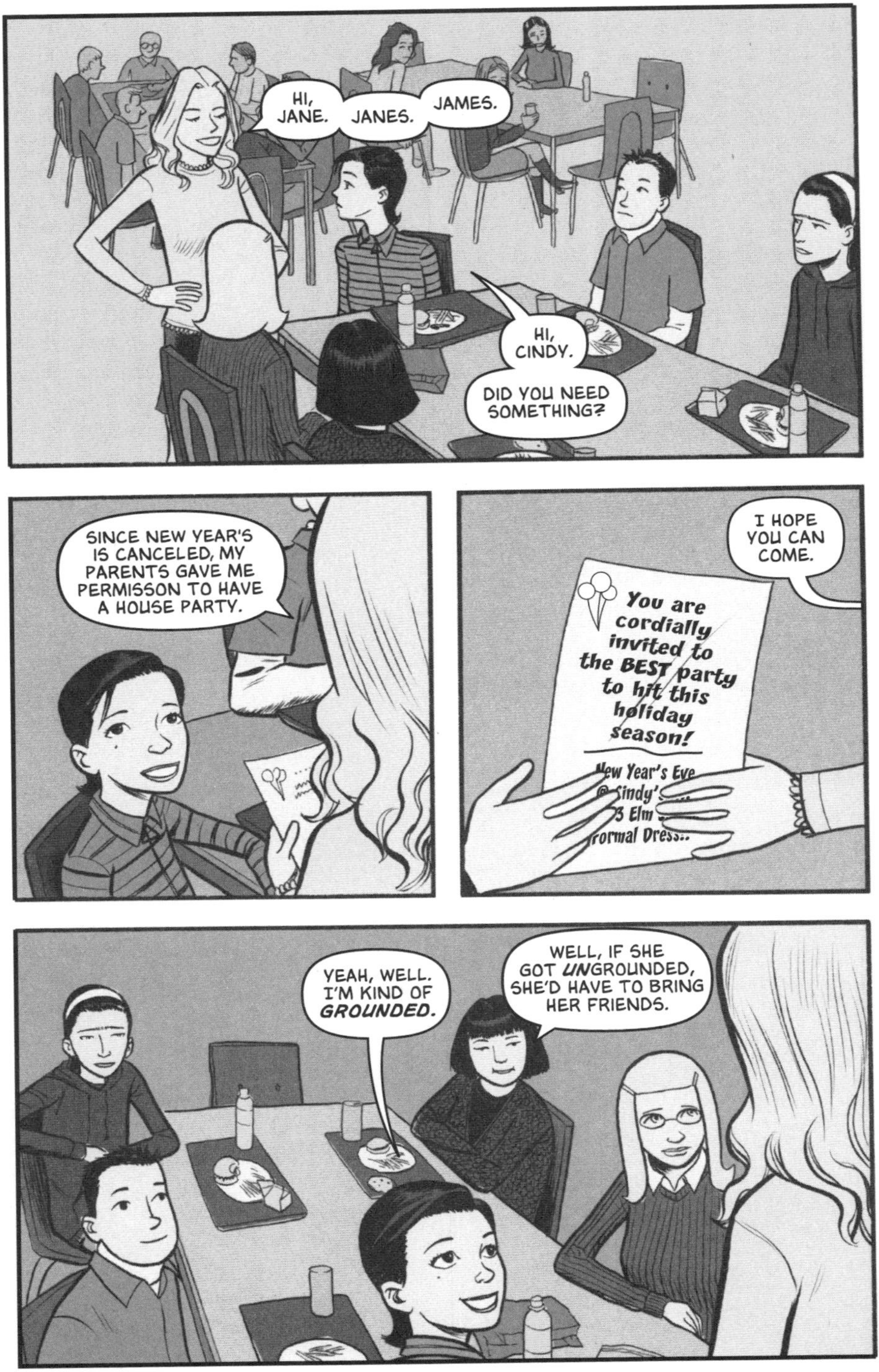
HI, JANE.
JANES.
JAMES.
HI, CINDY.
DID YOU NEED SOMETHING?
SINCE NEW YEAR'S IS CANCELED, MY PARENTS GAVE ME PERMISSON TO HAVE A HOUSE PARTY.
I HOPE YOU CAN COME.
You are cordially invited to the BEST party to hit this holiday season!
YEAH, WELL. I'M KIND OF *GROUNDED*.
WELL, IF SHE GOT *UN*GROUNDED, SHE'D HAVE TO BRING HER FRIENDS.

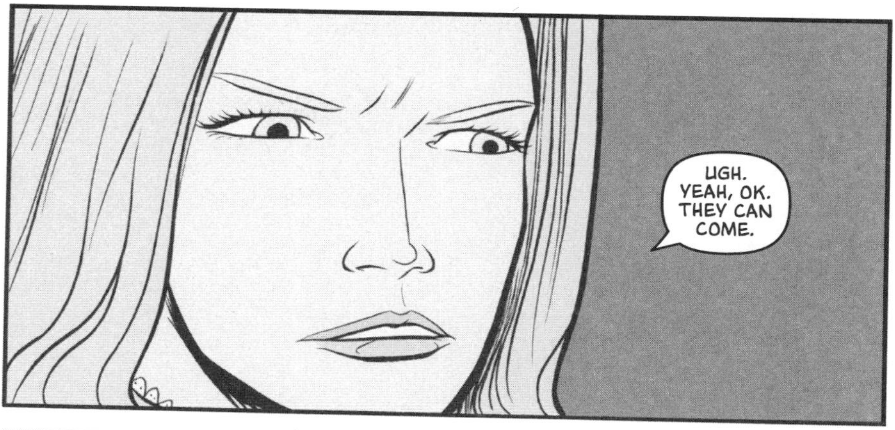
UGH.
YEAH, OK.
THEY CAN
COME.

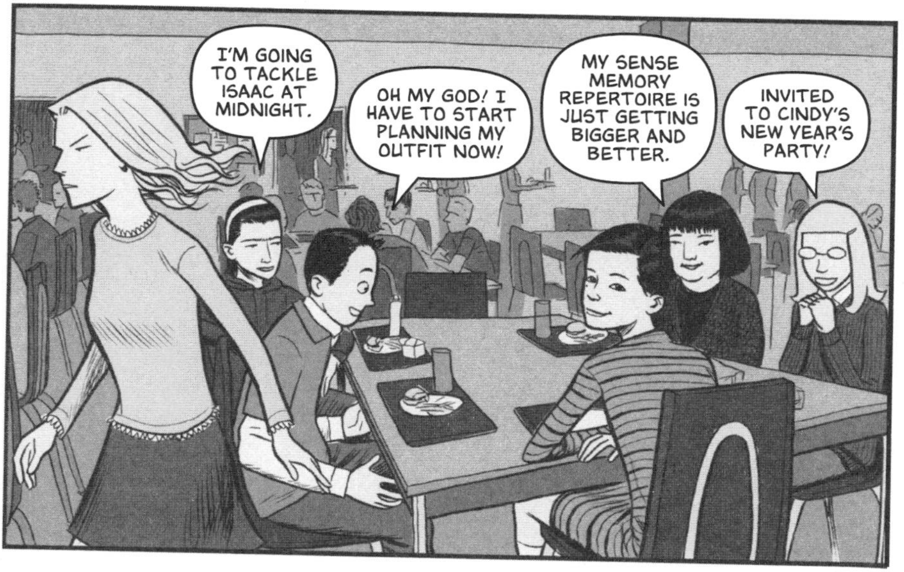
I'M GOING TO TACKLE ISAAC AT MIDNIGHT.
OH MY GOD! I HAVE TO START PLANNING MY OUTFIT NOW!
MY SENSE MEMORY REPERTOIRE IS JUST GETTING BIGGER AND BETTER.
INVITED TO CINDY'S NEW YEAR'S PARTY!

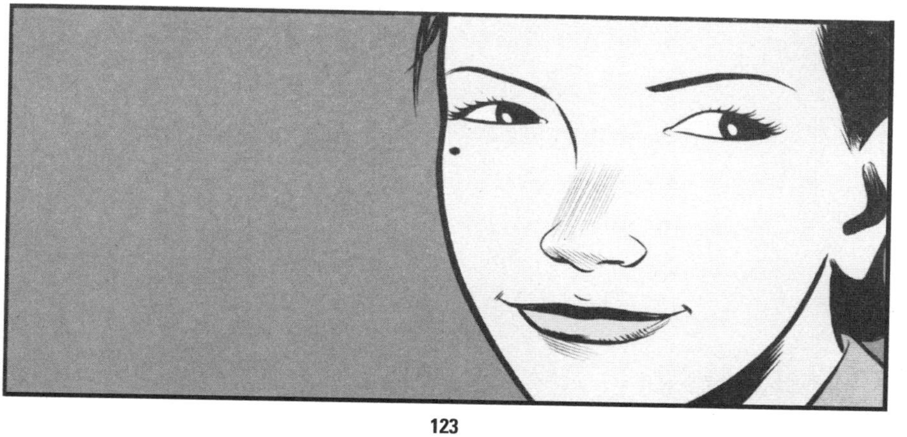

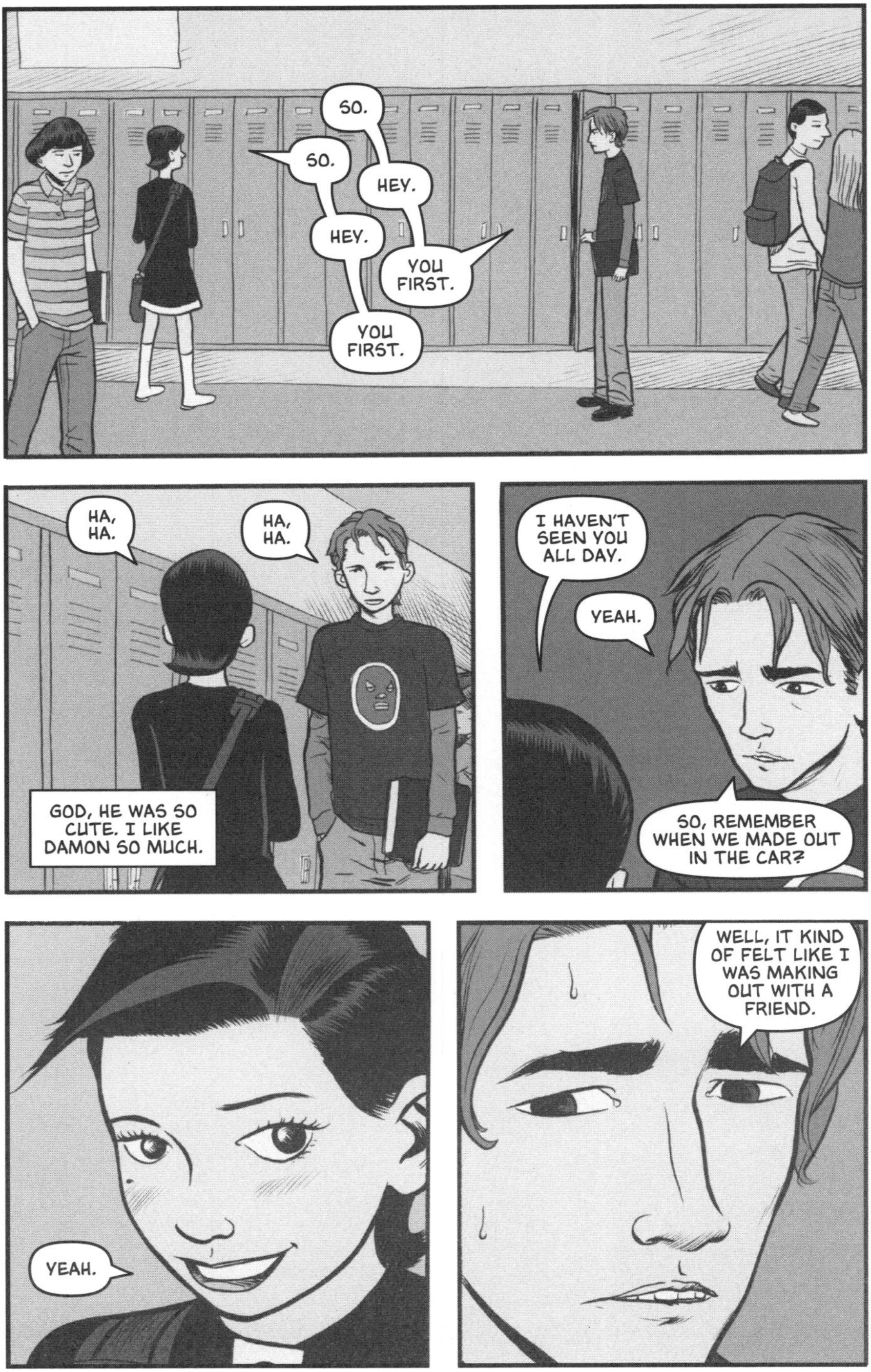
SO.
SO.
HEY.
HEY.
YOU FIRST.
YOU FIRST.
HA, HA.
HA, HA.
GOD, HE WAS SO CUTE. I LIKE DAMON SO MUCH.
I HAVEN'T SEEN YOU ALL DAY.
YEAH.
SO, REMEMBER WHEN WE MADE OUT IN THE CAR?
YEAH.
WELL, IT KIND OF FELT LIKE I WAS MAKING OUT WITH A FRIEND.

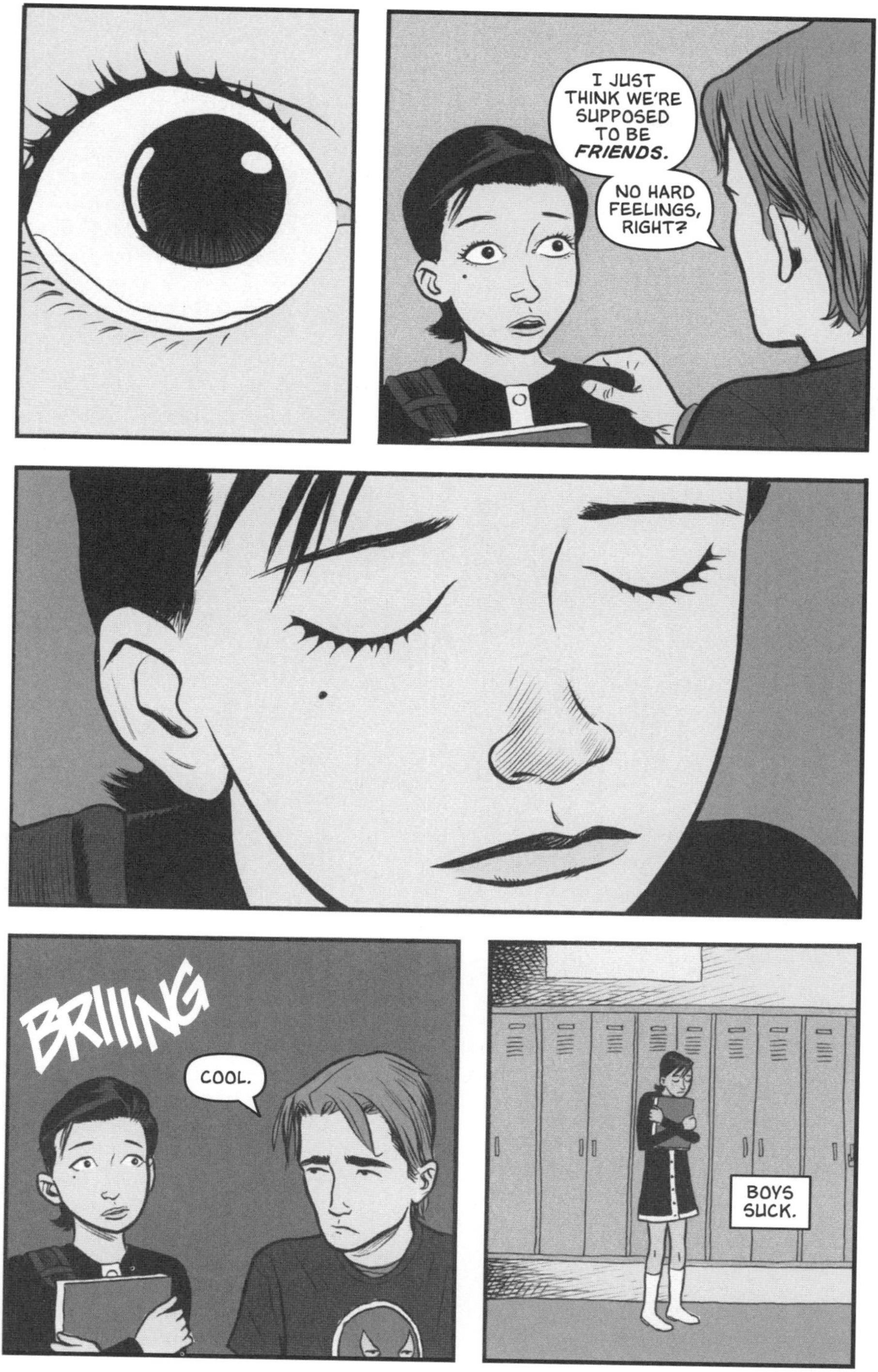
I JUST THINK WE'RE SUPPOSED TO BE *FRIENDS.*
NO HARD FEELINGS, RIGHT?
BRIIING
COOL.
BOYS SUCK.

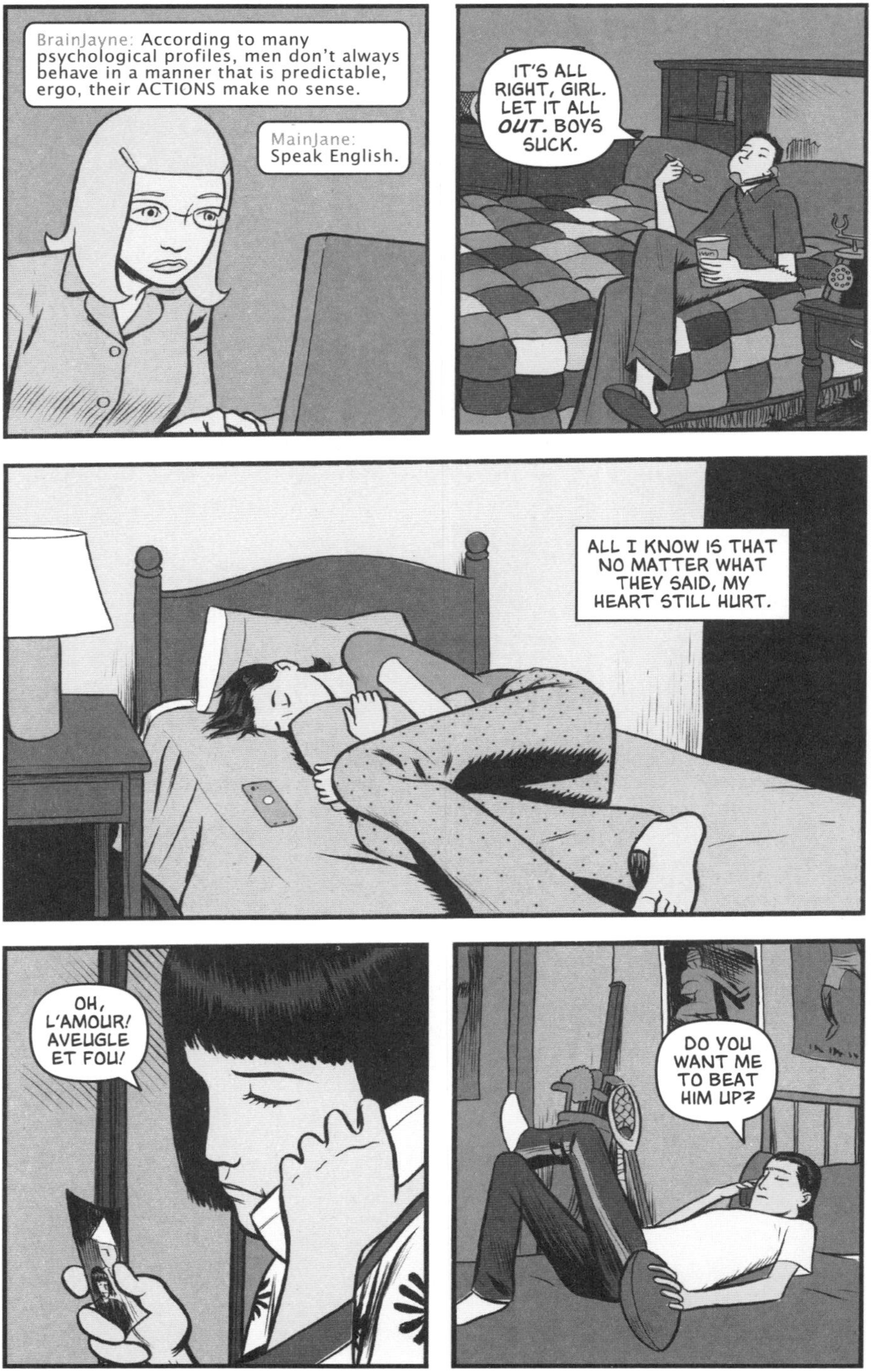
BrainJayne: According to many psychological profiles, men don't always behave in a manner that is predictable, ergo, their ACTIONS make no sense.
MainJane: Speak English.
IT'S ALL RIGHT, GIRL. LET IT ALL OUT. BOYS SUCK.
ALL I KNOW IS THAT NO MATTER WHAT THEY SAID, MY HEART STILL HURT.
OH, L'AMOUR! AVEUGLE ET FOU!
DO YOU WANT ME TO BEAT HIM UP?

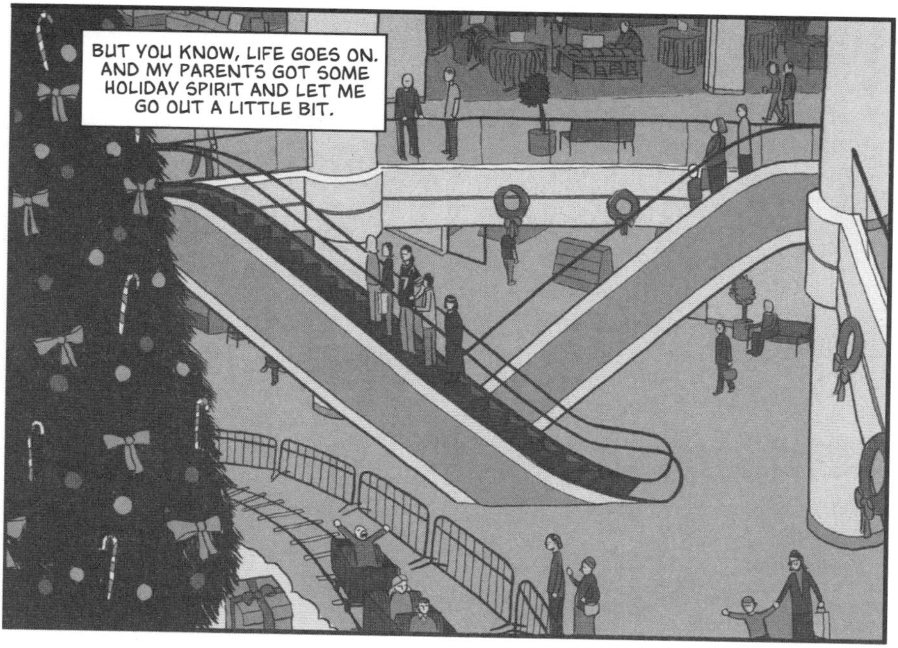
BUT YOU KNOW, LIFE GOES ON. AND MY PARENTS GOT SOME HOLIDAY SPIRIT AND LET ME GO OUT A LITTLE BIT.

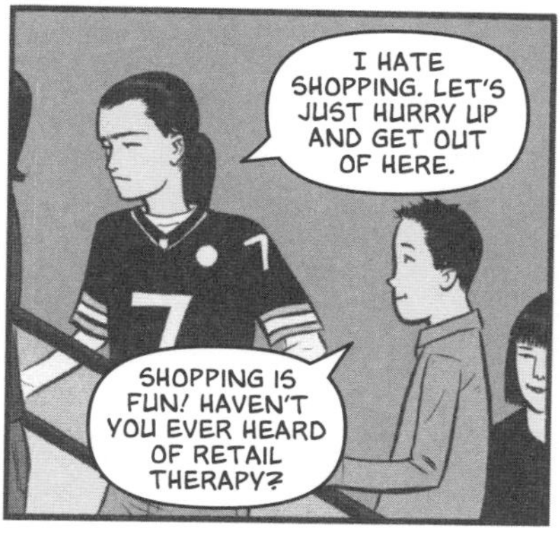
I HATE SHOPPING. LET'S JUST HURRY UP AND GET OUT OF HERE.
SHOPPING IS FUN! HAVEN'T YOU EVER HEARD OF RETAIL THERAPY?

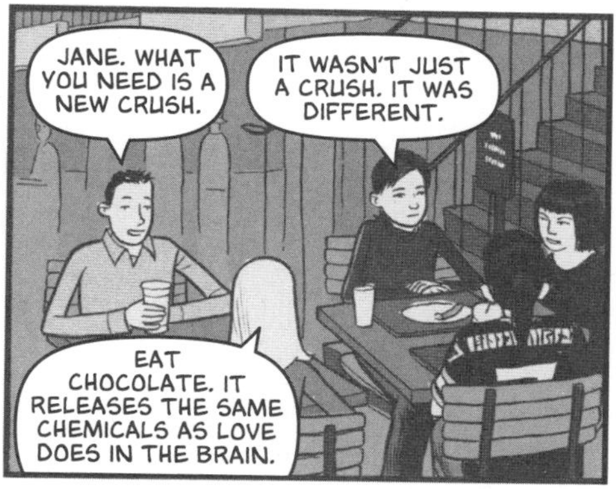
JANE. WHAT YOU NEED IS A NEW CRUSH.
IT WASN'T JUST A CRUSH. IT WAS DIFFERENT.
EAT CHOCOLATE. IT RELEASES THE SAME CHEMICALS AS LOVE DOES IN THE BRAIN.

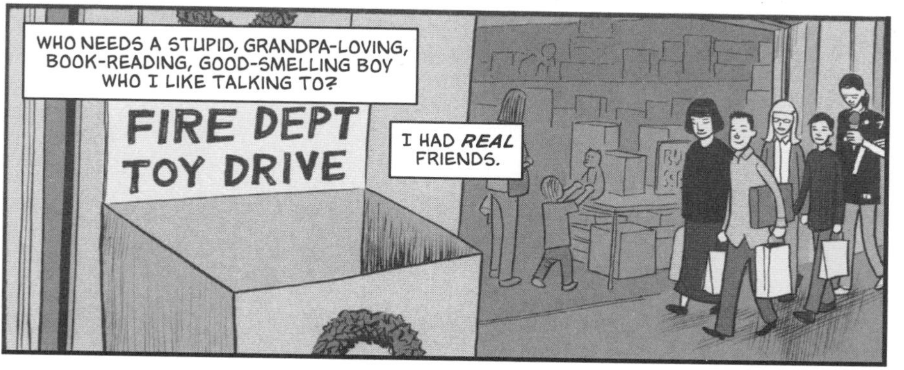
WHO NEEDS A STUPID, GRANDPA-LOVING, BOOK-READING, GOOD-SMELLING BOY WHO I LIKE TALKING TO?
FIRE DEPT TOY DRIVE
I HAD *REAL* FRIENDS.

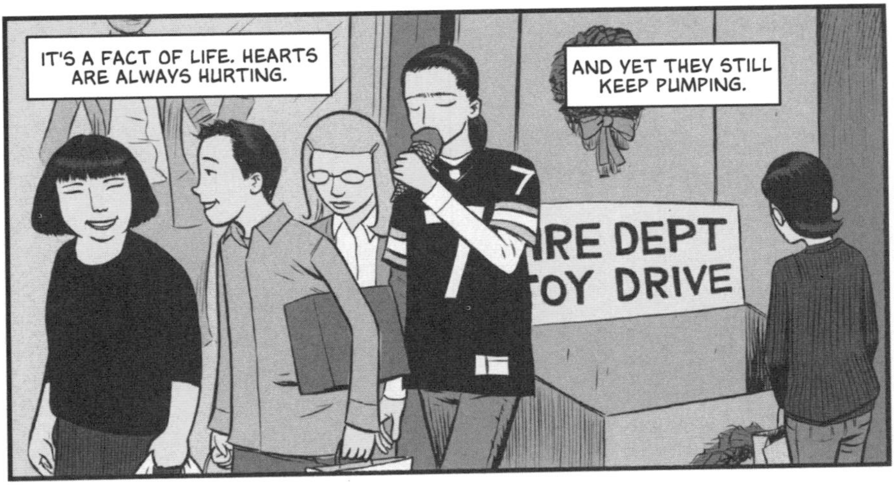
IT'S A FACT OF LIFE. HEARTS ARE ALWAYS HURTING.
AND YET THEY STILL KEEP PUMPING.
IRE DEPT
TOY DRIVE

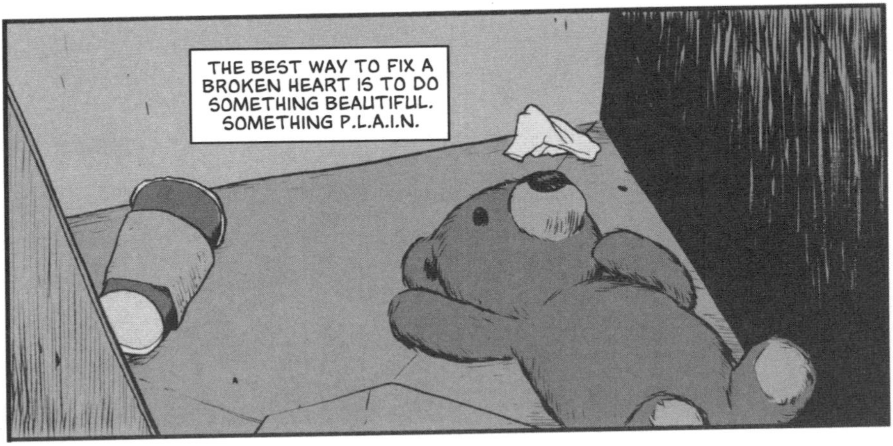
THE BEST WAY TO FIX A BROKEN HEART IS TO DO SOMETHING BEAUTIFUL. SOMETHING P.L.A.I.N.

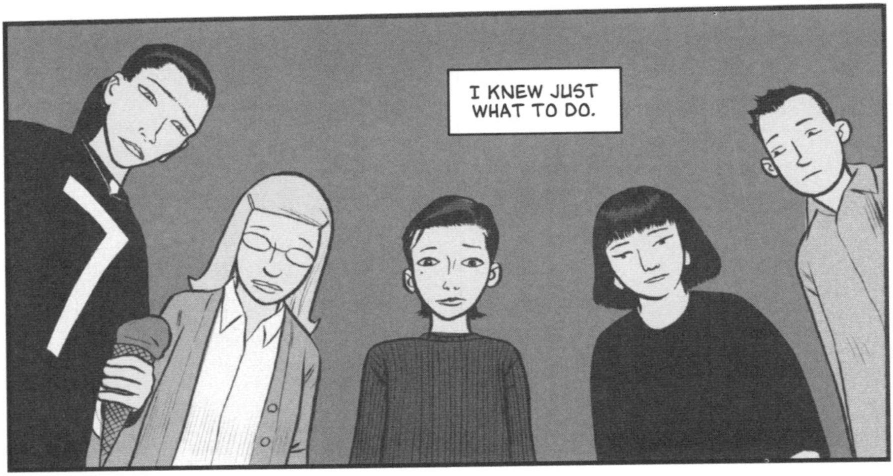
I KNEW JUST WHAT TO DO.

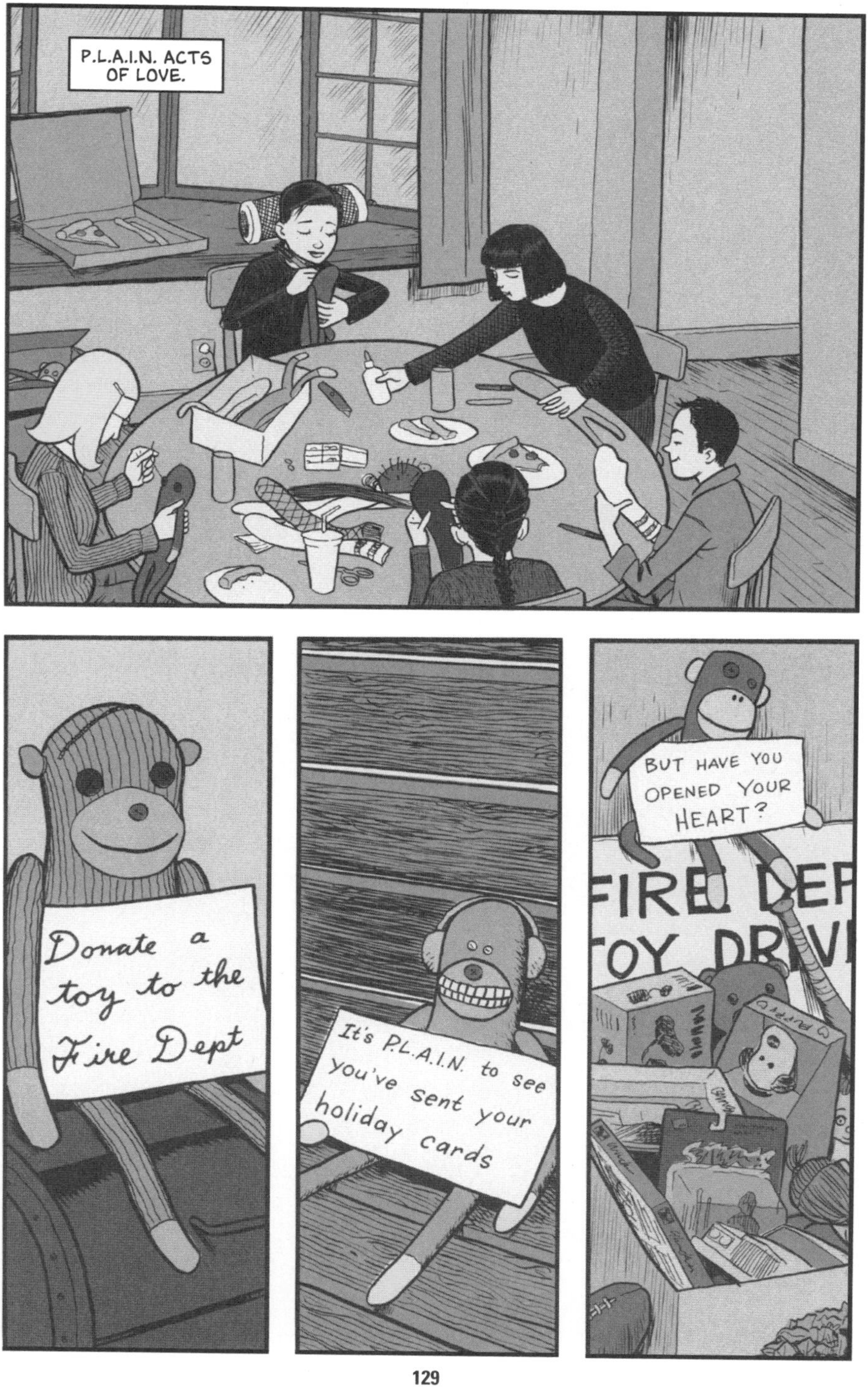
P.L.A.I.N. ACTS OF LOVE.
Donate a toy to the Fire Dept
It's P.L.A.I.N. to see you've sent your holiday cards
BUT HAVE YOU OPENED YOUR HEART?
FIRE DEP
TOY DRIV

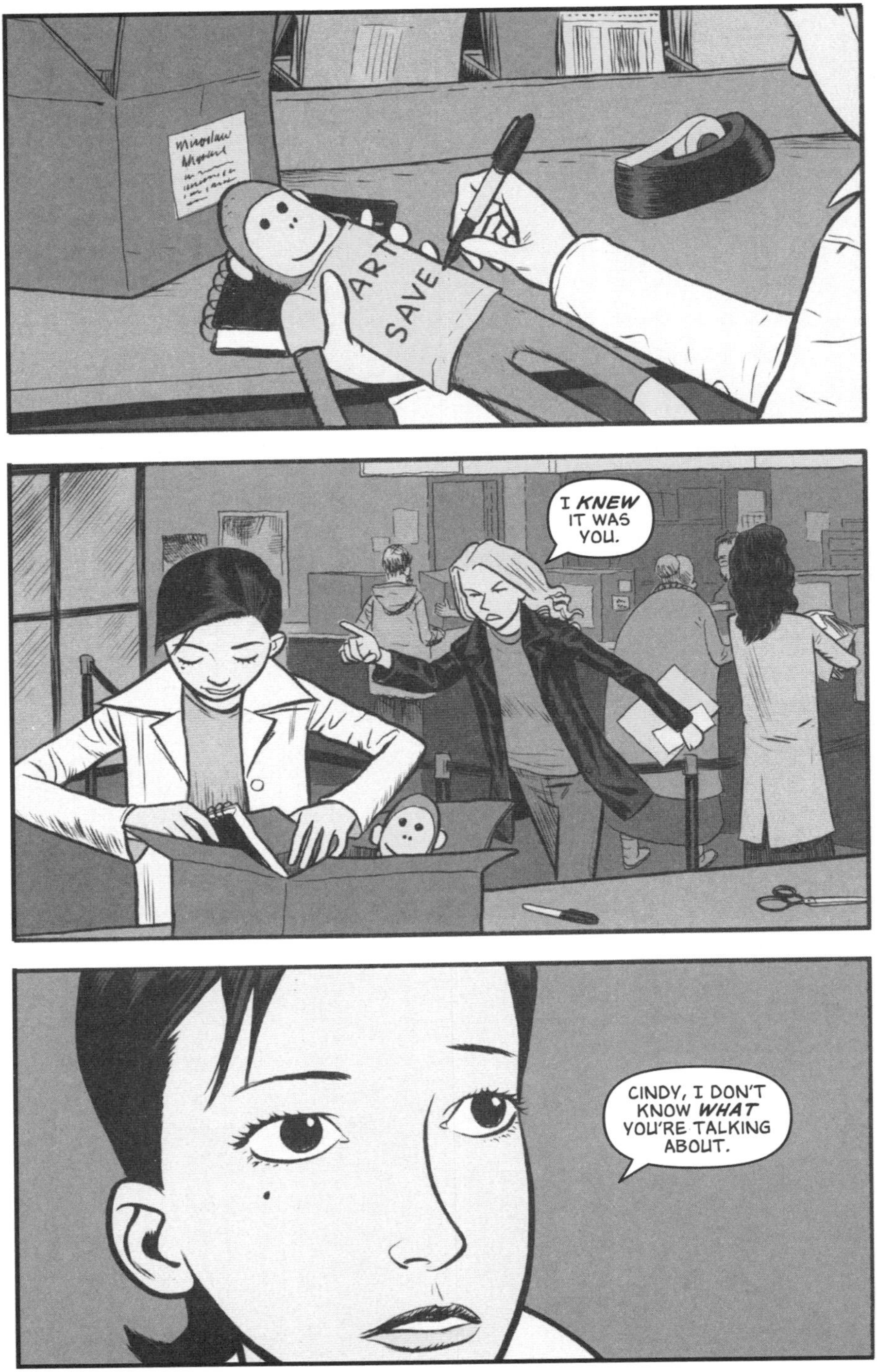
ART
SAVE
I KNEW IT WAS YOU.
CINDY, I DON'T KNOW WHAT YOU'RE TALKING ABOUT.

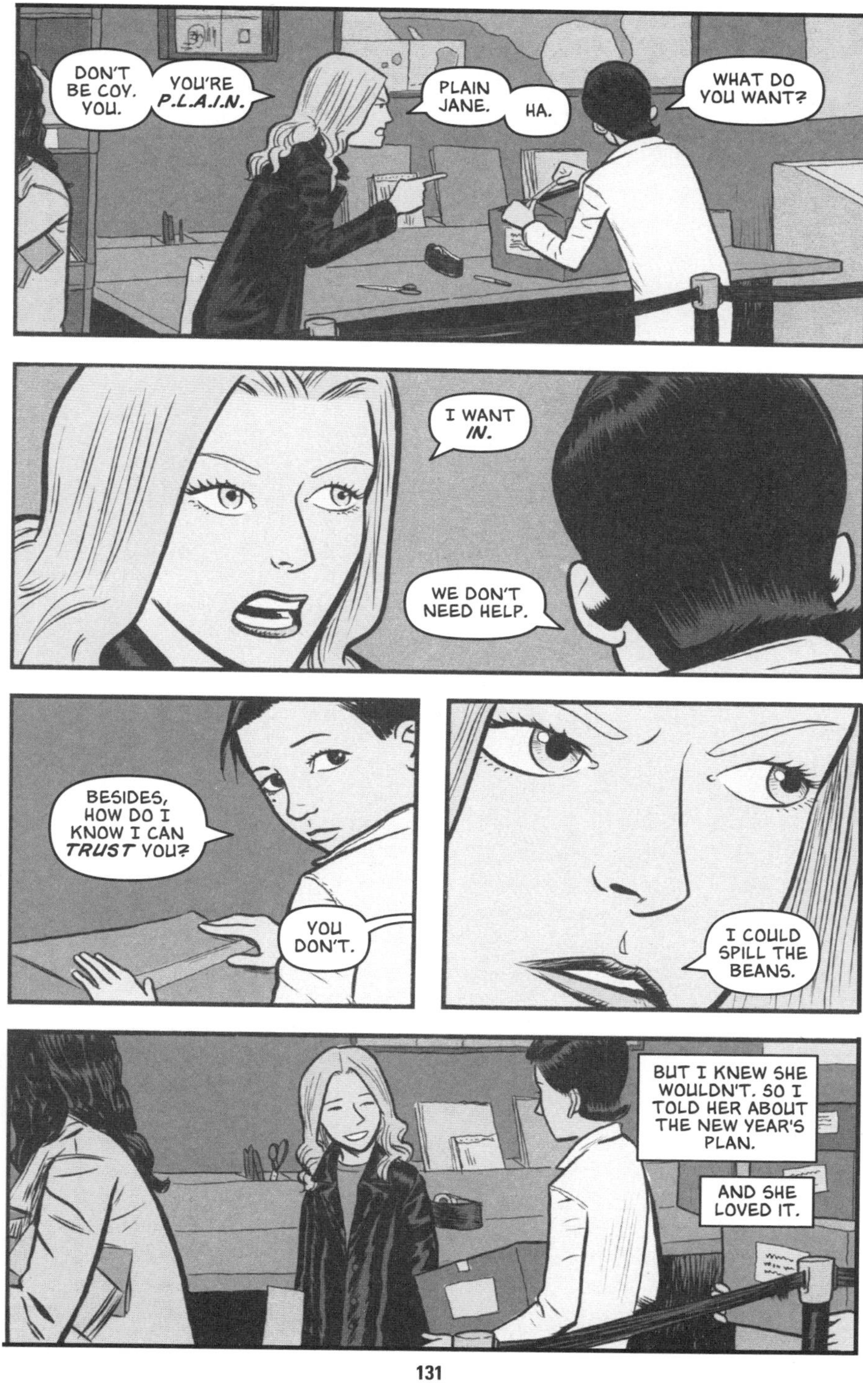
DON'T BE COY. YOU.
YOU'RE *P.L.A.I.N.*
PLAIN JANE.
HA.
WHAT DO YOU WANT?
I WANT *IN.*
WE DON'T NEED HELP.
BESIDES, HOW DO I KNOW I CAN *TRUST* YOU?
YOU DON'T.
I COULD SPILL THE BEANS.
BUT I KNEW SHE WOULDN'T. SO I TOLD HER ABOUT THE NEW YEAR'S PLAN.
AND SHE LOVED IT.

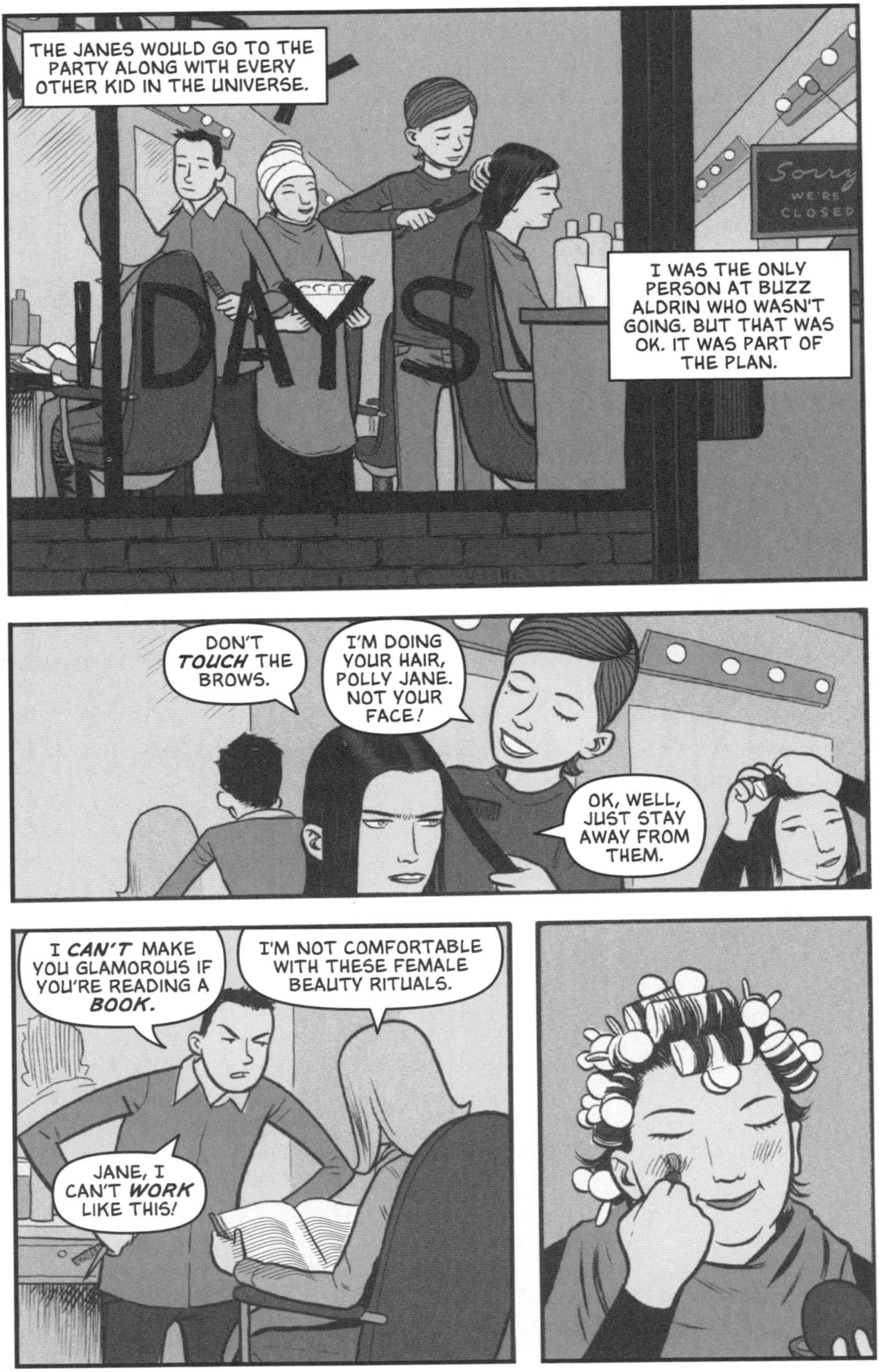
THE JANES WOULD GO TO THE PARTY ALONG WITH EVERY OTHER KID IN THE UNIVERSE.
Sorry WE'RE CLOSED
DAYS
I WAS THE ONLY PERSON AT BUZZ ALDRIN WHO WASN'T GOING. BUT THAT WAS OK. IT WAS PART OF THE PLAN.
DON'T *TOUCH* THE BROWS.
I'M DOING YOUR HAIR, POLLY JANE. NOT YOUR FACE!
OK, WELL, JUST STAY AWAY FROM THEM.
I *CAN'T* MAKE YOU GLAMOROUS IF YOU'RE READING A *BOOK*.
I'M NOT COMFORTABLE WITH THESE FEMALE BEAUTY RITUALS.
JANE, I CAN'T *WORK* LIKE THIS!

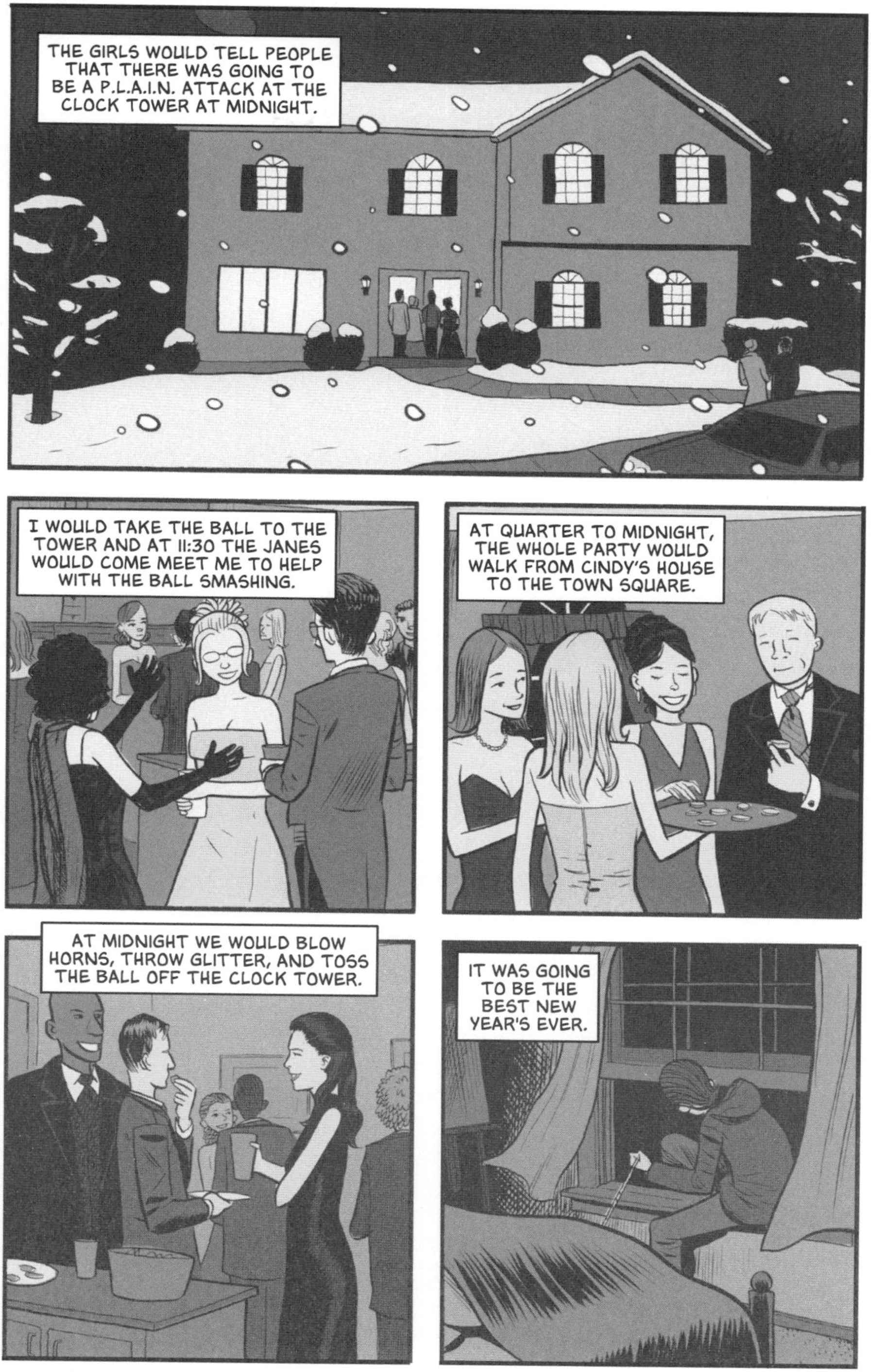
THE GIRLS WOULD TELL PEOPLE THAT THERE WAS GOING TO BE A P.L.A.I.N. ATTACK AT THE CLOCK TOWER AT MIDNIGHT.
I WOULD TAKE THE BALL TO THE TOWER AND AT 11:30 THE JANES WOULD COME MEET ME TO HELP WITH THE BALL SMASHING.
AT QUARTER TO MIDNIGHT, THE WHOLE PARTY WOULD WALK FROM CINDY'S HOUSE TO THE TOWN SQUARE.
AT MIDNIGHT WE WOULD BLOW HORNS, THROW GLITTER, AND TOSS THE BALL OFF THE CLOCK TOWER.
IT WAS GOING TO BE THE BEST NEW YEAR'S EVER.

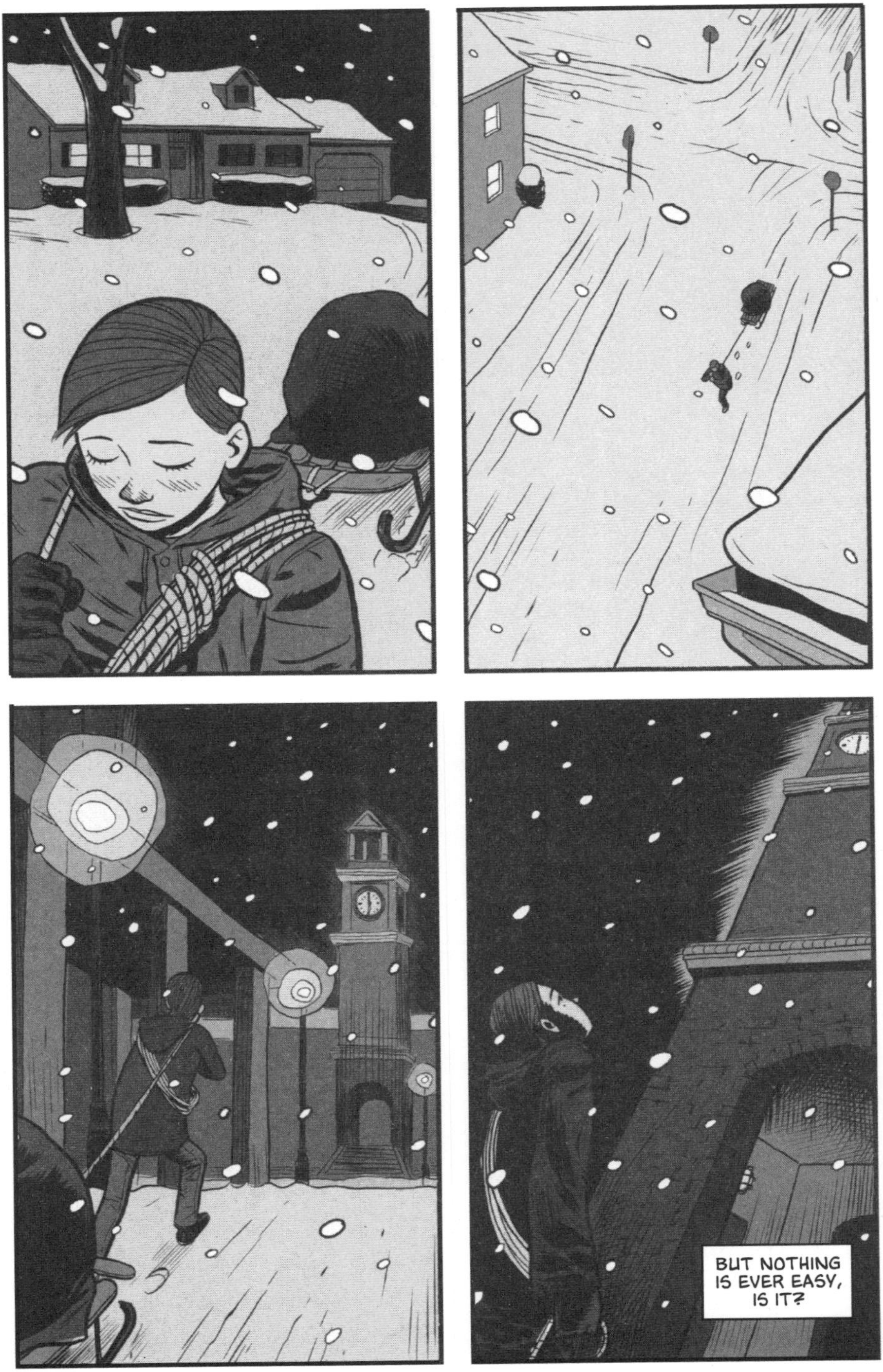
BUT NOTHING IS EVER EASY, IS IT?

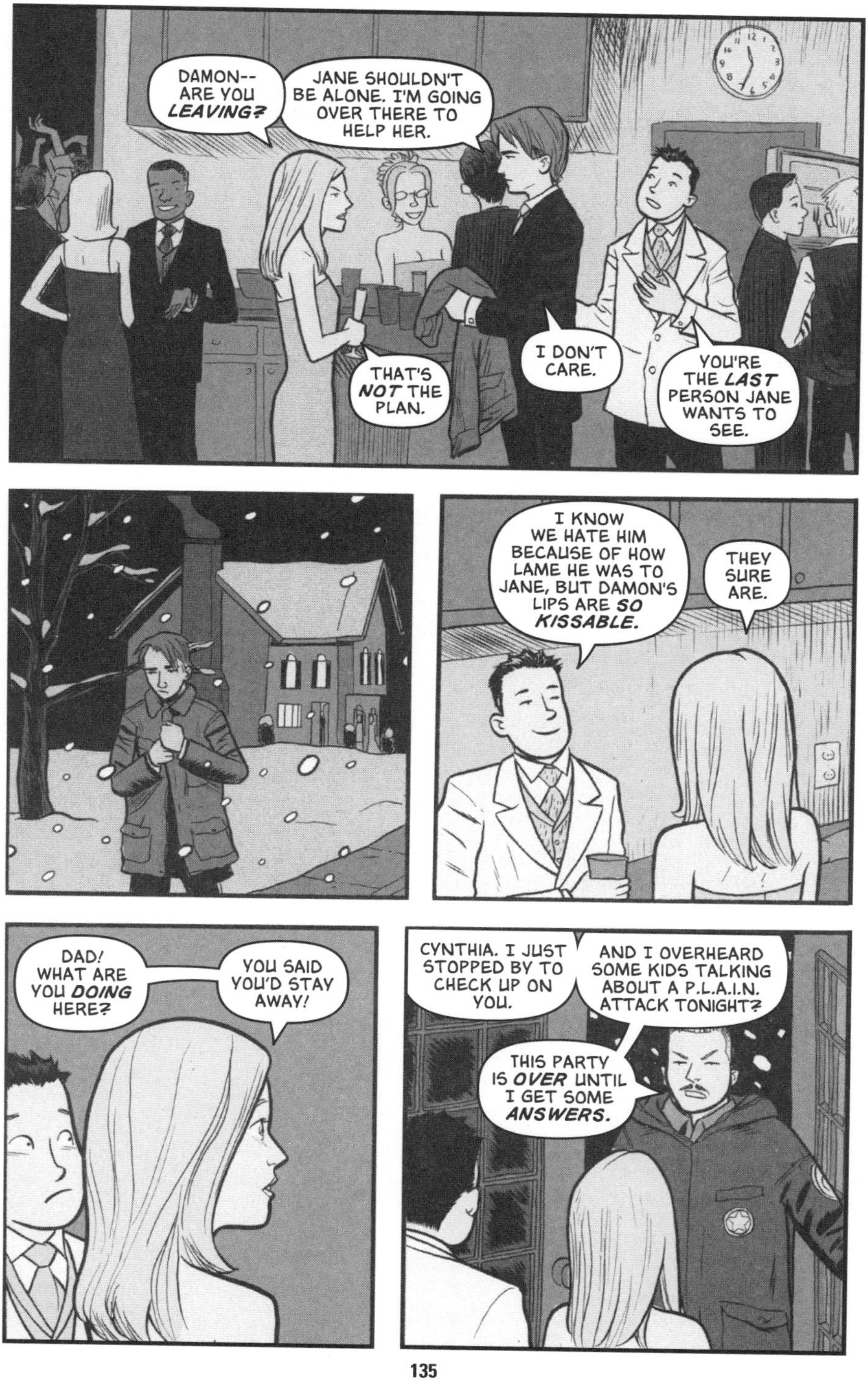
DAMON-- ARE YOU LEAVING?
JANE SHOULDN'T BE ALONE. I'M GOING OVER THERE TO HELP HER.
THAT'S NOT THE PLAN.
I DON'T CARE.
YOU'RE THE LAST PERSON JANE WANTS TO SEE.
I KNOW WE HATE HIM BECAUSE OF HOW LAME HE WAS TO JANE, BUT DAMON'S LIPS ARE SO KISSABLE.
THEY SURE ARE.
DAD! WHAT ARE YOU DOING HERE?
YOU SAID YOU'D STAY AWAY!
CYNTHIA. I JUST STOPPED BY TO CHECK UP ON YOU.
AND I OVERHEARD SOME KIDS TALKING ABOUT A P.L.A.I.N. ATTACK TONIGHT?
THIS PARTY IS OVER UNTIL I GET SOME ANSWERS.

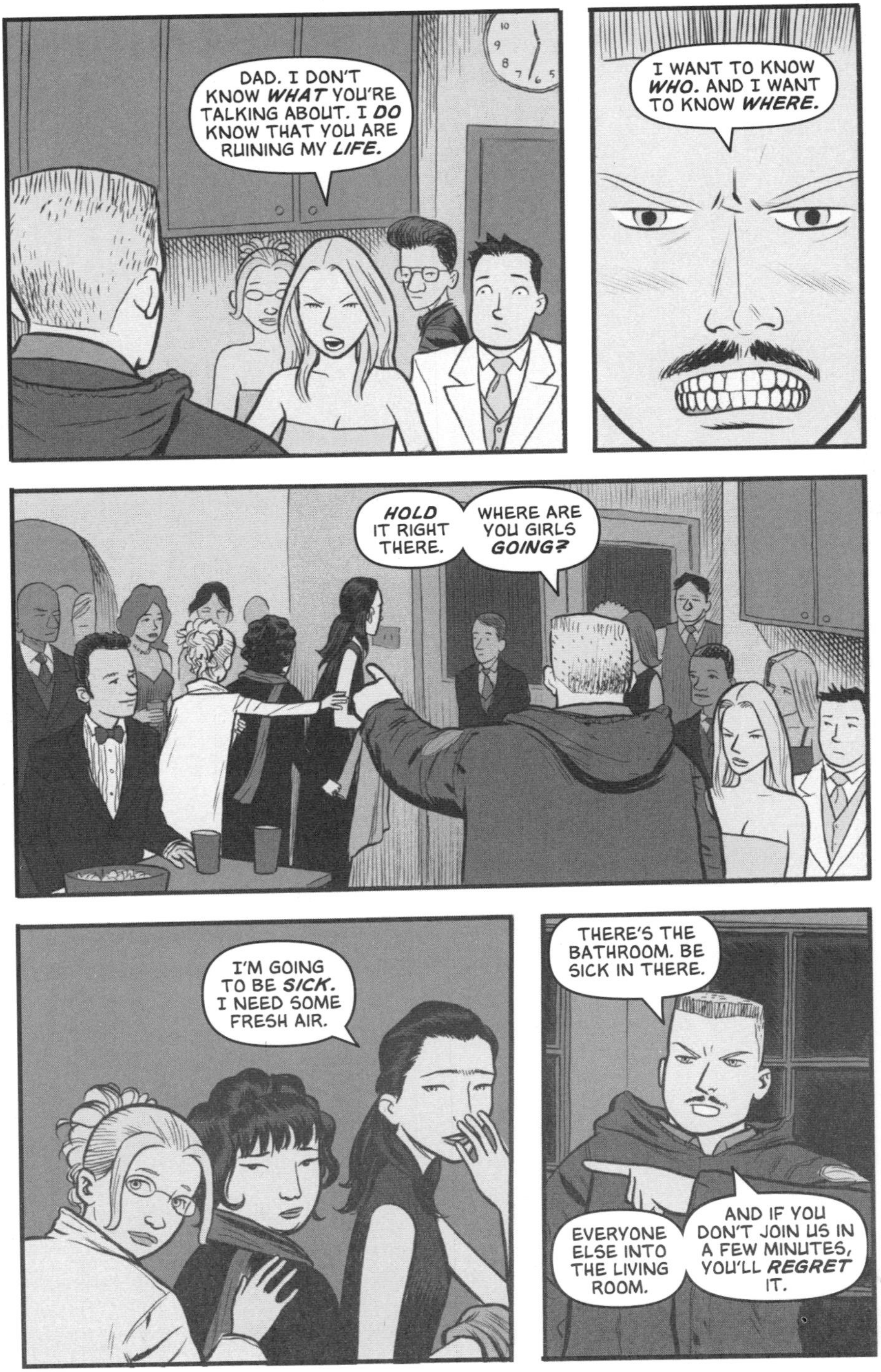
DAD. I DON'T KNOW WHAT YOU'RE TALKING ABOUT. I DO KNOW THAT YOU ARE RUINING MY LIFE.
I WANT TO KNOW WHO. AND I WANT TO KNOW WHERE.
HOLD IT RIGHT THERE.
WHERE ARE YOU GIRLS GOING?
I'M GOING TO BE SICK. I NEED SOME FRESH AIR.
THERE'S THE BATHROOM. BE SICK IN THERE.
EVERYONE ELSE INTO THE LIVING ROOM.
AND IF YOU DON'T JOIN US IN A FEW MINUTES, YOU'LL REGRET IT.

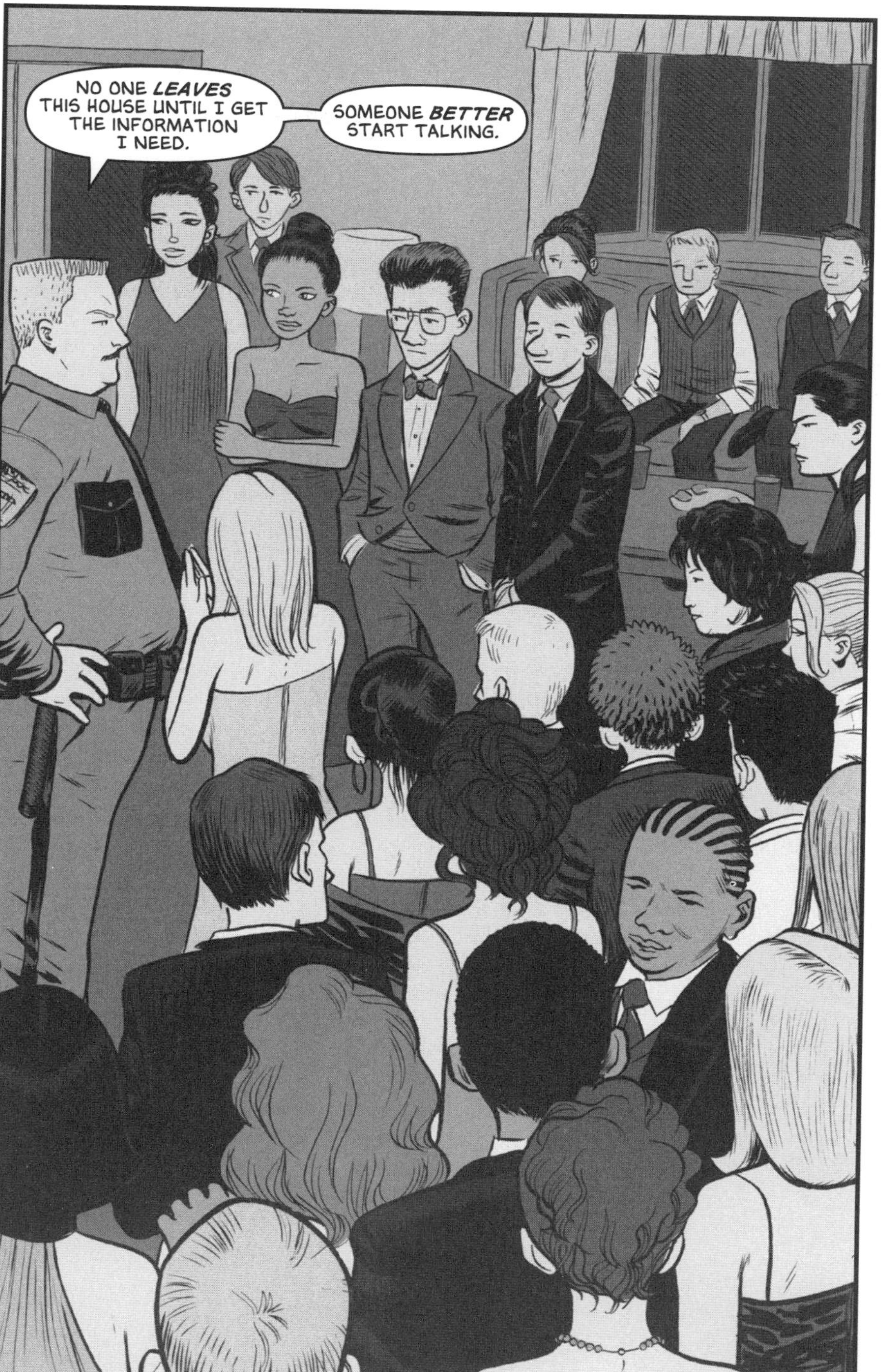
NO ONE LEAVES THIS HOUSE UNTIL I GET THE INFORMATION I NEED.
SOMEONE BETTER START TALKING.

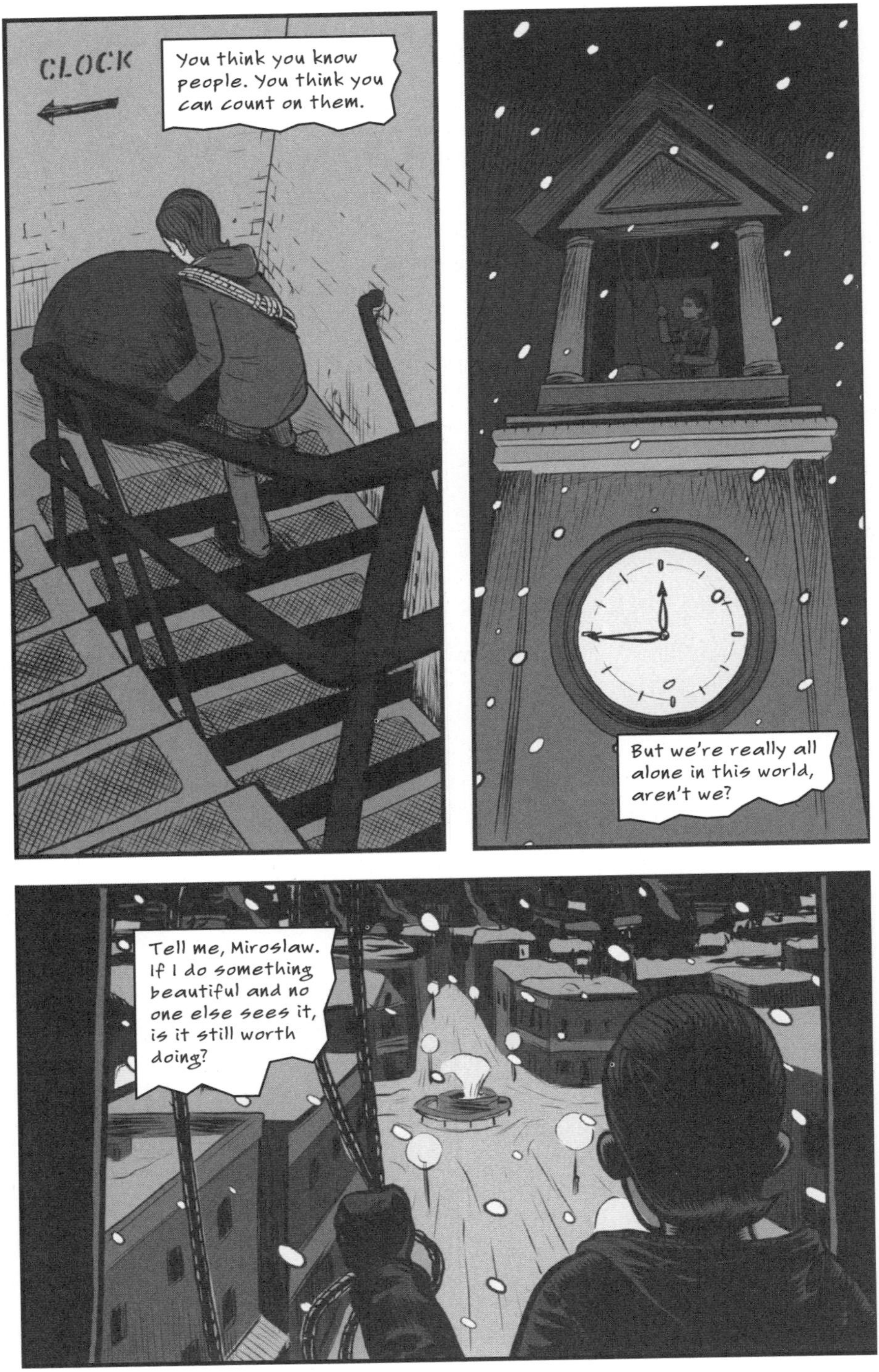
CLOCK
You think you know people. You think you can count on them.
But we're really all alone in this world, aren't we?
Tell me, Miroslaw. If I do something beautiful and no one else sees it, is it still worth doing?

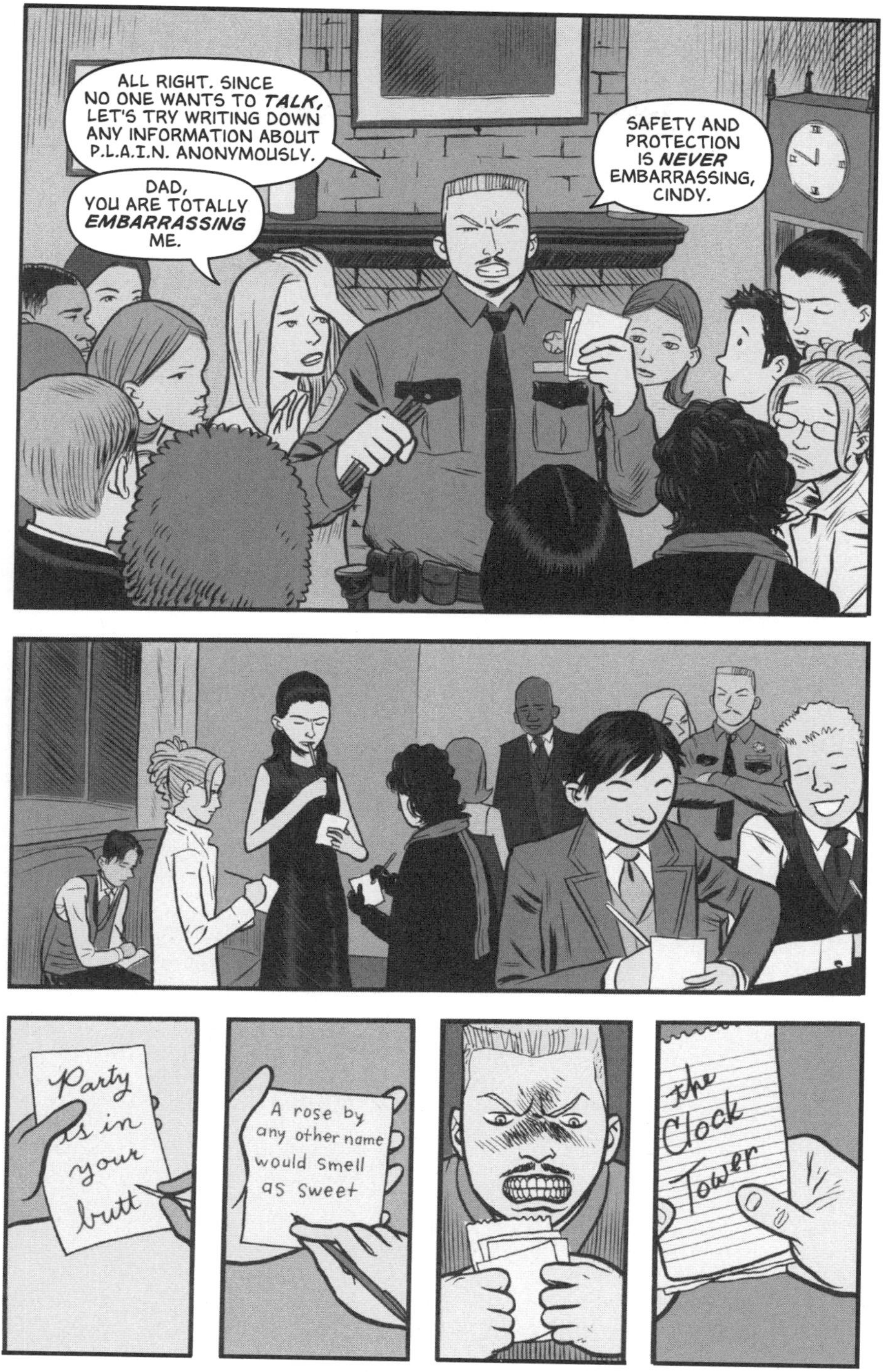
ALL RIGHT. SINCE NO ONE WANTS TO *TALK,* LET'S TRY WRITING DOWN ANY INFORMATION ABOUT P.L.A.I.N. ANONYMOUSLY.
DAD, YOU ARE TOTALLY *EMBARRASSING* ME.
SAFETY AND PROTECTION IS *NEVER* EMBARRASSING, CINDY.
Party is in your butt
A rose by any other name would smell as sweet
the Clock Tower

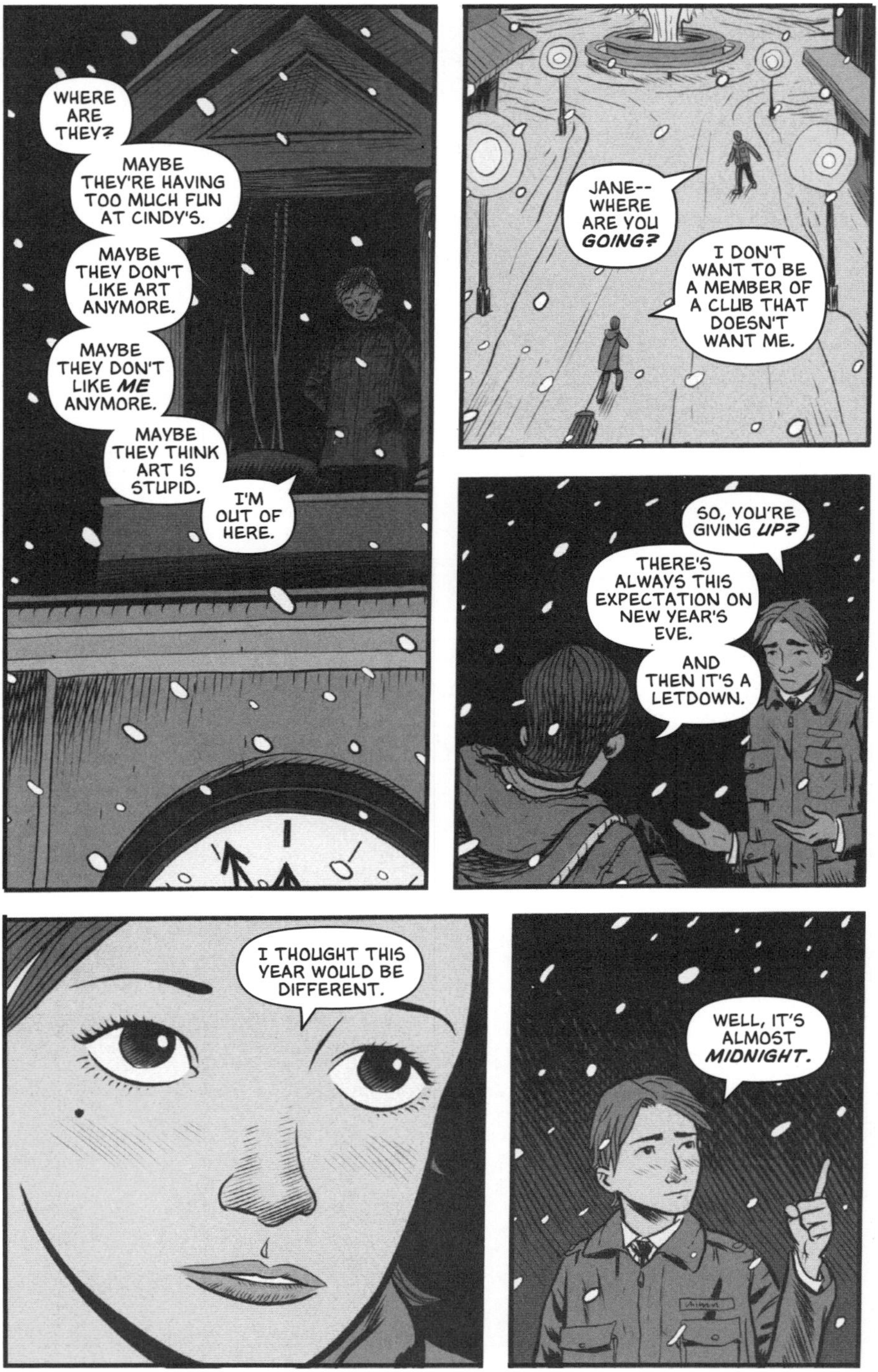
WHERE ARE THEY?
MAYBE THEY'RE HAVING TOO MUCH FUN AT CINDY'S.
MAYBE THEY DON'T LIKE ART ANYMORE.
MAYBE THEY DON'T LIKE *ME* ANYMORE.
MAYBE THEY THINK ART IS STUPID.
I'M OUT OF HERE.
JANE-- WHERE ARE YOU *GOING?*
I DON'T WANT TO BE A MEMBER OF A CLUB THAT DOESN'T WANT ME.
SO, YOU'RE GIVING *UP?*
THERE'S ALWAYS THIS EXPECTATION ON NEW YEAR'S EVE.
AND THEN IT'S A LETDOWN.
I THOUGHT THIS YEAR WOULD BE DIFFERENT.
WELL, IT'S ALMOST *MIDNIGHT.*

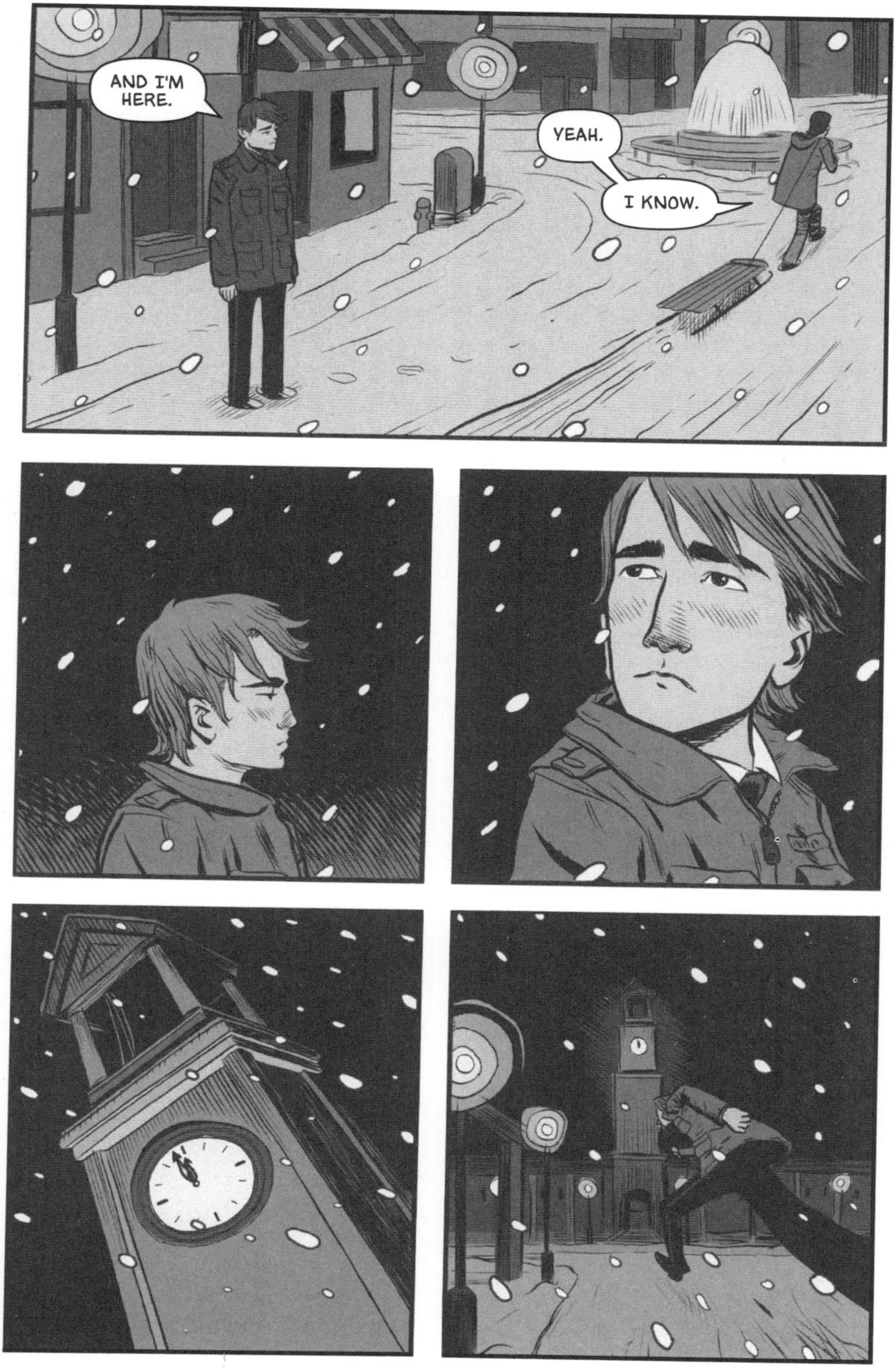
AND I'M HERE.
YEAH.
I KNOW.

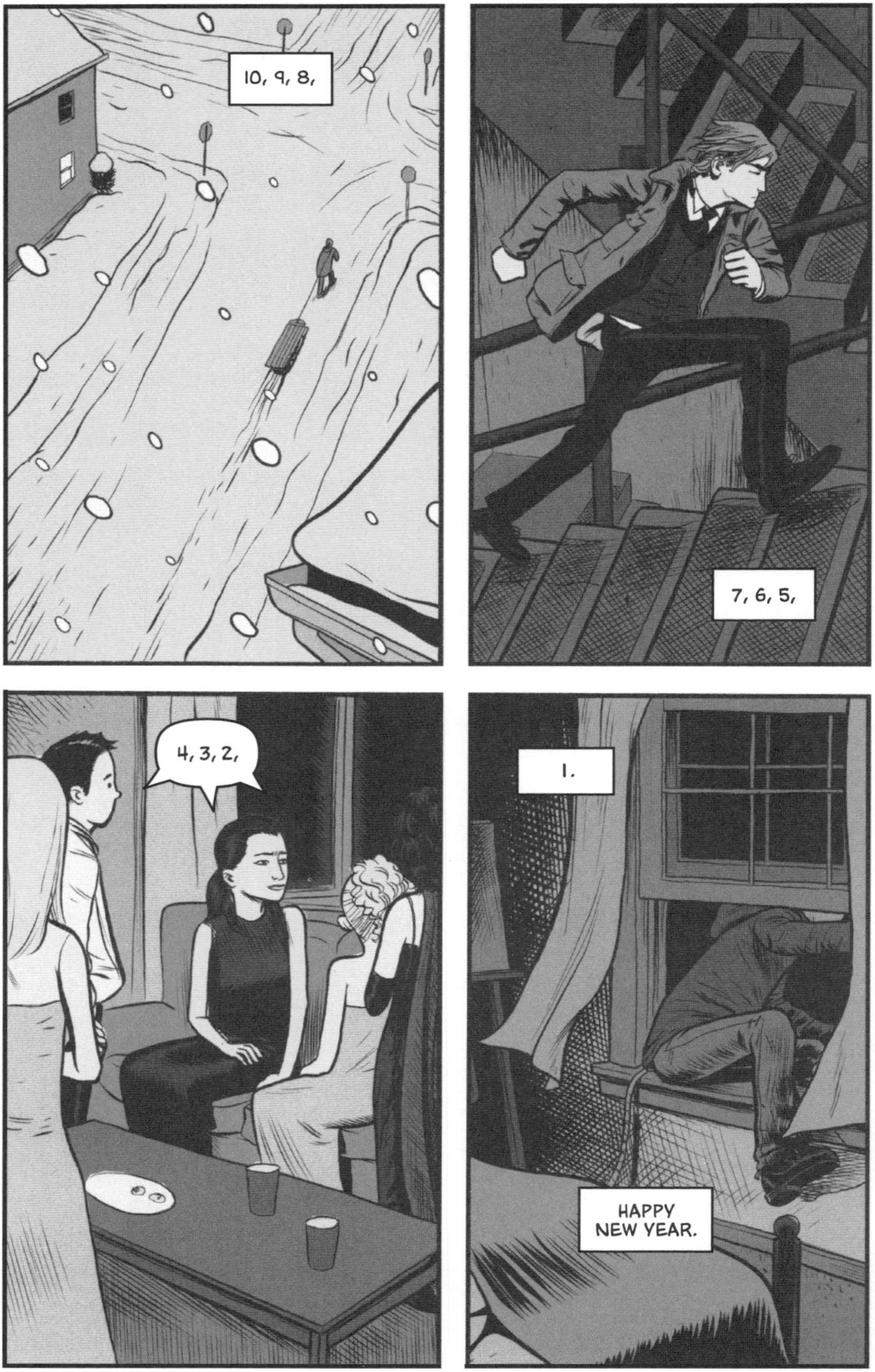
10, 9, 8,
7, 6, 5,
4, 3, 2,
1.
HAPPY NEW YEAR.

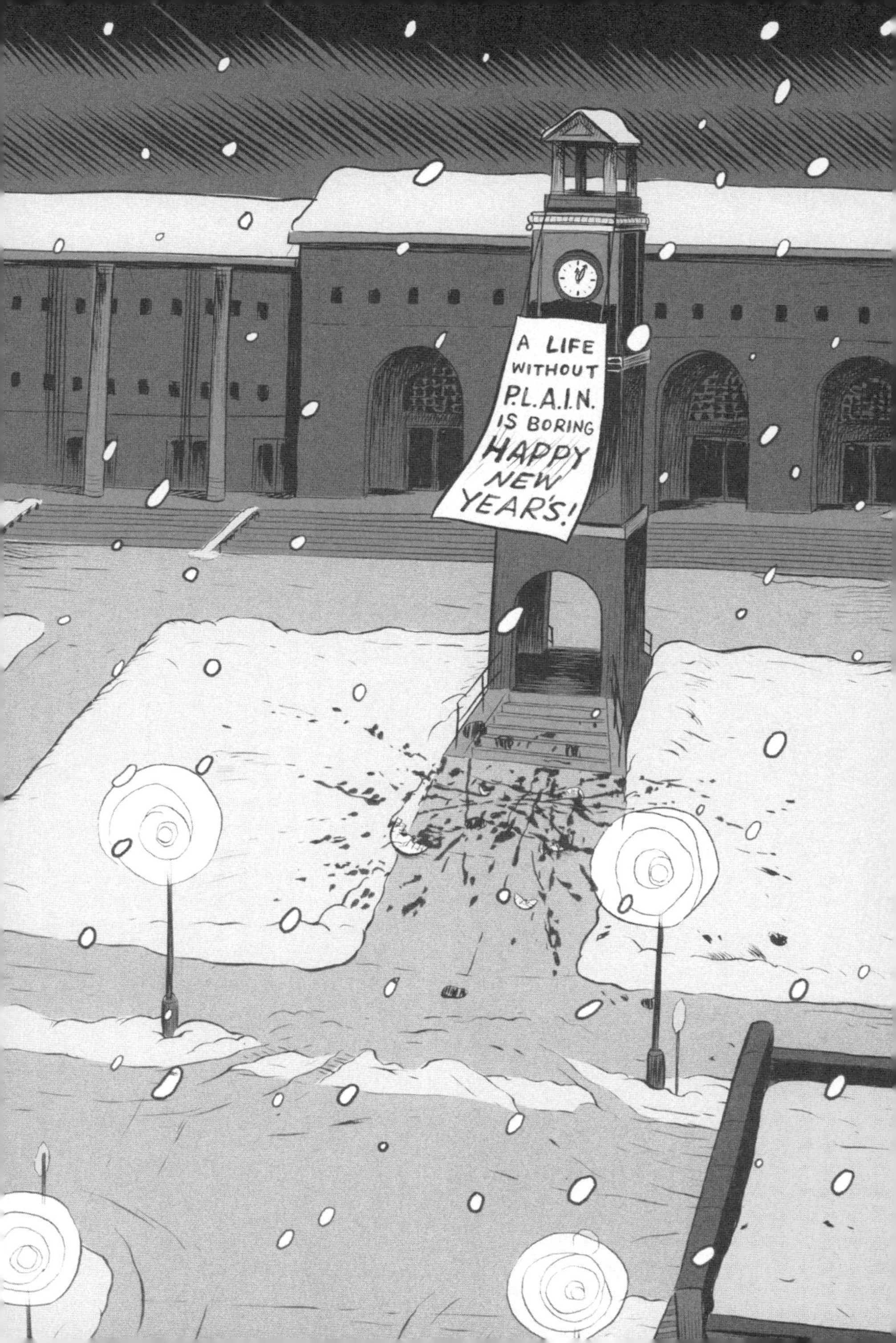
A LIFE WITHOUT P.L.A.I.N. IS BORING HAPPY NEW YEAR'S!

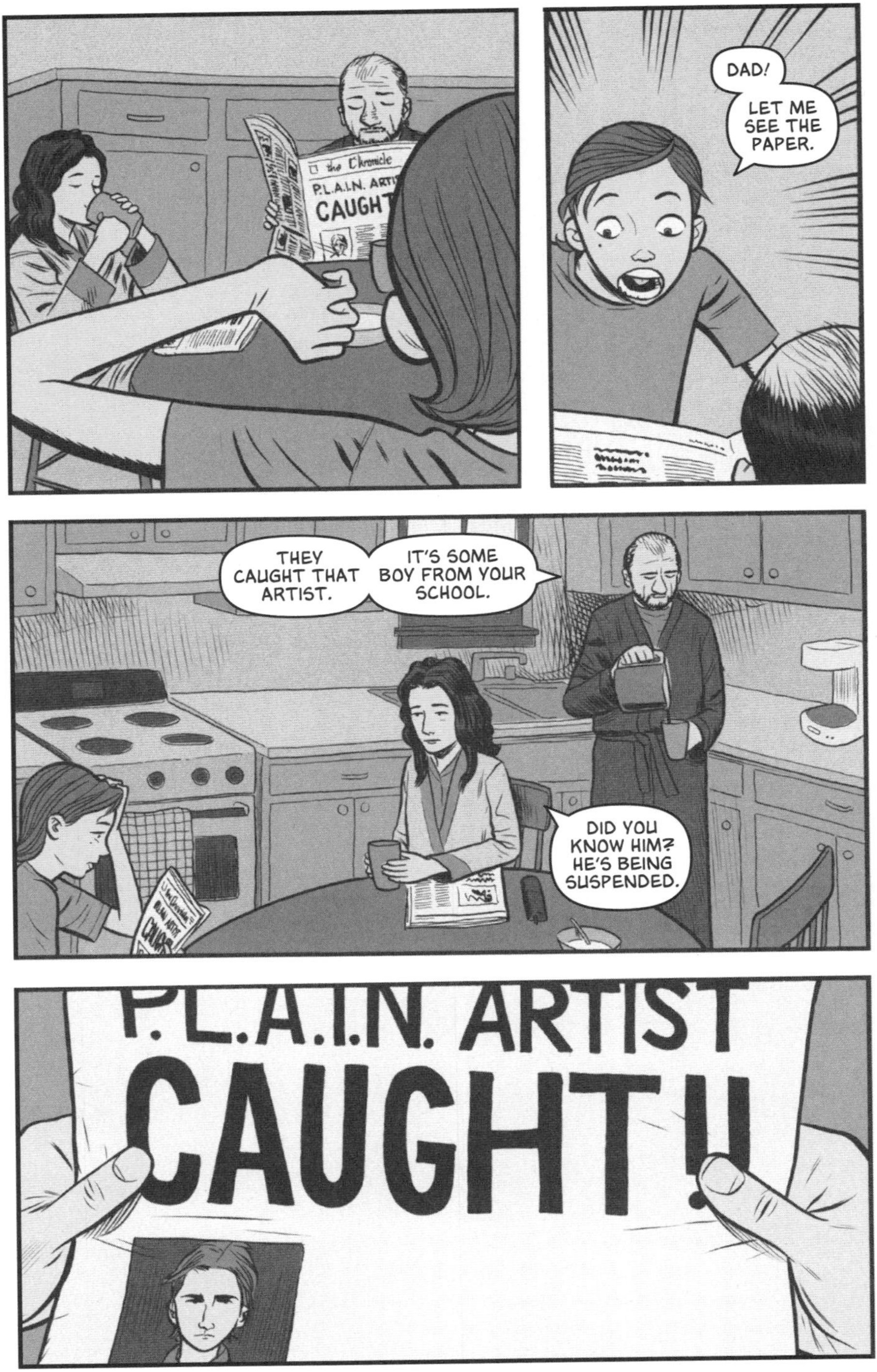
the Chronicle
P.L.A.I.N. ARTI
CAUGHT
DAD!
LET ME SEE THE PAPER.
THEY CAUGHT THAT ARTIST.
IT'S SOME BOY FROM YOUR SCHOOL.
DID YOU KNOW HIM? HE'S BEING SUSPENDED.
P.L.A.I.N. ARTIST
CAUGHT!

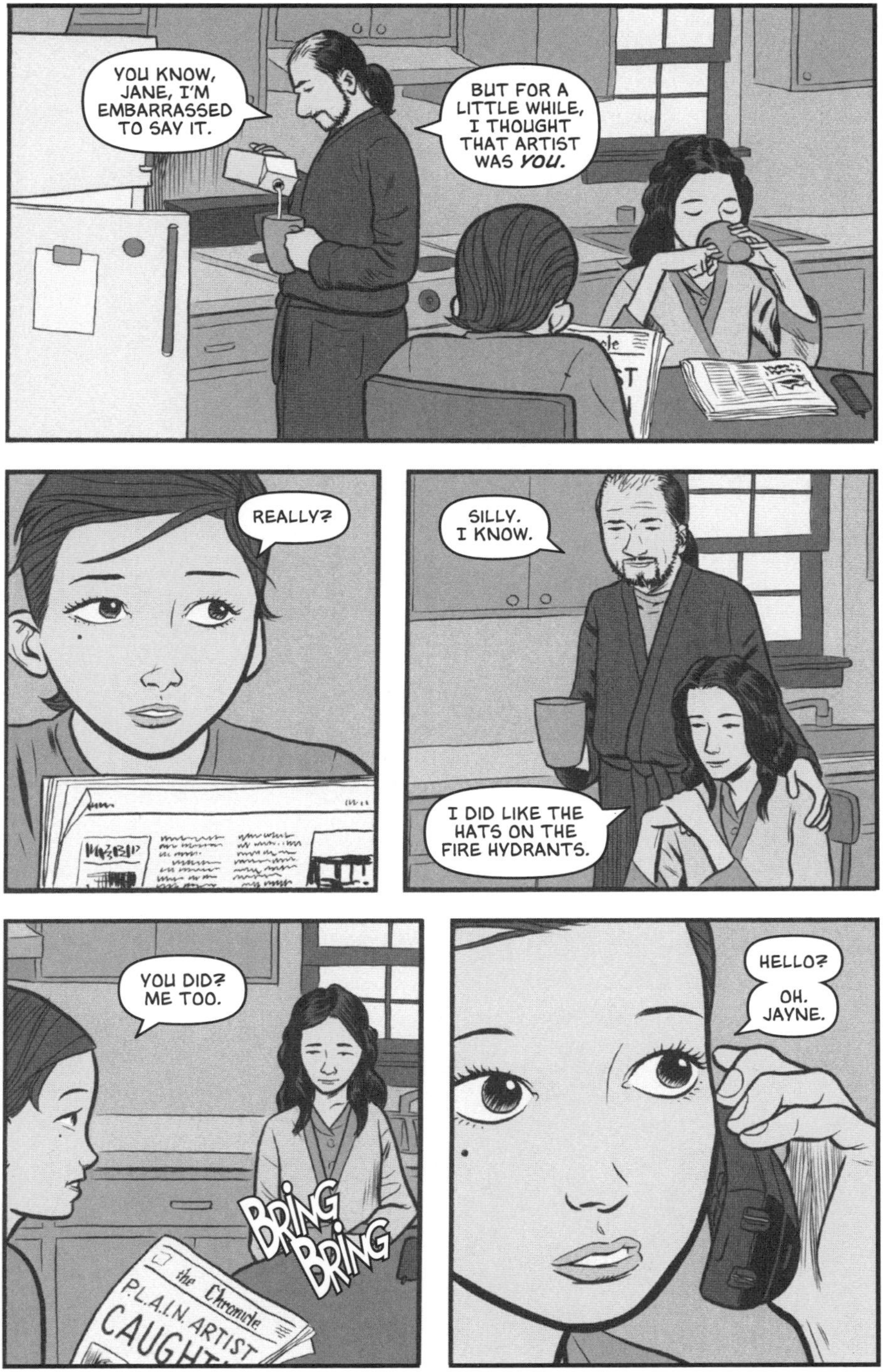
YOU KNOW, JANE, I'M EMBARRASSED TO SAY IT.
BUT FOR A LITTLE WHILE, I THOUGHT THAT ARTIST WAS *YOU.*
REALLY?
SILLY. I KNOW.
I DID LIKE THE HATS ON THE FIRE HYDRANTS.
YOU DID? ME TOO.
BRING BRING
the Chronicle
P.L.A.I.N. ARTIST CAUGHT
HELLO?
OH. JAYNE.

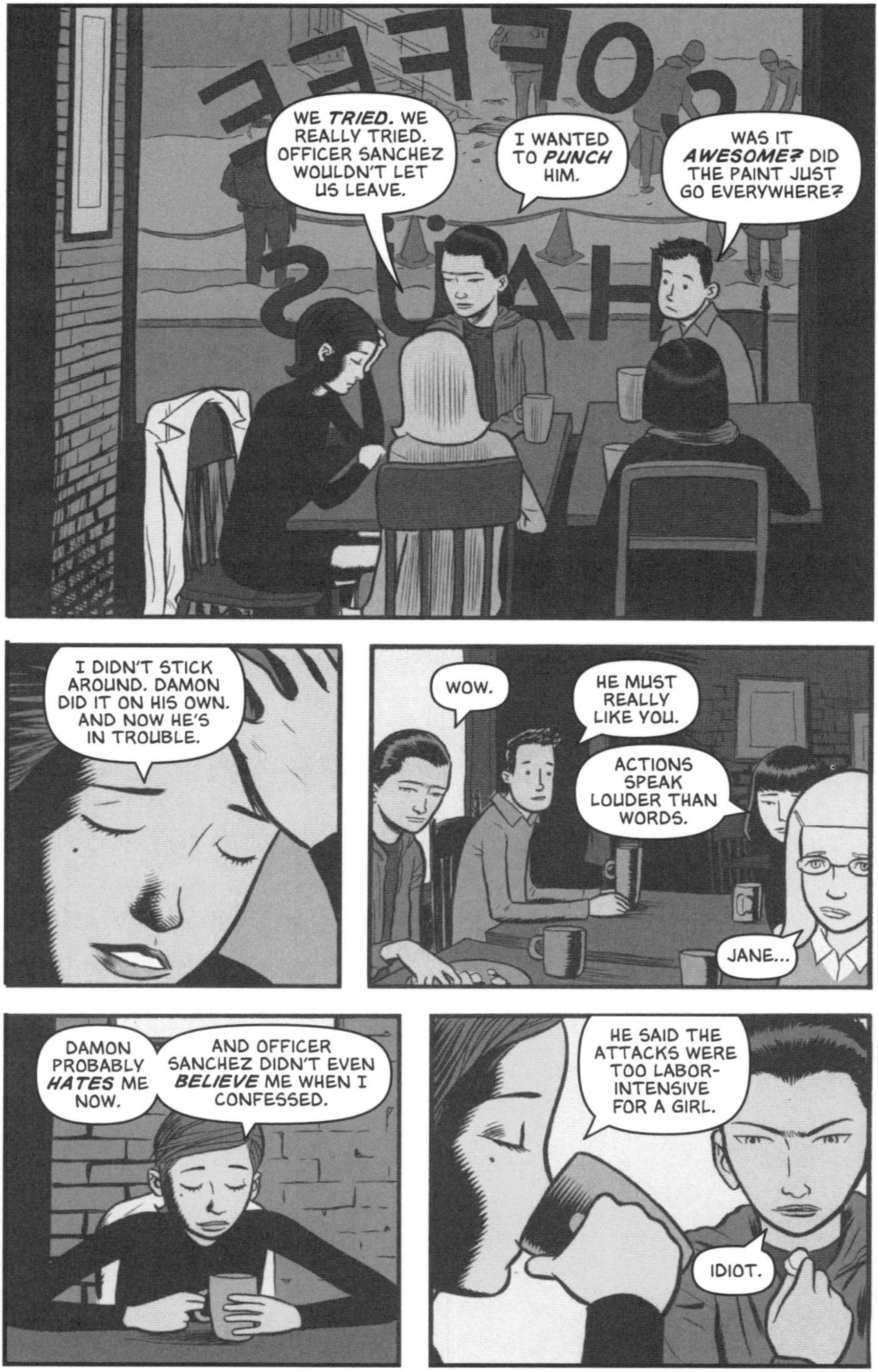
WE *TRIED.* WE REALLY TRIED. OFFICER SANCHEZ WOULDN'T LET US LEAVE.
I WANTED TO *PUNCH* HIM.
WAS IT *AWESOME?* DID THE PAINT JUST GO EVERYWHERE?
I DIDN'T STICK AROUND. DAMON DID IT ON HIS OWN. AND NOW HE'S IN TROUBLE.
WOW.
HE MUST REALLY LIKE YOU.
ACTIONS SPEAK LOUDER THAN WORDS.
JANE...
DAMON PROBABLY *HATES* ME NOW.
AND OFFICER SANCHEZ DIDN'T EVEN *BELIEVE* ME WHEN I CONFESSED.
HE SAID THE ATTACKS WERE TOO LABOR-INTENSIVE FOR A GIRL.
IDIOT.

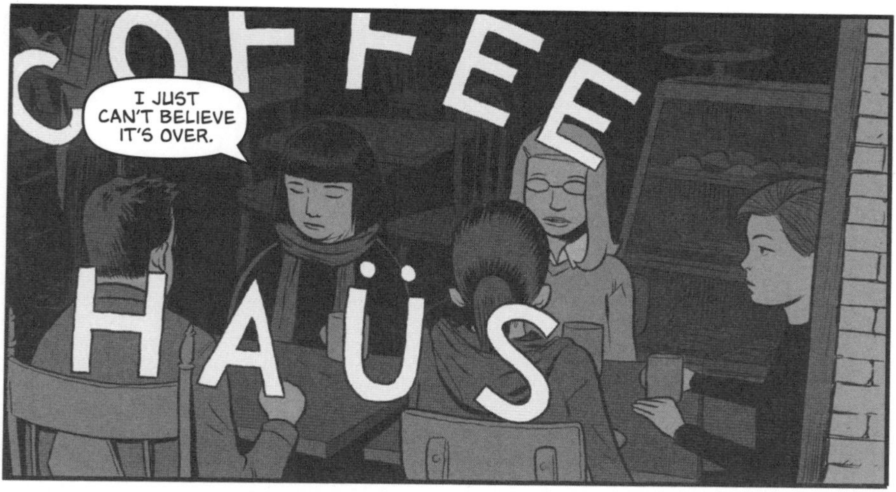
COFFEE HAÜS
I JUST CAN'T BELIEVE IT'S OVER.

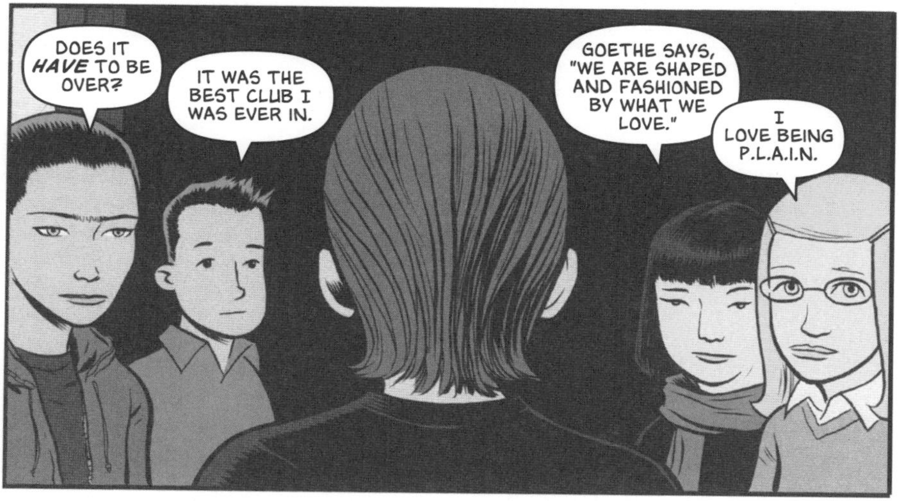
DOES IT *HAVE* TO BE OVER?
IT WAS THE BEST CLUB I WAS EVER IN.
GOETHE SAYS, "WE ARE SHAPED AND FASHIONED BY WHAT WE LOVE."
I LOVE BEING P.L.A.I.N.

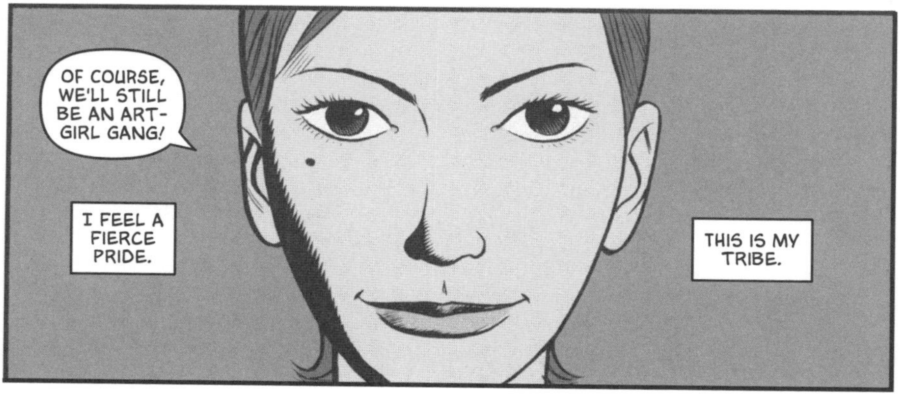
OF COURSE, WE'LL STILL BE AN ART-GIRL GANG!
I FEEL A FIERCE PRIDE.
THIS IS MY TRIBE.

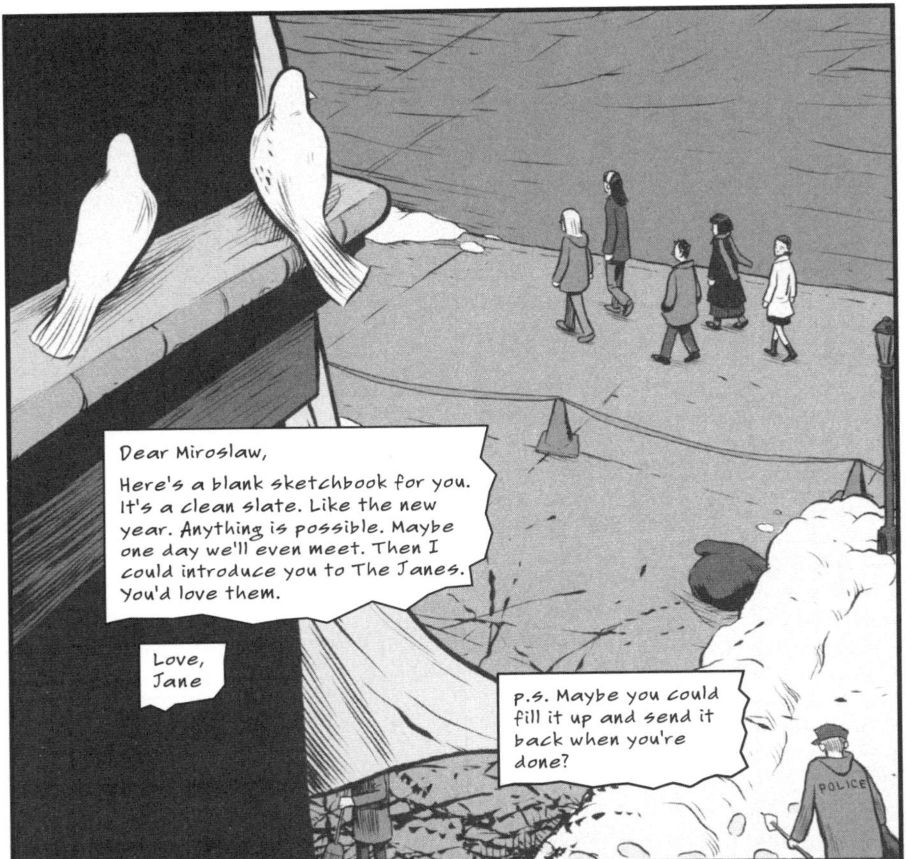
Dear Miroslaw,
Here's a blank sketchbook for you. It's a clean slate. Like the new year. Anything is possible. Maybe one day we'll even meet. Then I could introduce you to The Janes. You'd love them.
Love, Jane
p.s. Maybe you could fill it up and send it back when you're done?
POLICE

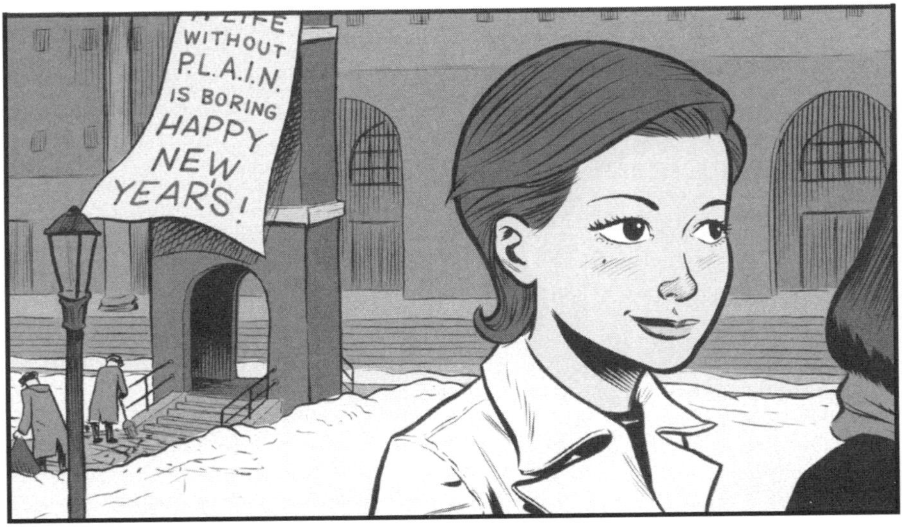
WITHOUT P.L.A.I.N. IS BORING HAPPY NEW YEAR'S!

Early Concepts for Main Jane

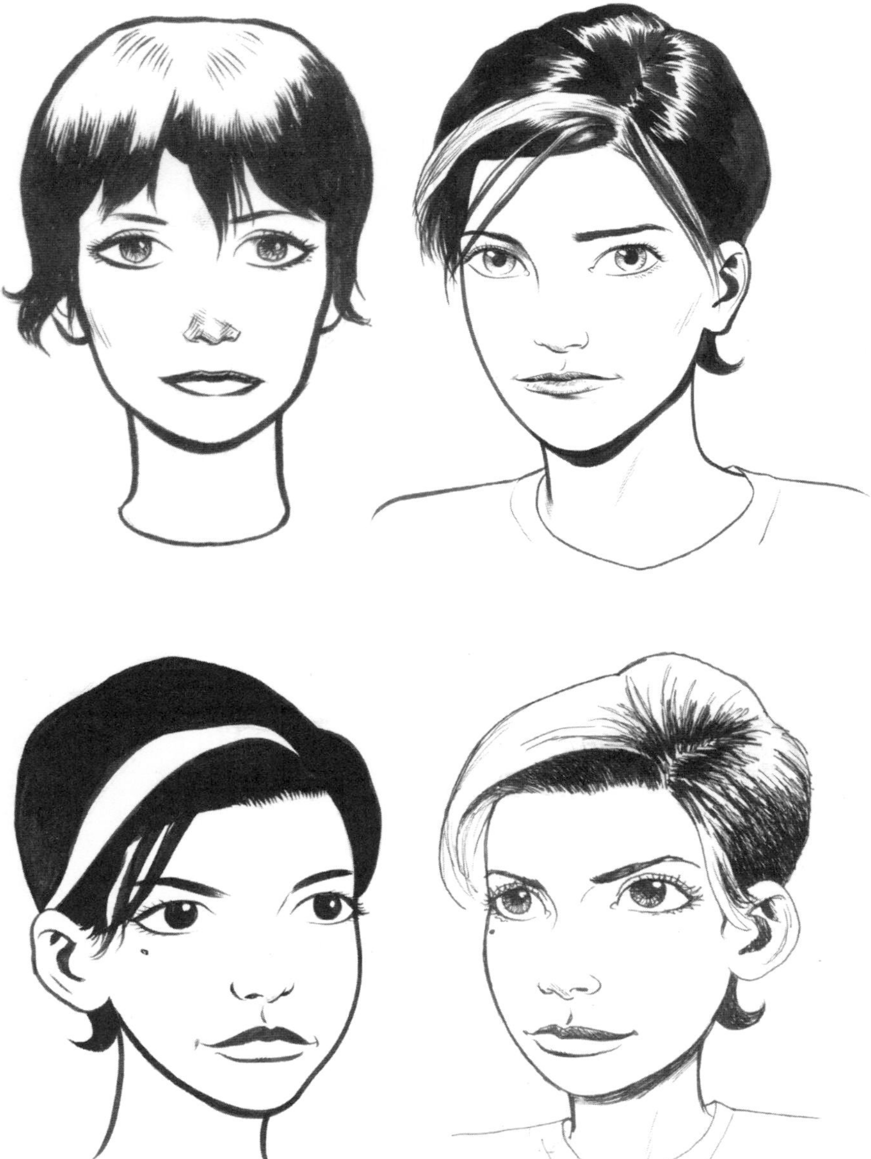

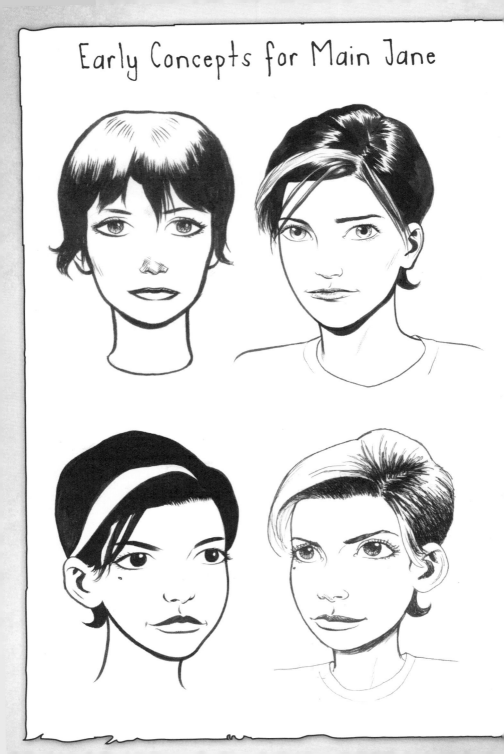

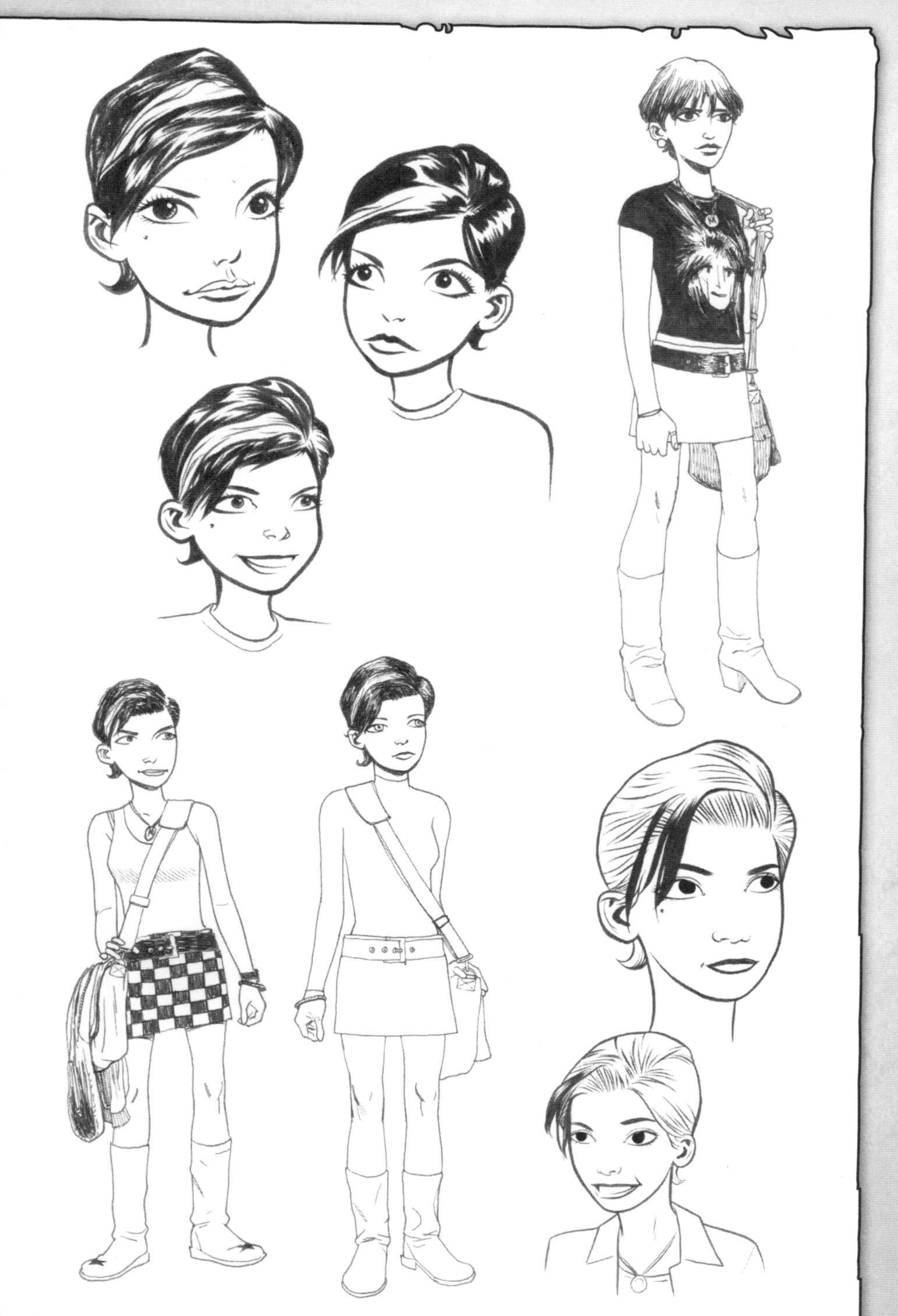

Part 2
Janes in Love

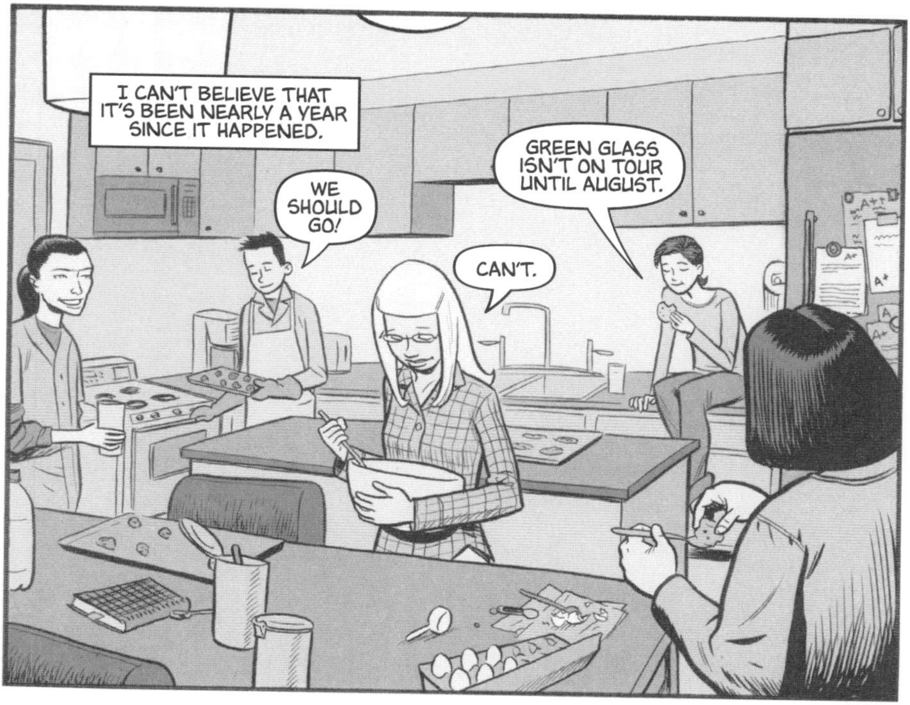

I CAN'T BELIEVE THAT IT'S BEEN NEARLY A YEAR SINCE IT HAPPENED.
WE SHOULD GO!
GREEN GLASS ISN'T ON TOUR UNTIL AUGUST.
CAN'T.

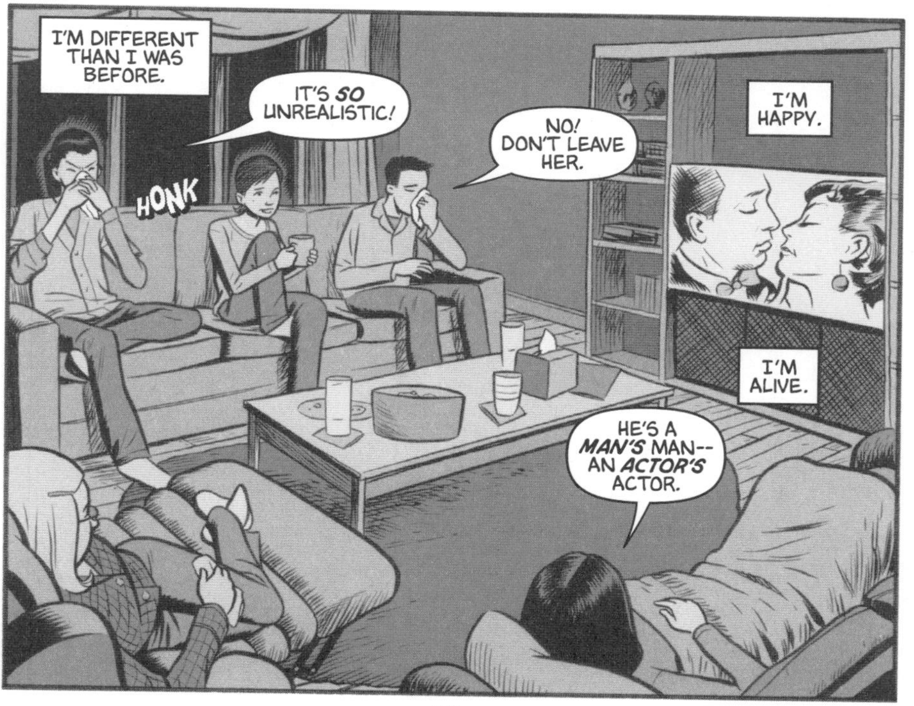

I'M DIFFERENT THAN I WAS BEFORE.
IT'S *SO* UNREALISTIC!
HONK
NO! DON'T LEAVE HER.
I'M HAPPY.
I'M ALIVE.
HE'S A ***MAN'S*** MAN-- AN ***ACTOR'S*** ACTOR.

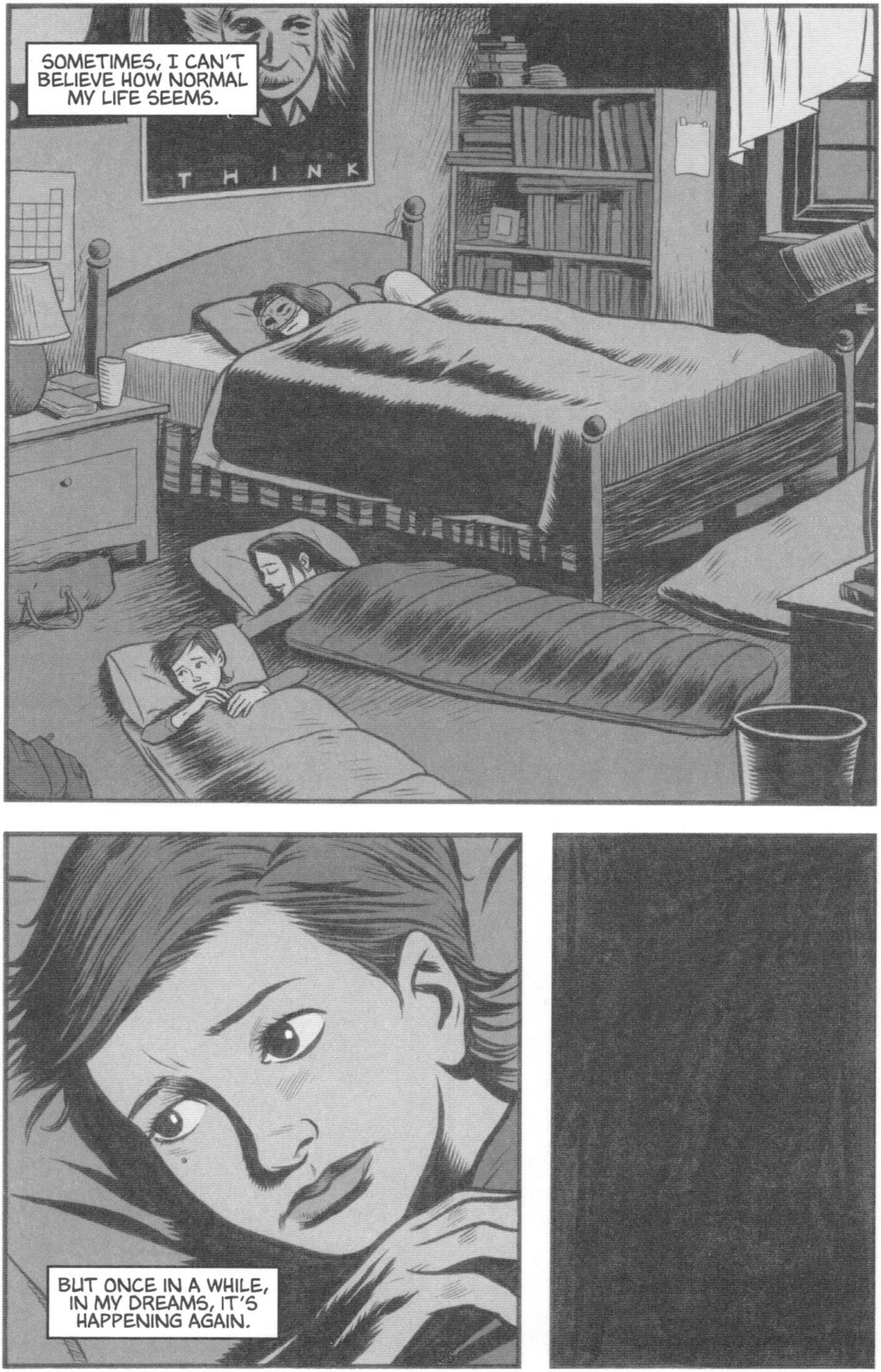
SOMETIMES, I CAN'T BELIEVE HOW NORMAL MY LIFE SEEMS.
THINK
BUT ONCE IN A WHILE, IN MY DREAMS, IT'S HAPPENING AGAIN.

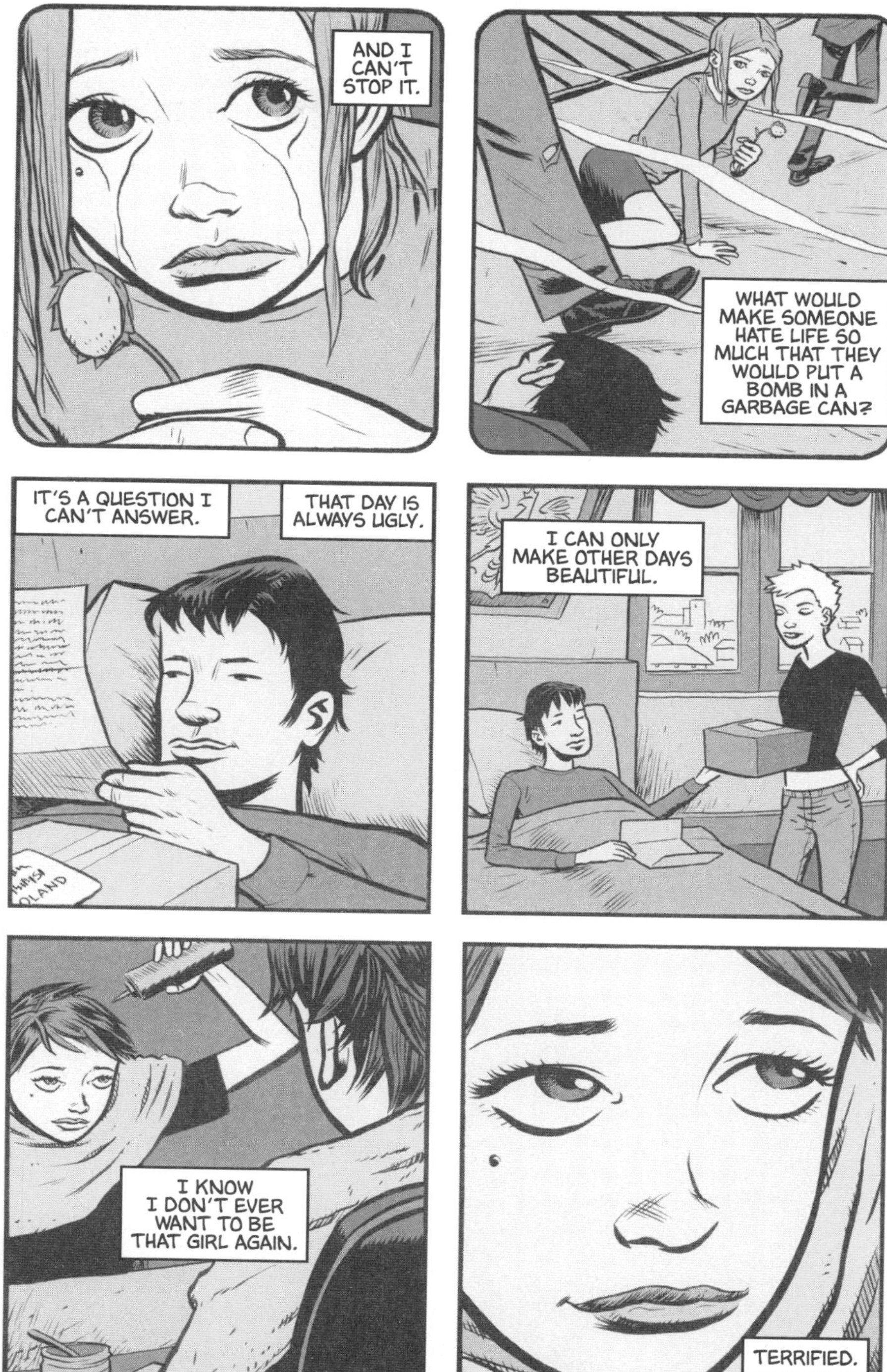
AND I CAN'T STOP IT.
WHAT WOULD MAKE SOMEONE HATE LIFE SO MUCH THAT THEY WOULD PUT A BOMB IN A GARBAGE CAN?
IT'S A QUESTION I CAN'T ANSWER.
THAT DAY IS ALWAYS UGLY.
I CAN ONLY MAKE OTHER DAYS BEAUTIFUL.
I KNOW I DON'T EVER WANT TO BE THAT GIRL AGAIN.
TERRIFIED.

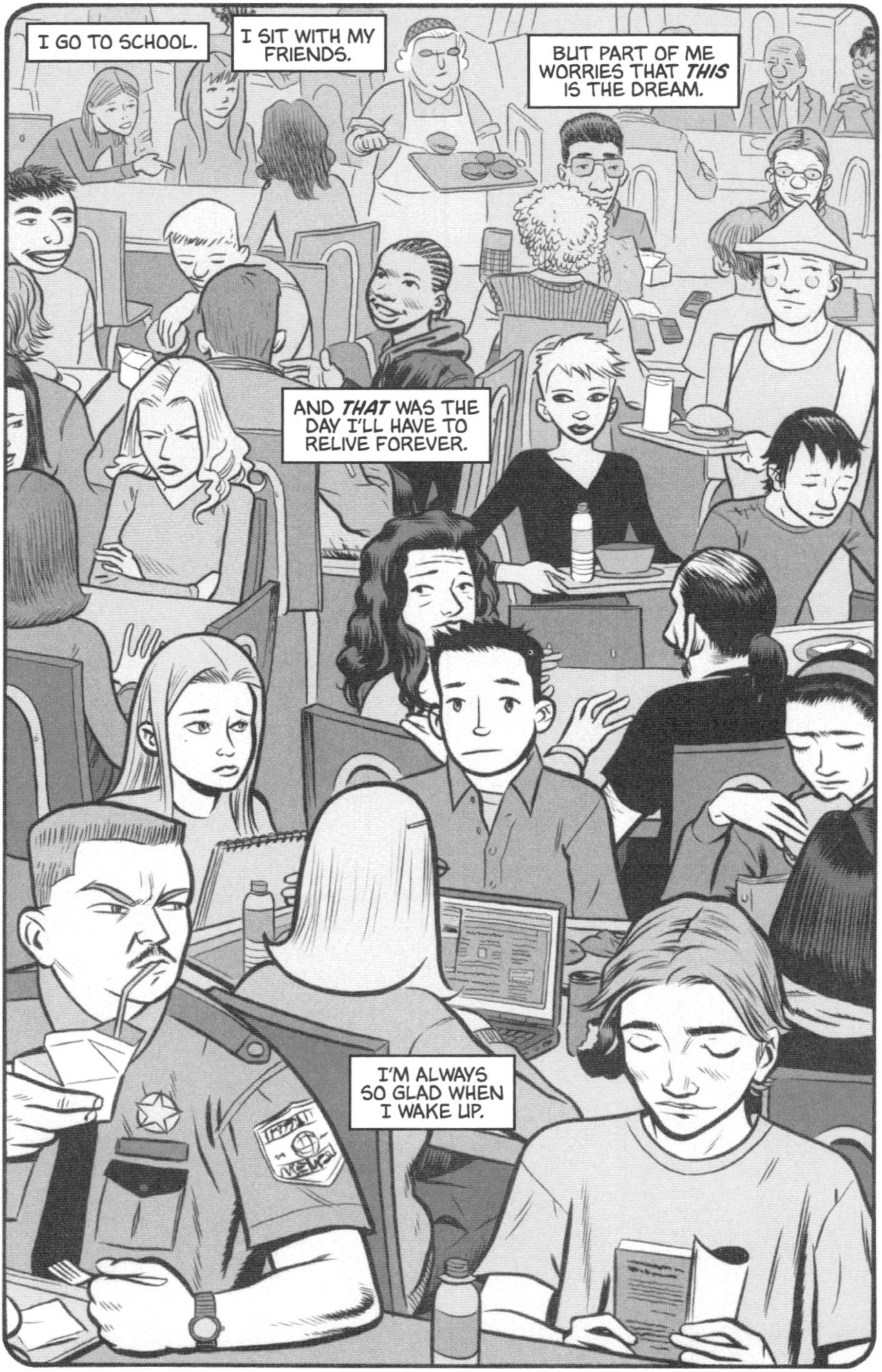

I GO TO SCHOOL.
I SIT WITH MY FRIENDS.
BUT PART OF ME WORRIES THAT *THIS* IS THE DREAM.
AND *THAT* WAS THE DAY I'LL HAVE TO RELIVE FOREVER.
I'M ALWAYS SO GLAD WHEN I WAKE UP.

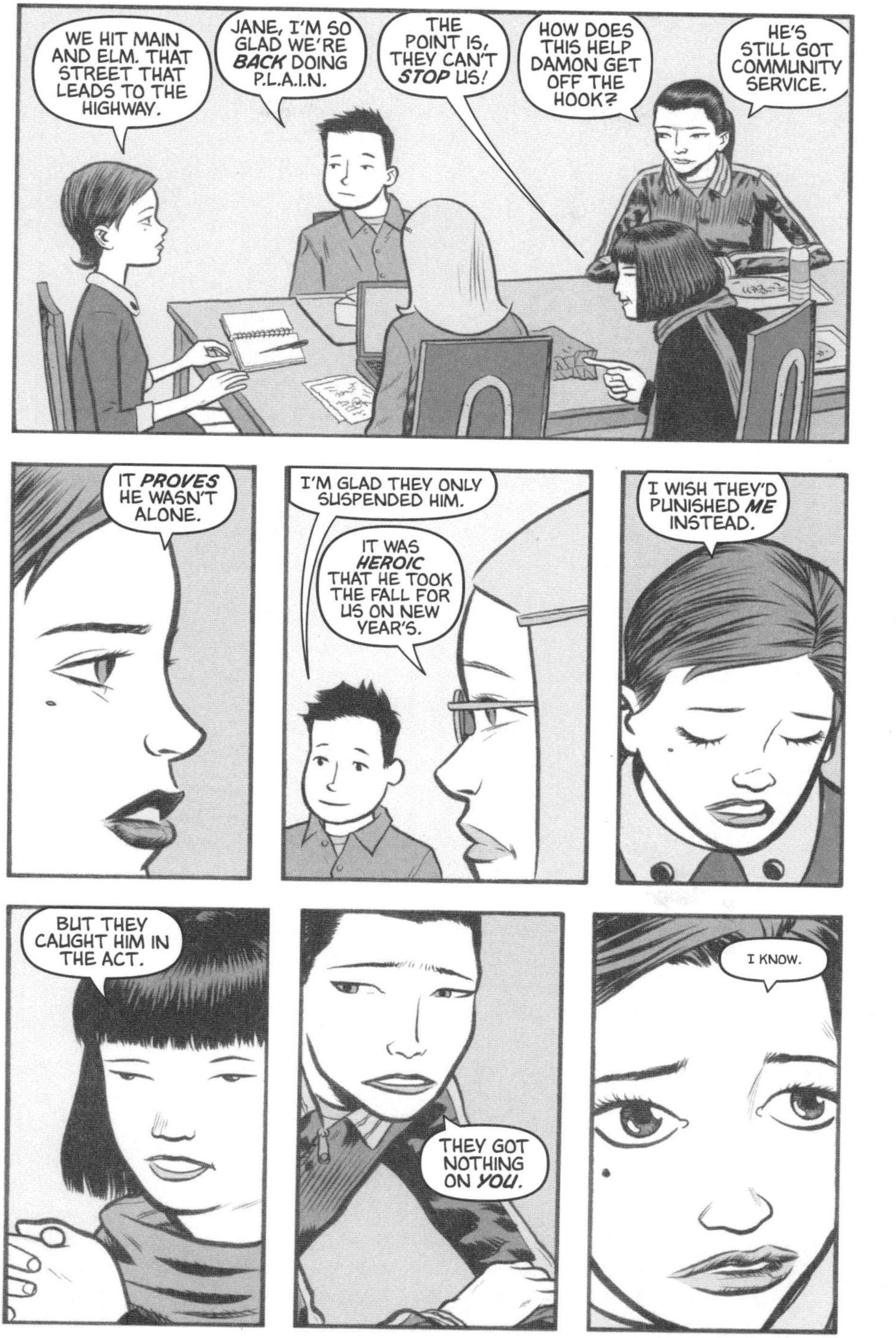
WE HIT MAIN AND ELM. THAT STREET THAT LEADS TO THE HIGHWAY.
JANE, I'M SO GLAD WE'RE **BACK** DOING P.L.A.I.N.
THE POINT IS, THEY CAN'T **STOP** US!
HOW DOES THIS HELP DAMON GET OFF THE HOOK?
HE'S STILL GOT COMMUNITY SERVICE.
IT **PROVES** HE WASN'T ALONE.
I'M GLAD THEY ONLY SUSPENDED HIM.
IT WAS **HEROIC** THAT HE TOOK THE FALL FOR US ON NEW YEAR'S.
I WISH THEY'D PUNISHED **ME** INSTEAD.
BUT THEY CAUGHT HIM IN THE ACT.
THEY GOT NOTHING ON **YOU**.
I KNOW.

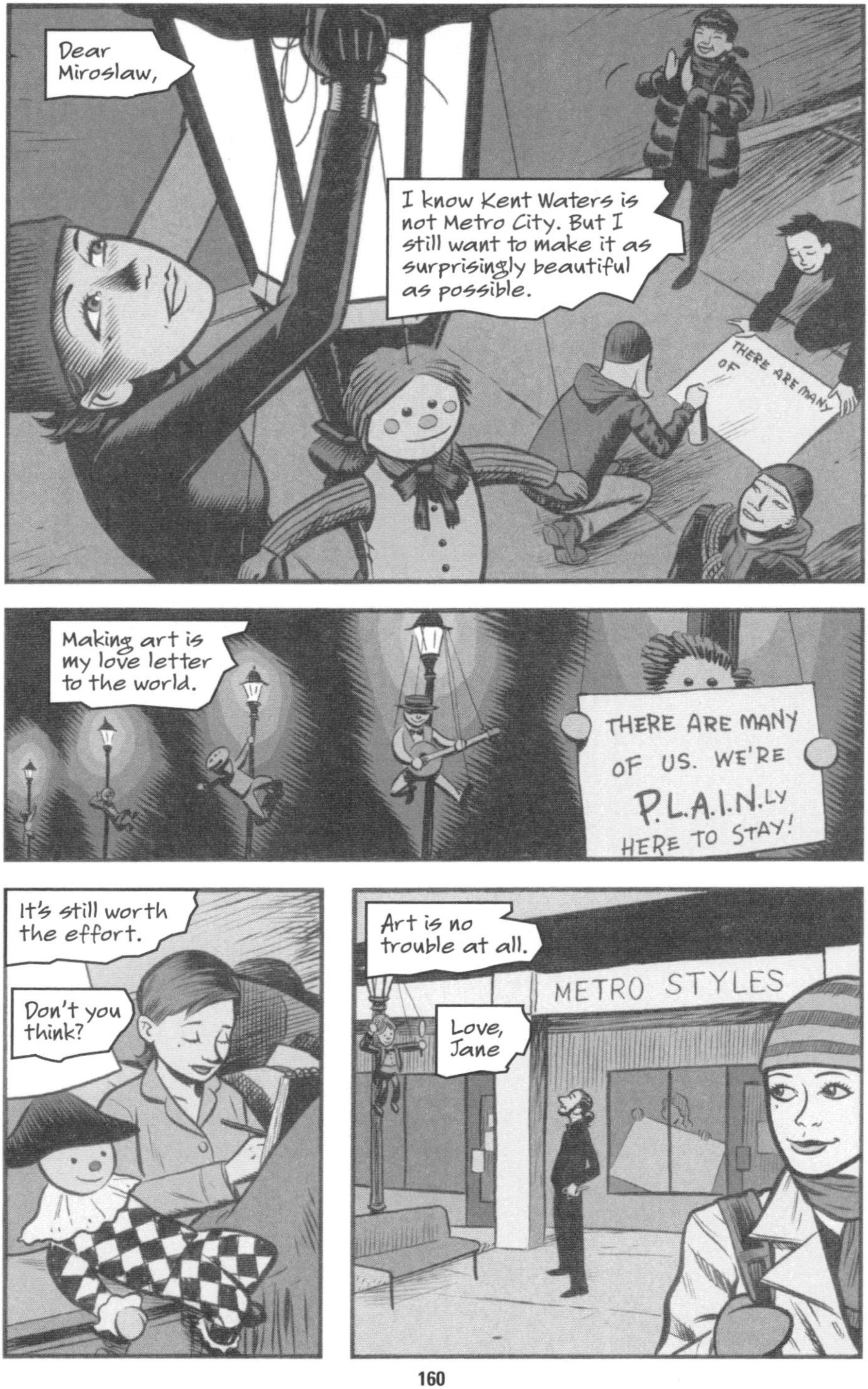
Dear Miroslaw,
I know Kent Waters is not Metro City. But I still want to make it as surprisingly beautiful as possible.
THERE ARE MANY OF
Making art is my love letter to the world.
THERE ARE MANY OF US. WE'RE P.L.A.I.N.LY HERE TO STAY!
It's still worth the effort.
Don't you think?
Art is no trouble at all.
METRO STYLES
Love, Jane

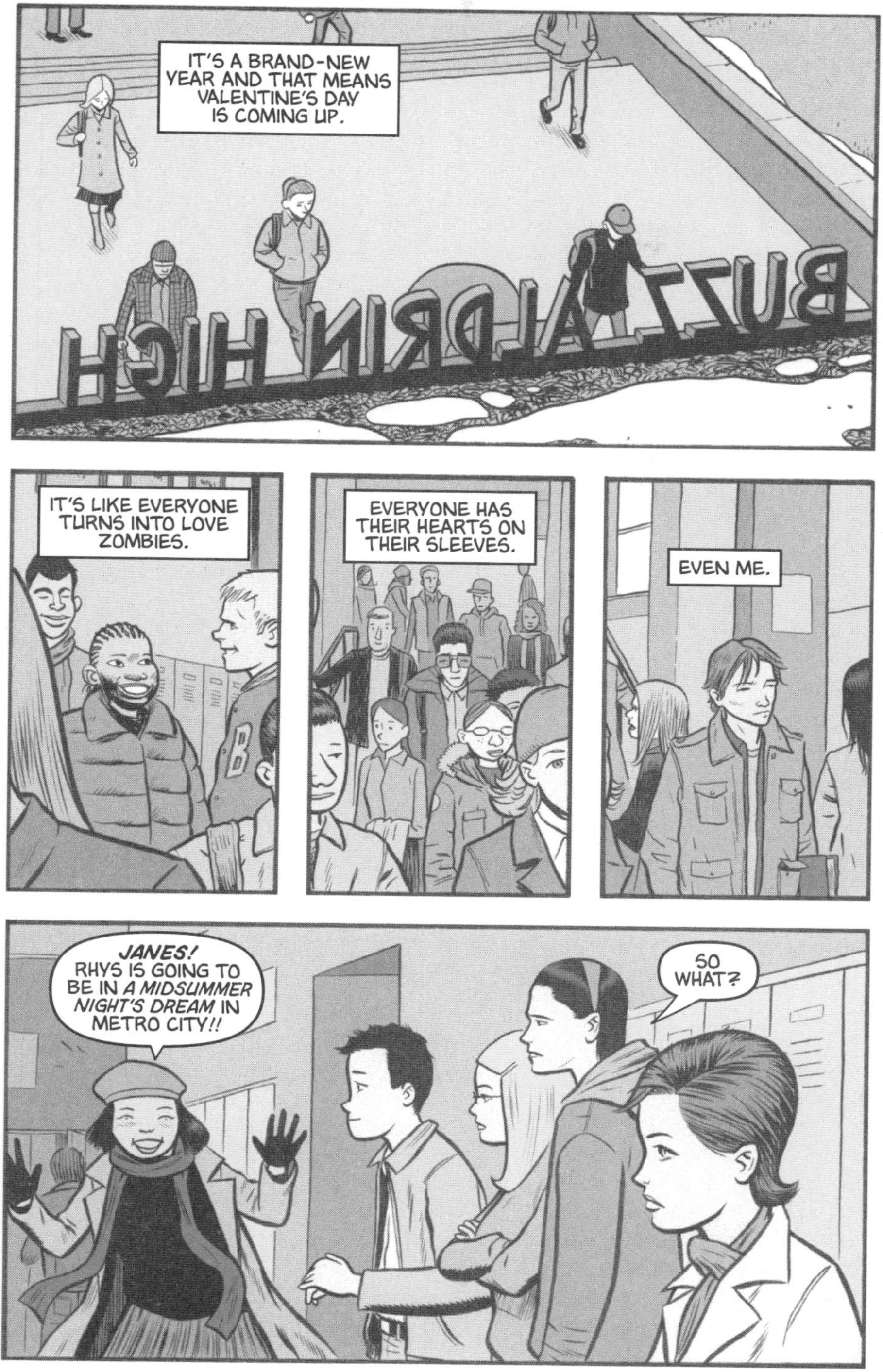
IT'S A BRAND-NEW YEAR AND THAT MEANS VALENTINE'S DAY IS COMING UP.
IT'S LIKE EVERYONE TURNS INTO LOVE ZOMBIES.
EVERYONE HAS THEIR HEARTS ON THEIR SLEEVES.
EVEN ME.
JANES! RHYS IS GOING TO BE IN *A MIDSUMMER NIGHT'S DREAM* IN METRO CITY!!
SO WHAT?

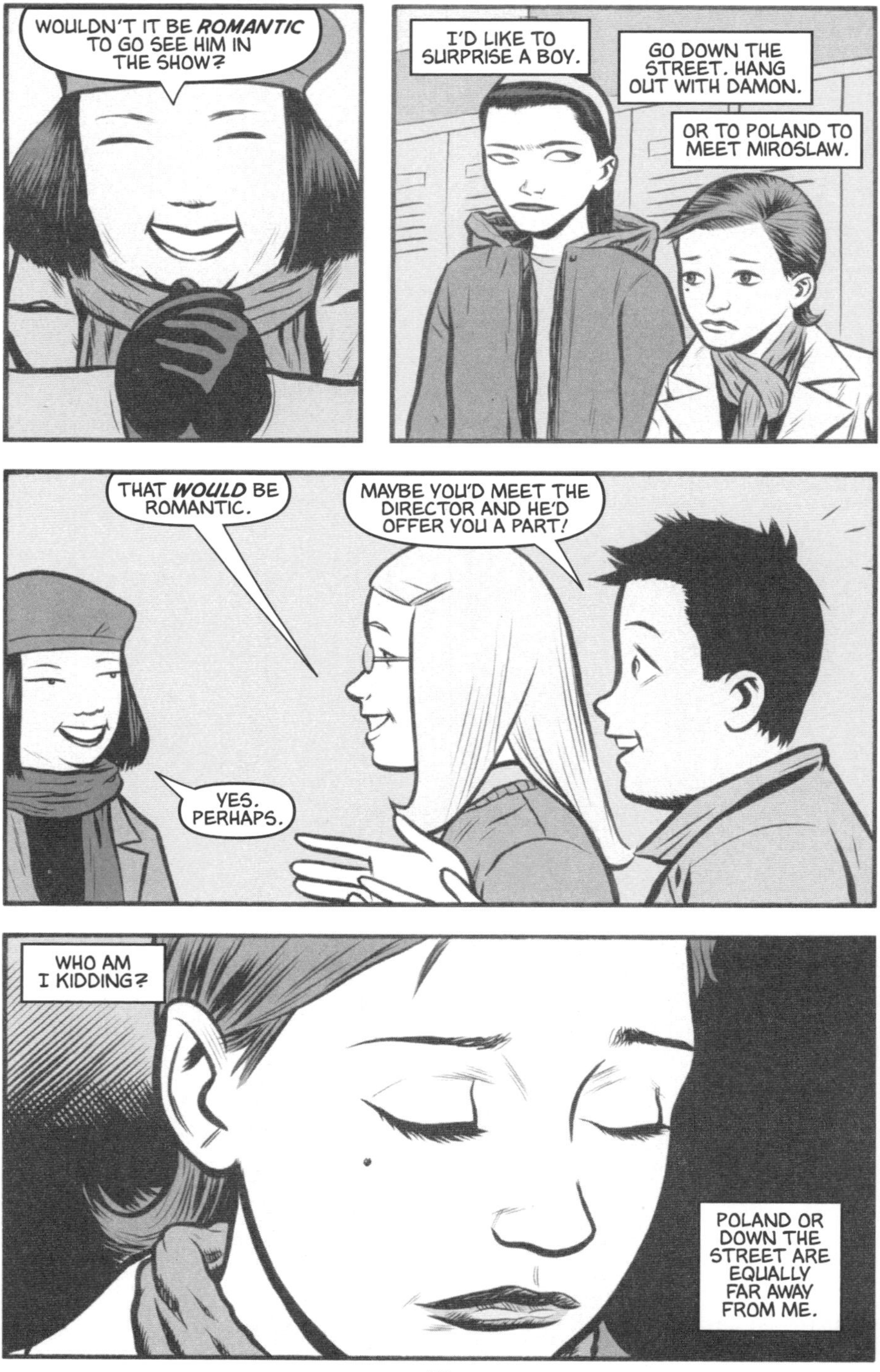
WOULDN'T IT BE ***ROMANTIC*** TO GO SEE HIM IN THE SHOW?
I'D LIKE TO SURPRISE A BOY.
GO DOWN THE STREET. HANG OUT WITH DAMON.
OR TO POLAND TO MEET MIROSLAW.
THAT ***WOULD*** BE ROMANTIC.
MAYBE YOU'D MEET THE DIRECTOR AND HE'D OFFER YOU A PART!
YES. PERHAPS.
WHO AM I KIDDING?
POLAND OR DOWN THE STREET ARE EQUALLY FAR AWAY FROM ME.

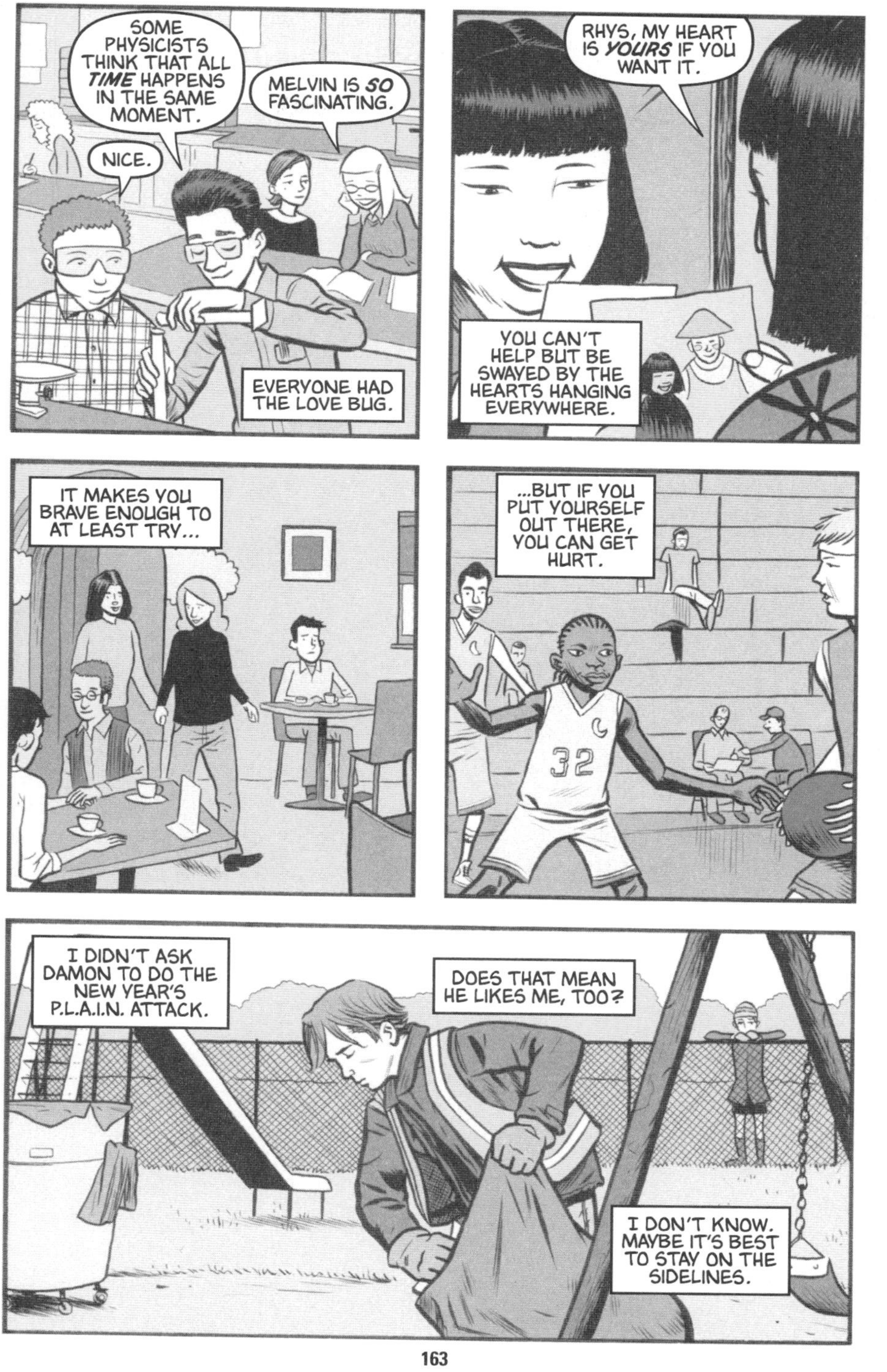
SOME PHYSICISTS THINK THAT ALL *TIME* HAPPENS IN THE SAME MOMENT.
MELVIN IS *SO* FASCINATING.
NICE.
EVERYONE HAD THE LOVE BUG.
RHYS, MY HEART IS *YOURS* IF YOU WANT IT.
YOU CAN'T HELP BUT BE SWAYED BY THE HEARTS HANGING EVERYWHERE.
IT MAKES YOU BRAVE ENOUGH TO AT LEAST TRY...
...BUT IF YOU PUT YOURSELF OUT THERE, YOU CAN GET HURT.
32
I DIDN'T ASK DAMON TO DO THE NEW YEAR'S P.L.A.I.N. ATTACK.
DOES THAT MEAN HE LIKES ME, TOO?
I DON'T KNOW. MAYBE IT'S BEST TO STAY ON THE SIDELINES.

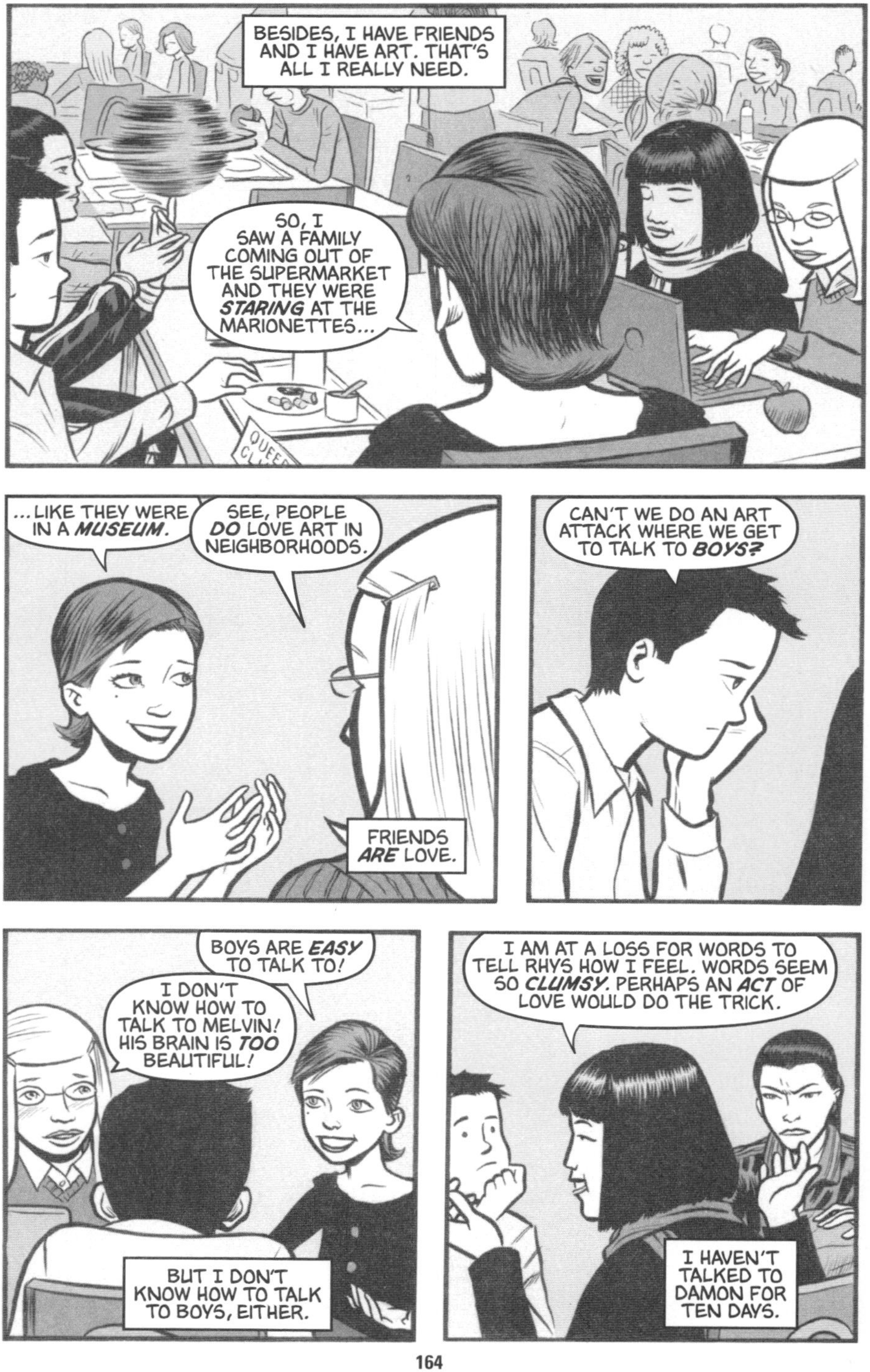
BESIDES, I HAVE FRIENDS AND I HAVE ART. THAT'S ALL I REALLY NEED.
SO, I SAW A FAMILY COMING OUT OF THE SUPERMARKET AND THEY WERE *STARING* AT THE MARIONETTES...
...LIKE THEY WERE IN A *MUSEUM*.
SEE, PEOPLE *DO* LOVE ART IN NEIGHBORHOODS.
FRIENDS *ARE* LOVE.
CAN'T WE DO AN ART ATTACK WHERE WE GET TO TALK TO *BOYS?*
BOYS ARE *EASY* TO TALK TO!
I DON'T KNOW HOW TO TALK TO MELVIN! HIS BRAIN IS *TOO* BEAUTIFUL!
BUT I DON'T KNOW HOW TO TALK TO BOYS, EITHER.
I AM AT A LOSS FOR WORDS TO TELL RHYS HOW I FEEL. WORDS SEEM SO *CLUMSY*. PERHAPS AN *ACT* OF LOVE WOULD DO THE TRICK.
I HAVEN'T TALKED TO DAMON FOR TEN DAYS.

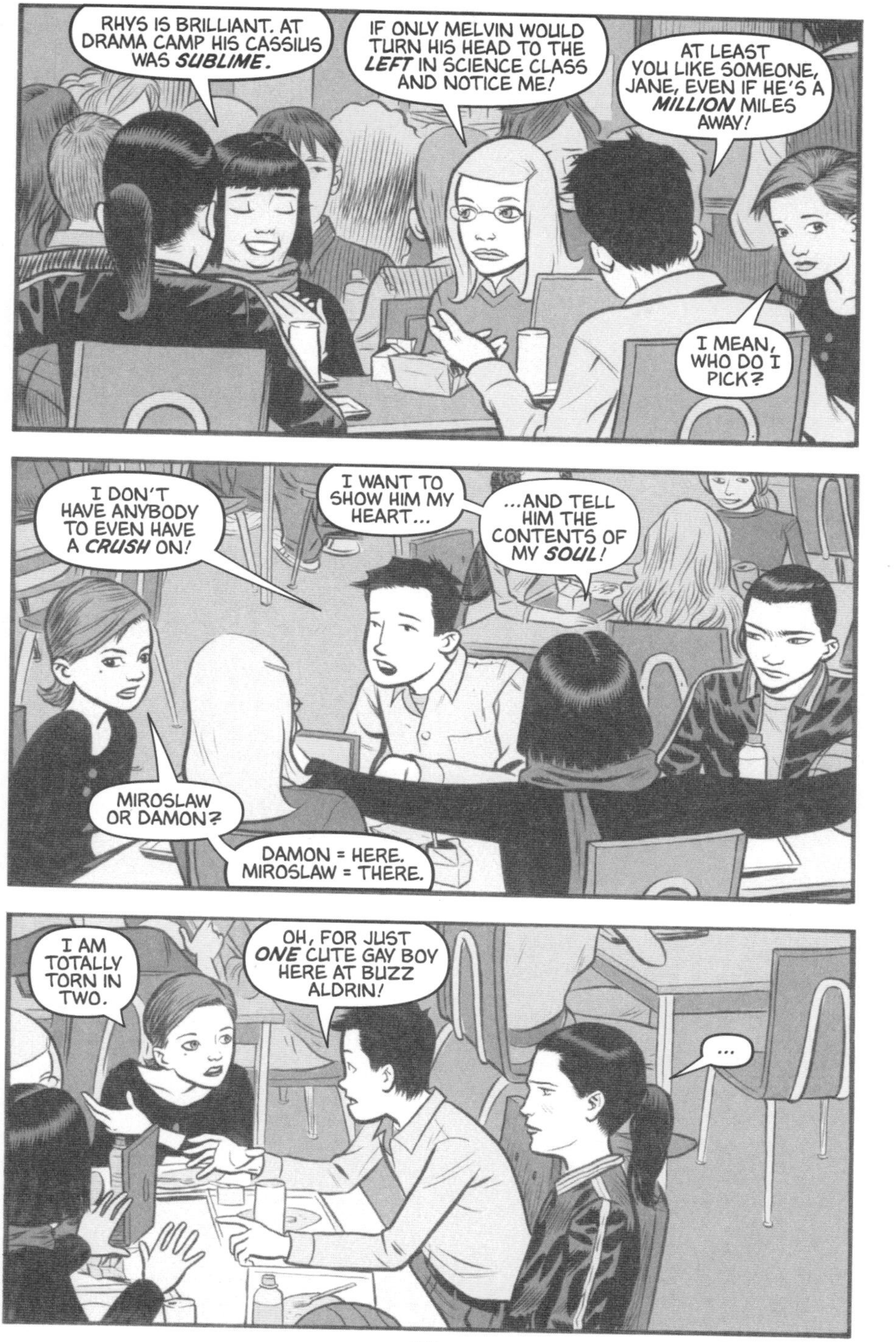
RHYS IS BRILLIANT. AT DRAMA CAMP HIS CASSIUS WAS *SUBLIME*.
IF ONLY MELVIN WOULD TURN HIS HEAD TO THE *LEFT* IN SCIENCE CLASS AND NOTICE ME!
AT LEAST YOU LIKE SOMEONE, JANE, EVEN IF HE'S A *MILLION* MILES AWAY!
I MEAN, WHO DO I PICK?
I DON'T HAVE ANYBODY TO EVEN HAVE A *CRUSH* ON!
I WANT TO SHOW HIM MY HEART...
...AND TELL HIM THE CONTENTS OF MY *SOUL*!
MIROSLAW OR DAMON?
DAMON = HERE. MIROSLAW = THERE.
I AM TOTALLY TORN IN TWO.
OH, FOR JUST *ONE* CUTE GAY BOY HERE AT BUZZ ALDRIN!
...

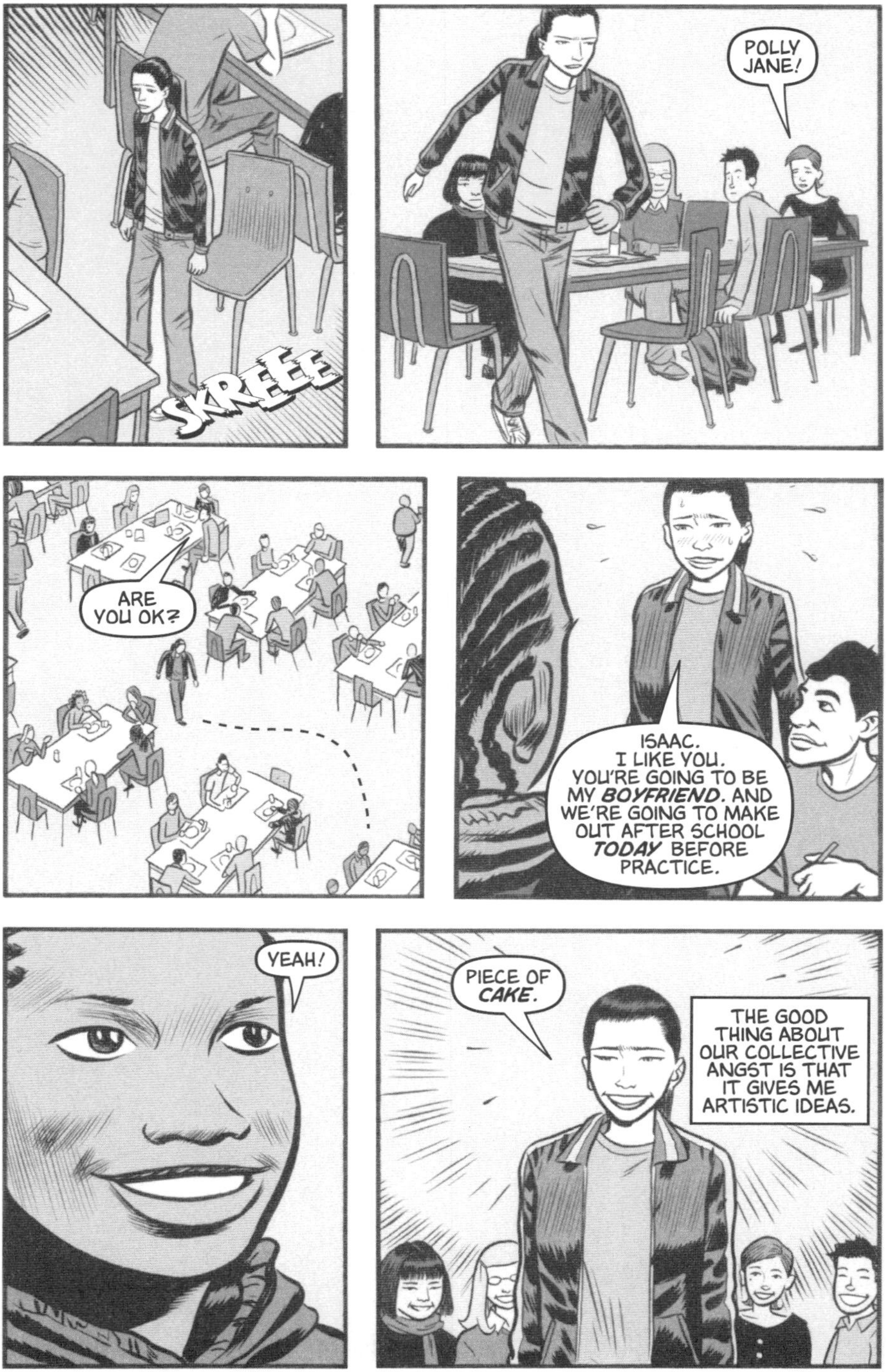
SKREEE
POLLY JANE!
ARE YOU OK?
ISAAC. I LIKE YOU. YOU'RE GOING TO BE MY **BOYFRIEND**. AND WE'RE GOING TO MAKE OUT AFTER SCHOOL **TODAY** BEFORE PRACTICE.
YEAH!
PIECE OF **CAKE**.
THE GOOD THING ABOUT OUR COLLECTIVE ANGST IS THAT IT GIVES ME ARTISTIC IDEAS.

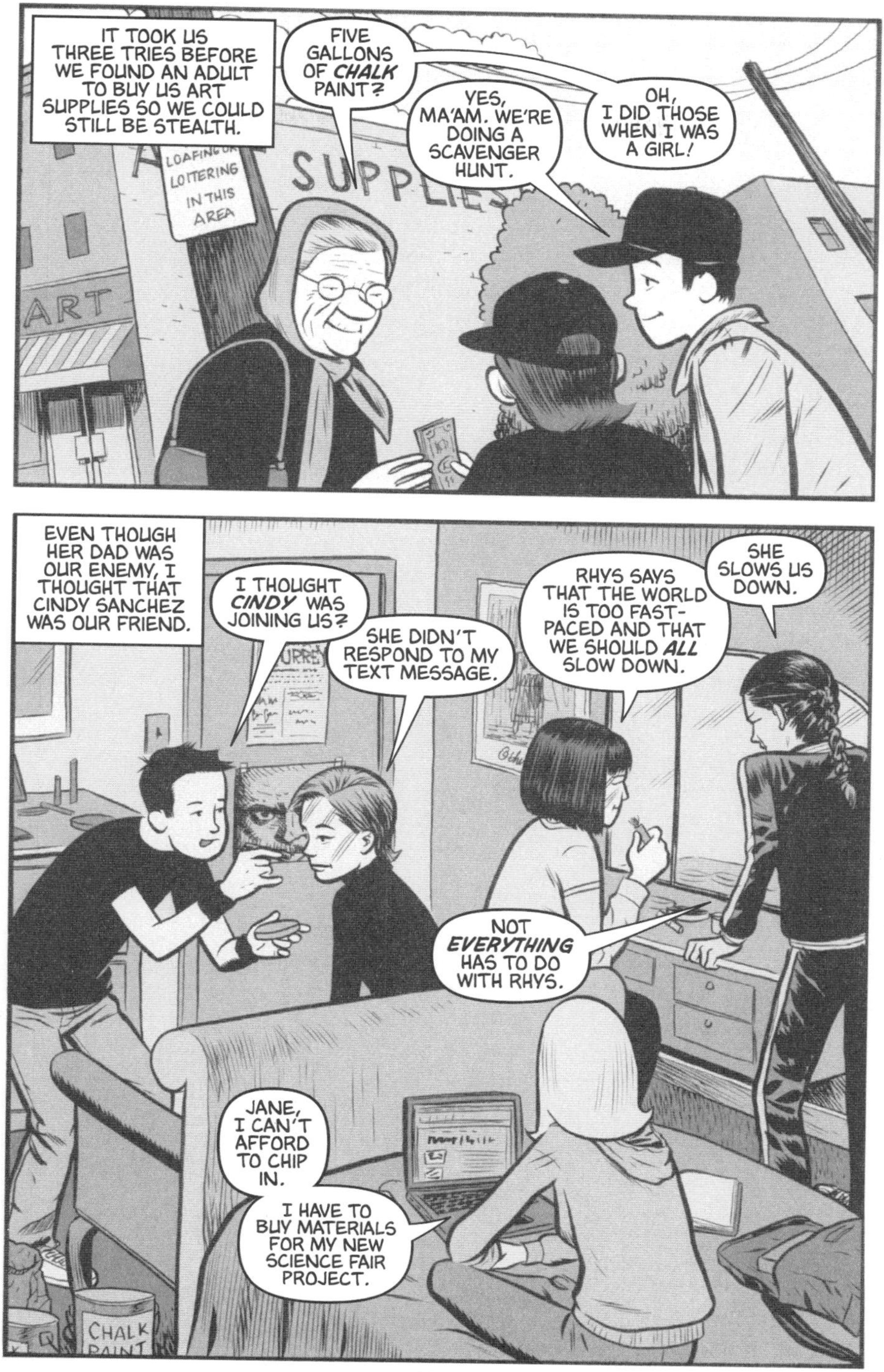
IT TOOK US THREE TRIES BEFORE WE FOUND AN ADULT TO BUY US ART SUPPLIES SO WE COULD STILL BE STEALTH.
FIVE GALLONS OF *CHALK* PAINT?
YES, MA'AM. WE'RE DOING A SCAVENGER HUNT.
OH, I DID THOSE WHEN I WAS A GIRL!
LOAFING OR LOITERING IN THIS AREA
SUPPLIES
ART
EVEN THOUGH HER DAD WAS OUR ENEMY, I THOUGHT THAT CINDY SANCHEZ WAS OUR FRIEND.
I THOUGHT *CINDY* WAS JOINING US?
SHE DIDN'T RESPOND TO MY TEXT MESSAGE.
RHYS SAYS THAT THE WORLD IS TOO FAST-PACED AND THAT WE SHOULD *ALL* SLOW DOWN.
SHE SLOWS US DOWN.
NOT *EVERYTHING* HAS TO DO WITH RHYS.
JANE, I CAN'T AFFORD TO CHIP IN.
I HAVE TO BUY MATERIALS FOR MY NEW SCIENCE FAIR PROJECT.
CHALK PAINT

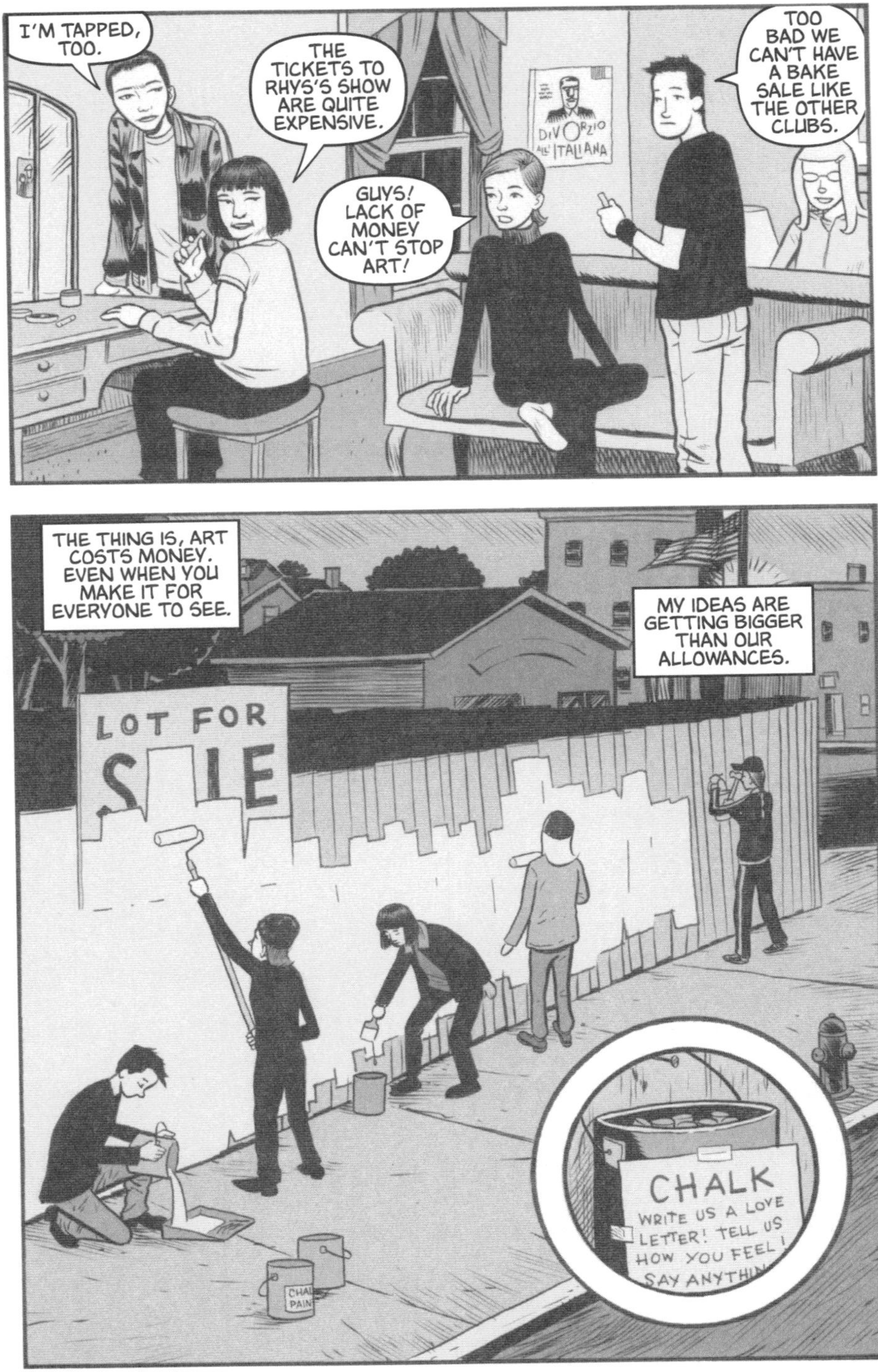

I'M TAPPED, TOO.
THE TICKETS TO RHYS'S SHOW ARE QUITE EXPENSIVE.
DIVORZIO ALL'ITALIANA
TOO BAD WE CAN'T HAVE A BAKE SALE LIKE THE OTHER CLUBS.
GUYS! LACK OF MONEY CAN'T STOP ART!
THE THING IS, ART COSTS MONEY. EVEN WHEN YOU MAKE IT FOR EVERYONE TO SEE.
MY IDEAS ARE GETTING BIGGER THAN OUR ALLOWANCES.
LOT FOR
CHALK
WRITE US A LOVE LETTER! TELL US HOW YOU FEEL!

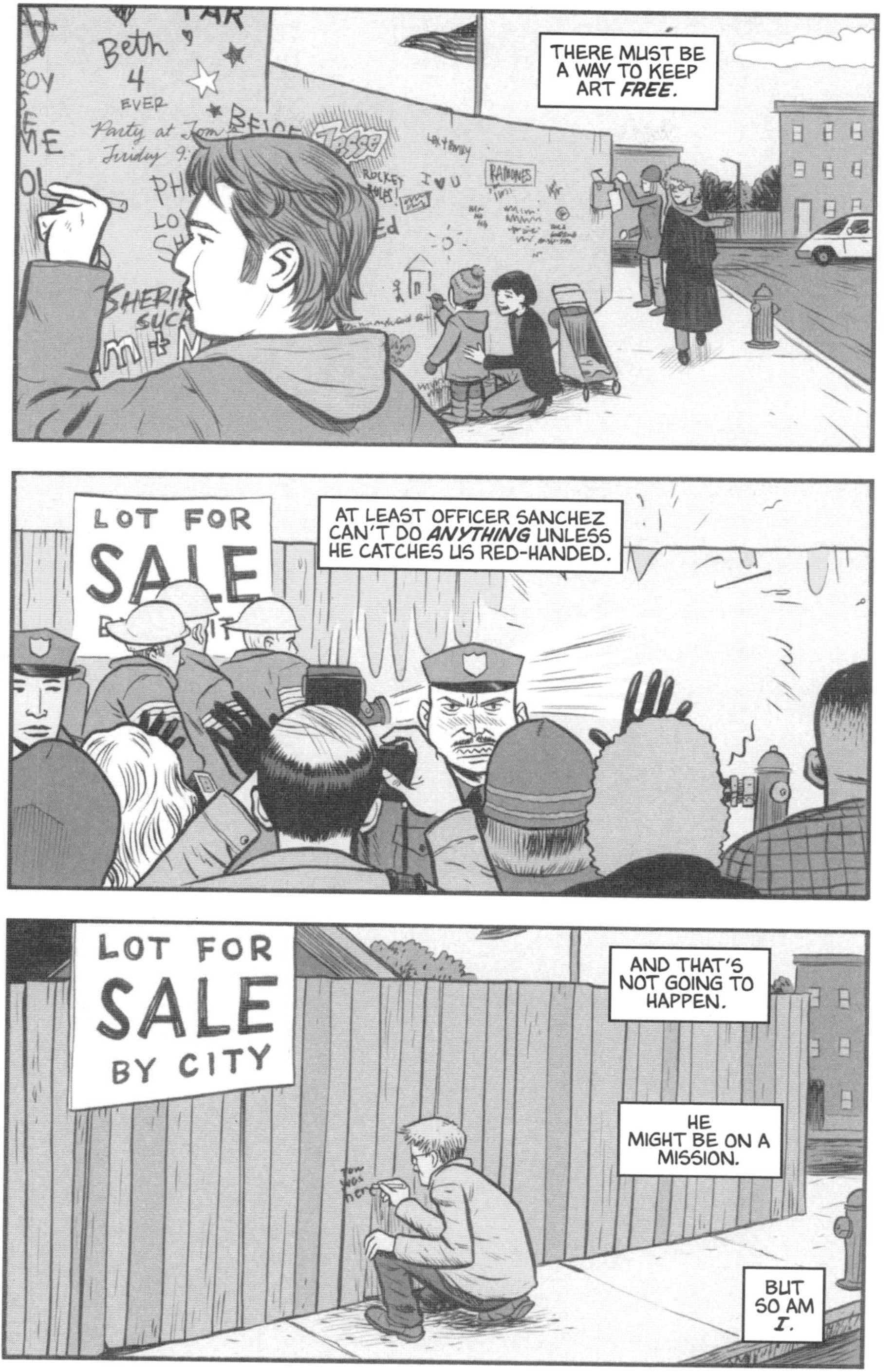
THERE MUST BE A WAY TO KEEP ART *FREE*.
Beth
4
EVER
LOT FOR SALE
AT LEAST OFFICER SANCHEZ CAN'T DO *ANYTHING* UNLESS HE CATCHES US RED-HANDED.
LOT FOR SALE BY CITY
AND THAT'S NOT GOING TO HAPPEN.
HE MIGHT BE ON A MISSION.
BUT SO AM *I*.

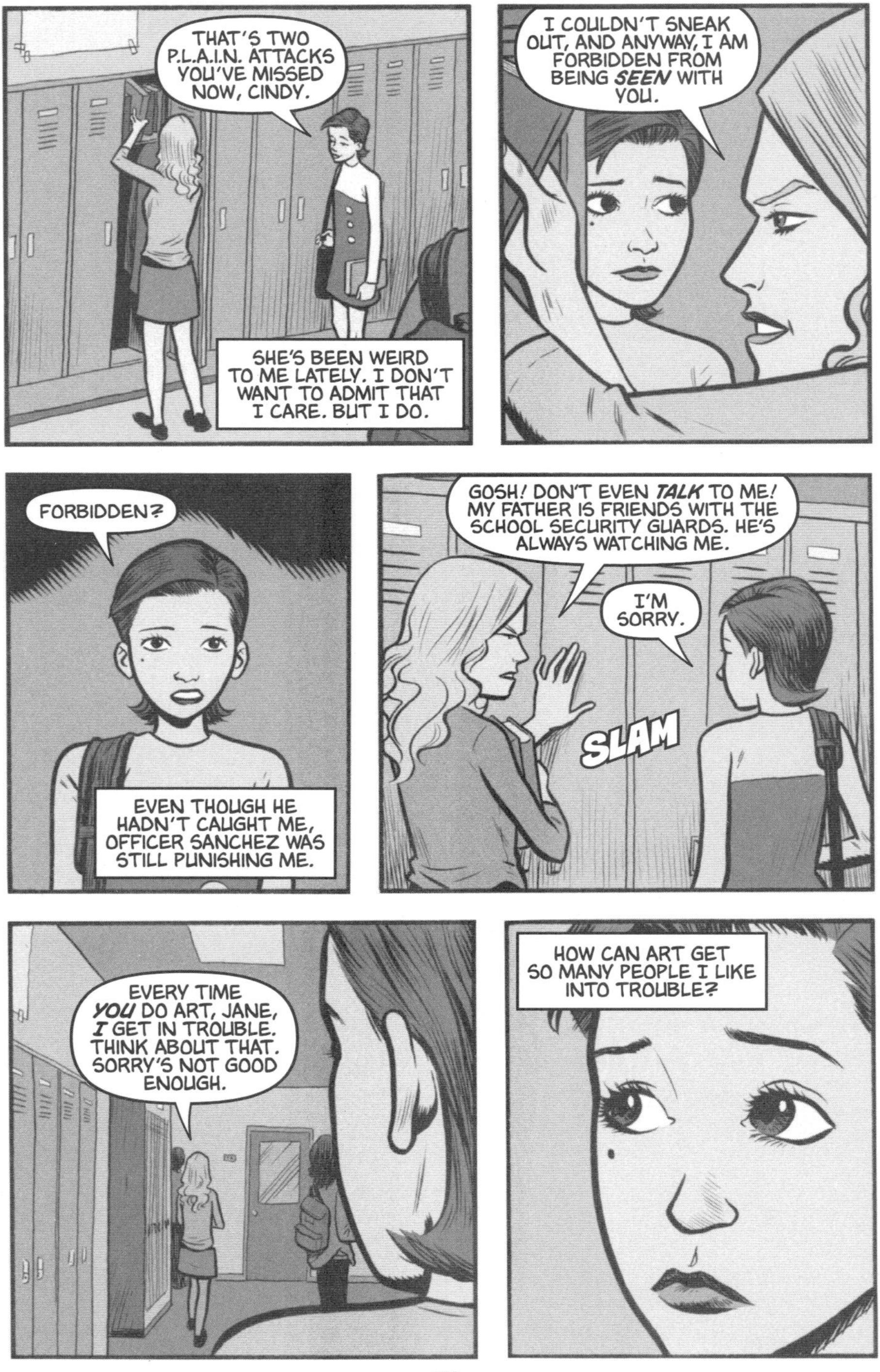
THAT'S TWO P.L.A.I.N. ATTACKS YOU'VE MISSED NOW, CINDY.
SHE'S BEEN WEIRD TO ME LATELY. I DON'T WANT TO ADMIT THAT I CARE. BUT I DO.
I COULDN'T SNEAK OUT, AND ANYWAY, I AM FORBIDDEN FROM BEING SEEN WITH YOU.
FORBIDDEN?
EVEN THOUGH HE HADN'T CAUGHT ME, OFFICER SANCHEZ WAS STILL PUNISHING ME.
GOSH! DON'T EVEN TALK TO ME! MY FATHER IS FRIENDS WITH THE SCHOOL SECURITY GUARDS. HE'S ALWAYS WATCHING ME.
I'M SORRY.
SLAM
EVERY TIME YOU DO ART, JANE, I GET IN TROUBLE. THINK ABOUT THAT. SORRY'S NOT GOOD ENOUGH.
HOW CAN ART GET SO MANY PEOPLE I LIKE INTO TROUBLE?

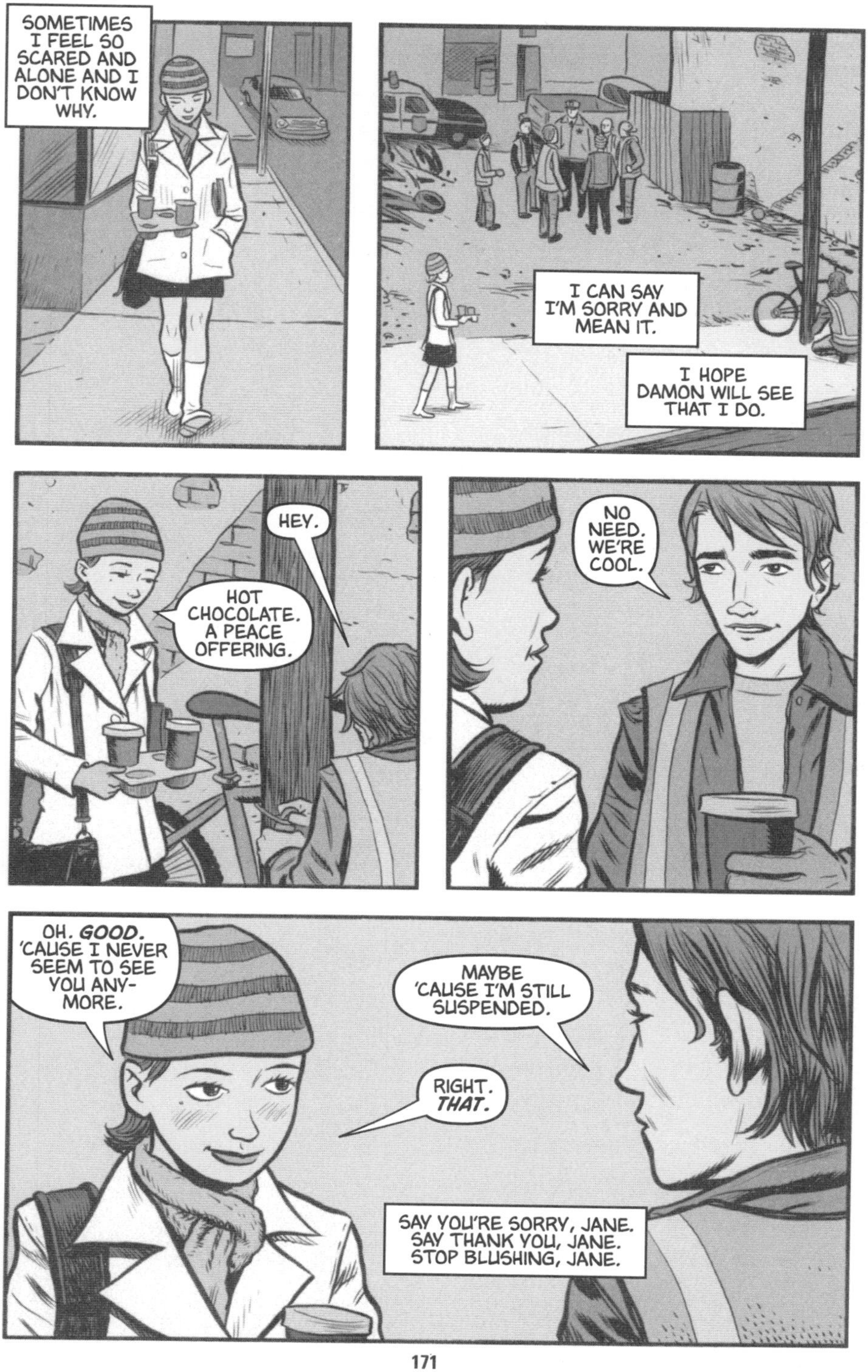
SOMETIMES I FEEL SO SCARED AND ALONE AND I DON'T KNOW WHY.
I CAN SAY I'M SORRY AND MEAN IT.
I HOPE DAMON WILL SEE THAT I DO.
HEY.
HOT CHOCOLATE. A PEACE OFFERING.
NO NEED. WE'RE COOL.
OH. **GOOD.** 'CAUSE I NEVER SEEM TO SEE YOU ANY-MORE.
MAYBE 'CAUSE I'M STILL SUSPENDED.
RIGHT. ***THAT.***
SAY YOU'RE SORRY, JANE. SAY THANK YOU, JANE. STOP BLUSHING, JANE.

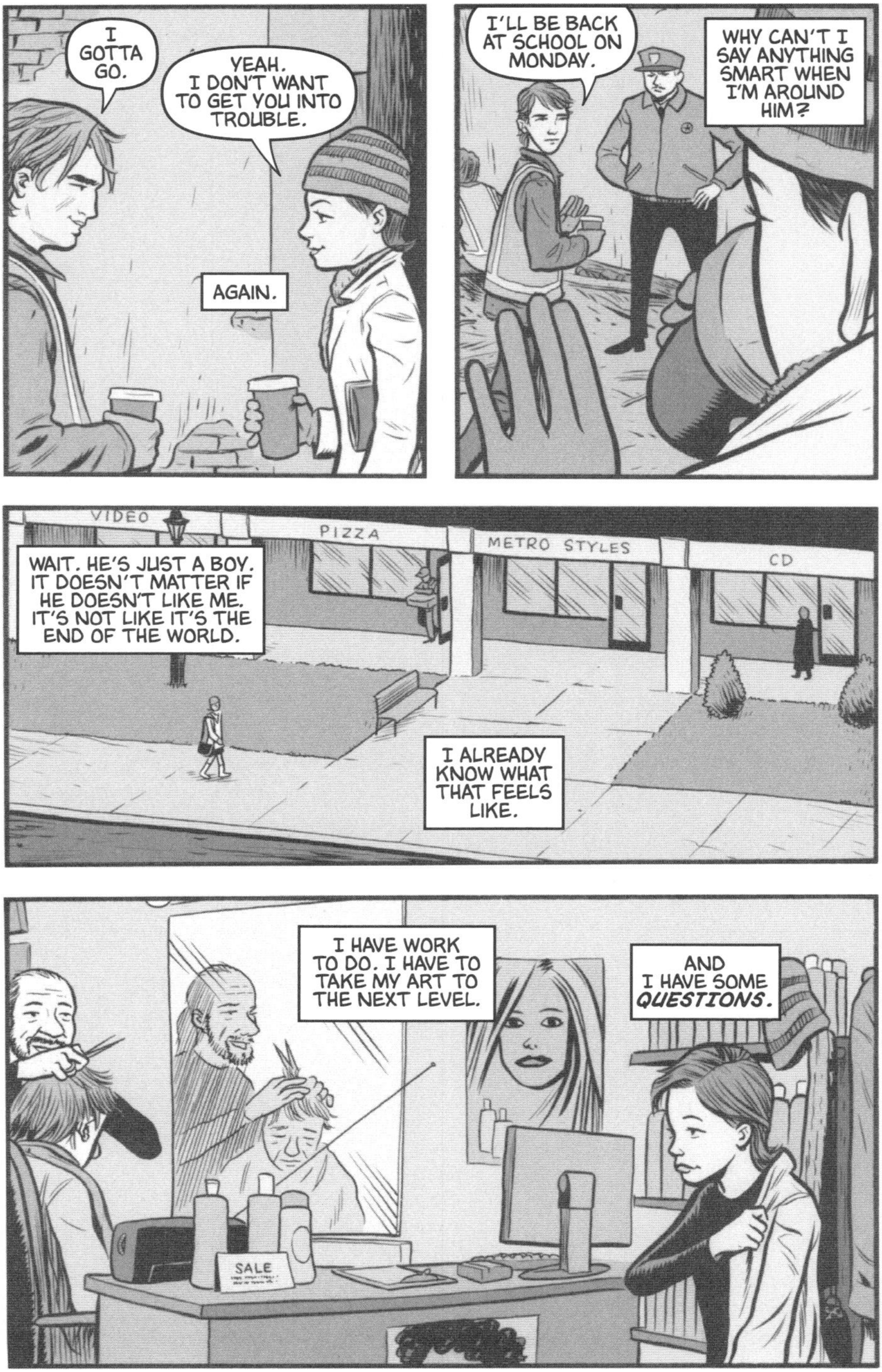
I GOTTA GO.
YEAH. I DON'T WANT TO GET YOU INTO TROUBLE.
AGAIN.
I'LL BE BACK AT SCHOOL ON MONDAY.
WHY CAN'T I SAY ANYTHING SMART WHEN I'M AROUND HIM?
VIDEO
PIZZA
METRO STYLES
CD
WAIT. HE'S JUST A BOY. IT DOESN'T MATTER IF HE DOESN'T LIKE ME. IT'S NOT LIKE IT'S THE END OF THE WORLD.
I ALREADY KNOW WHAT THAT FEELS LIKE.
I HAVE WORK TO DO. I HAVE TO TAKE MY ART TO THE NEXT LEVEL.
AND I HAVE SOME ***QUESTIONS.***
SALE

LIKE WHO DECIDES WHO'S A SERIOUS ARTIST?

HOW CAN I MAKE MY ART NOT GET PEOPLE I LIKE INTO TROUBLE?

AND HOW CAN I GET MONEY FOR ART SUPPLIES?

BUT JUST WHEN I THINK I CAN MAKE PLANS TO MAKE THINGS BETTER--

AND NOW THE NEWS--METRO CITY REPORTER FATALLY STRICKEN WITH *ANTHRAX* IN A NEW WAVE OF WHAT'S BEING LABELED HOMEGROWN TERROR.

--THE WORLD FALLS FURTHER APART.

Foundation for the American Arts

The

Call for Ent

Proposals for the 100 best and most innovative artists in the country will be selected for the largest public art projects. Each artist or art collective will propose an ...lation to be erected in the

BEVERLY DORAN, AN ALUMNA OF METRO CITY UNIVERSITY, HAD WON ACCOLADES IN THE FIELD OF REPORTING.

WE HERE AT KCCK ARE SADDENED BY THE LOSS OF ONE OF OUR BRETHREN. REST IN PEACE.

MOM!

I DIDN'T SEE ANY FLASH OR HEAR THAT WEIRD ABSENCE OF NOISE LIKE WHEN THE BOMB WENT OFF.

ALL I KNEW WAS THAT SOMETHING WAS TERRIBLY WRONG.

WHAT'S GOING ON? WHAT'S *WRONG*?

HELP ME GET HER TO THAT CHAIR.

MY HEART. OH, MY HEART IS BURSTING.

173

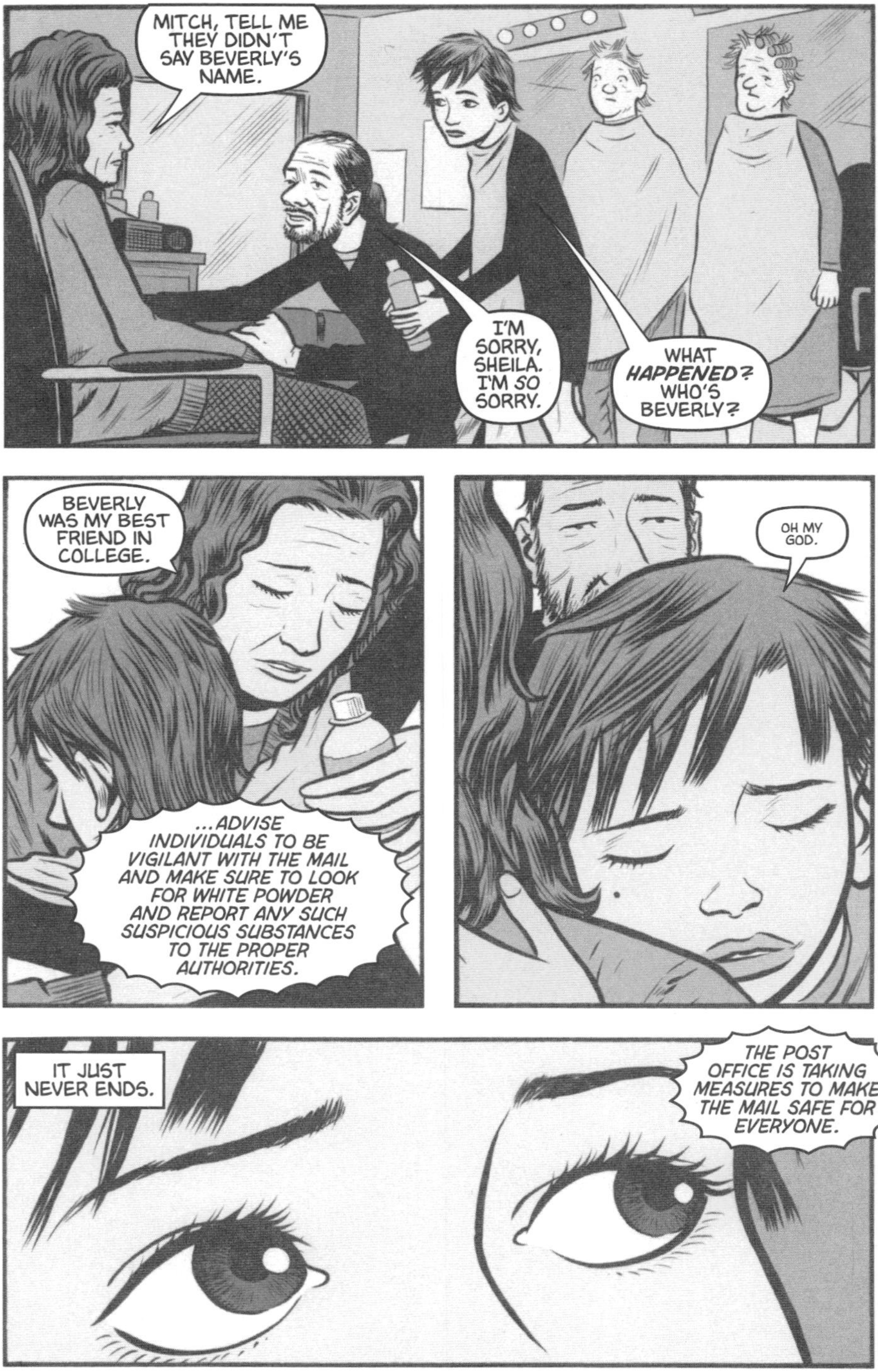
MITCH, TELL ME THEY DIDN'T SAY BEVERLY'S NAME.
I'M SORRY, SHEILA. I'M *SO* SORRY.
WHAT ***HAPPENED***? WHO'S BEVERLY?
BEVERLY WAS MY BEST FRIEND IN COLLEGE.
...ADVISE INDIVIDUALS TO BE VIGILANT WITH THE MAIL AND MAKE SURE TO LOOK FOR WHITE POWDER AND REPORT ANY SUCH SUSPICIOUS SUBSTANCES TO THE PROPER AUTHORITIES.
OH MY GOD.
IT JUST NEVER ENDS.
THE POST OFFICE IS TAKING MEASURES TO MAKE THE MAIL SAFE FOR EVERYONE.

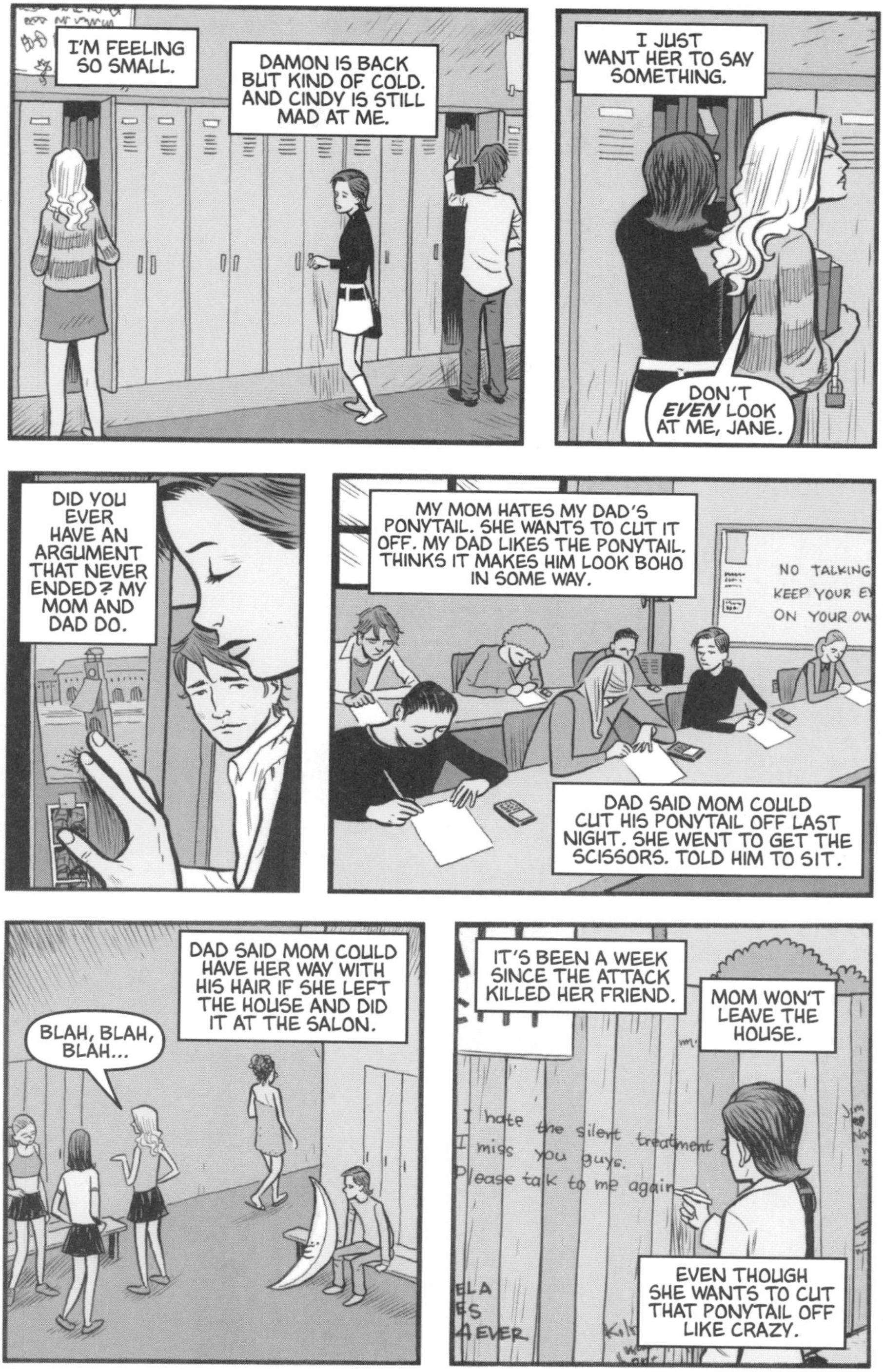

I'M FEELING SO SMALL.
DAMON IS BACK BUT KIND OF COLD. AND CINDY IS STILL MAD AT ME.
I JUST WANT HER TO SAY SOMETHING.
DON'T *EVEN* LOOK AT ME, JANE.
DID YOU EVER HAVE AN ARGUMENT THAT NEVER ENDED? MY MOM AND DAD DO.
MY MOM HATES MY DAD'S PONYTAIL. SHE WANTS TO CUT IT OFF. MY DAD LIKES THE PONYTAIL. THINKS IT MAKES HIM LOOK BOHO IN SOME WAY.
NO TALKING
DAD SAID MOM COULD CUT HIS PONYTAIL OFF LAST NIGHT. SHE WENT TO GET THE SCISSORS. TOLD HIM TO SIT.
DAD SAID MOM COULD HAVE HER WAY WITH HIS HAIR IF SHE LEFT THE HOUSE AND DID IT AT THE SALON.
BLAH, BLAH, BLAH...
IT'S BEEN A WEEK SINCE THE ATTACK KILLED HER FRIEND.
MOM WON'T LEAVE THE HOUSE.
I hate the silent treatment
I miss you guys.
Please talk to me again
EVEN THOUGH SHE WANTS TO CUT THAT PONYTAIL OFF LIKE CRAZY.

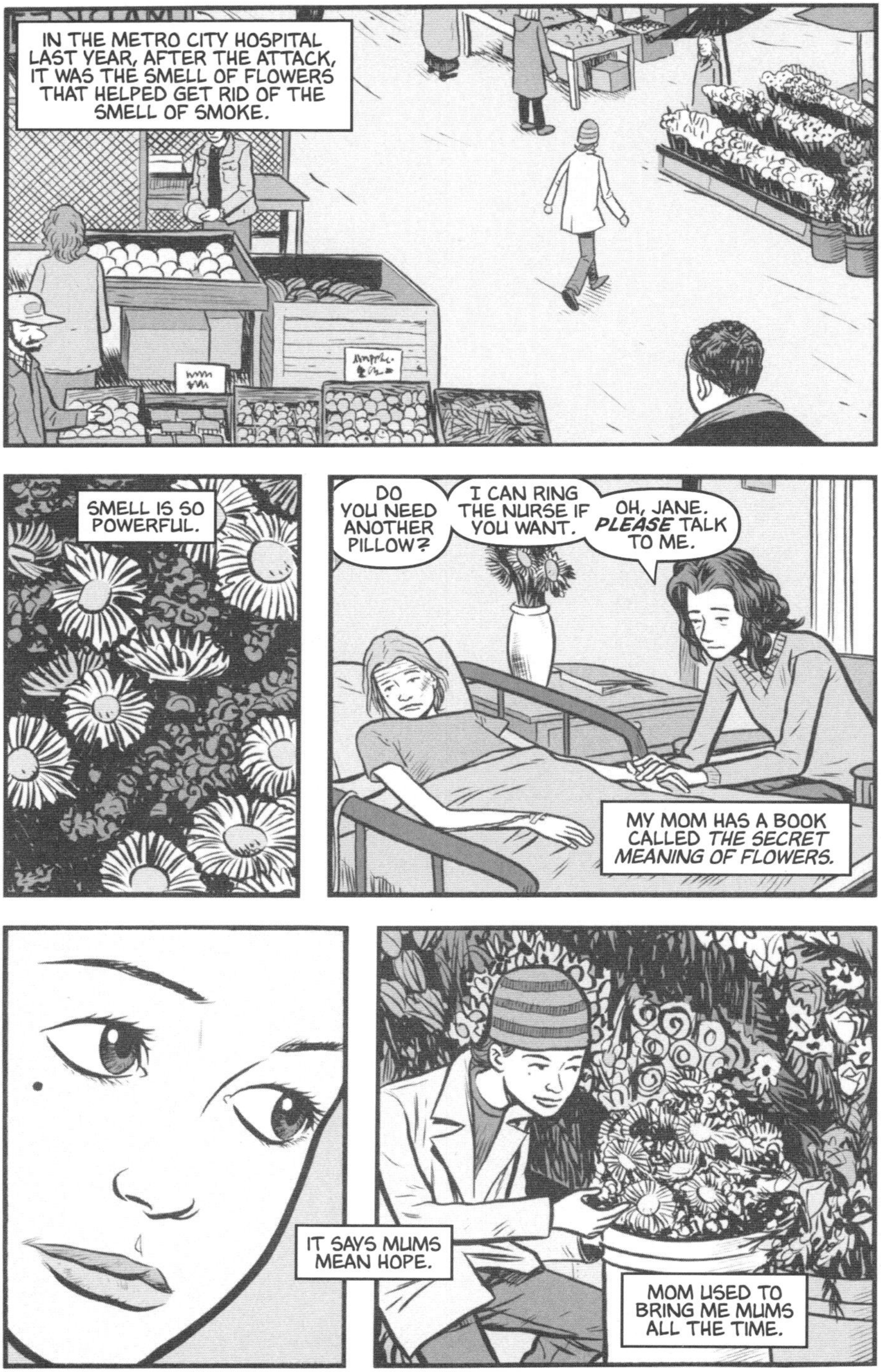
IN THE METRO CITY HOSPITAL LAST YEAR, AFTER THE ATTACK, IT WAS THE SMELL OF FLOWERS THAT HELPED GET RID OF THE SMELL OF SMOKE.
SMELL IS SO POWERFUL.
DO YOU NEED ANOTHER PILLOW?
I CAN RING THE NURSE IF YOU WANT.
OH, JANE. *PLEASE* TALK TO ME.
MY MOM HAS A BOOK CALLED *THE SECRET MEANING OF FLOWERS.*
IT SAYS MUMS MEAN HOPE.
MOM USED TO BRING ME MUMS ALL THE TIME.

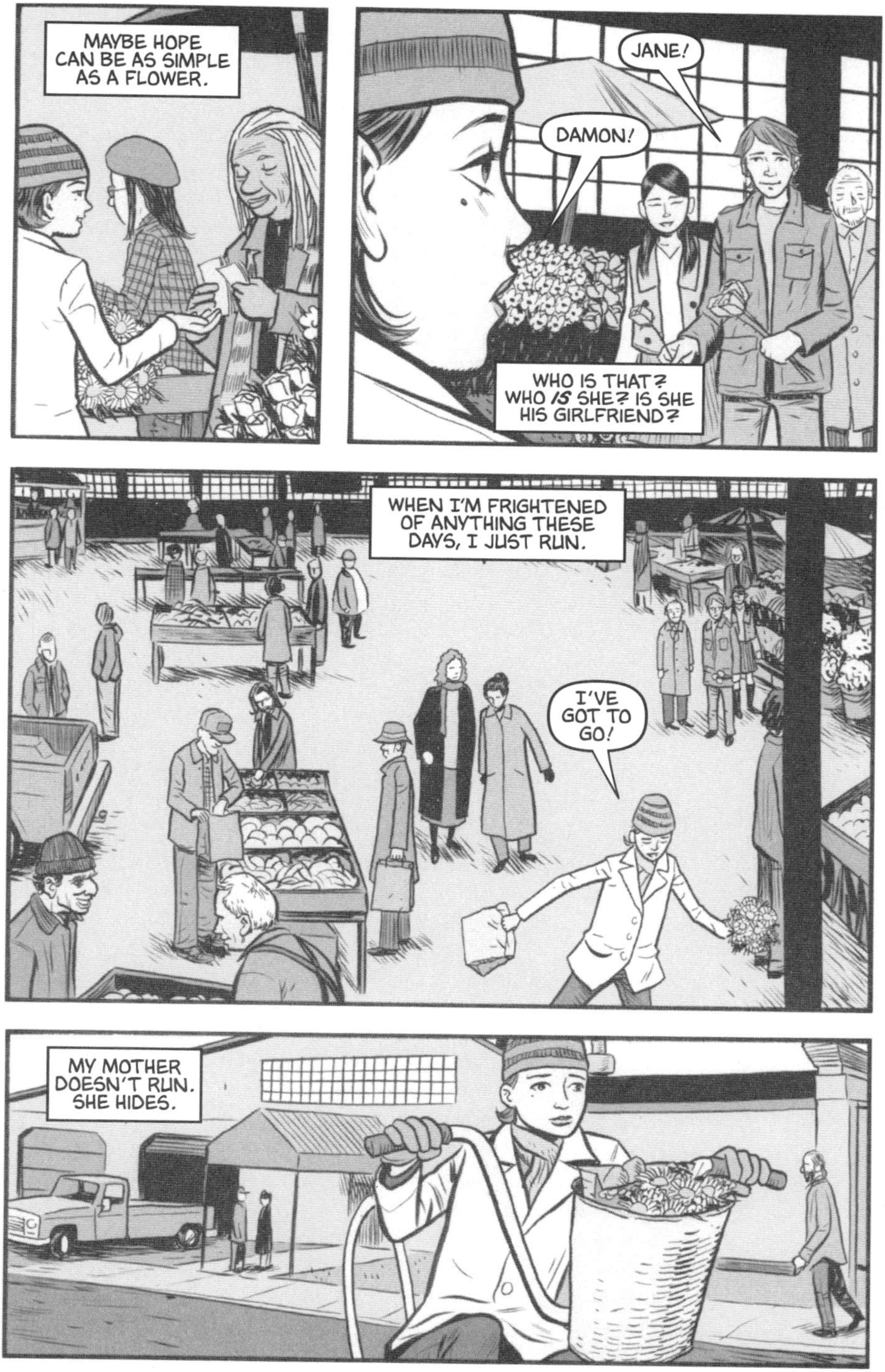
MAYBE HOPE CAN BE AS SIMPLE AS A FLOWER.
JANE!
DAMON!
WHO IS THAT? WHO *IS* SHE? IS SHE HIS GIRLFRIEND?
WHEN I'M FRIGHTENED OF ANYTHING THESE DAYS, I JUST RUN.
I'VE GOT TO GO!
MY MOTHER DOESN'T RUN. SHE HIDES.

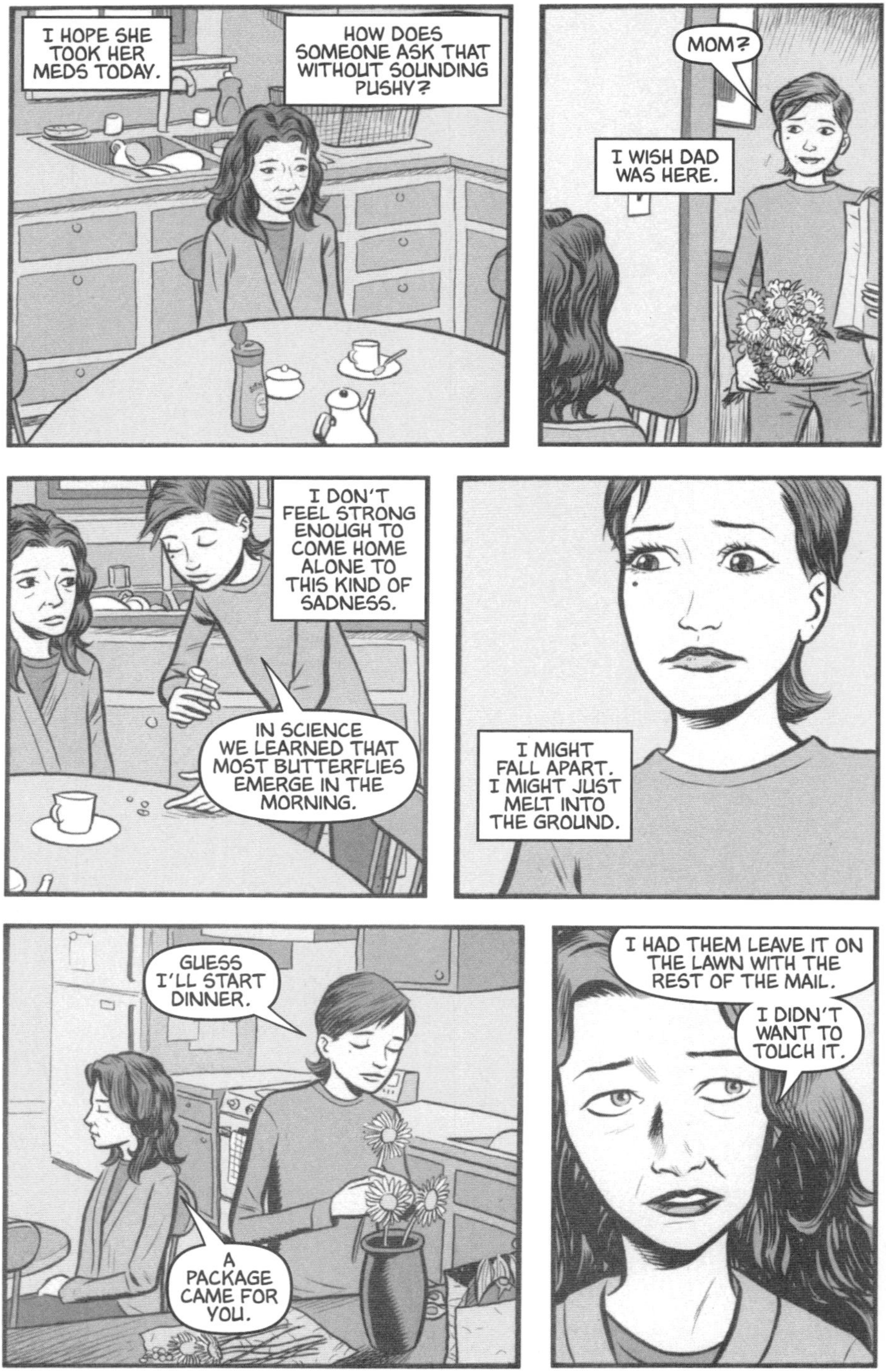
I HOPE SHE TOOK HER MEDS TODAY.
HOW DOES SOMEONE ASK THAT WITHOUT SOUNDING PUSHY?
MOM?
I WISH DAD WAS HERE.
I DON'T FEEL STRONG ENOUGH TO COME HOME ALONE TO THIS KIND OF SADNESS.
IN SCIENCE WE LEARNED THAT MOST BUTTERFLIES EMERGE IN THE MORNING.
I MIGHT FALL APART. I MIGHT JUST MELT INTO THE GROUND.
GUESS I'LL START DINNER.
A PACKAGE CAME FOR YOU.
I HAD THEM LEAVE IT ON THE LAWN WITH THE REST OF THE MAIL.
I DIDN'T WANT TO TOUCH IT.

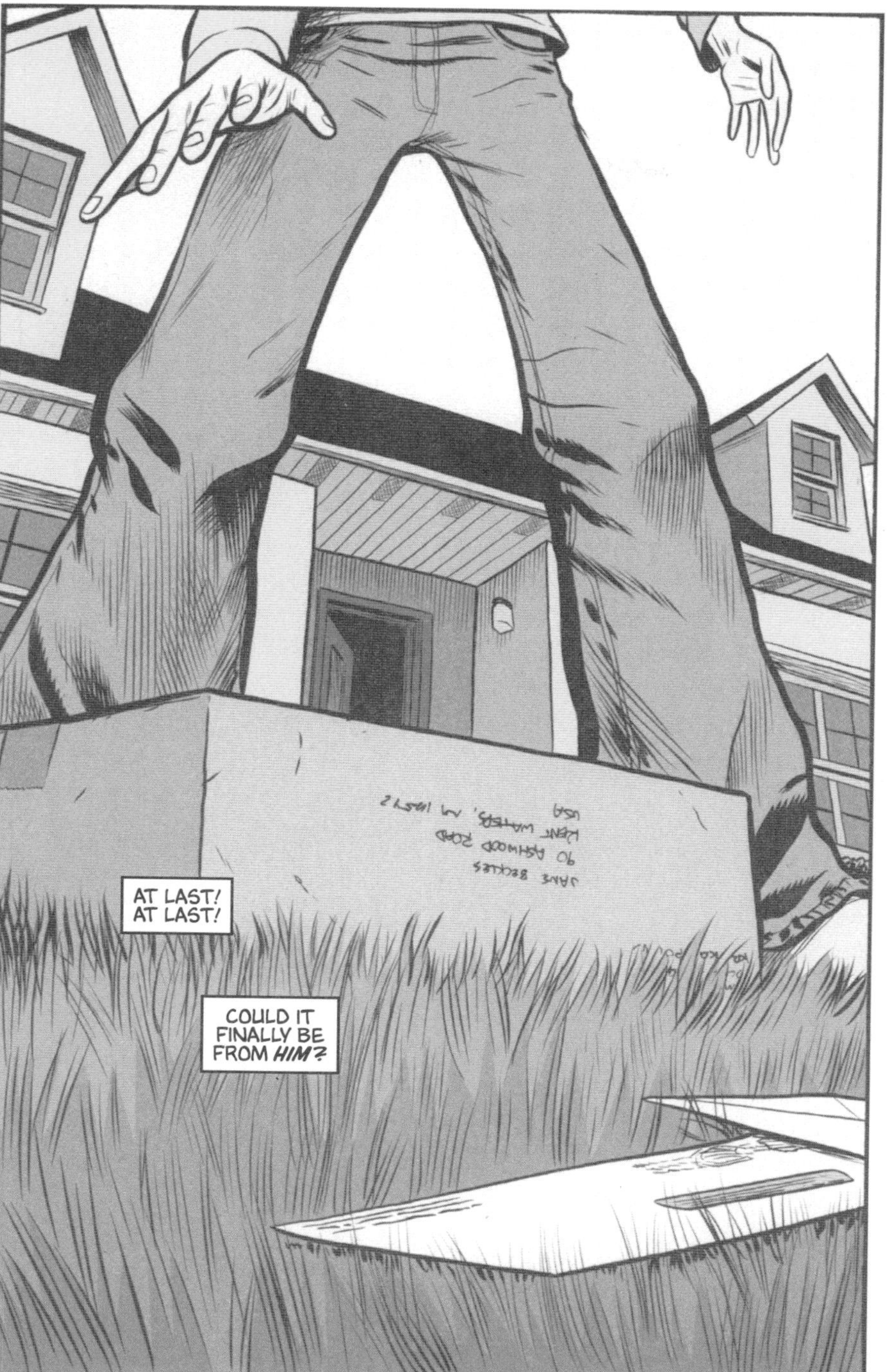
AT LAST! AT LAST!
COULD IT FINALLY BE FROM *HIM*?

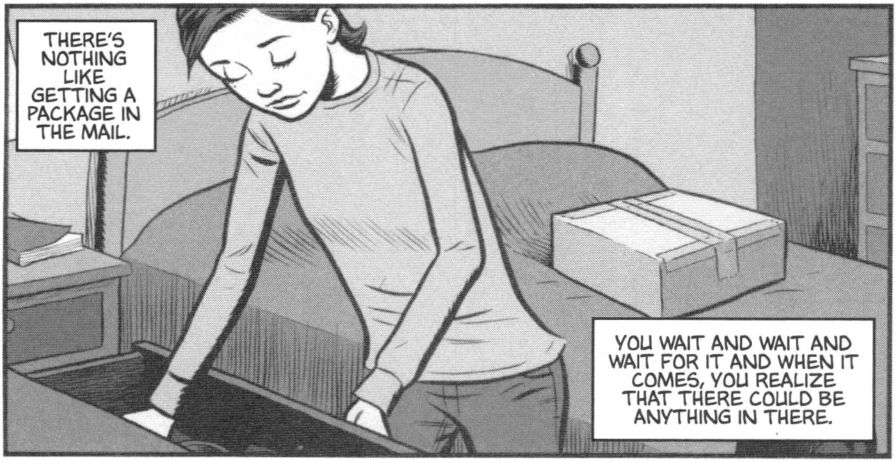
THERE'S NOTHING LIKE GETTING A PACKAGE IN THE MAIL.
YOU WAIT AND WAIT AND WAIT FOR IT AND WHEN IT COMES, YOU REALIZE THAT THERE COULD BE ANYTHING IN THERE.

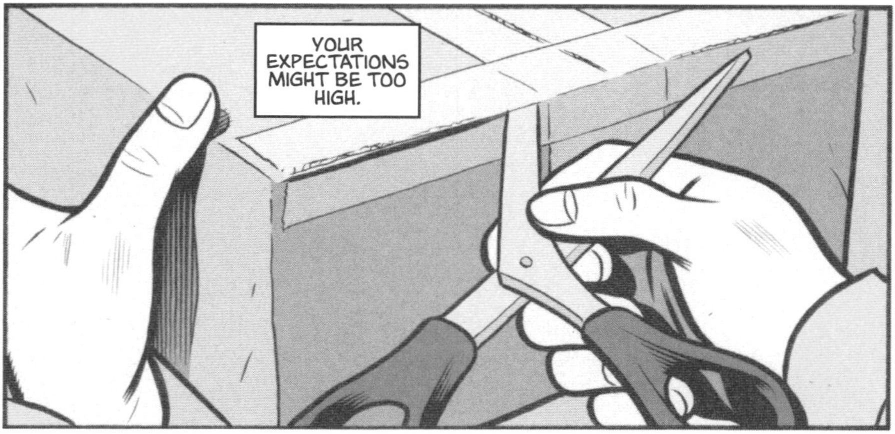
YOUR EXPECTATIONS MIGHT BE TOO HIGH.

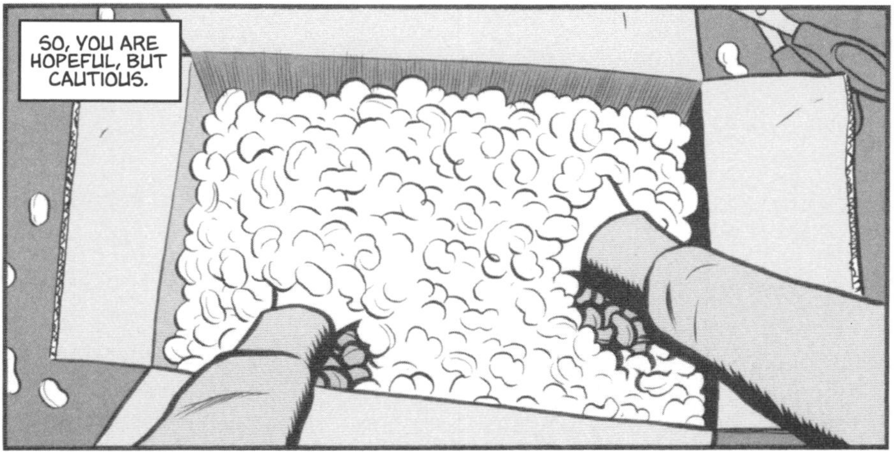
SO, YOU ARE HOPEFUL, BUT CAUTIOUS.

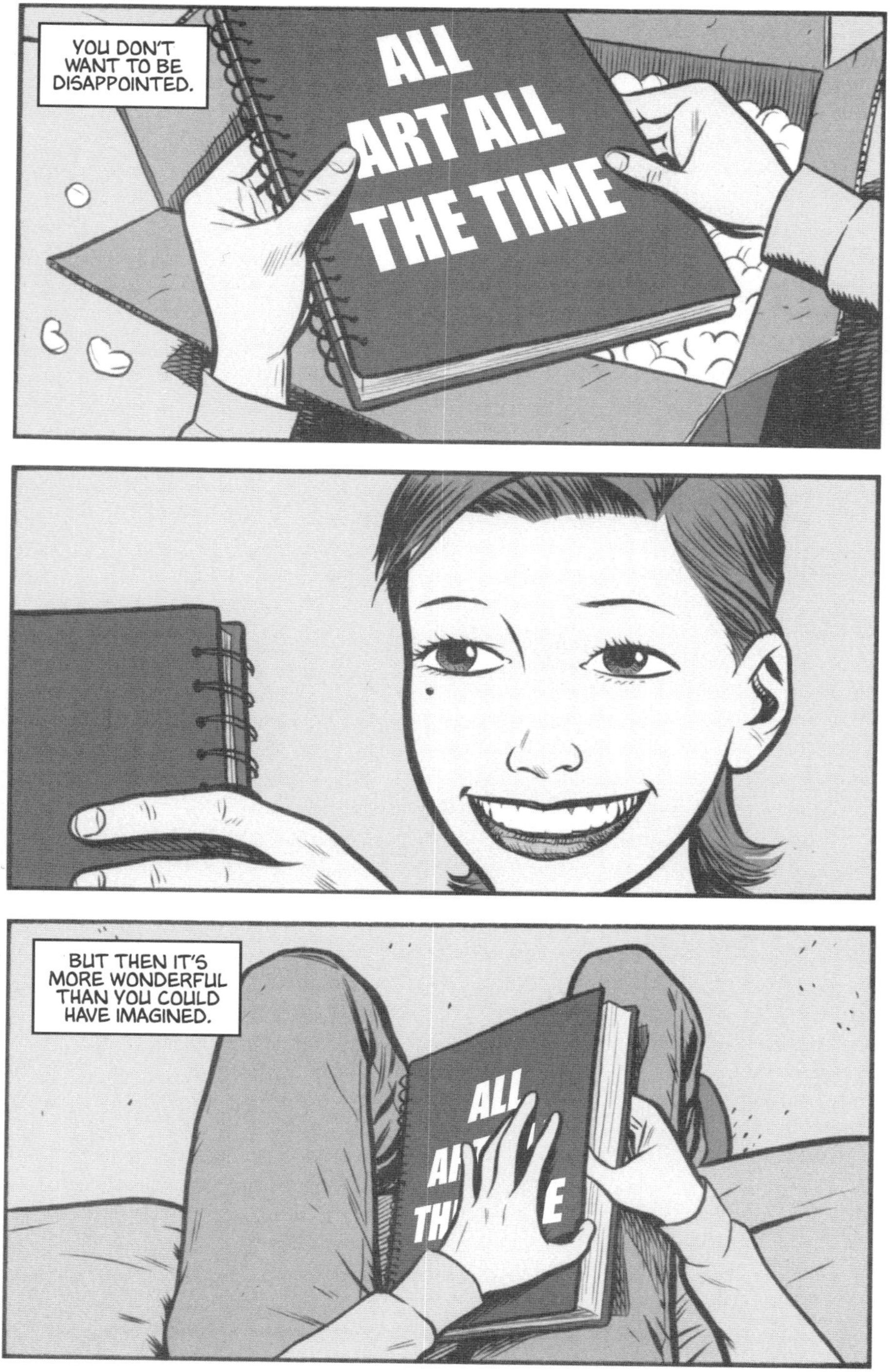
YOU DON'T WANT TO BE DISAPPOINTED.
ALL ART ALL THE TIME
BUT THEN IT'S MORE WONDERFUL THAN YOU COULD HAVE IMAGINED.
ALL

DEAR JANE

Hello. How wonderful to be able to say these words to you.
Hello, dear Jane. Light of my life.

Slow is the world
I have to take things
At a slower pace
Thoughts like molasses
Careful steps
Cautious
When I speak I slur
And the soup my mother feeds me
Dribbles out the left corner of my mouth.
I am safe now
Back again in the world of light

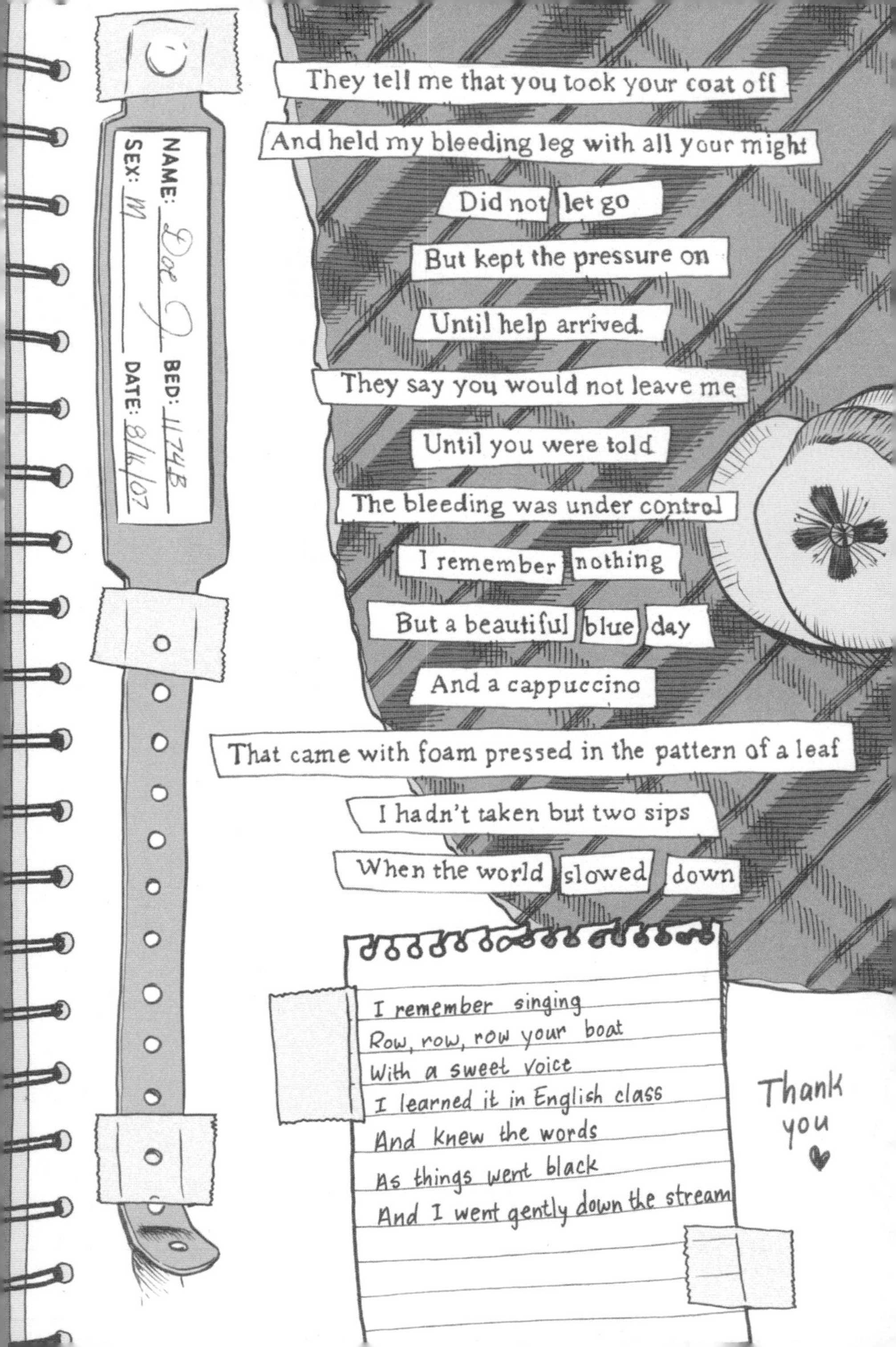

NAME: Doe J.
SEX: M
BED: 1174B
DATE: 8/16/07
They tell me that you took your coat off
And held my bleeding leg with all your might
Did not let go
But kept the pressure on
Until help arrived.
They say you would not leave me
Until you were told
The bleeding was under control
I remember nothing
But a beautiful blue day
And a cappuccino
That came with foam pressed in the pattern of a leaf
I hadn't taken but two sips
When the world slowed down
I remember singing
Row, row, row your boat
With a sweet voice
I learned it in English class
And knew the words
As things went black
And I went gently down the stream
Thank you

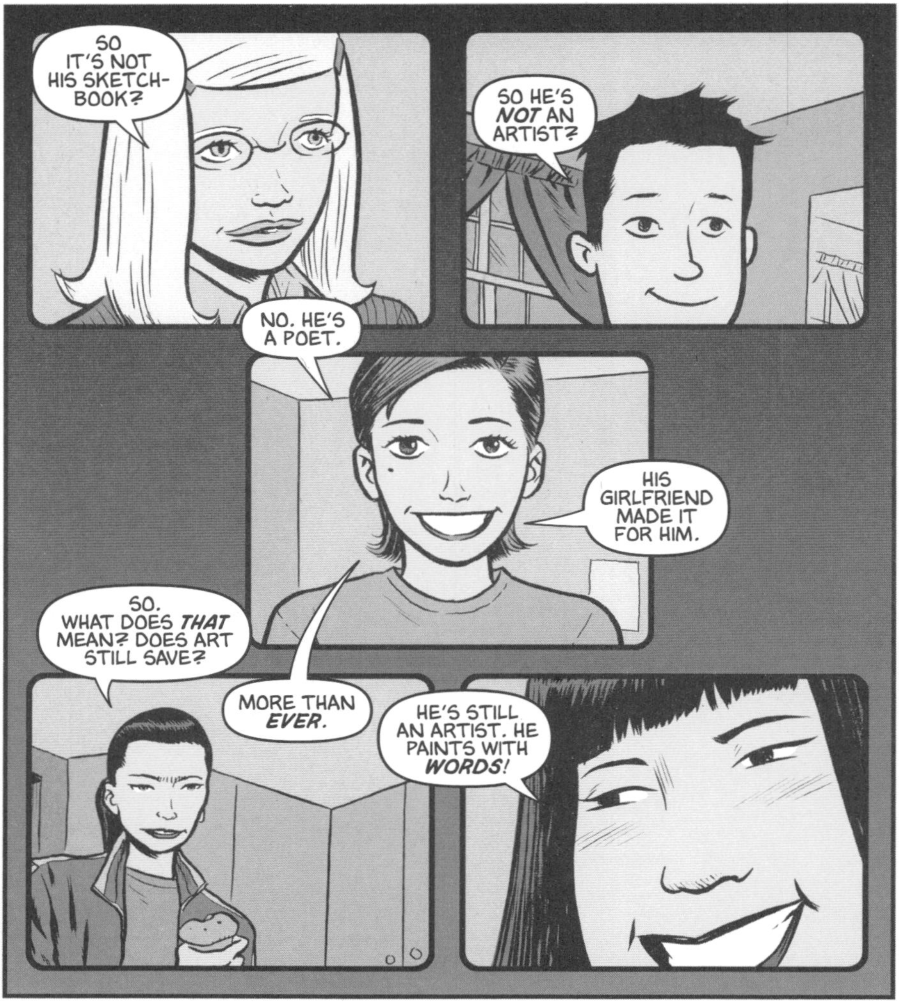
SO IT'S NOT HIS SKETCH-BOOK?
SO HE'S *NOT* AN ARTIST?
NO. HE'S A POET.
HIS GIRLFRIEND MADE IT FOR HIM.
SO. WHAT DOES *THAT* MEAN? DOES ART STILL SAVE?
MORE THAN *EVER*.
HE'S STILL AN ARTIST. HE PAINTS WITH *WORDS*!

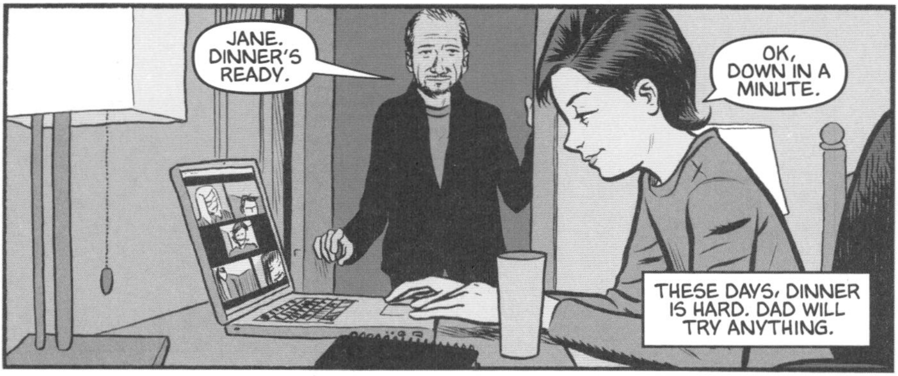
JANE. DINNER'S READY.
OK, DOWN IN A MINUTE.
THESE DAYS, DINNER IS HARD. DAD WILL TRY ANYTHING.

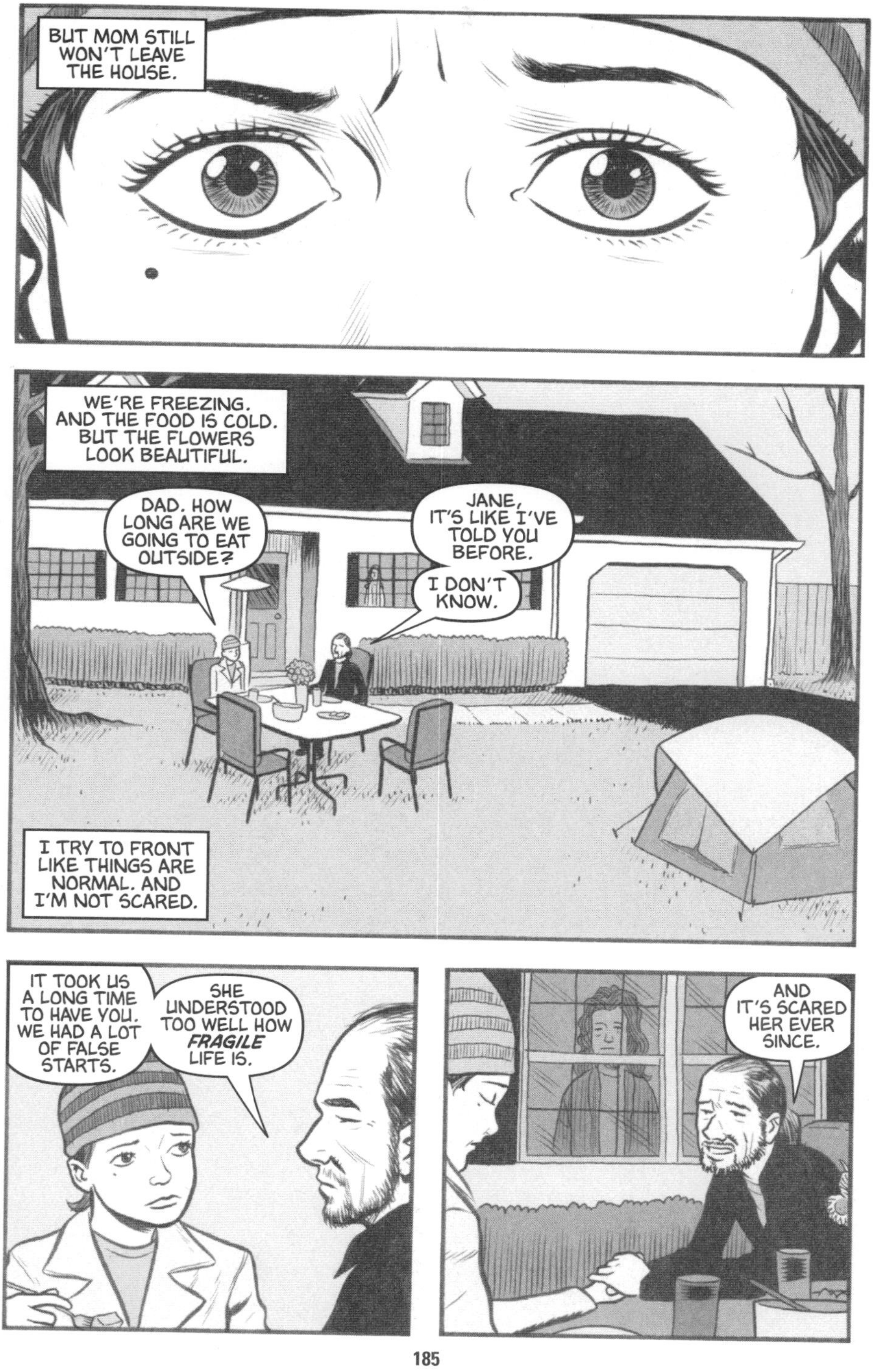
BUT MOM STILL WON'T LEAVE THE HOUSE.
WE'RE FREEZING. AND THE FOOD IS COLD. BUT THE FLOWERS LOOK BEAUTIFUL.
DAD. HOW LONG ARE WE GOING TO EAT OUTSIDE?
JANE, IT'S LIKE I'VE TOLD YOU BEFORE.
I DON'T KNOW.
I TRY TO FRONT LIKE THINGS ARE NORMAL. AND I'M NOT SCARED.
IT TOOK US A LONG TIME TO HAVE YOU. WE HAD A LOT OF FALSE STARTS.
SHE UNDERSTOOD TOO WELL HOW *FRAGILE* LIFE IS.
AND IT'S SCARED HER EVER SINCE.

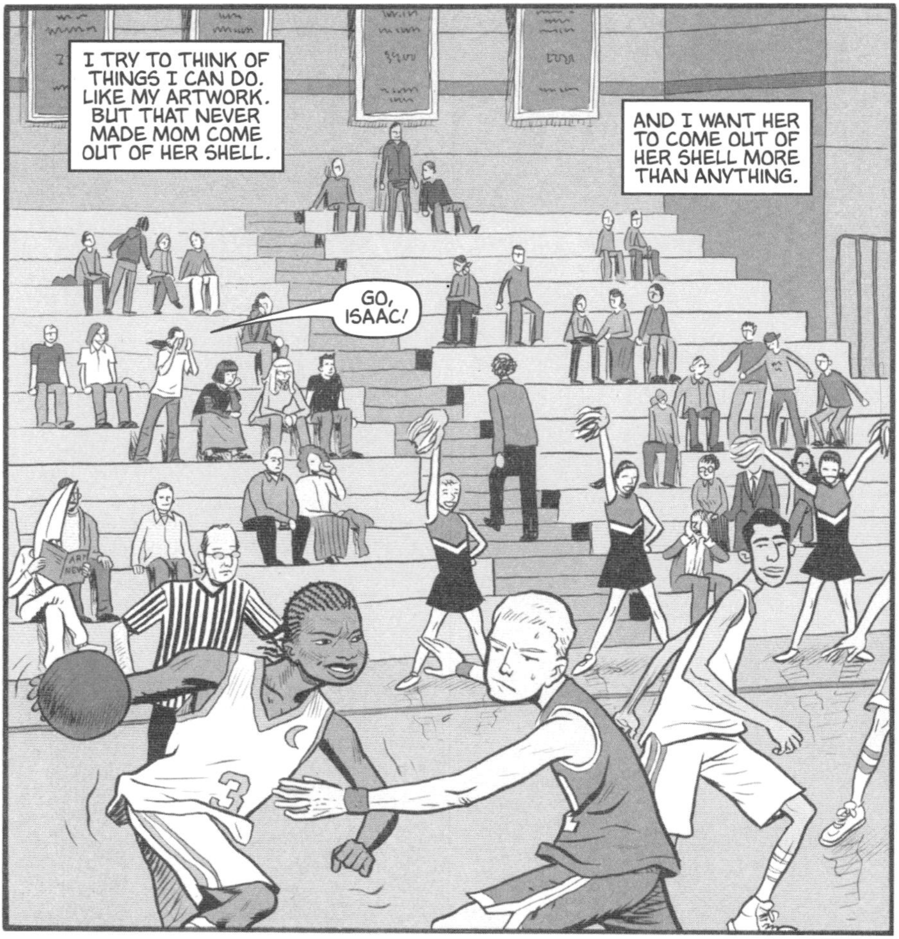
I TRY TO THINK OF THINGS I CAN DO. LIKE MY ARTWORK. BUT THAT NEVER MADE MOM COME OUT OF HER SHELL.
AND I WANT HER TO COME OUT OF HER SHELL MORE THAN ANYTHING.
GO, ISAAC!
3

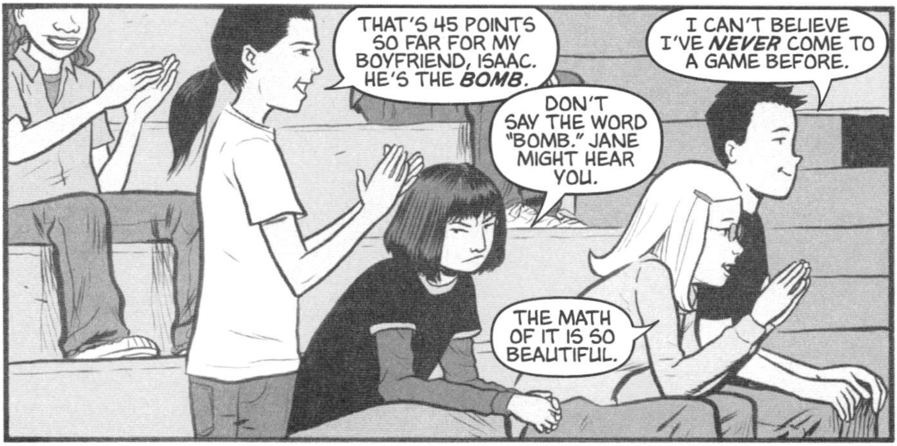
THAT'S 45 POINTS SO FAR FOR MY BOYFRIEND, ISAAC. HE'S THE *BOMB*.
DON'T SAY THE WORD "BOMB." JANE MIGHT HEAR YOU.
I CAN'T BELIEVE I'VE *NEVER* COME TO A GAME BEFORE.
THE MATH OF IT IS SO BEAUTIFUL.

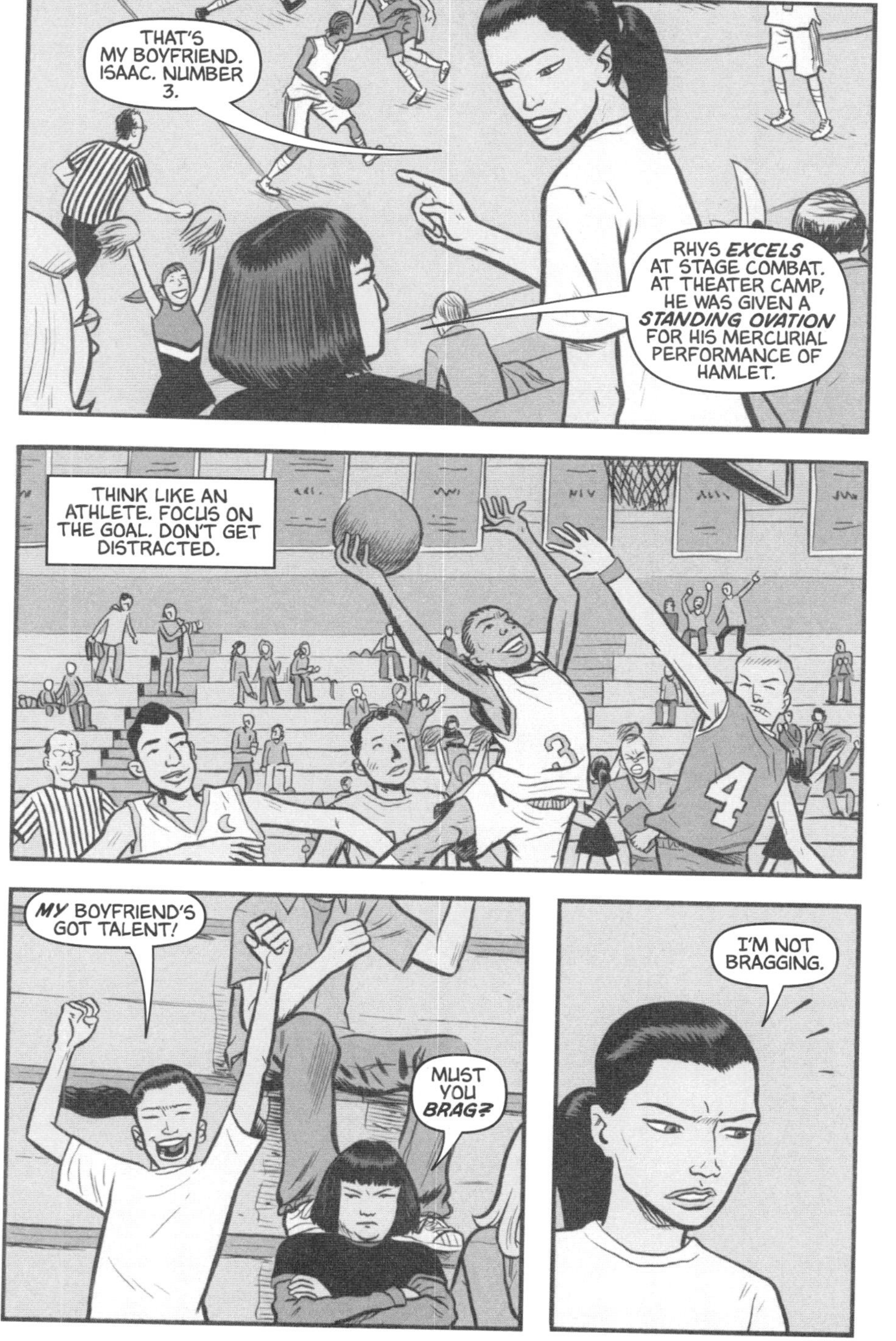
THAT'S MY BOYFRIEND. ISAAC. NUMBER 3.
RHYS *EXCELS* AT STAGE COMBAT. AT THEATER CAMP, HE WAS GIVEN A ***STANDING OVATION*** FOR HIS MERCURIAL PERFORMANCE OF HAMLET.
THINK LIKE AN ATHLETE. FOCUS ON THE GOAL. DON'T GET DISTRACTED.
MY BOYFRIEND'S GOT TALENT!
MUST YOU *BRAG?*
I'M NOT BRAGGING.

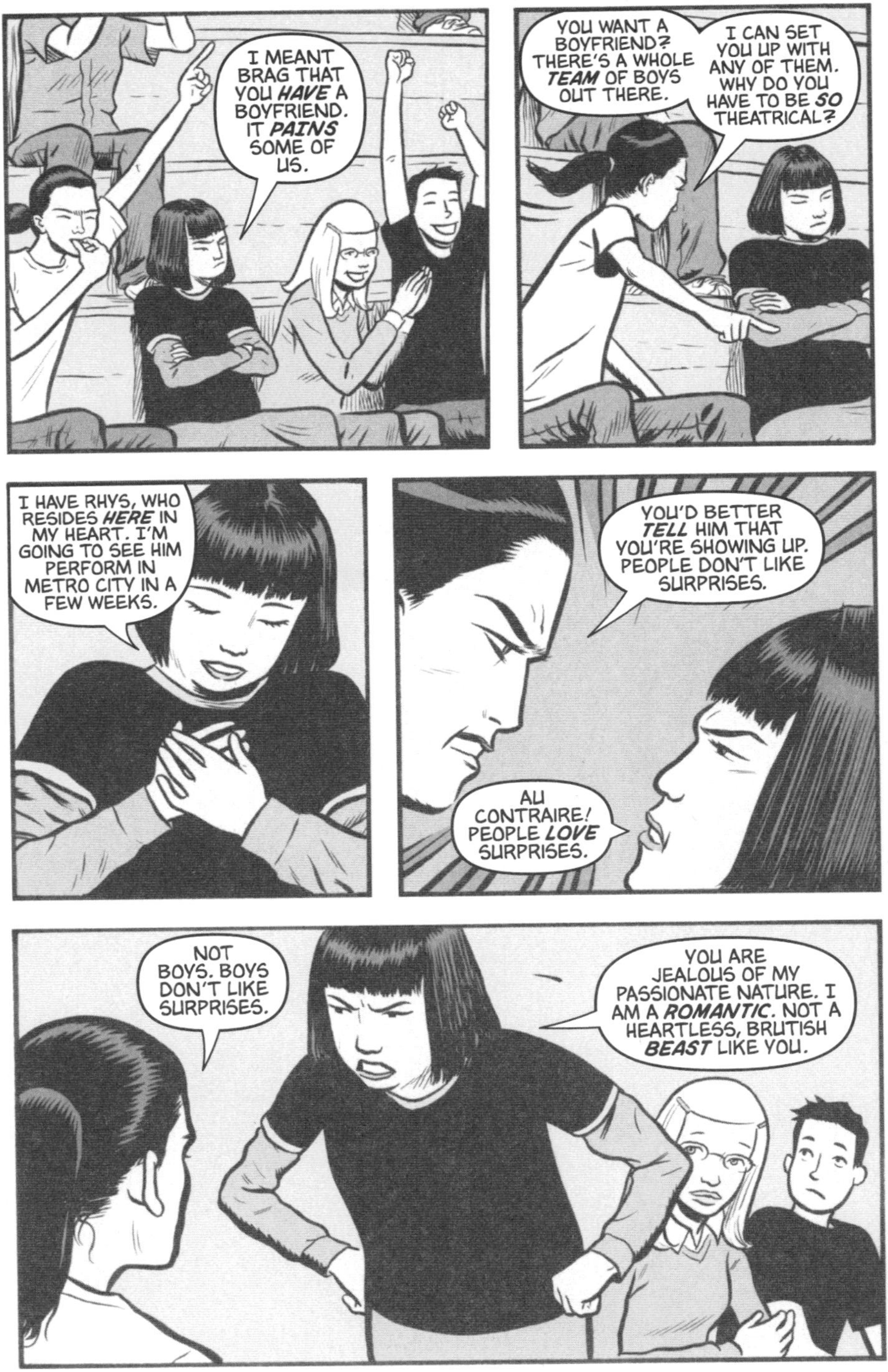
I MEANT BRAG THAT YOU *HAVE* A BOYFRIEND. IT *PAINS* SOME OF US.
YOU WANT A BOYFRIEND? THERE'S A WHOLE *TEAM* OF BOYS OUT THERE.
I CAN SET YOU UP WITH ANY OF THEM. WHY DO YOU HAVE TO BE *SO* THEATRICAL?
I HAVE RHYS, WHO RESIDES *HERE* IN MY HEART. I'M GOING TO SEE HIM PERFORM IN METRO CITY IN A FEW WEEKS.
YOU'D BETTER *TELL* HIM THAT YOU'RE SHOWING UP. PEOPLE DON'T LIKE SURPRISES.
AU CONTRAIRE! PEOPLE *LOVE* SURPRISES.
NOT BOYS. BOYS DON'T LIKE SURPRISES.
YOU ARE JEALOUS OF MY PASSIONATE NATURE. I AM A *ROMANTIC*. NOT A HEARTLESS, BRUTISH *BEAST* LIKE YOU.

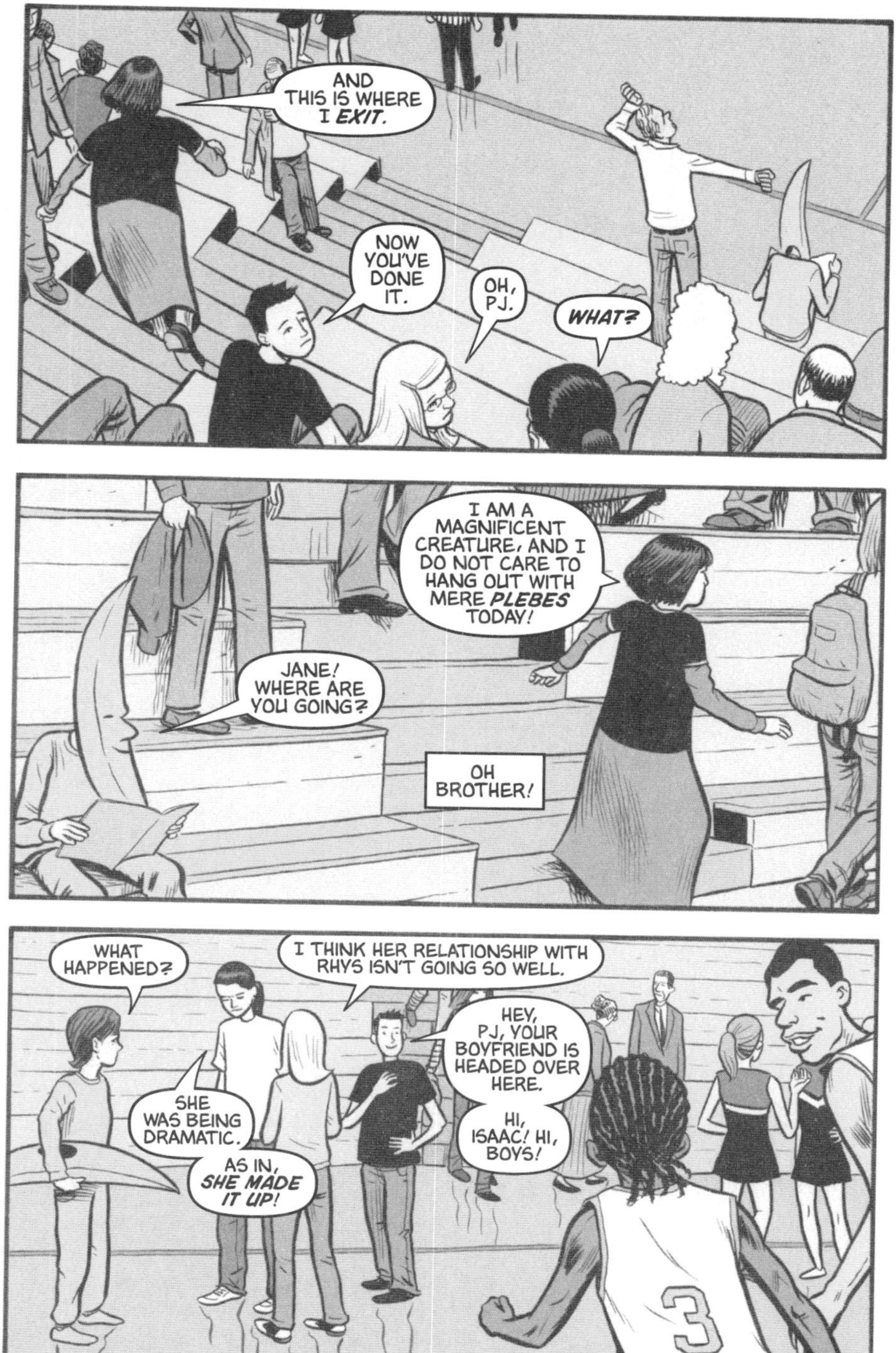
AND THIS IS WHERE I *EXIT.*
NOW YOU'VE DONE IT.
OH, PJ.
WHAT?
I AM A MAGNIFICENT CREATURE, AND I DO NOT CARE TO HANG OUT WITH MERE *PLEBES* TODAY!
JANE! WHERE ARE YOU GOING?
OH BROTHER!
WHAT HAPPENED?
I THINK HER RELATIONSHIP WITH RHYS ISN'T GOING SO WELL.
SHE WAS BEING DRAMATIC.
AS IN, *SHE MADE IT UP!*
HEY, PJ, YOUR BOYFRIEND IS HEADED OVER HERE.
HI, ISAAC! HI, BOYS!
3

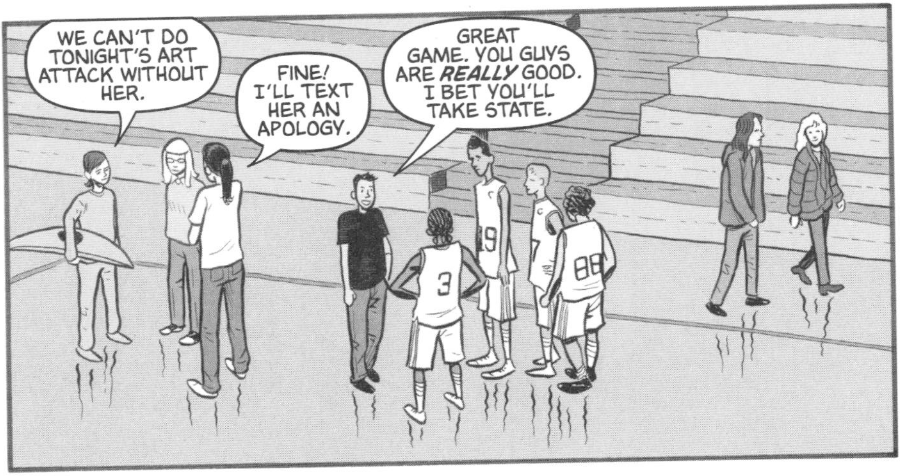
WE CAN'T DO TONIGHT'S ART ATTACK WITHOUT HER.
FINE! I'LL TEXT HER AN APOLOGY.
GREAT GAME. YOU GUYS ARE *REALLY* GOOD. I BET YOU'LL TAKE STATE.

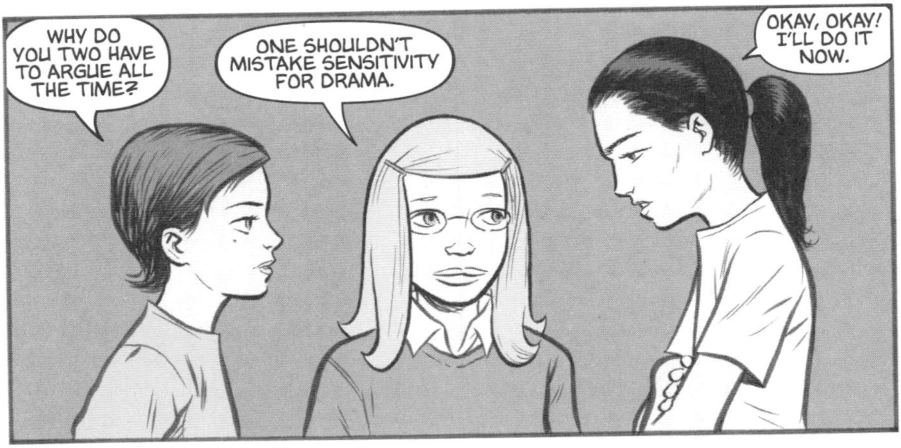
WHY DO YOU TWO HAVE TO ARGUE ALL THE TIME?
ONE SHOULDN'T MISTAKE SENSITIVITY FOR DRAMA.
OKAY, OKAY! I'LL DO IT NOW.

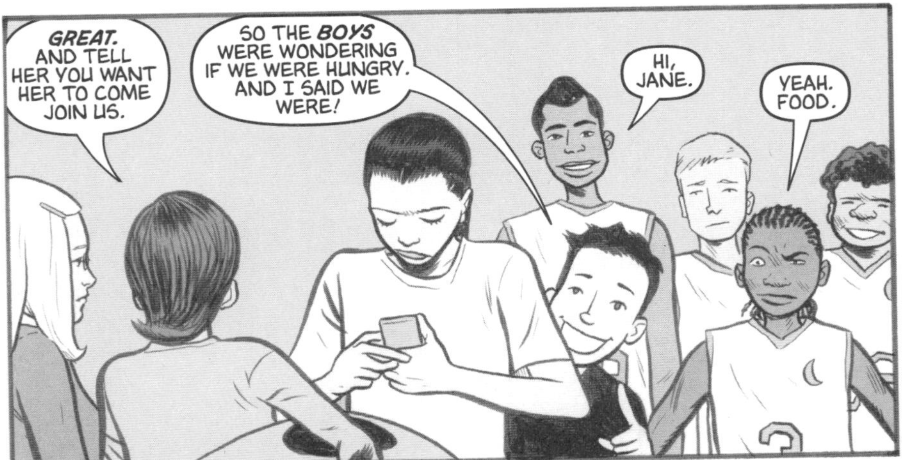
GREAT. AND TELL HER YOU WANT HER TO COME JOIN US.
SO THE *BOYS* WERE WONDERING IF WE WERE HUNGRY. AND I SAID WE WERE!
HI, JANE.
YEAH. FOOD.

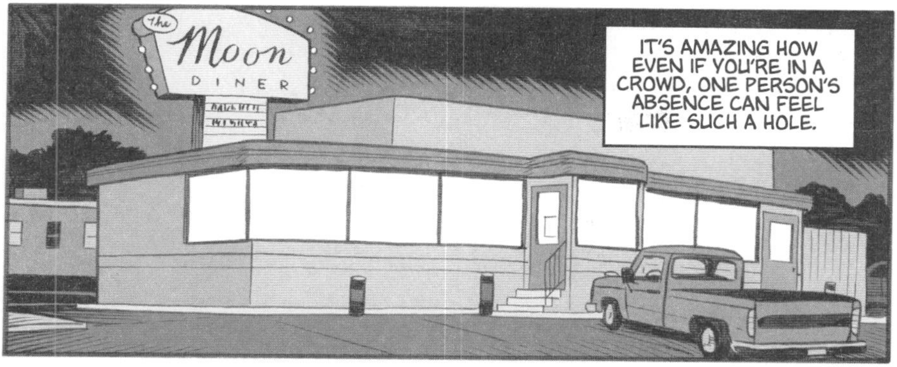
The Moon DINER
IT'S AMAZING HOW EVEN IF YOU'RE IN A CROWD, ONE PERSON'S ABSENCE CAN FEEL LIKE SUCH A HOLE.

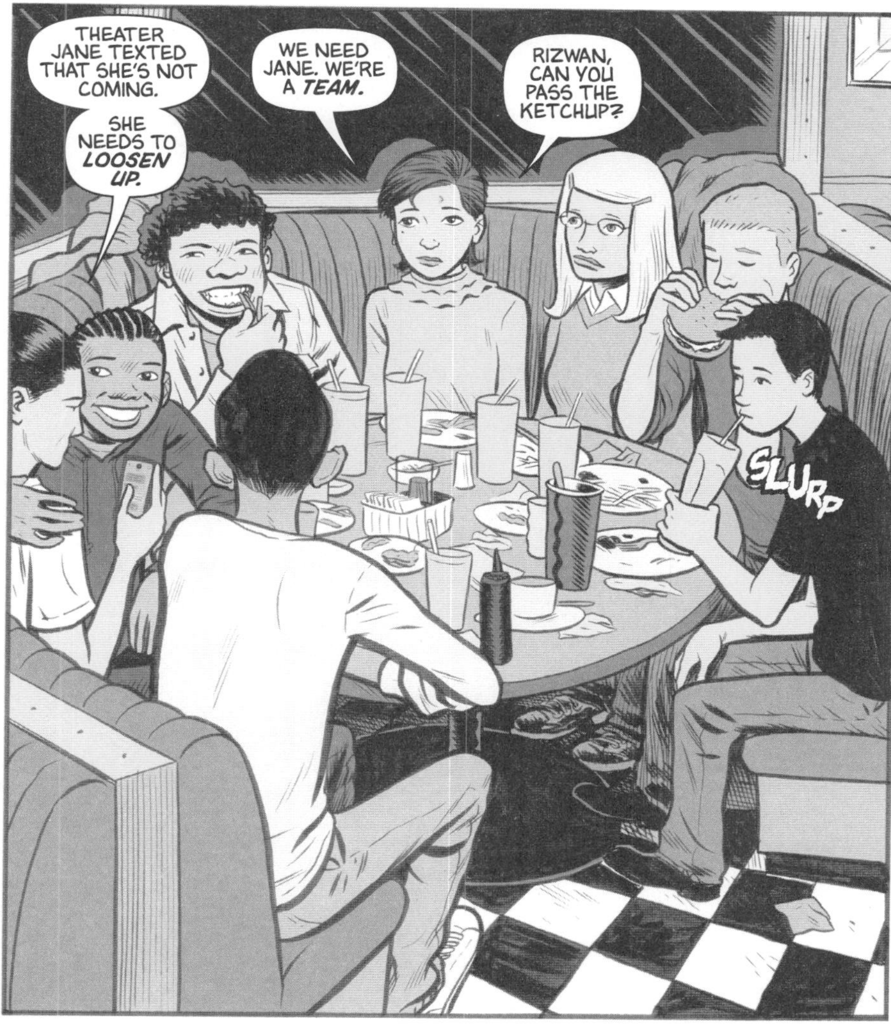
THEATER JANE TEXTED THAT SHE'S NOT COMING.
SHE NEEDS TO ***LOOSEN UP.***
WE NEED JANE. WE'RE A ***TEAM.***
RIZWAN, CAN YOU PASS THE KETCHUP?
SLURP

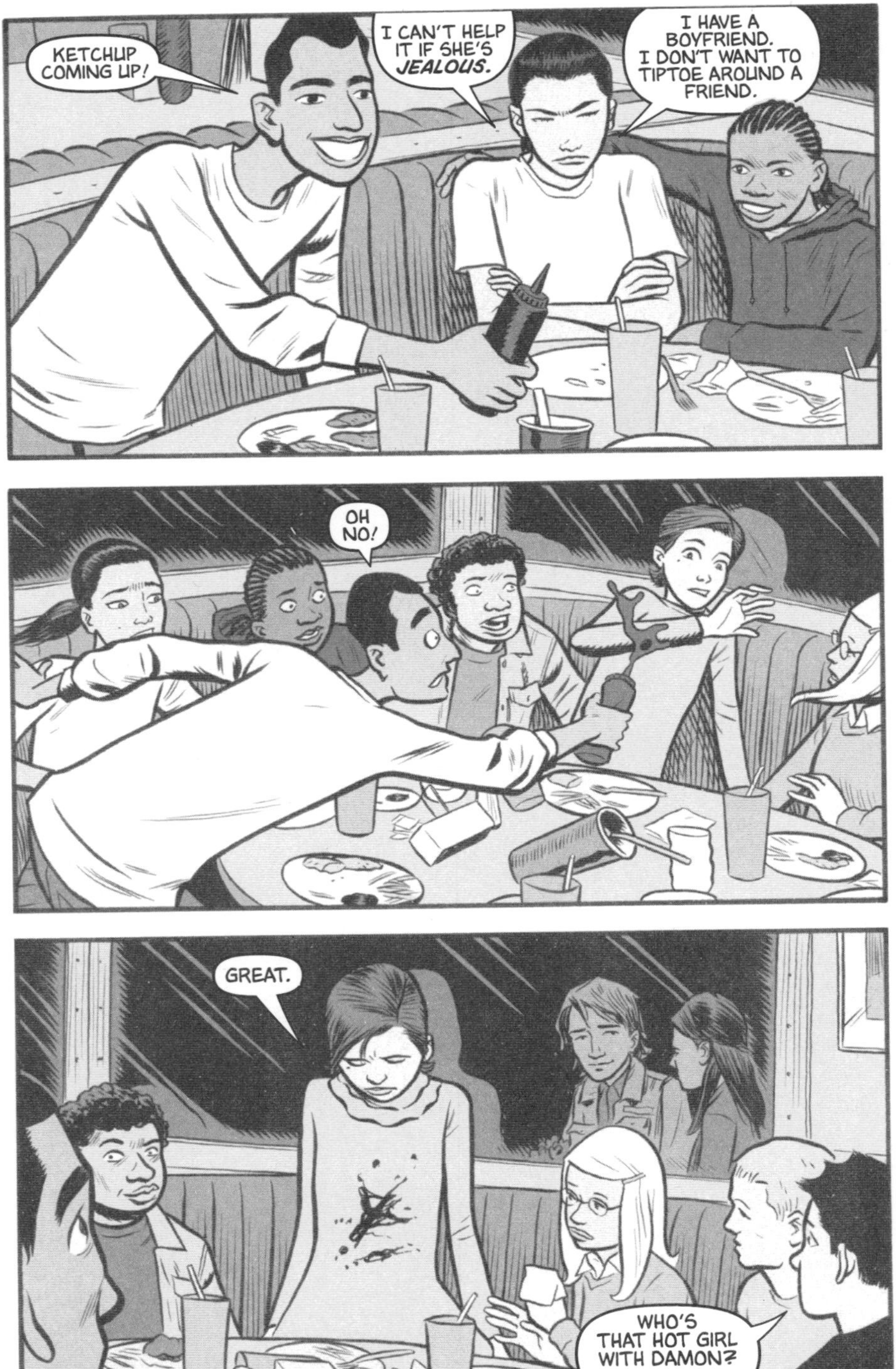
KETCHUP COMING UP!
I CAN'T HELP IT IF SHE'S *JEALOUS.*
I HAVE A BOYFRIEND. I DON'T WANT TO TIPTOE AROUND A FRIEND.
OH NO!
GREAT.
WHO'S THAT HOT GIRL WITH DAMON?

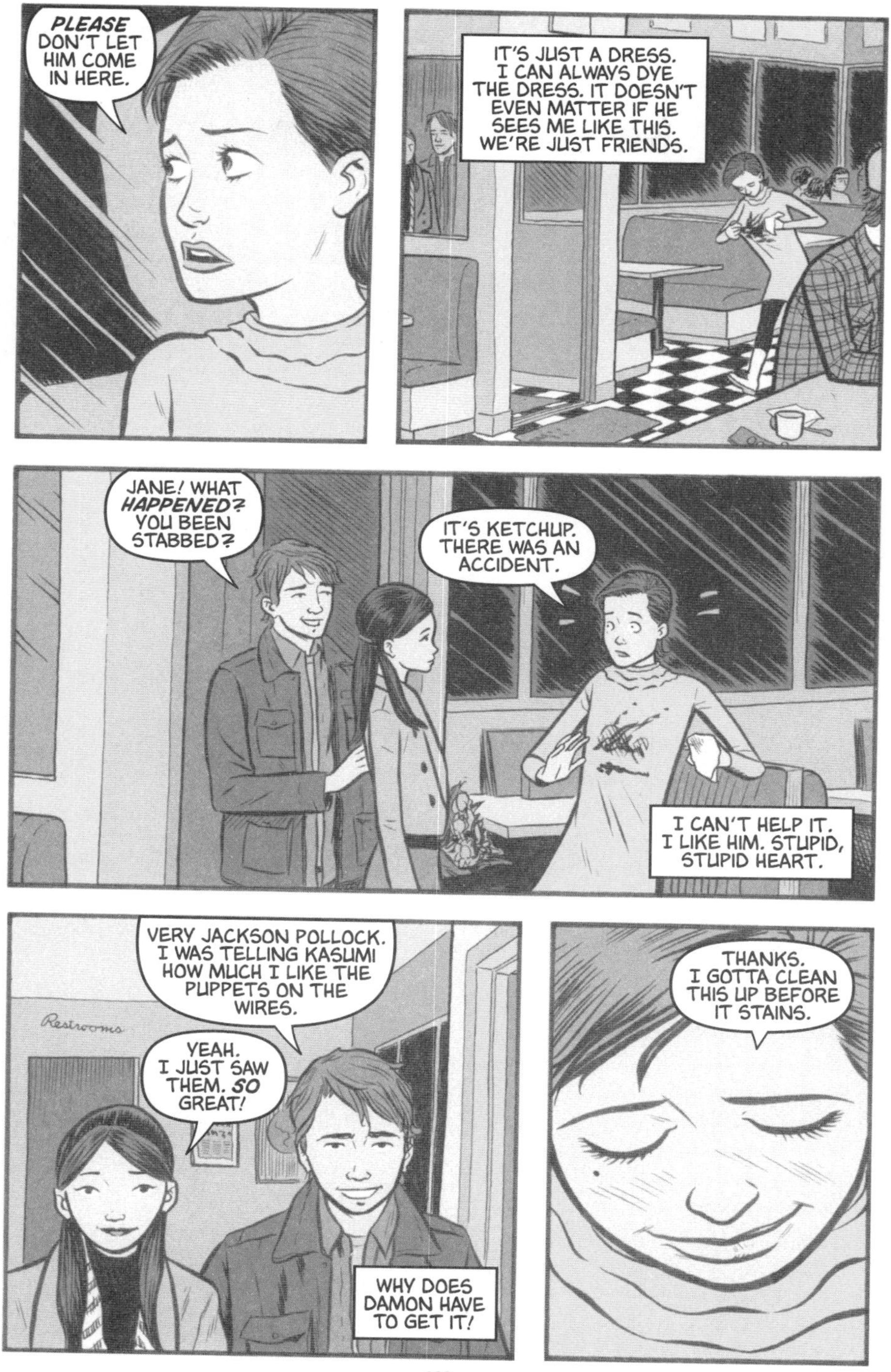
PLEASE DON'T LET HIM COME IN HERE.
IT'S JUST A DRESS. I CAN ALWAYS DYE THE DRESS. IT DOESN'T EVEN MATTER IF HE SEES ME LIKE THIS. WE'RE JUST FRIENDS.
JANE! WHAT *HAPPENED*? YOU BEEN STABBED?
IT'S KETCHUP. THERE WAS AN ACCIDENT.
I CAN'T HELP IT. I LIKE HIM. STUPID, STUPID HEART.
VERY JACKSON POLLOCK. I WAS TELLING KASUMI HOW MUCH I LIKE THE PUPPETS ON THE WIRES.
Restrooms
YEAH. I JUST SAW THEM. *SO* GREAT!
WHY DOES DAMON HAVE TO GET IT!
THANKS. I GOTTA CLEAN THIS UP BEFORE IT STAINS.

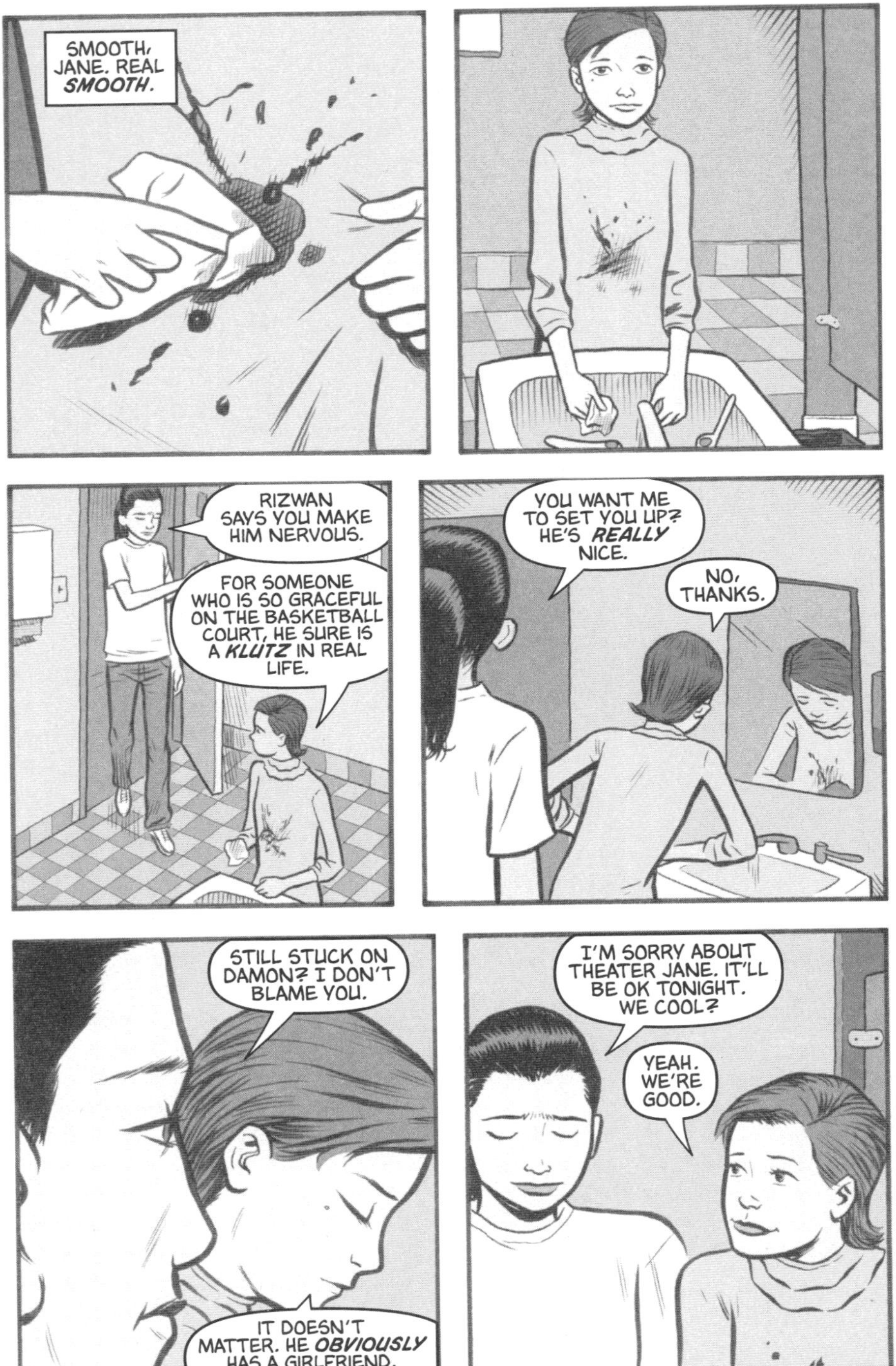
SMOOTH, JANE. REAL *SMOOTH*.
RIZWAN SAYS YOU MAKE HIM NERVOUS.
FOR SOMEONE WHO IS SO GRACEFUL ON THE BASKETBALL COURT, HE SURE IS A *KLUTZ* IN REAL LIFE.
YOU WANT ME TO SET YOU UP? HE'S *REALLY* NICE.
NO, THANKS.
STILL STUCK ON DAMON? I DON'T BLAME YOU.
IT DOESN'T MATTER. HE *OBVIOUSLY* HAS A GIRLFRIEND.
I'M SORRY ABOUT THEATER JANE. IT'LL BE OK TONIGHT. WE COOL?
YEAH. WE'RE GOOD.

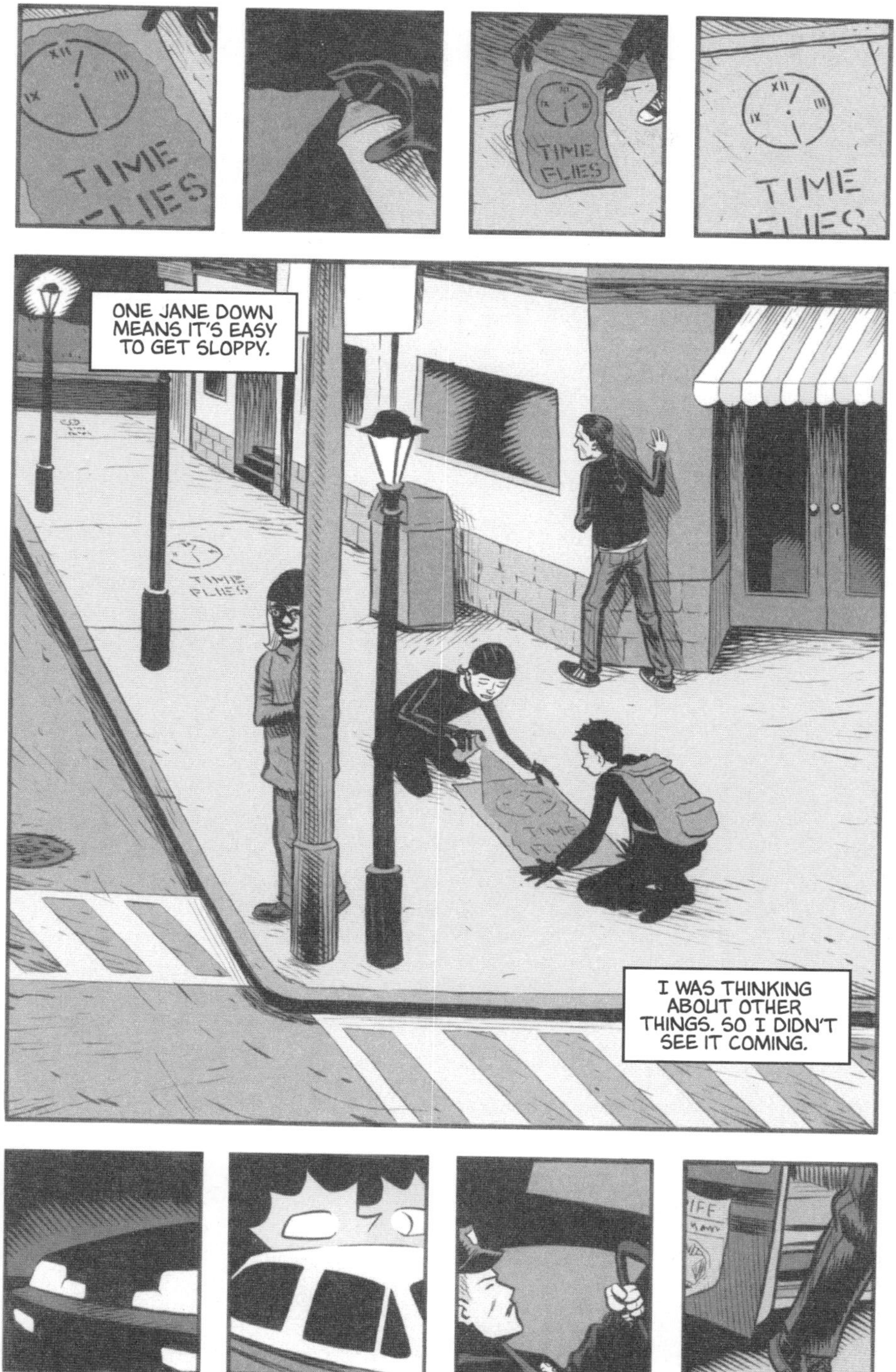
TIME FLIES
TIME FLIES
TIME FLIES
ONE JANE DOWN MEANS IT'S EASY TO GET SLOPPY.
TIME FLIES
I WAS THINKING ABOUT OTHER THINGS. SO I DIDN'T SEE IT COMING.

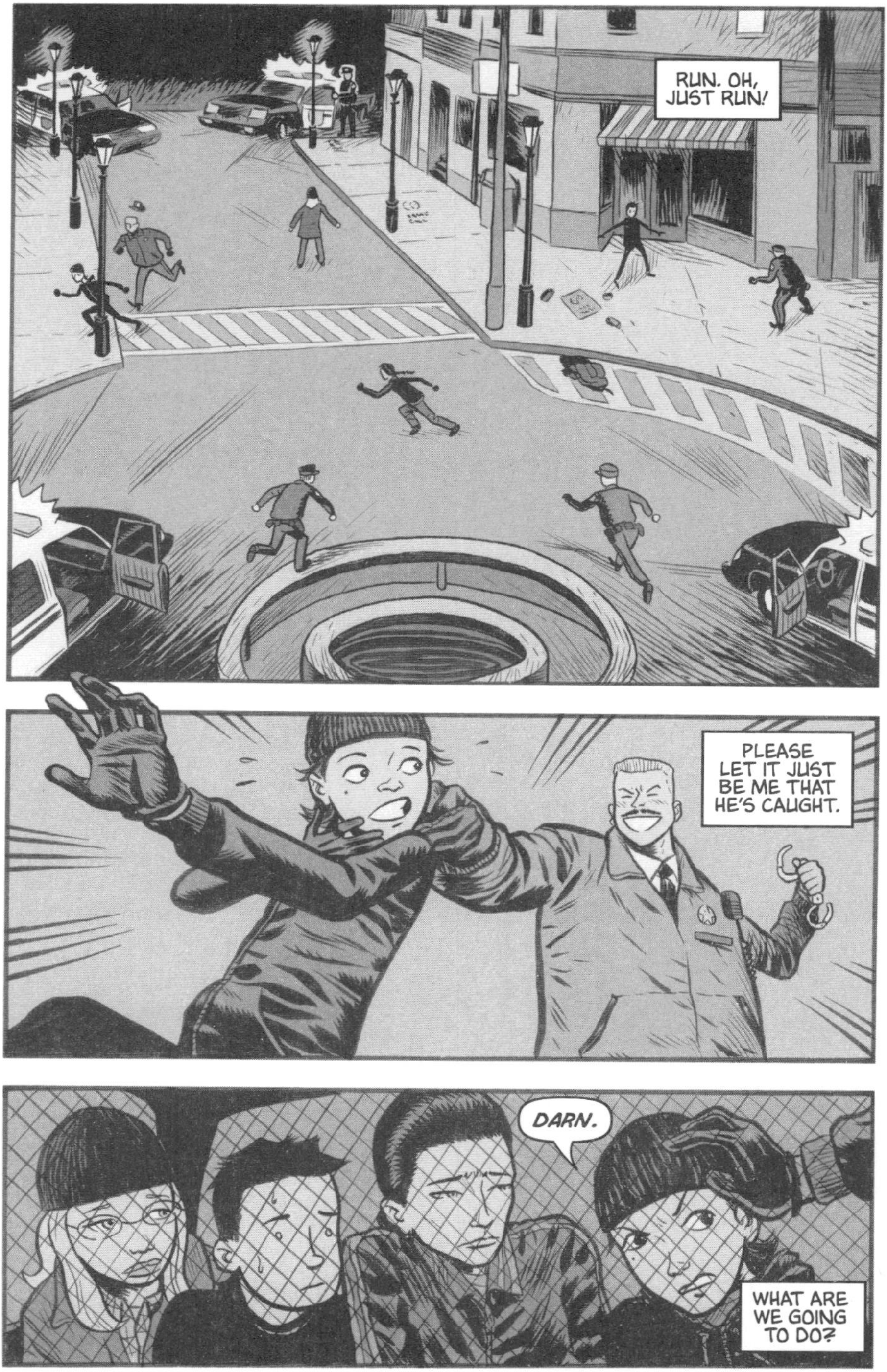
RUN. OH, JUST RUN!
PLEASE LET IT JUST BE ME THAT HE'S CAUGHT.
DARN.
WHAT ARE WE GOING TO DO?

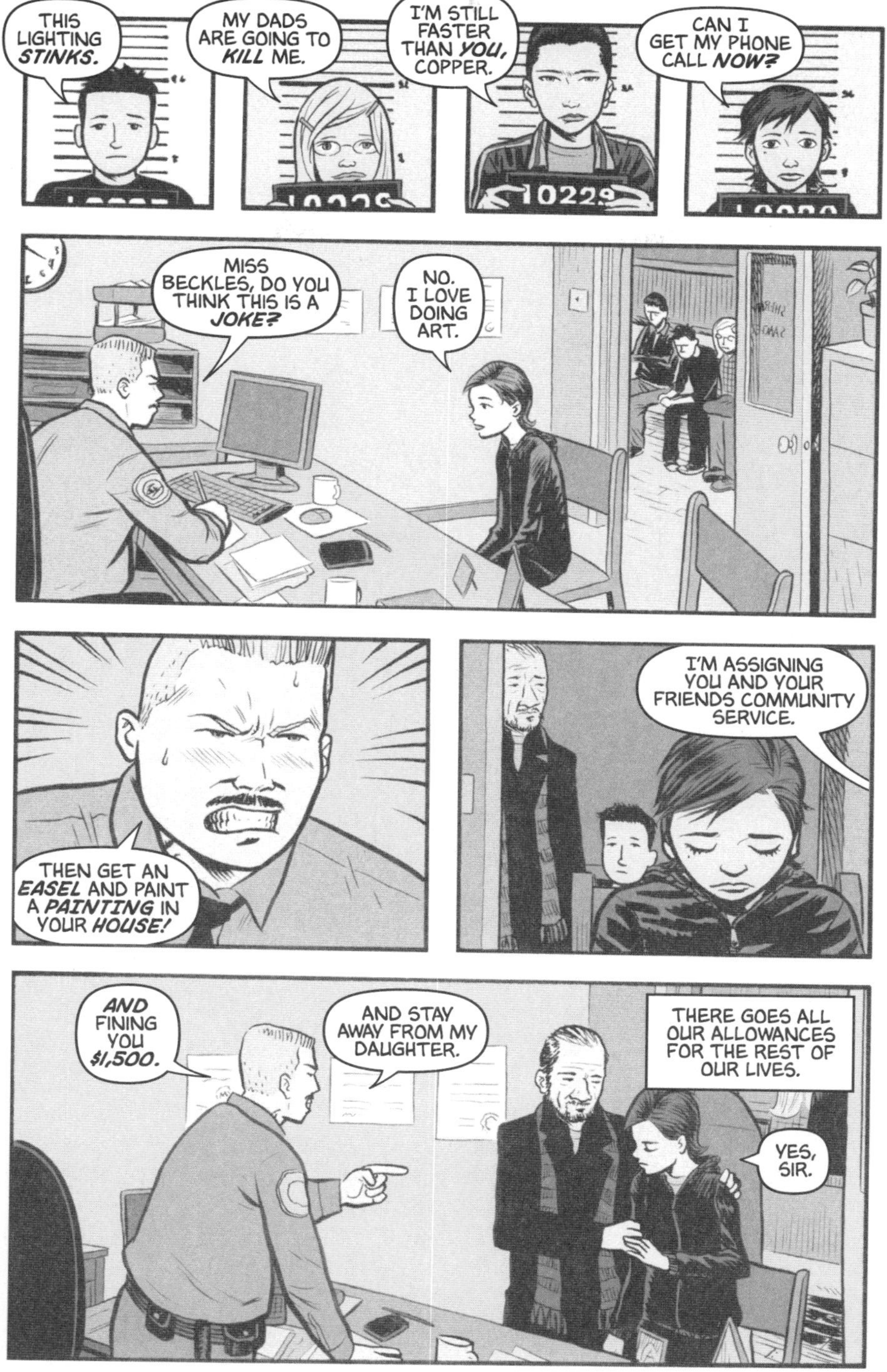
THIS LIGHTING STINKS.
MY DADS ARE GOING TO KILL ME.
I'M STILL FASTER THAN YOU, COPPER.
CAN I GET MY PHONE CALL NOW?
MISS BECKLES, DO YOU THINK THIS IS A JOKE?
NO. I LOVE DOING ART.
THEN GET AN EASEL AND PAINT A PAINTING IN YOUR HOUSE!
I'M ASSIGNING YOU AND YOUR FRIENDS COMMUNITY SERVICE.
AND FINING YOU $1,500.
AND STAY AWAY FROM MY DAUGHTER.
THERE GOES ALL OUR ALLOWANCES FOR THE REST OF OUR LIVES.
YES, SIR.

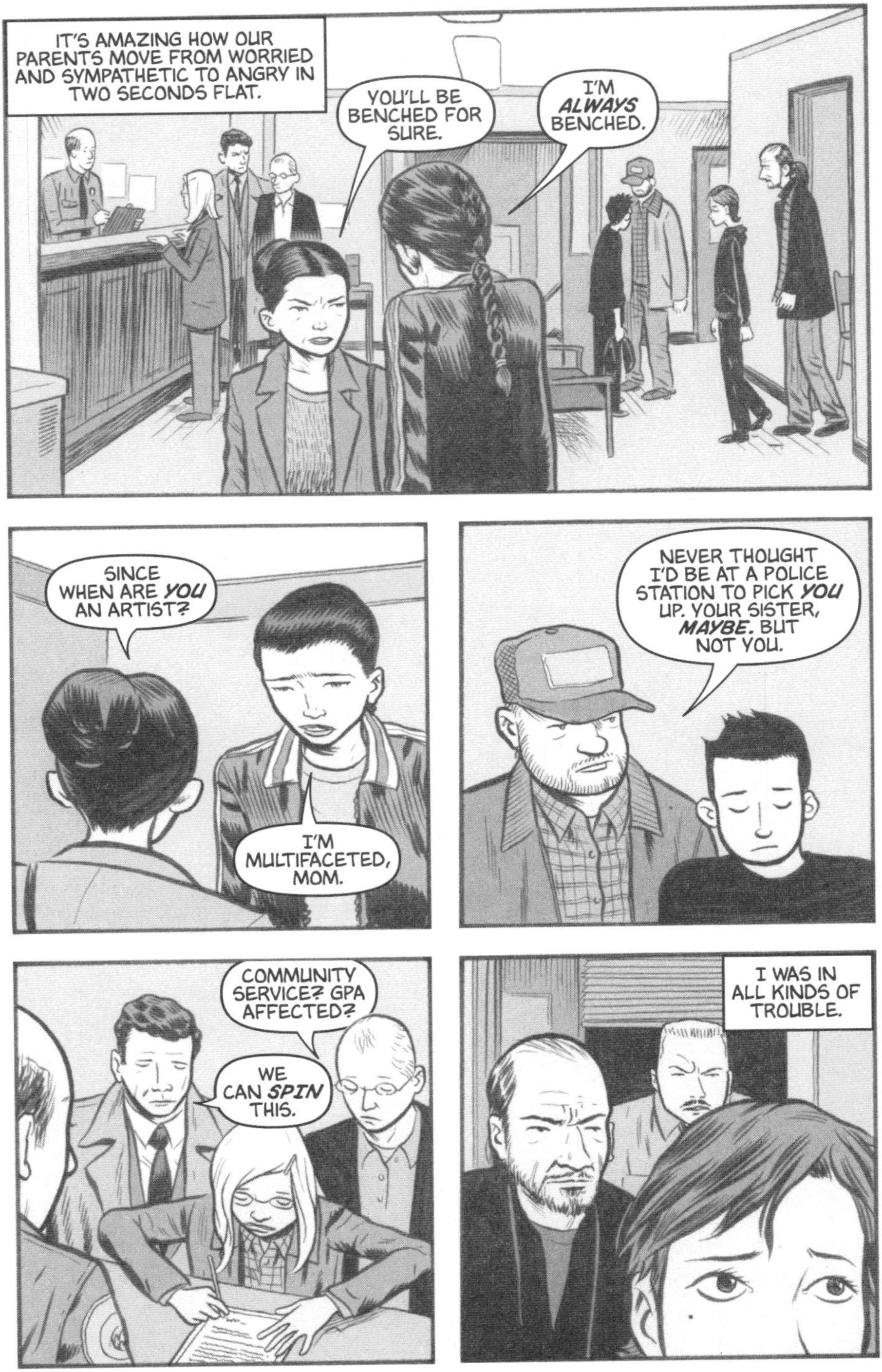
IT'S AMAZING HOW OUR PARENTS MOVE FROM WORRIED AND SYMPATHETIC TO ANGRY IN TWO SECONDS FLAT.
YOU'LL BE BENCHED FOR SURE.
I'M *ALWAYS* BENCHED.
SINCE WHEN ARE *YOU* AN ARTIST?
I'M MULTIFACETED, MOM.
NEVER THOUGHT I'D BE AT A POLICE STATION TO PICK *YOU* UP. YOUR SISTER, *MAYBE*. BUT NOT YOU.
COMMUNITY SERVICE? GPA AFFECTED?
WE CAN *SPIN* THIS.
I WAS IN ALL KINDS OF TROUBLE.

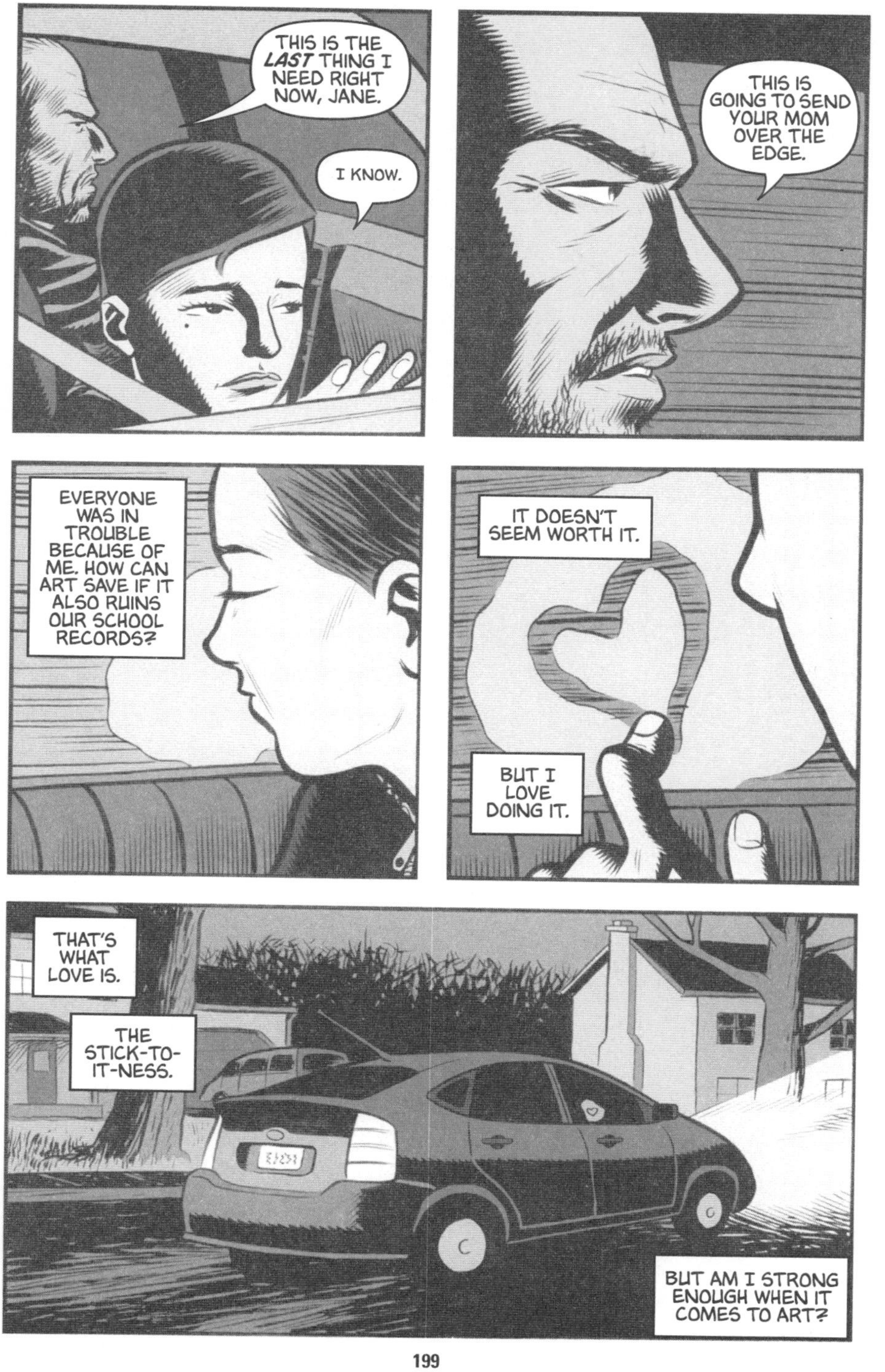
THIS IS THE *LAST* THING I NEED RIGHT NOW, JANE.
I KNOW.
THIS IS GOING TO SEND YOUR MOM OVER THE EDGE.
EVERYONE WAS IN TROUBLE BECAUSE OF ME. HOW CAN ART SAVE IF IT ALSO RUINS OUR SCHOOL RECORDS?
IT DOESN'T SEEM WORTH IT.
BUT I LOVE DOING IT.
THAT'S WHAT LOVE IS.
THE STICK-TO-IT-NESS.
BUT AM I STRONG ENOUGH WHEN IT COMES TO ART?

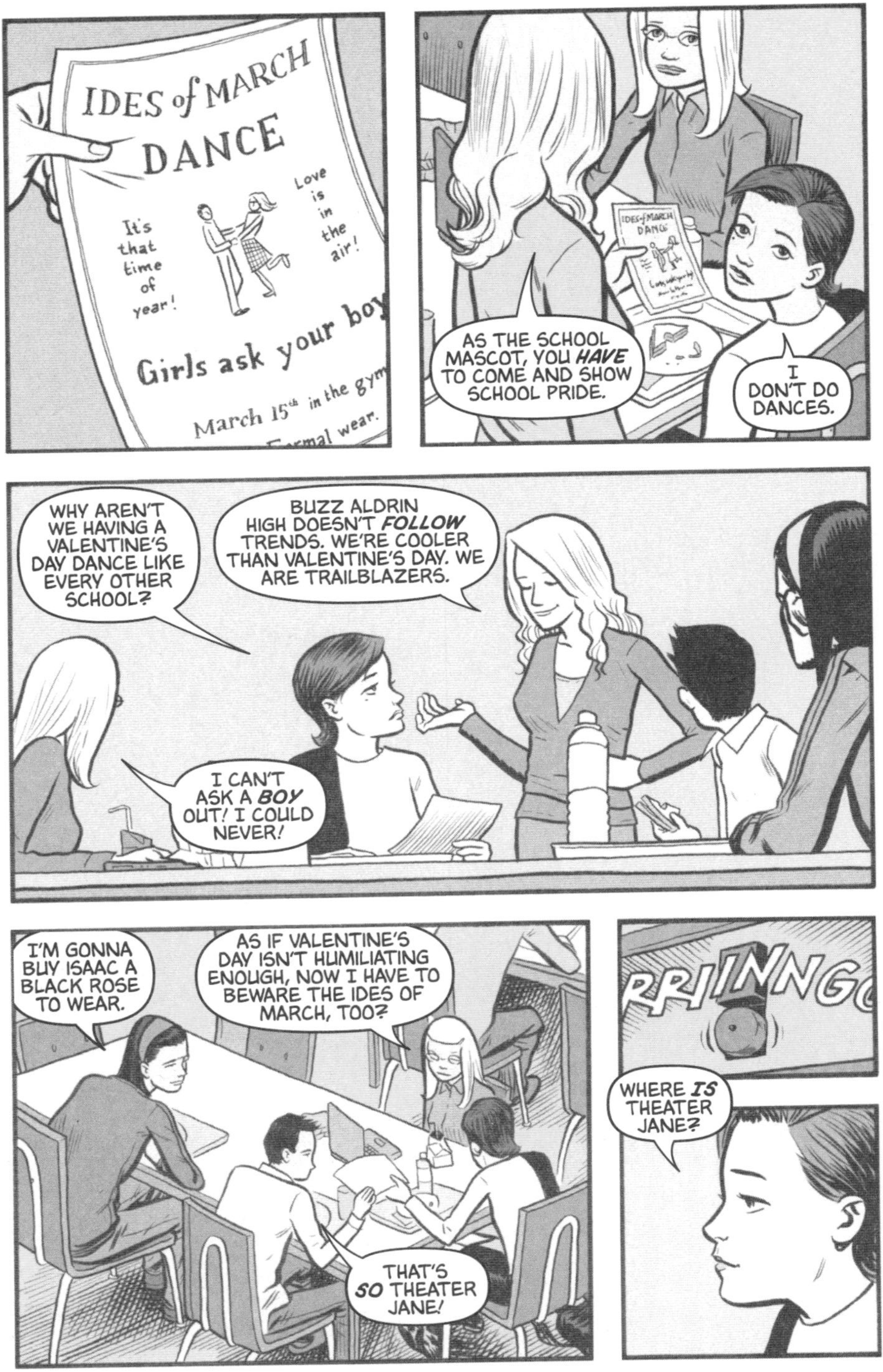
IDES of MARCH
DANCE
It's that time of year!
Love is in the air!
Girls ask your boy
March 15th in the gym
Formal wear.
AS THE SCHOOL MASCOT, YOU HAVE TO COME AND SHOW SCHOOL PRIDE.
I DON'T DO DANCES.
WHY AREN'T WE HAVING A VALENTINE'S DAY DANCE LIKE EVERY OTHER SCHOOL?
BUZZ ALDRIN HIGH DOESN'T FOLLOW TRENDS. WE'RE COOLER THAN VALENTINE'S DAY. WE ARE TRAILBLAZERS.
I CAN'T ASK A BOY OUT! I COULD NEVER!
I'M GONNA BUY ISAAC A BLACK ROSE TO WEAR.
AS IF VALENTINE'S DAY ISN'T HUMILIATING ENOUGH, NOW I HAVE TO BEWARE THE IDES OF MARCH, TOO?
THAT'S SO THEATER JANE!
RRIINNG
WHERE IS THEATER JANE?

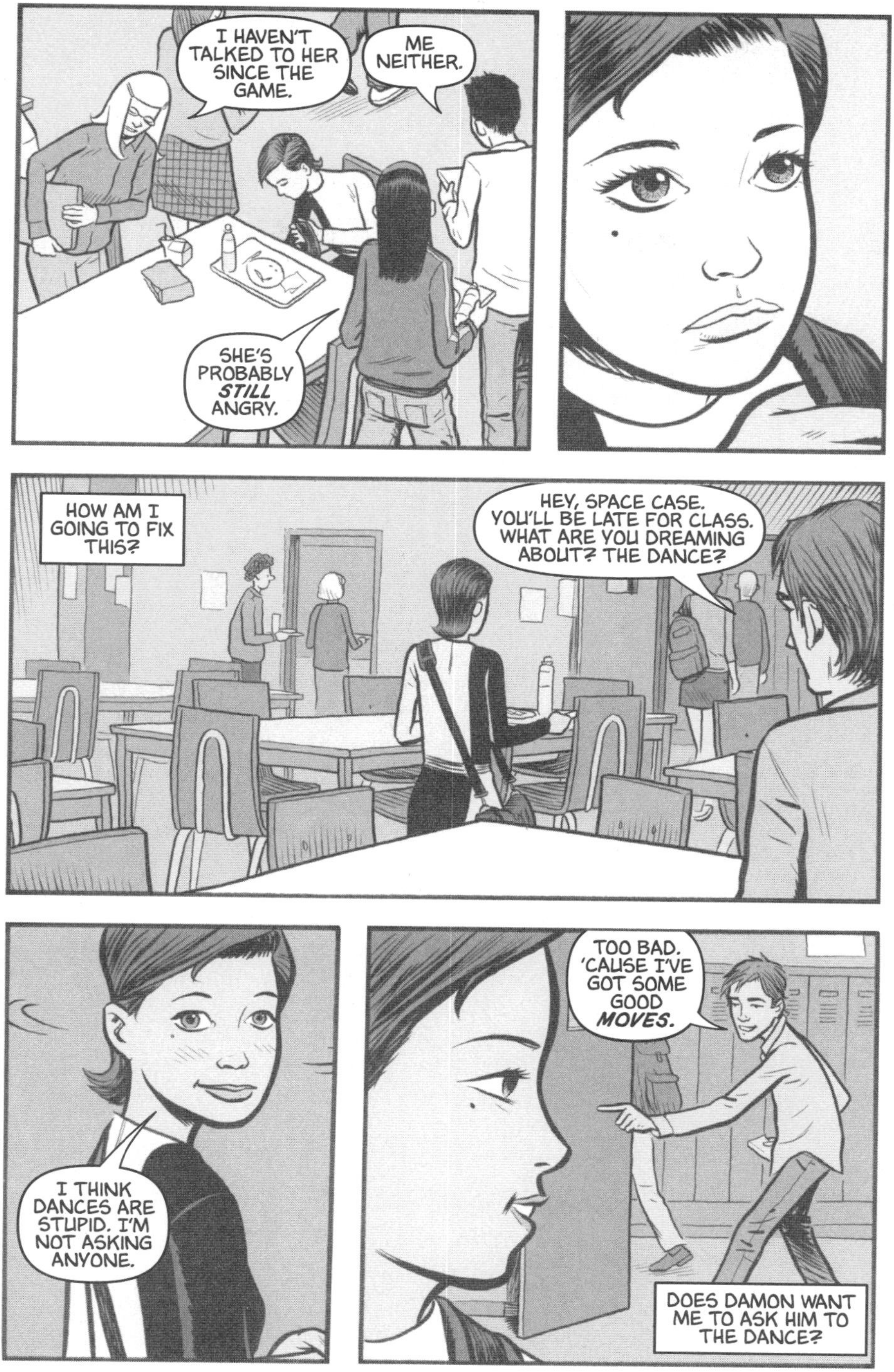
I HAVEN'T TALKED TO HER SINCE THE GAME.
ME NEITHER.
SHE'S PROBABLY STILL ANGRY.
HOW AM I GOING TO FIX THIS?
HEY, SPACE CASE. YOU'LL BE LATE FOR CLASS. WHAT ARE YOU DREAMING ABOUT? THE DANCE?
I THINK DANCES ARE STUPID. I'M NOT ASKING ANYONE.
TOO BAD. 'CAUSE I'VE GOT SOME GOOD MOVES.
DOES DAMON WANT ME TO ASK HIM TO THE DANCE?

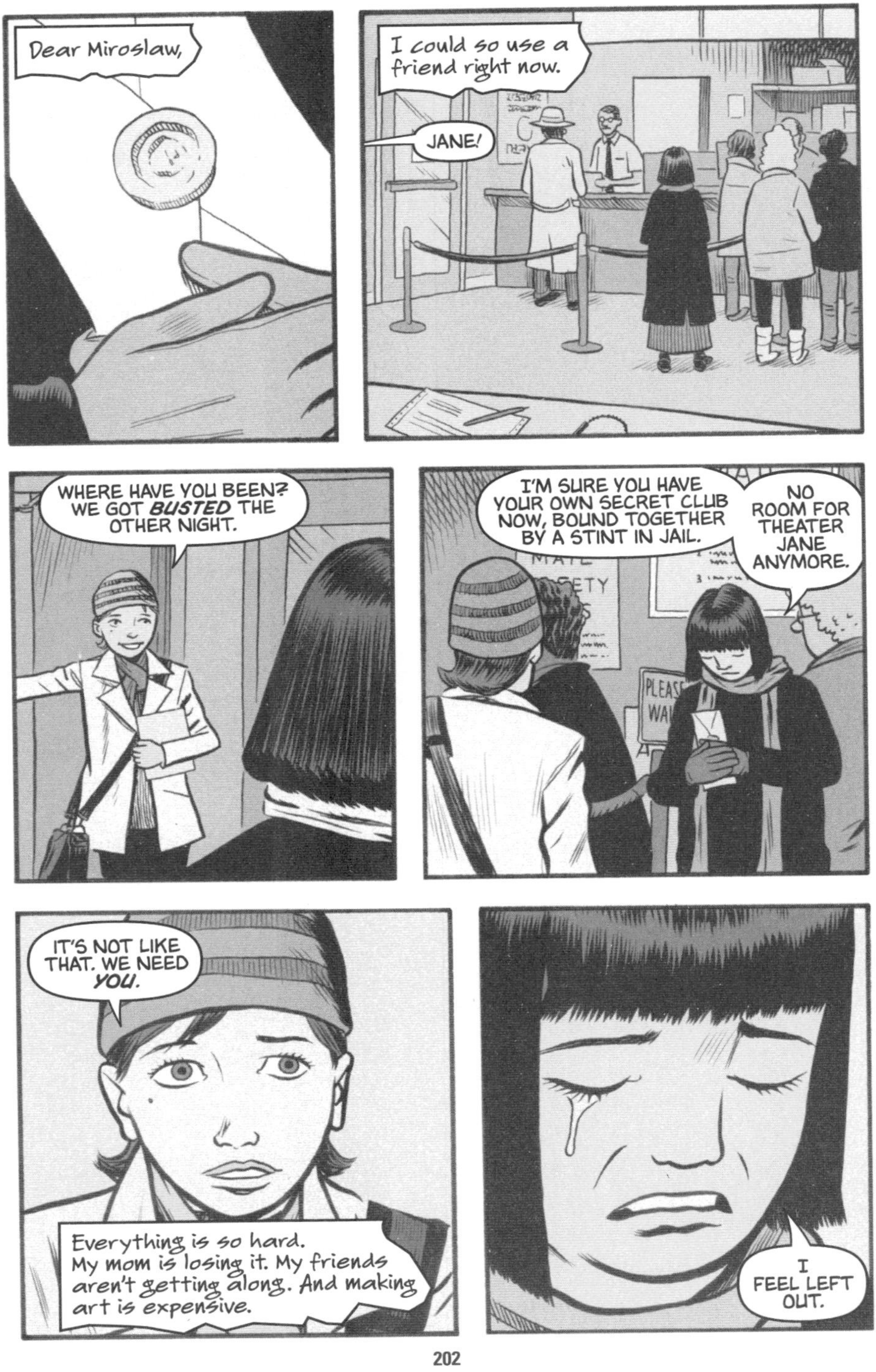
Dear Miroslaw,
I could so use a friend right now.
JANE!
WHERE HAVE YOU BEEN? WE GOT BUSTED THE OTHER NIGHT.
I'M SURE YOU HAVE YOUR OWN SECRET CLUB NOW, BOUND TOGETHER BY A STINT IN JAIL.
NO ROOM FOR THEATER JANE ANYMORE.
IT'S NOT LIKE THAT. WE NEED YOU.
Everything is so hard. My mom is losing it. My friends aren't getting along. And making art is expensive.
I FEEL LEFT OUT.

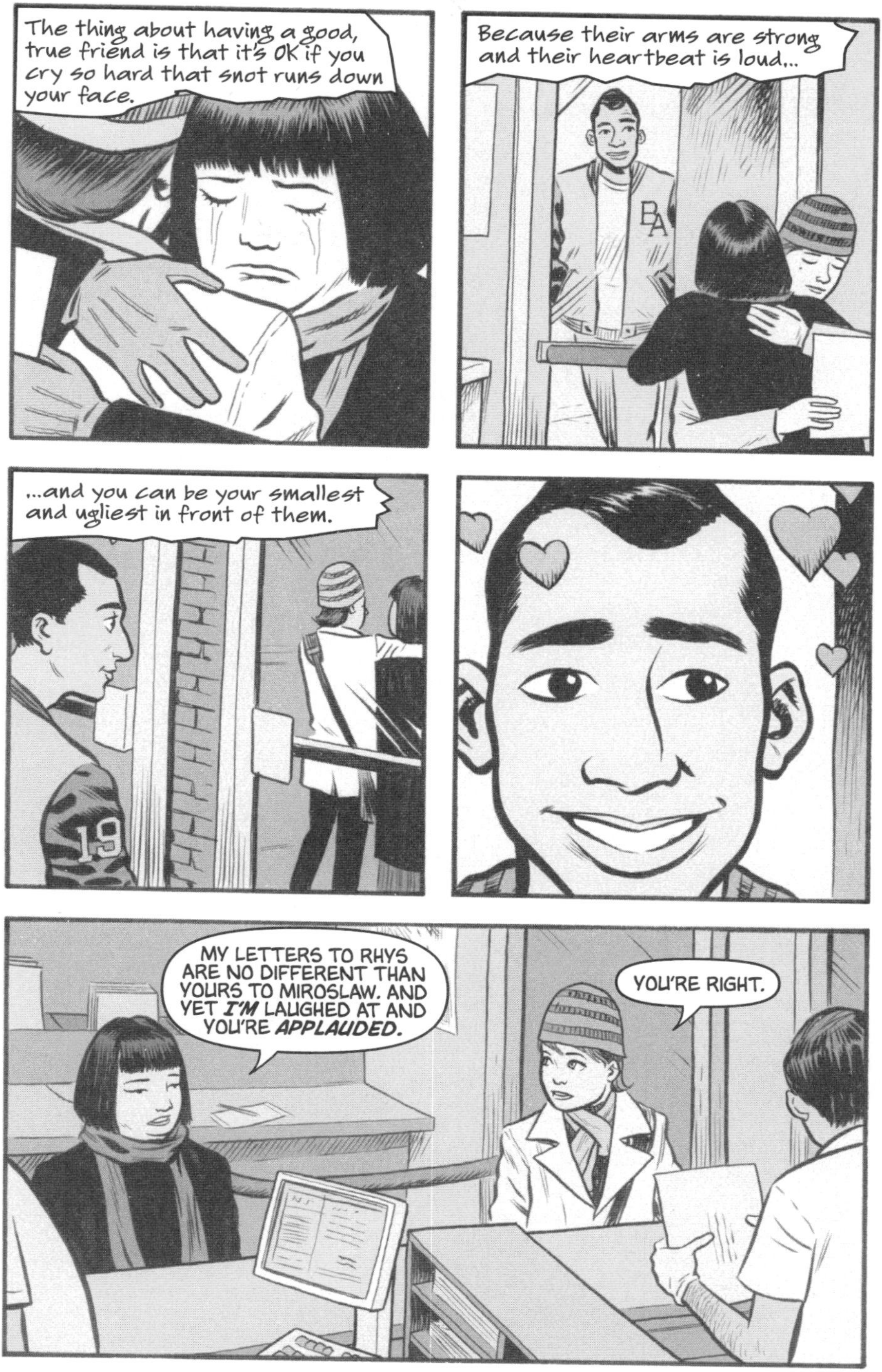
The thing about having a good, true friend is that it's OK if you cry so hard that snot runs down your face.
Because their arms are strong and their heartbeat is loud...
BA
...and you can be your smallest and ugliest in front of them.
19
MY LETTERS TO RHYS ARE NO DIFFERENT THAN YOURS TO MIROSLAW. AND YET *I'M* LAUGHED AT AND YOU'RE ***APPLAUDED.***
YOU'RE RIGHT.

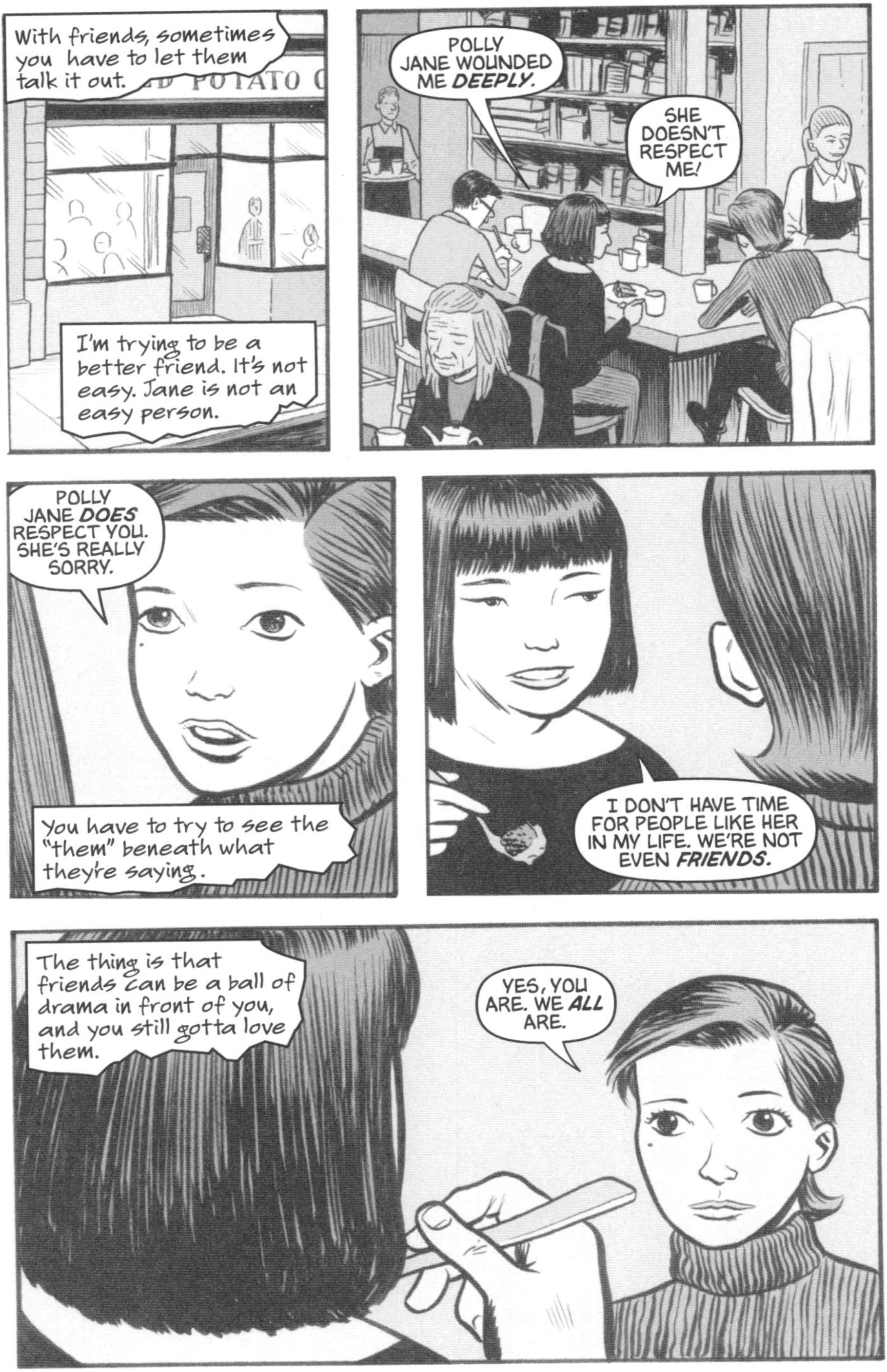
With friends, sometimes you have to let them talk it out.
I'm trying to be a better friend. It's not easy. Jane is not an easy person.
POLLY JANE WOUNDED ME *DEEPLY.*
SHE DOESN'T RESPECT ME!
POLLY JANE *DOES* RESPECT YOU. SHE'S REALLY SORRY.
You have to try to see the "them" beneath what they're saying.
I DON'T HAVE TIME FOR PEOPLE LIKE HER IN MY LIFE. WE'RE NOT EVEN *FRIENDS.*
The thing is that friends can be a ball of drama in front of you, and you still gotta love them.
YES, YOU ARE. WE *ALL* ARE.

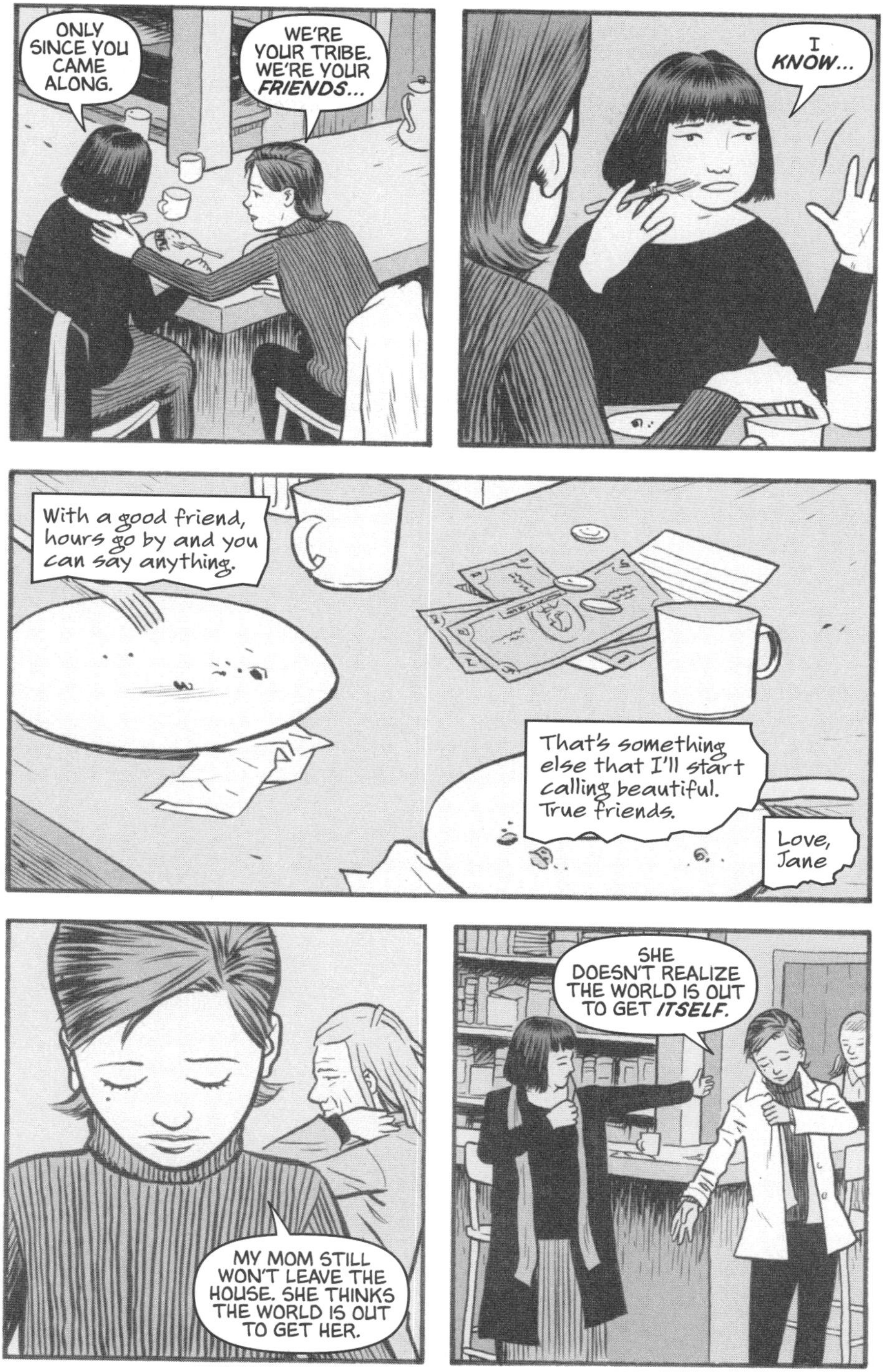
ONLY SINCE YOU CAME ALONG.
WE'RE YOUR TRIBE. WE'RE YOUR *FRIENDS*...
I *KNOW*...
With a good friend, hours go by and you can say anything.
That's something else that I'll start calling beautiful. True friends.
Love, Jane
MY MOM STILL WON'T LEAVE THE HOUSE. SHE THINKS THE WORLD IS OUT TO GET HER.
SHE DOESN'T REALIZE THE WORLD IS OUT TO GET *ITSELF*.

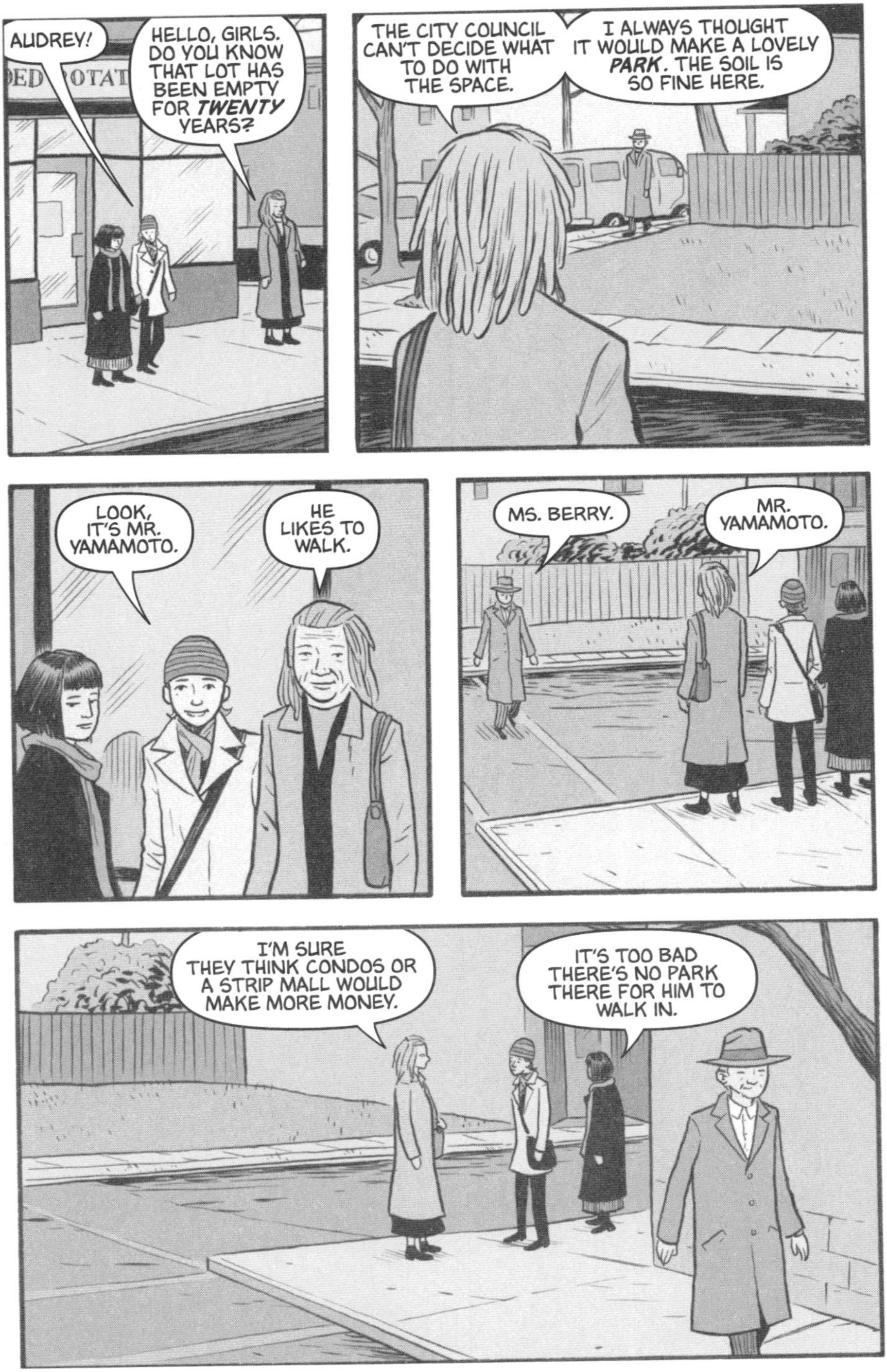
AUDREY!
HELLO, GIRLS. DO YOU KNOW THAT LOT HAS BEEN EMPTY FOR **TWENTY** YEARS?
DED ROTAT
THE CITY COUNCIL CAN'T DECIDE WHAT TO DO WITH THE SPACE.
I ALWAYS THOUGHT IT WOULD MAKE A LOVELY **PARK**. THE SOIL IS SO FINE HERE.
LOOK, IT'S MR. YAMAMOTO.
HE LIKES TO WALK.
MS. BERRY.
MR. YAMAMOTO.
I'M SURE THEY THINK CONDOS OR A STRIP MALL WOULD MAKE MORE MONEY.
IT'S TOO BAD THERE'S NO PARK THERE FOR HIM TO WALK IN.

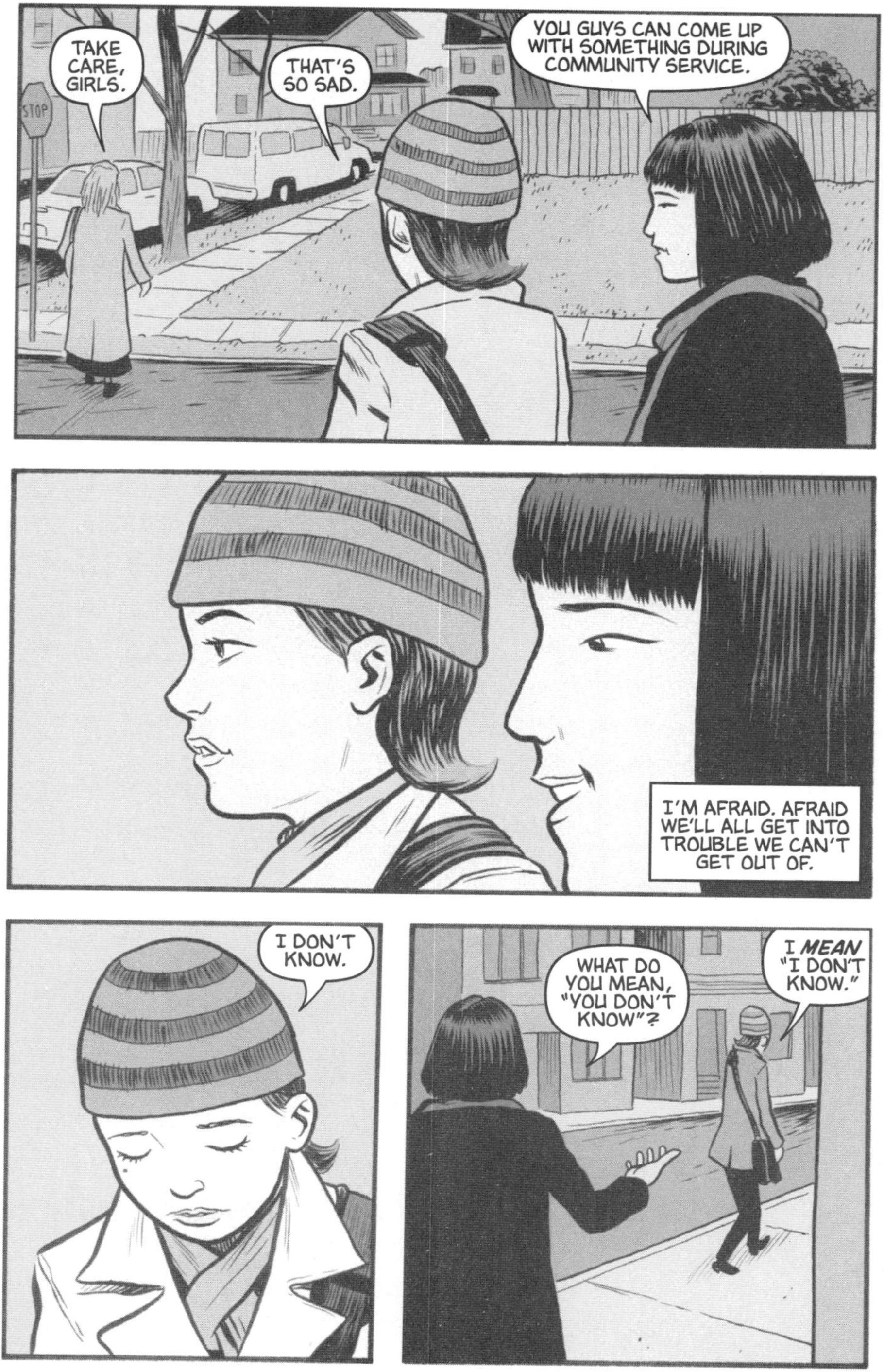
TAKE CARE, GIRLS.
THAT'S SO SAD.
YOU GUYS CAN COME UP WITH SOMETHING DURING COMMUNITY SERVICE.
STOP
I'M AFRAID. AFRAID WE'LL ALL GET INTO TROUBLE WE CAN'T GET OUT OF.
I DON'T KNOW.
WHAT DO YOU MEAN, "YOU DON'T KNOW"?
I *MEAN* "I DON'T KNOW."

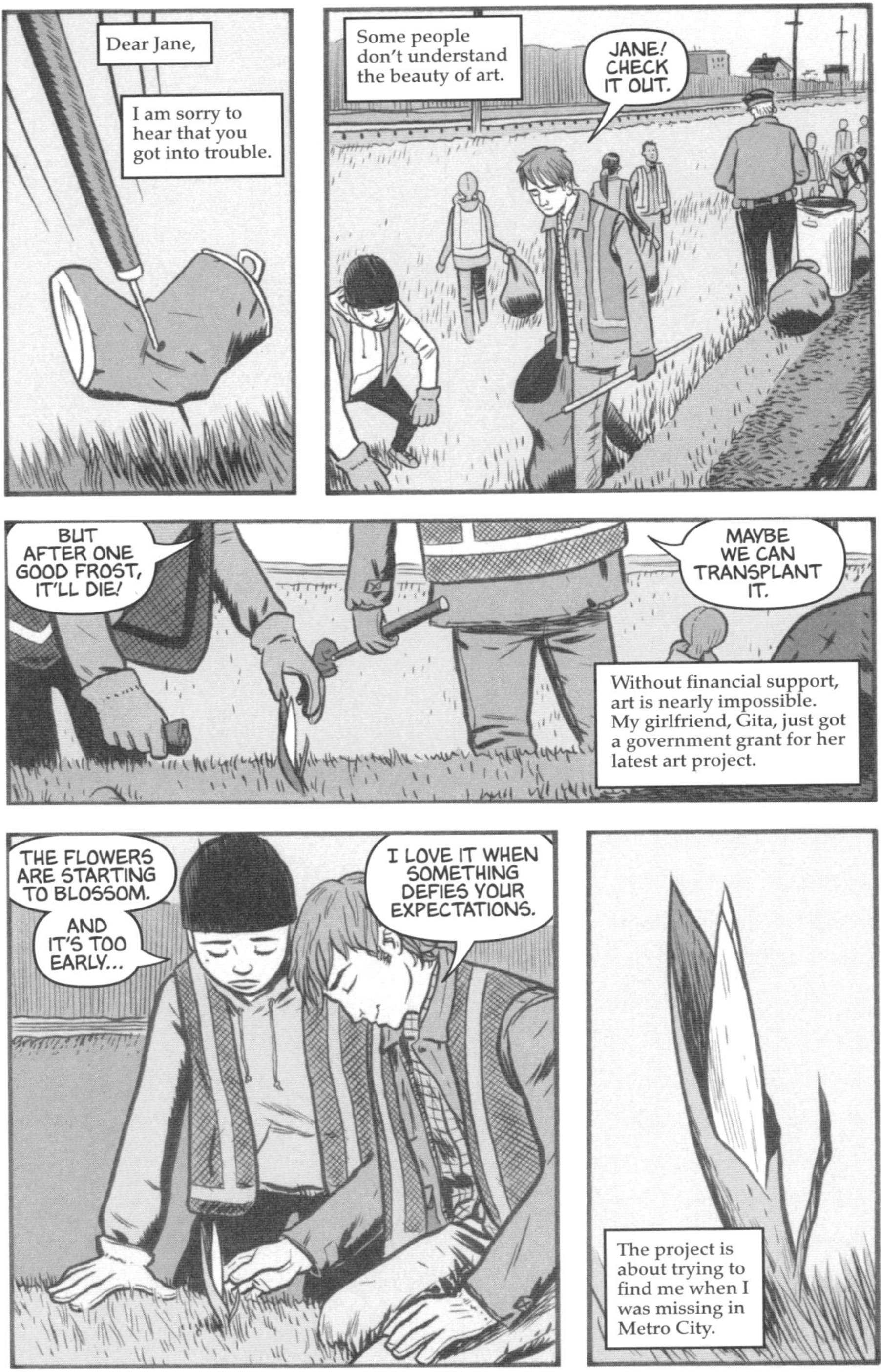
Dear Jane,
I am sorry to hear that you got into trouble.
Some people don't understand the beauty of art.
JANE! CHECK IT OUT.
BUT AFTER ONE GOOD FROST, IT'LL DIE!
MAYBE WE CAN TRANSPLANT IT.
Without financial support, art is nearly impossible. My girlfriend, Gita, just got a government grant for her latest art project.
THE FLOWERS ARE STARTING TO BLOSSOM.
AND IT'S TOO EARLY...
I LOVE IT WHEN SOMETHING DEFIES YOUR EXPECTATIONS.
The project is about trying to find me when I was missing in Metro City.

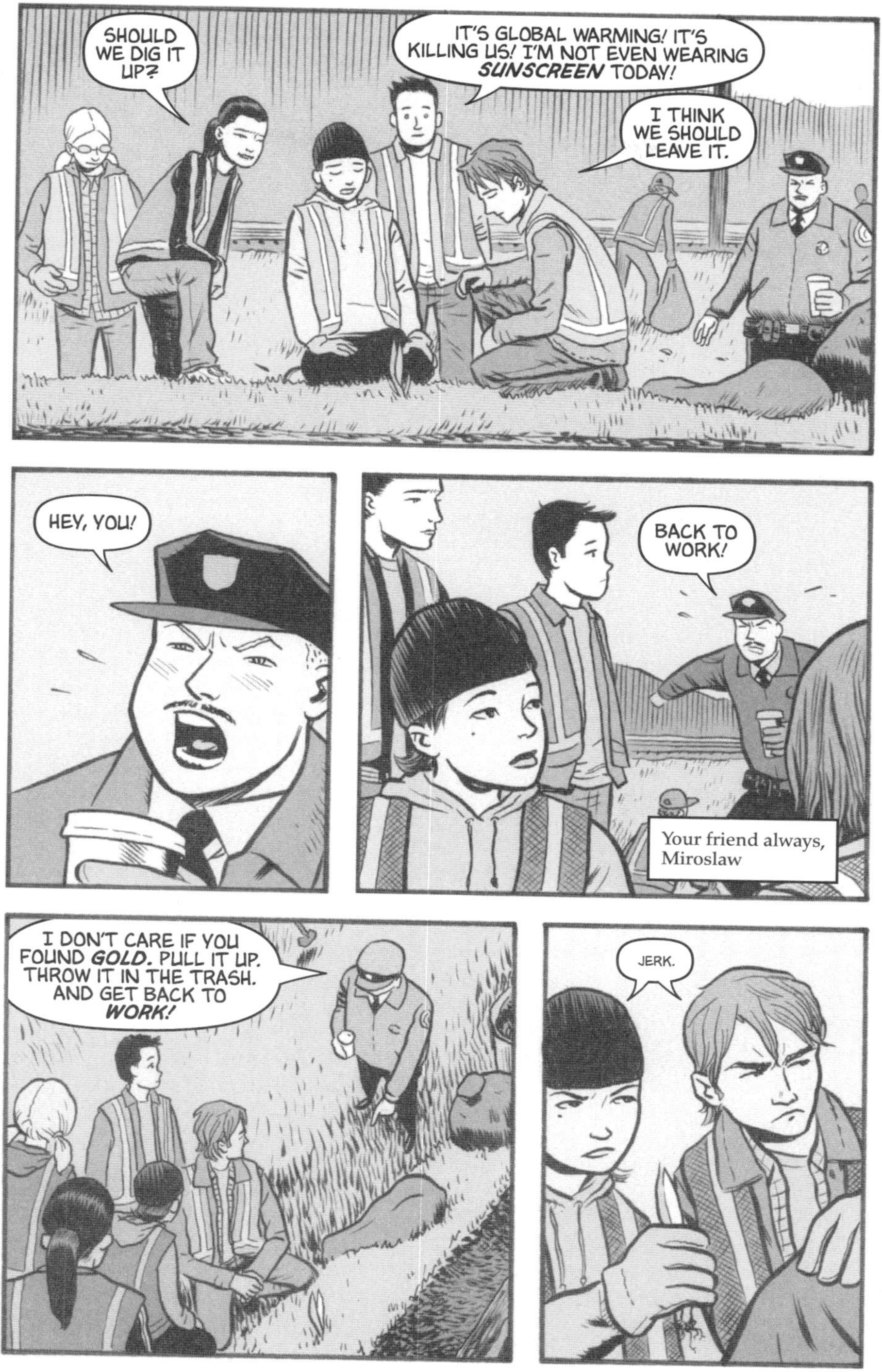
SHOULD WE DIG IT UP?
IT'S GLOBAL WARMING! IT'S KILLING US! I'M NOT EVEN WEARING SUNSCREEN TODAY!
I THINK WE SHOULD LEAVE IT.
HEY, YOU!
BACK TO WORK!
Your friend always, Miroslaw
I DON'T CARE IF YOU FOUND GOLD. PULL IT UP. THROW IT IN THE TRASH. AND GET BACK TO WORK!
JERK.

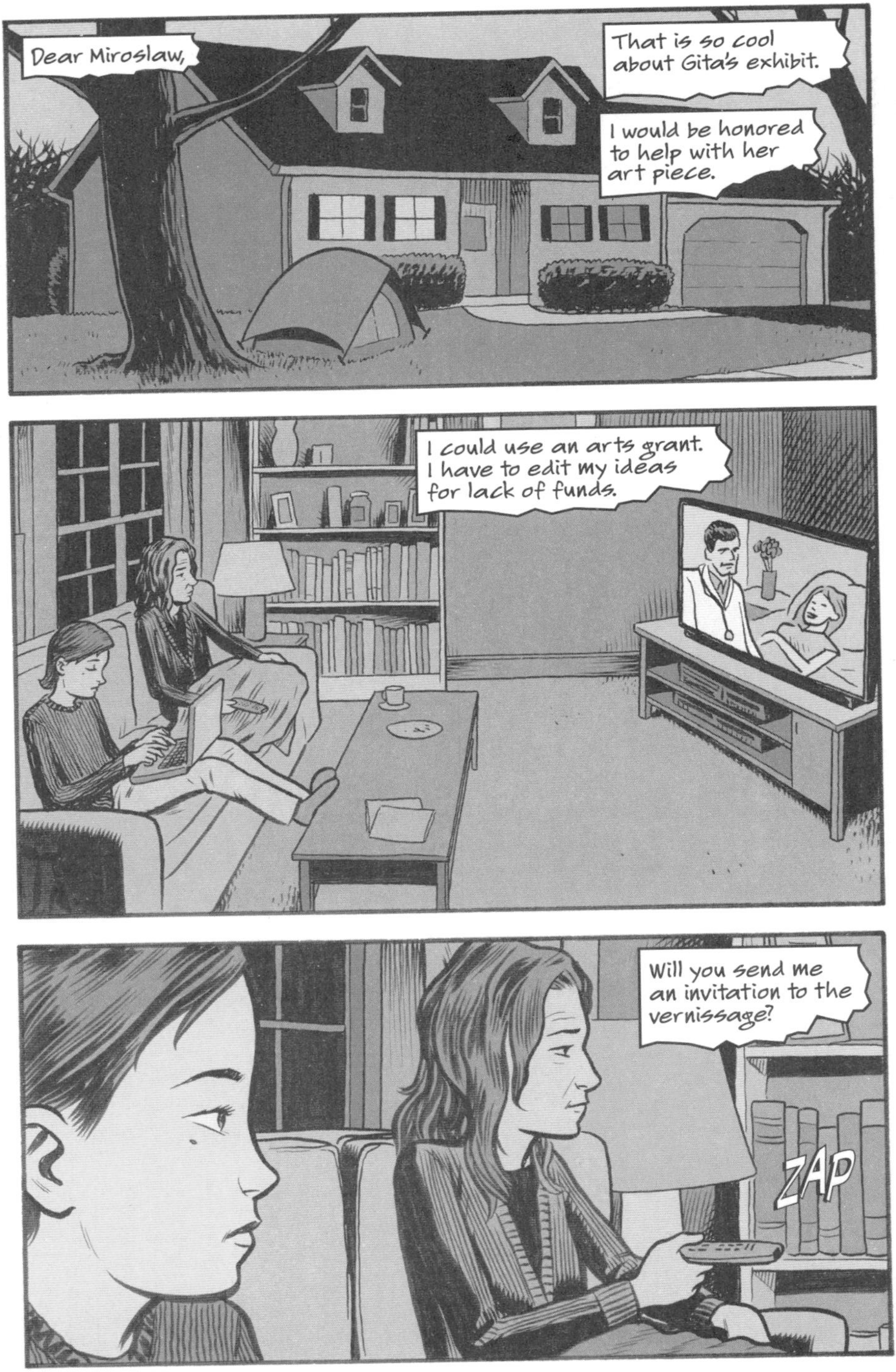
Dear Miroslaw,
That is so cool about Gita's exhibit.
I would be honored to help with her art piece.
I could use an arts grant. I have to edit my ideas for lack of funds.
Will you send me an invitation to the vernissage?
ZAP

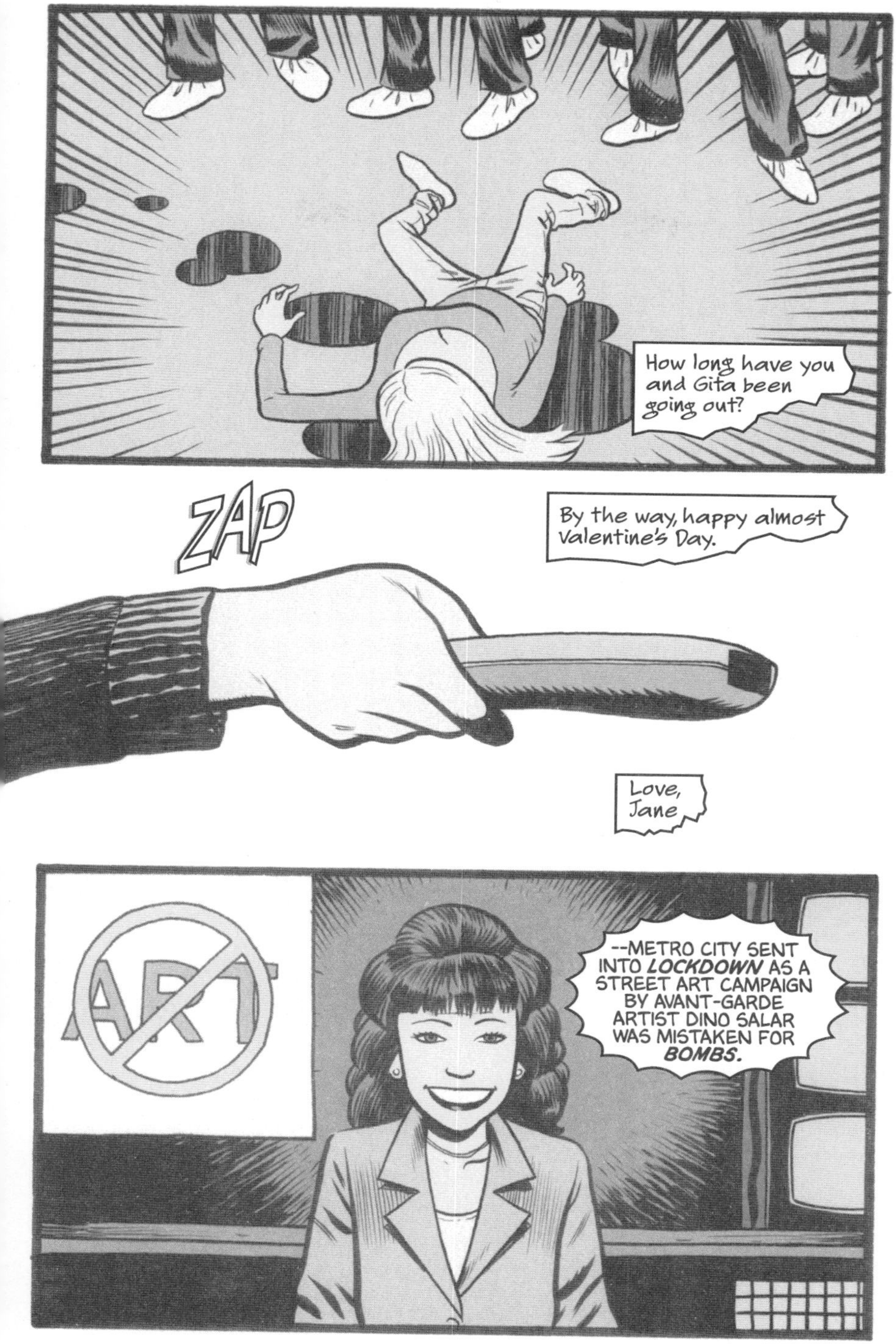
How long have you and Gita been going out?
ZAP
By the way, happy almost Valentine's Day.
Love, Jane
ART
--METRO CITY SENT INTO *LOCKDOWN* AS A STREET ART CAMPAIGN BY AVANT-GARDE ARTIST DINO SALAR WAS MISTAKEN FOR *BOMBS.*

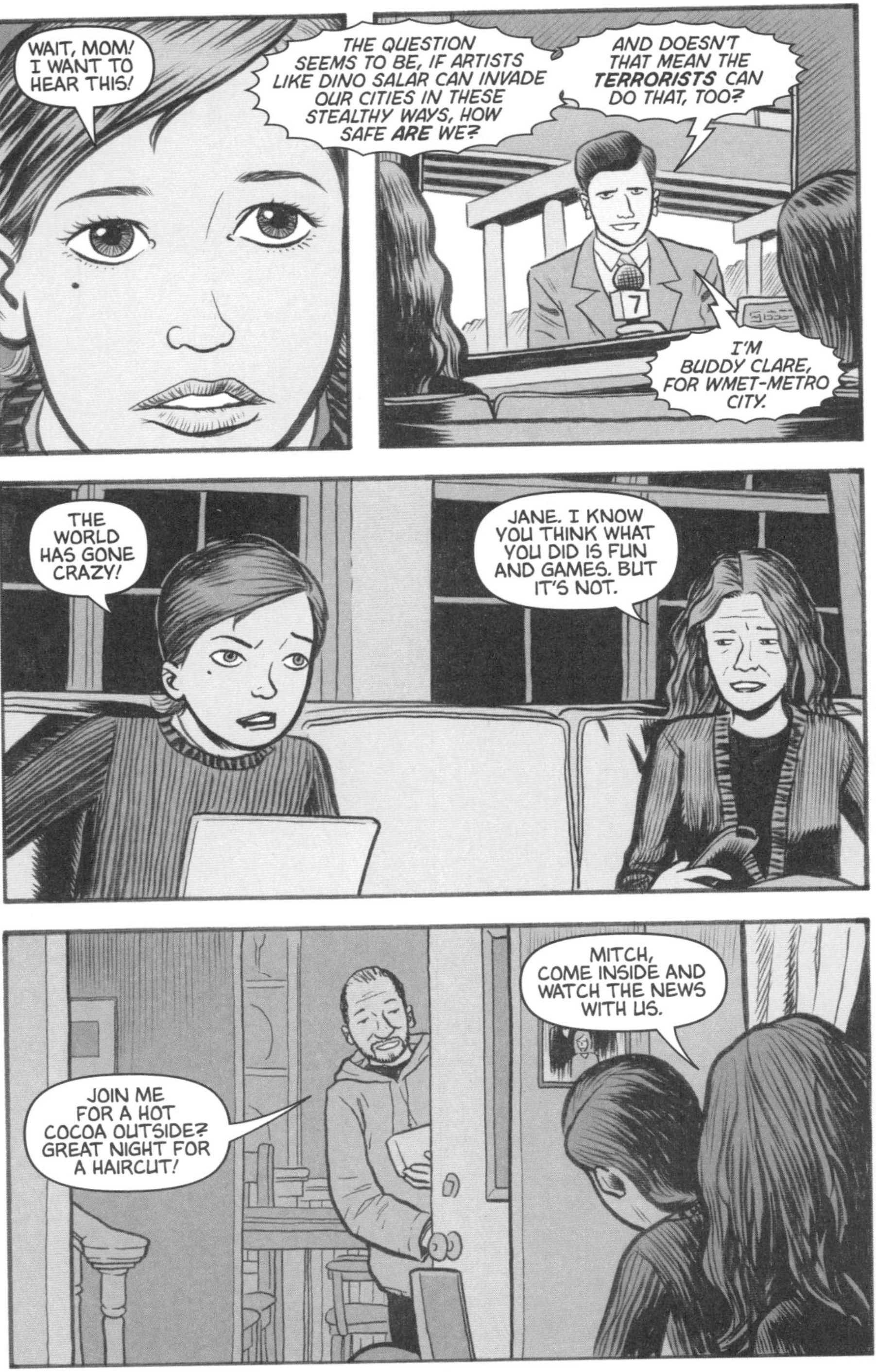
WAIT, MOM! I WANT TO HEAR THIS!
THE QUESTION SEEMS TO BE, IF ARTISTS LIKE DINO SALAR CAN INVADE OUR CITIES IN THESE STEALTHY WAYS, HOW SAFE **ARE** WE?
AND DOESN'T THAT MEAN THE **TERRORISTS** CAN DO THAT, TOO?
I'M BUDDY CLARE, FOR WMET-METRO CITY.
THE WORLD HAS GONE CRAZY!
JANE. I KNOW YOU THINK WHAT YOU DID IS FUN AND GAMES. BUT IT'S NOT.
MITCH, COME INSIDE AND WATCH THE NEWS WITH US.
JOIN ME FOR A HOT COCOA OUTSIDE? GREAT NIGHT FOR A HAIRCUT!

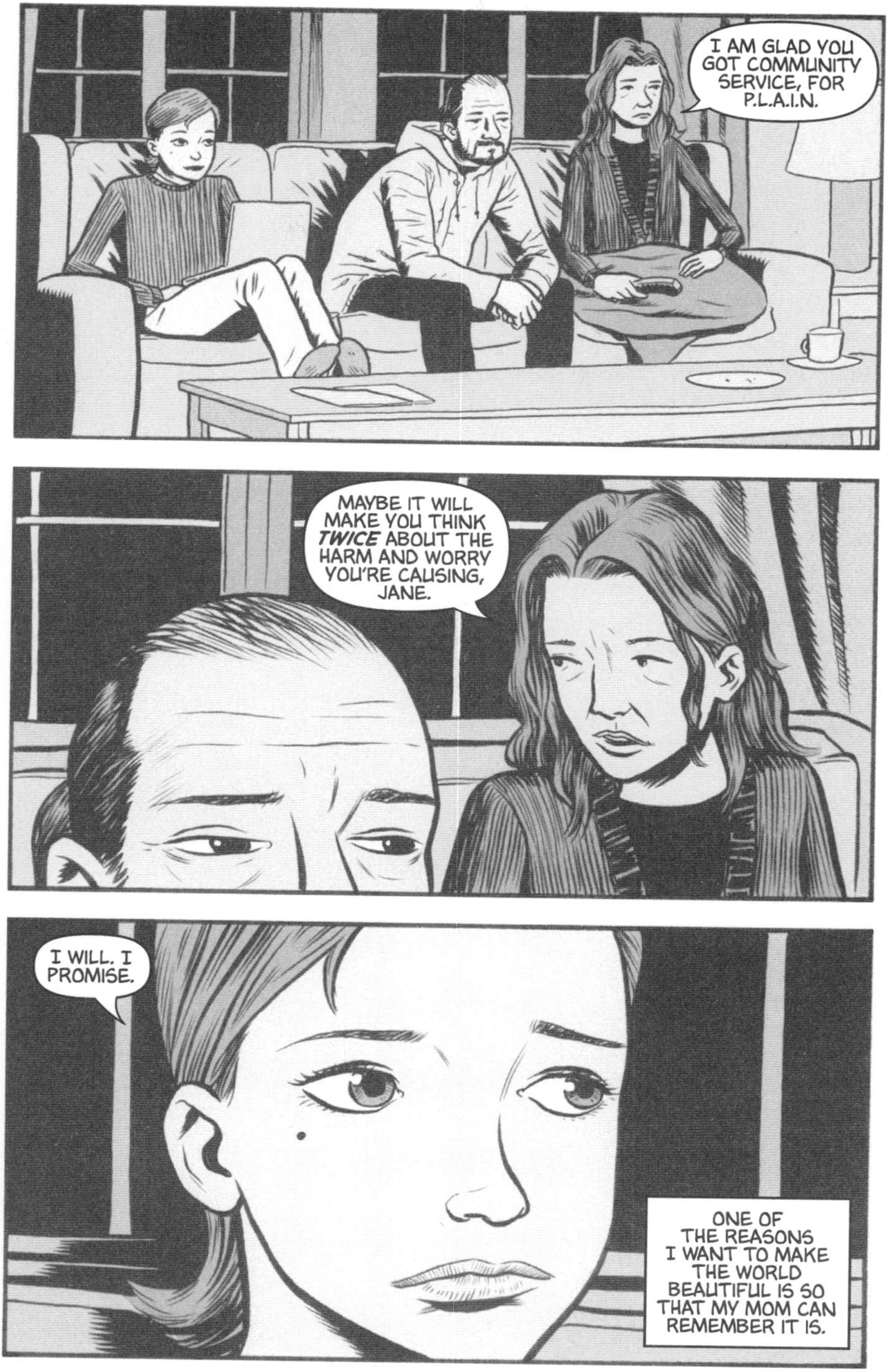
I AM GLAD YOU GOT COMMUNITY SERVICE, FOR P.L.A.I.N.
MAYBE IT WILL MAKE YOU THINK *TWICE* ABOUT THE HARM AND WORRY YOU'RE CAUSING, JANE.
I WILL. I PROMISE.
ONE OF THE REASONS I WANT TO MAKE THE WORLD BEAUTIFUL IS SO THAT MY MOM CAN REMEMBER IT IS.

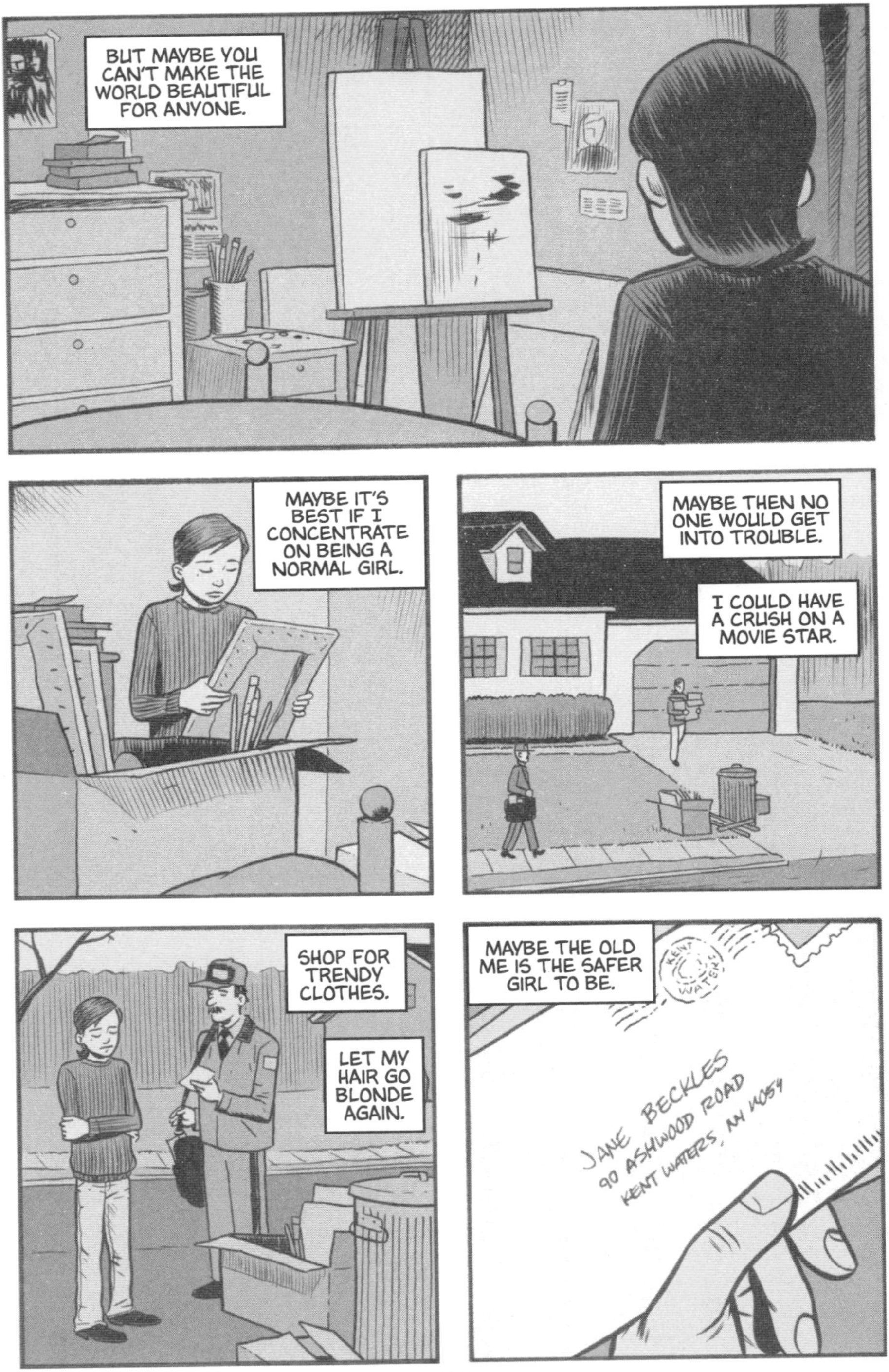

BUT MAYBE YOU CAN'T MAKE THE WORLD BEAUTIFUL FOR ANYONE.
MAYBE IT'S BEST IF I CONCENTRATE ON BEING A NORMAL GIRL.
MAYBE THEN NO ONE WOULD GET INTO TROUBLE.
I COULD HAVE A CRUSH ON A MOVIE STAR.
SHOP FOR TRENDY CLOTHES.
LET MY HAIR GO BLONDE AGAIN.
MAYBE THE OLD ME IS THE SAFER GIRL TO BE.
JANE BECKLES
90 ASHWOOD ROAD
KENT WATERS, NY 11054

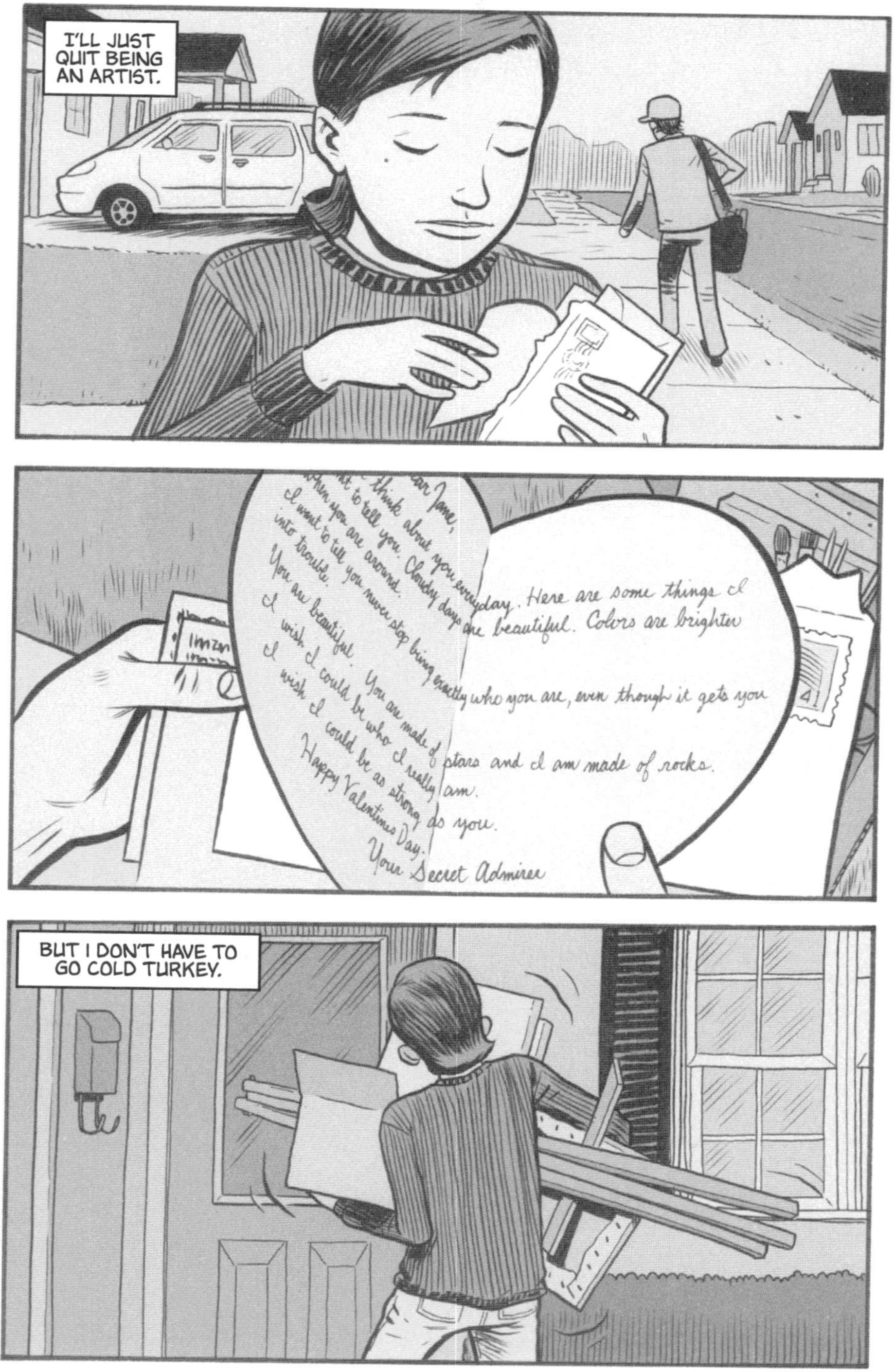
I'LL JUST QUIT BEING AN ARTIST.
ar Jane,
think about you everyday. Here are some things I
nt to tell you. Cloudy days are beautiful. Colors are brighter
hen you are around.
I want to tell you never stop being exactly who you are, even though it gets you
into trouble.
You are beautiful. You are made of stars and I am made of rocks.
I wish I could be who I really am.
I wish I could be as strong as you.
Happy Valentines Day.
Your Secret Admirer
BUT I DON'T HAVE TO GO COLD TURKEY.

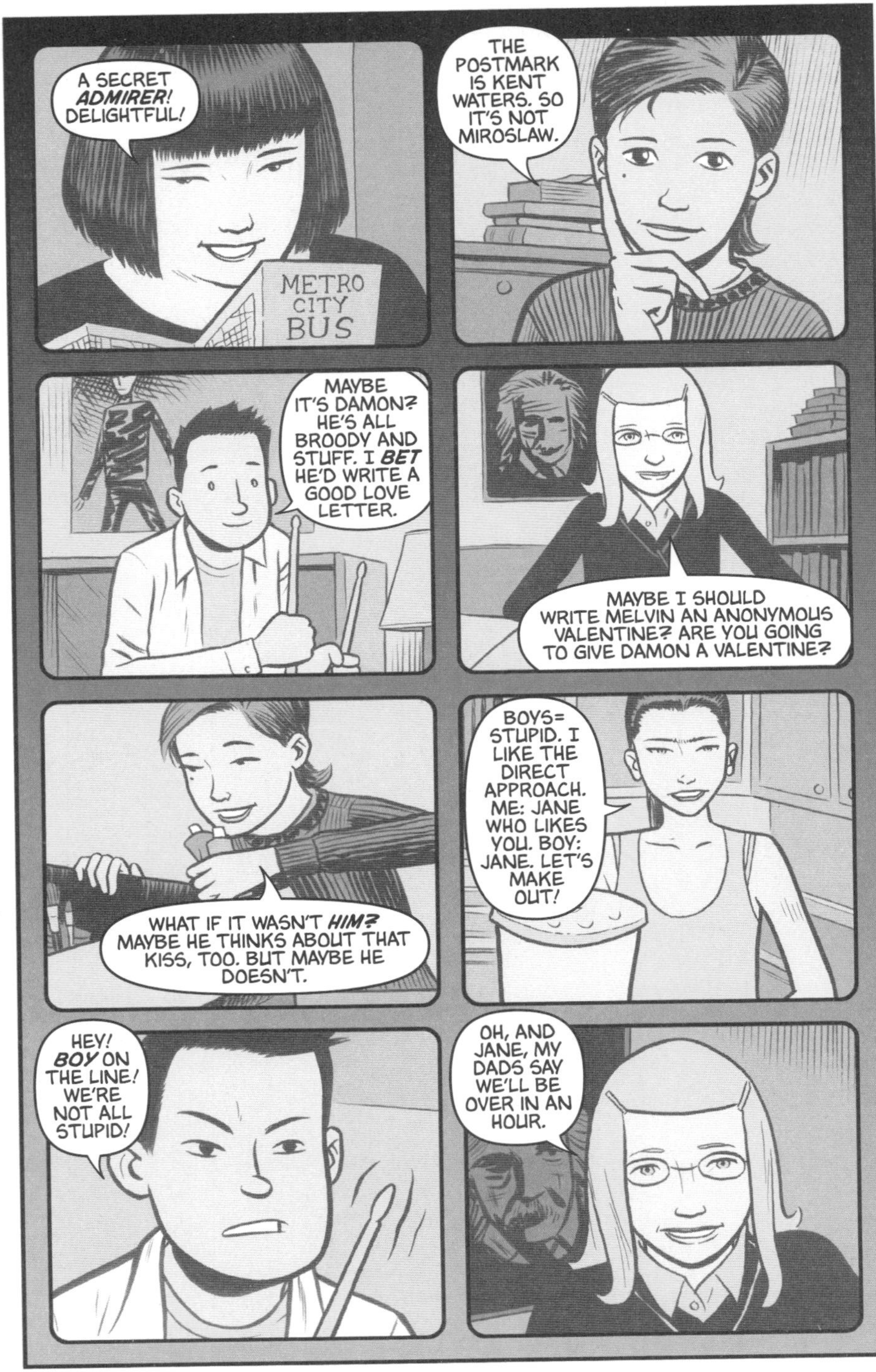
A SECRET *ADMIRER*! DELIGHTFUL!
METRO CITY BUS
THE POSTMARK IS KENT WATERS. SO IT'S NOT MIROSLAW.
MAYBE IT'S DAMON? HE'S ALL BROODY AND STUFF. I *BET* HE'D WRITE A GOOD LOVE LETTER.
MAYBE I SHOULD WRITE MELVIN AN ANONYMOUS VALENTINE? ARE YOU GOING TO GIVE DAMON A VALENTINE?
WHAT IF IT WASN'T *HIM*? MAYBE HE THINKS ABOUT THAT KISS, TOO. BUT MAYBE HE DOESN'T.
BOYS= STUPID. I LIKE THE DIRECT APPROACH. ME: JANE WHO LIKES YOU. BOY: JANE. LET'S MAKE OUT!
HEY! *BOY* ON THE LINE! WE'RE NOT ALL STUPID!
OH, AND JANE, MY DADS SAY WE'LL BE OVER IN AN HOUR.

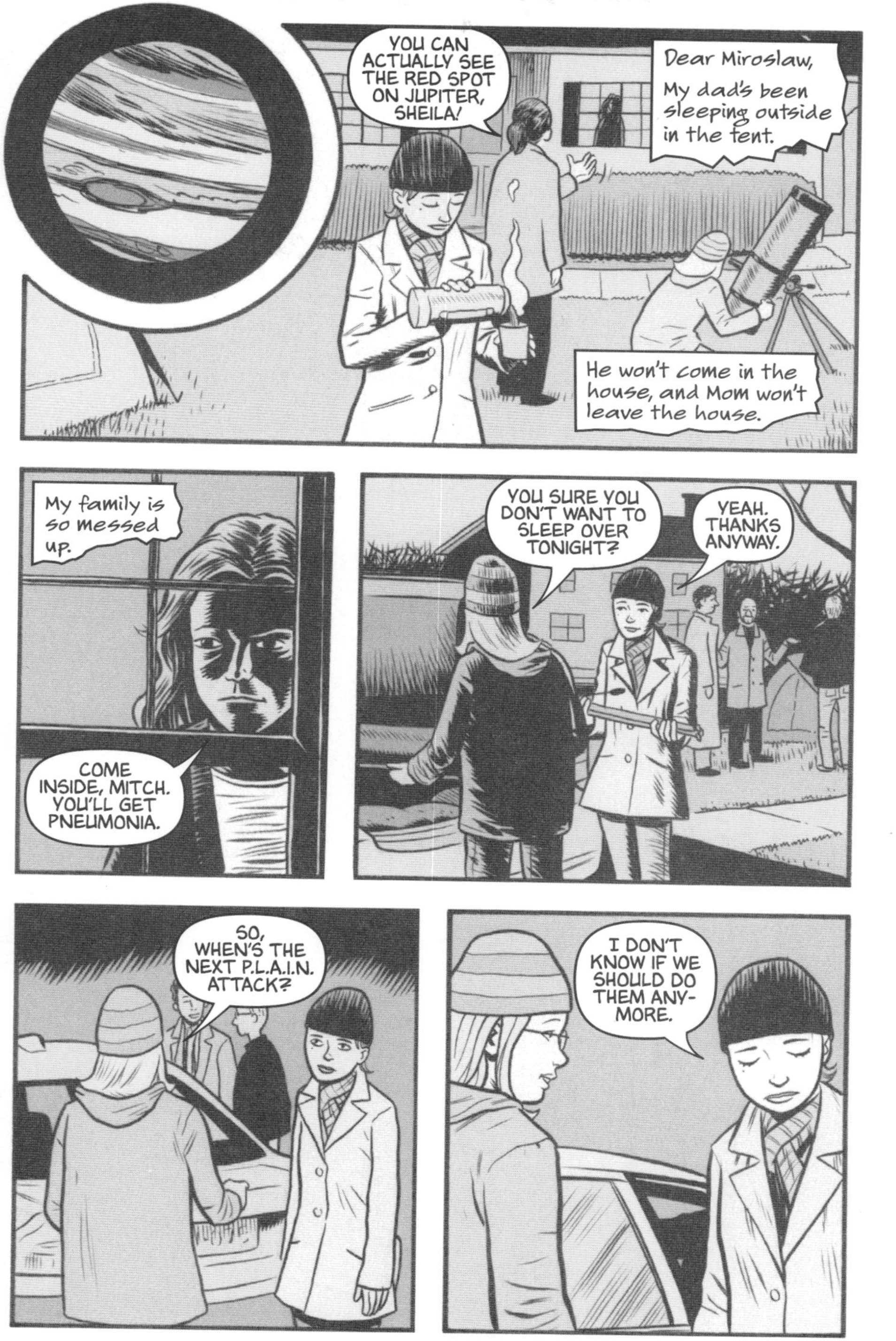
YOU CAN ACTUALLY SEE THE RED SPOT ON JUPITER, SHEILA!
Dear Miroslaw,
My dad's been sleeping outside in the tent.
He won't come in the house, and Mom won't leave the house.
My family is so messed up.
COME INSIDE, MITCH. YOU'LL GET PNEUMONIA.
YOU SURE YOU DON'T WANT TO SLEEP OVER TONIGHT?
YEAH. THANKS ANYWAY.
SO, WHEN'S THE NEXT P.L.A.I.N. ATTACK?
I DON'T KNOW IF WE SHOULD DO THEM ANY-MORE.

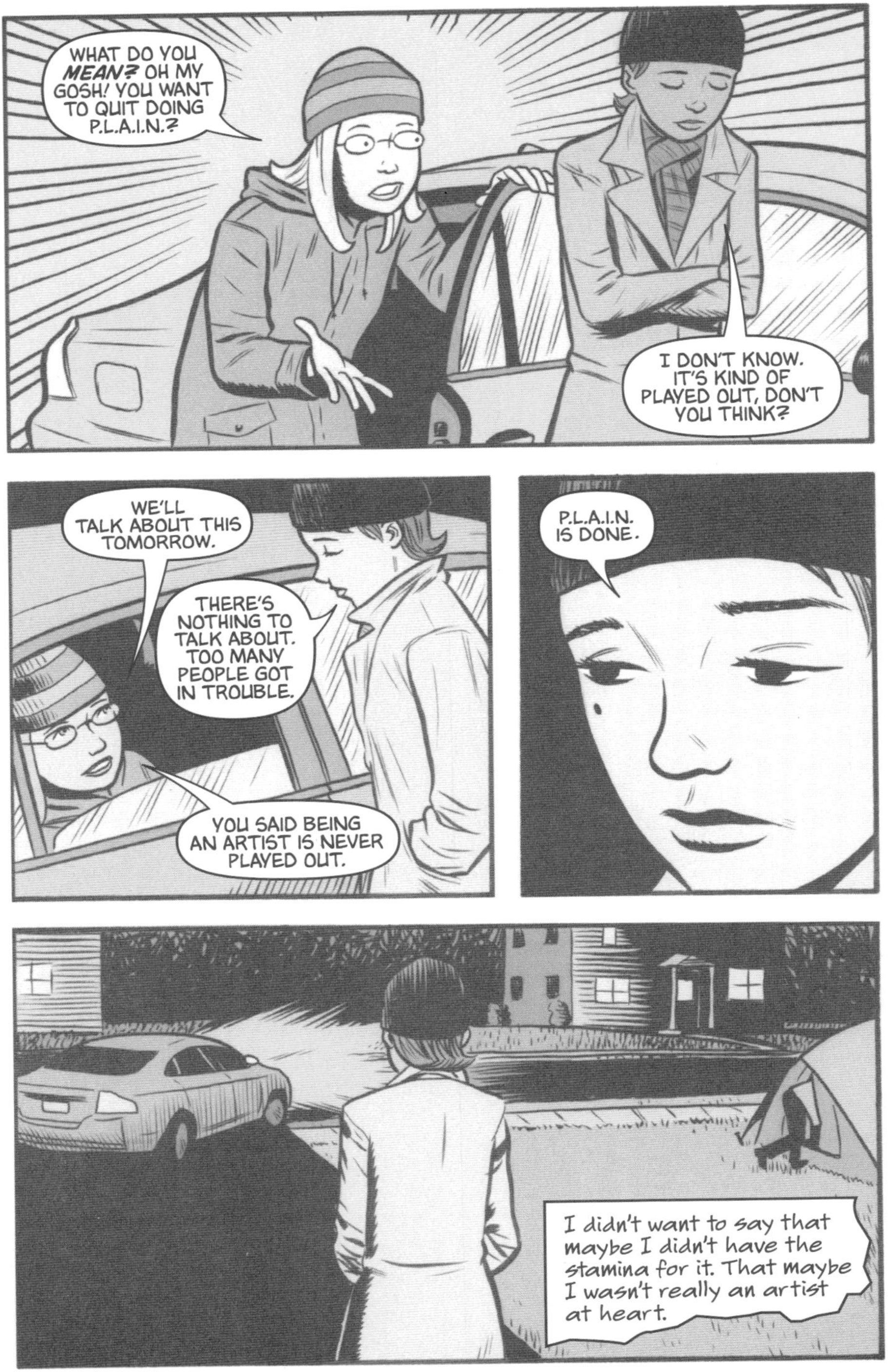
WHAT DO YOU *MEAN?* OH MY GOSH! YOU WANT TO QUIT DOING P.L.A.I.N.?
I DON'T KNOW. IT'S KIND OF PLAYED OUT, DON'T YOU THINK?
WE'LL TALK ABOUT THIS TOMORROW.
THERE'S NOTHING TO TALK ABOUT. TOO MANY PEOPLE GOT IN TROUBLE.
YOU SAID BEING AN ARTIST IS NEVER PLAYED OUT.
P.L.A.I.N. IS DONE.
I didn't want to say that maybe I didn't have the stamina for it. That maybe I wasn't really an artist at heart.

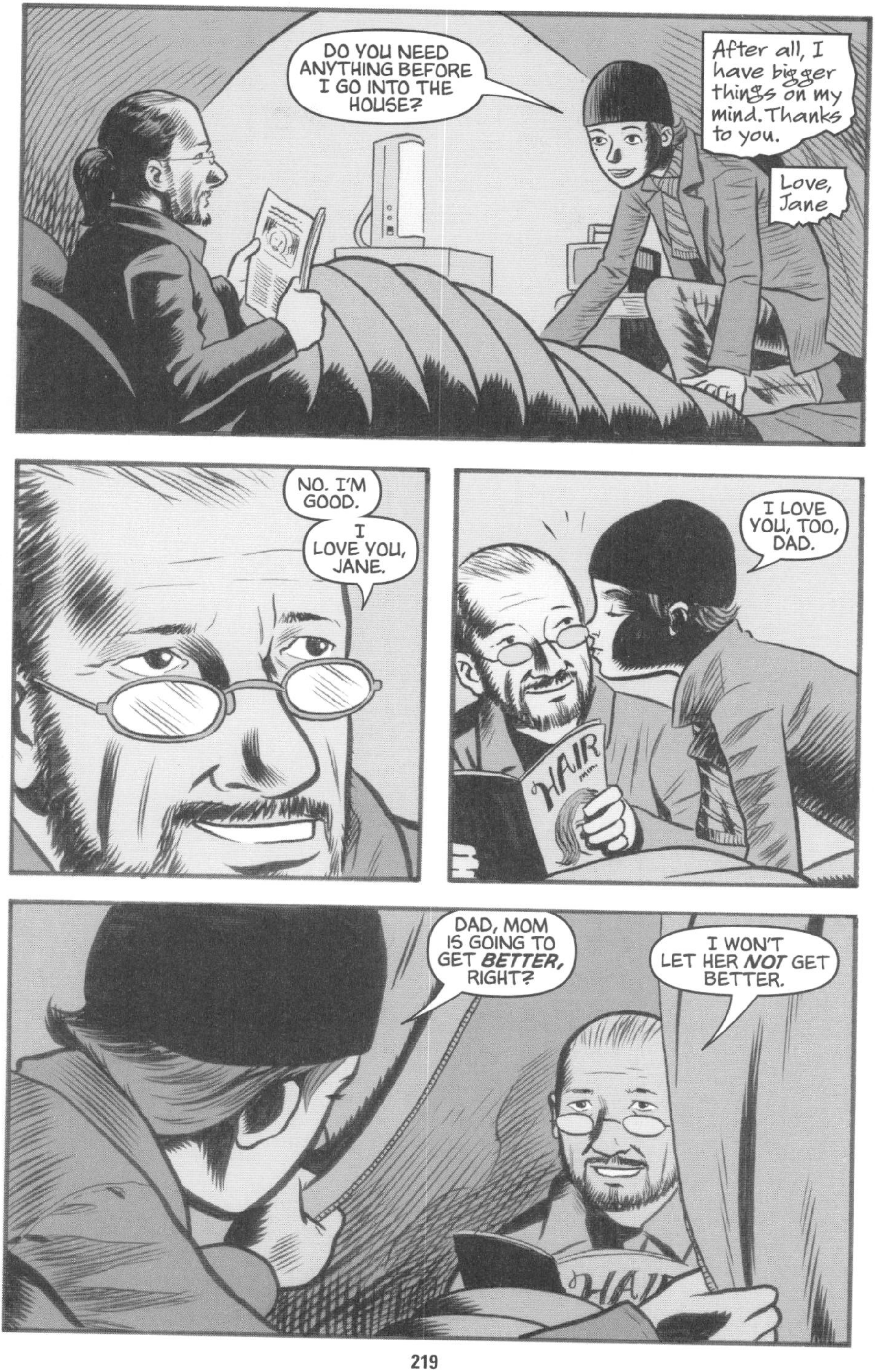

DO YOU NEED ANYTHING BEFORE I GO INTO THE HOUSE?
After all, I have bigger things on my mind. Thanks to you.
Love, Jane
NO. I'M GOOD.
I LOVE YOU, JANE.
I LOVE YOU, TOO, DAD.
HAIR
DAD, MOM IS GOING TO GET *BETTER*, RIGHT?
I WON'T LET HER *NOT* GET BETTER.

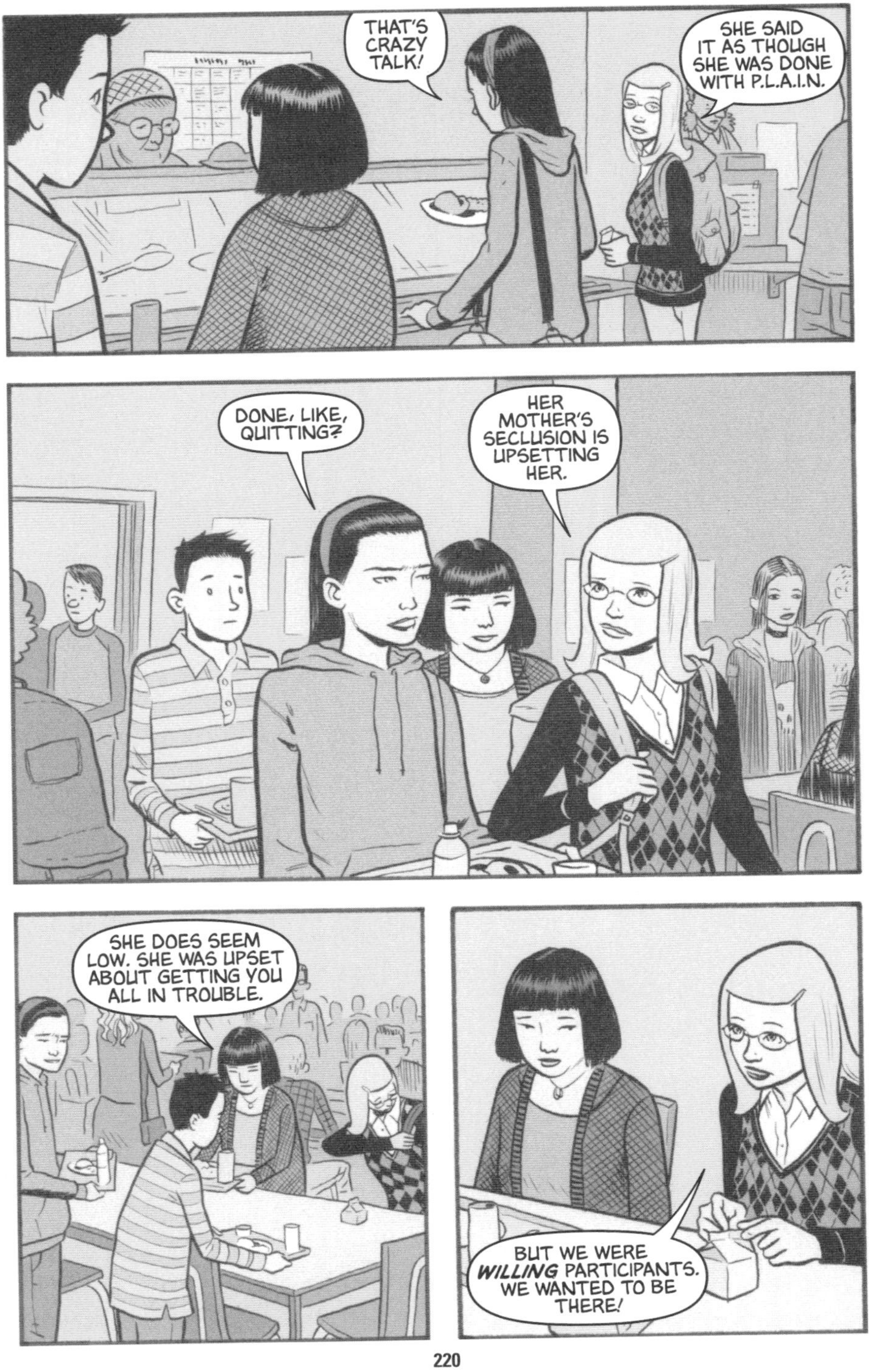
THAT'S CRAZY TALK!
SHE SAID IT AS THOUGH SHE WAS DONE WITH P.L.A.I.N.
DONE, LIKE, QUITTING?
HER MOTHER'S SECLUSION IS UPSETTING HER.
SHE DOES SEEM LOW. SHE WAS UPSET ABOUT GETTING YOU ALL IN TROUBLE.
BUT WE WERE *WILLING* PARTICIPANTS. WE WANTED TO BE THERE!

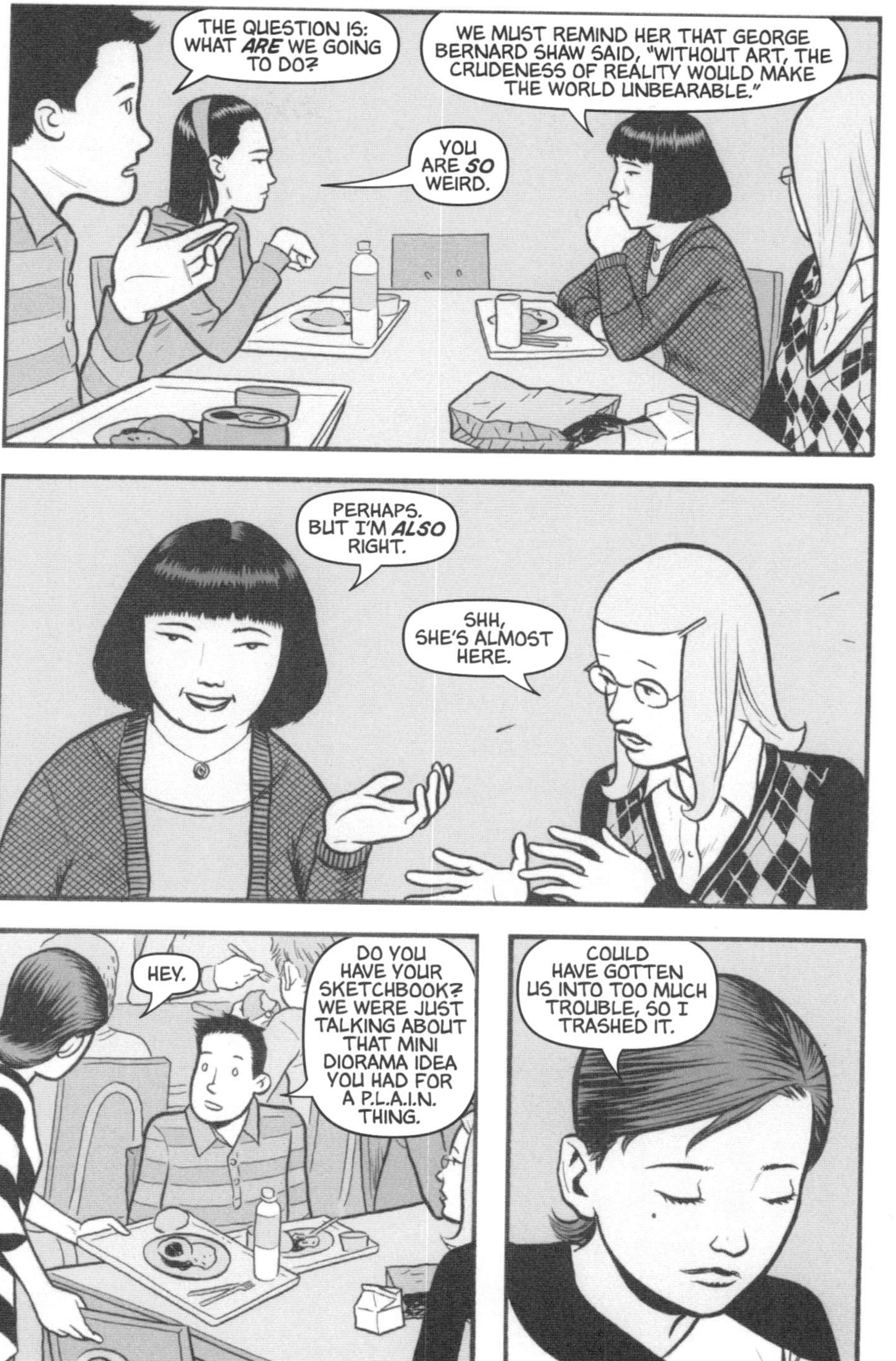
THE QUESTION IS: WHAT ARE WE GOING TO DO?
WE MUST REMIND HER THAT GEORGE BERNARD SHAW SAID, "WITHOUT ART, THE CRUDENESS OF REALITY WOULD MAKE THE WORLD UNBEARABLE."
YOU ARE SO WEIRD.
PERHAPS. BUT I'M ALSO RIGHT.
SHH, SHE'S ALMOST HERE.
HEY.
DO YOU HAVE YOUR SKETCHBOOK? WE WERE JUST TALKING ABOUT THAT MINI DIORAMA IDEA YOU HAD FOR A P.L.A.I.N. THING.
COULD HAVE GOTTEN US INTO TOO MUCH TROUBLE, SO I TRASHED IT.

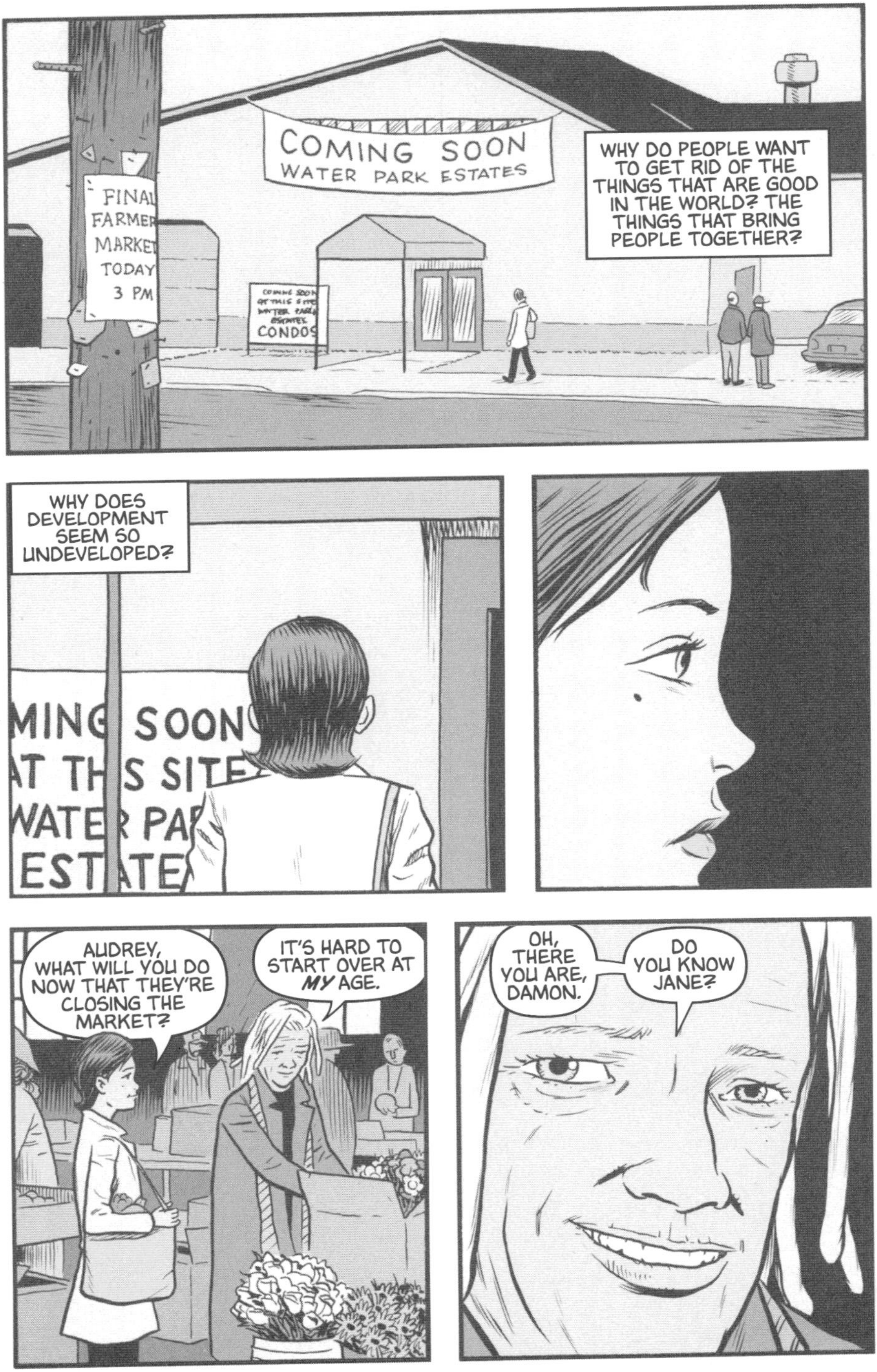

COMING SOON
WATER PARK ESTATES
FINAL FARMER MARKET TODAY 3 PM
CONDOS
WHY DO PEOPLE WANT TO GET RID OF THE THINGS THAT ARE GOOD IN THE WORLD? THE THINGS THAT BRING PEOPLE TOGETHER?
WHY DOES DEVELOPMENT SEEM SO UNDEVELOPED?
MING SOON
AT TH S SITE
WATER PAR
ESTATE
AUDREY, WHAT WILL YOU DO NOW THAT THEY'RE CLOSING THE MARKET?
IT'S HARD TO START OVER AT *MY* AGE.
OH, THERE YOU ARE, DAMON.
DO YOU KNOW JANE?

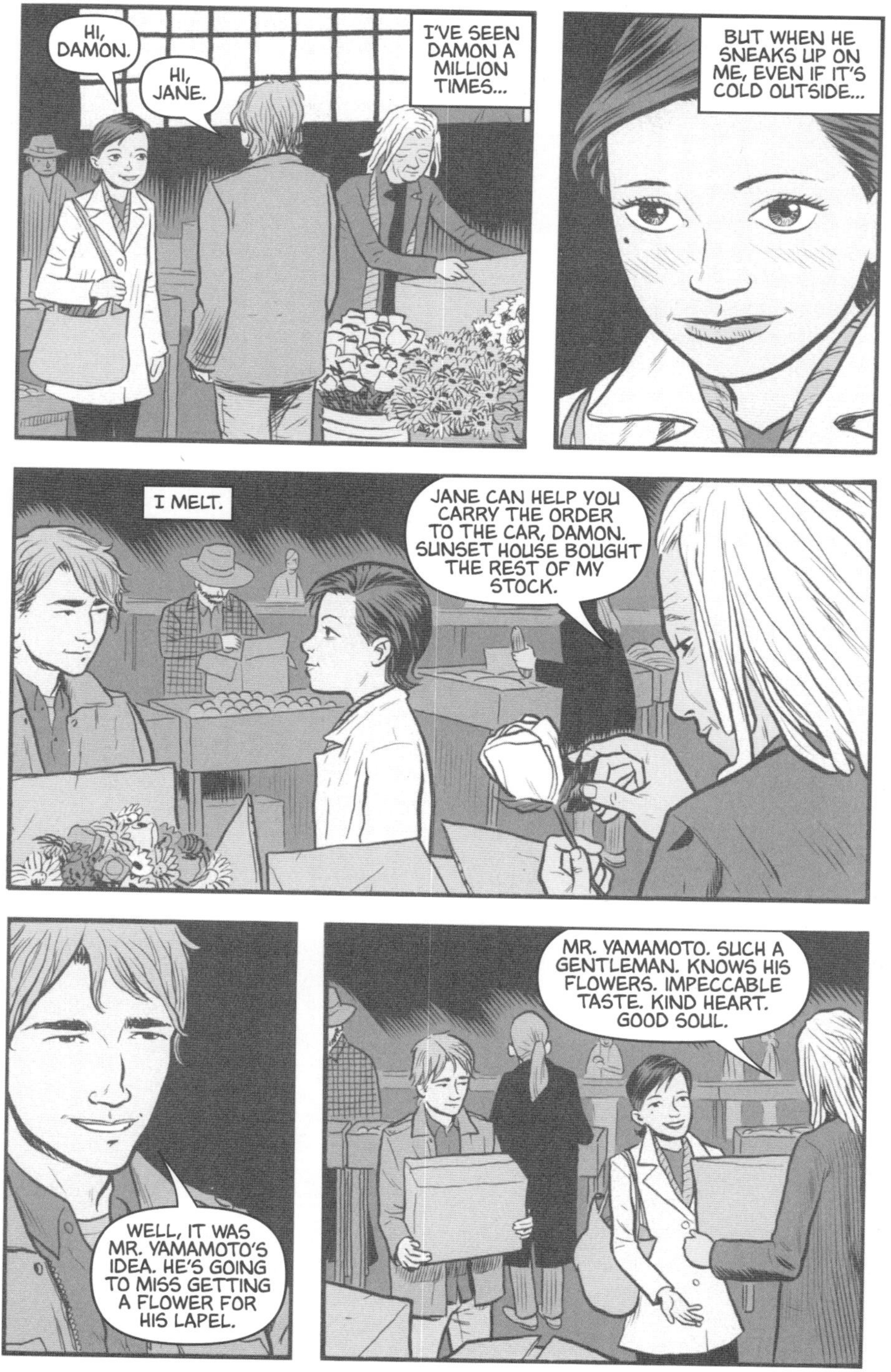
HI, DAMON.
HI, JANE.
I'VE SEEN DAMON A MILLION TIMES...
BUT WHEN HE SNEAKS UP ON ME, EVEN IF IT'S COLD OUTSIDE...
I MELT.
JANE CAN HELP YOU CARRY THE ORDER TO THE CAR, DAMON. SUNSET HOUSE BOUGHT THE REST OF MY STOCK.
WELL, IT WAS MR. YAMAMOTO'S IDEA. HE'S GOING TO MISS GETTING A FLOWER FOR HIS LAPEL.
MR. YAMAMOTO. SUCH A GENTLEMAN. KNOWS HIS FLOWERS. IMPECCABLE TASTE. KIND HEART. GOOD SOUL.

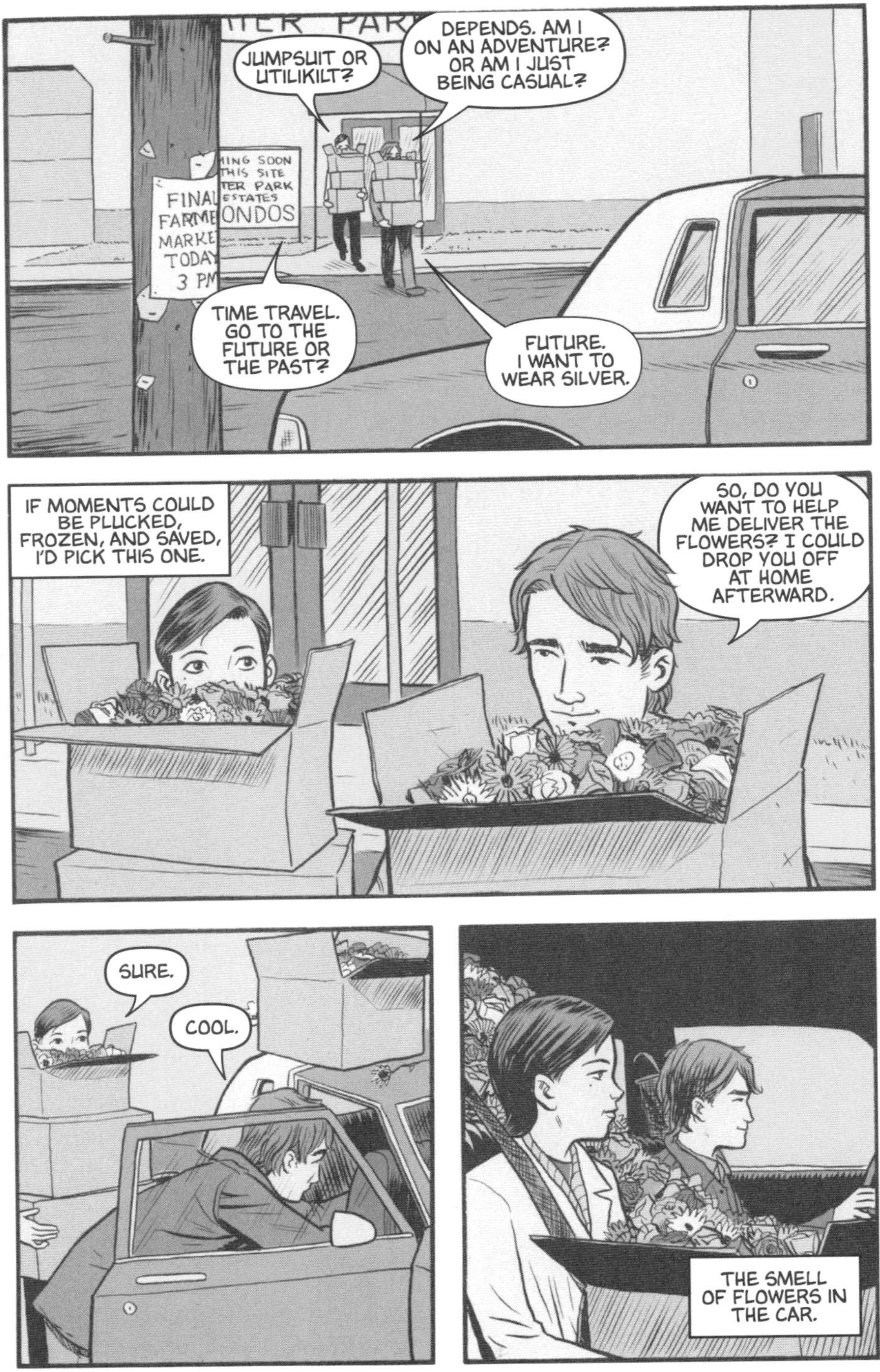
JUMPSUIT OR UTILIKILT?
DEPENDS. AM I ON AN ADVENTURE? OR AM I JUST BEING CASUAL?
TIME TRAVEL. GO TO THE FUTURE OR THE PAST?
FUTURE. I WANT TO WEAR SILVER.
IF MOMENTS COULD BE PLUCKED, FROZEN, AND SAVED, I'D PICK THIS ONE.
SO, DO YOU WANT TO HELP ME DELIVER THE FLOWERS? I COULD DROP YOU OFF AT HOME AFTERWARD.
SURE.
COOL.
THE SMELL OF FLOWERS IN THE CAR.

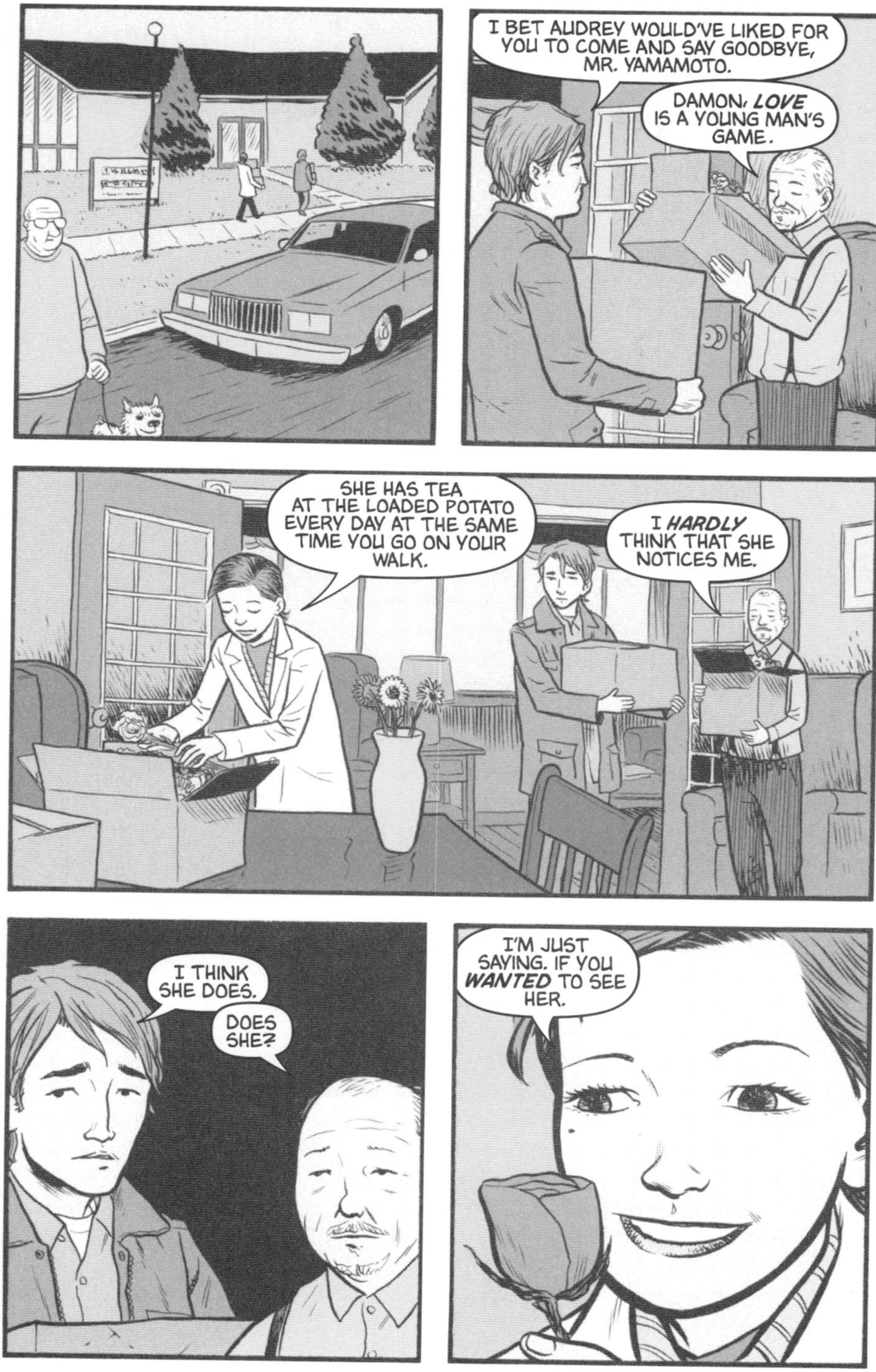
I BET AUDREY WOULD'VE LIKED FOR YOU TO COME AND SAY GOODBYE, MR. YAMAMOTO.
DAMON, LOVE IS A YOUNG MAN'S GAME.
SHE HAS TEA AT THE LOADED POTATO EVERY DAY AT THE SAME TIME YOU GO ON YOUR WALK.
I HARDLY THINK THAT SHE NOTICES ME.
I THINK SHE DOES.
DOES SHE?
I'M JUST SAYING. IF YOU WANTED TO SEE HER.

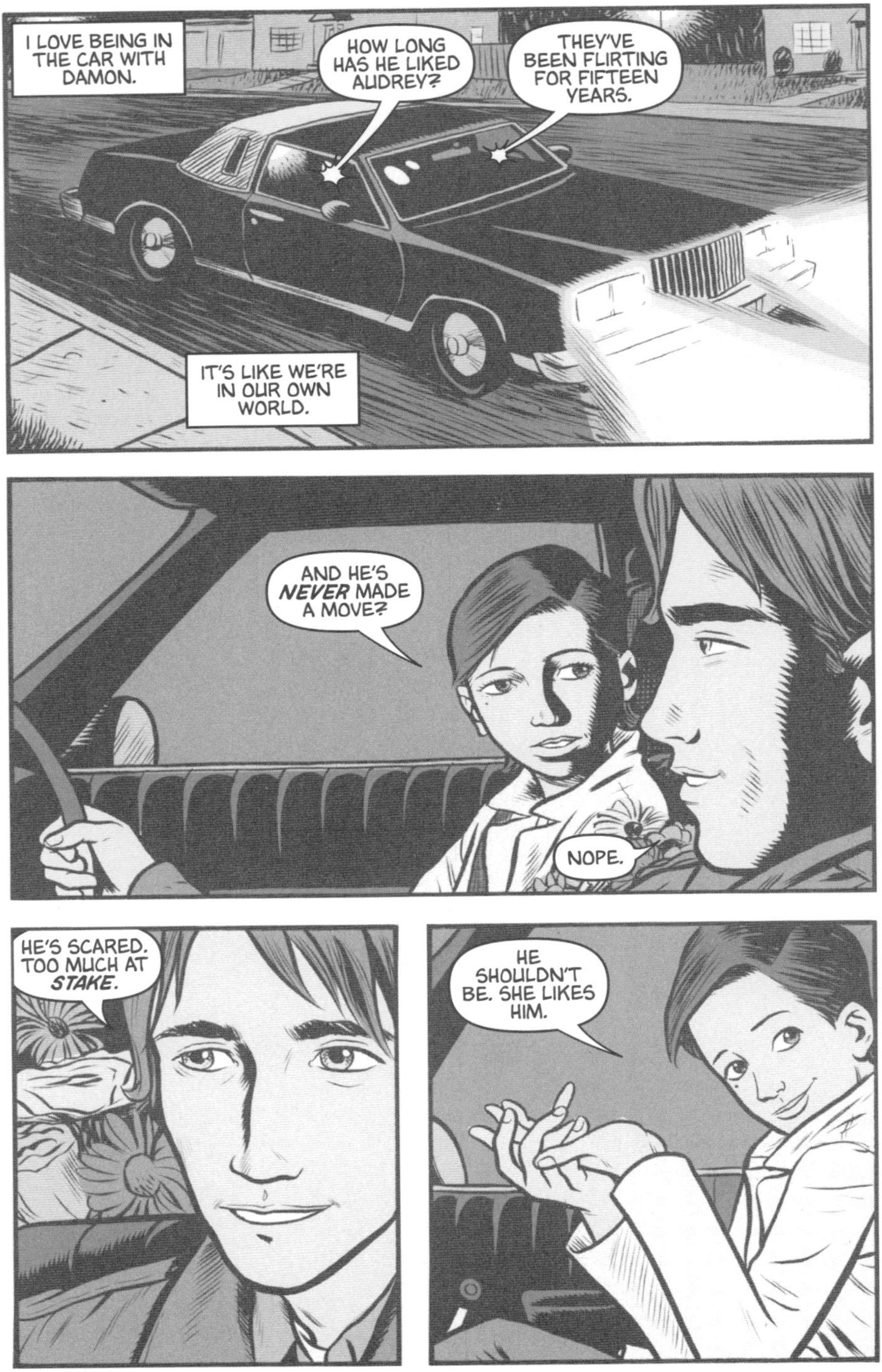
I LOVE BEING IN THE CAR WITH DAMON.
HOW LONG HAS HE LIKED AUDREY?
THEY'VE BEEN FLIRTING FOR FIFTEEN YEARS.
IT'S LIKE WE'RE IN OUR OWN WORLD.
AND HE'S *NEVER* MADE A MOVE?
NOPE.
HE'S SCARED. TOO MUCH AT *STAKE*.
HE SHOULDN'T BE. SHE LIKES HIM.

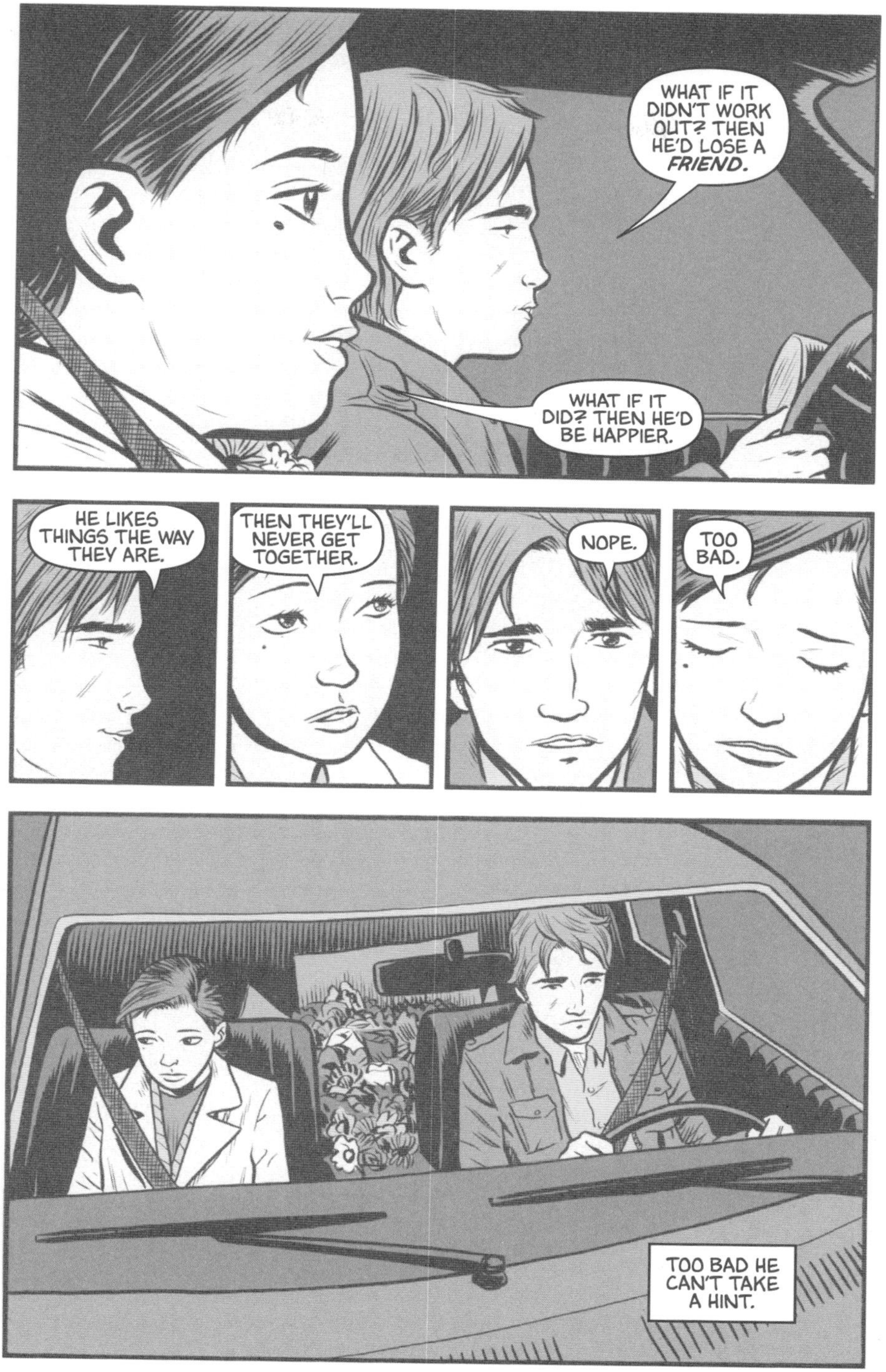
WHAT IF IT DIDN'T WORK OUT? THEN HE'D LOSE A *FRIEND.*
WHAT IF IT DID? THEN HE'D BE HAPPIER.
HE LIKES THINGS THE WAY THEY ARE.
THEN THEY'LL NEVER GET TOGETHER.
NOPE.
TOO BAD.
TOO BAD HE CAN'T TAKE A HINT.

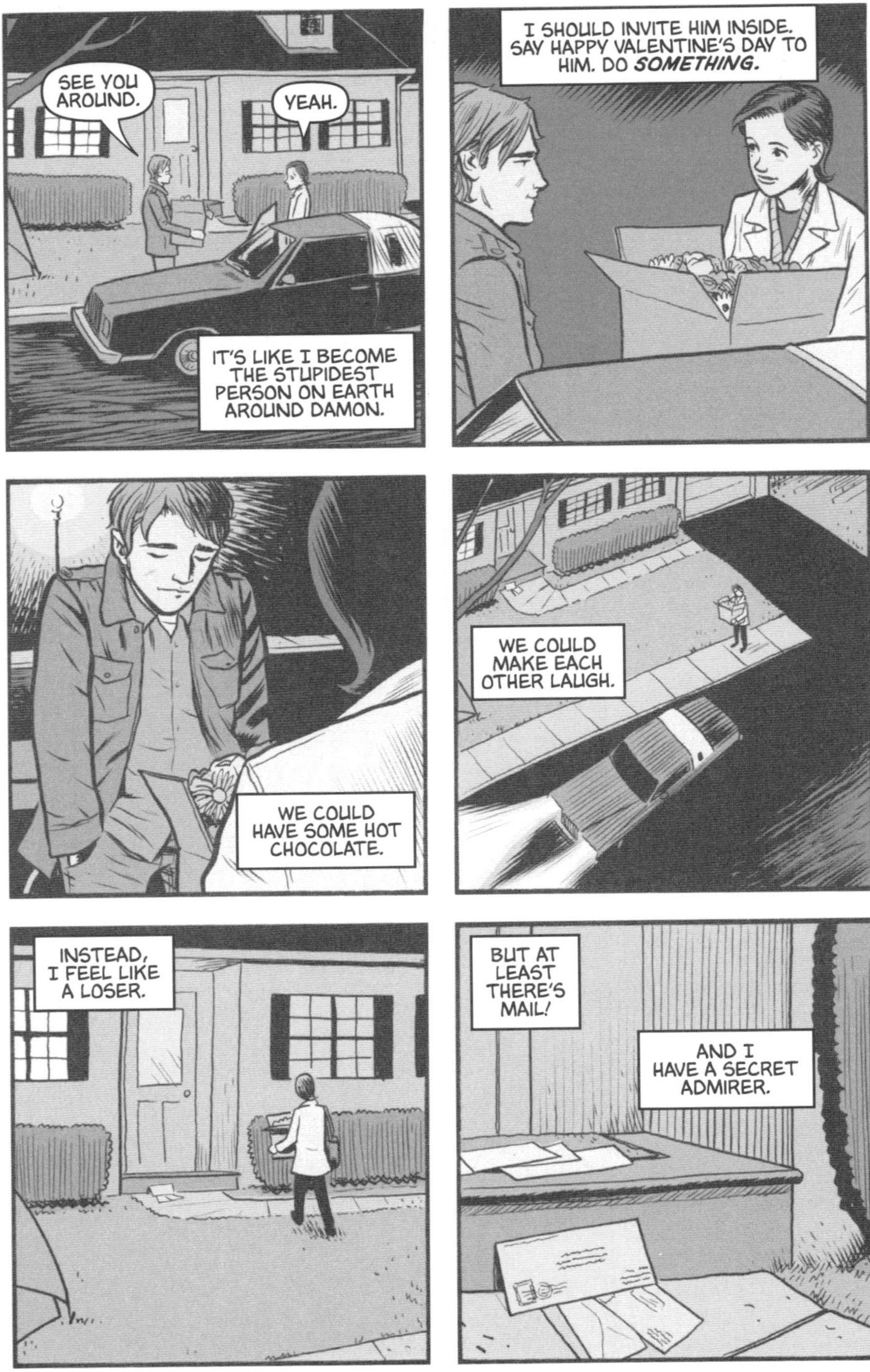
SEE YOU AROUND.
YEAH.
IT'S LIKE I BECOME THE STUPIDEST PERSON ON EARTH AROUND DAMON.
I SHOULD INVITE HIM INSIDE. SAY HAPPY VALENTINE'S DAY TO HIM. DO SOMETHING.
WE COULD HAVE SOME HOT CHOCOLATE.
WE COULD MAKE EACH OTHER LAUGH.
INSTEAD, I FEEL LIKE A LOSER.
BUT AT LEAST THERE'S MAIL!
AND I HAVE A SECRET ADMIRER.

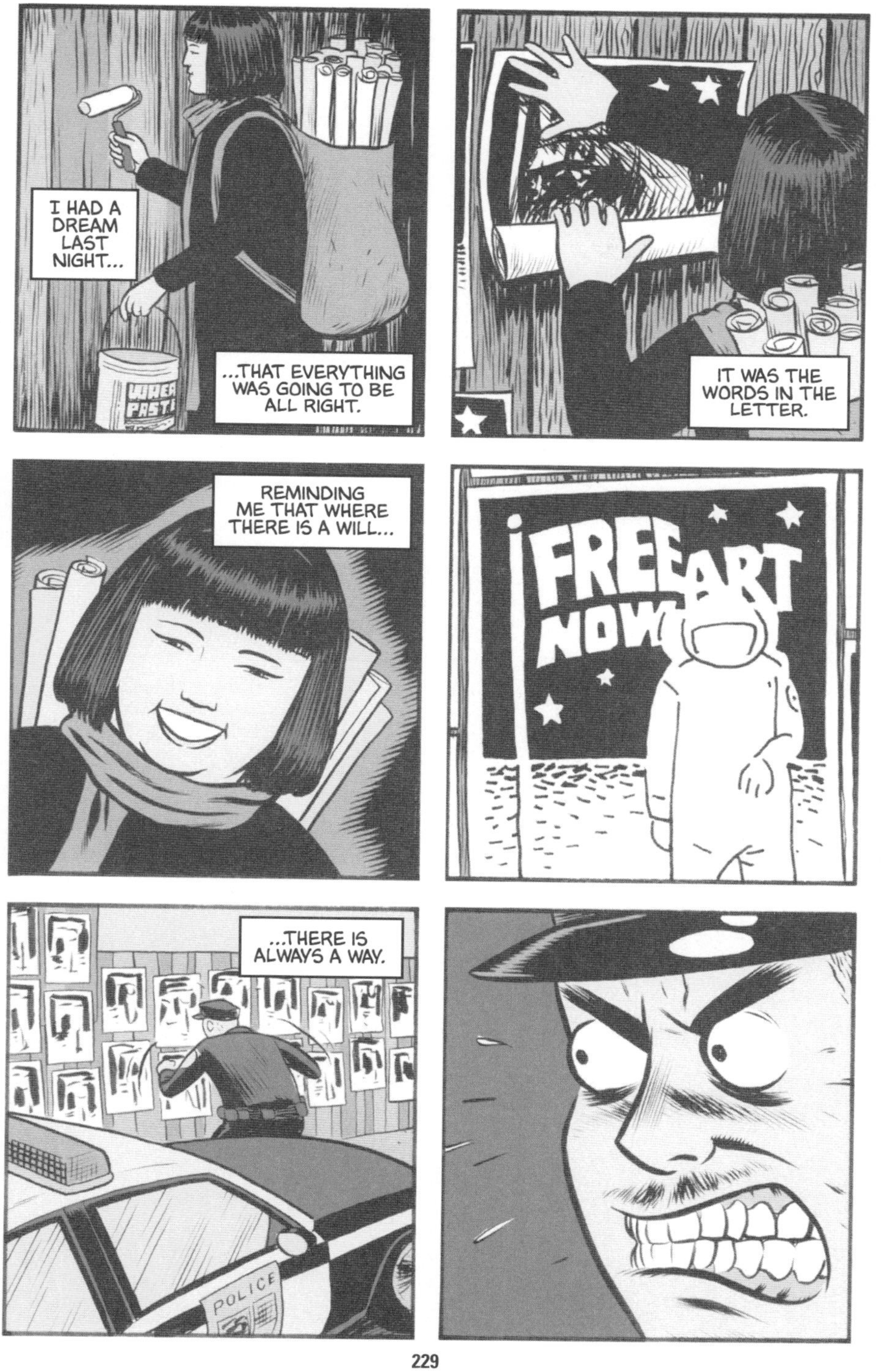
I HAD A DREAM LAST NIGHT...
...THAT EVERYTHING WAS GOING TO BE ALL RIGHT.
IT WAS THE WORDS IN THE LETTER.
REMINDING ME THAT WHERE THERE IS A WILL...
¡FREE ART NOW
...THERE IS ALWAYS A WAY.
POLICE

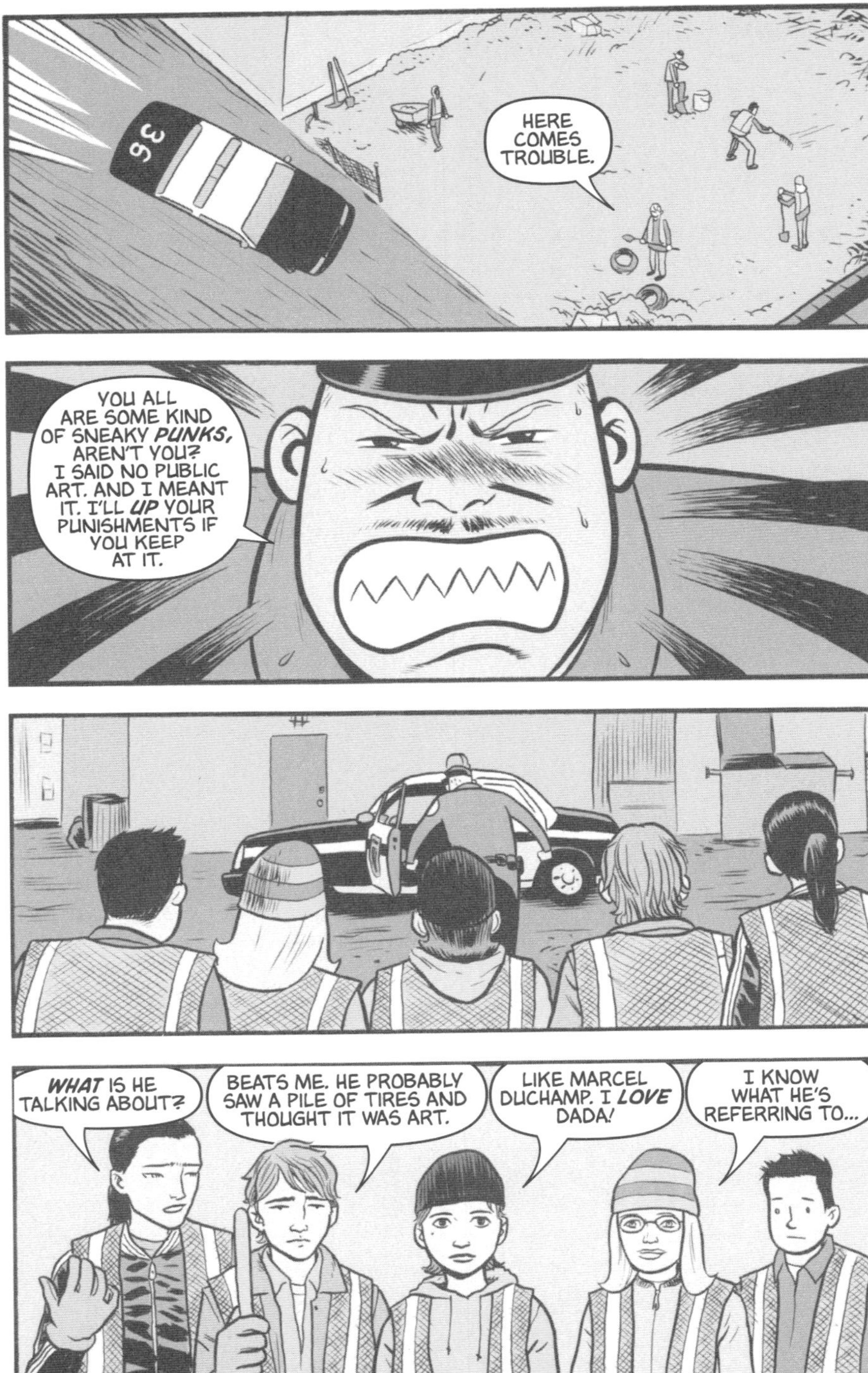
HERE COMES TROUBLE.
YOU ALL ARE SOME KIND OF SNEAKY *PUNKS,* AREN'T YOU? I SAID NO PUBLIC ART. AND I MEANT IT. I'LL *UP* YOUR PUNISHMENTS IF YOU KEEP AT IT.
WHAT IS HE TALKING ABOUT?
BEATS ME. HE PROBABLY SAW A PILE OF TIRES AND THOUGHT IT WAS ART.
LIKE MARCEL DUCHAMP. I *LOVE* DADA!
I KNOW WHAT HE'S REFERRING TO...

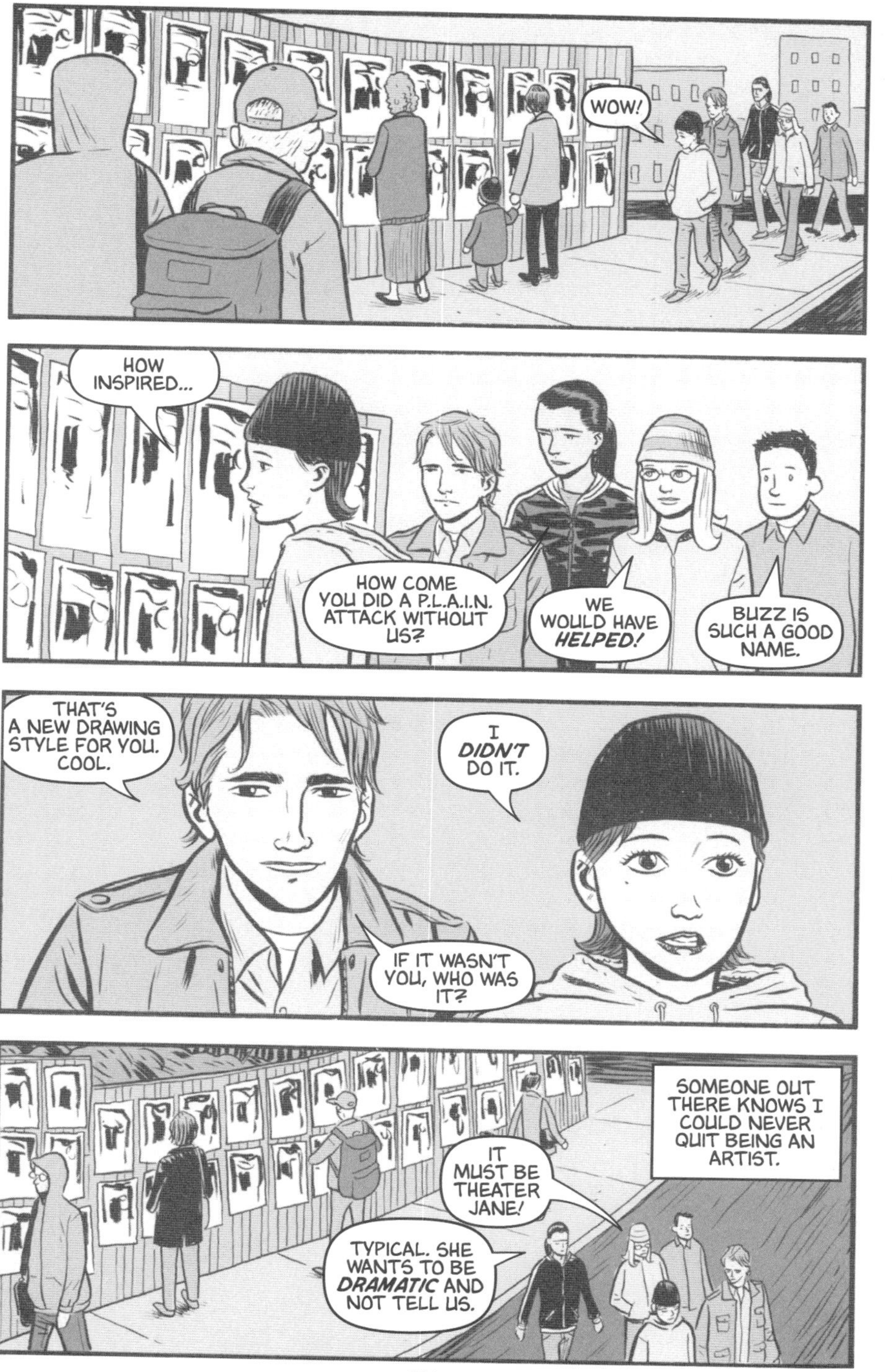
WOW!
HOW INSPIRED...
HOW COME YOU DID A P.L.A.I.N. ATTACK WITHOUT US?
WE WOULD HAVE HELPED!
BUZZ IS SUCH A GOOD NAME.
THAT'S A NEW DRAWING STYLE FOR YOU. COOL.
I DIDN'T DO IT.
IF IT WASN'T YOU, WHO WAS IT?
SOMEONE OUT THERE KNOWS I COULD NEVER QUIT BEING AN ARTIST.
IT MUST BE THEATER JANE!
TYPICAL. SHE WANTS TO BE DRAMATIC AND NOT TELL US.

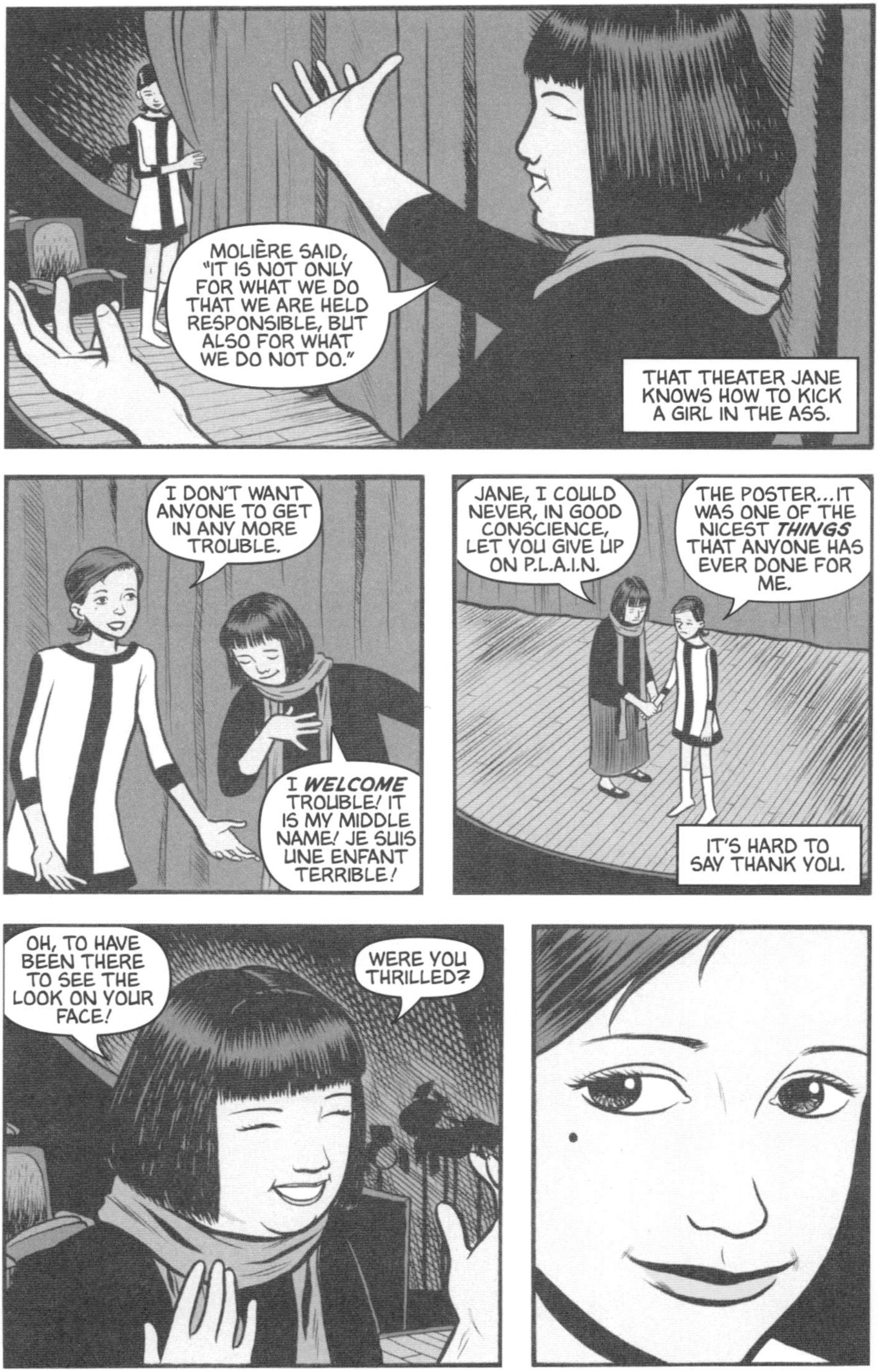
MOLIÈRE SAID, "IT IS NOT ONLY FOR WHAT WE DO THAT WE ARE HELD RESPONSIBLE, BUT ALSO FOR WHAT WE DO NOT DO."
THAT THEATER JANE KNOWS HOW TO KICK A GIRL IN THE ASS.
I DON'T WANT ANYONE TO GET IN ANY MORE TROUBLE.
I *WELCOME* TROUBLE! IT IS MY MIDDLE NAME! JE SUIS UNE ENFANT TERRIBLE!
JANE, I COULD NEVER, IN GOOD CONSCIENCE, LET YOU GIVE UP ON P.L.A.I.N.
THE POSTER...IT WAS ONE OF THE NICEST *THINGS* THAT ANYONE HAS EVER DONE FOR ME.
IT'S HARD TO SAY THANK YOU.
OH, TO HAVE BEEN THERE TO SEE THE LOOK ON YOUR FACE!
WERE YOU THRILLED?

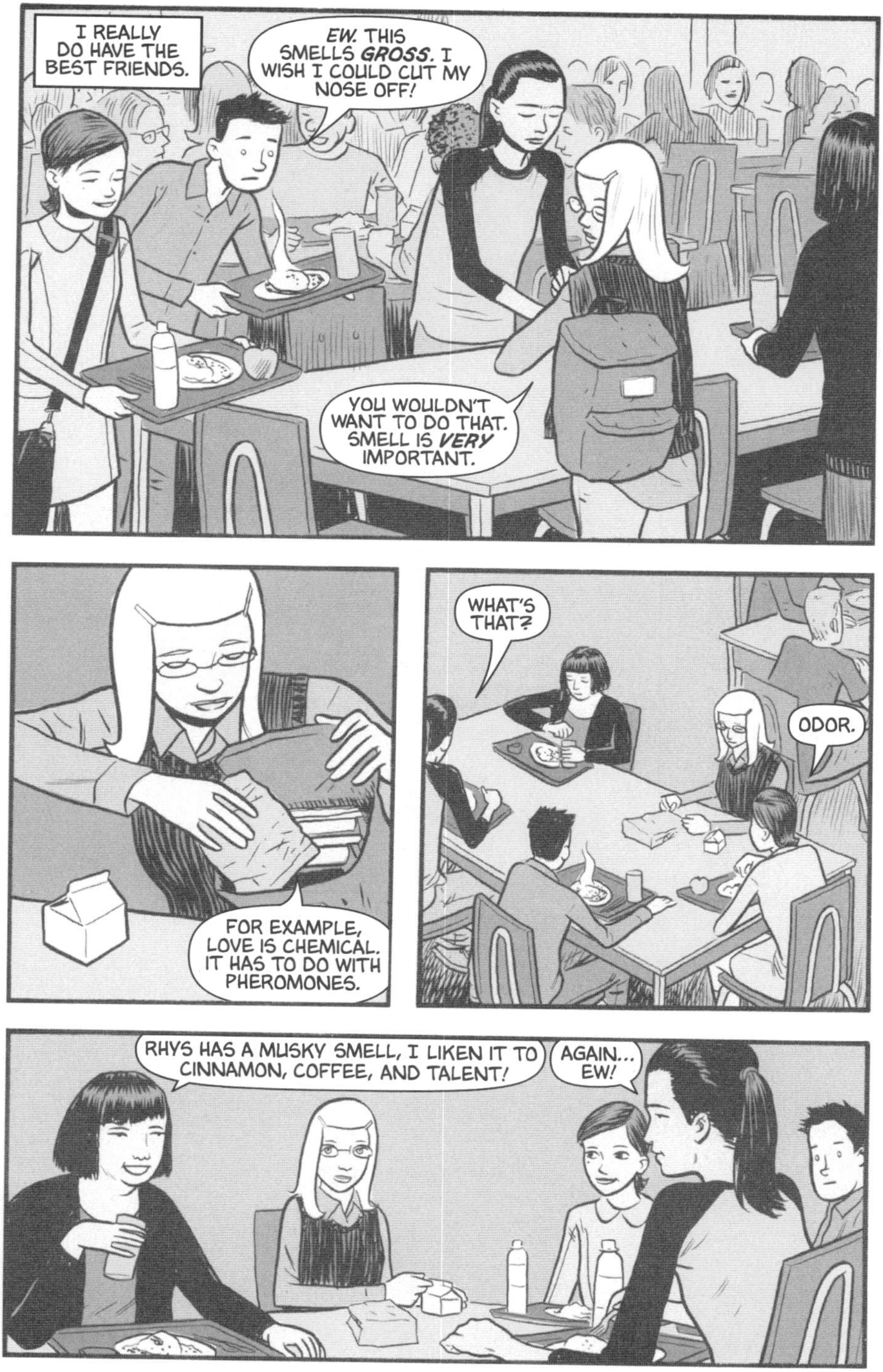

I REALLY DO HAVE THE BEST FRIENDS.
EW. THIS SMELLS GROSS. I WISH I COULD CUT MY NOSE OFF!
YOU WOULDN'T WANT TO DO THAT. SMELL IS VERY IMPORTANT.
FOR EXAMPLE, LOVE IS CHEMICAL. IT HAS TO DO WITH PHEROMONES.
WHAT'S THAT?
ODOR.
RHYS HAS A MUSKY SMELL, I LIKEN IT TO CINNAMON, COFFEE, AND TALENT!
AGAIN... EW!

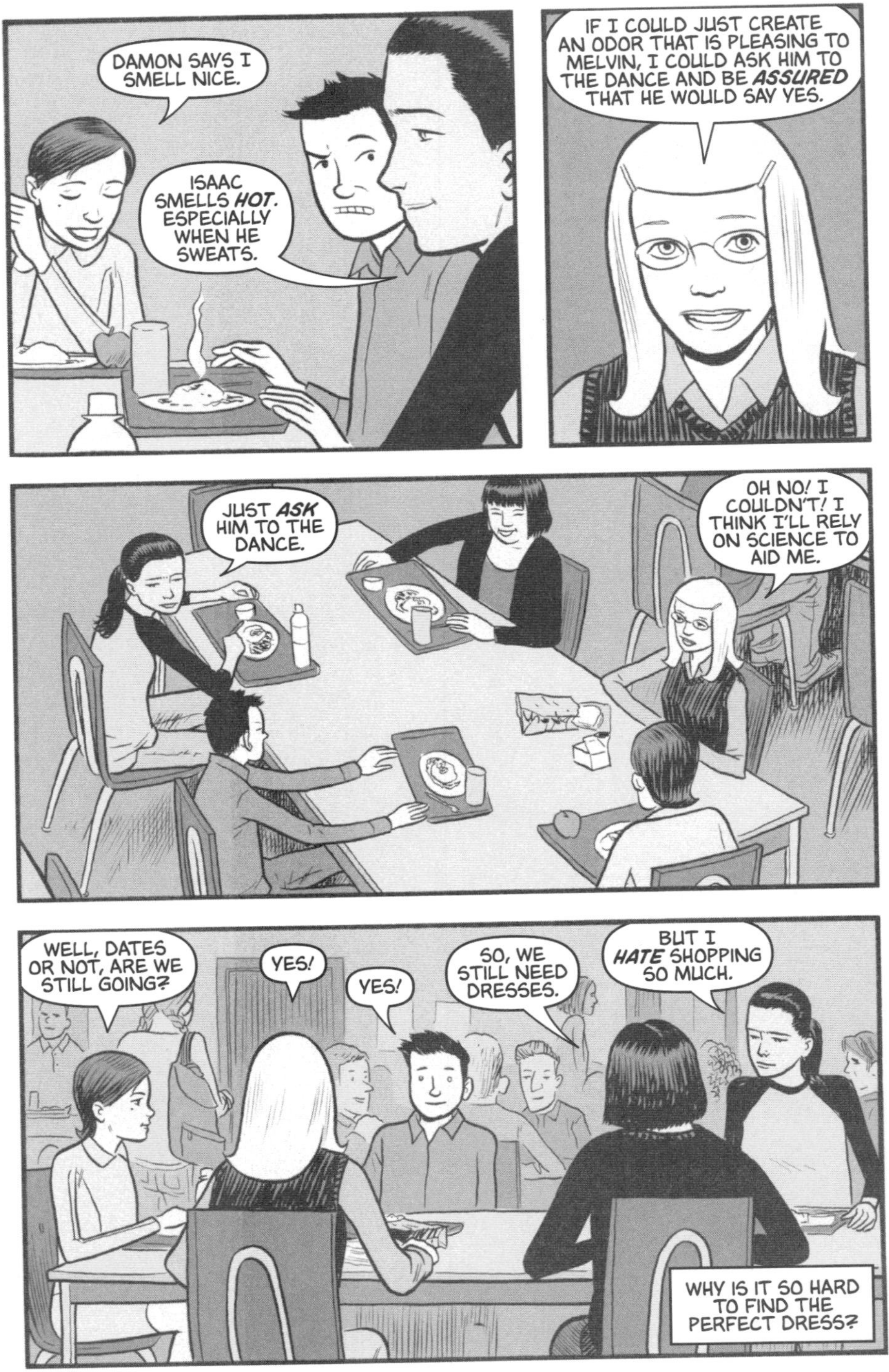
DAMON SAYS I SMELL NICE.
ISAAC SMELLS **HOT**. ESPECIALLY WHEN HE SWEATS.
IF I COULD JUST CREATE AN ODOR THAT IS PLEASING TO MELVIN, I COULD ASK HIM TO THE DANCE AND BE **ASSURED** THAT HE WOULD SAY YES.
JUST **ASK** HIM TO THE DANCE.
OH NO! I COULDN'T! I THINK I'LL RELY ON SCIENCE TO AID ME.
WELL, DATES OR NOT, ARE WE STILL GOING?
YES!
YES!
SO, WE STILL NEED DRESSES.
BUT I **HATE** SHOPPING SO MUCH.
WHY IS IT SO HARD TO FIND THE PERFECT DRESS?

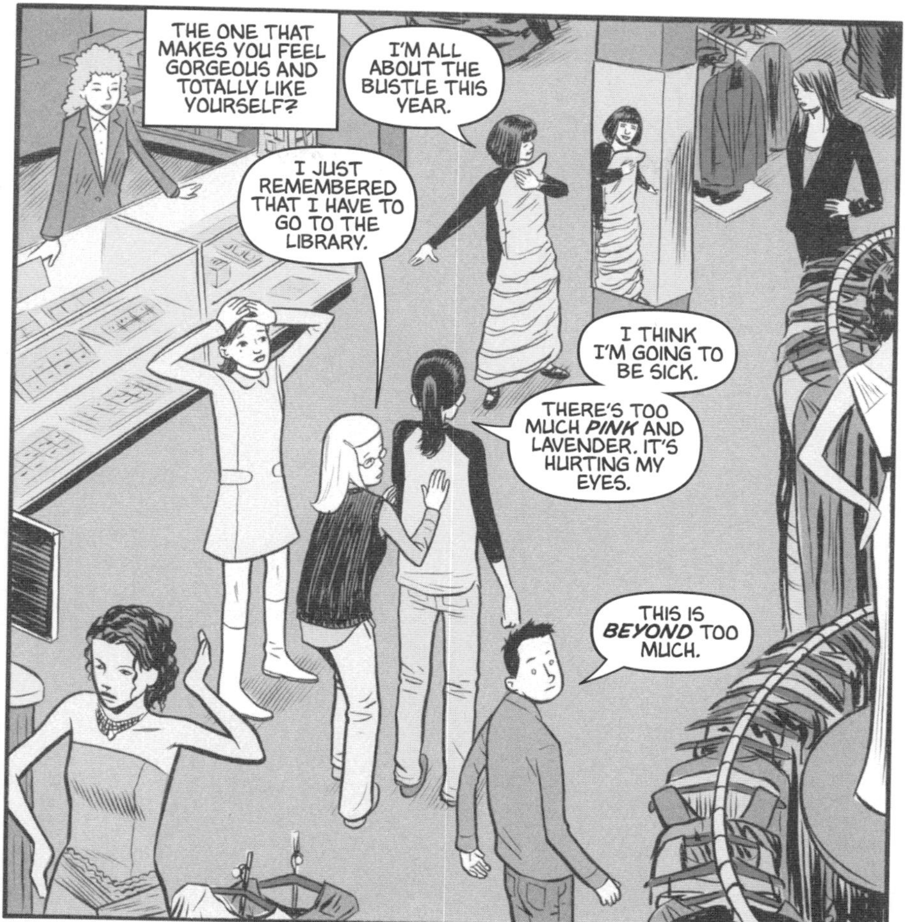
THE ONE THAT MAKES YOU FEEL GORGEOUS AND TOTALLY LIKE YOURSELF?
I'M ALL ABOUT THE BUSTLE THIS YEAR.
I JUST REMEMBERED THAT I HAVE TO GO TO THE LIBRARY.
I THINK I'M GOING TO BE SICK.
THERE'S TOO MUCH PINK AND LAVENDER. IT'S HURTING MY EYES.
THIS IS BEYOND TOO MUCH.

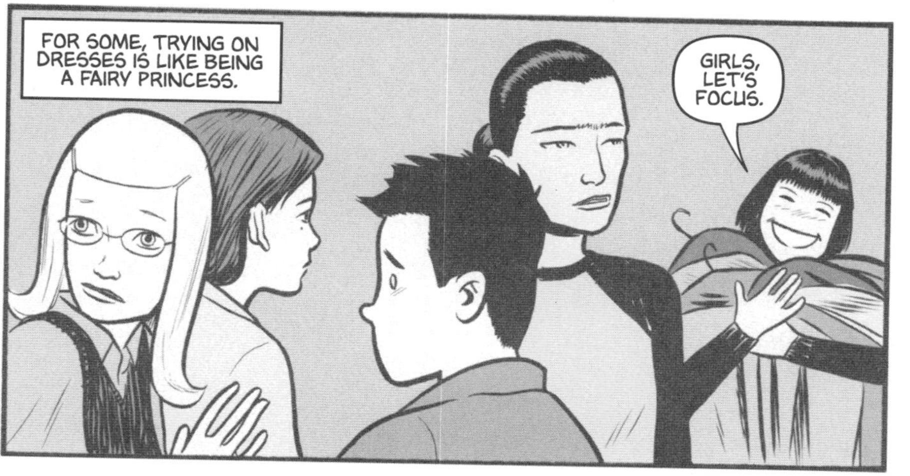
FOR SOME, TRYING ON DRESSES IS LIKE BEING A FAIRY PRINCESS.
GIRLS, LET'S FOCUS.

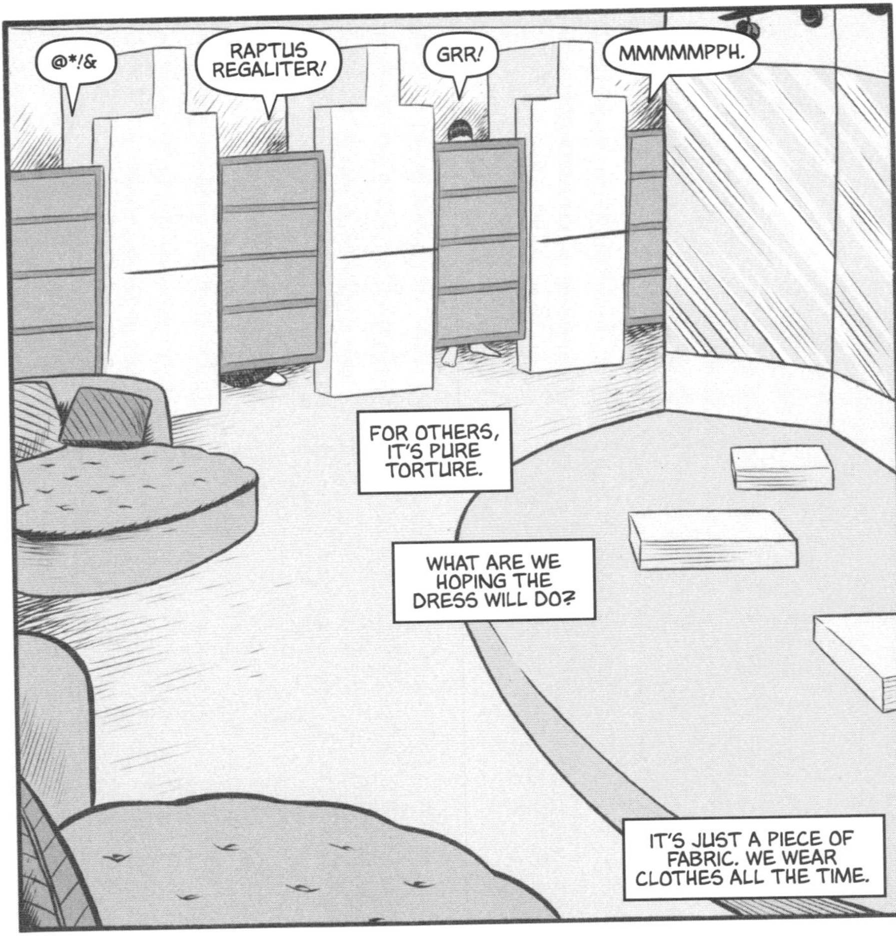
@*!&
RAPTUS REGALITER!
GRR!
MMMMMPPH.
FOR OTHERS, IT'S PURE TORTURE.
WHAT ARE WE HOPING THE DRESS WILL DO?
IT'S JUST A PIECE OF FABRIC. WE WEAR CLOTHES ALL THE TIME.

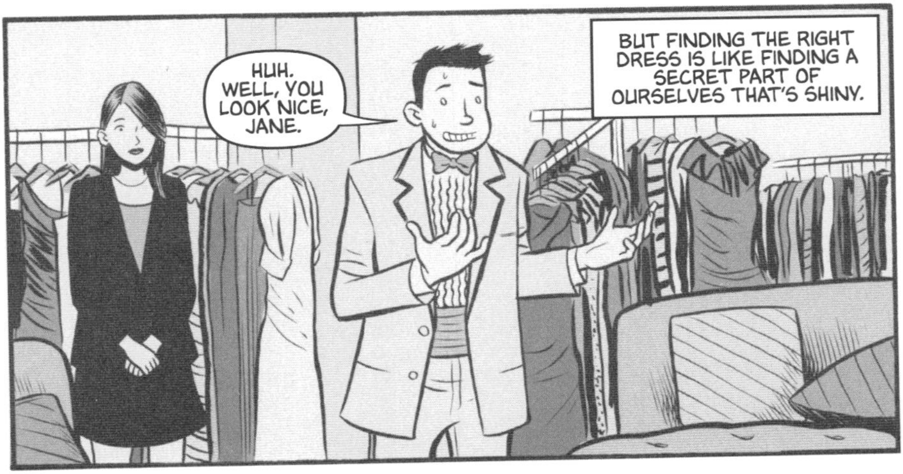
HUH. WELL, YOU LOOK NICE, JANE.
BUT FINDING THE RIGHT DRESS IS LIKE FINDING A SECRET PART OF OURSELVES THAT'S SHINY.

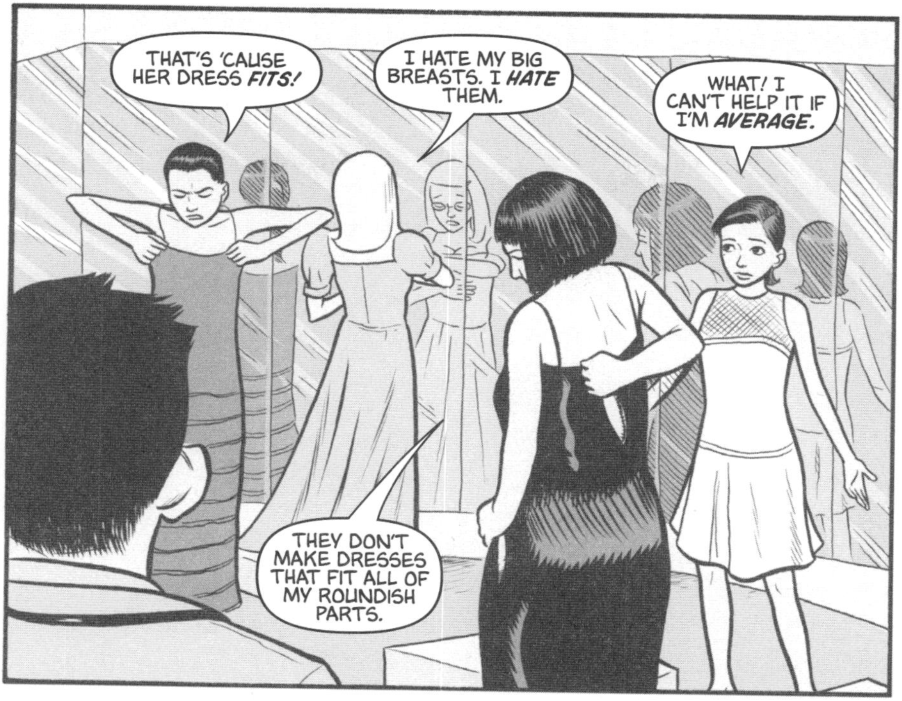
THAT'S 'CAUSE HER DRESS *FITS!*
I HATE MY BIG BREASTS. I *HATE* THEM.
WHAT! I CAN'T HELP IT IF I'M *AVERAGE*.
THEY DON'T MAKE DRESSES THAT FIT ALL OF MY ROUNDISH PARTS.

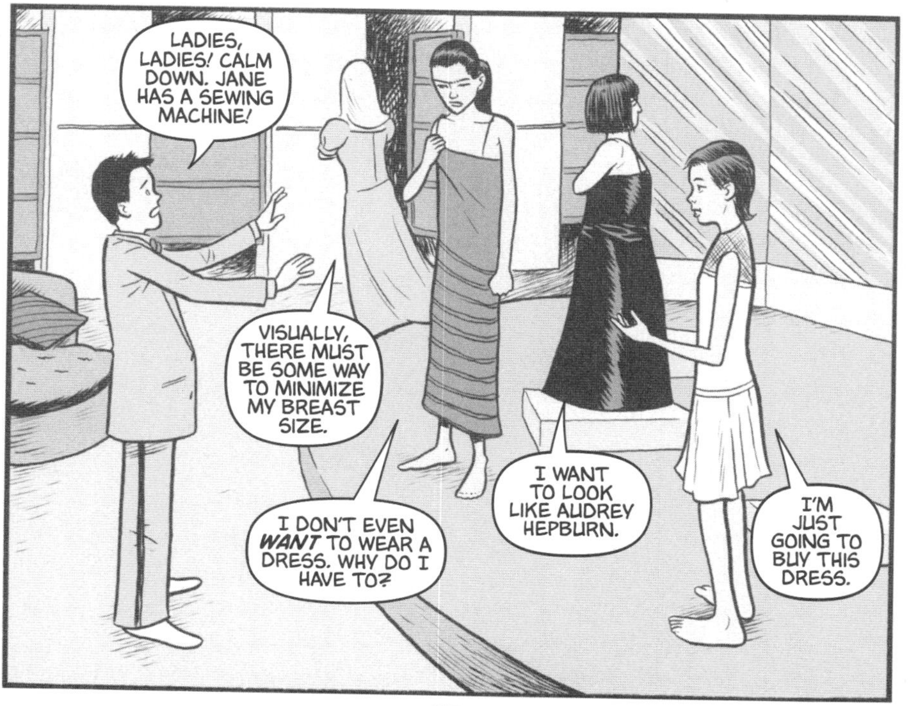
LADIES, LADIES! CALM DOWN. JANE HAS A SEWING MACHINE!
VISUALLY, THERE MUST BE SOME WAY TO MINIMIZE MY BREAST SIZE.
I DON'T EVEN *WANT* TO WEAR A DRESS. WHY DO I HAVE TO?
I WANT TO LOOK LIKE AUDREY HEPBURN.
I'M JUST GOING TO BUY THIS DRESS.

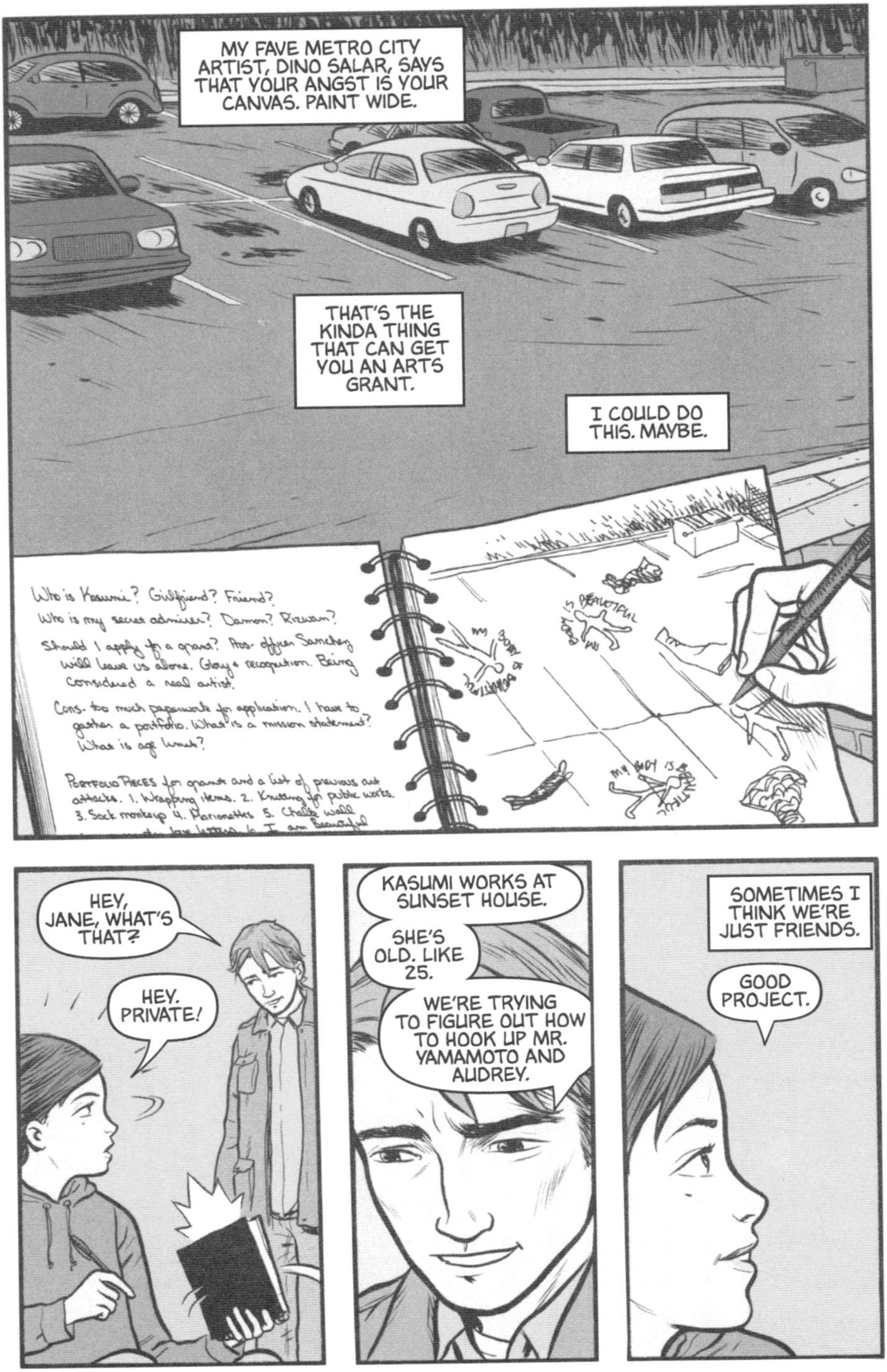
MY FAVE METRO CITY ARTIST, DINO SALAR, SAYS THAT YOUR ANGST IS YOUR CANVAS. PAINT WIDE.
THAT'S THE KINDA THING THAT CAN GET YOU AN ARTS GRANT.
I COULD DO THIS. MAYBE.
Who is Kasumi? Girlfriend? Friend?
Who is my secret admirer? Damon? Rizwan?
Should I apply for a grant? Pros- officer Sanchez will leave us alone. Glory + recognition. Being considered a real artist.
Cons- too much paperwork for application. I have to gather a portfolio. What is a mission statement? What is age limit?
PORTFOLIO PIECES for grant and a list of previous art attacks. 1. Wrapping items. 2. Knitting for public works. 3. Sock monkeys 4. Marionettes 5. Chalk wall
HEY, JANE, WHAT'S THAT?
HEY. PRIVATE!
KASUMI WORKS AT SUNSET HOUSE.
SHE'S OLD. LIKE 25.
WE'RE TRYING TO FIGURE OUT HOW TO HOOK UP MR. YAMAMOTO AND AUDREY.
SOMETIMES I THINK WE'RE JUST FRIENDS.
GOOD PROJECT.

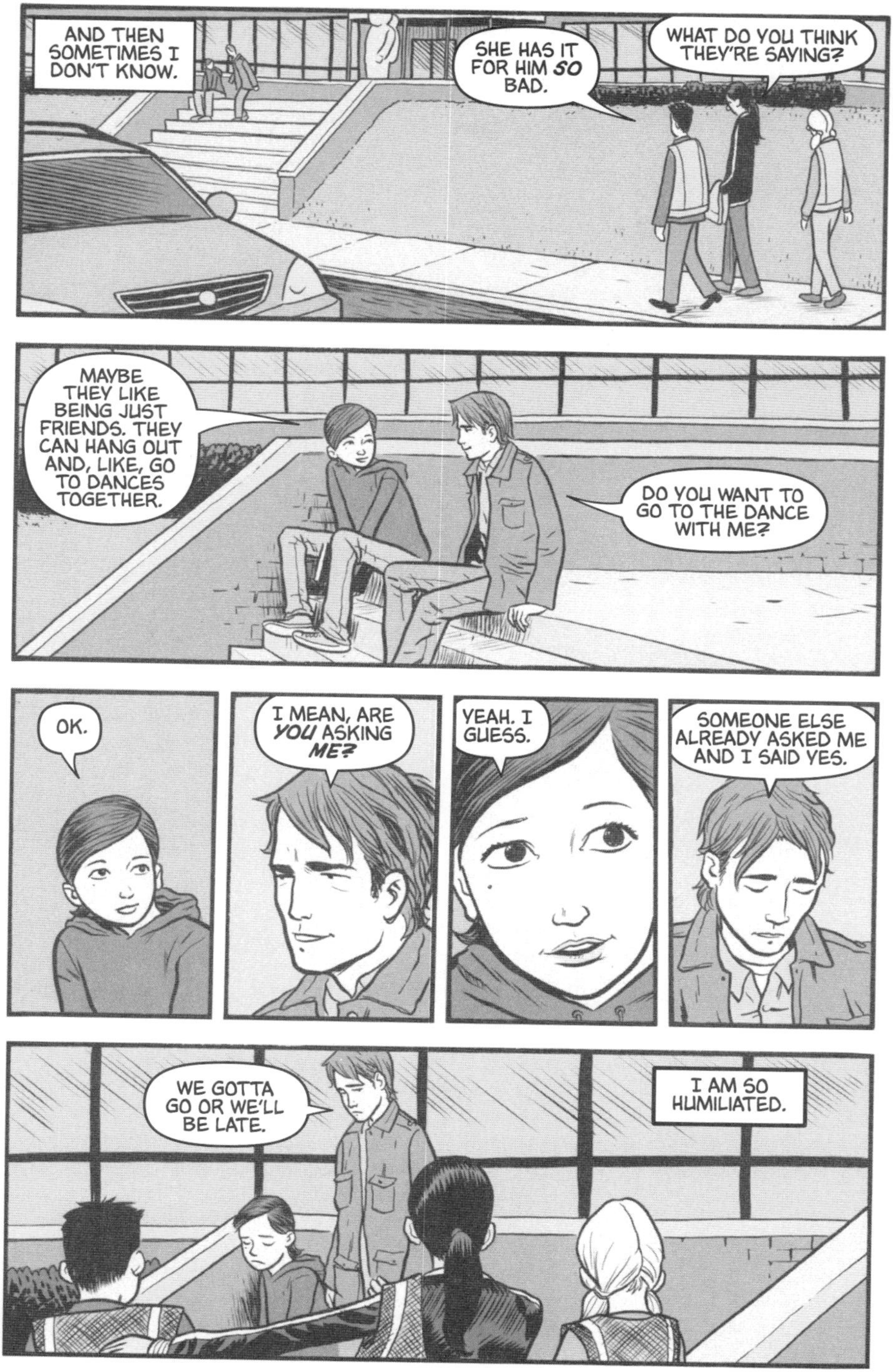
AND THEN SOMETIMES I DON'T KNOW.
SHE HAS IT FOR HIM SO BAD.
WHAT DO YOU THINK THEY'RE SAYING?
MAYBE THEY LIKE BEING JUST FRIENDS. THEY CAN HANG OUT AND, LIKE, GO TO DANCES TOGETHER.
DO YOU WANT TO GO TO THE DANCE WITH ME?
OK.
I MEAN, ARE YOU ASKING ME?
YEAH. I GUESS.
SOMEONE ELSE ALREADY ASKED ME AND I SAID YES.
WE GOTTA GO OR WE'LL BE LATE.
I AM SO HUMILIATED.

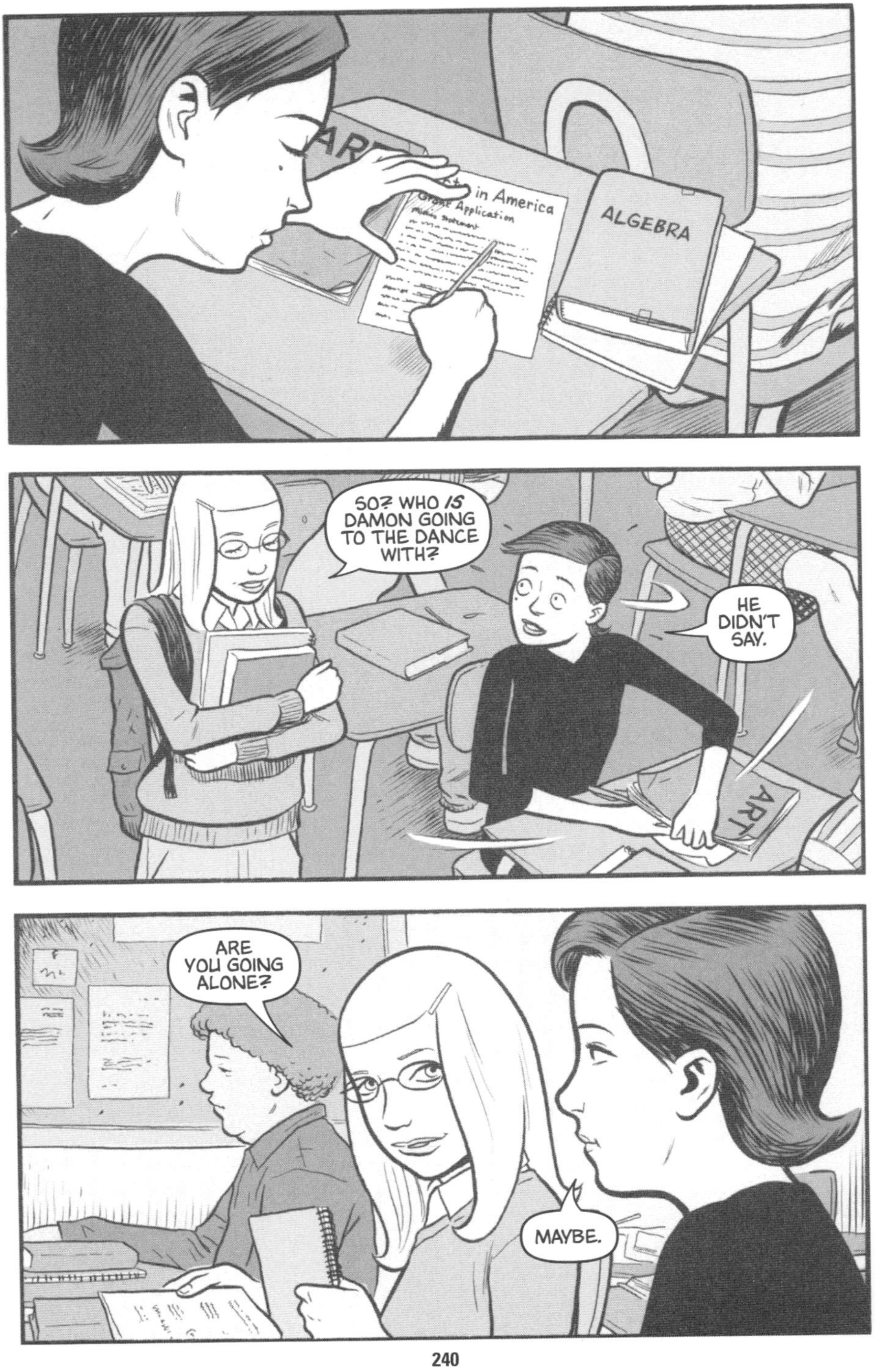
in America
Grant Application
ALGEBRA
SO? WHO *IS* DAMON GOING TO THE DANCE WITH?
HE DIDN'T SAY.
ART
ARE YOU GOING ALONE?
MAYBE.

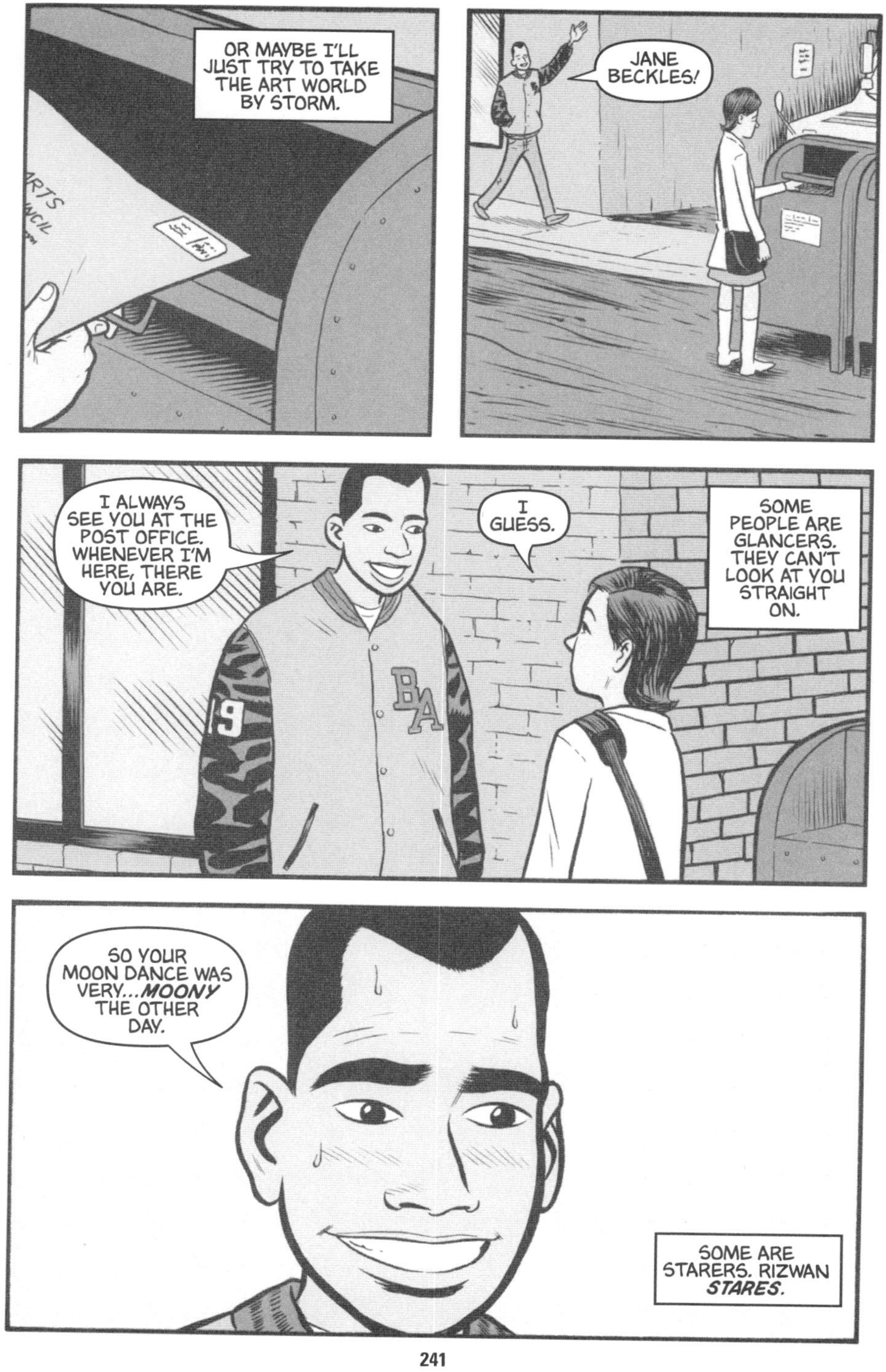
OR MAYBE I'LL JUST TRY TO TAKE THE ART WORLD BY STORM.
JANE BECKLES!
I ALWAYS SEE YOU AT THE POST OFFICE. WHENEVER I'M HERE, THERE YOU ARE.
I GUESS.
SOME PEOPLE ARE GLANCERS. THEY CAN'T LOOK AT YOU STRAIGHT ON.
SO YOUR MOON DANCE WAS VERY...*MOONY* THE OTHER DAY.
SOME ARE STARERS. RIZWAN ***STARES.***

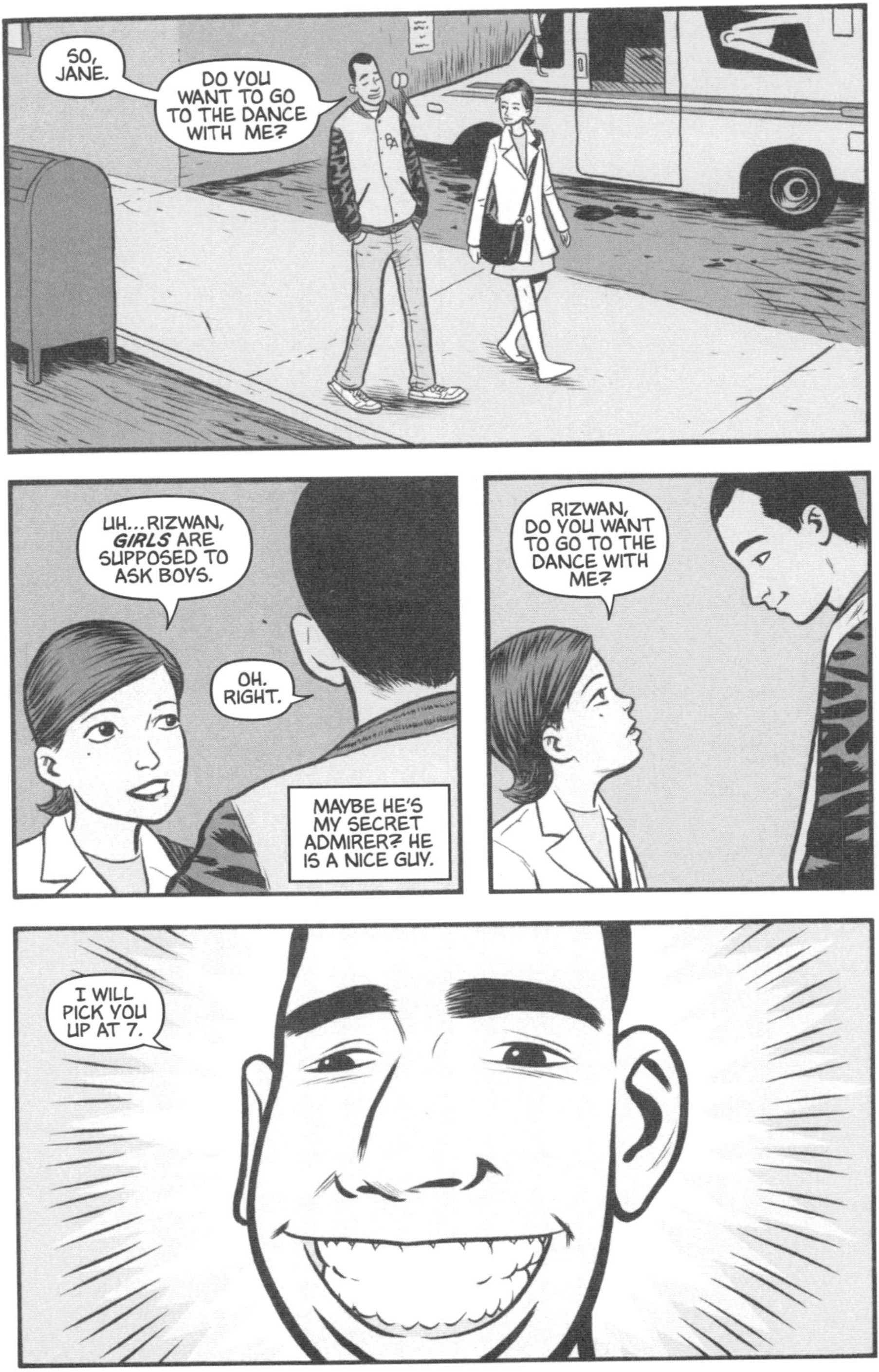
SO, JANE.
DO YOU WANT TO GO TO THE DANCE WITH ME?
UH...RIZWAN, *GIRLS* ARE SUPPOSED TO ASK BOYS.
OH. RIGHT.
MAYBE HE'S MY SECRET ADMIRER? HE IS A NICE GUY.
RIZWAN, DO YOU WANT TO GO TO THE DANCE WITH ME?
I WILL PICK YOU UP AT 7.

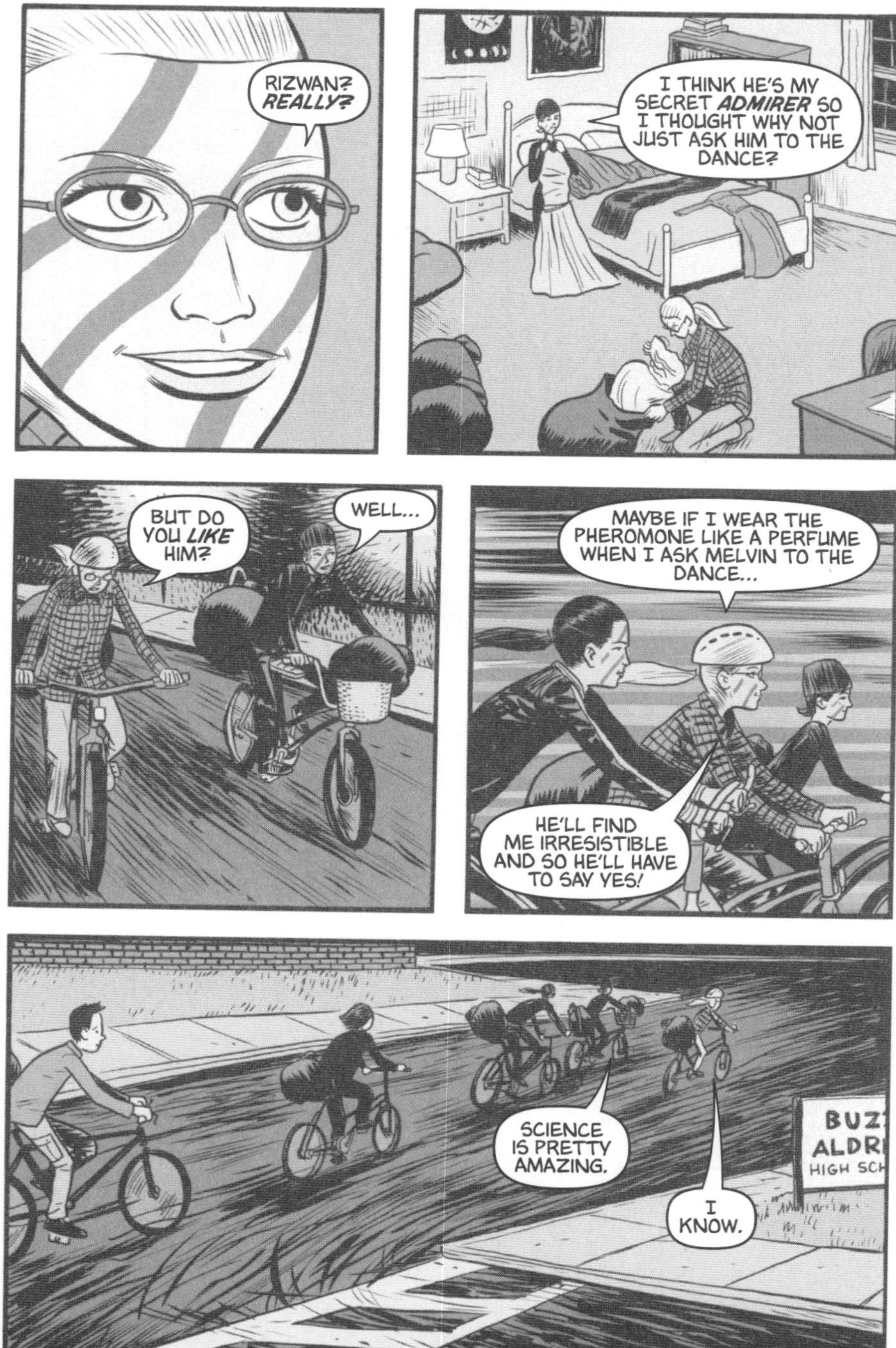
RIZWAN? *REALLY?*
I THINK HE'S MY SECRET *ADMIRER* SO I THOUGHT WHY NOT JUST ASK HIM TO THE DANCE?
BUT DO YOU *LIKE* HIM?
WELL...
MAYBE IF I WEAR THE PHEROMONE LIKE A PERFUME WHEN I ASK MELVIN TO THE DANCE...
HE'LL FIND ME IRRESISTIBLE AND SO HE'LL HAVE TO SAY YES!
SCIENCE IS PRETTY AMAZING.
I KNOW.

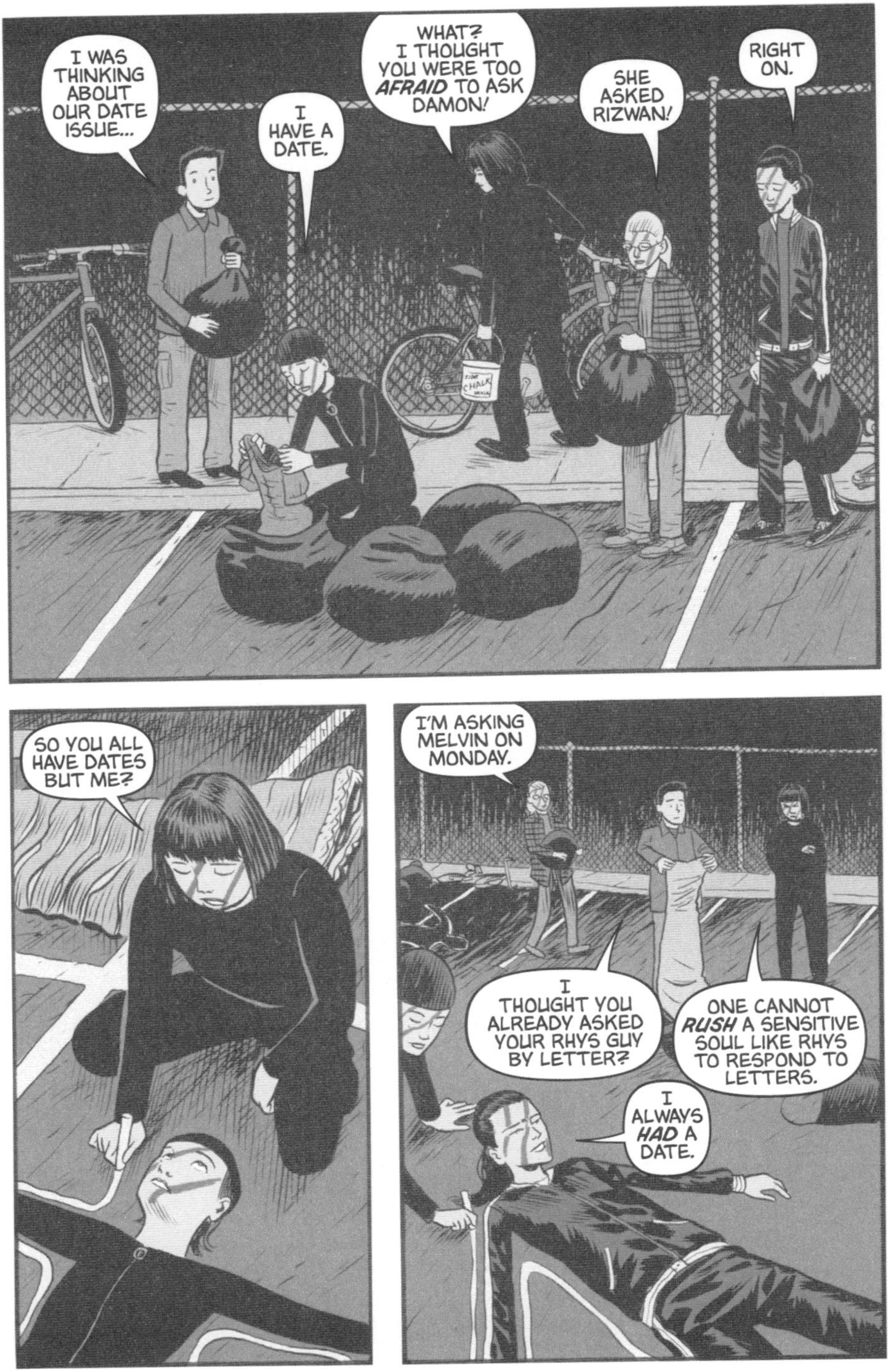
I WAS THINKING ABOUT OUR DATE ISSUE...
I HAVE A DATE.
WHAT? I THOUGHT YOU WERE TOO AFRAID TO ASK DAMON!
SHE ASKED RIZWAN!
RIGHT ON.
SO YOU ALL HAVE DATES BUT ME?
I'M ASKING MELVIN ON MONDAY.
I THOUGHT YOU ALREADY ASKED YOUR RHYS GUY BY LETTER?
ONE CANNOT RUSH A SENSITIVE SOUL LIKE RHYS TO RESPOND TO LETTERS.
I ALWAYS HAD A DATE.

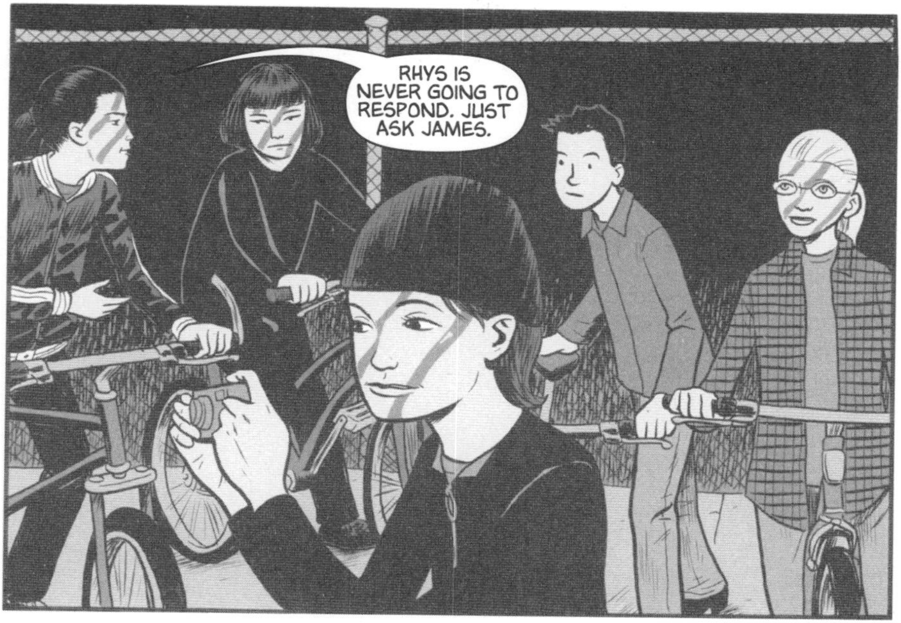
RHYS IS NEVER GOING TO RESPOND. JUST ASK JAMES.

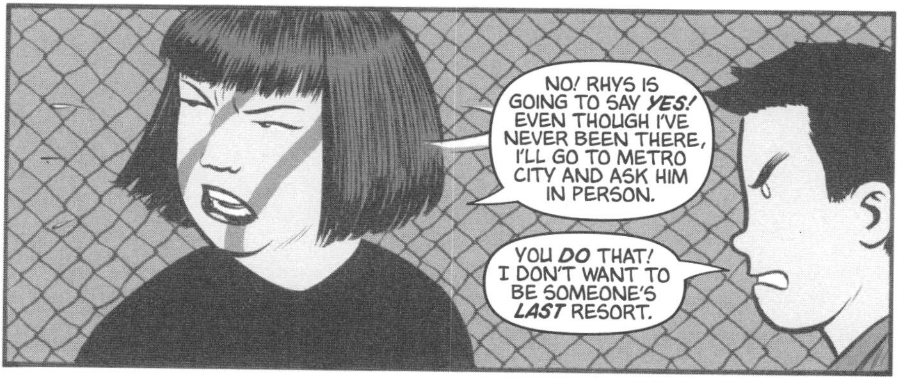
NO! RHYS IS GOING TO SAY *YES!* EVEN THOUGH I'VE NEVER BEEN THERE, I'LL GO TO METRO CITY AND ASK HIM IN PERSON.
YOU *DO* THAT! I DON'T WANT TO BE SOMEONE'S *LAST* RESORT.

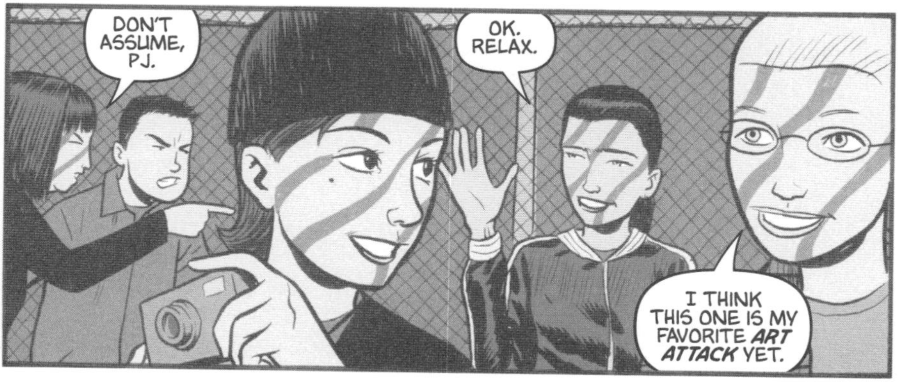
DON'T ASSUME, PJ.
OK. RELAX.
I THINK THIS ONE IS MY FAVORITE *ART ATTACK* YET.

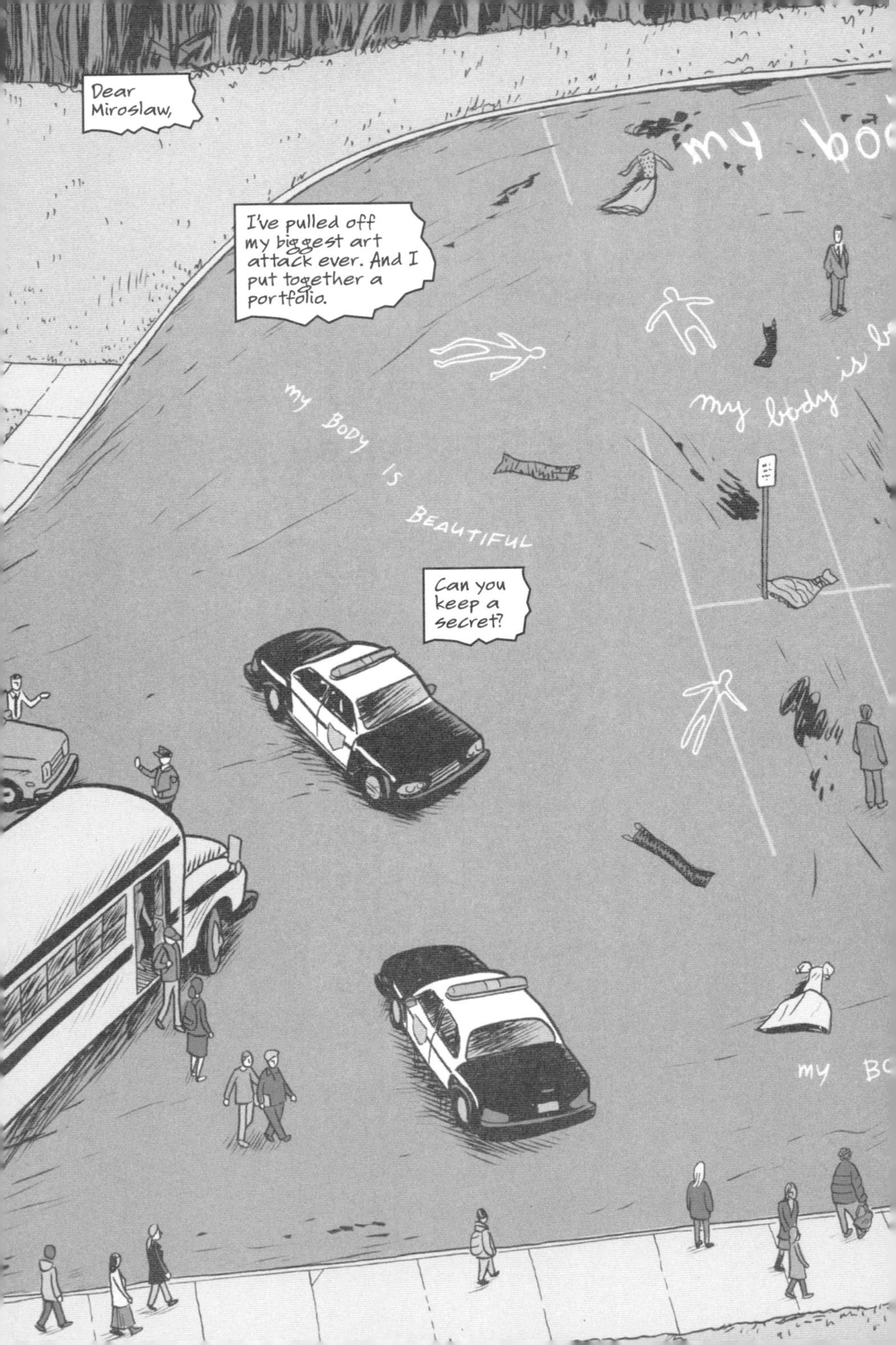
Dear Miroslaw,
I've pulled off my biggest art attack ever. And I put together a portfolio.
my BODY IS BEAUTIFUL
my body is
Can you keep a secret?

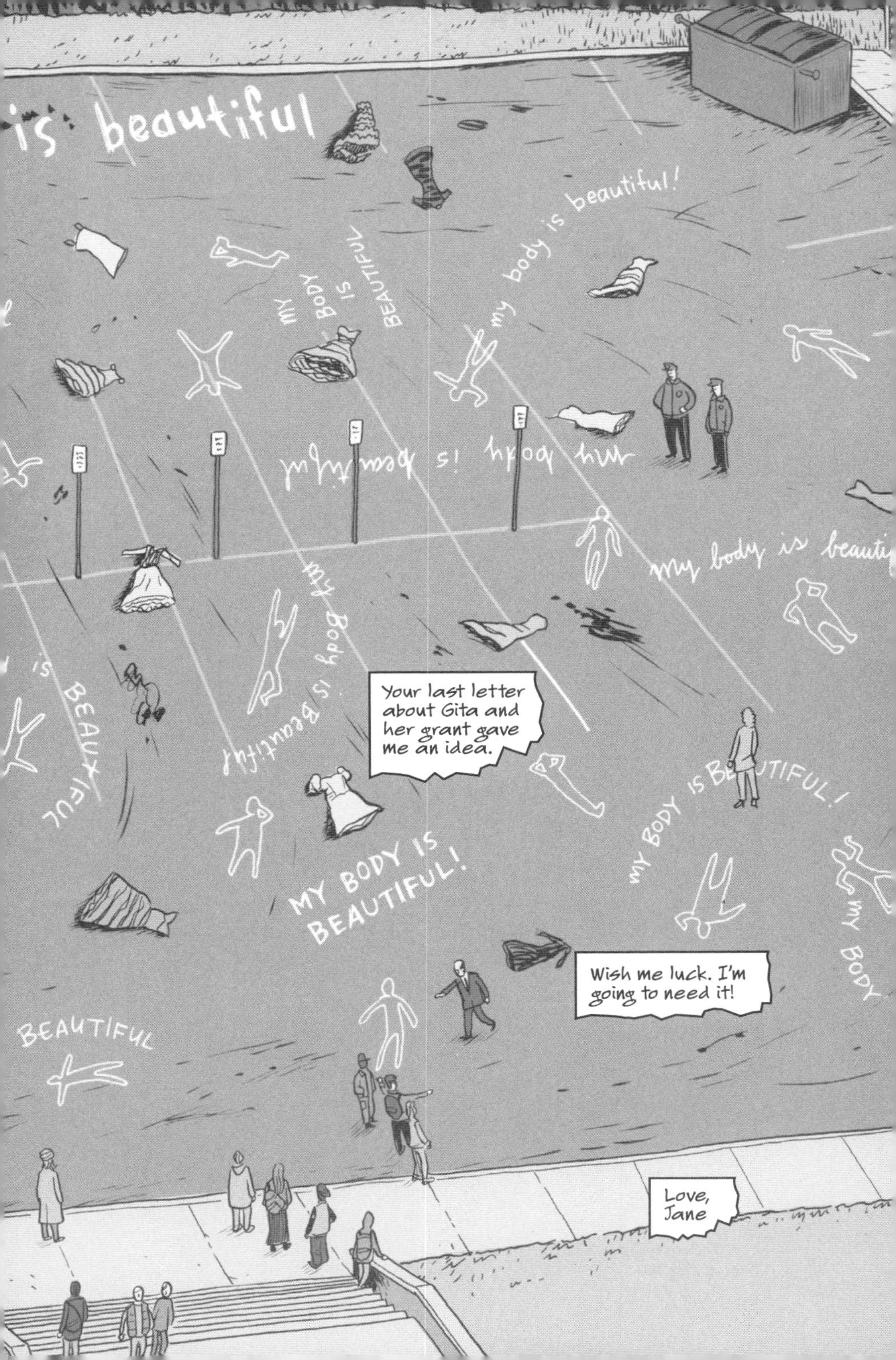
is beautiful
my body is beautiful!
MY BODY IS BEAUTIFUL
my body is beautiful
my body is beautiful
my body is beauti
my body is beautiful
IS BEAUTIFUL
Your last letter about Gita and her grant gave me an idea.
MY BODY IS BEAUTIFUL!
MY BODY IS BEAUTIFUL!
MY BODY
BEAUTIFUL
Wish me luck. I'm going to need it!
Love, Jane

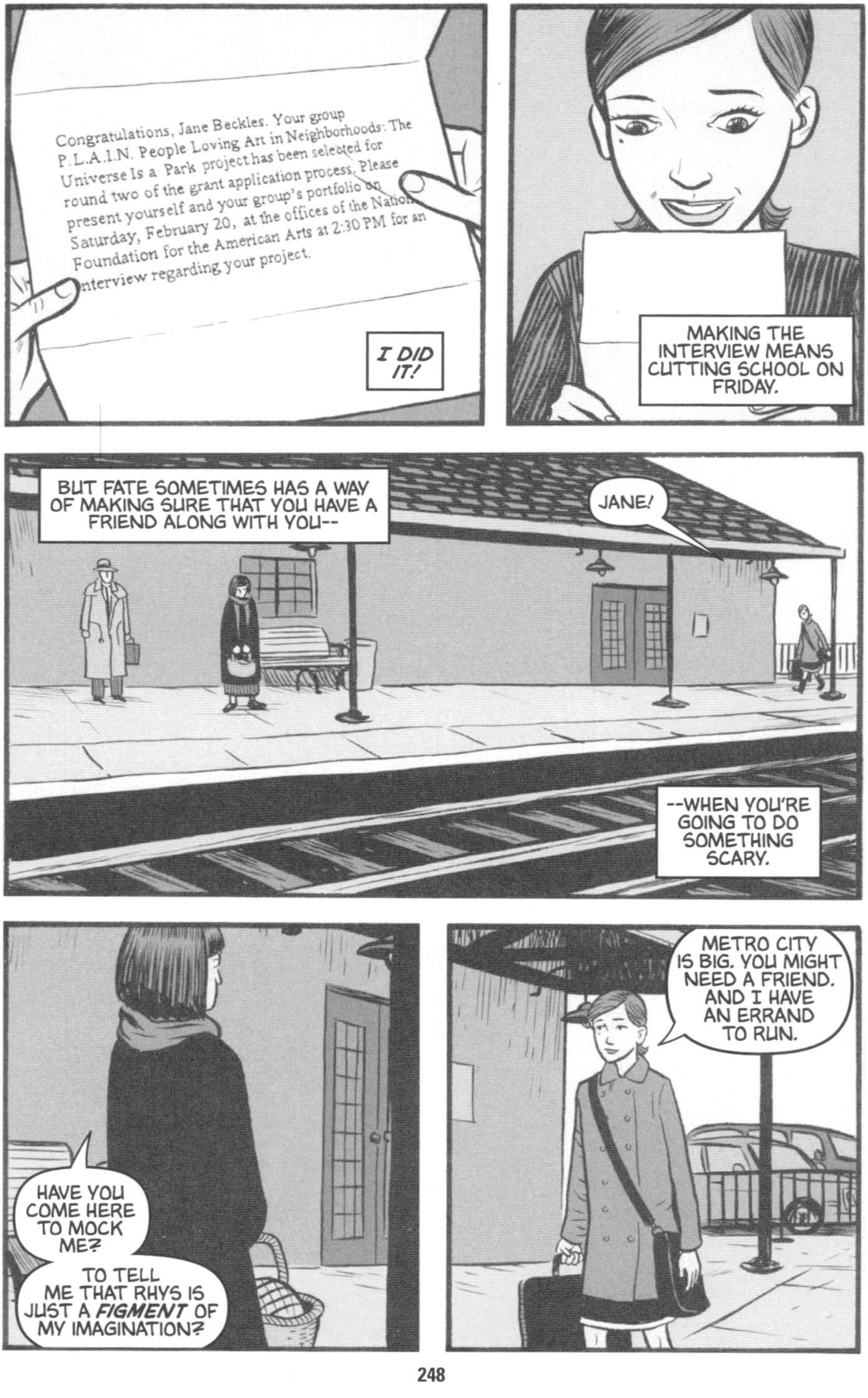
Congratulations, Jane Beckles. Your group
P.L.A.I.N. People Loving Art in Neighborhoods: The
Universe Is a Park project has been selected for
round two of the grant application process. Please
present yourself and your group's portfolio on
Saturday, February 20, at the offices of the Natio
Foundation for the American Arts at 2:30 PM for an
interview regarding your project.
I DID IT!
MAKING THE INTERVIEW MEANS CUTTING SCHOOL ON FRIDAY.
BUT FATE SOMETIMES HAS A WAY OF MAKING SURE THAT YOU HAVE A FRIEND ALONG WITH YOU--
JANE!
--WHEN YOU'RE GOING TO DO SOMETHING SCARY.
HAVE YOU COME HERE TO MOCK ME?
TO TELL ME THAT RHYS IS JUST A *FIGMENT* OF MY IMAGINATION?
METRO CITY IS BIG. YOU MIGHT NEED A FRIEND. AND I HAVE AN ERRAND TO RUN.

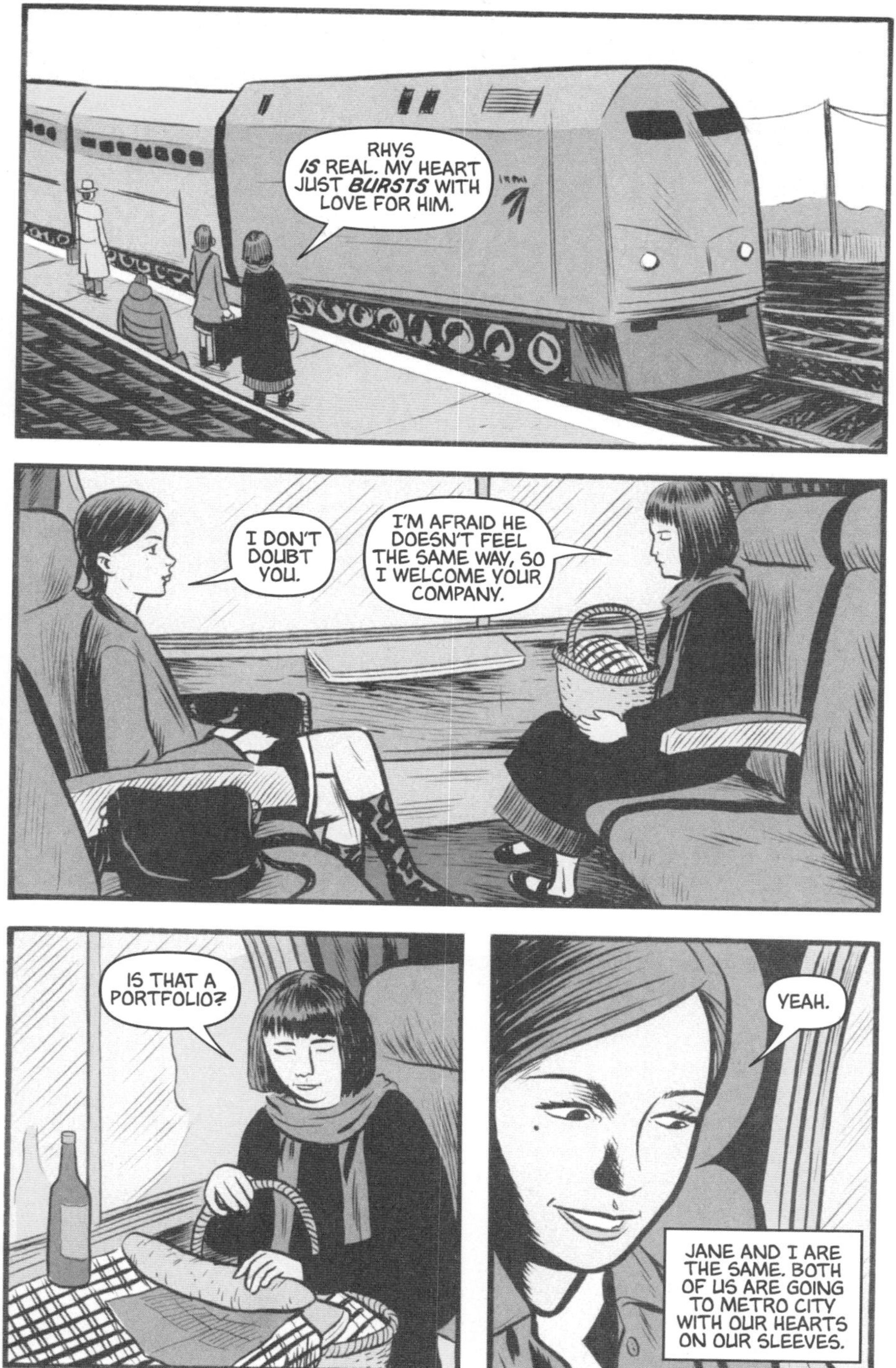
RHYS *IS* REAL. MY HEART JUST ***BURSTS*** WITH LOVE FOR HIM.
I'M AFRAID HE DOESN'T FEEL THE SAME WAY, SO I WELCOME YOUR COMPANY.
I DON'T DOUBT YOU.
IS THAT A PORTFOLIO?
YEAH.
JANE AND I ARE THE SAME. BOTH OF US ARE GOING TO METRO CITY WITH OUR HEARTS ON OUR SLEEVES.

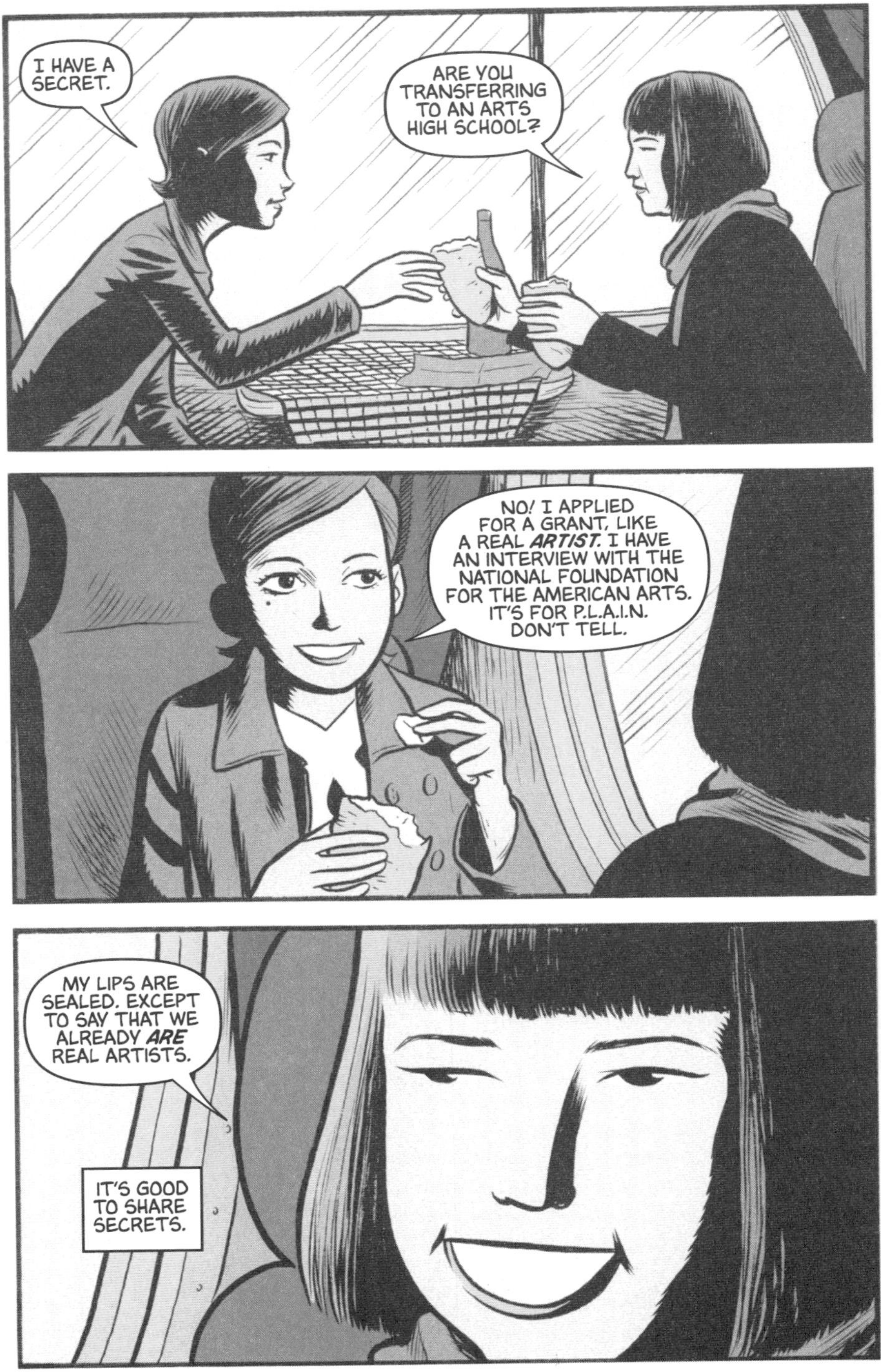
I HAVE A SECRET.
ARE YOU TRANSFERRING TO AN ARTS HIGH SCHOOL?
NO! I APPLIED FOR A GRANT, LIKE A REAL ARTIST. I HAVE AN INTERVIEW WITH THE NATIONAL FOUNDATION FOR THE AMERICAN ARTS. IT'S FOR P.L.A.I.N. DON'T TELL.
MY LIPS ARE SEALED. EXCEPT TO SAY THAT WE ALREADY ARE REAL ARTISTS.
IT'S GOOD TO SHARE SECRETS.

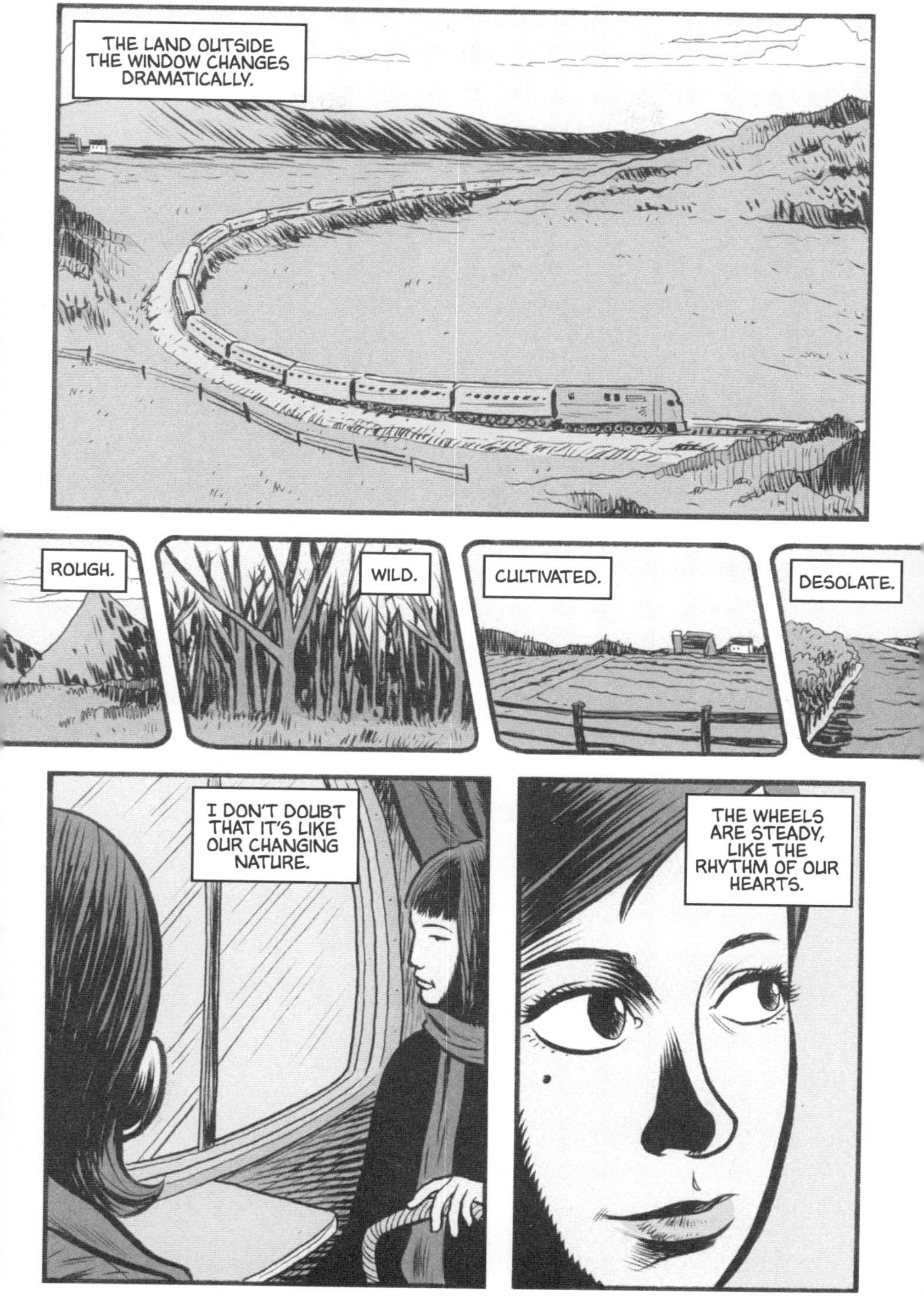
THE LAND OUTSIDE THE WINDOW CHANGES DRAMATICALLY.
ROUGH.
WILD.
CULTIVATED.
DESOLATE.
I DON'T DOUBT THAT IT'S LIKE OUR CHANGING NATURE.
THE WHEELS ARE STEADY, LIKE THE RHYTHM OF OUR HEARTS.

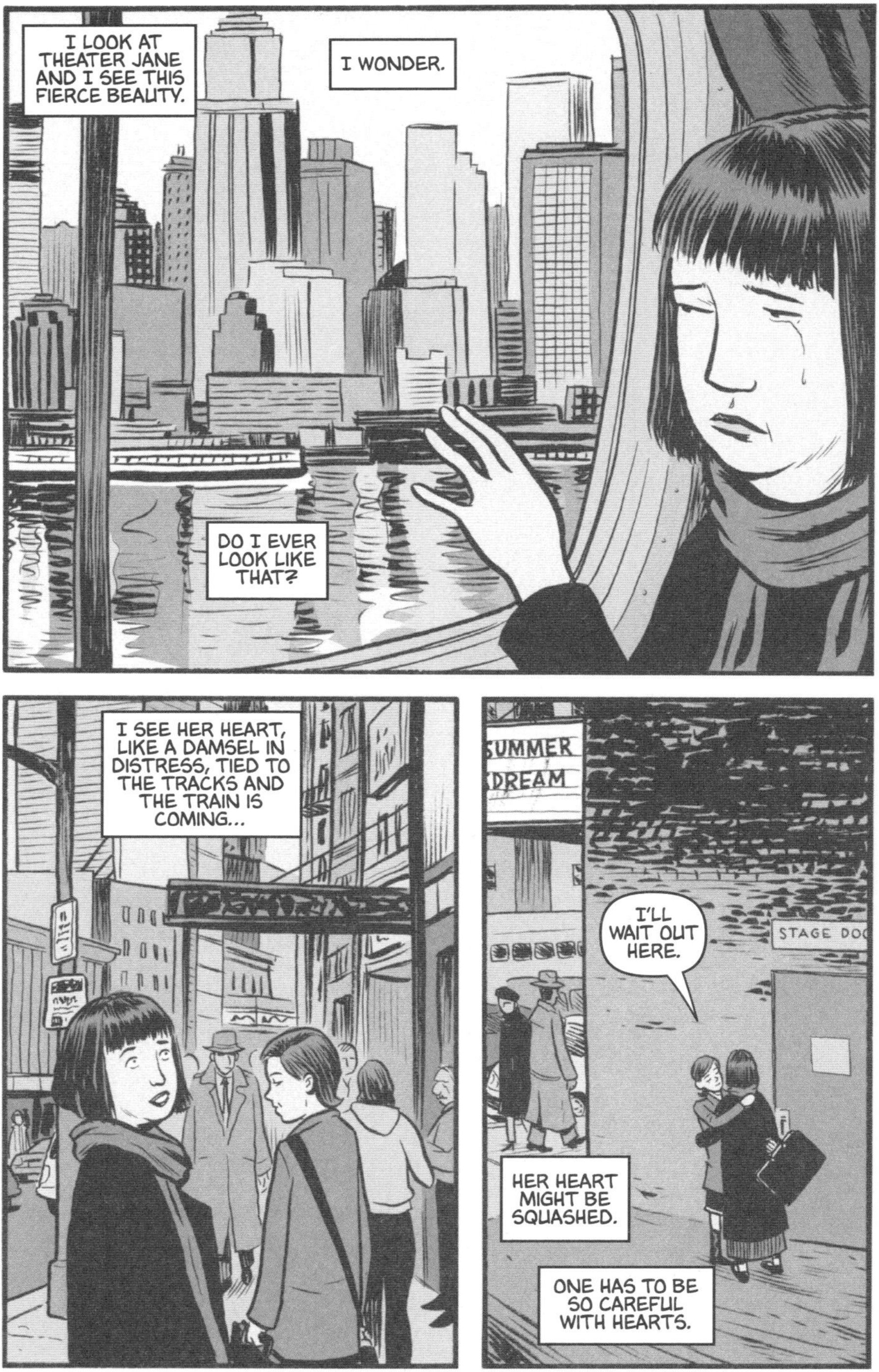
I LOOK AT THEATER JANE AND I SEE THIS FIERCE BEAUTY.
I WONDER.
DO I EVER LOOK LIKE THAT?
I SEE HER HEART, LIKE A DAMSEL IN DISTRESS, TIED TO THE TRACKS AND THE TRAIN IS COMING...
SUMMER
DREAM
I'LL WAIT OUT HERE.
HER HEART MIGHT BE SQUASHED.
ONE HAS TO BE SO CAREFUL WITH HEARTS.

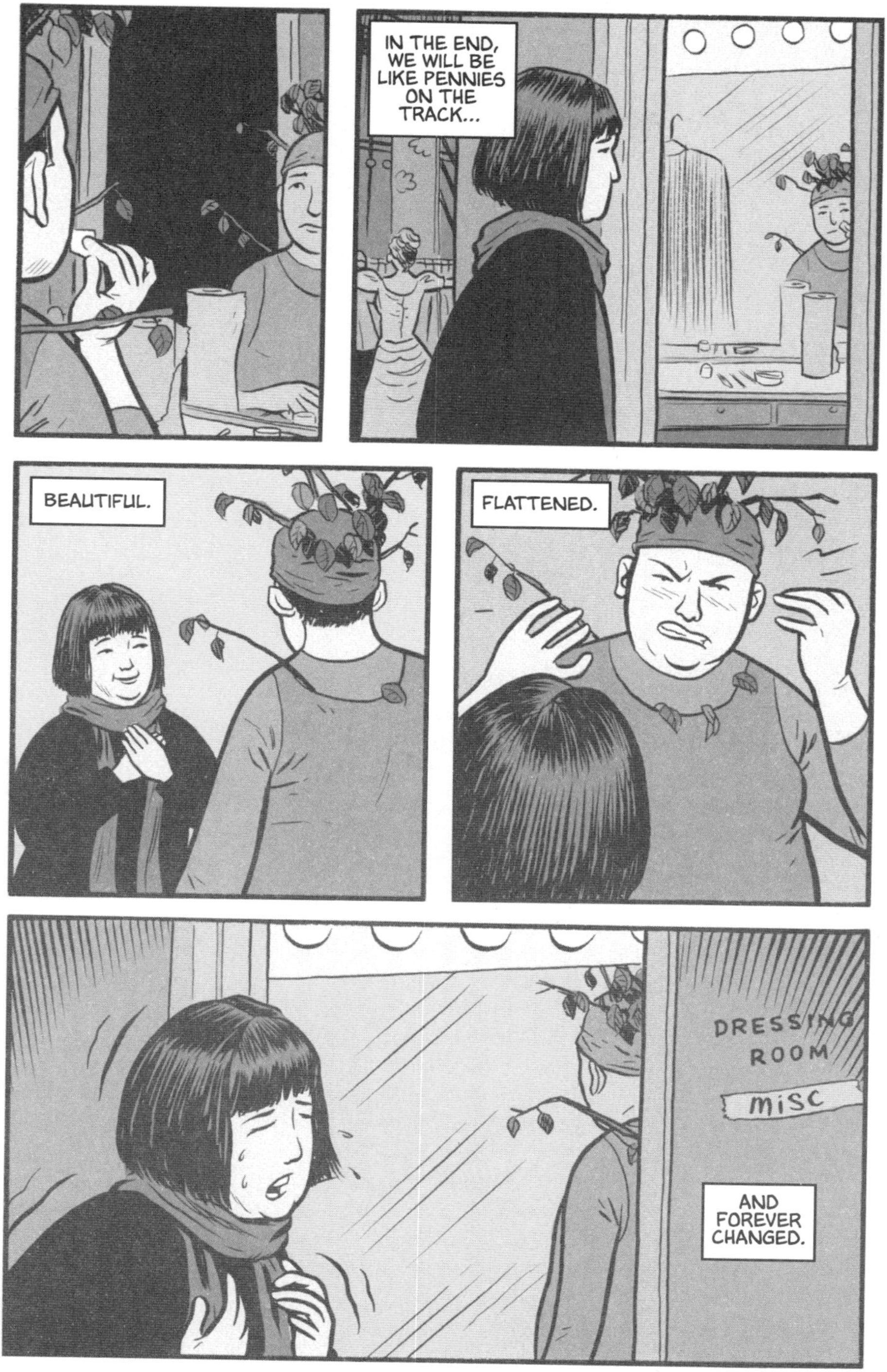
IN THE END, WE WILL BE LIKE PENNIES ON THE TRACK...
BEAUTIFUL.
FLATTENED.
DRESSING ROOM
MISC
AND FOREVER CHANGED.

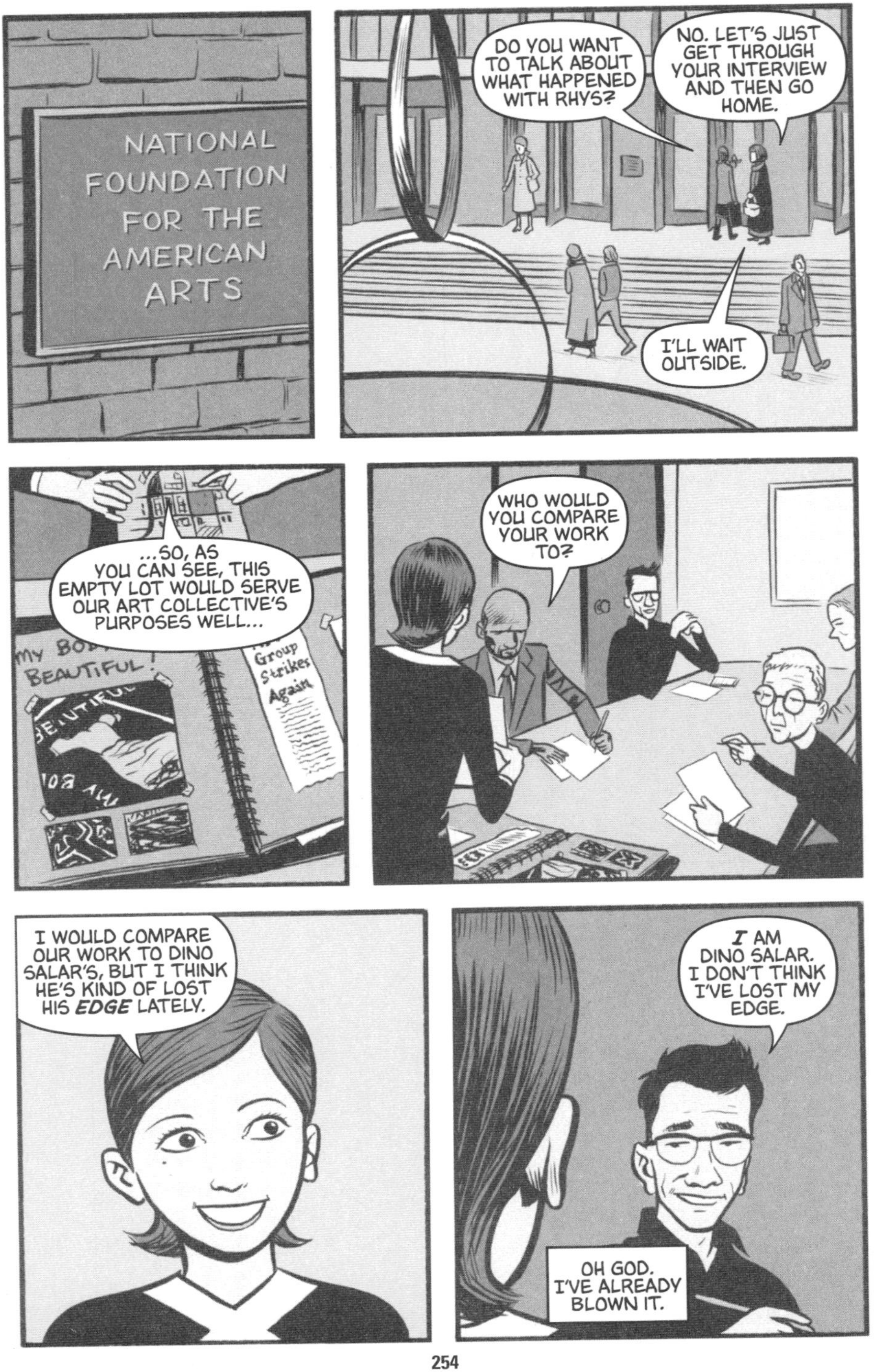
NATIONAL FOUNDATION FOR THE AMERICAN ARTS
DO YOU WANT TO TALK ABOUT WHAT HAPPENED WITH RHYS?
NO. LET'S JUST GET THROUGH YOUR INTERVIEW AND THEN GO HOME.
I'LL WAIT OUTSIDE.
...SO, AS YOU CAN SEE, THIS EMPTY LOT WOULD SERVE OUR ART COLLECTIVE'S PURPOSES WELL...
BEAUTIFUL!
Group Strikes Again
WHO WOULD YOU COMPARE YOUR WORK TO?
I WOULD COMPARE OUR WORK TO DINO SALAR'S, BUT I THINK HE'S KIND OF LOST HIS *EDGE* LATELY.
I AM DINO SALAR. I DON'T THINK I'VE LOST MY EDGE.
OH GOD. I'VE ALREADY BLOWN IT.

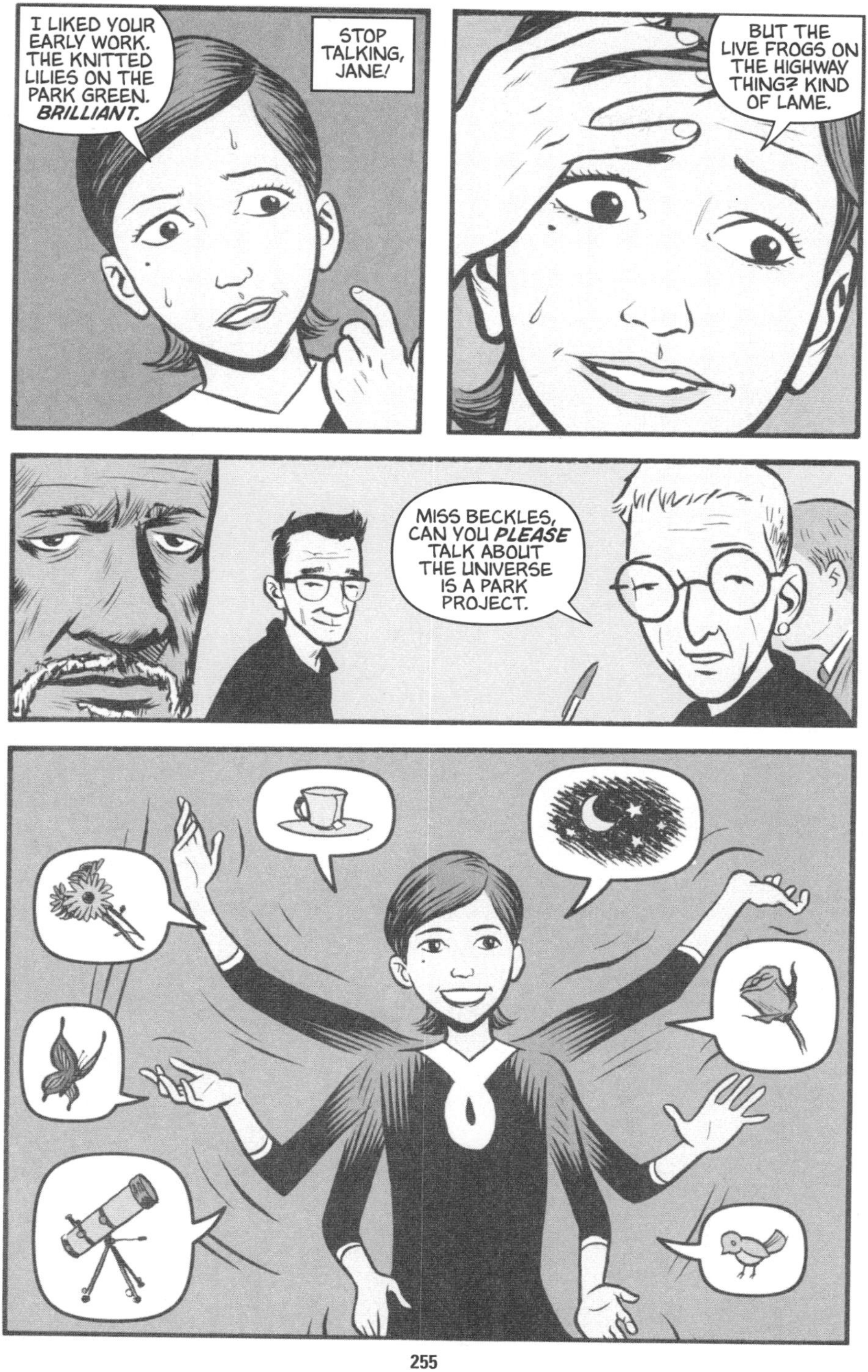
I LIKED YOUR EARLY WORK. THE KNITTED LILIES ON THE PARK GREEN. *BRILLIANT.*
STOP TALKING, JANE!
BUT THE LIVE FROGS ON THE HIGHWAY THING? KIND OF LAME.
MISS BECKLES, CAN YOU *PLEASE* TALK ABOUT THE UNIVERSE IS A PARK PROJECT.

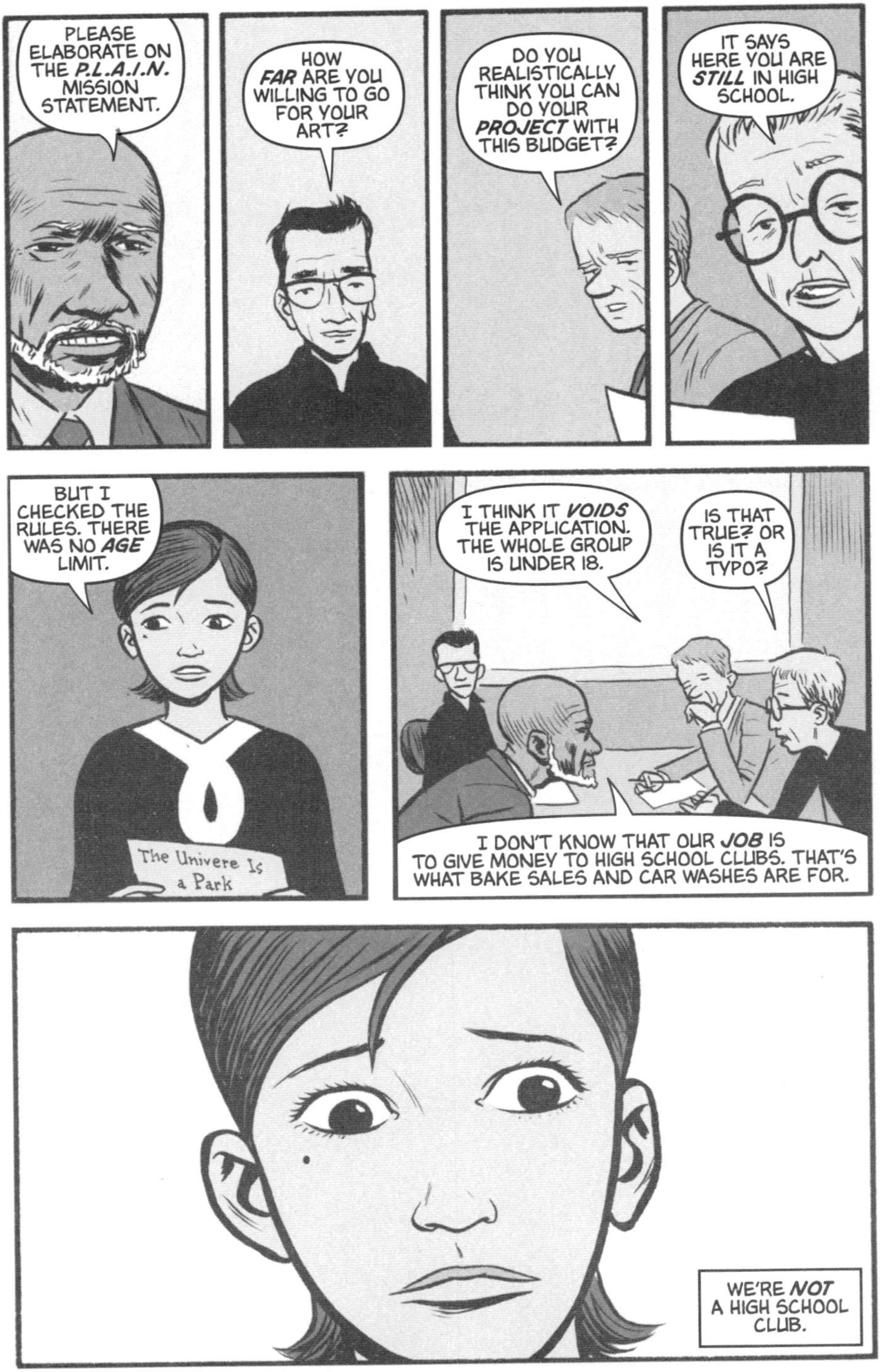
PLEASE ELABORATE ON THE P.L.A.I.N. MISSION STATEMENT.
HOW FAR ARE YOU WILLING TO GO FOR YOUR ART?
DO YOU REALISTICALLY THINK YOU CAN DO YOUR PROJECT WITH THIS BUDGET?
IT SAYS HERE YOU ARE STILL IN HIGH SCHOOL.
BUT I CHECKED THE RULES. THERE WAS NO AGE LIMIT.
The Univere Is a Park
I THINK IT VOIDS THE APPLICATION. THE WHOLE GROUP IS UNDER 18.
IS THAT TRUE? OR IS IT A TYPO?
I DON'T KNOW THAT OUR JOB IS TO GIVE MONEY TO HIGH SCHOOL CLUBS. THAT'S WHAT BAKE SALES AND CAR WASHES ARE FOR.
WE'RE NOT A HIGH SCHOOL CLUB.

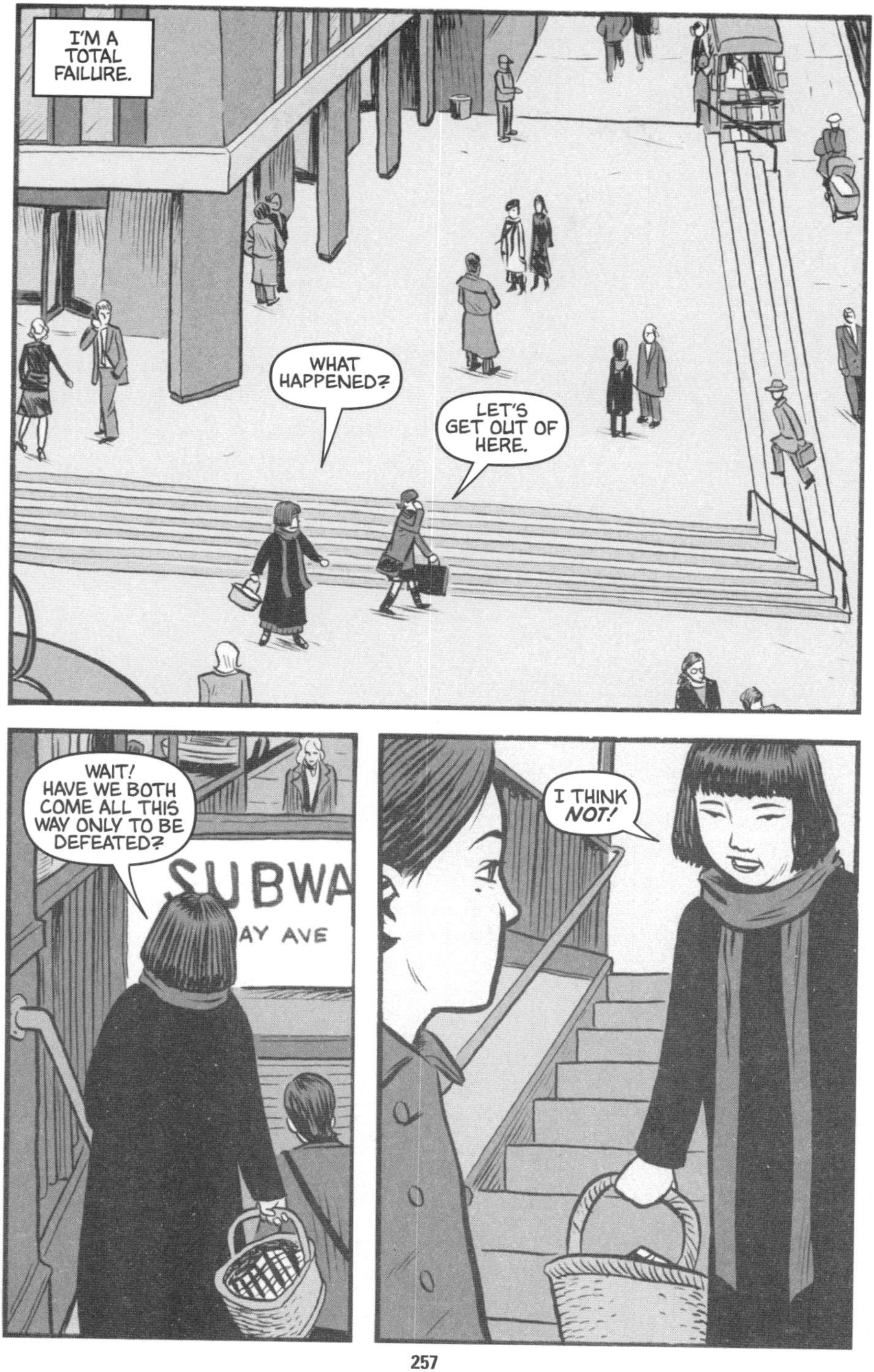
I'M A TOTAL FAILURE.
WHAT HAPPENED?
LET'S GET OUT OF HERE.
WAIT! HAVE WE BOTH COME ALL THIS WAY ONLY TO BE DEFEATED?
SUBWA
AY AVE
I THINK *NOT!*

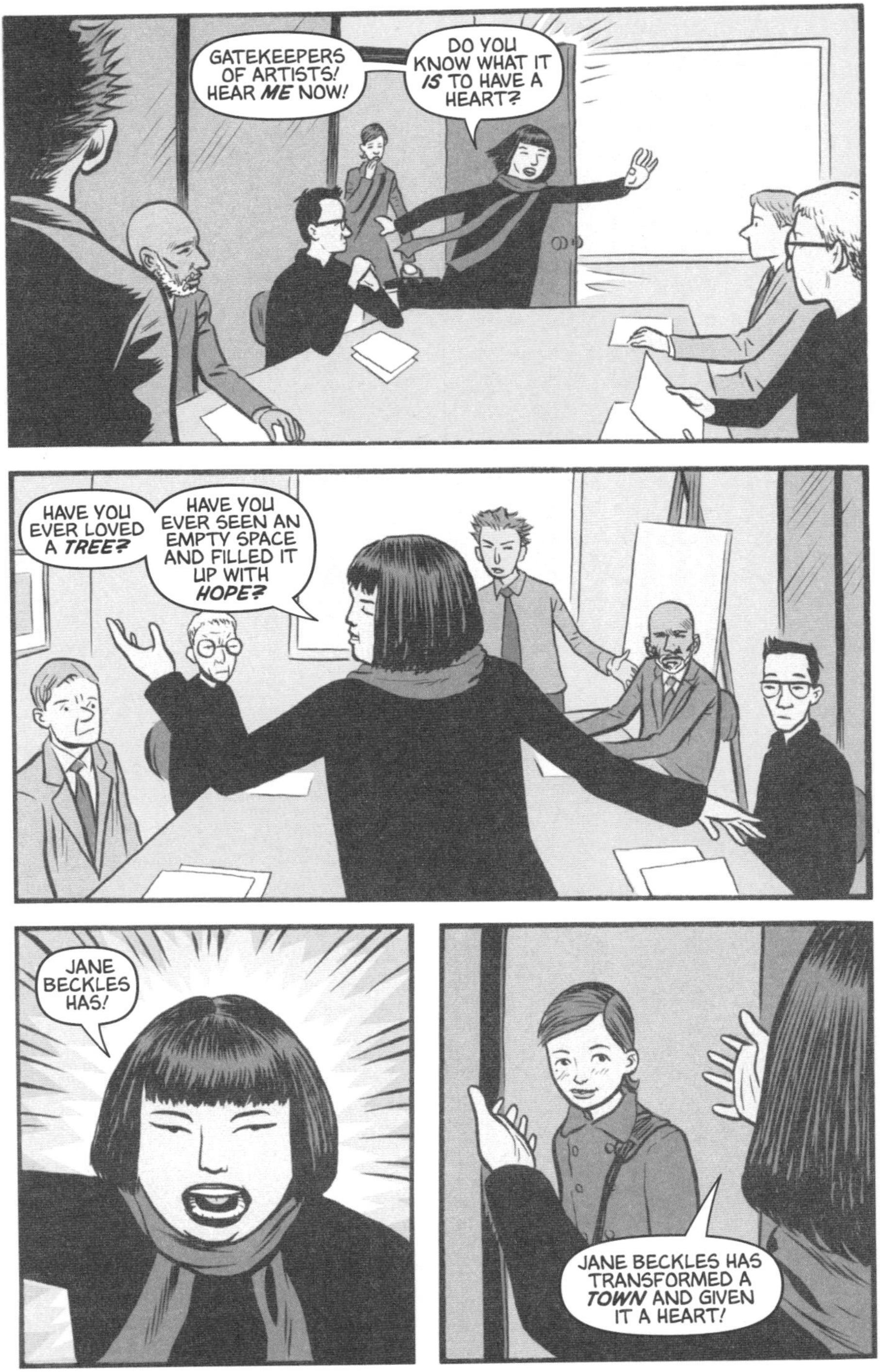
GATEKEEPERS OF ARTISTS! HEAR *ME* NOW!
DO YOU KNOW WHAT IT *IS* TO HAVE A HEART?
HAVE YOU EVER LOVED A *TREE?*
HAVE YOU EVER SEEN AN EMPTY SPACE AND FILLED IT UP WITH *HOPE?*
JANE BECKLES HAS!
JANE BECKLES HAS TRANSFORMED A *TOWN* AND GIVEN IT A HEART!

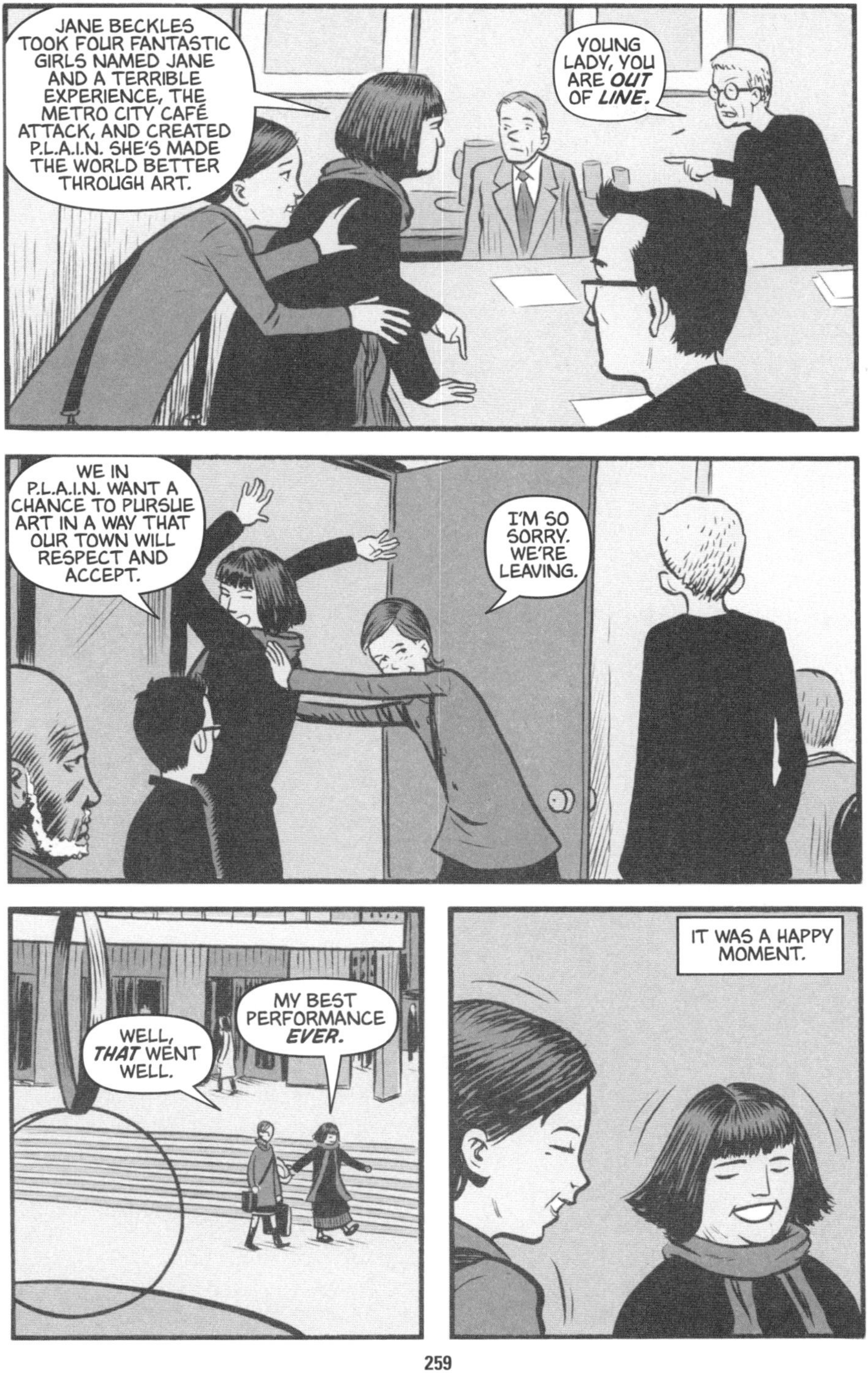
JANE BECKLES TOOK FOUR FANTASTIC GIRLS NAMED JANE AND A TERRIBLE EXPERIENCE, THE METRO CITY CAFÉ ATTACK, AND CREATED P.L.A.I.N. SHE'S MADE THE WORLD BETTER THROUGH ART.
YOUNG LADY, YOU ARE *OUT* OF *LINE*.
WE IN P.L.A.I.N. WANT A CHANCE TO PURSUE ART IN A WAY THAT OUR TOWN WILL RESPECT AND ACCEPT.
I'M SO SORRY. WE'RE LEAVING.
WELL, *THAT* WENT WELL.
MY BEST PERFORMANCE *EVER*.
IT WAS A HAPPY MOMENT.

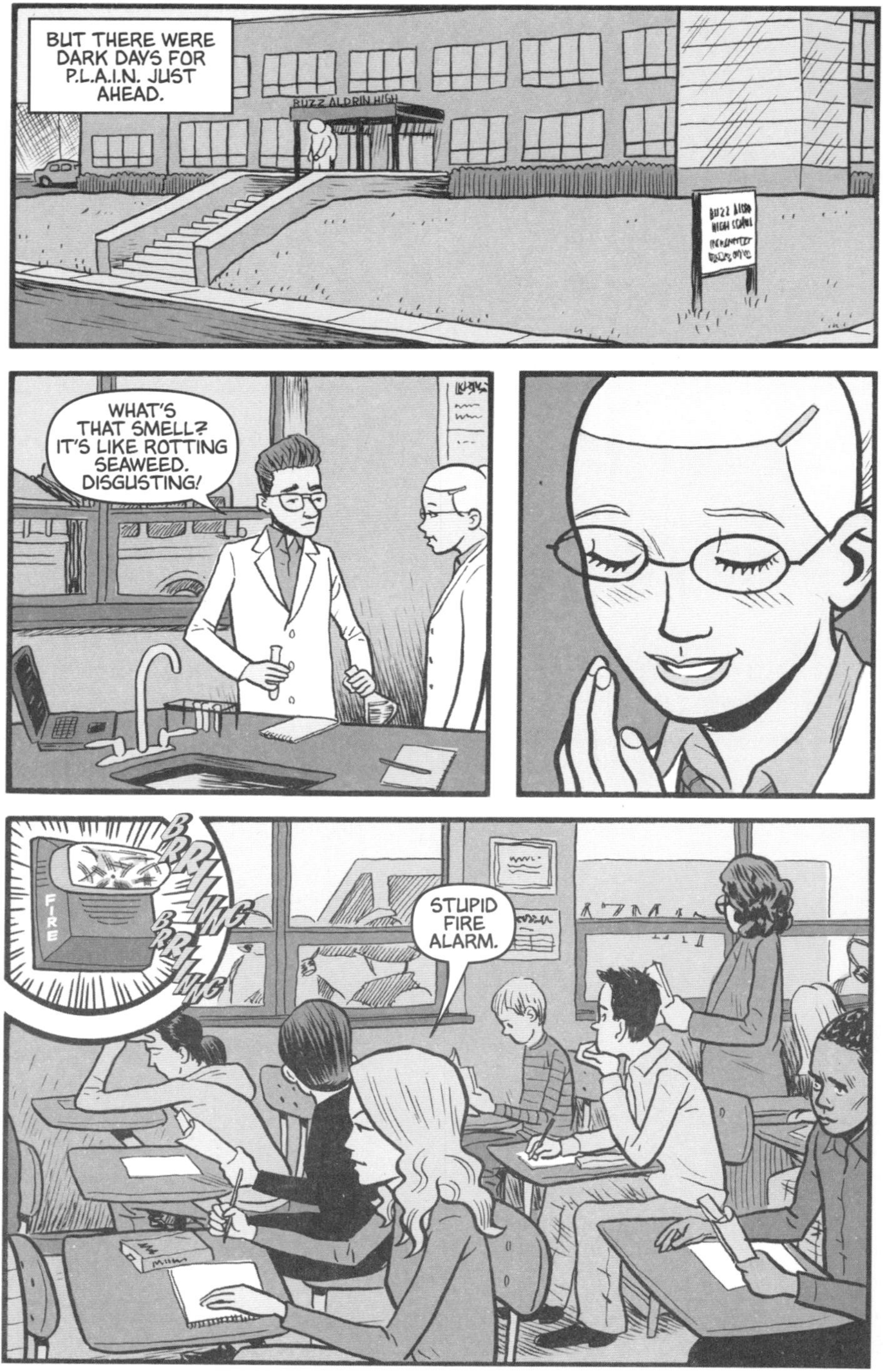
BUT THERE WERE DARK DAYS FOR P.L.A.I.N. JUST AHEAD.
BUZZ ALDRIN HIGH
WHAT'S THAT SMELL? IT'S LIKE ROTTING SEAWEED. DISGUSTING!
FIRE
STUPID FIRE ALARM.

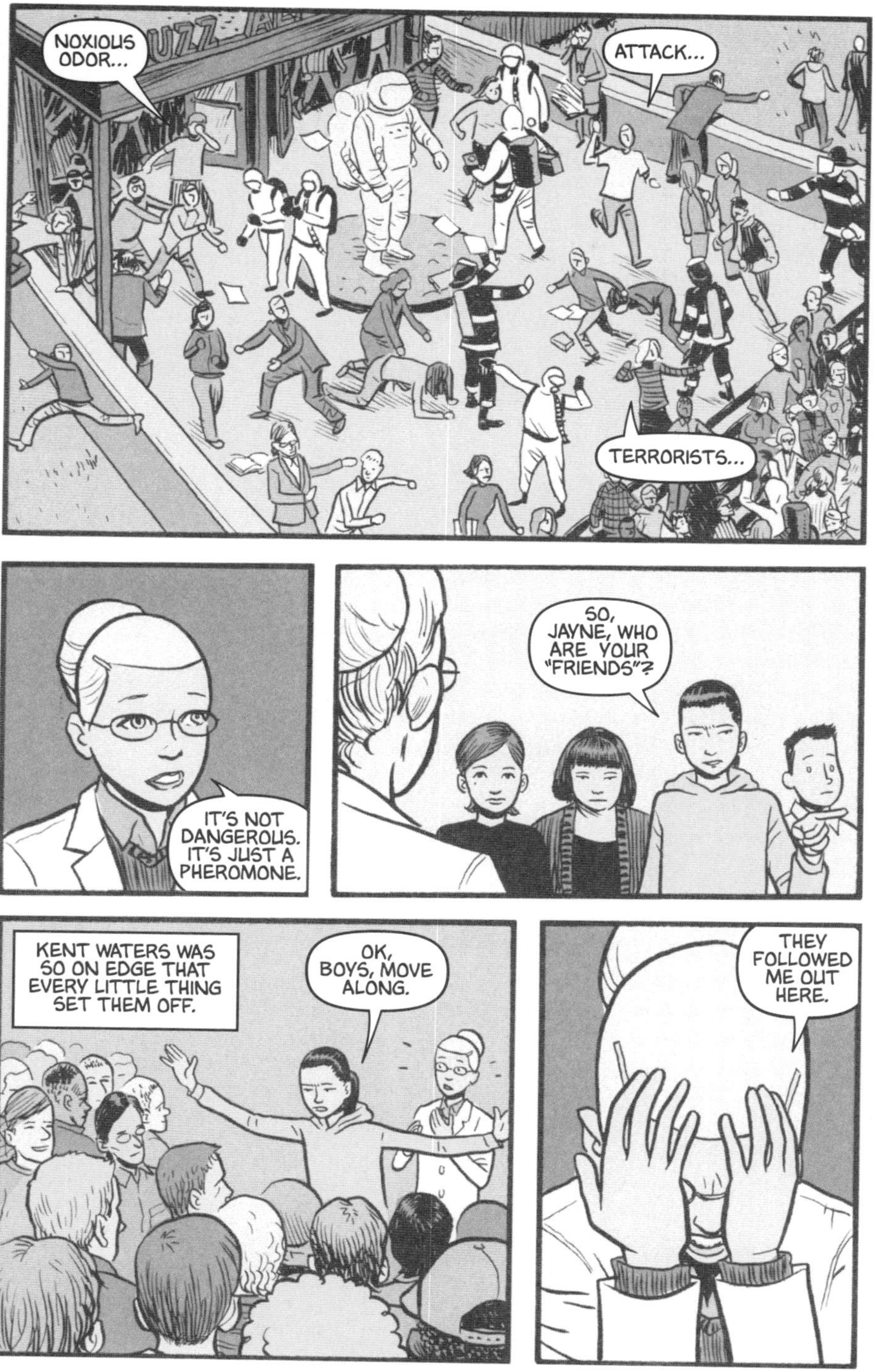
NOXIOUS ODOR...
ATTACK...
TERRORISTS...
IT'S NOT DANGEROUS. IT'S JUST A PHEROMONE.
SO, JAYNE, WHO ARE YOUR "FRIENDS"?
KENT WATERS WAS SO ON EDGE THAT EVERY LITTLE THING SET THEM OFF.
OK, BOYS, MOVE ALONG.
THEY FOLLOWED ME OUT HERE.

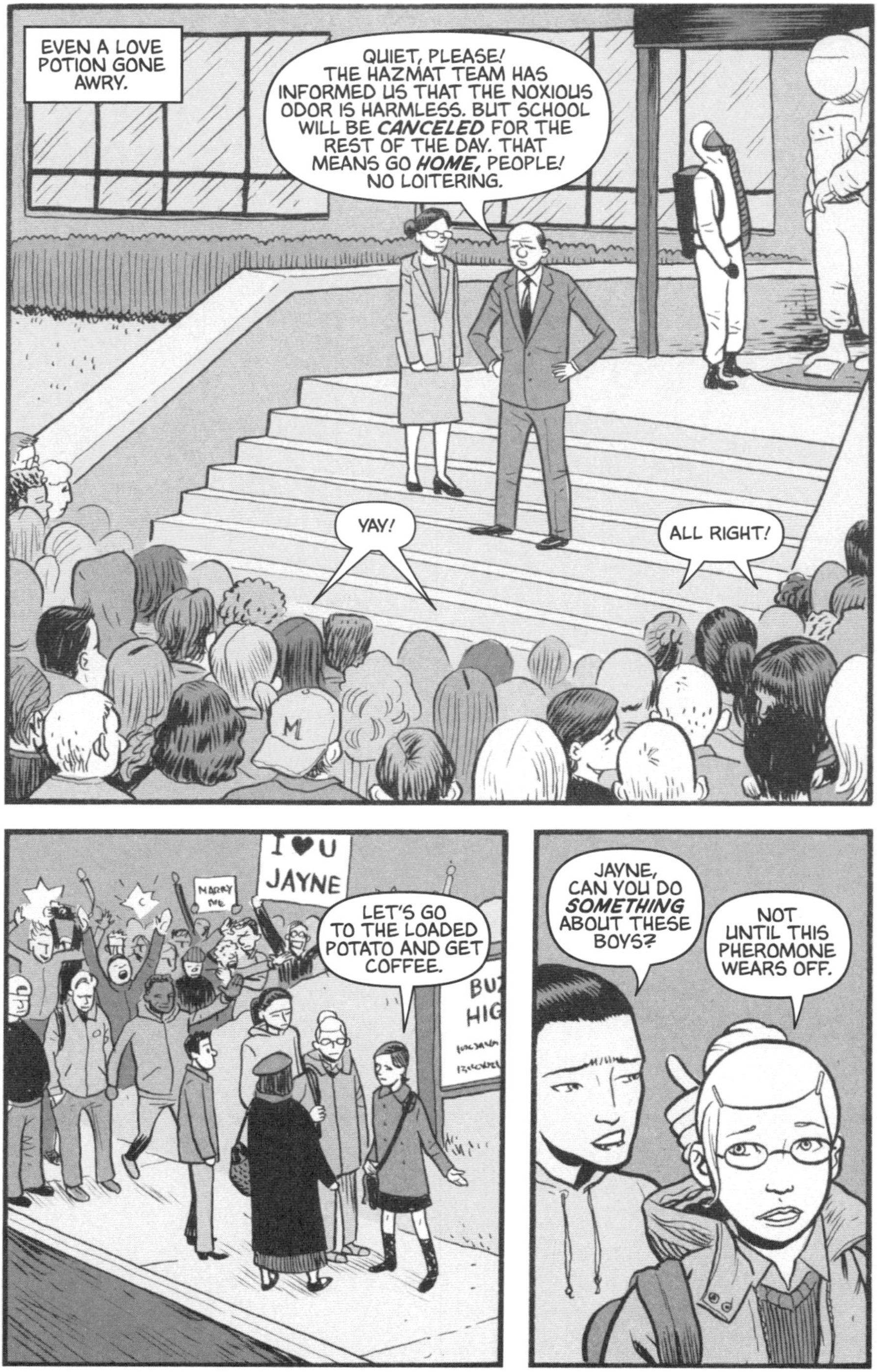
EVEN A LOVE POTION GONE AWRY.
QUIET, PLEASE! THE HAZMAT TEAM HAS INFORMED US THAT THE NOXIOUS ODOR IS HARMLESS. BUT SCHOOL WILL BE ***CANCELED*** FOR THE REST OF THE DAY. THAT MEANS GO ***HOME,*** PEOPLE! NO LOITERING.
YAY!
ALL RIGHT!
I ♥ U JAYNE
MARRY ME
LET'S GO TO THE LOADED POTATO AND GET COFFEE.
JAYNE, CAN YOU DO ***SOMETHING*** ABOUT THESE BOYS?
NOT UNTIL THIS PHEROMONE WEARS OFF.

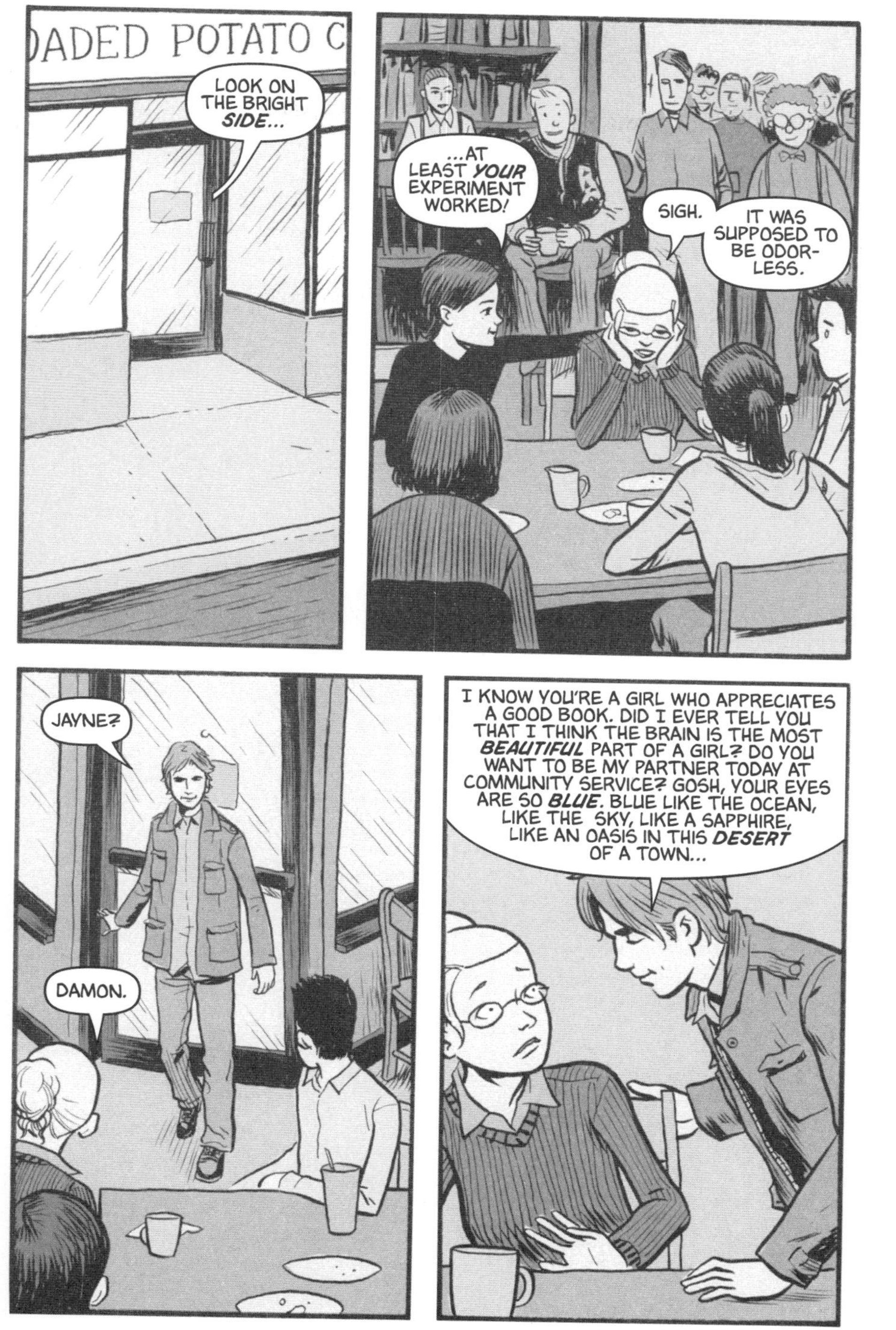
OADED POTATO C
LOOK ON THE BRIGHT SIDE...
...AT LEAST YOUR EXPERIMENT WORKED!
SIGH.
IT WAS SUPPOSED TO BE ODORLESS.
JAYNE?
DAMON.
I KNOW YOU'RE A GIRL WHO APPRECIATES A GOOD BOOK. DID I EVER TELL YOU THAT I THINK THE BRAIN IS THE MOST BEAUTIFUL PART OF A GIRL? DO YOU WANT TO BE MY PARTNER TODAY AT COMMUNITY SERVICE? GOSH, YOUR EYES ARE SO BLUE. BLUE LIKE THE OCEAN, LIKE THE SKY, LIKE A SAPPHIRE, LIKE AN OASIS IN THIS DESERT OF A TOWN...

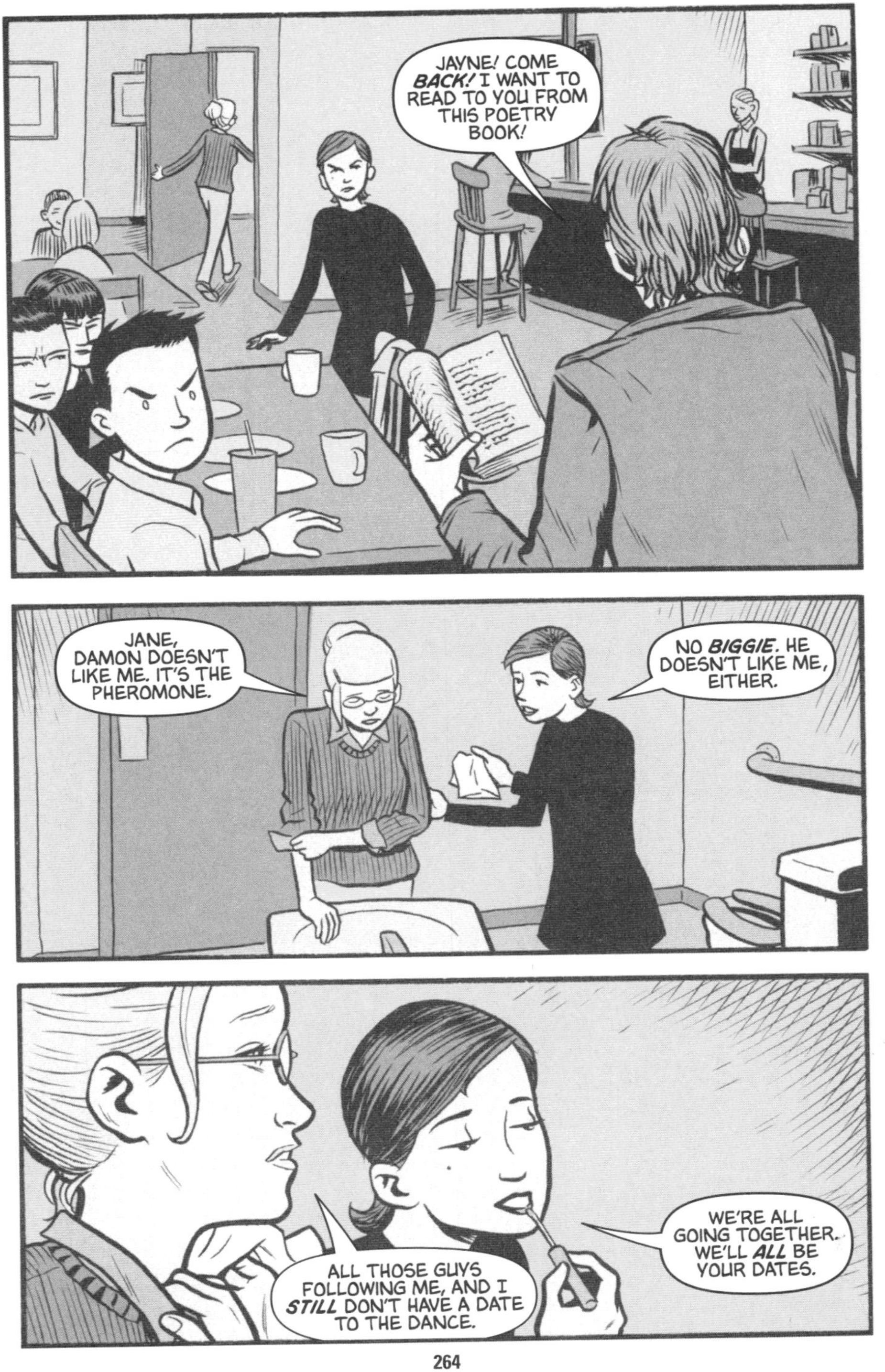
JAYNE! COME BACK! I WANT TO READ TO YOU FROM THIS POETRY BOOK!
JANE, DAMON DOESN'T LIKE ME. IT'S THE PHEROMONE.
NO BIGGIE. HE DOESN'T LIKE ME, EITHER.
ALL THOSE GUYS FOLLOWING ME, AND I STILL DON'T HAVE A DATE TO THE DANCE.
WE'RE ALL GOING TOGETHER. WE'LL ALL BE YOUR DATES.

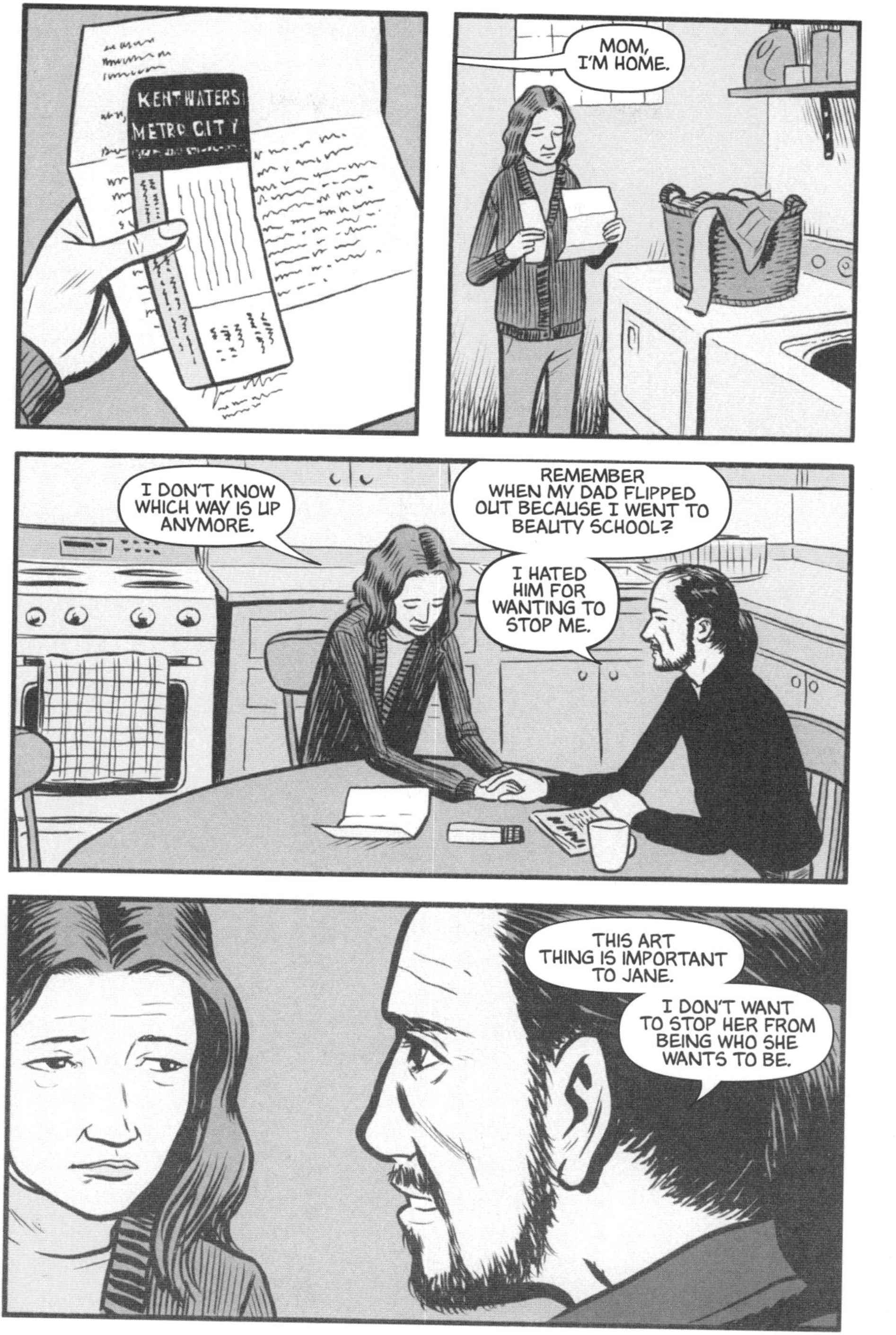
KENT WATERS
METRO CITY
MOM, I'M HOME.
I DON'T KNOW WHICH WAY IS UP ANYMORE.
REMEMBER WHEN MY DAD FLIPPED OUT BECAUSE I WENT TO BEAUTY SCHOOL?
I HATED HIM FOR WANTING TO STOP ME.
THIS ART THING IS IMPORTANT TO JANE.
I DON'T WANT TO STOP HER FROM BEING WHO SHE WANTS TO BE.

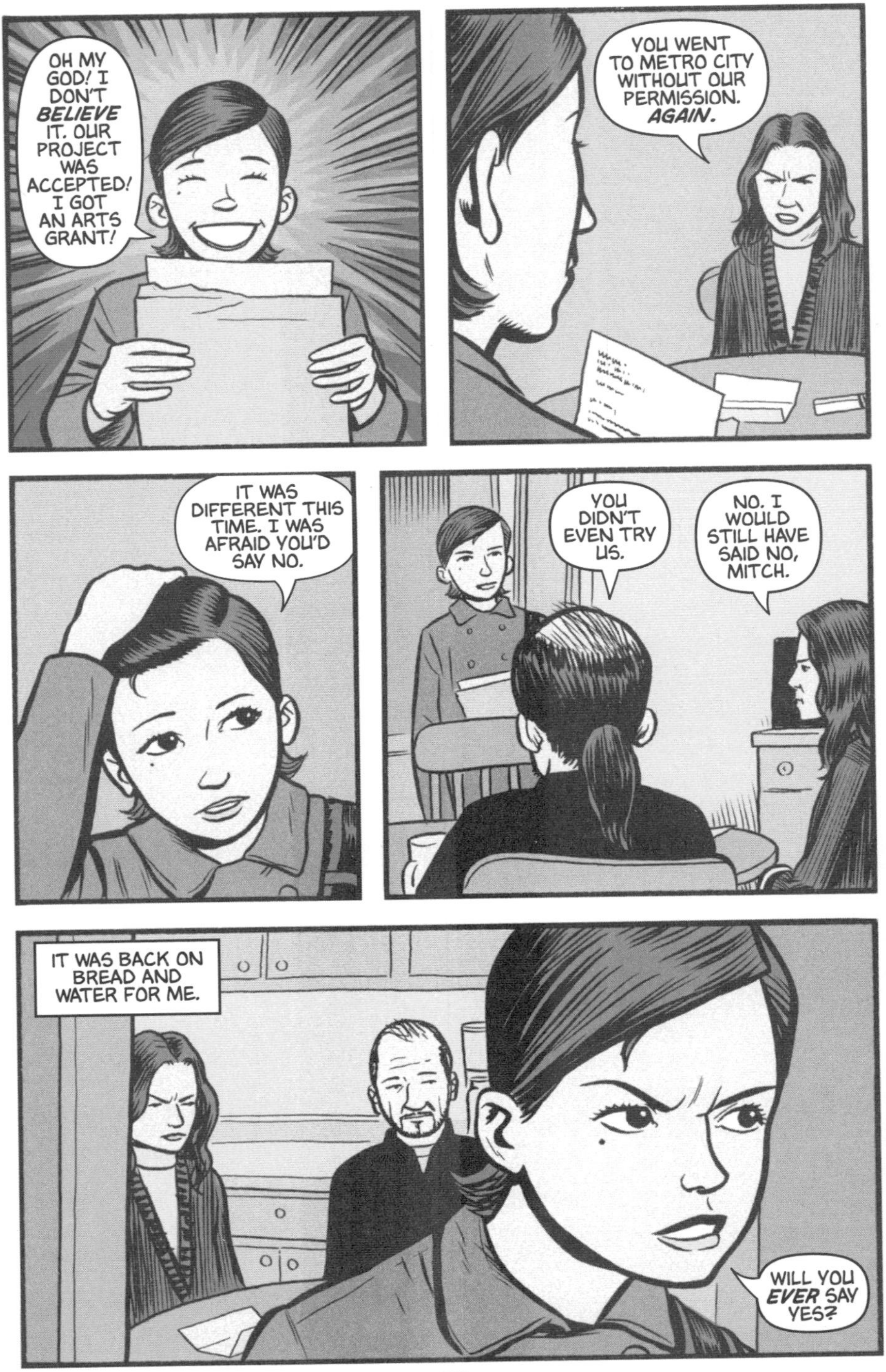
OH MY GOD! I DON'T *BELIEVE* IT. OUR PROJECT WAS ACCEPTED! I GOT AN ARTS GRANT!
YOU WENT TO METRO CITY WITHOUT OUR PERMISSION. *AGAIN.*
IT WAS DIFFERENT THIS TIME. I WAS AFRAID YOU'D SAY NO.
YOU DIDN'T EVEN TRY US.
NO. I WOULD STILL HAVE SAID NO, MITCH.
IT WAS BACK ON BREAD AND WATER FOR ME.
WILL YOU *EVER* SAY YES?

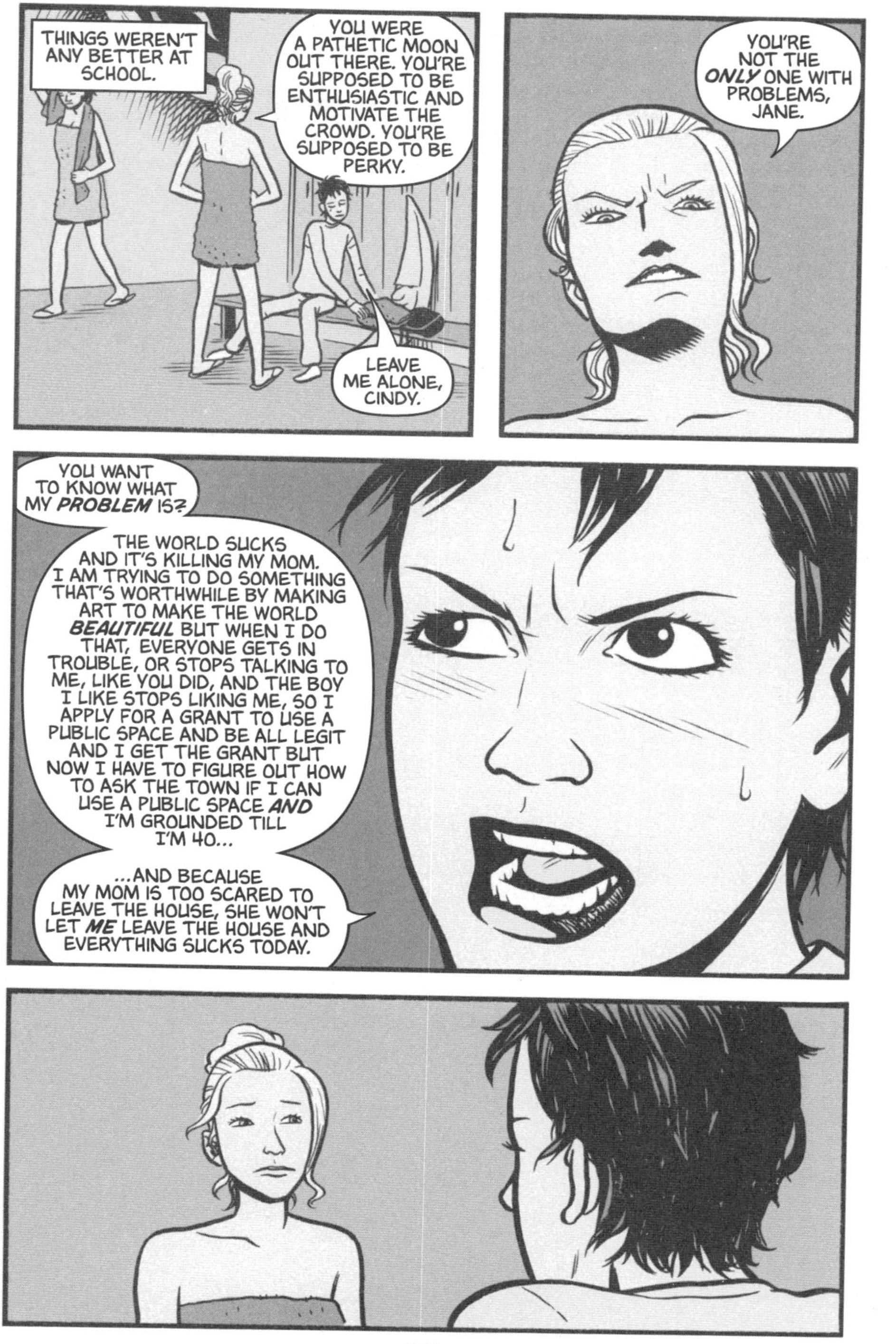
THINGS WEREN'T ANY BETTER AT SCHOOL.
YOU WERE A PATHETIC MOON OUT THERE. YOU'RE SUPPOSED TO BE ENTHUSIASTIC AND MOTIVATE THE CROWD. YOU'RE SUPPOSED TO BE PERKY.
LEAVE ME ALONE, CINDY.
YOU'RE NOT THE *ONLY* ONE WITH PROBLEMS, JANE.
YOU WANT TO KNOW WHAT MY *PROBLEM* IS?
THE WORLD SUCKS AND IT'S KILLING MY MOM. I AM TRYING TO DO SOMETHING THAT'S WORTHWHILE BY MAKING ART TO MAKE THE WORLD *BEAUTIFUL* BUT WHEN I DO THAT, EVERYONE GETS IN TROUBLE, OR STOPS TALKING TO ME, LIKE YOU DID, AND THE BOY I LIKE STOPS LIKING ME, SO I APPLY FOR A GRANT TO USE A PUBLIC SPACE AND BE ALL LEGIT AND I GET THE GRANT BUT NOW I HAVE TO FIGURE OUT HOW TO ASK THE TOWN IF I CAN USE A PUBLIC SPACE *AND* I'M GROUNDED TILL I'M 40...
...AND BECAUSE MY MOM IS TOO SCARED TO LEAVE THE HOUSE, SHE WON'T LET *ME* LEAVE THE HOUSE AND EVERYTHING SUCKS TODAY.

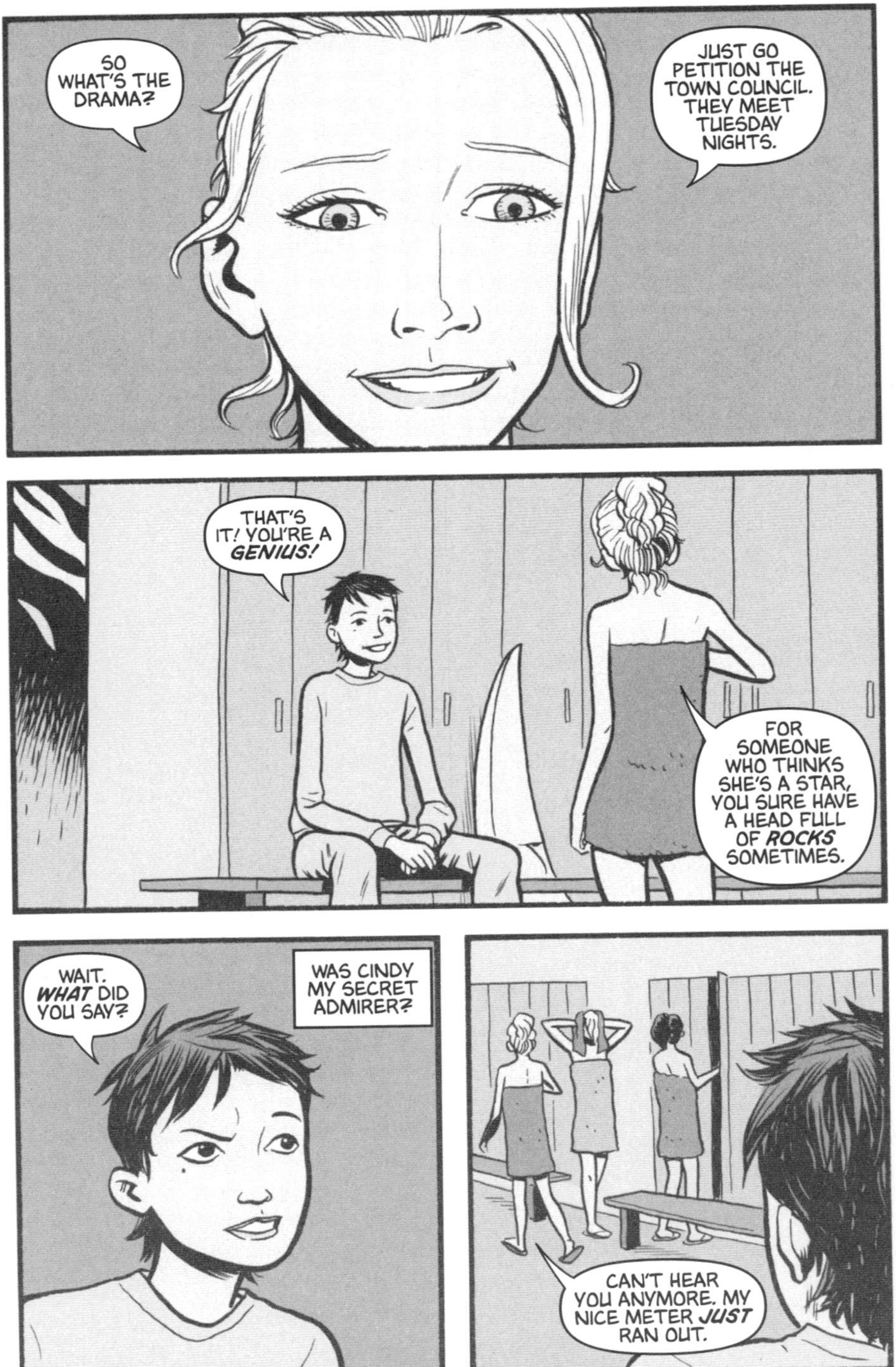
SO WHAT'S THE DRAMA?
JUST GO PETITION THE TOWN COUNCIL. THEY MEET TUESDAY NIGHTS.
THAT'S IT! YOU'RE A **GENIUS!**
FOR SOMEONE WHO THINKS SHE'S A STAR, YOU SURE HAVE A HEAD FULL OF **ROCKS** SOMETIMES.
WAIT. **WHAT** DID YOU SAY?
WAS CINDY MY SECRET ADMIRER?
CAN'T HEAR YOU ANYMORE. MY NICE METER **JUST** RAN OUT.

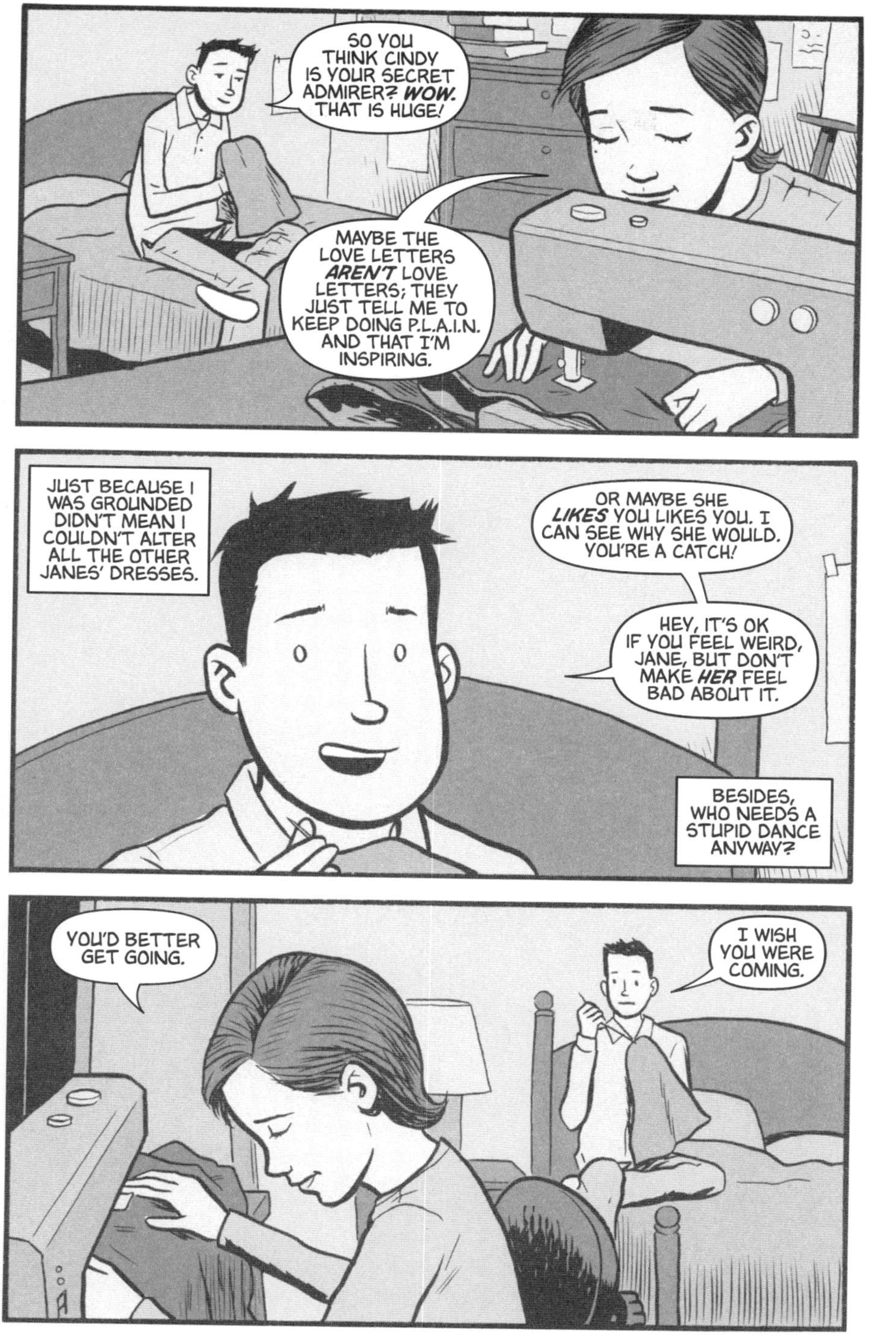
SO YOU THINK CINDY IS YOUR SECRET ADMIRER? WOW. THAT IS HUGE!
MAYBE THE LOVE LETTERS AREN'T LOVE LETTERS; THEY JUST TELL ME TO KEEP DOING P.L.A.I.N. AND THAT I'M INSPIRING.
JUST BECAUSE I WAS GROUNDED DIDN'T MEAN I COULDN'T ALTER ALL THE OTHER JANES' DRESSES.
OR MAYBE SHE LIKES YOU LIKES YOU. I CAN SEE WHY SHE WOULD. YOU'RE A CATCH!
HEY, IT'S OK IF YOU FEEL WEIRD, JANE, BUT DON'T MAKE HER FEEL BAD ABOUT IT.
BESIDES, WHO NEEDS A STUPID DANCE ANYWAY?
YOU'D BETTER GET GOING.
I WISH YOU WERE COMING.

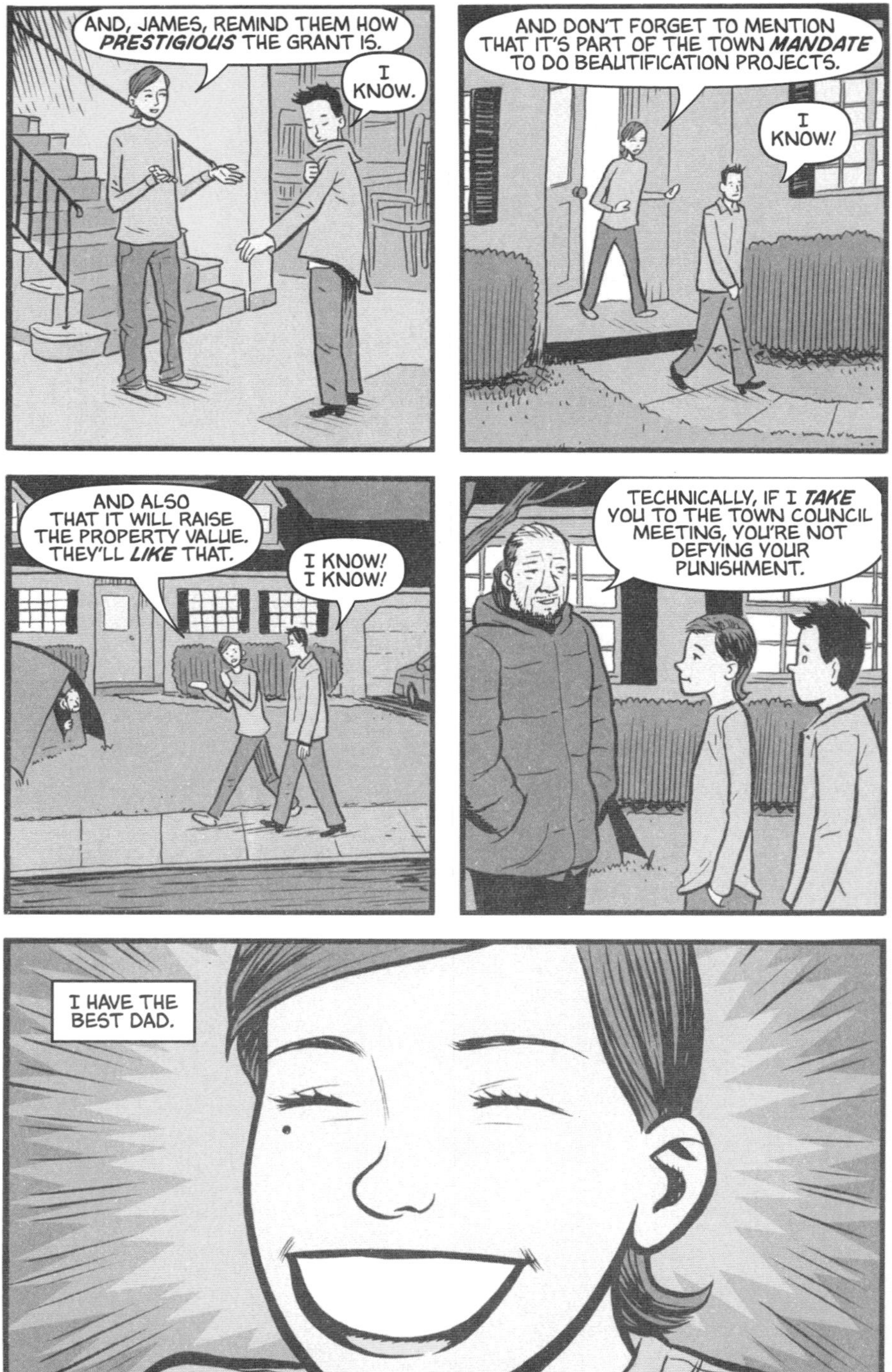

AND, JAMES, REMIND THEM HOW PRESTIGIOUS THE GRANT IS.
I KNOW.
AND DON'T FORGET TO MENTION THAT IT'S PART OF THE TOWN MANDATE TO DO BEAUTIFICATION PROJECTS.
I KNOW!
AND ALSO THAT IT WILL RAISE THE PROPERTY VALUE. THEY'LL LIKE THAT.
I KNOW! I KNOW!
TECHNICALLY, IF I TAKE YOU TO THE TOWN COUNCIL MEETING, YOU'RE NOT DEFYING YOUR PUNISHMENT.
I HAVE THE BEST DAD.

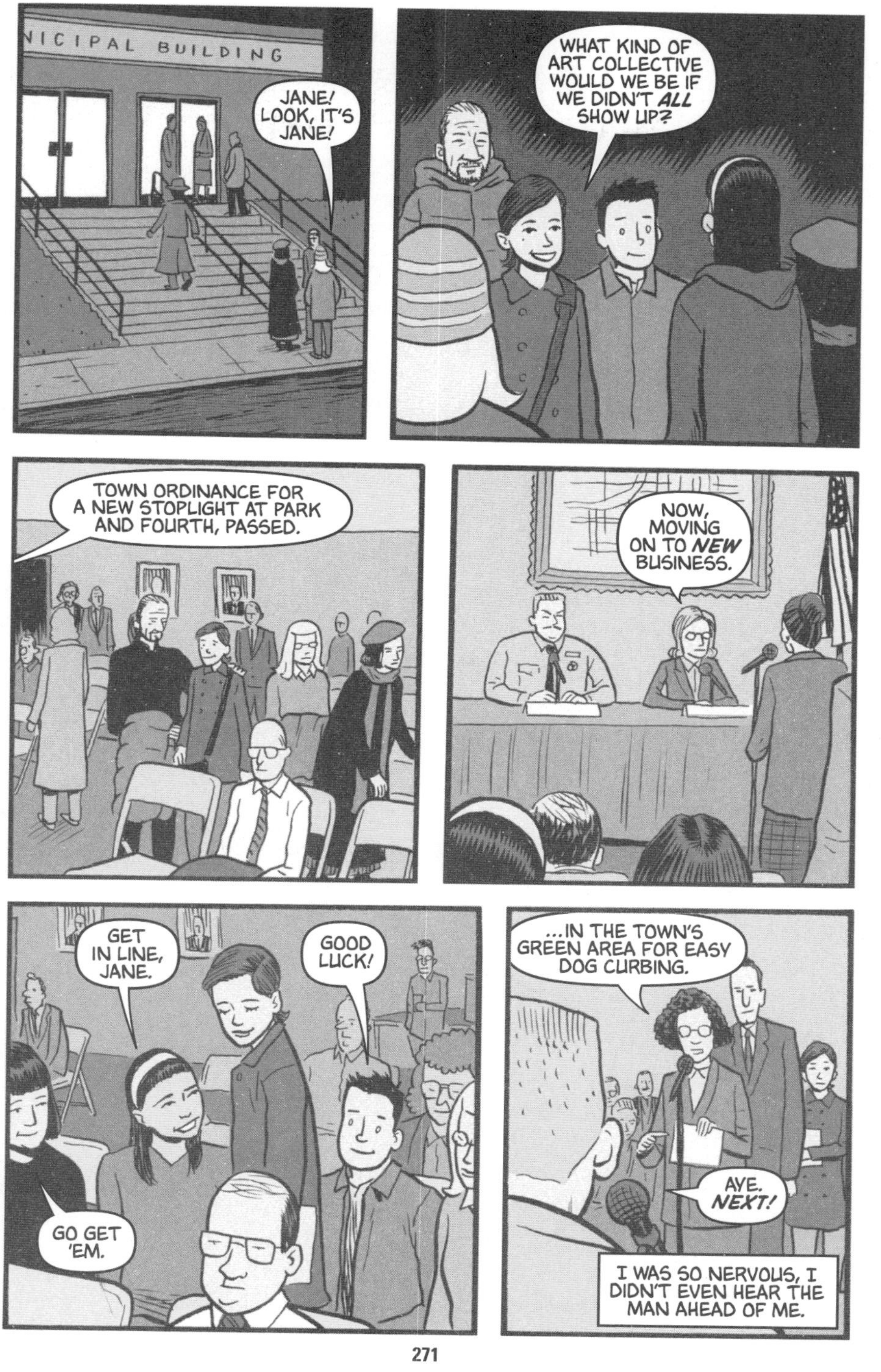

...NICIPAL BUILDING
JANE! LOOK, IT'S JANE!
WHAT KIND OF ART COLLECTIVE WOULD WE BE IF WE DIDN'T *ALL* SHOW UP?
TOWN ORDINANCE FOR A NEW STOPLIGHT AT PARK AND FOURTH, PASSED.
NOW, MOVING ON TO *NEW* BUSINESS.
GET IN LINE, JANE.
GOOD LUCK!
GO GET 'EM.
...IN THE TOWN'S GREEN AREA FOR EASY DOG CURBING.
AYE. *NEXT!*
I WAS SO NERVOUS, I DIDN'T EVEN HEAR THE MAN AHEAD OF ME.

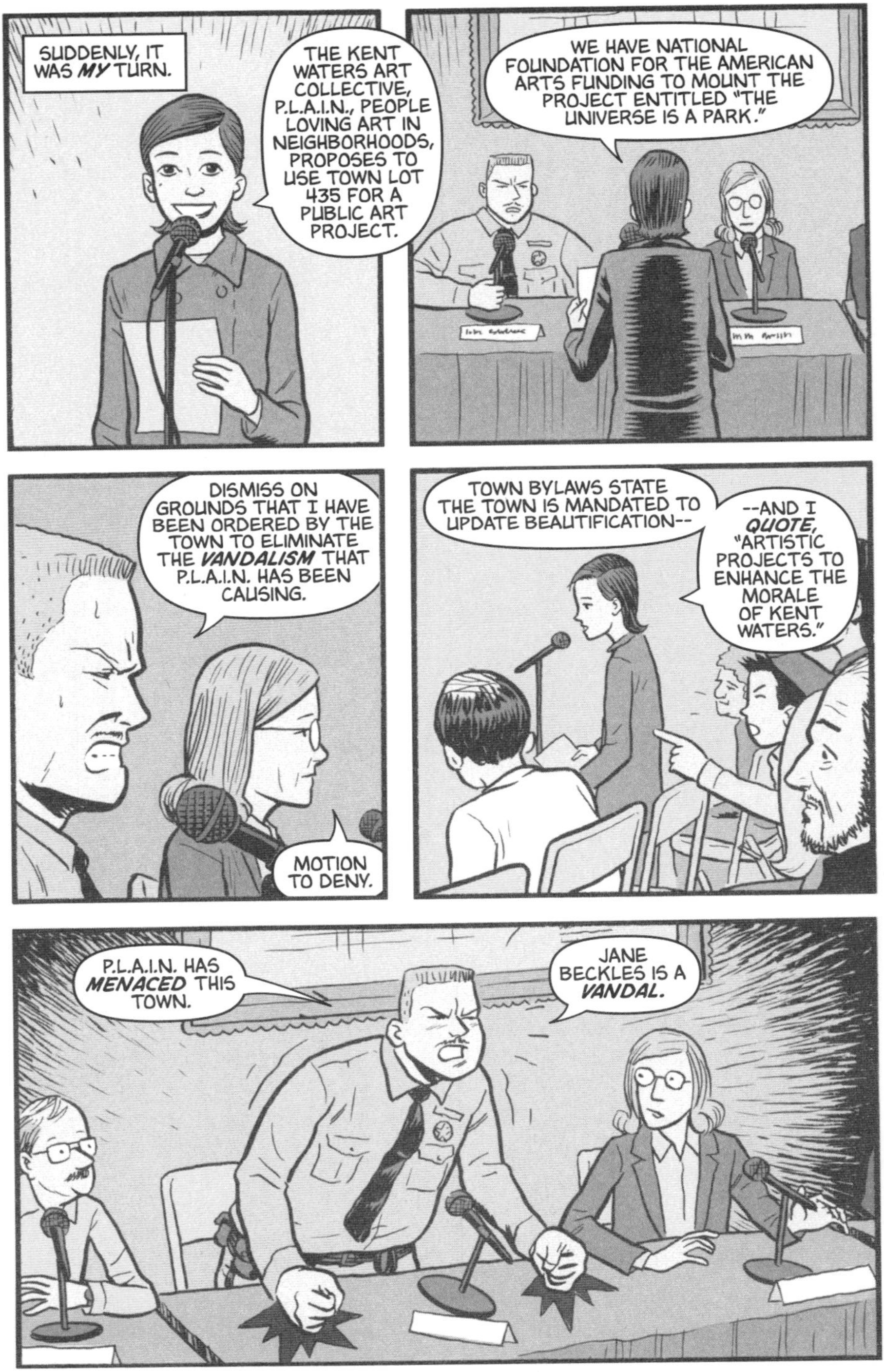
SUDDENLY, IT WAS *MY* TURN.
THE KENT WATERS ART COLLECTIVE, P.L.A.I.N., PEOPLE LOVING ART IN NEIGHBORHOODS, PROPOSES TO USE TOWN LOT 435 FOR A PUBLIC ART PROJECT.
WE HAVE NATIONAL FOUNDATION FOR THE AMERICAN ARTS FUNDING TO MOUNT THE PROJECT ENTITLED "THE UNIVERSE IS A PARK."
DISMISS ON GROUNDS THAT I HAVE BEEN ORDERED BY THE TOWN TO ELIMINATE THE *VANDALISM* THAT P.L.A.I.N. HAS BEEN CAUSING.
MOTION TO DENY.
TOWN BYLAWS STATE THE TOWN IS MANDATED TO UPDATE BEAUTIFICATION--
--AND I *QUOTE,* "ARTISTIC PROJECTS TO ENHANCE THE MORALE OF KENT WATERS."
P.L.A.I.N. HAS *MENACED* THIS TOWN.
JANE BECKLES IS A *VANDAL.*

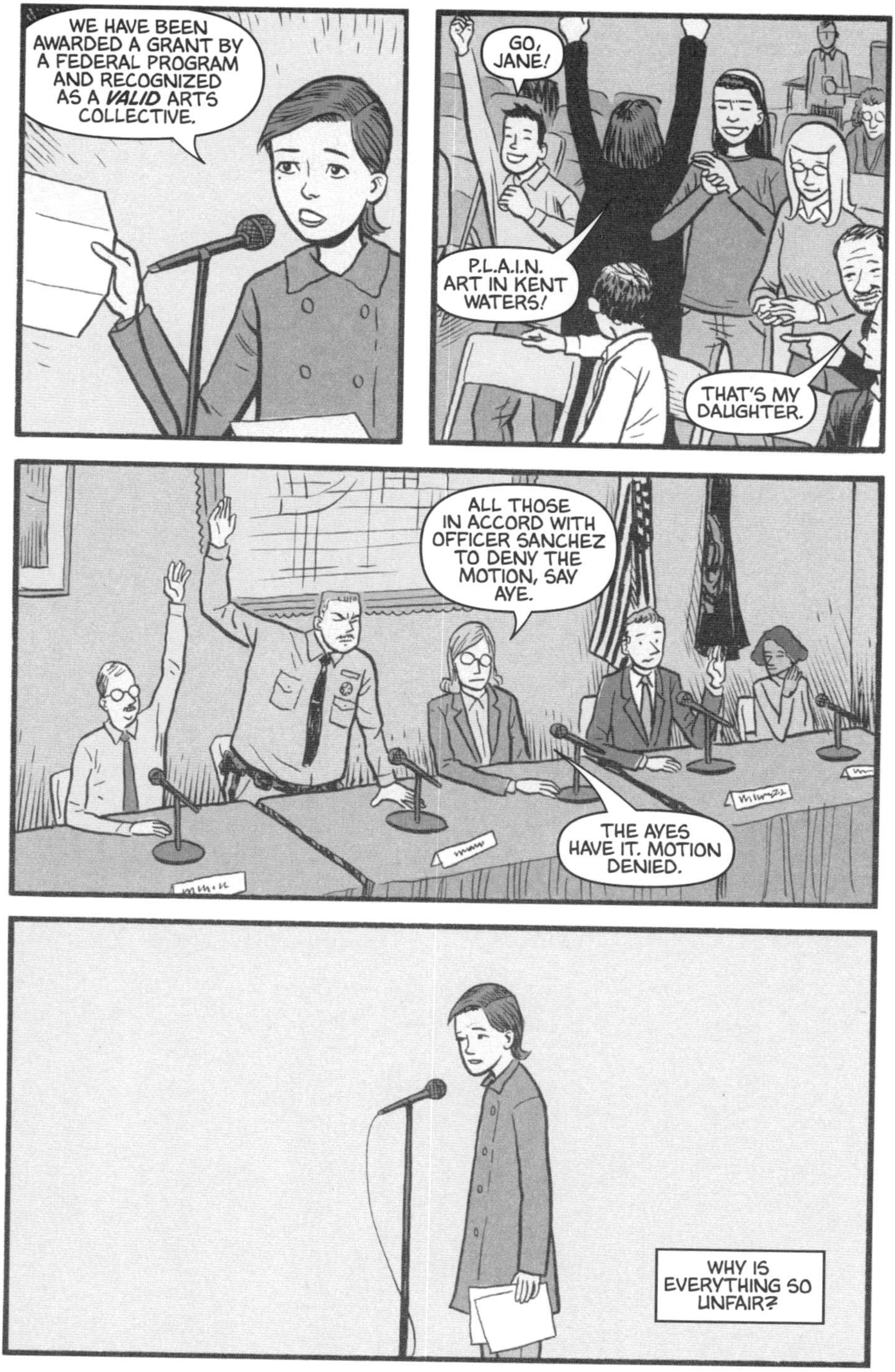
WE HAVE BEEN AWARDED A GRANT BY A FEDERAL PROGRAM AND RECOGNIZED AS A *VALID* ARTS COLLECTIVE.
GO, JANE!
P.L.A.I.N. ART IN KENT WATERS!
THAT'S MY DAUGHTER.
ALL THOSE IN ACCORD WITH OFFICER SANCHEZ TO DENY THE MOTION, SAY AYE.
THE AYES HAVE IT. MOTION DENIED.
WHY IS EVERYTHING SO UNFAIR?

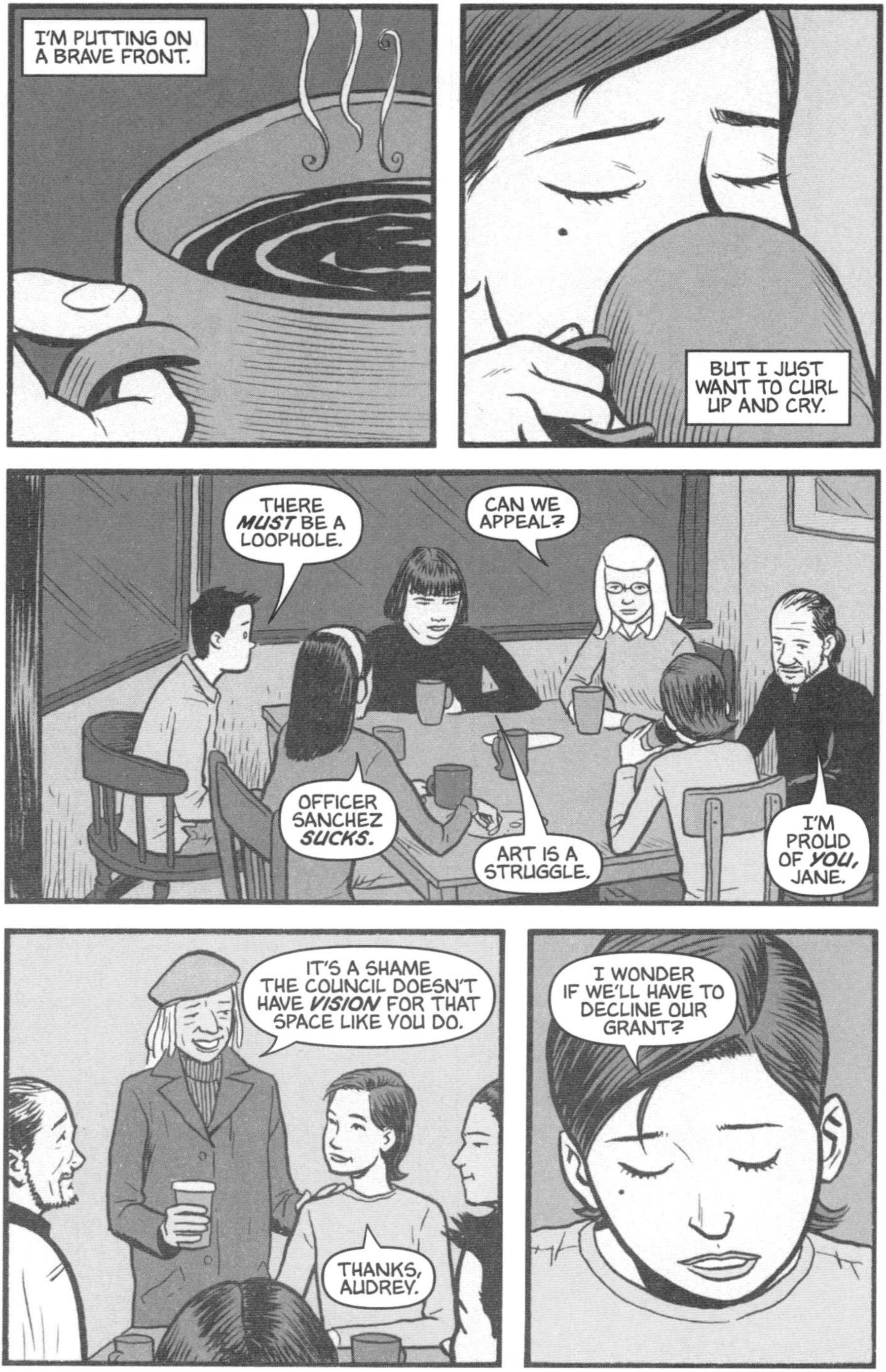
I'M PUTTING ON A BRAVE FRONT.
BUT I JUST WANT TO CURL UP AND CRY.
THERE MUST BE A LOOPHOLE.
CAN WE APPEAL?
OFFICER SANCHEZ SUCKS.
ART IS A STRUGGLE.
I'M PROUD OF YOU, JANE.
IT'S A SHAME THE COUNCIL DOESN'T HAVE VISION FOR THAT SPACE LIKE YOU DO.
THANKS, AUDREY.
I WONDER IF WE'LL HAVE TO DECLINE OUR GRANT?

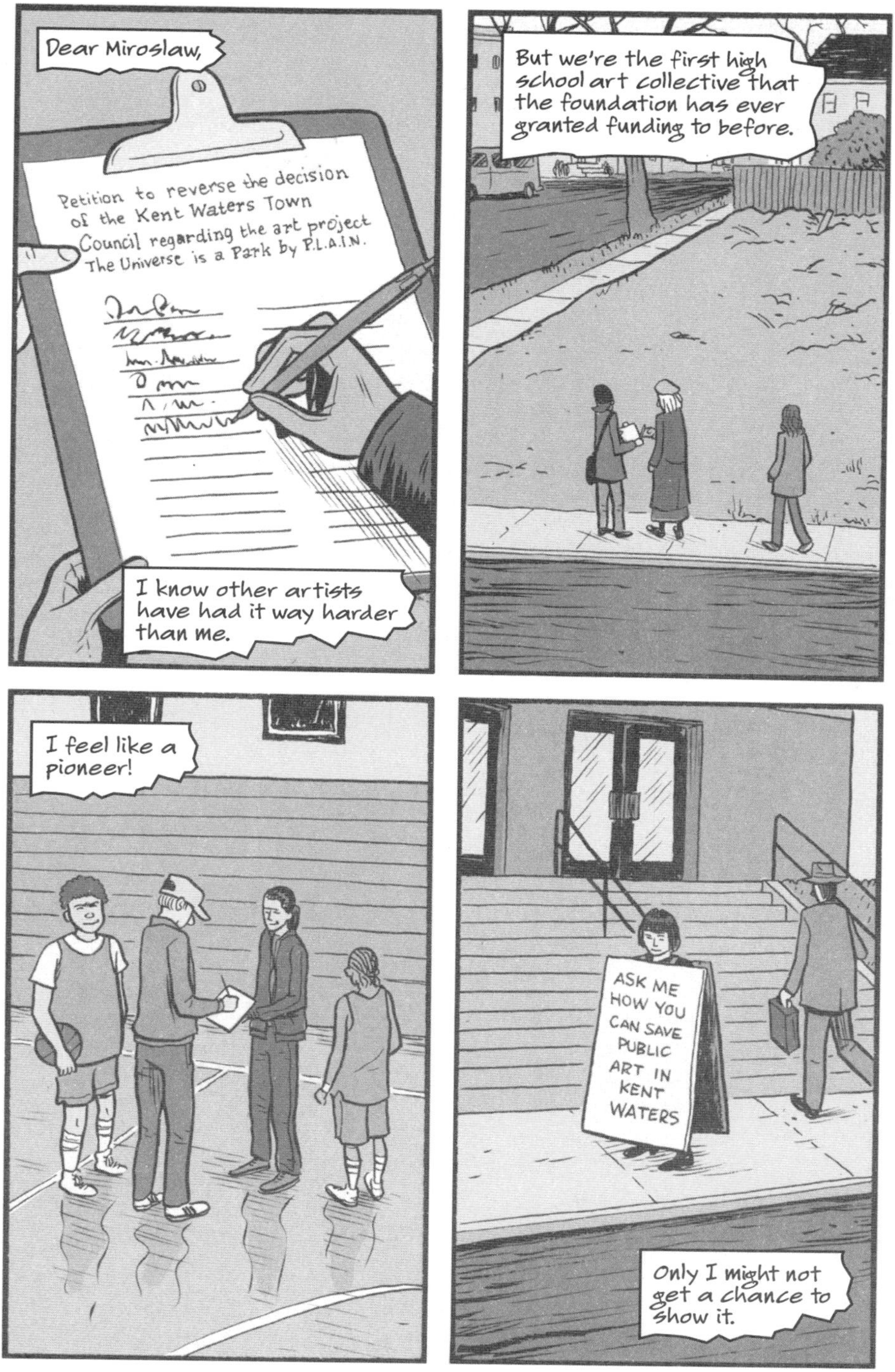

Dear Miroslaw,
Petition to reverse the decision of the Kent Waters Town Council regarding the art project The Universe is a Park by P.L.A.I.N.
I know other artists have had it way harder than me.
But we're the first high school art collective that the foundation has ever granted funding to before.
I feel like a pioneer!
ASK ME HOW YOU CAN SAVE PUBLIC ART IN KENT WATERS
Only I might not get a chance to show it.

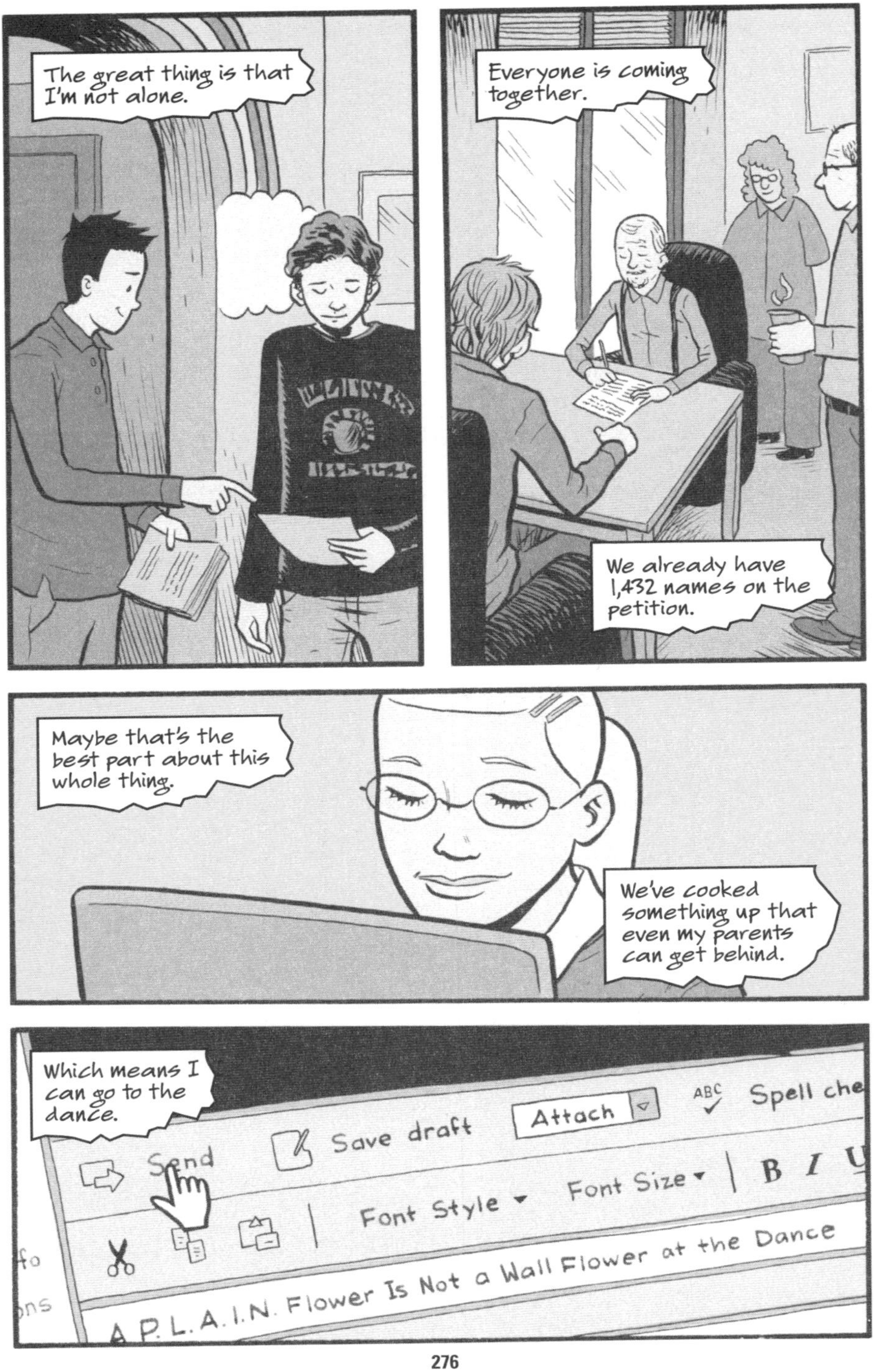

The great thing is that I'm not alone.
Everyone is coming together.
We already have 1,432 names on the petition.
Maybe that's the best part about this whole thing.
We've cooked something up that even my parents can get behind.
Which means I can go to the dance.
Attach
ABC
Spell che
Save draft
Send
Font Size
B I U
Font Style
A.P.L.A.I.N. Flower Is Not a Wall Flower at the Dance

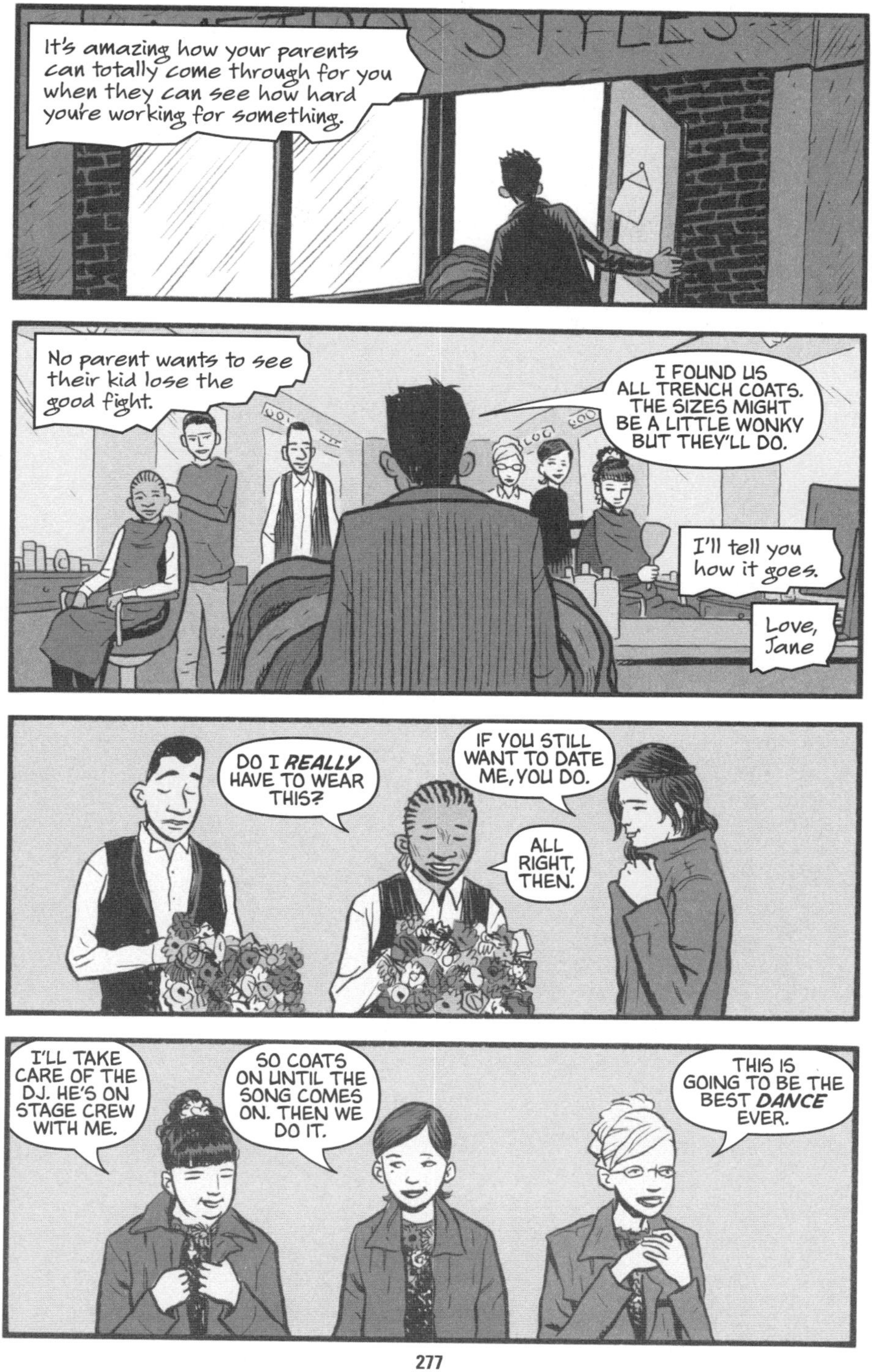
STYLES
It's amazing how your parents can totally come through for you when they can see how hard you're working for something.
No parent wants to see their kid lose the good fight.
I FOUND US ALL TRENCH COATS. THE SIZES MIGHT BE A LITTLE WONKY BUT THEY'LL DO.
I'll tell you how it *goes*.
Love, Jane
DO I ***REALLY*** HAVE TO WEAR THIS?
IF YOU STILL WANT TO DATE ME, YOU DO.
ALL RIGHT, THEN.
I'LL TAKE CARE OF THE DJ. HE'S ON STAGE CREW WITH ME.
SO COATS ON UNTIL THE SONG COMES ON. THEN WE DO IT.
THIS IS GOING TO BE THE BEST ***DANCE*** EVER.

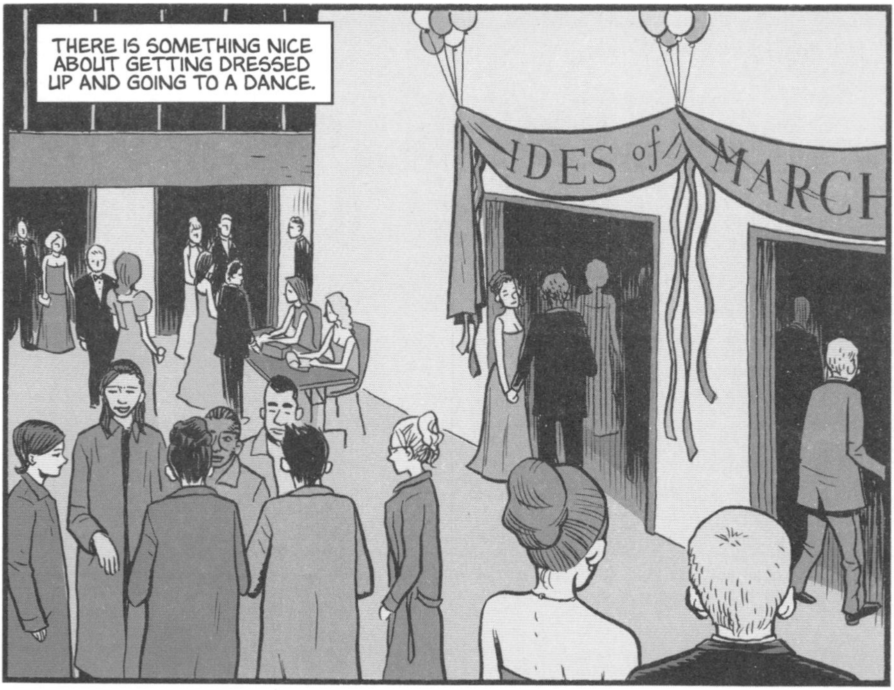
THERE IS SOMETHING NICE ABOUT GETTING DRESSED UP AND GOING TO A DANCE.
IDES of MARCH

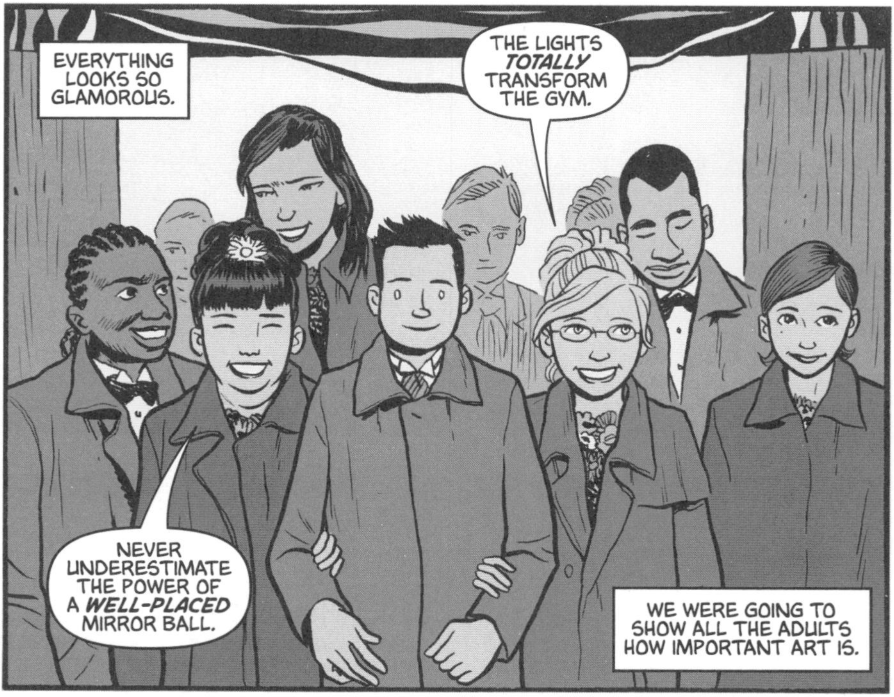
EVERYTHING LOOKS SO GLAMOROUS.
THE LIGHTS *TOTALLY* TRANSFORM THE GYM.
NEVER UNDERESTIMATE THE POWER OF A *WELL-PLACED* MIRROR BALL.
WE WERE GOING TO SHOW ALL THE ADULTS HOW IMPORTANT ART IS.

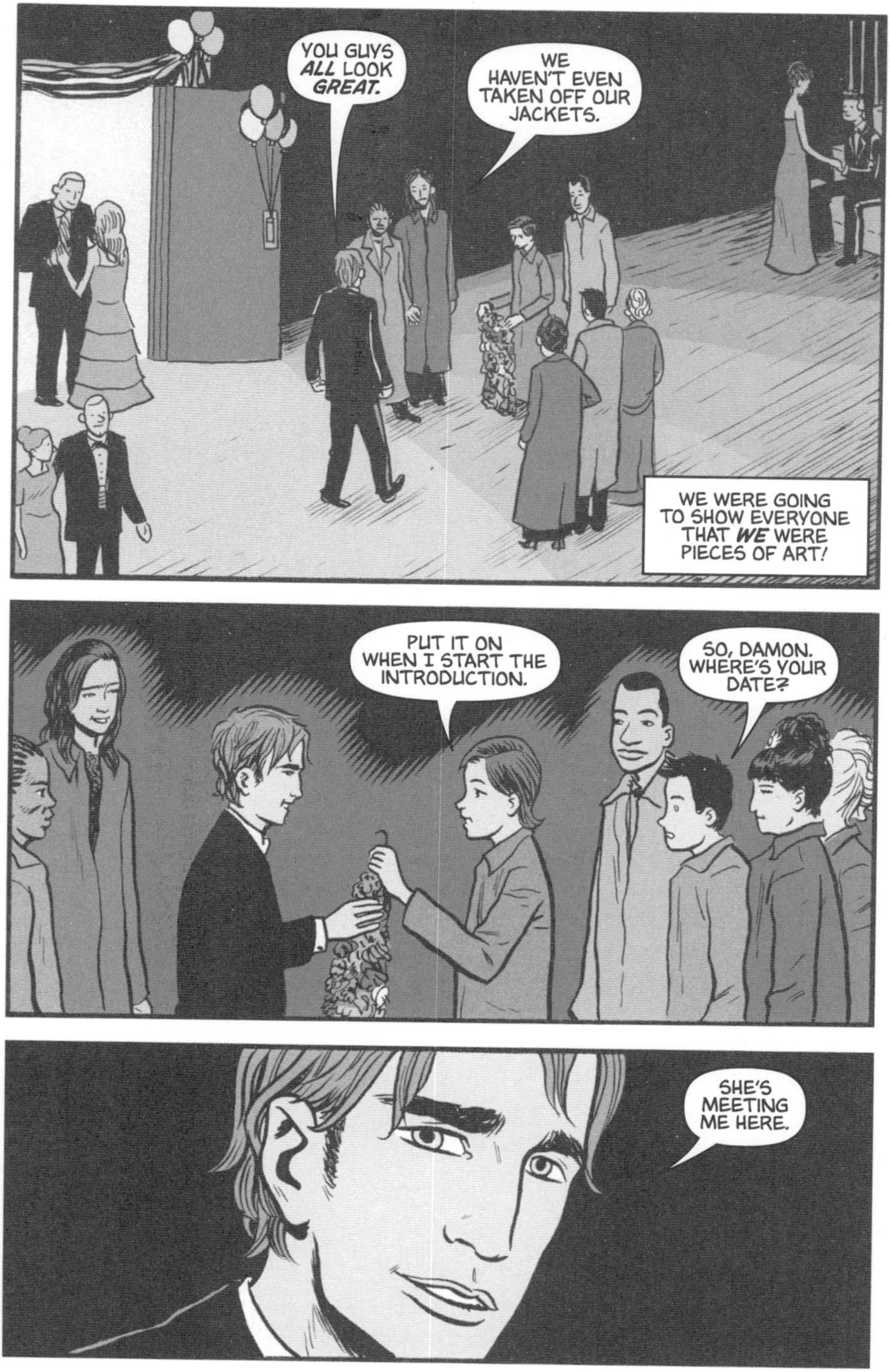
YOU GUYS ALL LOOK GREAT.
WE HAVEN'T EVEN TAKEN OFF OUR JACKETS.
WE WERE GOING TO SHOW EVERYONE THAT WE WERE PIECES OF ART!
PUT IT ON WHEN I START THE INTRODUCTION.
SO, DAMON. WHERE'S YOUR DATE?
SHE'S MEETING ME HERE.

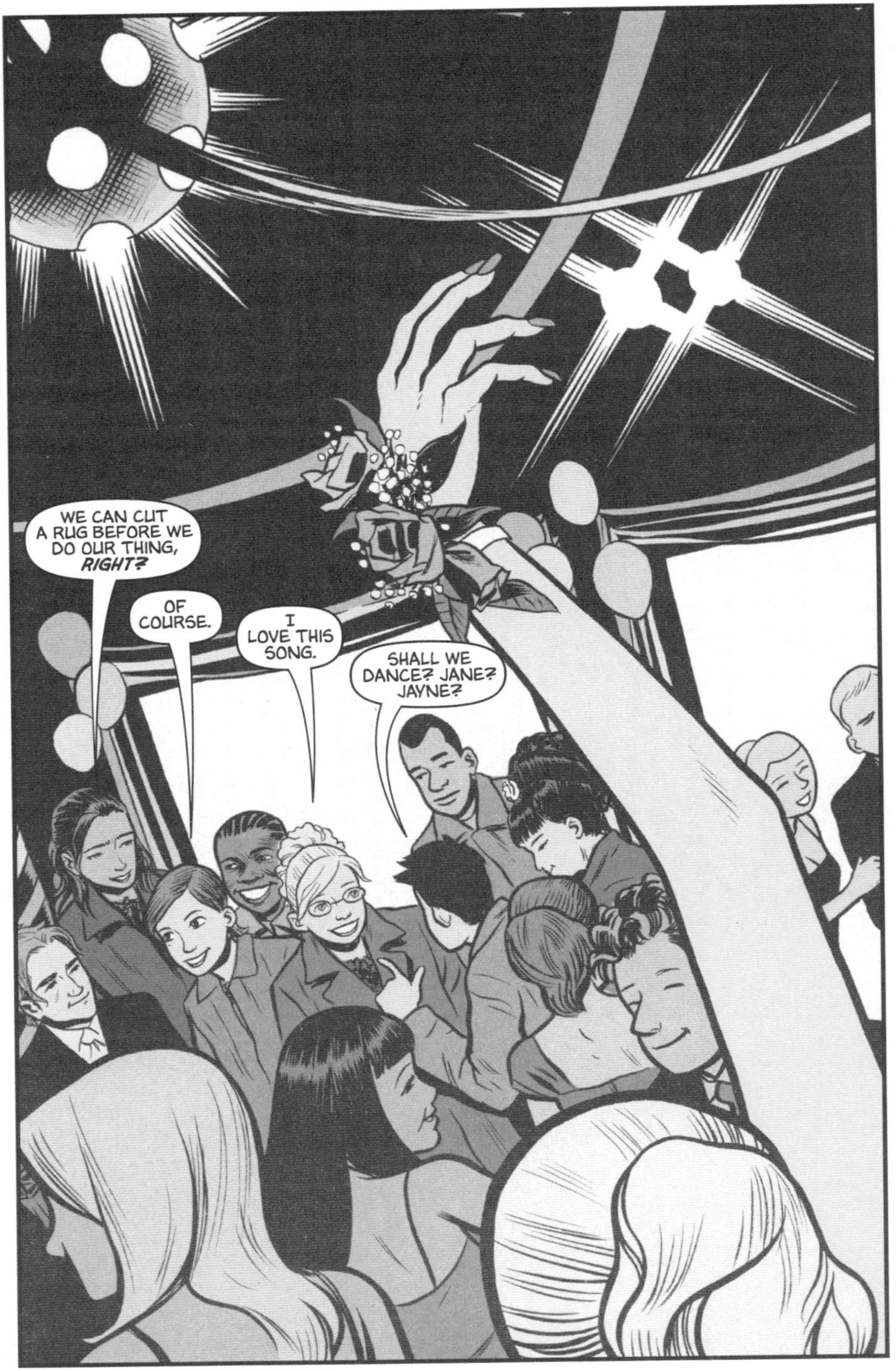
WE CAN CUT A RUG BEFORE WE DO OUR THING, RIGHT?
OF COURSE.
I LOVE THIS SONG.
SHALL WE DANCE? JANE? JAYNE?

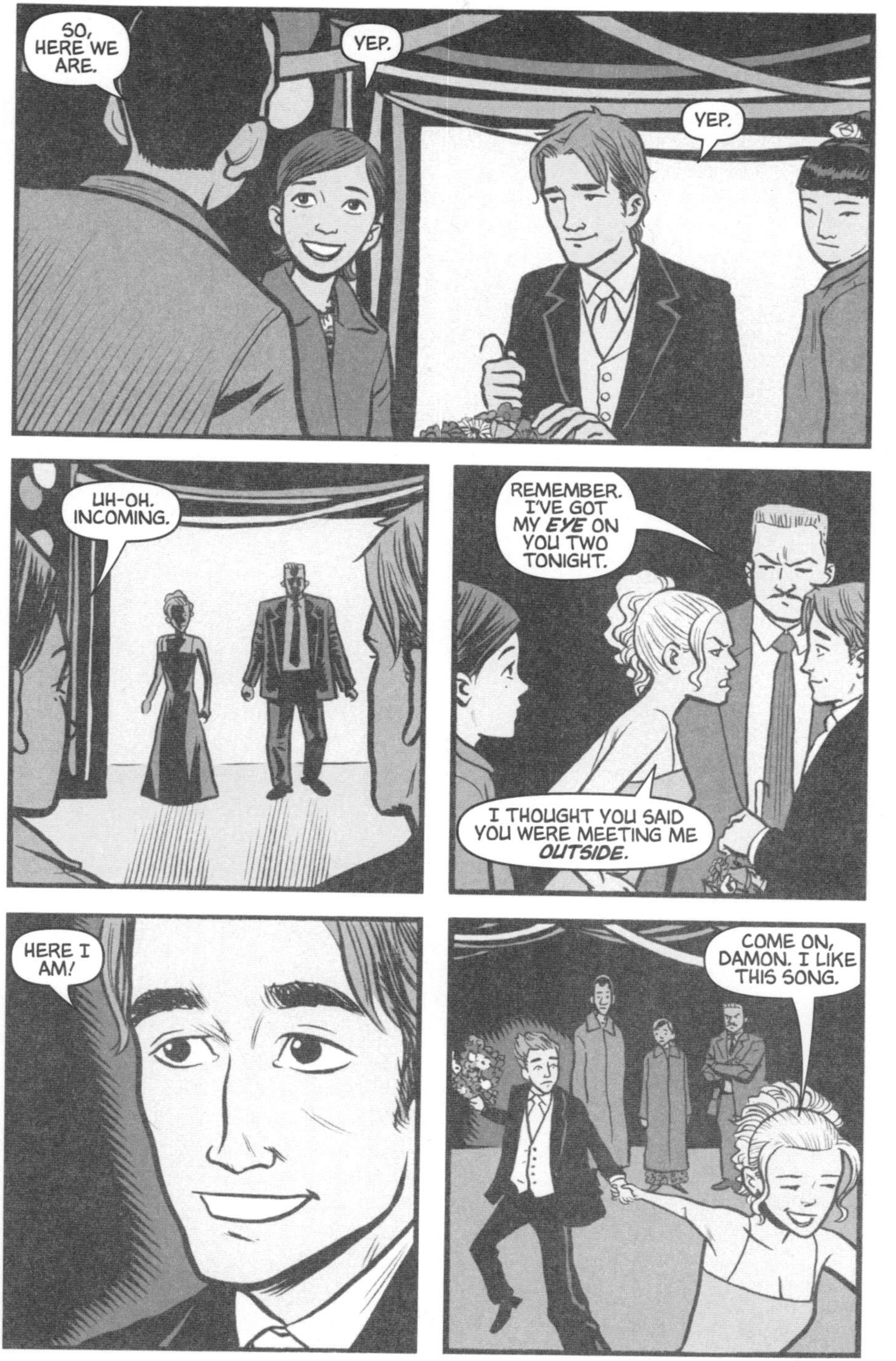
SO, HERE WE ARE.
YEP.
YEP.
UH-OH. INCOMING.
REMEMBER. I'VE GOT MY *EYE* ON YOU TWO TONIGHT.
I THOUGHT YOU SAID YOU WERE MEETING ME *OUTSIDE*.
HERE I AM!
COME ON, DAMON. I LIKE THIS SONG.

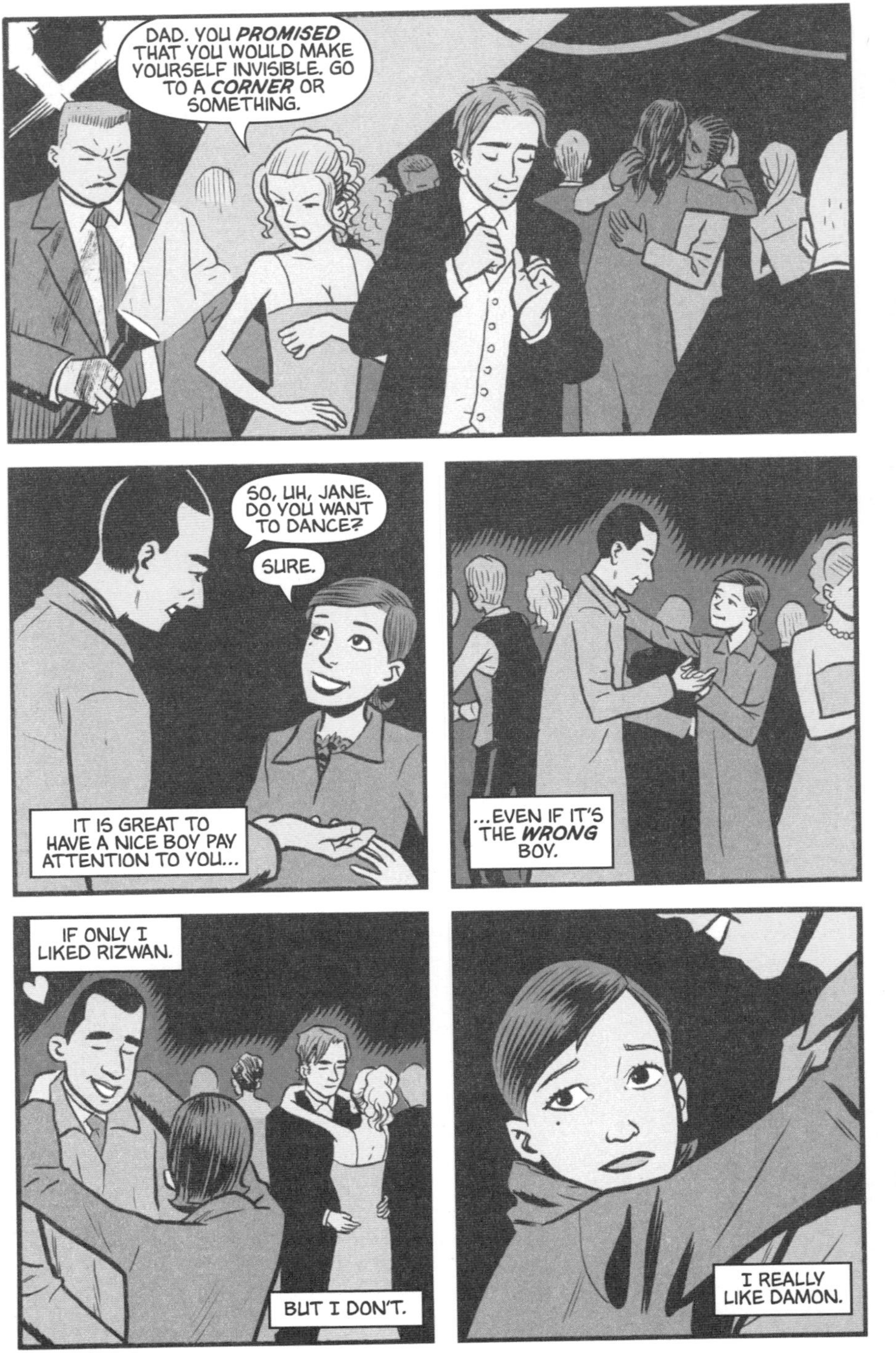
DAD. YOU PROMISED THAT YOU WOULD MAKE YOURSELF INVISIBLE. GO TO A CORNER OR SOMETHING.
SO, UH, JANE. DO YOU WANT TO DANCE?
SURE.
IT IS GREAT TO HAVE A NICE BOY PAY ATTENTION TO YOU...
...EVEN IF IT'S THE WRONG BOY.
IF ONLY I LIKED RIZWAN.
BUT I DON'T.
I REALLY LIKE DAMON.

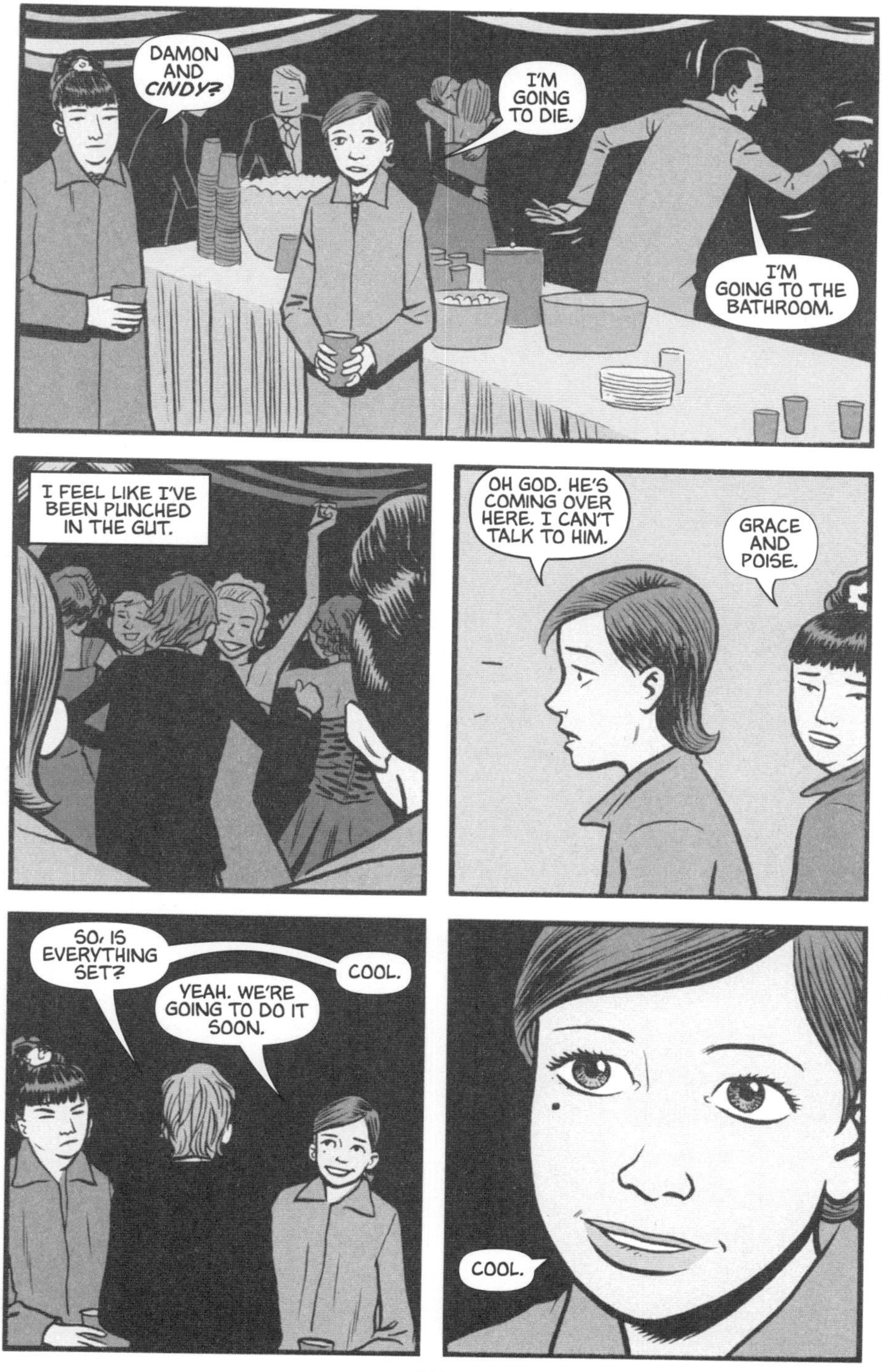
DAMON AND CINDY?
I'M GOING TO DIE.
I'M GOING TO THE BATHROOM.
I FEEL LIKE I'VE BEEN PUNCHED IN THE GUT.
OH GOD. HE'S COMING OVER HERE. I CAN'T TALK TO HIM.
GRACE AND POISE.
SO, IS EVERYTHING SET?
YEAH. WE'RE GOING TO DO IT SOON.
COOL.
COOL.

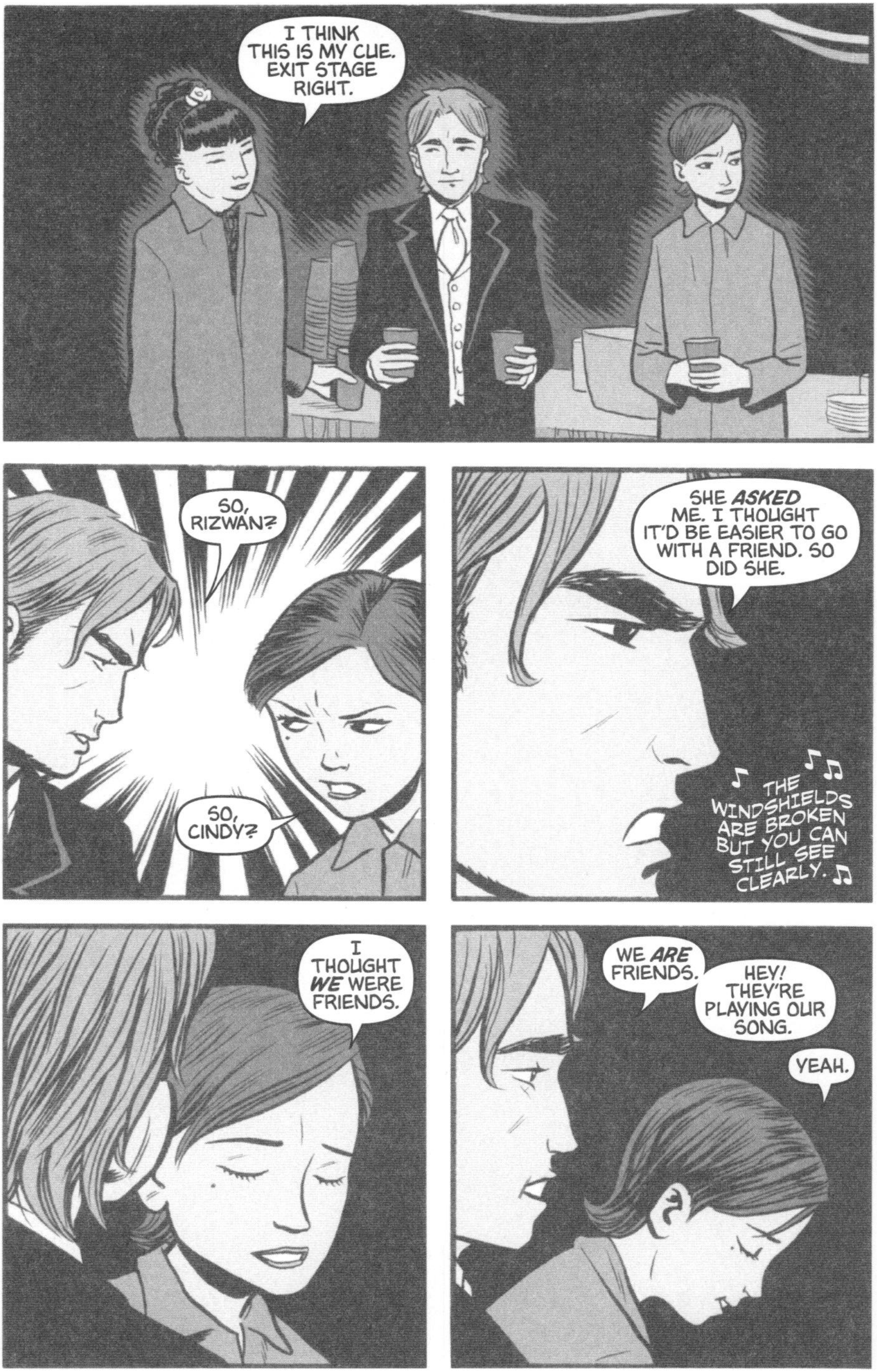
I THINK THIS IS MY CUE. EXIT STAGE RIGHT.
SO, RIZWAN?
SO, CINDY?
SHE ASKED ME. I THOUGHT IT'D BE EASIER TO GO WITH A FRIEND. SO DID SHE.
♪ THE WINDSHIELDS ARE BROKEN BUT YOU CAN STILL SEE CLEARLY. ♫
I THOUGHT WE WERE FRIENDS.
WE ARE FRIENDS.
HEY! THEY'RE PLAYING OUR SONG.
YEAH.

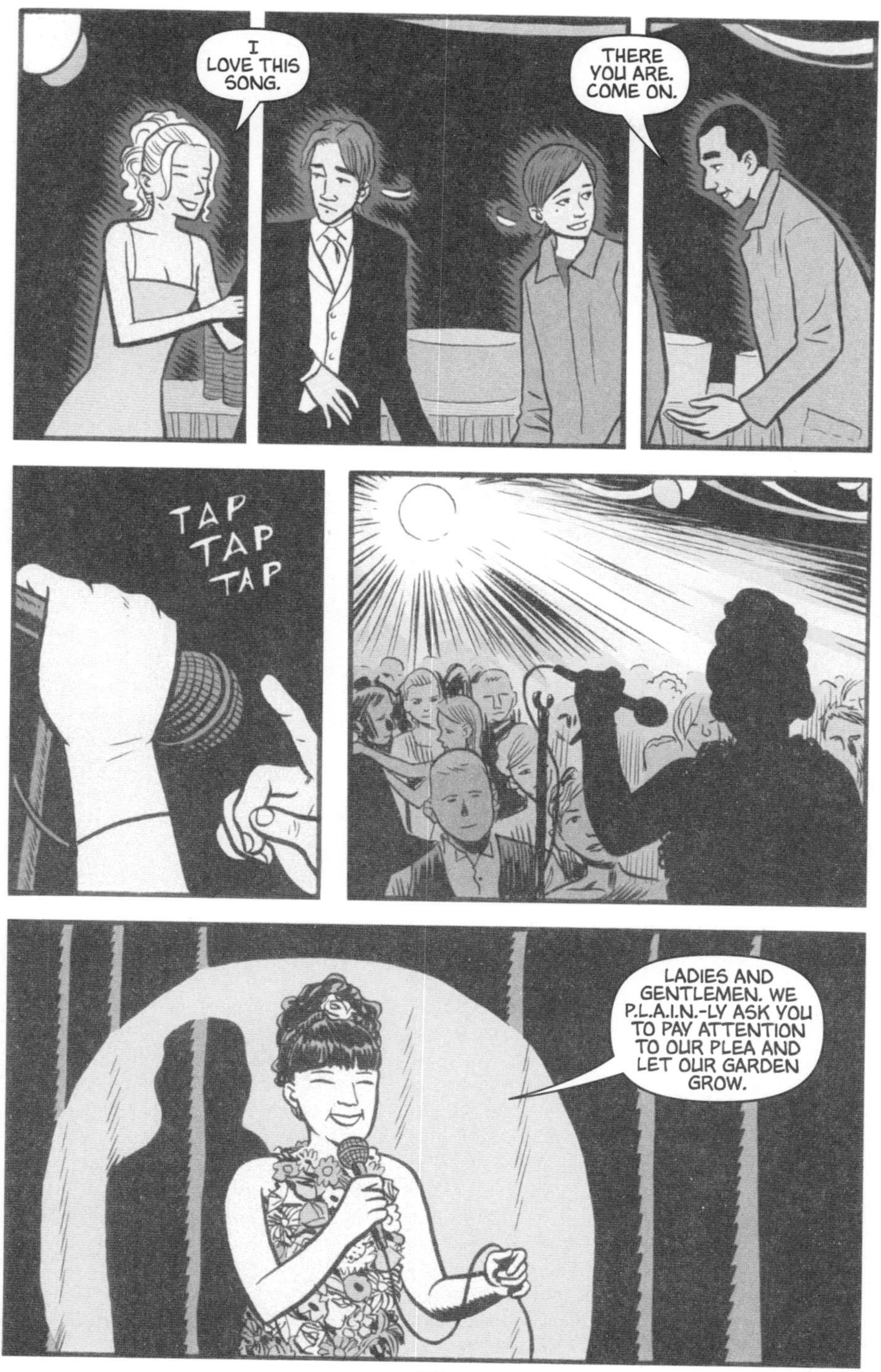
I LOVE THIS SONG.
THERE YOU ARE. COME ON.
TAP TAP TAP
LADIES AND GENTLEMEN. WE P.L.A.I.N.-LY ASK YOU TO PAY ATTENTION TO OUR PLEA AND LET OUR GARDEN GROW.

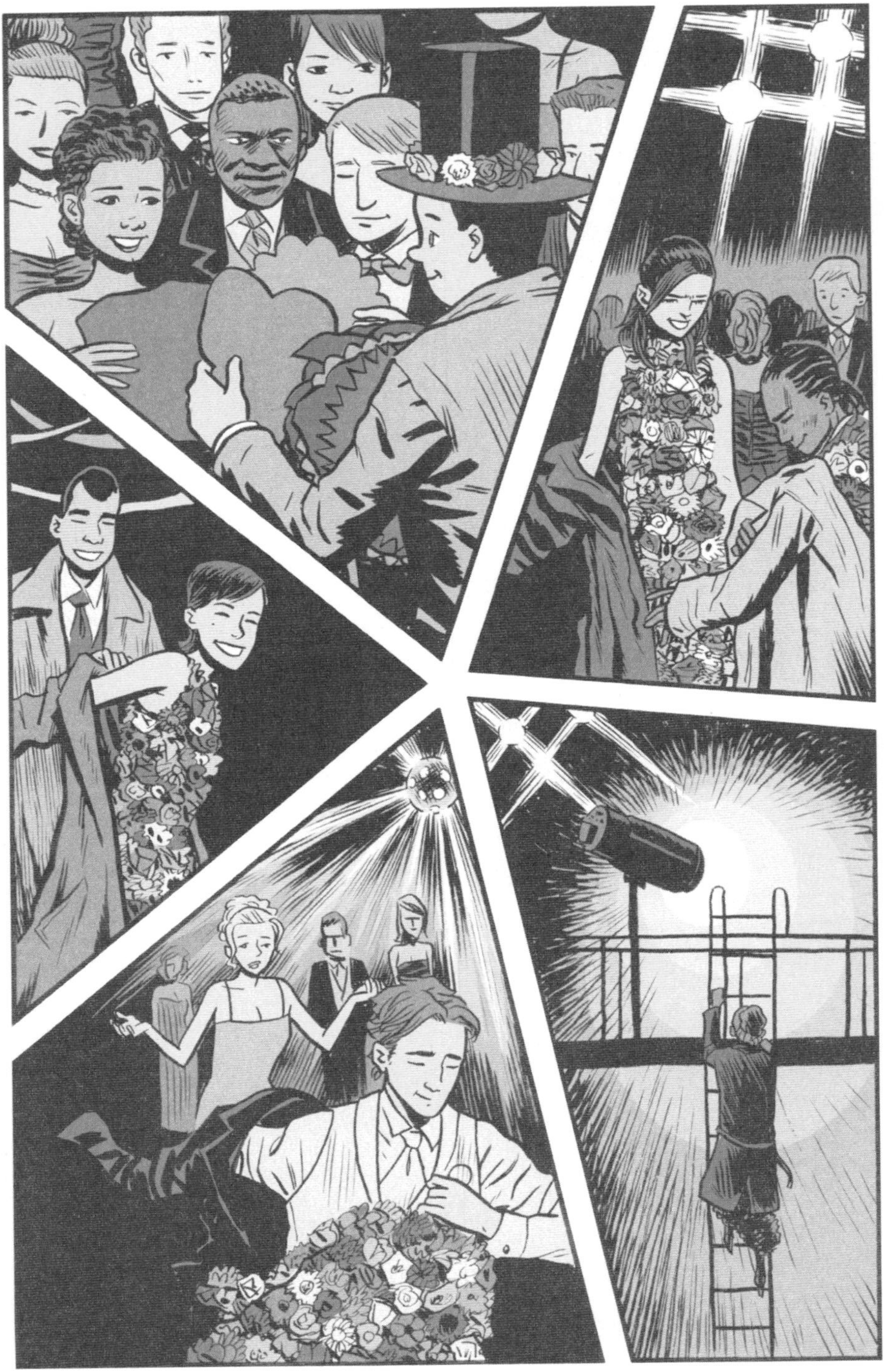

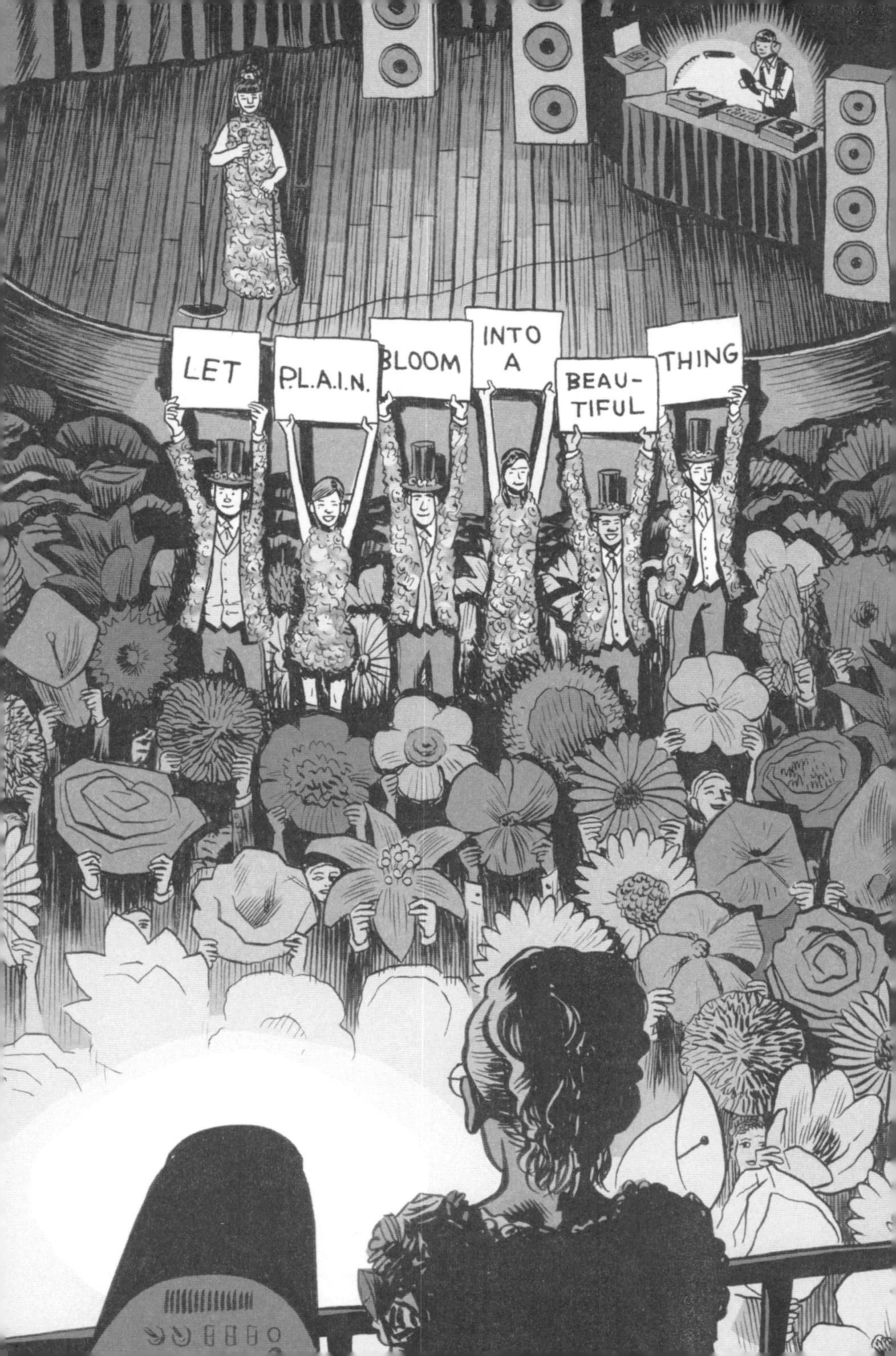
LET
P.L.A.I.N.
BLOOM
INTO A
BEAU-TIFUL
THING

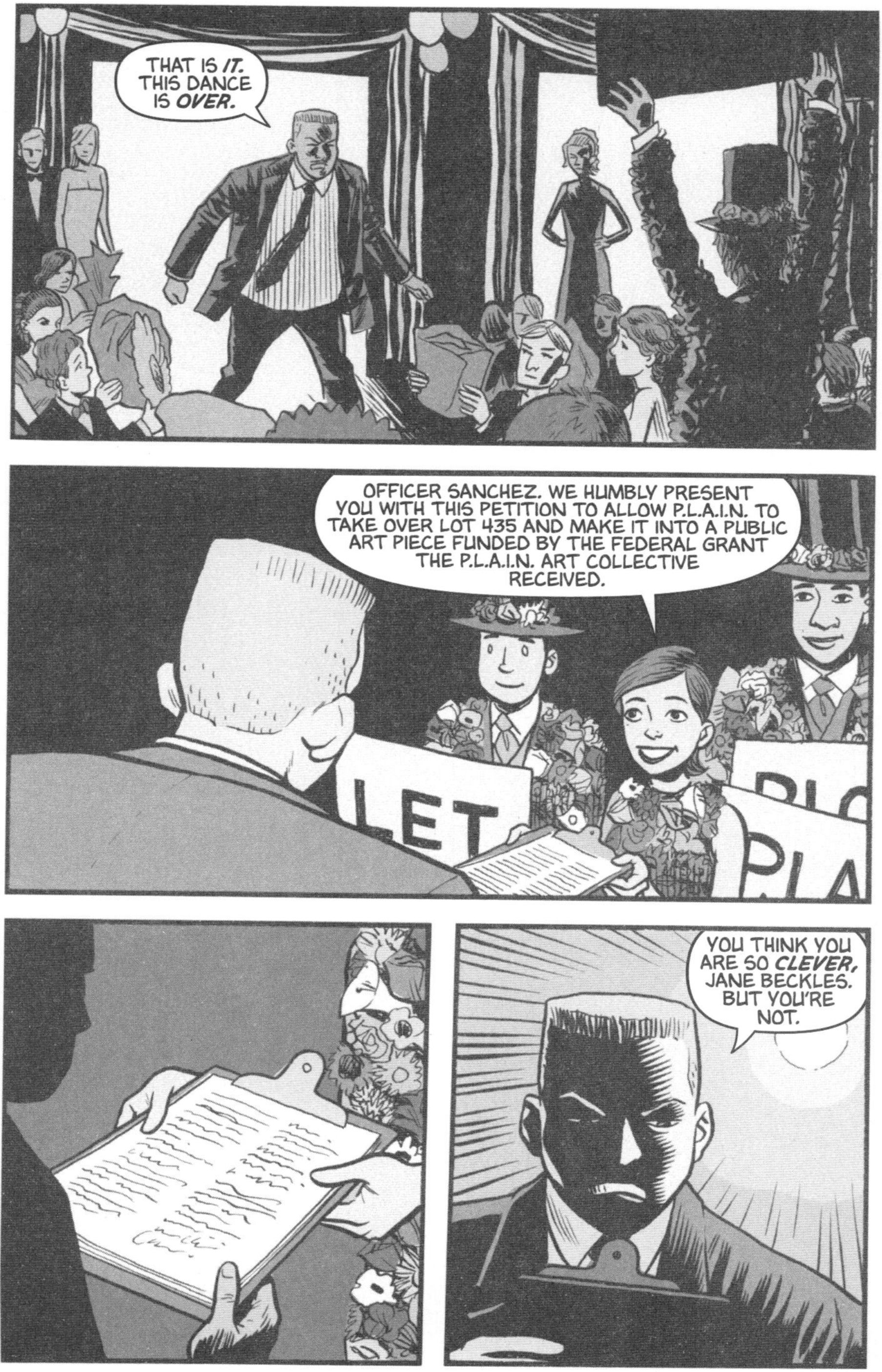
THAT IS *IT.* THIS DANCE IS *OVER.*
OFFICER SANCHEZ. WE HUMBLY PRESENT YOU WITH THIS PETITION TO ALLOW P.L.A.I.N. TO TAKE OVER LOT 435 AND MAKE IT INTO A PUBLIC ART PIECE FUNDED BY THE FEDERAL GRANT THE P.L.A.I.N. ART COLLECTIVE RECEIVED.
LET
YOU THINK YOU ARE SO *CLEVER,* JANE BECKLES. BUT YOU'RE NOT.

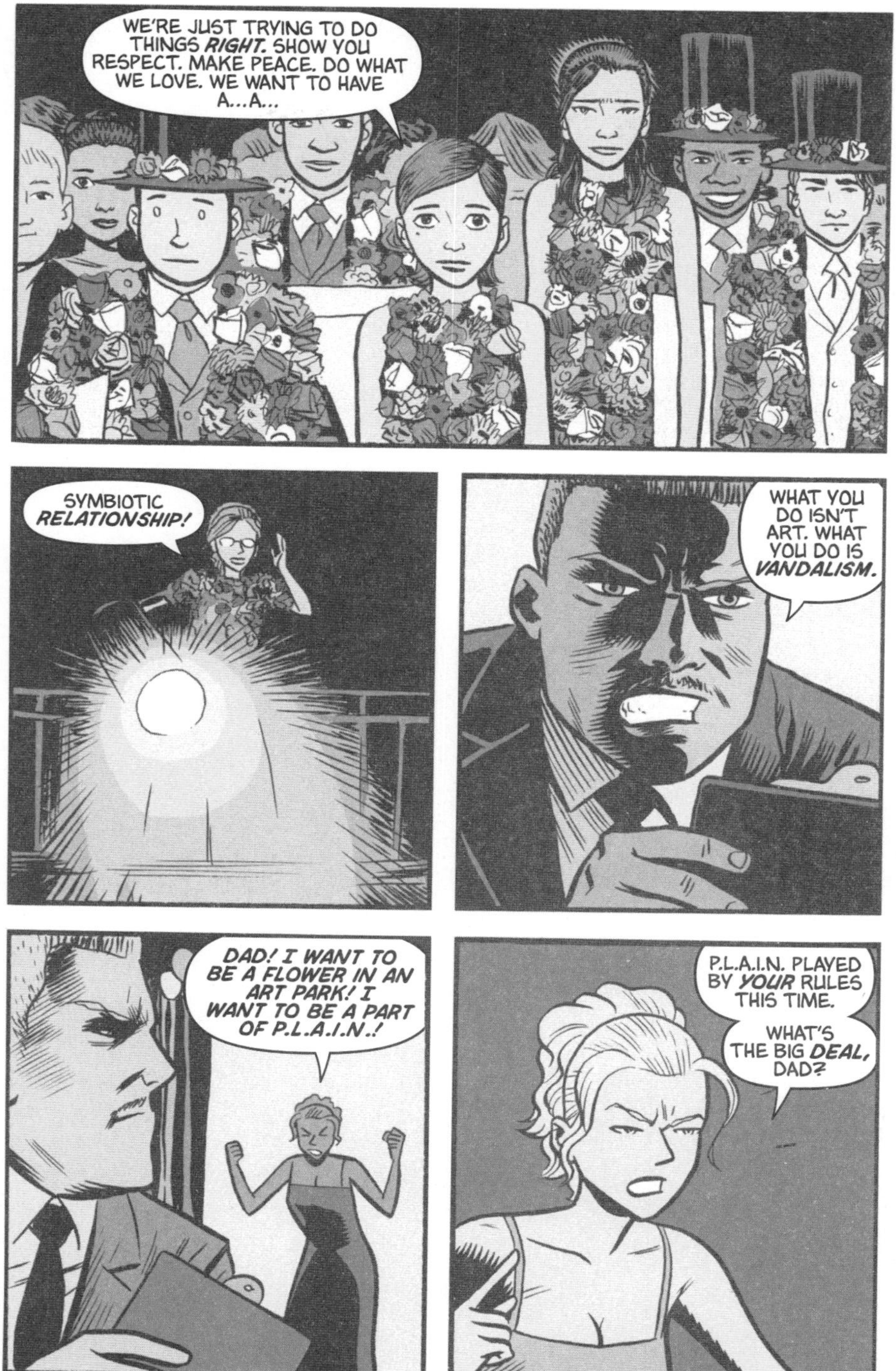

WE'RE JUST TRYING TO DO THINGS RIGHT. SHOW YOU RESPECT. MAKE PEACE. DO WHAT WE LOVE. WE WANT TO HAVE A...A...
SYMBIOTIC RELATIONSHIP!
WHAT YOU DO ISN'T ART. WHAT YOU DO IS VANDALISM.
DAD! I WANT TO BE A FLOWER IN AN ART PARK! I WANT TO BE A PART OF P.L.A.I.N.!
P.L.A.I.N. PLAYED BY YOUR RULES THIS TIME.
WHAT'S THE BIG DEAL, DAD?

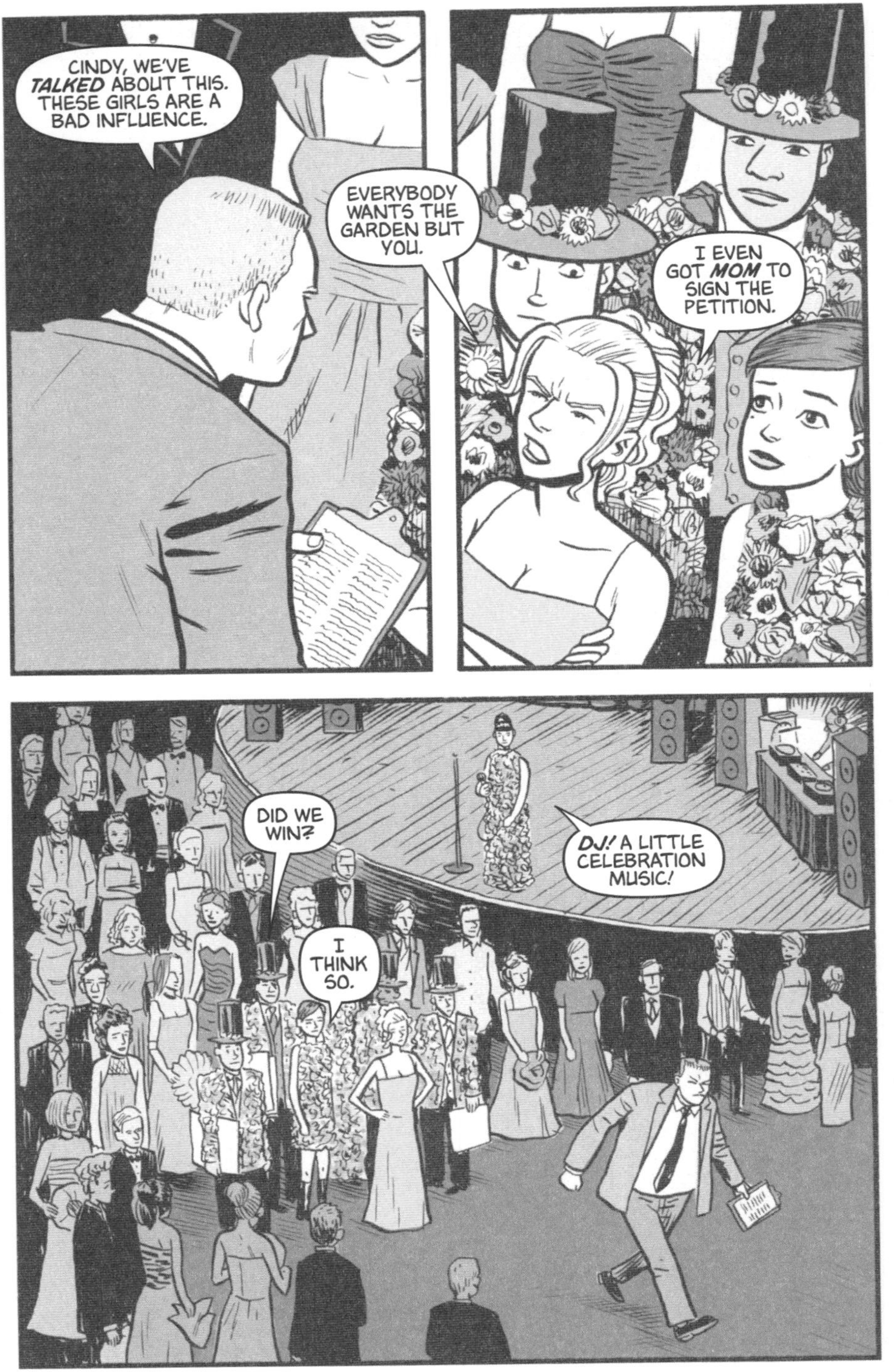
CINDY, WE'VE TALKED ABOUT THIS. THESE GIRLS ARE A BAD INFLUENCE.
EVERYBODY WANTS THE GARDEN BUT YOU.
I EVEN GOT MOM TO SIGN THE PETITION.
DID WE WIN?
I THINK SO.
DJ! A LITTLE CELEBRATION MUSIC!

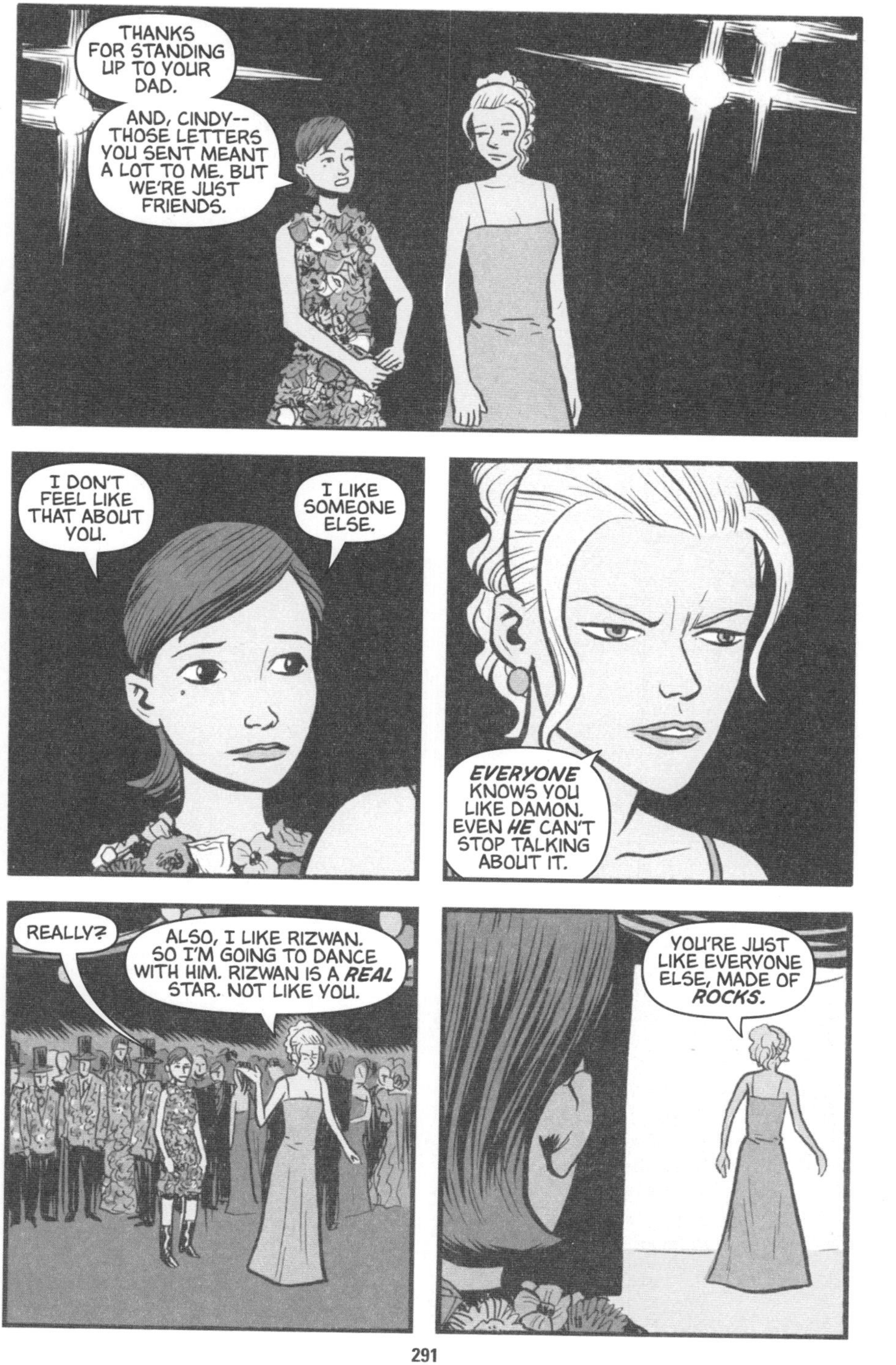
THANKS FOR STANDING UP TO YOUR DAD.
AND, CINDY-- THOSE LETTERS YOU SENT MEANT A LOT TO ME. BUT WE'RE JUST FRIENDS.
I DON'T FEEL LIKE THAT ABOUT YOU.
I LIKE SOMEONE ELSE.
EVERYONE KNOWS YOU LIKE DAMON. EVEN HE CAN'T STOP TALKING ABOUT IT.
REALLY?
ALSO, I LIKE RIZWAN. SO I'M GOING TO DANCE WITH HIM. RIZWAN IS A REAL STAR. NOT LIKE YOU.
YOU'RE JUST LIKE EVERYONE ELSE, MADE OF ROCKS.

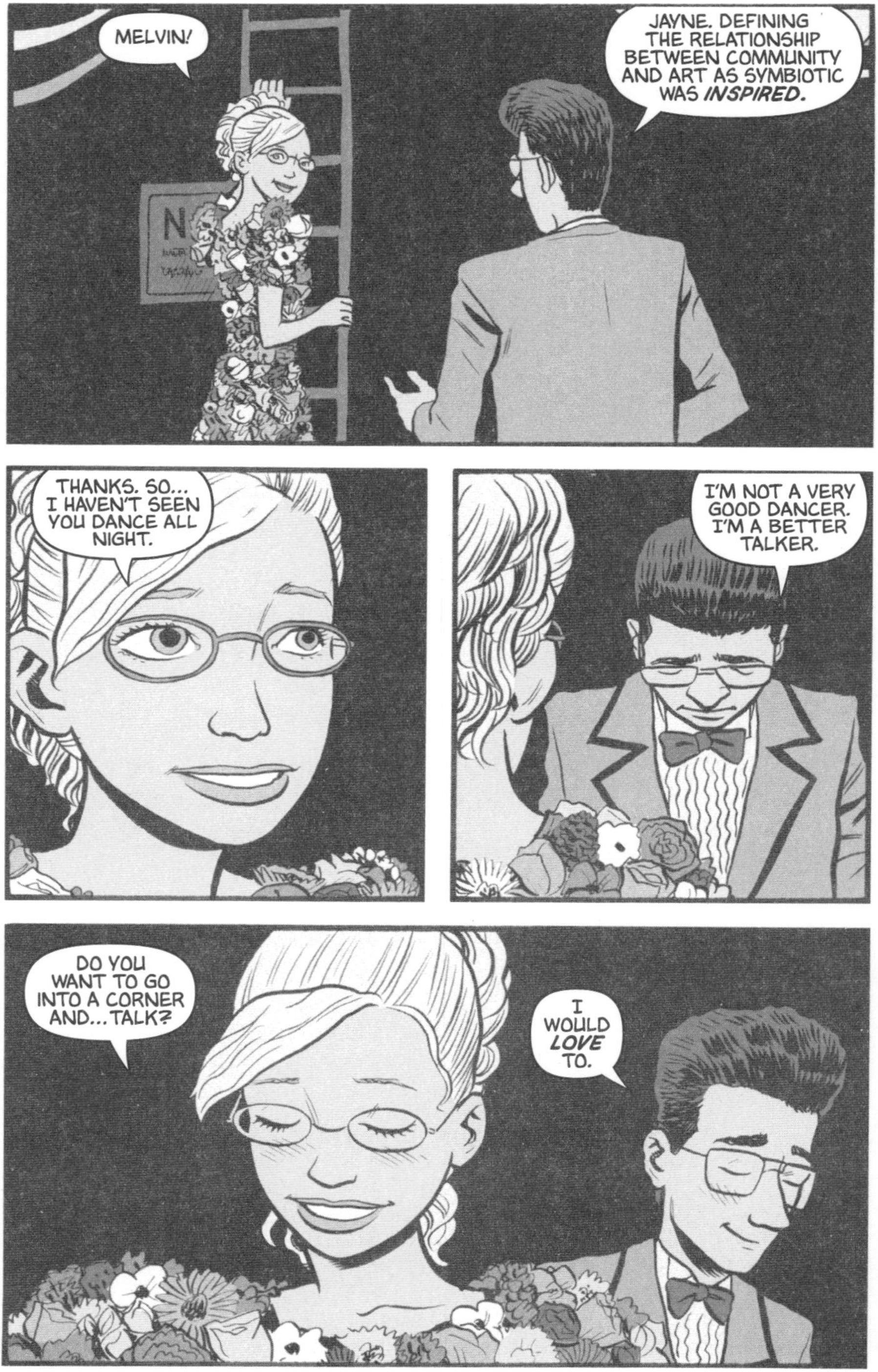
MELVIN!
JAYNE. DEFINING THE RELATIONSHIP BETWEEN COMMUNITY AND ART AS SYMBIOTIC WAS *INSPIRED.*
THANKS. SO... I HAVEN'T SEEN YOU DANCE ALL NIGHT.
I'M NOT A VERY GOOD DANCER. I'M A BETTER TALKER.
DO YOU WANT TO GO INTO A CORNER AND... TALK?
I WOULD *LOVE* TO.

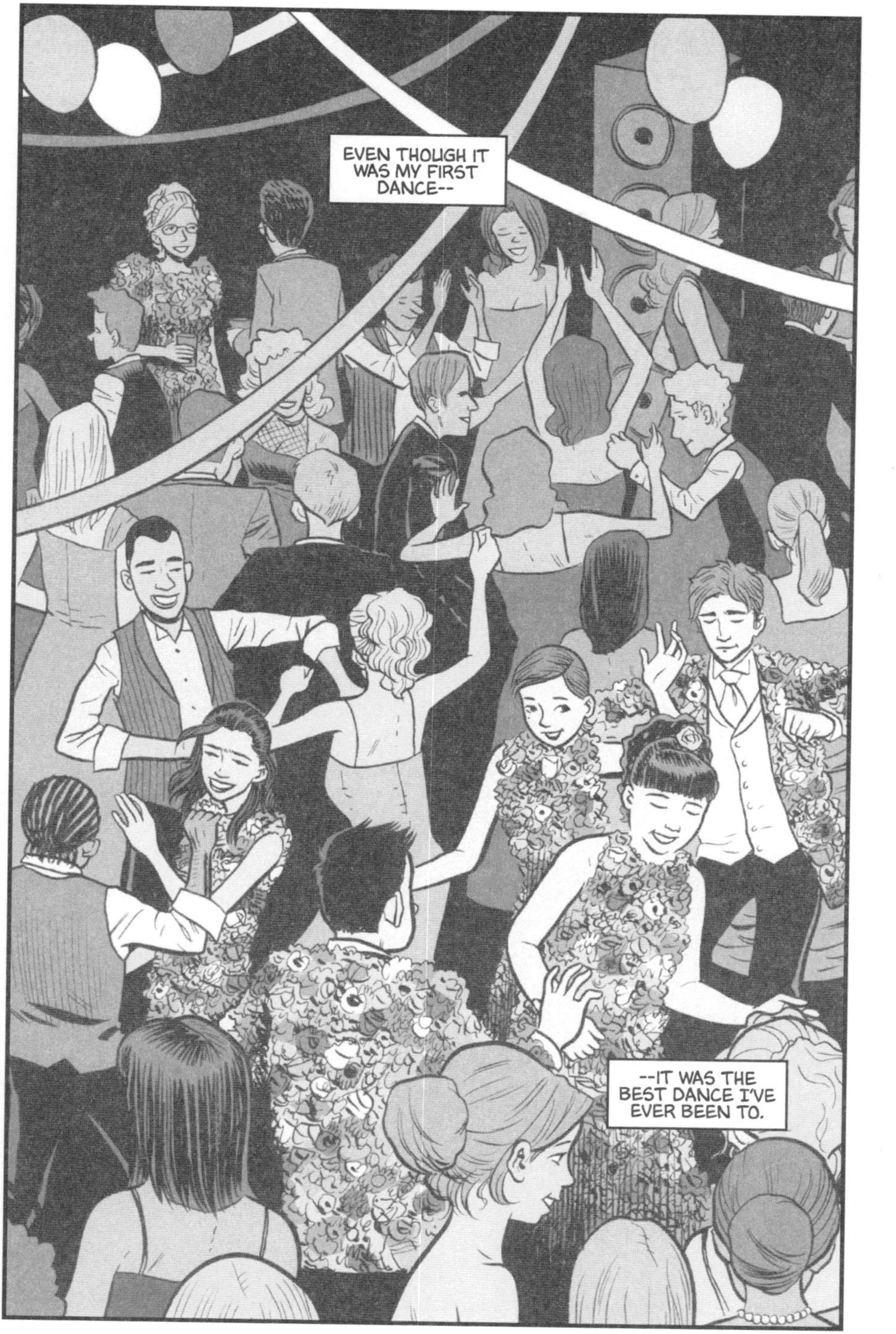
EVEN THOUGH IT WAS MY FIRST DANCE--
--IT WAS THE BEST DANCE I'VE EVER BEEN TO.

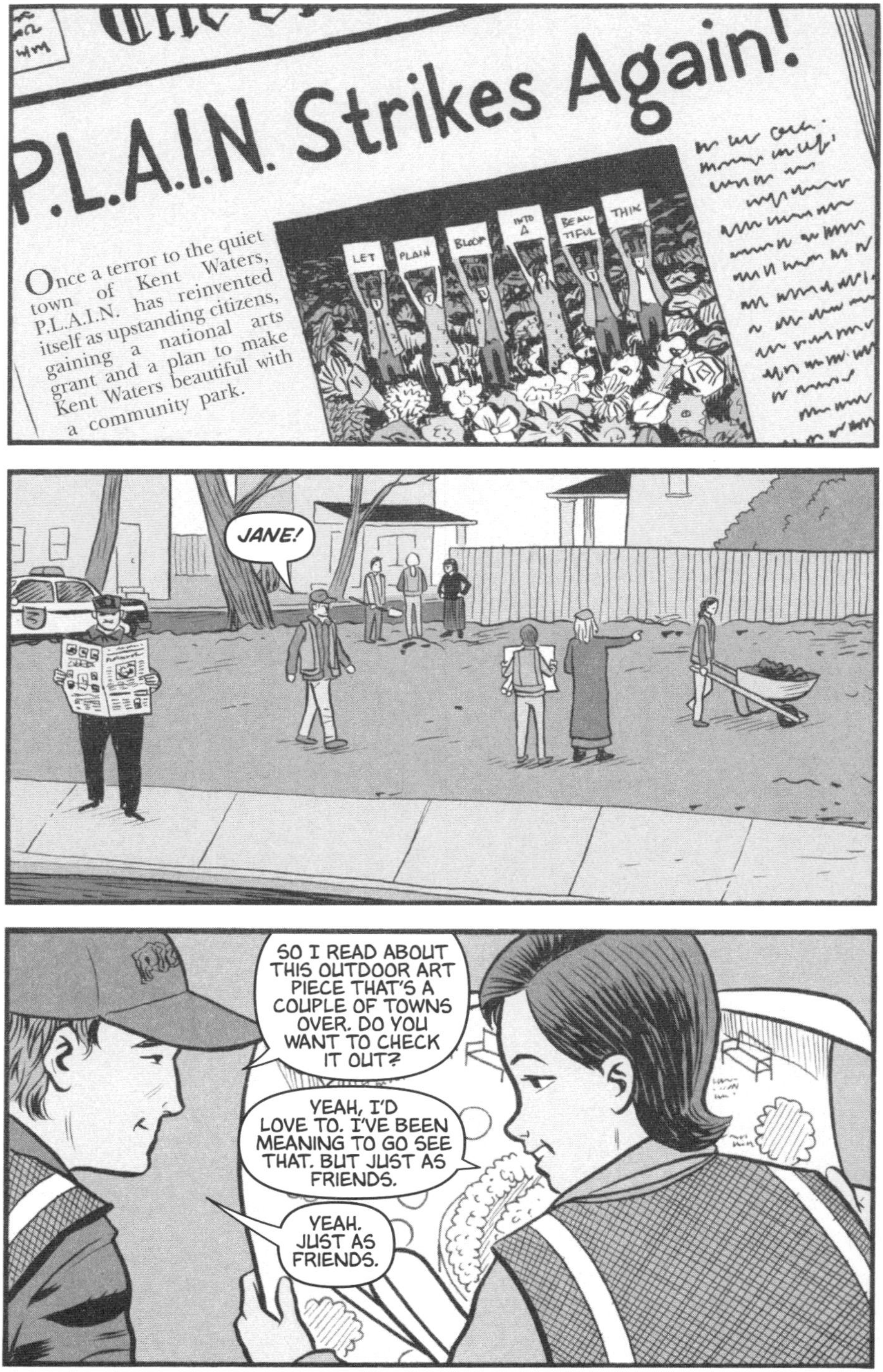
P.L.A.I.N. Strikes Again!
Once a terror to the quiet town of Kent Waters, P.L.A.I.N. has reinvented itself as upstanding citizens, gaining a national arts grant and a plan to make Kent Waters beautiful with a community park.
LET
PLAIN
BLOOM
INTO
A
BEAUTIFUL
THING
JANE!
SO I READ ABOUT THIS OUTDOOR ART PIECE THAT'S A COUPLE OF TOWNS OVER. DO YOU WANT TO CHECK IT OUT?
YEAH, I'D LOVE TO. I'VE BEEN MEANING TO GO SEE THAT. BUT JUST AS FRIENDS.
YEAH. JUST AS FRIENDS.

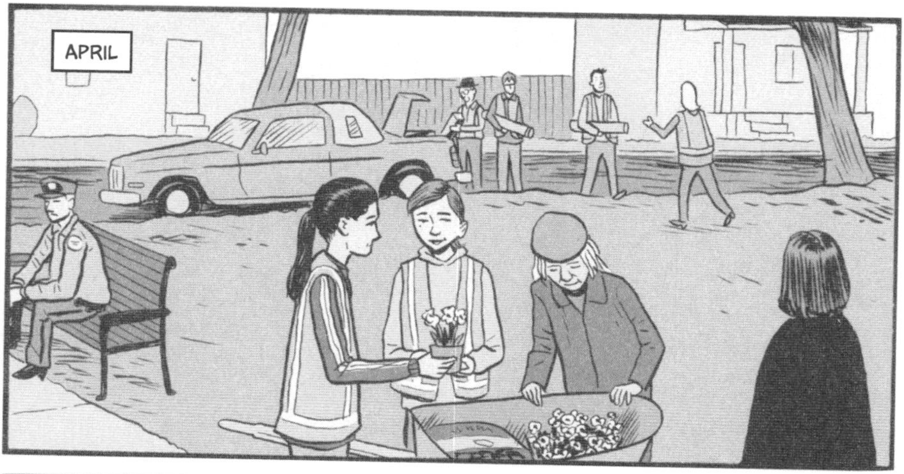
APRIL

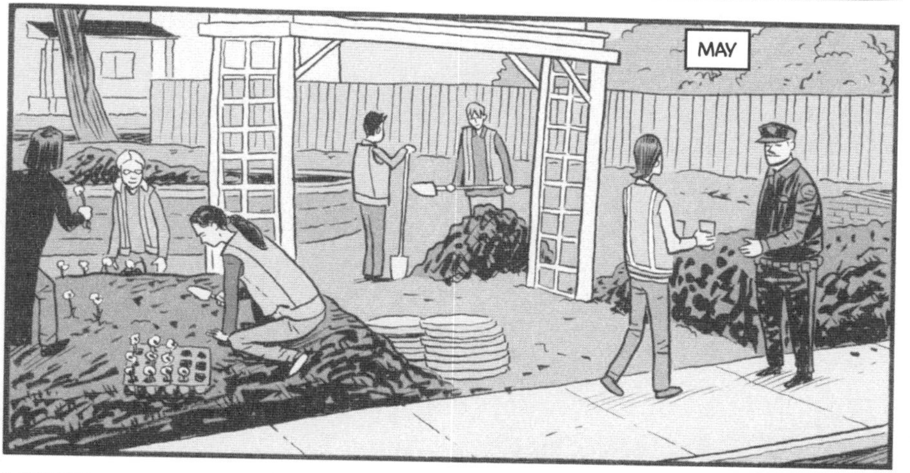
MAY

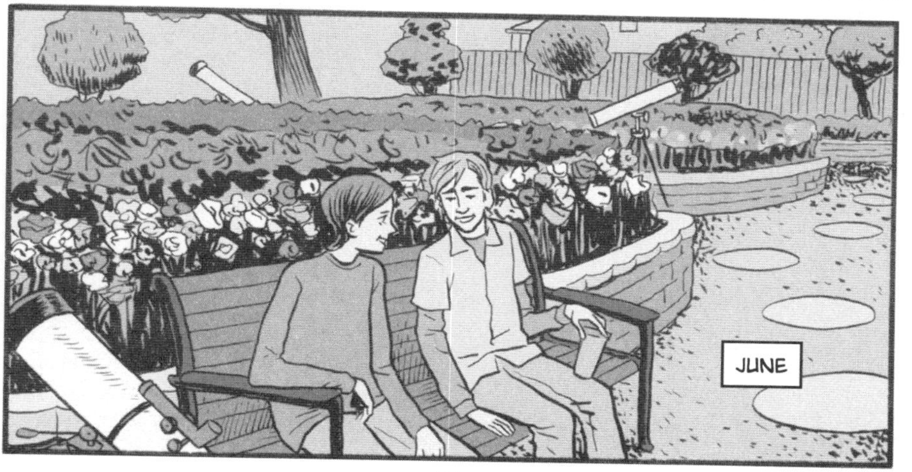
JUNE

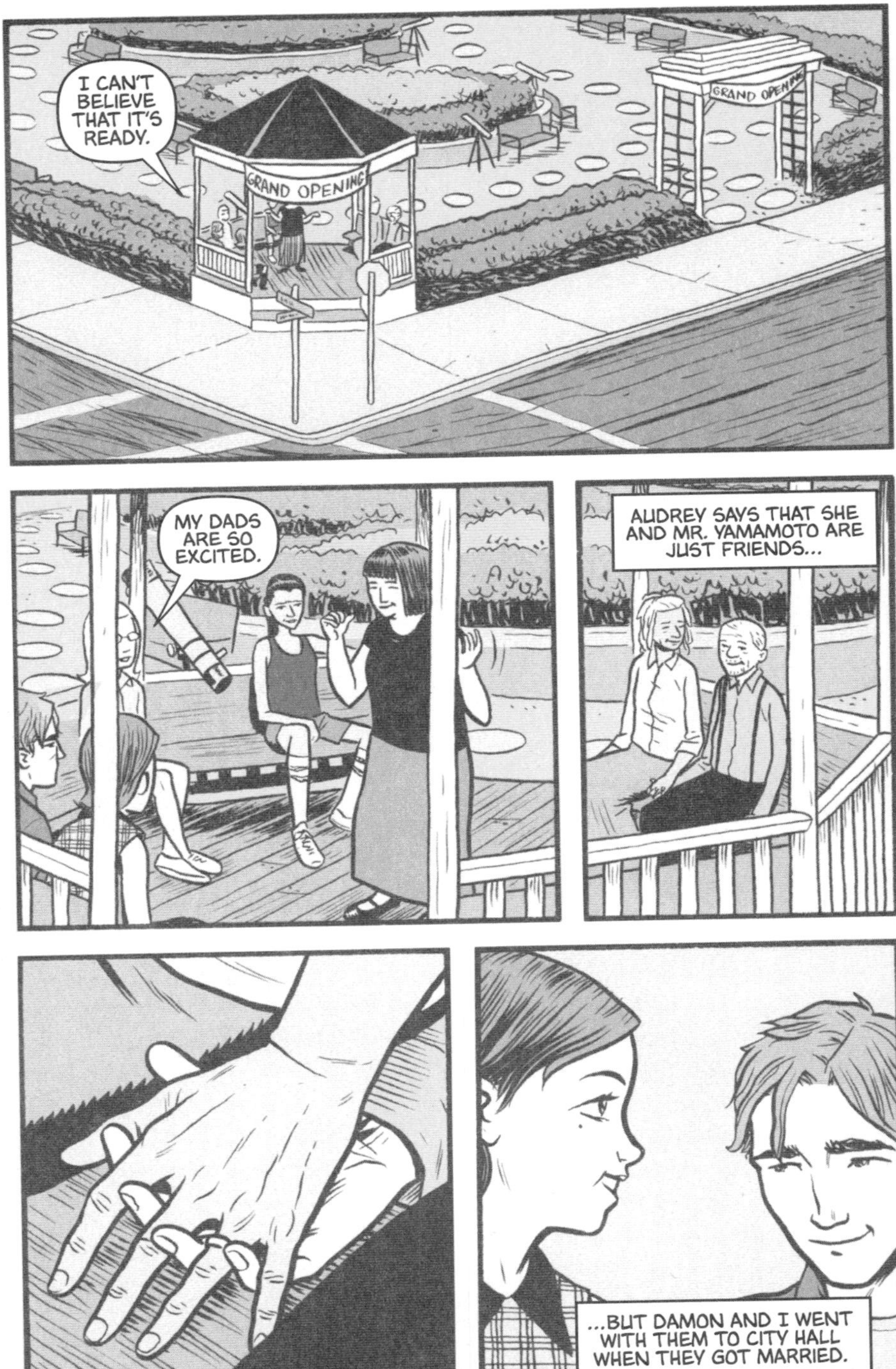

I CAN'T BELIEVE THAT IT'S READY.
GRAND OPENING
GRAND OPENING
MY DADS ARE SO EXCITED.
AUDREY SAYS THAT SHE AND MR. YAMAMOTO ARE JUST FRIENDS...
...BUT DAMON AND I WENT WITH THEM TO CITY HALL WHEN THEY GOT MARRIED.

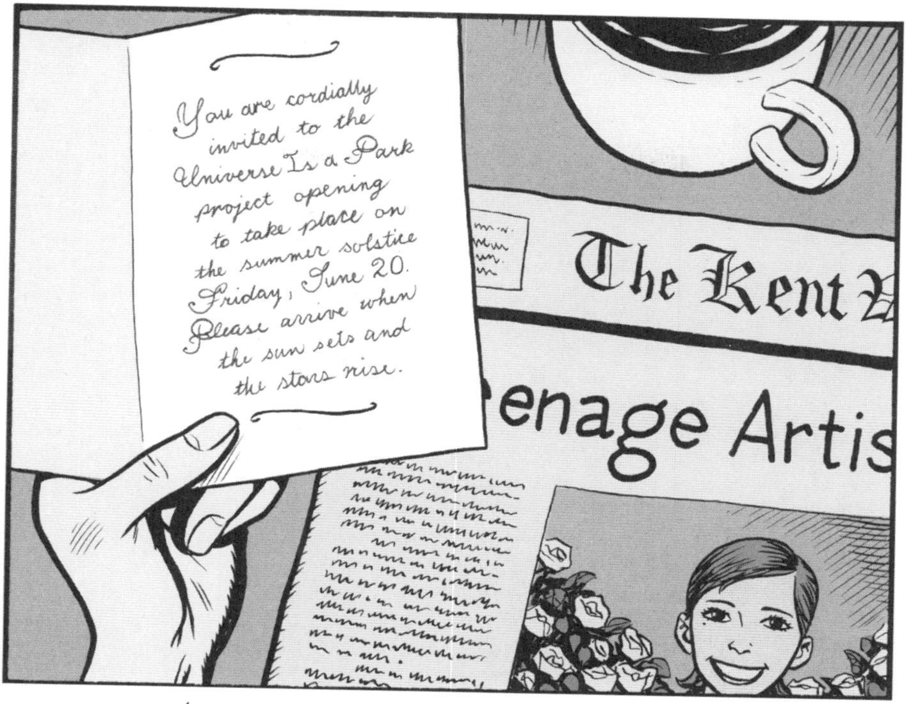
You are cordially invited to the Universe Is a Park project opening to take place on the summer solstice Friday, June 20. Please arrive when the sun sets and the stars rise.
The Kent
enage Artis

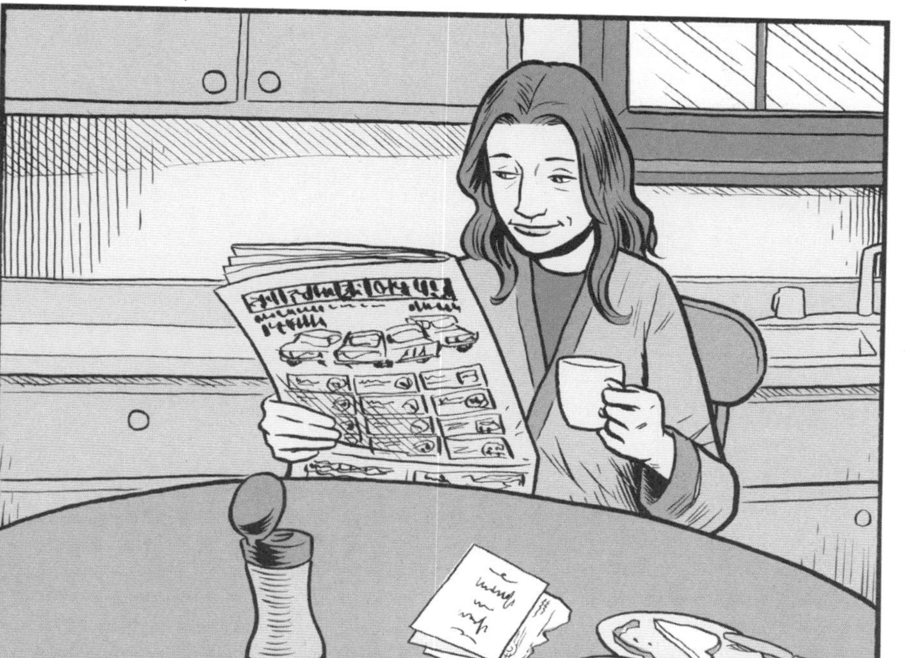

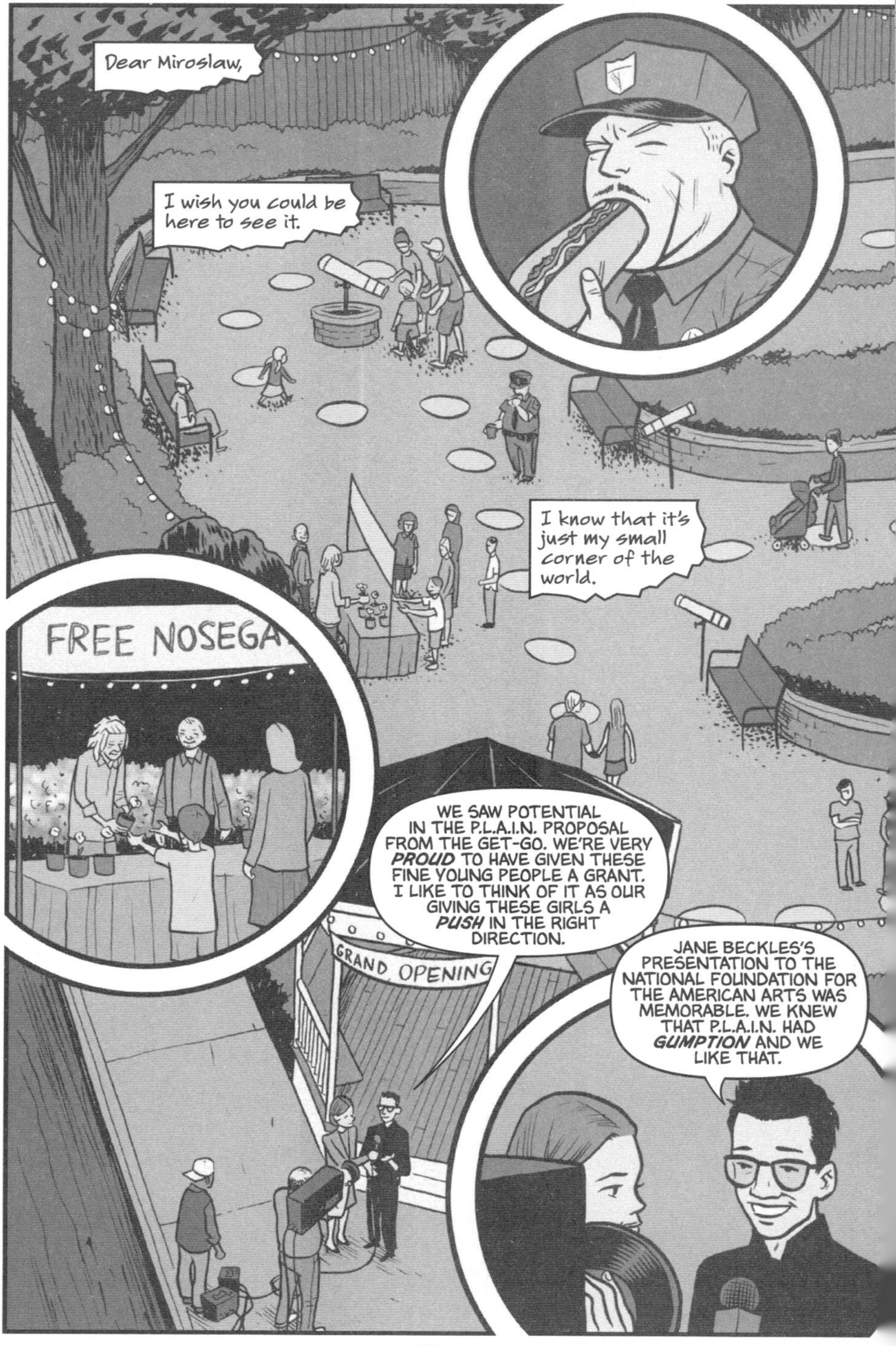
Dear Miroslaw,
I wish you could be here to see it.
I know that it's just my small corner of the world.
FREE NOSEGA
WE SAW POTENTIAL IN THE P.L.A.I.N. PROPOSAL FROM THE GET-GO. WE'RE VERY *PROUD* TO HAVE GIVEN THESE FINE YOUNG PEOPLE A GRANT. I LIKE TO THINK OF IT AS OUR GIVING THESE GIRLS A *PUSH* IN THE RIGHT DIRECTION.
GRAND OPENING
JANE BECKLES'S PRESENTATION TO THE NATIONAL FOUNDATION FOR THE AMERICAN ARTS WAS MEMORABLE. WE KNEW THAT P.L.A.I.N. HAD *GUMPTION* AND WE LIKE THAT.

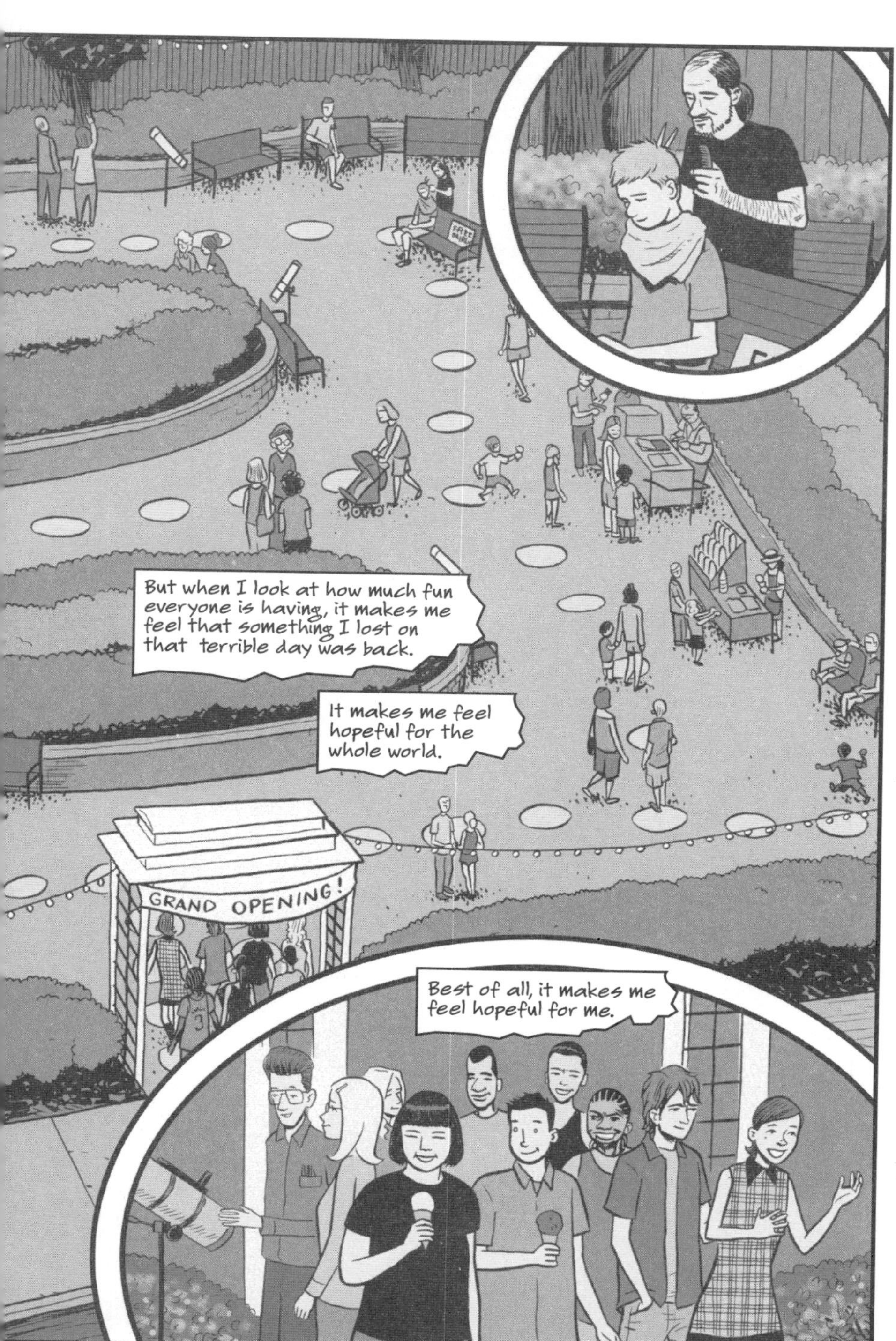
But when I look at how much fun everyone is having, it makes me feel that something I lost on that terrible day was back.
It makes me feel hopeful for the whole world.
GRAND OPENING!
Best of all, it makes me feel hopeful for me.

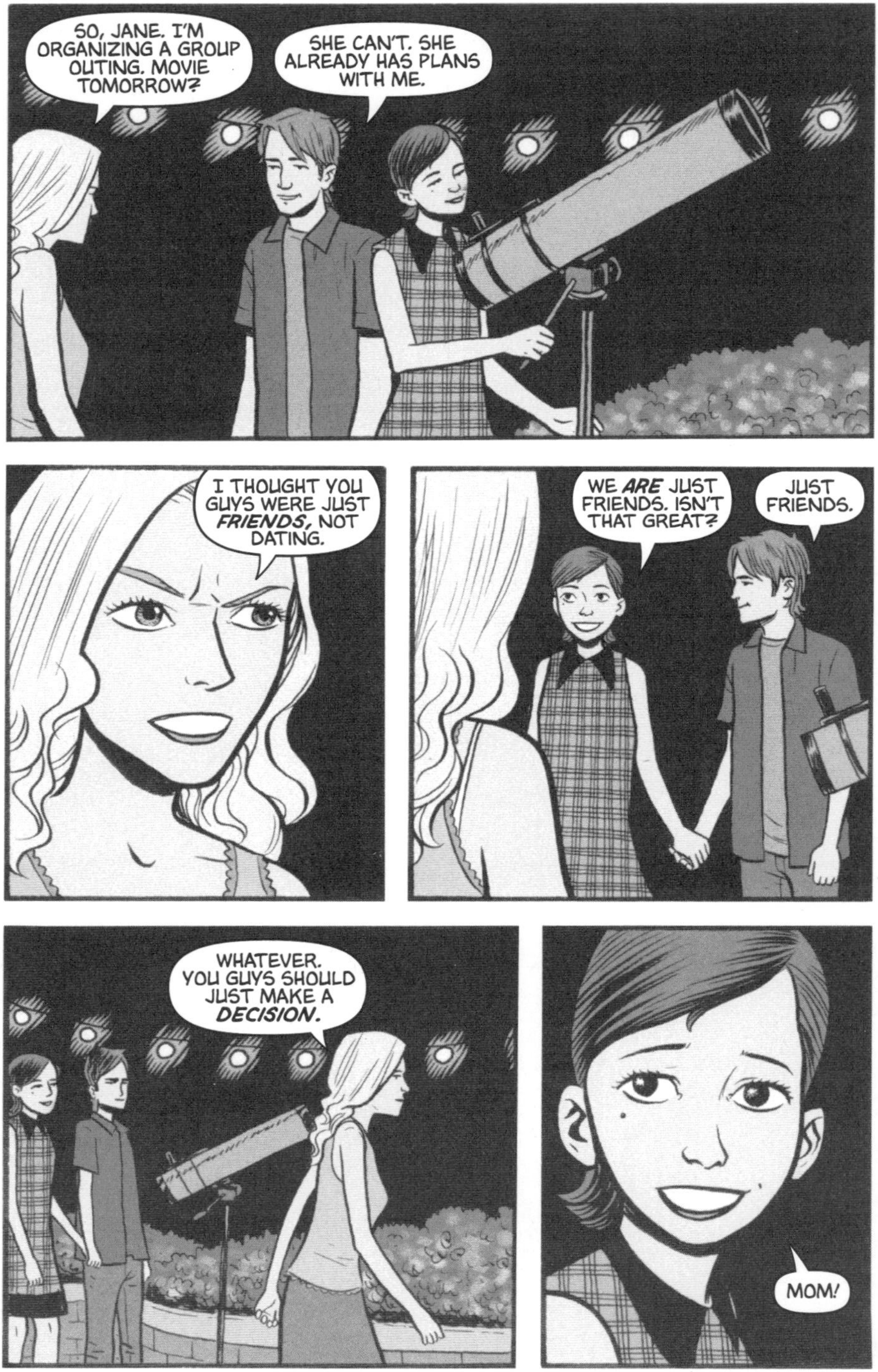
SO, JANE. I'M ORGANIZING A GROUP OUTING. MOVIE TOMORROW?
SHE CAN'T. SHE ALREADY HAS PLANS WITH ME.
I THOUGHT YOU GUYS WERE JUST FRIENDS, NOT DATING.
WE ARE JUST FRIENDS. ISN'T THAT GREAT?
JUST FRIENDS.
WHATEVER. YOU GUYS SHOULD JUST MAKE A DECISION.
MOM!

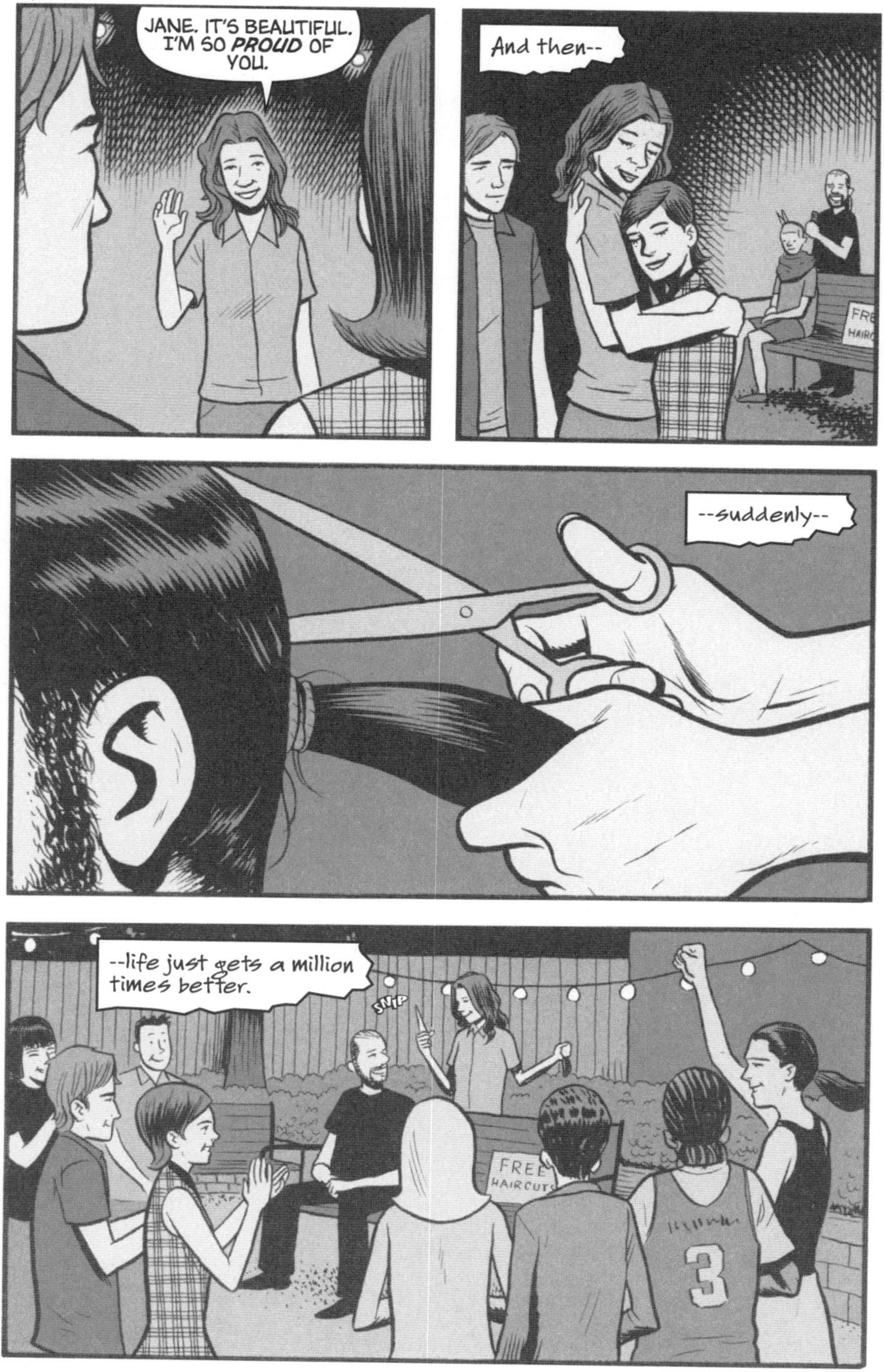
JANE. IT'S BEAUTIFUL. I'M SO *PROUD* OF YOU.
And then--
--suddenly--
--life just gets a million times better.
SNIP
FREE
3

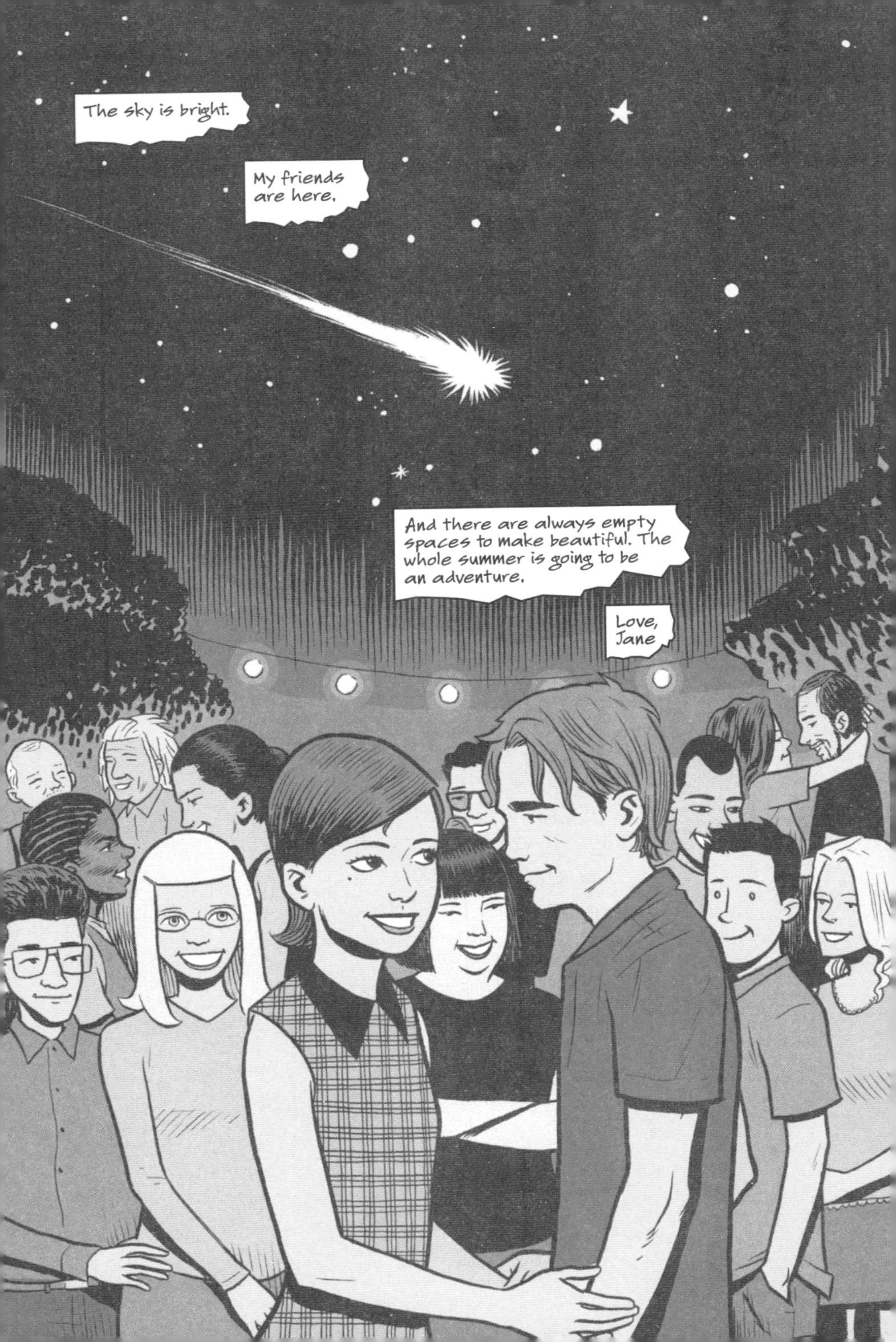
The sky is bright.
My friends are here.
And there are always empty spaces to make beautiful. The whole summer is going to be an adventure.
Love, Jane

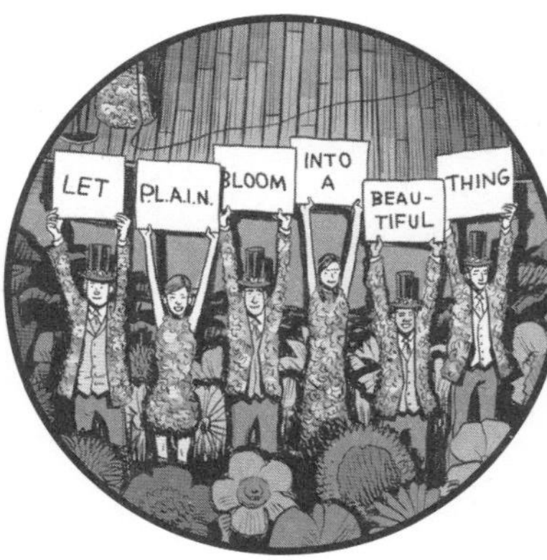
LET
P.L.A.I.N.
BLOOM
INTO A
BEAU-TIFUL
THING

The Evolution of a Graphic Novel
Step 1: The Manuscript

JANES IN LOVE – pgs 1 -40   3/12/07
Writer: Cecil Castellucci

CAPTION: Dear Miroslaw,

Making Art is a like my love letter to the everyone.

Panel 2

Long and skinny, we see that there are the puppets hanging beautifully from street lamps along the street. A sign taped to the pole. There are many of us. We're PLAINly here to stay.

CAPTION: This is my world. I know it's not Metro City.   But that doesn't mean I can't make Kent Waters interesting.

Panel 3

Jane is in bed she's smiling. One of the marionettes she's saved, is hanging above her or maybe it's on the night table next to her.

CAPTION: I want to make it as surprisingly beautiful as possible.

It's still worth the effort.

Don't you think?

Panel 4

Jane is outside of her parents salon on her way to school, she's waving goodbye.   Her dad is looking up at one of the marionettes.   He's smiling. Jane's Mom is in the window of the store hanging up a poster that says "New Salon Rules for Valentines Day Season: If you've just broken up with your boyfriend / girlfriend / significant other we will NOT CUT your hair."

CAPTION: Art is no trouble at all.

Love, Jane

Page 6

Panel 1

Jane outside of Buzz Aldrin as all the kids are spilling into the building. It's the first week of January.   Pretty much, I think here, we should see each of the Jane's sort of standing together looking sadly at all of their crushes. (James has no crush, poor guy. He's bummed about that.) So, that is Isaac, Melvin, Damon. Theater Jane is holding up a postcard from Rhys (from a Midsummer nights dream).
This should be the biggest panel on the page. It's also still winter.

JANES IN LOVE – pgs 1 -40   3/12/07
Writer: Cecil Castellucci

CAPTION: It's a brand new year. That always means just one thing. Valentines day is coming up.

Everyone's hearts is on their sleeves.

Panel 2

Theater Jane is taking up the center stage. She's very excited. Polly Jane is probably, like eating.

THEATER JANE: Janes! I've had a note! In February Rhys is going to be in Midsummer Nights Dream in Metro City in an off off off Grandway Theater!!

POLLY JANE: So what?

Panel 3

Close up of Theater Jane. She's kind of swooning. She's in the romantic theatrical zone.

THEATER JANE: Wouldn't it be romantic to surprise him and go to the city to see him in the show?

Panel 4

Polly Jane is rolling her eyes. She is standing next to Jane. Who is having romantic thoughts of her own.

CAPTION: I'd like to surprise a boy.

Go to Poland. Meet Miroslaw.

Or down the street. Hang out with Damon.

Panel 5

Back to Brain Jayne. She's being as scientifically romantic as she can. Of course James is very interested in boys. Theater boys.

BRAIN JAYNE: Oh that would be romantic.

JAMES: Does Rhys have any cute friends?

Panel 6

On our Jane again.

Step 2: Thumbnail Sketches

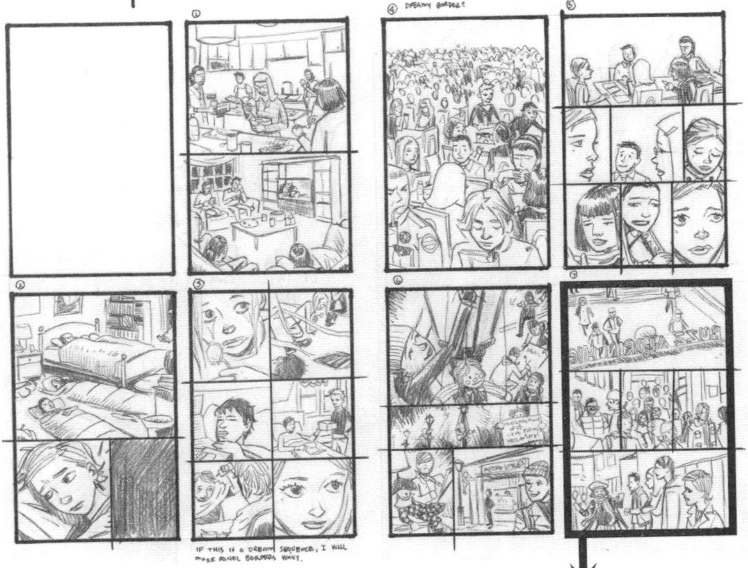

DREAMY BORDER?
IF THIS IS A DREAM SEQUENCE, I WILL MAKE PANEL BORDERS WAVY.

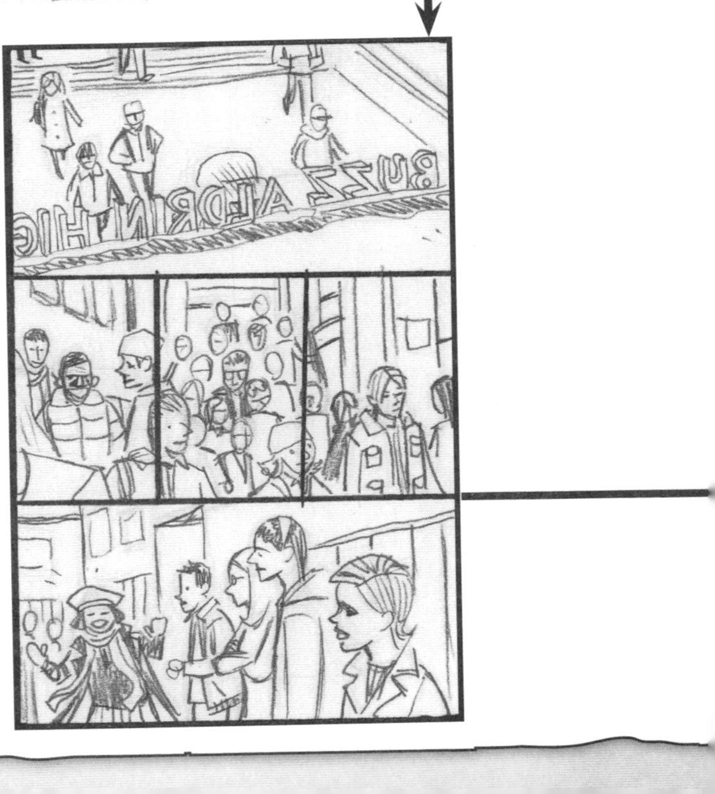

BUZZ ALDRIN HIG

Step 3: Inked Sketches

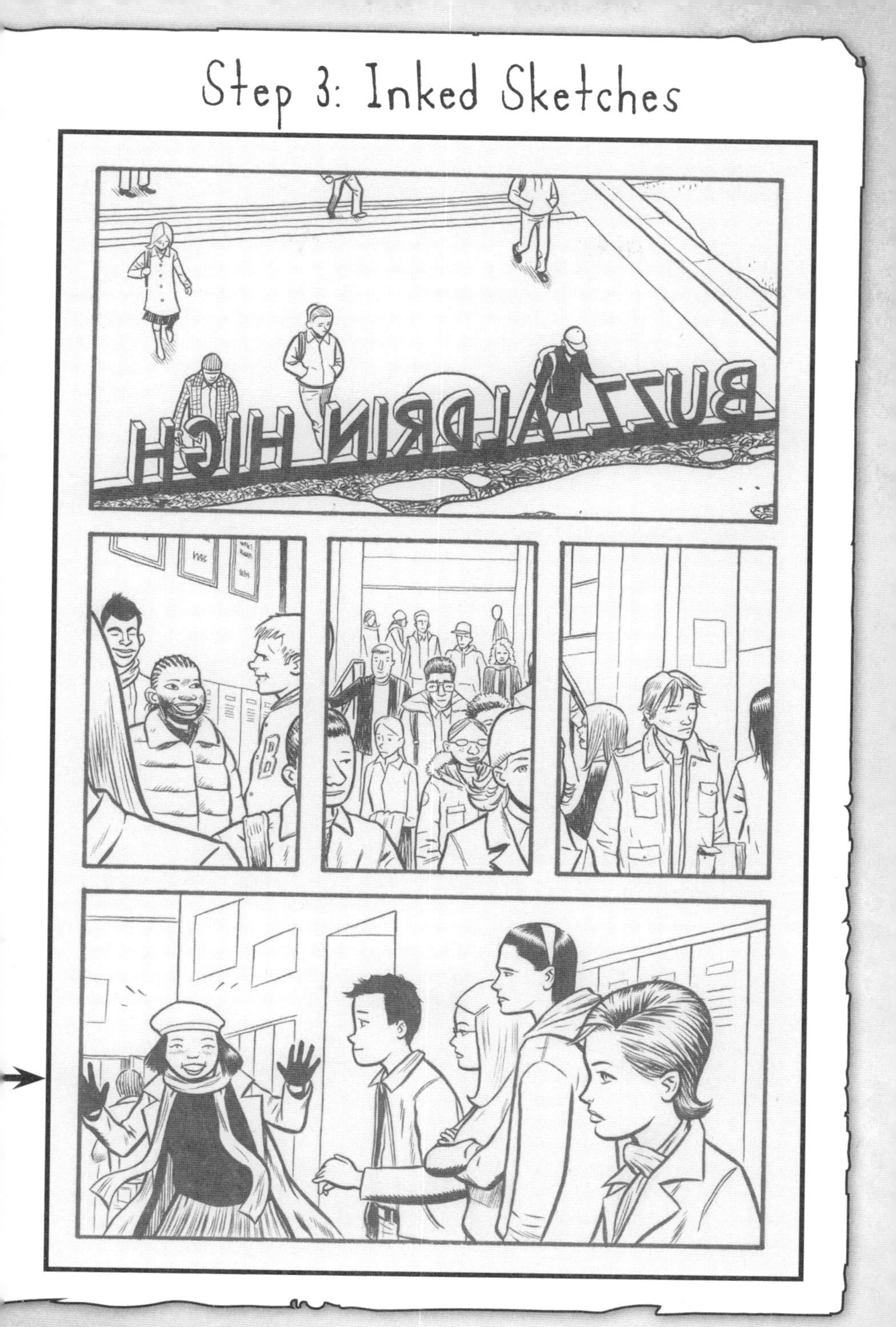
BUZZ ALDRIN HIGH

Step 4: Final Art

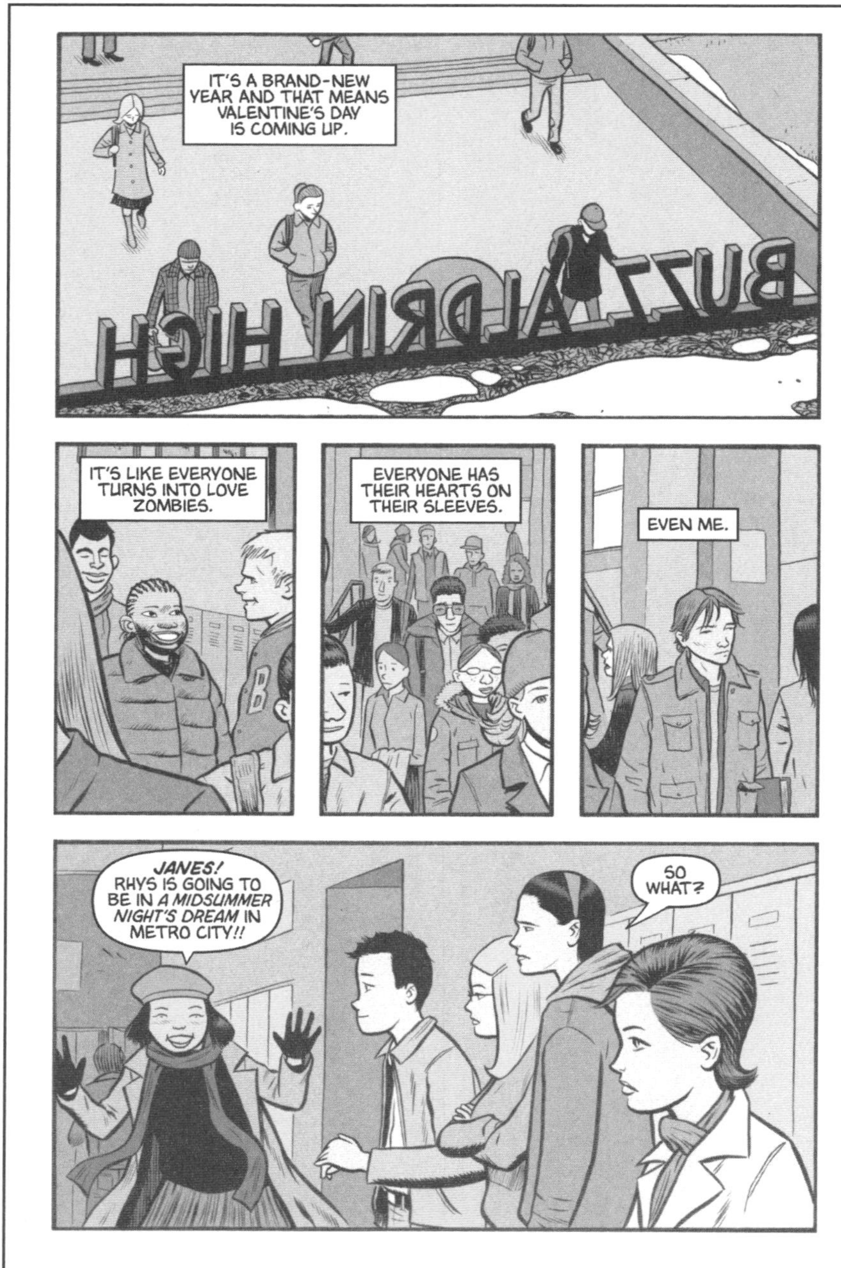
IT'S A BRAND-NEW YEAR AND THAT MEANS VALENTINE'S DAY IS COMING UP.
BUZZ ALDRIN HIGH
IT'S LIKE EVERYONE TURNS INTO LOVE ZOMBIES.
EVERYONE HAS THEIR HEARTS ON THEIR SLEEVES.
EVEN ME.
JANES! RHYS IS GOING TO BE IN *A MIDSUMMER NIGHT'S DREAM* IN METRO CITY!!
SO WHAT?

Original Cover Sketches for *Janes in Love*

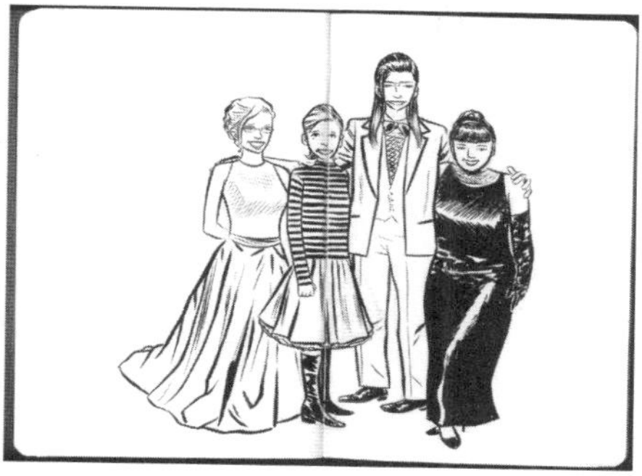

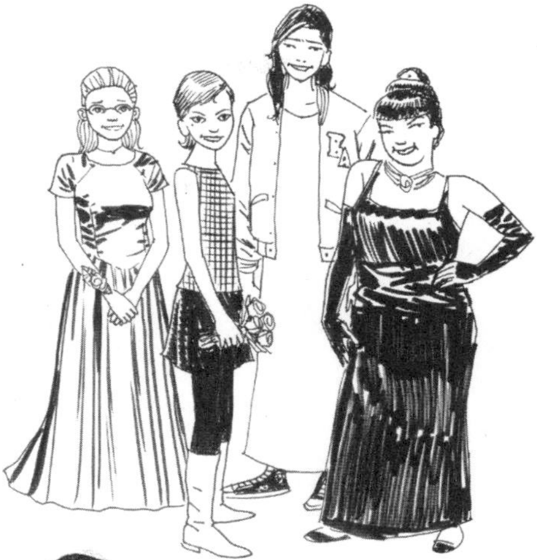

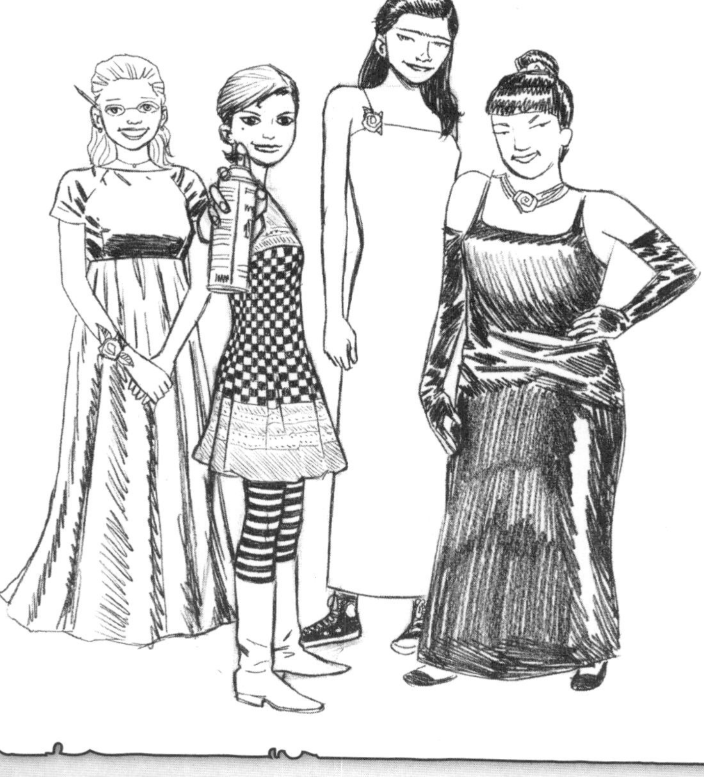

BA

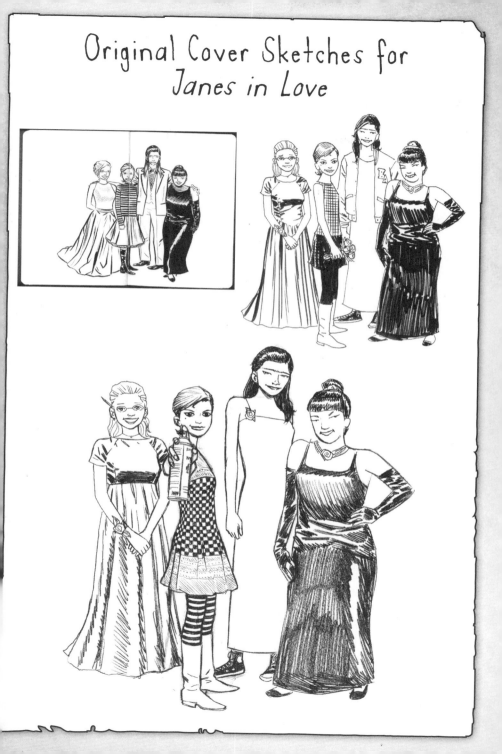

Cover Options

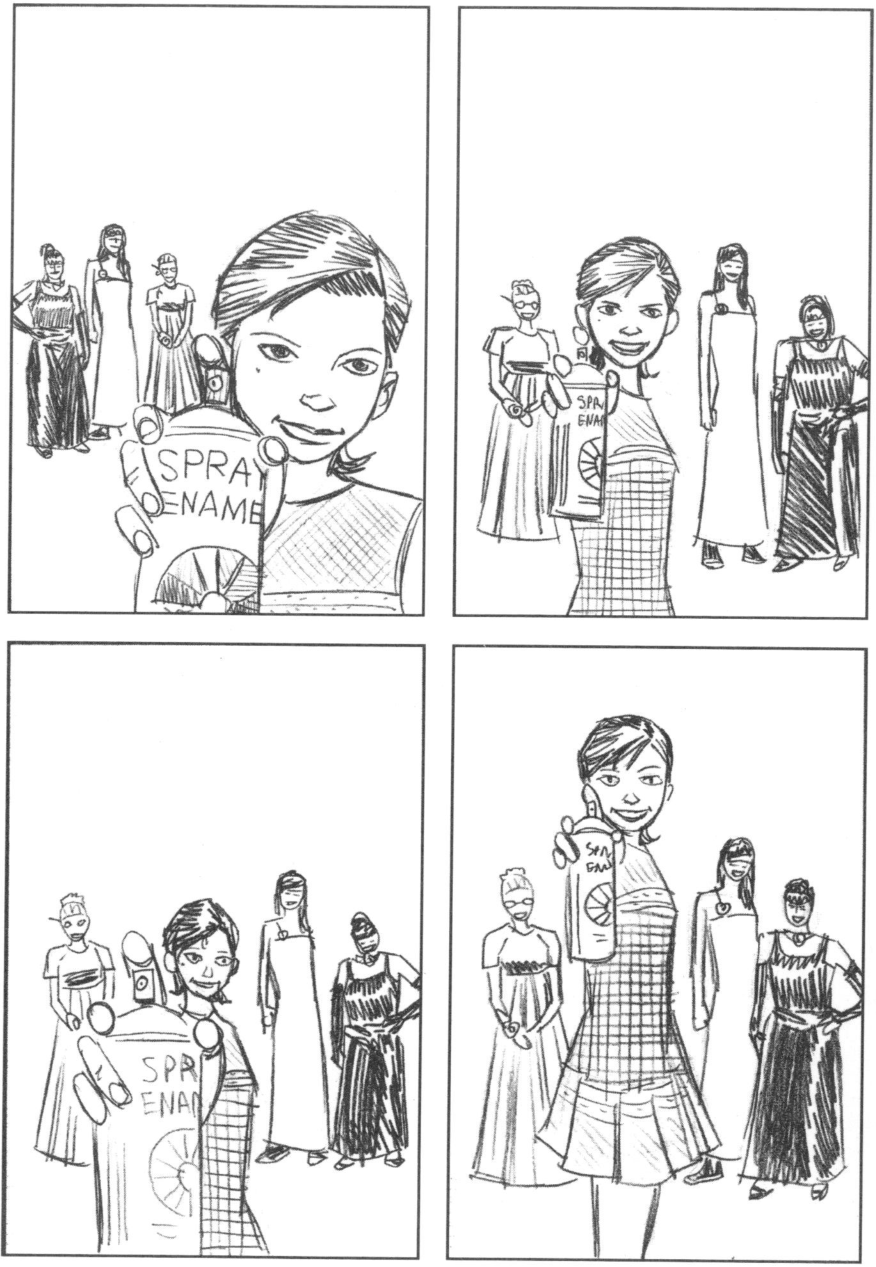

SPRAY ENAME
SPRA ENAM
SPR ENAM
SPR ENAM

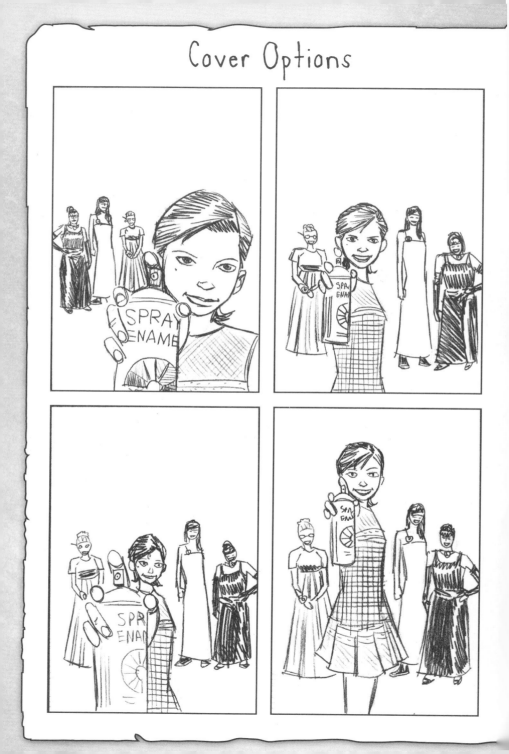

More Cover Options

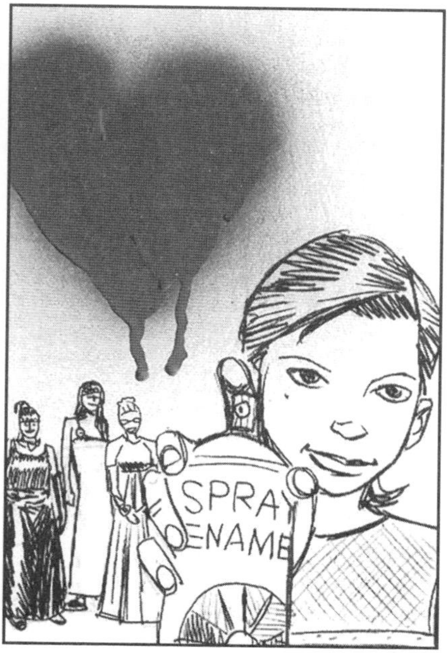
SPRAY
ENAME

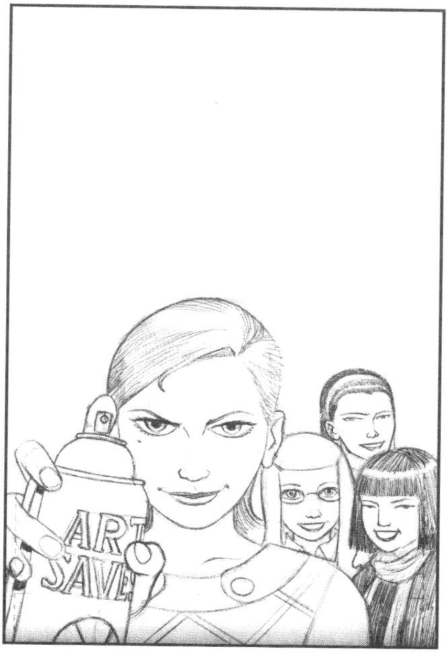
ART
SAVE

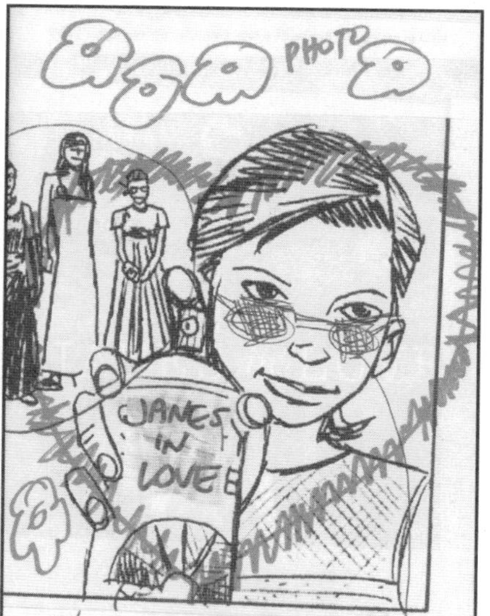
PHOTO
JANES IN LOVE
dressed for attack
CECIL CASTELLUCCI
and JIM RUGG
cool sunglasses

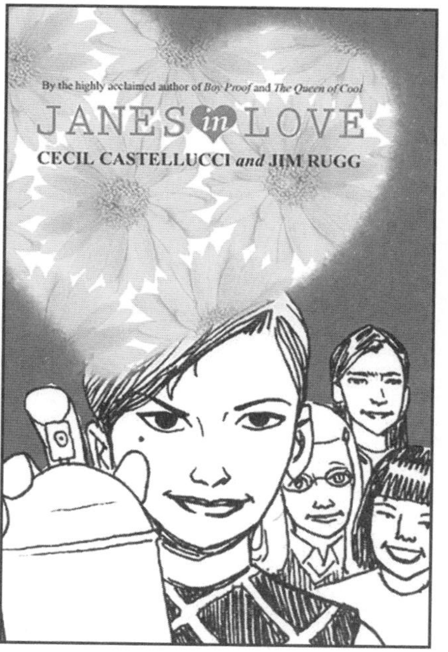
By the highly acclaimed author of Boy Proof and The Queen of Cool
JANES in LOVE
CECIL CASTELLUCCI and JIM RUGG

Part 3
Janes Attack Back

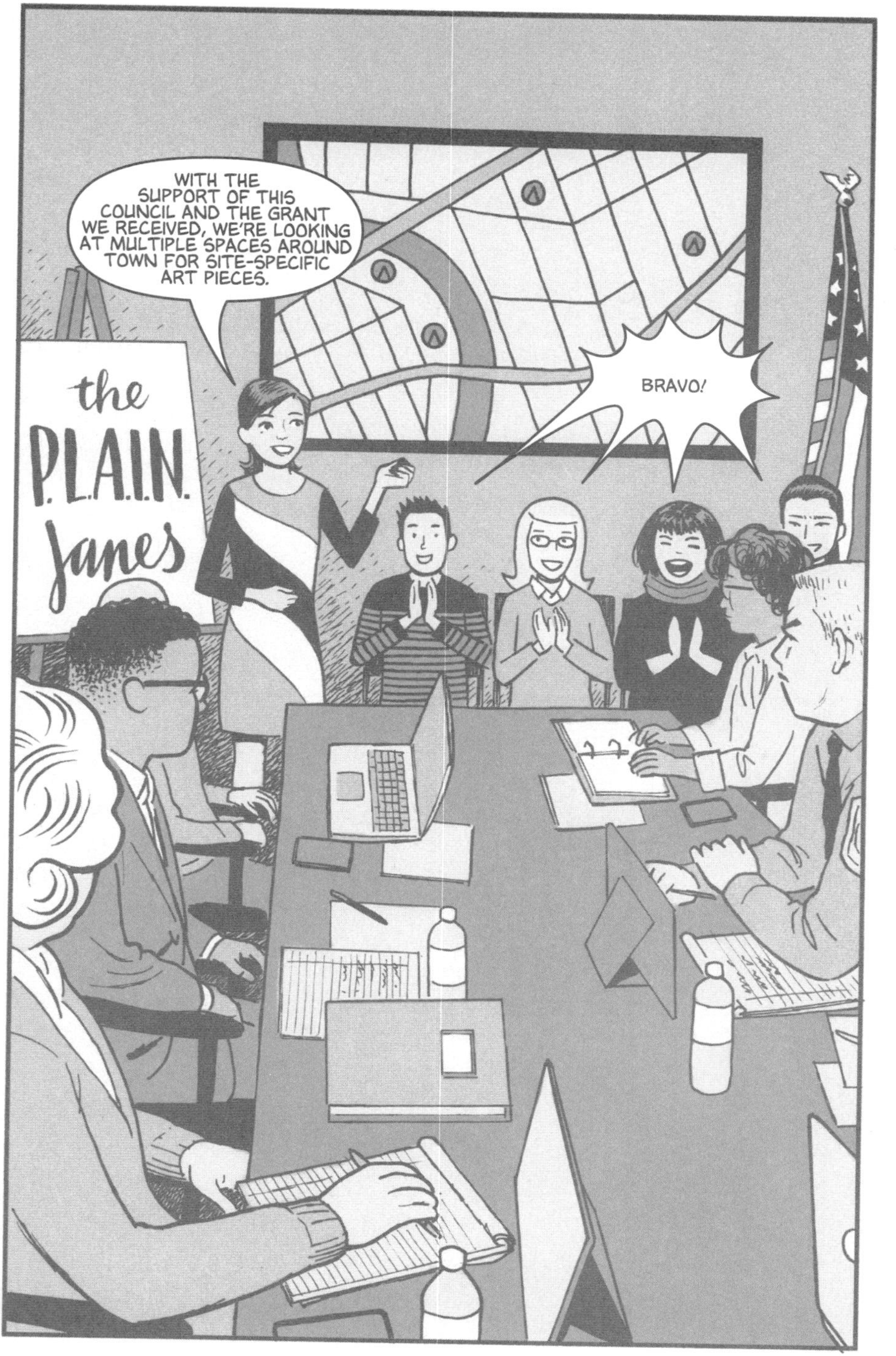
WITH THE SUPPORT OF THIS COUNCIL AND THE GRANT WE RECEIVED, WE'RE LOOKING AT MULTIPLE SPACES AROUND TOWN FOR SITE-SPECIFIC ART PIECES.
the P.L.A.I.N. Janes
BRAVO!

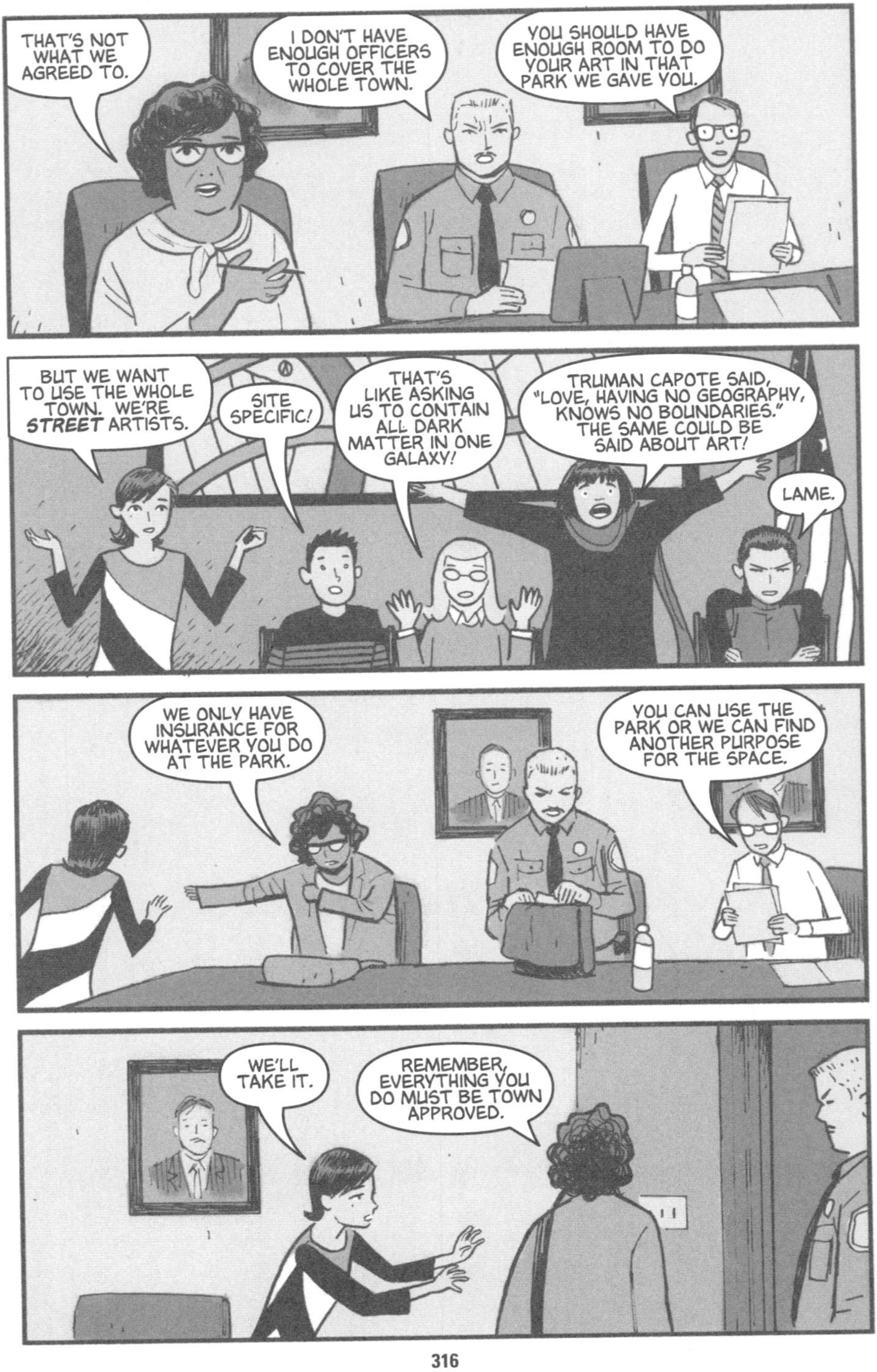
THAT'S NOT WHAT WE AGREED TO.
I DON'T HAVE ENOUGH OFFICERS TO COVER THE WHOLE TOWN.
YOU SHOULD HAVE ENOUGH ROOM TO DO YOUR ART IN THAT PARK WE GAVE YOU.
BUT WE WANT TO USE THE WHOLE TOWN. WE'RE *STREET* ARTISTS.
SITE SPECIFIC!
THAT'S LIKE ASKING US TO CONTAIN ALL DARK MATTER IN ONE GALAXY!
TRUMAN CAPOTE SAID, "LOVE, HAVING NO GEOGRAPHY, KNOWS NO BOUNDARIES." THE SAME COULD BE SAID ABOUT ART!
LAME.
WE ONLY HAVE INSURANCE FOR WHATEVER YOU DO AT THE PARK.
YOU CAN USE THE PARK OR WE CAN FIND ANOTHER PURPOSE FOR THE SPACE.
WE'LL TAKE IT.
REMEMBER, EVERYTHING YOU DO MUST BE TOWN APPROVED.

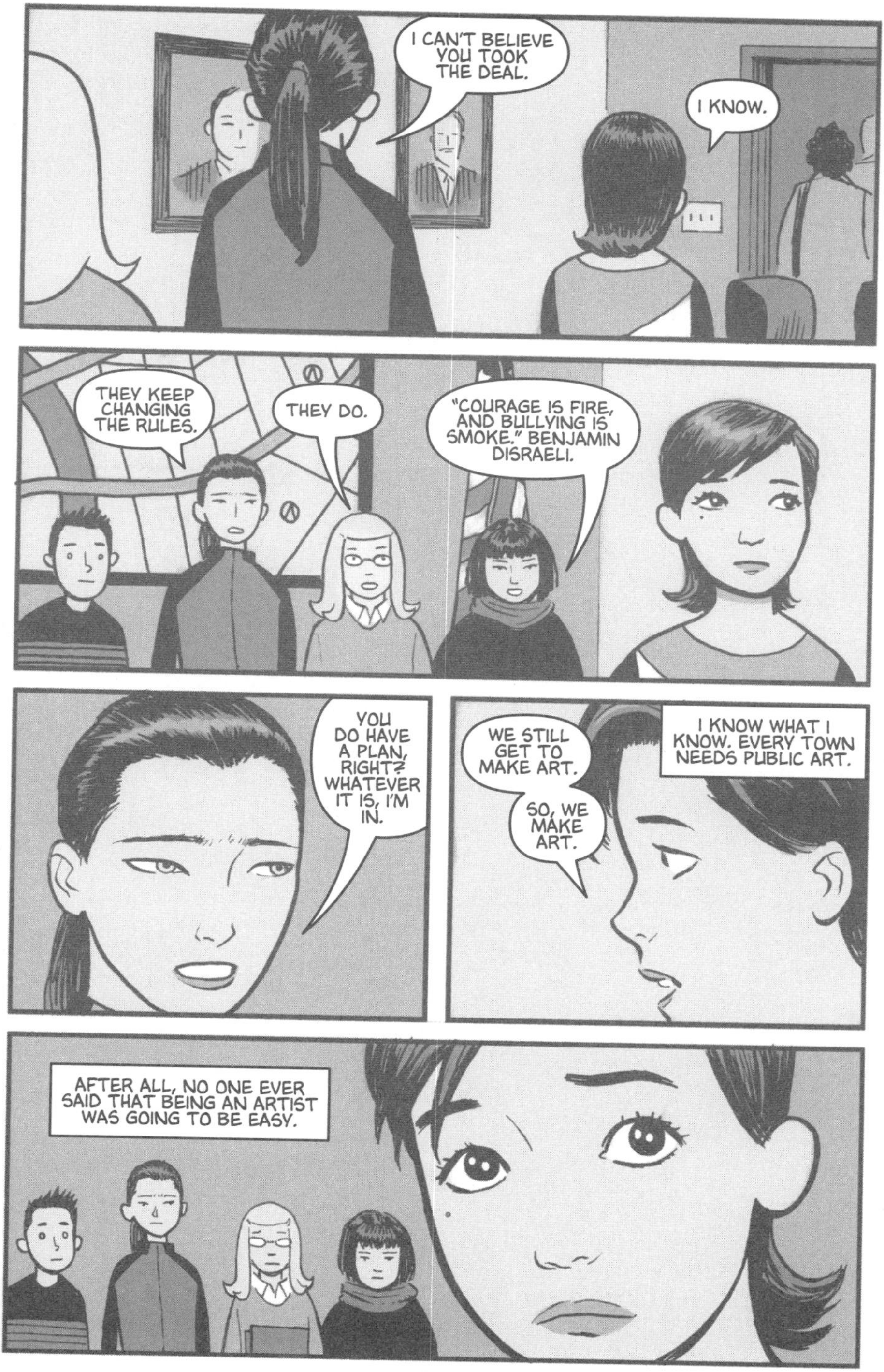
I CAN'T BELIEVE YOU TOOK THE DEAL.
I KNOW.
THEY KEEP CHANGING THE RULES.
THEY DO.
"COURAGE IS FIRE, AND BULLYING IS SMOKE." BENJAMIN DISRAELI.
YOU DO HAVE A PLAN, RIGHT? WHATEVER IT IS, I'M IN.
WE STILL GET TO MAKE ART.
SO, WE MAKE ART.
I KNOW WHAT I KNOW. EVERY TOWN NEEDS PUBLIC ART.
AFTER ALL, NO ONE EVER SAID THAT BEING AN ARTIST WAS GOING TO BE EASY.

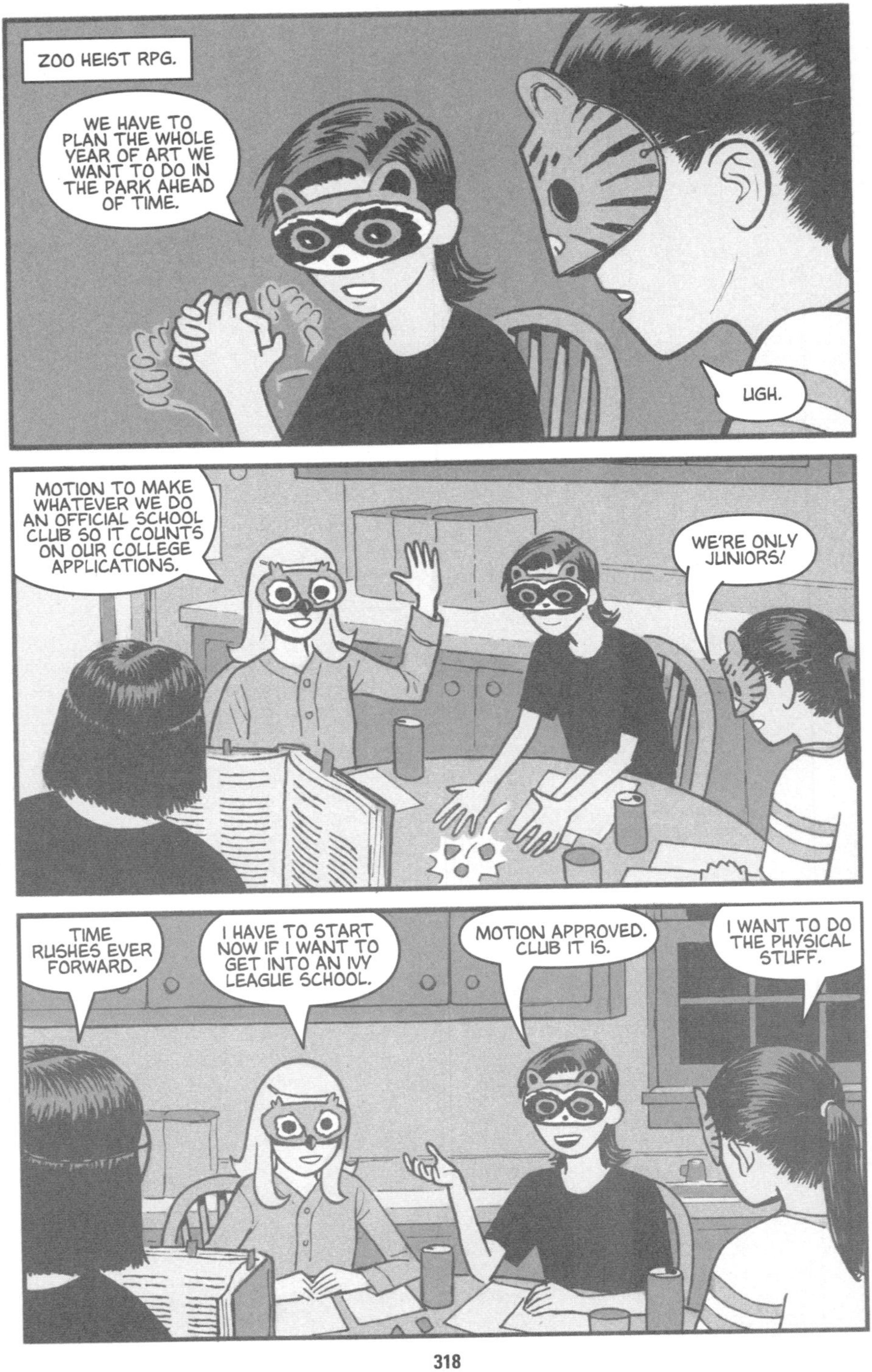
ZOO HEIST RPG.
WE HAVE TO PLAN THE WHOLE YEAR OF ART WE WANT TO DO IN THE PARK AHEAD OF TIME.
UGH.
MOTION TO MAKE WHATEVER WE DO AN OFFICIAL SCHOOL CLUB SO IT COUNTS ON OUR COLLEGE APPLICATIONS.
WE'RE ONLY JUNIORS!
TIME RUSHES EVER FORWARD.
I HAVE TO START NOW IF I WANT TO GET INTO AN IVY LEAGUE SCHOOL.
MOTION APPROVED. CLUB IT IS.
I WANT TO DO THE PHYSICAL STUFF.

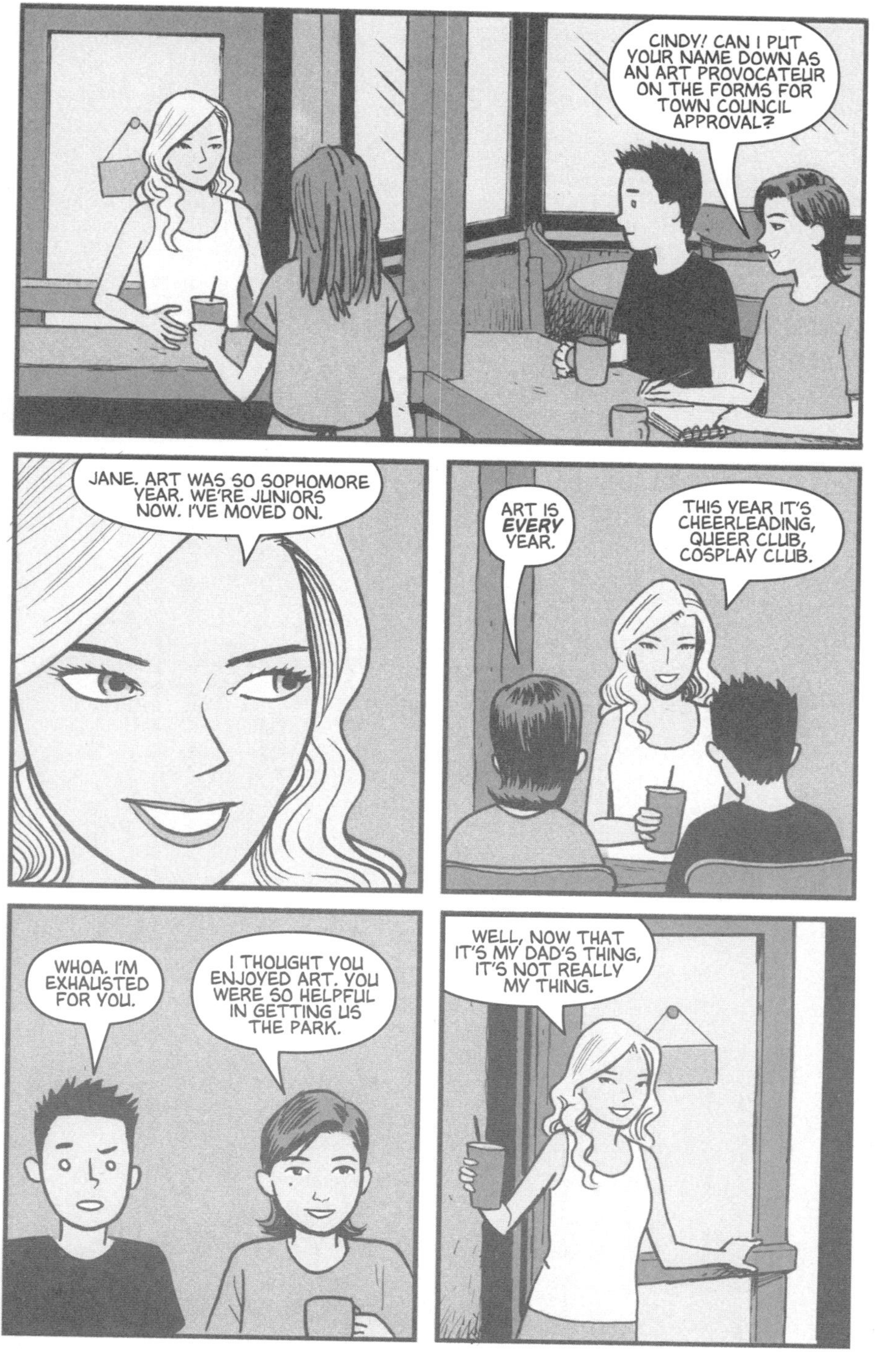
CINDY! CAN I PUT YOUR NAME DOWN AS AN ART PROVOCATEUR ON THE FORMS FOR TOWN COUNCIL APPROVAL?
JANE. ART WAS SO SOPHOMORE YEAR. WE'RE JUNIORS NOW. I'VE MOVED ON.
ART IS **EVERY** YEAR.
THIS YEAR IT'S CHEERLEADING, QUEER CLUB, COSPLAY CLUB.
WHOA. I'M EXHAUSTED FOR YOU.
I THOUGHT YOU ENJOYED ART. YOU WERE SO HELPFUL IN GETTING US THE PARK.
WELL, NOW THAT IT'S MY DAD'S THING, IT'S NOT REALLY MY THING.

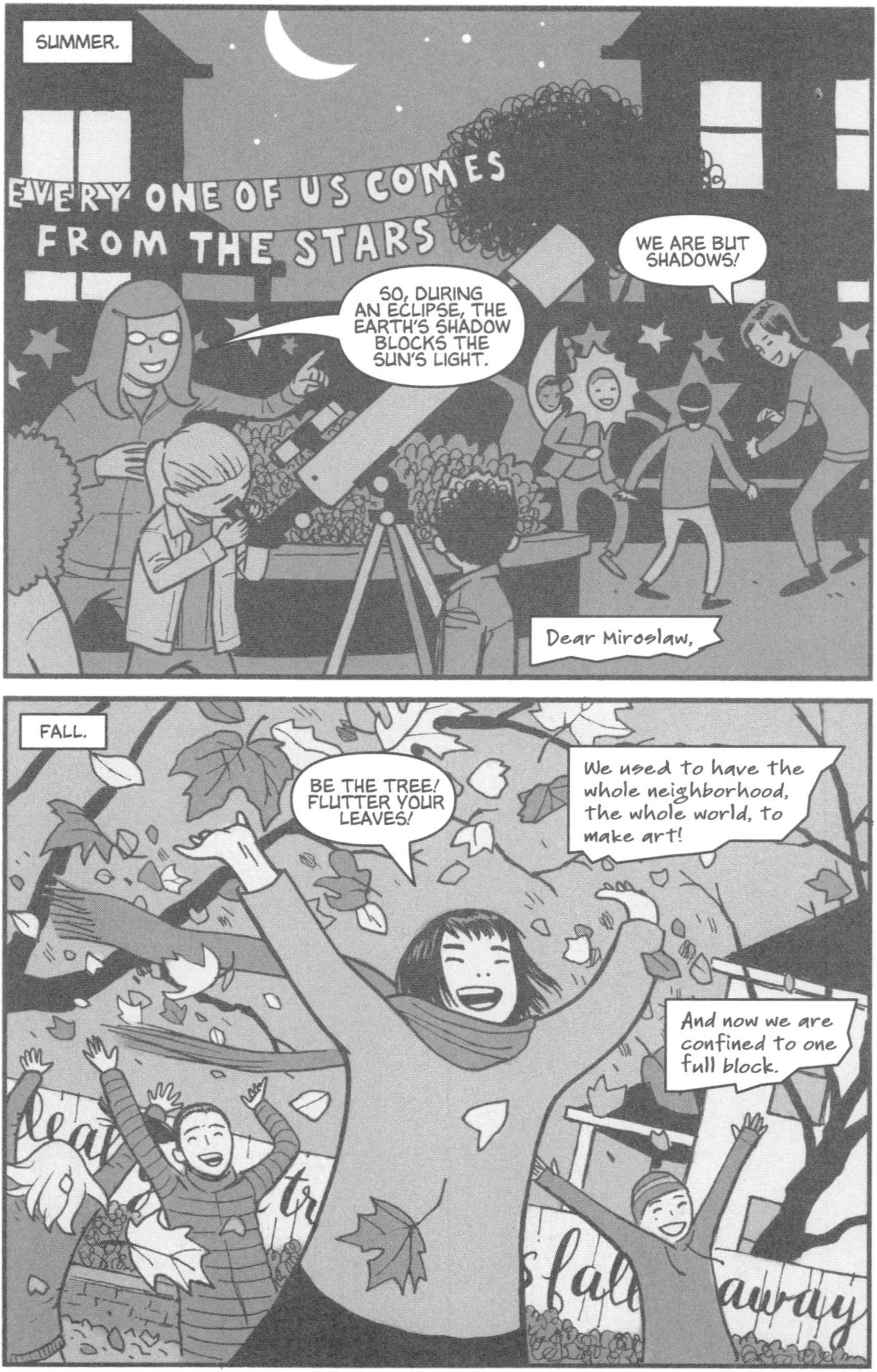
SUMMER.
EVERY ONE OF US COMES FROM THE STARS
SO, DURING AN ECLIPSE, THE EARTH'S SHADOW BLOCKS THE SUN'S LIGHT.
WE ARE BUT SHADOWS!
Dear Miroslaw,
FALL.
BE THE TREE! FLUTTER YOUR LEAVES!
We used to have the whole neighborhood, the whole world, to make art!
And now we are confined to one full block.

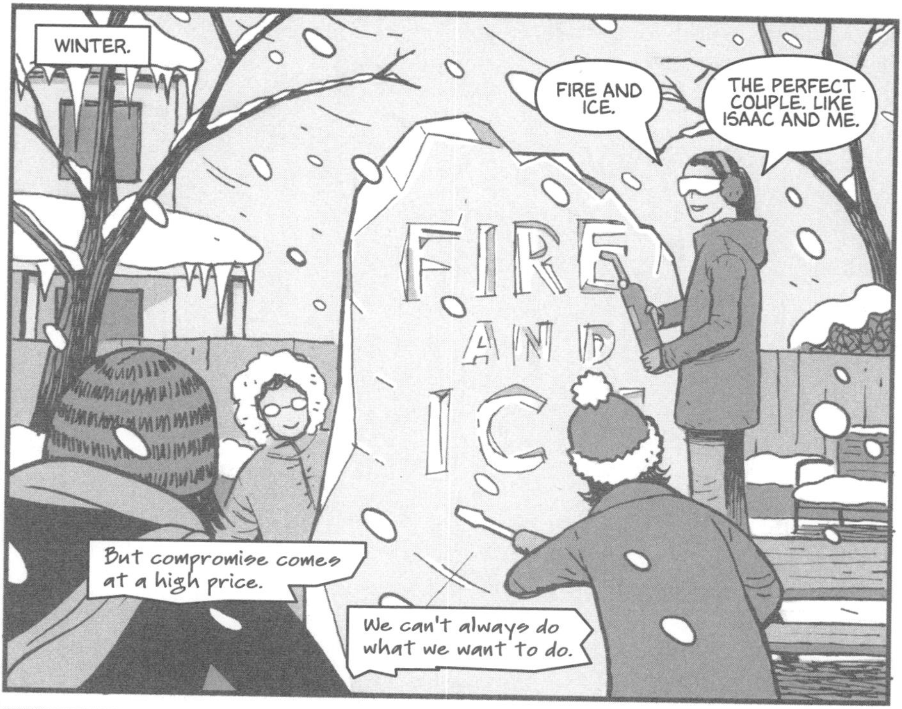
WINTER.
FIRE AND ICE.
THE PERFECT COUPLE. LIKE ISAAC AND ME.
FIRE AND ICE
But compromise comes at a high price.
We can't always do what we want to do.

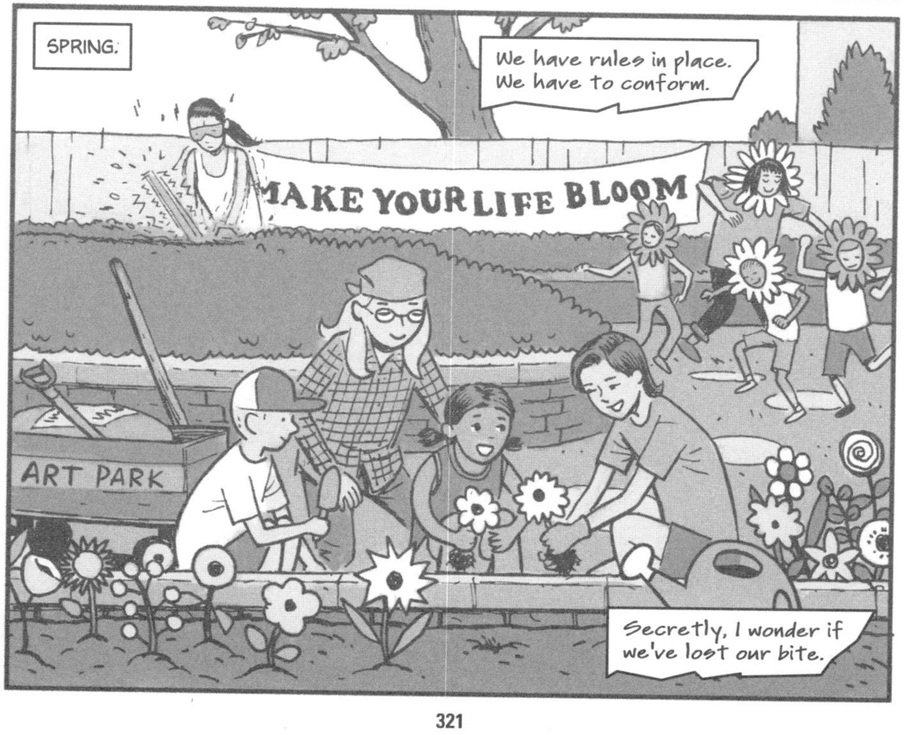
SPRING.
We have rules in place. We have to conform.
MAKE YOUR LIFE BLOOM
ART PARK
Secretly, I wonder if we've lost our bite.

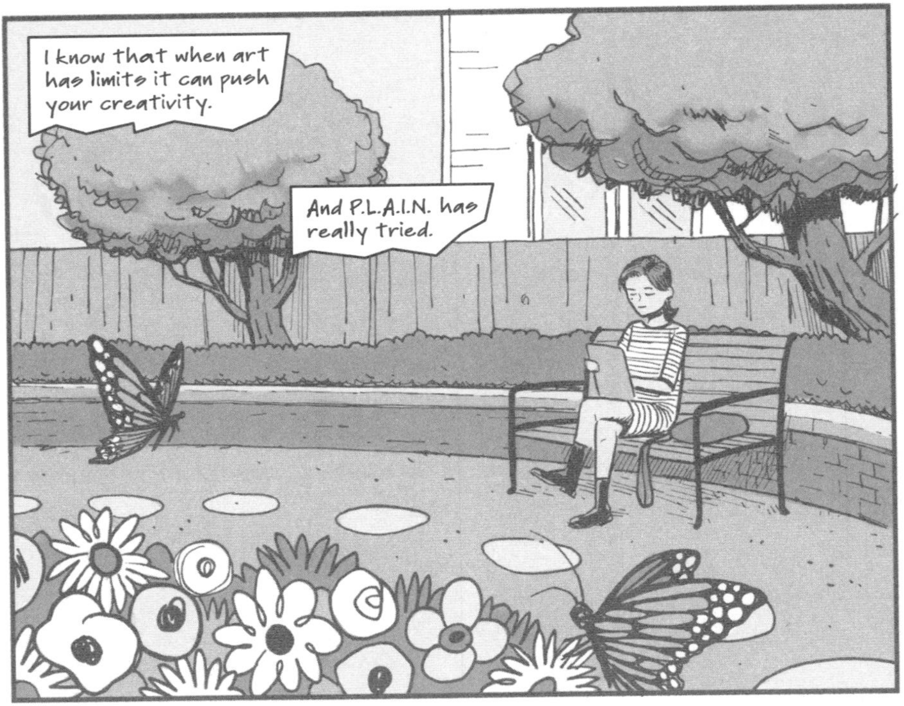
I know that when art has limits it can push your creativity.
And P.L.A.I.N. has really tried.

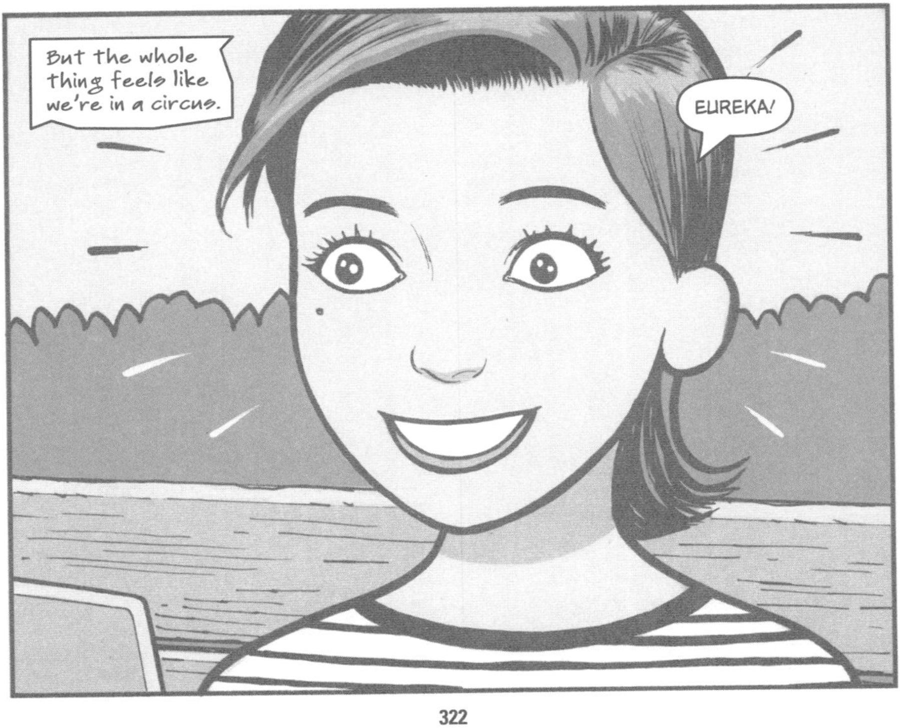
But the whole thing feels like we're in a circus.
EUREKA!

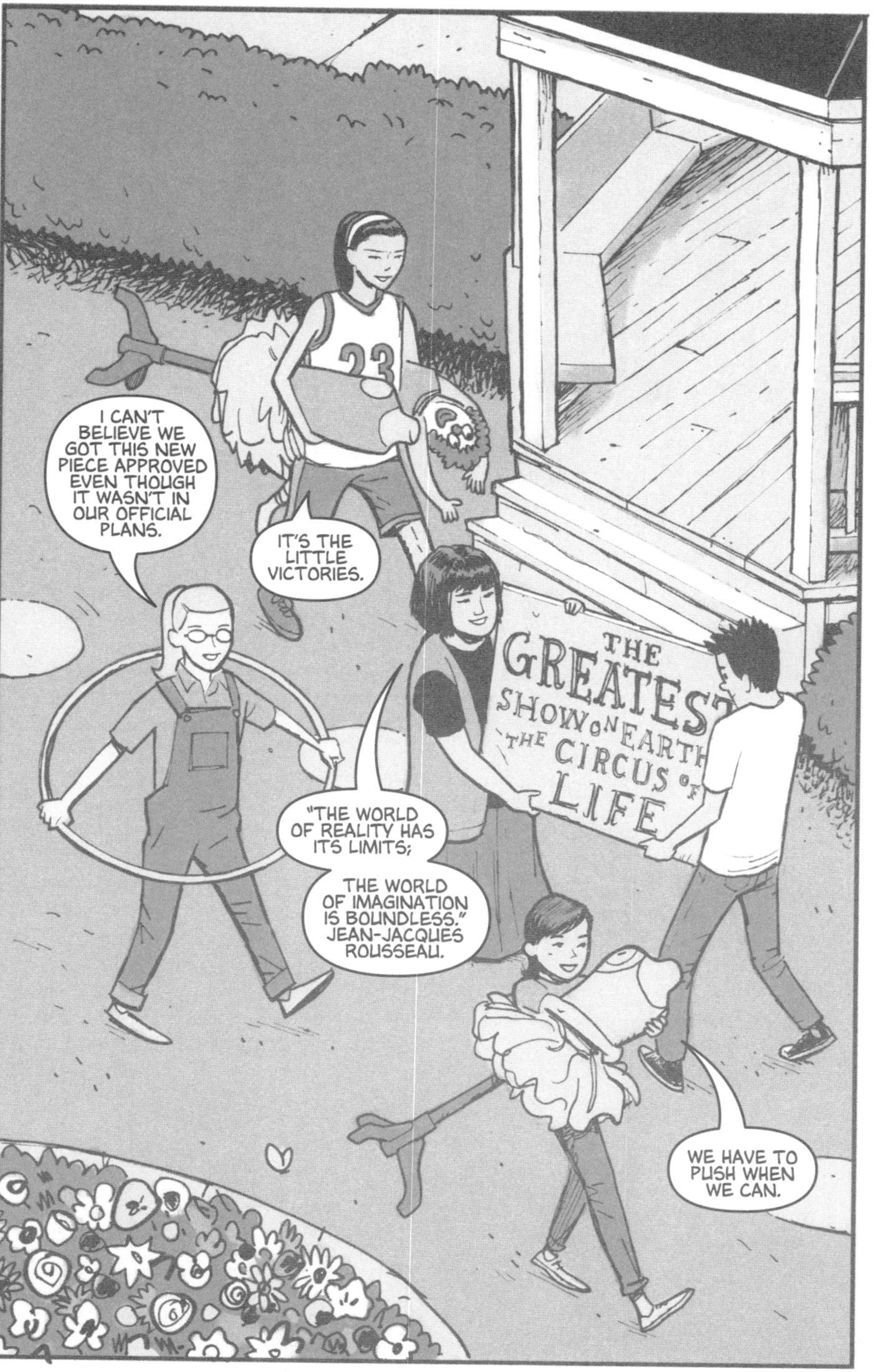
I CAN'T BELIEVE WE GOT THIS NEW PIECE APPROVED EVEN THOUGH IT WASN'T IN OUR OFFICIAL PLANS.
IT'S THE LITTLE VICTORIES.
THE GREATEST SHOW ON EARTH THE CIRCUS OF LIFE
"THE WORLD OF REALITY HAS ITS LIMITS;
THE WORLD OF IMAGINATION IS BOUNDLESS." JEAN-JACQUES ROUSSEAU.
WE HAVE TO PUSH WHEN WE CAN.

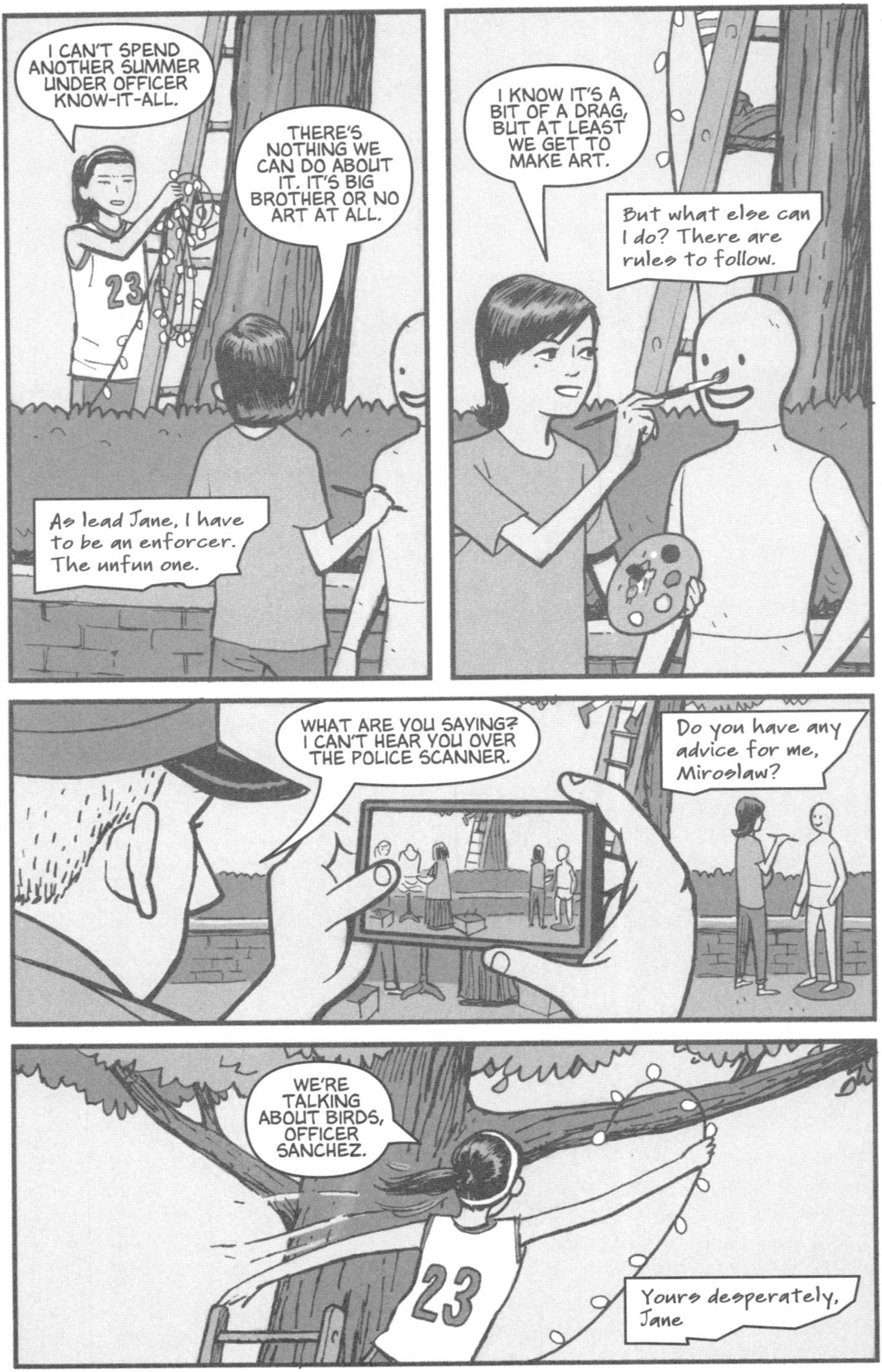
I CAN'T SPEND ANOTHER SUMMER UNDER OFFICER KNOW-IT-ALL.
THERE'S NOTHING WE CAN DO ABOUT IT. IT'S BIG BROTHER OR NO ART AT ALL.
As lead Jane, I have to be an enforcer. The unfun one.
I KNOW IT'S A BIT OF A DRAG, BUT AT LEAST WE GET TO MAKE ART.
But what else can I do? There are rules to follow.
WHAT ARE YOU SAYING? I CAN'T HEAR YOU OVER THE POLICE SCANNER.
Do you have any advice for me, Miroslaw?
WE'RE TALKING ABOUT BIRDS, OFFICER SANCHEZ.
Yours desperately, Jane

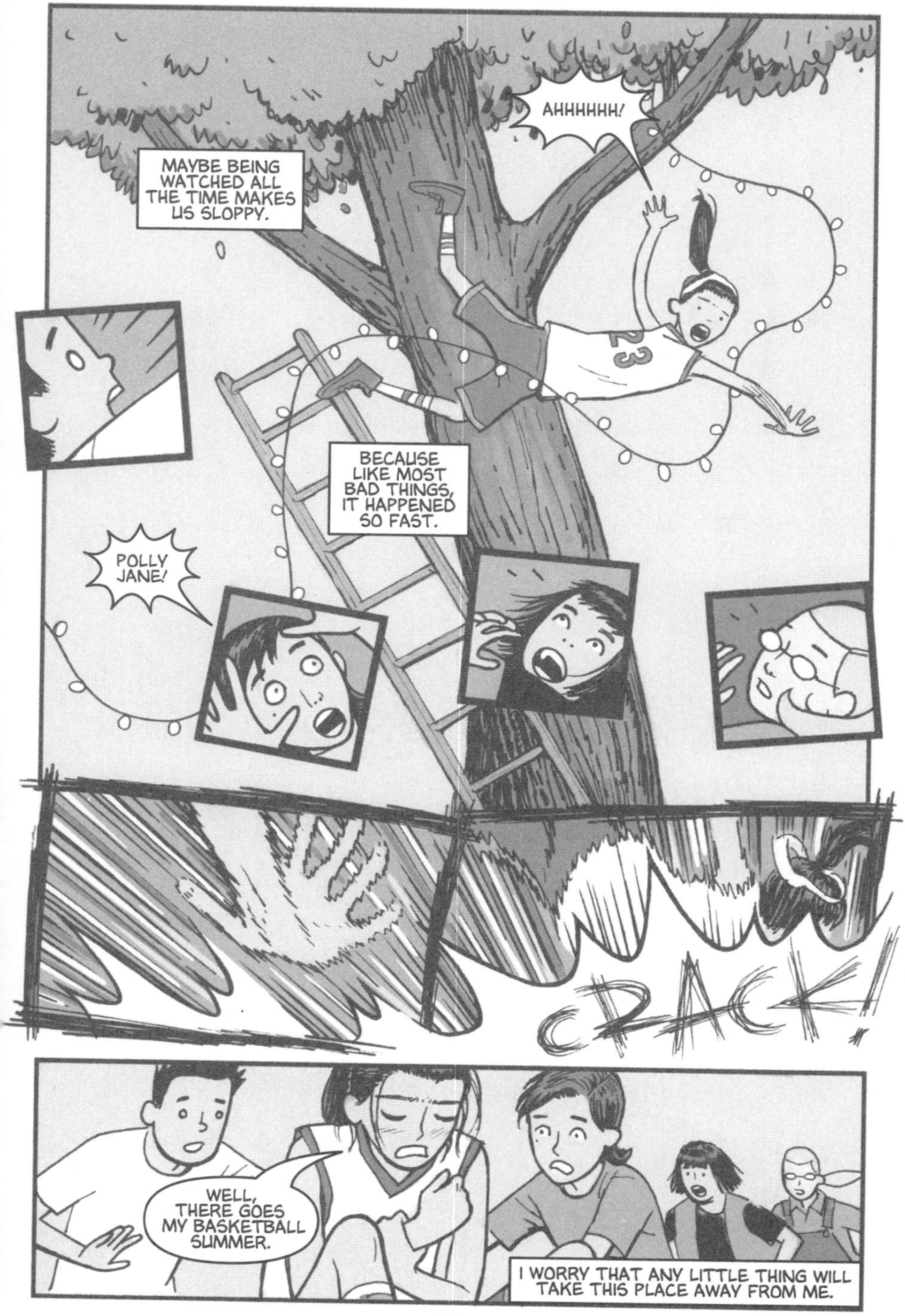

AHHHHHH!
MAYBE BEING WATCHED ALL THE TIME MAKES US SLOPPY.
BECAUSE LIKE MOST BAD THINGS, IT HAPPENED SO FAST.
POLLY JANE!
CRACK!
WELL, THERE GOES MY BASKETBALL SUMMER.
I WORRY THAT ANY LITTLE THING WILL TAKE THIS PLACE AWAY FROM ME.

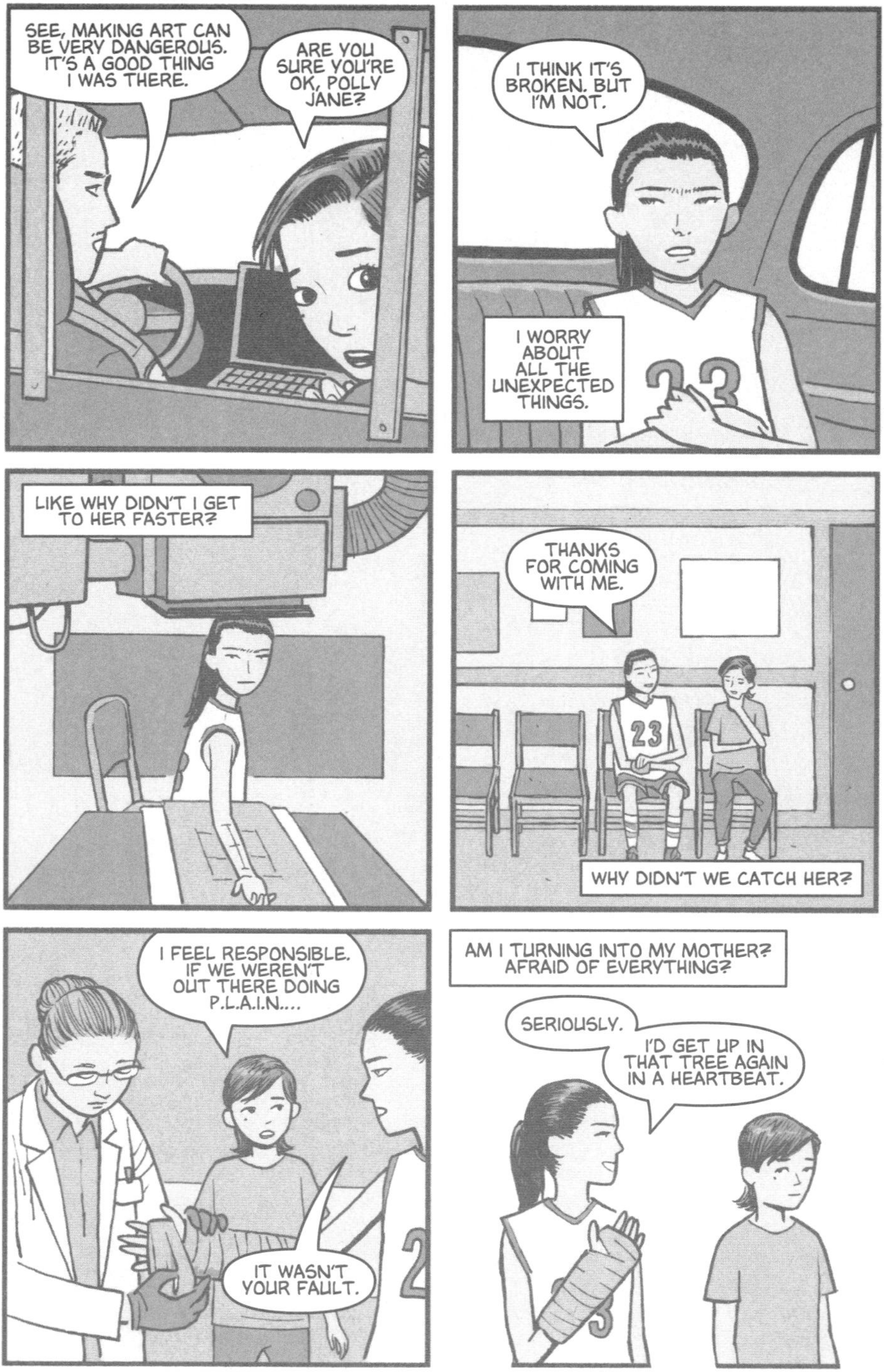
SEE, MAKING ART CAN BE VERY DANGEROUS. IT'S A GOOD THING I WAS THERE.
ARE YOU SURE YOU'RE OK, POLLY JANE?
I THINK IT'S BROKEN. BUT I'M NOT.
I WORRY ABOUT ALL THE UNEXPECTED THINGS.
23
LIKE WHY DIDN'T I GET TO HER FASTER?
THANKS FOR COMING WITH ME.
23
WHY DIDN'T WE CATCH HER?
I FEEL RESPONSIBLE. IF WE WEREN'T OUT THERE DOING P.L.A.I.N....
IT WASN'T YOUR FAULT.
AM I TURNING INTO MY MOTHER? AFRAID OF EVERYTHING?
SERIOUSLY.
I'D GET UP IN THAT TREE AGAIN IN A HEARTBEAT.

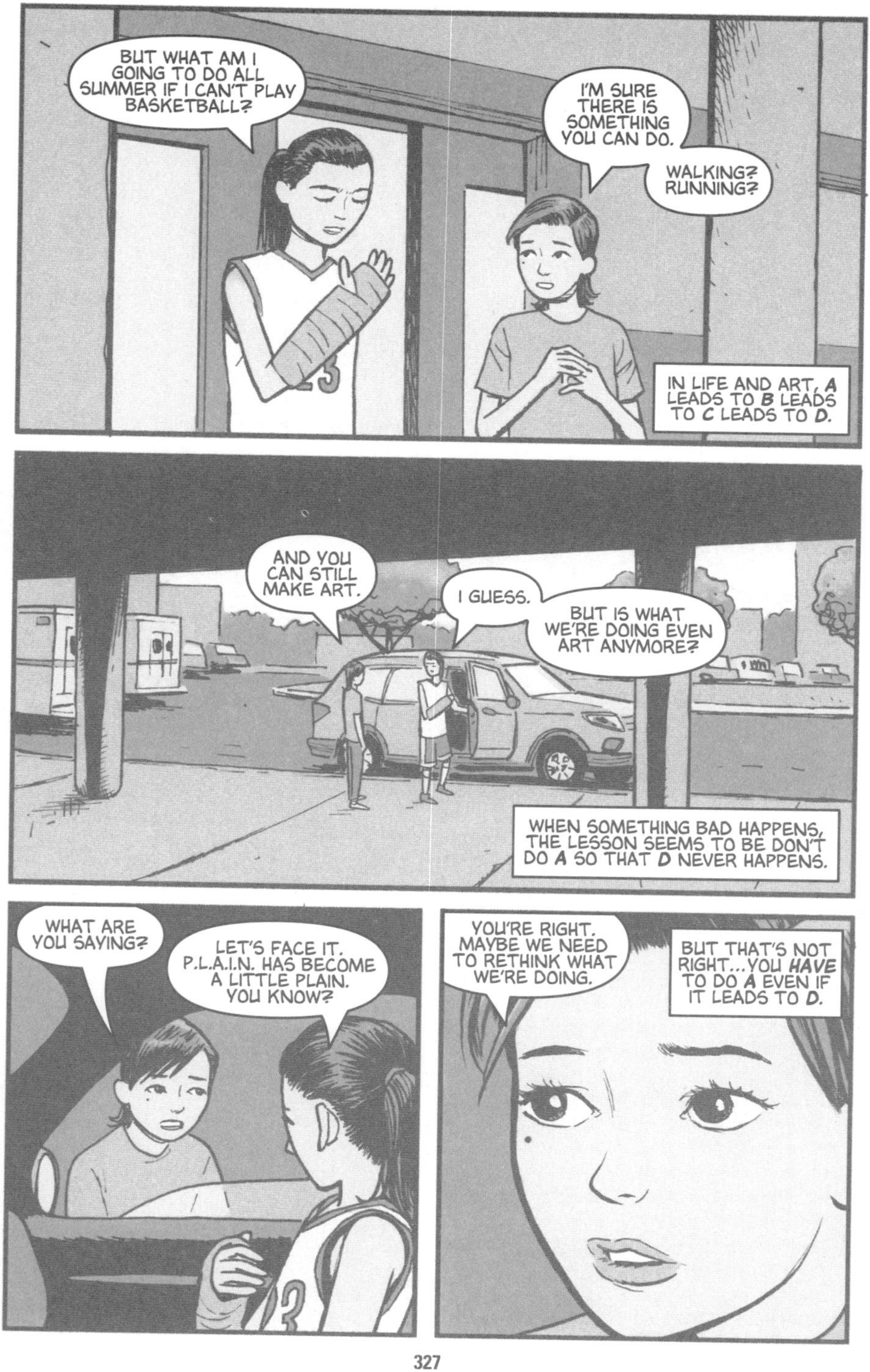
BUT WHAT AM I GOING TO DO ALL SUMMER IF I CAN'T PLAY BASKETBALL?
I'M SURE THERE IS SOMETHING YOU CAN DO.
WALKING? RUNNING?
IN LIFE AND ART, A LEADS TO B LEADS TO C LEADS TO D.
AND YOU CAN STILL MAKE ART.
I GUESS.
BUT IS WHAT WE'RE DOING EVEN ART ANYMORE?
WHEN SOMETHING BAD HAPPENS, THE LESSON SEEMS TO BE DON'T DO A SO THAT D NEVER HAPPENS.
WHAT ARE YOU SAYING?
LET'S FACE IT. P.L.A.I.N. HAS BECOME A LITTLE PLAIN. YOU KNOW?
YOU'RE RIGHT. MAYBE WE NEED TO RETHINK WHAT WE'RE DOING.
BUT THAT'S NOT RIGHT...YOU HAVE TO DO A EVEN IF IT LEADS TO D.

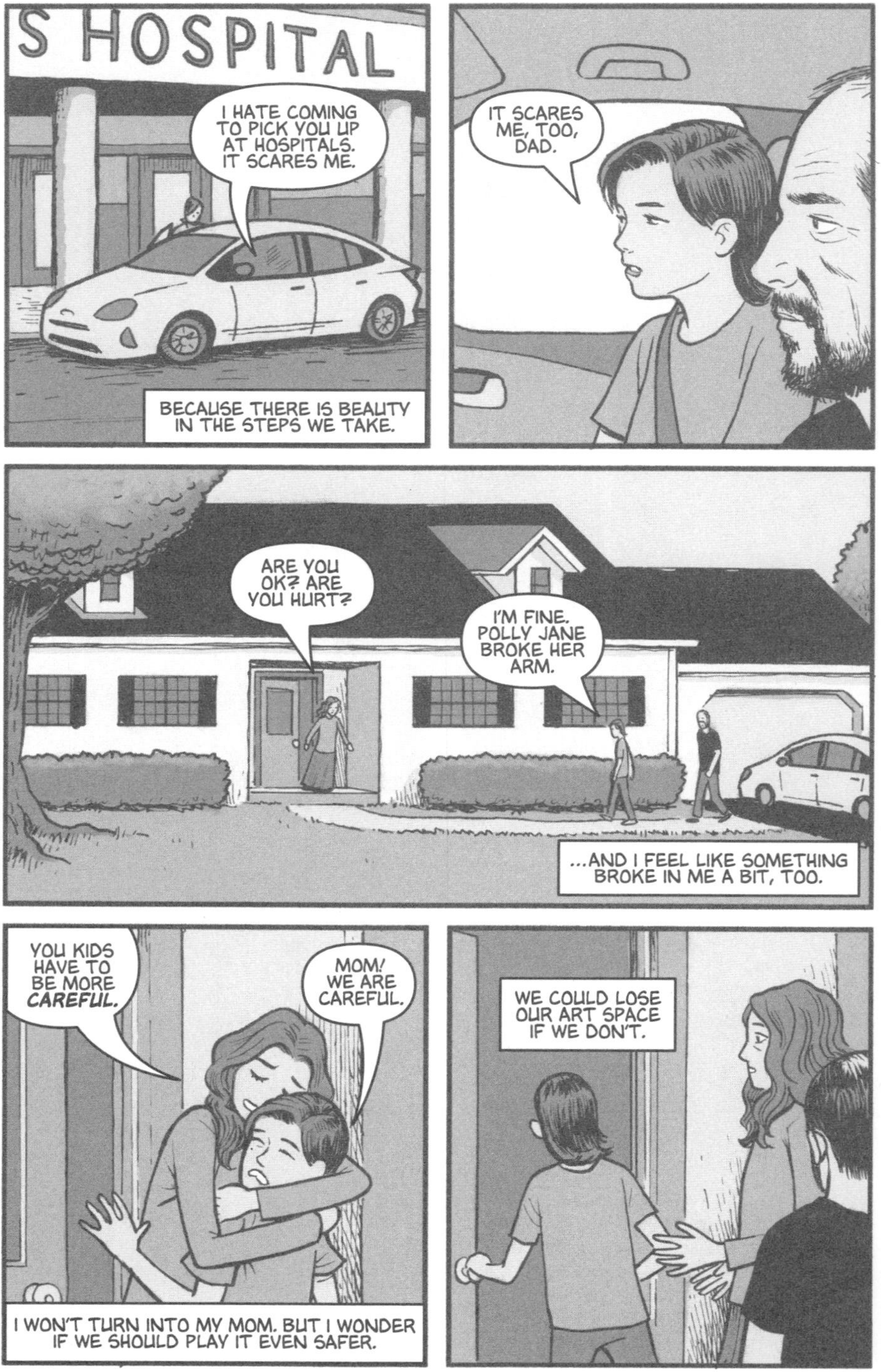
S HOSPITAL
I HATE COMING TO PICK YOU UP AT HOSPITALS. IT SCARES ME.
BECAUSE THERE IS BEAUTY IN THE STEPS WE TAKE.
IT SCARES ME, TOO, DAD.
ARE YOU OK? ARE YOU HURT?
I'M FINE. POLLY JANE BROKE HER ARM.
...AND I FEEL LIKE SOMETHING BROKE IN ME A BIT, TOO.
YOU KIDS HAVE TO BE MORE CAREFUL.
MOM! WE ARE CAREFUL.
I WON'T TURN INTO MY MOM. BUT I WONDER IF WE SHOULD PLAY IT EVEN SAFER.
WE COULD LOSE OUR ART SPACE IF WE DON'T.

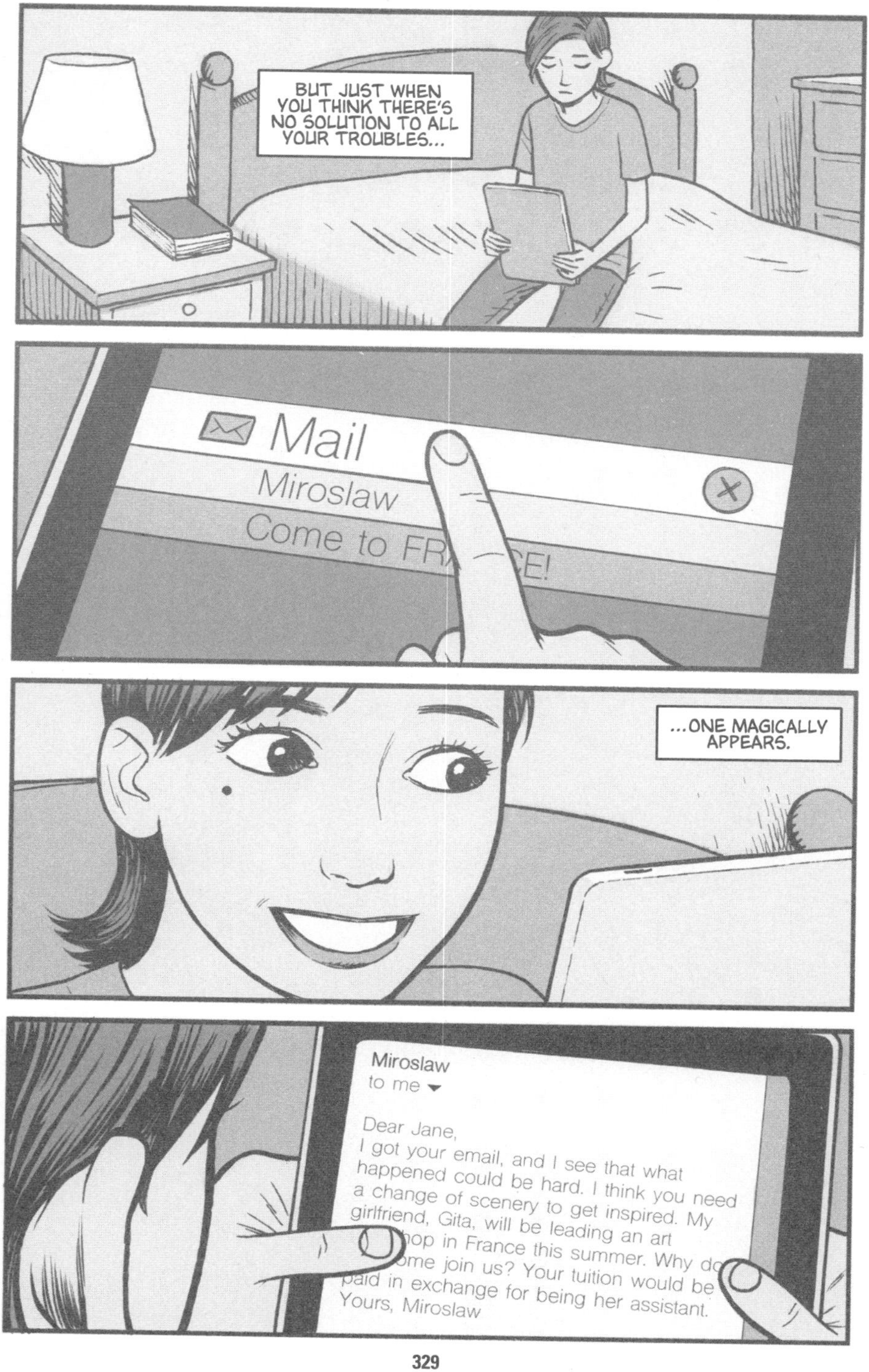
BUT JUST WHEN YOU THINK THERE'S NO SOLUTION TO ALL YOUR TROUBLES...
Mail
Miroslaw
Come to FR
CE!
...ONE MAGICALLY APPEARS.
Miroslaw
to me
Dear Jane,
I got your email, and I see that what
happened could be hard. I think you need
a change of scenery to get inspired. My
girlfriend, Gita, will be leading an art
hop in France this summer. Why do
ome join us? Your tuition would be
paid in exchange for being her assistant.
Yours, Miroslaw

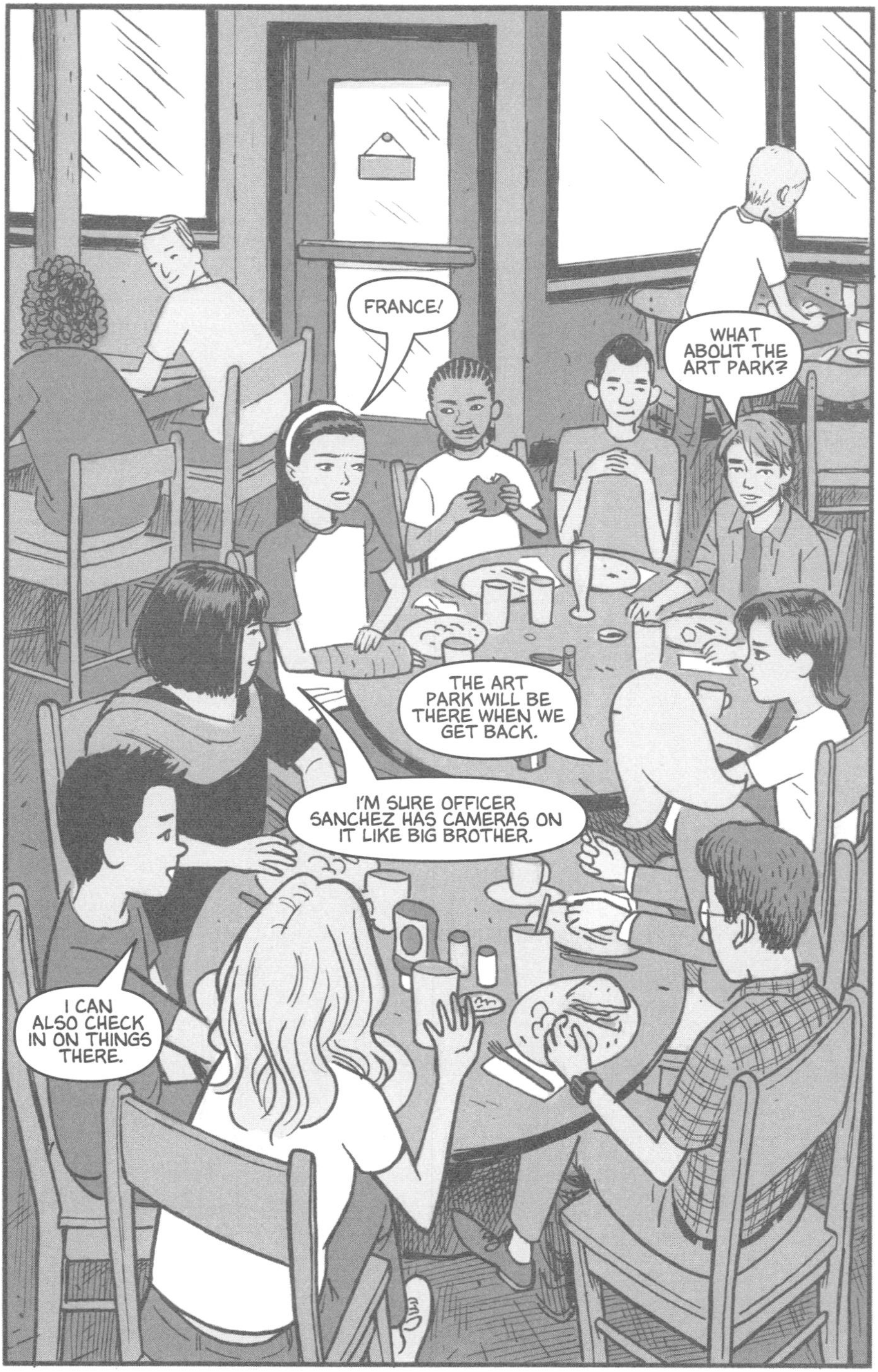
FRANCE!
WHAT ABOUT THE ART PARK?
THE ART PARK WILL BE THERE WHEN WE GET BACK.
I'M SURE OFFICER SANCHEZ HAS CAMERAS ON IT LIKE BIG BROTHER.
I CAN ALSO CHECK IN ON THINGS THERE.

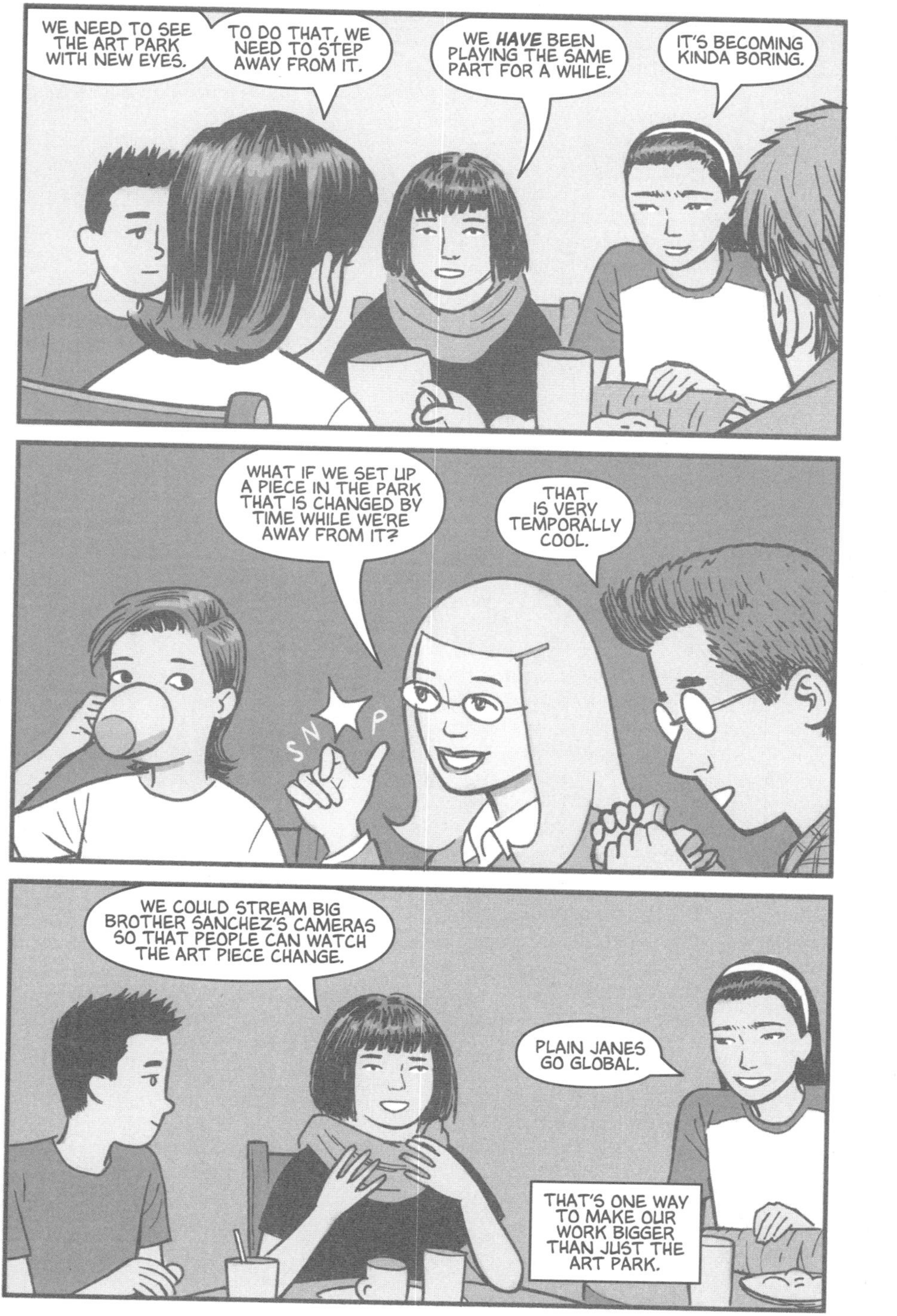
WE NEED TO SEE THE ART PARK WITH NEW EYES.
TO DO THAT, WE NEED TO STEP AWAY FROM IT.
WE **HAVE** BEEN PLAYING THE SAME PART FOR A WHILE.
IT'S BECOMING KINDA BORING.
WHAT IF WE SET UP A PIECE IN THE PARK THAT IS CHANGED BY TIME WHILE WE'RE AWAY FROM IT?
SNAP
THAT IS VERY TEMPORALLY COOL.
WE COULD STREAM BIG BROTHER SANCHEZ'S CAMERAS SO THAT PEOPLE CAN WATCH THE ART PIECE CHANGE.
PLAIN JANES GO GLOBAL.
THAT'S ONE WAY TO MAKE OUR WORK BIGGER THAN JUST THE ART PARK.

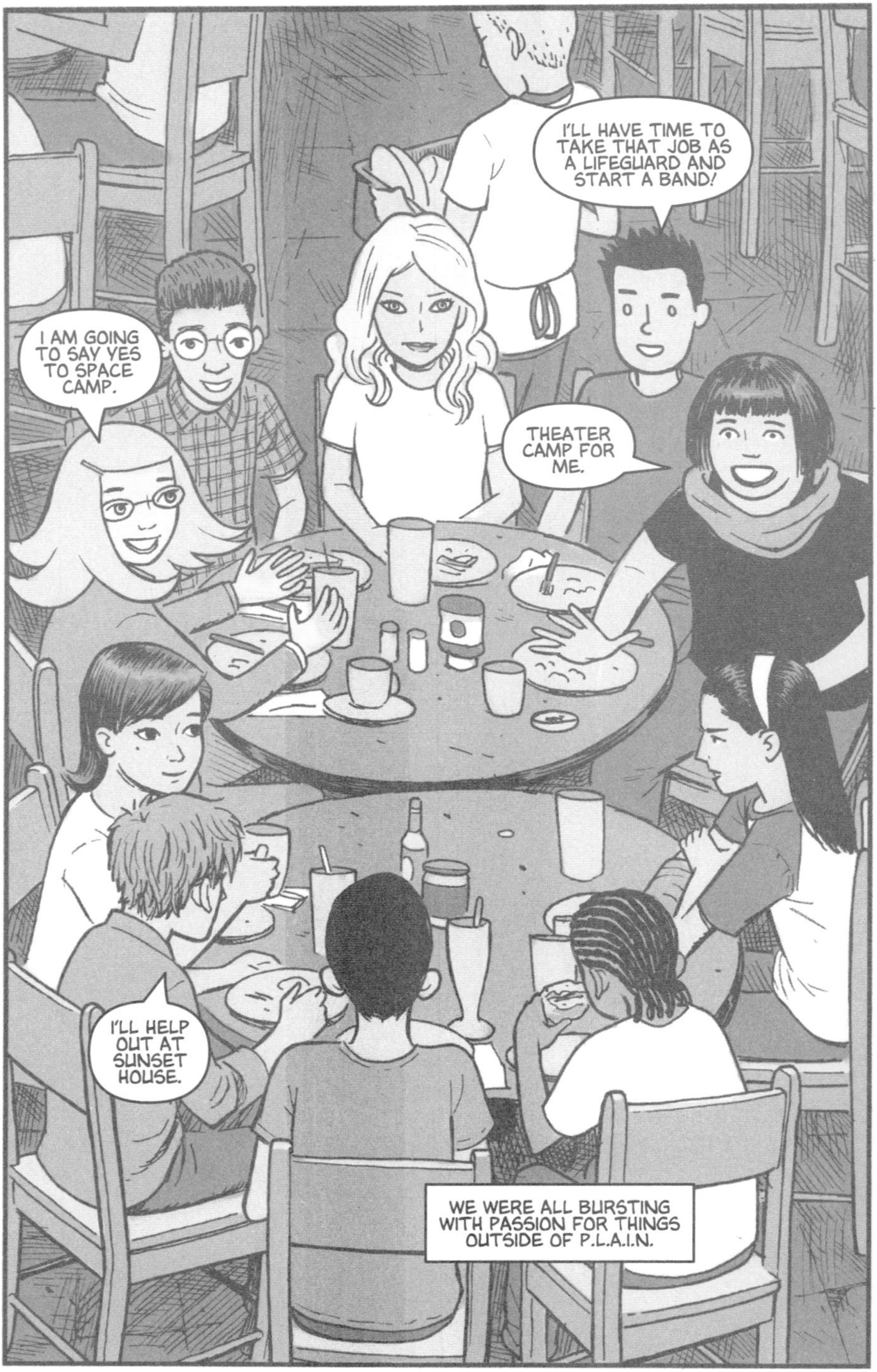
I'LL HAVE TIME TO TAKE THAT JOB AS A LIFEGUARD AND START A BAND!
I AM GOING TO SAY YES TO SPACE CAMP.
THEATER CAMP FOR ME.
I'LL HELP OUT AT SUNSET HOUSE.
WE WERE ALL BURSTING WITH PASSION FOR THINGS OUTSIDE OF P.L.A.I.N.

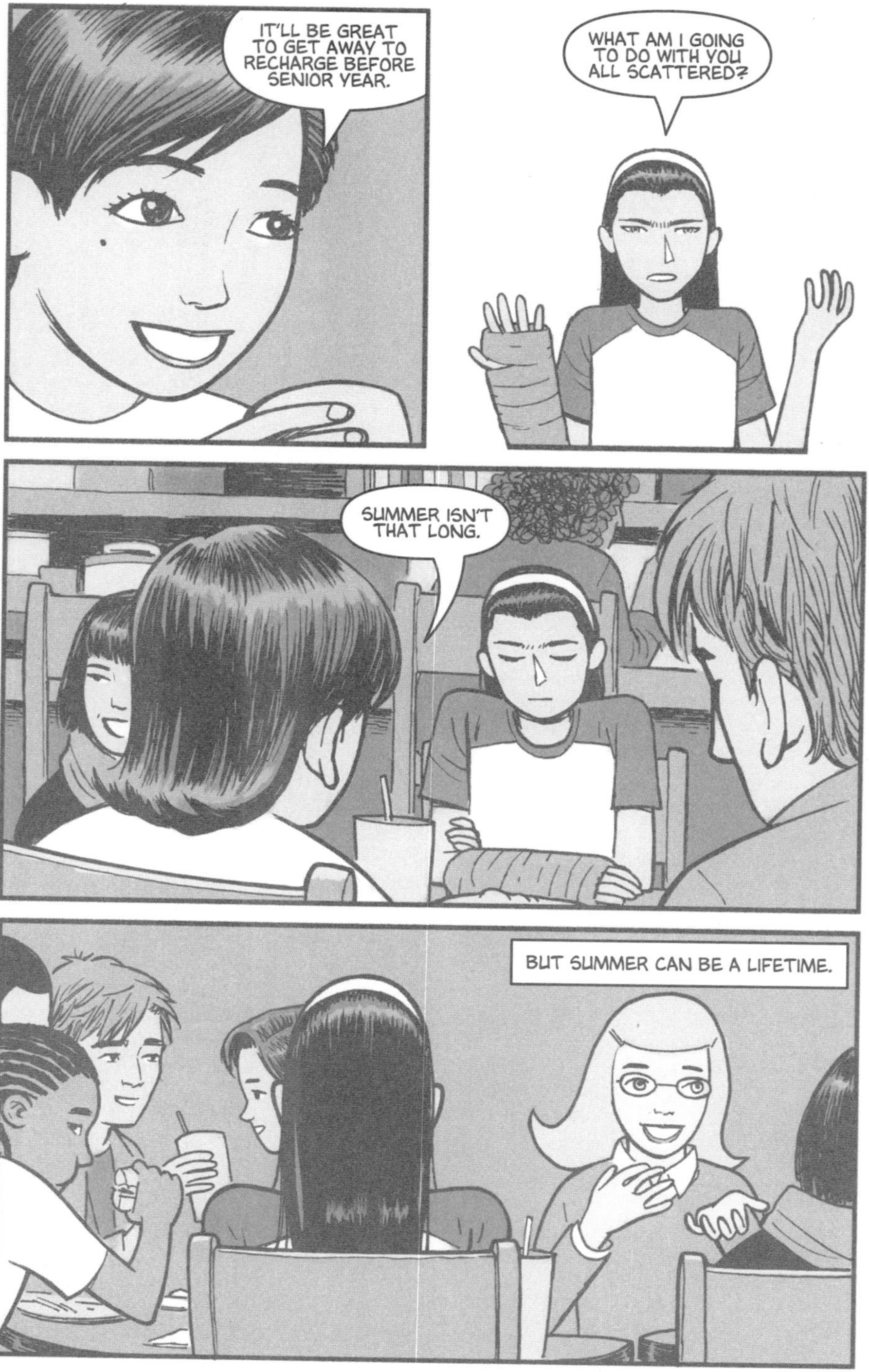
IT'LL BE GREAT TO GET AWAY TO RECHARGE BEFORE SENIOR YEAR.
WHAT AM I GOING TO DO WITH YOU ALL SCATTERED?
SUMMER ISN'T THAT LONG.
BUT SUMMER CAN BE A LIFETIME.

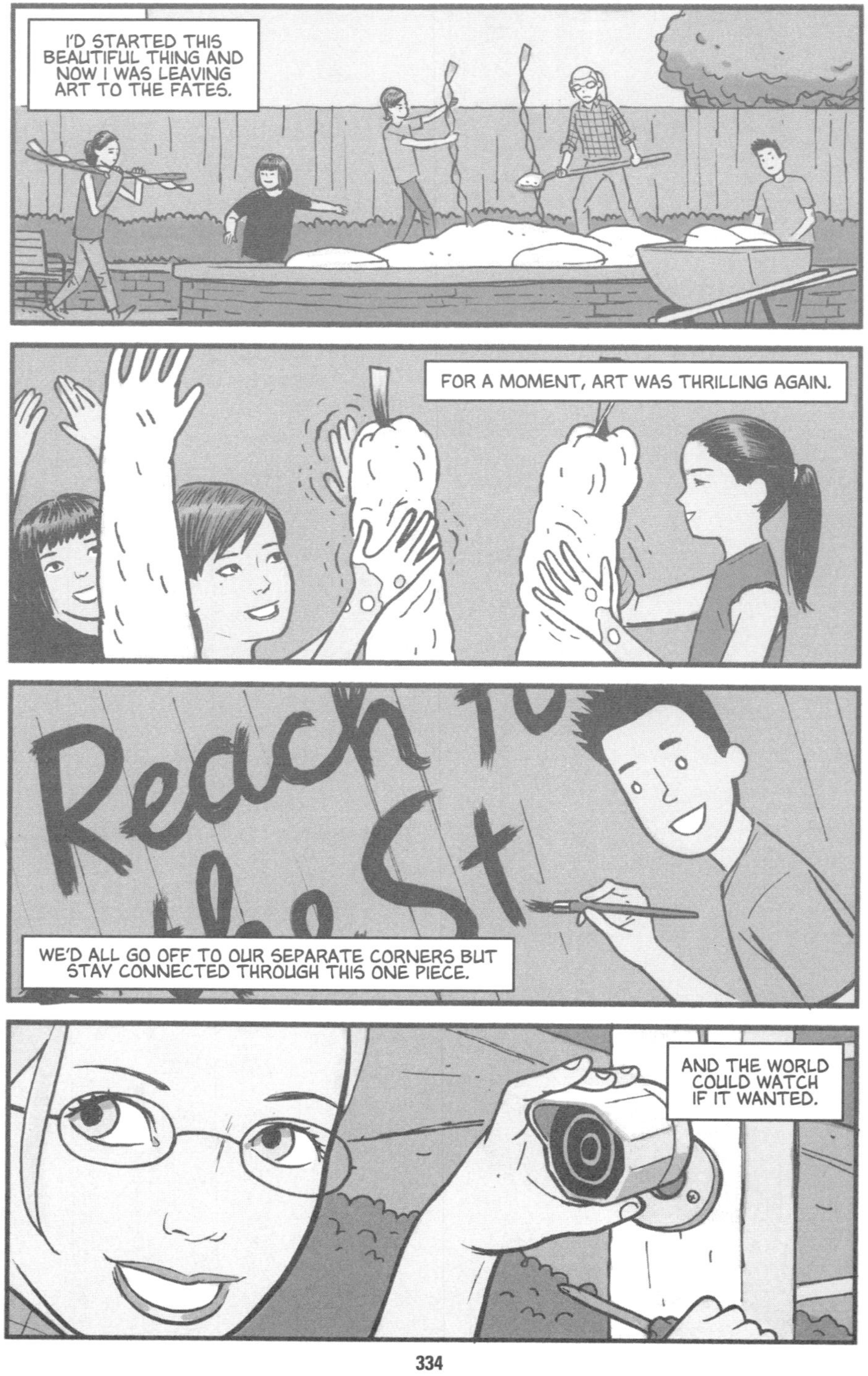
I'D STARTED THIS BEAUTIFUL THING AND NOW I WAS LEAVING ART TO THE FATES.
FOR A MOMENT, ART WAS THRILLING AGAIN.
Reach
WE'D ALL GO OFF TO OUR SEPARATE CORNERS BUT STAY CONNECTED THROUGH THIS ONE PIECE.
AND THE WORLD COULD WATCH IF IT WANTED.

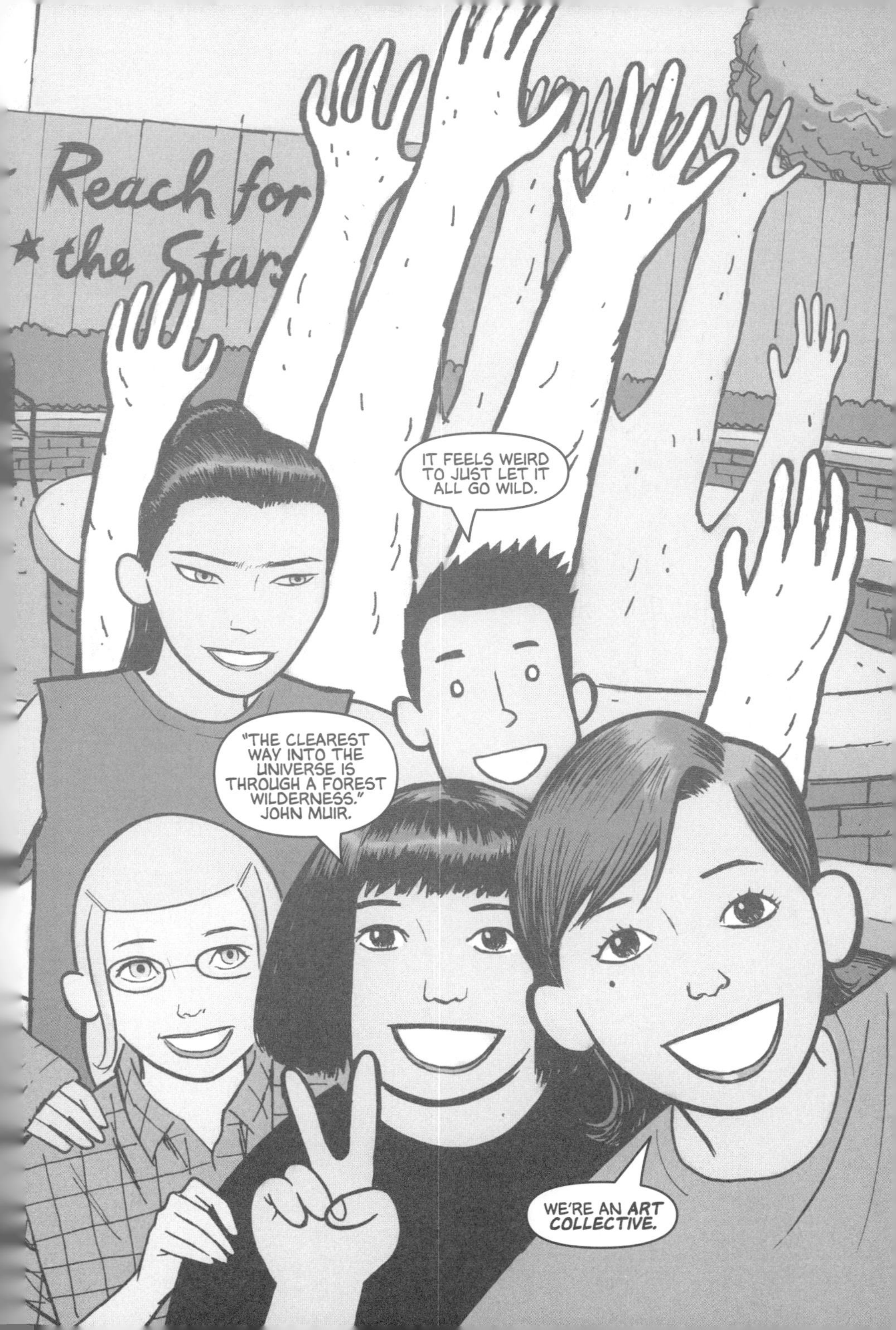
Reach for the Stars
IT FEELS WEIRD TO JUST LET IT ALL GO WILD.
"THE CLEAREST WAY INTO THE UNIVERSE IS THROUGH A FOREST WILDERNESS." JOHN MUIR.
WE'RE AN *ART COLLECTIVE*.

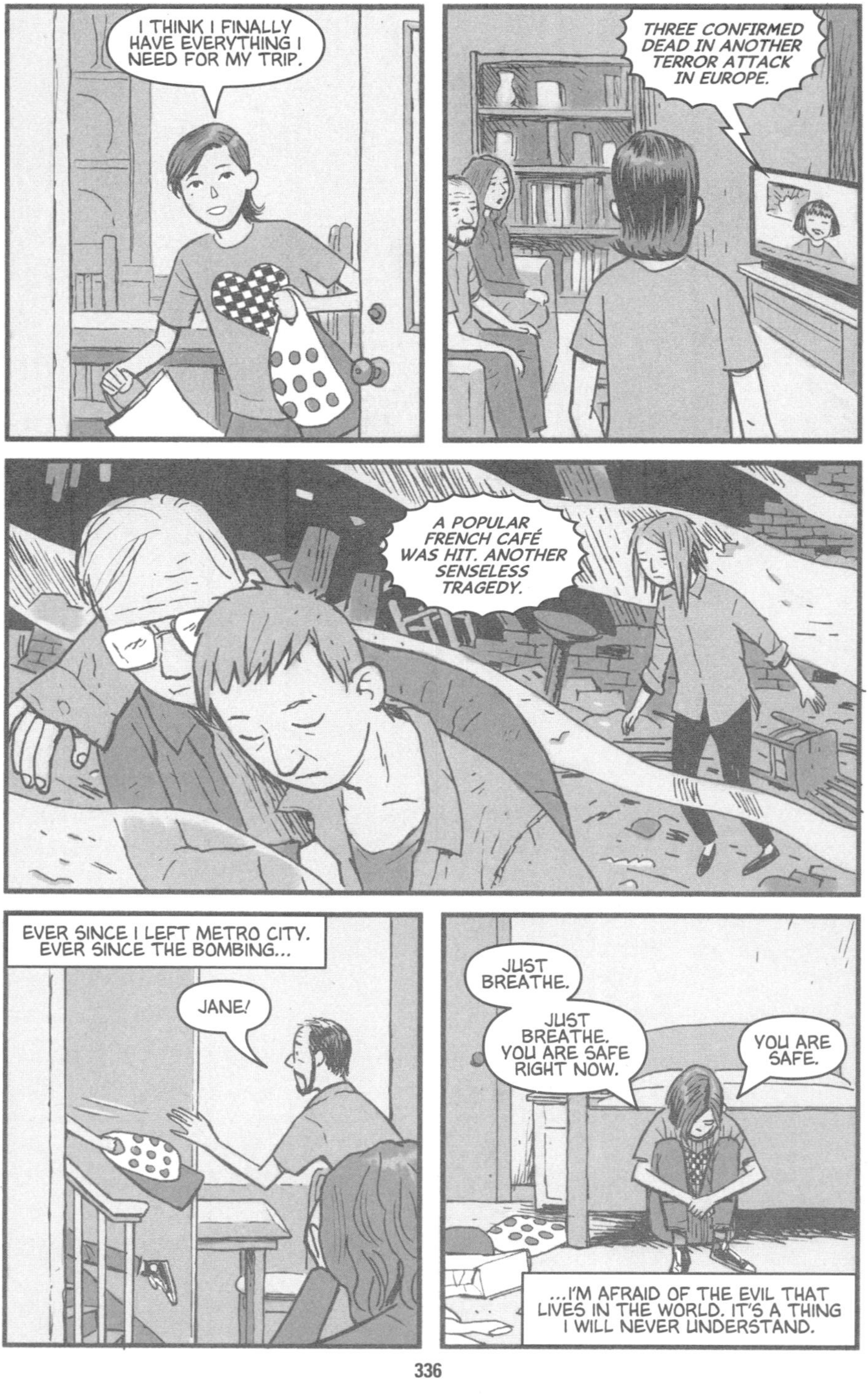
I THINK I FINALLY HAVE EVERYTHING I NEED FOR MY TRIP.
THREE CONFIRMED DEAD IN ANOTHER TERROR ATTACK IN EUROPE.
A POPULAR FRENCH CAFÉ WAS HIT. ANOTHER SENSELESS TRAGEDY.
EVER SINCE I LEFT METRO CITY. EVER SINCE THE BOMBING...
JANE!
JUST BREATHE.
JUST BREATHE. YOU ARE SAFE RIGHT NOW.
YOU ARE SAFE.
...I'M AFRAID OF THE EVIL THAT LIVES IN THE WORLD. IT'S A THING I WILL NEVER UNDERSTAND.

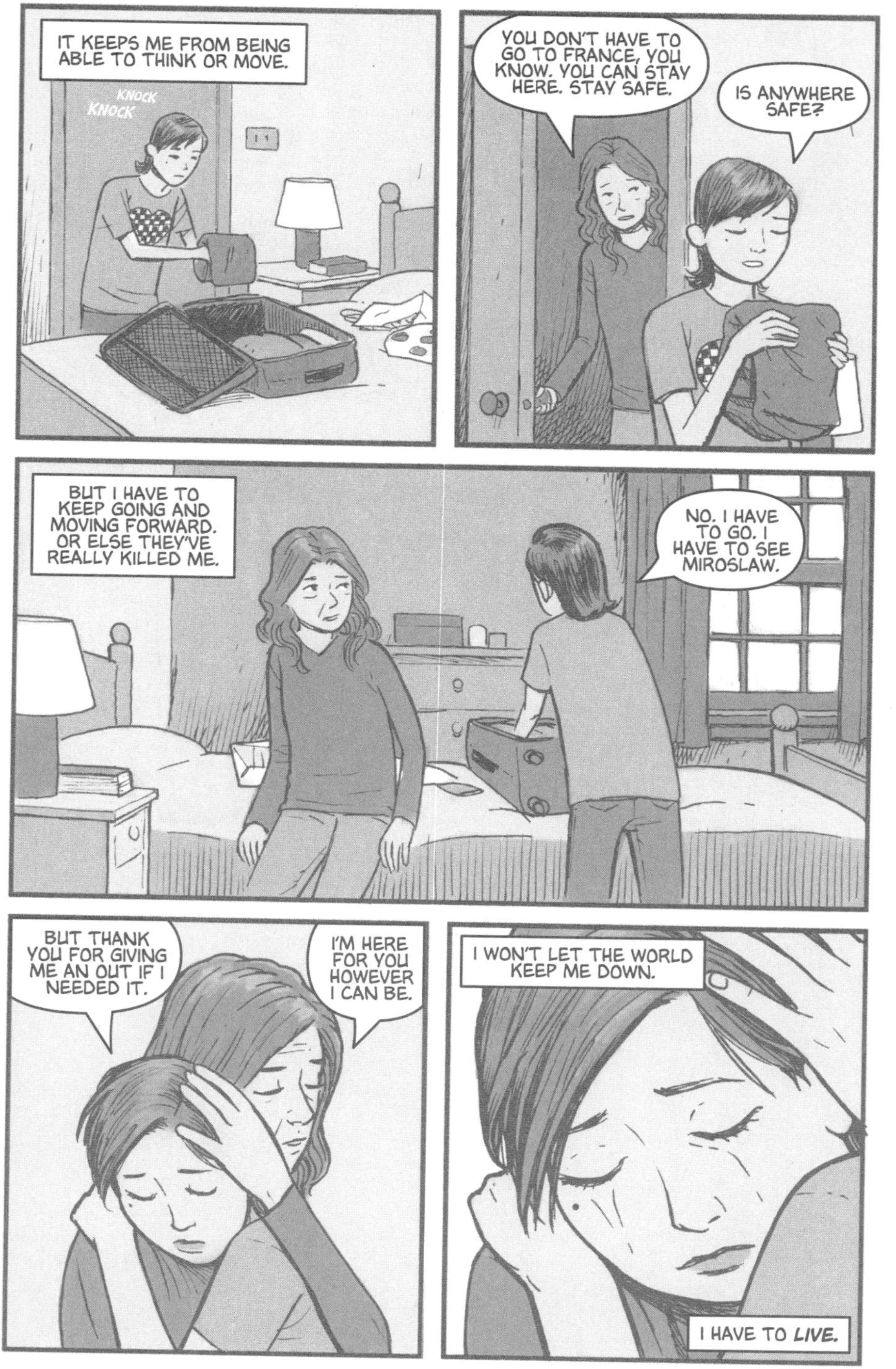
IT KEEPS ME FROM BEING ABLE TO THINK OR MOVE.
KNOCK KNOCK
YOU DON'T HAVE TO GO TO FRANCE, YOU KNOW. YOU CAN STAY HERE. STAY SAFE.
IS ANYWHERE SAFE?
BUT I HAVE TO KEEP GOING AND MOVING FORWARD. OR ELSE THEY'VE REALLY KILLED ME.
NO. I HAVE TO GO. I HAVE TO SEE MIROSLAW.
BUT THANK YOU FOR GIVING ME AN OUT IF I NEEDED IT.
I'M HERE FOR YOU HOWEVER I CAN BE.
I WON'T LET THE WORLD KEEP ME DOWN.
I HAVE TO *LIVE.*

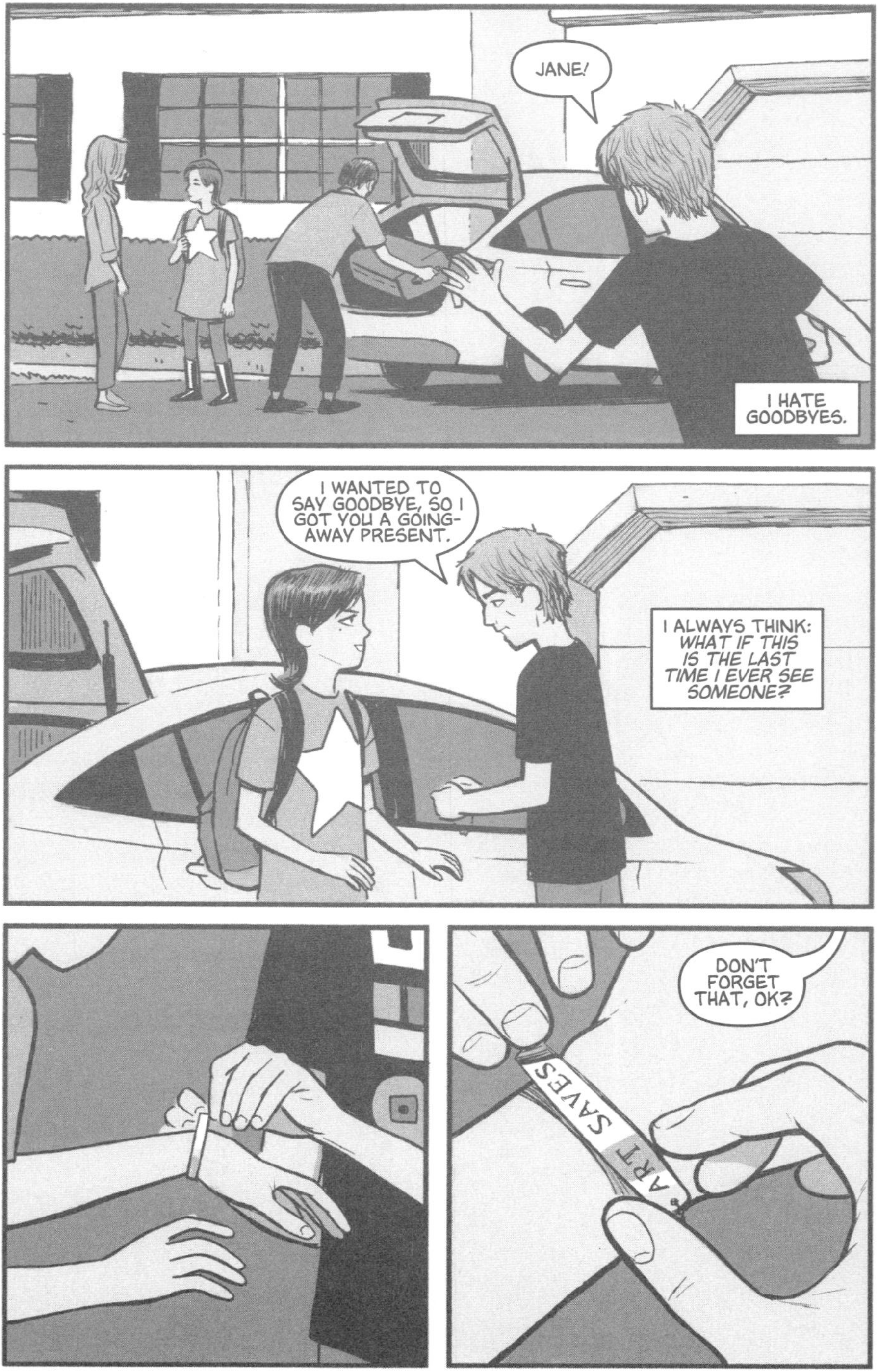
JANE!
I HATE GOODBYES.
I WANTED TO SAY GOODBYE, SO I GOT YOU A GOING-AWAY PRESENT.
I ALWAYS THINK: *WHAT IF THIS IS THE LAST TIME I EVER SEE SOMEONE?*
DON'T FORGET THAT, OK?
ART SAVES

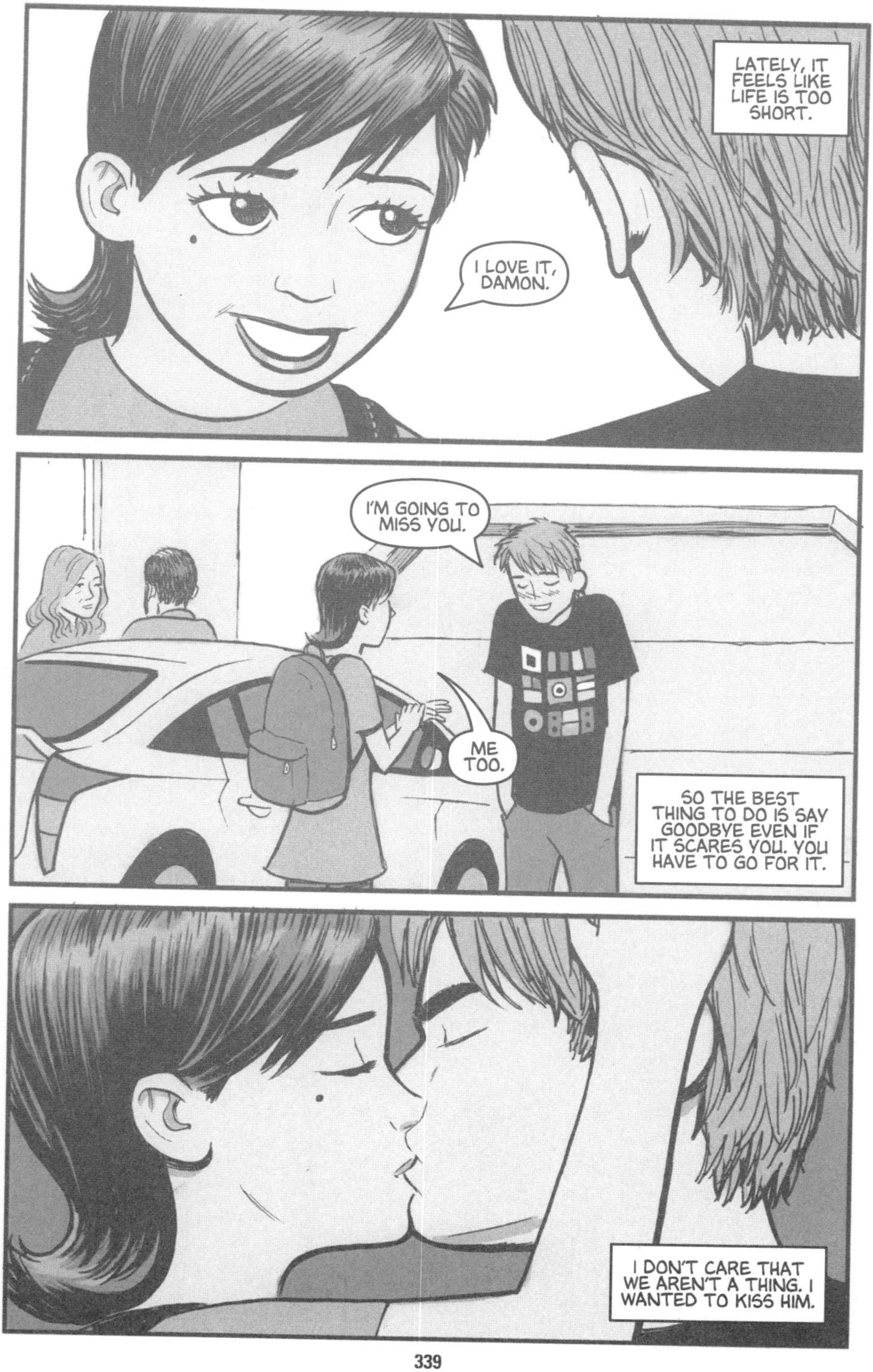
LATELY, IT FEELS LIKE LIFE IS TOO SHORT.
I LOVE IT, DAMON.
I'M GOING TO MISS YOU.
ME TOO.
SO THE BEST THING TO DO IS SAY GOODBYE EVEN IF IT SCARES YOU. YOU HAVE TO GO FOR IT.
I DON'T CARE THAT WE AREN'T A THING. I WANTED TO KISS HIM.

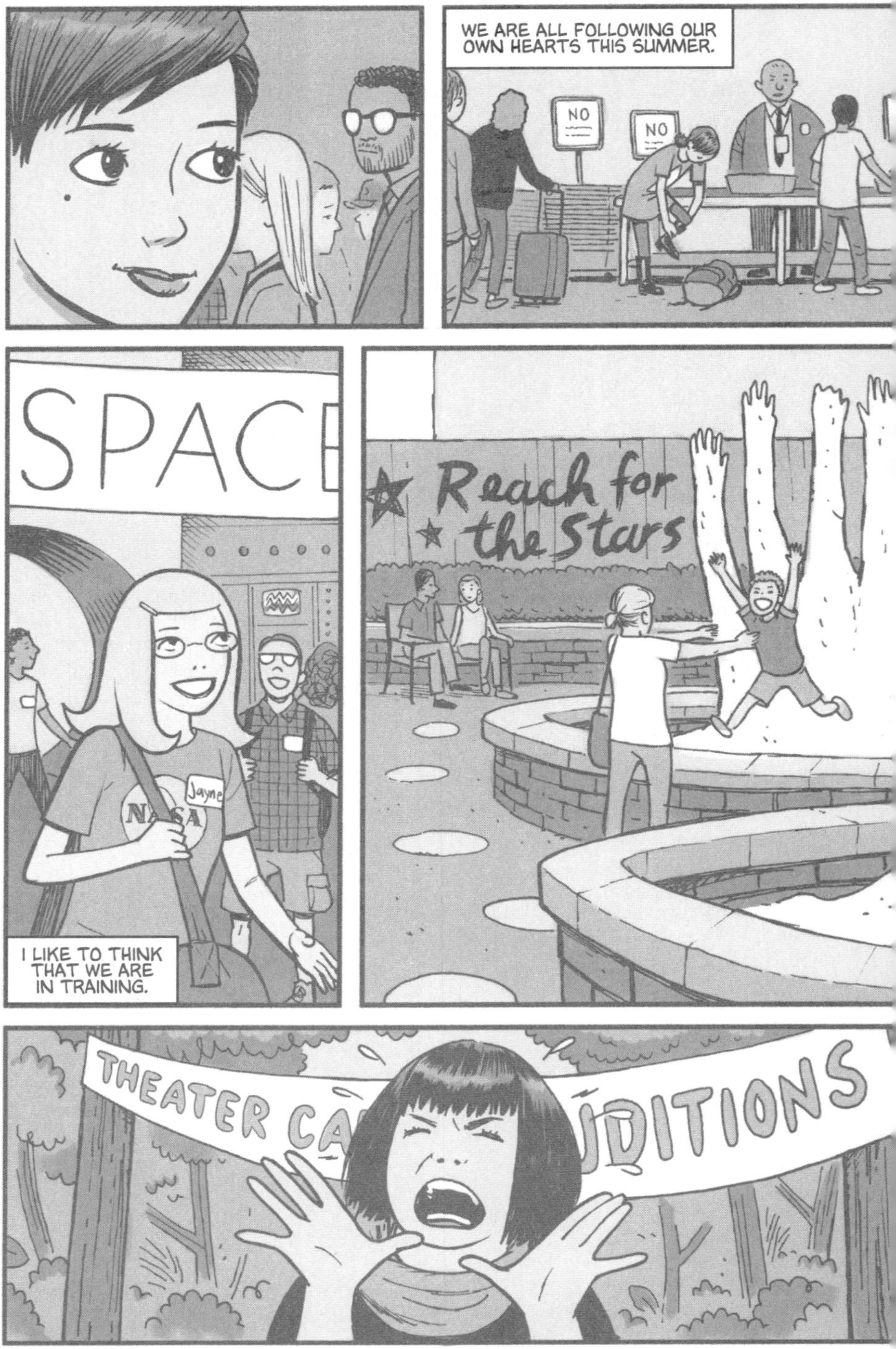
WE ARE ALL FOLLOWING OUR OWN HEARTS THIS SUMMER.
NO
NO
SPACE
Jayne
NASA
I LIKE TO THINK THAT WE ARE IN TRAINING.
Reach for the Stars
THEATER CA
UDITIONS

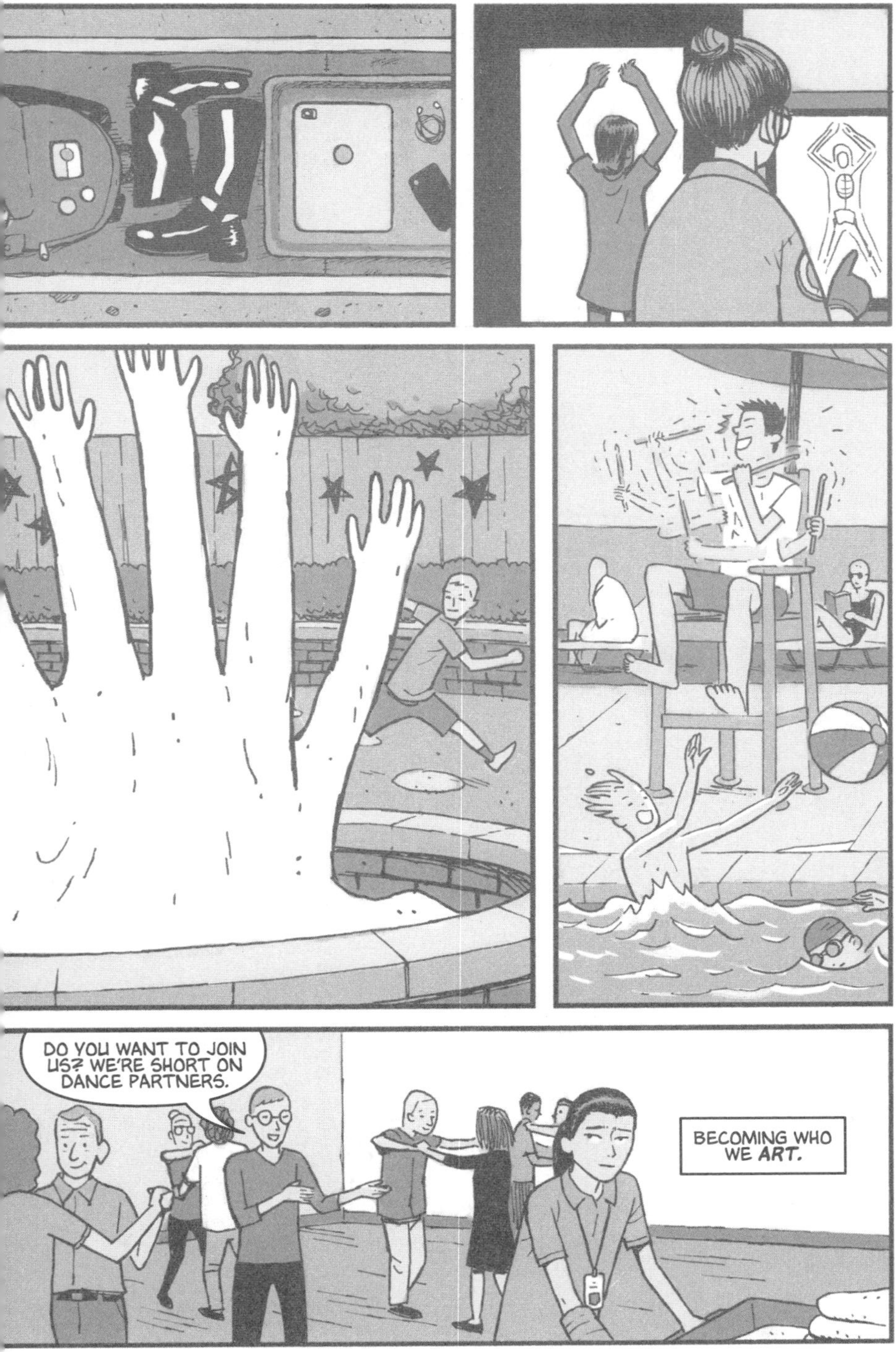
DO YOU WANT TO JOIN US? WE'RE SHORT ON DANCE PARTNERS.
BECOMING WHO WE *ART.*

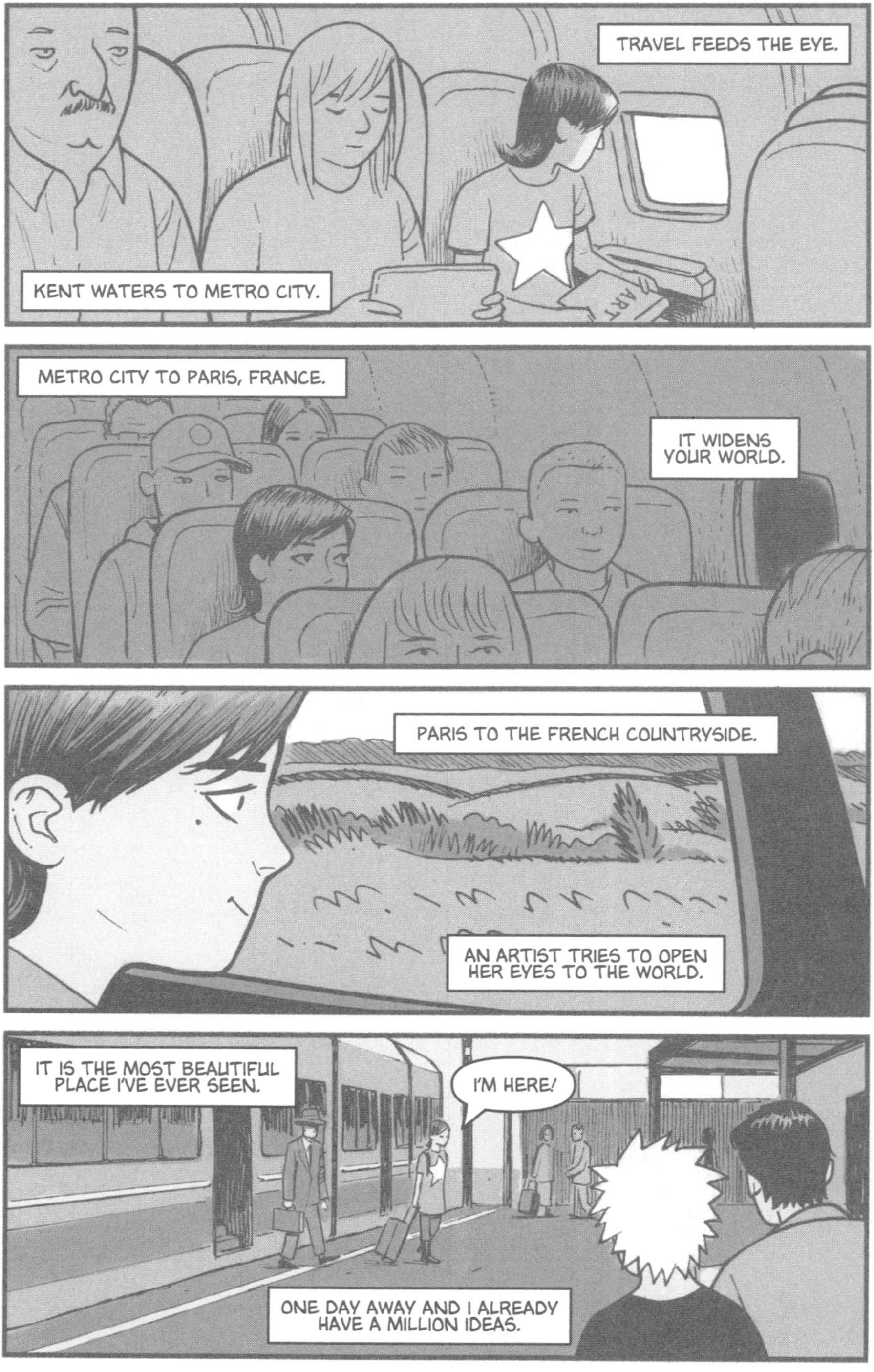
TRAVEL FEEDS THE EYE.
KENT WATERS TO METRO CITY.
ART
METRO CITY TO PARIS, FRANCE.
IT WIDENS YOUR WORLD.
PARIS TO THE FRENCH COUNTRYSIDE.
AN ARTIST TRIES TO OPEN HER EYES TO THE WORLD.
IT IS THE MOST BEAUTIFUL PLACE I'VE EVER SEEN.
I'M HERE!
ONE DAY AWAY AND I ALREADY HAVE A MILLION IDEAS.

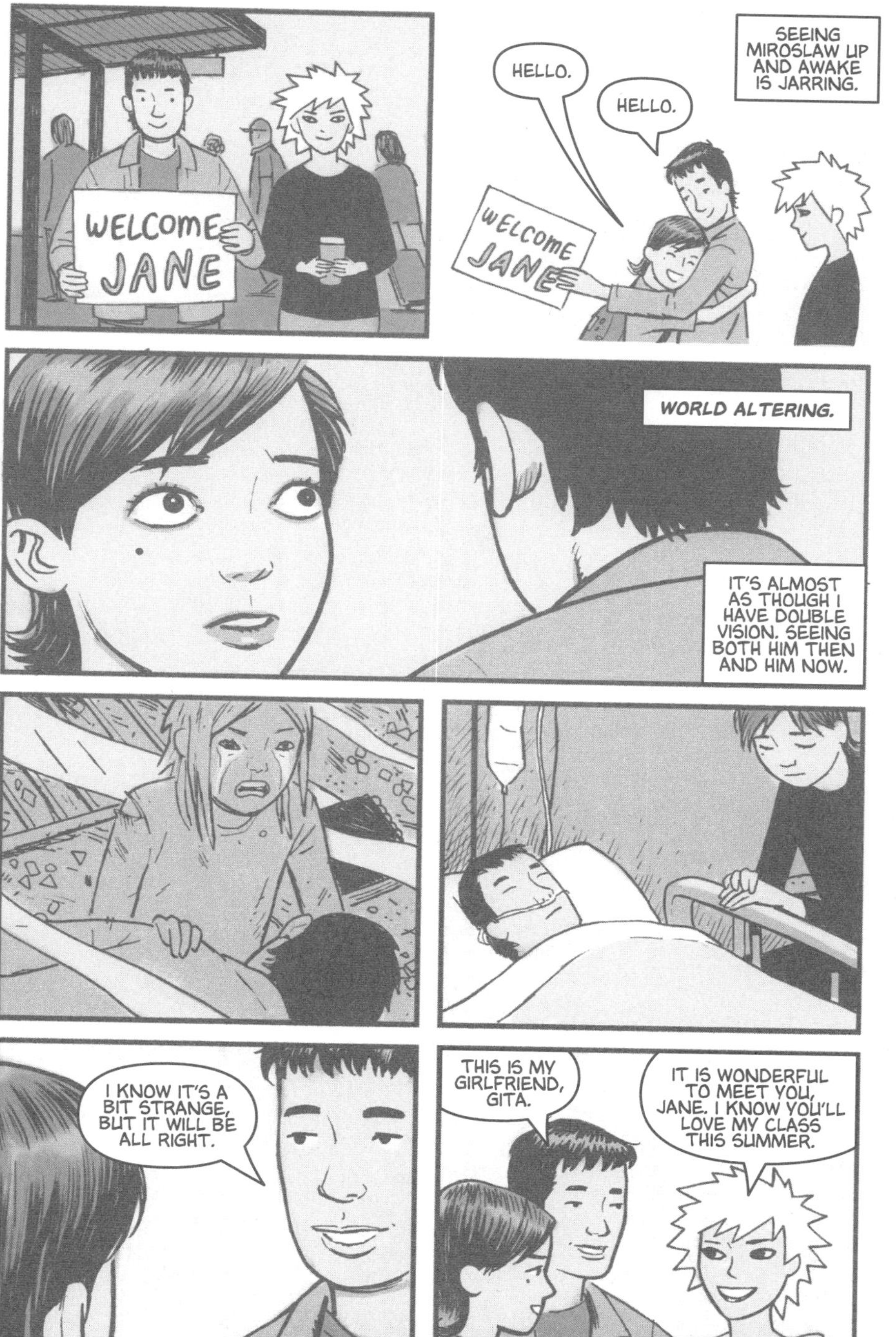
WELCOME JANE
HELLO.
HELLO.
SEEING MIROSLAW UP AND AWAKE IS JARRING.
WELCOME JANE
WORLD ALTERING.
IT'S ALMOST AS THOUGH I HAVE DOUBLE VISION. SEEING BOTH HIM THEN AND HIM NOW.
I KNOW IT'S A BIT STRANGE, BUT IT WILL BE ALL RIGHT.
THIS IS MY GIRLFRIEND, GITA.
IT IS WONDERFUL TO MEET YOU, JANE. I KNOW YOU'LL LOVE MY CLASS THIS SUMMER.

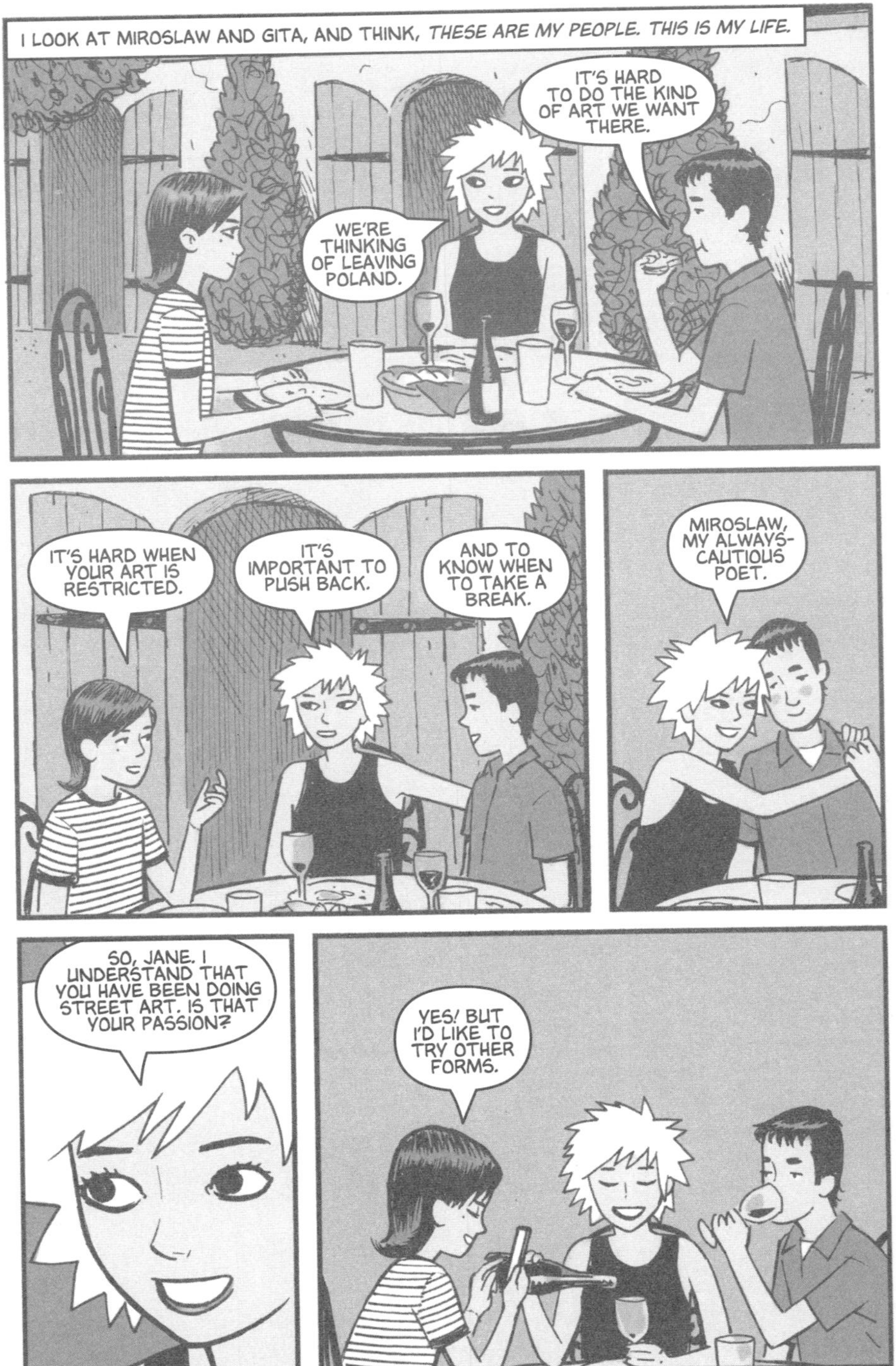
I LOOK AT MIROSLAW AND GITA, AND THINK, *THESE ARE MY PEOPLE. THIS IS MY LIFE.*
WE'RE THINKING OF LEAVING POLAND.
IT'S HARD TO DO THE KIND OF ART WE WANT THERE.
IT'S HARD WHEN YOUR ART IS RESTRICTED.
IT'S IMPORTANT TO PUSH BACK.
AND TO KNOW WHEN TO TAKE A BREAK.
MIROSLAW, MY ALWAYS-CAUTIOUS POET.
SO, JANE. I UNDERSTAND THAT YOU HAVE BEEN DOING STREET ART. IS THAT YOUR PASSION?
YES! BUT I'D LIKE TO TRY OTHER FORMS.

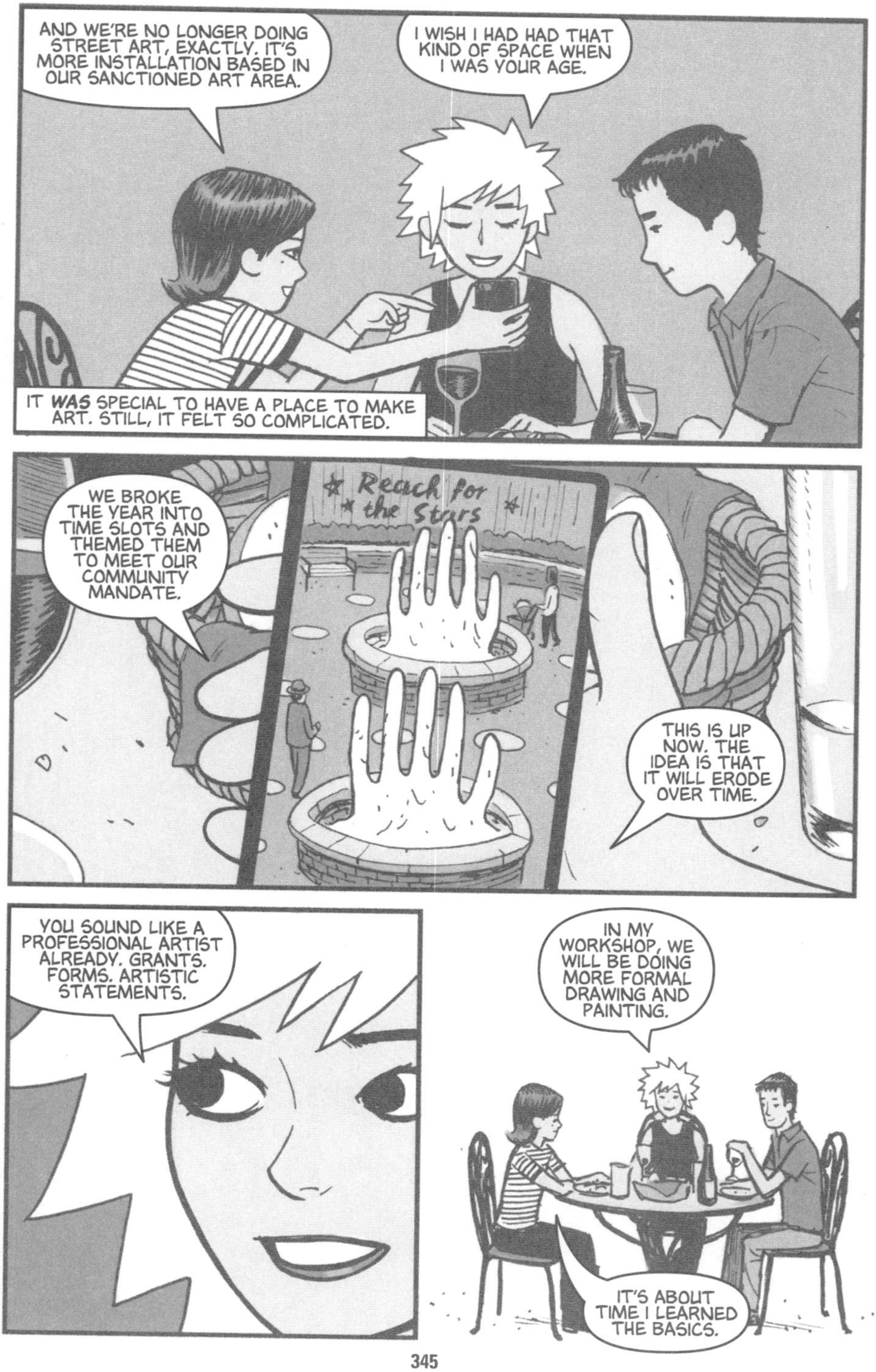
AND WE'RE NO LONGER DOING STREET ART, EXACTLY. IT'S MORE INSTALLATION BASED IN OUR SANCTIONED ART AREA.
I WISH I HAD HAD THAT KIND OF SPACE WHEN I WAS YOUR AGE.
IT *WAS* SPECIAL TO HAVE A PLACE TO MAKE ART. STILL, IT FELT SO COMPLICATED.
WE BROKE THE YEAR INTO TIME SLOTS AND THEMED THEM TO MEET OUR COMMUNITY MANDATE.
Reach for the Stars
THIS IS UP NOW. THE IDEA IS THAT IT WILL ERODE OVER TIME.
YOU SOUND LIKE A PROFESSIONAL ARTIST ALREADY. GRANTS. FORMS. ARTISTIC STATEMENTS.
IN MY WORKSHOP, WE WILL BE DOING MORE FORMAL DRAWING AND PAINTING.
IT'S ABOUT TIME I LEARNED THE BASICS.

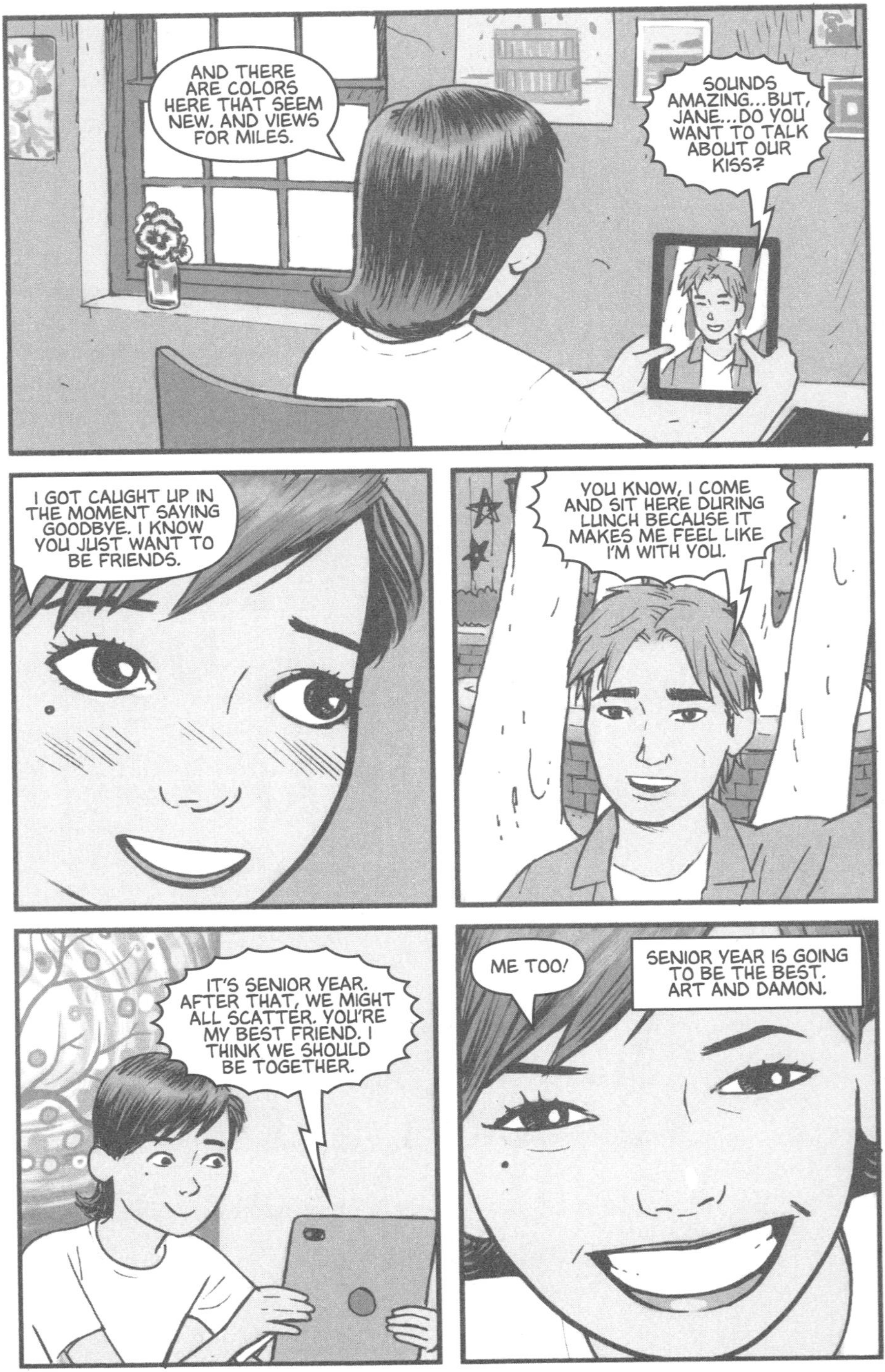
AND THERE ARE COLORS HERE THAT SEEM NEW. AND VIEWS FOR MILES.
SOUNDS AMAZING...BUT, JANE...DO YOU WANT TO TALK ABOUT OUR KISS?
I GOT CAUGHT UP IN THE MOMENT SAYING GOODBYE. I KNOW YOU JUST WANT TO BE FRIENDS.
YOU KNOW, I COME AND SIT HERE DURING LUNCH BECAUSE IT MAKES ME FEEL LIKE I'M WITH YOU.
IT'S SENIOR YEAR. AFTER THAT, WE MIGHT ALL SCATTER. YOU'RE MY BEST FRIEND. I THINK WE SHOULD BE TOGETHER.
ME TOO!
SENIOR YEAR IS GOING TO BE THE BEST. ART AND DAMON.

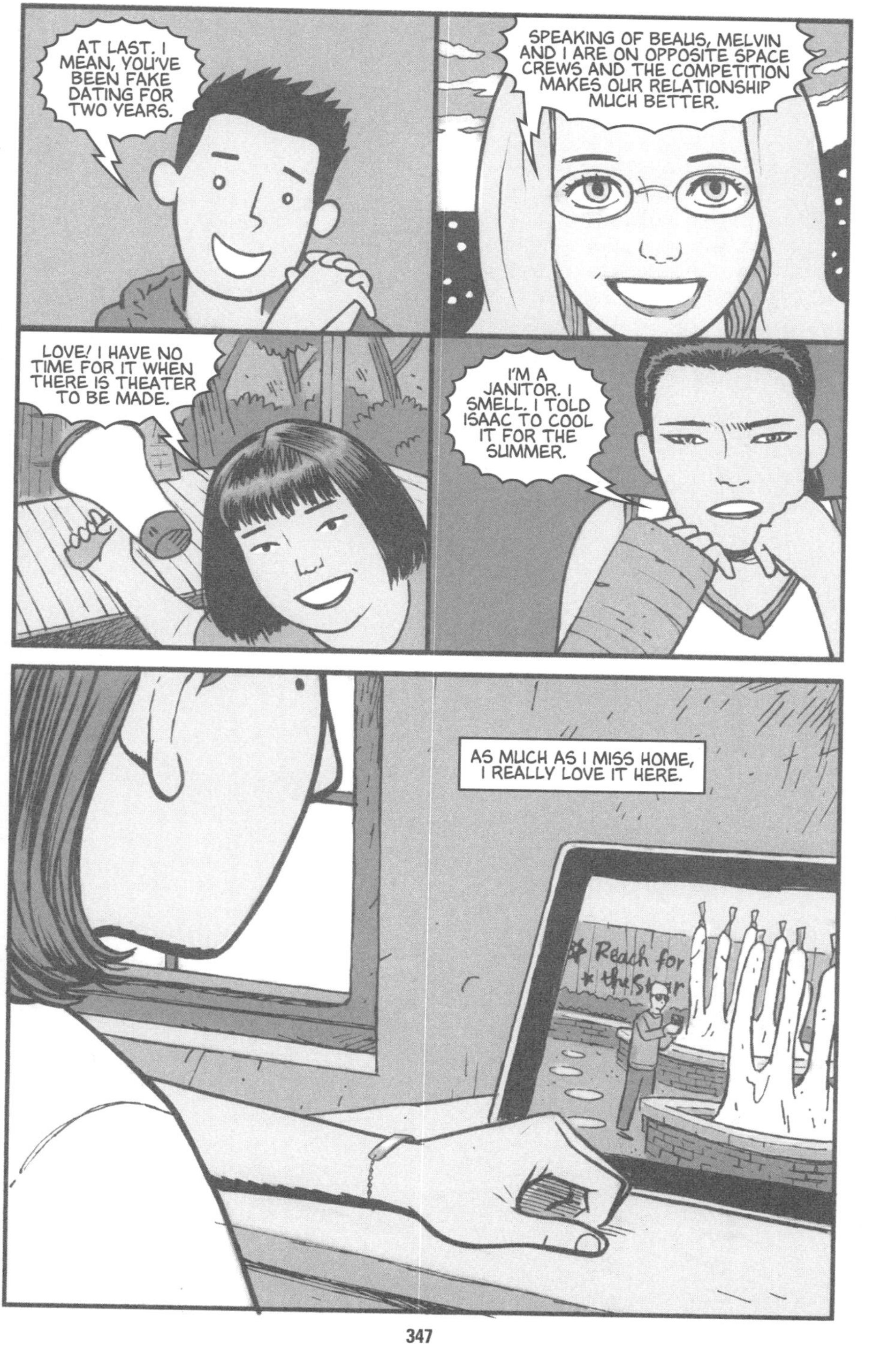
AT LAST. I MEAN, YOU'VE BEEN FAKE DATING FOR TWO YEARS.
SPEAKING OF BEAUS, MELVIN AND I ARE ON OPPOSITE SPACE CREWS AND THE COMPETITION MAKES OUR RELATIONSHIP MUCH BETTER.
LOVE! I HAVE NO TIME FOR IT WHEN THERE IS THEATER TO BE MADE.
I'M A JANITOR. I SMELL. I TOLD ISAAC TO COOL IT FOR THE SUMMER.
AS MUCH AS I MISS HOME, I REALLY LOVE IT HERE.
Reach for the Star

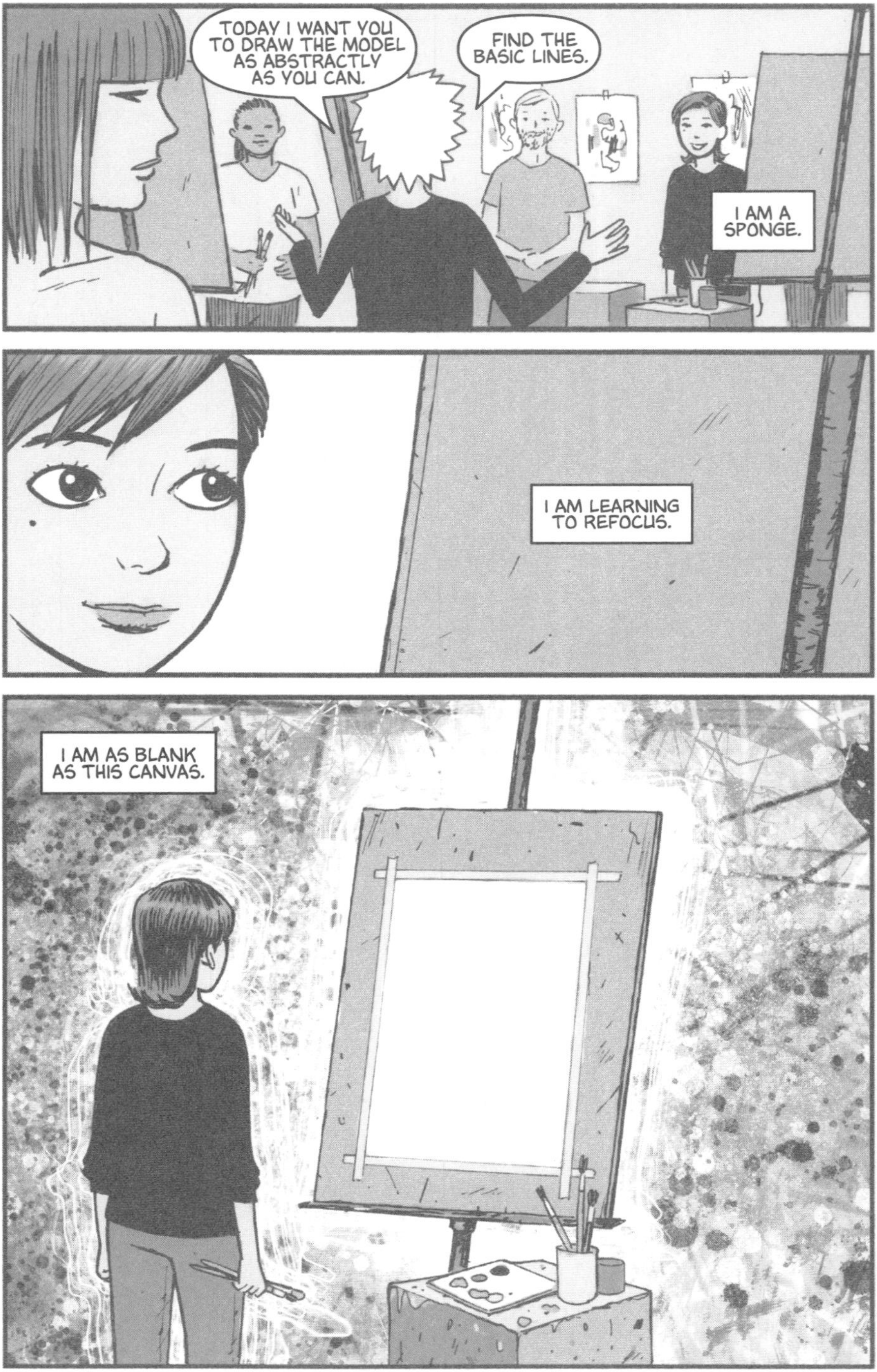
TODAY I WANT YOU TO DRAW THE MODEL AS ABSTRACTLY AS YOU CAN.
FIND THE BASIC LINES.
I AM A SPONGE.
I AM LEARNING TO REFOCUS.
I AM AS BLANK AS THIS CANVAS.

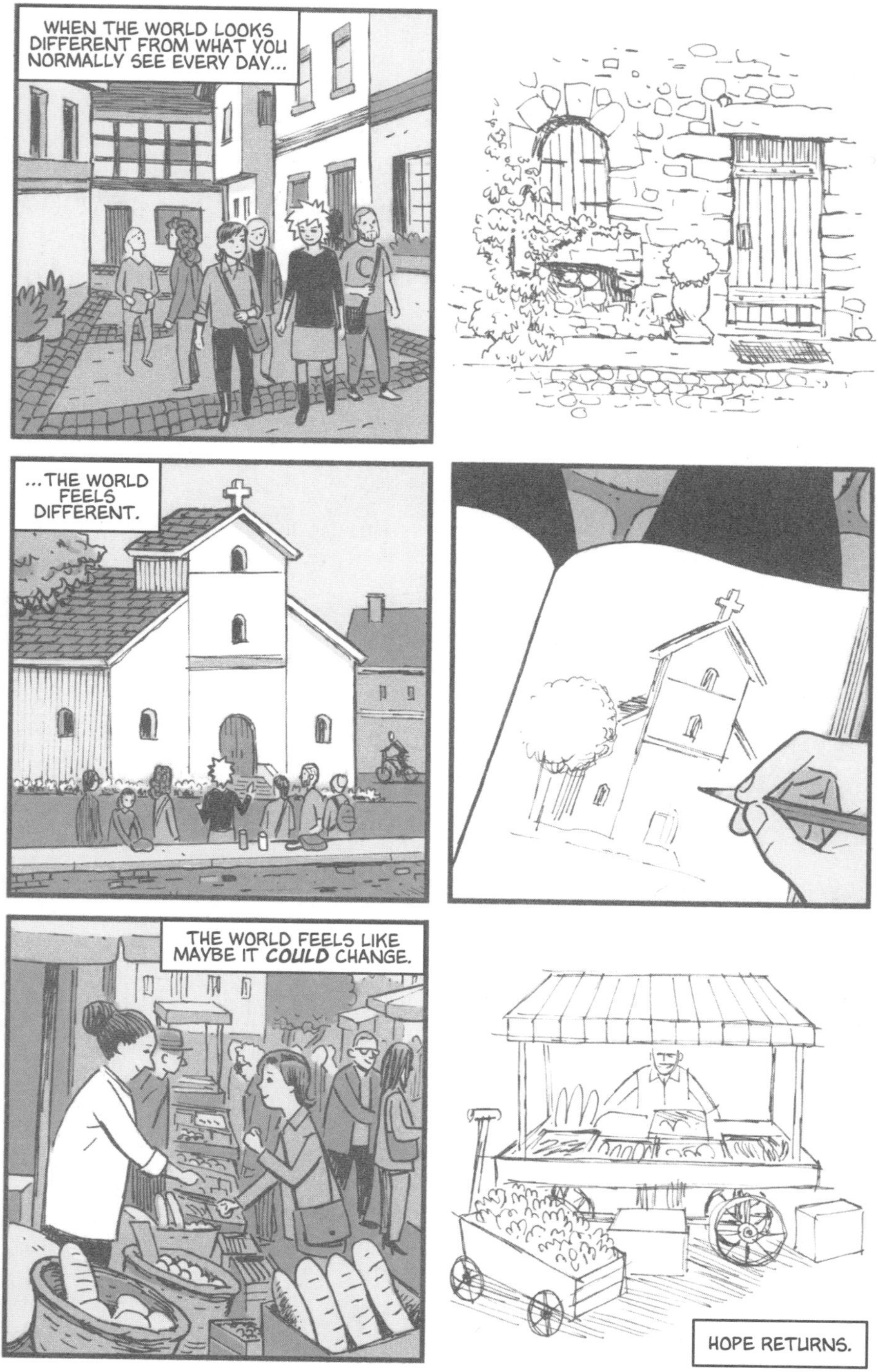
WHEN THE WORLD LOOKS DIFFERENT FROM WHAT YOU NORMALLY SEE EVERY DAY...
...THE WORLD FEELS DIFFERENT.
THE WORLD FEELS LIKE MAYBE IT COULD CHANGE.
HOPE RETURNS.

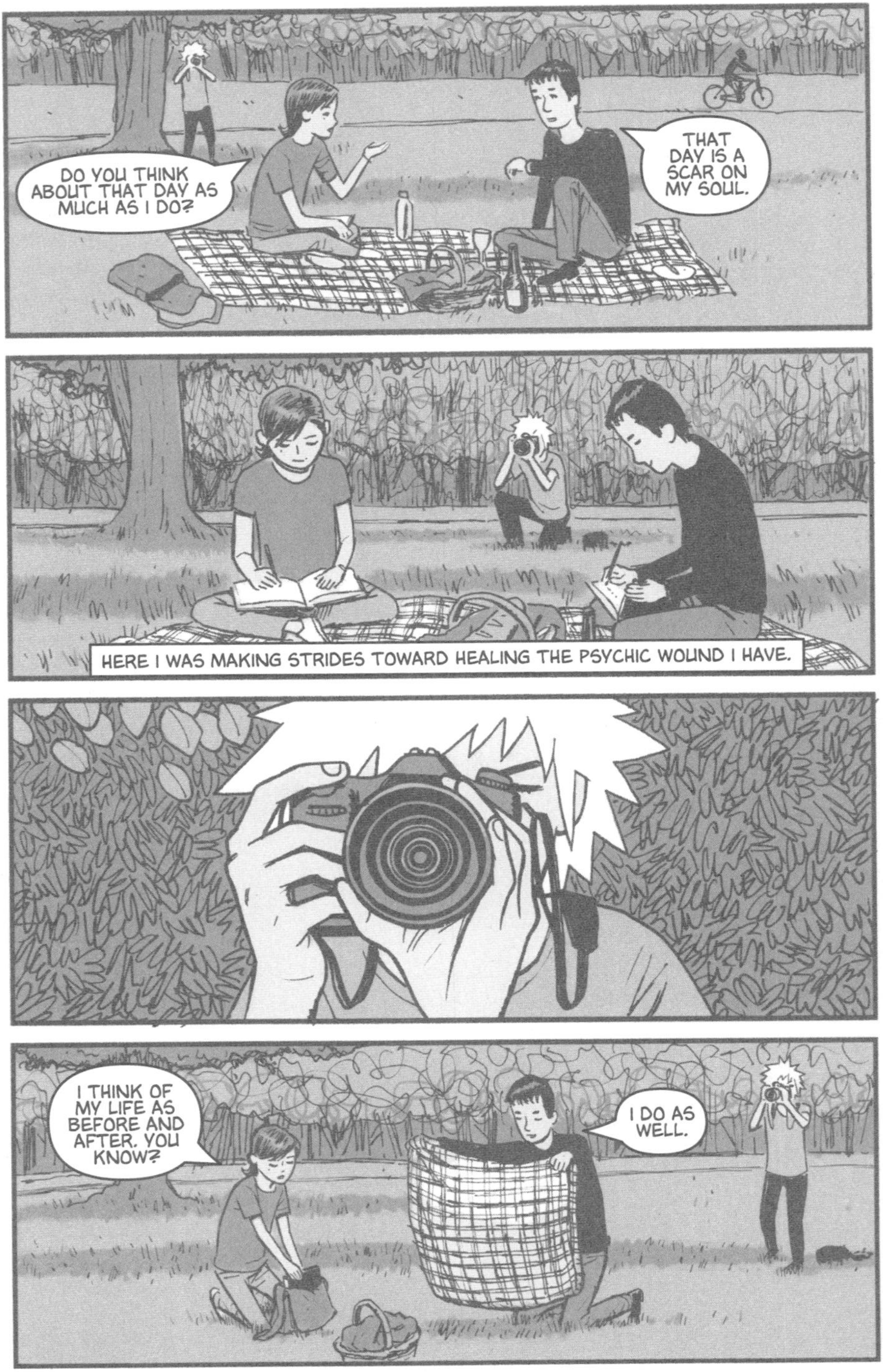
DO YOU THINK ABOUT THAT DAY AS MUCH AS I DO?
THAT DAY IS A SCAR ON MY SOUL.
HERE I WAS MAKING STRIDES TOWARD HEALING THE PSYCHIC WOUND I HAVE.
I THINK OF MY LIFE AS BEFORE AND AFTER. YOU KNOW?
I DO AS WELL.

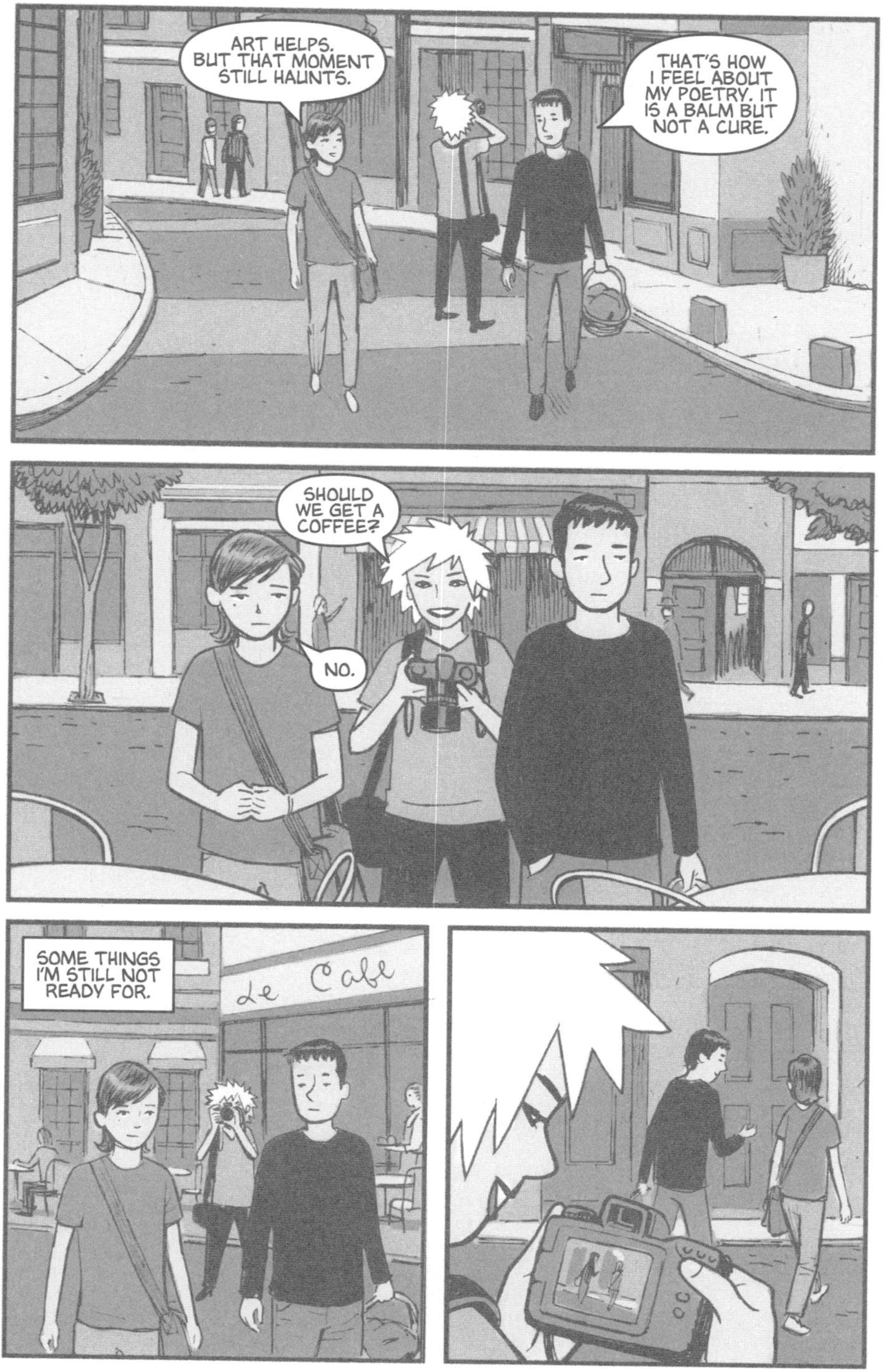
ART HELPS. BUT THAT MOMENT STILL HAUNTS.
THAT'S HOW I FEEL ABOUT MY POETRY. IT IS A BALM BUT NOT A CURE.
SHOULD WE GET A COFFEE?
NO.
SOME THINGS I'M STILL NOT READY FOR.
Le Cafe

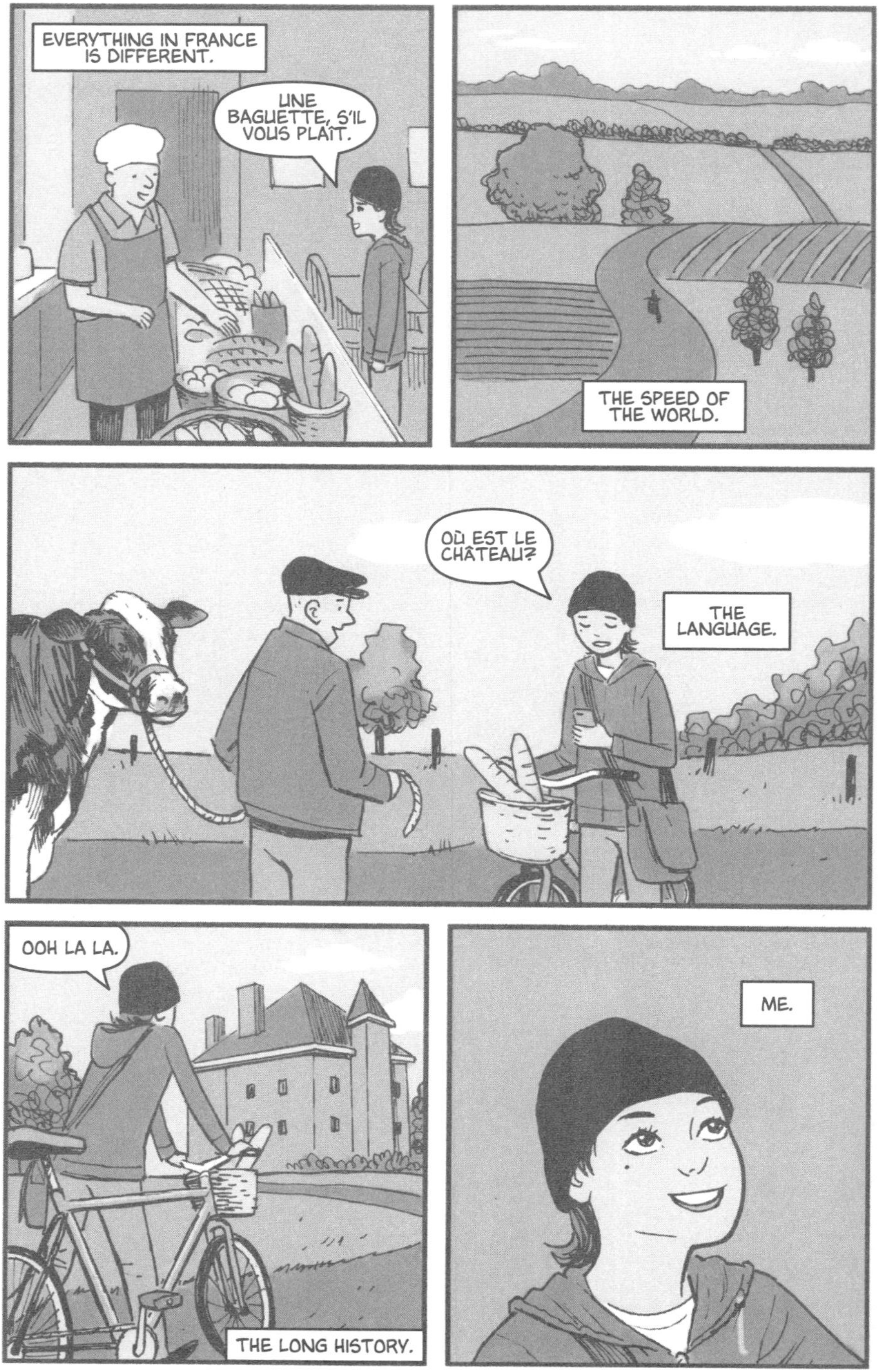
EVERYTHING IN FRANCE IS DIFFERENT.
UNE BAGUETTE, S'IL VOUS PLAÎT.
THE SPEED OF THE WORLD.
OÙ EST LE CHÂTEAU?
THE LANGUAGE.
OOH LA LA.
THE LONG HISTORY.
ME.

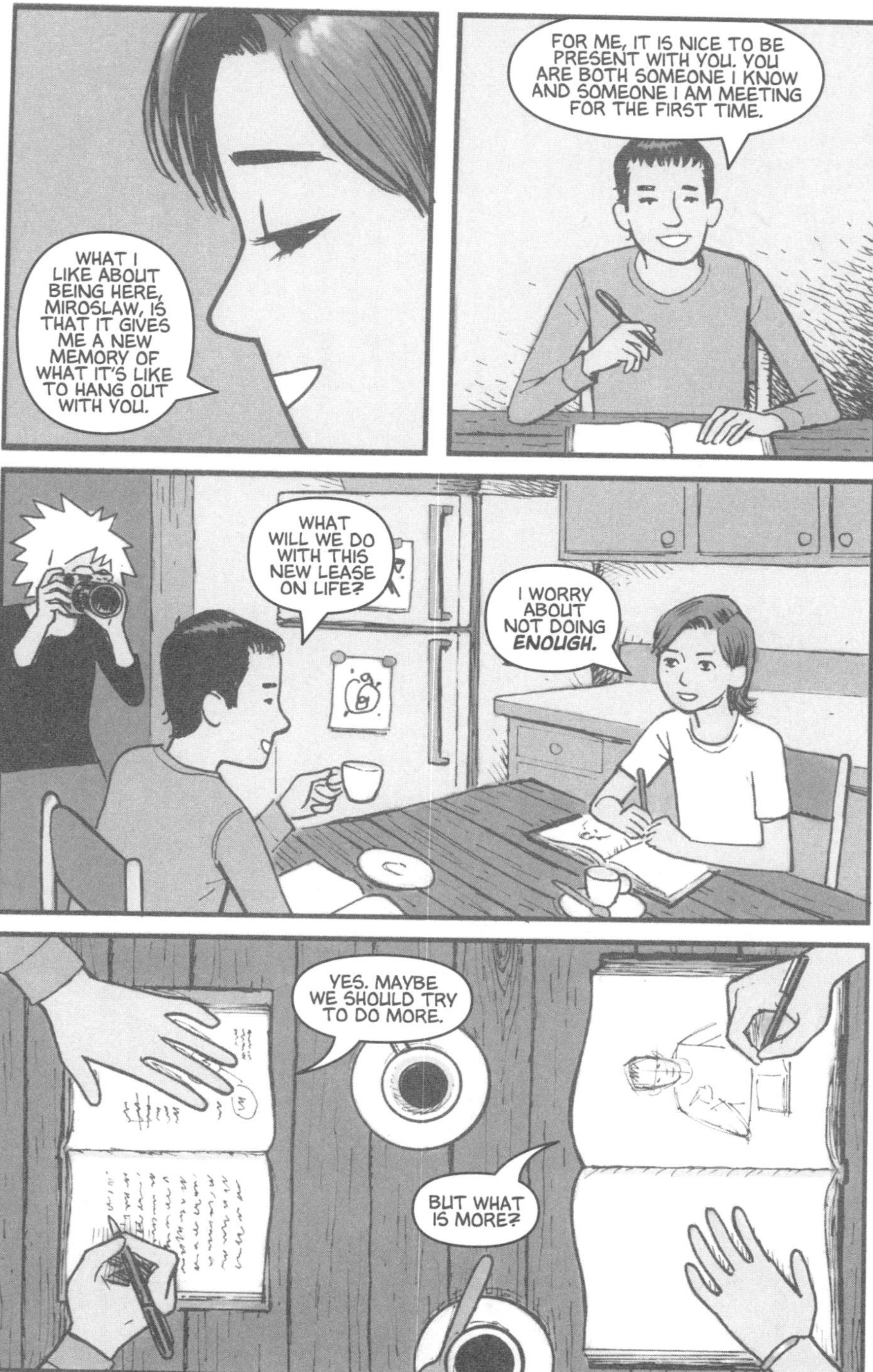
WHAT I LIKE ABOUT BEING HERE, MIROSLAW, IS THAT IT GIVES ME A NEW MEMORY OF WHAT IT'S LIKE TO HANG OUT WITH YOU.
FOR ME, IT IS NICE TO BE PRESENT WITH YOU. YOU ARE BOTH SOMEONE I KNOW AND SOMEONE I AM MEETING FOR THE FIRST TIME.
WHAT WILL WE DO WITH THIS NEW LEASE ON LIFE?
I WORRY ABOUT NOT DOING ***ENOUGH.***
YES. MAYBE WE SHOULD TRY TO DO MORE.
BUT WHAT IS MORE?

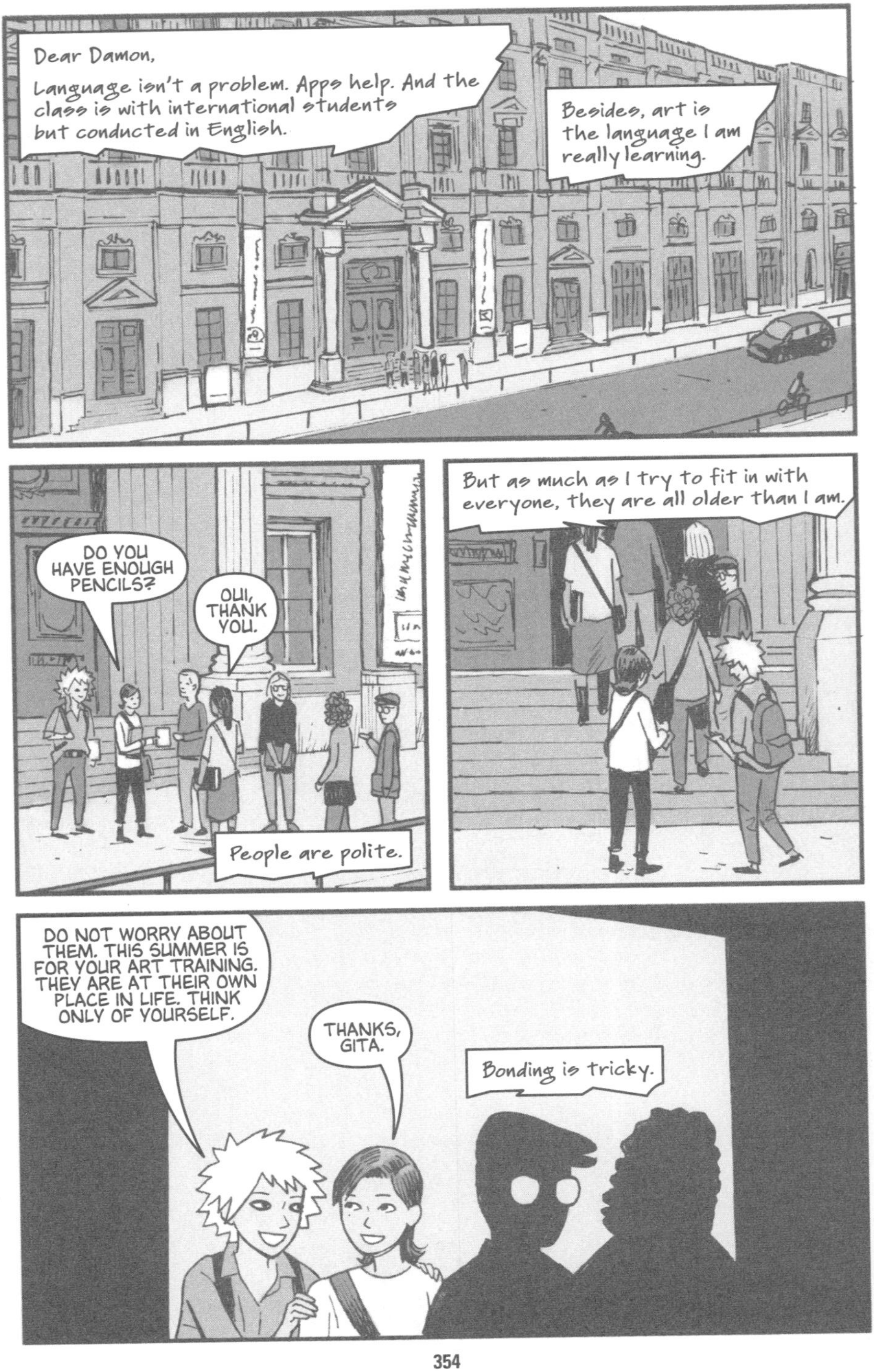
Dear Damon,
Language isn't a problem. Apps help. And the class is with international students but conducted in English.
Besides, art is the language I am really learning.
DO YOU HAVE ENOUGH PENCILS?
OUI, THANK YOU.
People are polite.
But as much as I try to fit in with everyone, they are all older than I am.
DO NOT WORRY ABOUT THEM. THIS SUMMER IS FOR YOUR ART TRAINING. THEY ARE AT THEIR OWN PLACE IN LIFE. THINK ONLY OF YOURSELF.
THANKS, GITA.
Bonding is tricky.

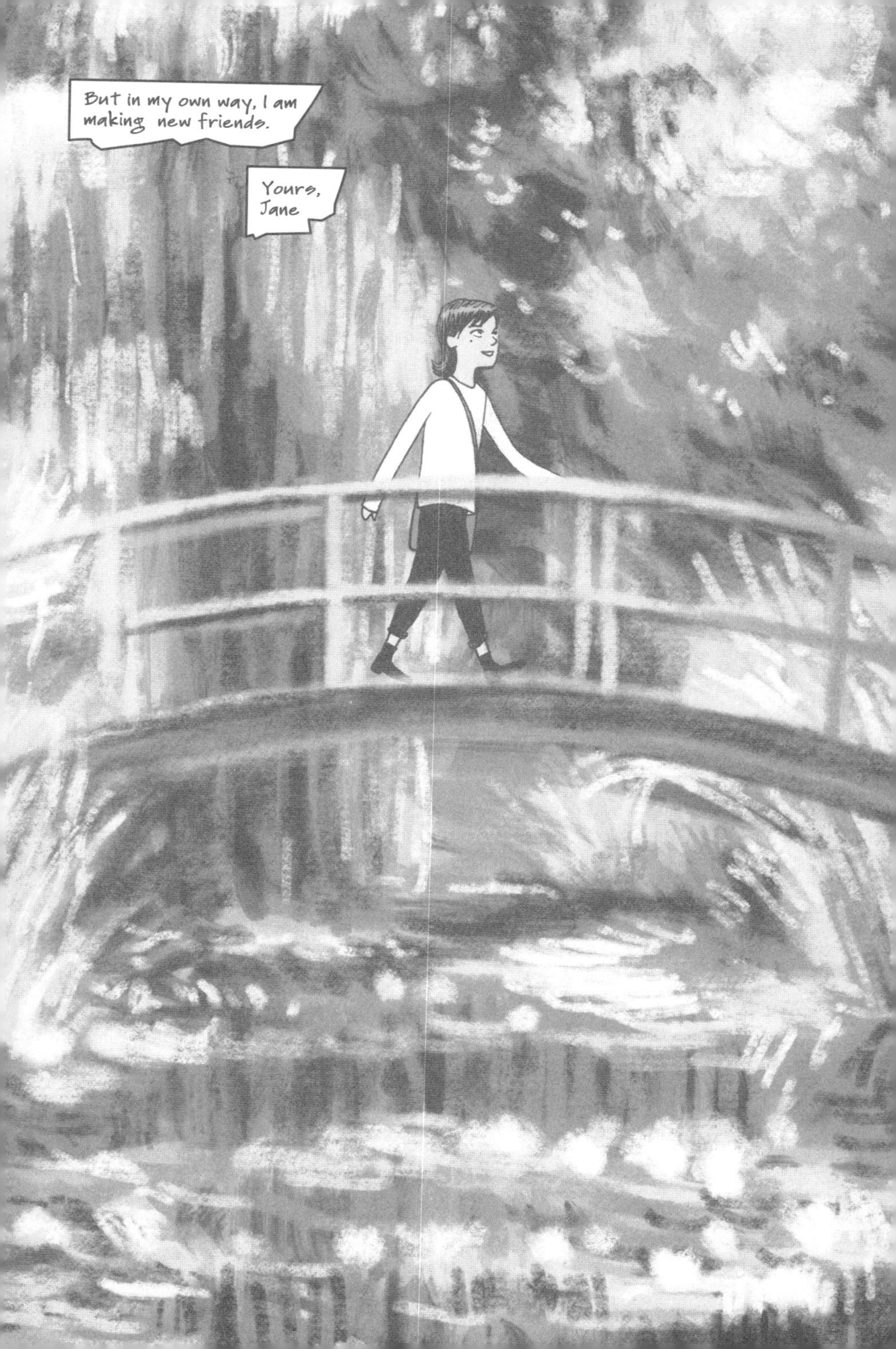
But in my own way, I am making new friends.
Yours, Jane

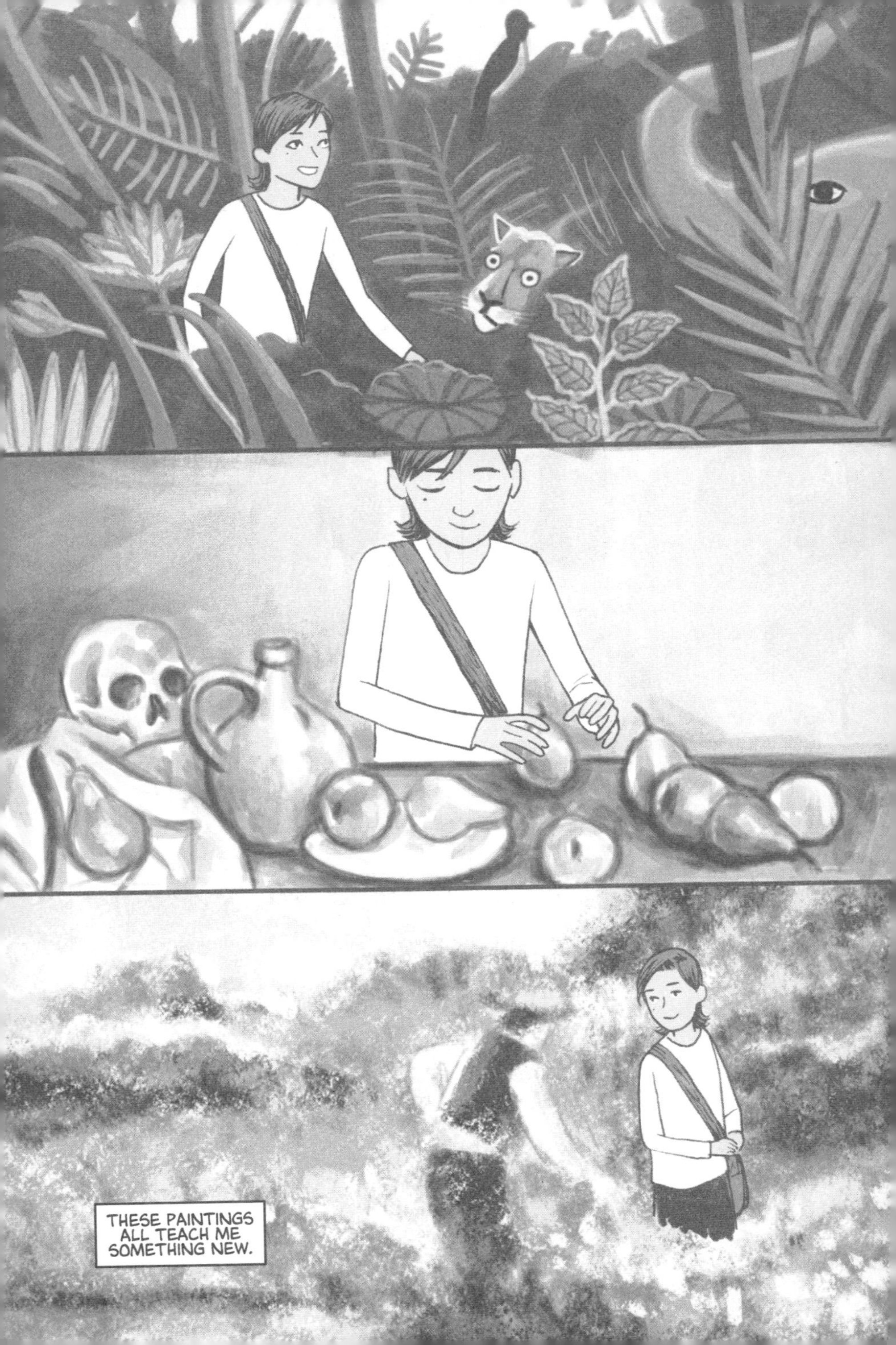
THESE PAINTINGS ALL TEACH ME SOMETHING NEW.

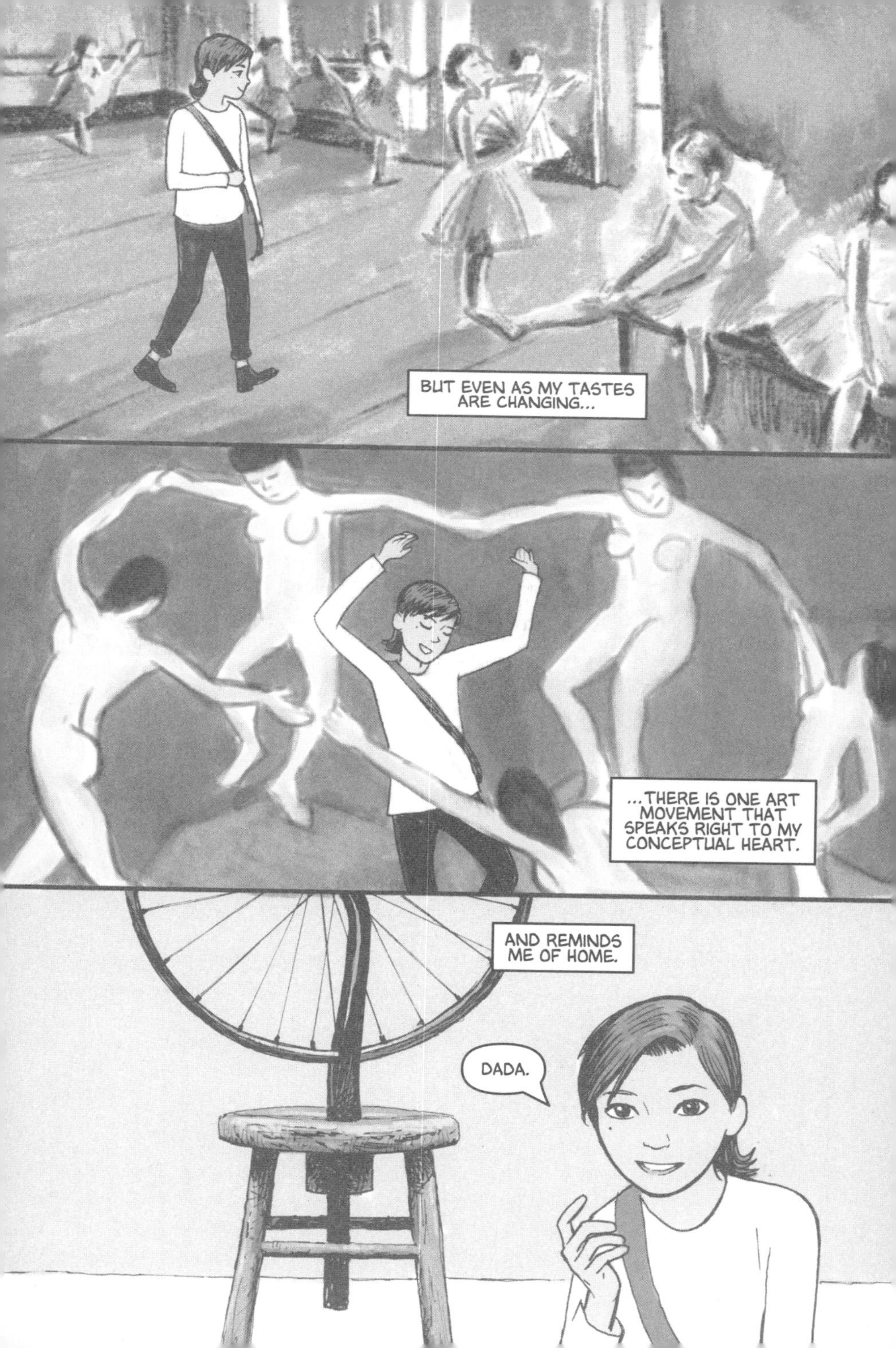
BUT EVEN AS MY TASTES ARE CHANGING...
...THERE IS ONE ART MOVEMENT THAT SPEAKS RIGHT TO MY CONCEPTUAL HEART.
AND REMINDS ME OF HOME.
DADA.

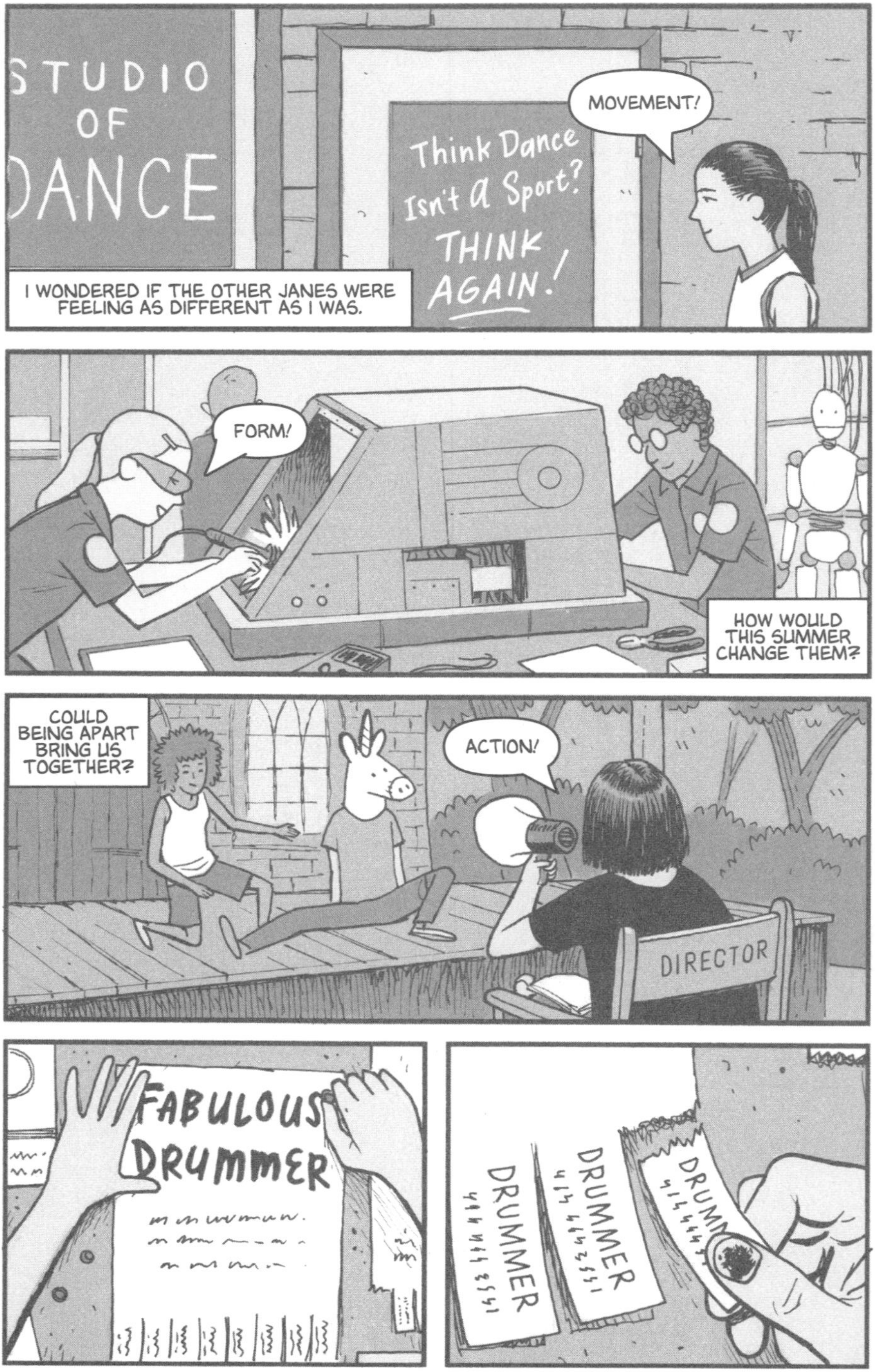
STUDIO OF DANCE
Think Dance Isn't a Sport? THINK AGAIN!
I WONDERED IF THE OTHER JANES WERE FEELING AS DIFFERENT AS I WAS.
MOVEMENT!
FORM!
HOW WOULD THIS SUMMER CHANGE THEM?
COULD BEING APART BRING US TOGETHER?
ACTION!
DIRECTOR
FABULOUS DRUMMER
DRUMMER
DRUMMER
DRUMM

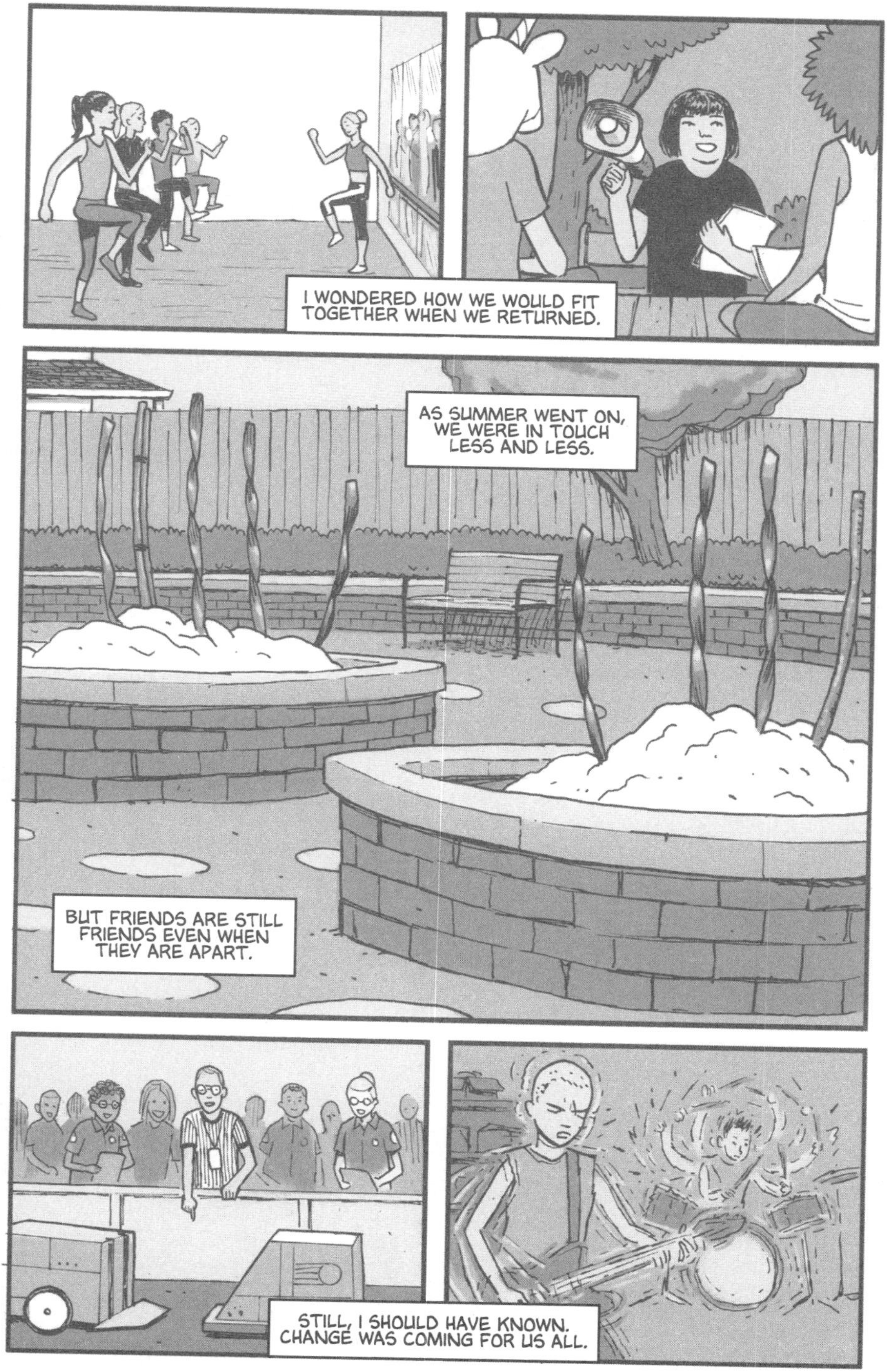
I WONDERED HOW WE WOULD FIT TOGETHER WHEN WE RETURNED.
AS SUMMER WENT ON, WE WERE IN TOUCH LESS AND LESS.
BUT FRIENDS ARE STILL FRIENDS EVEN WHEN THEY ARE APART.
STILL, I SHOULD HAVE KNOWN. CHANGE WAS COMING FOR US ALL.

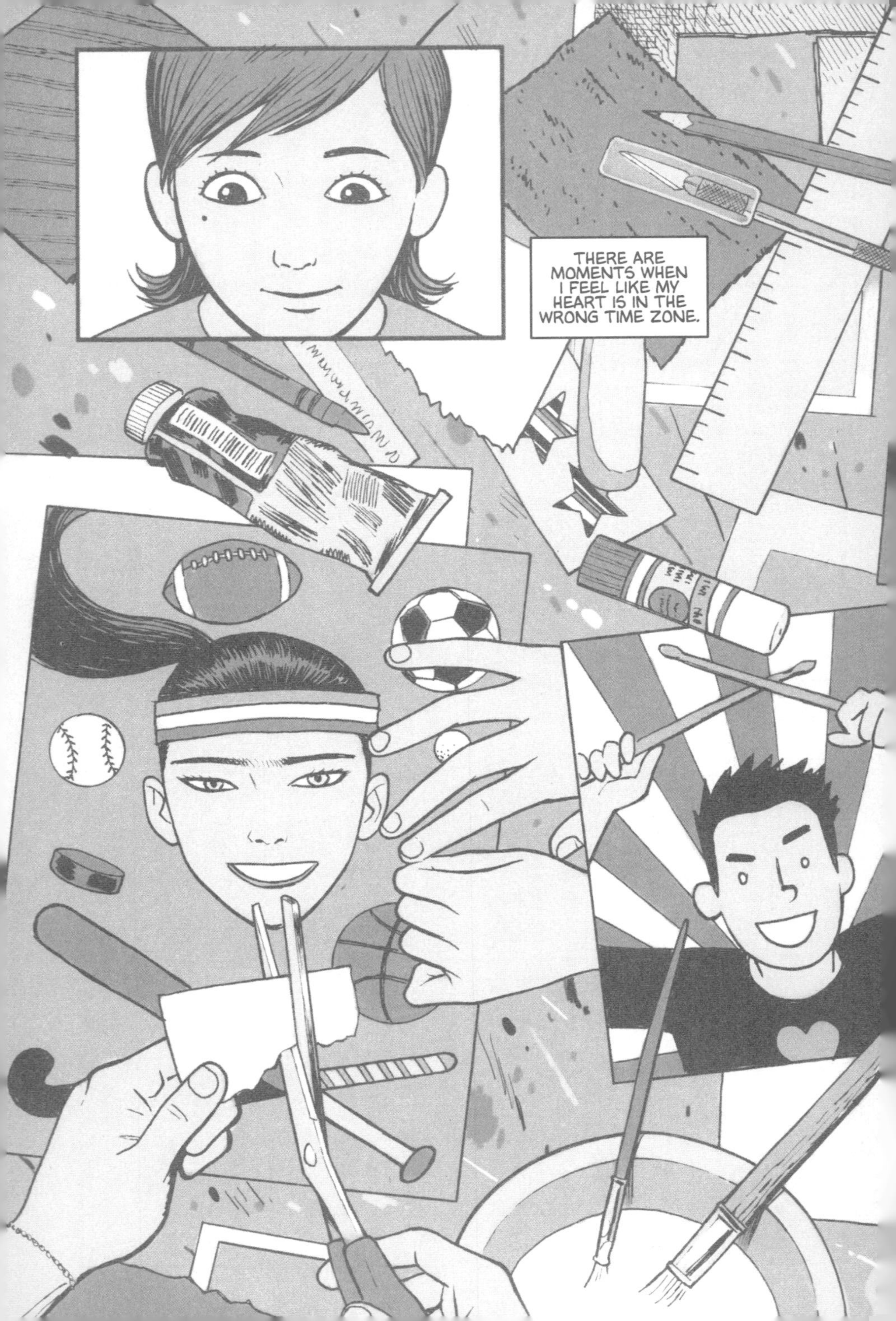
THERE ARE MOMENTS WHEN I FEEL LIKE MY HEART IS IN THE WRONG TIME ZONE.

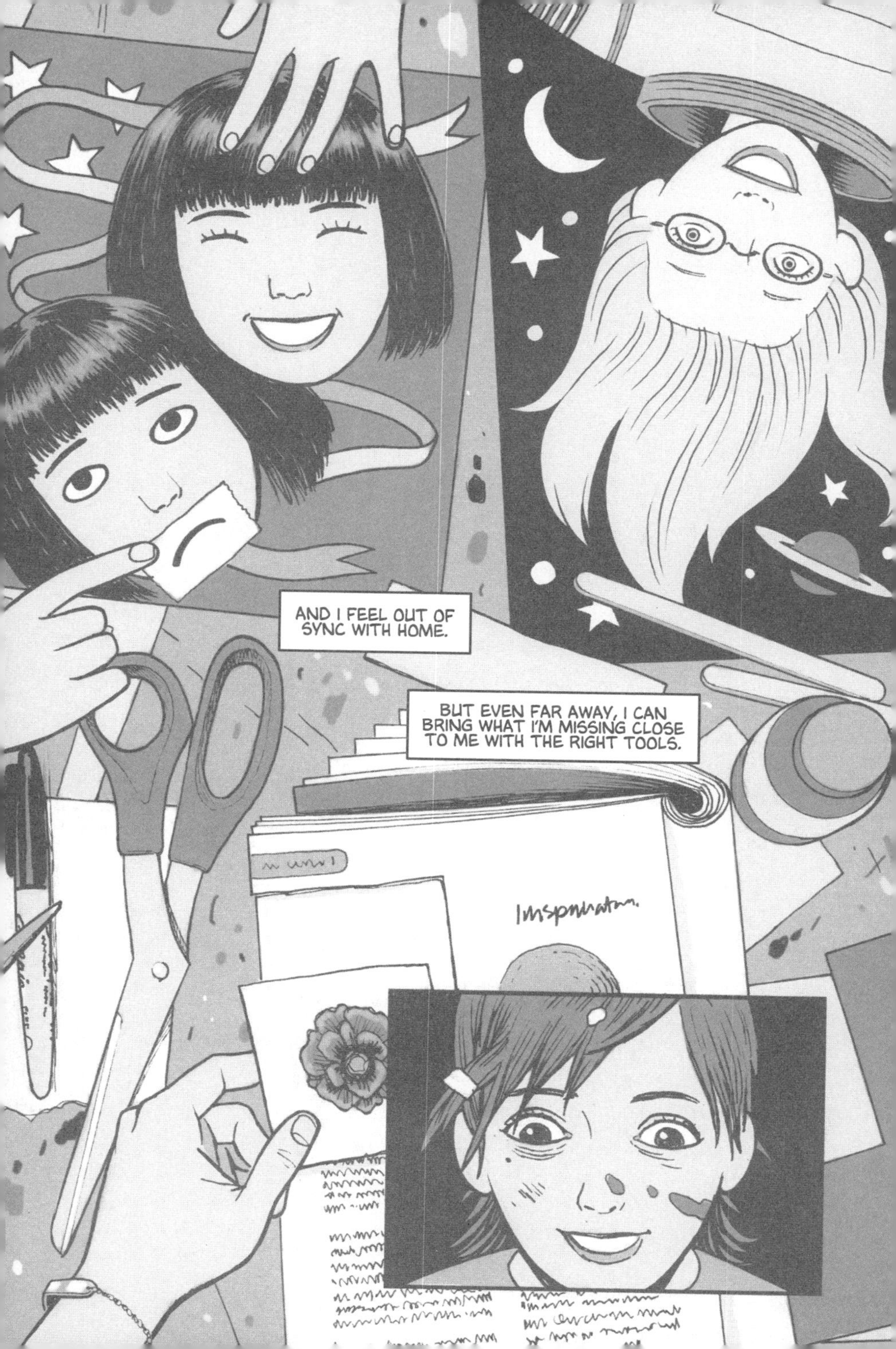
AND I FEEL OUT OF SYNC WITH HOME.
BUT EVEN FAR AWAY, I CAN BRING WHAT I'M MISSING CLOSE TO ME WITH THE RIGHT TOOLS.

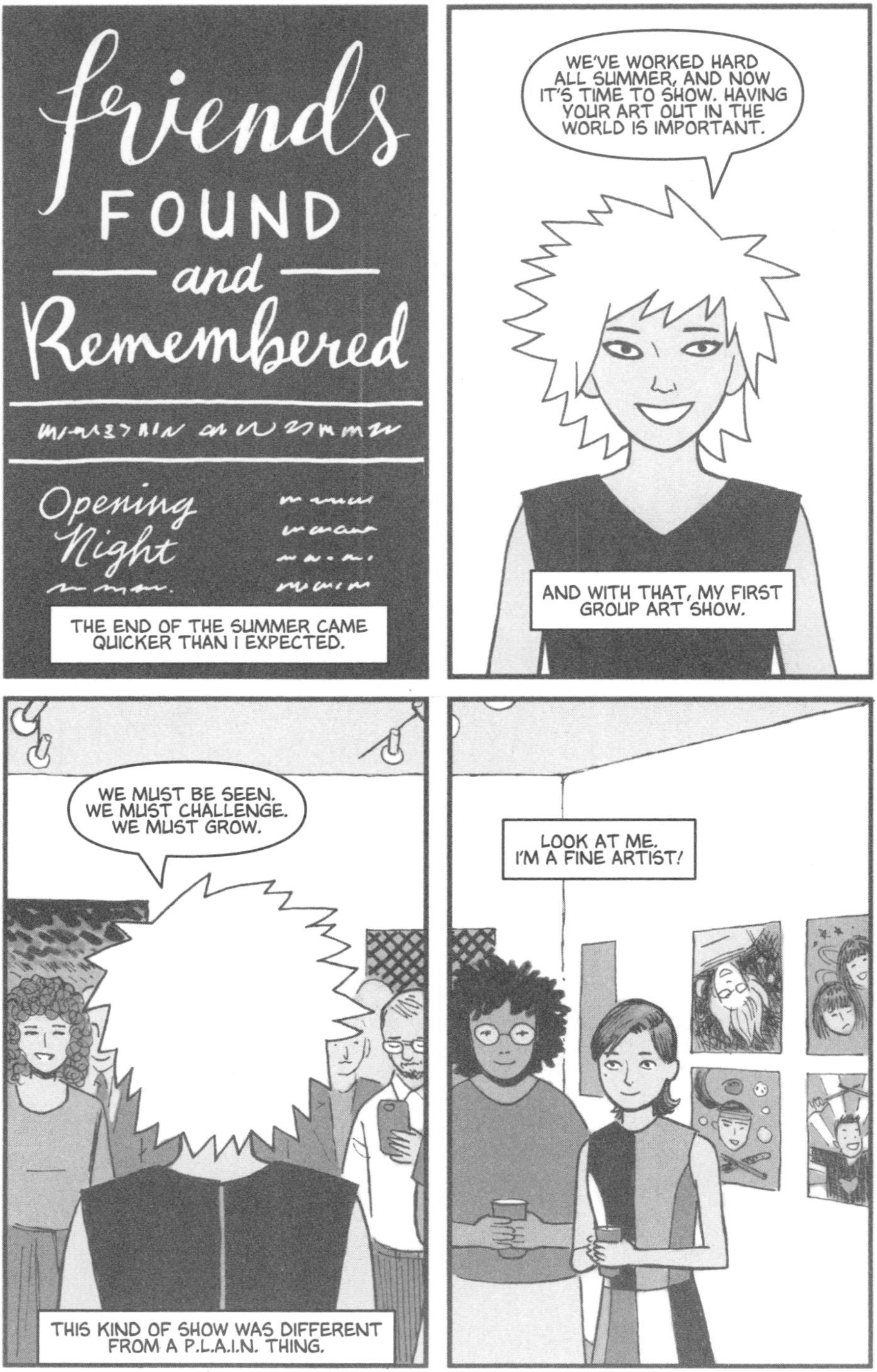
friends
FOUND
and
Remembered
Opening
Night
THE END OF THE SUMMER CAME QUICKER THAN I EXPECTED.
WE'VE WORKED HARD ALL SUMMER, AND NOW IT'S TIME TO SHOW. HAVING YOUR ART OUT IN THE WORLD IS IMPORTANT.
AND WITH THAT, MY FIRST GROUP ART SHOW.
WE MUST BE SEEN. WE MUST CHALLENGE. WE MUST GROW.
THIS KIND OF SHOW WAS DIFFERENT FROM A P.L.A.I.N. THING.
LOOK AT ME. I'M A FINE ARTIST!

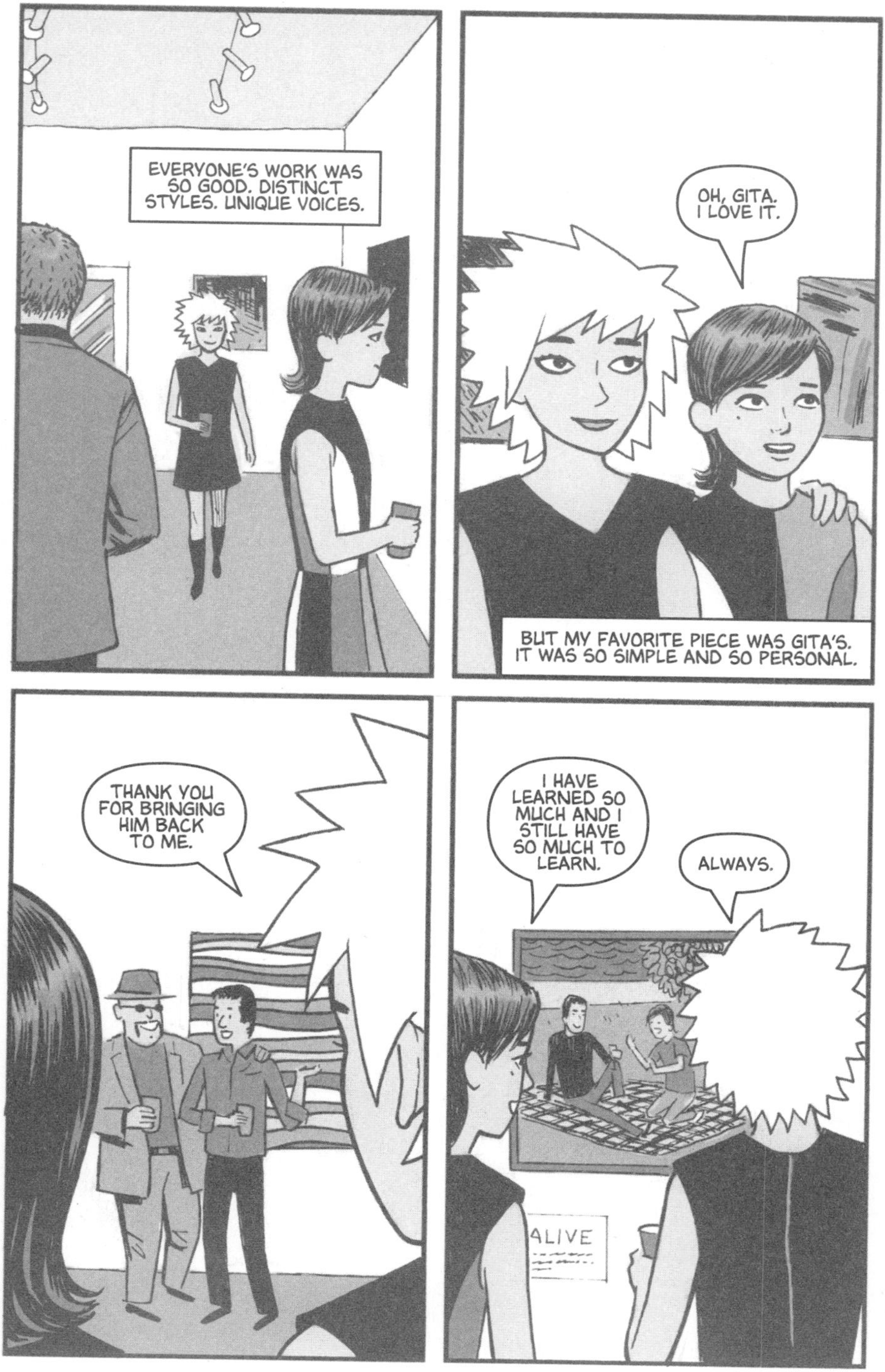
EVERYONE'S WORK WAS SO GOOD. DISTINCT STYLES. UNIQUE VOICES.
OH, GITA. I LOVE IT.
BUT MY FAVORITE PIECE WAS GITA'S. IT WAS SO SIMPLE AND SO PERSONAL.
THANK YOU FOR BRINGING HIM BACK TO ME.
I HAVE LEARNED SO MUCH AND I STILL HAVE SO MUCH TO LEARN.
ALWAYS.
ALIVE

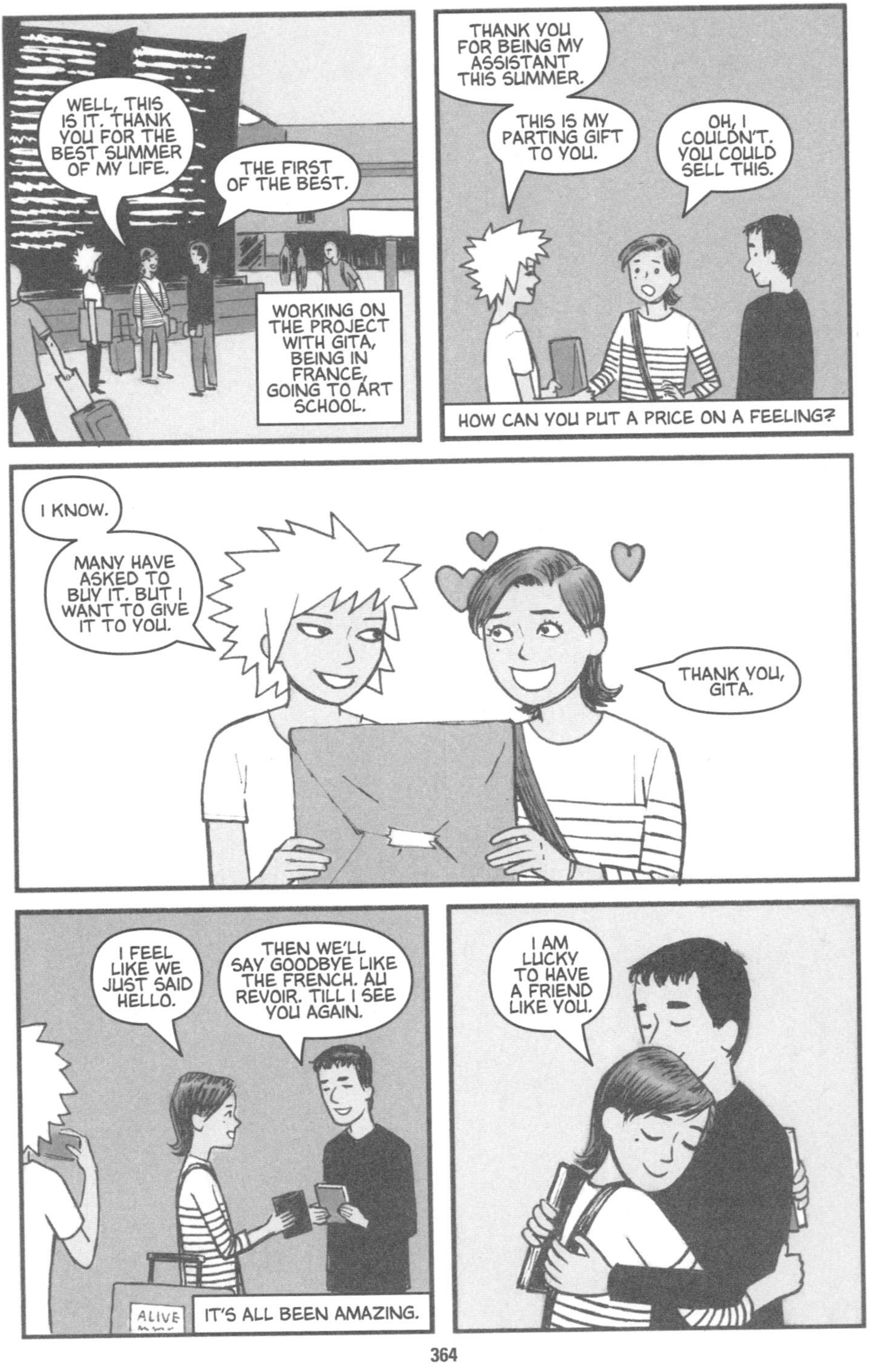
WELL, THIS IS IT. THANK YOU FOR THE BEST SUMMER OF MY LIFE.
THE FIRST OF THE BEST.
WORKING ON THE PROJECT WITH GITA, BEING IN FRANCE, GOING TO ART SCHOOL.
THANK YOU FOR BEING MY ASSISTANT THIS SUMMER.
THIS IS MY PARTING GIFT TO YOU.
OH, I COULDN'T. YOU COULD SELL THIS.
HOW CAN YOU PUT A PRICE ON A FEELING?
I KNOW.
MANY HAVE ASKED TO BUY IT. BUT I WANT TO GIVE IT TO YOU.
THANK YOU, GITA.
I FEEL LIKE WE JUST SAID HELLO.
THEN WE'LL SAY GOODBYE LIKE THE FRENCH. AU REVOIR. TILL I SEE YOU AGAIN.
ALIVE
IT'S ALL BEEN AMAZING.
I AM LUCKY TO HAVE A FRIEND LIKE YOU.

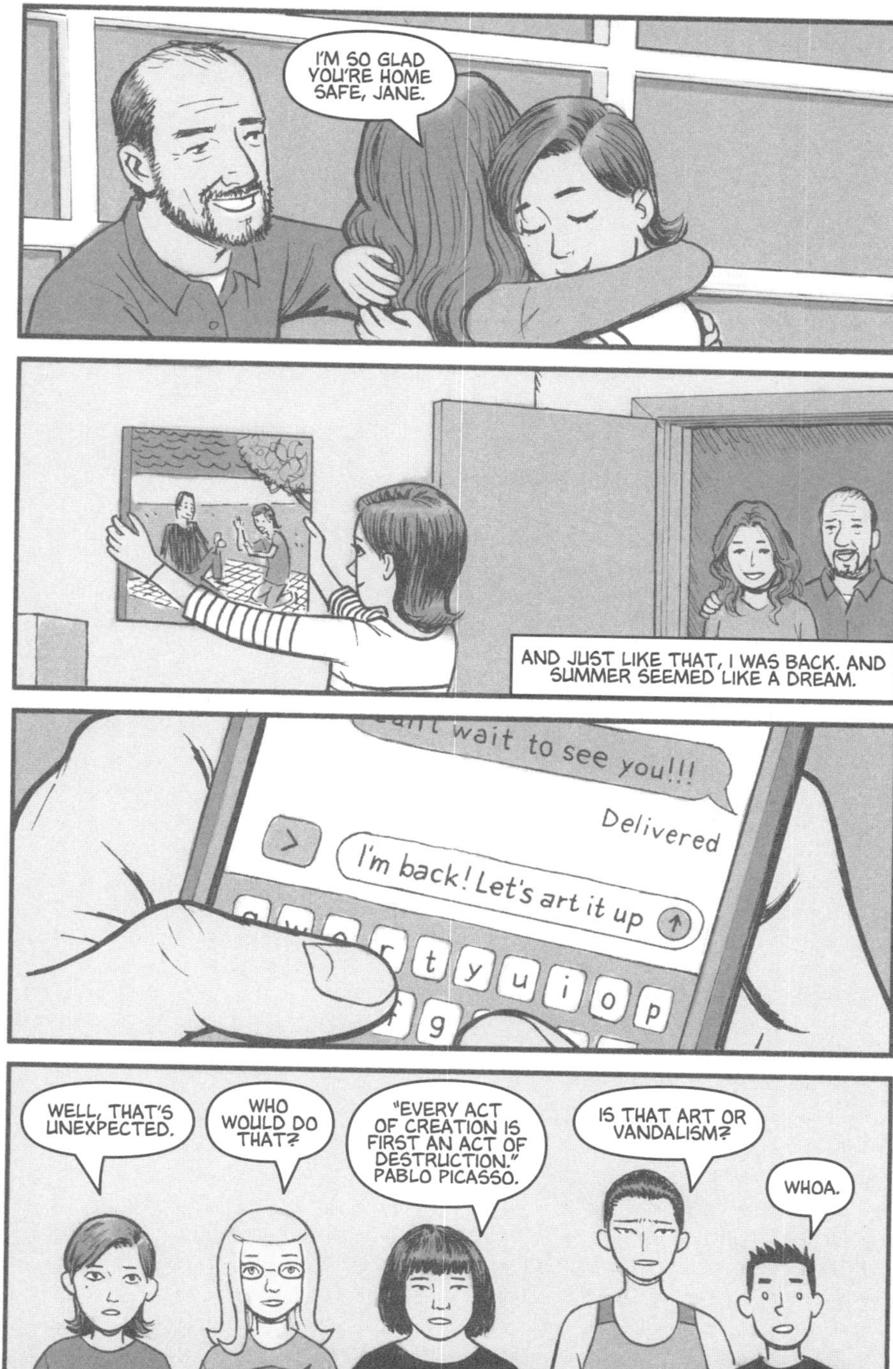
I'M SO GLAD YOU'RE HOME SAFE, JANE.
AND JUST LIKE THAT, I WAS BACK. AND SUMMER SEEMED LIKE A DREAM.
wait to see you!!!
Delivered
I'm back! Let's art it up
WELL, THAT'S UNEXPECTED.
WHO WOULD DO THAT?
"EVERY ACT OF CREATION IS FIRST AN ACT OF DESTRUCTION." PABLO PICASSO.
IS THAT ART OR VANDALISM?
WHOA.

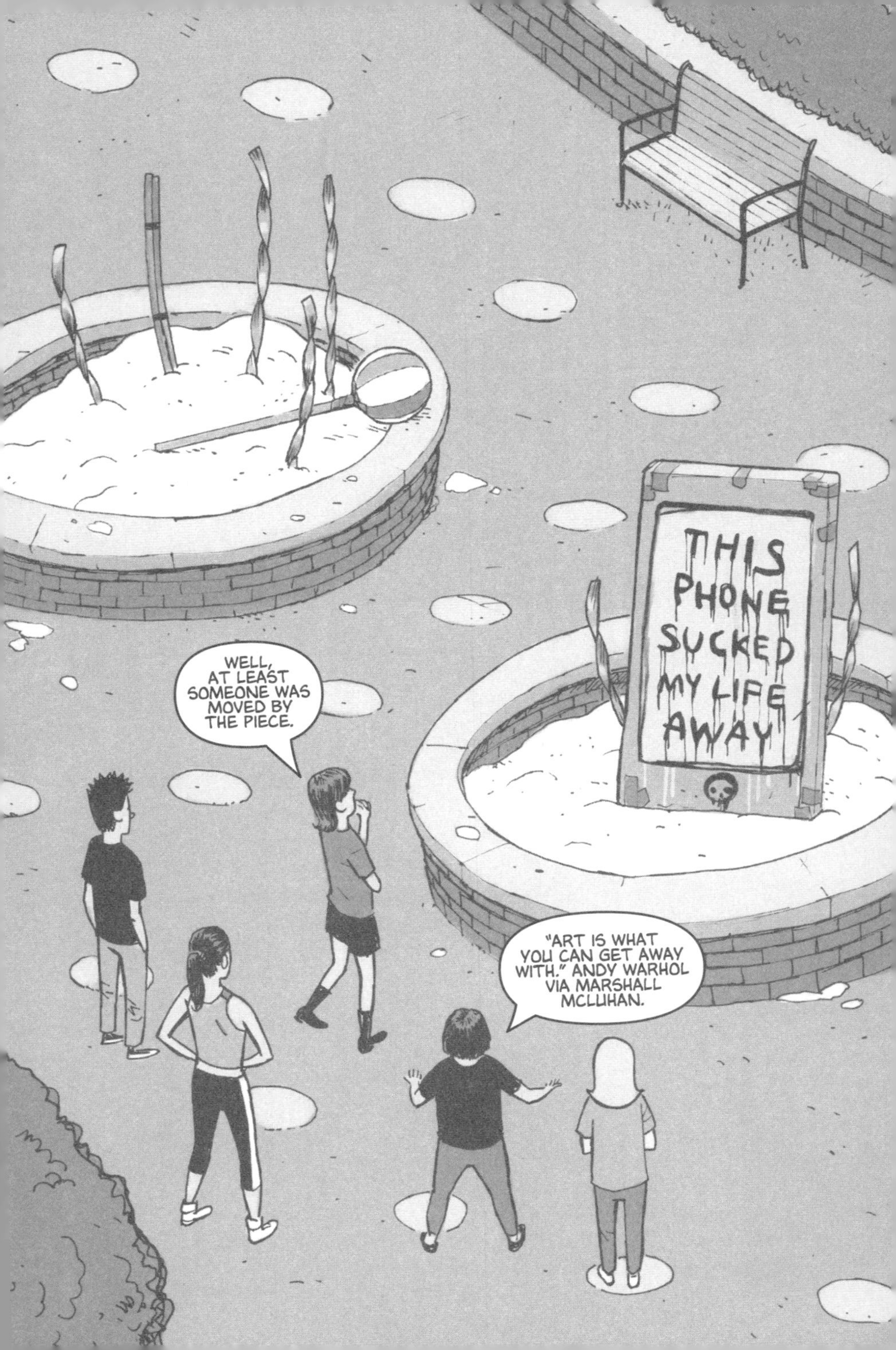
THIS PHONE SUCKED MY LIFE AWAY
WELL, AT LEAST SOMEONE WAS MOVED BY THE PIECE.
"ART IS WHAT YOU CAN GET AWAY WITH." ANDY WARHOL VIA MARSHALL MCLUHAN.

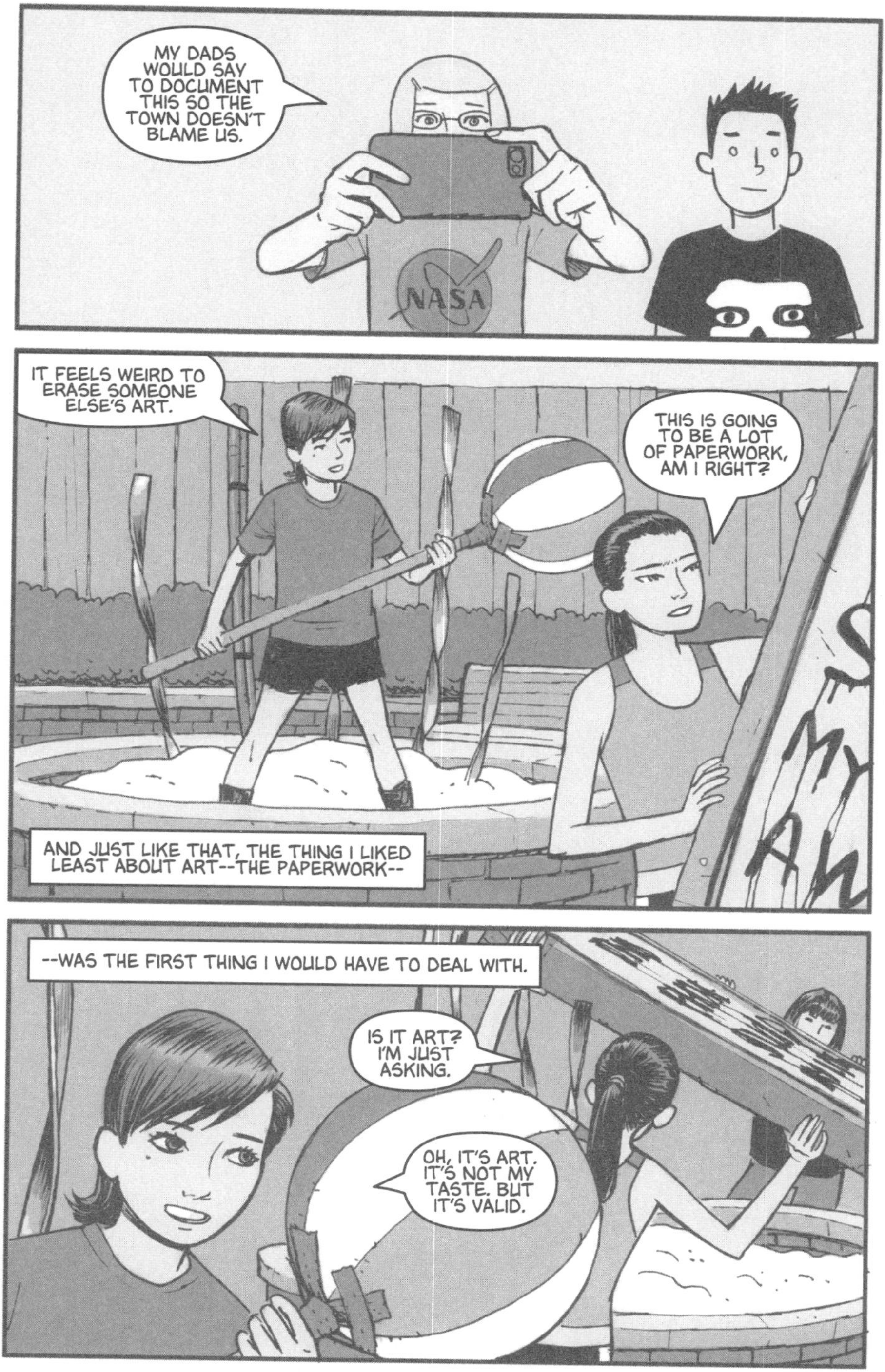
MY DADS WOULD SAY TO DOCUMENT THIS SO THE TOWN DOESN'T BLAME US.
NASA
IT FEELS WEIRD TO ERASE SOMEONE ELSE'S ART.
THIS IS GOING TO BE A LOT OF PAPERWORK, AM I RIGHT?
AND JUST LIKE THAT, THE THING I LIKED LEAST ABOUT ART--THE PAPERWORK--
--WAS THE FIRST THING I WOULD HAVE TO DEAL WITH.
IS IT ART? I'M JUST ASKING.
OH, IT'S ART. IT'S NOT MY TASTE. BUT IT'S VALID.

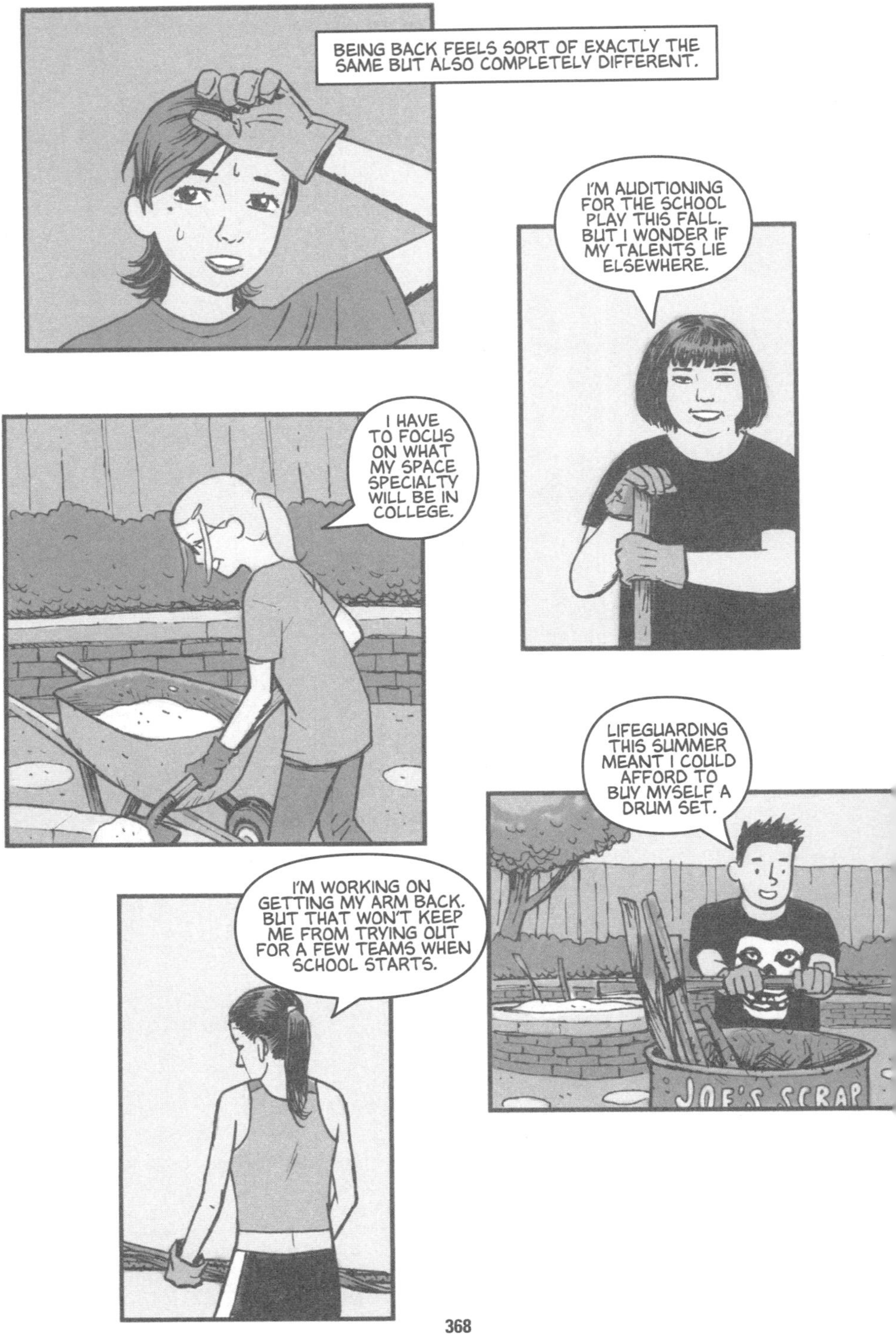
BEING BACK FEELS SORT OF EXACTLY THE SAME BUT ALSO COMPLETELY DIFFERENT.
I'M AUDITIONING FOR THE SCHOOL PLAY THIS FALL. BUT I WONDER IF MY TALENTS LIE ELSEWHERE.
I HAVE TO FOCUS ON WHAT MY SPACE SPECIALTY WILL BE IN COLLEGE.
LIFEGUARDING THIS SUMMER MEANT I COULD AFFORD TO BUY MYSELF A DRUM SET.
JOE'S SCRAP
I'M WORKING ON GETTING MY ARM BACK. BUT THAT WON'T KEEP ME FROM TRYING OUT FOR A FEW TEAMS WHEN SCHOOL STARTS.

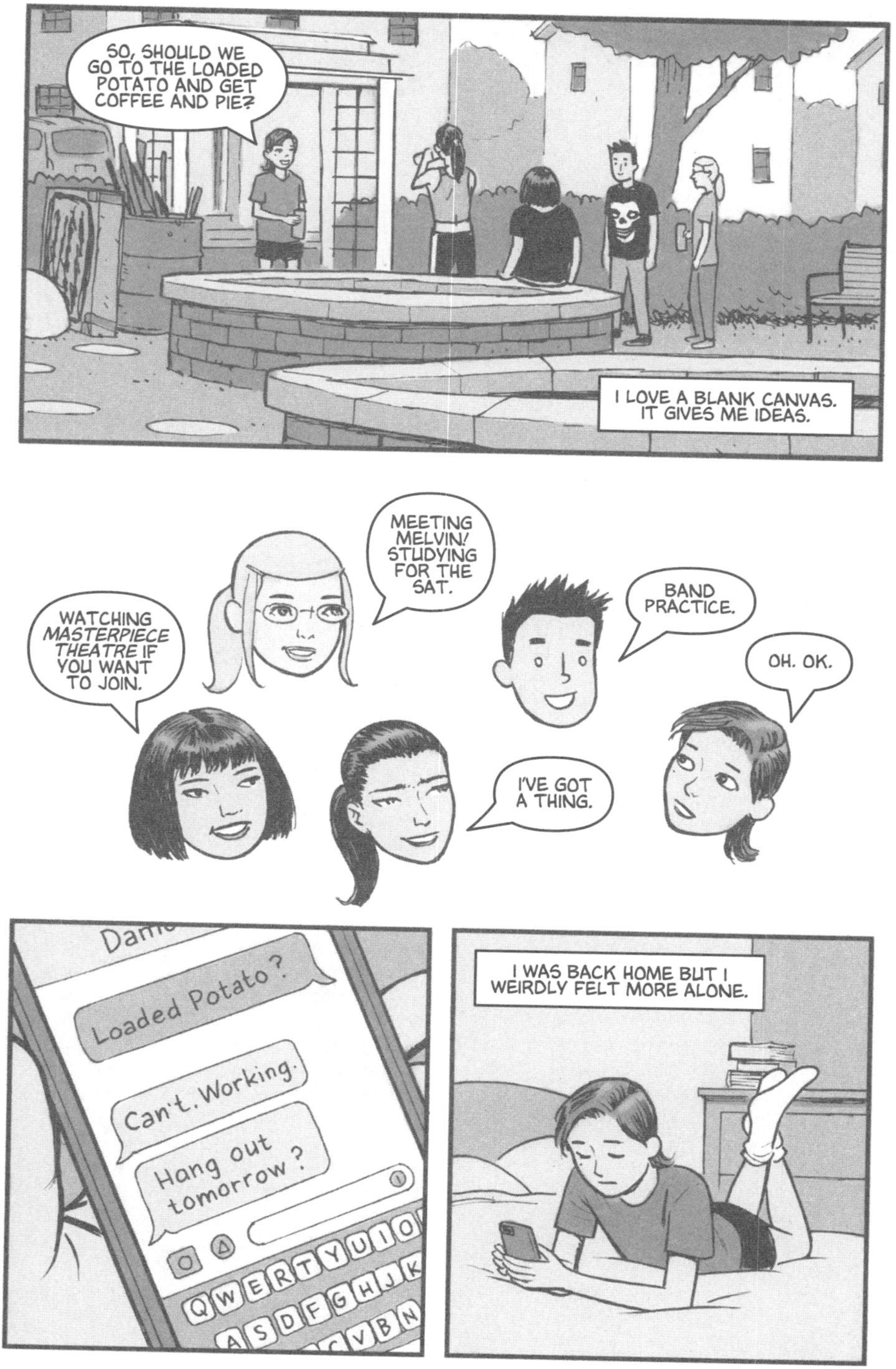

SO, SHOULD WE GO TO THE LOADED POTATO AND GET COFFEE AND PIE?
I LOVE A BLANK CANVAS. IT GIVES ME IDEAS.
MEETING MELVIN! STUDYING FOR THE SAT.
WATCHING *MASTERPIECE THEATRE* IF YOU WANT TO JOIN.
BAND PRACTICE.
I'VE GOT A THING.
OH. OK.
Loaded Potato?
Can't. Working.
Hang out tomorrow?
I WAS BACK HOME BUT I WEIRDLY FELT MORE ALONE.

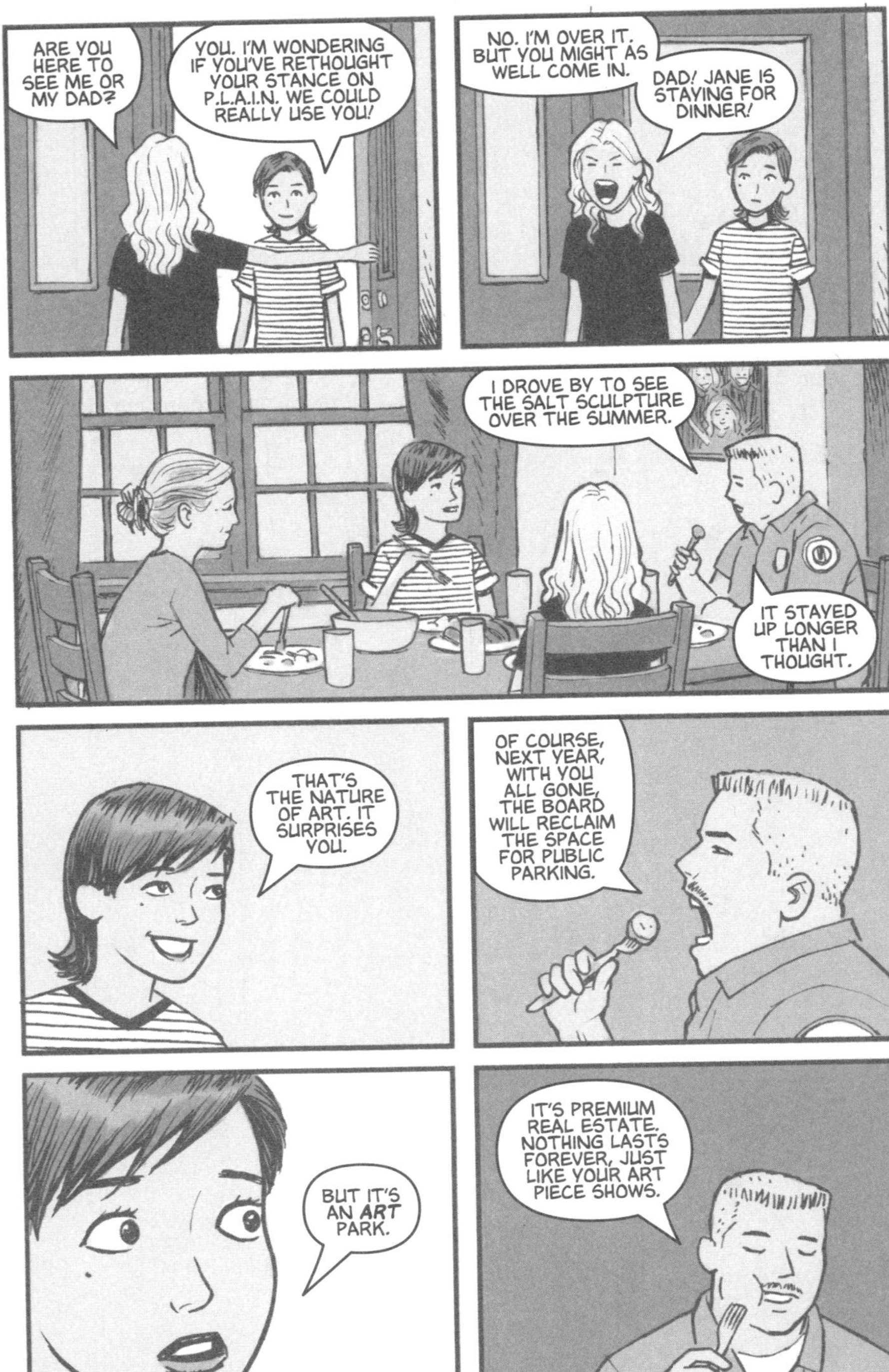
ARE YOU HERE TO SEE ME OR MY DAD?
YOU. I'M WONDERING IF YOU'VE RETHOUGHT YOUR STANCE ON P.L.A.I.N. WE COULD REALLY USE YOU!
NO. I'M OVER IT. BUT YOU MIGHT AS WELL COME IN.
DAD! JANE IS STAYING FOR DINNER!
I DROVE BY TO SEE THE SALT SCULPTURE OVER THE SUMMER.
IT STAYED UP LONGER THAN I THOUGHT.
THAT'S THE NATURE OF ART. IT SURPRISES YOU.
OF COURSE, NEXT YEAR, WITH YOU ALL GONE, THE BOARD WILL RECLAIM THE SPACE FOR PUBLIC PARKING.
BUT IT'S AN ART PARK.
IT'S PREMIUM REAL ESTATE. NOTHING LASTS FOREVER, JUST LIKE YOUR ART PIECE SHOWS.

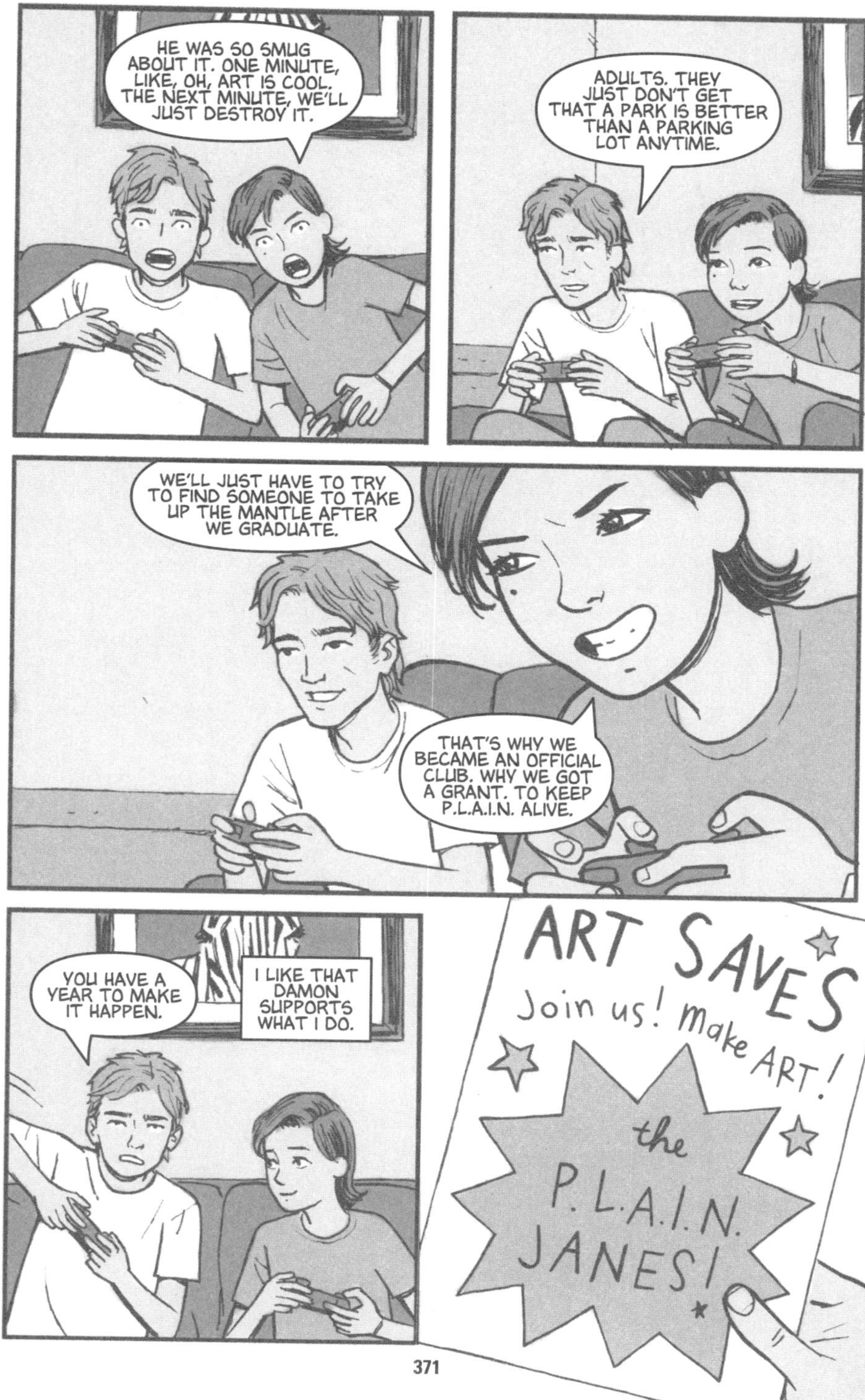
HE WAS SO SMUG ABOUT IT. ONE MINUTE, LIKE, OH, ART IS COOL. THE NEXT MINUTE, WE'LL JUST DESTROY IT.
ADULTS. THEY JUST DON'T GET THAT A PARK IS BETTER THAN A PARKING LOT ANYTIME.
WE'LL JUST HAVE TO TRY TO FIND SOMEONE TO TAKE UP THE MANTLE AFTER WE GRADUATE.
THAT'S WHY WE BECAME AN OFFICIAL CLUB. WHY WE GOT A GRANT. TO KEEP P.L.A.I.N. ALIVE.
YOU HAVE A YEAR TO MAKE IT HAPPEN.
I LIKE THAT DAMON SUPPORTS WHAT I DO.
ART SAVES
Join us! Make ART!
the P.L.A.I.N. JANES!

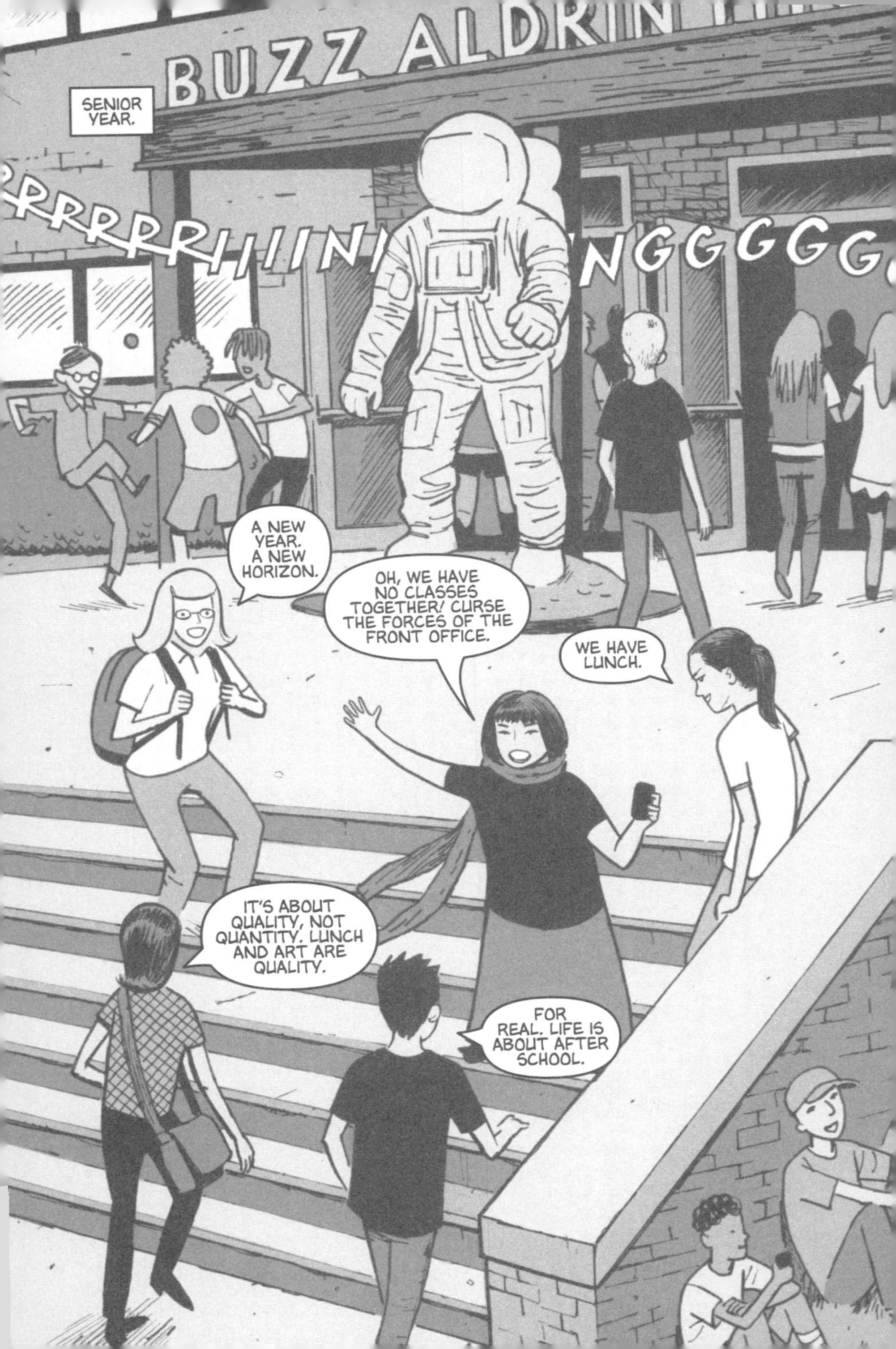
BUZZ ALDRIN
SENIOR YEAR.
RRRRRRIIIIINNGGGGG
A NEW YEAR. A NEW HORIZON.
OH, WE HAVE NO CLASSES TOGETHER! CURSE THE FORCES OF THE FRONT OFFICE.
WE HAVE LUNCH.
IT'S ABOUT QUALITY, NOT QUANTITY. LUNCH AND ART ARE QUALITY.
FOR REAL. LIFE IS ABOUT AFTER SCHOOL.

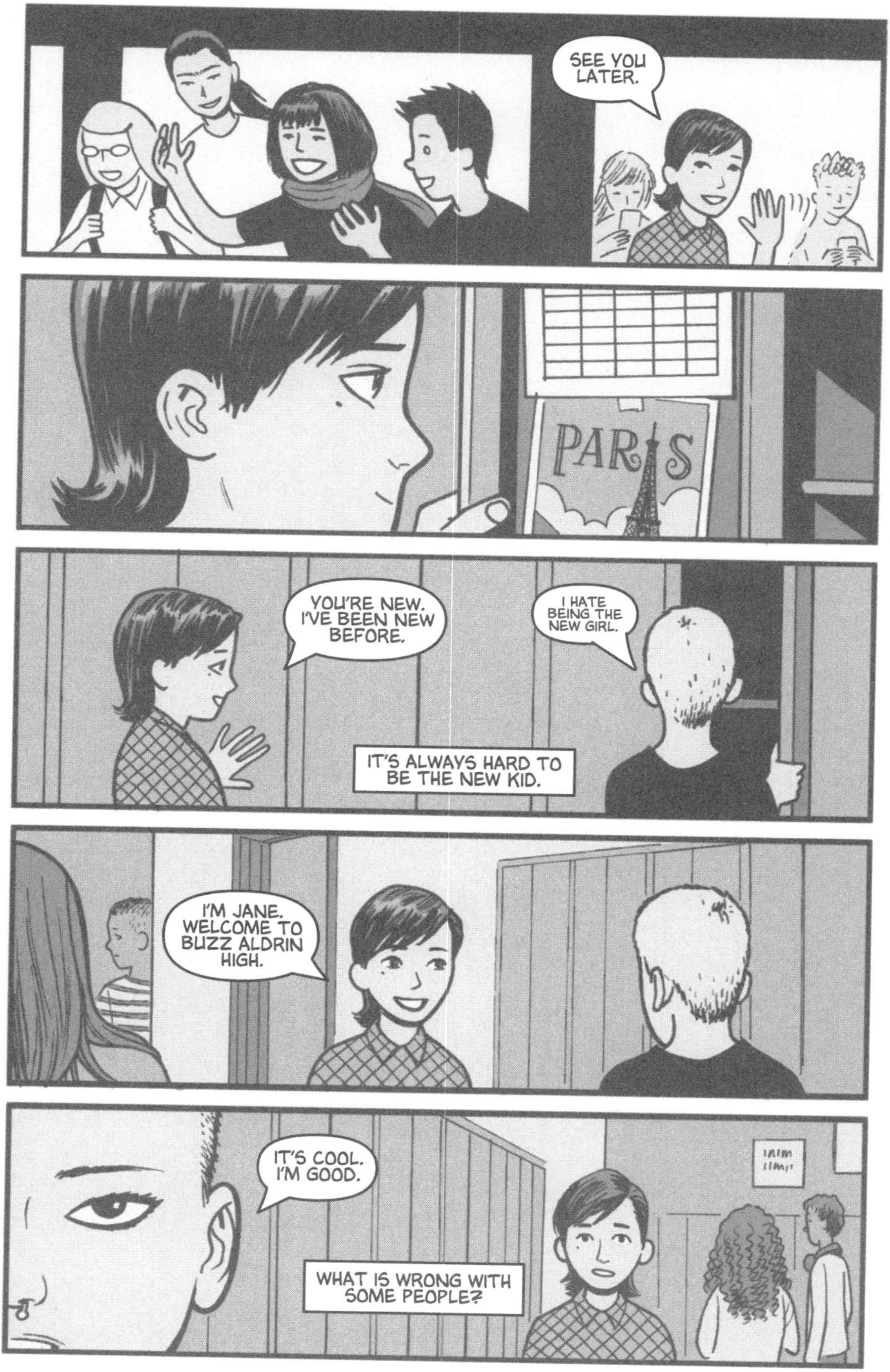
SEE YOU LATER.
PARIS
YOU'RE NEW. I'VE BEEN NEW BEFORE.
I HATE BEING THE NEW GIRL.
IT'S ALWAYS HARD TO BE THE NEW KID.
I'M JANE. WELCOME TO BUZZ ALDRIN HIGH.
IT'S COOL. I'M GOOD.
WHAT IS WRONG WITH SOME PEOPLE?

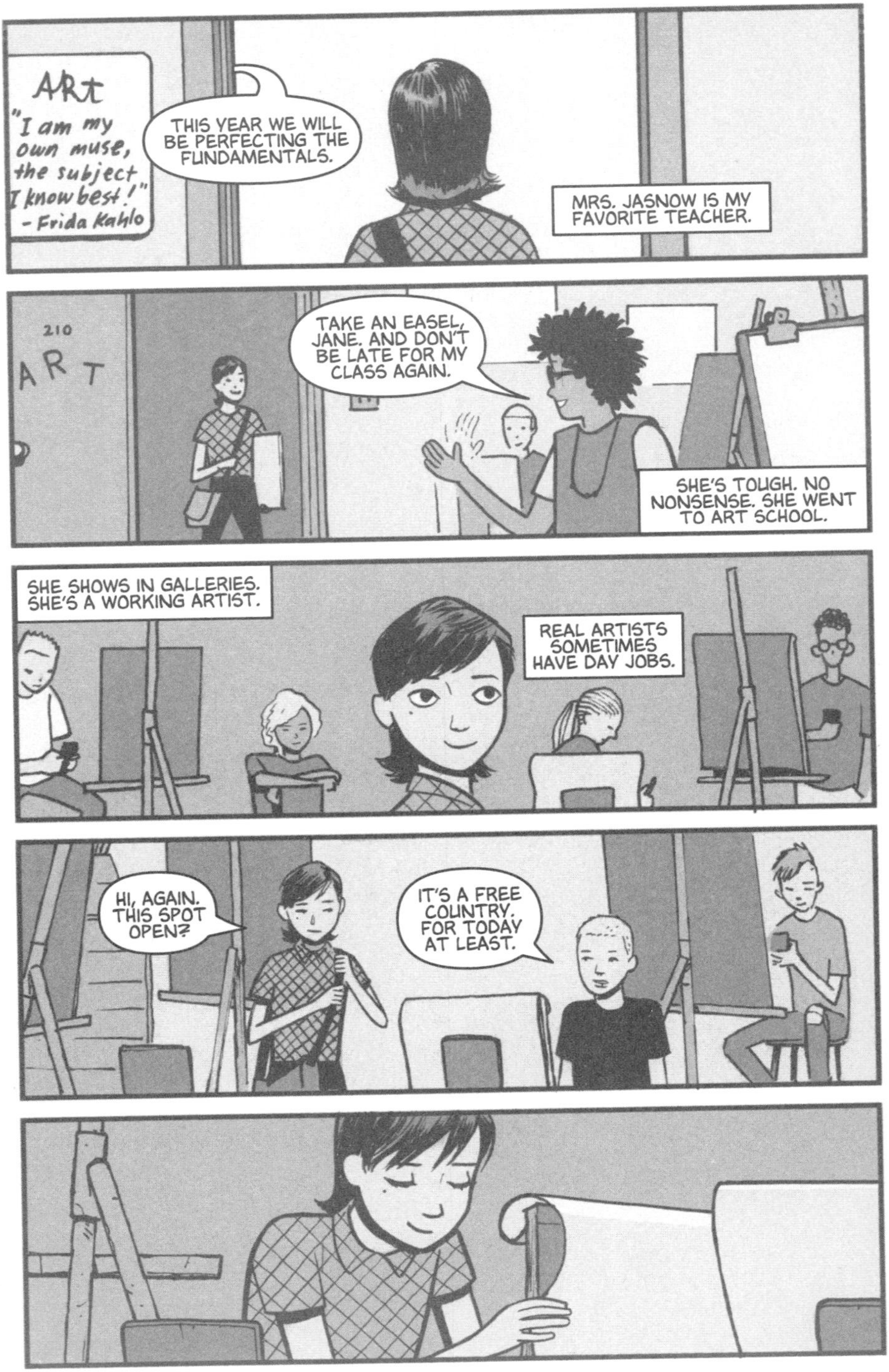
ART
"I am my own muse, the subject I know best!"
- Frida Kahlo
THIS YEAR WE WILL BE PERFECTING THE FUNDAMENTALS.
MRS. JASNOW IS MY FAVORITE TEACHER.
210
ART
TAKE AN EASEL, JANE. AND DON'T BE LATE FOR MY CLASS AGAIN.
SHE'S TOUGH. NO NONSENSE. SHE WENT TO ART SCHOOL.
SHE SHOWS IN GALLERIES. SHE'S A WORKING ARTIST.
REAL ARTISTS SOMETIMES HAVE DAY JOBS.
HI, AGAIN. THIS SPOT OPEN?
IT'S A FREE COUNTRY. FOR TODAY AT LEAST.

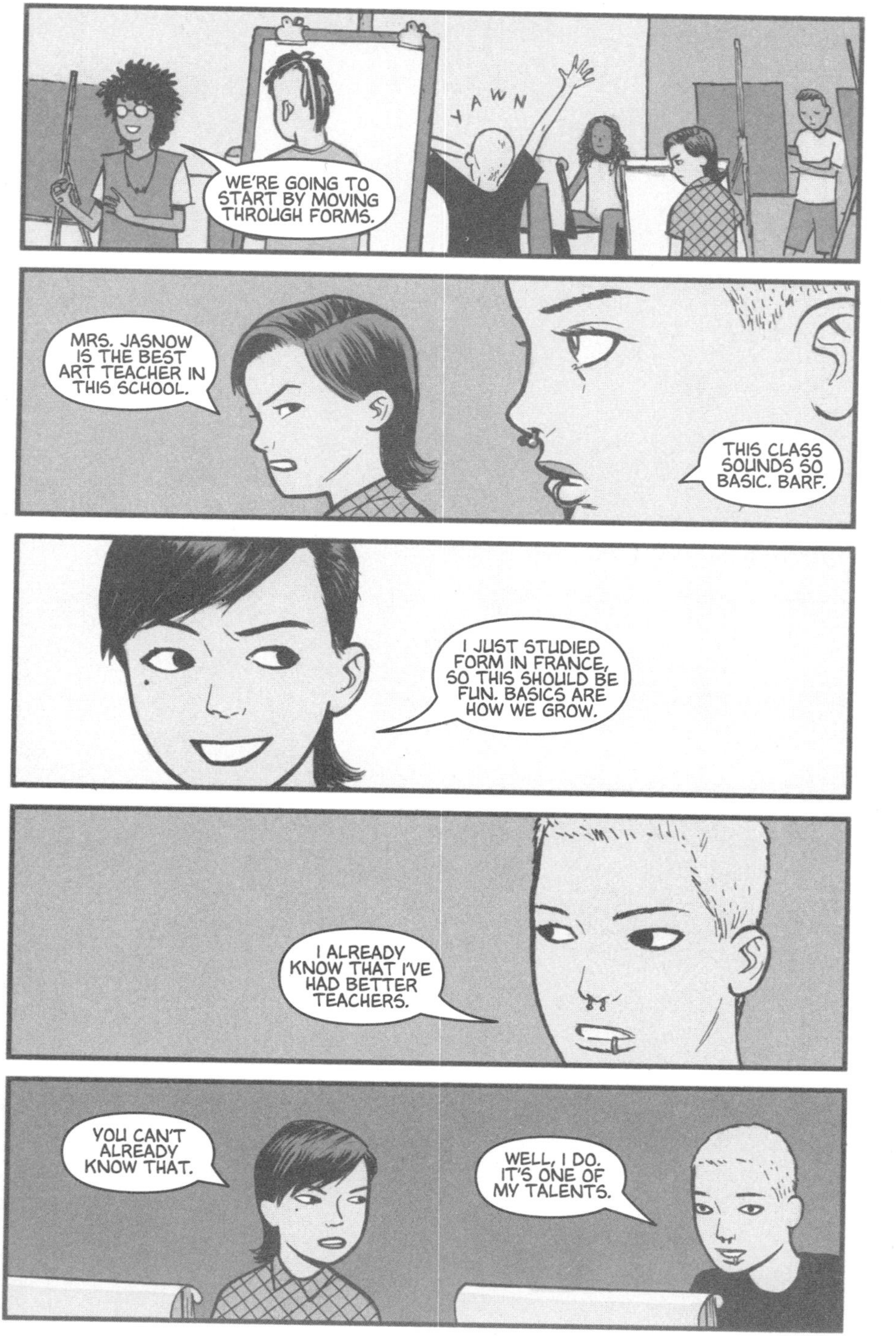
WE'RE GOING TO START BY MOVING THROUGH FORMS.
YAWN
MRS. JASNOW IS THE BEST ART TEACHER IN THIS SCHOOL.
THIS CLASS SOUNDS SO BASIC. BARF.
I JUST STUDIED FORM IN FRANCE, SO THIS SHOULD BE FUN. BASICS ARE HOW WE GROW.
I ALREADY KNOW THAT I'VE HAD BETTER TEACHERS.
YOU CAN'T ALREADY KNOW THAT.
WELL, I DO. IT'S ONE OF MY TALENTS.

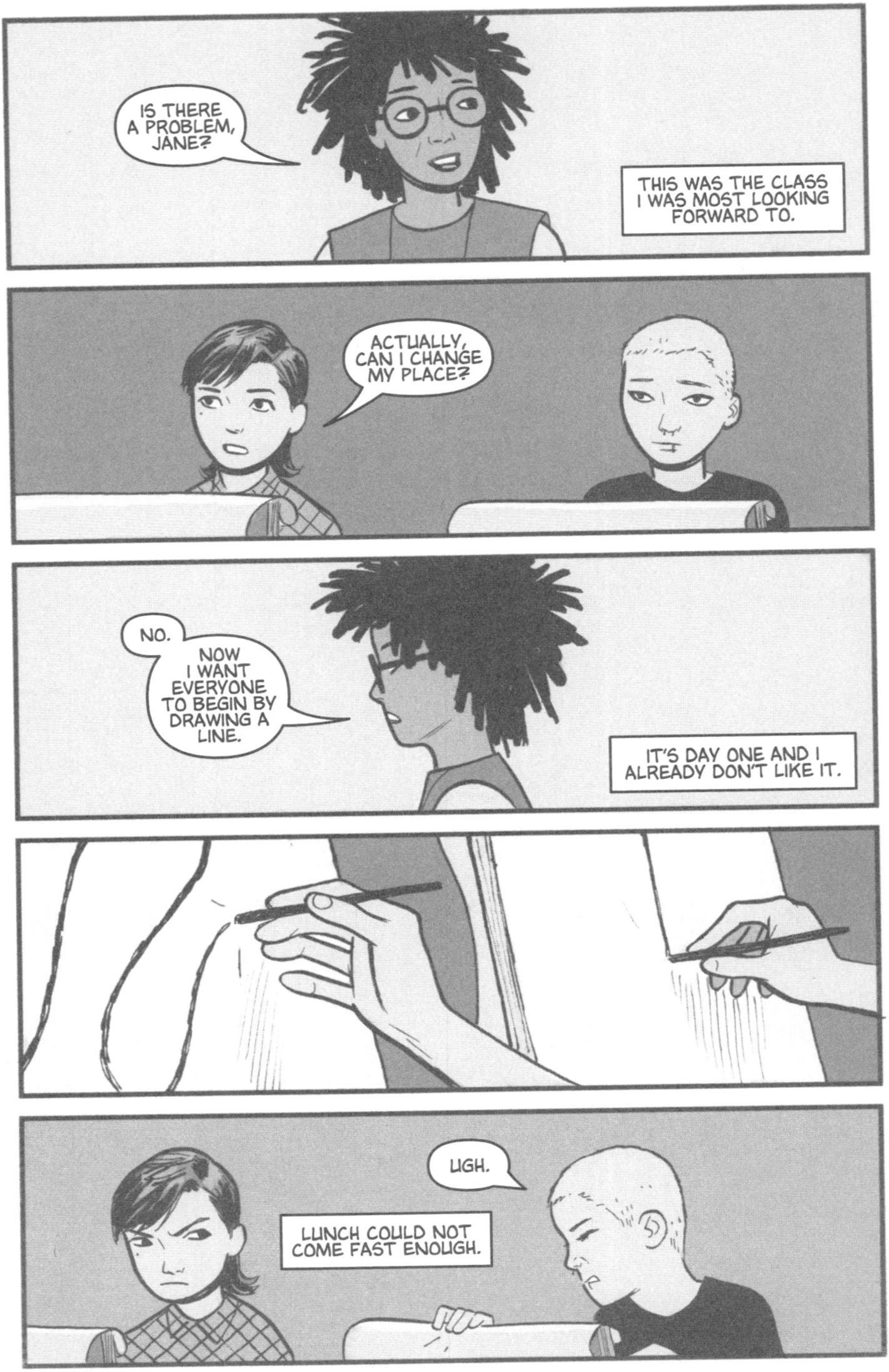
IS THERE A PROBLEM, JANE?
THIS WAS THE CLASS I WAS MOST LOOKING FORWARD TO.
ACTUALLY, CAN I CHANGE MY PLACE?
NO.
NOW I WANT EVERYONE TO BEGIN BY DRAWING A LINE.
IT'S DAY ONE AND I ALREADY DON'T LIKE IT.
UGH.
LUNCH COULD NOT COME FAST ENOUGH.

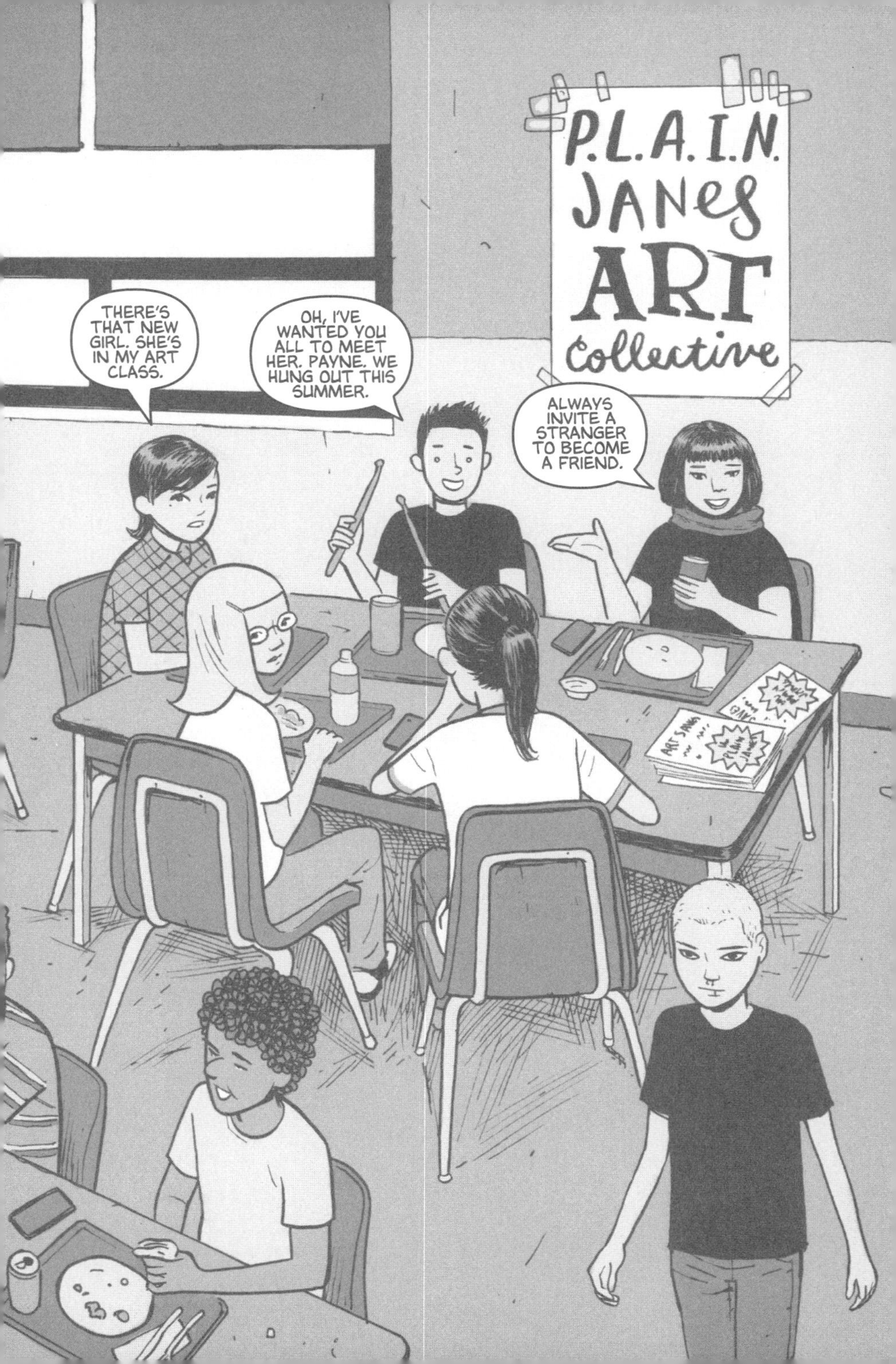
P.L.A.I.N. Janes ART Collective
THERE'S THAT NEW GIRL. SHE'S IN MY ART CLASS.
OH, I'VE WANTED YOU ALL TO MEET HER. PAYNE. WE HUNG OUT THIS SUMMER.
ALWAYS INVITE A STRANGER TO BECOME A FRIEND.

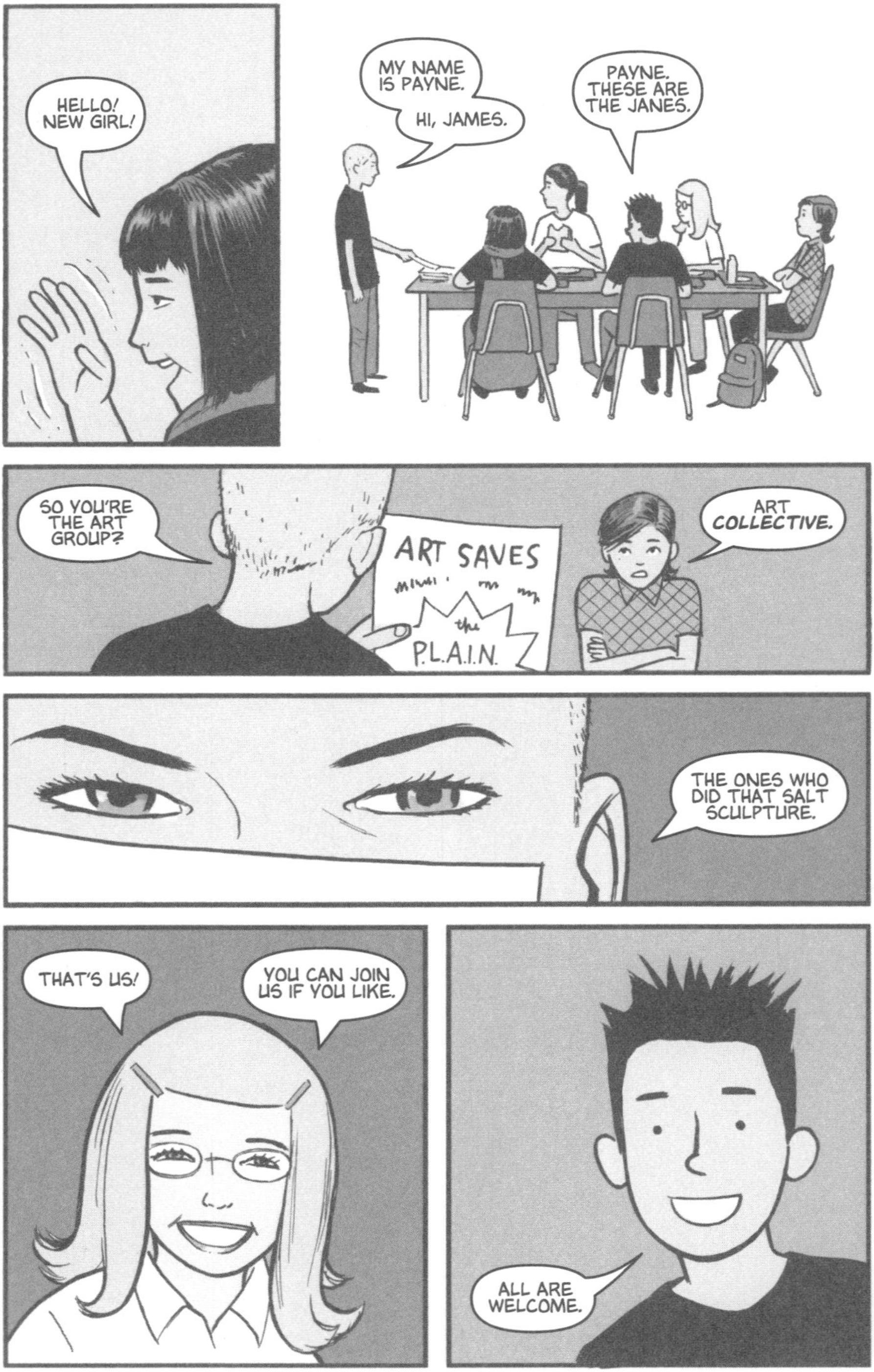
HELLO! NEW GIRL!
MY NAME IS PAYNE.
HI, JAMES.
PAYNE. THESE ARE THE JANES.
SO YOU'RE THE ART GROUP?
ART SAVES
the
P.L.A.I.N.
ART COLLECTIVE.
THE ONES WHO DID THAT SALT SCULPTURE.
THAT'S US!
YOU CAN JOIN US IF YOU LIKE.
ALL ARE WELCOME.

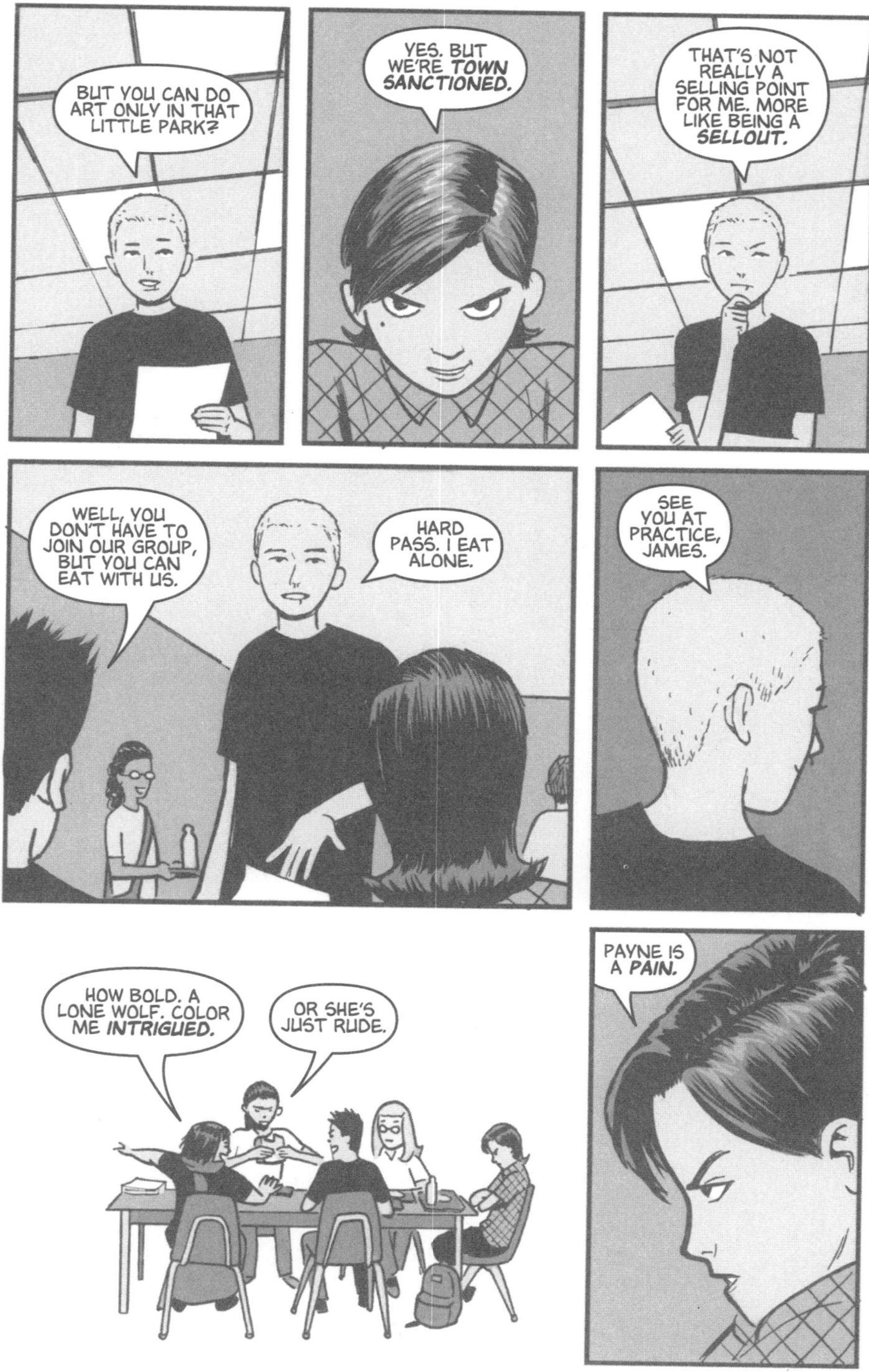
BUT YOU CAN DO ART ONLY IN THAT LITTLE PARK?
YES. BUT WE'RE **TOWN SANCTIONED.**
THAT'S NOT REALLY A SELLING POINT FOR ME. MORE LIKE BEING A **SELLOUT.**
WELL, YOU DON'T HAVE TO JOIN OUR GROUP, BUT YOU CAN EAT WITH US.
HARD PASS. I EAT ALONE.
SEE YOU AT PRACTICE, JAMES.
HOW BOLD. A LONE WOLF. COLOR ME **INTRIGUED.**
OR SHE'S JUST RUDE.
PAYNE IS A **PAIN.**

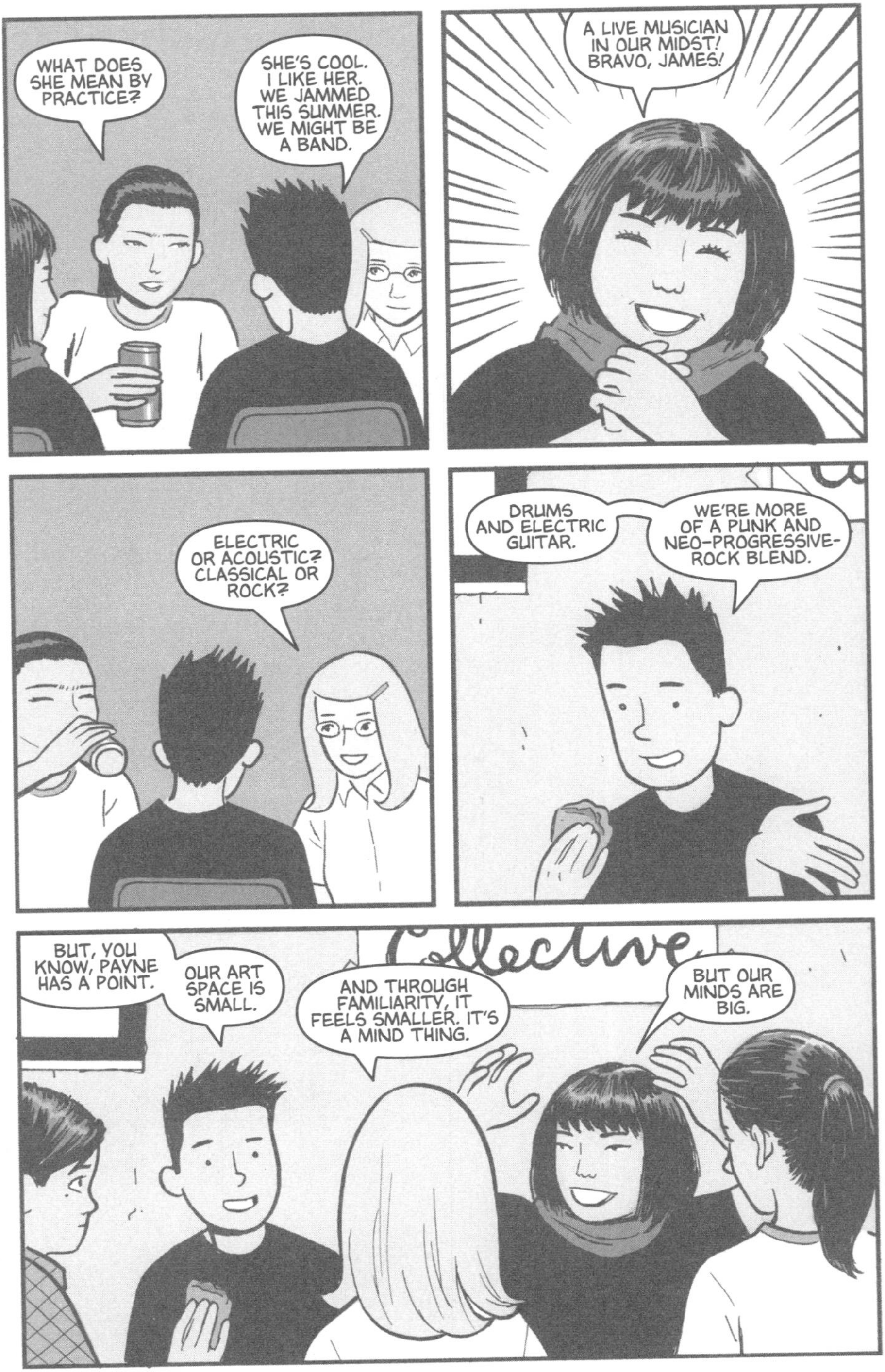
WHAT DOES SHE MEAN BY PRACTICE?
SHE'S COOL. I LIKE HER. WE JAMMED THIS SUMMER. WE MIGHT BE A BAND.
A LIVE MUSICIAN IN OUR MIDST! BRAVO, JAMES!
ELECTRIC OR ACOUSTIC? CLASSICAL OR ROCK?
DRUMS AND ELECTRIC GUITAR.
WE'RE MORE OF A PUNK AND NEO-PROGRESSIVE-ROCK BLEND.
Collective
BUT, YOU KNOW, PAYNE HAS A POINT.
OUR ART SPACE IS SMALL.
AND THROUGH FAMILIARITY, IT FEELS SMALLER. IT'S A MIND THING.
BUT OUR MINDS ARE BIG.

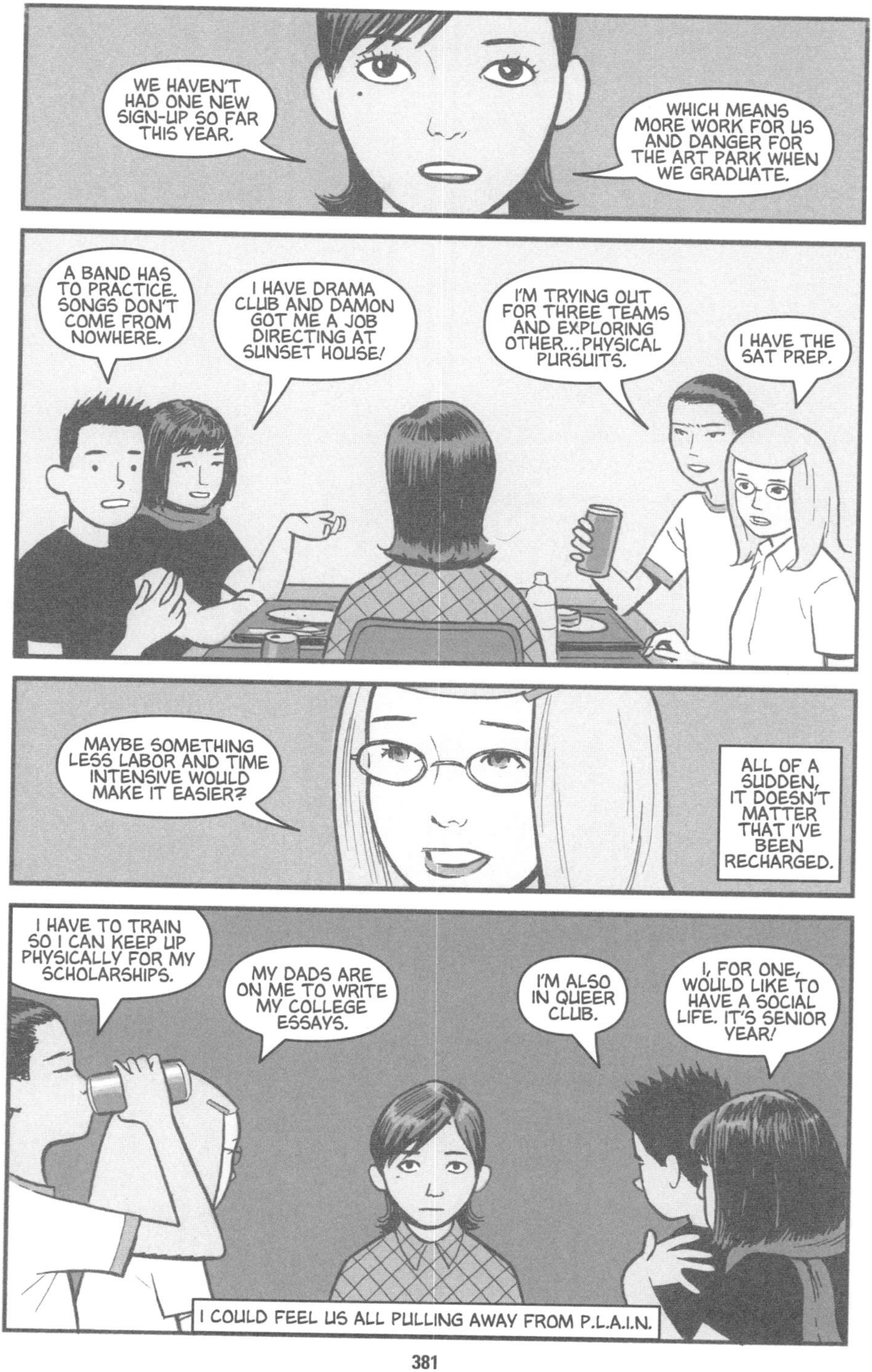
WE HAVEN'T HAD ONE NEW SIGN-UP SO FAR THIS YEAR.
WHICH MEANS MORE WORK FOR US AND DANGER FOR THE ART PARK WHEN WE GRADUATE.
A BAND HAS TO PRACTICE. SONGS DON'T COME FROM NOWHERE.
I HAVE DRAMA CLUB AND DAMON GOT ME A JOB DIRECTING AT SUNSET HOUSE!
I'M TRYING OUT FOR THREE TEAMS AND EXPLORING OTHER...PHYSICAL PURSUITS.
I HAVE THE SAT PREP.
MAYBE SOMETHING LESS LABOR AND TIME INTENSIVE WOULD MAKE IT EASIER?
ALL OF A SUDDEN, IT DOESN'T MATTER THAT I'VE BEEN RECHARGED.
I HAVE TO TRAIN SO I CAN KEEP UP PHYSICALLY FOR MY SCHOLARSHIPS.
MY DADS ARE ON ME TO WRITE MY COLLEGE ESSAYS.
I'M ALSO IN QUEER CLUB.
I, FOR ONE, WOULD LIKE TO HAVE A SOCIAL LIFE. IT'S SENIOR YEAR!
I COULD FEEL US ALL PULLING AWAY FROM P.L.A.I.N.

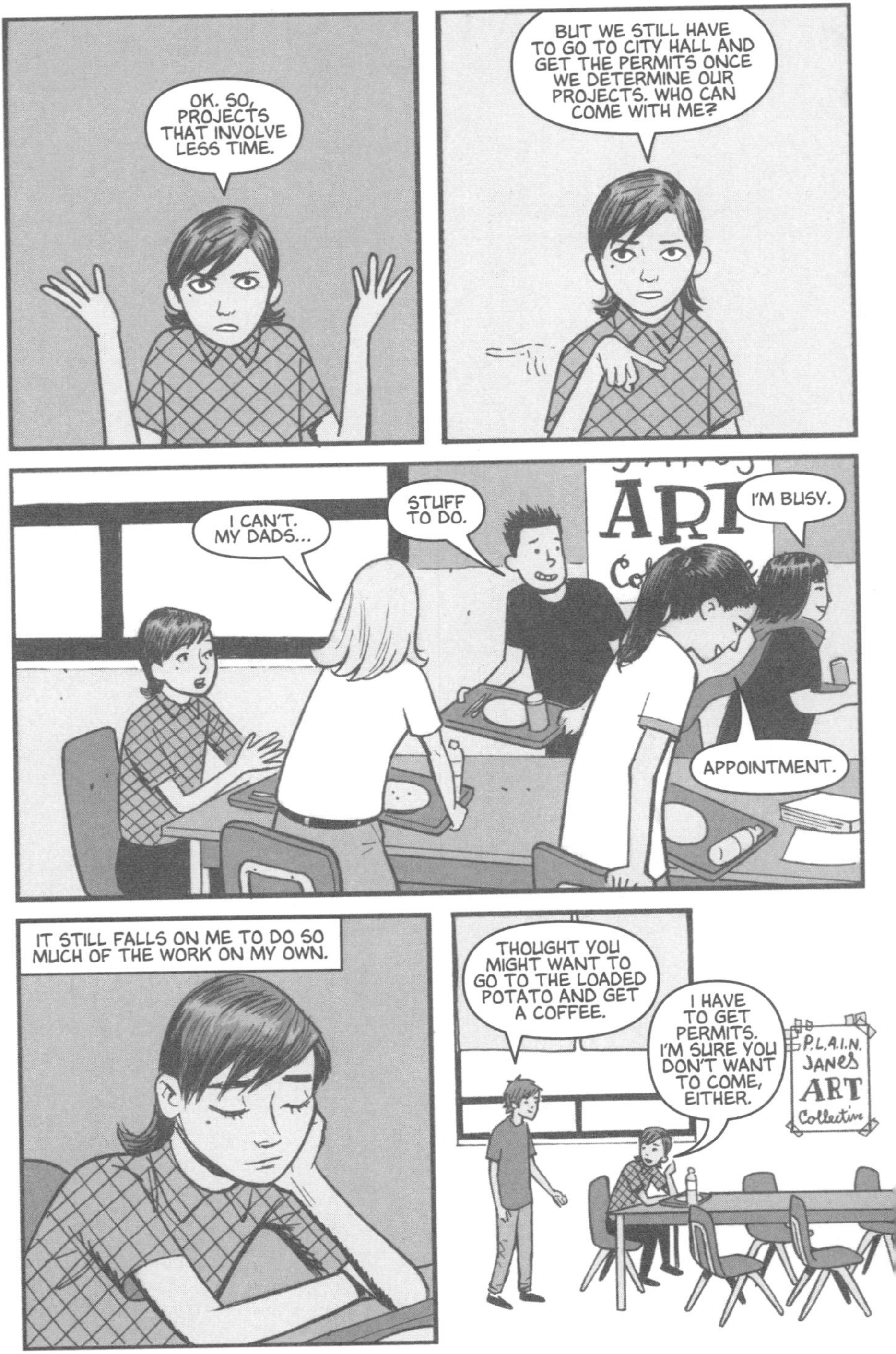
OK. SO, PROJECTS THAT INVOLVE LESS TIME.
BUT WE STILL HAVE TO GO TO CITY HALL AND GET THE PERMITS ONCE WE DETERMINE OUR PROJECTS. WHO CAN COME WITH ME?
I CAN'T. MY DADS...
STUFF TO DO.
I'M BUSY.
APPOINTMENT.
ART
IT STILL FALLS ON ME TO DO SO MUCH OF THE WORK ON MY OWN.
THOUGHT YOU MIGHT WANT TO GO TO THE LOADED POTATO AND GET A COFFEE.
I HAVE TO GET PERMITS. I'M SURE YOU DON'T WANT TO COME, EITHER.
P.L.A.I.N. JANES ART Collective

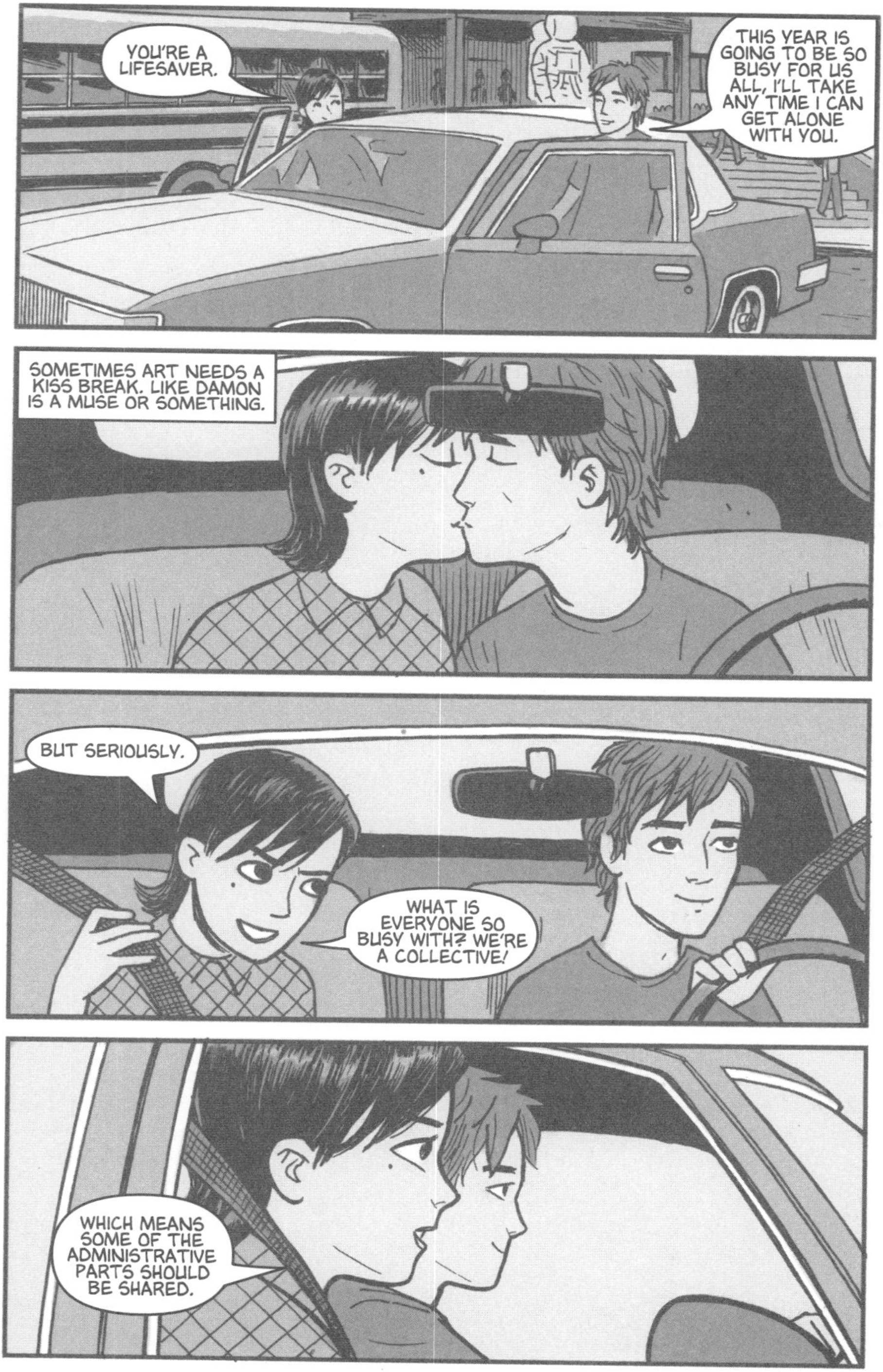
YOU'RE A LIFESAVER.
THIS YEAR IS GOING TO BE SO BUSY FOR US ALL, I'LL TAKE ANY TIME I CAN GET ALONE WITH YOU.
SOMETIMES ART NEEDS A KISS BREAK. LIKE DAMON IS A MUSE OR SOMETHING.
BUT SERIOUSLY.
WHAT IS EVERYONE SO BUSY WITH? WE'RE A COLLECTIVE!
WHICH MEANS SOME OF THE ADMINISTRATIVE PARTS SHOULD BE SHARED.

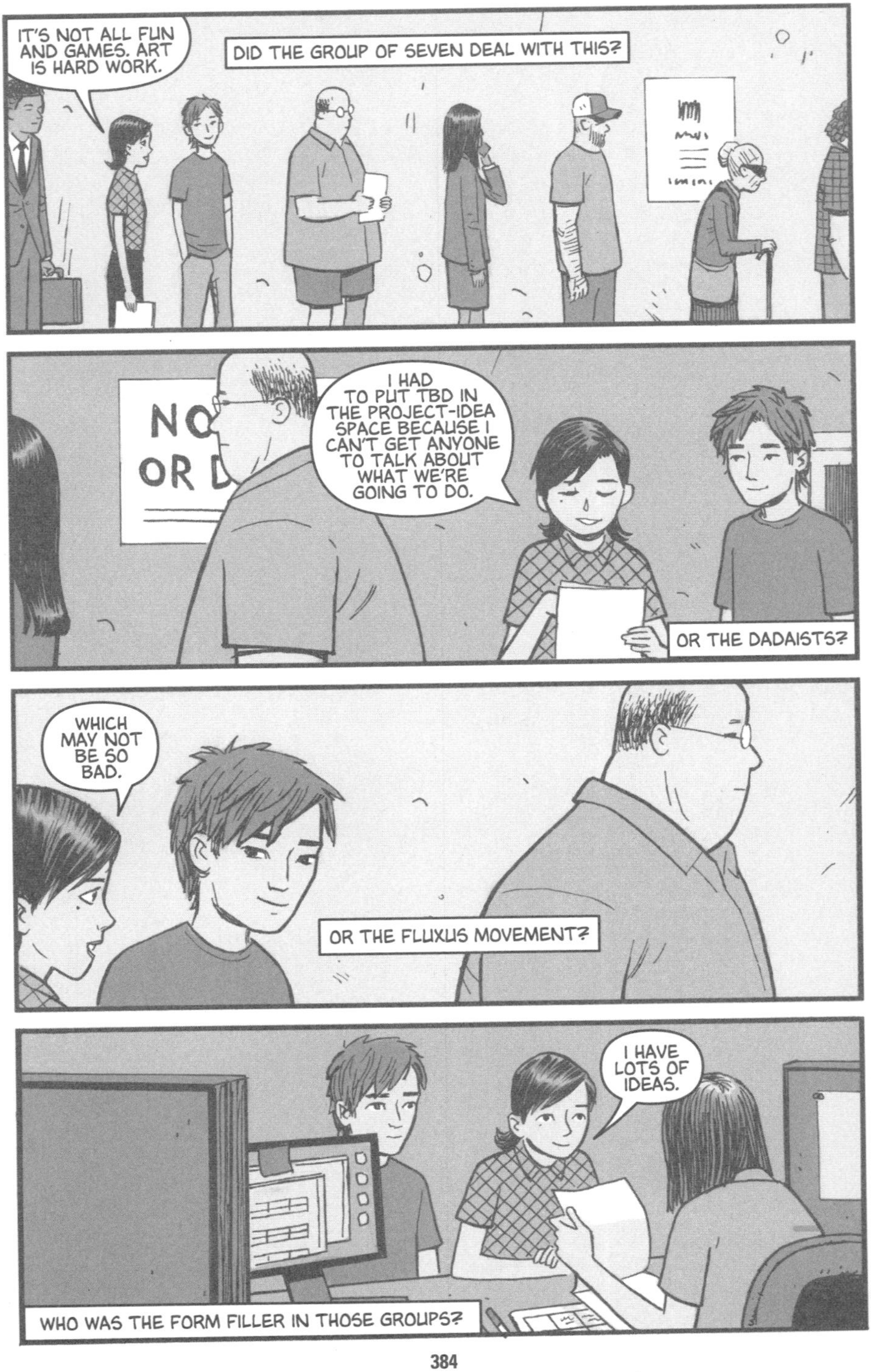
IT'S NOT ALL FUN AND GAMES. ART IS HARD WORK.
DID THE GROUP OF SEVEN DEAL WITH THIS?
I HAD TO PUT TBD IN THE PROJECT-IDEA SPACE BECAUSE I CAN'T GET ANYONE TO TALK ABOUT WHAT WE'RE GOING TO DO.
OR THE DADAISTS?
WHICH MAY NOT BE SO BAD.
OR THE FLUXUS MOVEMENT?
I HAVE LOTS OF IDEAS.
WHO WAS THE FORM FILLER IN THOSE GROUPS?

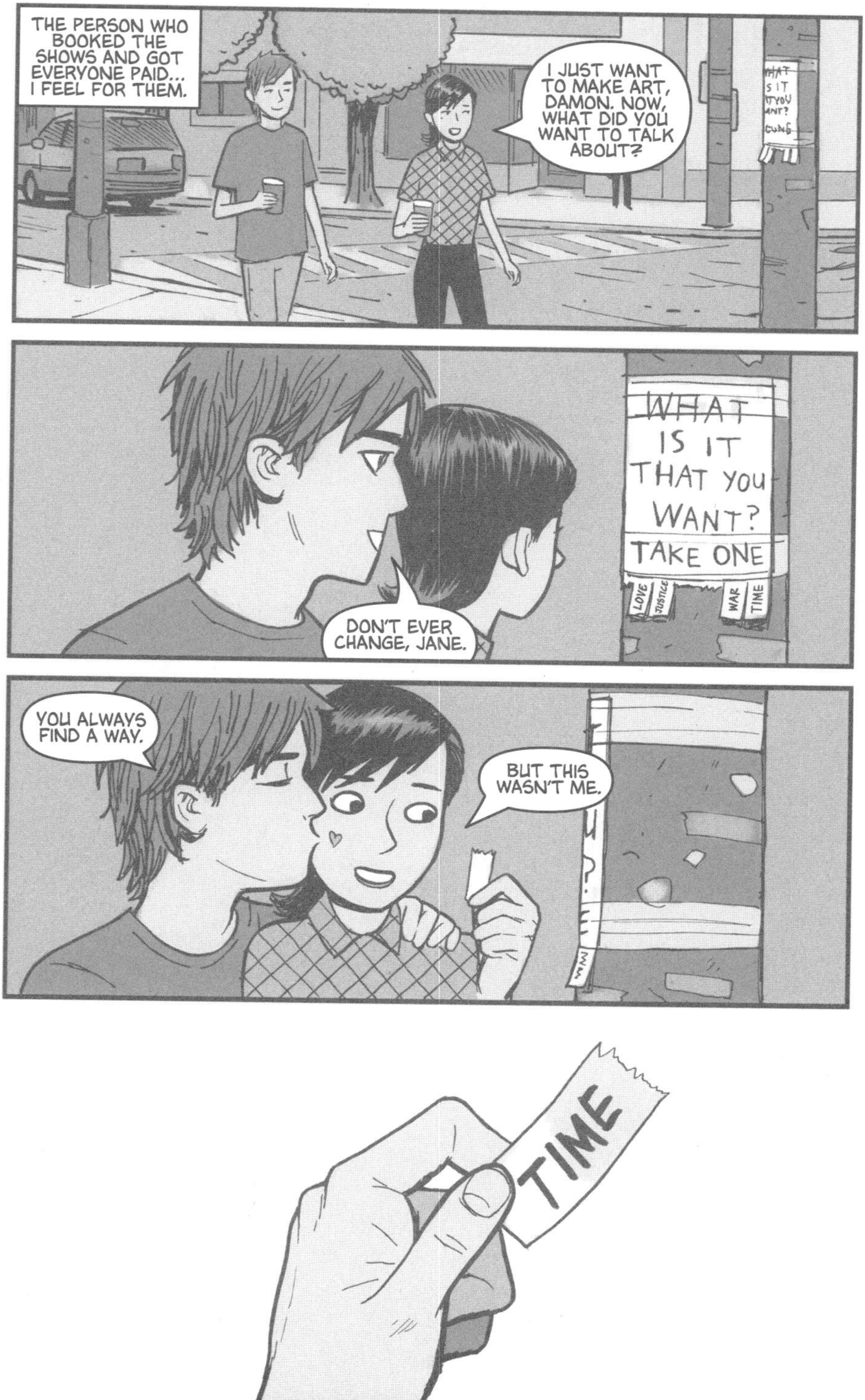
THE PERSON WHO BOOKED THE SHOWS AND GOT EVERYONE PAID... I FEEL FOR THEM.
I JUST WANT TO MAKE ART, DAMON. NOW, WHAT DID YOU WANT TO TALK ABOUT?
WHAT IS IT THAT YOU WANT?
TAKE ONE
LOVE
JUSTICE
WAR
TIME
DON'T EVER CHANGE, JANE.
YOU ALWAYS FIND A WAY.
BUT THIS WASN'T ME.
TIME

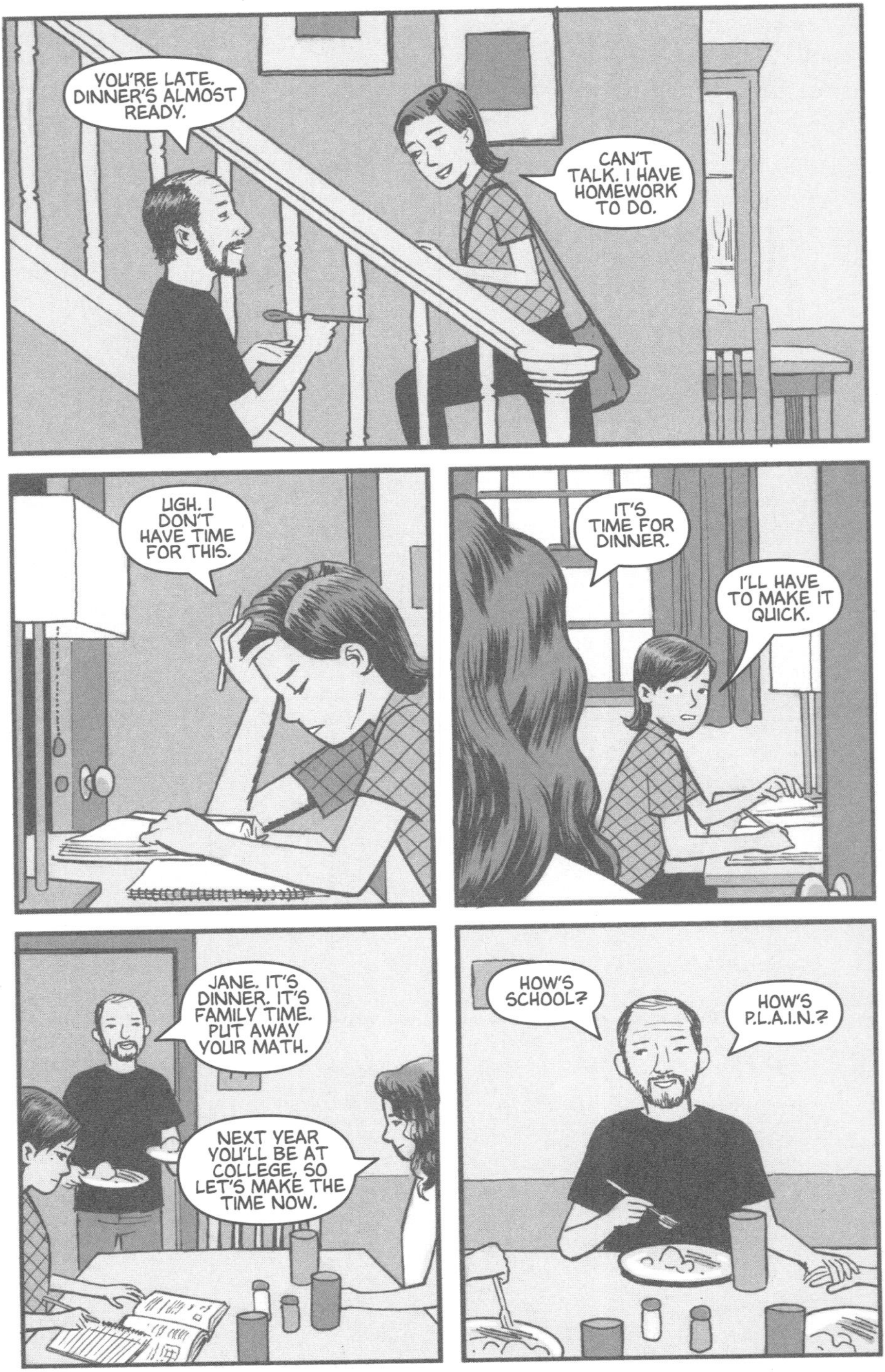
YOU'RE LATE. DINNER'S ALMOST READY.
CAN'T TALK. I HAVE HOMEWORK TO DO.
UGH. I DON'T HAVE TIME FOR THIS.
IT'S TIME FOR DINNER.
I'LL HAVE TO MAKE IT QUICK.
JANE. IT'S DINNER. IT'S FAMILY TIME. PUT AWAY YOUR MATH.
NEXT YEAR YOU'LL BE AT COLLEGE, SO LET'S MAKE THE TIME NOW.
HOW'S SCHOOL?
HOW'S P.L.A.I.N.?

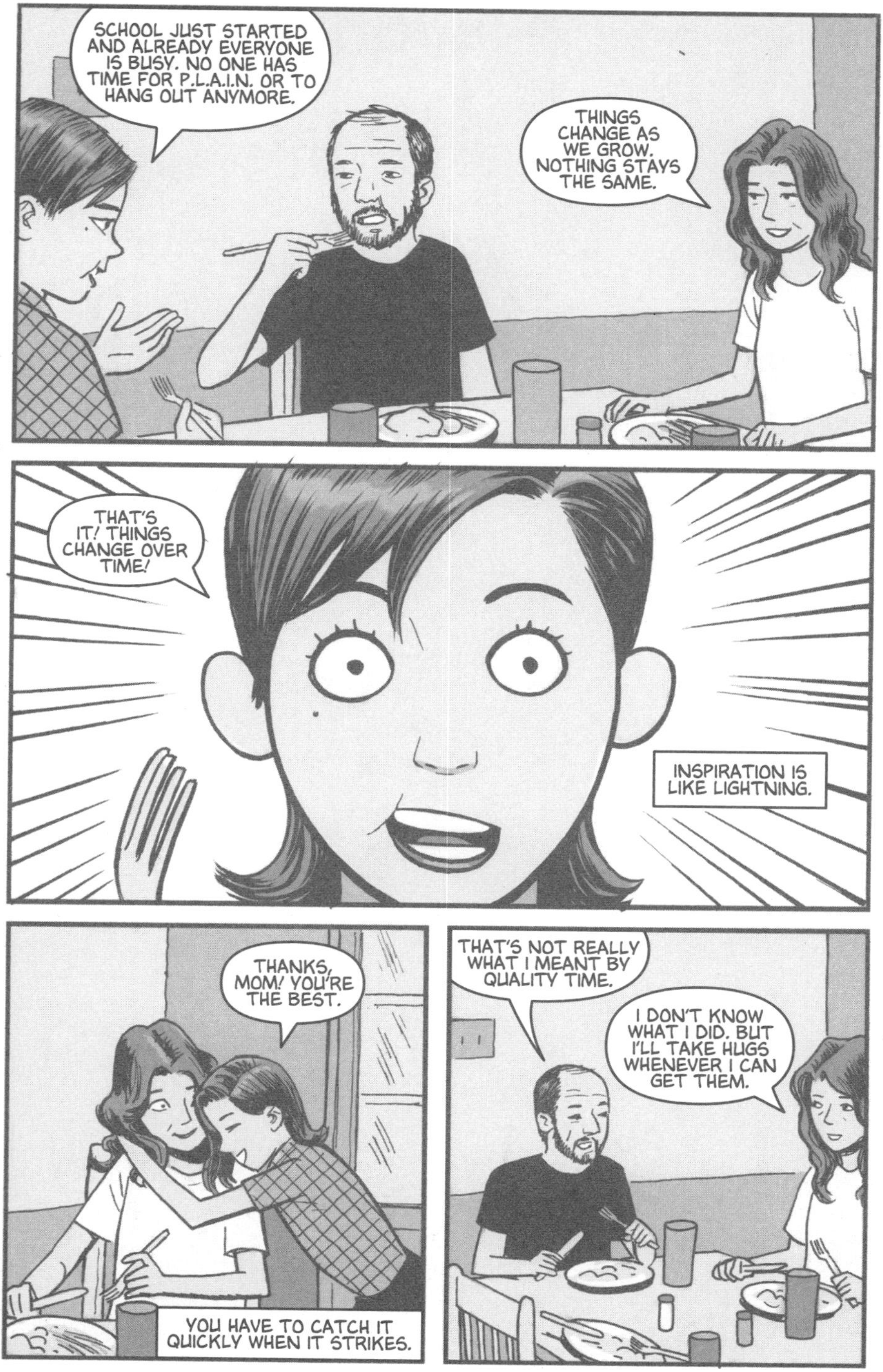
SCHOOL JUST STARTED AND ALREADY EVERYONE IS BUSY. NO ONE HAS TIME FOR P.L.A.I.N. OR TO HANG OUT ANYMORE.
THINGS CHANGE AS WE GROW. NOTHING STAYS THE SAME.
THAT'S IT! THINGS CHANGE OVER TIME!
INSPIRATION IS LIKE LIGHTNING.
THANKS, MOM! YOU'RE THE BEST.
YOU HAVE TO CATCH IT QUICKLY WHEN IT STRIKES.
THAT'S NOT REALLY WHAT I MEANT BY QUALITY TIME.
I DON'T KNOW WHAT I DID. BUT I'LL TAKE HUGS WHENEVER I CAN GET THEM.

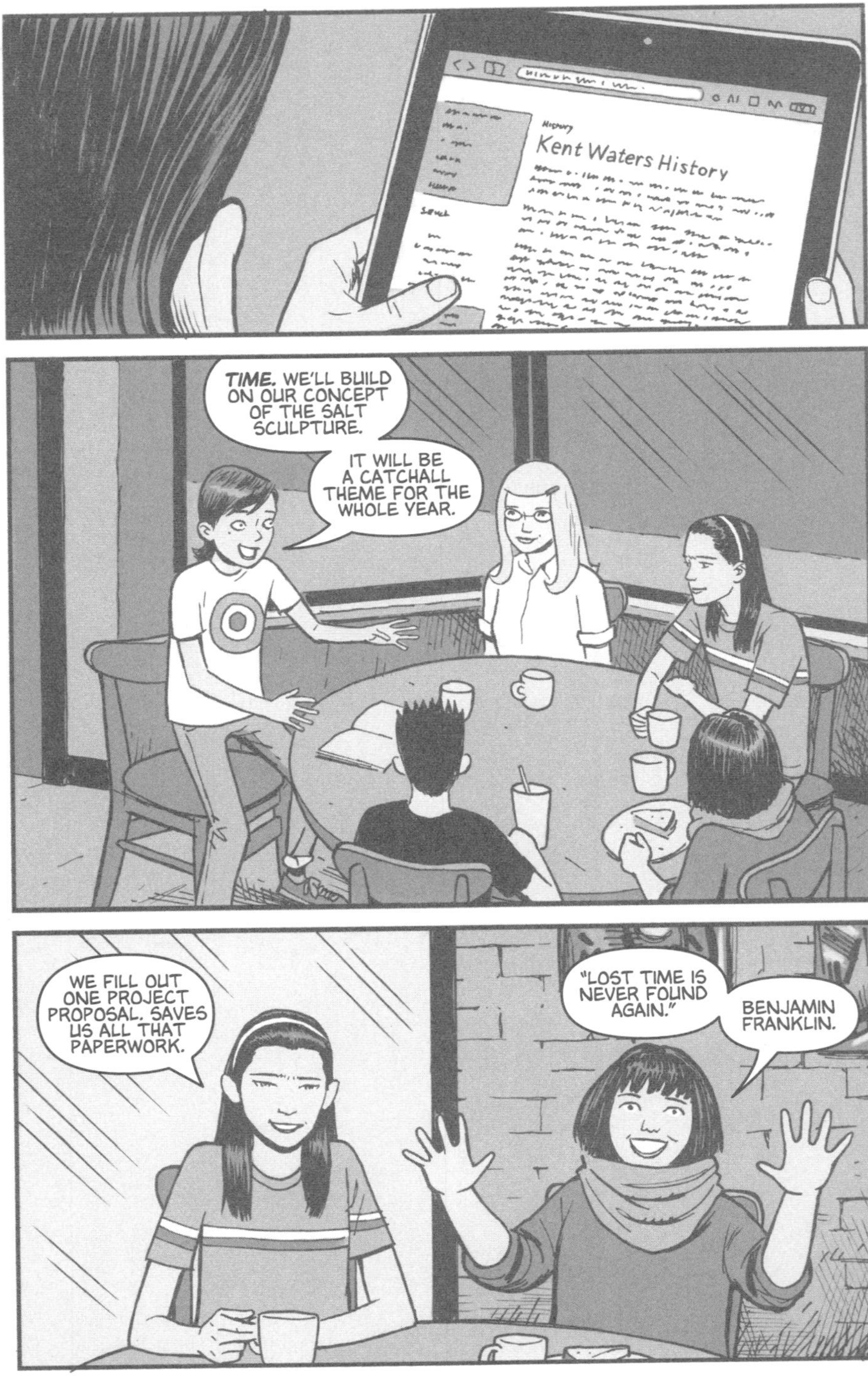
History
Kent Waters History
TIME. WE'LL BUILD ON OUR CONCEPT OF THE SALT SCULPTURE.
IT WILL BE A CATCHALL THEME FOR THE WHOLE YEAR.
WE FILL OUT ONE PROJECT PROPOSAL. SAVES US ALL THAT PAPERWORK.
"LOST TIME IS NEVER FOUND AGAIN."
BENJAMIN FRANKLIN.

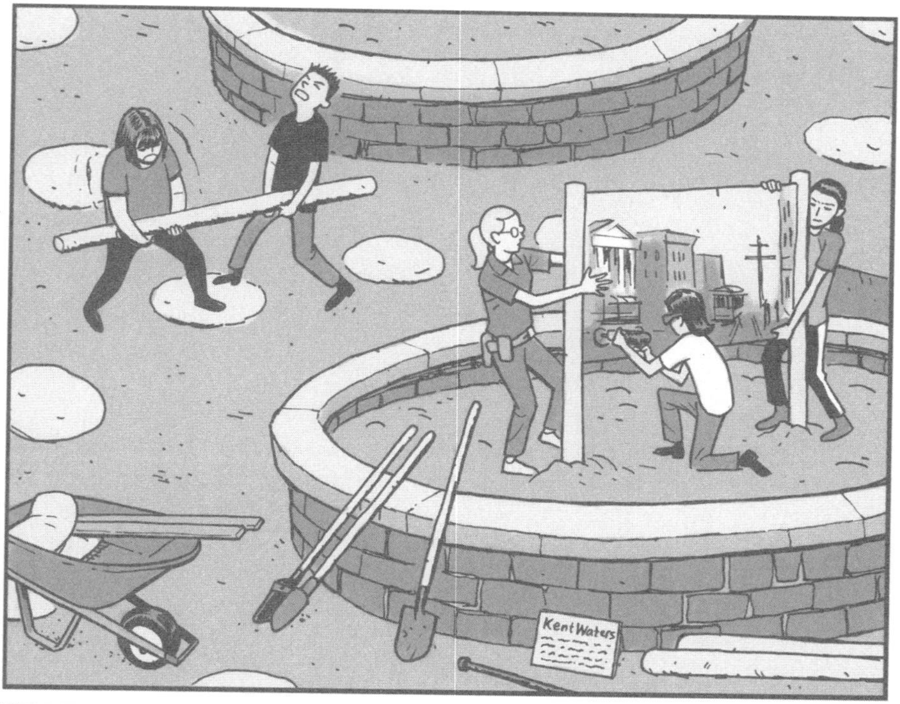
Kent Waters

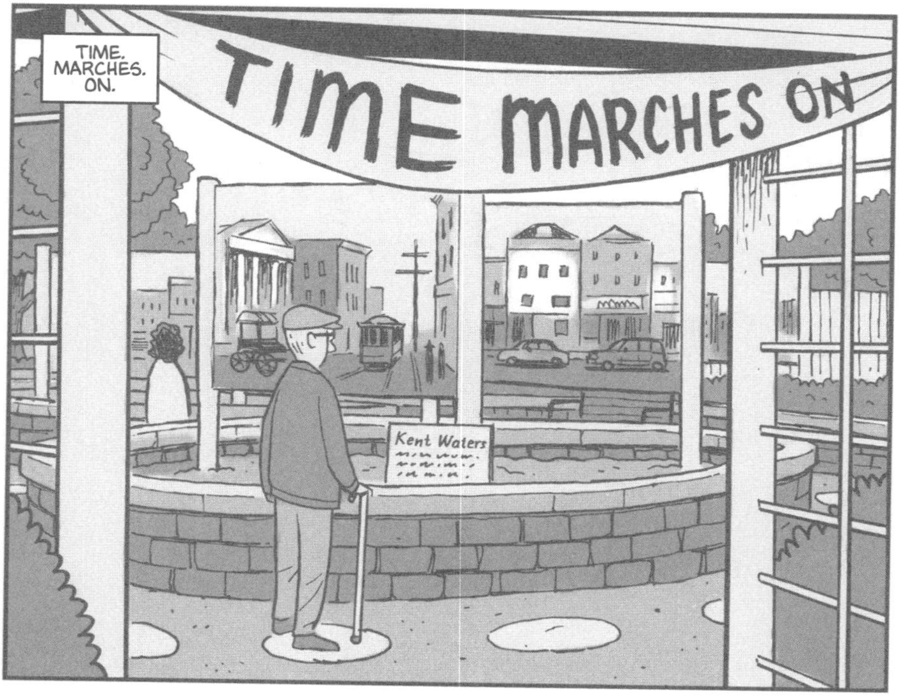
TIME. MARCHES. ON.
TIME MARCHES ON
Kent Waters

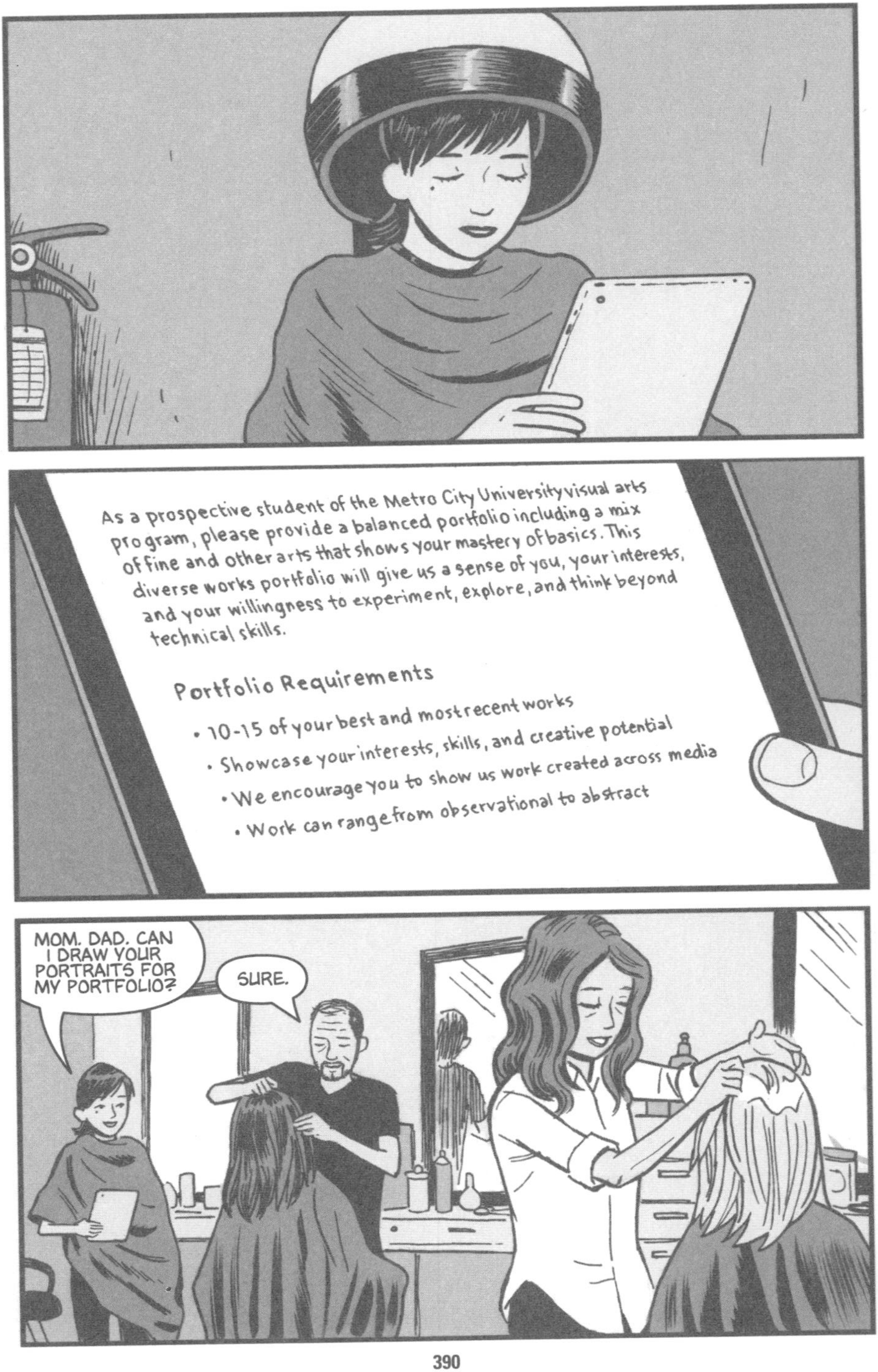
As a prospective student of the Metro City University visual arts
program, please provide a balanced portfolio including a mix
of fine and other arts that shows your mastery of basics. This
diverse works portfolio will give us a sense of you, your interests,
and your willingness to experiment, explore, and think beyond
technical skills.
Portfolio Requirements
• 10-15 of your best and most recent works
• Showcase your interests, skills, and creative potential
• We encourage you to show us work created across media
• Work can range from observational to abstract
MOM. DAD. CAN I DRAW YOUR PORTRAITS FOR MY PORTFOLIO?
SURE.

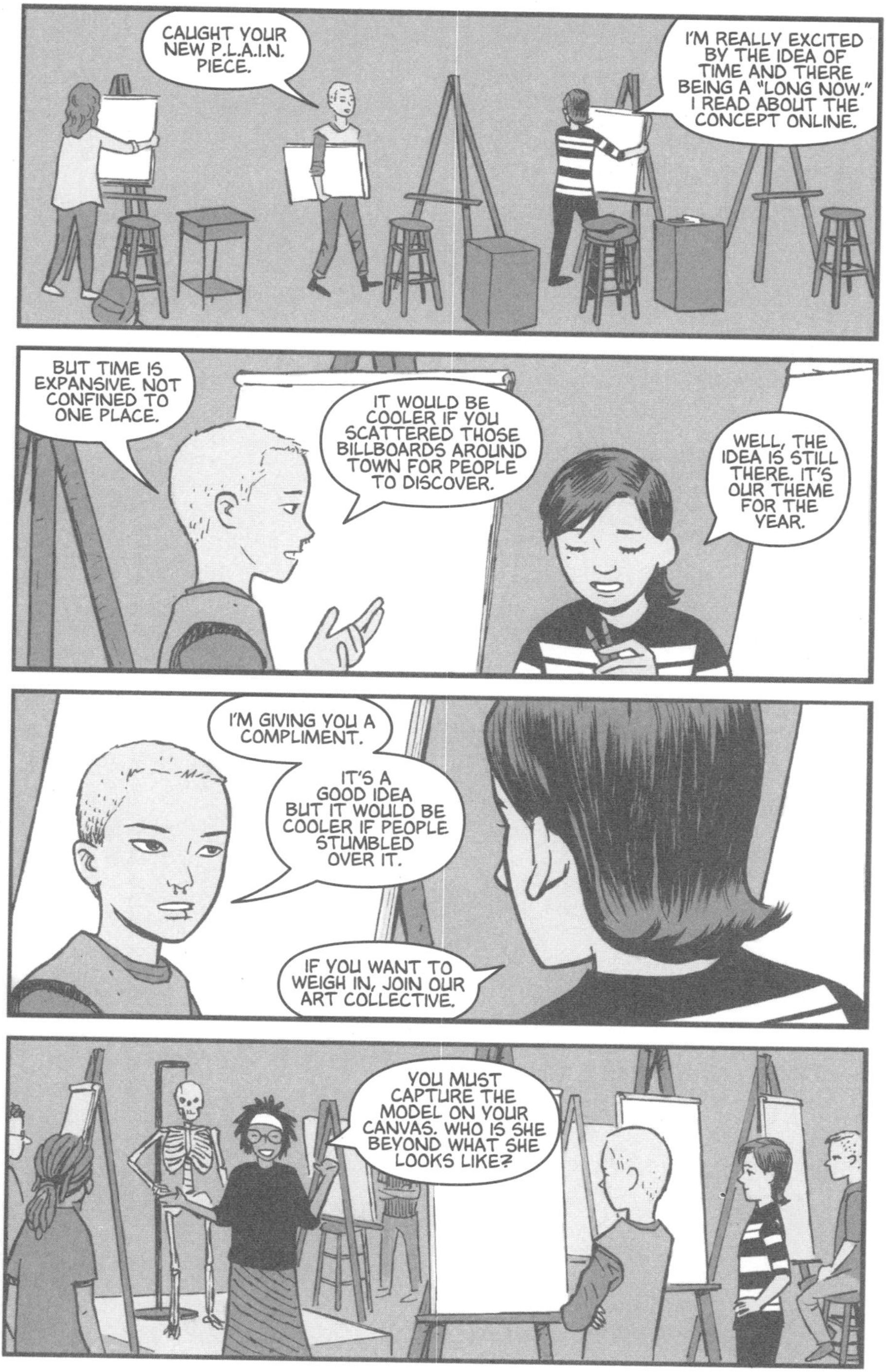
CAUGHT YOUR NEW P.L.A.I.N. PIECE.
I'M REALLY EXCITED BY THE IDEA OF TIME AND THERE BEING A "LONG NOW." I READ ABOUT THE CONCEPT ONLINE.
BUT TIME IS EXPANSIVE. NOT CONFINED TO ONE PLACE.
IT WOULD BE COOLER IF YOU SCATTERED THOSE BILLBOARDS AROUND TOWN FOR PEOPLE TO DISCOVER.
WELL, THE IDEA IS STILL THERE. IT'S OUR THEME FOR THE YEAR.
I'M GIVING YOU A COMPLIMENT.
IT'S A GOOD IDEA BUT IT WOULD BE COOLER IF PEOPLE STUMBLED OVER IT.
IF YOU WANT TO WEIGH IN, JOIN OUR ART COLLECTIVE.
YOU MUST CAPTURE THE MODEL ON YOUR CANVAS. WHO IS SHE BEYOND WHAT SHE LOOKS LIKE?

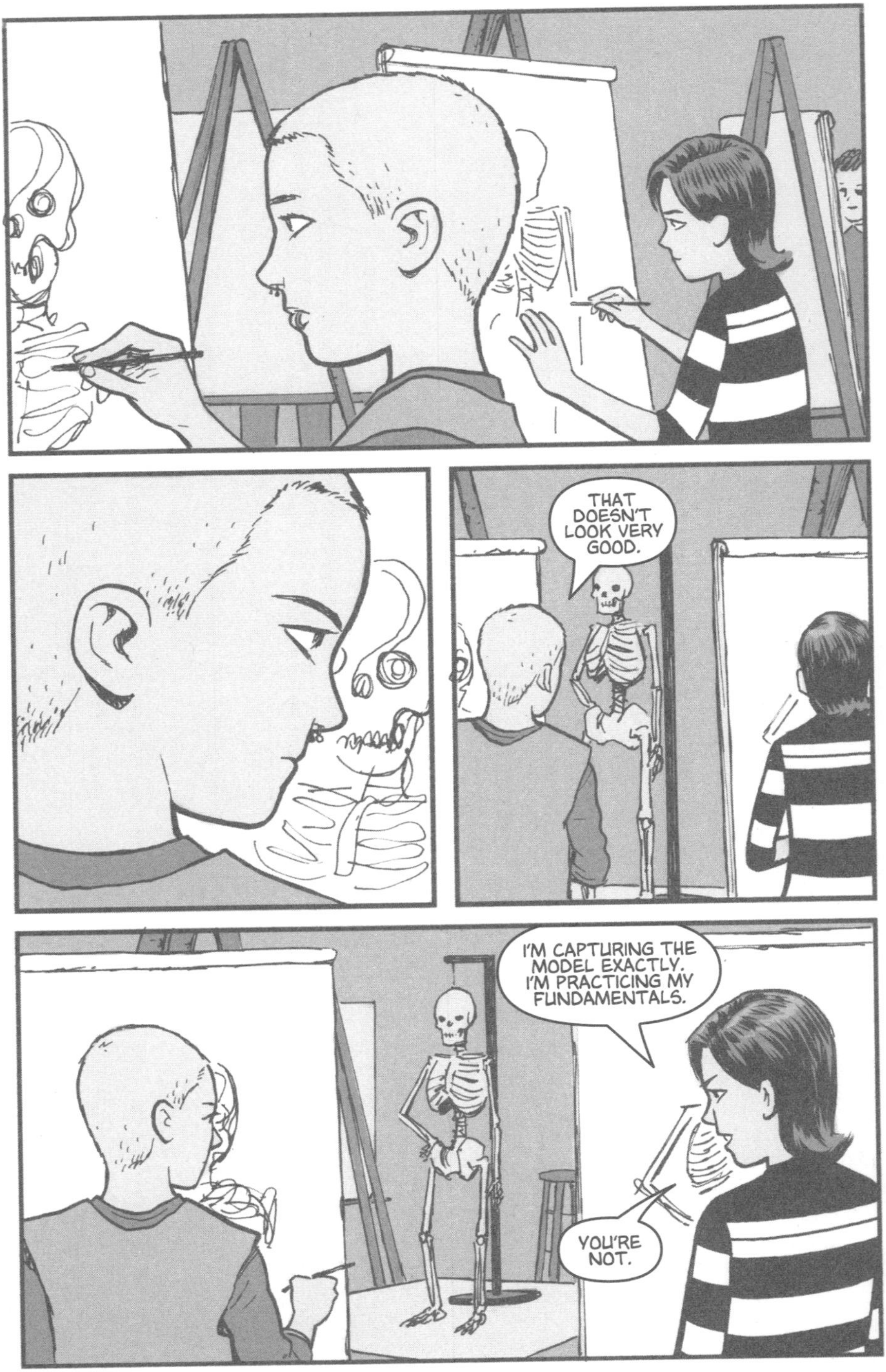
THAT DOESN'T LOOK VERY GOOD.
I'M CAPTURING THE MODEL EXACTLY. I'M PRACTICING MY FUNDAMENTALS.
YOU'RE NOT.

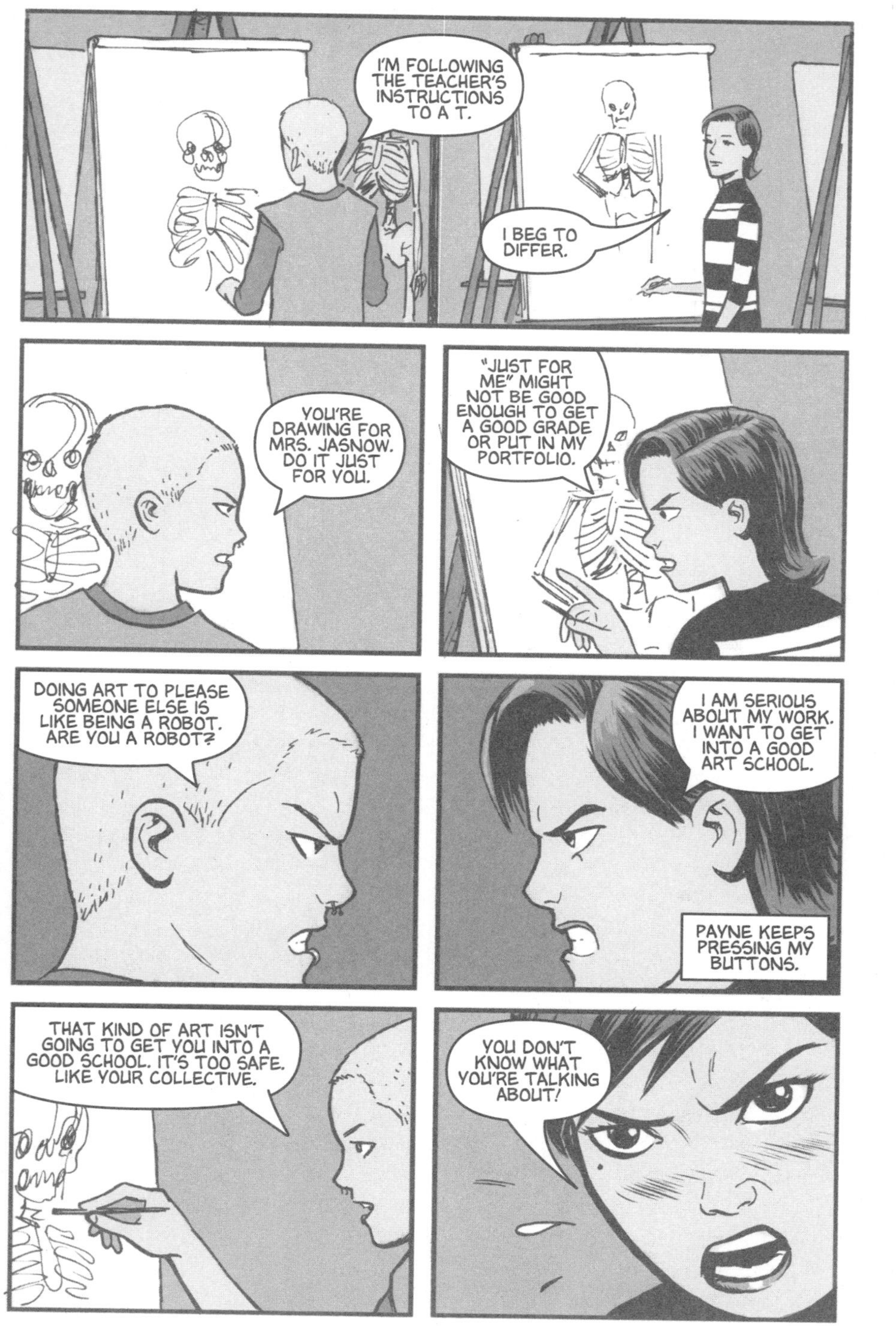
I'M FOLLOWING THE TEACHER'S INSTRUCTIONS TO A T.
I BEG TO DIFFER.
YOU'RE DRAWING FOR MRS. JASNOW. DO IT JUST FOR YOU.
"JUST FOR ME" MIGHT NOT BE GOOD ENOUGH TO GET A GOOD GRADE OR PUT IN MY PORTFOLIO.
DOING ART TO PLEASE SOMEONE ELSE IS LIKE BEING A ROBOT. ARE YOU A ROBOT?
I AM SERIOUS ABOUT MY WORK. I WANT TO GET INTO A GOOD ART SCHOOL.
PAYNE KEEPS PRESSING MY BUTTONS.
THAT KIND OF ART ISN'T GOING TO GET YOU INTO A GOOD SCHOOL. IT'S TOO SAFE. LIKE YOUR COLLECTIVE.
YOU DON'T KNOW WHAT YOU'RE TALKING ABOUT!

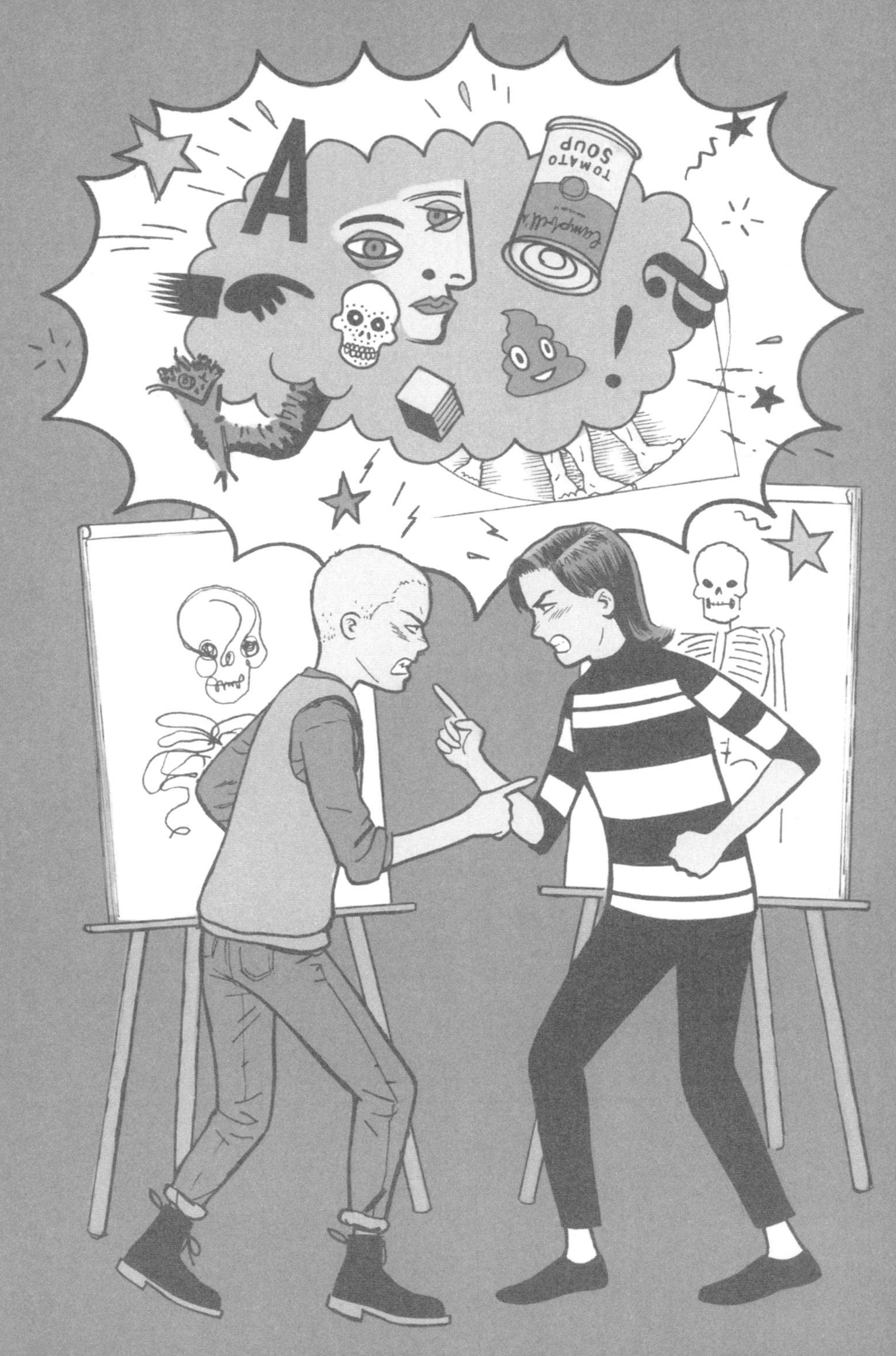
TOMATO SOUP

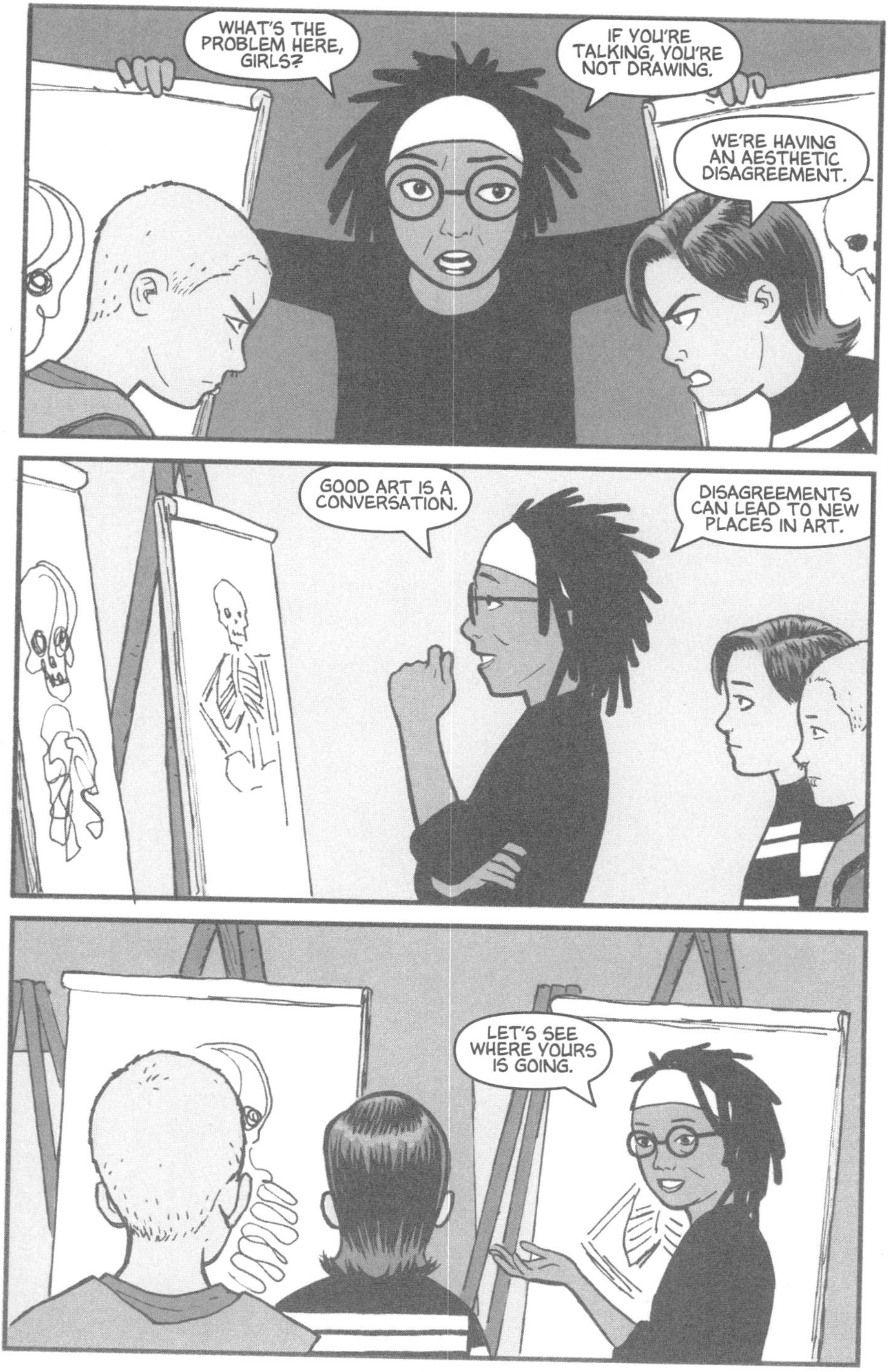
WHAT'S THE PROBLEM HERE, GIRLS?
IF YOU'RE TALKING, YOU'RE NOT DRAWING.
WE'RE HAVING AN AESTHETIC DISAGREEMENT.
GOOD ART IS A CONVERSATION.
DISAGREEMENTS CAN LEAD TO NEW PLACES IN ART.
LET'S SEE WHERE YOURS IS GOING.

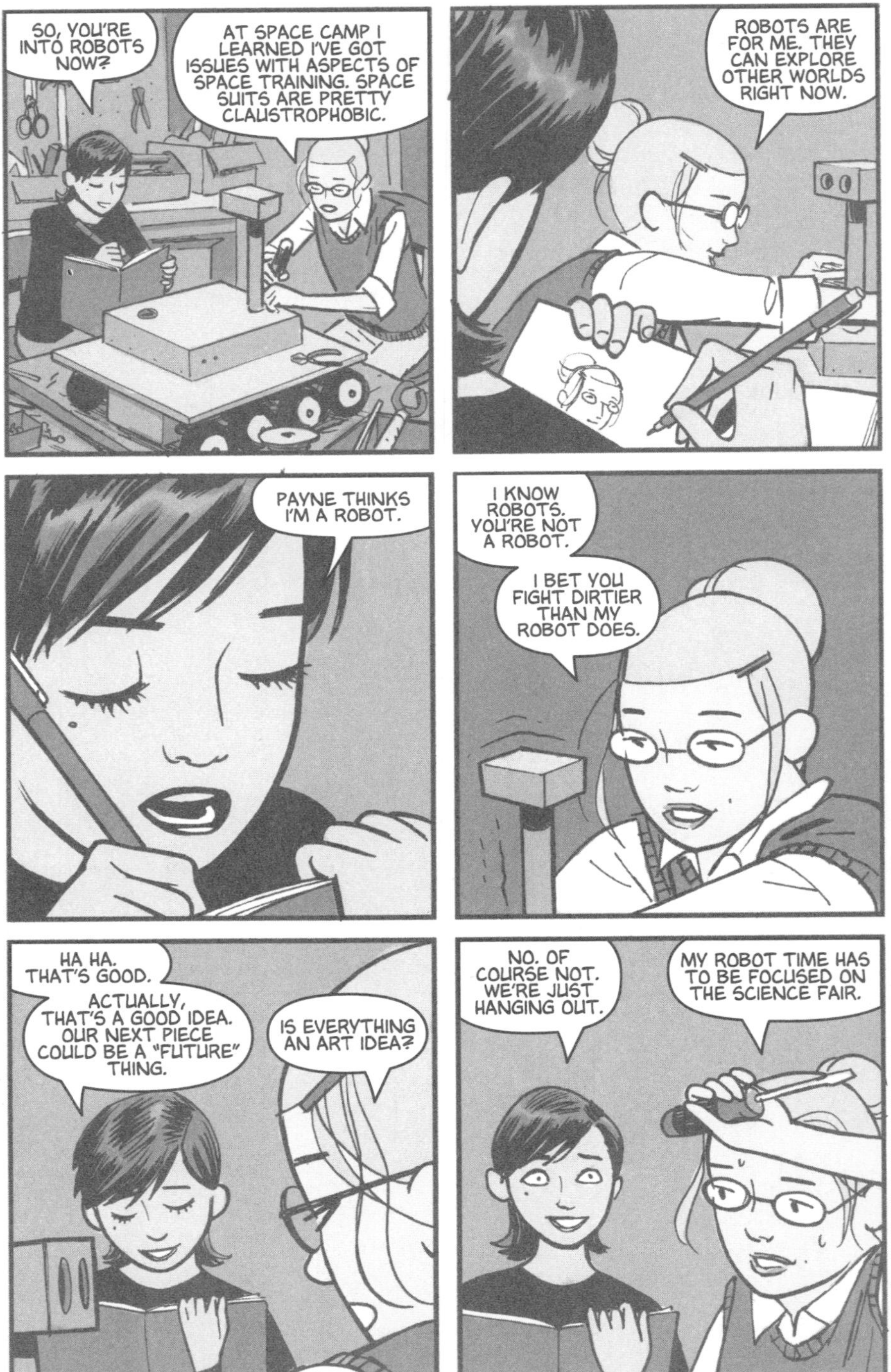
SO, YOU'RE INTO ROBOTS NOW?
AT SPACE CAMP I LEARNED I'VE GOT ISSUES WITH ASPECTS OF SPACE TRAINING. SPACE SUITS ARE PRETTY CLAUSTROPHOBIC.
ROBOTS ARE FOR ME. THEY CAN EXPLORE OTHER WORLDS RIGHT NOW.
PAYNE THINKS I'M A ROBOT.
I KNOW ROBOTS. YOU'RE NOT A ROBOT.
I BET YOU FIGHT DIRTIER THAN MY ROBOT DOES.
HA HA. THAT'S GOOD.
ACTUALLY, THAT'S A GOOD IDEA. OUR NEXT PIECE COULD BE A "FUTURE" THING.
IS EVERYTHING AN ART IDEA?
NO. OF COURSE NOT. WE'RE JUST HANGING OUT.
MY ROBOT TIME HAS TO BE FOCUSED ON THE SCIENCE FAIR.

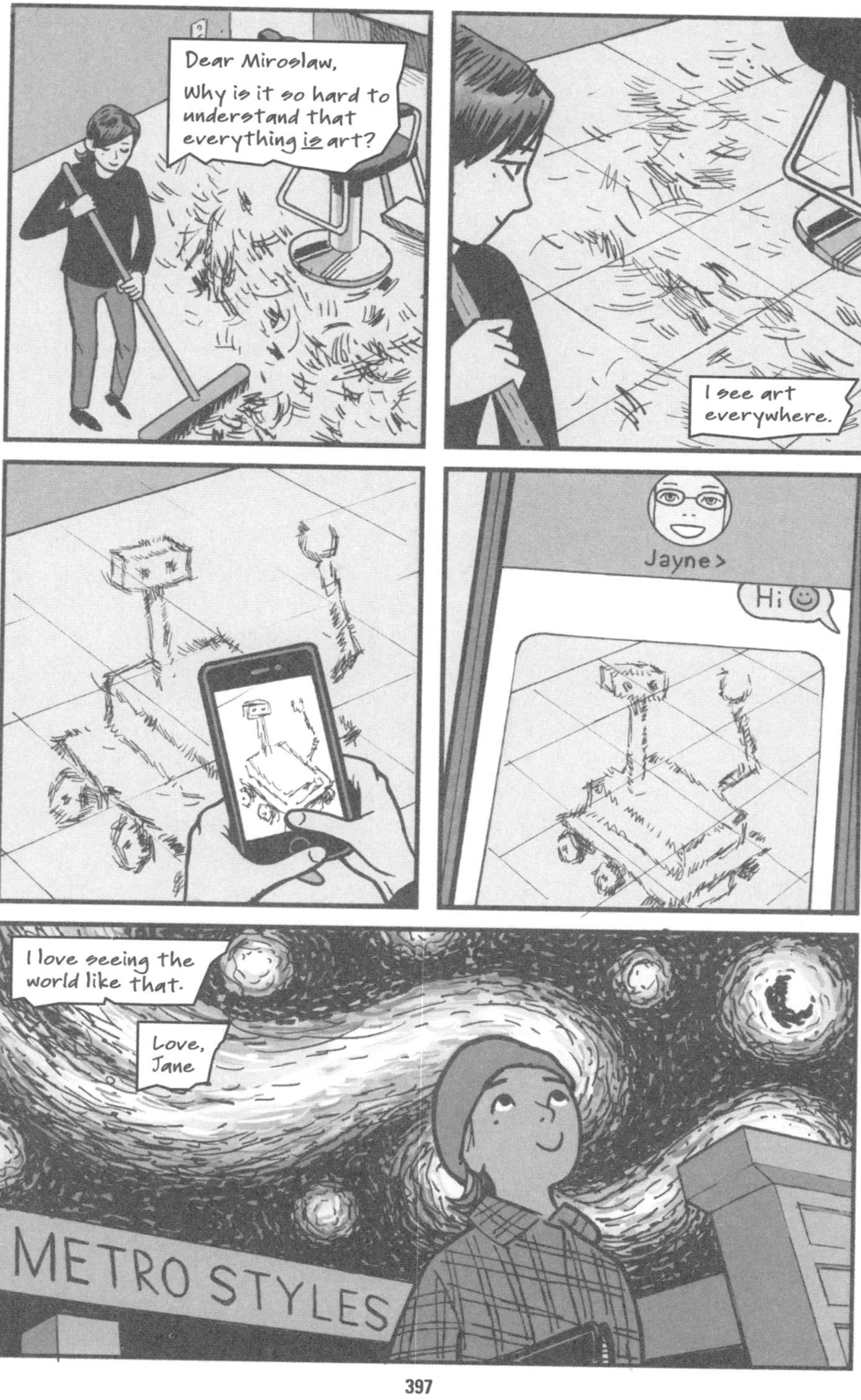
Dear Miroslaw,
Why is it so hard to understand that everything is art?
I see art everywhere.
Jayne >
Hi
I love seeing the world like that.
Love, Jane
METRO STYLES

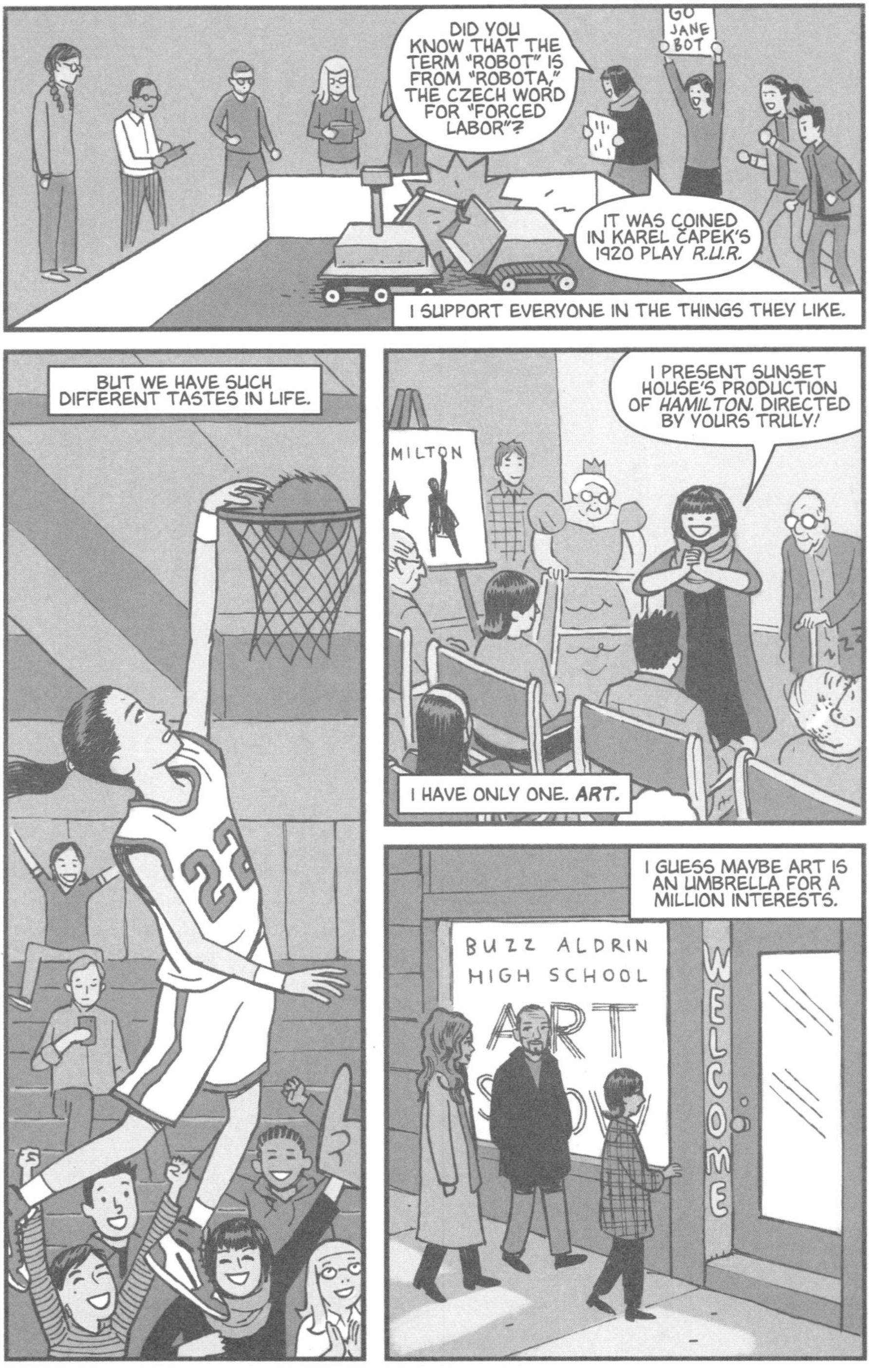
DID YOU KNOW THAT THE TERM "ROBOT" IS FROM "ROBOTA," THE CZECH WORD FOR "FORCED LABOR"?
GO JANE BOT
IT WAS COINED IN KAREL ČAPEK'S 1920 PLAY *R.U.R.*
I SUPPORT EVERYONE IN THE THINGS THEY LIKE.
BUT WE HAVE SUCH DIFFERENT TASTES IN LIFE.
22
MILTON
I PRESENT SUNSET HOUSE'S PRODUCTION OF *HAMILTON.* DIRECTED BY YOURS TRULY!
I HAVE ONLY ONE. **ART.**
I GUESS MAYBE ART IS AN UMBRELLA FOR A MILLION INTERESTS.
BUZZ ALDRIN HIGH SCHOOL
ART
WELCOME

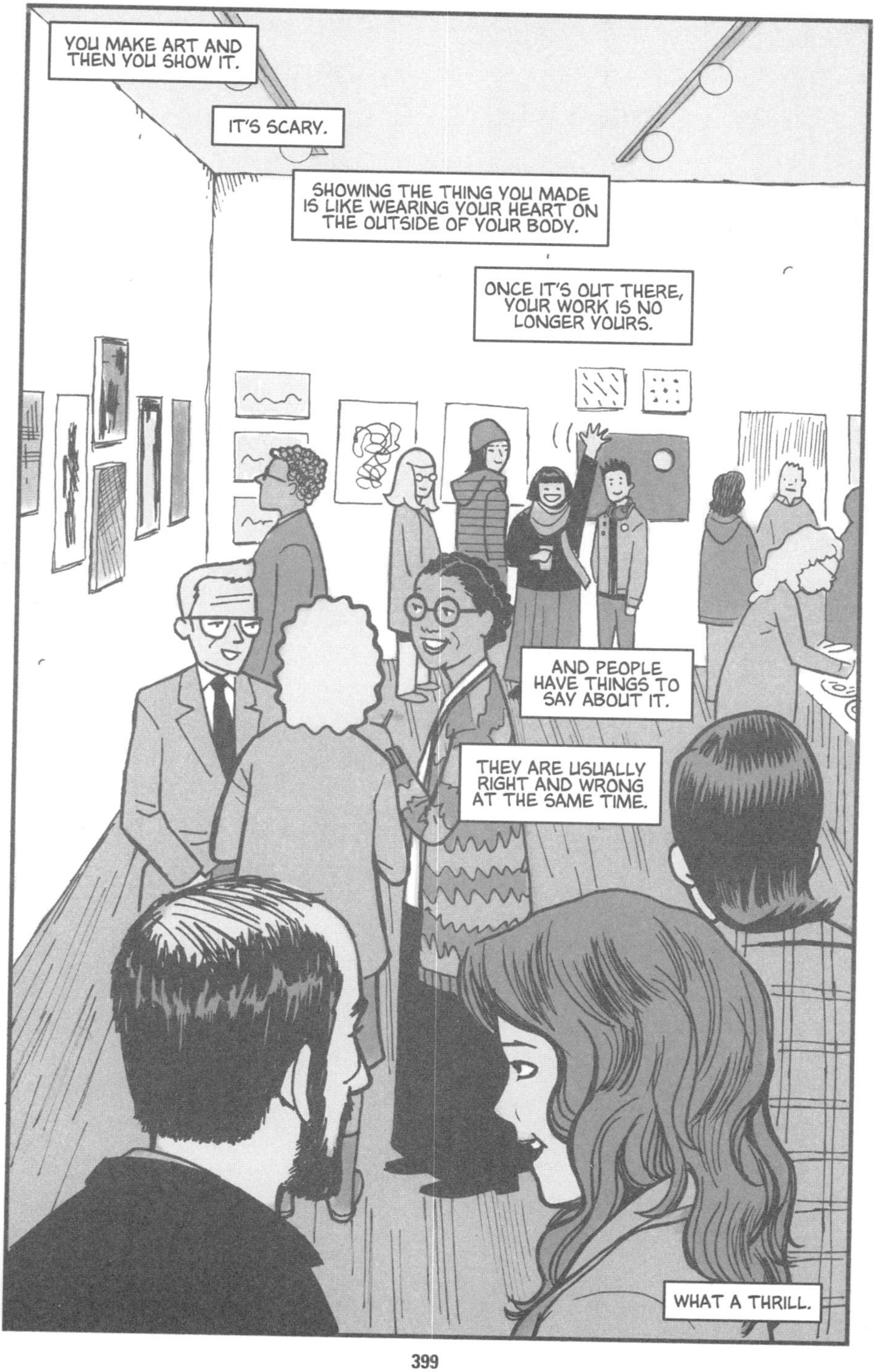
YOU MAKE ART AND THEN YOU SHOW IT.
IT'S SCARY.
SHOWING THE THING YOU MADE IS LIKE WEARING YOUR HEART ON THE OUTSIDE OF YOUR BODY.
ONCE IT'S OUT THERE, YOUR WORK IS NO LONGER YOURS.
AND PEOPLE HAVE THINGS TO SAY ABOUT IT.
THEY ARE USUALLY RIGHT AND WRONG AT THE SAME TIME.
WHAT A THRILL.

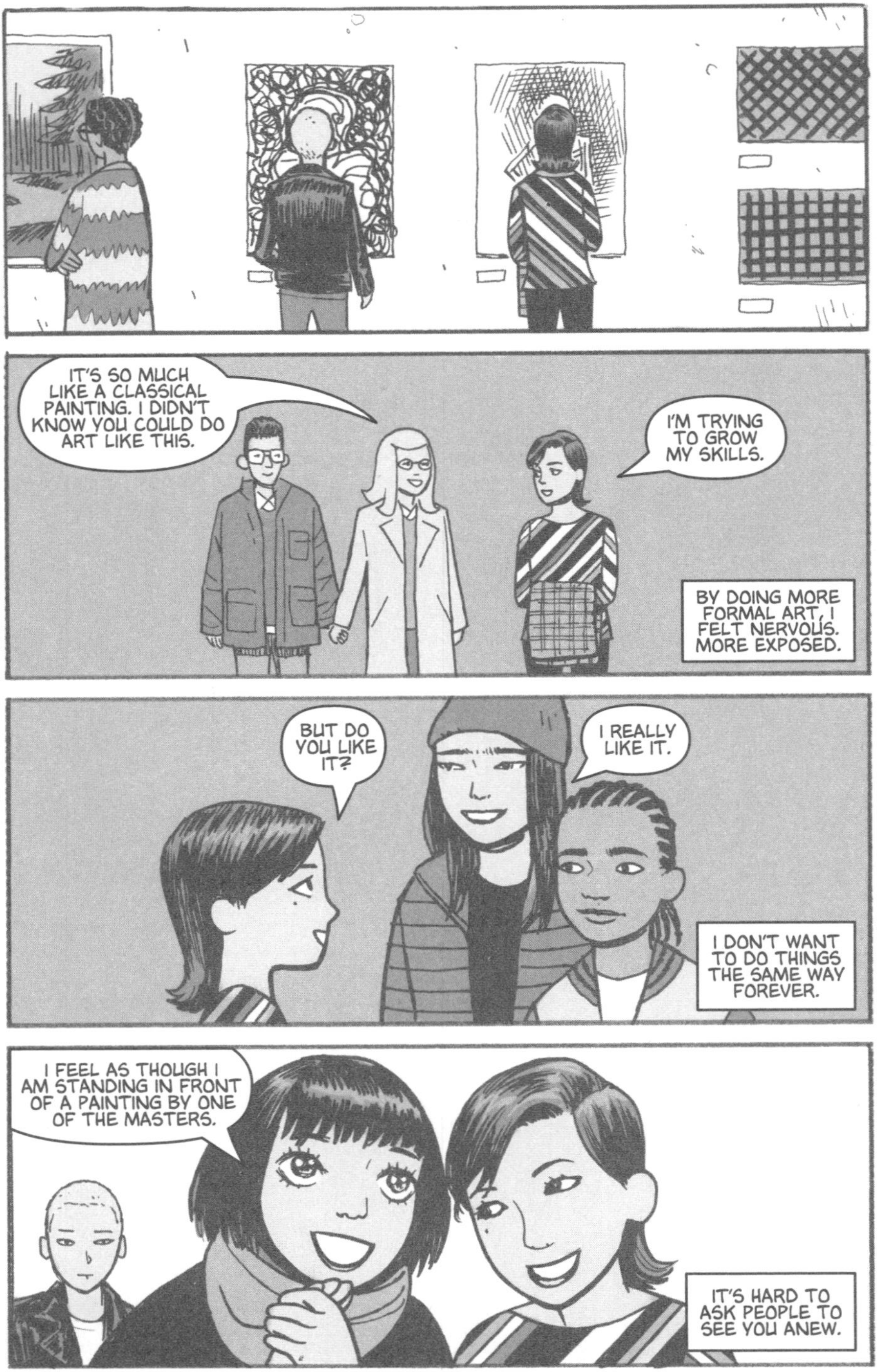
IT'S SO MUCH LIKE A CLASSICAL PAINTING. I DIDN'T KNOW YOU COULD DO ART LIKE THIS.
I'M TRYING TO GROW MY SKILLS.
BY DOING MORE FORMAL ART, I FELT NERVOUS. MORE EXPOSED.
BUT DO YOU LIKE IT?
I REALLY LIKE IT.
I DON'T WANT TO DO THINGS THE SAME WAY FOREVER.
I FEEL AS THOUGH I AM STANDING IN FRONT OF A PAINTING BY ONE OF THE MASTERS.
IT'S HARD TO ASK PEOPLE TO SEE YOU ANEW.

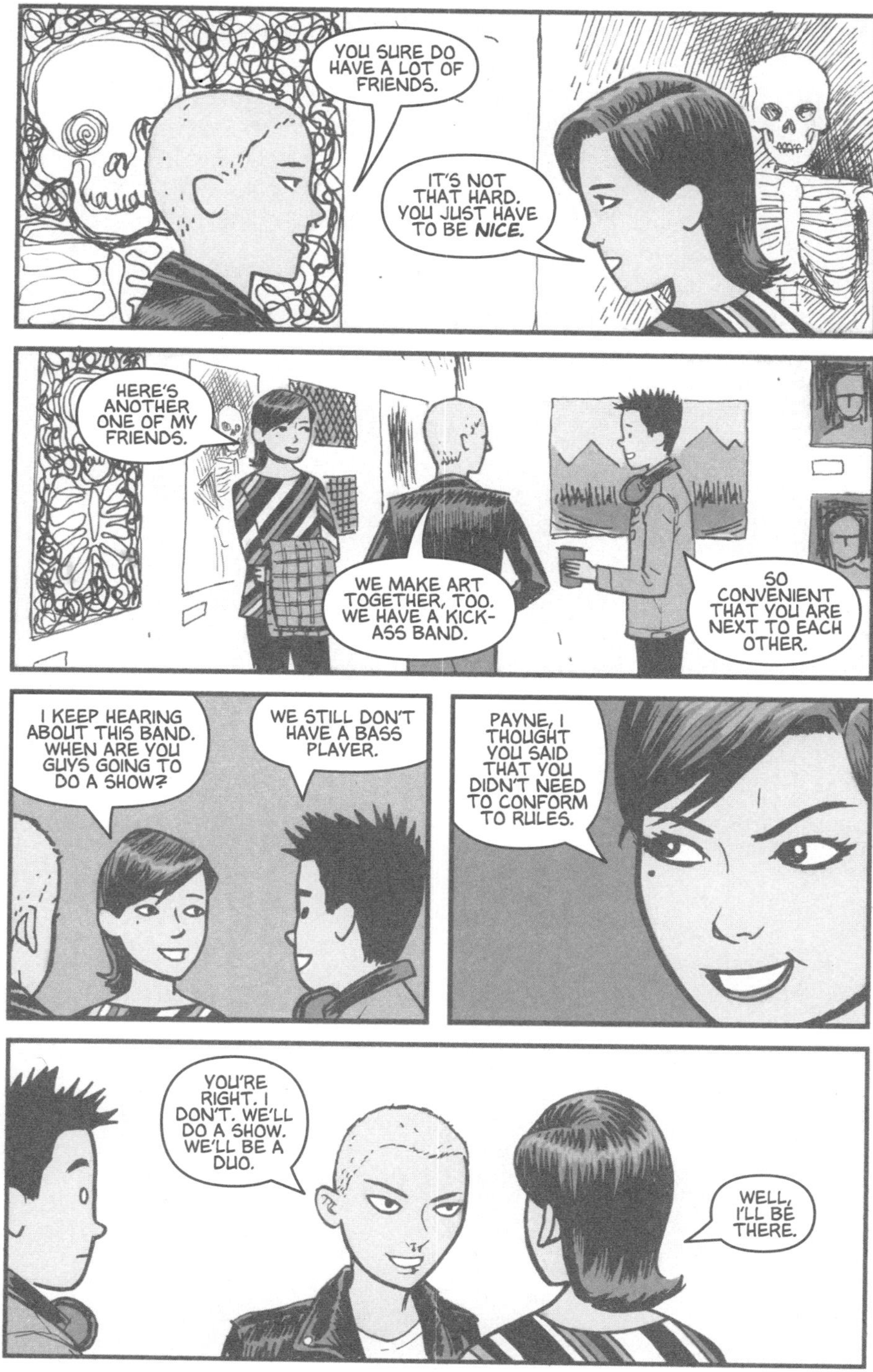
YOU SURE DO HAVE A LOT OF FRIENDS.
IT'S NOT THAT HARD. YOU JUST HAVE TO BE *NICE.*
HERE'S ANOTHER ONE OF MY FRIENDS.
WE MAKE ART TOGETHER, TOO. WE HAVE A KICK-ASS BAND.
SO CONVENIENT THAT YOU ARE NEXT TO EACH OTHER.
I KEEP HEARING ABOUT THIS BAND. WHEN ARE YOU GUYS GOING TO DO A SHOW?
WE STILL DON'T HAVE A BASS PLAYER.
PAYNE, I THOUGHT YOU SAID THAT YOU DIDN'T NEED TO CONFORM TO RULES.
YOU'RE RIGHT. I DON'T. WE'LL DO A SHOW. WE'LL BE A DUO.
WELL, I'LL BE THERE.

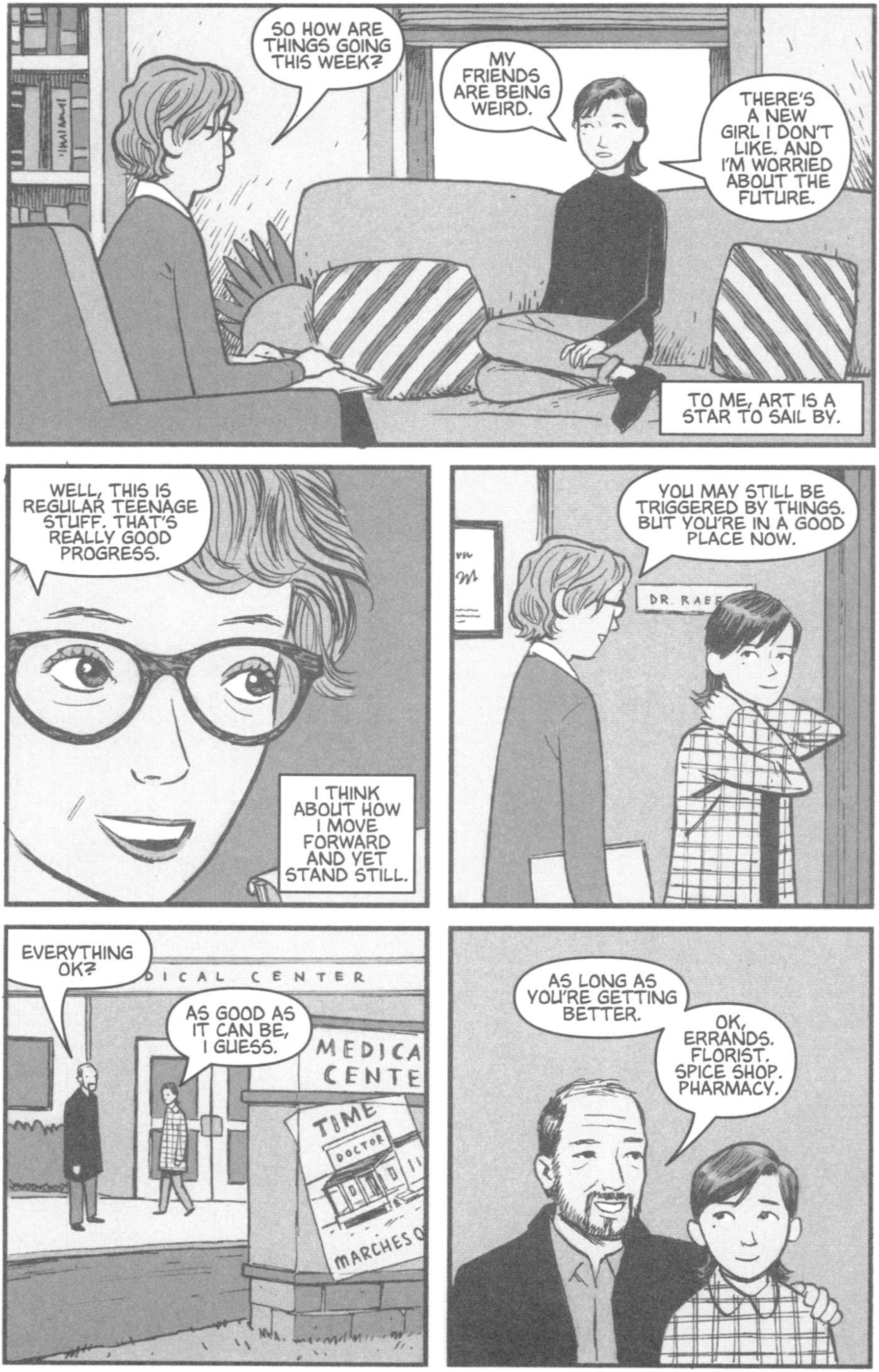
SO HOW ARE THINGS GOING THIS WEEK?
MY FRIENDS ARE BEING WEIRD.
THERE'S A NEW GIRL I DON'T LIKE. AND I'M WORRIED ABOUT THE FUTURE.
TO ME, ART IS A STAR TO SAIL BY.
WELL, THIS IS REGULAR TEENAGE STUFF. THAT'S REALLY GOOD PROGRESS.
I THINK ABOUT HOW I MOVE FORWARD AND YET STAND STILL.
YOU MAY STILL BE TRIGGERED BY THINGS. BUT YOU'RE IN A GOOD PLACE NOW.
DR. RAE
EVERYTHING OK?
DICAL CENTER
AS GOOD AS IT CAN BE, I GUESS.
MEDICA CENTE
TIME
DOCTOR
MARCHES O
AS LONG AS YOU'RE GETTING BETTER.
OK, ERRANDS. FLORIST. SPICE SHOP. PHARMACY.

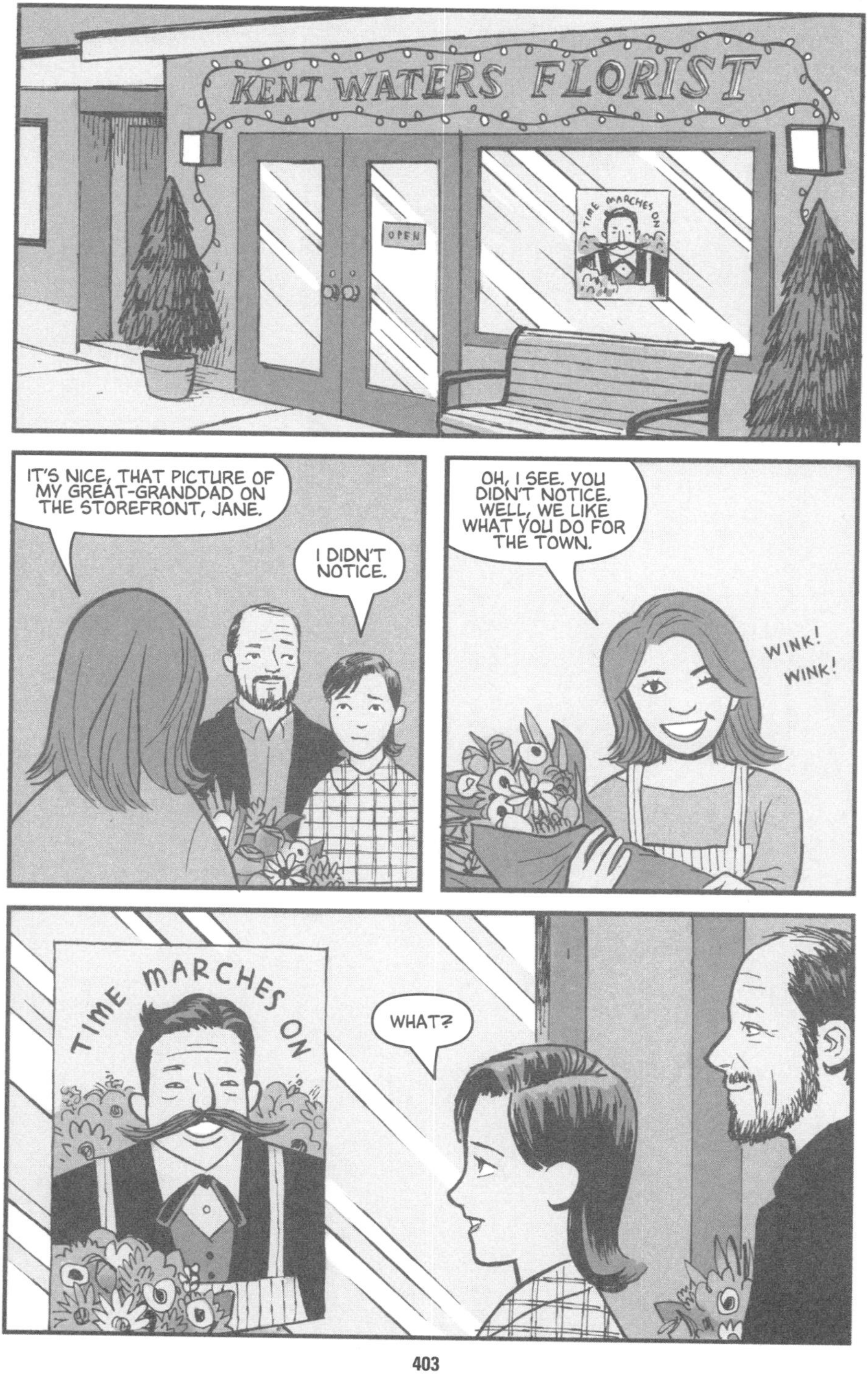
KENT WATERS FLORIST
OPEN
TIME MARCHES ON
IT'S NICE, THAT PICTURE OF MY GREAT-GRANDDAD ON THE STOREFRONT, JANE.
I DIDN'T NOTICE.
OH, I SEE. YOU DIDN'T NOTICE. WELL, WE LIKE WHAT YOU DO FOR THE TOWN.
WINK!
WINK!
TIME MARCHES ON
WHAT?

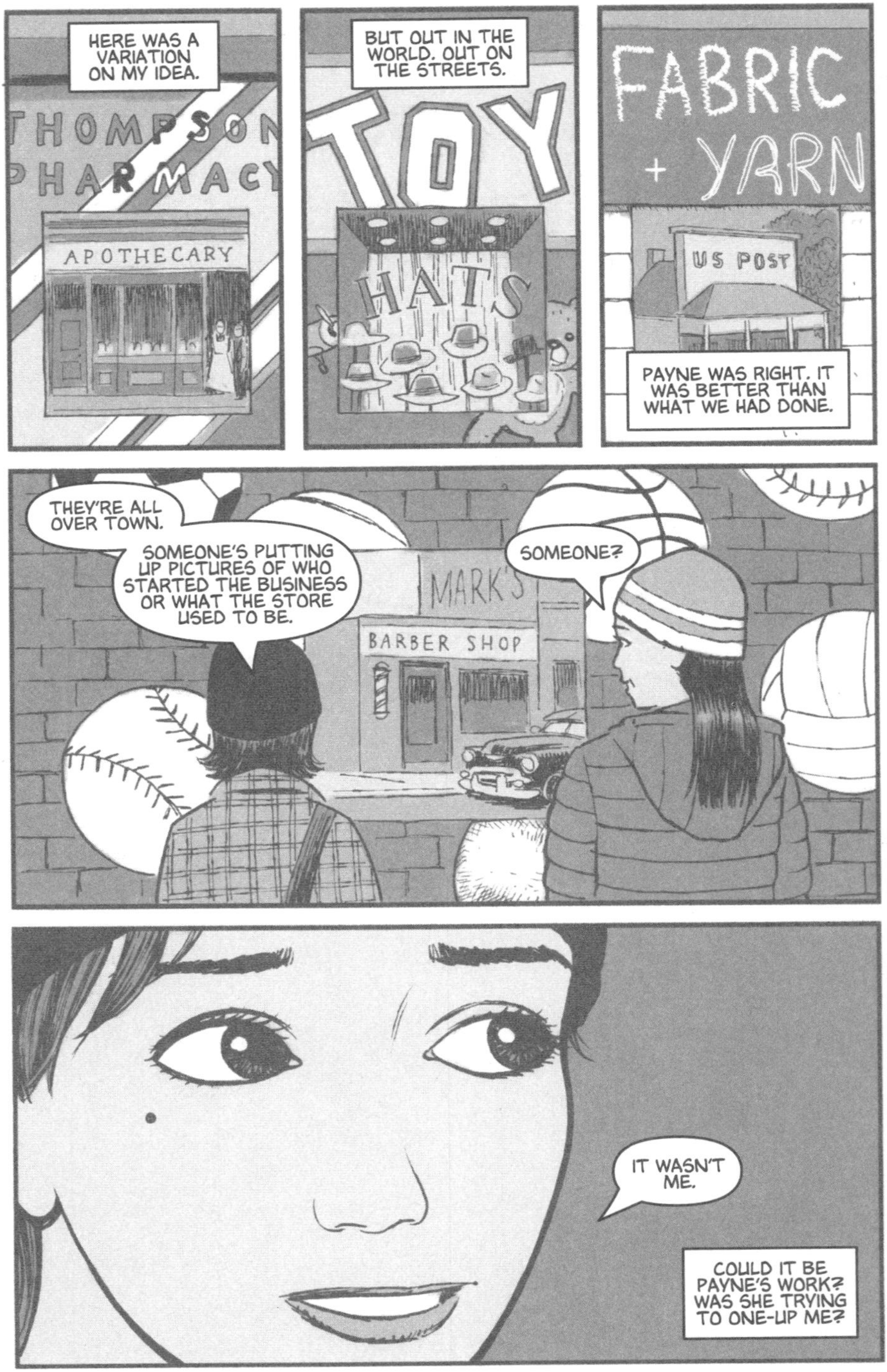
HERE WAS A VARIATION ON MY IDEA.
THOMPSON PHARMACY
APOTHECARY
BUT OUT IN THE WORLD. OUT ON THE STREETS.
TOY
HATS
FABRIC + YARN
US POST
PAYNE WAS RIGHT. IT WAS BETTER THAN WHAT WE HAD DONE.
THEY'RE ALL OVER TOWN.
SOMEONE'S PUTTING UP PICTURES OF WHO STARTED THE BUSINESS OR WHAT THE STORE USED TO BE.
SOMEONE?
MARK'S
BARBER SHOP
IT WASN'T ME.
COULD IT BE PAYNE'S WORK? WAS SHE TRYING TO ONE-UP ME?

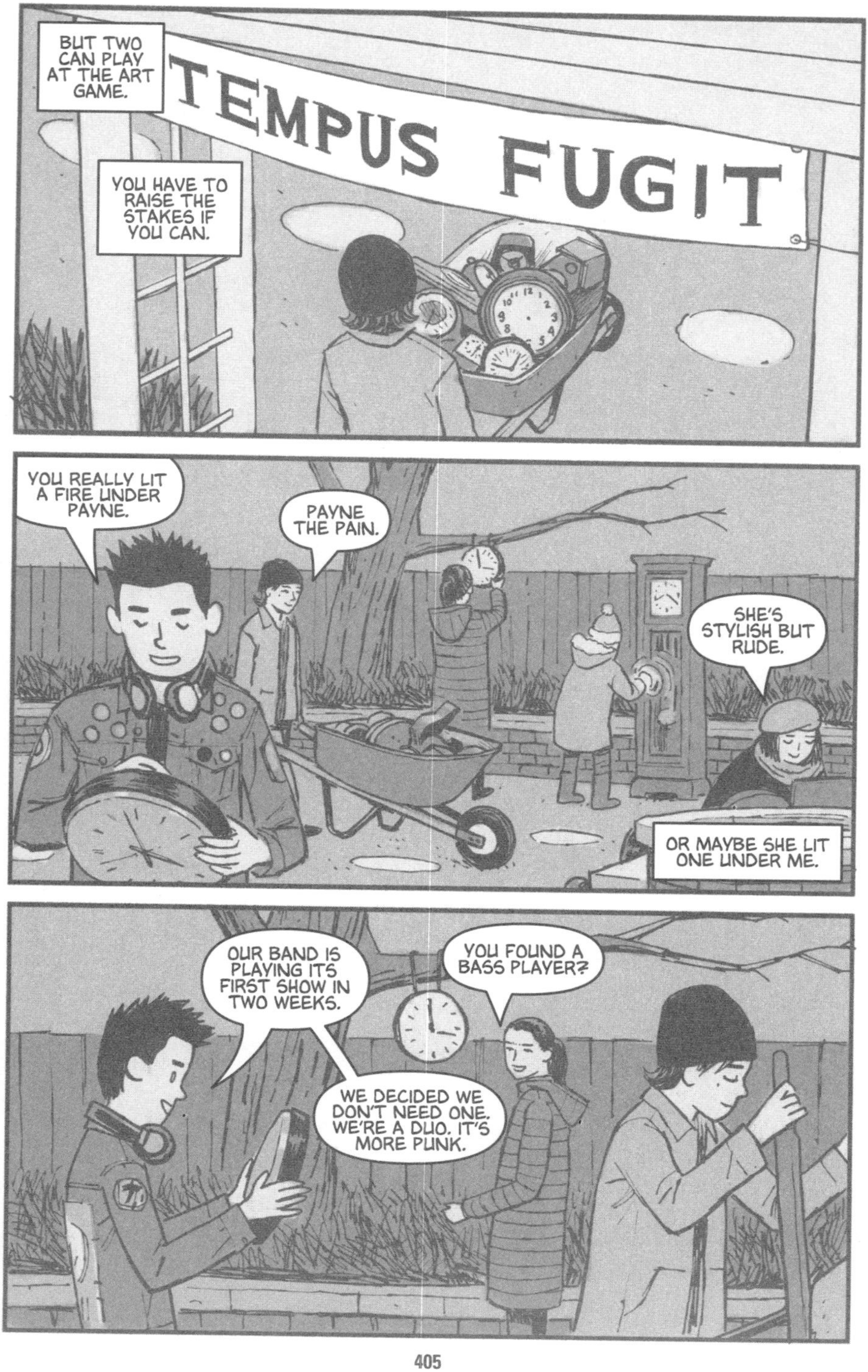
BUT TWO CAN PLAY AT THE ART GAME.
TEMPUS FUGIT
YOU HAVE TO RAISE THE STAKES IF YOU CAN.
YOU REALLY LIT A FIRE UNDER PAYNE.
PAYNE THE PAIN.
SHE'S STYLISH BUT RUDE.
OR MAYBE SHE LIT ONE UNDER ME.
OUR BAND IS PLAYING ITS FIRST SHOW IN TWO WEEKS.
YOU FOUND A BASS PLAYER?
WE DECIDED WE DON'T NEED ONE. WE'RE A DUO. IT'S MORE PUNK.

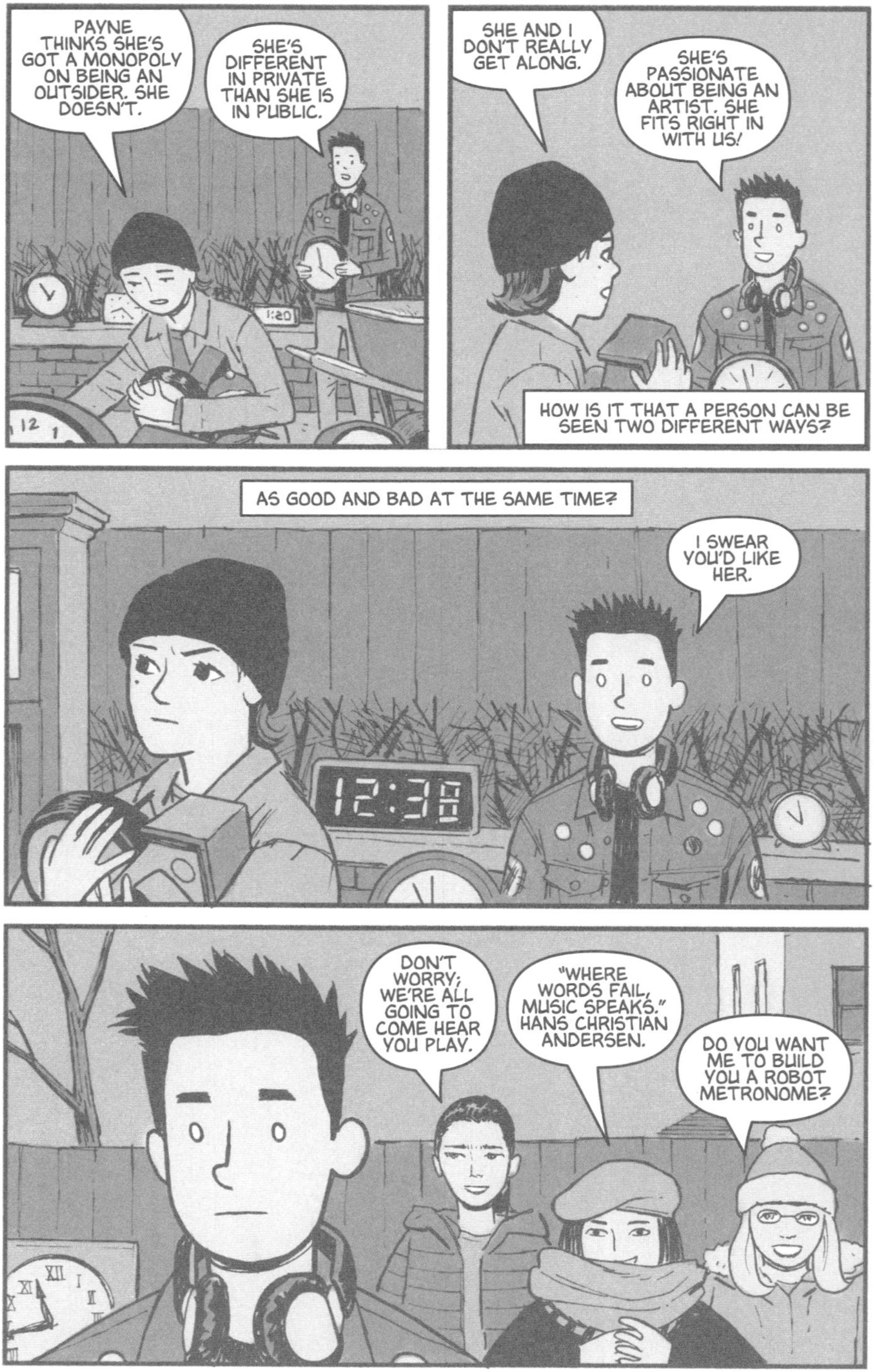
PAYNE THINKS SHE'S GOT A MONOPOLY ON BEING AN OUTSIDER. SHE DOESN'T.
SHE'S DIFFERENT IN PRIVATE THAN SHE IS IN PUBLIC.
SHE AND I DON'T REALLY GET ALONG.
SHE'S PASSIONATE ABOUT BEING AN ARTIST. SHE FITS RIGHT IN WITH US!
HOW IS IT THAT A PERSON CAN BE SEEN TWO DIFFERENT WAYS?
AS GOOD AND BAD AT THE SAME TIME?
I SWEAR YOU'D LIKE HER.
DON'T WORRY; WE'RE ALL GOING TO COME HEAR YOU PLAY.
"WHERE WORDS FAIL, MUSIC SPEAKS." HANS CHRISTIAN ANDERSEN.
DO YOU WANT ME TO BUILD YOU A ROBOT METRONOME?

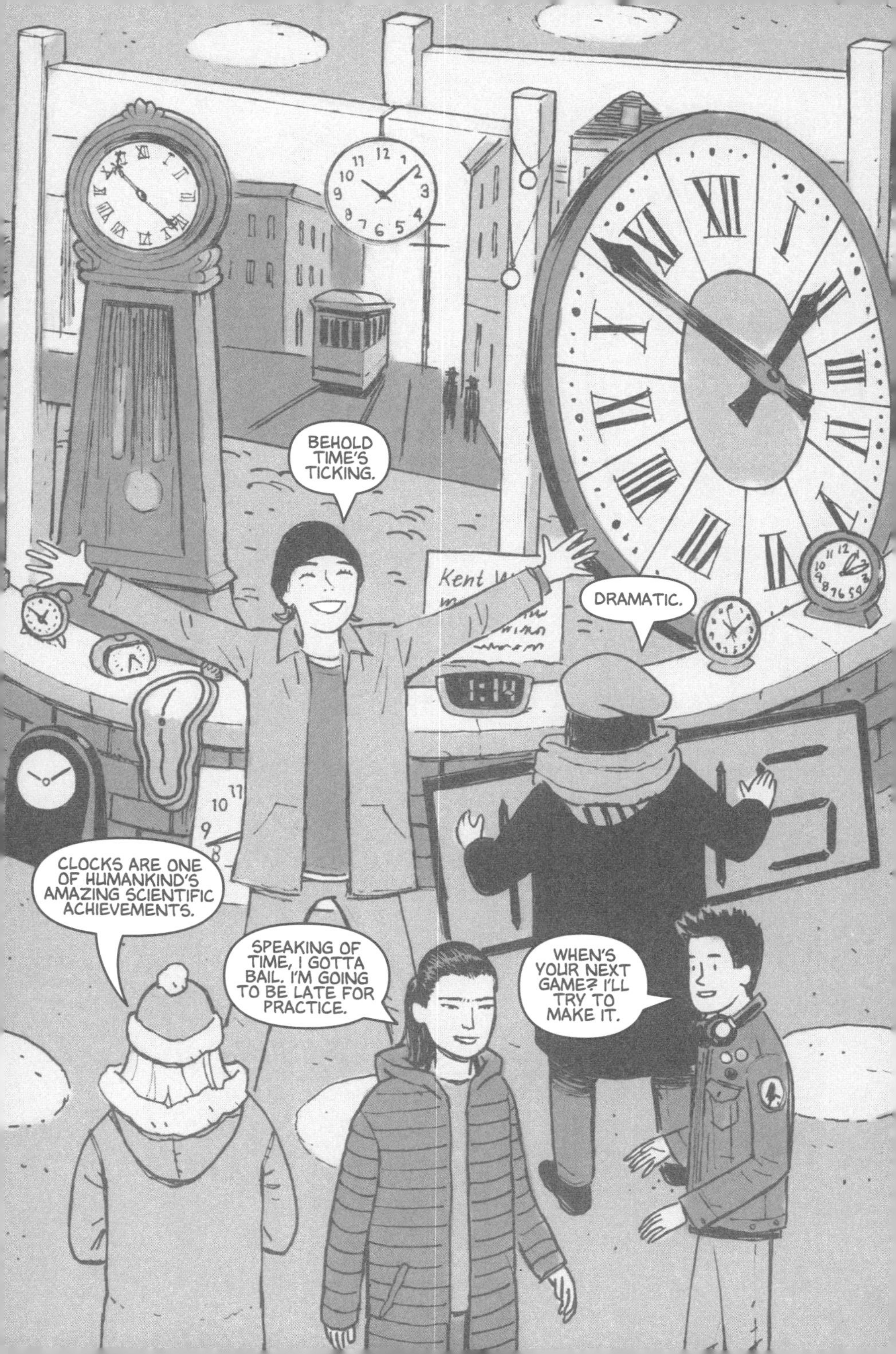
BEHOLD TIME'S TICKING.
DRAMATIC.
CLOCKS ARE ONE OF HUMANKIND'S AMAZING SCIENTIFIC ACHIEVEMENTS.
SPEAKING OF TIME, I GOTTA BAIL. I'M GOING TO BE LATE FOR PRACTICE.
WHEN'S YOUR NEXT GAME? I'LL TRY TO MAKE IT.

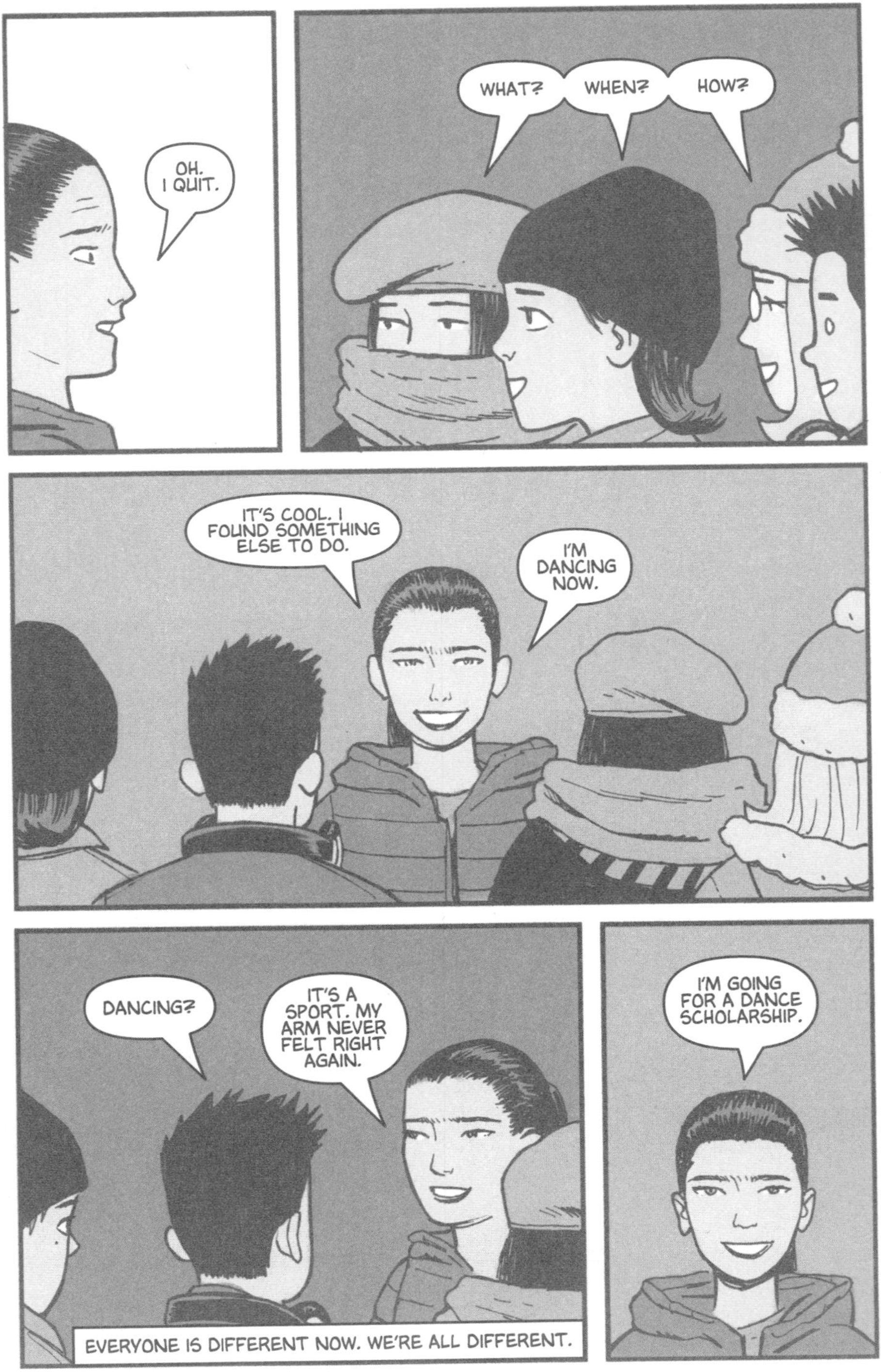
OH. I QUIT.
WHAT?
WHEN?
HOW?
IT'S COOL. I FOUND SOMETHING ELSE TO DO.
I'M DANCING NOW.
DANCING?
IT'S A SPORT. MY ARM NEVER FELT RIGHT AGAIN.
EVERYONE IS DIFFERENT NOW. WE'RE ALL DIFFERENT.
I'M GOING FOR A DANCE SCHOLARSHIP.

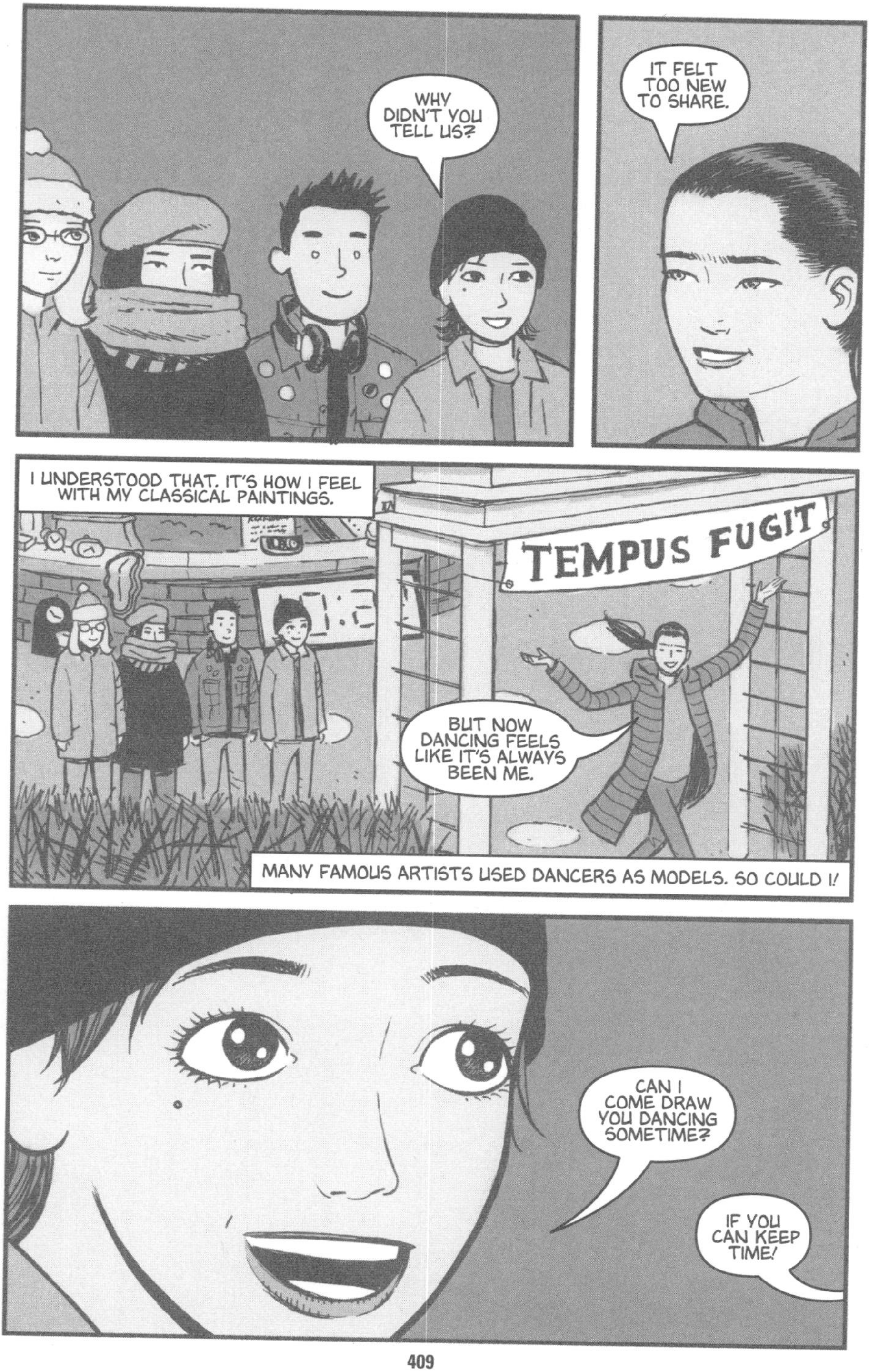

WHY DIDN'T YOU TELL US?
IT FELT TOO NEW TO SHARE.
I UNDERSTOOD THAT. IT'S HOW I FEEL WITH MY CLASSICAL PAINTINGS.
TEMPUS FUGIT
BUT NOW DANCING FEELS LIKE IT'S ALWAYS BEEN ME.
MANY FAMOUS ARTISTS USED DANCERS AS MODELS. SO COULD I!
CAN I COME DRAW YOU DANCING SOMETIME?
IF YOU CAN KEEP TIME!

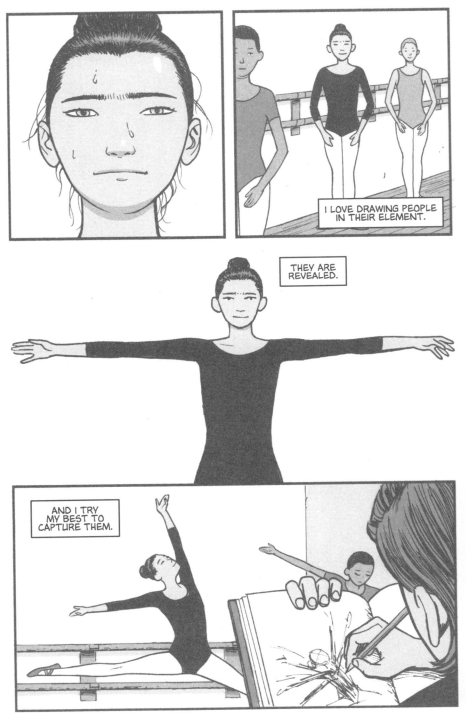

I LOVE DRAWING PEOPLE IN THEIR ELEMENT.

THEY ARE REVEALED.

AND I TRY MY BEST TO CAPTURE THEM.

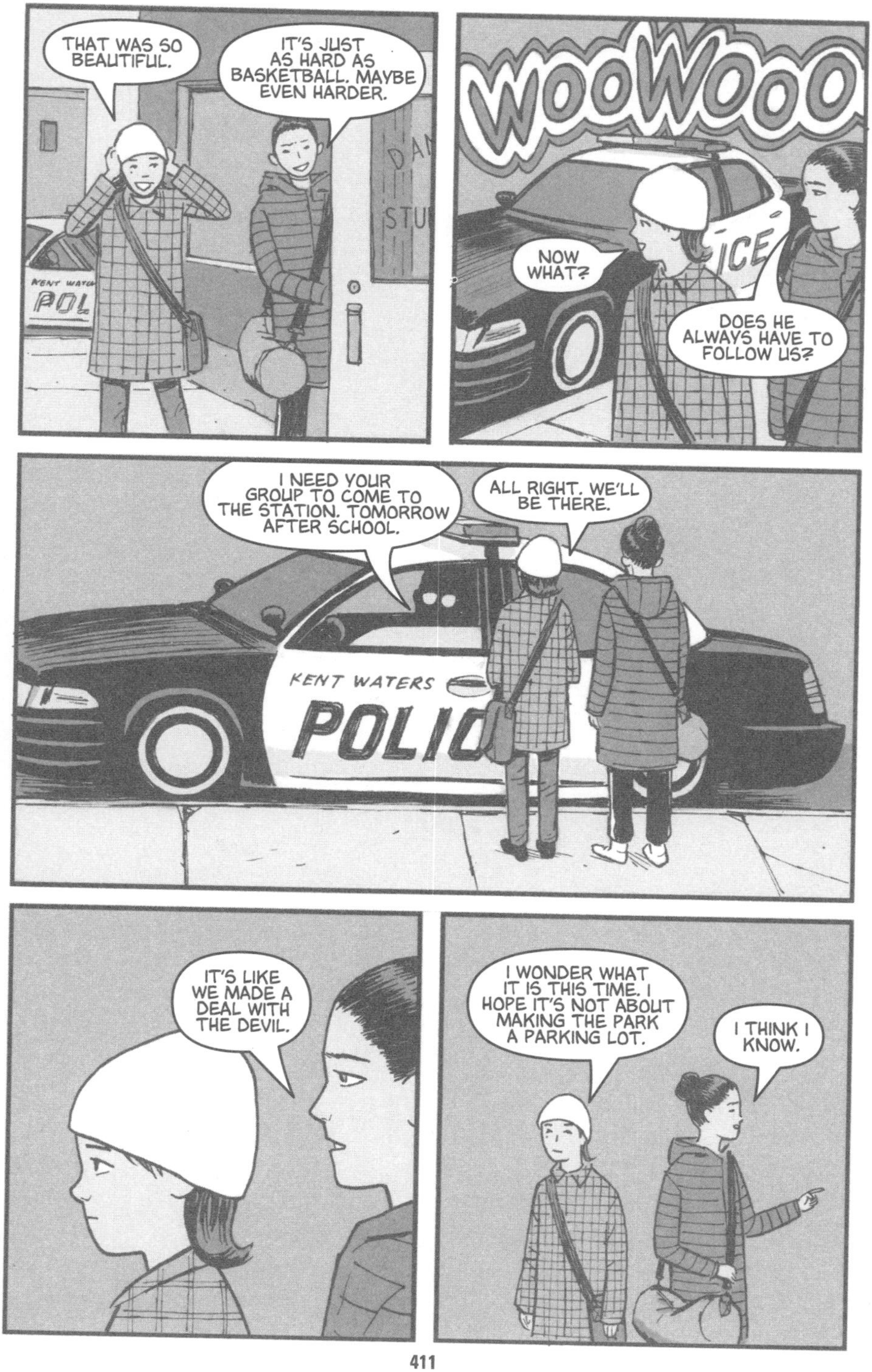
THAT WAS SO BEAUTIFUL.
IT'S JUST AS HARD AS BASKETBALL. MAYBE EVEN HARDER.
KENT WATC
POL
WOOWOOO
ICE
NOW WHAT?
DOES HE ALWAYS HAVE TO FOLLOW US?
I NEED YOUR GROUP TO COME TO THE STATION. TOMORROW AFTER SCHOOL.
ALL RIGHT. WE'LL BE THERE.
KENT WATERS
POLIC
IT'S LIKE WE MADE A DEAL WITH THE DEVIL.
I WONDER WHAT IT IS THIS TIME. I HOPE IT'S NOT ABOUT MAKING THE PARK A PARKING LOT.
I THINK I KNOW.

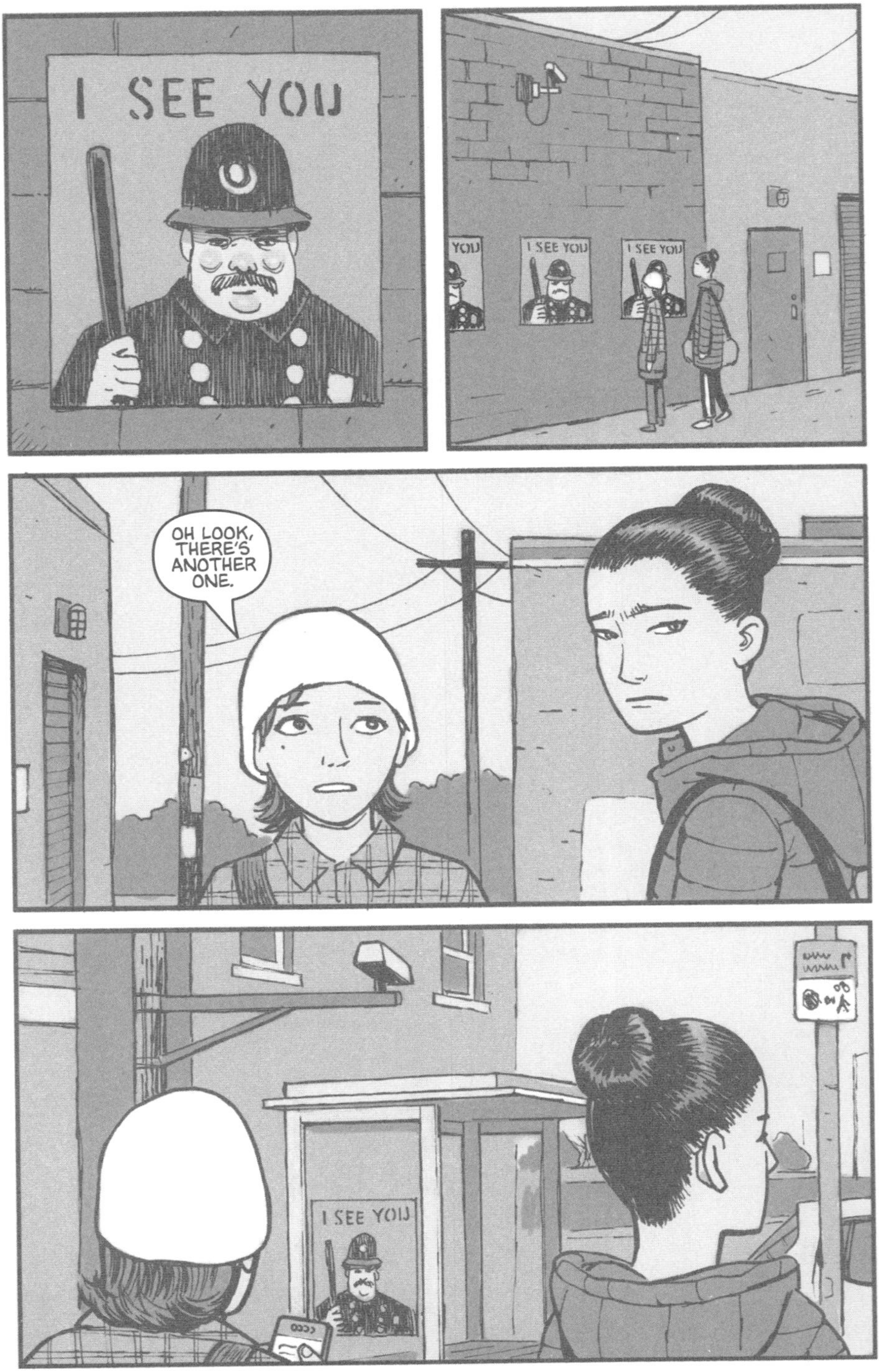
I SEE YOU
YOU
I SEE YOU
I SEE YOU
OH LOOK, THERE'S ANOTHER ONE.
I SEE YOU

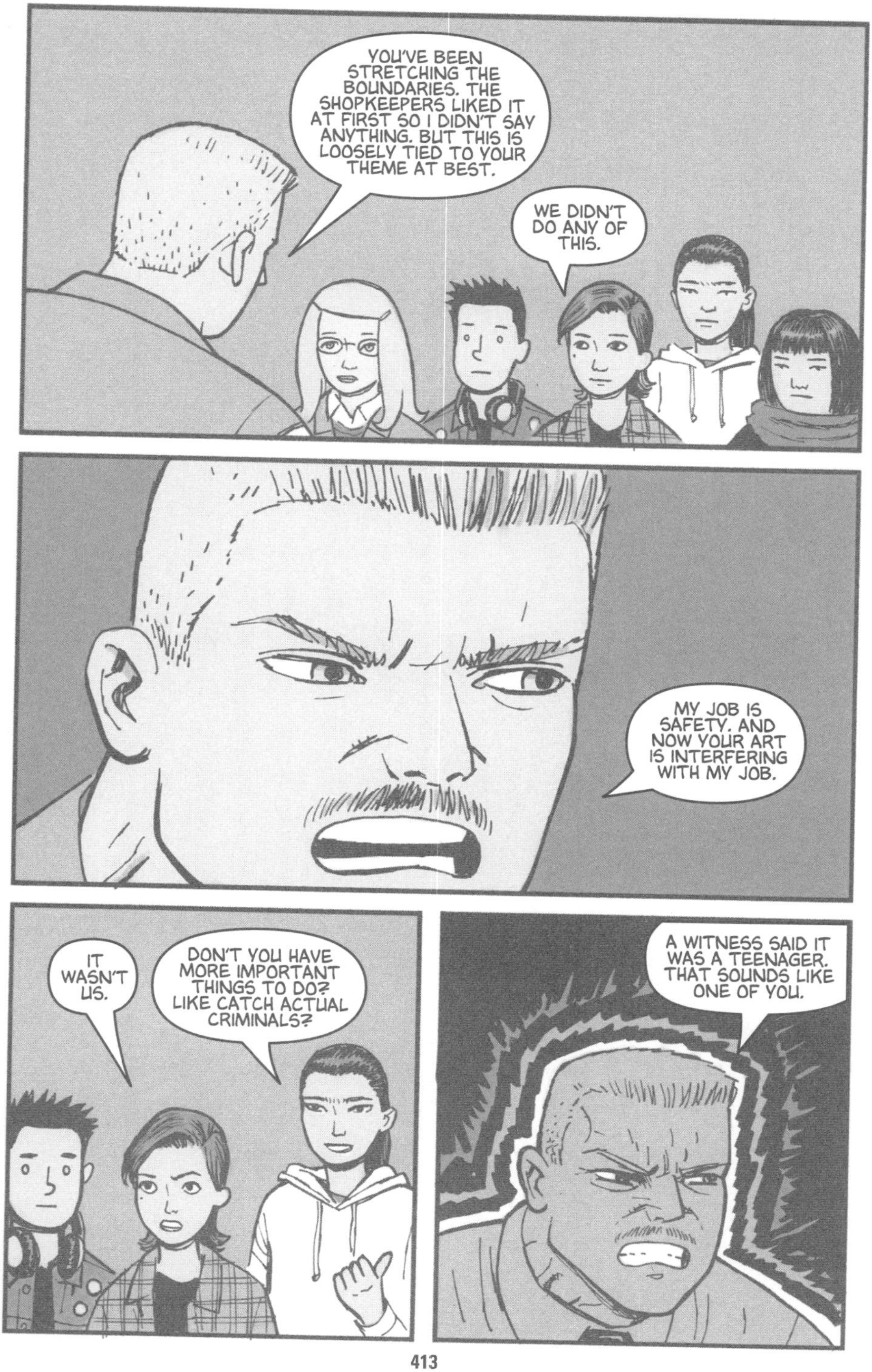
YOU'VE BEEN STRETCHING THE BOUNDARIES. THE SHOPKEEPERS LIKED IT AT FIRST SO I DIDN'T SAY ANYTHING. BUT THIS IS LOOSELY TIED TO YOUR THEME AT BEST.
WE DIDN'T DO ANY OF THIS.
MY JOB IS SAFETY. AND NOW YOUR ART IS INTERFERING WITH MY JOB.
IT WASN'T US.
DON'T YOU HAVE MORE IMPORTANT THINGS TO DO? LIKE CATCH ACTUAL CRIMINALS?
A WITNESS SAID IT WAS A TEENAGER. THAT SOUNDS LIKE ONE OF YOU.

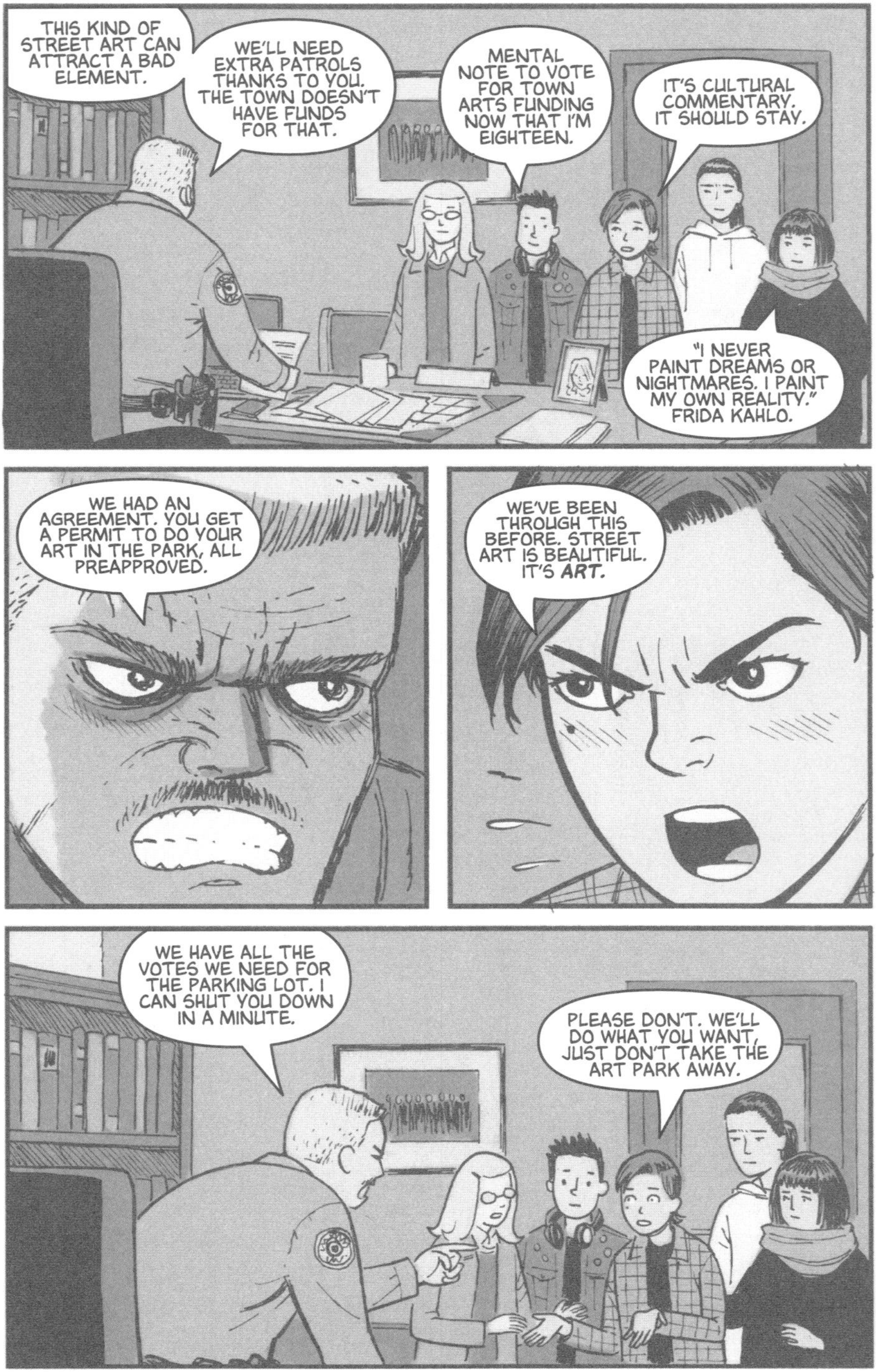
THIS KIND OF STREET ART CAN ATTRACT A BAD ELEMENT.
WE'LL NEED EXTRA PATROLS THANKS TO YOU. THE TOWN DOESN'T HAVE FUNDS FOR THAT.
MENTAL NOTE TO VOTE FOR TOWN ARTS FUNDING NOW THAT I'M EIGHTEEN.
IT'S CULTURAL COMMENTARY. IT SHOULD STAY.
"I NEVER PAINT DREAMS OR NIGHTMARES. I PAINT MY OWN REALITY." FRIDA KAHLO.
WE HAD AN AGREEMENT. YOU GET A PERMIT TO DO YOUR ART IN THE PARK, ALL PREAPPROVED.
WE'VE BEEN THROUGH THIS BEFORE. STREET ART IS BEAUTIFUL. IT'S ART.
WE HAVE ALL THE VOTES WE NEED FOR THE PARKING LOT. I CAN SHUT YOU DOWN IN A MINUTE.
PLEASE DON'T. WE'LL DO WHAT YOU WANT, JUST DON'T TAKE THE ART PARK AWAY.

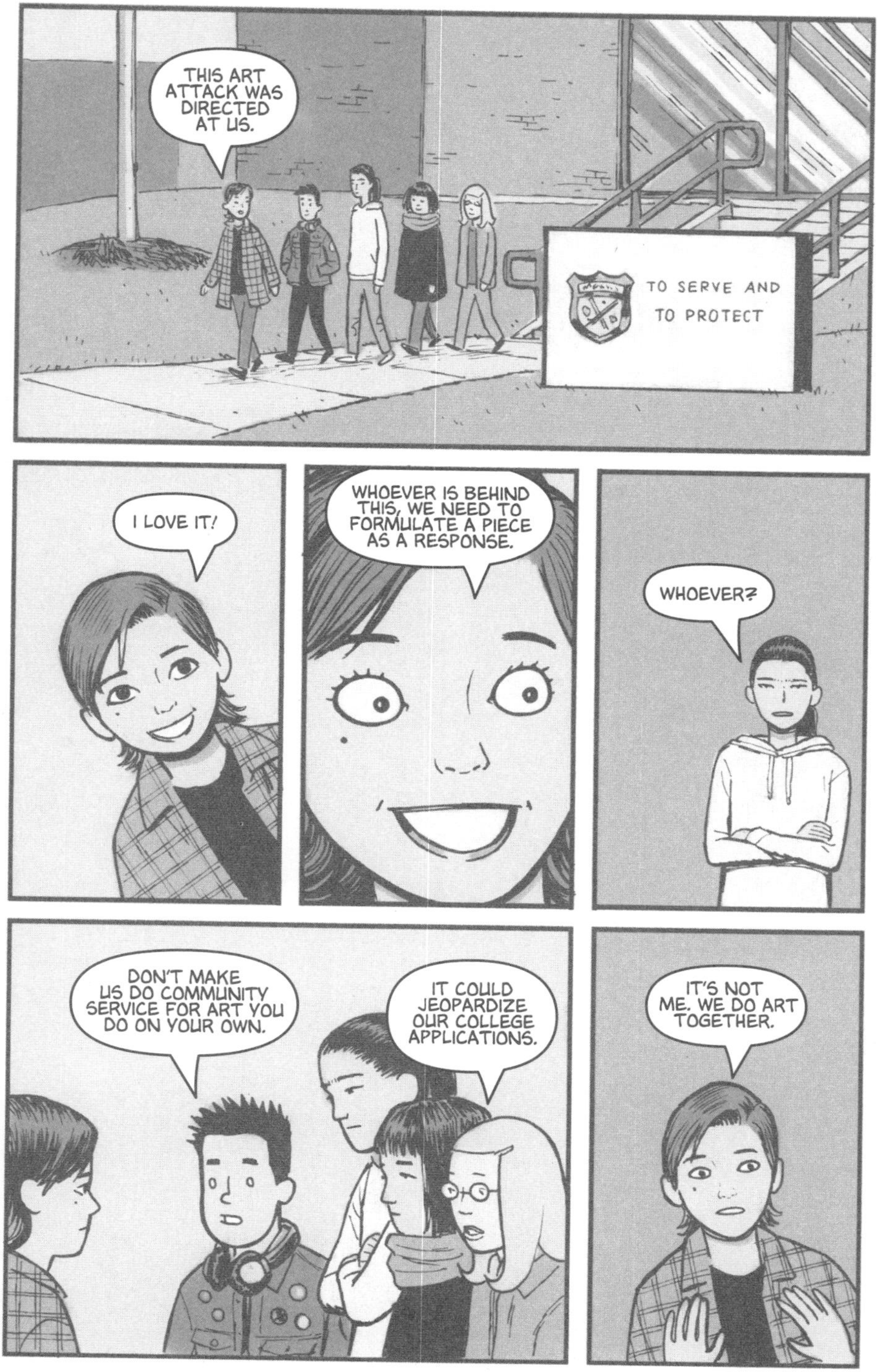
THIS ART ATTACK WAS DIRECTED AT US.
TO SERVE AND TO PROTECT
I LOVE IT!
WHOEVER IS BEHIND THIS, WE NEED TO FORMULATE A PIECE AS A RESPONSE.
WHOEVER?
DON'T MAKE US DO COMMUNITY SERVICE FOR ART YOU DO ON YOUR OWN.
IT COULD JEOPARDIZE OUR COLLEGE APPLICATIONS.
IT'S NOT ME. WE DO ART TOGETHER.

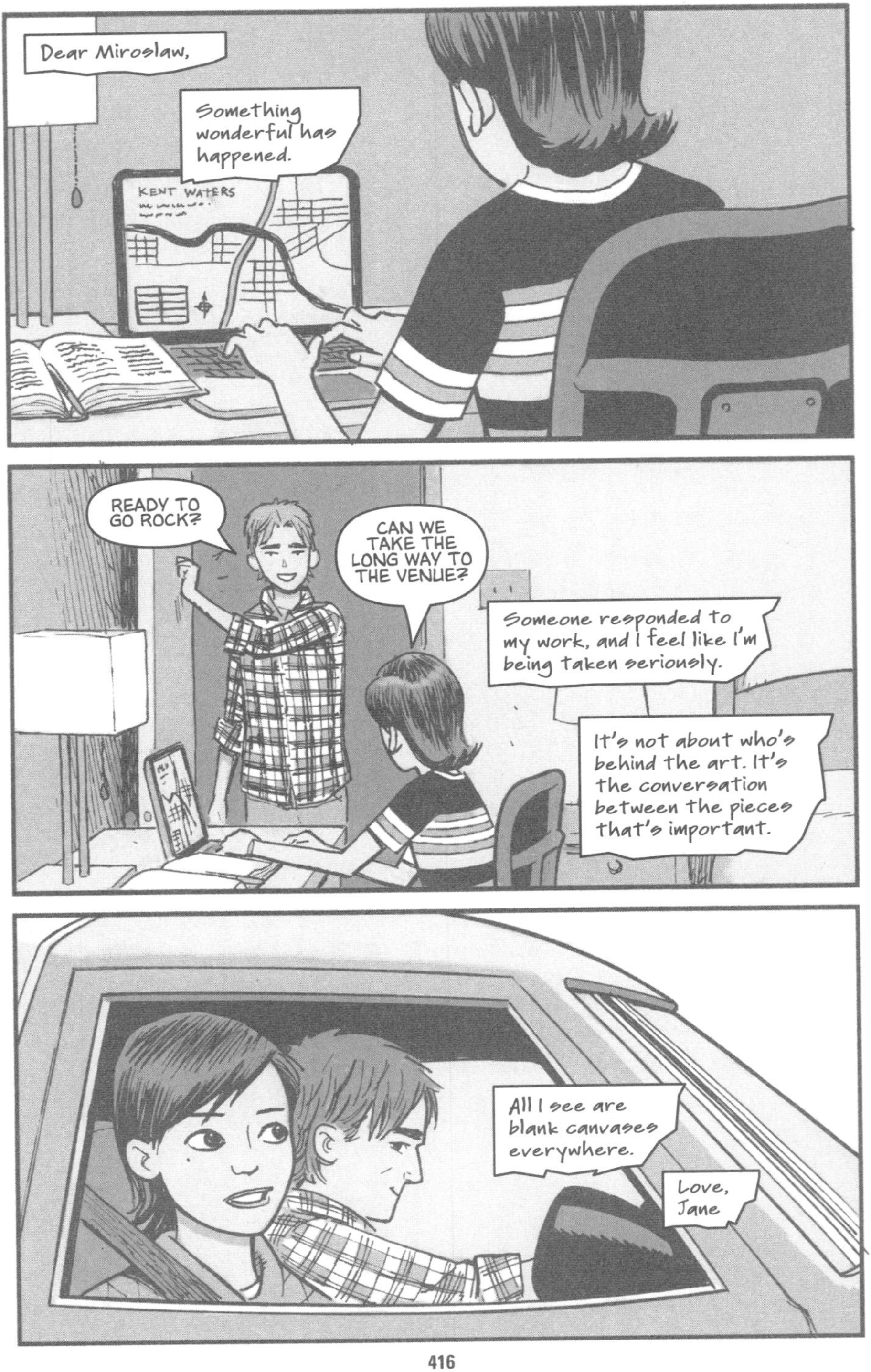
Dear Miroslaw,
Something wonderful has happened.
KENT WATERS
READY TO GO ROCK?
CAN WE TAKE THE LONG WAY TO THE VENUE?
Someone responded to my work, and I feel like I'm being taken seriously.
It's not about who's behind the art. It's the conversation between the pieces that's important.
All I see are blank canvases everywhere.
Love, Jane

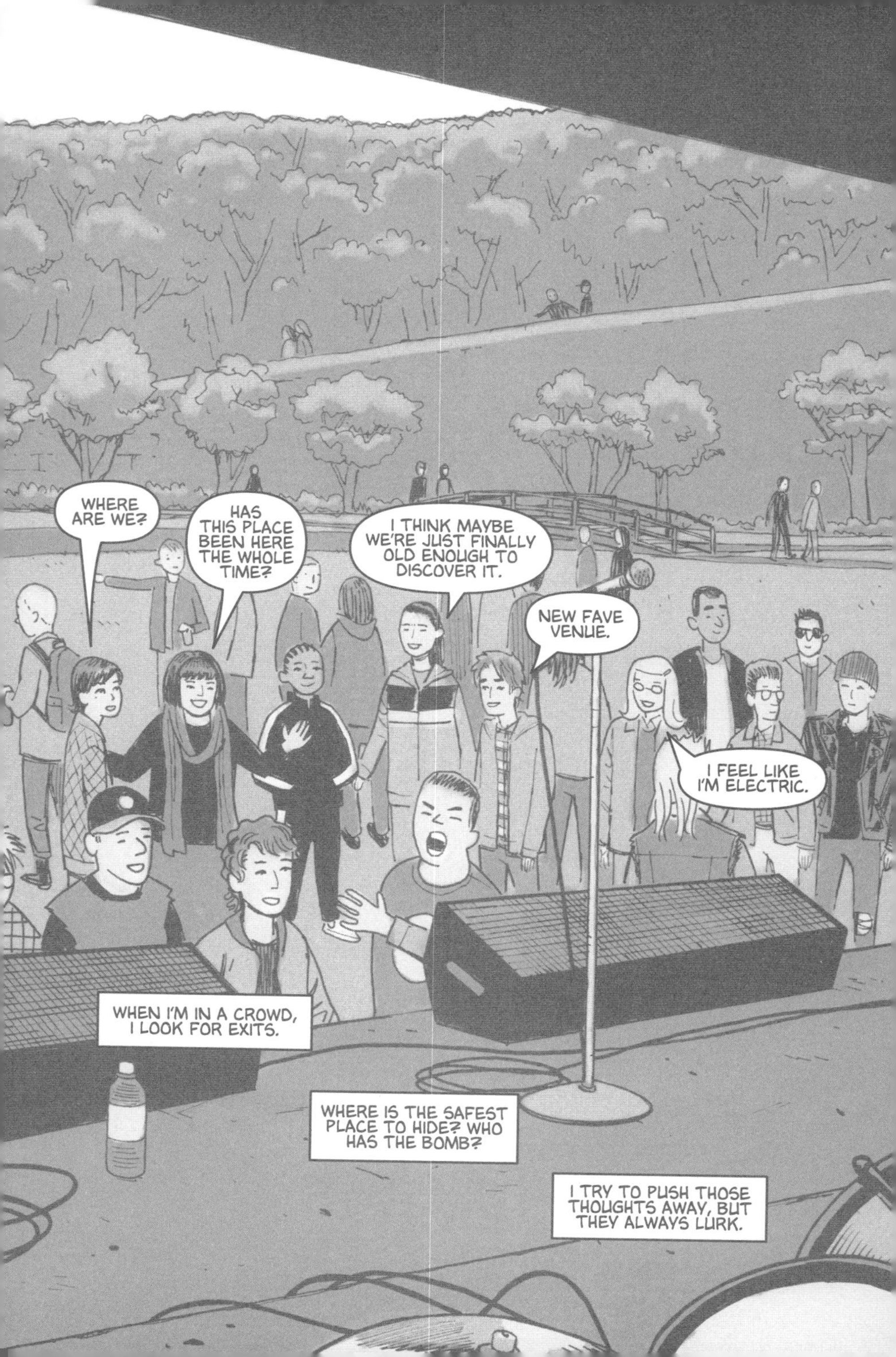
WHERE ARE WE?
HAS THIS PLACE BEEN HERE THE WHOLE TIME?
I THINK MAYBE WE'RE JUST FINALLY OLD ENOUGH TO DISCOVER IT.
NEW FAVE VENUE.
I FEEL LIKE I'M ELECTRIC.
WHEN I'M IN A CROWD, I LOOK FOR EXITS.
WHERE IS THE SAFEST PLACE TO HIDE? WHO HAS THE BOMB?
I TRY TO PUSH THOSE THOUGHTS AWAY, BUT THEY ALWAYS LURK.

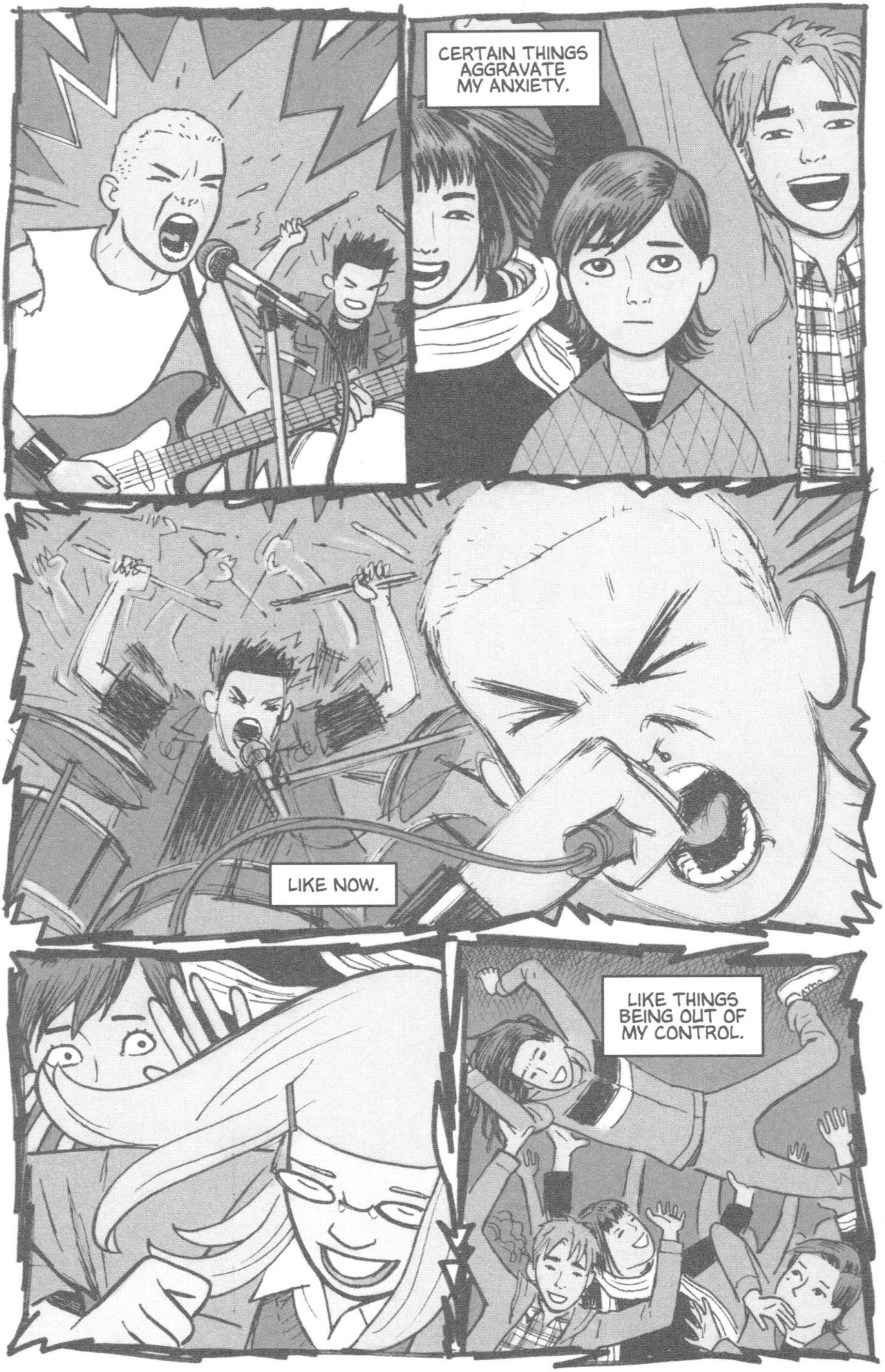
CERTAIN THINGS AGGRAVATE MY ANXIETY.
LIKE NOW.
LIKE THINGS BEING OUT OF MY CONTROL.

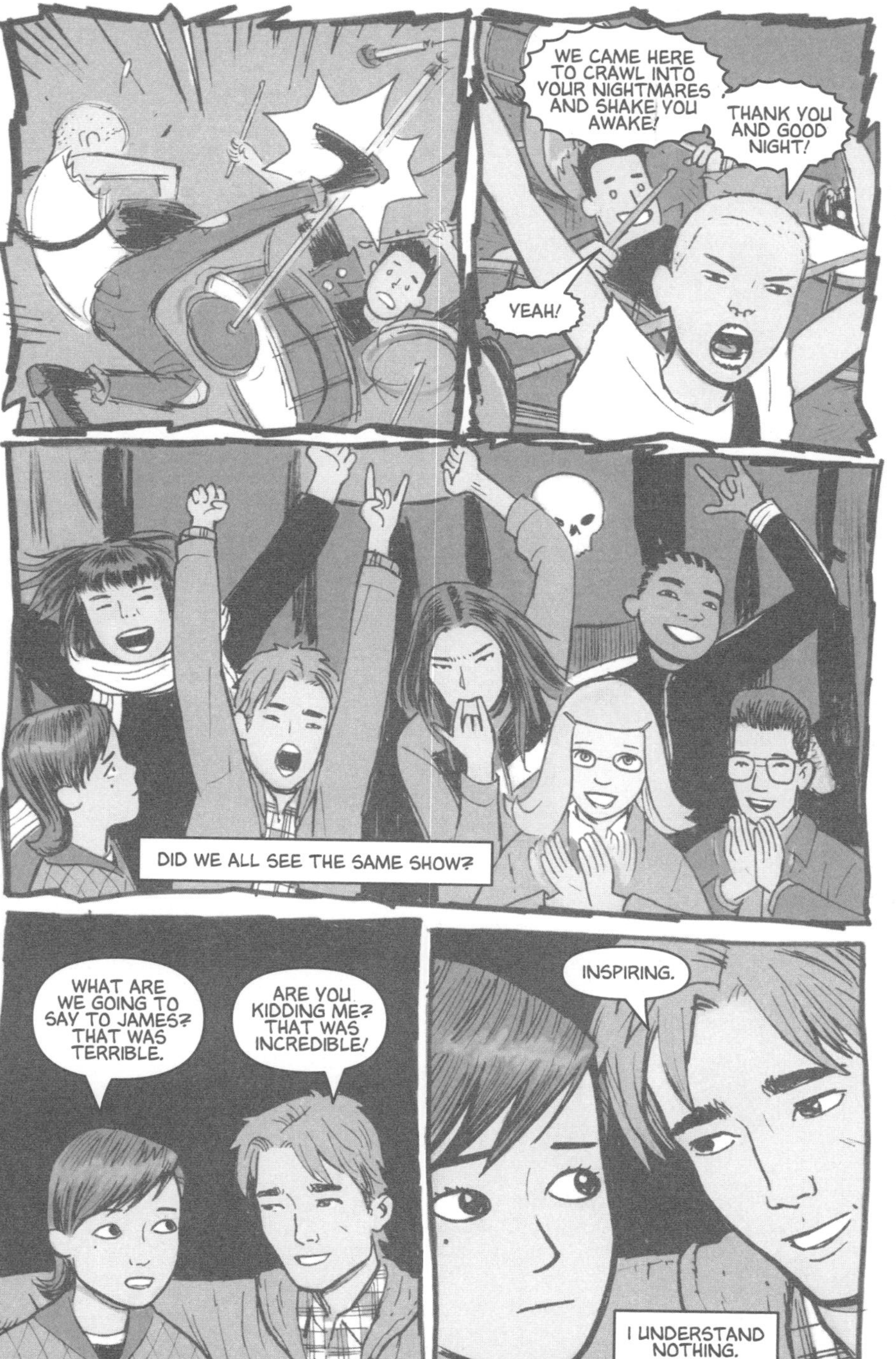
WE CAME HERE TO CRAWL INTO YOUR NIGHTMARES AND SHAKE YOU AWAKE!
THANK YOU AND GOOD NIGHT!
YEAH!
DID WE ALL SEE THE SAME SHOW?
WHAT ARE WE GOING TO SAY TO JAMES? THAT WAS TERRIBLE.
ARE YOU KIDDING ME? THAT WAS INCREDIBLE!
INSPIRING.
I UNDERSTAND NOTHING.

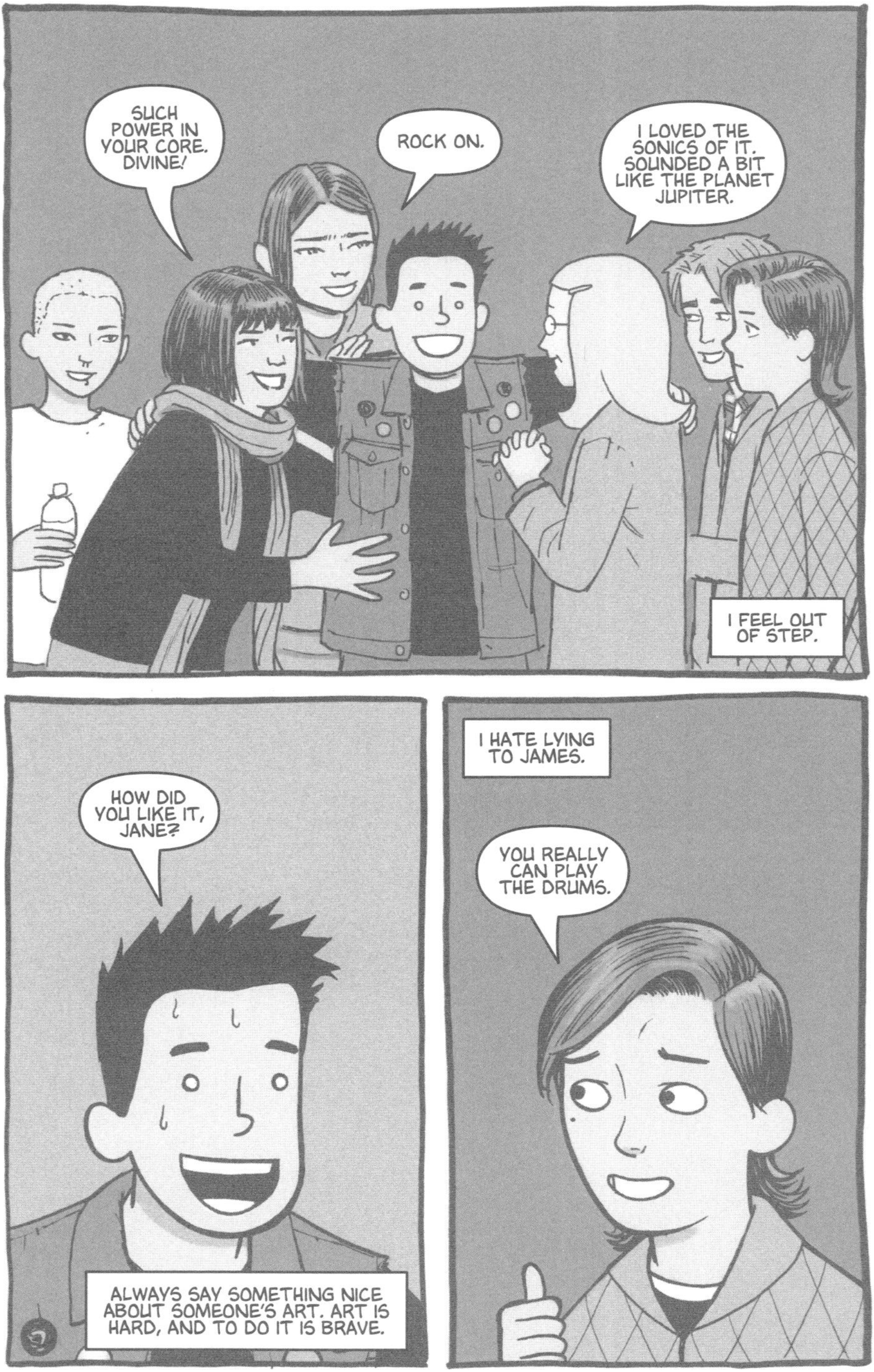
SUCH POWER IN YOUR CORE. DIVINE!
ROCK ON.
I LOVED THE SONICS OF IT. SOUNDED A BIT LIKE THE PLANET JUPITER.
I FEEL OUT OF STEP.
HOW DID YOU LIKE IT, JANE?
ALWAYS SAY SOMETHING NICE ABOUT SOMEONE'S ART. ART IS HARD, AND TO DO IT IS BRAVE.
I HATE LYING TO JAMES.
YOU REALLY CAN PLAY THE DRUMS.

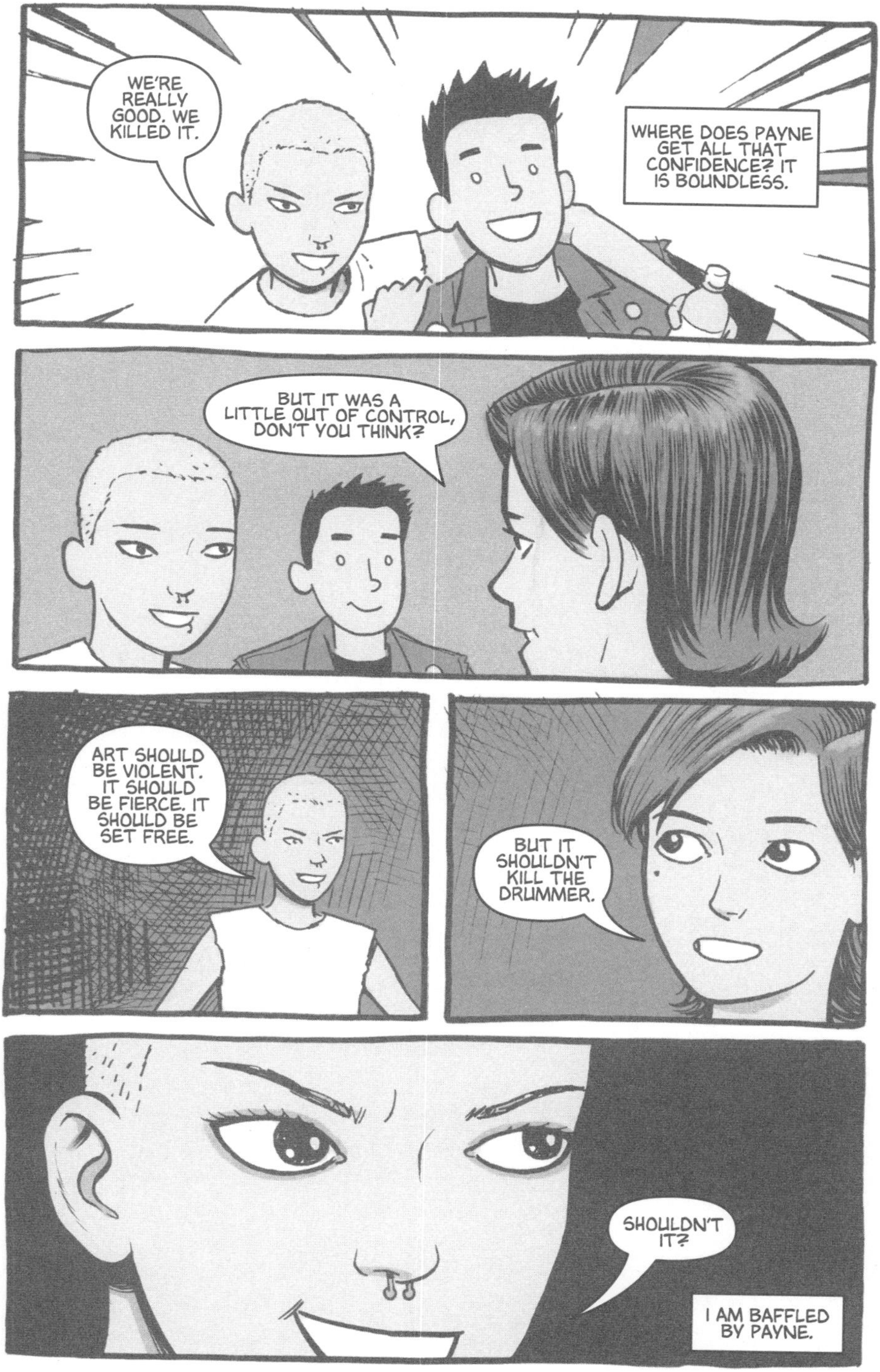
WE'RE REALLY GOOD. WE KILLED IT.
WHERE DOES PAYNE GET ALL THAT CONFIDENCE? IT IS BOUNDLESS.
BUT IT WAS A LITTLE OUT OF CONTROL, DON'T YOU THINK?
ART SHOULD BE VIOLENT. IT SHOULD BE FIERCE. IT SHOULD BE SET FREE.
BUT IT SHOULDN'T KILL THE DRUMMER.
SHOULDN'T IT?
I AM BAFFLED BY PAYNE.

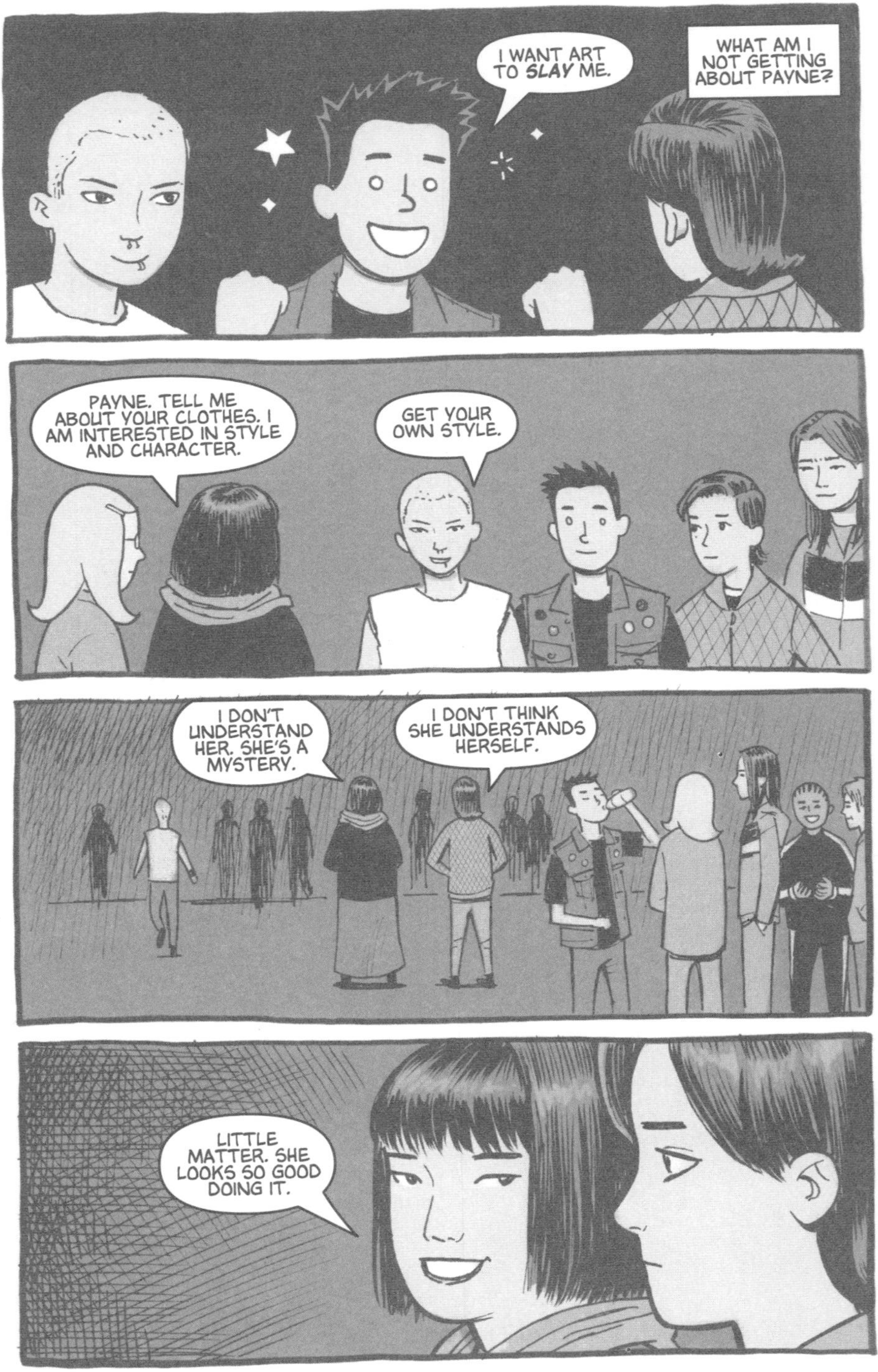

I WANT ART TO SLAY ME.
WHAT AM I NOT GETTING ABOUT PAYNE?
PAYNE. TELL ME ABOUT YOUR CLOTHES. I AM INTERESTED IN STYLE AND CHARACTER.
GET YOUR OWN STYLE.
I DON'T UNDERSTAND HER. SHE'S A MYSTERY.
I DON'T THINK SHE UNDERSTANDS HERSELF.
LITTLE MATTER. SHE LOOKS SO GOOD DOING IT.

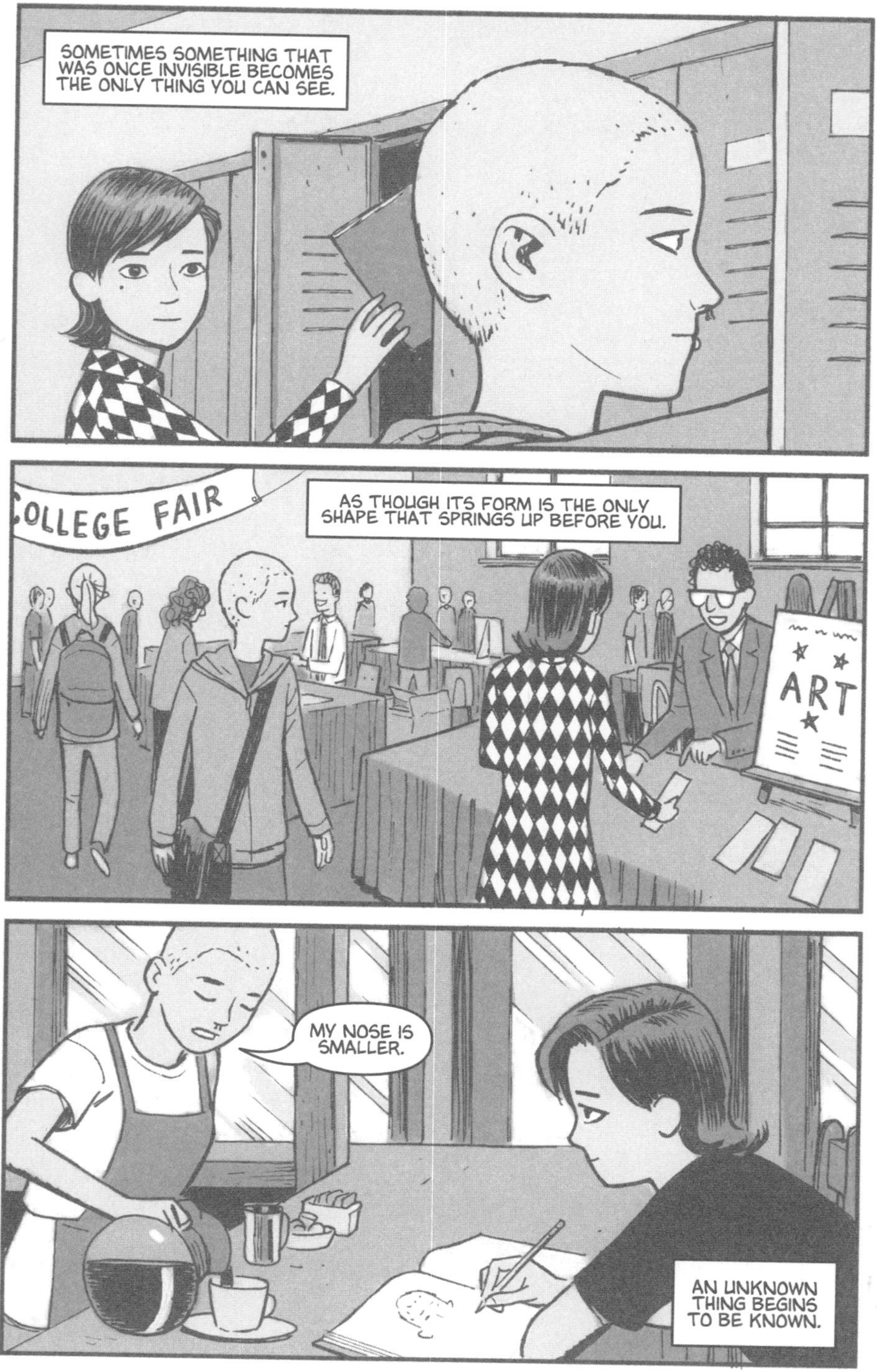
SOMETIMES SOMETHING THAT WAS ONCE INVISIBLE BECOMES THE ONLY THING YOU CAN SEE.
COLLEGE FAIR
AS THOUGH ITS FORM IS THE ONLY SHAPE THAT SPRINGS UP BEFORE YOU.
ART
MY NOSE IS SMALLER.
AN UNKNOWN THING BEGINS TO BE KNOWN.

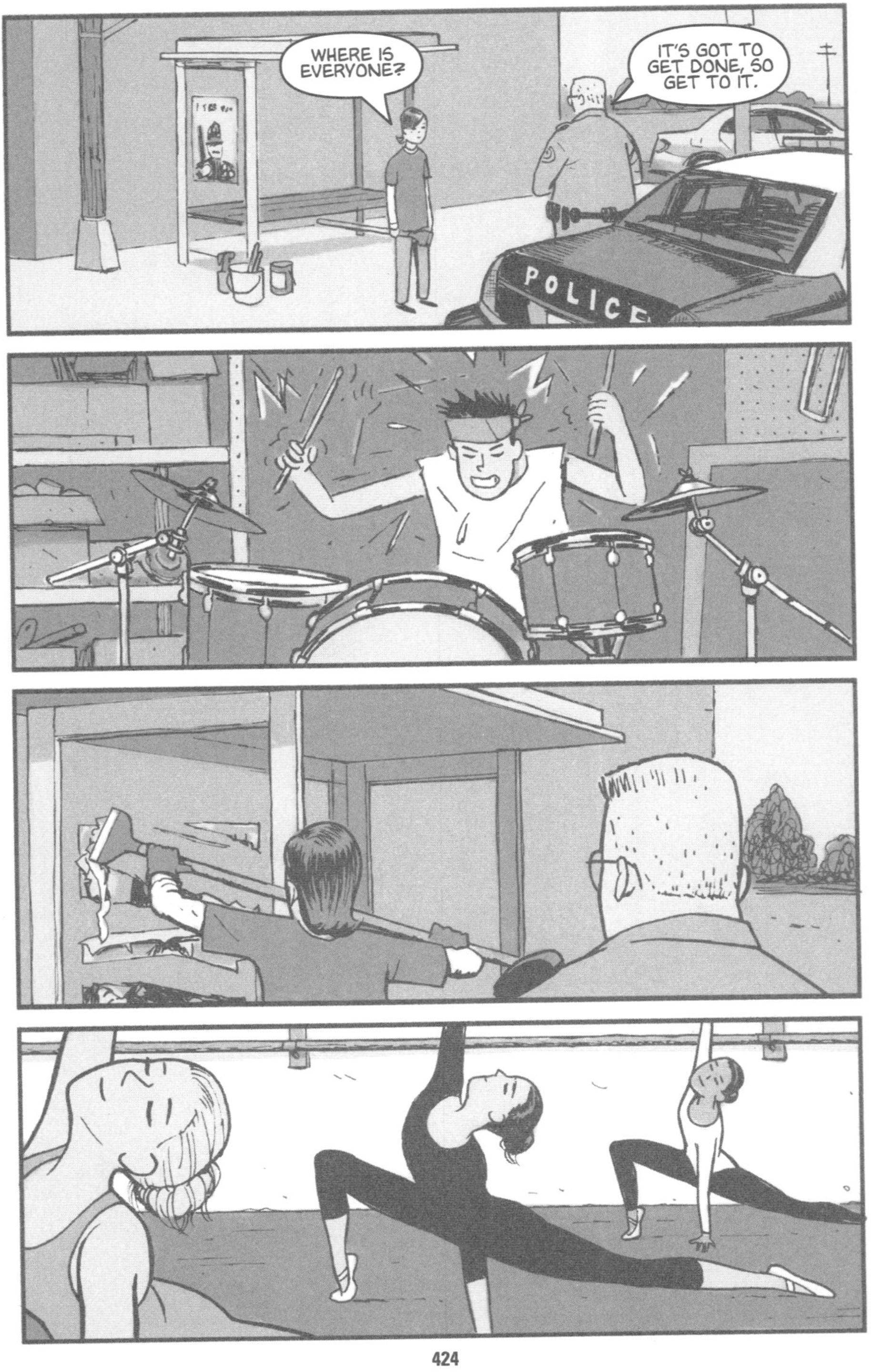
WHERE IS EVERYONE?
IT'S GOT TO GET DONE, SO GET TO IT.
POLICE

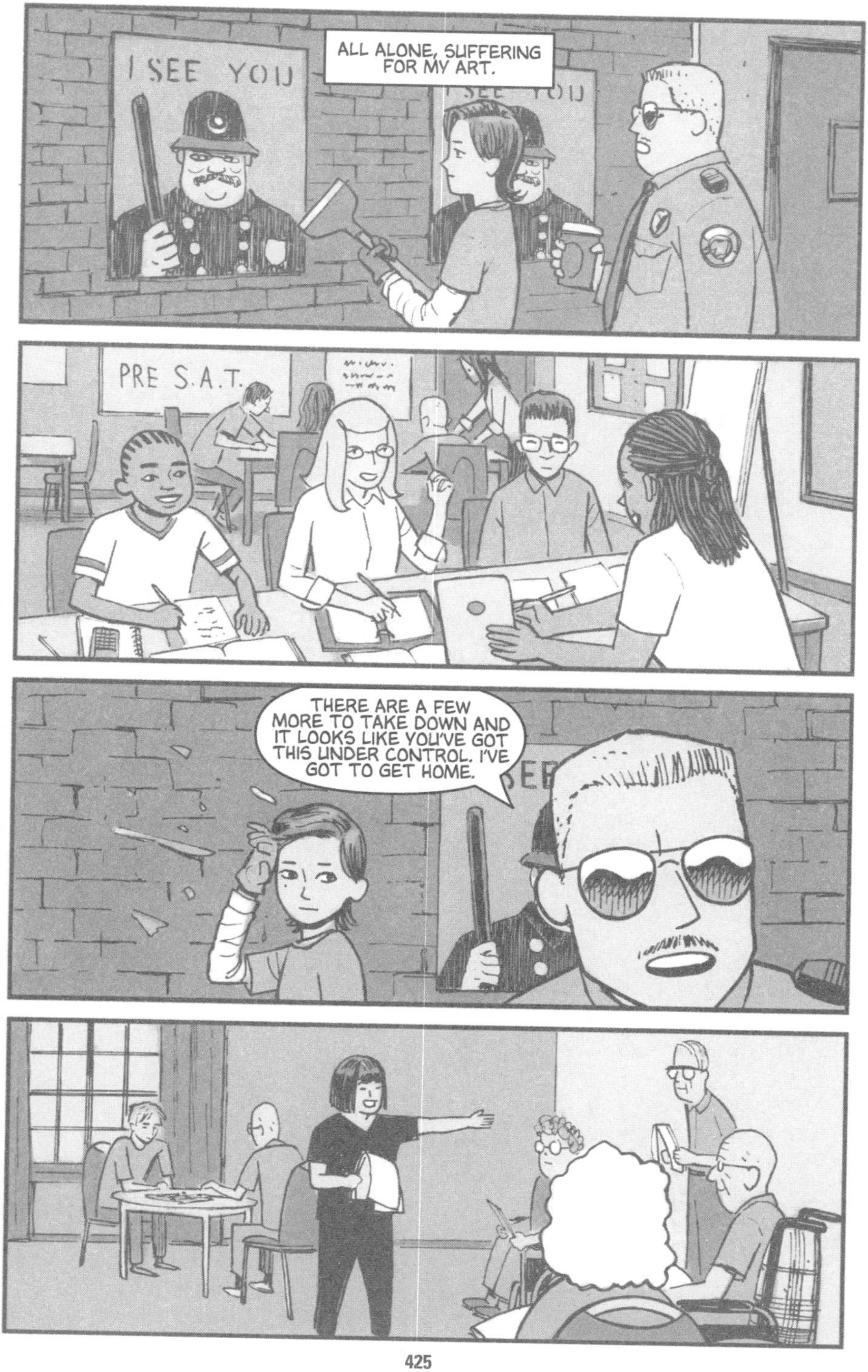

ALL ALONE, SUFFERING FOR MY ART.
I SEE YOU
PRE S.A.T.
THERE ARE A FEW MORE TO TAKE DOWN AND IT LOOKS LIKE YOU'VE GOT THIS UNDER CONTROL. I'VE GOT TO GET HOME.

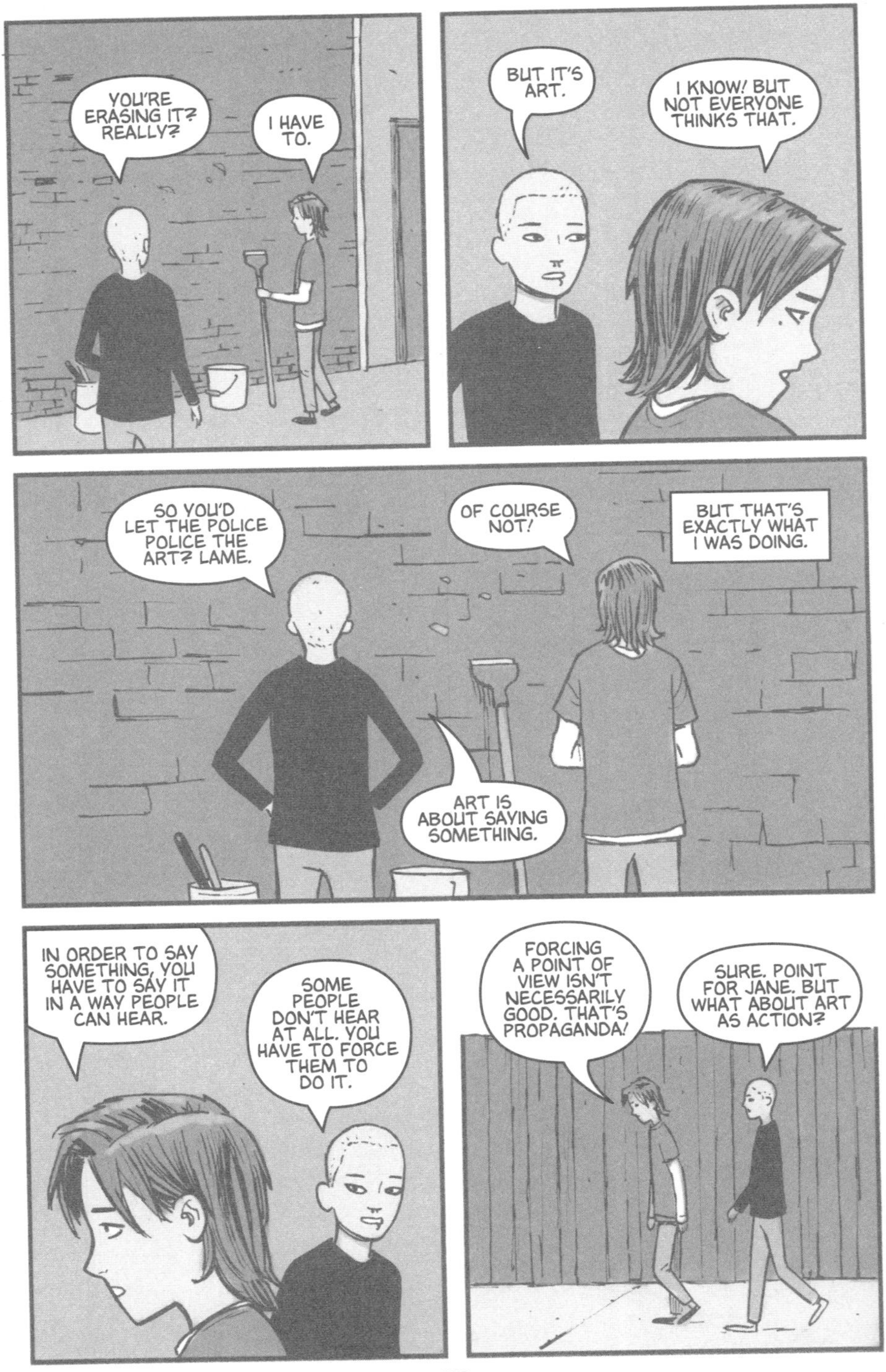
YOU'RE ERASING IT? REALLY?
I HAVE TO.
BUT IT'S ART.
I KNOW! BUT NOT EVERYONE THINKS THAT.
SO YOU'D LET THE POLICE POLICE THE ART? LAME.
OF COURSE NOT!
BUT THAT'S EXACTLY WHAT I WAS DOING.
ART IS ABOUT SAYING SOMETHING.
IN ORDER TO SAY SOMETHING, YOU HAVE TO SAY IT IN A WAY PEOPLE CAN HEAR.
SOME PEOPLE DON'T HEAR AT ALL. YOU HAVE TO FORCE THEM TO DO IT.
FORCING A POINT OF VIEW ISN'T NECESSARILY GOOD. THAT'S PROPAGANDA!
SURE. POINT FOR JANE. BUT WHAT ABOUT ART AS ACTION?

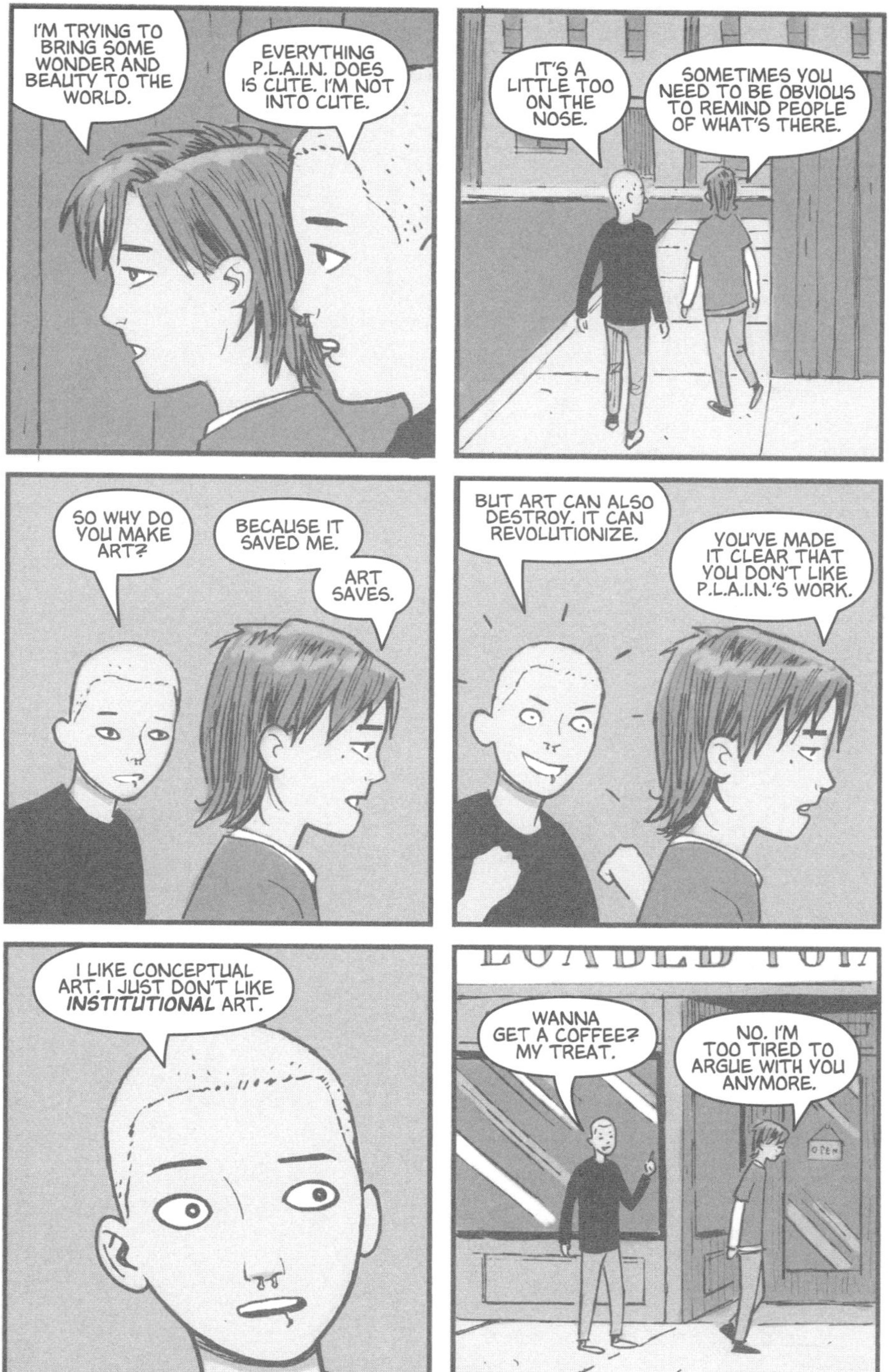
I'M TRYING TO BRING SOME WONDER AND BEAUTY TO THE WORLD.
EVERYTHING P.L.A.I.N. DOES IS CUTE. I'M NOT INTO CUTE.
IT'S A LITTLE TOO ON THE NOSE.
SOMETIMES YOU NEED TO BE OBVIOUS TO REMIND PEOPLE OF WHAT'S THERE.
SO WHY DO YOU MAKE ART?
BECAUSE IT SAVED ME.
ART SAVES.
BUT ART CAN ALSO DESTROY. IT CAN REVOLUTIONIZE.
YOU'VE MADE IT CLEAR THAT YOU DON'T LIKE P.L.A.I.N.'S WORK.
I LIKE CONCEPTUAL ART. I JUST DON'T LIKE *INSTITUTIONAL* ART.
WANNA GET A COFFEE? MY TREAT.
NO. I'M TOO TIRED TO ARGUE WITH YOU ANYMORE.

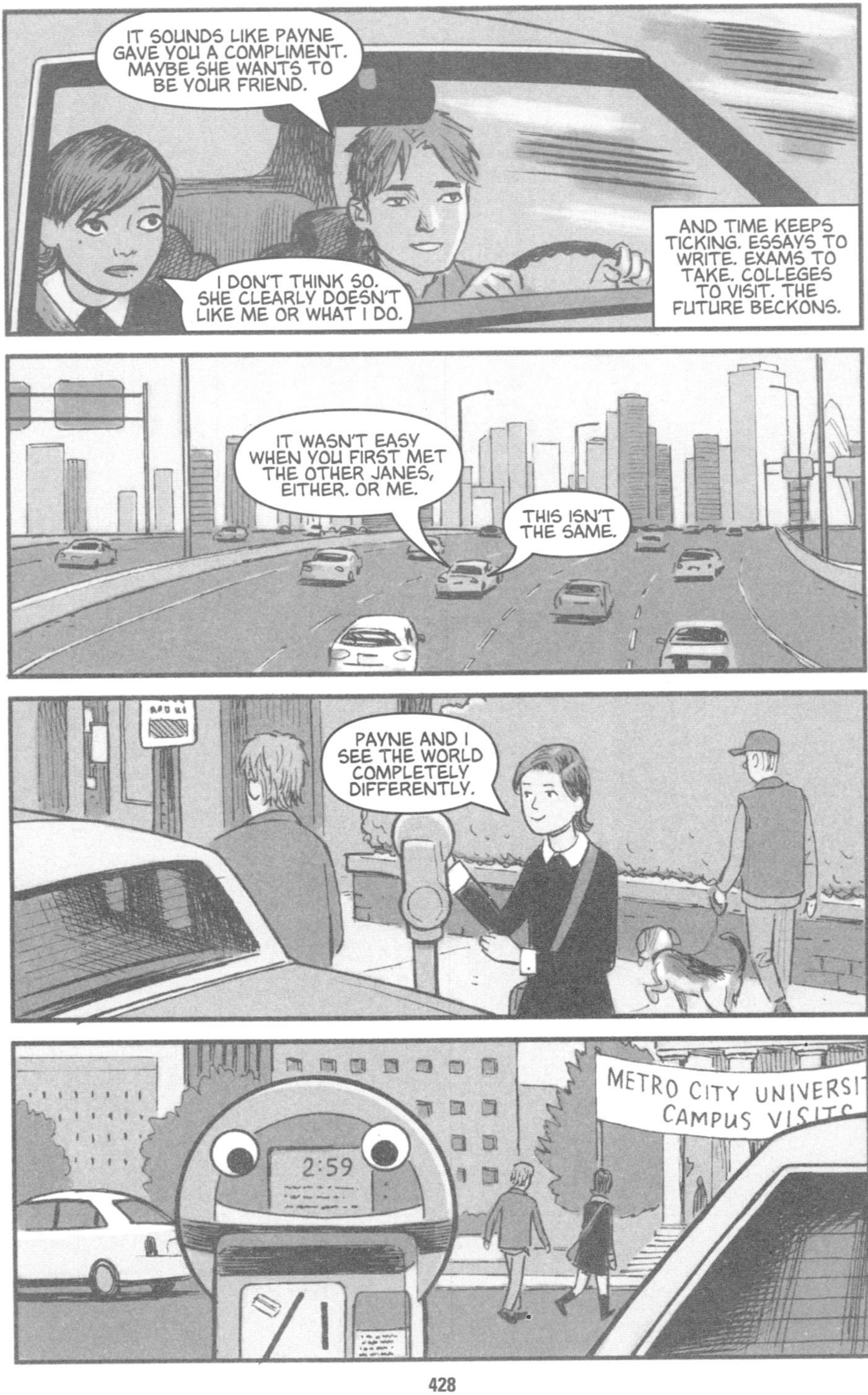
IT SOUNDS LIKE PAYNE GAVE YOU A COMPLIMENT. MAYBE SHE WANTS TO BE YOUR FRIEND.
I DON'T THINK SO. SHE CLEARLY DOESN'T LIKE ME OR WHAT I DO.
AND TIME KEEPS TICKING. ESSAYS TO WRITE. EXAMS TO TAKE. COLLEGES TO VISIT. THE FUTURE BECKONS.
IT WASN'T EASY WHEN YOU FIRST MET THE OTHER JANES, EITHER. OR ME.
THIS ISN'T THE SAME.
PAYNE AND I SEE THE WORLD COMPLETELY DIFFERENTLY.
METRO CITY UNIVERSIT
CAMPUS VISIT
2:59

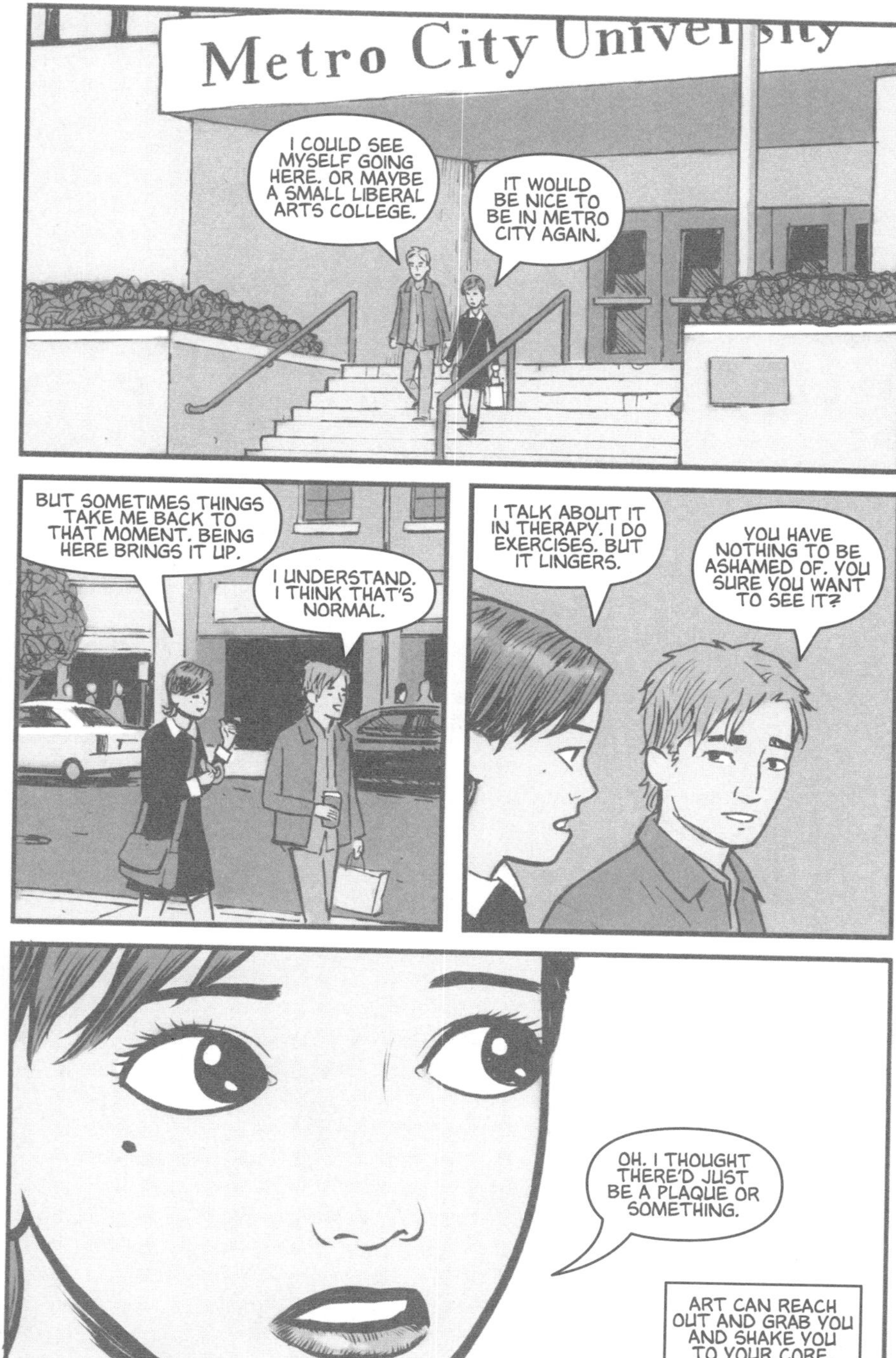
Metro City University
I COULD SEE MYSELF GOING HERE. OR MAYBE A SMALL LIBERAL ARTS COLLEGE.
IT WOULD BE NICE TO BE IN METRO CITY AGAIN.
BUT SOMETIMES THINGS TAKE ME BACK TO THAT MOMENT. BEING HERE BRINGS IT UP.
I UNDERSTAND. I THINK THAT'S NORMAL.
I TALK ABOUT IT IN THERAPY. I DO EXERCISES. BUT IT LINGERS.
YOU HAVE NOTHING TO BE ASHAMED OF. YOU SURE YOU WANT TO SEE IT?
OH. I THOUGHT THERE'D JUST BE A PLAQUE OR SOMETHING.
ART CAN REACH OUT AND GRAB YOU AND SHAKE YOU TO YOUR CORE.

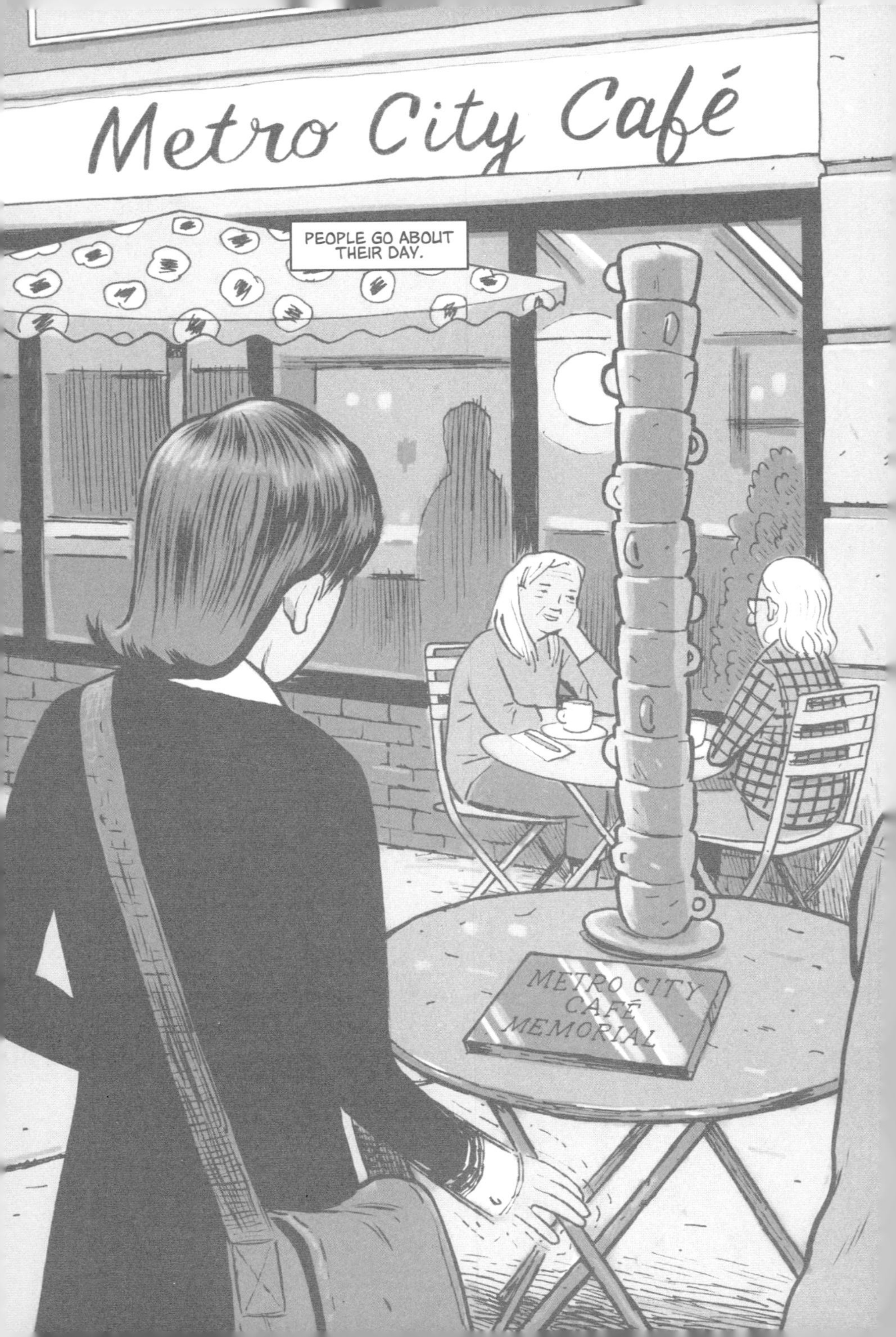
Metro City Café
PEOPLE GO ABOUT THEIR DAY.
METRO CITY CAFÉ MEMORIAL

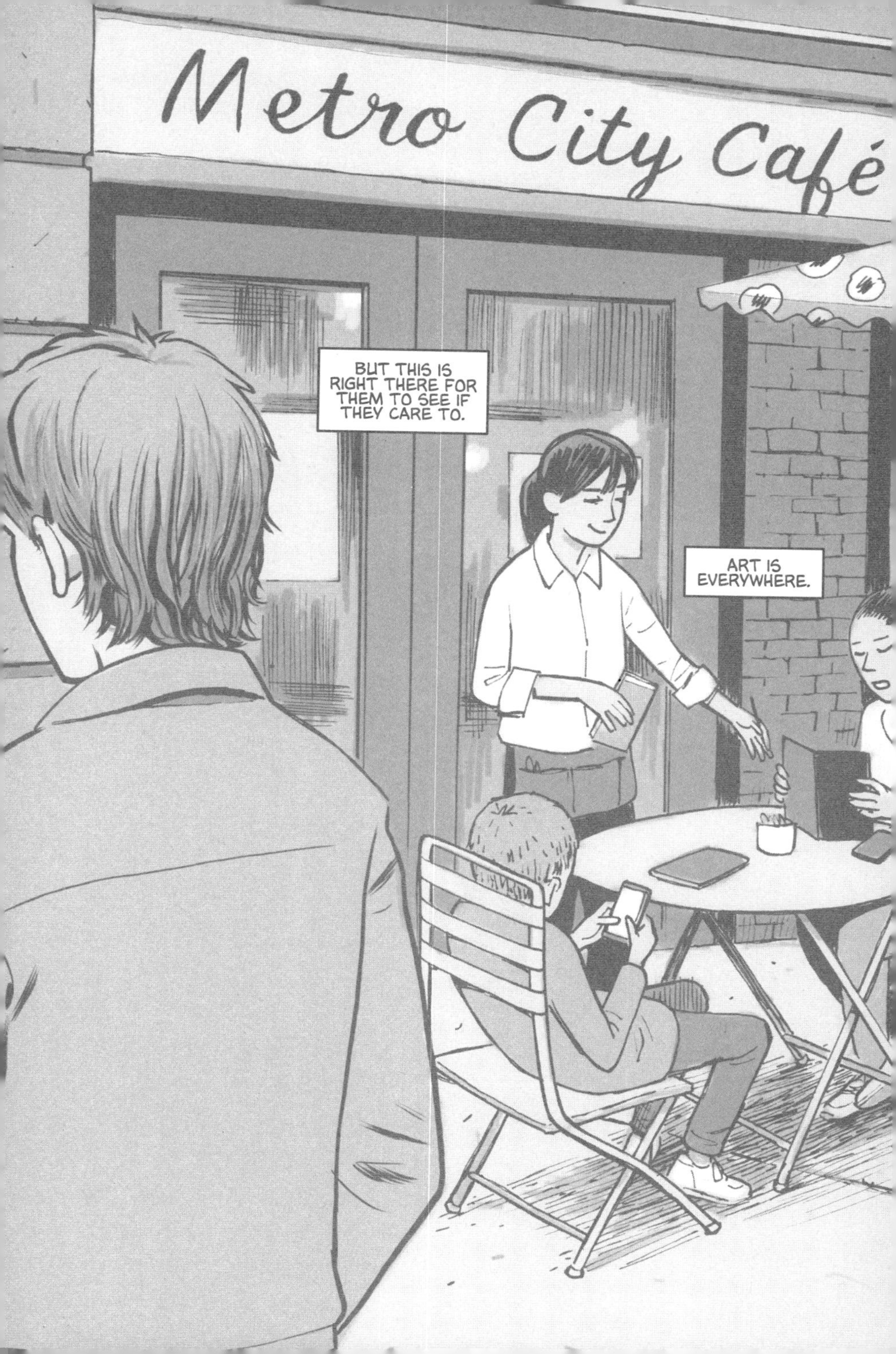
Metro City Café
BUT THIS IS RIGHT THERE FOR THEM TO SEE IF THEY CARE TO.
ART IS EVERYWHERE.

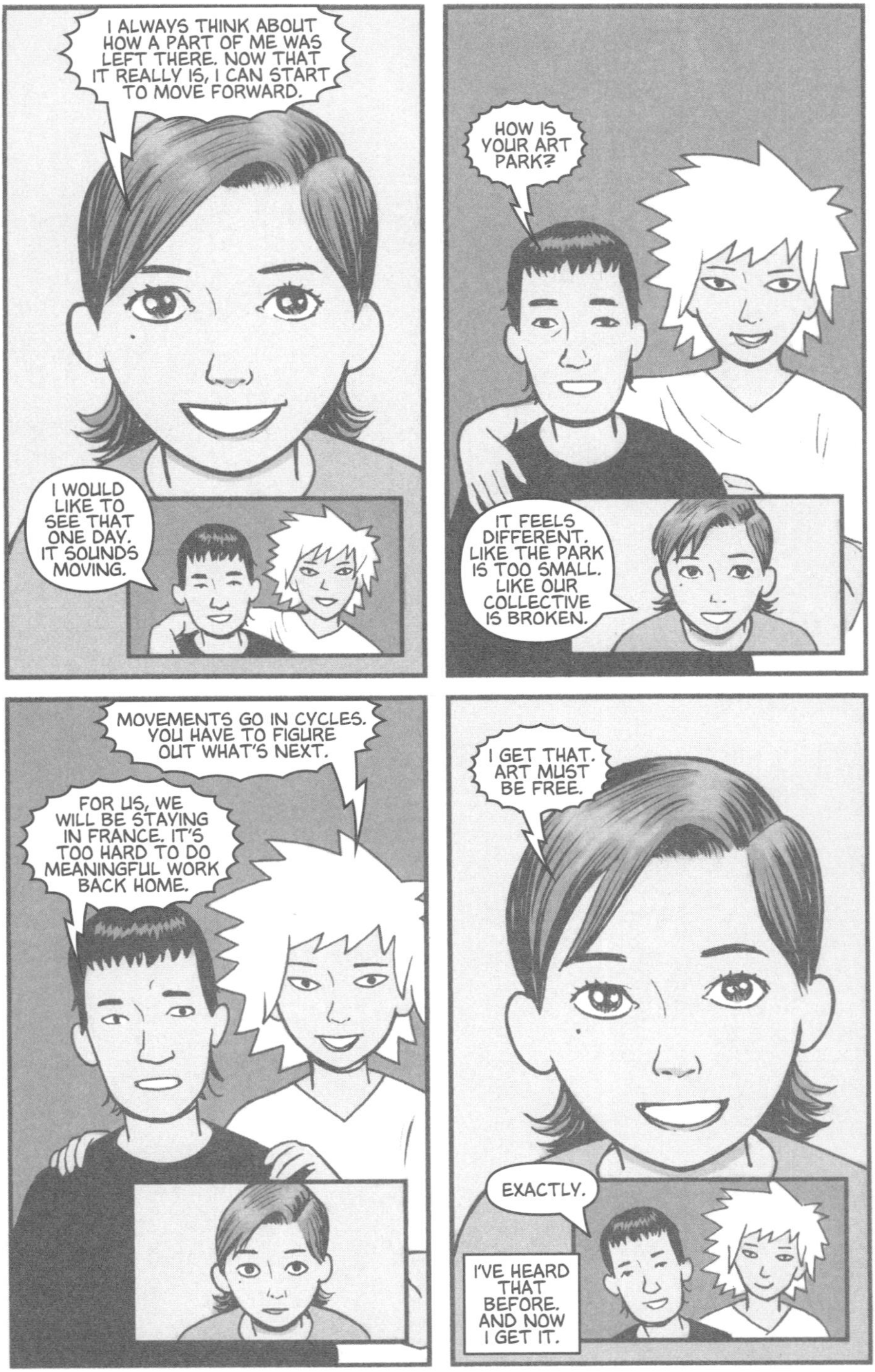
I ALWAYS THINK ABOUT HOW A PART OF ME WAS LEFT THERE. NOW THAT IT REALLY IS, I CAN START TO MOVE FORWARD.
I WOULD LIKE TO SEE THAT ONE DAY. IT SOUNDS MOVING.
HOW IS YOUR ART PARK?
IT FEELS DIFFERENT. LIKE THE PARK IS TOO SMALL. LIKE OUR COLLECTIVE IS BROKEN.
MOVEMENTS GO IN CYCLES. YOU HAVE TO FIGURE OUT WHAT'S NEXT.
FOR US, WE WILL BE STAYING IN FRANCE. IT'S TOO HARD TO DO MEANINGFUL WORK BACK HOME.
I GET THAT. ART MUST BE FREE.
EXACTLY.
I'VE HEARD THAT BEFORE. AND NOW I GET IT.

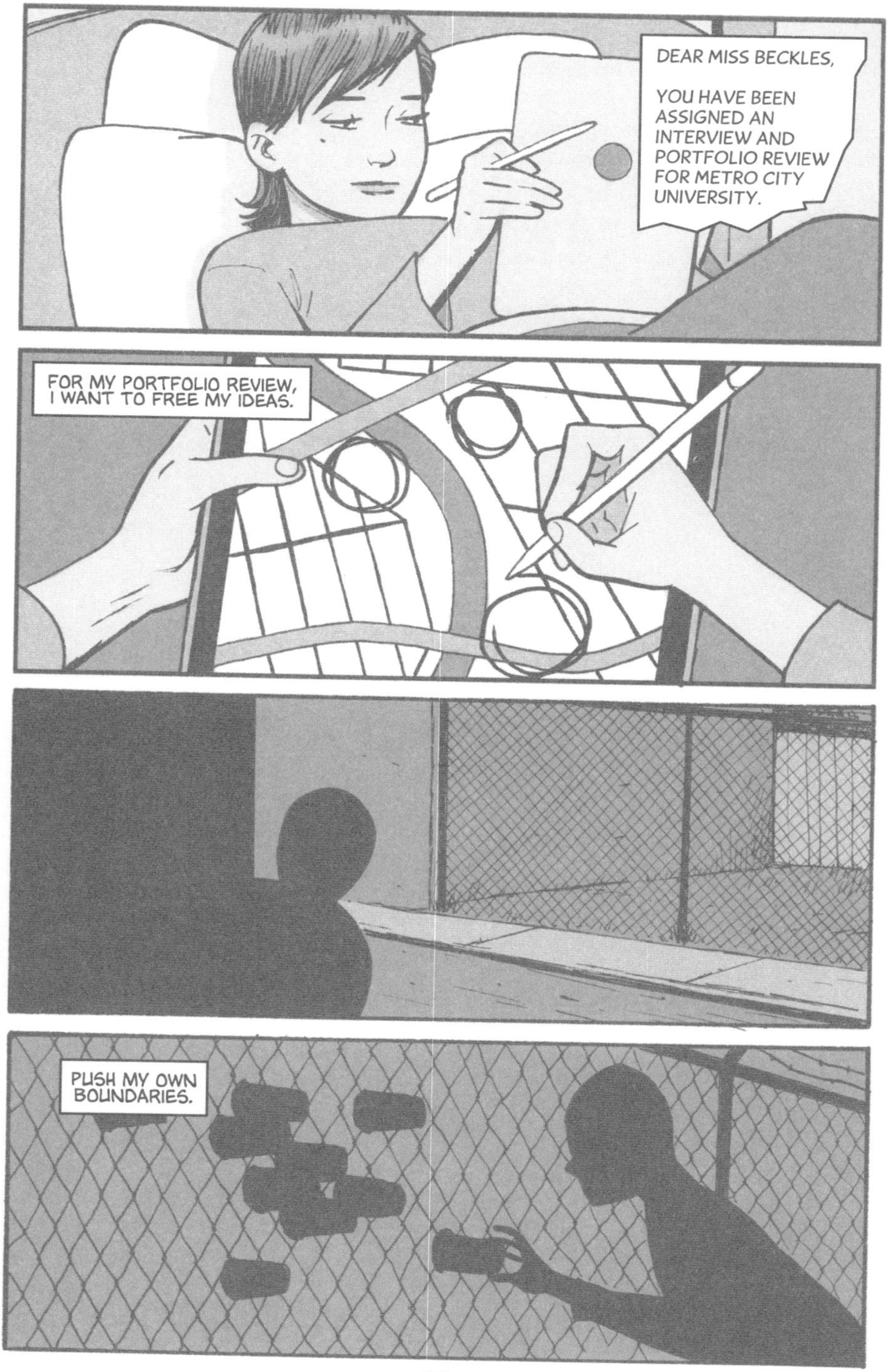
DEAR MISS BECKLES,
YOU HAVE BEEN ASSIGNED AN INTERVIEW AND PORTFOLIO REVIEW FOR METRO CITY UNIVERSITY.
FOR MY PORTFOLIO REVIEW, I WANT TO FREE MY IDEAS.
PUSH MY OWN BOUNDARIES.

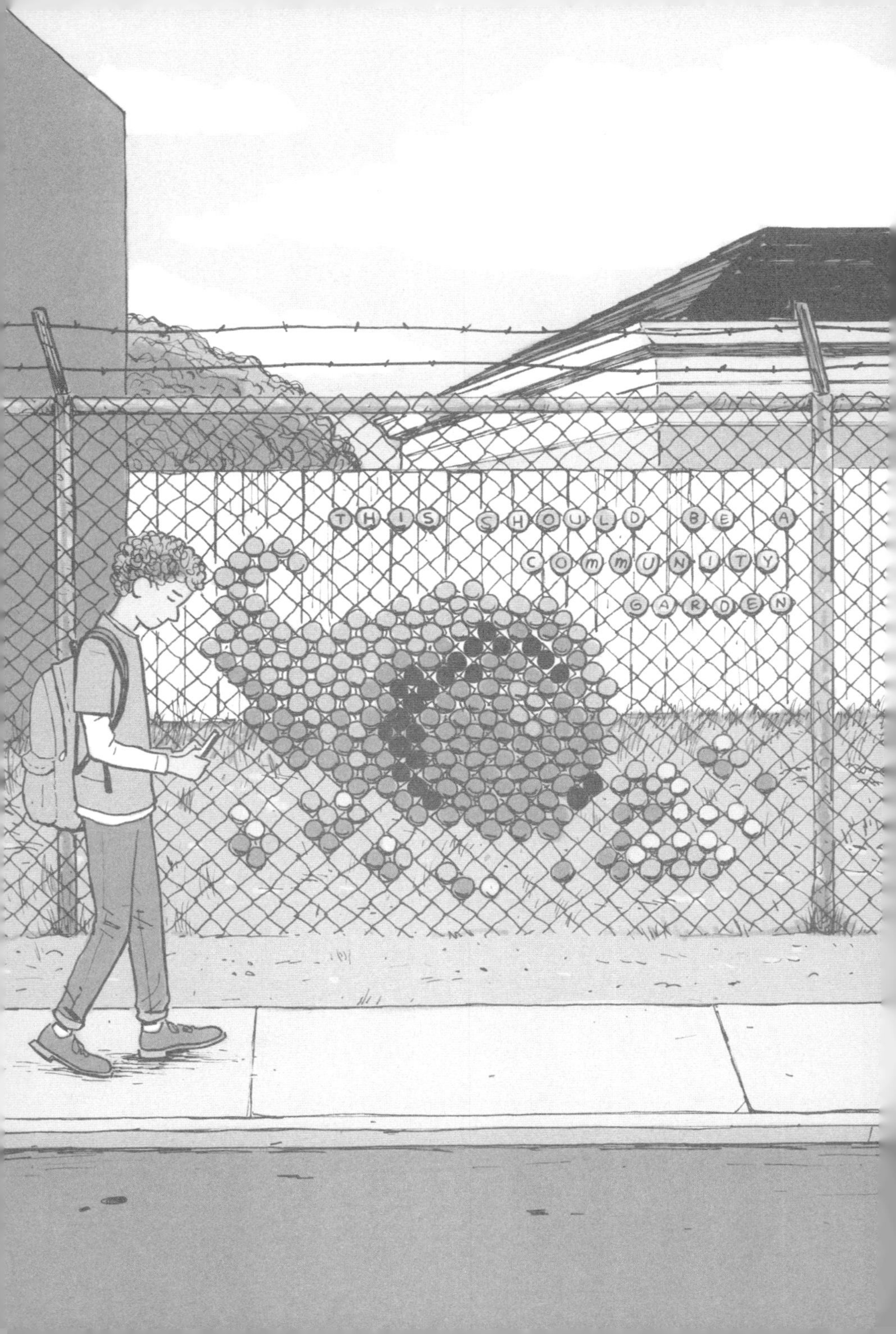
THIS SHOULD BE A
COMMUNITY
GARDEN

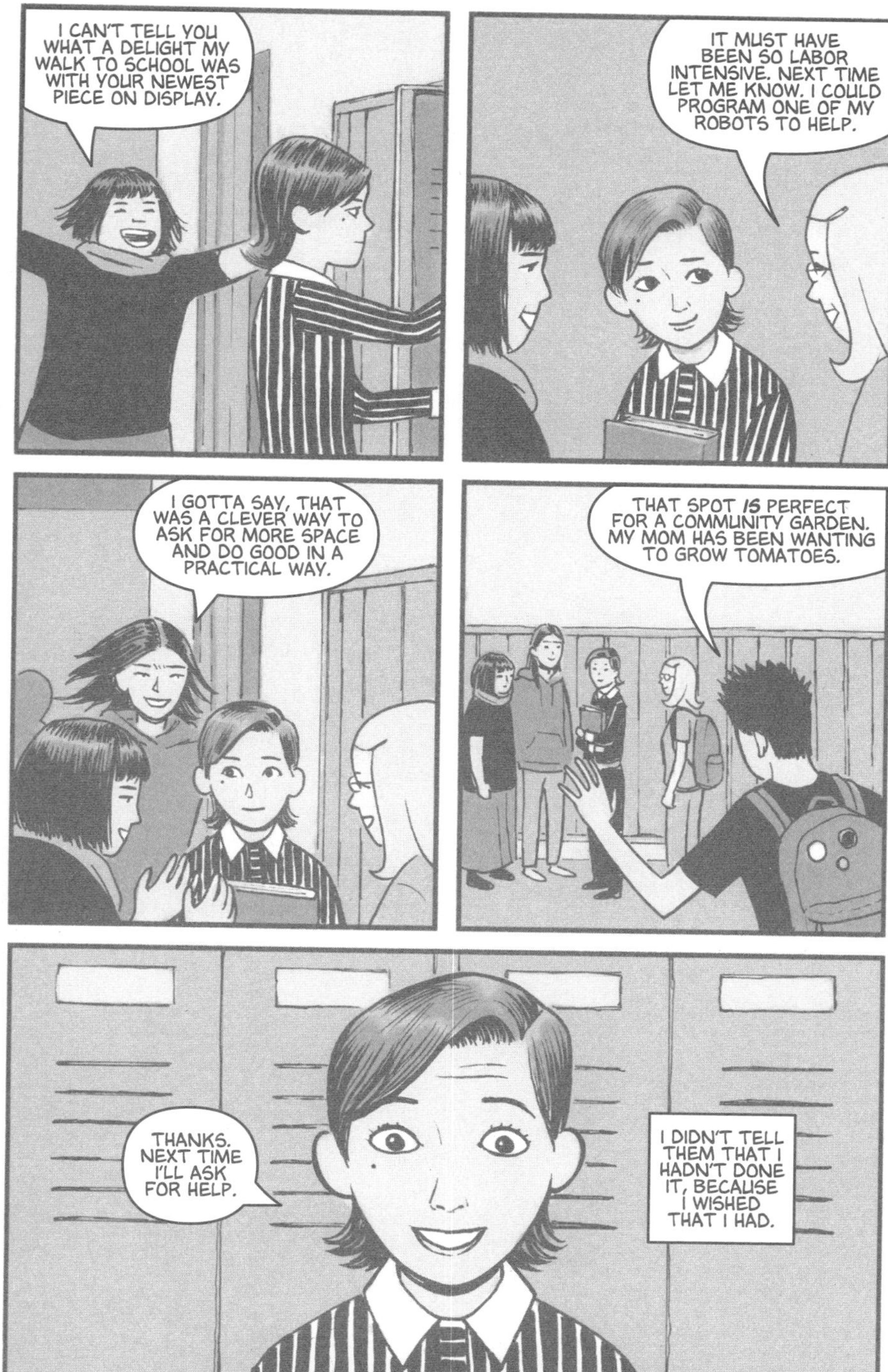
I CAN'T TELL YOU WHAT A DELIGHT MY WALK TO SCHOOL WAS WITH YOUR NEWEST PIECE ON DISPLAY.
IT MUST HAVE BEEN SO LABOR INTENSIVE. NEXT TIME LET ME KNOW. I COULD PROGRAM ONE OF MY ROBOTS TO HELP.
I GOTTA SAY, THAT WAS A CLEVER WAY TO ASK FOR MORE SPACE AND DO GOOD IN A PRACTICAL WAY.
THAT SPOT *IS* PERFECT FOR A COMMUNITY GARDEN. MY MOM HAS BEEN WANTING TO GROW TOMATOES.
THANKS. NEXT TIME I'LL ASK FOR HELP.
I DIDN'T TELL THEM THAT I HADN'T DONE IT, BECAUSE I WISHED THAT I HAD.

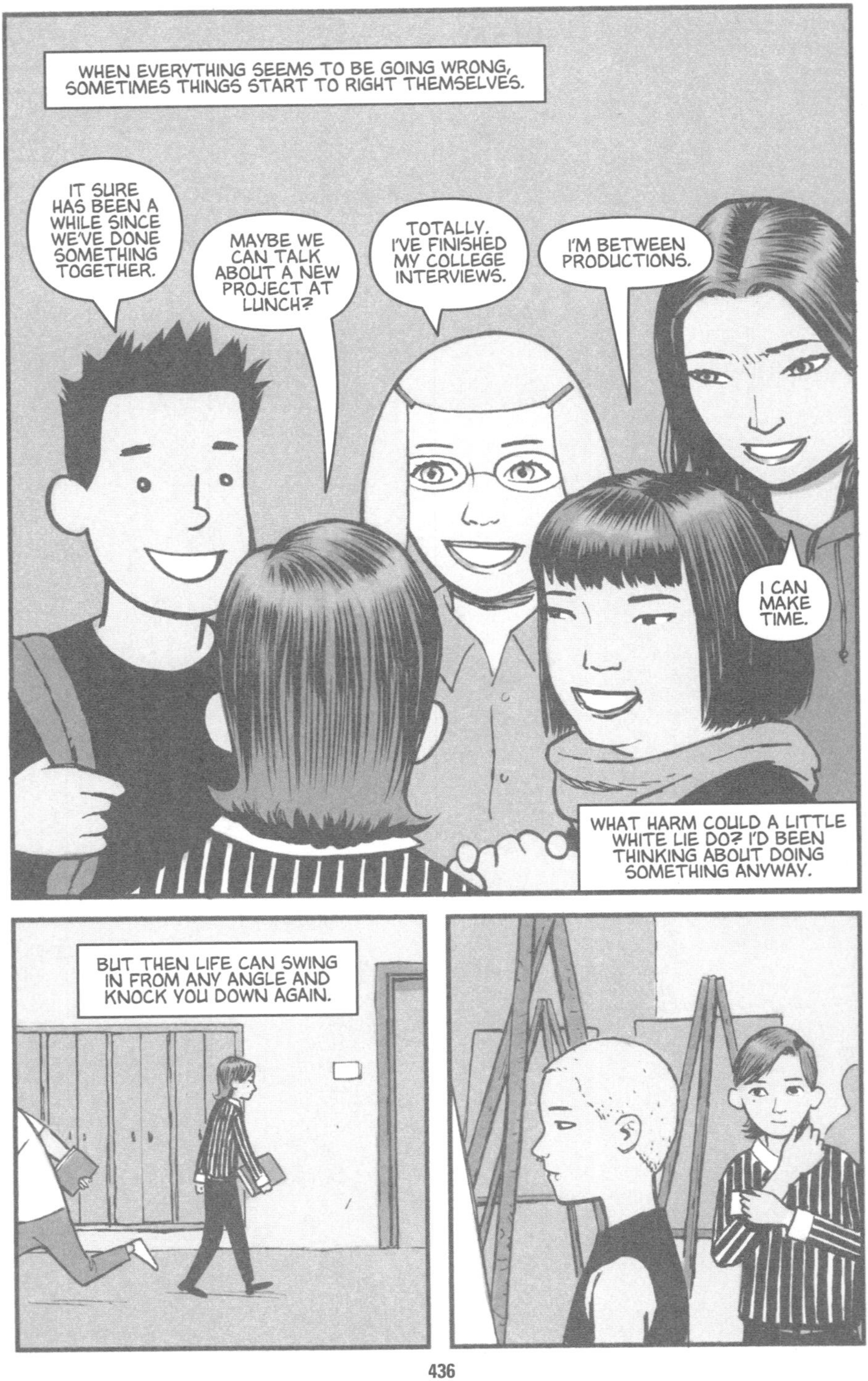
WHEN EVERYTHING SEEMS TO BE GOING WRONG, SOMETIMES THINGS START TO RIGHT THEMSELVES.
IT SURE HAS BEEN A WHILE SINCE WE'VE DONE SOMETHING TOGETHER.
MAYBE WE CAN TALK ABOUT A NEW PROJECT AT LUNCH?
TOTALLY. I'VE FINISHED MY COLLEGE INTERVIEWS.
I'M BETWEEN PRODUCTIONS.
I CAN MAKE TIME.
WHAT HARM COULD A LITTLE WHITE LIE DO? I'D BEEN THINKING ABOUT DOING SOMETHING ANYWAY.
BUT THEN LIFE CAN SWING IN FROM ANY ANGLE AND KNOCK YOU DOWN AGAIN.

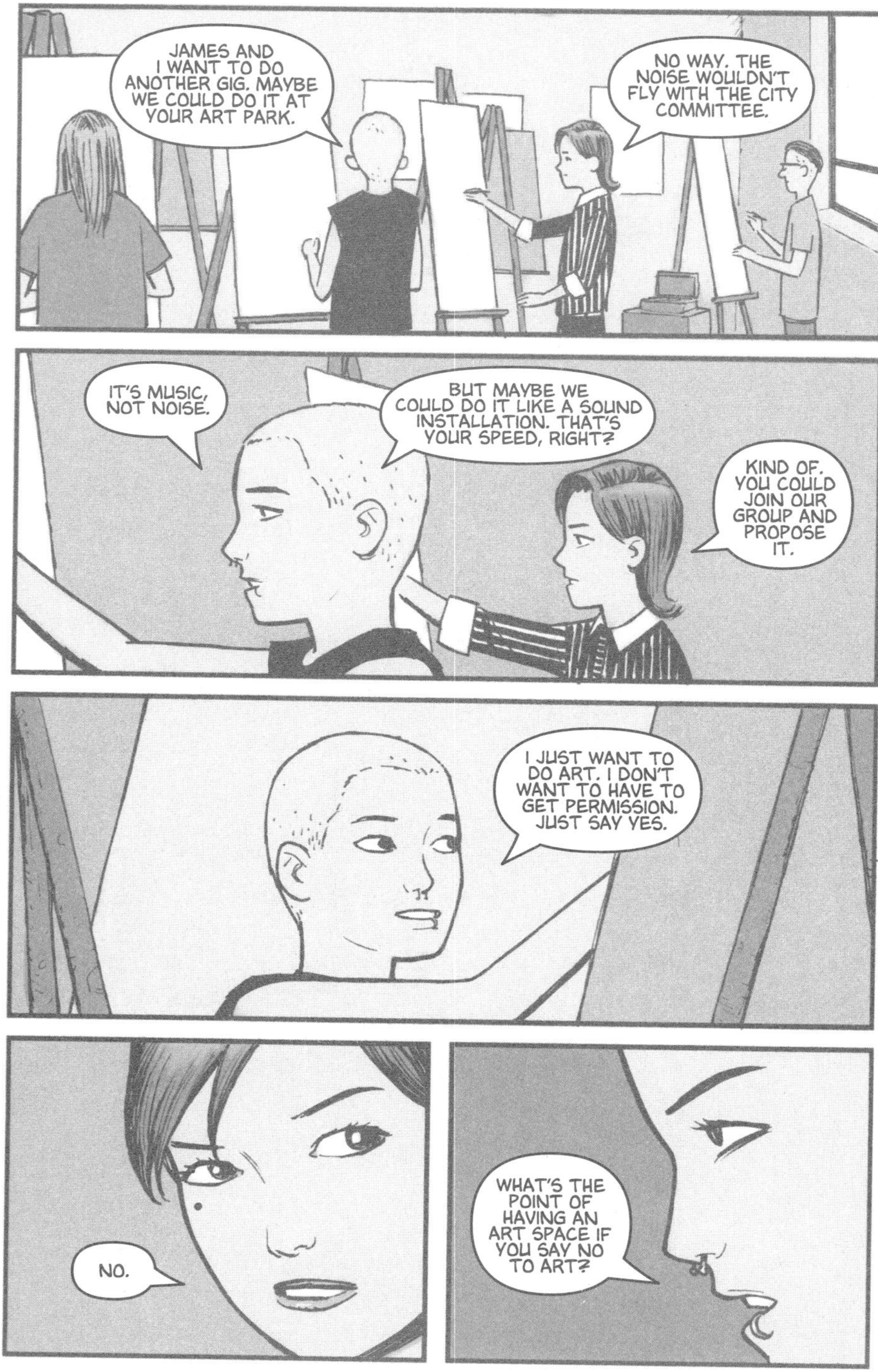
JAMES AND I WANT TO DO ANOTHER GIG. MAYBE WE COULD DO IT AT YOUR ART PARK.
NO WAY. THE NOISE WOULDN'T FLY WITH THE CITY COMMITTEE.
IT'S MUSIC, NOT NOISE.
BUT MAYBE WE COULD DO IT LIKE A SOUND INSTALLATION. THAT'S YOUR SPEED, RIGHT?
KIND OF. YOU COULD JOIN OUR GROUP AND PROPOSE IT.
I JUST WANT TO DO ART. I DON'T WANT TO HAVE TO GET PERMISSION. JUST SAY YES.
NO.
WHAT'S THE POINT OF HAVING AN ART SPACE IF YOU SAY NO TO ART?

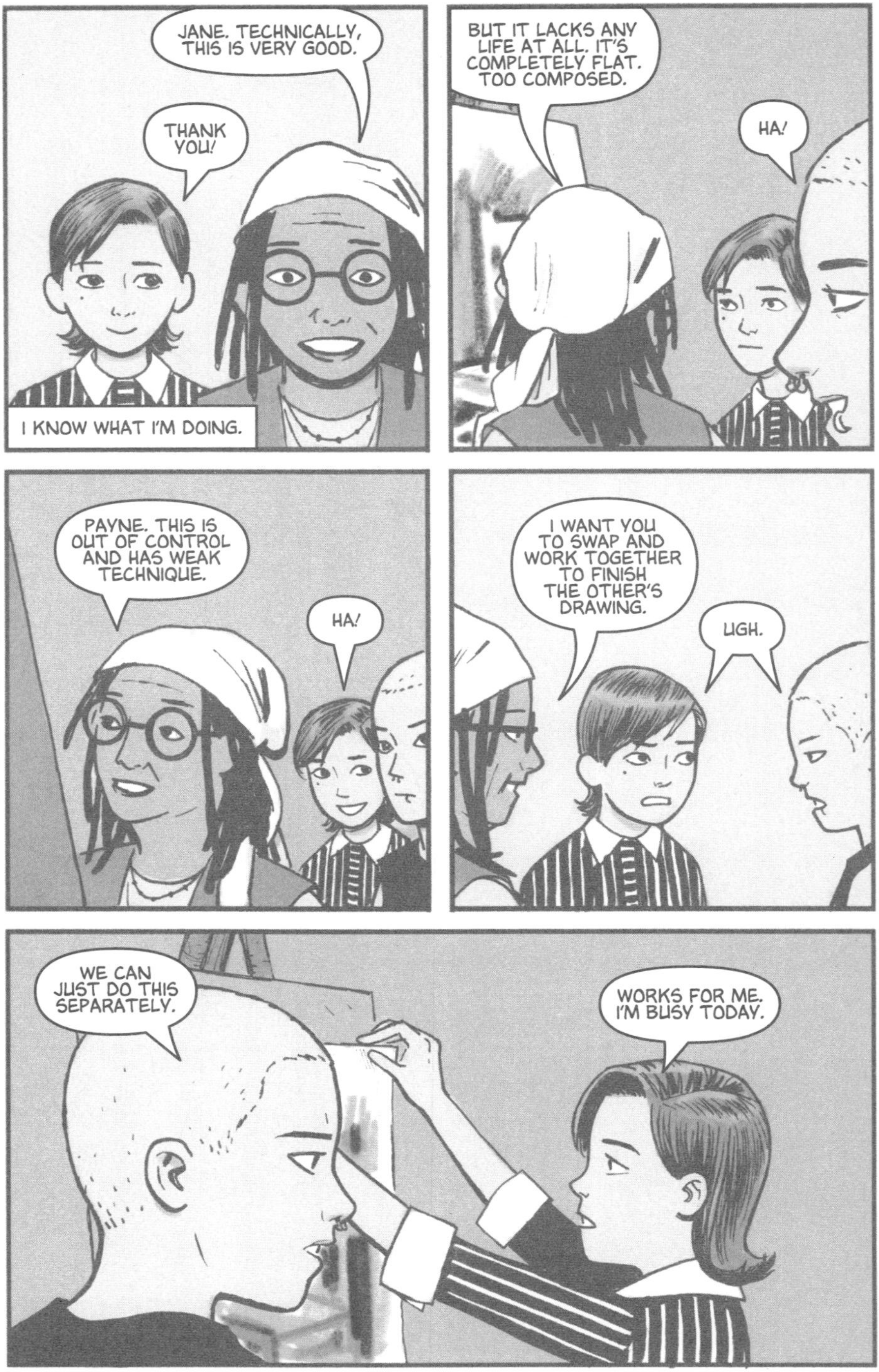
JANE. TECHNICALLY, THIS IS VERY GOOD.
THANK YOU!
I KNOW WHAT I'M DOING.
BUT IT LACKS ANY LIFE AT ALL. IT'S COMPLETELY FLAT. TOO COMPOSED.
HA!
PAYNE. THIS IS OUT OF CONTROL AND HAS WEAK TECHNIQUE.
HA!
I WANT YOU TO SWAP AND WORK TOGETHER TO FINISH THE OTHER'S DRAWING.
UGH.
WE CAN JUST DO THIS SEPARATELY.
WORKS FOR ME. I'M BUSY TODAY.

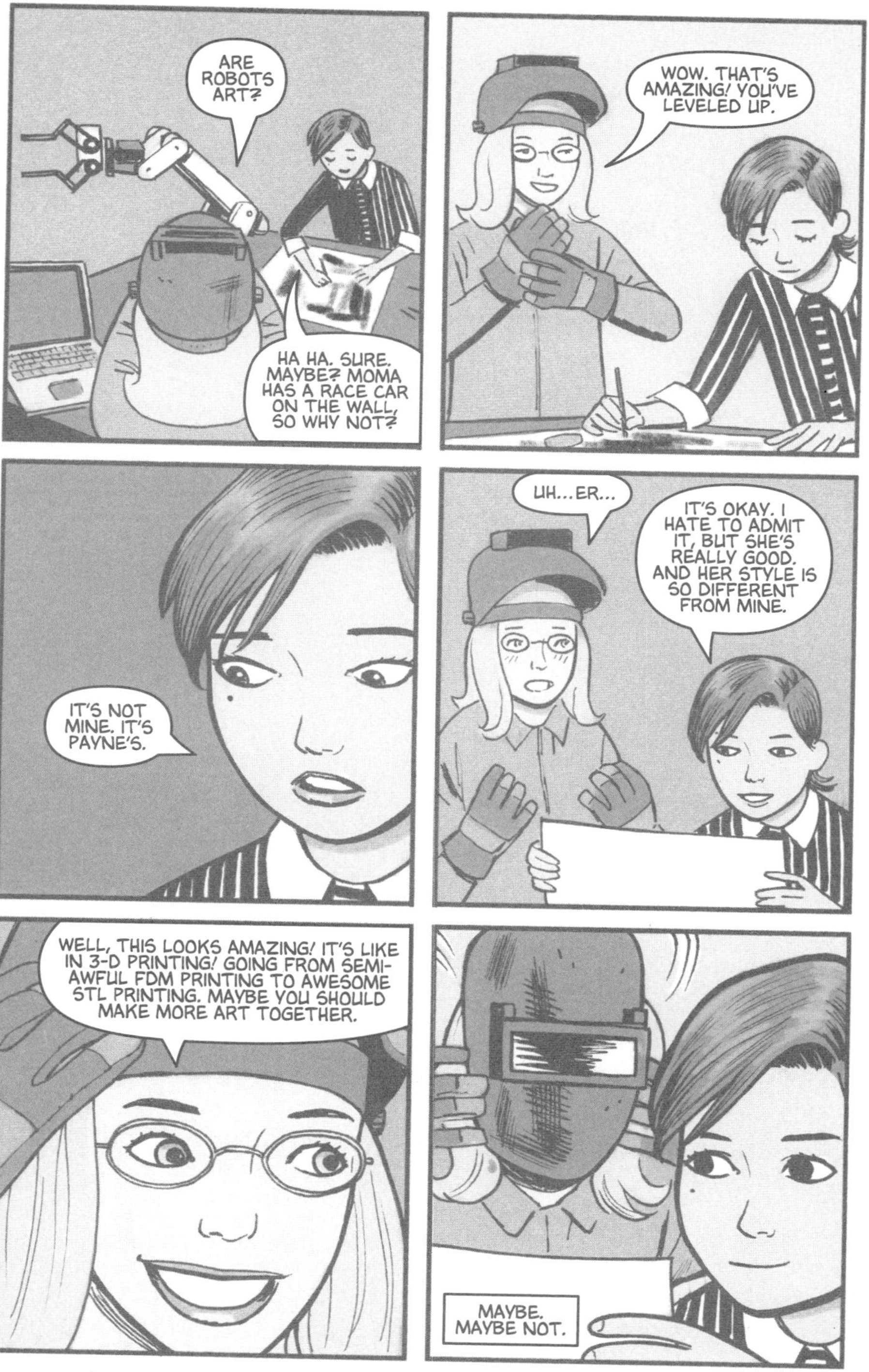
ARE ROBOTS ART?
HA HA. SURE. MAYBE? MOMA HAS A RACE CAR ON THE WALL, SO WHY NOT?
WOW. THAT'S AMAZING! YOU'VE LEVELED UP.
IT'S NOT MINE. IT'S PAYNE'S.
UH...ER...
IT'S OKAY. I HATE TO ADMIT IT, BUT SHE'S REALLY GOOD. AND HER STYLE IS SO DIFFERENT FROM MINE.
WELL, THIS LOOKS AMAZING! IT'S LIKE IN 3-D PRINTING! GOING FROM SEMI-AWFUL FDM PRINTING TO AWESOME STL PRINTING. MAYBE YOU SHOULD MAKE MORE ART TOGETHER.
MAYBE. MAYBE NOT.

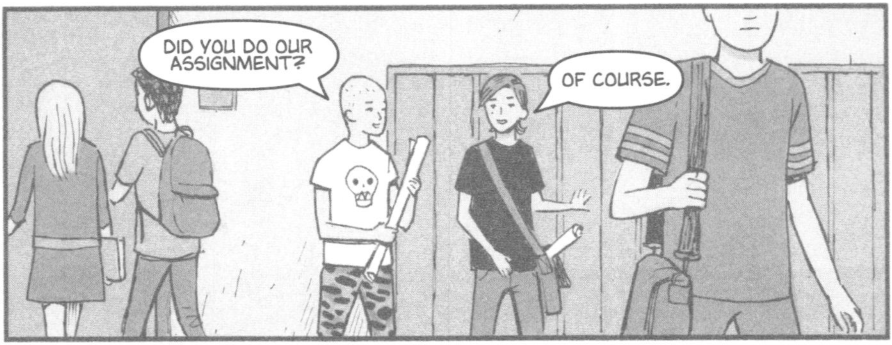
DID YOU DO OUR ASSIGNMENT?
OF COURSE.

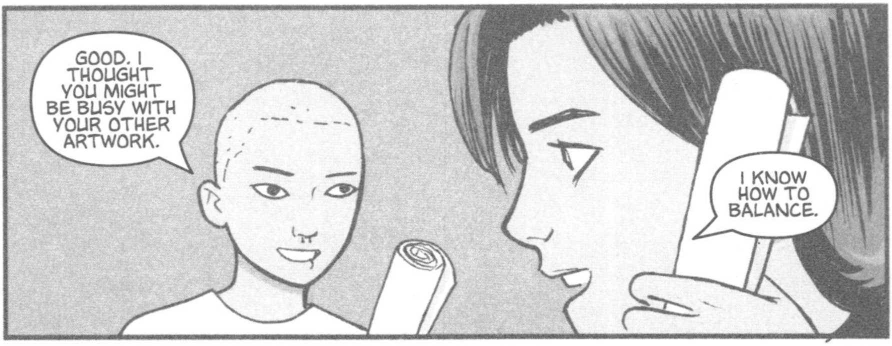
GOOD. I THOUGHT YOU MIGHT BE BUSY WITH YOUR OTHER ARTWORK.
I KNOW HOW TO BALANCE.

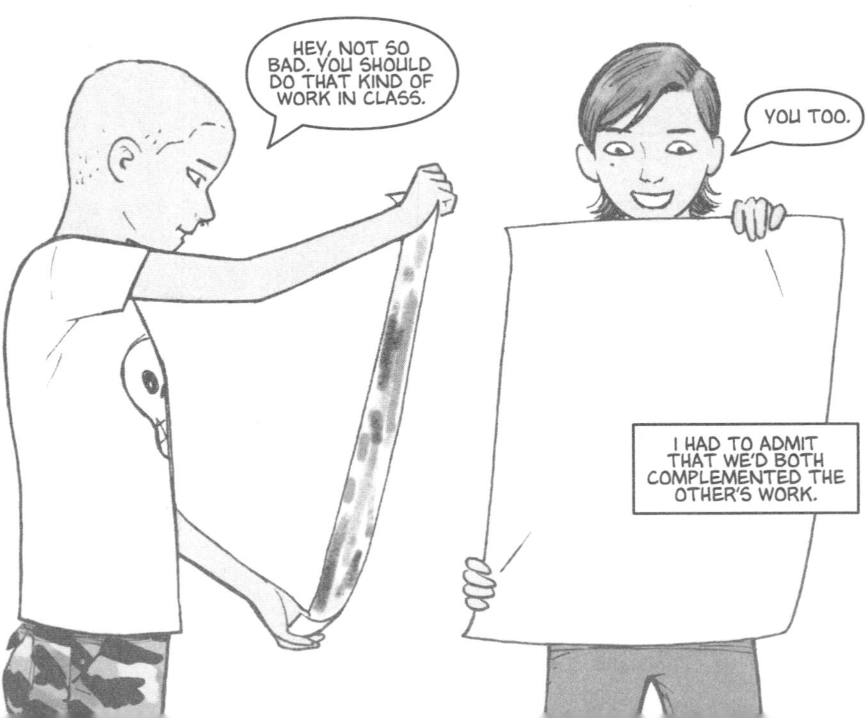
HEY, NOT SO BAD. YOU SHOULD DO THAT KIND OF WORK IN CLASS.
YOU TOO.
I HAD TO ADMIT THAT WE'D BOTH COMPLEMENTED THE OTHER'S WORK.

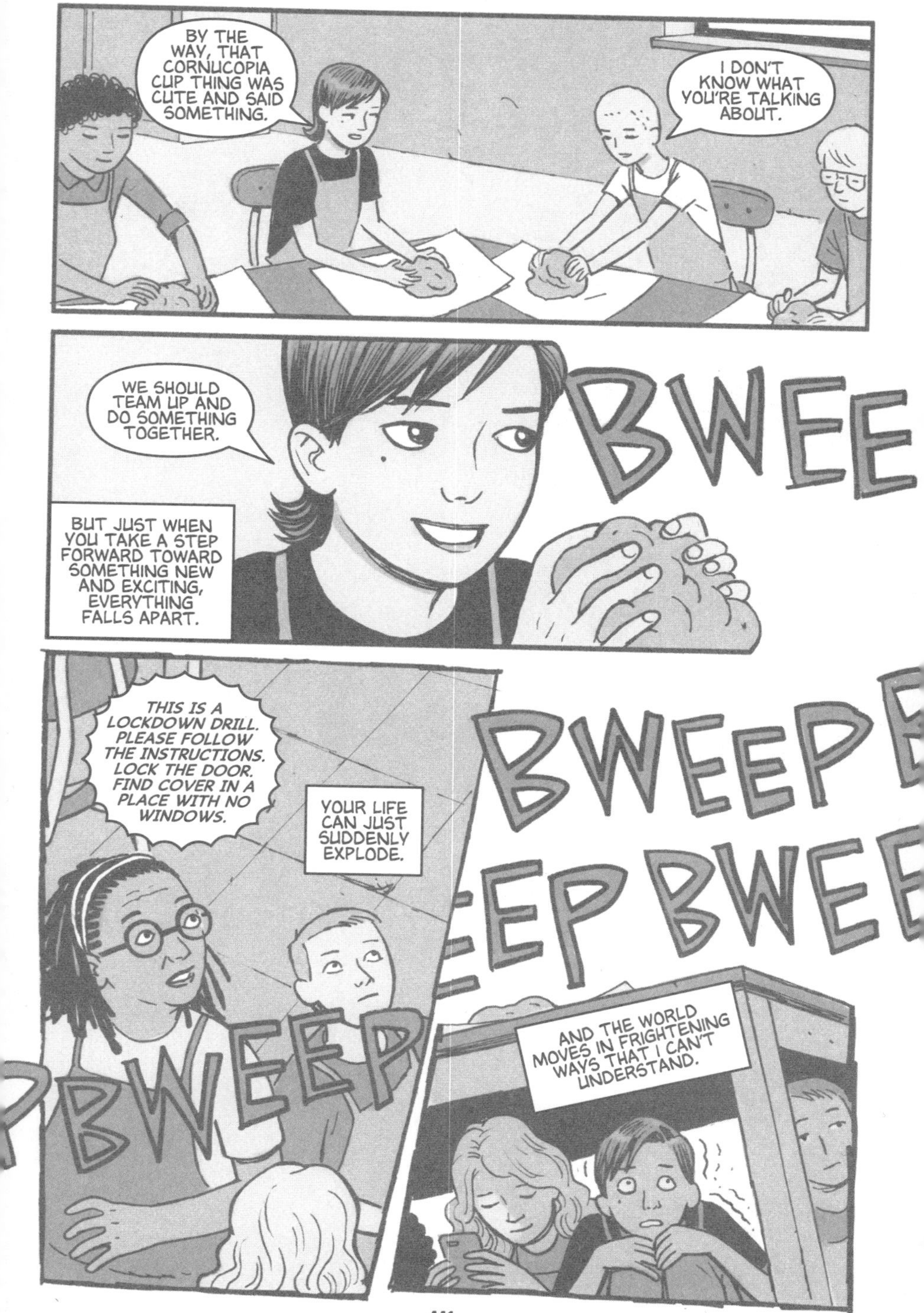

BY THE WAY, THAT CORNUCOPIA CUP THING WAS CUTE AND SAID SOMETHING.
I DON'T KNOW WHAT YOU'RE TALKING ABOUT.
WE SHOULD TEAM UP AND DO SOMETHING TOGETHER.
BUT JUST WHEN YOU TAKE A STEP FORWARD TOWARD SOMETHING NEW AND EXCITING, EVERYTHING FALLS APART.
BWEE
BWEEPB
EEP BWEE
PBWEEP
THIS IS A LOCKDOWN DRILL. PLEASE FOLLOW THE INSTRUCTIONS. LOCK THE DOOR. FIND COVER IN A PLACE WITH NO WINDOWS.
YOUR LIFE CAN JUST SUDDENLY EXPLODE.
AND THE WORLD MOVES IN FRIGHTENING WAYS THAT I CAN'T UNDERSTAND.

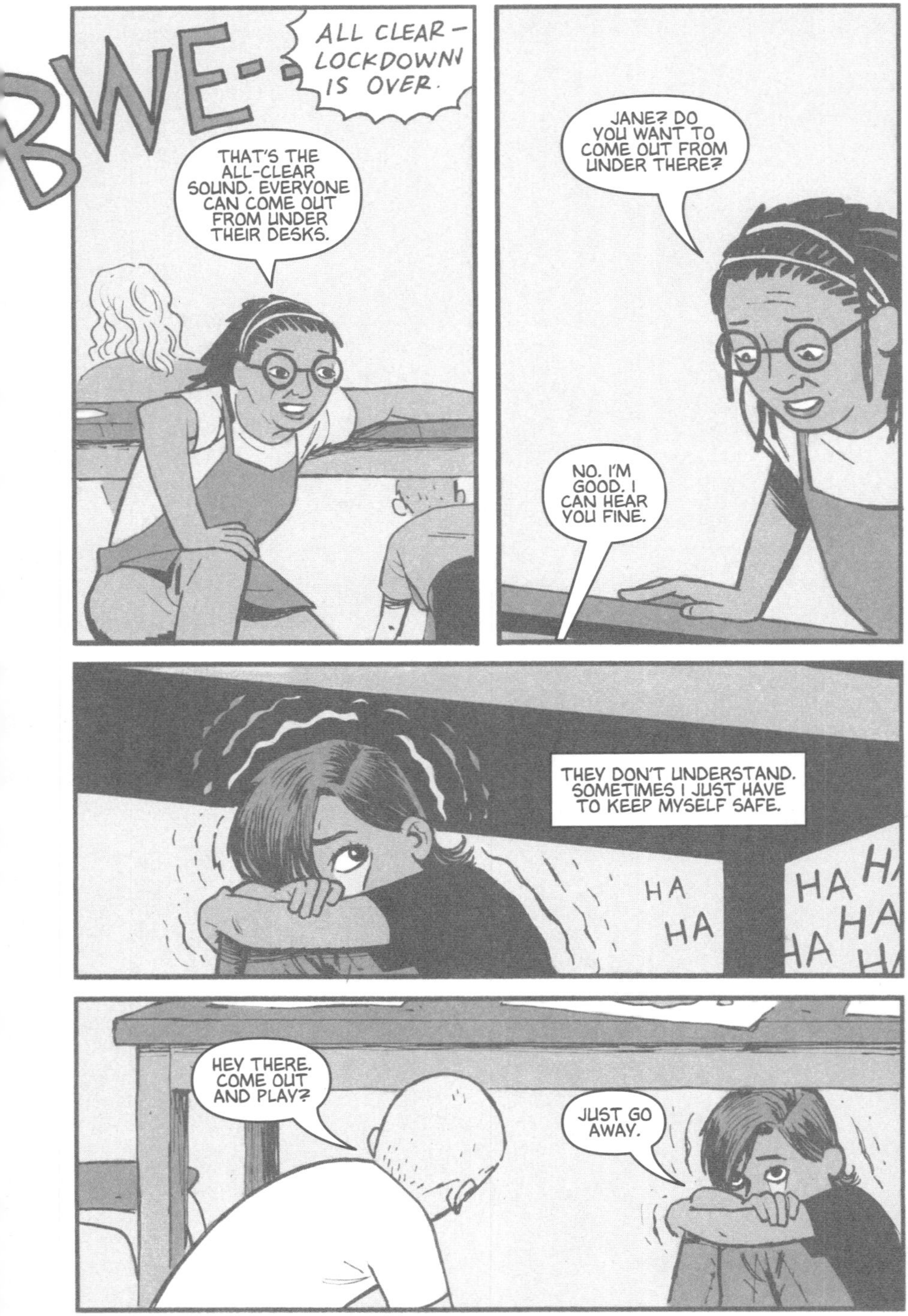
BWE-
ALL CLEAR—LOCKDOWN IS OVER.
THAT'S THE ALL-CLEAR SOUND. EVERYONE CAN COME OUT FROM UNDER THEIR DESKS.
JANE? DO YOU WANT TO COME OUT FROM UNDER THERE?
NO. I'M GOOD. I CAN HEAR YOU FINE.
THEY DON'T UNDERSTAND. SOMETIMES I JUST HAVE TO KEEP MYSELF SAFE.
HA HA
HA HA HA HA HA HA
HEY THERE. COME OUT AND PLAY?
JUST GO AWAY.

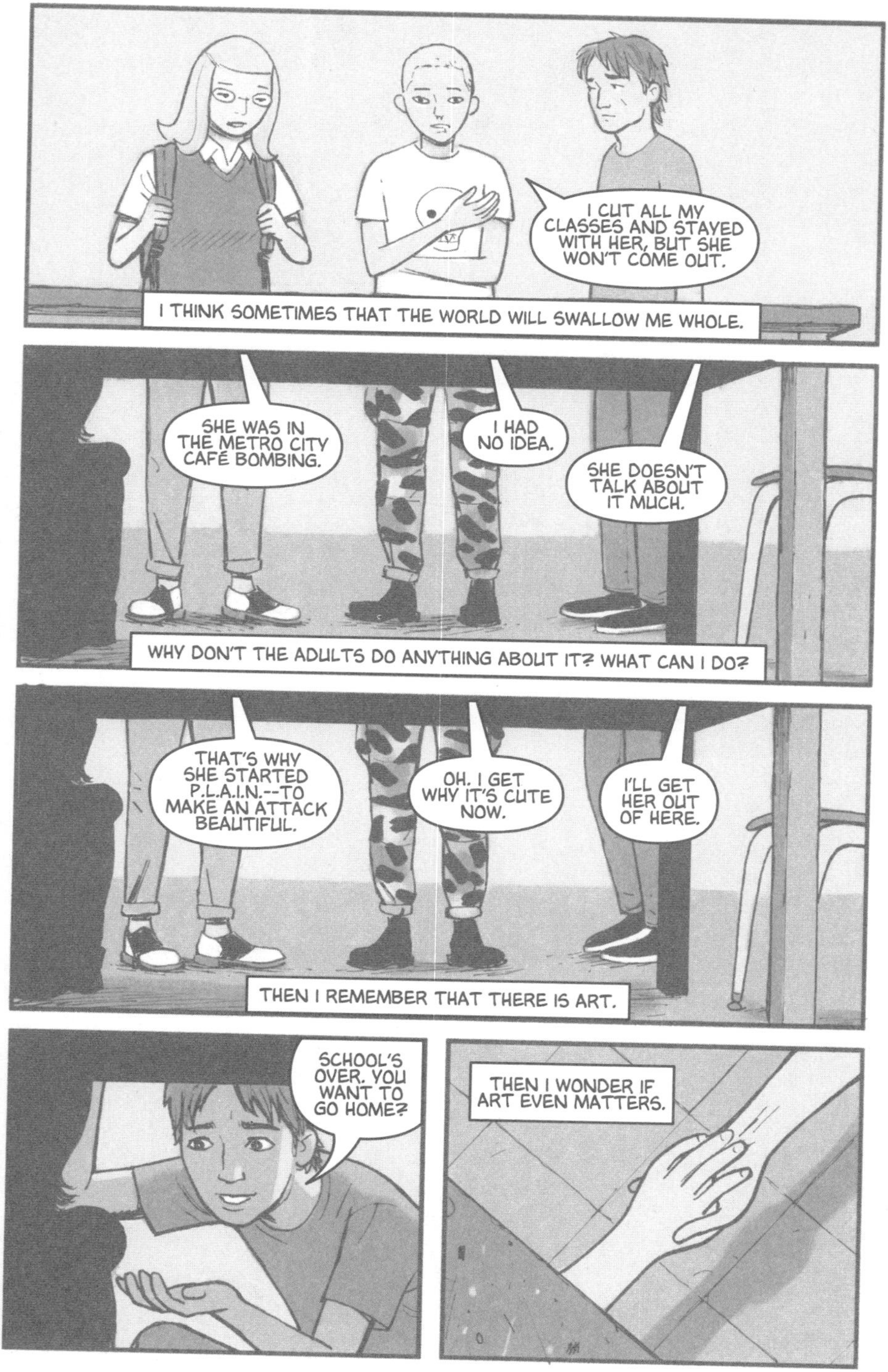
I CUT ALL MY CLASSES AND STAYED WITH HER, BUT SHE WON'T COME OUT.
I THINK SOMETIMES THAT THE WORLD WILL SWALLOW ME WHOLE.
SHE WAS IN THE METRO CITY CAFÉ BOMBING.
I HAD NO IDEA.
SHE DOESN'T TALK ABOUT IT MUCH.
WHY DON'T THE ADULTS DO ANYTHING ABOUT IT? WHAT CAN I DO?
THAT'S WHY SHE STARTED P.L.A.I.N.--TO MAKE AN ATTACK BEAUTIFUL.
OH. I GET WHY IT'S CUTE NOW.
I'LL GET HER OUT OF HERE.
THEN I REMEMBER THAT THERE IS ART.
SCHOOL'S OVER. YOU WANT TO GO HOME?
THEN I WONDER IF ART EVEN MATTERS.

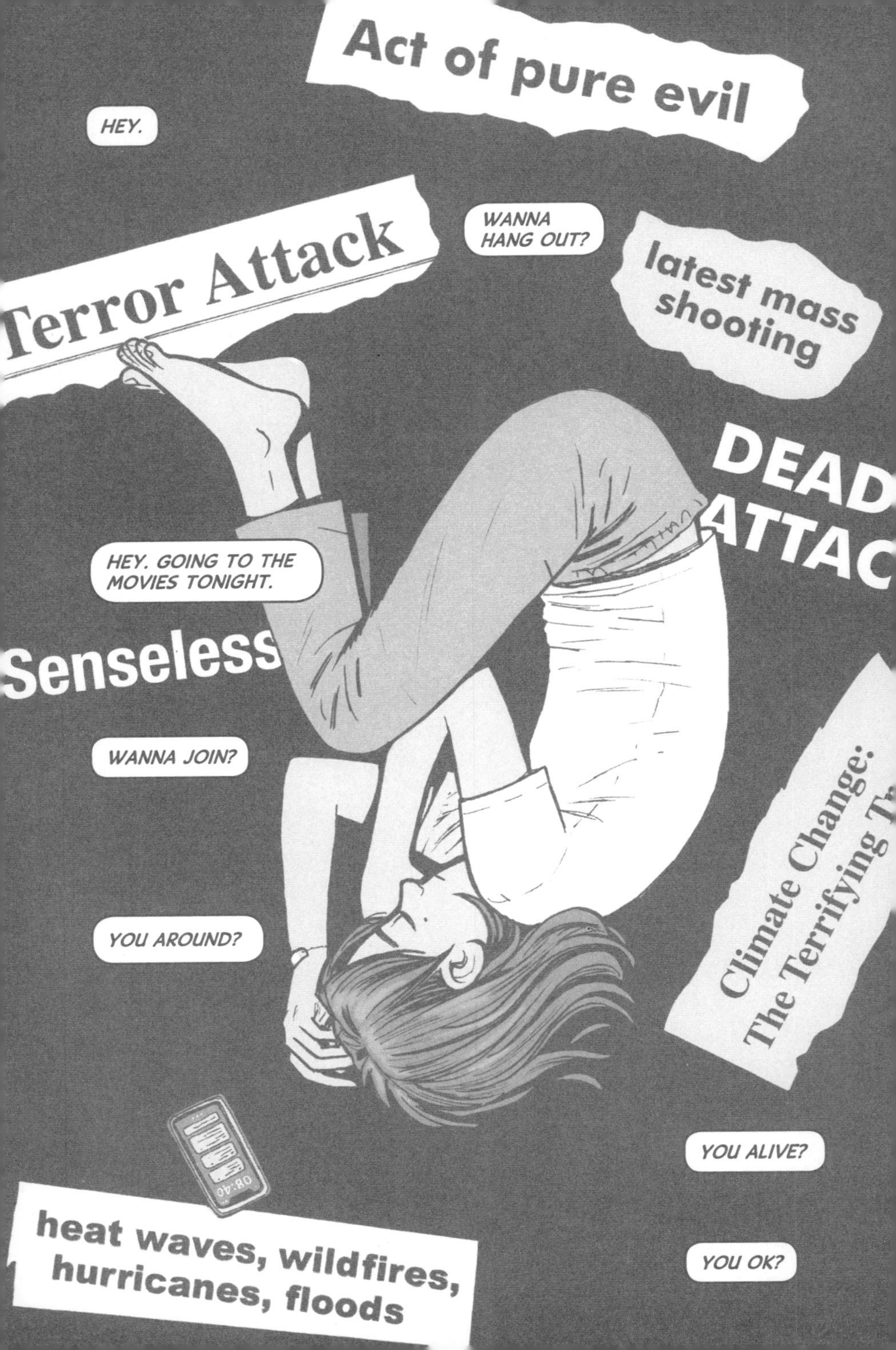
Act of pure evil
HEY.
Terror Attack
WANNA HANG OUT?
latest mass shooting
DEAD
ATTAC
HEY. GOING TO THE MOVIES TONIGHT.
Senseless
WANNA JOIN?
Climate Change: The Terrifying T
YOU AROUND?
08:40
YOU ALIVE?
heat waves, wildfires, hurricanes, floods
YOU OK?

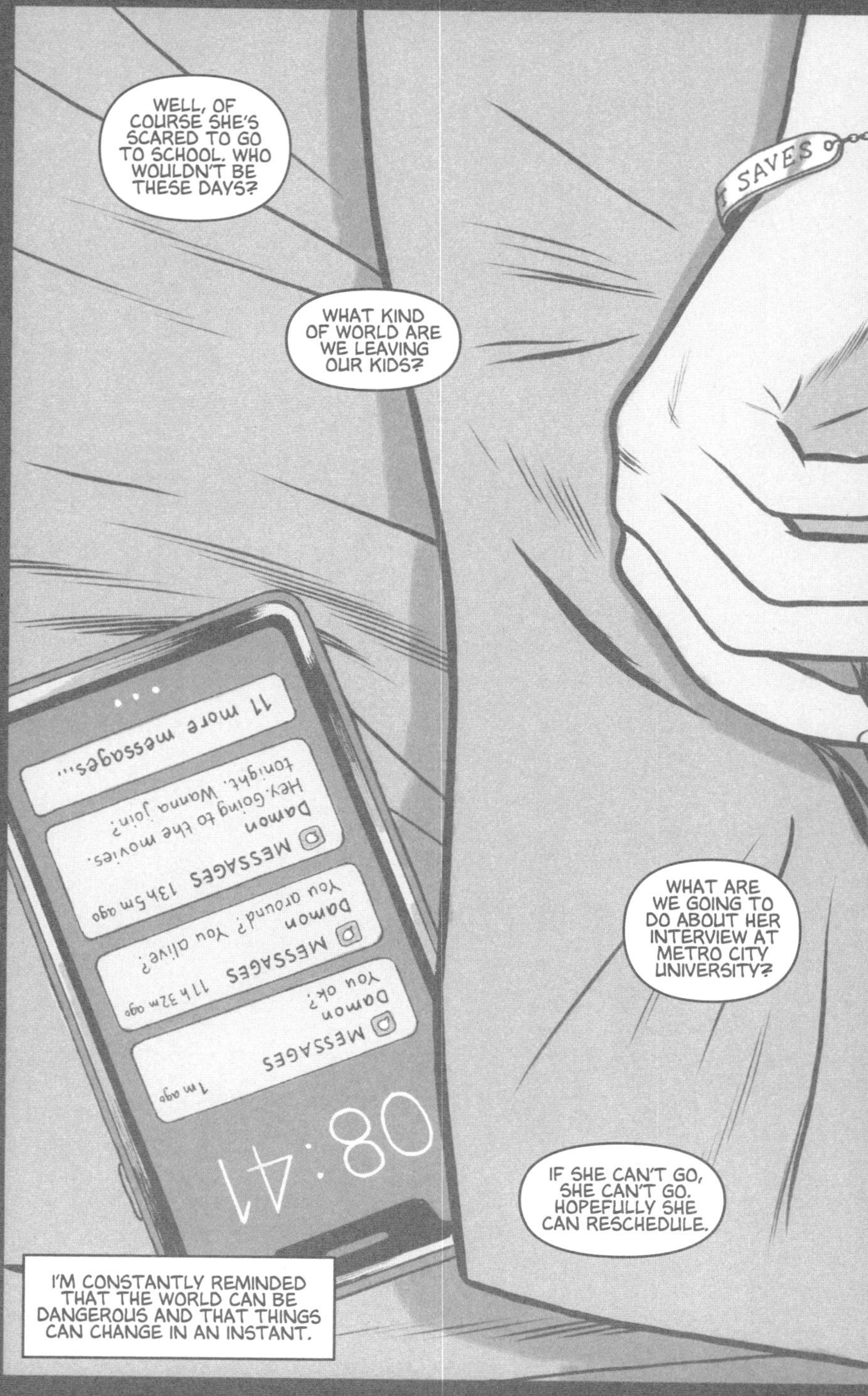
WELL, OF COURSE SHE'S SCARED TO GO TO SCHOOL. WHO WOULDN'T BE THESE DAYS?
WHAT KIND OF WORLD ARE WE LEAVING OUR KIDS?
SAVES
08:41
MESSAGES 1m ago
Damon
You ok?
MESSAGES 11h 32m ago
Damon
You around? You alive?
MESSAGES 13h 5m ago
Damon
Hey. Going to the movies tonight. Wanna join?
messages...
11 more messages
WHAT ARE WE GOING TO DO ABOUT HER INTERVIEW AT METRO CITY UNIVERSITY?
IF SHE CAN'T GO, SHE CAN'T GO. HOPEFULLY SHE CAN RESCHEDULE.
I'M CONSTANTLY REMINDED THAT THE WORLD CAN BE DANGEROUS AND THAT THINGS CAN CHANGE IN AN INSTANT.

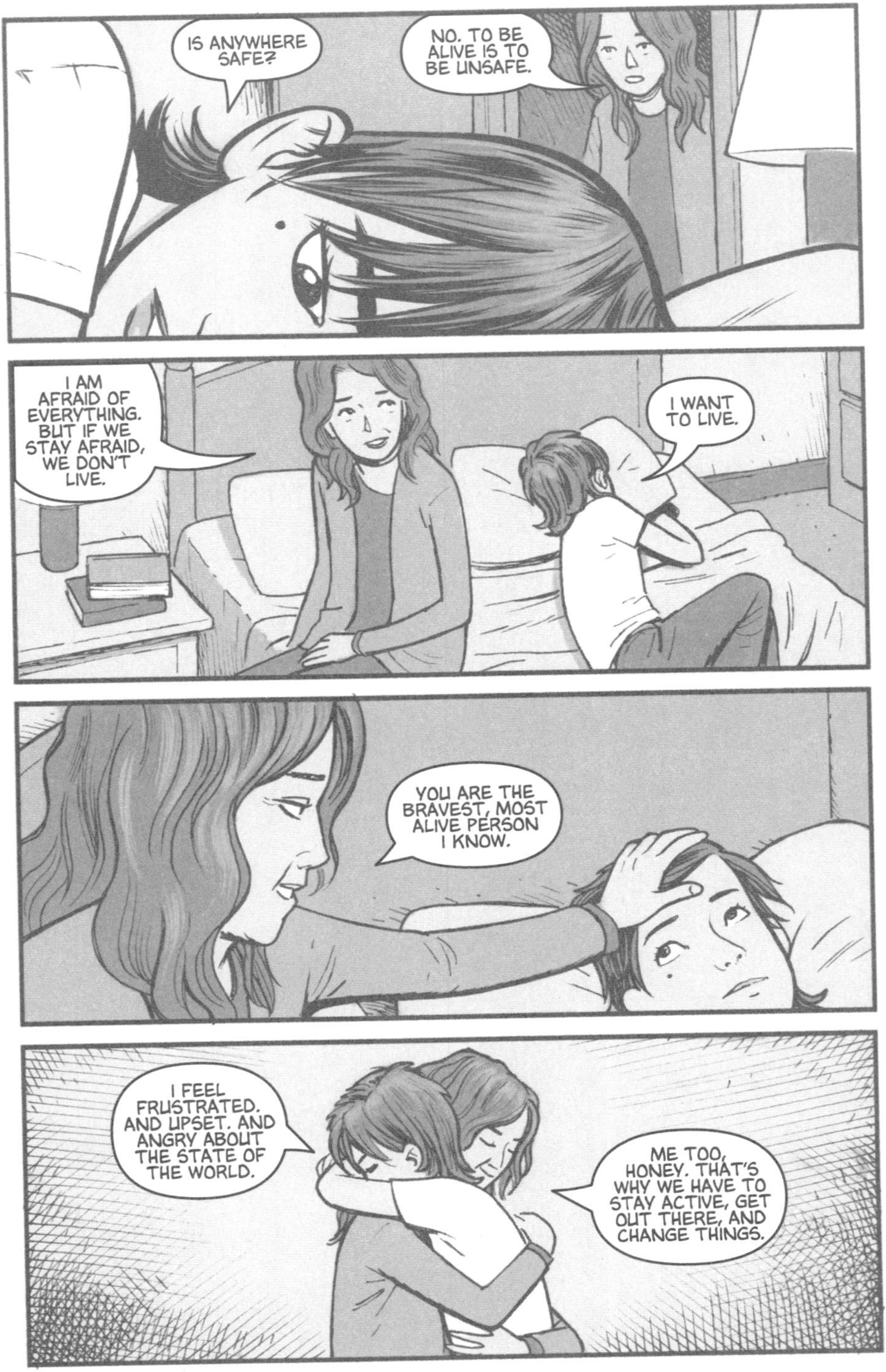
IS ANYWHERE SAFE?
NO. TO BE ALIVE IS TO BE UNSAFE.
I AM AFRAID OF EVERYTHING. BUT IF WE STAY AFRAID, WE DON'T LIVE.
I WANT TO LIVE.
YOU ARE THE BRAVEST, MOST ALIVE PERSON I KNOW.
I FEEL FRUSTRATED. AND UPSET. AND ANGRY ABOUT THE STATE OF THE WORLD.
ME TOO, HONEY. THAT'S WHY WE HAVE TO STAY ACTIVE, GET OUT THERE, AND CHANGE THINGS.

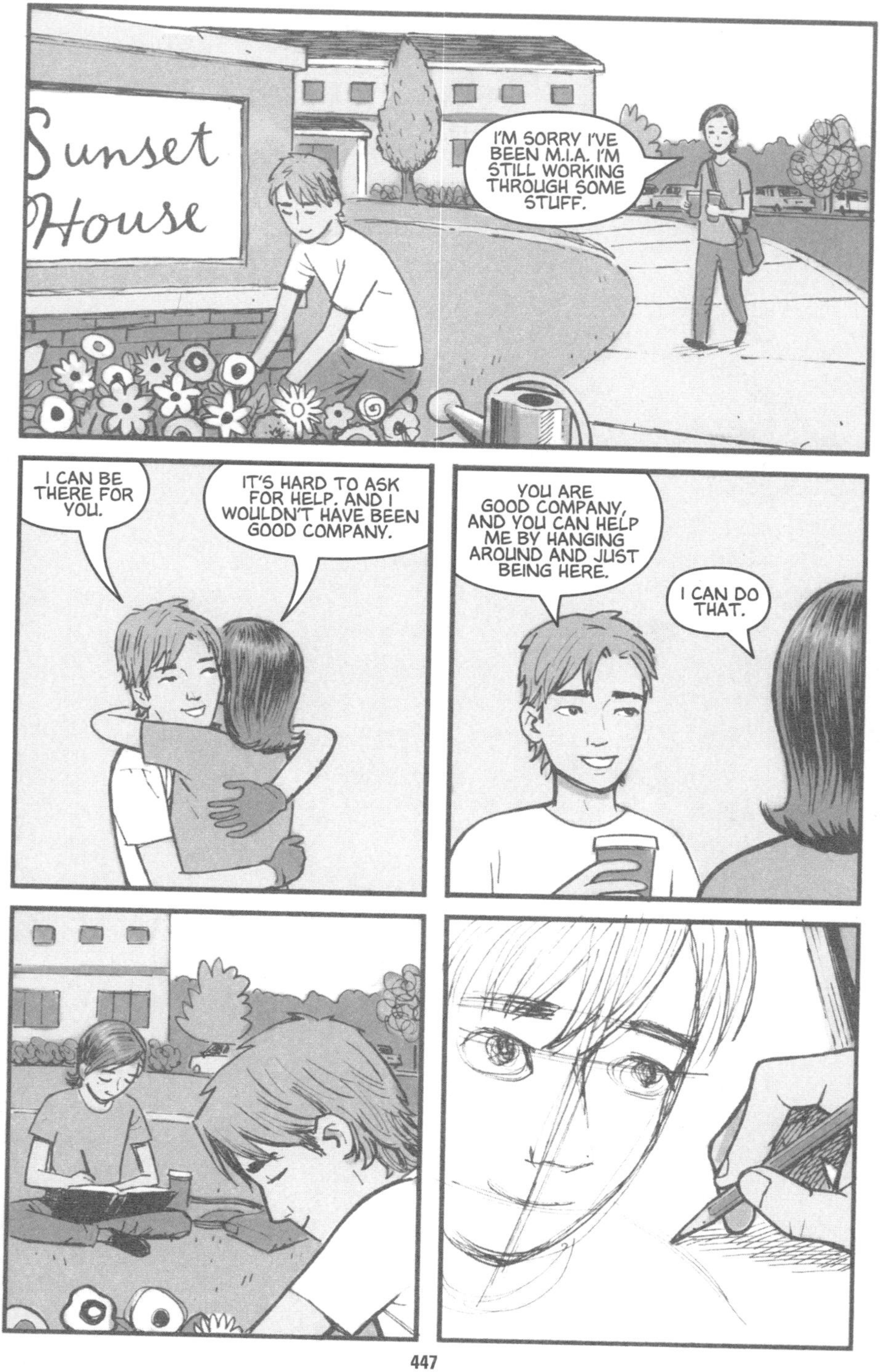
Sunset House
I'M SORRY I'VE BEEN M.I.A. I'M STILL WORKING THROUGH SOME STUFF.
I CAN BE THERE FOR YOU.
IT'S HARD TO ASK FOR HELP. AND I WOULDN'T HAVE BEEN GOOD COMPANY.
YOU ARE GOOD COMPANY, AND YOU CAN HELP ME BY HANGING AROUND AND JUST BEING HERE.
I CAN DO THAT.

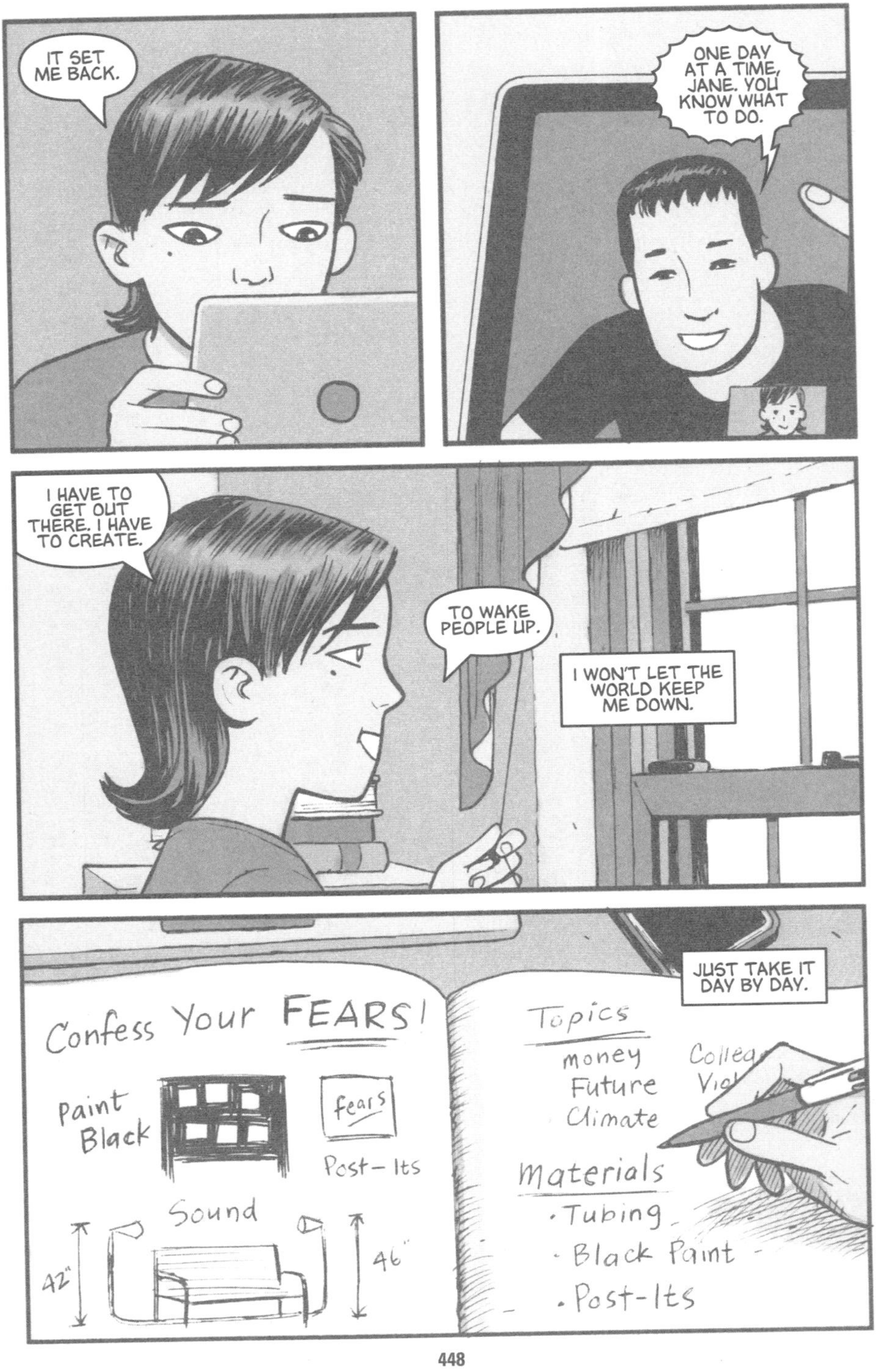
IT SET ME BACK.
ONE DAY AT A TIME, JANE. YOU KNOW WHAT TO DO.
I HAVE TO GET OUT THERE. I HAVE TO CREATE.
TO WAKE PEOPLE UP.
I WON'T LET THE WORLD KEEP ME DOWN.
JUST TAKE IT DAY BY DAY.
Confess Your FEARS!
Paint Black
fears
Post-Its
Sound
42"
46"
Topics
money
Future
Climate
Materials
· Tubing
· Black Paint
· Post-Its

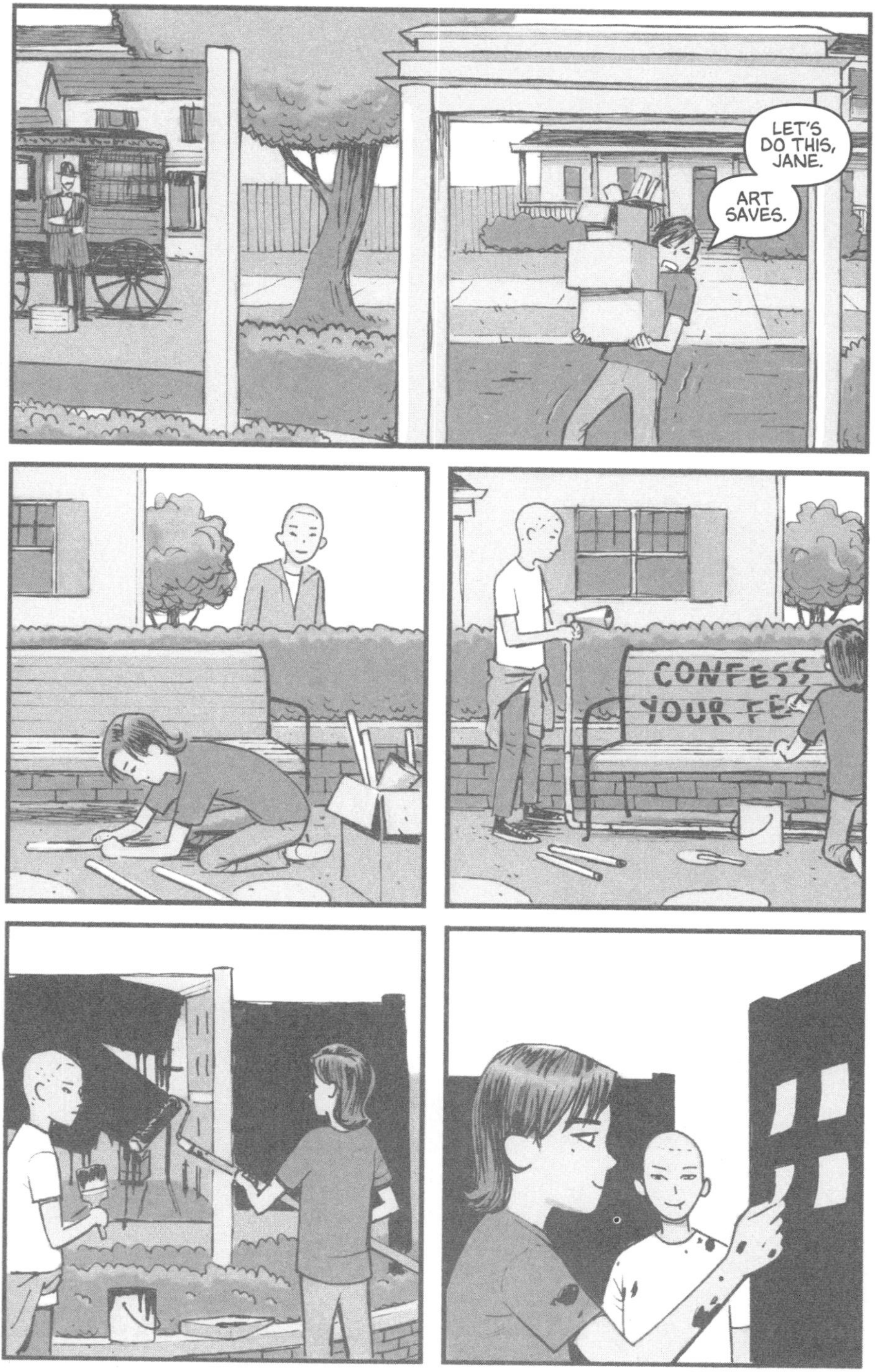
LET'S DO THIS, JANE.
ART SAVES.
CONFESS YOUR FE

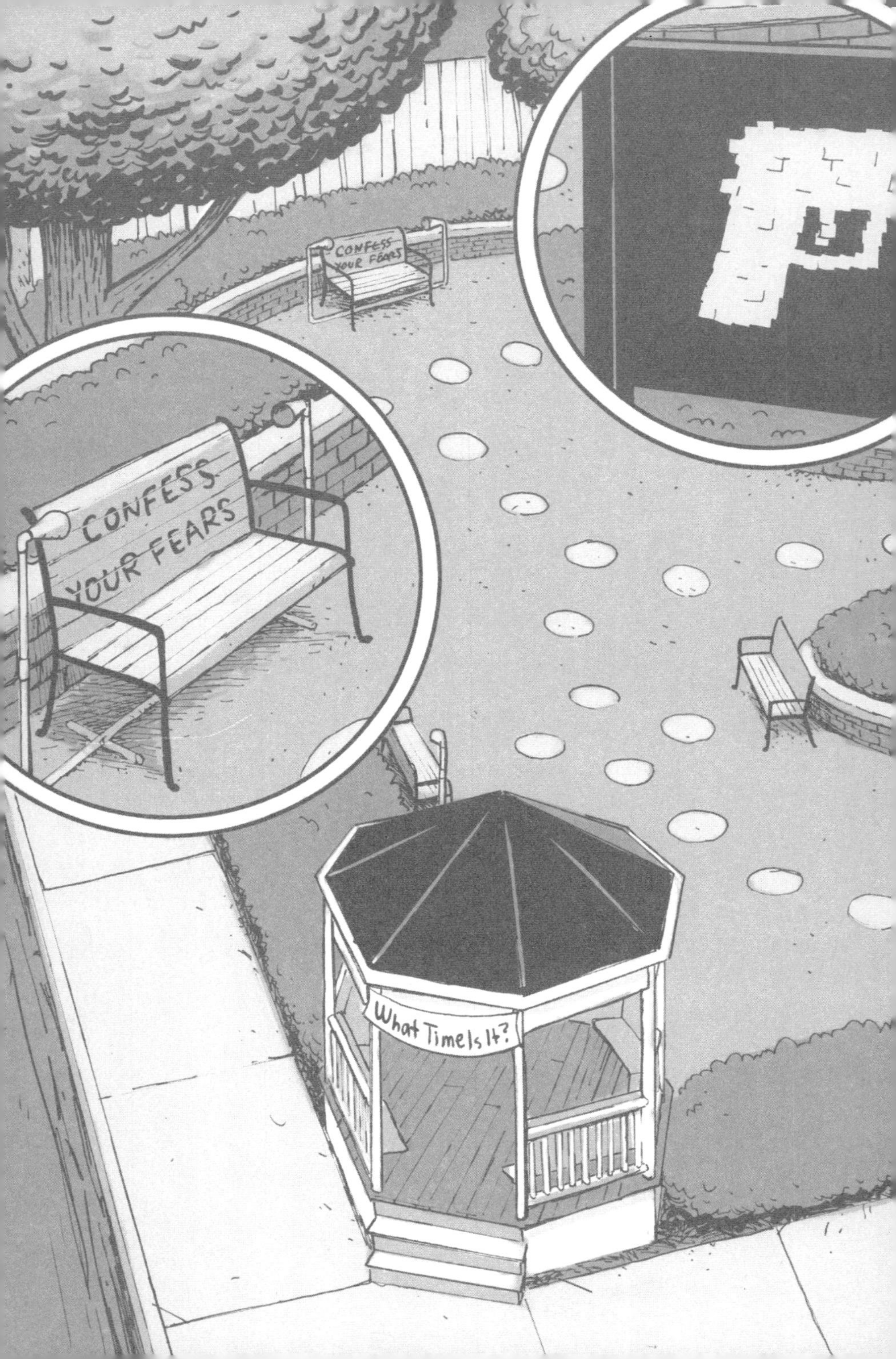
CONFESS
YOUR FEARS
CONFESS
YOUR FEARS
What Time Is It?

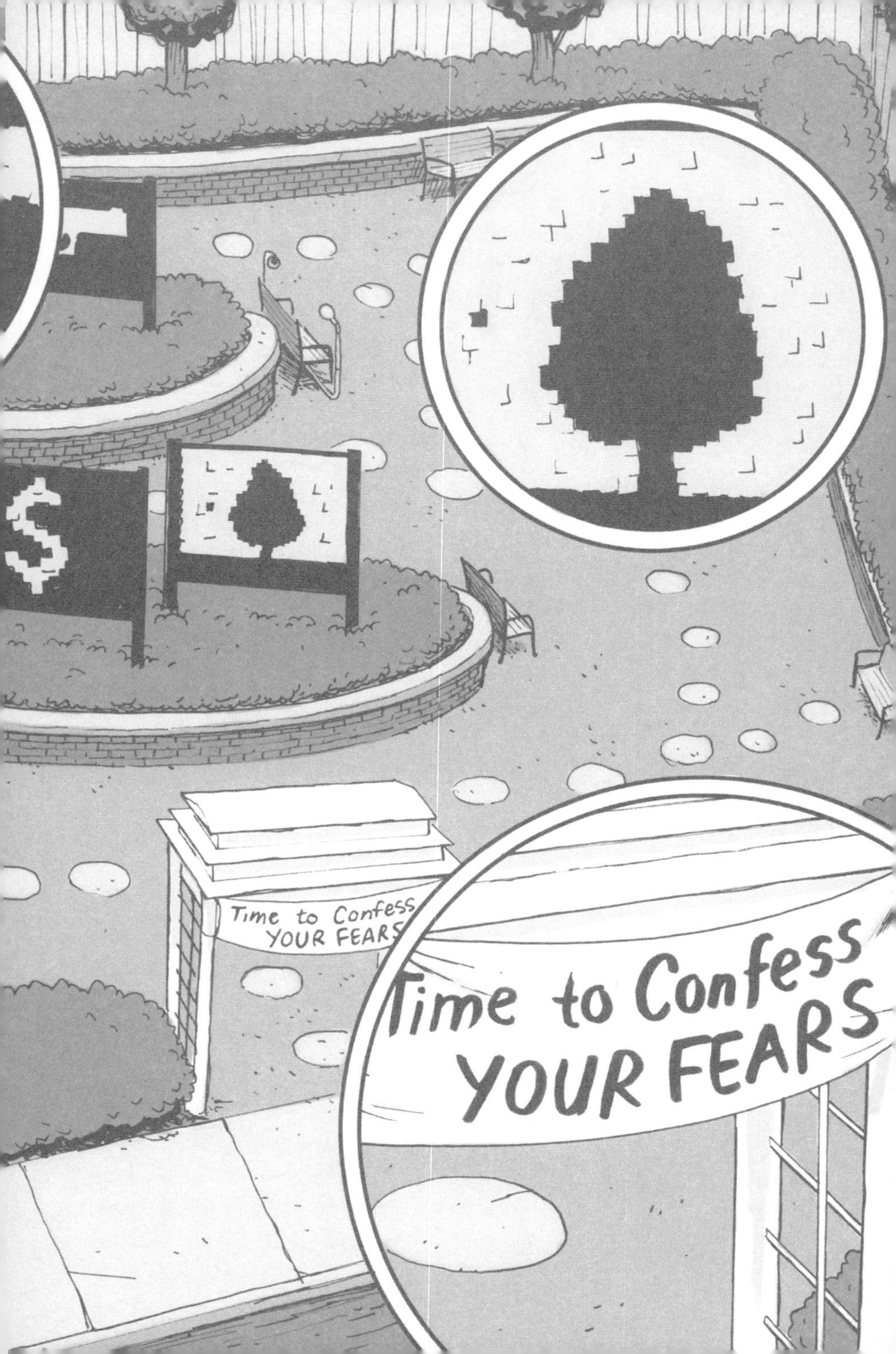
Time to Confess YOUR FEARS
Time to Confess YOUR FEARS

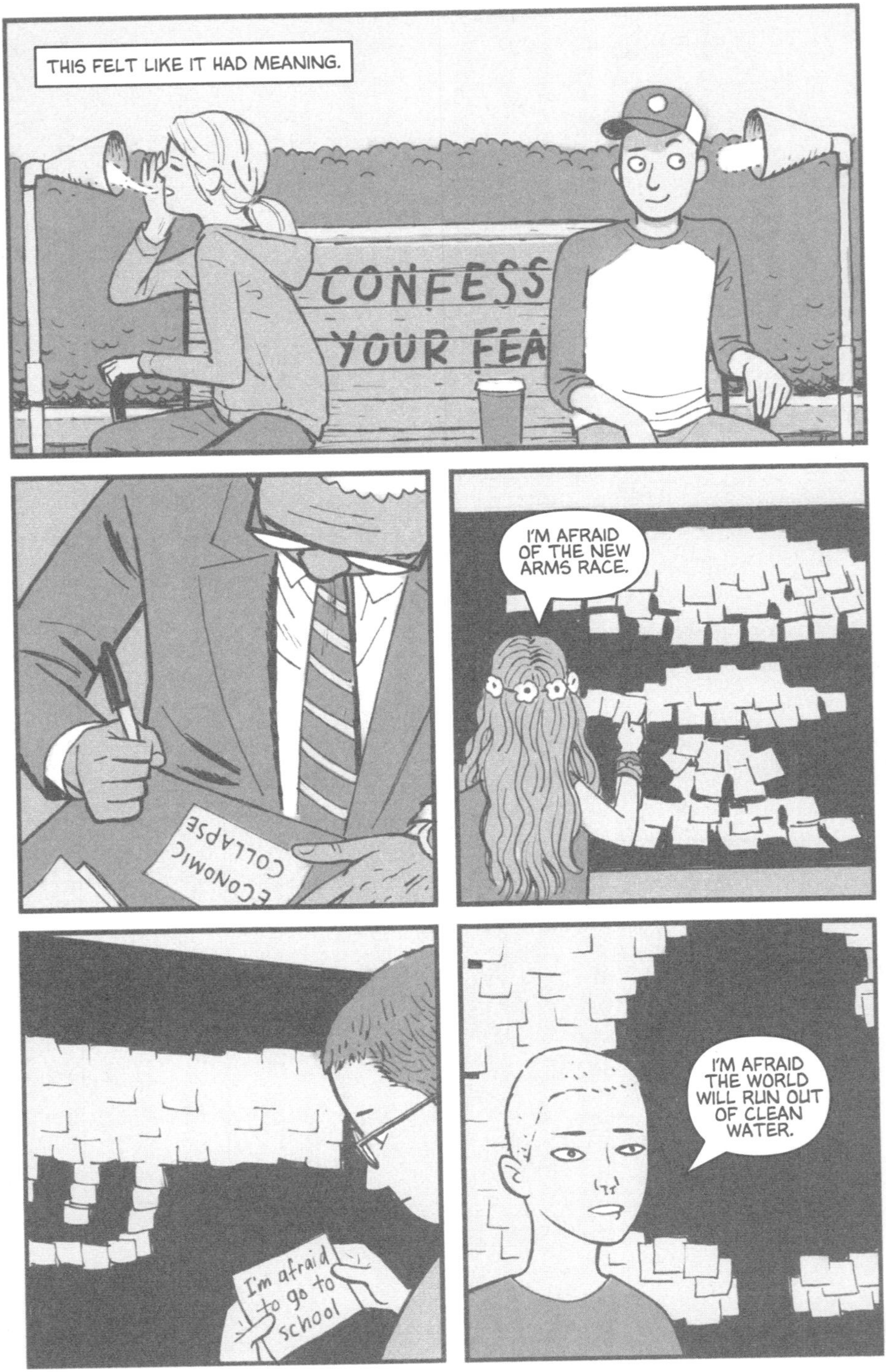
THIS FELT LIKE IT HAD MEANING.
CONFESS YOUR FEA
ECONOMIC COLLAPSE
I'M AFRAID OF THE NEW ARMS RACE.
I'm afraid to go to school
I'M AFRAID THE WORLD WILL RUN OUT OF CLEAN WATER.

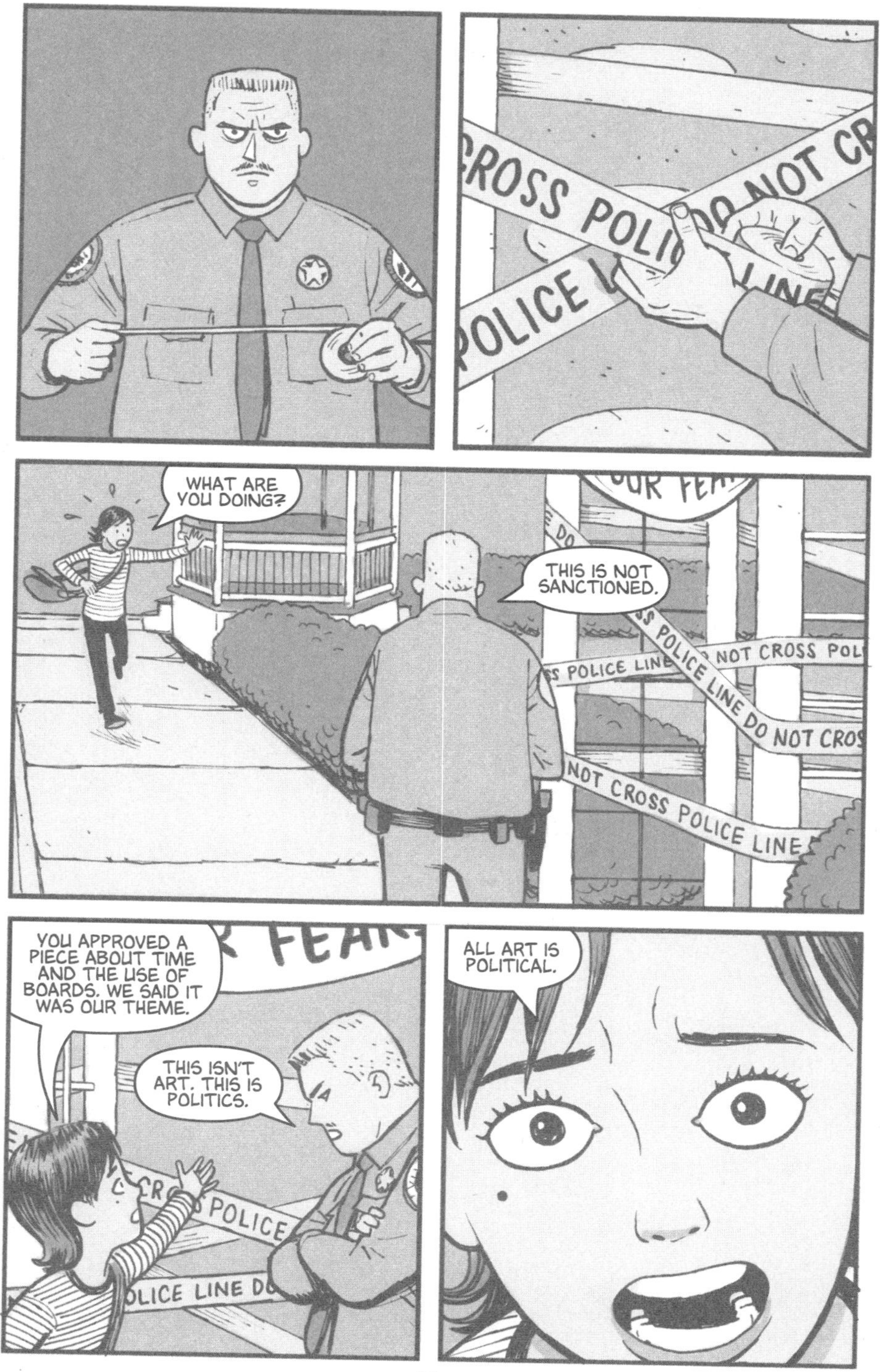
CROSS POLICE LINE DO NOT CR
POLICE LINE
WHAT ARE YOU DOING?
THIS IS NOT SANCTIONED.
POLICE LINE DO NOT CROSS POL
POLICE LINE
LINE DO NOT CROS
NOT CROSS POLICE LINE
YOU APPROVED A PIECE ABOUT TIME AND THE USE OF BOARDS. WE SAID IT WAS OUR THEME.
THIS ISN'T ART. THIS IS POLITICS.
POLICE
POLICE LINE DO
ALL ART IS POLITICAL.

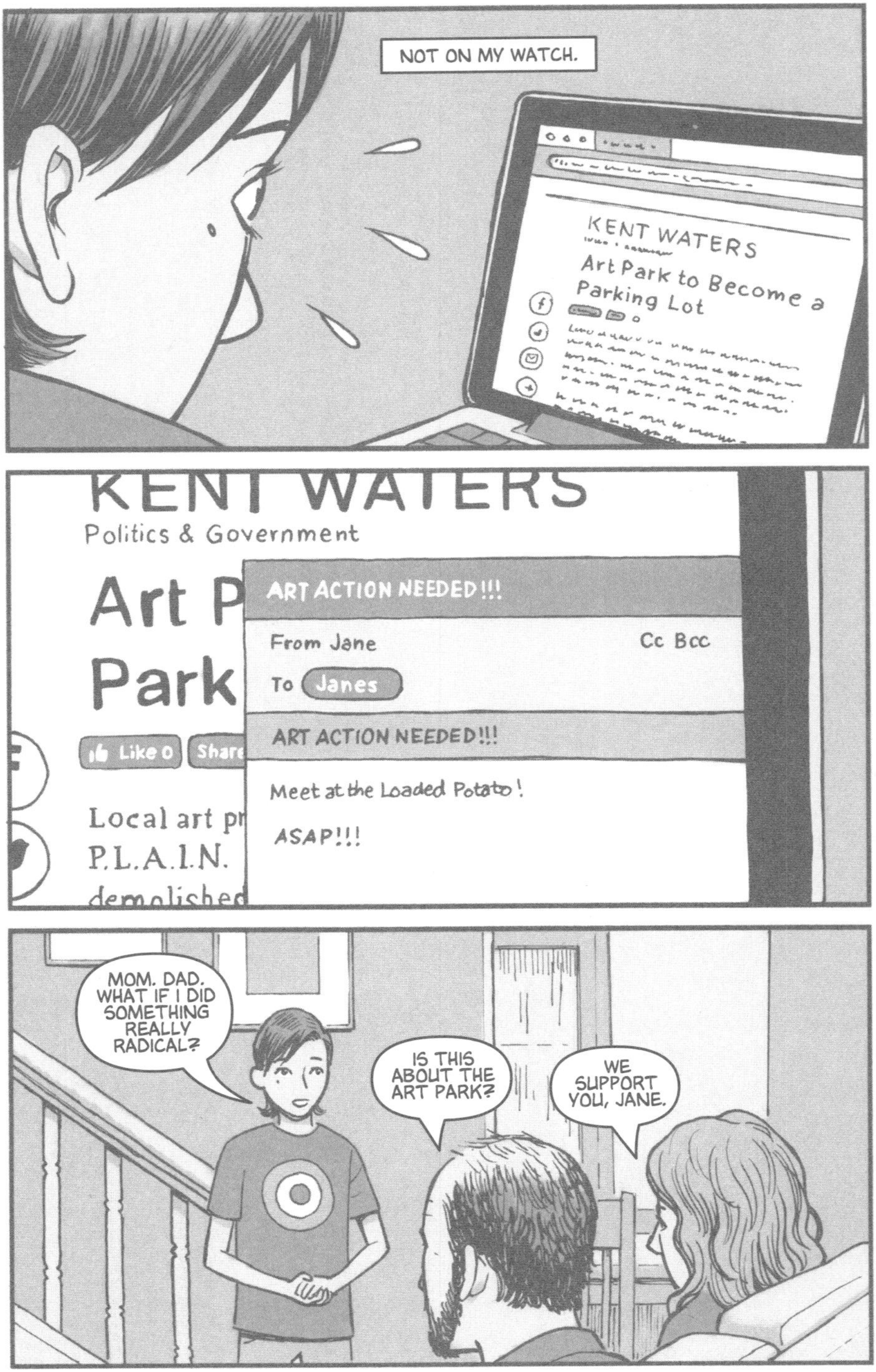

NOT ON MY WATCH.
KENT WATERS
Art Park to Become a Parking Lot
KENT WATERS
Politics & Government
Art P
Park
Like 0
Share
Local art pr
P.L.A.I.N.
demolished
ART ACTION NEEDED!!!
From Jane
Cc Bcc
To Janes
ART ACTION NEEDED!!!
Meet at the Loaded Potato!
ASAP!!!
MOM. DAD. WHAT IF I DID SOMETHING REALLY RADICAL?
IS THIS ABOUT THE ART PARK?
WE SUPPORT YOU, JANE.

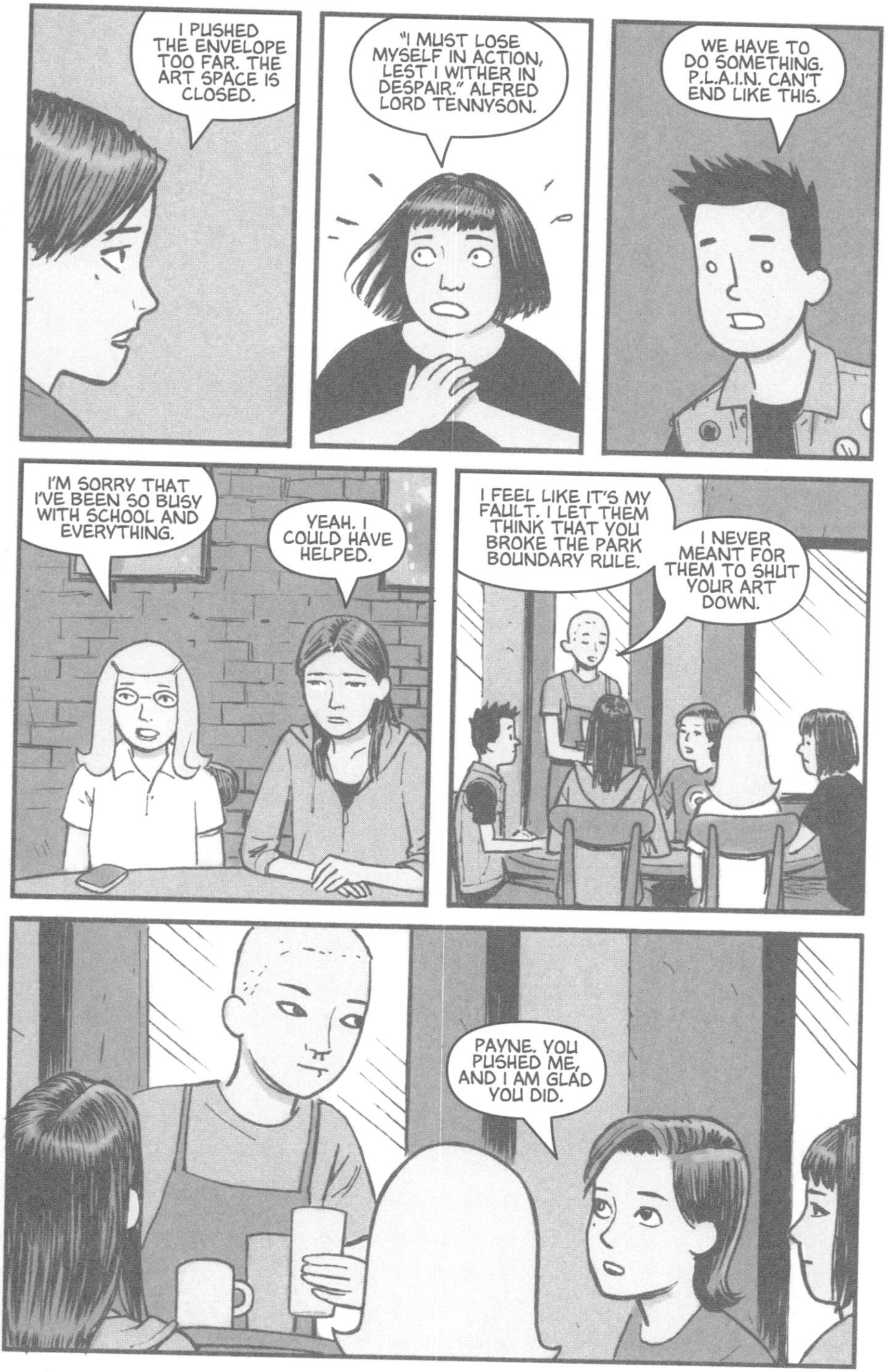
I PUSHED THE ENVELOPE TOO FAR. THE ART SPACE IS CLOSED.
"I MUST LOSE MYSELF IN ACTION, LEST I WITHER IN DESPAIR." ALFRED LORD TENNYSON.
WE HAVE TO DO SOMETHING. P.L.A.I.N. CAN'T END LIKE THIS.
I'M SORRY THAT I'VE BEEN SO BUSY WITH SCHOOL AND EVERYTHING.
YEAH. I COULD HAVE HELPED.
I FEEL LIKE IT'S MY FAULT. I LET THEM THINK THAT YOU BROKE THE PARK BOUNDARY RULE.
I NEVER MEANT FOR THEM TO SHUT YOUR ART DOWN.
PAYNE. YOU PUSHED ME, AND I AM GLAD YOU DID.

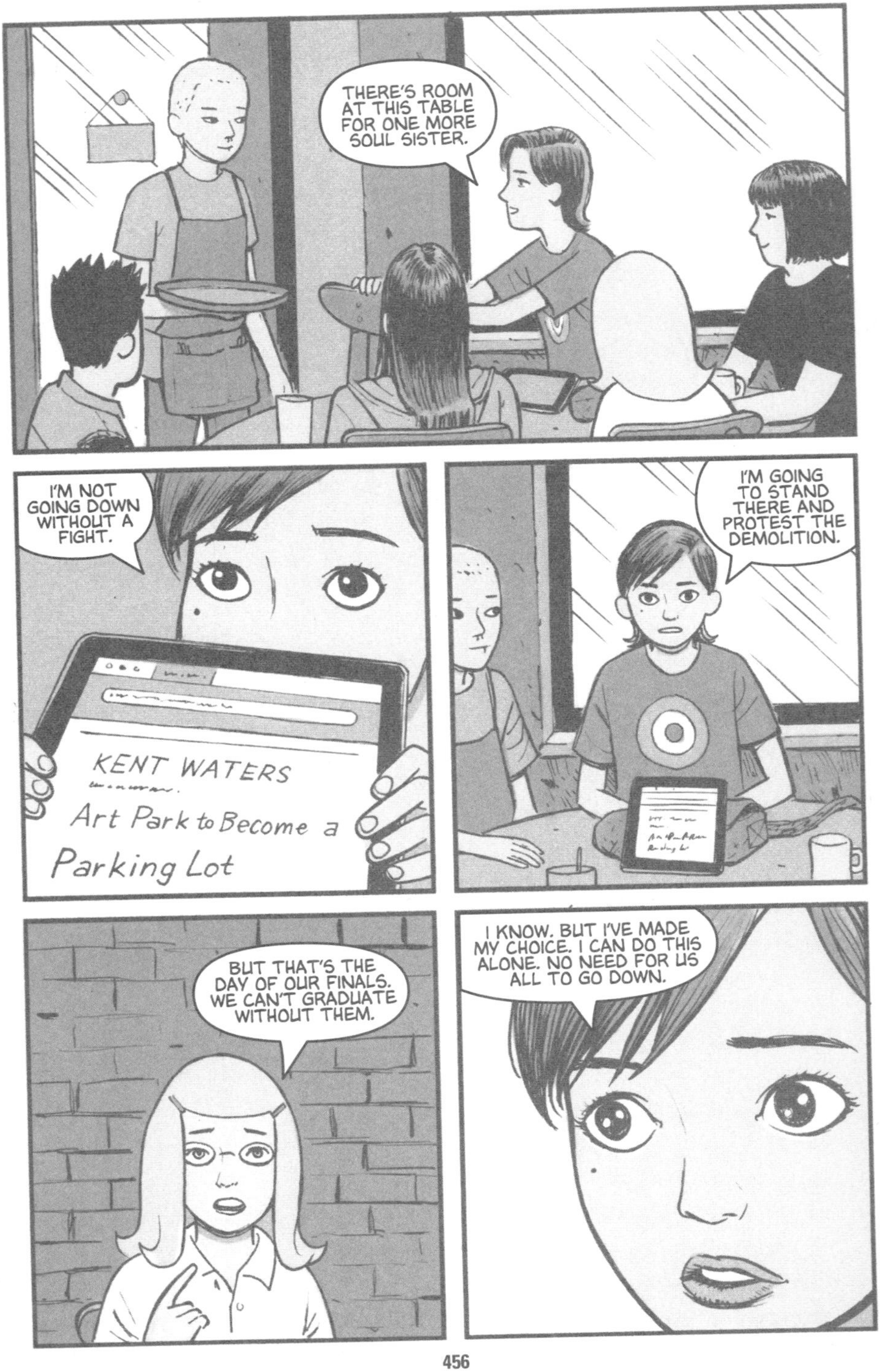
THERE'S ROOM AT THIS TABLE FOR ONE MORE SOUL SISTER.
I'M NOT GOING DOWN WITHOUT A FIGHT.
KENT WATERS
Art Park to Become a Parking Lot
I'M GOING TO STAND THERE AND PROTEST THE DEMOLITION.
BUT THAT'S THE DAY OF OUR FINALS. WE CAN'T GRADUATE WITHOUT THEM.
I KNOW. BUT I'VE MADE MY CHOICE. I CAN DO THIS ALONE. NO NEED FOR US ALL TO GO DOWN.

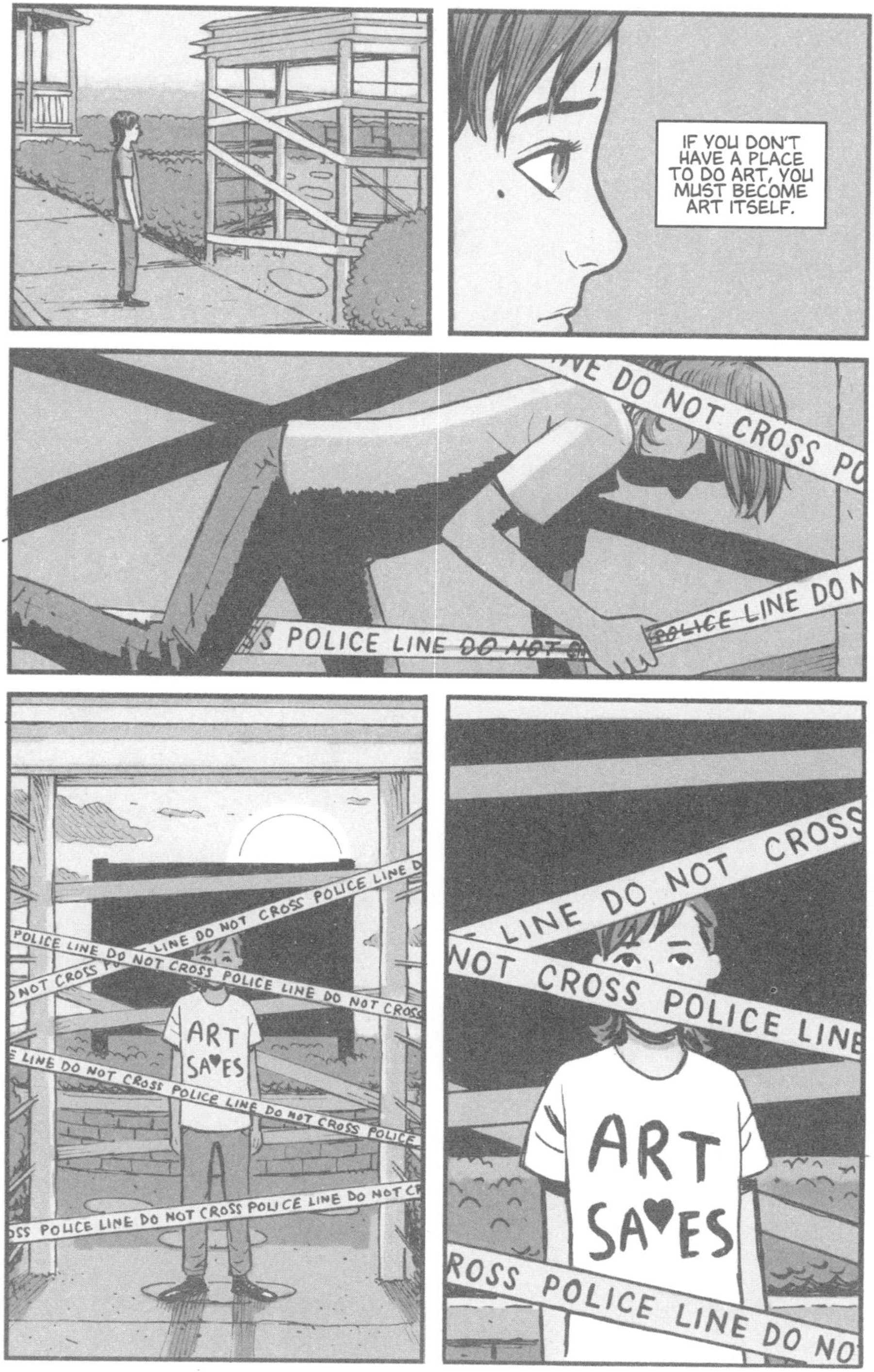
IF YOU DON'T HAVE A PLACE TO DO ART, YOU MUST BECOME ART ITSELF.
DO NOT CROSS PO
SS POLICE LINE DO NOT
POLICE LINE DO N
POLICE LINE DO NOT CROSS POLICE LINE
ART SA♥ES
LINE DO NOT CROSS
NOT CROSS POLICE LINE
ART SA♥ES
ROSS POLICE LINE DO NO

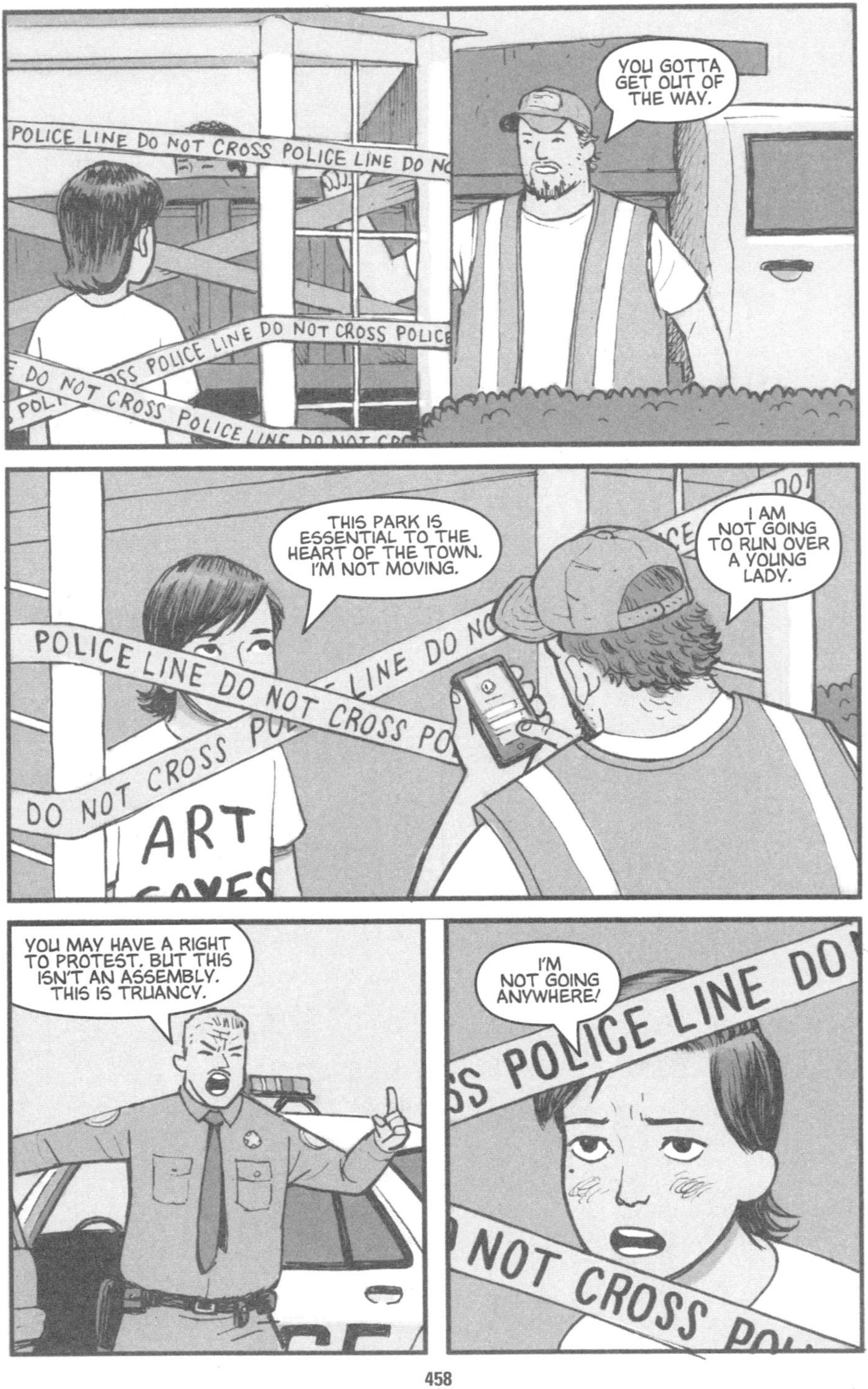
YOU GOTTA GET OUT OF THE WAY.
THIS PARK IS ESSENTIAL TO THE HEART OF THE TOWN. I'M NOT MOVING.
I AM NOT GOING TO RUN OVER A YOUNG LADY.
ART
YOU MAY HAVE A RIGHT TO PROTEST. BUT THIS ISN'T AN ASSEMBLY. THIS IS TRUANCY.
I'M NOT GOING ANYWHERE!

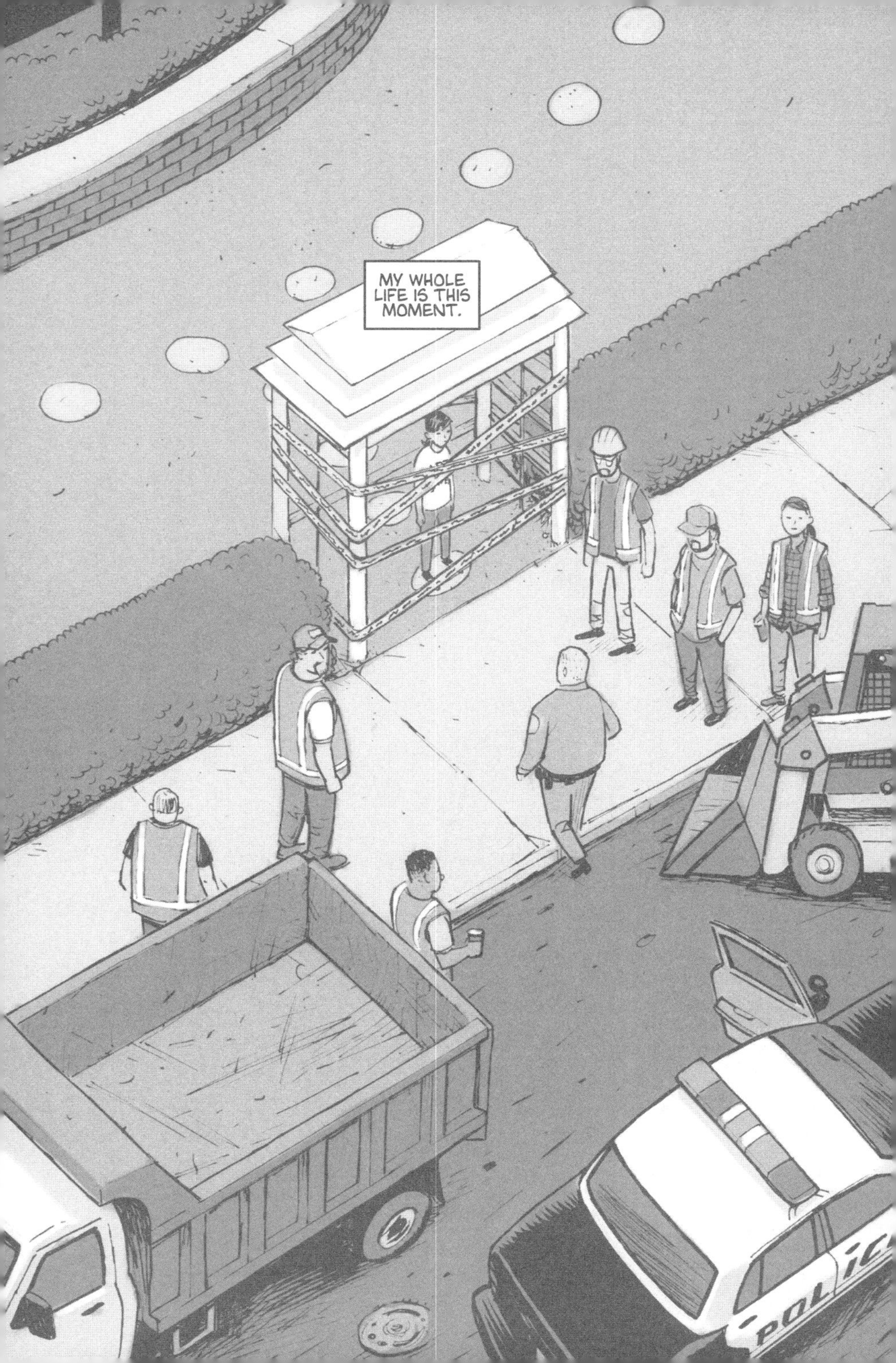
MY WHOLE LIFE IS THIS MOMENT.
POLIC

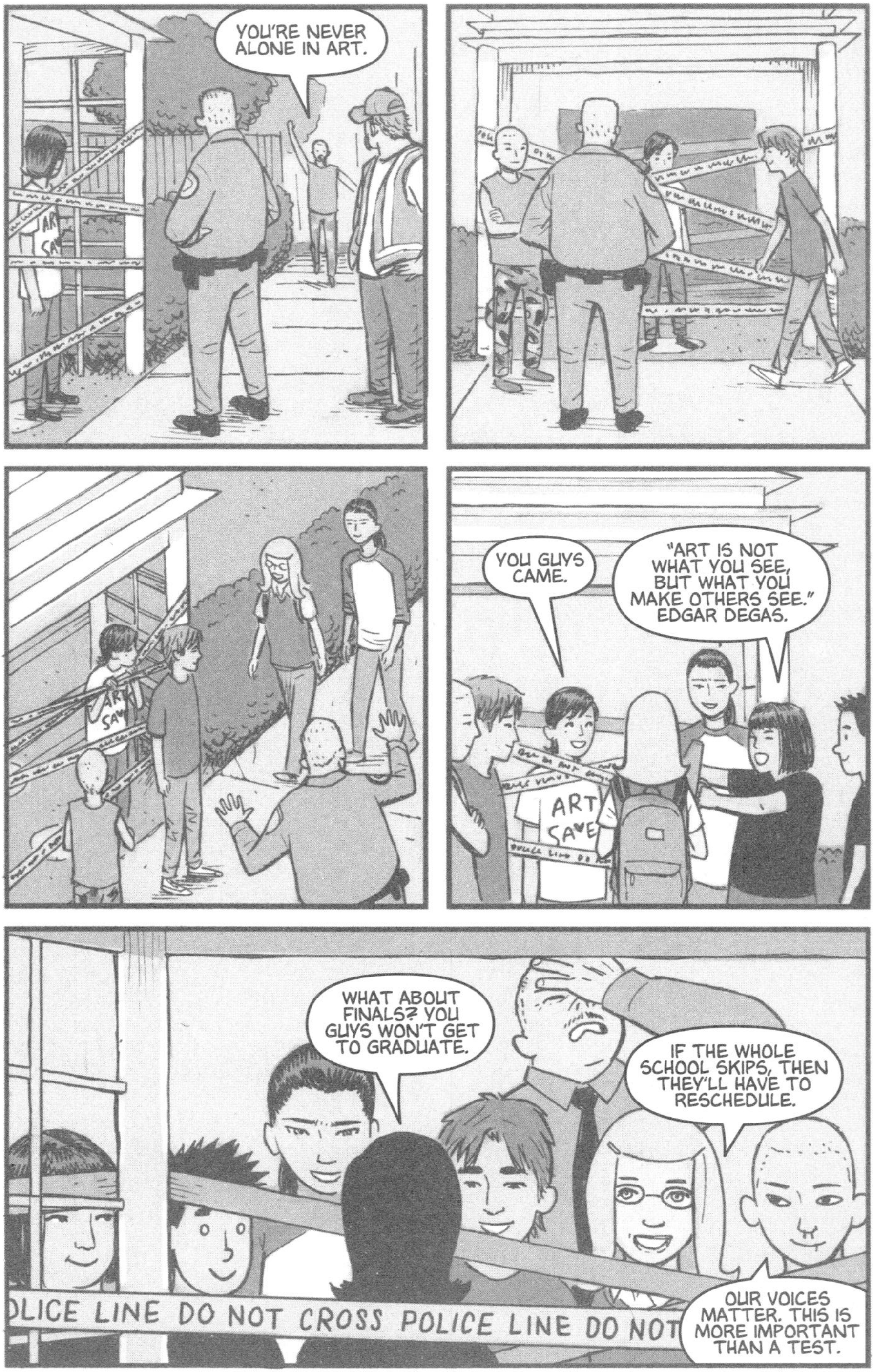
YOU'RE NEVER ALONE IN ART.
YOU GUYS CAME.
"ART IS NOT WHAT YOU SEE, BUT WHAT YOU MAKE OTHERS SEE." EDGAR DEGAS.
ART SAVE
WHAT ABOUT FINALS? YOU GUYS WON'T GET TO GRADUATE.
IF THE WHOLE SCHOOL SKIPS, THEN THEY'LL HAVE TO RESCHEDULE.
OLICE LINE DO NOT CROSS POLICE LINE DO NOT
OUR VOICES MATTER. THIS IS MORE IMPORTANT THAN A TEST.

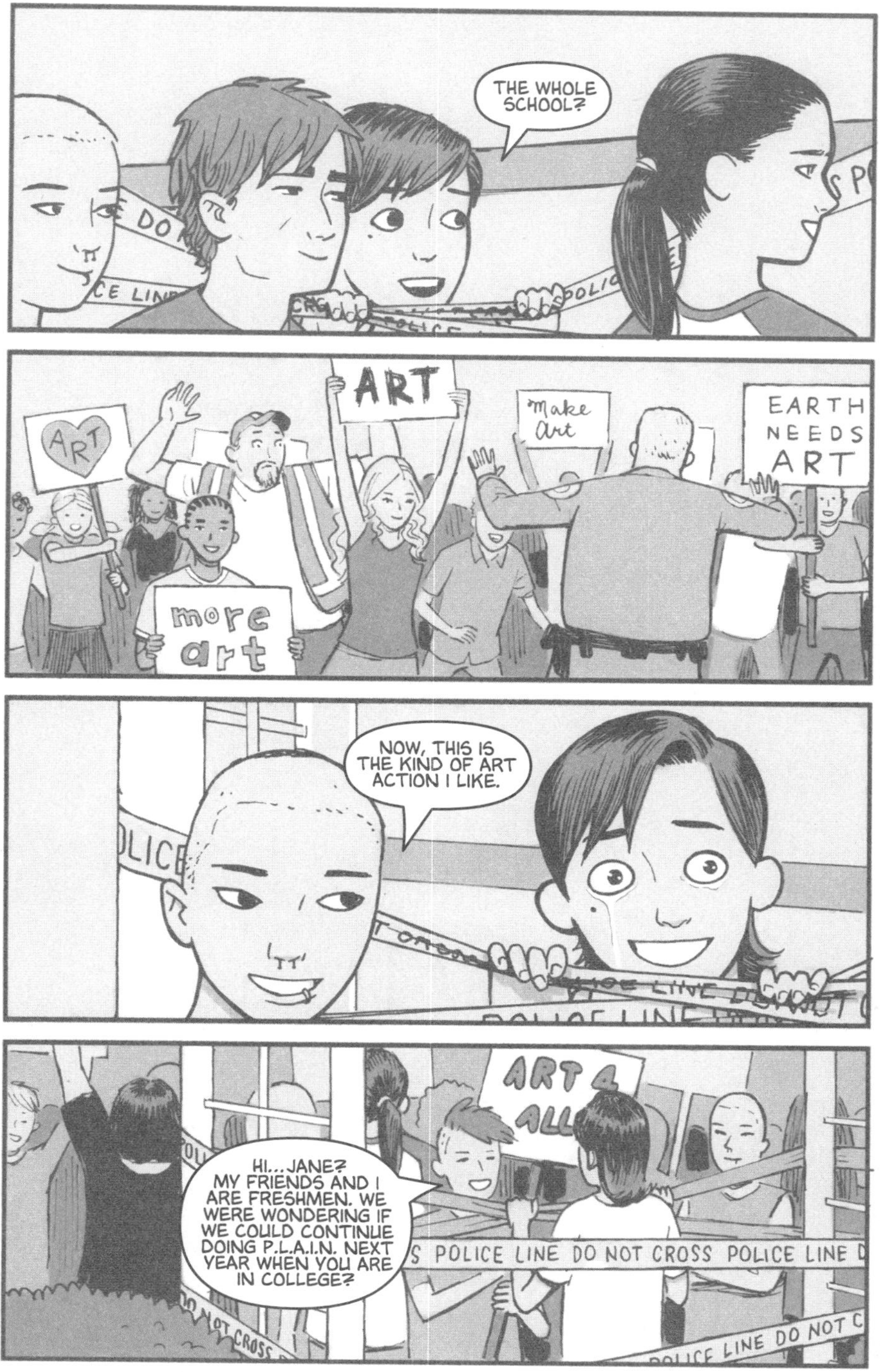
THE WHOLE SCHOOL?
ART
ART
Make Art
EARTH NEEDS ART
more art
NOW, THIS IS THE KIND OF ART ACTION I LIKE.
ART 4 ALL
HI... JANE? MY FRIENDS AND I ARE FRESHMEN. WE WERE WONDERING IF WE COULD CONTINUE DOING P.L.A.I.N. NEXT YEAR WHEN YOU ARE IN COLLEGE?
POLICE LINE DO NOT CROSS POLICE LINE
POLICE LINE DO NOT

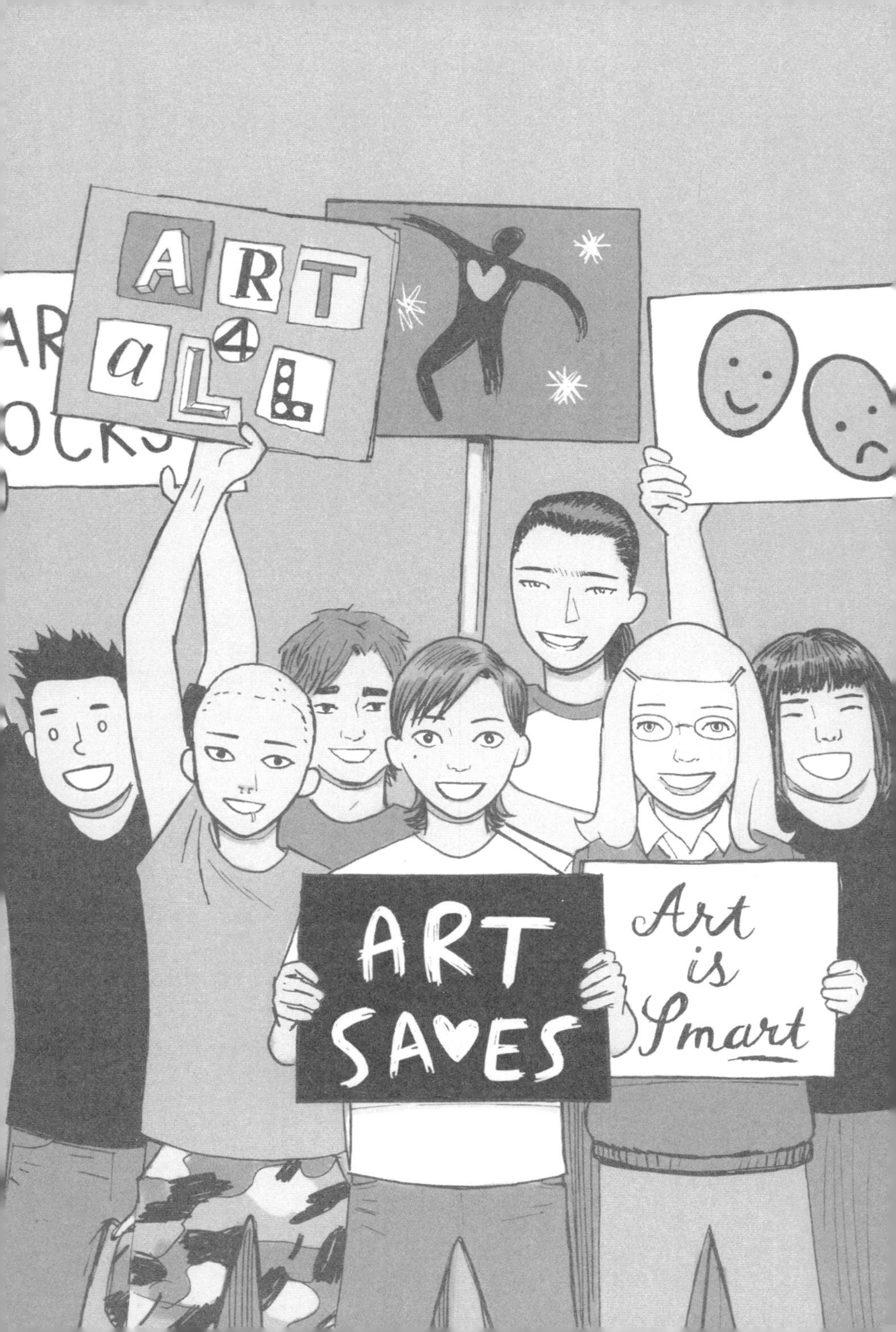
ART 4 aLL
ART SAVES
Art is Smart

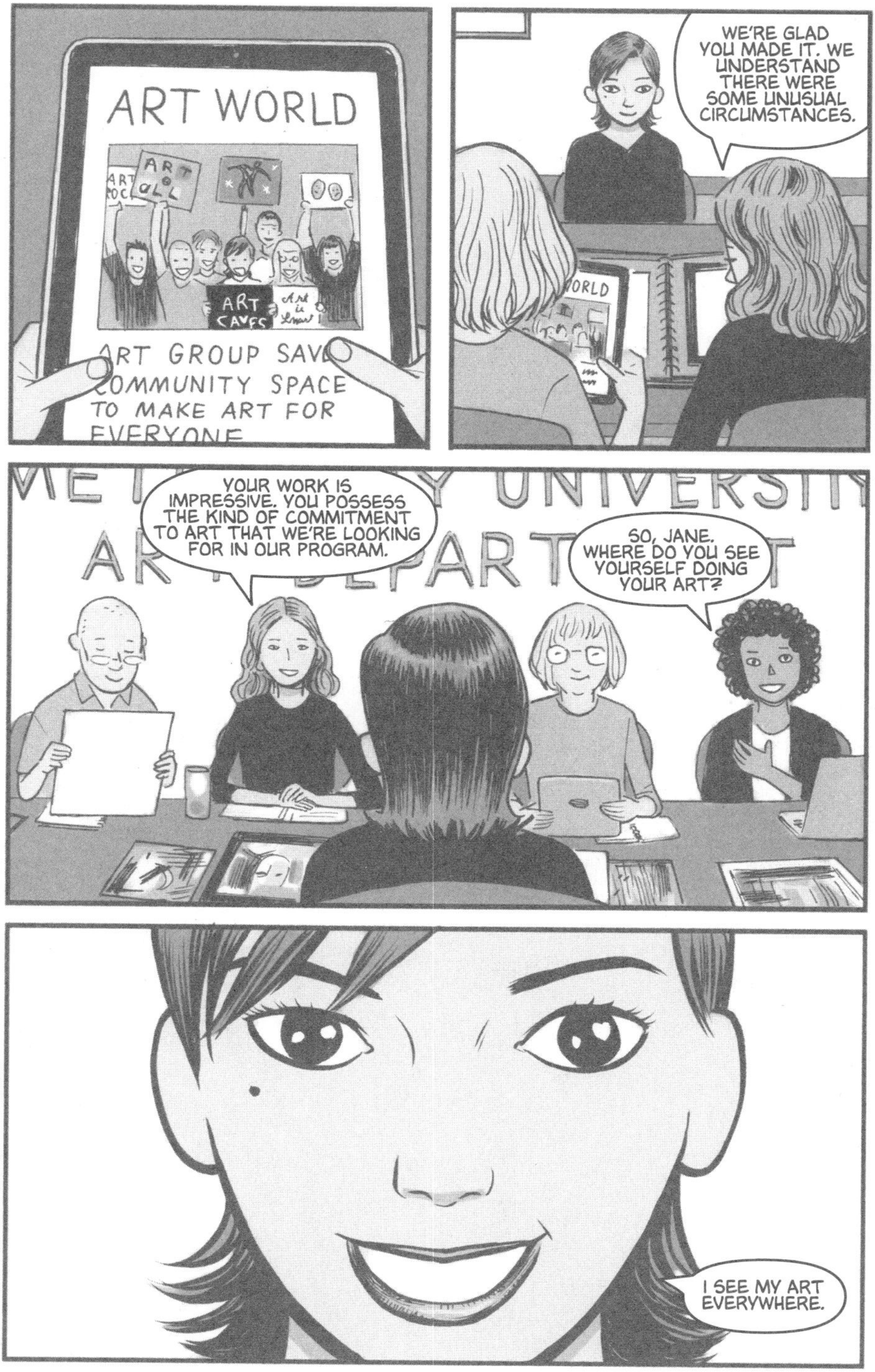
ART WORLD
ART CAVES
ART GROUP SAV
COMMUNITY SPACE
TO MAKE ART FOR
EVERYONE
WE'RE GLAD YOU MADE IT. WE UNDERSTAND THERE WERE SOME UNUSUAL CIRCUMSTANCES.
UNIVERSITY
YOUR WORK IS IMPRESSIVE. YOU POSSESS THE KIND OF COMMITMENT TO ART THAT WE'RE LOOKING FOR IN OUR PROGRAM.
SO, JANE. WHERE DO YOU SEE YOURSELF DOING YOUR ART?
I SEE MY ART EVERYWHERE.

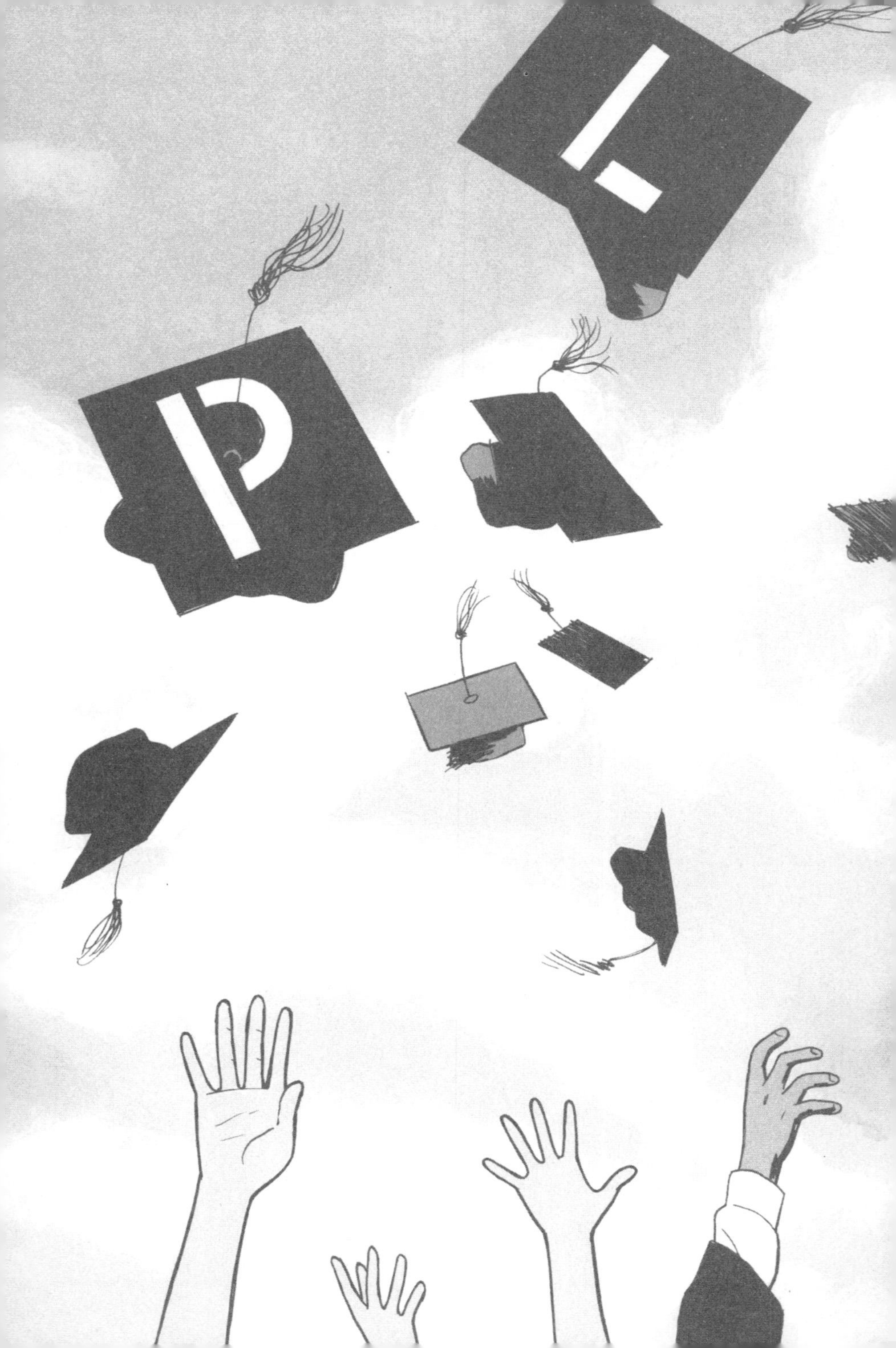

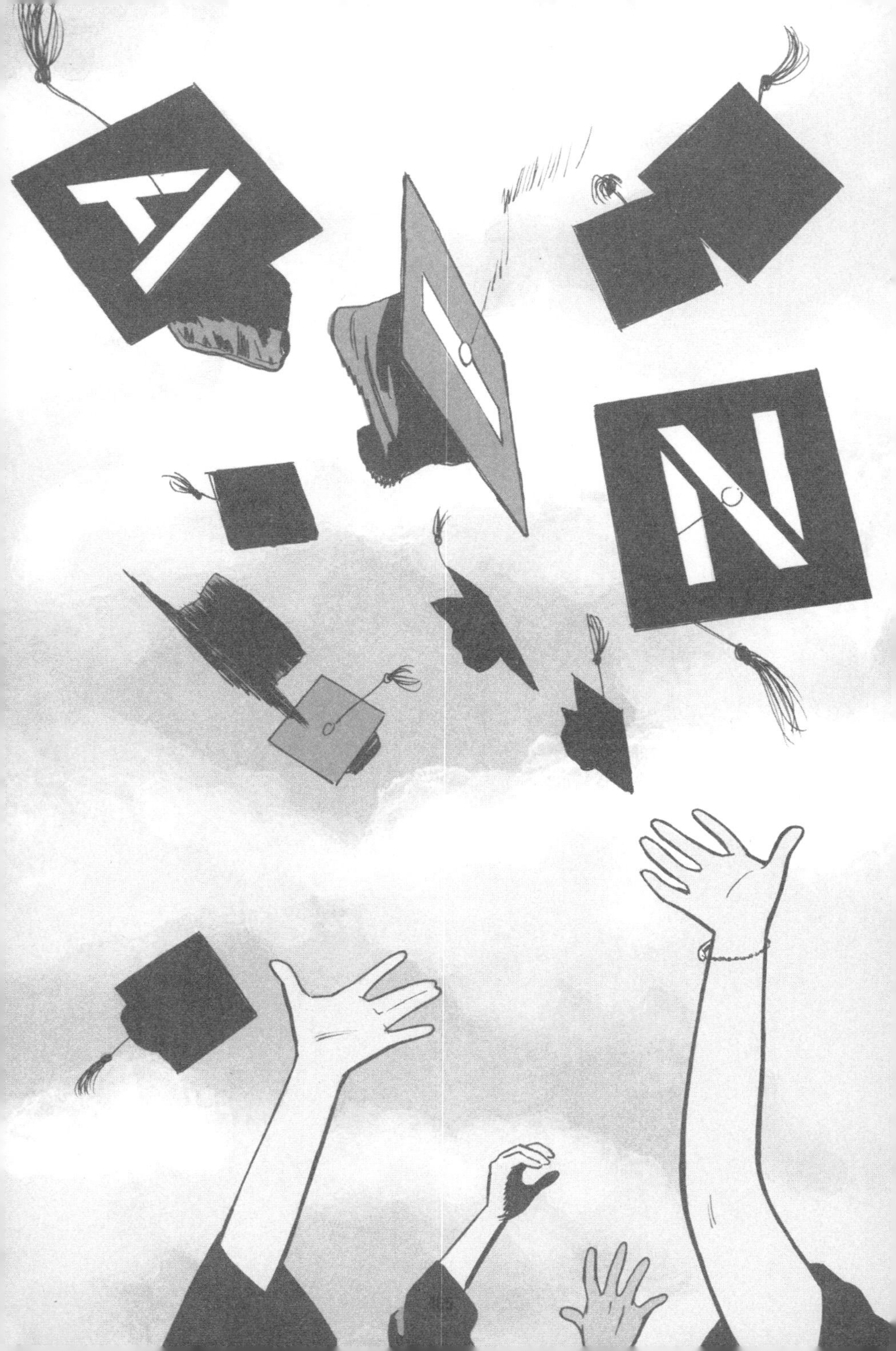
A
N

Other Artists Draw the Janes

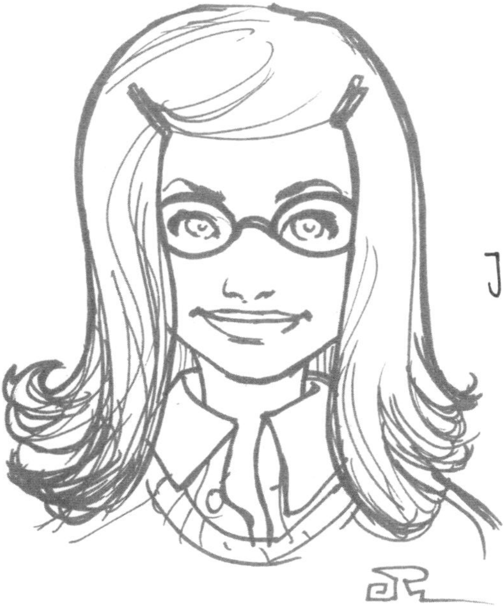

Art by
Joshua Middleton

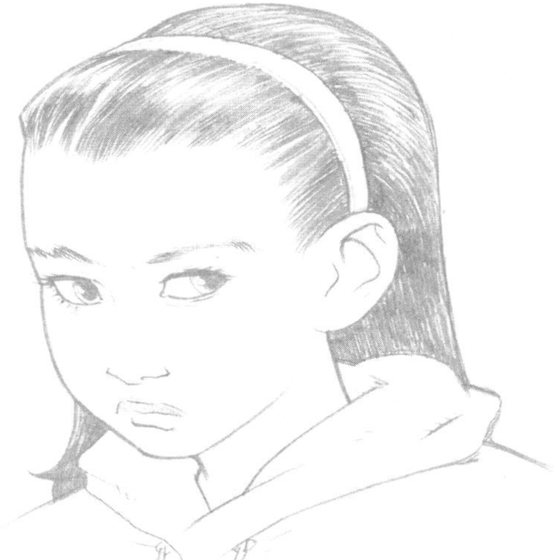
2009

Art by
Sophie Campbell

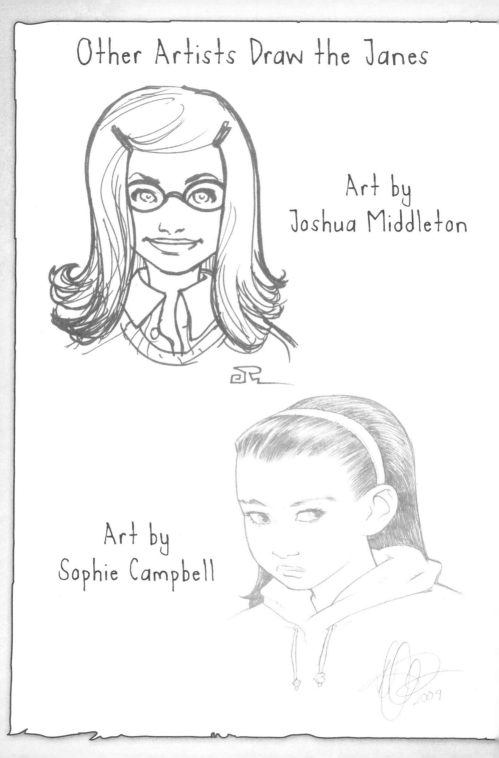

Art by
Becky Cloonan

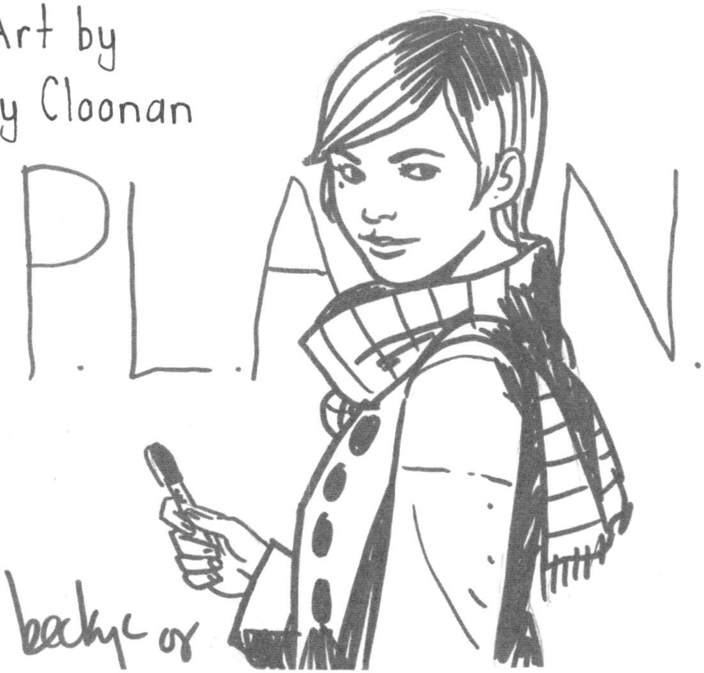
P.L.A.N.
beckyc 08

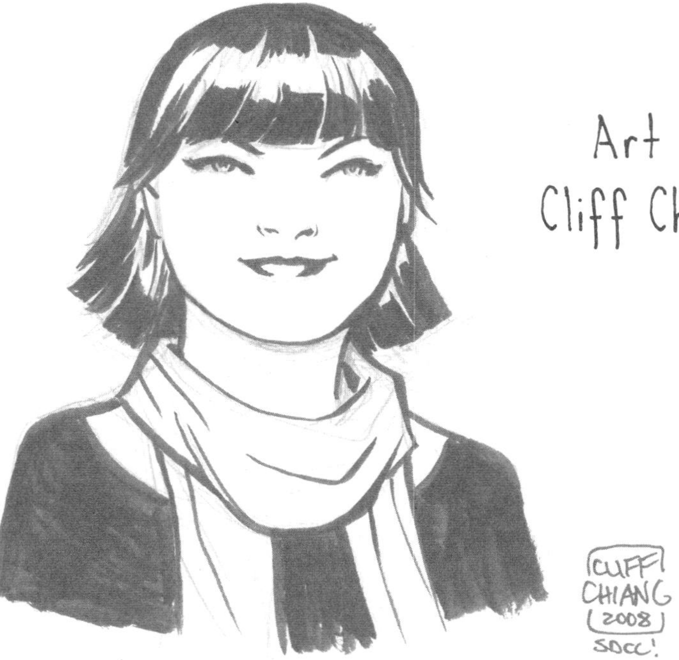
CLIFF
CHIANG
2008
SDCC!

Art by
Cliff Chiang

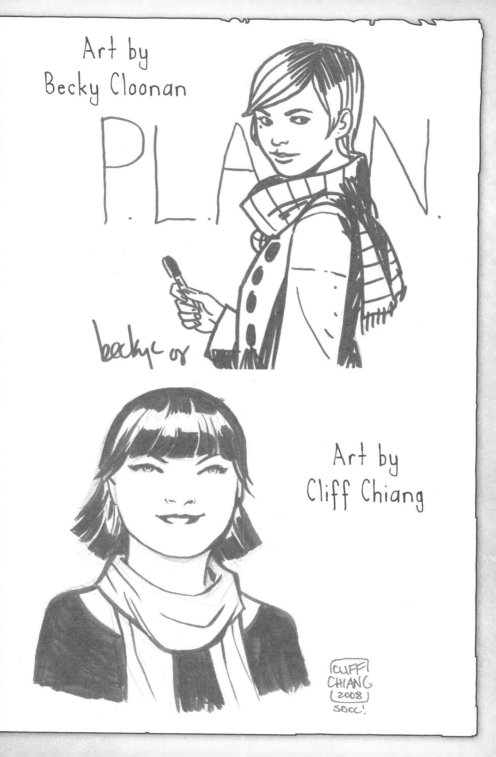

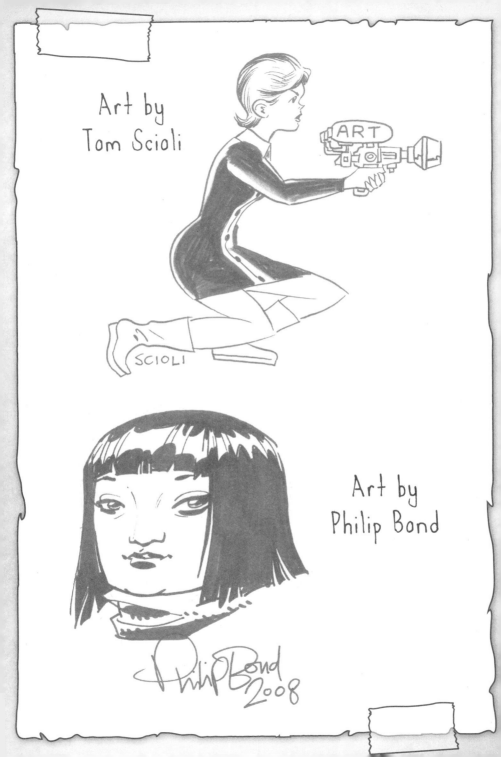

Art by
Tom Scioli

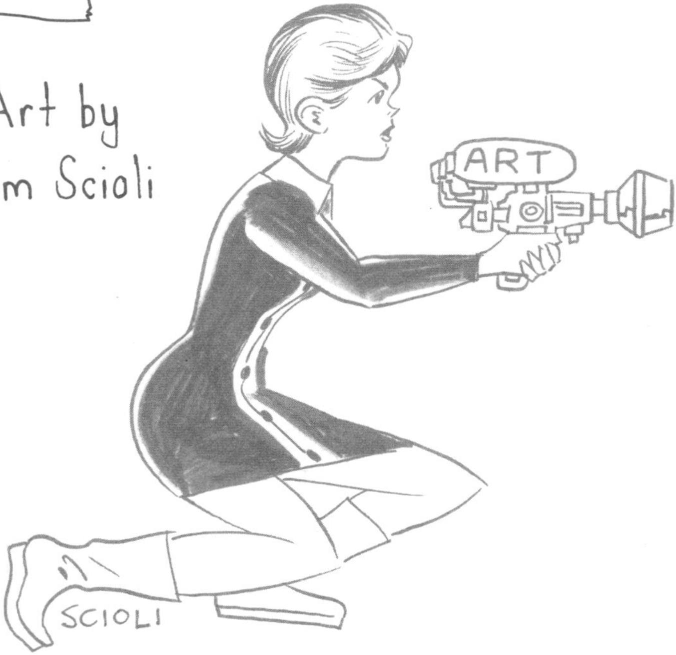
ART
SCIOLI

Art by
Philip Bond

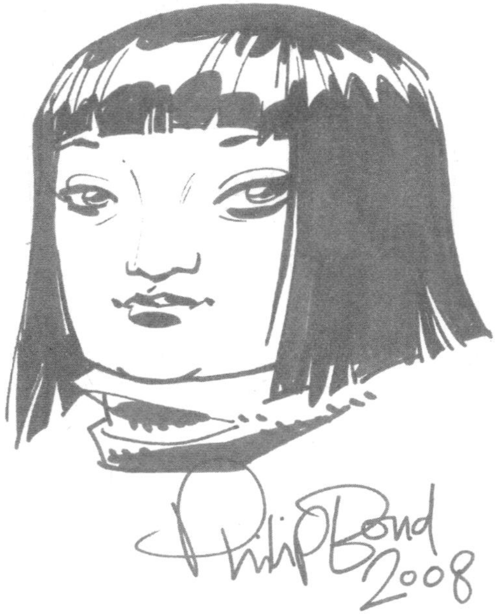
Philip Bond
2008

Acknowledgments

Thank you to:

Shelly Bond

DC Comics, Dan DiDio,
and Jack Mahan

Kirby Kim

Jared Fletcher

Pam Gruber and Little, Brown Books
for Young Readers

Street Art Everywhere

Photograph by Eric Charles

Cecil Castellucci is an Eisner, EGL, and Harvey Award—nominated, *New York Times* bestselling author of books and graphic novels for young adults, including *Shade, The Changing Girl, Soupy Leaves Home, The Year of the Beasts, Tin Star,* and *Odd Duck.* She has also written for DC Comics, and her short stories and short comics have been published in many literary journals and comics anthologies. In a former life, she was known as Cecil Seaskull in the '90s indie band Nerdy Girl. She is a two-time MacDowell Fellow and the founding YA editor at the *Los Angeles Review of Books.* She lives in Los Angeles.

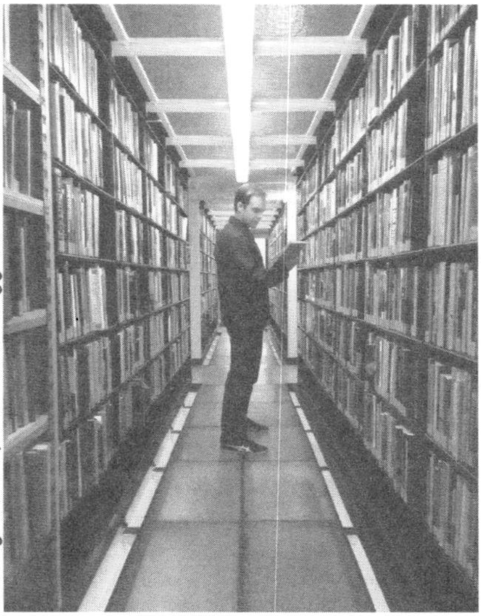

Photograph by Natalie Rugg

Jim Rugg is a comic book artist, book maker, illustrator, designer, and cat dad. His books include *Street Angel*, *The PLAIN Janes*, *Afrodisiac*, *Notebook Drawings*, *Rambo 3.5*, and *Supermag*. He is the winner of an Eisner Award and an Ignatz Award, and he was recognized as part of the AIGA 50/50. His YouTube channel, Cartoonist Kayfabe, will make you love comics even more!